THE CUYAHOGA STORIES

Five Dr. Fairchild Mysteries
Sequels to Valley of the Gray Moon

KEN BROWNLEE

These works are entirely fictional. The names, places and events are drawn from the author's imagination, and any similarity to actual events or persons (other than historical persons, events or references to cities or towns) is entirely coincidental and unintended. Fremont College is a fictional location, although the Plumbrook NASA facility does exist, but is no longer nuclear. See *Introduction* for a summary of the *Valley of the Gray Moon* stories, events referred to in *The Cuyahoga Stories*.

Other *Dr. Fairchild* Stories: *Valley of the Gray Moon (A Trilogy)* (1993)

Other Books By Ken Brownlee:
Collections: Poems and Short Stories (2002) (Valley Enterprises)
Casualty Insurance Claims, 4th Ed., Vol. 1-3 (Thomson Reuters West Group)
Excess Liability - Rights and Duties of Commercial Risk Insureds and Insurers, 4th, Vol. 1 + 2
Casualty Fire & Marine Investigation Checklists, 9th Ed., (Both, Thomson Reuters West)
Winning By the Rules: Ethics and Success in the Insurance Profession (National Underwriter Co.)
The Year in Liturgy and Church History Through a Cathedral Window (Cathedral of St. Philip)
*Call of the Fishermen (*Christ United Methodist Church, St. Petersburg, windows)
Ghost Railroads of Carroll County, Indiana
From Clipper Ships to Rocket Ships – History of American Transportation

Copyright 2016, By Ken Brownlee

IBSN 13-978-1537077741, 10-1537077740

                        Valley Enterprises
                        P.O. Box 421633
                        Atlanta, Ga. 30342

Soft Cover Edition Photo:
The Cuyahoga River from below the High Level Bridge

THE CUYAHOGA STORIES

Five Dr. Fairchild Mysteries
Sequels to Valley of the Gray Moon

- Shoeless George
- 'Q'
- Sandusky Bay
- Solemn Evensong
- Fire and Ice

Ken Brownlee

Table of Contents

Introduction i
Shoeless George 1
   Prologue to Shoeless George 1
   Chapter 1 4
   Chapter 2 12
   Chapter 3 24
   Chapter 4 29
   Chapter 5 38
   Chapter 6 48
   Chapter 7 57
   Chapter 8 72
   Chapter 9 78
   Chapter 10 91
   Chapter 11 105
   Chapter 12 114
   Chapter 13 123
   Chapter 14 132
   Chapter 15 139
   Chapter 16 148
   Chapter 17 160
   Chapter 18 170
"Q" 175
   Prologue to "Q" 175
   Chapter 1 178
   Chapter 2 196
   Chapter 3 203
   Chapter 4 211
   Chapter 5 219
   Chapter 6 229
   Chapter 7 243
   Chapter 8 254
   Chapter 9 263
   Chapter 10 276

- Chapter 11 288
- Chapter 12 299
- Chapter 13 318
- Chapter 14 330
- Chapter 15 345
- Chapter 16 358
- Chapter 17 366

Sandusky Bay 376
- Prologue to Sandusky Bay 376
- Chapter 1 378
- Chapter 2 389
- Chapter 3 404
- Chapter 4 411
- Chapter 5 424
- Chapter 6 431
- Chapter 7 436
- Chapter 8 445
- Chapter 9 458
- Chapter 10 474
- Chapter 11 489
- Chapter 12 498
- Chapter 13 503
- Chapter 14 507
- Chapter 15 517
- Chapter 16 531

Solemn Evensong 540
- Part One – A Death in the Cathedral 540
- Chapter 1 541
- Chapter 2 549
- Chapter 3 556
- Chapter 4 566
- Chapter 5 573
- Chapter 6 588
- Part Two 598
- Chapter 7 598

- Chapter 8 603
- Chapter 9 615
- Chapter 10 623
- Chapter 11 633
- Chapter 12 636
- Chapter 13 643
- Chapter 14 650

Fire & Ice 655
- Chapter 1 655
- Chapter 2 665
- Chapter 3 672
- Chapter 4 684
- Chapter 5 689
- Chapter 6 701
- Chapter 7 705
- Chapter 8 716
- Chapter 9 719
- Chapter 10 725
- Chapter 11 733
- Chapter 12 745
- Chapter 13 761
- Chapter 14 780
- Chapter 15 784
- Chapter 16 789
- Chapter 17 800
- Chapter 18 808

Introduction

The following are five sequels to *Valley of the Gray Moon,*
a trilogy set in the Firelands of Northern Ohio
during 1959 and the early 1960s

Valley of the Gray Moon is told in the first person by Robert Merriam, who is to become the Associate Professor of Religions at Freemont College. This trilogy of mysteries begins in 1959 with the discovery of a 1920s trolley car in an Ohio quarry with its final passenger still inside. Professor Richard Fairchild, Ph.D., dispatches his beautiful secretary, Sally White, and Merriam to help research the history of the car. During the venture, the two fall in love and get engaged. Merriam also begins his search for a legendary valley where a Sulpician missionary was alleged to have converted Native Americans, located somewhere south of Lake Erie.

The second story takes place partly on an island in Lake Erie and also in England and France and involves a World War II German spy. The island, West Bass, is owned by a corporation based in Germany, and the old winery in the basement of a large mansion on the island contains a secret. During the story the Merriams get married and spend their honeymoon in England doing research, which helps to resolve a questionable death on the island.

The third tale combines a radical domestic terrorist's plot against a civil rights leader, and a mysterious man who "haunts" an old inn on the Ohio Canal that is opened by one of Sally's friends. During these adventures Dr. Fairchild acquires for Fremont College the island resort and winery and a Texan's large yacht, both of which are involved in *The Cuyahoga Stories*.

The stories, although taking place between 1959 and 1961 with factors going back into the 1920s, 30s and 40s, are wrapped in the legend of the 16th century Sulpician friar who lived among the Indians in a mystic valley of the gray moon. Others who play a prominent role in the stories include Esther Fairchild, the professor's wife, who writes and illustrates children's stories, Dean Harding, who gets frustrated by his famous professor, and members of Sally White Merriam's family.

Shoeless George

Prologue to Shoeless George

Ohio -- The Early 1960s. Ohio is a land of transition. Once it was The Far West – out beyond the Alleghenies, Indian Lands of the Shawnee, Huron, Erie, and Wyandots. For the French and the English it was the Great Northwest, wet and forested, unexplored, full of riches and wealth for those who would conquer it. By the early 1800s it was a new state, but it had two personalities, separated by the watershed created by ancient glaciers. To the south the rivers flowed to the Ohio; commerce tended to run northeastward or southwestward, as did that great river of commerce. North of that watershed the rivers were prone to wander, then flow northward to Lake Erie – an inland sea of fresh water – providing dockage along their banks. Commerce flowed in an east/west direction, with links between the port cities to industrial cities to their south. On one of these rivers, the Cuyahoga, grew the port city of Cleveland, the Industrial Heart of the Great Lakes. To its harbor and rail yards came iron ore, chemicals, coal, and immigrants to work its mills and factories. From its mighty manufacturing enterprises flowed every imaginable product.

Bridges over the Cuyahoga also bridged the East with the rest of the Industrial Great Lakes, the agriculture and mining of the Midwest. Some spanned the valley, others, at water level, were draw bridges, opening and closing like the valves of a heart to allow the lifeblood of the nation, its commerce, to flow. Yet it had not always been so. For many eons the river had carved its valley and followed its course without the regulation of man. After man came to the river, for how long was he subject to the whims of the water before making the water subject to himself?

The river, the water, the bridges, and the machinery all become a part of the story of those who worked on the Cuyahoga's banks. It is a story of many peoples and races and kinds, a story of love, of war, of fear and greed, and perhaps the story of the constant search for freedom by an industrious people. Their roots and their faith were of many other lands and rivers and bridges, but those valleys, too, were bridged by the Cuyahoga.

The sounds of the Cuyahoga are many: train whistles, steam blasts, clanking and sloshing, deep bellowing boat signals, sirens, bells and the roar of traffic. The river is never quiet, never at peace. A rich milieu of people, lights, chemicals, smells and sounds make the river unique, and those who know it love it for that uniqueness.

Autumn in Northern Ohio in the early Kennedy Era was much more a beginning than an ending of routine life. Although the shipping season was from spring until late fall, when the Great Lakes iced over and prevented the long ore boats from traveling through Superior, Huron and Erie, Labor Day beckoned a return to routine. It marked the time when farmers were bringing in their harvest, setting aside silage for feeding cattle in the winter. It signaled a wrap-up of the baseball season for the Cleveland Indians and the beginning of football season for the Browns and for the many college teams across the region. It meant a return to school or college, an end of vacation, a new concert season for the Cleveland Symphony Orchestra. It warned of the return to dull, gray days and snowstorms, the migration of birds to the south, and the advent of hunting season. It meant pumpkins in the meadows, plans for family get-togethers for Thanksgiving and Christmas. In short, it was one of the best times of the entire year.

Northern Ohio is blessed with an excess of colleges, universities and various special institutes of higher education. Only a few are known for athletic programs. They are places of learning, usually set in small towns and often associated with a religious denomination. Most are simply referred to as "liberal arts" schools, places where Ohioans and others obtain a quality education and prepare for a life hopefully better than their immigrant or farmer or factory worker parents had endured along the river banks.

To some students in Ohio's colleges and universities in the 1960s, success meant going elsewhere, to New York City, Washington, D. C., or Chicago. It meant escaping the gray and grime of industrial Northern Ohio. Success, they hoped, lay elsewhere, in Boston, Philadelphia, or California. Ultimately most found that success lay right where they were, on that bridge between East and West, in those port cities of Northern Ohio that took the raw materials of the world and converted them to usable products. Though it seemed gray and dull, the valleys and plains of Northern Ohio were rich in ways that those in other places would envy. Its valleys were parks, its farms rich in the products of the soil and the land, and its quarries produced minerals that kept the cities strong.

In the basement of an old sandstone building on the campus of Fremont College were the offices of the Religions Department. Richard F. Fairchild, M.Th., Ph.D., was not only chairman of that department, but was also the assistant chaplain of that non-denominational college. He shared the cramped quarters with Dr. Mortimer Simon, Professor of Geology at Fremont, and with Dr. Robert Merriam, his Assistant Professor.

Fremont was a relatively small college, built in the mid-1800s on the east bank of the Sandusky River, but it had an international reputation, largely through the work of several of its professors, including Fairchild. Although he was a very gentle man, now in his forties, Fairchild had a reputation of being severe with his students. Nevertheless, they competed to take his classes, and every seat in his classroom was always filled. Each summer Dr. Fairchild conducted a foreign seminar, usually in Europe, for his upper level religion students. He had a farm on the Portage River near Port Cleland, and worked hard on it all summer raising beef cattle, other than for the few weeks he spent with students on the tour, conducted for college credit. In autumn the professor became more sedentary, and the leather belts he wore tended to move to the outer notches. Dressed in a brown sports coat, bow tie and gray sweater, he gave the impression of what a portly professor ought to look like as he surveyed his students through his brown horn-rimmed glasses.

Fairchild taught most of the upper and graduate level courses, but had turned many of the lower level undergraduate survey courses over to his young associate, who was married to the department's secretary, Sally White Merriam. Tall, stately, and emerald-eyed, Sally's long blond hair usually hung loosely below the base of her slender neck, and it was often difficult for Bob Merriam to concentrate on work when he was in close proximity to his wife. They were, after all, still newly-weds.

A year earlier the Languages and Religions Departments, along with the History, Geography, Political Science and Business Departments, had launched the college's International Studies program, enticing new students from around the country and even from Canada. A combination of languages and social sciences, with an emphasis on both politics and an understanding of the world's major religions, this degree program helped prepare students for a variety of work in international relations, including employment with the State Department or other governmental agencies. The college also had a hotel management department, and even had classes in wine making, as it owned a vineyard.

Chapter 1

November 20, 1960
The Old Harbor Post Office, Overlooking Lake Erie

Sam Whitaker stood outside the old Harbor Post Office smoking a cigarette. His shoulders, wrapped in a light tan wool-lined raincoat, were hunched against the cold, misty fog blowing in from the waterfront down the embankment behind the post office building, a stained red brick building probably dating from the 1920s. It was nearly midnight. The cloudy mist carried the sound of Old Beulah, the foghorn on one of the two small lighthouses that guarded the sandstone breakwater entrance to the Cleveland harbor. In the distance a long ore boat, the *Dudley J. Roswell*, was passing northward from the Cuyahoga River into the harbor behind the breakwater on its way back to Duluth for another load of iron ore. Sam pulled his rumpled hat tighter on his head as a gust of wind blew up from the icy chop within the harbor's deep water.

He knew from experience that no one ever came to that post office after midnight. It was a safe, warm place, and he had discovered a long cupboard beneath a work shelf in the postal box room – the only part of the building never locked – that was about seven feet long and three feet wide. IRS forms were stored there between January and April, but the rest of the year the secluded location made a secure, warm bed. Sam had discovered it when he had obtained a box in the Post Office for whatever mail he might receive. With dinner at St. Vincent House and a warm place to sleep, Sam was comfortable, but lonely.

It had not always been this way for the brown-eyed 39-year old six footer, his brown hair a bit longer than it ought to have been. A successful advertising manager with a degree in marketing from the state university, Sam had once had all the luxuries of the American Dream: A plush office, fancy car, Carolyn, his shapely blond wife, and little Courtney, now eleven. His old home, a pillared Colonial with five bedrooms in a suburb outside town, overlooked a valley. Promotions had come regularly, and Sam had few complaints. Then trouble began.

Sam's ad agency had been taken over by a larger New York firm. At first Sam hoped for promotions, but he soon learned that the role of mergers was what management called "downsizing." Sam's accounts were transferred to New York and Sam transferred to the unemployment line. Despite his qualifications, no other ad agency in town needed him. He was too well qualified, too expensive. Too eager. With the lost job went all the perks and trimmings, including health insurance. When Courtney was injured at school and incurred some high medical bills he had to dip into what little savings he had upon being dismissed, and he quickly found that he and Carolyn were hopelessly in debt. He could no longer meet the mortgage payments on the Valleyview house, Courtney was transferred from the private school she had been attending to public school, and Sam spent every day hunting for a job. That's when he started drinking.

Carolyn had found a job as a teacher, but it was still not enough to cover all the debts. After three months she announced she'd had enough, and was returning to her parent's home in Connecticut, where she had lined up another teaching job. Courtney was going with her, and Sam could do whatever the hell he wanted, which, in her opinion, was to become a drunk. A week after she left, the bank foreclosed on the house. The car had already been traded in on an older model, and Carolyn had taken that. Sam was now not only jobless, but homeless, and the state unemployment benefit was about to expire.

Sam had drifted for months, living on what he had left of his assets in fleabag hotels, drinking in neighborhood bars, and spending the days in endless search for a job. At last he had found one, as a salesman in a small marine insurance office down by the harbor. It paid very little, only an hourly wage, yet it allowed Sam to get cleaned up and salvage what was left of his business clothes. But he still had no place to stay.

It was then that he had learned about St. Vincent House, a shelter down along the waterfront run by a man everyone called Brother Amos. It was located in an old three-story storefront building on River Street. The river ran behind it, and a collection of sleazy bars, pawn shops, warehouses and day labor offices surrounded it. Sam had visited the shelter, and was accepted by Brother Amos. Only twenty-five men, black, white, Hispanic, Native American or Asian, could spend the night, but up to fifty could get dinner and breakfast.

Sam had spent three weeks at the shelter before finding the cupboard in the Post Office. Free housing allowed him to bank most of his earnings so that he could eventually get a down payment on another house, or at least the rent on an apartment. He had already arranged to have half his wages sent to Connecticut. Carolyn had filed for divorce, and Sam figured he was now going to have to live a life much different from that of his recent past. Even with his college degree, he was still a man without a home, and now without a family. He planned to fight the divorce, if he could afford to do so.

Brother Amos was a bearded man in his mid-fifties, an employee of a religious order based in New York. He had been hired because he was a professional social worker as well as a lay member of the order. He generally wore work trousers and a tee-shirt, except when he conducted either Morning or Evening Prayer, when he would don a gray robe of some sort that had a hood and a white rope for a belt. "Guests," as the men were called at the shelter, were encouraged to attend these services, but it was not mandatory. As many of the men worked during the day, attendance was usually very sparse. Brother Amos – Sam had not learned his last name – was a professional social worker with a master's degree. His counseling was gentle and sincere, never in a "you ought to" tone.

Various churches around the city provided dinner each evening at seven, along with sandwiches, cookies and fruit for the men's' lunch the next day. Brother Amos was in charge, but unless a church group forgot to come and he had to prepare a meal from what was in the pantry, those church members did the work. He instructed the meal providers to prepare and serve the "guests" and to clean up afterwards. Most of the men in the shelter did participate in some way, either helping to wash dishes, scrub the showers, change the bedding or sweep the floor of the shelter, which was in an area called "the Flats," near where the river flowed into the harbor.

Then the church volunteers were assigned to various other tasks such as sorting, mending and handing out donated clothing, running the laundry, which contained two washers and two dryers, or simply mingling with the "guests." At least three were required to spend the night, arising at five in the morning to prepare the breakfast for the men at six. They were also required to attend both Evening Prayer the evening before and Morning Prayer at seven, after which most of the men left for the day.

Brother Amos controlled what food the churches were allowed to bring. Left on their own, most would bring fried chicken or spaghetti, or some noodle casserole. While the men always liked those dishes, Brother Amos insisted on nourishing, yet tasteful, meals: Salads, large portions of meat, lots of vegetables, few starches, and something tasty for dessert. The lunch sandwiches were to be wholesome and healthy, but without mayonnaise or other spreads that might spoil. The breakfasts were to include a variety of cereals, meat and eggs – no donuts or pastry. Brother Amos argued that well-nourished men had less craving for alcohol or drugs, and did his best to prove it.

Some of the more conservative church members complained that such rules were ridiculous for "a bunch of bums," but Brother Amos always sat them down and had them read the 25th Chapter of *Matthew*. They usually got the point and either never returned, or never complained again.

Brother Amos kept the men in the shelter busy in other ways. If they were on drugs or alcohol, they had to agree to participate in AA or a drug therapy program. If they were illiterate, they had to take reading classes. Hispanics attended an English as a Second Language class held in the basement of a nearby Catholic church. St. Vincent House provided an address where the men could receive mail or use as a reference. There was a large library where those who wished could read after the ten o'clock "lights out." There was also an arrangement with a small gym in the neighborhood for those who wished to work out or play basketball. Once a week a local physician from the County Health Department visited the shelter to see about any medical problems the men might be experiencing. Brother Amos kept a file on each man, and provided letters of recommendation whenever one of them had an opportunity for a job that would lift him out of homelessness.

There were rules. No smoking, another reason Sam had moved out. If one of the men showed up in the evening drunk, he was thrown out. Brother Amos said, "If you've money to drink or burn, you don't need to be here." After dinner each night there was a television lounge, but Brother Amos had the station locked on the local educational channel. There were tables where the men could play cards or chess, or write a letter, and one phone for personal calls – with a five minute limit. Brother Amos was strict, yet no one complained.

But it was not all these developments that were on Sam's mind as he stood in the misty wind, smoking his final cigarette of the night. He gazed off across the blurry lights of the harbor, and muttered to himself, "Why? Why old Shoeless George? What had he ever done to anyone?"

Sam knew of no answers. He was a man who liked to solve problems, but this one was unsolvable. Over the months at St. Vincent House Sam had gotten to know and love many of the other men who were in similar situations. Some, like him, had become drunks, and Brother Amos, as had his predecessor, helped countless men to overcome that addiction. Others had been on drugs, some to the point of ruining their brains. Still others were ex-convicts, parolees who were unable to find jobs because no one would hire a worker with a criminal record. Many were simply unemployed blue-collar – and a handful of white-collar – victims of recession, men like himself who had lost their jobs when the factories and mills had shut down or businesses merged.

Still others were like George, men who in a different era might have been institutionalized due to disabilities, mental illness or retardation, but who were marginally functional and therefore put on the streets to fend for themselves. George had two problems, a physical deformity and a slow mind – what some might have considered to be mild retardation. He seemed a hopeless figure, but he was often able to find work through the day-labor pool doing gardening or picking up trash.

George's main problem was that his feet were deformed. Some said that as a teenager a car had ran over his feet, crushing the bones. As George said his family consisted of only himself and an elderly aunt, now dead, there was no money for medical care, and the feet grew back deformed. But what feet! They were at least size fourteen. Yet because of the width of the two feet, either from birth defect or the accident, George's feet were diamond-shaped, nearly as wide as they were long. No shoes could fit him. He had hardly any arch in the feet, and they constantly hurt him. The best he was able to do was to wrap his feet in plastic bags and fashion cardboard and plywood boxes to fit around his feet. Thus he waddled more than walked, with a slap-slap-slap sound that would wake others in the shelter whenever George got up at night, which, unfortunately, was frequently.

George tired of the complaints from the others in the shelter and found another place to live, under the ramp to the harbor viaduct. It was a noisy place most of the time, especially when large trucks went up the ramp, but after midnight it generally was quiet until about five in the morning, and George had become accustomed to the racket of the traffic. He'd fixed up a nest for himself from plywood boxes and a few old blankets from the shelter. He had started a collection of junk and trash he called his treasures, things he picked up as he wandered around the inner city or worked an occasional job.

As the ramp was only open at one end, his little hideaway was mostly hidden from all but a few pedestrians who might walk along Sixth Street to a small parking lot underneath the viaduct. Twice the police had forced George out of his ramshackle home, but they had not called in the city Refuse Department to haul away the palace George had fashioned, and George had returned. After the second time the police tended to ignore him, for they knew that there were other homeless men and women living under other bridges and in corners and tunnels all over the city. The end of the recession and "new economy" was making the stock markets soar, but for the poor, the world just got a little more difficult every day.

Brother Amos had referred George to the state welfare department, and those like Sam at the shelter who knew him hoped that he might get some sort of monthly disability check. But the state had not yet qualified him for benefits, and George remained in his nest, enjoying breakfast and dinner at St. Vincent House. He spent most of each day in the waiting room at Downtown Labor, Inc., one of several local day labor firms that fed like parasites on the homeless.

DLI, as the men called it, did provide work for many of the homeless, but it was always hard, heavy work such as loading or unloading furniture, heavy labor at a cold, wet construction site, or cleaning up old buildings before they were either torn down or restored to something else. The pay was minimum wage, but from it DLI kept various amounts including withholding tax, Social Security, and what they called "insurance." Damned little insurance it was – no workers compensation in event of an injury, no health benefits, no other benefits at all. DLI was not even subsistence, but it kept the men out of the bars during the day and gave them pocket money for whatever their other needs might be at evening or on weekends.

Because of George's feet and the box-like contraptions he wore, he got the nickname "Shoeless." Few jobs came along that George could perform. Trash jobs, a few gardening jobs – mostly pulling weeds – and sweeping were about all he was capable of doing. But it did not affect his cheerfulness. George was the happiest person Sam had ever known. He was always smiling, happy with whatever little he got, and always first at the door of St. Vincent House for Evening Prayer, dinner, breakfast, and Morning Prayer. He had about six jokes, and he would re-tell them at every meal. The other men would always laugh, even if they had heard the jokes a hundred times. While they called him Shoeless, nobody made fun of George. Rather, the men tended to protect him, giving him clothing and his favorite, Hershey bars, before he left the shelter each night for his home under the ramp.

That George did not show up every day at the shelter was not unusual. He would occasionally sleep late, or if he had found work that had paid him a few dollars he might walk downtown to buy a hamburger and see a movie at one of the old theaters that still survived on the side streets. Therefore Sam had not paid any attention those first early November mornings when George did not appear in the line for breakfast.

Even that evening at supper Sam had thought little about it when one of the other men commented, "Wonder where Old Shoeless is. Haven't seen him down at DLI for a couple of days now."

"Well, he'd been working out there at that old warehouse the city's restoring. Maybe he struck it rich and moved into a hotel."

"George? Naw, he wouldn't leave that place he's got under the bridge. He's always finding stuff and hauling it back in there. Calls it his treasure house, but it's just a pile of junk. He's probably just sleeping late."

"Maybe he's sick," Brother Amos suggested. "Sam, you go by there on your way to your office, don't you? Take a peek up in there and see if he's okay."

Sam had readily agreed to check on George, and the viaduct ramp was only a block from his route to the dockside office where he worked. After breakfast he left the shelter and started down Sixth Street toward the ramp. In the cold November air he thought about how uncomfortable it must be trying to survive amidst a pile of clutter underneath a bridge. Then his mind wandered to a childhood story about the troll who lived under a bridge and the Billy goat "gruff." He considered that anyone who met George crawling out from under his bridge might well think him to be a troll.

As Sam approached the ramp he noticed a sickly smell that seemed to emanate from under the bridge. When he reached the darkened entrance to George's hideaway, he called out, "George? George, are you there?"

There was no response. Sam had visited George's "nest" several times before, and had noted that while the collection of junk was growing, it nevertheless was neat and orderly. As he entered this time, however, he noted that all of the junk was scattered around like it had been pulled apart in a tornado. Cautiously he approached the blanketed entrance to where

George slept. He noticed a blackened stream of something hard and caked that seemed to have flowed from inside.

In the dim light he pulled back the blanket and peered in. On a pile of rags lay George, his eyes staring blankly upward, a black, crusted hole in the middle of his forehead above his eyes. His body was starting to puff up like a loaf of bread, and fluids were beginning to ooze from his flesh. The smell of death surrounded Sam and he began to gag. He backed out of the passageway beneath the ramp and ran back to the shelter.

* * *

As one might well have predicted, the police took little notice of the murder of George Antopholis. Only Brother Amos had known his last name, a matter of the records he kept on all the regular "guests." George had no living relatives, the file revealed, or so Amos said. At the funeral paid for by the county only a handful of men from the shelter had shown up. There was one vase of flowers. The card read, "From Billy, Downtown Labor, Inc."

Sam had left work early that afternoon to attend the service. George's remains were cremated, and his ashes given to Brother Amos for disposal. That afternoon the city backed a garbage truck up the entrance to the ramp and two city jail trustees had shoveled the trash and treasures of George's nest into the truck. George and his big, square shoeless feet were now just a memory.

Yet it was a memory that Sam could not forget. The police had decided that robbery was the motive, and that some other homeless person had decided to rummage through George's trash collection, and shot George first. As far as the police and the city were concerned, it was a matter of "good riddance."

Sam was unconvinced. He had been homeless long enough to know that most of the men did not own or keep any firearms. A gun would be too valuable. It would be pawned for whatever little cash it would provide. Further, any of the homeless in the downtown or harbor area of the city would have known George, and would know that he was totally harmless. He might well have enjoyed having someone plow through his trash heap, for George loved everyone, and wanted to share everything he had – which wasn't much – with anyone he met. That George was the victim of another homeless person seemed to Sam to be totally bizarre.

Sam stubbed out the cigarette, shook his shoulders to dislodge the moisture from the mist, and entered the lobby of the post office. To one side was the locked entrance to the counters. On the other was a bank of mail slots and post office boxes of various sizes. Below the front window was the long work shelf with the cupboard beneath it. One old milky-white glass globe burned in the center of the room, providing just enough light for those who might enter at night to drop something in the mail slots or to check the contents of their post office box.

Sam opened the cupboard door and crawled inside. He had borrowed a blanket and pad from the shelter, which no one had yet discovered inside the cabinet, and soon he was asleep. His internal clock would awake him about five thirty in the morning, and he would make his way to the shelter for breakfast and a visit to the shower room to shave and clean up for work.

Chapter 2

The fall semester at Fremont College was always exciting for the three permanent members of the Religions Department staff. The small liberal arts college, located east of Toledo near the back of Sandusky Bay, was vibrant with new and excited freshmen, a fairly successful intercollegiate football team, and the prospect of a four day vacation for Thanksgiving during which students could study for December examinations.

Fremont College took its name from the town that was most famous for being the home of President Rutherford B. Hayes. At a nearby fort General William Henry Harrison had received a dispatch in September of 1813 from Commodore Oliver Hazard Perry stating that "we have met the enemy, and they are ours, two ships, two brigs, one schooner and one sloop."

The college operated on a three-semester system, the summer session having longer classes. The Religions Department shared the small corner of the basement in Hayes Hall, across from the Gothic-like chapel, with the Geology and Geography Department, whose chairman, Dr. Simon, usually was traveling or worked at home. The sandstone surfaces of both buildings were now nearly black with decades of smoke, mold and ivy.

Richard Fairchild, although a great scholar and teacher, was often a frustration to the Dean of Fremont College, Dr. Ralph Harding. His star professor had a hobby that occasionally caused the Dean to fear for both the life of Dr. Fairchild and the reputation of the college. Richard Fairchild had a penchant for getting involved in criminal investigations. Local and federal police often called for the professor's assistance in solving some crime or other, and the results often led to headlines that the Dean feared would cast the college in a negative light. He never knew what to expect from his professor of religion and assistant chaplain.

Neither did the professor's wife, Esther, who had been the victim of retaliation against the professor on more than one occasion. She would beg him to not get involved, but his innate curiosity and need to know what lay at the root of every question drove him to chip away at each problem until it was solved. He did his best to please Esther and the Dean, but too often the source of a problem found him before he found it.

While the college's Board of Trustees considered Fairchild the one who best gave an international reputation to the school, Dean Harding found Fairchild to be his most aggravating subordinate. Fairchild seemed to constantly be involved in some matter of criminal intrigue, being physically threatened, injured, or having his home or office ransacked. Yet every time there was such an event, the college seemed to gain only positive public relations. Fairchild was simply a mystery to the Dean, one he was having to learn to tolerate.

Fairchild had a growing national reputation as both a religious history scholar and as a detective who was often able to help the police find the solution to unsolved mysteries. Fairchild's investigative skills had brought both fame and some degree of fortune to Fremont College. But the Dean, often at emotional odds with his famous professor, was not quite in favor of the way that fame or fortune had been acquired. Only the gratitude of the Board, along with Fairchild's international scholastic reputation, kept Dean Harding from putting a lock and chain on his famous professor.

Dr. Fairchild, "Richie" to his friends, was in his autumnal weight-gaining phase. Whenever he became overly absorbed in any academic project he became too busy -- or simply forgot -- to exercise, and it often showed. Esther, a children's book artist, would occasionally rant and rail at him without much success, just as she scolded him about getting overly involved in criminal matters, where results affected her almost as much as it did her forgetful husband. The couple had no children of their own, so the light-haired professor's wife tended to act somewhat like a mother hen to her academically-absorbed spouse. But neither Bob, a former infantry soldier who had kept his tall, slender shape, nor Sally Merriam, who were constantly around the often gruff bespectacled professor, took notice or made comment.

"What has you so intent lately," Bob asked the portly scholar one morning.

"A new course for the January semester," he replied. "I need to get it finished by mid-December so Dean Harding will approve it for registration. It will be called 'Religion and International Politics,' part of the International Studies Program, and I want it to have at least a 300 level rating.

"I suspect our nation gets into difficulty overseas because our leaders do not totally understand how important religious issues are in many countries," Fairchild said, almost ranting. "Look, for example, at the Hindu and Muslim clashes in India and Pakistan, or the Sunni versus Shiite disputes within Islam. Then there are the Muslim, Orthodox and Catholic conflicts -- for centuries -- in the Balkans. And there's Israel. Good Lord, that could be a course in and of itself!"

"Is that where your summer tour will be this year, Israel?"

"No, it had already been planned for Greece, so we'll have to stick to the schedule." Richard Fairchild and his wife led an annual tour, usually to Europe, for upper level classmen who were religion or International Studies majors. The tours were popular and counted for three hours of credit, but fewer than half of those who applied to go were actually selected. Generally those with some foreign language ability were picked first.

"What textbook are you going to use?" Merriam asked.

"That's what I'm working on. There really isn't any. I think what we'll do the first year is use a good syllabus, and then write a textbook for future use. I've talked to Dean Harding about it, and he agrees that we ought to have our own little publishing company here at the college. He's going to bring it up at the next board meeting. This text may be the first. Want to help write it?" That Fairchild was apparently receiving approval for his new course from Dean Harding was significant.

"Sure! Do an outline and assign me some chapters."

Fairchild had simply grunted his appreciation of his assistant's agreement to help, and handed a stack of scribbled notes to Merriam's wife to decipher and type. Sally, who had been department secretary before Merriam had arrived at the college, had finally talked her boss into getting her an electric typewriter, replacing the old Remington manual that had produced sermons, textbooks, academic papers and class notes for eons before she had arrived in the department as a part-time student and employee.

* * *

Thanksgiving, along with other major holidays, was always special at St. Vincent House. One of the downtown hotels always donated enough turkey and trimmings for the fifty men, and some of the churches sent whole cadres of volunteers to serve the meal and to clean up afterwards. The next day the men spent most of the day decorating the shelter for Christmas, putting up a large tree in the chapel, and stringing lights around the entrance and over the façade in front of the roof.

On Saturday the men who had no families to visit spent the day like most other Saturdays, loafing around the shelter, reading a book, or walking uptown to see a movie. There was always a temptation to Sam to stop in a local bar and have a drink, but he knew that it would be a fatal mistake, that he could not prevent himself from getting drunk again and losing all that he had gained since finding St. Vincent House. Sundays, likewise, were lazy days for the men. After Morning Prayer Brother Amos usually changed into a suit and went to one of the big downtown churches. While he had both a bedroom and a small parlor, as well as his office, in his little apartment at the back of the second floor, he seldom left the shelter except to shop or attend church. Those who wished could join him, but few ever did. Brother Amos was from Boston, and had no family in the Cleveland area.

On that particular Sunday after Thanksgiving at supper that evening after the dinner prayer was said, Brother Amos made an announcement.

Those who had been at the shelter for more than a year might have expected it, but to the others it was news.

"As you all know," he began, "each year I take a few weeks off. I visit with some of my family over Christmas, then take a trip somewhere for a week or so, and then go on a retreat at our order's friary in New York. One of the others from the order usually comes down to watch over you guys while I'm away, but this year none of them are available. "So, I think you are in for a treat. One of the professors – he's also a chaplain – at Fremont College west of here has agreed to come down over the school's year end break and mind the store for us. He's been here a few times before, so some of you may remember him. His name is Richard Fairchild."

"Is he the fat guy with the glasses?" one of the regulars asked. "He was a lot of fun, and had a lot of great stories. He's like a detective or something."

"Well, I guess he's a bit chubby, but that sounds like Richie. Now, I don't want you guys calling him 'Richie.' To you he will be either 'Professor,' or 'Doctor' Fairchild. And I've warned him that he's not to put up with any shenanigans. He also works as a prison chaplain sometimes, so he knows how to keep control. But then, I'm not worried. You're a great bunch of guys, and I'm proud of you."

"When's he coming?" another asked.

"At the end of the third week in December. I guess his wife is going to be visiting her family in Pennsylvania. While he may sneak over there for a day, he wants to let his wife spend more time with her sisters, and I guess they don't need him around!"

Several of the men, those who had been or still were married, chuckled. Then one of the men asked, "Where are you going this year?"

"Oh, I've got some cousins that are taking a trip to the Caribbean and have asked me along. I'm not sure of the itinerary, but if I go, I'll send you guys a postcard. But I've got some other plans, too. Not quite sure what may develop."

"Send us one of those bikinied island girls!" another joked.

Dinner over, the men returned to whatever activity was at hand, and Brother Amos retired to his apartment. From a locked cupboard he pulled out a bottle of single malt Scotch and poured a glassful, then relaxed in his reclining chair to read a novel.

* * *

Thanksgiving was special to the Merriams. Before he had married Sally, Bob had gone to his home in the Philadelphia suburbs for Thanksgiving. But he found that the festivities there among his parent's friends somewhat cold and remote from the warmth and hospitality he had come to love in the Northern Ohio world of his wife. His father's business associates were uninterested in the social sciences that encrusted Robert Merriam, Ph.D., Associate Professor of Religions at Fremont College. Their day, following a catered turkey dinner, would probably consist of some business chatter and the traditional Army-Navy game. Some Thanksgiving, he knew, he would have to take Sally to Philadelphia. But then he imagined how his father's business associates would respond to having Sally in their midst -- he suspected that she would create quite a distraction from their usual interests.

Much better was the invitation to his in-law's home in Norwell, where the White's presented a home-cooked dinner fit for a king. George White, his father-in-law, always seemed to be interested in whatever project Bob and Sally had going, and was especially interested in any adventure in which Richard Fairchild was involved. He, too, had been drawn into several of them, and the idea of "being there" when the professor solved the mysteries he encountered stimulated White's natural curiosity. In one of Fairchild's cases George White had accompanied the professor, whose hobby was investigating old crimes, in a search for the location of an old rail car. The next year he had been present when a former Nazi was arrested by the Coast Guard while fleeing the country with a case of gold bullion. That, too, had occurred on a Thanksgiving Day.

The White's home, an older multi-story house on a shady side street, was crowded when the Merriams arrived. Two of Sally's older brothers and their families were also visiting, and young children were romping around the living room and dashing into the kitchen to check on the progress of the dinner. Sally's mother quickly put her to work setting the table, and she assisted her two sisters-in-law with other kitchen tasks. It was the first time that Bob had met one of his brothers-in-law, and, as George served them each a bourbon-on-the-rocks, the four men conversed in the living room.

"What's the Professor up to this fall?" George White asked Bob.

"He's planning some new courses for the next semester. As if we haven't enough courses now!"

"I hear your Professor Fairchild is quite a detective," Jim White, Sally's oldest brother, said.

"Yes, he does manage to get into a few criminal cases now and then."

"Dad said he had helped capture the guys who tried to murder that civil rights leader last year," Jack White, the next oldest brother, added. "Was he really that involved?"

"We all were, but I didn't know it at the time," Bob replied. "Yes, he was actually with the assassins aboard their yacht and with them when they planted the bomb that was supposed to go off during Thomas Jefferson Singletary's speech at the hotel in Fremont. I saw them in the lobby, but Richie -- that's what we call Fairchild -- pretended he didn't know me. I almost blew his cover! The FBI were right there, too, and picked them all up as they left town."

"And Richie sued the bastards and got their yacht and a lot of money!" George White added. "Gave the big cabin cruiser to the College. But after all, they'd blown his house apart."

"What?" Jim exclaimed.

"Yeah," Bob answered. "They'd stolen a truckload of dynamite, killed the driver and removed much of the dynamite to a warehouse to use in the assassination attempt, then left the truck with the dynamite on it across the railroad tracks behind Richie's farmhouse. A passenger train hit the truck, and the explosion half demolished the Fairchild's home, and killed several people on the train."

"Good heavens! What did they do?" Jack inquired.

"First, they helped the passengers and crew. But Richie and Esther, his wife, were taking a group of students to Europe a few days later, so they stayed with us until then. By the time they got back, their house had been repaired," Bob explained.

"What are the Fairchilds doing this Christmas?" George asked. "Maybe they could come here for Christmas and the boys could get to meet them."

"No, I heard that Esther was going to visit her sister, and Richie's going to run some shelter down in Cleveland over the holidays, while the regular guy takes a vacation. He works down there occasionally on a weekend. It's some church-related thing, I guess."

After another hour of conversation and refilled drinks, the dinner was finally ready and the men joined the rest of the family around the dining room table. George said a grace that was traditional in the White family, and they all sat down to heaping platters of food and great conversation.

* * *

The blizzard that hit that night left the city in a snowy white tomb. Eight inches of soft flaky snow had clogged the streets and paralyzed the arteries in and out of town, stranding many who had planned to return home that night or the next morning after the Thanksgiving holiday. The airport was closed, and only the trains were running on schedule. The men in the shelter were delighted, as they knew most would find work the next day shoveling snow. Blizzards always brought calls to DLI for snow shovelers.

Sam wondered whether his office would even be open the next morning. But it didn't matter. He had a key, and if he were the only one there, available for business, his boss would be pleased.

Before leaving the shelter for the post office, Sam stopped by the clothing closet, being manned by a young dark-haired girl from one of the suburban churches. "Any rubber boots in there?" he asked. "Large size?"

"I think I did see a pair," she replied, turning toward a shelf at the back of the closet. "Yes, here they are. Try these on."

The boots slipped easily over Sam's shoes. Although just slightly too large, they were warm and comfortable, and Sam was grateful for the protection they would offer against the ever-deepening snow outside. He thanked the girl, and then asked if there were any warm scarves. This, too, she found, and though it was a bit worn — most of the clothing were donations of used items — it was just what Sam needed. Those who could contributed something to the clothing fund, and Sam stuffed a five dollar bill into the box on the closet shelf, then bid everyone good night, and headed out into the cold.

The only vehicle Sam saw on his four block walk to the harbor post office was a city truck with a snow plow up front and a salt spreader on the back. The sidewalk was clogged deep with snow, and with every step Sam thought the suction would pull the boots off his feet. He crossed into the street and walked along the plowed area until he reached the post office. It was too cold that night for a smoke, so he entered and stored the boots at the far end of the cupboard.

On Monday morning only a gray glow represented daylight. Fortunately the furnace in the post office had kept going all night, and Sam's bed beneath the counter was cozy and warm. He crawled out, stretched, and put his shoes and the rubber boots back on his feet. Nothing was moving outside. The path that the plow had made the night before had drifted over, and was barely visible. Still, what remained of it was easier to travel than the sidewalk, and Sam retraced his steps to St. Vincent House for breakfast.

That morning he stayed for Morning Prayer, saying the *Venite* and other prayers along with those who had not yet departed for DLI or, for the church volunteers, their homes in the suburbs. Then he again entered the frigid air outside the shelter and started down Sixth Street toward the Harbor. As he passed the entrance to the ramp he thought about Shoeless George, and wondered how George had managed to survive cold nights such as that of the past evening.

His mind was still on George as he reached the wharf area and entered the door at the side of General Dock #7, climbing the steps to the second floor office of the Taylor Marine Insurance Agency. He noted that the little restaurant on the ground floor — usually open from about six in the morning to six at night, was locked and unlighted. Sam unlocked the door of the office, switched on the light, and immediately went to the thermostat, which had been set low for the weekend, to increase the heat in the suite of rooms that constituted the Taylor Agency.

At his desk he found the papers on which he had been working the previous week, and began afresh to calculate some of the numbers needed to place coverage for a client. About forty minutes later the phone rang. It was Harry Taylor, who owned the agency.

"Sam!" he replied as Sam answered the phone. "Glad you made it in. No way in hell I'll be able to get in today. Our street is completely blocked, and the weather report says another dose is on the way tonight. County says the roads may be blocked all week, and to stay off them if you don't have somewhere urgent to go. Think you can man the shop for a few days?"

"Of course, Mr. Taylor! There's light and heat — at least so far — and I think I'm familiar enough with all the various coverages that I can get along okay. In fact, I'm glad to be here."

"Yeah. Well, how was your Thanksgiving?"

"Oh, great. I spent it with friends here in the city. How was yours?"

"Oh, the usual. Ate too much, drank too much, and laid around.

"Say," he continued, "where the hell you staying these days. Last address I had for you was some dump down in the Flats. You still there?"

"Oh, I stop in there for meals, but have moved to a better location downtown." Sam did not want his boss to know he was living in a cupboard in a post office.

"Oh. Well, I'm glad you're close by. Takes a lot off my mind to know someone will be there."

"Don't worry, Mr. Taylor. And if anything comes along that I'm not sure about, I'll give you a call. I suspect, however, that most of the inquiries are going to be about claims — shipment delays and that sort of thing."

"You're right. Do you know where the claim forms are?"

"I've a pad at my desk, and there's more in the supply room, I think."

"Yeah, second shelf on the left. Well, Sam, you hold the fort, and I'll try to make it in before the end of the week if I can."

"Okay. Bye."

Sam hung up the phone, slid his chair back and put his feet up on the desk as he looked out the window toward the west. The heavy gray clouds hung low in the sky. As the temperature had dropped after the snow fell there was no slush or ice yet, except where the salt spreaders had melted some of the snow. From the window Sam could see both the harbor and the city skyline. There was no movement visible in either, no traffic outside, no trucks backing up to the warehouses, no ships berthed at the docks. The city was cold and silent. If new snow fell that night, it would remain a dead city for a week.

Sam's mind again returned to his old friend, George. Sam had never seen a murder before, except in the movies. He'd seen deceased people in funeral homes, but not before the morticians had performed their art. Finding a dead body — especially of someone he knew — had been a shock. He kept coming back to the same old question: Why? Why poor old helpless George, who had never hurt anyone.

* * *

By Friday of the following week the city had returned to normal. The first week streets remained clogged by snow and ice, but by the next week people had become accustomed to the ice and cold, had absorbed the crisp spirit in the air promising a White Christmas, and the city seemed cheerful. The big department stores downtown had decorated their windows, and on Saturday, after breakfast, Sam had wandered around the downtown area looking at the toy trains, mechanical elves, blinking lights and the delighted children who were excited about seeing Santa Claus.

Sam longed to see Courtney, but could not afford the trip to Connecticut. He had already purchased, wrapped and mailed a number of packages to her, as well as to Carolyn. But with more than half his salary going to Carolyn for child support, no vacation time, and no other benefits, Sam was barely existing on the meager remains of his earnings. His savings account was growing very slowly.

Harry Taylor had been delighted with Sam's effort during the blizzard, one of the worst, the newscasters reported, in decades. But then they always claimed such storms were "the worst." Taylor had invited Sam to join him and his family for Christmas dinner, and Sam had accepted. For that he would need a new suit, something other than an ill-fitting recycle from the clothing closet at the shelter. He spent the morning searching for one that would fit both his body and his budget, and by noon had purchased a dark gray suit, new white shirt, and a subdued maroon tie to go with it.

Like so many of the residents – full and part time – of St. Vincent House, Sam had a locker in the dormitory where he kept his valuables. It gave him a sense of permanency and security at the shelter. As the lockers were all padlocked, there was none of the pilferage so common in other street shelters. Sam walked back to the little storefront in the Flats with his purchases to place them in the locker.

He arrived just as Brother Amos was getting ready to leave. A taxi awaited him, and he was carrying a large suitcase as he came out the front door.

"So you're off, then, Brother Amos?"

"Oh, hello, Sam. Yes, off to the airport. Richard got here about an hour ago, so I'm leaving the place in good hands. What you got there? New clothes?"

"My boss invited me to Christmas dinner. Couldn't go in that old brown suit I've been wearing to the office, so I had to make a purchase."

"Well, good. One of these days you're going to be successful again and be leaving us. I wish all the men were as ambitious and eager as you, Sam. Many of them are their own worst enemies."

"I was too, if you remember when I first arrived."

"Yes, but you have an objective. You want your family back, and that's important. I hope you accomplish that. Well, I'm away, so have a great Christmas, Sam, and keep me in your prayers, as I will you."

"Thank you, Brother Amos. And Merry Christmas to you, too."

As the taxi drove off Sam entered the building and started up the front stairway to the dormitory. There were about thirty lockers at the front, then twenty-five small cubicles, each containing an army cot, a locker, a straight-back chair, and a small dresser. A thick dark curtain enclosed each, providing the guests with relative privacy. Beyond that were the shower rooms and lavatories, and a back stairway leading to another exit. As a licensed shelter, various governmental departments periodically inspected St. Vincent House, including the Fire Department. It was as much a halfway house as it was a shelter, and was considered one of the better such facilities in the city.

Sam placed his suit and shirt in his locker, pulled out a thick book he had been reading, and headed for the lounge downstairs. As he entered, another man, somewhat rotund with wire rimmed glasses and a wide smile, who was sitting in the lounge looked up and said "Hello." He was a man in his mid-fifties, with thick graying hair.

"Hi," Sam answered. "You must be Dr. Fairchild. Brother Amos said you had arrived."

"Guilty!" the professor answered. "And you are ...."

"Sam Whitaker. I've been here about eight months, but I spend the nights elsewhere. It frees up a bed, and I sleep better."

"Where do you stay?"

"Believe it or not, in a cupboard at the post office. It's dry, warm, and available. No one else has discovered it, and I don't want the other men to know where I go, as they tend to talk a lot at DLI, and guys from other shelters would be there in an instant."

"DLI?"

"Downtown Labor. It's a day labor pool, where a lot of the guys get temporary work, usually heavy labor jobs. But I have a job with an insurance agency down on the docks, so the shelter here and the post office are very convenient."

"Interesting. What are you reading, Sam?"

"It's called *A Distant Mirror*. It's all about the middle ages."

"I know. In fact, I've met its author, Barbara Tuchman. What got you interested in that?"

"Well, I minored in history in college, and have always been interested in it, especially medieval history. Brother Sam said you were a professor. What do you teach, Dr. Fairchild?"

"Medieval history is one of my subjects. I'm head of the religion department at Fremont. Where did you go to school?"

"The state university in Kent. Say, you're not the man who wrote that book about the French monastic republics, are you?"

"Oh, you do have an interest in the subject! Yes. I've written several on the topic. Often take our more senior students on a field trip over to Europe each summer. Well, I can see we're going to have some interesting chats over the next month. By the way, Sam, please call me 'Richie'."

"Brother Amos said not to."

"Ha! He would. Well, then, call me 'Doc.' When people call me Dr. Fairchild I seem to want to reach for my grade book."

"Okay, Doc. Brother Amos said you'd been here a few times before, so I guess you know the routine."

"I hope so. Most of the men are probably new since I was here last, but I recognize a few names on the list. But I didn't see George's name. Did he move out?"

"George is dead. Someone shot him – murdered him – about a month ago, up in a little nest he'd made for himself under the ramp to the viaduct."

"Murdered him?"

"Shot him between the eyes, and rummaged through what he called his treasure house, a pile of junk he'd collected from all over the city."

"Who…"

"The police said it must have been another homeless person but, Doc, I don't believe that. Most of the homeless men are harmless, unless they're drunk, and in that case, they're more apt to use a knife as a weapon, not a gun. Guns get pawned quickly. I'm the one who found George, and it didn't look to me like any drunken brawl."

"Why was George out on the street at night?"

"Well, as you know, he had feet that wouldn't fit in shoes, and when he would get up at night the guys complained that he made too much noise paddling around. I experienced it. He was a great guy, but he snored and made a lot of noise at night. He would get tired of the complaints and move into the park for a while. He moved under the bridge about the same time I moved to the post office. But he kept a locker here, and we both came here for our meals, like about half the guys do."

"Hmm. What did he do during the day?"

"He practically lived at DLI, waiting to be sent out on a job. When he got work it was usually just pulling weeds or picking up trash, things he could do with his disabled feet. He didn't get much work, but it kept him out of mischief."

"Had he been working before he was killed?"

"I don't know, Doc. One of the guys said he'd been on a job for the city. They might know, but I doubt they know where he had actually been working."

"Who would?"

"Probably the guys that run DLI. They keep records on all the men. You sound like you're interested, Doc. I remember now that one of the men said you were some sort of detective. Are you?"

"A detective? No, not hardly," the professor laughed. "But I have been involved in some criminal investigations and have been of some assistance to the police in solving some crimes. I guess it's just my nature to be inquisitive and to want to dig out facts."

"Doc, if you want to dig out facts on who shot George, I'd like to help."

"Thank you, Sam. But we'll have to wait and see how busy I am around here before we go off playing Sherlock Holmes."

The professor sat quietly for a moment, then asked, "Did George have any family?"

"I guess not. Only some of the fellows from here were at his funeral. Brother Amos knew his last name. Had some sort of file on him. But I understand that an aunt had raised him, and she was already dead when he came here. He had applied for disability payments, but you know how slow that process is. It might have provided him enough for a hotel room in one of the flophouses downtown, if he would have left that place under the bridge."

"Did you ever hear his last name?"

"Yes, but I don't recall what it was. It sounded Greek. But it would be in his file in Brother Amos's office."

"I'll have a look sometime."

The two men chatted for over an hour, the subject switching to families, colleges, medieval history, and finally to what church group was bringing the dinner that evening. About four a group from a suburban church arrived and unloaded their food into the kitchen. Dr. Fairchild then rang a bell to indicate the start of Evening Prayer, and the church group, Sam, and about a dozen others who were in the shelter moved into the chapel for the brief service.

Chapter 3

Mildred and Fred Rogers were planning their New Year's Eve party. All Fred's business associates at the Rogers Chemical Company would be invited, along with some of the Environmental Protection Agency men Fred had been dealing with for several years. With their wives it would be a group of at least forty, but such parties fit well in the Rogers' large shoreline mansion in Lakewood. Mildred was arranging for the caterer and the decorations. Fred was in charge of the liquor.

Fred hated these annual parties. He hated holidays in general, found them boring, expensive and generally unproductive. He much preferred private dinner parties, with only one or two other couples, but Mildred had started a tradition, and he had to comply for another year. Mildred, however, loved the affair – it gave her the chance to show off the Rogers' home, with its view of the water and the festive decorations placed in the terraced garden. But it was all just "a damned nuisance" to Fred.

Mildred was going over Fred's address book, deciding who to ask and who to exclude. From year to year the list changed as new clients were added and former ones deleted. Mildred's own friends would be invited to a separate Christmas party, to be held in the afternoon a few days before Christmas. The New Year's party was strictly for Fred's business.

"What about the Abbottsons this year? Is Larry still buying from you?" Mildred asked Fred as he sat making out a list of all the different liquors he would need.

"Yes. Don't exclude Larry and what's-her-name ..."

"Judy."

"Yeah, Judy. Good lookin' dame. Their son's in the business now, too. Larry Junior. Better add him and his date."

"Who's this Billy Aronso? His name has the word 'George' in brackets after it."

"What?"

"Aronso. You want to invite him?"

"Let me see that." Fred took the address book and studied the name. It had no address, just a phone number.

"No, you don't want him," he replied, handing her back his address book. "He occasionally does some work for the company, but he's not a customer or anyone we'd want at our party. That's the guy where we got George. Remember? He did some yard work for us. The crippled guy."

"Oh yes, George," she replied. "Poor man. I always felt sorry for him, but he was always singing and happy. Okay, that's all the As. How about the Bentons?"

"Yeah, include the Bentons. I'll have to get some fruit juices or soft drinks. Jimmy Benton doesn't drink. Makes a big point about it. But he eats a lot." Fred wrote "soft drinks for Jimmy" on his pad.

"The Boyles?"

"Oh God, yeah. Tim Boyle will drink a bottle of Scotch all by himself. But we can't leave the Boyles out."

As the guest list went on to the other letters of the alphabet, Fred finished his own list. This would be an expensive party, but it had been a good year for Rogers Chemical Company, and Fred had many debts to pay. His annual party was a good way to pay most of them.

Mildred had come to the last pages of the address book. "Gary Williams and his wife?"

"Of course. Oh, and also invite that boy of theirs, Eddie. He's around Kelly's age, gone off to college, and I suspect Gary's going to try to get him to come work at the plant when he graduates. Supposed to be going to Yale, I think. May as well let him see what the thing's all about."

"Okay. What about the Youngs?"

"No. Otto doesn't buy anything from us any longer. Cross them off."

* * *

It was several days before Richard Fairchild had an opportunity to do any research into the murder of George Antopholis. He had reviewed the file that Brother Amos kept on the disabled man, but found very little in it. There was only the form Brother Amos filled out on each resident when they arrived, along with copies of two letters Brother Amos had sent to the welfare department on George's behalf and a reply from the welfare department advising that they would look into George's case.

Although the file was thin, the professor learned that George was thirty-five years old at the time of his death. He had been born in Buffalo to Greek immigrant parents who were killed in an auto accident when he was ten. His father's sister, also an immigrant, had taken care of him. He had left school at age fourteen as he could not pass any of the courses. The aunt, Anna Bergeman, had died when George was about thirty. All his widowed aunt's money had gone to pay her final medical bills, and she died broke. George had claimed no knowledge of any other family.

George had drifted from city to city after that, seeking work, and finding little that he could do with his disabled feet and weak mental abilities. Brother Amos had found him in the park sleeping on a bench, and brought him back to the shelter, where he had lived for more than a year before moving under the bridge. He said that he had been at the shelter before, some months ahead of when Amos became the manager. Several months before George's murder Brother Amos had filled in forms for the state welfare department on his behalf as George could neither read nor write very well, only a few simple words, and the state promised to investigate. George was dead before they completed their investigation.

The county had picked up the funeral bill. There had not been much of an autopsy beyond recovery and classification of the bullet lodged in George's skull, a .45-caliber slug. His locker at the shelter had contained only a cap and a pair of the cardboard and plywood boxes George wore on his feet, Brother Amos told the police. The next day he scattered George's ashes into the harbor. George was at peace and his feet no longer hurt.

Getting information from the man who ran Downtown Labor, Inc. was going to be difficult, Richard Fairchild discovered the morning he stopped in at the small office on River Street. First, the man in charge was busy. Fairchild anticipated that he would also be suspicious of anyone who asked too many questions. The manager had no reason to answer inquiries about the men who worked out of their firm, and to the professor's first inquiry he responded, "All that information is confidential and can't be released."

Dr. Fairchild considered his options. He could continue attempting to win the confidence of the DLI manager in hopes of getting the information he wanted. He could perhaps use some subterfuge to obtain the data, or he could take a hostile approach, relying on the word of the men that DLI was withholding too much from their pay, and threatening them with an official investigation.

He decided on a direct approach. "Look, Mr. Ahh...."

"Aronso. Billy Aronso."

"Aronso, I'm a professor doing some research. One of your clients here was of Greek parentage, and I'm trying to trace his family. I'm sure you would remember him. His name was George Antopholis, a man with disabled feet."

"Yeah, we all knew George. He was one of the guys. The clients are the ones that hire them through us. But I don't know nothin' about George, except it was hard to get him a job he could do."

"George was killed, and...."

"Yeah, somebody shot the poor bugger. The guys told me, an' I sent some flowers to his funeral. Sort of miss the guy. He was always telling jokes. We'd all heard them before, but they were always new to George. Poor dumb guy."

"What I'd like to know is where George was working before he was killed."

"Well, like I said, Mister, our records are confidential. We don't give out information on the guys, because we're never sure who's asking, and if they get garnished, it's a whole hell of a lot of paper work for us. But I can tell you this. George didn't get much work, but when he did, it was generally for the city Refuse Department, cleaning out old buildings. They'd come around every so often, pick up a bunch of guys, and where they took 'em, I don't know. Nor care. We bill the city from when they leave until they get delivered back, and that's all the records we would have."

"No one else? Just the City?"

"Ahh, hell! Let me look." Aronso moved over to an index file and shuffled through it for a few moments, finally pulling out a card.

"Yeah," he continued. "He usually worked for the City. But there are a couple of entries here in the last couple months for the Rogers Chemical Company. They've a big plant down on the river, and some sort of garden. Believe they had George working in that, as I recall. He worked hard, and they liked him, so they asked for him the next time they needed someone. Look, I shouldn't be telling you this. My partner'd have a tizzy if he knew I was giving out information on the guys. I don't know what you're researching, but it's probably a dead end if it involves George."

"This will be very helpful, Mr. Aronso. I do appreciate your help."

"You say you're a professor. You ain't that new guy runnin' that shelter down here in the Flats, are you? The guys living there said some professor was coming in for a month while the guy that runs it is away."

"Yes," Fairchild replied. "I'm helping out at St. Vincent House while Brother Amos is out of town."

"Well, hell! That's where George used to stay. I bet the guys can tell you where he was working. They're like a bunch of gossiping old women over there!"

* * *

After dinner that evening Richard Fairchild signaled to Sam Whitaker to come to the office. Sam had been reading his thick history book, but did not mind the interruption.

"What's up?" he asked as he entered the small room and sat down in the chair across the desk from the professor.

"I went down to the day labor office today, and talked to one of the owners about George."

"Which one?"

"A man named Aronso."

"Billy. Yes, he'd talk with you, but the other guy, Jack something-or-other, is a skunk. Did you learn anything?"

"Apparently most of the jobs George got were for the city, but he also had a couple of assignments to a company called Rogers Chemical. He did some gardening there, Aronso thought. Do you know anything about them?"

"The city hires a lot of the guys, mostly for labor. I've heard a couple of the fellows mention Rogers Chemical, but it's usually warehouse work, loading and unloading trucks. The place is up the river from here, a couple of miles. One of those smokestack places that looks like a jungle gym."

"Would any of the men here know when he worked there?"

"I doubt it, Doc. After George was killed we all talked about him, and I remember asking if anyone knew where he had been working. All they knew was that he'd done some work for the city. Remember, a lot of those guys at the labor pool are from other shelters or just out on the street. If any of them had worked with George, it would be like trying to find a needle in a haystack to locate him. Half those guys don't even give their right names to DLI. There are more Smiths, Joneses and Garcias down there than in the phone book."

"I see. But from what you told me, it would seem logical that George might have found something, picked it up, and taken it back to his place under the bridge. Someone saw him, wanted whatever it was, and came to get it."

"That's how I read it, too, Doc. But what was it, and where did it come from?"

"Maybe the city would have some records of places they cleaned out."

"That would be worth a try, I guess. Somebody at the Refuse Department has got to remember Shoeless," Sam agreed.

Chapter 4

Another heavy snow fell the week before Christmas. With it came a blow that Sam Whitaker had half expected – the arrival of the IRS forms, which completely filled the cupboard beneath the work counter in the post office. On Monday evening when he arrived back at the post office after dinner at the shelter he found the cupboard stuffed full of various forms. His blanket was gone, obviously discarded by whoever filled the cupboard, but also alerting the postal workers that someone might be occupying the place at night. Still, it was a lot warmer on the floor than outside in the snow, but it would be uncomfortable without his blanket. He couldn't return to the shelter, as all the bunks were claimed, although he anticipated that the professor might bend the rules for him and let him sleep in one of the cots for the volunteers.

Sam was standing outside the post office smoking a cigarette and trying to decide what to do when a police car stopped in front, and the officer rolled down his window.

"Anything wrong?" the police officer called.

"No, just checking my post office box before I go home," Sam replied.

"Oh, well, we got a report that someone might be staying inside at nights. Have you seen anyone around?"

"Not a soul. Who'd want to stay here?"

"Probably some bum. You got a car?"

"No."

"Well, the buses are all late 'cause of the snow. You want a lift somewhere?"

Sam decided it was time to make a move. He needed to start living like a normal person once again. His savings would more than cover the first and last month deposit on a small apartment he had seen advertised that was within walking distance of the docks, and he had enough in his wallet to cover a night or two in one of the cheaper hotels in town. He decided quickly.

"Do you know the Craythorn Hotel, a couple blocks from here?"

"Yeah, I can drop you there. Come on."

Sam and the policeman chatted briefly on the short drive to the small, inexpensive three-story brick hotel where Sam had stayed a few times before. "You look familiar," the policeman said as Sam had climbed into the car.

"Oh? Ahh, don't know why, Officer…."

"Segretti. Andy Segretti."

"Oh, I do know why," Sam exclaimed. "You were the officer who came when I found old Shoeless George dead under the viaduct ramp."

"Yeah, that's right! That's where I saw you. The crime unit took over, but I was first on the scene. Heck of a thing. All of us in the precinct knew George, of course, but, hell, a pile of junk under a bridge is no place for a man to live. We'd run him out, and a day later he was back. Whatever happened?"

"Apparently nothing. Your police department thinks he was killed by some other homeless guy, but I don't believe that." By this time the police car had pulled up in front of the Craythorn, but Sam waited while the policeman replied.

"You don't?" he said. "Why not."

"First, and I confess I've spent a night or two in a shelter, the guys don't have guns. Too valuable. It's the first thing they'd pawn if they had one. Second, if someone had wanted something George had, he'd have given it to him. He was always wanting people to take things he had found. If it was a homeless guy who killed him, most likely he'd have used a knife. I mean, who's going to shoot old harmless George between the eyes, for God's sake?"

"Yeah, that's logical," Officer Segretti replied. "So who do you think did it?"

"Well, there's this new guy running the shelter down there in the Flats. I stop in occasionally, and this new guy, he's a college professor, and I were talking about George, and we think that perhaps George found something someplace where he was sent to work, you know, cleaning out old buildings or pulling weeds, things that George was able to do. Whatever he found someone wanted back, and killed him for it."

"Hmm. Where had he been working?"

"The professor went down to the day labor office, and as far as he could find out, most of George's recent work assignments were with the city's Refuse Department, clearing out old buildings. The professor said he would try to find out if the city has any records of where George might have been assigned."

"This is fascinating, mister. I'm no detective, but what you're saying makes a lot of sense. Tell you what. Let me talk to the Lieutenant tomorrow and see if I can get them to take another look at George's file. Maybe I can get your professor friend an appointment with the guys at Refuse to see what they have. Give me your name, and where I can reach you."

"Sam Whitaker. I'm planning to move to an apartment over on Ninth in a day or so, but you can reach me at my office, the Taylor Marine Insurance Agency, down on the docks in the daytime."

"I know the place. Eat in that little café there all the time. Well, thanks, Whitaker. Have a great Christmas, and I'll keep in touch."

The next morning Sam called the landlord of the apartment house on Ninth from his office, and made arrangements to stop by at noon to see the furnished apartment that had been advertised, and, if he liked it, to sign a lease. The distance from the apartment to his office was about the same as from the shelter to his office, but the distance between the apartment and the shelter was now twice as far. He'd have to take the bus to bring his belongings from his locker at St. Vincent House.

* * *

By Wednesday afternoon Sam had completed his move, even stopping in a local grocery store to purchase some things for his meals. Harry Taylor had given Sam an extra hour at lunch to transfer his property — Sam had not told him from where — and Richard Fairchild had helped him pack his few possessions, including his new suit and shirt, in a box. Sam told the professor about his visit with Officer Segretti.

"That would be great if he can get me into the Refuse Department files," Dr. Fairchild had said. "I didn't get a chance to tell you, but I drove by the Rogers Chemical Company, down on the river. They have a big office in front of the plant, and the whole front area is nicely landscaped. Of course, it was covered with snow, but I can't imagine what George might have found if he was simply there to pull weeds. Of course, there are a lot of warehouses around there, and several did have the Rogers name on them, so he might also have been working in one of those."

"Sure is a mystery." Sam replied. "Have any of the other guys said anything about having worked with George?"

"I asked, but they all say no, that they usually get sent out first, and George was usually still at DLI when they left."

"Well, I'll let you know if Officer Segretti contacts me, Professor. Looks like I'll be on my own now, and I have an invite for Christmas, so tell the guys I wish them all the best, and if I get a chance, I'll drop in occasionally."

"Thanks, Sam. And Merry Christmas. Hope you hear from that family of yours up in, where did you say? Connecticut."

"Yeah. That would be a merry Christmas gift. So long."

* * *

Christmas fell on a Friday that year. Although the city buses were running only a holiday schedule, Sam was able to get one that dropped him three blocks from the Taylor's home, a fairly large frame house on the West Side of town, surrounded with trees and lawn. He'd stopped at the train station the night before for a shoeshine, and had also visited the barber. In his new suit, with his new address, Sam felt like a new man. He had also stopped and bought a big tin of Christmas cookies, which was wrapped with a multicolored ribbon, and also had purchased a bottle of the brand of bourbon that he knew Harry Taylor liked.

Marilyn Taylor was an attractive dark-haired lady in her mid-forties. She made Sam feel very much at home. Harry Taylor offered Sam a drink, which he declined, opting for plain eggnog instead. The Taylor's fifteen-year-old daughter, Margaret, joined them for dinner, a roast turkey with all the trimmings. Sam ate eagerly, truthfully stating that it was the best meal he had eaten in years.

Although Marilyn made a few inquiries about Sam and his family, Sam was able to skirt most of the unpleasant aspects. He truthfully revealed that his wife and daughter were in Connecticut with her family at present, where she was attending school. Sam said he had moved to his new apartment as his old lodgings "had become a bit cramped." If only the Taylors had known how cramped, they would have had a good laugh.

After the dinner Harry invited Sam into his small office he kept at home. It was lined with insurance books, photos of ships and other memorabilia of the marine insurance business.

"How do you like the marine business?" Taylor asked.

"I've really enjoyed it. It is an aspect of business I never got in college. I guess the university professors didn't think selling insurance was marketing, but it sure is. And what I like most is the historical aspects."

"Historical?"

"Dealing with Lloyd's of London, and other famous old insurers. I'm a history buff."

"Oh, I didn't know that. Well, Sam, I've got an offer for you. You don't have to accept if you don't want, and I know you're anxious to get back to New England to be with your family, but I really need a partner down at the agency. You're only part time now, but you've been putting in better than forty hours a week for months, and you are reliable. I know you have nothing to invest, but that's not what I'm after. I need someone I can trust down there to run the place if I'm away, or even when I'm there. We can make much more money if I could spend more time getting new clients, and you seem to be great with the paper work, applications, claims and so forth.

"It would be a salaried position. Say, twice what you're getting now for forty hours. Plus benefits. We've a little group policy on the full time employees. Even a little pension plan. You'd have the title of assistant vice president. What do you say, Sam?"

"Golly, what can I say? That would be great. Thank you, Mr. Taylor."

"Mr. Taylor hell! Call me Harry."

"Well, Harry, I really appreciate this. You're right that I'm anxious to see my family in Connecticut, but I have no plans to move there. I'd just like to go up for a few days."

"Tell you what, Sam. You take next week off – with pay, at the new rate – and go on over there to New England, see that wife and kid of yours, and be back the following Monday. It's going to be a slow week anyway, and I doubt you'd have had much to do. You keep your desk pretty current. But after the holidays I bet there'll be a pile of stuff when you get back."

"Oh, thank you again, Harry. I wish I had something I could give you in exchange."

"Your reliability, my boy! That's what you're giving me. I think you're going to be a name in the marine insurance business some day, and that's good for me and the Taylor agency."

The two chatted for over an hour. Harry Taylor asked Whitaker what sort of interests he had, and Sam told him about his interest in medieval history, and about the Fremont professor with whom he had become friends. Then he told his boss about how they were looking into the murder of 'Shoeless George,' explaining who George was, and how he had been killed. Taylor asked him a number of questions about the professor, and seemed interested in him.

"I seem to recall seeing something about some professor at Fremont who was involved in helping in the arrest of some terrorists awhile back," Taylor said. "They'd blown up a train. I'll bet it's the same guy."

"Yes, the professor told me about that. The terrorists were going to assassinate that civil rights leader, Thomas Jefferson Singletary."

"Yeah, that's right. And now you say he's working on this, what, street person's murder? Huh. What's he got so far?"

"Oh, just some theories. We think maybe George found something while he was out working somewhere, and took it to his place under the bridge, and someone shot him for it. The police may reopen the case, and one of the officers is going to try to get Fairchild into the city Refuse Department to see if they have any records as to where he was working. Of course, I have no time or talent for such. Don't know how the professor goes about his research."

"Interesting. And you say his name is Fairchild?"

* * *

It took almost all the cash Sam had to buy a round coach trip ticket on the railroad to get to Stamford, Connecticut. He had called Carolyn, and she had agreed to meet him at the train. She was standing on the platform as he stepped off, only slightly rumpled after sitting in a coach seat into Grand Central, then catching a Boston-bound train to Stamford. Carolyn, on the other hand, looked gorgeous, wrapped warmly in a mink jacket Sam had bought her several Christmases earlier. She allowed him to hug and kiss her, but he detected coldness in her response.

"So, what are you up to these days? Still living in a homeless shelter?"

"Oh, no!" he replied. "I've got my own apartment now, and a very good promotion at the insurance agency. I'm an assistant vice president. The monthly checks should be about double now.

"Where's Courtney?" Sam added.

"With her grandparents. I didn't tell her you were coming, because I didn't think you would. We couldn't have survived without Dad, you know."

"I know, Carolyn. I'm truly sorry, but I've been dry for months now. I have a good job, a future, and I'm still in love with you. I want you and Courtney back."

"Hmff. We'll see. Mother said you could stay in the spare bedroom while you're here, so come on, and we'll drive on out there." She looked at the rather small valise Sam was carrying, and said, "Is that all the luggage you have?"

"That's it," he admitted.

Carolyn led him to her car, the same one she had left in a year earlier, a mid-sized Ford now six years old. The interior was still in good condition, although six winters had taken a toll on the body, and spots of rust were showing.

"Are you still teaching?" Sam asked.

"Of course. We pay our own way with my parents. I give them most of what I earn in exchange for Courtney's and my keep. I will admit that your checks do help."

"Carolyn, I know this is awkward, and maybe not the time, but I must tell you that I still love you very much, miss you very much, and want you to come home with me as soon as I get a place for us, which shouldn't be long now."

"It is the wrong time, Sam. Let's wait and see how the next few days go. I have another appointment with my attorney next week, and I understand he has not heard from yours yet...."

"I don't have one. Carolyn, I'd fight like hell to keep you, but it's silly to fight in court. I'd give you whatever you want – everything I have or ever will have. But what I really want is you and Courtney together again with me. I've overcome my demons. They're not there anymore. The only love I have is for you two."

Within a few minutes they arrived at a rambling big house a few blocks from the Sound. Carolyn parked on the street in front, and Sam got out and started up the walk beside her. As they approached the door it flew open and Courtney came running out.

"Daddy!" she cried. "Oh, Daddy! You've come to take us home!"

"Oh, not quite yet, Dear," he responded, gathering the tall eleven-year-old into his arms. "But soon, I hope. Did you get the packages I sent for Christmas?"

"Yes, they were wonderful presents. I loved the matching coat and hat you sent, and the game box. I wrote you a letter. Did you get it?"

"It must not have arrived yet. But I'll look forward to reading it when I get home. How was your Christmas?"

"We had a big dinner, Daddy, but I missed you. Santa came, but it just wasn't the same. Where did you have Christmas?"

"At my boss's home. He's got a daughter, too, just a few years older than you are. And he gave me a promotion, so...."

"Careful what you say, Sam," Carolyn interrupted, whispering in his ear.. "Don't build her hopes and then smash them again. It's happened too often."

By this time they were inside the house, and Sam received a half-hearted welcome from his father-in-law, Harvey Frist. His mother-in-law, Maggie, was a bit more cordial. The rest of the day Sam tried to listen rather than talk. He'd spoken with Carolyn only a few times over the past year, but Courtney's letters had kept him somewhat current on what was happening. He had written to her weekly, but suspected, from unanswered questions he had posed, that his letters were being censored before his daughter got them.

That evening Sam luxuriated in the hot shower in the guest bathroom. After all night on the train he was exhausted. He had only a few more nights until he had to return home, again all night in a coach. Because he would be traveling on a New Year's weekend he was only able to get a reservation for Friday, the First of January.

On Wednesday morning Sam asked to use the phone. He called the Taylor Agency and spoke with Harry Taylor for a few minutes. He knew his father-in-law was listening, and was grateful that Harry had some good questions for Sam. The answers made him sound authoritative, and seemed to reassure Frist that he really was an executive with whomever he was conversing. When Sam hung up, he immediately offered to reimburse Harvey the cost of the call.

"Ah, not at all, Sam. I'm just damned glad you've gotten yourself straightened out and have a boss to call. What is it you're doing?"

"It's a marine insurance agency," Sam explained. "We write coverage on ships and cargo, mostly cargo, and some inland marine things like machinery. I've learned a lot about it, and am really enjoying the work. I do a bit of selling, but mostly process the applications, verifying values and things, and handle all the claims that come in. It's just a small office, six full time employees, in one of the pier buildings down on the wharf. I'm able to walk to work from my apartment."

"No car?"

"Haven't really needed one. Everything's handy, and cheap."

"Well, I hope it goes okay for you. Sam, I'll be quite honest, but I don't want Carolyn or Maggie to hear me say this, but I'm hoping you and Carolyn can get things worked out and get her home again. I was as disappointed as she was when you took to drinking, but having lived through the Depression and seeing what happened to men who lost everything due to unemployment, I understood better than she did.

"I think she's really sorry she filed that divorce action," Harvey Frist continued. "She spent weeks sobbing and blubbering around here, and, frankly, I'm sick of it. Don't let her coolness keep you away. It's the only protection she has, if things aren't working out. But if you're sincere in wanting the two of them back – and that girl of yours needs her father – let Carolyn know."

"Thank you, Harvey. That's what I'd hoped, but I wasn't sure. I need a bit more time to get settled, and there won't be any big house in the suburbs for a good long time again, no big cars or private schools, but with my new promotion I think in a few months it might be possible for me to get someplace for us, if Carolyn will work with me."

"Let's make that our goal, then, Sam. I'll work from this end, you from yours, and maybe we can get you two together by spring."

* * *

The following Monday Sam was at his desk before seven. The week in Connecticut had gone far better than he hoped. By Thursday night Carolyn had invited him to her bedroom "for a chat," but, with the door closed, it had soon evolved into hugging and kissing, along with expressions of love from both that were like when they had first become engaged. Sam felt a certain feeling of trust on Carolyn's part that had not been there since he had lost his job and began drinking. The memory of their love now encouraged him, and he attacked the stack of work on his desk with renewed vigor.

Late that afternoon a policeman entered the Taylor agency and asked for Sam. The receptionist, Harriet Anderson, a tall, middle aged woman with a short haircut, came to his office and said, "Sam, there's a policeman here to see you."

Sam got up, and went out into the reception area, but immediately recognized the officer. "Andy Segretti!" he said. "Come on in my office. How was your holiday?"

"Great. And yours?"

"Wonderful. The best I've ever had. What brings you up here?" Sam had deliberately left his door open as he knew the receptionist and Harry Taylor's secretary, Audrey Campbell, would be listening out of curiosity, and would report everything to Harry.

"As agreed, I talked to Lieutenant Fochee about George. He wouldn't agree to reopen the case, but did agree to let you or your friend review the Refuse Department records to see what you can find. He got the name of the department head, a Greg Millerman, whose office is up above the Public Works garage on South Eighth. It's a big place, near the embankment. Give him a call at 487-2445, and he'll see what he can do to find out where George might have worked."

Sam made a note of the name and phone number, and thanked the officer for helping. The policeman quickly left again, and the office settled back to normal, although it was obvious that both Harriet and Audrey were wondering what had initiated the visit from the police.

That evening after work Sam returned to St. Vincent House to talk with Richard Fairchild. The professor insisted that Sam stay for dinner, and though it would be a long hike back to his apartment in the cold, he agreed. He conveyed the message Officer Segretti had left, and Richard said he would follow up on it.

Chapter 5

It was the second week of January before Sam heard from Dr. Fairchild again. Sam was in his office discussing a cargo claim with a client when Richard Fairchild entered the office and asked for him.

Harriet Anderson advised that Sam was with a client, but would not be very long, and invited the professor to have a seat in a small reception area. Richard Fairchild sat down, and picked up a copy of the *International Shipping Weekly* newspaper that was sitting on a table. It was over a month old, and most of the news had to do with arrivals and departures of cargo ships, ads for intermodal transportation or freight lines, and a few classifieds. One of the articles caught his interest, however, and he was just starting to read it when Sam came out with his client and saw the professor.

"Oh, hi, Doc!" he said. "Didn't know you were waiting."

To his client, he added, "Bill, I'll get that claim filed this afternoon, and they should have an adjuster on it by tomorrow, or the next day at the latest. From what you say, I don't have any doubt it's covered, but, of course, there is a fairly high deductible on that policy."

"Sam, I know it's in good hands. Say hello to Harry Taylor for me, eh?" the client replied as he donned his hat and coat and started out the door.

"Come on in, Professor," Sam said, pointing toward his office door.

"Sam, I've gotten interested in an article in this newspaper. Okay if I keep that page?"

"Keep the whole thing if you want. It's an old issue, and probably should have been thrown out weeks ago."

Once inside Sam's office Sam directed Fairchild to a chair, and asked, "Any news?"

"Actually, quite a bit. As you know, this is my last week at St. Vincent House. I've got to get back to Fremont as the winter session starts Monday, and I have at least six classes scheduled this semester.

"But yesterday," he continued, "I got a call from the BSV – the Brothers of St. Vincent – in New York. They told me that Brother Amos has resigned and they will be sending one of their friars down to run the shelter until a new permanent director can be found. I asked why Amos had resigned, and they said it was apparently some personal matter. They seemed to suggest that he couldn't afford to survive on the meager salary. As he was a lay member, he was under no vows that might otherwise have had a bearing on his staying. The new brother is to arrive tomorrow, and I'll leave the next day."

"That *is* news. Do the guys know yet? They all loved Brother Amos."

"I'm to tell them tonight. Actually nothing will change. The Order has shelters like St. Vincent House all over the country, and try to staff them with professional social workers like Amos. But I imagine it's a hard job with little pay."

"I'd agree. He was a hard worker," Sam agreed. "Have you had a chance to meet with that guy at the Refuse Department?"

"Yes, that's the other reason I stopped by, as well as to say good bye. I got over to the department's office yesterday, and the director, a Greg Millerman, was very helpful. He said he remembered George, because of his feet, and while he does not go out on the jobs very often, he did see George working on a few of the cleanup jobs. Most of them were buildings that had been abandoned.

"He reviewed his records for the last six months, and found four assignments that he thought George might have been on. Two were buildings that had burned and the work was mostly outside debris. One was an abandoned city pumping station that had been used for storage years ago, and the fourth was a warehouse. Interesting, in that it had once been owned by the Rogers Chemical Company, and was just south of their plant, next to another warehouse. Rogers had sold it to some other firm several years ago, and that firm was using it to store returned merchandise. But they went bankrupt, and the warehouse sat for a couple of years, and was finally placed for sale by the city for back taxes. That's when the Refuse Department was called in to clean it out. It was sometime in late October, according to Millerman's records. "When I got back, I stopped in at Downtown Labor and talked with Billy again. He checked his records, and they matched. George had gone out on a job for the city on October 29. It was the last time he worked for the city, in fact, for anyone."

"George seemed to keep coming back to the vicinity of Rogers Chemical Company, didn't he," Sam commented.

"Yes, but there certainly is very little to indicate how they might be involved, and if they sold the warehouse to someone else, it's doubtful they would have had anything still in it that George could have found. I'm afraid it's a bit of a dead end."

"Well, Doc, I appreciate your looking into it. If I see Andy Segretti, I'll let him know what you found. Now, I want your address at the college so I can keep in touch. Maybe I can even take one of your classes some time, especially when Carolyn and I get back together, if we stay here in Ohio."

"That would be wonderful, Sam. I hope you do." Richard Fairchild quickly scribbled his address on a pad Sam had handed him, and stood up to shake hands. He had the folded *Shipping Weekly* tucked under his arm as he left the office and walked back to St. Vincent House.

* * *

Gunther Harcourt sat in the plush eighth floor London office of Marcus Staley, just south of Threadneedle Street. The Staley Syndicate was lead underwriter on the marine policy for an American company located in Cleveland, Ohio, holding a 17.5% portion of the risk for hull, indemnity and cargo. It was a policy that had been transferred when the vessel was sold to the American company by its former Greek owners. As lead underwriter, it was that syndicate's responsibility to monitor the claim for the others subscribed on the risk. They would rely on whatever decision Staley would make.

Harcourt had just returned from Canada, and was providing a first-hand report to supplement a brief written report he had submitted a month earlier on the claim. "It's one of the strangest cases I've ever investigated," he explained. "I talked to Hammerman, the captain of the vessel *Chem Queen*, and he said that it was the usual procedure that they would bring the ship into the Cleveland harbor and down the river to the plant dock on Friday afternoons. The crew, including Hammerman, all live in Cleveland, so they tie up the vessel and leave it to be unloaded on Saturday mornings. A land crew does the off-loading, using the on-board hoses and pumps to pump the stuff into their holding tanks. Only the ship's master, a Johnnie Franklin, was left aboard.

"On Saturday morning they found Franklin unconscious on the dock, and the ship was gone. Because of the dangerous chemical aboard, a petroleum-based acid of some sort that they produce at their plant in Sarnia, Ontario, they immediately contacted the Coast Guard. I also interviewed the Cleveland Harbormaster, but they have no record of seeing the ship departing between Friday evening and Saturday morning. The records show that it was a very foggy October night, but several large ore boats did depart that evening, and the Harbormaster said it would be entirely possible for a tanker the size of the *Chem Queen* to leave without the harbormaster's knowledge.

"United States Customs were also brought in to investigate, as the ship had entered Cleveland from Canada. One of their agents had met the ship while it entered the harbor Friday afternoon, and processed the crew while the ship was towed up the river."

"The vessel has to be towed up the river?" Staley interrupted.

"Yes. Here, let me show you on this map," Harcourt replied, unrolling a map of the Cleveland harbor and Cuyahoga River. "See, the river has several bends in it. Many of the long ore boats are able to navigate at least a mile or more up the river. The insured's plant is further up the river just beyond these steel mills and refineries. The river narrows quite a bit at that point, and there is not sufficient room to turn the ship there, so rather than turn it further down the river and risk backing it some distance to their dock, they turn it in the harbor and have it towed backwards up the river. Then, on departure, no tow is needed."

"I see. So a tow would not be needed to get the vessel away from the dock and down the river?"

"No. But the Customs records do show that the tanks were full when the ship arrived in port Friday afternoon. It got in about four, and tied up at the dock around six, just as it was getting dark."

"What about at the plant? Are there any guards? Lights, or cameras?"

"Yes, there are guards, but they don't regularly patrol the dock area. It is immediately behind several large tanks – here, let me show you on this map – and the entire area is fenced. The guards patrol the parking area accessible by roads around the plant, but don't check the rear area that is fenced. The Coast Guard confirmed that the fence had been cut open at a point near the river, just north of the dock. I inspected it. They've since repaired the fence, but you can see where the cut had been made, and the area just opposite it is vacant. There had been a warehouse there, but it had burned down, so the area was just weeds and debris. There are no cameras that I know of."

"What is south of this plant, or across the river?" Staley asked.

"South? There are just a couple large warehouses. The insured owns several of them, and the others are vacant. Across the river is the back of a steel mill. There's an open hearth furnace there, and always a glow in the sky at night, so it is almost like daylight. There are some lights around the perimeter of the plant, but they are not really needed, even on a dark night.

"Anyway, I checked all the tank records. There were 350,000 gallons of chemical on the ship that was supposed to be unloaded the next day into tanks One and Two, both of which hold 200,000 gallons of this product. The records show that there were only 20,000 gallons in Tank B, and Tank A was empty on that Saturday morning. The chemical is needed for production of the various products your insured sells, and they had to curtail production later that week until another shipment of the chemical could be received. I don't believe your policy covers any indirect loss like that, so I did not get any details on their alleged loss of revenue due to this theft."

"That's correct. We have no business interruption coverage."

"The Coast Guard alerted the United States Federal Bureau of Investigation, their FBI, and they, in turn, contacted the Royal Canadian Mounted Police, which is the Canadian national police force, and they both had their field offices check all possible ports for the ship. It's a fairly big tanker. The insured purchased it three years ago from the Suez-Arabian Line, owned by that Greek, who sold it when he had those super-tankers built to ship oil to the U.K. Of course it wasn't so large it wouldn't...."

"I know that, Gunther," Staley interrupted. "That's how we got on the risk, as we insured the vessel when it was owned by Suez-Arabian. We knew it was a sound ship. I've got all its dimensions and capacity here. It was certainly large enough to be noticed if it arrived in someone's harbor."

"But it never passed the Welland Canal locks in Ontario that link Lake Erie with Lake Ontario, never passed the Soo Locks, and neither the American nor Canadian officials on the St. Claire and Detroit Rivers recall seeing it pass through their checkpoints. They know the ship and its schedule. It's got to still be somewhere on Lake Erie, or one of the lake ports.

"I also checked the insured's plant in Sarnia," Harcourt continued. "Their records show that 350,000 gallons of the chemical were loaded on Wednesday afternoon, and that the ship departed Thursday morning."

"Any danger of pollution?" the Lloyd's underwriter asked. "We've got P&I, too."

"Plenty. I asked what this chemical they haul in the holds would do, and was told that, as a petroleum-based product, it is not only highly toxic, but is lighter than water, hence would float on the surface. The Coast Guard has found no indication of any sort of oil slick that might have resulted if the ship had been scuttled, especially if it was still full of the product it was hauling. They crisscrossed Lake Erie looking for one. That's the mystery of it, Mr. Staley. The ship simply has disappeared. That's why the insured is alleging it was sunk."

"How would you hide something like that? If it wasn't seen passing Detroit, and didn't pass the canal to Canadian waters – which seems logical if it was pirated, as papers would be required to enter Canada – where else could it be but on Lake Erie. What Lake Erie ports could a ship that size enter?"

"Several, not counting those in Canada. Toledo, Sandusky, Lorain, Ashtabula, Conneaut, Erie, even Buffalo. But it's not in any of those places as far as we can tell."

"I still want to delay paying this claim. Can't believe it won't be found. I suppose those diesel engines aboard are never really shut down," Staley said, posing his comment as much as a question.

"No, that's correct. The ship's not new, but it's well mechanized. Hammerman told me it could operate with a crew as small as four. They usually have eleven aboard."

Staley sighed, and looked out his window at the afternoon sun beating down on The City. He was not yet ready to commit millions on the ship and its cargo. "Keep digging," he instructed the investigator. "I'm not quite ready to settle yet."

He thought about the wording of the Lloyd's policy, language that had been used for nearly three hundred years: 'Touching the adventures and perils which the underwriters are contented to bear and take upon themselves, they are of the seas, men-of-war, fire, lightning, earthquake, jettisons, enemies, rovers, assailing thieves, pirates. ..' In all his years of underwriting, except for boarded vessels during time of war, he had never encountered piracy of a commercial vessel, especially in inland domestic waters. He wondered how long it would be before the matter hit the press.

* * *

Sally Merriam, Fremont College Religion Department's secretary, had spent the first two weeks of January preparing for the winter semester. It was her role, along with other departmental secretaries, to schedule the classes and assist at registration. The secretaries had to work among themselves to align classes so they would not conflict with related courses, or with their instructors' own schedules.

Sally had been through the process many times. She knew that the religion classes could not have schedule conflicts with certain history classes or the International Studies Program that the Religions, Languages and Geography Departments had put together.

By the time Richard Fairchild again ensconced himself in his small, cramped office in the basement of Hayes Hall on the third Monday in January, the scheduling and registration were complete. Fairchild's classes, among the most popular at the college, were always fully registered. Fistfights over remaining slots in his classes had been known to occur on the gym floor where registration took place. It was not that Fairchild was an "easy grade." Quite the opposite. His were among the toughest of the courses in the school outside of math, sciences and engineering.

All students had to take at least one religion or philosophy course along with a list of other required arts and sciences, but many became addicted to the religion classes after even one low level survey course. With only two professors in the department – aided occasionally by the college chaplain, Dr. Stephen Boldt – the small department got considerable attention from students despite their size and overall importance at Fremont.

Dr. Fairchild kept two calendars. One was on his desk. If Sally added anything to it while he was not there, she left him a note as to what and when it was – usually a conference with a student, or a faculty meeting called by Dean Harding. Fairchild would then incorporate the desk calendar into the personal one he carried with him.

The professor sat at his desk incorporating the new class schedule into his two calendars. The wide array of classes left him little free time for preparation and his own studies, but he was used to that. There were to be two sessions of Basic Islam 402 this semester, but Dr. Merriam was to teach the second. Merriam's Native American Religions 312 class was new this semester. It fell during one of Fairchild's free sessions, and he hoped to sit in on it, although the class was fully registered. Only Fairchild's own class on Asian Religions 408 had any space left, and there were only two

43

vacancies. Both of his Medieval Christianity 307 classes were full, along with several basic Bible Survey 101 and 102 classes. It would be a busy semester.

As he finished filling in his schedule, he opened the three-month-old copy of the International Shipping Weekly that he had brought back from the Taylor agency office and turned to a story entitled, "Israeli Shippers Dispute Work Stoppage on Muslim Holy Days." It was a fitting issue to illustrate how important understanding religions could be in the modern world. He carefully cut the article out of the paper, adding the masthead to show the date and publication, and flipped to another page on which the story was continued, clipping that out also. Just as his eye caught the headline of another article, the bell rang and the professor was off to his first class of the new semester.

* * *

Fred Rogers, Chairman and Chief Executive Officer of the Rogers Chemical Company asked his secretary to have Garrett Williams, the Chief Financial Officer, come to his office. As Williams came to the door Rogers motioned him to a chair and said, "Close the door."

The younger executive, a tall man with dark hair dressed in a conservative business suit, said nothing, but closed the door and sat down as instructed.

"Gary, I was going over last year's calendar and got to thinking about that ship situation back in October. Are we positive that the insurer will pay up?"

"Yes sir, the claim was filed within a couple of weeks after the thing was confirmed as lost."

"Well, they better pay soon. And what about the costs of that warehouse mess?"

"That's been taken care of, too. In fact, the city even picked up most of the costs involved. Trash disposal and all."

"Good. I don't want to leave too many loose ends hanging around, but I don't want to know the details. I suspect our board of directors will inquire about that claim at the next meeting, and want to be sure everything is okay."

"Nothing to worry about, Fred. Our agent got involved in the claim personally. It's all being taken care of. There is one little hitch he's heard about, but he's ...."

"Well, whatever it is, Gary, see that he gets it taken care of. And quick. I don't want *any* loose ends before that board meeting. Say, how's that boy of yours, Eddie? He still going to Yale?"

"Yes, probably partying and drinking more than studying, but that's typical, I guess. But the tuition! I'll be sent to the poor house after paying for it. Be glad your Kelly went to a less expensive college."

"Yeah, I was afraid there for a while that she was going to run off with some pimple-faced kid in a leather jacket on a motorcycle, but she finally dumped him and picked Fremont College, out west of here, for a school. They've got some international program that she likes, and she seems to be doing well. Seems to have forgotten boys for a while," Rogers said.

"Think so, ehh? You should have seen her and my Eddie at your New Year's Eve party, then! I thought for a while Eddie'd be telling me he wanted to go to Fremont instead of Yale. How I wish! But I guess all they did was exchange addresses."

"Really! Sorry I missed it. Too busy tending bar. Man, that would be some combination, your Eddie and my Kelly. Ha!"

* * *

The man registering at the small London hotel off Kensington Avenue smiled as he wrote his name on the registration card. Edgar A. Latimer. He gave an address in Boston, Massachusetts.

"And how many nights?" asked the clerk in a crisp English accent.

"I'm not entirely sure. At least four or five, but perhaps as long as a fortnight," Latimer replied, using the British term for two weeks. "I'll let you know as soon as my plans are complete."

"That would be satisfactory, Sir. A breakfast comes with the room," the clerk continued. "It is served in the parlor here on the ground floor between seven and ten in the morning. Can we arrange a rental car or tour for you, Mr. Latimer?"

"No, thank you. But perhaps you could tell me which tube line to use that would get me closest to the marine offices near the Tower."

"The Circle Line should take you the entire way, Mr. Latimer. Just a bit up the street to Kensington High, and then exit at Tower Hill. It's the stop after Monument."

"Thank you."

The clerk handed Edgar Latimer the key, and he proceeded to the small elevator that took him to the third floor, which was actually the fourth floor of the six story hotel.. The doorman also served as a bell hop, but with only one medium sized suitcase, Latimer did not need any help. Once at his room, he unpacked the contents of his suitcase and placed the empty case in a closet. The room was small, but adequate. A double bed occupied the middle. There was a small writing table and chair on one side, and another larger chair with a lamp beside it on the other, plus a small dresser. In the small lavatory was a sink and shower. It was adequate for

Latimer's needs, even though there was no television, and no telephone. He had only one call to make, and that could be made from the lobby.

As it was a Friday afternoon, Latimer did not expect to find anyone at the shipping office when he phoned, other than perhaps a few clerks. However, when he asked for the manager, he was put through directly to a man with a broken accent.

"'Allo?" the manager said upon answering the call.

"Good afternoon," Latimer began. "Are you the manager of the Suez-Arabian and the Cyprus-Hellenic Lines?"

"Yes. Vat can I do for you?"

"I have some information for your senior people, but I do not know how to reach them."

"Vat kynt of information?"

"About ownership. Inheritances. I was wondering if I might make an appointment to meet with you next week."

"Yes. Certainly. Ven do you vans to come?"

"Would Monday be okay? I just got into London."

"Yes, dat would be fine. Say at ten o'clock. Ant your name, Sir?"

"Latimer. Edgar Latimer, of Boston. And your name?"

"Phillip Hercell. Vee vill see you Monday, den."

Edgar Latimer smiled as he hung up the phone and walked outside to a red Royal Mail postal box. He had the rest of the weekend to relax, and by the end of the following week he should be well on his way toward greatly improving his life.

* * *

Tillman Farmer, one of the oldest of the six partners in the law firm of Freeze, Farmer & Rivera, opened up the airmail envelope that had just been delivered to him by his secretary. It was postmarked in London, but had no return address.

Inside was just one piece of paper. It was a certified copy of a death certificate, but there was no message written on it. The paper stated that George Antopholis, age 36, last known address of 62 River Street, Cleveland, had died on or before November 7 due to trauma to the forehead, skull and brain caused by a .45-calibur bullet. No "next of kin" was known. The certificate was signed by the county coroner.

Tillman Farmer turned the paper over, but nothing was on the back. He then stapled the death certificate to the envelope in which it had come, and walked over to a file cabinet at the side of his office, pulling open the top drawer and removing a file from behind the letter A that read "Antopholis."

Inside the file was a last will and testament, a copy of a welfare department application form that showed Antopholis's date of birth and

Social Security Number, some correspondence with the welfare department, and a page of notes that Farmer had taken that day he had met with Antopholis and his friend, to whom Antopholis had willed all of his worldly possessions – which at the time had consisted of absolutely nothing. The original of his bill was still in the file, unsent and unpaid.

Farmer reviewed the notes, but found that he did not have any sort of permanent address for this friend who was to inherit the *nothing* his client apparently was leaving. He shook his head, wondering what his legal obligation might be to find and advise that person. Anticipating that the friend – someone who apparently lived with George, he seemed to recall – would already know of his death, he replaced the file, and returned to his desk to review the rest of the mail his secretary had delivered.

Chapter 6

Edgar Latimer was determined to enliven a friendship with an English girl he had been in love with in graduate school back in Boston, and with whom he had kept in contact. They had shared a room for several months, and though he was seven years her senior, she was a very mature and wise – as well as beautiful – young lady. With dark hair and eyes, dimples and a sleek, well-shaped body, Terri Bookley made the perfect roommate.

They had kept in touch over the last four years, and Latimer, who in his mid-thirties already had a receding hairline above his thick glasses, felt a surge of excitement as he dialed the phone number he had kept in his wallet.

"Hello?" the cheery voice said.

"Terri?"

"Yes, who is it?"

"Ed. Ed Latimer."

"Ed!" the girl exclaimed. "Where are you?"

"Here in London. Are you free tonight for dinner? A nice pub someplace."

"For you, always!" she bubbled. "When did you get in?"

"Just this afternoon. The flight from Boston was late leaving last night, and a storm in the Atlantic drove us way up north. We had to refuel in Iceland."

"Iceland! Good Lord, Ed. You must be exhausted. Why not just come over here for supper. I've a bit of fish, and we can have that and chips."

"You're sure I won't be imposing."

"Not at all. Your letter at Christmas said you might be coming, and I was delighted. You have the address, but where are you?"

"At a small hotel on Kensington."

"Are you near Notting Hill Gate?"

"I think so."

"Get to there, and then take the East London line about four stops west to East Acton. I'll meet you at the tube station. Say, in twenty minutes?"

"Fine. I'm on my way."

The kisses and hugs Latimer received upon exiting the tube station brought glances and smiles from others exiting or entering the station. Terri led him to a low building containing about ten flats that was only three blocks from the station. She unlocked the front door, then headed up a flight of stairs to another door on the first floor. Inside was a neatly decorated apartment with one bedroom, decorated in soft pink, a small kitchen and dinette, and a comfortable living room with a sofa, tables and two matching chairs, all facing the television. In the bedroom Terri also had a desk at which she kept her telephone. It was a full bathroom, complete with a large tub.

"Have you had a chance to relax any since you got in?" she asked.

"No, I went straight to the hotel after Heathrow, and then called you."

"While I'm fixing supper, why don't you take a bath, and relax in the tub a bit?" she suggested. "That big fluffy robe of yours that you left behind when you left Boston is still in my closet. Let me get it for you. And I've got some ice, so let me fix you a little whiskey, too."

Pleasant memories filled Ed Latimer's head as he lay soaking in the warm, steamy water in the big tub, sipping on the Scotch she had poured for him. His mind brought back images of he and Terri together in bed, lying close together, embraced in love for hours at a time. It has been years since he had experienced that kind of love, despite all the one night stands he had encountered since then.

As he drained the water and dried himself with a rather stiff but large towel, Terri called that the meal was ready. He donned the large robe and padded barefoot to the kitchen, coming up behind Terri as she stood at the stove, placing his arms around her.

'Mmm, oh, it's good to see you again, Ed. I've no one here in London. A few dates now and then, but the blokes are idiots. How I remember those days in Boston, and the trips we used to take on weekends."

"I've missed them, too, Terri. But maybe again, soon."

"What brings you to London?"

"A little business deal. If it works out, I could be wealthy," Latimer said casually.

"Really?!! I didn't know you were into 'business.'"

"Oh, everything is business, when you get right down to it. But this deal just came along, and, as they say, 'opportunity knocks only once.'"

"I hope it works out. These fish are ready, so if you'll have a seat, I'll bring your plate to you."

While not the world's best cook, Terri Booklet's fish and chips were passable. To Ed Latimer they were gourmet. Both ate slowly, sipping a white wine Terri had opened and poured. Dinner over, they washed up the dishes and moved to the sofa where Terri quickly curled up next to Ed, who was still in the fluffy robe.

"They'll miss you at the hotel," she laughed.

"So what. They get paid whether I sleep there or not, and it is a place to keep my stuff. I've a meeting Monday morning, so will have to go back Sunday night."

"Or Monday morning."

"We'll see."

Jet lag was wearing heavily on Ed. He had not slept on the plane. Sleeping on a plane had always been difficult for him, although he'd not flown that much. He had dozed off for a few moments, during which Terri had gone into her bedroom and put on a very short nightgown. He awoke as she returned, and curled up beside him.

"Oh, sorry!" he said.

"I understand. I know just the place for you. Come on, let's go to bed."

It was an invitation Ed was not about to refuse. Now fully alert, every nerve in his body responded to Terri, and they were quickly entwined in each other's arms.

* * *

After his final class on Friday morning Professor Richard Fairchild had a free afternoon. He used the time to mark grade books on each of his students in each class, and to prepare his notes for the following week, a task he would continue through Saturday, unless the weather was suitable for fishing. Given that it was the middle of January and Lake Erie was frozen solid, and further that Fairchild hated ice fishing, he knew he would spend the next morning in class preparation.

After working for several hours, he started assembling the various texts and notes on his desk to place in his large leather briefcase to take home with him. At the bottom of the stack was the old copy of the *International Shipping News* from which he had clipped an article. He was about to gather it up and throw it in the trash when he again noticed the article that had caught his eye five days earlier, and leaned back in his old wooden swivel chair to read it.

"*Heirs Sought for Greek Shipping Company*," the headline read. "London. Lawyers for the Cyprus-Hellenic Ship Lines have advised that they have few leads in finding heirs to the Antopholis dynasty founded in Limassol, Cyprus, and headquartered in Athens. The last known member of the wealthy shipping family, Demetrius Antopholis, died in September in an Athens Hospital of heart disease. He was 78. His will, according to the London solicitors who are working in conjunction with attorneys in Greece, leaves the entire estate, estimated to be one of the fourth richest in that nation, to his sister in Buffalo, New York, or to her heirs.

"The will specifically excludes his former wife, Sophia Chigaren, who resides in London. The couple was childless. Contacted by reporters, Miss Chigaren stated that as far as she knew, her former sister-in-law who had emigrated to Buffalo, New York, had died, but she believed that there was a nephew living somewhere in the United States. Anyone with information about the Antopholis family is asked to contact Ian Sherling of Beckelsley & Durand, 27 Brewster House, Leicester Square, London EW7 2XK."

The professor ripped the article from the old newspaper, folded it and placed it in his inside suitcoat pocket. He then pulled on his overcoat, grabbed a warm cap off his coat rack, and stepped out of his office. Sally Merriam was still at her desk, typing a report for her husband, who sat in his office just opposite that of Fairchild's.

"Good night, you two," he said, heading toward the wooden door with frosted glass windows. "Don't hang around too long. I hear there's another storm brewing for this evening."

"We're about through," Bob Merriam replied. "Thanks for the warning, though. Our drive to Sandusky is bad enough without a blizzard. You be careful, too. Good night, and give our love to Esther."

"Yes, good night, Dr. Fairchild. See you Sunday at chapel," Sally added.

* * *

Phillip Hercell stood up and extended his hand as Ed Latimer entered his office at ten o'clock on Monday morning. "Mr. Latimer," he said, pointing to a chair in front of his desk. "Vat can ve do for you?"

The man from Boston pulled an envelope out of his pocket and handed it to the shipping company manager. It was from a firm of solicitors in London, Beckelsley & Durand, with offices on Leicester Square. The letter was addressed to George Antopholis at an address in Buffalo, New York. It had been forwarded to another address in Boston. The original postmark showed September 26, but the Buffalo postmark was October 19, and was marked "Last Known Address."

The letter was very formal. It identified the Beckelsley & Durand firm as representing the Estate of Demetrius Antopholis, late of Piraeus, Greece, and Limassol, Cyprus. They were seeking the whereabouts of any heirs of his sister, Anna, who had resided at the address shown in Buffalo, New York, after her marriage to one Sidney Bergeman, now also deceased. The letter further stated that the writer believed that there was an heir to Anna Antopholis Bergeman, a nephew "named Georgio or some version such as Jorge or George." If the letter recipient was – or knew – such a person, they were to contact Ian Sherling at the London firm as soon as possible.

A copy was shown to another law firm in Athens, and to several executives of the Cyprus-Hellenic Ship Lines in both Greece and London.

Hercell read the letter, then handed it back to Latimer and looked at him. "You are dis Georgio?"

"No, he is dead, I believe. But if so, I am the beneficiary of his estate."

"Vhy are you telling me dis, Mr. Latimer? You should contact dees solicitors who wrote dah letter."

"Oh, I will, I will. But first, I have a few questions about this ship line, Cyprus Hellenic. Did you know this Demetreus Antopholis?"

"No. I knew of him, but ve never met."

"What exactly is Cyprus Hellenic? A ferry service between Greece and Cyprus?"

Hercell roared with laughter. "No, no! Ve have a fleet of more dan fifty ships, in tree divisions. One, as you suggest, does serve the Piraeus to Cyprus trade. Da second is da old Adriatic Steamship Lines dat Antopholis bought ten, twelve years ago. It is a vorld-vide line of large freighters, and tree cruise ships for da Mediterranean trade. Da tird division is da Suez-Arabian Line, vich Antopholis bought six years ago. It is da primary carrier of crude oil between da Persian Gulf and Britain, vit sixteen super tankers. Dis is a very big operation, Mr. Latimer."

"I see. No chance it's in debt, or that there are creditors to the Antopholis estate?"

"Debt? Vell, I am not da company accountant, Mr. Latimer, but I am a stockholder, ant da dividends are pretty good. No, I don't tink der are any debts."

After thanking Phillip Hercell for his time, Ed Latimer left the offices of Cyprus Hellenic Lines and took a taxi to Leicester Square. He had called earlier that morning and had an eleven thirty appointment with Ian Sherling.

Brewster House was a large office building on Leicester Square containing a number of firms. The Beckelsley & Durand firm was on the sixth floor, in a large suite opposite the elevators. Edgar Latimer approached the receptionist, a trim red headed girl with freckles and a short haircut, and asked to see Ian Sherling.

"Righto," she responded. "I'll let him know you are here, Mister...."

"Latimer. I have an eleven thirty appointment."

The girl rang a number on the phone from her desk, and advised that a Mr. Latimer was there to see Mr. Sherling. As she hung up, she pointed down a hallway, and said, "Second door on the left. Mr. Sherling is expecting you."

Latimer thanked her, and headed for the appointed door, about thirty feet away. As he came to it, a tall, thin, balding man about fifty was rising from a desk within.

"Ah, Mr. Latimer. Do come in. I see you found us with no difficulty."

Ed Latimer shook hands and sat down in the chair across from Ian Sherling.

"What can we do for you, Mr. Latimer?" the solicitor asked.

Latimer did not respond, but simply handed Sherling the envelope he had shown earlier that morning to Phillip Hercell. The solicitor opened it, placed a pair of half-lens reading glasses on his nose and ears and read it quickly. He then set it on the desk in front of him and looked intensely at Latimer.

"Are you George Antopholis?" Sherling asked.

"No, but I knew George. He is dead. I have reason to believe that he may have left a will, and that I may be a beneficiary of that will," Ed Latimer replied.

"I see. Do you have any documentation or other proof of these facts? Or that this is the same George Antopholis we are seeking?"

Not with me, of course. But an attorney in Cleveland, Ohio, in the United States, has all that. I would be grateful if you would contact him and verify what I've said."

Sherling looked at Latimer for a few seconds, his eyes bearing into the other's. "You have an address for this attorney?" he inquired.

"Yes, his name is Tillman Farmer, of the firm of Freeze, Farmer & Rivera, on the 29th floor of the Guardian Building in downtown Cleveland. Unfortunately I do not have that street address or a phone number."

"Oh, I'm sure we can find that, Mr. Latimer. Do you know if there were other beneficiaries?"

"I don't know, but I doubt it. George was a homeless man with deformed feet who appeared somewhat retarded. He lived... well, he stayed under a bridge and collected junk. Someone shot him apparently in a fight over the junk, and it was several days until his body was found. I had known George several years earlier when he first arrived in Cleveland from Buffalo He used my address in Boston for any mail, which I would then forward to him at a street shelter in Cleveland, where George ate his meals. I received this letter, but when I tried to contact him, I learned he was dead."

"But how do you know this is the same man as we were seeking?"

"I would anticipate that you will have to check some records in Buffalo, which is a city in New York State. I also believe that the Ohio welfare people were doing some background checking on George to see if he had any relatives, so they may also be able to help you confirm that he was Demetrius Antopholis's nephew. I don't believe George knew about his uncle, however. He told me he had no family other than his aunt who had died."

"This is very interesting, Mr. Latimer," the solicitor said, writing notes as he spoke. "If what you say is verified, you could become a very rich person. How do we contact you?"

"I'm staying at the Farley Hotel on Kensington. Here, I've got the number on a card," Latimer replied, pulling a card from the hotel out of his wallet and handing it to the solicitor, who jotted down the phone number. "I also have a friend in the city, with whom I may stay part of the time, but I will check the hotel for any messages, or let you know if I move.

"I'm not a man of means, Mr. Sherling," he continued. "I came to London at great personal expense to try to assist you, since I knew George. I knew nothing about this Demetrius Antopholis who died, but have come to learn that he was apparently in the shipping business. Whether he was wealthy or penniless is of no concern to me, but I would like to settle whatever needs to be settled quickly so that I can return to America.

"You could have written to us," the solicitor suggested.

"I intended to. But then, you had a postal strike. By the time I got here, the strike was over. Also, I needed a vacation, and a week in London will not hurt me. And as I said, I do have a friend here."

"I see. We are certainly grateful to you, Mr. Latimer. I will contact this fellow in Cleveland by telephone today and see what we can do. I should be in touch with you in a day or so."

Ed Latimer arose, again shook hands, and turned toward the door. The solicitor watched him leave, then sat down at his desk and dialed a number. In a moment his secretary, a gray-haired lady about sixty, came to his door.

"Get me a phone number in the States, would you, Helen. It is the number of a lawyer named Tillman Farmer, of the firm of Freeze, Farmer and Rivera in Cleveland, Ohio. Some building called the Guardian. Thank you."

* * *

After hearing what the London solicitor had to say, Tillman Farmer agreed that considerable investigation would have to be conducted. After pulling the file, he had confirmed to Ian Sherling that he had indeed a last will and testament in his file, that George Antopholis had been born in Buffalo, New York, to parents who were immigrants from Greece, that he had been raised by an aunt in Buffalo who had died, that he was a disabled homeless street person, and that, yes, he had been murdered.

Did Tillman Farmer think that he might have been murdered because of the will? He said he certainly had no reason to think so, that the only reason he, as an attorney, had been contacted at all was because a friend was helping George apply for welfare, and needed help because the welfare department had delayed in their investigation. The attorney had even suggested a guardianship, but George had rejected the idea. The will had, he recalled, been an afterthought.

Tillman agreed to contact someone in Buffalo to obtain a copy of Antopholis's birth certificate, and also agreed to check on his parents' immigration documents, his aunt's death certificate (a copy of which Sherling said he already had), and any other information he could find on George Antopholis. He would also get a verification of the Social Security Number, and check with the welfare department to see what information they may have found to verify Antopholis's application. He agreed to get back to the London solicitor as soon as possible, but questioned whether there was any chance that someone might oppose the will that he had drawn for George.

"If there are no other legitimate heirs," Sherling had replied, "it is likely that the Greek government will claim a right to the Estate. Whatever transpires, Demetrius Antopholis died in Greece, and his estate is held in Greece. Hence, it is likely that the Greek court may take control of the situation. Would the heir named in this will fight the Greek government for control of the estate?"

"I don't know. The will is valid, and I believe it would be upheld by the Ohio courts. Why would the Greek government not have to file any opposition to the inheritance in Ohio?"

Sherling laughed. "I can see this is going to be a long process! Our firm simply represents the ship lines owned by the estate. Obviously it would be to our advantage to have a person inherit rather than to have the government take it over. Right now the Greek government is not all that stable, so their takeover might well mean the end of the ship lines. We have a man in Greece who works with our firm in any negotiations with the government there. So we would certainly be willing to assist you and your client, whom I assume and you seem to confirm, is this Edgar Latimer, if he wishes to pursue the matter in the courts."

"I'd have no choice but to encourage him to do so," Farmer replied. The two lawyers discussed a few additional points, and agreed to keep in touch. As he hung up, Tillman Farmer also decided to look further into the murder of George Antopholis.

Farmer immediately placed a call to an attorney friend in Buffalo and outlined the situation. He envisioned what might be a very long international legal battle, probably fought only on the basis that he and his firm would be paid a percentage – a very large percentage – of the estate value if they were successful, but very little if they were not. He needed the best information he could get, and instructed his friend to hire the best investigator to look into Antopholis's background in Buffalo, including his school records, his parents' immigration status, the aunt's status and death, and Antopholis's birth certificate. He, in turn, would file the will with the County Probate Court in order to establish jurisdiction.

Later that afternoon Tillman Farmer called another friend at the police department and explained that he had become interested in the murder of a client, George Antopholis, the previous November. He requested any information the friend might provide. Within an hour the friend at the police department called back to advise that the case had been closed, unsolved. The police theory was that Antopholis had been murdered because of something he had in the collection of junk he kept at his unauthorized campsite underneath the viaduct ramp, and that the murderer was most likely another homeless person who had probably left town.

* * *

Sam Whitaker stood in the old Harbor Post Office examining the certified letter that had arrived in his box. It was from a bank in New York. He could not imagine what it might be.

He carefully tore it open and found a number of documents inside. The letter was from the trust department of the bank that had all the accounts for the advertising agency that had taken over the one for which Sam had worked. It explained that at the time of Sam's termination, his vesting in his pension had not been taken into account. For the twelve years Sam had worked for the acquired agency, he had been building a fund of retirement benefits paid for by the agency. These accounts had now been calculated, and Sam was to advise the bank trustees as soon as possible whether he wished to obtain the benefits in the form of a cash settlement of $32,789.84, an annuity policy purchased for that amount which would continue to grow, or the equivalent amount in common stock of the acquiring agency at the value of that stock at the time Sam's firm had been acquired, which would represent 1821.6 shares at $18. Neither the cash settlement nor the annuity, the letter stated, would represent taxable income at this time. The stock, however, would be paid without any accrued dividends; any future dividends would be taxable, as would any capital gains on the original price, should Sam sell it.

Sam walked over to the newsstand across from the Post Office and purchased an afternoon paper that had the closing stock quotes. He ran through the listings until he found the ad agency. The stock was now selling for $24.40. Sam floated back to his hotel, then immediately placed a call to Carolyn in Connecticut. With the stock as collateral, he could make a down-payment on a new home, and Carolyn and Courtney could be home by Easter.

Carolyn, however, was not as enthusiastic. "Let's see the stock, first," she said. "Then let's discuss it with a bank, and see what they suggest. The idea of a long term mortgage doesn't really appeal to me, and we've got to be saving for Courtney's college tuition," she warned. But compared to her usual reactions since they had separated, Sam knew she was seriously considering coming home. He went to dinner that night quite content, and slept well until morning.

Chapter 7

That winter was one of the most severe to strike Northern Ohio in a decade. After one all-day snowstorm the three members of the Religion Department of Fremont College were obliged to spend the night in their office, as the roads to their homes were entirely blocked. Dr. Fairchild lived on a farm along the Portage River south of Port Cleland, at least a fifteen mile drive. The Merriams lived in a Sandusky garden apartment, an even longer and more hazardous drive. The snow had not entirely closed the campus, but enough classes had to be canceled that the students living in the dorms, fraternity or sorority houses had declared a mid-winter frolic. It was the men against the women in an all-out snowball fight, and the women appeared to have the upper hand.

Richard Fairchild was not about to waste such an opportunity to work on anything as frivolous as letting his secretary and his assistant professor join the frolic. Instead he determined that it the perfect time to complete plans for the summer educational tour. This summer the theme was to be Ancient Greece and the Travels of Paul. Only twenty-eight students, mostly from the upper classes who were religion, history or international studies majors, would be permitted to apply.

The two-week tour would be based in Athens, but the students would travel to Thessaloniki, Corinth, Meteora, Patmos, and Ephesus in Turkey. The travel agent who had handled the previous Fremont College tours was already hard at work on the arrangements, but it was now necessary to line up the students, get their deposits, and make sure they had all the proper passports, visas, and inoculations. Although it was only early March, the June departure would be upon them sooner than they would want, and there was a hectic half of a semester left to complete before that.

Sally Merriam had taken special courses in her own college career at Fremont to learn about the travel agency business, hotel management and similar skills needed to assist in scheduling the departmental tours. It was her job to be sure everything and every traveler were ready to go when the appointed day arrived. After six years of arranging such tours, however, she had become an expert.

Richard Fairchild, however, was working on a slightly different project, one that had nothing to do with the college or the trip to Greece, although Greece did figure into the matter. Dr. Fairchild had received a reply to an inquiry he had sent, and while the Merriams were busy planning itineraries and lining up hotel reservations, he was enjoying a moment of peace to read the letter he had just received that day from Ian Sherling, a London solicitor in the firm of Beckelsley & Durand.

The letter surprised the professor. It thanked him for his letter advising that he had encountered someone who possibly might fit the description of the Antopholis heir he was seeking, and confirmed that it did appear that the person he referenced, one George Antopholis, who had been murdered the previous November, might, indeed, be the missing heir. However, he also advised that there was a further will, signed by that heir before his death that left any estate to a friend, a certain Edgar Latimer.

"Would you happen to know this Edgar Latimer?" the letter inquired. "He apparently resides, or once resided, in Boston, but was with the deceased, George or Georgio Antopholis, when the will was prepared by a Cleveland attorney, Tillman Farmer. Mr. Farmer is currently providing us with further documentation on the relationship of the deceased George or Georgio Antopholis to Demetrius Antopholis. He has also filed the will with the Cuyahoga County Probate Court, as that is where the death of the American heir occurred."

Fairchild reread the letter, but could not think of who Edgar Latimer might be. He knew of no such person, but of course, he had barely known George, and it was only through Sam Whitaker that he knew about George's murder.

On the outside chance that Whitaker might still be in his office, Fairchild picked up his phone and asked the operator to place the long distance call to the Taylor Marine Insurance Agency in Cleveland. Although Harry Taylor was standing at Sam's desk when the phone rang, he nodded to Sam to go ahead and answer the phone.

"Taylor Marine," he said.

"Sam? Sam Whitaker?"

"Yes?"

"Sam, this is Richard Fairchild. I wasn't sure I'd get you on a stormy day like this."

"Doc! Good to hear from you. Yep, Mr. Taylor and I are all alone here. The others went home hours ago, but, as you know I don't have — well, that's another story, and a good one, too. But what can I do for you. You gonna move the insurance on that boat of yours up in Port Cleland to our agency?"

"Oh, I hadn't thought about that, but I guess I could get the college to consider it. What's your good news that has you so excited? Are you still living in that little hotel?"

"Yes, but not for long. Seems that when I was terminated from the ad agency they forgot to reimburse me my pension funds. It's enough for me to get another house, and I think Carolyn and Courtney will come home. They're going to come down over the spring school break and we'll look at houses. She's dropped the divorce action, too."

"Well, that's wonderful news, Sam." Fairchild replied. "What I called about, however, is George. Have you ever heard of a Edgar Latimer?"

"Latimer? No, it doesn't sound familiar. Who is he?"

"It appears George had a rich uncle in Greece, some tycoon who owned a bunch of ship lines. Before George was killed he apparently went to an attorney and had a will made that left anything he had to this Edgar Latimer."

"George? George wouldn't have known how to find a lawyer!"

"Maybe it was this Latimer that took him to the lawyer. Were any of the guys at the shelter especially friendly with George?"

"Oh, a couple of the guys looked out for him, like I did, but I don't think they'd have been the kind of friends that George would have named in a will. What the heck, he had nothing to will to anyone that any of us knew about. I seriously doubt he knew anything about a rich uncle in Greece."

"That's about what I thought. What's the name of the new man at St. Vincent House? Maybe he could check the records and see if there was an Edgar Latimer."

"The new guy calls himself 'Brother Fred.' He's not as friendly as Amos was, but he might give you that information. Do you have the phone number there?"

"Yes. I guess I'll give Brother Fred a call. Thanks, Sam, and congratulations on your great news. I'll keep in touch."

As Sam hung up the phone his boss said, "'Doc?' Is that your friend, Richard Fairchild, the detective professor?"

"Yes. He has learned that the homeless man that was murdered, George, was the heir to some big shipping company in Greece. Odd. Shoeless George never had a cent."

"Hmm. That is interesting. So your friend is still investigating that murder?

"Yes, I guess so. I figured he'd forget about it after the holidays."

* * *

When he disconnected from the first call the professor again rang the college operator and asked for a second long distance call to Cleveland, this time to St. Vincent House, to the phone number in the office. In a few moments a man answered.

"St. Vincent House, Brother Fred," said the soft voice.

"Brother Fred, my name is Richard Fairchild. I believe you arrived just as I was leaving last January, having supervised the shelter while Brother Amos was away."

"Oh, yes, I recognize your name. You're the professor from Fremont. But the fellow who was here in January was Brother Jerome, one of the friars. I'm just a lay brother, like Amos. A trained group counselor. But what can I do for you? Do you want to join us again?"

"No, no, not right away, anyway!" Fairchild laughed. He then explained about George, and asked if there might be any records on a "guest" named Edgar Latimer. The new man in charge of the shelter quickly rifled through the files kept on all of the guests, but could not find one in that name.

"No 'Edgars' and no 'Latimers'," Brother Fred reported.

"Hmm. You don't happen to know what Brother Amos's last name is, do you?"

"No, I never met Amos. The Order would know. I do seem to recall hearing it once, something like Watts or Waters I believe it was."

"How would I contact the Order?"

"They're located in Geneva, New York, on the Canandaigua Road. Brother James is in charge of the shelter program. Here, let me give you the number."

The college switchboard operator was used to placing a number of long distance calls for the Religion Department – although they seemed to have more than most of the other departments. The operator lived in town, and was not as urgent to get home as many of the other staff members who lived outside of town, and who would be affected by the storm. After several rings a man with a deep voice answered.

"Brothers of St. Vincent."

Fairchild identified himself, and explained why he was calling.

"We don't usually give out information on our brothers, or our lay employees, Dr. Fairchild," the man, who called himself Brother Peter, explained. "However, I know Brother Amos slightly, from retreats he has made here, and I don't believe his name was Latimer. It might have been, but I just don't recall that name. We don't have the personnel files here. We screen and hire the lay brothers who run our shelters, but the paperwork is all handled by an outside employment service that issues the paychecks, keeps track of taxes and Social Security, health insurance and things like that. It's called Northern New York Employee Services, up in Rochester, but they have instructions not to release information on our employees without written permission of the employee. I'm sorry I can't help you further, Dr. Fairchild."

"Does the name Watts or Waters sound familiar, perhaps in association with Brother Amos?"

"No, I don't know anyone with those names. I do recall that Amos was from the Boston area, at least he went to graduate school up there. But I don't know which one. He was only with us a couple of years."

"Well, thank you, Brother Peter. I'm at a dead end, but I do appreciate your help."

"Not at all. Your name is also familiar to us here. We have you on our regular prayer cycle. I do hope that you will continue to volunteer at St. Vincent House in Cleveland, and that you will come visit us on a retreat some time. We really do have a nice setting here on the Finger Lakes."

"Thank you. I enjoy working at the shelter, and I may take you up on that offer of a retreat some day. Right now my schedule is so hectic I could use a retreat!"

The professor sat staring at his phone after he had hung up. It was indeed a dead end. He scribbled a little note back to the London solicitor, Ian Sherling, addressed and stamped the envelope, and threw it in his outgoing mailbox. The rest of the day he spent working on his class notes for the remainder of the winter/spring semester

* * *

"Daddy!" Fred Rogers heard as he answered his office phone. "Daddy, I'm so glad I reached you."

"Is anything wrong, Kelly?" he urgently inquired.

"No, everything's fine. But listen. This class I'm in is one of the ones approved for a summer trip to Greece. It's a credit course, and I want to go. They only take twenty eight, and there aren't many vacancies left. I need a deposit of $300 by Tuesday."

"Greece? Why would you want to go to Greece?"

"It's a history tour, Daddy. All the ancient cities, and the mountains, and even some ancient city in Turkey. This great professor, one of the best here at Fremont, will be leading it, and I hear his tours are fabulous."

"Whoa! You sound like a salesman. Let's think this through. I thought you were going to spend your summer here at the plant so you could earn some money for a car. And when we went to Paris you went on a family passport. You'd need your own now."

"But Daddy, it's just for two weeks. I could work at the plant for the weeks ahead of and after the tour. And a passport is no problem. The secretary helps the students get what they need."

"Employees don't just come and go as they please, Kelly. You can't work a week or so and then take a two-week vacation. Real life isn't like that. It's a full time commitment."

"*Daddy!*"

"Daddy nothing. I can't have you coming in here for a week and then taking off again, just because you're the boss's daughter."

"Well, then, I'll start work after the trip. I can use the couple of weeks ahead of that to learn a little Greek, or study the texts we're supposed to study before we go."

Fred Rogers knew he would lose this discussion, but decided to play the game. "I doubt your mother will agree, Kelly. How much is this trip?"

"Only $2800, including air fare, all meals and hotels."

"You're surely not going to get very good hotels and meals for $2800, dear."

"We have roommates."

"Who would be your roommate?"

"I don't know."

"Are there boys on this tour too?"

"I suppose. But Daddy, it's a lifetime opportunity. I'll work for free when I get back if you'll loan me the money now."

"But you wouldn't earn $2800 in just two months of work, Kelly. The job you would have only earns minimum wage."

"But I have savings…."

"You know your mother would never let you touch your savings, dear."

"*Daddy…,*" Kelly pleaded.

Kelly had always been a sensible kid. A strikingly beautiful auburn-haired green-eyed girl, much like her mother, she had always gotten good grades, and had never even hinted a desire to get into the kind of mischief other kids seemed to enjoy. Yet Fred had always tried to teach her respect for money, and the fact that her father's success was not necessarily her success. She needed independence, and he could see where such a trip might help her to learn such independence.

"Kelly, I'll discuss this with your mother. If she agrees, we'll cover the $2800 for you, and you can work here after you get back, no reimbursement necessary. You seem to have your heart set on this, and it could well be a good experience."

"Oh, Daddy! Thank you. You won't be sorry. Besides, don't you have clients in Greece?"

"No clients, but one of our transportation companies, a ship line, is there."

"Maybe you and Mom could come over and meet us somewhere?"

"It's something to think about, but I'd doubt that, dear. Do you have the $300 left in your checking account?"

"I'm afraid not, Daddy. You know, books and all…."

"Okay. I'll transfer $500 into it today, and you can make your deposit. I think I can convince your mother that the trip is a good idea. Now, you take care, dear, and we'll be out to pick you up for the spring break."

"Thanks, Daddy. I love you."

"I love you, too, dear." Fred knew he was a pushover for his daughter.

* * *

Ian Sherling and Tillman Farmer were discussing the litigation filed by the Greek government in Athens. "I've had our office in Athens retain one of the best law firms in Greece," Sherling said. "They won't be cheap, but I believe that they will be effective. There's a lot at risk."

"What is their name?" the Cleveland lawyer inquired.

"Kenopoulos and Associates. 15 Acropolis Way."

"Exactly what does the Greek lawsuit allege?" the American asked.

"First, they allege that full jurisdiction of the Estate of Demetrius Antopholis is in Greece, as he was a Greek citizen and died in Greece. Under Greek law, only qualified heirs in foreign nations can inherit under a will. The suit disputes that Latimer is a qualified heir, hence the Estate should revert to the government."

"On what basis do they make this allegation that Latimer is not a qualified heir?"

"Their legal reasoning is not very clear. As you know, they don't follow the common law as we do, so have not cited previous cases. Their arguments will focus primarily on the fact that Latimer is not a Greek resident, and that he is not related in any way to the deceased, hence should not inherit."

"Our probate court should rule on our motion for approval of the will here within a week. As soon as I get that order – which should be favorable as no one opposed it – I'll send it to the firm in Athens, with a copy to you there in London. Have you heard anything further from Latimer?"

"He moved out of his hotel and apparently is staying with his girlfriend in her flat. I understand he has applied for a work visa, as he apparently had not anticipated the time it was going to take to complete this matter. I guess he thought that all he had to do was show up, advise of the Ohio will, and take over. I fear he was a bit naïve."

"To say the least. Ian, I'll forward the order from here as soon as I get it."

"Bye."

* * *

Ed Latimer stood behind the children's clothing counter in an East Acton neighborhood branch department store. It was the only job he had been able to find since being issued his six-month work visa, and while he loathed selling, he especially loathed selling children's clothing.

"Would these fit a two-year-old?" a customer asked, holding up a pair of short pants.

"Depends on the two-year-old, Madam. Is he chubby or thin?"

"About average."

"Then they ought to fit. Those are listed for 18 to 36 months, I believe."

"Do you have them in other colors?"

"I could check, Madam," he replied, moving over to the table where the pants had been to look in the cupboard beneath. She held the green ones. He pulled out a pair of blue ones and held them up for her to examine.

"Oh, these are lovely," she exclaimed. " Jolly good, I'll take them both."

"Thank you, Madam," he replied as he rang up the sale and placed the two pairs of pants in a bag.

"American, are you?" the customer asked.

"Yes, staying with a friend for a while," he replied. It was a constant question. He had no West End accent, and his New England twang gave him away. But it would not be long, he believed. Ian Sherling was encouraging, and it appeared that the case in Athens might collapse.

He had been warned, however, that it would be necessary to go to Greece for the trial, and that it would be conducted entirely in Greek. In his spare time he had been endeavoring to learn some Greek phrases, things that might help him sway the judges who would decide his case. He could win all the cases he wanted in America, but it was the Greek court that would make the final decision.

That night at dinner he told Terri Bookley that he would soon have to go to Greece for a trial. Up to that point she had known very little of why he was in England, or what it was he had been awaiting.

"A trial? What kind of a trial?"

"That business matter I said brought me here."

"I thought that had fallen through. Isn't that why you got the work visa and a job?"

"Oh, that's just to tide me over. No, what is at hand is big. Very big. Have you ever heard of the Cyprus-Hellenic Lines, a ship line?"

"Don't they operate the *Helen of Troy*, that Mediterranean cruise ship? I planned to take a trip on it a couple of years ago, but wasn't able to get away."

"Yes, that, and the *Ulysses Voyager* and a couple of smaller vessels, plus most of the tankers bringing oil into Britain."

"How are you involved with that?" Terri asked.

"I may own them," he casually replied.

"Own them?" she exclaimed. "How?"

"The old guy who owned all of them in Greece died. The estate went to his nephew in America, but before they found the nephew he was killed. I was named the heir to his estate, so I inherit the ship line."

"My God! When? It must be worth millions."

"Many millions. But the Greek government has contested the will, and is trying to claim that the ship lines, there are three of them, should be taken over by the Greek government. That's what the trial is about.

"I have lawyers here in London, in Ohio and in Athens all working on my behalf, for a big piece of the money if they are successful, but in the meantime, I have very little cash, which is why I had to take a job. The trial is supposed to be in June, just a few months from now, and I'll have to be there."

Terri looked at him, just a bit starry-eyed. "I'll not miss this!" she said. "I'll go with you."

"I hoped you would, Terri."

* * *

Fremont College faculty usually only got a few days off at the spring break, although students got a full week. It was long enough, however, for Richard and Esther Fairchild to take a long weekend drive. As they had no children, and the farm on which the professor lived had only beef cattle, there were no daily chores to keep him home.

On the Friday afternoon before the long four-day holiday he and Esther loaded up their late model Ford station wagon and headed east, picking up Interstate 90 east of Cleveland, and by dusk they were just west of Buffalo. By 7:30 that evening they had exited the New York State Thruway near Rochester, and found a motel for three nights.

Dr. Fairchild had explained his mission to his wife, and she had approved his concern and nosiness, although she was usually disapproving of his frequent forays into the world of crime and danger. Too often he had become a target, and after even she had been mugged, blown out of her bed, and hunted down like an animal, Esther had said, "No more!" But she knew that her husband thrived on such drama. She only prayed that this would not turn out to be another wild goose chase where Richard was the goose being chased.

On Saturday the Fairchilds awoke to a sunny morning. The hills around the Finger Lakes were starting to turn green with the first buds of spring, and they spent the day driving around Lake Canandaigua, stopping at one of the wineries to purchase a few bottles of the locally grown wines for their wine cellar back in Ohio. That evening they drove into Rochester and attended a concert at the Eastman Conservatory.

On Sunday morning they drove over to the St. Vincent Friary west of Geneva and attended the morning service held by the brothers in their chapel. This was the order that operated the shelter where Fairchild occasionally substituted as manager. After the service he introduced Esther and himself to Brother Peter.

"I'm glad you came to visit us, Dr. Fairchild," the brown-robed, gray-bearded friar said. "Why didn't you let us know? We had plenty of room in our guest house this weekend."

"Maybe we'll do that again some time. But I did want to tell you that I have been in touch with the Northern New York Employee Services in Rochester, and they have agreed to meet with me tomorrow morning. I'm hopeful that they can verify what I need to know."

"Still concerned about Brother Amos?" the friar asked.

"Yes. I'm hoping to confirm that his last name is not 'Latimer.'"

"What if it is? Why would that be important?"

"Well, there is a murder involved, the murder last November of a man named George Antopholis. One of the persons who could have profited by that murder was named Latimer. Edgar Latimer. I pray that Brother Amos is not Edgar Latimer."

"I see. As I explained, we had no information on him here. He had been screened by our people, selected for his knowledge and training for group social work and his interest in conducting a religious shelter, with all the daily offices we require. He has a master's in social work, as do all our shelter managers, but, of course, as a lay employee who is not really paid all that much, it was not unusual, or unexpected, that Amos would leave us. Our lay employees have their own lives and families apart from the Order. But I would certainly concur with you that I hope Amos was not involved in any murder."

On Monday morning Richard and Esther Fairchild checked out of their motel and drove into downtown Rochester, to an office on East Broad Street. While Esther went to a nearby department store, Richard entered the tall office building and took an elevator to the fifth floor, finally finding the offices of the Northern New York Employee Services. He had spoken earlier by phone with the manager, Jim Schiff, and asked for him. In a few minutes a short man with dark rimmed glasses appeared, and invited the professor into his office.

"Dr. Fairchild, good morning. Thank you for coming. I'm Jim Schiff," he said, holding out his hand.

"I just had a call from Brother Peter at the friary. He said he knew you were coming, and that given the circumstances of your mission and the potential public relations impact on their order, that I could share whatever information I might have with you. I've pulled the file in question," he continued. "Exactly what is it you would like to know?"

"First, I'd like to know the full name of Brother Amos. And his address."

"Okay," Schiff said, opening the manila-colored file folder on his desk. "Let's see. Amos Fowler Waterman, age 54, well, about to turn 55. Home address is 16 Barkley Street, Boston, Massachusetts. Master's degree in social work from the University of Massachusetts. Assigned to St. Vincent House for three years, resigned after only two, and, as far as we know, returned to that address in Boston. Would you like his Social Security Number?"

Richard Fairchild had been taking notes, and nodded in the affirmative, writing down the nine digits as Schiff read them. "Thank goodness!" he said.

"What was it you feared?" the employment service manager asked.

"I was afraid his name was Latimer."

"We had a Latimer here. A number of years ago," Schiff replied.

"What? Who?"

"He was the manager of the Cleveland shelter, just ahead of Waterman, I believe. Let me get his file." Jim Schiff arose, left his office and returned in a minute with another manila folder.

"Why are you concerned about Latimer?" Schiff inquired.

"He was named in the will of a man who was murdered," Fairchild explained. "He could be a suspect, I suppose."

"Goodness!" the other man replied. "I would hope not."

Schiff opened the folder, and withdrew several papers inside. One was an employment application, much like that in Waterman's file. Edgar A. Latimer, it indicated, would now be in his late thirties; he also had a master's degree in social work from the University of Massachusetts, and an original address in Boston. His last known address, after resigning from employment with the religious order, was 47 Forestwood Avenue, Lakewood, Ohio. Fairchild also copied down his Social Security Number. There was little else in the file, except a note in his letter of resignation that Latimer recommended Amos Waterman for the position he was leaving.

"This is all very helpful," Fairchild said. He then stood up, and added, "But I've taken you away from your work long enough, Mr. Schiff, and I do appreciate your help."

"Glad we were able to be of assistance, Dr. Fairchild. I hope that your fears or suspicions are not confirmed."

"So do I. I'd hate for any bad publicity to fall on the order. They do so much good in the inner cities. Thank you again."

Once he had collected Esther from the department store, where they stopped and had an early lunch, the Fairchilds headed west again, bypassing Buffalo on the Thruway and stopping only once for gas. It was early afternoon when they reached the point east of Cleveland where Interstate 90 and the Cleveland Shoreway merged, and Fairchild rolled along the waterfront, past the Burke Lakefront Airport, the wharves along the harbor, and the Stadium, climbing up onto the viaduct over the Cuyahoga River. He exited the expressway at Lake Avenue, driving past all of the expensive high-rises overlooking Lake Erie, and at 117th Street entered the City of Lakewood.

There he slowed until he came to a cross street named Forestwood. Number 47 was to the right, on the very end of the street, on a bluff overlooking the lake. A white fence surrounded the yard. Fairchild parked his station wagon in front of the large, expensive-looking house. Esther remained in the car while the professor went to the door.

A pleasant-looking auburn-haired woman in her forties came to the door, inquiring what the man standing outside wanted.

"I'm looking for an Edgar Latimer," Fairchild replied.

"Ed Latimer?" the woman repeated. "Gosh, Ed hasn't lived here for a couple of years now. Last I heard, he'd moved back to Boston. He was only a tenant, living in the little apartment above our garage. It has been years."

"Would you have a forwarding address?"

"I think we did, for a while. Sent some mail and stuff on to him in Boston, but I don't know where that would be now."

"If you could find it, I would certainly appreciate it," Fairchild said. "Here, let me leave you my card. If you find the address, or any other information on how I might contact Latimer, please let me know."

"He worked at a shelter downtown, I believe," the woman at the door added. "Perhaps they may know."

"I've already checked there, Mrs. ...."

"Rogers."

Fairchild then noticed the two letters on the fancy wrought iron frame door: FR.

"Fred Rogers?" he asked.

"Yes. Do you know my husband?"

"No, but I've heard of a Fred Rogers who is in the chemical business."

"Yes, that's Fred. He owns the Rogers Chemical Company."

"I see," the professor replied. "Well, thank you, Mrs. Rogers. I appreciate your help, and hope you can find that forwarding address."

* * *

From his farm on the Portage River the next morning Richard Fairchild made several more phone calls. The first was to Sam Whitaker. He told Sam what he had found out at the employment services office, and that he was trying to trace Ed Latimer, the previous shelter manager. Sam said that he had once heard George mention a "Brother Ed," but had not really understood about whom George was talking. Sam agreed to pass the information on to Officer Andy Segretti.

Fairchild's next call was to the state welfare department in Cleveland. After going through several underlings, the professor was finally connected to the manager. He explained who he was, and why he was calling.

"Yes, I seem to recall the case," the manager, a Ralph Winter, said. "It was the man's second application. He'd made one several years earlier, but the investigators found he had some wealthy relatives somewhere, and put his application on hold. Just a minute, let me get that file."

After a long wait, Winter again picked up his phone. "Hello? Dr. Fairchild? Yes, I have that file here. It was marked 'pending,' as there had been an inquiry to the New York welfare department for background investigation of an aunt, apparently now deceased. She apparently had a will. In the file here I see a note on the first application that any information is to be conveyed to an Ed Latimer through some attorney named Farmer. On the second application, the information was to go to a Brother Amos, at St. Vincent House. We did write a letter to that attorney advising why the application was being delayed, but never heard back. That was about two and a half years ago. The second application was made about a year ago."

"In the application, is there any listing of 'next of kin'?" Fairchild inquired.

"Yes, let me see. On the first application it simply lists this Ed Latimer. On the second," he hesitated while he flipped through the pages, "the second shows that as the Brothers of St. Vincent, in care of St. Vincent House."

"Would that have the same effect as a will?"

"Now, that's an interesting question, Dr. Fairchild. I do seem to recall a case where a previous will was disputed on the basis of a welfare application, but, of course, I'm not a lawyer, so I couldn't really say. Had we been paying benefits, we would have a right of lien, of course."

"Is the second application dated and signed by George Antopholis?"

"Yes, it is. It's not a very clear handwriting, but that appears to be the name signed on the application, last August."

"Thank you, Mr. Winter. I really appreciate your looking into this for me."

Fairchild's next call was to an attorney in Sandusky. He asked the attorney to research Ohio law on the subject of wills and agency. Then he placed another call to Geneva, New York, and spoke at length with Brother Peter, informing him of the way the state application had been completed.

Dr. Fairchild's final long distance call that afternoon was to a number in Boston. A woman answered the phone, and advised that the party with whom Fairchild wished to speak would not be in until that evening. The professor agreed to call back that evening.

At eight that evening Fairchild again called Boston, this time connecting with Amos Waterman. The former shelter manager immediately recognized Fairchild's name and voice, and inquired about Esther and the men at the shelter. Waterman explained that after he had left the shelter for his vacation he had been offered a position as an instructor in group social work at a small Boston college, and couldn't refuse the offer because it paid so much better than the shelter work. "Besides," he added, "I was never cut out to live like a monk. That's hard on one's love life!"

After several minutes of such discussion Fairchild asked, "Amos, you apparently were a good friend of Edgar Latimer, the man who was manager of St. Vincent House ahead of you. Have you been in touch with him recently?"

"Ed Latimer? No, I've not seen or heard from Ed in months. I think he's working for the state here in Massachusetts. Last time I spoke with him was in November. He called me trying to find George, and I told him George had been killed. Why?"

"I'm trying to locate him. It seems he was named in George Antopholis's will, and stands to inherit a very valuable Greek shipping company."

"What! Our 'Shoeless George'? Why, he hadn't anything to leave to anyone."

"He didn't know he had a 'rich uncle'."

"A rich uncle? George? You've got to be kidding!"

"I wish I were. It's just possible that this was why George was murdered."

"But I thought the police believe another homeless person shot George."

"Do you think that?"

"Well, it did seem sort of out of keeping with the guys. None of them ever had a gun, as far as I knew. But George was out there on the street. Why, anyone could have shot him."

"No, I think George was deliberately murdered, either for something he found, or because he was about to become very rich."

"Something he found?"

"Yes, Sam Whitaker and I had a theory that on one of George's assignments through the labor pool he may have found something that could become evidence of some sort of crime, and someone involved saw him take it. He was, I understand, always collecting 'treasures' in that junk-pile under the bridge."

"There wasn't anything of real value there, as far as I know, but, of course, I never looked at any of it."

"Who knows what George might have found. But that is just one theory. The business about the will is the other. Apparently Edgar Latimer was from Boston," the professor continued, "but I don't have a specific address. I thought you might. I'd like to talk with him. Would you be willing to do a little research for me?"

"Research?"

"George was shot apparently sometime around November 7. The exact day is unknown because he wasn't missed right away."

"That's right."

"I want to know where Edgar Latimer was the entire first week of November. If you can find that out for me, it will go a long way toward showing whether Latimer should be a suspect or not in George's murder."

"Good God! I can't believe Ed would.... But I wouldn't know where to start."

"Start by trying to find out where Latimer lives. You said he apparently has a job with the state, so someone must kept track of his working hours."

"Okay, I'll try. I think I know where he works. How do I reach you, Richard?"

Fairchild left his address and phone numbers and hung up. He thought to himself that even if Latimer had been out of Boston the first week in November, it would be difficult to prove he had been in Cleveland, especially if he had tried to hide his travel.

* * *

Harry Taylor sat at his desk overlooking the pier next to the one in which his insurance agency was located. It was late in the afternoon, a gray, misty day, and only Sam Whitaker was still working. He had in front of him one of his claim files, a file that concerned him greatly. The claim had not yet been paid. The insurers had certainly had enough time to investigate, but still there was no word from them. He had written twice for a status report, and his client was anxious to collect.

The delay in settlement of the claim alarmed Taylor. There was so much money involved, too much at stake for his client. His brow wrinkled as he thought about all the possible things that could go wrong. Then his mind wandered to what Sam had told him about Sam's friend, this college professor, who was intent on solving a murder. He wondered what motivated someone to do that after even the police had abandoned the case. Sam had related to him what they had done, and how Sam was passing information along to one of the policemen he'd seen eating in the restaurant below the agency offices.

Harry closed the file. No sense writing another letter to London. Sooner or later they would have to respond. He gathered up the rather thick file and carried it back to the claim file cabinet, where he stuffed it in back of a number of older, closed files.

Chapter 8

It was several weeks later when Richard Fairchild was sitting in his office reviewing the applications of the students who had made deposits for the summer seminar in Greece and Turkey that he made the connection between one of the applicants and the matter that had been his avocation for the past five months. The application showed the address of Kelly Rogers as 47 Forestwood Avenue, Lakewood. What a coincidence, he thought.

For those students under the age of 21, which included Kelly, the professor always wrote a letter to the parents advising of the application and requesting the parents' consent for the trip. There was also a release for each to sign. Fairchild debated whether he should include a note with his letter to the Rogers inquiring again about a forwarding address for Edgar Latimer, but decided against it.

However, when the forms came back to him two weeks later, Mildred Rogers had added a note of her own, expressing surprise when she had realized that the professor had been the man at her door inquiring about Ed Latimer, and confirming that she had been unable to find any forwarding address. She also advised that she and Fred Rogers might possibly also be in Athens while Kelly was on the tour as her husband had business there, and that perhaps their paths might cross again.

Fairchild wrote a short personal note back, thanking her for the information and stating that he, too, was surprised at the coincidence, but that he would look forward to seeing them in Athens. He enclosed a copy of their itinerary, including all of the hotels at which the tour would be staying.

* * *

"We've got problems!" Tillman Farmer stated when Ian Sherling answered his phone in London.

"What is the matter?" the British solicitor inquired.

"There has been a challenge made to the Ohio will," the Cleveland attorney explained. "It seems that when our client, Latimer, met with Antopholis and me three years ago he did not explain that he was working within his capacity as the manager of a homeless shelter where Antopholis was living at the time. The shelter was owned by a religious order in New York, and they have filed an appeal to the order confirming Latimer as the heir. To support their claim, they have provided a certified copy of a later welfare department application in which Antopholis lists their shelter as 'next of kin.'

"I don't believe that carries the same value as a true last will and testament," Farmer continued, "but my people are researching it at present. It could, at the least, throw some doubt on the validity of the will, if in fact there could be sufficient evidence brought that Antopholis was not of 'sound mind and body' when he signed the will. If there is such evidence, as this application for welfare seems to state, that he was retarded, then a guardianship should have been appointed to execute the will."

"That will play into the Greek government's hands, won't it?" Sherling said, not really expecting an answer. "But let's fight the Greeks first. If Latimer wins that, then we can take on this challenge in the States later. The trial is set for June. I've alerted Latimer, and he and his girlfriend are going to fly down there with me a few days before to meet with our attorneys in Athens. Are you coming to the trial?"

"No, I've got only a few weeks to respond to this appeal. But I'll keep in touch with you. I've spoken to the attorneys in Athens a couple of times, and have their number. Perhaps it would be better not to tell them about this appeal just yet. Let's see what happens first."

"Right. I won't say anything to Latimer at this point, either, until I hear from you. Christ, Tillman, do you think maybe Latimer did shoot Antopholis?"

"I don't know. The police here have not suspected him. But it looks awfully suspicious, the timing and all. Demetrius died before George was killed, so if the aunt's will was valid – which seems to be an uncontested factor – then George was the rightful heir, and his heirs should also inherit. But if George was murdered just for the inheritance, God, I really don't know. But suspicions are not convictions. We're a long way from that! You can't convict on a motive alone. There has to be proof beyond the shadow of a reasonable doubt in our courts, just as in yours."

"Keep me advised, Tillman, and I'll do likewise for you."

* * *

"Welcome to Athinai. Welcome to Hellas," the signs at the Athens International Airport read. Richard Fairchild had not realized that he and his student tour group had been on the same flight from London Heathrow to Athens with Edgar Latimer until he had seen one of the students, Kelly Rogers, speaking with a man and woman while they were waiting to clear customs.

Curious as to whom they were, he later saw Kelly at their hotel, the Attalos on Athinas Street, and said, "Hello, Miss Rogers. Are you enjoying the trip so far?"

"Oh, yes, Dr. Fairchild, very much. I've been to Europe before, but never to Greece. I so much appreciate your allowing me to join the tour."

"I noticed you were having a conversation with some people as we were clearing the customs. Did you see someone you knew?"

"Talk about a small world!" she laughed. "Came all this way, and bumped into a man who used to be my parents' tenant back in Lakewood. I hadn't seen Ed in years."

"Ed?"

"His name is Ed Latimer. He said he is here on some business deal. He and his girlfriend from London."

"Interesting. Did he say at which hotel they would be staying?"

"Yes. Said to give him a call if I had time. They are staying at the Titania − if that is how it's pronounced − and will be here a couple of weeks. Apparently it is near what is called Constitution Square."

"That isn't too far from our hotel," Fairchild said, before another student approached to ask him a question.

* * *

The courts in Greece, organized under Article 93 of the Constitution, are similar to those in the United States, except for the various levels of appeal. Lawyers, or *dikhgoros*, represent those appearing before the courts, which, except for the audit court that rules on governmental issues, are divided into administrative, civil and criminal matters. A three-judge panel had been assigned to hear the case of the *Estate of Demetrius Antopholis*.

News of the case, and its importance to both Greece and the international shipping industry, had been reported in several London newspapers, attracting worldwide attention in the week before the trial in Athens was to begin. That evening after supper Richard Fairchild, who had been so busy the few days before leaving Ohio that he had not had time to read the papers, relaxed in his room in the Attalos and glanced through the latest *International Herald Tribune* he had purchased in the lobby.

"Listen to this, Esther," he said as she continued to unpack some of her clothes from a suitcase. 'Trial to Determine Ownership of Antopholis Ship Lines Begins Tomorrow. Athens. Trial to determine the right of inheritance to the Estate of Demetrius Antopholis is scheduled to begin before a three-judge panel in Athens on Tuesday. The Estate includes ownership of the Cyprus-Hellenic Lines, including the former Adriatic Steamship Lines and the Suez-Arabian Line, a major oil transporter of crude oil to the U.K. Estimated value of the estate is near £800,000,000.

"London solicitors Beckelsley & Durand are representing the interests of Edgar Latimer, who was named in the will of Georgio Antopholis, a nephew of Demetrius Antopholis, who died in the United States after the death of his uncle. The government of Greece, however, argues that the right of inheritance died with Demetrius's sister, who was specifically named in Demetrius's will, and should not pass beyond that sister or her heir, Georgio. As Latimer has no direct relationship to any of the deceased Antopholis family, the government argues that the Estate should pass to the Greek people.

"Sources in the United States, however, note that a court in Ohio has already validated the Georgio, or George, Antopholis will naming Latimer. An appeal has recently been filed however, by a religious order in New York for which Latimer was employed at the time the will was made.

"Business interests in the U.K. argue that if the Greek government takes over the ship line, oil shipments to the U.K. could become subject to any political disputes that might arise in the future between Greece and Turkey or other Balkan nations. They argue that independence of the ship line is vitally important, and strongly oppose confiscation by the Greek government."

"We certainly got here at an interesting time," Esther commented.

"Yes," he replied, arising from his chair to stretch. "You know, I believe I will take a little walk this evening. Want to come along?"

"Richard!" Esther exclaimed. "I'm exhausted. You must be, too. We've been flying for, how many hours? I'm not even sure what day it is. You ought to go to bed, for you've got a big day tomorrow taking those kids up the Acropolis and lecturing all day."

"I won't be long. Just need to stretch my legs a little, so I'll sleep better," he answered, straightening his tie.

At the door to the hotel Fairchild climbed into a taxi and asked to be taken to the Hotel Titania on Panepistimiou Avenue. It was only a few short blocks away, but took several minutes in the heavy evening traffic. Athens is a city that becomes very active after dark, and it seemed that thousands were in the streets and restaurants and clubs, enjoying the warm summer air and sea breezes.

At the Titania Fairchild asked for Edgar Latimer. The desk clerk agreed to ring his room. "Whom may I say is visiting?" he asked the professor in perfect English.

"Tell Mr. Latimer I am Dr. Fairchild, an acquaintance of Fred Rogers."

The instruction worked, and within moments Fairchild was on the elevator to the fifth floor room of Edgar Latimer. Latimer was standing at his door down the hall as Fairchild exited the elevator.

"Dr. Fairchild?" Latimer said, holding out his hand. "The clerk said you were a friend of Fred Rogers. Come in."

Latimer followed the professor into the room, and introduced him to Terri Bookley, who, like Esther Fairchild, was still unpacking. They sat down in the two armchairs in the room.

"I'm not exactly a friend of Fred Rogers," Fairchild said. "However, his name is known to me, in connection with his chemical company, I've met Mrs. Rogers, and their daughter, Kelly, is on a college history tour I am conducting."

"Yes! I saw her this morning. You are not a medical doctor, then."

"No. I'm a religion professor. However, I am also a friend of the Brothers of St. Vincent, and have temporarily helped manage St. Vincent House in Cleveland. I believe you worked there at one time."

"Yes, that's correct," Latimer confirmed. "I managed the shelter for a couple of years. But it didn't pay very much, I'm afraid."

"It was during my first temporary stay at St. Vincent House a year and a half ago that I became familiar with a disabled man, George Antopholis," Fairchild continued. He watched Edgar Latimer's face and eyes for any reaction, but saw none.

"Shoeless George! What a pitiful character he was. You know that it is because of him that I am here, I gather," Latimer said.

"Yes. The upcoming trial was reported in the paper. They didn't report that George was murdered, however." This time Fairchild detected a slight wrinkling of Latimer's brow. Latimer was looking more intensely at the professor.

"George's murder interests me," Fairchild added.

"The police believe another homeless man shot George, I understand," Latimer said. They both noticed that Terri Bookley had stopped unpacking, and was sitting on the bed, listening to the conversation.

"I understand the police may reopen the case," Fairchild reported.

This time Latimer's brows raised a bit as he stared at Fairchild, who added, "I rather suspect that they may ask you where you were the first week in November last year, Mr. Latimer."

"Why, I was in Boston, where I was living then. I was working for a state social agency there since I am a trained social worker."

"The Massachusetts Department of Social Services, Alcoholic Rehabilitation Division, I understand," Fairchild responded.

"You seem to know a lot about me, Dr. Fairchild. What is your point? Why are you telling me all this? Do you think I had something to do with George's murder?"

"I would certainly hope not, but the fact that you stand to possibly profit very greatly from George's death certainly may create suspicion with the Cleveland police."

"I can't help that! George made that will years ago. How could I have envisioned what has happened?"

"That is a good question."

"I don't see how any of this is *your* business, Professor Fairchild. Right now I suggest that you get out of my room and mind your own business."

"George's death has become my business, I'm afraid, Mr. Latimer. I intend to find out who murdered him, whatever it takes. I certainly have no more reason to suspect you than anyone else. If you know nothing about George's murder, then you have nothing to fear from me, I assure you, nor I from you."

"I know nothing about his murder. I liked George, and tried to help him. I'm just as sorry as anyone that he was killed, but I had nothing to do with it. Now I'm asking you to leave."

Fairchild arose, but Latimer did not hold out his hand, but simply walked to the door and opened it. Within moments the professor was back on the elevator, down in the lobby and in a taxi back to the Attalos Hotel.

"Did you have a pleasant walk, dear?" Esther inquired as he returned to the hotel room where they were staying.

"Quite informative," he replied, opening his suitcase to do his own unpacking.

Chapter 9

It was three days later when Fred and Mildred Rogers arrived in Athens, and took a taxi to their plush first class hotel in the center of the city. They checked in, and Mildred immediately placed a call to Kelly at the Attalos. The clerk told her that the students in the Fremont tour group were on an excursion to Thessaloniki, some 500 kilometers north of Athens, and would not be back until very late that evening. Mildred left Kelly a message advising their arrival in Greece and in which hotel they stayed.

"I've some business calls," Fred Rogers said. "After you've finished unpacking, why not do some shopping, and we'll meet back here at six and plan for dinner?"

Mildred agreed, and was soon off to see the shops in the hotel and those in the surrounding neighborhood. Now alone, Fred picked up the telephone and placed a call to another Athens hotel. He spoke with the other person for about ten minutes, then hung up and made several additional phone calls.

Later that evening Fred and Mildred Rogers took a taxi to the Attalos Hotel to meet with their daughter after the tour group had returned from Thessaloniki. The Fairchilds were in the hotel dining room at a table next to where Kelly was sitting, the dinner almost completed. Mildred Rogers spotted the professor, and, after embracing her daughter, turned to Richard Fairchild.

"Dr. Fairchild, so nice to see you again. I understand the tour is going well."

"Hello, Mrs. Rogers," he answered, rising to his feet. "Yes, we have seen a lot, and learned a lot, and I think everyone is properly exhausted. Oh, and I'd like you to meet my wife, Esther."

Esther turned in her chair to take the hand Mildred Rogers extended as Fred Rogers, who had been leaning over his daughter's shoulder speaking with her, straightened and turned to the Fairchilds.

"Fred, this is the professor I was telling you about, Dr. Fairchild."

"Yes. Your name is becoming a familiar one in our family. My wife said you had stopped by the house once. If you ever need a public relations boost, just call Kelly. If I didn't know better, I'd say she had a crush on you!"

"Goodness!" Esther laughed. "I hope not."

"I am very glad to meet you, Mr. Rogers," Richard Fairchild replied. "Kelly said you were going to be in Athens. Do you have business interests here?"

"A few. Normally I would not have made the trip until the fall, but as Kelly was going to be here, we thought we'd come now."

"I met a mutual acquaintance of yours the other night," Fairchild said.

"Oh?" Rogers replied. "Who was that?"

"An Edgar Latimer."

"Oh, yes! Kelly said he was in town," Rogers responded. "Some trial or other."

Fairchild waited to see what else Rogers might say, but he added nothing. The professor then said, "I understand you knew a George Antopholis."

"Antopholis?" Rogers replied.

"A homeless man with bad feet and an odd accent."

"Oh! George!" Rogers exclaimed. "Yes, he did some work around our home a few times, and some gardening at the plant. Mostly just pulling weeds. Now that I come to think of it, I believe it was Ed Latimer who brought him out to my place. How do you know George?"

"George lived some of the time in a shelter down on River Road in the Flats. I occasionally helped out at the shelter when the manager was away, and got to know George. But he was murdered last November."

"Murdered?" Mildred Rogers gasped. "How? Why?"

"He was living under a bridge and someone shot him. The police don't know why," Fairchild answered. He watched Fred Rogers face, but there was no change in his expression.

"I hadn't heard," Rogers said, after a moment of hesitation. "That's too bad. He was an odd duck, but gentle."

Having finished her dinner, Kelly joined her parents at the Fairchilds' table, and said, "Daddy, Mom, come on up to my room. I want you to meet my roommate, Susan Kradell. She's really nice. But she was feeling tired after the trip today and left the dinner early. I know she'll want to meet you."

"Okay, Dear," Mildred Rogers replied. "Dr. Fairchild, so nice to see you again. I hope the rest of your trip is successful."

"Thank you, Mrs. Rogers," Fairchild said, and shook the hand of Fred Rogers, which the Cleveland businessman had extended to him. Esther also made a parting comment, and the Rogers and their daughter moved into the hotel lobby toward the bank of elevators.

* * *

The following day was to be an easy one for the Fremont students. Their tour bus was to pick them up at eight, and cover the ninety kilometers to Korinthos in less than two hours. The group would then spend the rest of the day there.

It was late afternoon as Richard Fairchild led the students around the ruins of the ancient city. He had been lecturing on the importance of Corinth both in Greek history and as a site of one of the early Christian communities, and in modern times its location on the canal that provided a shortcut around the lower part of Greece.

No one had noticed a dark, swarthy man who seemed to be following the tour group from point to point for the previous hour. The group had just turned, and Richard Fairchild was walking at the rear of the group when a small German-made car pulled up beside the swarthy man. The man then pointed something at Fairchild's back, and there was the sound of a soft *ping* that no one seemed to hear. The man quickly climbed into the car, which immediately drove away as Dr. Fairchild slumped to the ground.

As he fell, he exclaimed, "Oh!" Esther, who had been a few paces ahead of him talking with one of the students, turned, saw her husband on the ground, and screamed.

The others then turned, and quickly gathered around the professor, who was now unconscious. No one observed the small auto, with two people in it, leaving the scene.

One of the students ran to find a policeman, and soon an ambulance was at the scene. Blood was pouring from a large hole in Fairchild's upper back, just below his shoulder. The ambulance attendant quickly pressed a bandage over it, but the pressure did not seem to slow the flow of blood. He was placed into the ambulance, and an intravenous solution was started as the ambulance pulled away from the sidewalk where Fairchild had fallen. The ambulance raced off with its "whooohaww" siren screaming.

Esther Fairchild was torn between wanting to go to the hospital with her husband, and responsibilities for the students, since she was the next in charge. If someone was hunting them, she realized, she needed to get the students back to Athens as quickly as possible. They were to meet the bus at five, about forty-five minutes later, but she knew where the bus would be parked. After the policeman obtained her name, and the name of the hotel where they would be in Athens, she had the students go directly to the bus.

One of the students, the one who had summonsed the policeman, spoke fairly good Greek, and explained to the driver what had happened. He understood, and within minutes they were back on the main road to Athens.

Upon arrival, Esther placed a call to the hospital in Korinthos, and was advised that her husband was still unconscious, that he had suffered a considerable loss of blood, and that surgery would be needed to remove a shattered bullet from his right shoulder. He would, the doctor assured her, survive, and should fully recover.

The following day the students were to travel north toward Meteora, where they would spend the night in one of the ancient Orthodox monasteries atop one of the limestone mountains that make the area famous. There was little she could do but continue with the tour. She had access to Richard's lecture notes, and had been to most of the places on the tour before. She would carry on in his absence.

* * *

The courtroom was crowded and a bit noisy as the Greek government began their case. Athens attorney Paulos Kenopoulos, representing the interests of Edgar A. Latimer, of Boston, listened closely as Assistant Government Attorney Theo Patroris concluded his opening comments to the Court.

"Further," he summarized in Greek, "we have learned that the person whom we will concede was a rightful heir at the time of his death, Georgio Antopholis, nephew of the deceased, Demetrius Antopholis, was a retarded individual. At the time he signed and executed the purported 'last will and testament' he was not, as the will states, 'of sound mind.' The government, therefore, your honors, holds the position that Georgio Antopholis died intestate, and that the Estate of Demetrius Antopholis should revert to the Government."

In his opening statement, Kenopoulos again reviewed the facts, emphasizing those on which the government had conceded. "My learned opponent," he argued, "has suggested that the heir, Georgio Antopholis, was retarded and therefore not of 'sound mind.' We refute that assumption, your honors, and would point out that the evidence presented by my client demonstrates that while Georgio Antopholis was, shall we say, a bit slow-witted, he was not retarded to the extent that he could not reason on his own behalf. While his school records do show that he was unable to pass the various curricula of his schools, he was capable of both reading and writing at a basic level. Further, your honors, we have provided an affidavit from the attorney in the United States, one Tillman Farmer, Esquire, affirming that he had suggested a guardianship for Antopholis, but that Georgio Antopholis had rejected such an idea. This does not, your honors, sound like a man who was of unsound mind. He was grateful to his friend, my client, Edgar Latimer, for taking care of him. To whom else should he will any of his possessions?"

Following opening statements, which were eagerly absorbed by the reporters representing publications in Greece, Britain and America, the government opened its presentation, calling as a witness the attorney who had prepared Demetreus Antopholis's last will and testament. A small, balding man in his late fifties, he had also been one of the attorneys for the ship line, and had little interest in seeing the government take it from private hands.

The Late Demetrius Antopholis's attorney, Alexi Granopolis, explained in great detail to the Court how precise the old man had been when his final will had been drawn about six years earlier, while his sister, Anna Antopholis Bergeman, in Buffalo, New York, was still alive. Anna corresponded with him regularly, he said, and she and her husband, Sidney, returned to Greece for periodic visits. To his knowledge, she had never mentioned Demetrius's nephew, Georgio, the attorney testified. However, under later cross examination he admitted he "was vaguely aware" of the nephew's existence, but that the old man thought the nephew was so retarded that he would not survive his or his sister's lives, and therefore Georgio had not been mentioned specifically in the will, except in reference to Anna's own heirs.

Theo Patroris pressed his witness to testify that so much was at stake with the properties owned by the Antopholis estate that Demetrius would never have considered leaving it to a retarded person. Paulos Kenopoulos immediately challenged the government's attorney to prove that Georgio was, indeed, "retarded."

"We shall," Patroris assured the three judges.

The government's next witness was an American investigator from Buffalo who spoke fluent Greek. The investigator, Charlie Candelous, a rather large, bald man with a bushy mustache who was about fifty, testified that at Patroris's request he had researched all the documentation available in the United States on Anna Antopholis Bergeman and her nephew, Georgio, known as 'George'. His investigation confirmed that she was, indeed, the sister of Demetrius Antopholis, that she had told acquaintances that she had surrendered to her brother any interest in their father's small shipping company on Cyprus before she immigrated to the United States prior to World War II. She had become an American citizen before she met and married Sidney Bergeman. He further confirmed that there had been no children from that marriage.

Georgio's parents, Georgio, Senior, for whom his son was named, and Clea, had also immigrated to the United States shortly after Anna. They had been married in Greece. The father, Georgio, and his wife, Clea, had been killed in an auto accident when Georgio, the Junior, was still a young boy, the investigator stated. They had not yet become American citizens, although their son, born in Buffalo, was considered American by birth.

Candelous had no information on any of Georgio's father's interest in the boy's grandfather's ship company, but testified that he understood that Demetrius had purchased his brother's interest prior to his immigration to Buffalo. On this point Kenopoulos immediately contested, requesting proof of this allegation.

"How do we know," he asserted to the judges, "that Georgio's own father did not have as much interest in the ship business as did Demetrius himself? If that had been the case, then Georgio, the Junior, known in America as 'George,' would have been a direct heir to his grandfather's company, now known as Cyprus-Hellenic Lines, and could have disposed of those interests in any way he wished."

The Court duly noted the objection, and cautioned the government's attorney that they would require some evidence that Georgio's own father did not also have an interest in the ship line.

Candelous then testified that he had located records on Georgio, Junior, including his birth certificate, showing the parents as Georgio and Clea Antopholis, Greek citizens.

He had attended public schools in Buffalo, but had been held back in grades two, three, and five, finally dropping out of school when he was fourteen. The records showed consistent failing grades.

Theo Patroris suggested to the Court that this was certainly evidence that Georgio was retarded. Paulos Kenopoulos, however, disputed such a conclusion. "Remember," he suggested to the judges, "this boy was in an American school where English was spoken, but his parents were Greek speaking. Where is the government's evidence that these parents spoke enough English for the boy to learn the language of his nation of birth, and therefore possessed the ability to pass the various grades at the school where, undoubtedly, only English was spoken prior to the time that his parents were killed?"

The Court again cautioned the government's attorney that documentation of retardation would be needed.

"We have such evidence, your Honors" Patroris replied. He then continued his questioning of the Buffalo investigator. "Mr. Candelous, would you please discuss the document you have brought with you, which we have designated as an exhibit?"

The investigator then referred to a folder, a copy of which was presented to each of the judges and to Kenopoulos. "This," he said, "is a copy of an application for welfare assistance from the State of Ohio filed on behalf of the deceased, Georgio Antopholis, Junior, in June of last year. It states that Antopholis, the Junior, is disabled – he had oddly shaped large feet – and that he was, and I quote, 'retarded.' He was described as being homeless. The document was filed on his behalf by one Amos Waterman, who, as far as I was able to learn on my visit to Cleveland, was the manager of a shelter for homeless men operated by some religious organization."

On cross-examination, Kenopoulos pressed the investigator further on each point of the application. "Mr. Candelous, in whose handwriting is this application?"

"I presume that it is that of the shelter manager, Amos Waterman," he replied.

"What about the place on the form marked in English, 'Signature of Applicant'? Are you testifying that this is also the signature of Waterman?"

"No. That writing is clearly different. It appears to be the signature of the deceased, Georgio Antopholis, Junior."

"So you are saying that while he signed this application, he did not fill it out himself?"

"That is my assumption."

"That is what you assume. But do you know it of your own knowledge, sir? Have you ever seen the signature of Georgio Antopholis, the Junior, before?"

"Yes, I have," Candelous replied. "I have personally inspected the will that he signed in the office of a Cleveland attorney, Tillman Farmer."

"Is the signature the same?"

"Yes. I am not a handwriting expert, but I would say that the two signatures are basically identical."

"The writing on the application, other than the signature, is not by the same person?"

"No. It is entirely different handwriting, more professional. The form itself states that it is being filled out on Antopholis's behalf by Waterman."

"So it is this Amos Waterman who is suggesting that George Antopholis, the applicant, is 'retarded'?"

"It would appear so."

"Would you read the exact language that this Amos Waterman used in the application? Please read it in English. You may then translate it into Greek for the benefit of the Court, although I reserve the right to question your translation."

"It says, 'The applicant is physically disabled and barely able to walk. He is also slightly retarded, but quite functional and able to survive on his own,'" the investigator read in English. He then translated it into Greek.

"So the application states that he is only 'slightly retarded, but quite functional,' is that correct, Mr. Candelous?"

"How retarded is 'slightly retarded'?"

"I don't know. It would be a judgment factor...."

"Are you familiar with what is called Intelligence Quotients, or 'IQ'?" Kenopoulos interrupted.

"Yes, but I can't give ranges."

"Was this Amos Waterman qualified to administer IQ tests?"

"I don't know."

"So you cannot testify that by Waterman's stating in this application that Georgio Antopholis was 'slightly retarded' that Waterman had any actual evidence that he was even within a retarded range, is that correct?"

Ian Sherling smiled as his Greek counterpart appeared to rip the government's prime witness to shreds. He hoped that Theo Patroris would not pursue further investigation that Candelous might have conducted in

Cleveland, and was relieved when Candelous was finally dismissed. Patroris had several more witnesses, but none of them appeared to give much evidence that would shed light on why the government should lay claim to the Antopholis estate.

At the conclusion of the government's presentation, the three judges called a recess before the Latimer team presented their evidence. After the brief recess, they adjourned the trial until the following morning.

* * *

Raymond Ingersol, a dark, swarthy looking man about forty, was talking on the telephone in his room at the Titania Hotel. Curled up on the bed was his young, dark-haired girlfriend, Sheri Blake, who was perhaps twenty, at most. Shapely and thin, she wore only a flimsy mini-skirt and a light blue see-through blouse.

"No," Ingersol was telling the other party, "we only wounded the son-of-a-bitch. Yeah, they got him to a hospital and he apparently is going to survive. ... What? .... No, I don't think we can make another attempt here. The police think this one was a stray bullet, and are calling it an accident. Another attempt, and they're going to start investigating. Who knows what that might turn up? ... Yeah, we'll have to wait until he gets back to the States. ... Okay. See yah."

As he hung up, Ingersol looked over at Blake. "Looks like we're stuck here for a few days. What'd yah want to do, doll?"

"Let's go out on one of those speed boats again. I really liked that!" she replied.

* * *

Esther Fairchild purchased an English language Athens newspaper at the hotel newsstand the next morning before boarding the bus with the students for the long drive to Meteora. On page two she found the article. The headline read: American Scholar Mysteriously Wounded.

"Professor Richard Fairchild," it read, "was seriously wounded by what appears to have been a stray bullet while leading a group of American students on a tour of Corinth yesterday afternoon. The well-known religion professor from Fremont College in Ohio was guiding twenty-eight students around some of the Corinthian ruins when he collapsed after being struck in the right shoulder by a bullet. No one in the group nor in the vicinity reported hearing a gunshot, and no one saw anyone else in the area, other than the students who at the time were walking in front of the professor. His wife, Esther Fairchild, is continuing the students' tour while her husband recuperates in a Corinth hospital from surgery to remove the bullet. Doctors report that he is in stable condition.

"Corinth Police Inspector Mikel Malecki informed reporters that a search of the area where the injury occurred turned up no indication of what could have happened. They theorize that the bullet was fired from a considerable distance, and struck the professor totally by accident. 'This is a most unusual accident,' he said. 'It is a rare event, and tourists should certainly not fear coming to Corinth. We do not consider this a terrorist act.' A representative at the American Embassy in Athens confirmed that the Embassy had no knowledge of the shooting."

Esther Fairchild shook her head. She had spoken to Richard earlier that morning by phone, as he had regained consciousness and successfully underwent the surgery to remove the bullet. Although extremely weak, he encouraged her to continue the tour with the students, including the cruise the following week to the West Coast of Turkey. "I'll be fine," he assured her, but she worried none-the-less.

* * *

The trial continued the next day. Paulos Kenopoulos presented a certified copy of the will Shoeless George had signed, along with a copy of his death certificate. He also presented a copy of the probate court ruling in favor of Edgar A. Latimer. As he had feared, the government's attorney had learned of the appeal that challenged the will.

"That appeal is of little consequence," Kenopoulos told the Court. "While it presents a challenge, it, too, is based on the erroneous theory that Georgio Antopholis, the Junior, was 'retarded,' a fiction for which there is not the least evidence. As to the allegation in that appeal that my client, Edgar Latimer, was acting in his capacity as a manager of a shelter for the homeless at the time, again this is an erroneous theory that will not stand.

"Besides, your Honors, the matter is basically irrelevant, for if the Court determines that Georgio Antopholis, the Junior, was indeed the heir of the deceased, Demetrius Antopholis, at the time of his death, then the matter of the Estate is one for the courts in the United States, not here in Greece."

The three judges made notes on this point, which was unchallenged by the government's attorney. Kenopoulos then called Edgar Latimer as a witness, and he was sworn to tell the truth. A court translator was to immediately translate each question and answer for the Court.

"Your name?" Kenopoulos asked in English. The translator repeated it in Greek.

"Edgar Alvin Latimer."

"And you live where?"

"My home is in Boston, Massachusetts. However, I have been residing in London with a friend for the past several months."

"And you are employed where?"

"My employer in Massachusetts, from whom I have a leave of absence, was the state welfare department. I was a counselor in their alcoholic rehabilitation program, as I have a Master's degree in social work. In London I was temporarily employed as a salesman in a department store."

"Thank you. Could you please tell the Court how you came to know Georgio Antopholis, the Junior, also known, I understand, as 'Shoeless George.'?"

"'*Shoeless* George?'" asked one of the judges, as the other two and a number of people in the courtroom chuckled.

"As has been testified by others, I was the manager of a shelter for homeless men in a run-down neighborhood of Cleveland, Ohio. The shelter was operated by a religious order, the Brothers of St. Vincent. I was only a lay employee, not a member of the order, although I was required to conduct two daily religious services.

"As the manager, I would accept men into the program. I was known as 'Brother Ed.' We had twenty-five men who basically lived at the shelter, and another twenty-five for whom we provided meals. I would interview each, and as a trained social worker, would attempt to help each with whatever problem had made the man homeless.

"Some were drunks…." Latimer paused as the translator held up his hand to have him wait until he finished the previous comment. "Some were drunks," he repeated, "and some were on drugs. Others were on parole from prison, and still others had simply lost their jobs and had no place to go. Still others had mental or physical problems, and were basically unemployable, left on the street to rot.

"George was living on the street when I found him. He apparently had just arrived from Buffalo, although how he got to Cleveland I am not sure. He was disabled, as his feet had been crushed in an accident many years earlier, and had grown back in a deformed way. They were large feet, what we would say as fourteen or fifteen inches long – I'm not sure what that would be in centimeters, but somewhere around half a meter -- and because of their natural or accidental deformity, almost as wide. They were diamond shaped, hence George was unable to wear shoes. He simply wrapped his feet in rags, and had fashioned cardboard and plywood boxes for each foot. Obviously, this made him very awkward, and he could not find regular work"

"Was George retarded?"

"George spoke with an unusual accent, probably because of his Greek parents. He was not very bright, but he could read and write a little. He certainly did not have the appearance of one with a brain disorder from birth. In technical terms, he was not a moron or an imbecile."

"You were qualified to make that determination?"

"I never had George tested for intelligence, if that is what you mean, but as a professional social worker, I was trained enough in psychology to make such a distinction, yes."

"Why did you take 'George' to an attorney to have a will made?" Kenopoulos asked.

"As I was saying, George, because of his feet, was unemployable. He was basically totally disabled, and he had no resources for any medical care. He would spend all day at an employment office, but only got an occasional job pulling weeds or picking up trash somewhere. George needed help. On his behalf we filed an application for aid from the Ohio welfare department. I helped George fill out the form, and he signed it. The state never approved the application, and after more than a month of waiting, I took George to see an attorney I had heard about, to see if the attorney could help get George's application approved."

"Is this the application you assisted him in completing?" Kenopoulos asked, holding up the exhibit on which the Buffalo investigator had testified the previous day.

"No, that is another application, apparently filed a year or more after I left the shelter. I know Amos Waterman. In fact, I recommended him to the religious order that operated St. Vincent House as my replacement."

"Is this the application?" Kenopoulos asked, holding up a similar document.

"Yes, that appears to be it, or a copy of it," Latimer replied. The attorney then had the document cited as an exhibit, and copies presented to each judge and to the government's attorney.

"On this form you describe the disability as 'permanently crippled feet and a slow thinker, barely able to read or write.' Is that a reference to retardation?"

"No, although we later discussed with the attorney whether it might be better to allege that George was mentally retarded to see if that would help to get him the benefits he needed. We did that because the state could always allege that just because George had bad feet he could be employed in a sit-down job. We needed to show that George would not be qualified to do an office or clerical type of job."

"This form asks the question, 'Who is your next of kin?' Your name appears. Why is that?"

"George said he had no family at all. These forms had to be completed in full. The state could reject them for any blank answers, and as I was the only person in Cleveland that George knew, my name was entered."

"How did the will come to be drawn by the attorney in Cleveland, Tillman Farmer?"

"As I have stated, the state did not respond to George's application. We therefore went to the attorney to see if he could help get an acceptance from the state. In our conversation the attorney, Mr. Farmer suggested that perhaps a guardianship should be set up for George. I did not want that responsibility, and George also made it clear that he did not want a guardian. He said his aunt had been his guardian as a child, and had ruled his life. He knew what a guardianship meant." Latimer paused again, while the translator completed the comment.

"At that point," he then continued, "the attorney, Mr. Farmer, asked George if he had a will. George said he did not, as he had nothing to will. The attorney said something about having an executor if anything should happen to him, and suggested that a very simple will be prepared. I was to be the executor. The attorney specifically asked George, 'If you had something worth giving to someone, to whom would you want to give it?' or something of that sort. George said, 'Brother Ed here is my only friend. I have no one else.' So I was listed not only as George's executor, but also as his heir."

"I see. And this is a copy of that will?" Kenopoulos asked, holding up the document that had already been entered as evidence.

"Yes, I believe so."

"When did you find out that 'George,' Georgio Antopholis, the Junior, might be an heir to the Estate of Demetrius Antopholis?"

"It was in late October of last year. A letter that had been sent by some London solicitors to his aunt's old address in Buffalo was forwarded to my address in Boston."

"Why was mail from Buffalo forwarded to you?"

"That had been the attorney's suggestion."

"Mr. Farmer?"

"Yes. He suggested that we place a forwarding address at George's old home in Buffalo so that any correspondence that might come to him could be handled. At the time George was staying at the shelter, but was planning to move out as he was very noisy at night, because of his feet, and disturbed the other men. Also, I was planning on resigning from the shelter, hence I listed my family's home in Boston, where I still reside."

"What did you do when you got the letter from the London solicitors?"

"I was out of town at the time it arrived, so I did not get it until the last week in October. Because I was busy at work, I was unable to follow up on it until the second week in November, when I called the shelter in Cleveland to see if George was still there. I learned that he had been killed."

"So you knew that George – Georgio – might have a valuable inheritance before he was killed?"

"Yes. I understand he had been living on the street, under a bridge. I was told someone shot him."

"Your Honors," Kenopoulos said, turning to the three judges, "this is a copy of a Cleveland Police homicide report on the murder of Georgio Antopholis, the Junior. You will note that the perpetrator is 'unknown, most likely a transient,' and that the motive is shown as 'theft of junk the victim had collected.' My client is not in any way a suspect in this unfortunate crime."

Kenopoulos had covered every base that Patroris might question, from the will to the murder. Patroris then made a half-hearted attempt to cross-examine and raise questions, but by noon the judges suggested a recess.

* * *

The next morning Richard Fairchild was discharged from the hospital in Korinthos and caught one of the frequent trains back to Athens. His right arm was in a sling, his shoulder and back heavily bandaged, and he was presented with a sack of various medications, bandages and painkillers to take with him. The surgeon had also presented him the bullet that had been removed from his shoulder as a souvenir. In slightly more than two and a half hours he was back in the lobby of the Attalos Hotel.

Esther and the students were not due back from Meteora until late that evening. The next day would be one of leisure in Athens before the group embarked on the *Ulysses Voyager* for several days in Eastern Turkey.

Fairchild felt very tired, partly from the loss of blood and partly from all the medications, and his shoulder constantly ached. As he stood at the hotel desk awaiting his key, the clerk said, "Oh, there is a cablegram for you, Dr. Fairchild."

With his right arm disabled, he had to have the clerk tear open the envelope for him. The cable read, "Have verified, without doubt, Ed Latimer was in Boston entire first week of November. Stop. He attended several meetings. Stop. Amos. Stop."

In his discomfort Fairchild felt somewhat unhappy about the message. He knew he would have to apologize to Edgar Latimer for having suspected him, and for the way he had questioned him. Yet a bit of doubt remained in his mind. There were simply too many coincidences. With his left hand he folded the cablegram, placed it in his shirt pocket, and picked up the key to his room.

Chapter 10

It was mid-morning on a Saturday as Bob and Sally Merriam sat at their kitchen table in their Sandusky garden apartment reviewing the stack of mail the postman had just delivered to the apartment communal mailbox area.

"What's that bill?" Sally asked, looking at some invoice Bob had just opened.

"For the car repairs on my old Olds," he answered. "That jalopy is beginning to cost as much as a new car would. One of these days we'll have to invest in a new one."

"Oh, here's a letter from Esther," Sally said, tearing open an envelope that was marked Air Mail and had a Greek stamp. She carefully tore off the stamp and set it aside as one of her brother's sons collected stamps, and she saved any unusual ones she found for her nephew.

"'Dear Bob and Sally,'" she read. "'I don't know if you heard anything on the news over there, but we had a bit of bad luck yesterday in Corinth. Richie was shot in the shoulder....'"

"What?!" Bob exclaimed.

"'Richie was shot in the shoulder,'" Sally reread, "'but it was apparently an accidental stray bullet and he was not seriously injured. They rushed him to a hospital in Corinth, and he had surgery to remove the bullet, but the doctors say he will be okay. I've taken over the tour, and we are going along on schedule, up to the monasteries in Meteora tomorrow as planned. I suspect that the students will find that the highlight of the trip, although I wish Richie was going to be with us.

"'The Corinth police think the shooting was just an isolated thing. I can't imagine what else it might have been. It is just one of those circumstances that one has to accept when traveling. Otherwise the trip has been interesting and uneventful. The parents of one of our students are here in Athens, and we met them the other evening. Gosh, the world gets smaller and smaller!

"'How is your summer class coming, Bob? Don't work too hard. The two of you need to plan a little vacation before the busy fall semester starts.

"'Richie expects to be discharged from the hospital by tomorrow or the next day, so we'll be flying home on schedule. If you could meet us at the Cleveland airport, that would be great, and we would really appreciate it. Our flight is scheduled to get in about seven thirty in the evening, United Flight 131 from Idlewild in New York. I just don't know what I would do without you two. You've been so much involved in helping us. Anyway, we will see you next week. Esther.'"

Sally looked up as she finished reading the letter. "Poor Richie. If it isn't one thing it's another. I sure hope it was an accident and not some deliberate attempt on his life."

"Who would want to harm Richie?"

"Who knows? Maybe he's involved in some investigation again, like last year. Didn't he mention some murder down in Cleveland that had drawn his attention?"

"You mean the old homeless man? How could that have a connection to Greece? Besides, I don't think he has come up with anything. No, I'm sure it was just an accident."

* * *

The Fremont College tour was scheduled to fly home from Athens following their return from Turkey, by way of Paris on TWA's Flight 801, departing Athens at ten-thirty in the morning, and arriving in New York at eight that evening, flying with the sun. They had arrived in Athens the evening before on the *M.V. Epirus II* from Patras about nine.

While waiting in the departure lounge of the Athens Airport Dr. Fairchild purchased an English-language Greek newspaper. The headline read, "American Heir Wins Greek Ship Line." Fairchild quickly glanced through the article, which recited much of the testimony from the trial, which was of considerable importance to Greece.

"In a two to one decision," the article stated, "the Court has ruled that an American social worker, Edgar Latimer, has the right to inherit the Estate of Demetrius Antopholis. The wealthy estate, consisting of several homes and principal interest in the three divisions of the Cyprus-Hellenic Ship Lines, a Greek corporation, passed to his nephew, Georgio Antopholis, upon the death of Demetrius last summer. However, Georgio Antopholis was killed in an Ohio shooting in November. His will, filed in the United States, named a friend, Edgar Latimer, as executor and heir. The Government had challenged the inheritance, but the Court ruled in favor of the American."

The article continued to outline the arguments pressed by both sides in the trial, and quoted comments from various sources, including management of the ship line. After scanning the article, Fairchild went to a public phone and placed a local call. He was unsure he would get his party, but felt it worth a chance, as the matter hung heavily on his mind, and he wanted to correct an impression.

"Hello," the voice at the other end said, when the call was completed.

"Is this Edgar Latimer?"

"Yes, but if you are a reporter, you'll have to talk to my attorneys."

"No, it's Dr. Richard Fairchild. You may recall I came to visit you last week."

"Yes. I certainly remember *you*."

"Mr. Latimer, first I want to congratulate you on your victory in the Court." The professor heard a slight grunt of acknowledgment, and continued. "Secondly, I want to apologize for my suspicions and what must have sounded like an accusation that evening. I've since learned that you were in Boston that entire week, and therefore my questioning you was certainly premature."

There was a pause at the other end. Finally Latimer replied. "Dr. Fairchild, you actually did me a favor. I knew, of course, the date George was killed. I found out from Amos Waterman in Cleveland, a few weeks after I had received the letter for George from the solicitor in London, and called the shelter to see if I could locate him. So

I also knew by then that George might have inherited something, but I didn't then know what. It just never dawned on me that someone might think I had murdered George for that inheritance.

"In hindsight, it should have been obvious to me that I would be a suspect. But I'm a bit naive, I guess. By your questioning me I suddenly realized that the Greek government's attorney would probably ask the same questions, and I was able to prepare my attorney and myself for that. Those questions did arise in the trial, and I was able to testify truthfully. If you hadn't alerted me to your suspicions, I would not have been ready to reply to the Court any more than I was to you. So I must say thank you."

"And I must again say I'm sorry I questioned you so bluntly, Mr. Latimer."

"Dr. Fairchild, you said you were intent on finding out who murdered George. I don't know how to help you, but I hope you are successful."

"There is one question I have," Fairchild continued. "How familiar are you with a Fred Rogers, who owns a chemical company in Cleveland. He was in Athens last week, and may still be here."

"Yes, he *is* still here. He called me a few days ago. I hadn't seen him or heard from him in over a year. He was my landlord for a while after I left St. Vincent House, and we kept in touch occasionally, mostly through his wife, Mildred, forwarding my mail to Boston. He'd read about the trial and got the name of my hotel from the London attorneys, and gave me a call last week. Why, I even saw his daughter, Kelly, at the airport awhile back. She was on some sort of a college tour, so she was also here."

"She was on the tour I was conducting, before I was shot...."

"*Shot?*"

"In Corinth. Someone shot me in the shoulder. It was undoubtedly an accident," Fairchild explained. "Fred Rogers also knew George. Used to have George do some gardening work for him at his plant, and also at his home in Lakewood. Rogers told me you were the one who introduced him to George. I told him that George was dead. He said he had not known. "

Fairchild paused a moment and then added, "I imagine you will be here in Greece for a while. I read where you have inherited several large homes. Have you seen them?"

"Not yet, Dr. Fairchild. But, as the saying goes, I guess my ship has come in."

"Not only came in, but docked, unloaded, reloaded and is ready to sail again by the sound of it!" Fairchild laughed. "Oh, our plane is about to leave, so I'd better move on. Again, congratulations, and I hope you will keep in touch, perhaps through Amos."

"Thank you for your call, Dr. Fairchild. I will keep in touch," Latimer replied. "Have a safe flight home."

* * *

Both Esther and Richard Fairchild were exhausted from their tour. The professor had no other summer session classes scheduled beyond a two hour seminar with the tour group two weeks later to wrap up what they had learned, and to collect term papers each was to write on the tour in order to get credit.

The surgeon in Athens had insisted that Richard have his wound checked by his own doctor when he returned to the States, and doctor on the ship had changed his dressings several times during the voyage to Turkey. Esther had already made him an appointment with their physician in Port Cleland. The professor placed the bullet he had been given into a box on his dresser when he got home. Curious, he thought, picking it up again and holding it. It looks like a .45-caliber slug. A .45's a loud gun, he remembered. Strange that nobody heard the shot

He was tired. His wound had drained him of his usual boundless energy, and he simply felt like lying around the house for a few days. Even though they had been home for two days already, he was still feeling the lingering jet lag. For Fairchild, this was a new experience. He usually arrived at the opposite end of an ocean or continent fully alert and ready for action.

He lay down on his bed. In his mind he mulled the conversations he had held over the past few months, the articles on the Antopholis estate trial, and the murder of George. So many links. George did work for Rogers. Latimer knew Rogers. Latimer knew George. But it all meant nothing. If George had not been killed for the inheritance, and that now seemed probable, then why had he been killed? Could the police perhaps be correct? Could George simply have been shot by a transient in a senseless robbery?

* * *

In early July that same summer Sam and Carolyn Whitaker moved into a small home on the West Side of Cleveland. It was not as large as their former suburban home, but was neat and comfortable, in a good school district for Courtney, and convenient for Sam to get to work. The couple seemed to have completely reconciled their marriage, and both Sam and his wife felt happy for the first time in years. Harry and Mildred Taylor had taken the three weeks after the Fourth of July for a vacation in Canada, and Sam had been placed in charge of the agency.

Carolyn had brought her automobile, an older model Chevrolet that she had purchased in Connecticut, with her to Ohio, and on weekends the three planned to take drives in the country. One Wednesday evening Sam said at dinner, "Carolyn, I'd like you to meet a friend of mine I met at the shelter. Perhaps we could visit him this weekend?"

"A friend from the shelter," she repeated in a somewhat sarcastic tone. "What is he, a drunk or an ex-con?"

Sam laughed. "No, no, he wasn't one of the guys. He was a temporary manager of the place during Christmas last year. He's a professor of religion at Fremont College, a very famous historian."

Sam had not told Carolyn about the murder of Shoeless George – he avoided the subject of his time at the shelter with a passion, knowing how cynical Carolyn was about it – and he did not tell her that the professor and he were -- what could he call it? Investigating? Just curious? Trying to solve a murder case the police had already closed? She would really think he was nuts if he told her *that*.

"Oh. Fremont? That's a pretty well-known college. It won't be long before Courtney needs to be selecting a school. Does this professor live near the campus?"

"Frankly, I'm not sure where he lives, but I've got both his home and office phone numbers. Why don't I give him a call and maybe we could visit him this weekend?"

Carolyn agreed, and Sam reached Richard Fairchild at his farm on the Portage River. He explained that he and Carolyn had gotten back together, and that he would like the professor to meet Carolyn and his daughter, Courtney, and perhaps see the college.

As usual, Fairchild had a better idea. "Believe I've told you that I had access to a big cabin cruiser. You had wanted to insure it at the agency," he told Sam. "It was confiscated last year from a bigoted terrorist who was planning to blow up the college and kill Dr. Thomas Jefferson Singletary."

"The civil rights leader?" Sam exclaimed into the telephone. "I remember reading about that in the paper."

"Anyway, we confiscated this terrorist's yacht, which I then donated to the college, but I'm in charge of it, and we can take it out on the Lake, if you like, and tour the islands. Then we'll come back to the farm for some steaks – remember, I raise my own cattle – and you can spend the night with us. We have plenty of room, and love to have company. Then Sunday morning, say, by golly, I'm scheduled to conduct the service at the college chapel, so after that we can tour the campus and have dinner in town before you head home. Great idea, Sam! Have Courtney bring her swimsuit. You and Carolyn, too, if you want."

Carolyn was doubtful about spending such a lavish-sounding weekend with people she had never met, but finally agreed. When they arrived at the farm and Esther immediately took Carolyn and Courtney on a tour, Carolyn was completely won over and delighted with the Fairchilds. "I didn't know Sam had friends like you when he was living alone," she confessed to Esther. "I'm awfully glad he does."

"Actually, I've never met your husband before," Esther said, "but Richard seems to talk about him a lot, and thinks the world of him. They're both into medieval history, and that's the password to Richard's heart."

After the farm tour Richard packed the group into his station wagon and they drove up to the lagoon in Port Cleland and boarded the large two-decked cabin cruiser that had formerly belonged to Carter Anderson Swaine, III, a Texas millionaire who had headed a group of right-wing religious fanatics intent on assassinating liberal leaders and scholars, including Dr. Fairchild. It had been renamed *Castle Kent*.

Fairchild backed the large cruiser out of its birth at the dock and turned it into the channel, blasting the whistle for the drawbridge. Courtney, clad only in the skimpiest of swimsuits that her mother would allow her to wear, had found a spot at the front of the cruiser, well behind the railing, where she could see all that was ahead. As they passed under the bridge, opened to block traffic on the Toledo highway, she waved to people in their cars. They passed from the channel to the open water of Lake Erie, which had only a slight chop that morning. In the galley was a basket containing a picnic of cold fried chicken, sandwiches and salads, along with other goodies. Remembering that Sam was a recovering alcoholic, Fairchild had not included his usual bottle of Castle Kent Catawba.

In half an hour they had arrived at the harbor of Put-In-Bay and tied up at the municipal dock. Neither Sam nor Carolyn had been to the island before, so the Fairchilds suggested that their guests visit the top of the Perry Monument while they prepared lunch in the galley. Courtney, changing into a shirt and shorts, was especially excited by the stories Richard Fairchild told about the island. It had been the site of the Battle of Lake Erie in 1813, when Oliver Hazard Perry defeated the British and sent his message to General William Henry Harrison, "We have met the enemy, and they are ours: two ships, two sloops, a schooner and a frigate."

"Can we visit the caves under the island?" she asked.

"Sure. They're just south of town a bit. We'll take a walk down there after lunch," the professor replied.

By this time they were all on a first name basis. Sam had started calling Fairchild "Richie" instead of "Doc," although Courtney continued to call him "Dr. Fairchild." As it was a clear day, the view from the monument top was excellent, and Courtney could not believe that she had actually been able to see Canada. After the lunch the Fairchilds had prepared, the five walked through the charming little town, and south to Perry's Cave, a cavern formed in the limestone where Perry kept ammunition and other stocks during the preparation for the battle. Back on the cruiser, they stopped at a sand bar where Carolyn and Courtney went swimming, then changed back into their clothes in one of the large cabins below deck. They then motored around Middle and North Bass Islands, and crossed diagonally toward West Bass.

"Found gold there, a couple years ago," Fairchild casually said.

"Gold?" I didn't know there was gold mining around here," Sam replied.

"Nope. There isn't. It was mined in Canada, and shipped down Lake Huron by the British to finance the War in 1813. But they scuttled the treasure ship when Perry started winning the battle on Lake Erie, and a bunch of Nazis found it during World War II."

"Nazis? German Nazis?" Carolyn asked.

"Yes. I had a bit of a tangle with one of them myself. They were living in that big castle you see up on that bluff. That's Castle Kent. The college owns it now, for our viniculture program and our hotel management classes. There really was a spy nest here, and one of them got killed. It all came to light when I found his skeleton."

"My gracious!" Carolyn exclaimed. "Oh! Richie, you're putting us on!"

"No, you can read about it. It all happened." Esther confirmed.

"I know you've been involved in other investigations, Richie," Sam said. "How, or why, did you get interested in investigating?"

"Well, I was a chaplain in an Army Intelligence unit behind the lines in Germany during World War II, serving primarily as a translator as I spoke fluent German," Dr. Fairchild explained. "Even though I was just the chaplain and an interpreter, I had to take all the training the other Intelligence officers took, hence I've always had an interest in, what shall I say, finding out the answer to things?"

"He gets into too darned many things, if you ask me," Esther added. "If he'd stay home and tend to his knitting he'd not get into the pickles that he does, even getting shot last month."

"That was an accident," the professor interrupted.

"So they say. I certainly hope so."

"What other 'pickles,' Esther?"

"Well, the terrorist thing last year, for example. They nearly blew our house apart. And the year before that it was another attempt on his life, and once I was tied to a chair and gagged while a bunch of hoodlums searched the house."

"Good heavens!" Carolyn exclaimed. "Sam, thank God you're not into things like that!" she laughed.

"If he hangs around Richard long enough, don't count on it, Carolyn," Esther added with a wink.

"Truce!" the professor shouted. "We're almost back to the port. Prepare to man the ropes, crew, we're coming in."

* * *

Raymond Ingersol had sat in the parking area of the Port Cleland lagoon for over an hour before he and Sheri Blake gave up waiting and returned to their motel in Sandusky. Ingersol had promised to take Sheri to the amusement park at Cedar Point that afternoon, and she had been pestering him for over an hour.

"Ah, Ray, let's go. You can see that boat ain't here. Why, from what you say they could live on it for a month and not be back. Let's go to the motel so I can change for the park. I ain't been at an amusement park in years."

"Yeah, you're right, doll. No telling when they'll get back." Ingersol started the motor, and they exited the lagoon lot.

When Ingersol had again been contacted for this job in March, he had been busy on another assignment. He knew he would have to be more cautious with this contract. This was no bum living under a bridge -- it was a well-respected professor with a reputation as a detective. But Ingersol had done his homework well, determining where the professor's office was on campus, where his farm was located, and the fact that he had charge of a big cabin cruiser at the Port Cleland lagoon. Further digging had uncovered the fact that Fairchild would be traveling overseas in June. That, he reasoned, would be the best time to make the hit. But then, he had missed. Now he had to do the job in Fairchild's own territory, which made it much more difficult. The guy was unpredictable, back and forth between his farm and the college campus on an irregular basis, and now, on a weekend, not even at the farm.

Having found no one at the professor's home on the Portage River, Ingersol had suspected that the beautiful summer day might have led the professor to his cruiser, and he was right. But the yacht was gone, and there was no telling when it would return. He would just have to postpone the hit and wait for another opportunity.

Yet the idea of the cabin cruiser, which he had staked out a week earlier, appealed to Ingersol. If the professor went out on it alone and somehow didn't return, there would be no messy investigation, nothing to trace him to the disappearance. Perhaps he could manufacture a reason to get Fairchild on the boat alone. That would be tricky, but.... Patience, he thought to himself. Just be patient.

* * *

That evening while Esther Fairchild and Carolyn Whitaker cleaned up in the kitchen after supper and Courtney watched a television show, Sam and Richard sat in his library. "Richie, do you think the shooting in Greece had anything to do with George?" Sam asked.

"Oh, I'd seriously doubt it. The Greeks think it was just an accident, and no one heard a shot. But it looks like a .45 bullet they took out of me. Wasn't George killed with a .45?

"I believe that's what the police said. Do you think that maybe they could match the bullets?"

"That's quite a long shot, but I suppose it is worth a try. I'll give you my souvenir, if you want to pass it along to Andy Segretti and see if he can get it tested." Fairchild quickly ran up the back stairway to his bedroom and in a minute or two returned with the bullet wrapped in a tissue and gave it to Whitaker, who carefully placed it in his pocket.

"Well, Sam, how are things going at the Taylor Agency?" the professor asked. "Are you still enjoying marine insurance?"

"Very much so,' Sam replied. "In fact, I've been in charge for a couple of weeks while the boss is on vacation in Canada.

"I found something unusual the other day, though," he continued. "I was looking for an old closed claim file folder in the closed file drawer and came across an open claim the boss was handling. Obviously it had been misfiled. But what was of interest was that it was from last October, and the insured was the Rogers Chemical Company."

"That is interesting. What kind of a marine claim did they have?"

"Actually a very large one. They apparently have several good sized tankers that they use to haul various chemicals or raw material liquids. It's an account that Taylor handles personally, as you can imagine. Most of the insurance is with Underwriters at Lloyd's, in London. Anyway, on this claim, one of their tankers was allegedly hijacked and apparently sunk. It's a pretty big claim, several million dollars."

"Where did this happen?"

"Apparently somewhere around their plant on the Cuyahoga River in Cleveland."

"I don't recall reading about such an event. If this was a big chemical tanker, you would think it would have been big news," Fairchild replied.

"I didn't even hear about it in the office. Guess it's being kept under wraps."

"What about what was in it? Any chemicals?"

"The claim alleges there was several hundred thousand gallons of some kind of chemical aboard. I don't recall now what it was, but that it was valued at more than one million. The claim says that the tanker, with a claimed value in excess of one million, was stolen, the chemicals off-loaded, and the ship disposed of."

"Where?"

"No one knows. It didn't pass the Welland Canal, nor the Soo Locks, nor was it seen on the Detroit River, so it has to be somewhere on Lake Erie. But after a thorough search it hasn't shown up, hence the insured, Rogers, is reporting it as sunk."

"Most unusual! Was the Coast Guard informed?"

"Apparently so. They did an investigation, and even brought in the FBI, as some of the water where the vessel might be, like the Detroit River, or even Lake Erie, are international. There's been no trace, but the insurance company has not yet settled the claim. They still think it will be found."

"Is Lloyd's investigating themselves, or just relying on the government?"

"Apparently they have their own investigator, but they have only sent blank proof of loss forms for the insured to complete. Rogers' financial director, some guy named Williams, completed them with Harry Taylor's help and submitted them in February. But there has not been any formal reply, just an acknowledgment of the claim and a notice that the Underwriters are reserving their right to delay acceptance or denial of the claim until they complete their investigation. I left the file where I found it. I don't want Harry thinking I'm butting into his account, but it just seemed to be something very unusual."

"It certainly is! What is this 'proof of loss' you mentioned?"

"Oh, that's a claim document on which a formal claim is made, and it must be notarized, hence sworn to. Usually an insurer has about sixty days after the formal 'proof' document is filed to either pay or deny a claim, but they can reserve the right to extend that time, which is what they did here. Can't say as I blame them. It's a lot of money."

"I'm not about to go hunting pirated ships, but I would appreciate your keeping me advised of any developments."

As the two wives joined them in the library, the conversation switched to the plans for the following morning.

* * *

Bob and Sally Merriam had planned all summer to spend a whole day at Cedar Point, the large amusement park on a peninsula just east of Sandusky that was originally opened in the late 19th Century, but was modern in every way. They had been there before, often for picnics with some of the other young people who lived in the garden apartments where the Merriams resided. On this day Matt and Karen August, their neighbors, had been in Chicago visiting Karen's parents. After Sally and Bob finished a few cleaning chores around their apartment they drove out the causeway to the park, arriving in the early afternoon. Hotdogs had served for lunch, but by late in the afternoon their hunger was increasing, and they were beginning to make dinner plans.

There was a hotel in the park, and several restaurants that had service above the level of a hotdog stand; the Merriams made reservations at one of them for six that evening, which would allow them time later to go dancing at the park's dance hall.

At a quarter past five they were standing in a long line, awaiting their turn on the Cyclone, one of the park's many roller coasters, a ride with a drop so steep that it made the park internationally famous. Another couple, a dark, swarthy man about Bob's age, and a girl who would have been college age, was standing in the line ahead of them.

"Have you ridden this thing before?" the girl asked Sally.

"Oh, lots of times," she replied. "I grew up in a town just south of here, and we used to come over to Cedar Point a couple of times a year, ever since I was a little kid. It wouldn't be a trip to Cedar Point without at least one ride on the roller coasters. You're not scared, are you?

"No. But I did hear that it's a very steep drop, and that it goes real fast," the girl replied. By this time they had moved forward in the line a bit, and passed through a turnstile so that they would be able to board the next train.

"I always hang on tight," Bob added. "Sally screams her head off and raises her hands. Not me!"

"I'll probably hang on tight, too," the girl replied. The noise level increased as the next train roared into the little station, screeched to a halt, and the protective bars over the seats released to let the passengers out. Then the cars, three hooked together, each containing three seats for two each, rolled forward, stopped again, and the waiting riders climbed in. The girl and her older, swarthy friend entered the front seats of the second car, while Bob and Sally entered the seats behind them.

The protective bars fell over their laps, and the little three-car train jerked forward, hooking to the cog chain that would pull them to the top of the first drop. The clanking sound was so loud that Bob could not hear a word Sally or anyone else was saying. As the car reached the pinnacle of the latticed wooden structure it paused for a very slight moment, then dropped over the edge and flew down the first fall of the rickety ride, Sally and the girl ahead both screaming in mock terror.

As fast again the cars raced up the next hill, twisted around a curve, and dropped again in another screaming freefall. Then came a series of curves and dips and another long hill, followed by another drop, more curves and more dips. Within minutes that seemed like hours, the cars rolled to a stop at the station, the safety bars were raised, and the riders wobbly climbed onto the wooden deck. The cars then shunted forward for the next eighteen passengers.

"That was fun, Ray!" the girl said to her companion. "Let's ride it again."

"Oh, maybe later, doll, after dark. I'm hungry. We need to find some place to eat."

He and Bob were walking next to each other, and he turned to Bob and asked, "Are any of these restaurants around here any good?"

"We have reservations at one over by the hotel," Bob answered. "In fact, we're on our way there now. Would you two like to join us?"

"Sure," the man the girl had called 'Ray' replied. "My name's Ray. The doll, here, is Sheri Blake."

"We're Bob and Sally Merriam," Sally responded. "Are you from around here?"

"Naw, We're from the East. The doll's from Maryland, I've lived all over."

"On vacation?" Bob asked.

"Well, sort of. Have a little project here before we head back. Actually we just got back from Europe a couple of weeks ago."

"Really? Where were you in Europe?"

"Greece!" Sheri exclaimed. Neither Bob nor Sally saw the little poke she received from her companion, and she said nothing more.

"Oh, Greece," Sally repeated. "Our boss just got back from Greece. He was in Athens and Corinth."

Sheri wanted to say, "So were we," but fearing another poke, just said, "How interesting. What does he do?"

"He's a college professor," Sally replied. "So is my husband, and I'm the department secretary."

"A professor?" Ray asked, suddenly interested. "Where? What does he teach?"

"He's the head of the Religions Department at Fremont College," Sally answered.

"No kiddin'!" Ray replied, in almost a shocked voice. Then he added, "I seem to recall reading in an English newspaper when we were over there that some well-known religion professor from Ohio was shot."

"Yes," Bob said. "That was Dr. Fairchild. He had a group of students on a tour."

"How about that coincidence!" Ray added. By this time they had reached the restaurant. While Bob and Sally's reservation had been only for two, the hostess was easily able to find them a table for four.

102

"Was your trip to Greece business or vacation?" Sally asked after they had been seated and handed menus.

"A bit of both, I guess," Ray replied.

"What business are you in, Ray?" Bob asked.

"I'm an independent contractor. A consultant on difficult situations, you might say."

"Sounds interesting. What sort of situations?"

"Oh, just complex business deals where something gets in the way, that sort of thing." By this time the waitress had arrived to take their orders, and the four studied their menus and then told her what they wanted.

"Tell me more about your college professor," Ray said as the waitress left. "How is he doing?"

"Kind of you to ask," Sally answered. "He seems fully recuperated, back to his usual task of keeping me frantically busy all the time."

"Hard guy to work for, eh?"

"Oh, no, not really. We love him, as do his students. But he can be a 'no nonsense' taskmaster at times. He's quite a famous historian, but he also has a reputation of getting involved in criminal investigations, and the police are constantly asking for his assistance in local situations. Last year, for example, he helped capture some terrorists."

"No kiddin'!" Ray exclaimed. "What happened?"

"Well," Bob said, taking up the story, "he came across this terrorist who was planning to assassinate the civil rights leader, Singletary. It was the same guy who had tried to kill Fairchild a month or so earlier, but the terrorist didn't know that. So the terrorist invited our boss onto his big cabin cruiser until the hit on Singletary was planned, and the professor got word to the FBI, who were able to arrest all the terrorists."

"Yeah?" Ray said. "So what happened to the boat?"

"Fairchild sued the terrorist," Bob continued, "and was awarded it by the federal court. He then donated it to the college, but he is its official custodian."

"He sounds like quite a guy," Sherri said, overcoming her timidness.

"Does the professor use the boat often?" Ray asked.

"I don't really know," Bob replied. "I doubt it. It's diesel, but still expensive to operate on a long trip, I suppose, and like the rest of us in the department, he hasn't much spare time. But I would guess that this summer he's using it occasionally."

"I think he said he was taking some friends on it today," Sally added. "Someone he'd met in Cleveland."

"Boy, I'd love to be able to take a trip on a boat like that," Sherri said. "What does the college do with it?"

"They have a marine navigation course in the Engineering Department," Bob replied. "They take it out on field trips, and they also use it to ferry the viniculture students and the hotel management students and guests out to West Bass Island where the college operates the Castle Kent Inn and Winery."

"Hell, that's some college!" Ray laughed. "They have their own winery?"

"The Lake Erie islands are famous for their wines," Sally confirmed.

"And this professor, is he the one who takes people out to that island?" Ray asked.

"I think he has a few times," Sally said. "But several of the hotel management students usually do it. I guess it would depend on the circumstances."

"Interesting. Very interesting," Ray responded, just as the waitress arrived with the four dinners.

* * *

Gunther Harcourt again sat in the London office of Marcus Staley in London. He had explained to the Lloyd's underwriter that there was still no sign of the missing Chem-Queen that had disappeared from their insured's dock in Cleveland. "The FBI and Coast Guard have come up with absolutely nothing. But at least they have managed to keep it out of the newspapers. They are as puzzled as I am."

"Looks like we're going to have to pay the claim. That agent in Cleveland has been pestering us for months to make a decision on their proof of loss. I can't think of any reason to deny the claim. If the ship's master was aboard her when she was taken, there's no way to allege any policy violation."

"I'm sorry, Markus. I was certain it would show up. I just can't believe it.

Chapter 11

Richard Fairchild spent most of the next three days fishing in the Portage River and preparing for the new fall semester. While some of the basic courses were offered every semester, others were offered only on a cyclical basis, usually every other year. Every so often a course would be dropped and replaced with a different one if the subject failed to attract the requisite number of enrollees.

Bob Merriam was teaching two classes during the summer session, hence someone was always in the department's office in the basement of Hayes Hall. When Fairchild had returned from Greece, except for the final sessions with his tour group, he had chosen to work at home, resting his wounded shoulder. By mid-July, however, he felt fully recovered, regaining most of his strength, and he was able to do chores around his home and barn.

On the Thursday of the week after the Fairchilds and the Whitakers had gone out to the islands on the cruiser, the Fairchilds packed their station wagon and left early to drive to Pennsylvania. Esther's sister, Cecilia, had gotten sick, and her doctor felt that surgery might be needed. Esther agreed to come and spend a few weeks with her, and Richard felt that it would be good to drive her over to their home near Harrisburg and spend some time with his in-laws.

Cecilia was married to Roger Carpenter, who worked for the Pennsylvania Forestry Department. Although he usually occupied an office near the state capitol building, he periodically had to visit various state forests, or attend meetings with lumber industry representatives. Roger always enjoyed Fairchild's visits and tried to plan some interesting field trips whenever the professor visited. On this occasion he had arranged a meeting with some of his rangers in the Susquehannok State Forest in the upper central part of the state.

"You know," Carpenter said as they drove along the scenic West Branch of the Susquehanna west of Williamsport the following Monday, "there's a meadow just north of that forest where this big river begins as nothing more than a little brook. And in the same meadow, the Genesee River also starts as a brook. And on the far west side of that same meadow, the Allegheny River begins as a tiny stream. All in the same meadow. That meadow drains to the Chesapeake Bay, Lake Ontario and the St. Lawrence, and down the Ohio to the Mississippi and the Gulf of Mexico. Now, Richie, that's some meadow!"

"That's not where the canals came through, though, is it?"

"No, they were further south. They followed the Potomac, and then there was a pulley contraption that pulled the barges up a mountain and slid 'em down the other side to another canal that connected with the Allegheny north of Pittsburgh. Not much left to see of that, but there is a monument to the Portage Railroad around Cresson somewhere. Maybe we can go home that way and see if we can find it."

The two men spent the next four days visiting several state forests, finally arriving back in Harrisburg on Friday. On Saturday Fairchild returned to his Port Cleland farm, leaving Esther and Roger to take care of her ailing sister and the Carpenter's two teenage sons. As Fairchild was scheduled to conduct the college chapel service the following day, he left Harrisburg early in order to have the late afternoon and evening to complete his preparations for the Sunday service.

Attendance was always light in the summertime, but the non-denominational service processional was impressive nonetheless, with a verger, the ROTC honor guard, acolytes, the summer college glee club serving as choir, and the two clergymen in their robes and academic hoods following behind. The neo-gothic style chapel, with its booming bells and massive pipe organ, never failed to stir the professor's emotions as he proceeded slowly down the aisle behind the choir while the congregation sang some lively hymn. An hour later it was over. Fairchild declined an invitation to join the college chaplain, Dr. Stephen Boldt, and his wife for dinner, and opted to get back to his farm to complete some fence work on which he had been procrastinating. "My shoulder, you know," he explained. "I can't use that excuse for not mending the fence now that it is better! But I'm grateful that it got me out of a few chores for at least a week or two."

"Richard," the chaplain laughed, "I don't think anyone will ever accuse you of being lazy. You deserved a rest, and I'm glad you got one, even if it took someone to shoot you."

Fairchild had just arrived back at the farm when the phone rang. For all he knew it might have been ringing all week, but this time he was there to answer it.

"Is this Richard Fairchild?" a man at the other end asked.

"Yes."

"Ahh, Professor Fairchild, my name is Ray Southerland. Ahh, I have a reservation at that hotel the college operates out on that island, and I understand that you could run me out there."

"Well, yes. Maybe. When are you going?"

"This Thursday."

"There's a plane from the Port Cleland airport to the island on Thursdays. That would be faster for you."

"Well, the college said they had a boat and you could take me. Frankly, ahh, I don't like flying."

"I see. I'd have to charge you for the fuel to run out there. It's almost forty miles round trip. It would be $25, each way."
"That's okay with me."
"What time did you have in mind?"
"Oh, say in the morning. I'm staying in Sandusky right now, so maybe nine-thirty or ten?"
"Do you know where the boat is docked?"
"The college said some lagoon in Port Cleland."
"Yes. Follow the state highway into town and cross over the drawbridge. The entrance to the lagoon is just beyond that to the right. The cruiser is at the far end of the second row of slips. There's a sign that says Castle Kent posted at the entrance to that slip. That's the name of the cruiser. The sign also says 'Fremont College' on it. I'll be there at nine-thirty, but I'm fairly busy right now, so if you think you will be late, please give me a call well before nine."
"Okay, I'll do that. Ahh, thank you, Professor."
Unusual, the professor thought to himself as he hung up. But then, he'd taken a few others out to the old castle on West Bass before, and always enjoyed the trip. Maybe he'd have time to stop and visit his friends, the Forrakers, who lived in Kent Village on the island after his passengers departed. The Forrakers tended the inn and winery in the off season, and the Fairchilds had known them for many years.

* * *

On the following Tuesday morning, one of the final few days of July, Fairchild received another phone call, this time from someone who identified himself as Thomas Morris, an agent in the Cleveland field office of the Federal Bureau of Investigation. The man did not say what he wanted, but asked if he might visit the professor at his home that afternoon. Richard agreed, and told him how to find the farm. Fairchild was glad that Esther was away at her sister's home in Pennsylvania, as she often got upset when law enforcement officers came seeking the professor's counsel.

About one thirty a dark blue car pulled into the driveway of the Fairchild farm and a tall man about forty in a gray suit and gray hat got out and came to the door. Fairchild had heard the car, and met him at the door.

"Agent Morris?" he asked.

"Yes," replied the other, holding out his identification pad containing his badge and photo-identification card. "Dr. Fairchild?"

"Right. Come on in. Let's go down to the library. It's more comfortable in there," the professor replied, leading the FBI agent down the short hallway by the kitchen to the large, cluttered library.

"Goodness, a lot of books!" Agent Morris said.

"Tools of my trade, I guess," Fairchild replied, directing Morris to a chair and seating himself behind his desk. "What can I do for you?"

The agent began by asking Fairchild some questions. He had not known what kind of professor Fairchild was.

Fairchild explained. "I teach religions at Fremont College, and serve as assistant chaplain there."

"I see," the agent replied. "Actually, there is quite a file on you at the Bureau. Seems you and Special Agent Jim Slade have worked some operations before. He had some glowing comments about you in the file."

"Is he still in the Toledo office?"

"No, he's been transferred – promoted, really – to Chicago. I understand you have also worked with local police departments on cases."

"Oh, nothing big, just some little historical puzzles. I guess I'm like a little animal that likes to dig. I probably got the digging bug from having been in Army Intelligence during the War."

"Behind German lines, I understand."

"Golly, you guys do have quite a file on me, don't you," Fairchild laughed.

"Are you currently 'digging' into something?" the agent inquired. "Something like a murder investigation?"

"Well, no, not really doing much digging. Why?"

"You have a friend in Cleveland, Sam Whitaker, who is a friend of one of the Cleveland Police officers, Andy Segretti. Whitaker discovered the body of a murdered man, a homeless man named George Antopholis, and Segretti was the first policeman on the scene, so they got to know each other. Antopholis was shot with a .45 caliber gun. The Cleveland Police closed the case, anticipating that the crime had been committed by a transient intent on theft. But Whitaker told Segretti that he did not believe that, and Segretti got his precinct captain to reopen the case. They did, but they never learned anything further.

"Then, a little over a week ago, you gave Whitaker a bullet that had been removed from your back, I understand...."

"Right rear shoulder," Fairchild corrected.

"Yes. Whitaker told Segretti that you had been wounded while traveling in Greece. The Cleveland Police tried to match the bullet from Antopholis's murder with the one you gave Whitaker. They thought there was a match, but were not sure, so both were sent overnight to the FBI lab in Washington, where we were able to positively match the two. Both bullets were fired from the same gun. If, as Whitaker told Segretti, you were wounded in a foreign country, the matter comes under federal jurisdiction.

"Frankly, it sounds to us like someone tried to assassinate you, and it must have had something to do with Antopholis. Dr. Fairchild, what have you gotten into?"

"Well, I didn't know that I've gotten into anything, really. Sam told me about George when I asked where George was. Well, perhaps I'd better start at the beginning. You see, I occasionally help out at a homeless shelter in Cleveland called St. Vincent House. As an ordained clergyman, they are glad to have me substitute for their shelter managers if they are away, perhaps on vacation. I've been down there several times, and got to know George, who was known as 'Shoeless George' because of his disabled feet. When I was there over the Christmas holidays I didn't see George. I asked one of the other men, Sam Whitaker, about George, and he told me that George had been murdered, and that the police had closed the case. As you just said, he believed it was not a transient who shot George to rob him, because very few of the homeless have guns. If they do, they usually pawn them. Nobody would have to shoot George to rob him as he had nothing worth stealing. He was totally helpless.

"Sam and I could not think of any other reason why George would have been murdered. The only thing we could think of was that perhaps while he was wandering around the city or on some job – he occasionally got work picking up trash or gardening – that he had found something and was killed for it. But what it was, we had no idea.

"Then I discovered that George was actually the heir to a large Greek steamship line owned by an uncle in Greece. This uncle, Demetrius Antopholis, had died last September. He had named his sister in Buffalo in his will. She had raised George when his parents were killed. But this sister was dead, and, under her will, George was the inheritor of anything she had. So George would have inherited the ship line and estate in Greece as the sole remaining relative.

"It turned out that George had also made a will, and had named a previous manager of the shelter as his heir. I thought that perhaps that man, an Edgar Latimer...."

The agent, who was making notes, held up his hand.

"Is that Latimer with two 't's?" he asked.

"No, just one. Edgar A. Latimer. He lived in Boston. But I was able to learn that he was in Boston the week George was murdered, so I don't think he had anything to do with George's murder. I met with him in Athens – a trial was occurring on the inheritance of the estate in Greece when I was there with my college student study group – and he seems a very honest person. He did know about George having possibly inherited something – he didn't know what – a few weeks before George was killed, but at that time he didn't even know how to contact George."

"But it was while you were in Greece that you were wounded."

"Right. The Corinth police thought it was an accidental shooting. Now you say it probably wasn't. I know it was not Latimer who shot me as he was in a Greek courtroom that day at the trial. Actually, he won. The

Greek government had been trying to claim that they should be entitled to the Antopholis estate."

"Hmm. Who else knew you were investigating George's murder?"

"Oh, let's see. Sam, of course. And I don't know whom he may have told. And Amos Waterman, the manager of the shelter at the time George was killed." Fairchild thought for a second, then continued, "Brother Peter, at the Order's friary in New York. I understand they have filed a suit to challenge the will. Oh, and Andy Segretti, the Cleveland police officer, got me in touch with a Mr. Millerman, who runs the city refuse department that hired George occasionally on trash details. And then Billy Aronso, the manager of Downtown Labor, Incorporated."

"Mmm. And so far, you've found no connections?"

"No, none specifically. The only name that keeps coming up time and again is that of the Rogers Chemical Company. Ed Latimer had been a tenant of Fred Rogers in Lakewood after he quit as manager of the shelter and before he returned to Boston. And George often worked out at the chemical plant, doing gardening, or cleaning out warehouses that had belonged to the company. He may even have worked at Rogers' home in Lakewood as a gardener. Fred Rogers and his wife were in Athens at the same time as our tour. Their daughter, Kelly, was one of the students on the tour."

"Rogers Chemical. That's the one down on the River, just south of the refinery."

"Right. Say, you don't happen to be the agent investigating that missing ship at the Rogers Chemical Company, are you?"

"How the hell do you know about that?" the agent exclaimed. "There has been absolute press silence on that matter. Where on earth....?"

"I didn't know it was a secret," Fairchild explained. "Apparently the Taylor Marine Insurance Agency where Sam Whitaker works has the insurance on the ship. Sam mentioned it to me."

Agent Morris sat silent for a moment. Then he asked, "And you think there are some parallels, don't you?"

"The thought had crossed my mind, but.... I just don't see how. How could George's murder in November be connected with a ship that disappeared in September?"

"Ships don't just vanish in Lake Erie," Agent Morris replied. "The Coast Guard has even used sonar to see if they could find it. But I must swear you to confidentiality on that case, as it is still pending, and one of international importance. It might also interest you to know that the ship, the Chem Queen, was purchased from Antopholis's ship line."

"Really! But I can't see how that would be connected."

"Nor can I. But Professor Fairchild, what I came out here to tell you was that we believe you are in danger. Someone who apparently has already killed at least once has already made one attempt on your life. It's very likely another attempt will soon be made. The government is prepared to offer you asylum in our witness protection program where you and your wife will be safe."

"My wife is away for a few weeks with her sister in Pennsylvania. I'm sure she's safe there. You don't think I'd be safe here?"

"No. You need to get out of here as soon as possible. You can't stay here tonight!" Morris stated emphatically.

"What about Sam Whitaker? He may be in danger, too."

"We don't think so, although we do have a tail on him. Don't let him know that. Whitaker isn't as likely to put two and two together on this thing as you are. He has no reputation as a detective. You do. It isn't just the FBI that knows your reputation, and that's what puts you in danger. You've simply got to protect yourself."

"But I've got commitments all week, and need to finish my preparations for the fall term. I can't just pack up and leave."

"You must go now. If you won't go into the witness program, at least go somewhere where you will be safe," Morris insisted. "We can't force you to accept our offer of protection, but you ought to consider it.. Where do you think you might be safe?"

"I have access to a large cruiser. I could stay on that, and move about."

"I don't know. You'd have to keep your whereabouts very secret. You might discuss it with your wife. Maybe you could join her in Pennsylvania."

"Ha! I just got back from there!"

"Who else can you really trust as a contact?"

"Well, our assistant professor, Bob Merriam, and his wife, Sally, who is our department secretary. They live in Sandusky, and he's teaching during the summer session. Esther and I stayed with them a few days when our house was hit by the train."

"Yes, Merriam's name is in our file, I recall. Okay. Can we reach Merriam now?"

Fairchild called the college and reached Bob Merriam in his office. The situation was explained, and Merriam agreed to be the contact between Fairchild and the FBI. The agent then insisted that Fairchild pack a bag and get out of the house as quickly as possible. Fairchild called his neighbor, who looked after Fairchild's cattle while he was away, and said he'd be out of town for a couple of weeks. Then he called Esther and explained what was happening in a way that he hoped would not unduly alarm her. Morris then followed Fairchild's station wagon up to the lagoons at Port Cleland, and after seeing the professor aboard the cruiser, returned to the neighborhood of the farm to see if anyone was watching it.

Esther was furious when she hung up the phone after her husband's call. "I keep telling him to keep his nose out of these criminal things," she ranted to Cecelia Carpenter. "Does he listen? No. Always he's butting into these things and getting shot and beaten up and threatened. Now we're being chased out of our home again. This is the limit!" she complained. "You should be grateful Roger doesn't fancy himself as a policeman."

"But Esther," her sister replied, trying to calm her, "Richard is an exceptionally good citizen. He has helped both the FBI and the local police many times, and I'm sure they are always grateful. I understand your concern, though.

"Actually, Roger does have some police authority, through the state forest rangers." Cecelia continued. "I do worry when he has to get involved in some crime investigation. I think that's why Roger and Richie get along so well. They understand each other. Richie's just a brilliant detective."

"Brilliant," Esther repeated. "Too smart for his own good, you mean. Oh, what's the use? He's going to stay on that boat and move around, so maybe nobody will find him. In a way, I'm glad I'm not there."

"He'd maybe be better in the FBI's witness protection program."

"I know. But you'd never get Richard off that yacht."

* * *

Sheri Blake lay curled up on a bed in a room on the second floor of a Sandusky motel overlooking part of the harbor. She wore only skimpy blue satin bikini panties and a matching flimsy lace bra. Raymond Ingersol sat in a chair opposite to her in only his undershorts, smiling at his view of her while he talked on the telephone.

"Yeah, I finally got him on the phone. He must have been out of town or something. Anyway, I'm supposed to meet him at his boat in Port Cleland Thursday morning. That tip from his college partner and secretary really paid off. I made reservations at the college's inn out on some island, and Fairchild is supposed to take me out there. Said he'd charge me $25 to fuel his damned boat. ... Of course I used another name. What the hell you think I am, an idiot? ... No, no. We'll never reach that island. We've rented another boat for Sherri for that day, and she'll follow us out. When we get rid of him, I'll have a ride back, and it will be days before they find his empty boat. I'll see you by six Thursday night, so stick around till I get there. ... What? ... Yeah, I'll keep you posted. Bye."

Ingersol gave Blake a wink. "Well, doll," he continued after he had hung up the phone, "we've been looking for that needle in a haystack. But we've found it now. Let me put that 'do not disturb' sign on the door. Then...."

Ingersol felt surges of energy coursing throughout his body. He arose, went to the door and turned the short plastic sign to the outside, then placed the double lock on the door. It was mid-afternoon, and they'd had lunch in their room. The empty pizza box had been stuffed in a garbage can outside the door. Now they had the rest of the day, plus the entire next one, to play.

"Let's do that shower routine you seem to enjoy," Sheri Blake giggled. "I'll go run the water," she said, rolling off the bed and padding in her bare feet into the large motel bathroom. Ingersol followed closely behind her, shutting the door behind him.

* * *

The official-looking business letter from London came by registered mail. It required Harry Taylor's personal signature. As the postman left his office, delivering the rest of the mail to the receptionist, Taylor tore open the envelope. There was a letter and two checks payable to the Rogers Chemical Company, although one was also payable to the bank that was the lienholder on the vessel. The letter was short, and simply stated that the Underwriters were pleased to enclose payment of the claims under the Rogers policy, but that in the event of any recovery of either the vessel or the cargo, the Underwriters would be entitled to full refund, less any recovery expenses.

"Thank God!" he said aloud. Then he reached for the telephone, and placed a call to Garrett Williams, the Rogers Chemical Company Chief Financial Officer.

"They've settled!" he told his client. "I've got two certified checks here, drawn on a London bank, one payable to Rogers Chemical, and the other to Rogers and the Marine National Bank of Detroit for their lien on the ship."

"Good. I'll have one of my people stop by today and pick them up so we can get them in the bank," Williams replied.

Taylor walked into the file room where there was also a thermofax machine and made a copy of the two checks and the letter. Then he placed those in the thick file folder he had deliberately misfiled amongst the closed files. He stamped the file "closed,' and now filed it in its correct alphabetical order.

Chapter 12

It took a while for Esther to get over her anger at Richard for having to again leave home because of some investigation he had undertaken. Richard called her early the next morning, but both said very little and he realized how upset she was. He was grateful that this time the college itself was not at risk. That would have meant that Dean Harding would also have been mad at him. Having his wife on the warpath was enough turmoil.

Fairchild had filled the cruiser's diesel fuel tank in preparation to take the large vessel out to West Bass Island. That was also as good a place to hide, and fish, as any he could think of. Just to be safe, he called the college inn on the ship to shore phone and verified that a Ray Southerland did indeed have a reservation at the Inn the next day.

The Inn at Castle Kent had also been obtained by Fremont College through the activities of Richard Fairchild. When he and Merriam had discovered the remains of a German agent in the wine cellar of the old castle-like mansion and the transportation company that owned it had offered it for sale, Fairchild had encouraged the college to buy it and operate it for their growing hotel and restaurant management department, as well as for the several viniculture classes offered by the college's chemistry department. The Inn was staffed about eight months of the year now, and had become popular with both tourists and Northern Ohio boaters, who would visit the island to dine in the Inn's restaurant and purchase the several quality wines the students were producing.

The late July sun was baking down by nine o'clock. It was almost too hot to do much but sit in the shade of the upper deck. He had brought along enough books to last several weeks. It was an entire day before he had to take a passenger to the island.

Shortly after nine that morning, however, the marine radio advised of an approaching storm. Fairchild responded immediately, and headed the cruiser, the Castle Kent, toward the protection of Sandusky Bay. Anchoring well inside the Bay, he pulled the sheltering tarps around the open cabin area and awaited the storm.

The storm hit with the typical fury of a Lake Erie gale, with wind, water, lightning and thunder blasting around the boat and rocking it back and forth and up and down at the same time. Fairchild could do nothing but hang on to the chair in which he sat, which was bolted to the deck. It was the worst storm he had experienced in the cruiser.

Within an hour the storm had passed, and the marine radio channel was reporting fair skies to the west. Fairchild unhooked the tarps, mopped remaining water off the decks, and went down into the galley to prepare an early lunch.

After he had eaten, he thought to himself that he ought to cruise down the coast to Cleveland. It would break the monotony, and he could easily get back to Sandusky that evening in order to be available for his passenger to West Bass Island the next morning.

He got to Cleveland in the early afternoon, immediately heading the cruiser into the harbor and up the Cuyahoga River. About a quarter of a mile above the main railroad drawbridge, just slightly south of the Shoreway viaduct, he pulled the cruiser to the east bank of the channel and tied up at the two metal docking stubs at that location. It was the back of the St. Vincent House shelter, which at one time had been a marine supply store. There was a tugboat company to the north of the shelter, and they often tied one of their boats to the shelter's dock, but none was there that afternoon.

From the upper deck the professor was able to step onto the pavement behind the shelter. He was down in the Flats, in territory that Fairchild knew well from the times he had managed the shelter. He entered the shelter and went to the office of the manager, introducing himself and asking to use the phone. He then called a taxi, and within a few minutes it had delivered him to the Cuyahoga County Court Annex, across from the mammoth gray limestone pillared building that was the county's courthouse. The professor entered the more modern building, located on Lakeside Avenue at Ontario, and after scanning the directory, went to the second floor where the plat maps were kept.

In a room at the back of the building were large tables at which giant map books, about four feet wide and two and a half high, were kept. Another map on the wall gave the key to the books, and within moments Fairchild had found the one he wanted, pulled it out, and checked the index. He then fished through the pages until he found the correct map. It showed in great detail the ownership changes and dates, coordinates and other data about each parcel of land. This particular map showed a section of the Cuyahoga River valley.

He found the property that was now the Rogers Chemical Company. But he noted that Rogers once owned the section just south of that, but that this property was sold to another company. Now that name has been struck, and 'City' entered. Then he noticed another section just south of that, which was formerly owned by 'Gooding Company,' but had recently been changed to 'T&W Marine, Inc.' Fairchild made a note of this, and placed it in his wallet, then replaced the book in the shelf and went outside to find a taxi.

Back aboard the Castle Kent Fairchild followed the Goodtime, a tour boat that took people on a guided tour of the river. He could hear the announcements of what lay along the banks of the river, from Carter's cabin, the first structure on the river that served for years as an inn in the late 1700s, to the railroad depots, refineries, steel mills and the drawbridges that permitted land transportation to interact with river traffic. Early in the journey he passed behind the marine shops and bars that lined River Street. Further along he came to some of the better parts of the river, including the famous Jim's Steak House, where Richard and Esther had once stopped for dinner.

About two miles further up the river, just beyond the last refinery on the eastern bank and opposite the last steel mill on the western bank, the Goodtime made a wide turn and began its voyage back to the pier where it was docked. Fairchild carefully guided the Castle Kent a bit further, finally reaching the fenced area and tanks on the riverbank behind the Rogers Chemical Company.

Just beyond the chemical plant were a number of old warehouses, some that appeared to date from the time of the Ohio Canal, which intersected with the Cuyahoga a bit further up the river. Fairchild slowed the cruiser's speed. It was still in fairly deep water, but he had noticed various items of debris sticking up, hence was concerned about hitting something submerged.

About three warehouses beyond the chemical plant there was a vacant lot where it appeared a building had burned down. Next to that was another very tall and wide brick warehouse that had only a few dirty windows on one side, which backed right up to the river. He could make out the faint lettering of the word 'Gooding' on the river side of the building. Fairchild pulled up next to the warehouse, and examined the part of the brick wall that appeared to extend down under the water. There was something very unusual about the wall, but he could not quite tell what it was in the late afternoon sunlight and his distance from the wall. He did, however, climb out on the deck with his sounding pole, and probed the water in front of the warehouse. The pole, ten feet long, did not strike the bottom.

Fairchild replaced the pole and returned to the wheel and controls to the cruiser, which was drifting in neutral. He shifted the engine to reverse, pushed the throttle forward slightly, and the cruiser swung around in the river until it faced north. Then he placed the engine back into the forward gear, and again pressed the throttle forward, heading the cruiser out into the middle of the river. As it again passed the chemical plant heading down the river he noticed a man standing beside one of the tanks on the Rogers property, watching the cruiser through binoculars.

A few minutes later he approached the tie-up dock for the steakhouse, which was built on one of the bends -- just east of the famous Collision Bend -- of the Cuyahoga, directly below the Terminal Tower complex. Tempted to have an early dinner, Fairchild pulled up to the dock, and tied the ropes from the cruiser to it. His table, at a window in the restaurant, looked out on the river and he enjoyed watching a variety of ships and pleasure craft go up and downstream.

Although tempted to spend the night in Cleveland's harbor and return for his passenger in the early morning, the professor decided he had better head back to the Sandusky area for the night in case another storm might roll in from the west. Perhaps he would dock somewhere along the Marblehead or Catawba Peninsulas for the night, he thought as the cruiser cut along the lake shore at about twenty-two knots.

* * *

The next morning Raymond Ingersol dropped Sherri at a small marina just east of Port Cleland, where they had arranged to rent a fairly large and fast speedboat for the day. He and Sherri had rented several boats while in Greece, and one the previous week while they were planning their move against the professor, and she had become a skilled navigator, now quite familiar with the channel leading from the Port Cleland lagoons.

As soon as he saw Sherri depart in the rented speedboat he got back into his rented automobile and drove the remaining three miles into Port Cleland, turning right at the far end of the drawbridge. It was almost exactly nine-thirty when he parked in a slot at the end of the slips and locked the car. He had only one case, which looked like luggage but did not contain clothing. He quickly walked to the end of the slip, where the engine of the Castle Kent, was already burbling and Dr. Richard Fairchild was waiting.

"Hello," he called as he approached.

"Ray Southerland?" the professor asked.

"Yes. Are we ready?"

"You're right on time, mate!" Fairchild answered, reaching out for the case Ingersol was carrying. "I'll set this below, but stay on the dock there until you can unhook that front line for me, then hop onto the bow." Fairchild set the case inside the cabin, then unfastened the rope at the rear of the cruiser, and throttled slightly forward so that the front rope slackened. Ingersol pulled it from the hooks that held it and threw it aboard.

"Done like a true sailor!" Fairchild added.

"Oh, I've done a bit of boating. How far is this island?" Ingersol asked, although he already knew from the charts that it was eighteen miles to the northwest.

"Just a little over eighteen miles to the inn's new dock. There's another dock at the village on the north end of the island. I may spend the rest of the day up there. How long are you going to be staying at the inn?

"I'm not sure," Ingersol replied. "Thought I'd wait until I got there and then decide. The college said somebody on the island would probably be able to run me back."

"Yes, the students keep a boat out there, but it's just a little one, and the Lake can get rough at times. Too bad you don't like flying."

By this time the Castle Kent had cleared the harbor, and Fairchild set a course to the northwest. About a mile further out from land he noted another boat approaching from the east, but it appeared to be running parallel to the Kent. A young girl was at the controls. It appeared to the professor that the other boat was capable of much greater speed than it was using, which somewhat surprised him, given the calm water that morning. There was not even a very great chop.

Ingersol asked if there was a "head" on the boat, and Fairchild told him where the two bathrooms on the cruiser were located, and to have a look around below if he wished. Ingersol went below, then came back into the main cabin and opened his case, carefully turning it away from Fairchild, who remained at the spoked mahogany wheel. By this time the cruiser was about eight miles from shore, and shoreline features could barely be seen, but they still were far enough away that they could not yet see West Bass Island.

The speedboat was still paralleling the cruiser to starboard, but edging a bit closer. Ingersol again came onto the deck, his jacket now zipped part way up. He looked over at the speedboat and waved. The girl waved back. Fairchild initially thought it was just a friendly gesture, but now the speedboat seemed to be coming closer.

"Someone you know, Ray?" he asked.

"Yeah, maybe it is, Professor." With that, he unzipped his jacket and pulled out a .45 caliber revolver. He pointed it at Fairchild.

"Just idle the engine down to a stop, Professor. You'll be getting off soon." Fairchild did as instructed, and the speedboat quickly churned up beside the cruiser. "You know, Fairchild, you've been the devil to find."

"Who are you and what are you doing?" Fairchild demanded.

"Never mind who I am. Just sit down on that deck chair over there, and keep your mouth shut, Doctor Professor." Richard Fairchild said nothing.

"Understand you're a preacher man," Ingersol continued. "Pretty soon I'll let you say your prayers. First things first, though. My boss wants to know what you know, so you can tell me nicely, or, if you don't, I'll beat the crap out'a you, so it's your choice."

"Know about what? I know about lots of things," Fairchild replied.

"Don't be cute with me, Jackass. You know very well what I mean. What were you doin' poking around those warehouses up that river yesterday afternoon, eh? Sightseeing?"

"Yes. The old canal comes in somewhere around there. I was looking for it."

"Oh, bull! You're lookin' for canals like I'm lookin' for daffodils! Tell me what you know, and it will go a lot easier on you."

"No, I'm not going to tell you. I'll tell Fred Rogers, your boss, though," Fairchild replied. "We can just go on down to his place in Lakewood, and I'll tell him directly. That way you won't get any of it wrong."

"What are you pullin'? I don't know any Fred Rogers."

"Sure you do. You obviously know about his chemical plant, you or someone you deal with, or you wouldn't know where I'd been yesterday. Whoever it is won't be very happy if you come back today with no information and only one more murder on your – and his – hands."

"So who's this Rogers guy you're telling me I know? He's the guy who owns the warehouses?"

"He's that 'guy.'" Fairchild said. "I think this boss of yours suspects what I know, but he needs proof."

"Rogers ain't the guy who hired me. I never heard of him."

"Oh? That's interesting. So who's your boss?"

"Come on, Jackass. Quit stalling. What do you know, and who have you told?"

"So, you've got two bosses, and you didn't even know it! I can see exactly what they were setting you up for. Boy! And you are stepping right into it. Brother! Have they taken you for a ride."

"What'd yah mean?"

"Have they paid you yet?"

"That's none of your business."

"Unhuh. Paid your expenses to Greece and back, and probably got you holed up in some fancy hotel and you don't get paid until you prove I'm dead. But you can't prove that unless you've got a body to show, plus the information they want, and you don't know how to get it."

"How'd you know I'd been in Greece?"

"Because that's where you shot me. You followed our tour down to Corinth, and when you had the opportunity you tried to shoot me in the back. Your lady friend, in the next boat here, probably drove the car. Well, you lucked out, because the Greek police thought it was an accident."

"Yeah, well, how do you know it was me?"

"Look, Mister.... No, you won't give me your name. But give me your first name. Is it really 'Ray'?"

"Yeah, it's 'Ray'."

"Good, now look, Ray, you shot me with the same gun you used to shoot that homeless, helpless George, undoubtedly the same .45 you're holding in your hand right now. That gun is lethal to you. The FBI has already traced it. They know where I am, and they're probably watching us right now."

"You're bluffing! There ain't nobody within miles of here. There ain't no FBI trace. You're just making that up to stall."

"Think so, eh. Then how do I know what I've already told you."

"Guesswork."

"No, Ray. You're in very hot water, but I can get you out of some of it. Let's go see Fred Rogers and see if he's the one behind all this. Good Lord, Ray, his own daughter was in that group of students I had down there in Corinth. If you had missed me and hit her, you'd be the one he'd be wanting killed right now."

"You're bullin' me!"

"No I'm not, Ray, and you know it. If you really think I am, then shoot me now, and just see how much money you get, and how far away you can get before you are arrested. At this point I can help you. Beyond this point, I can't."

"Get up!" Ingersol demanded, and the professor arose from the chair. Ingersol raised the revolver, preparing to strike Fairchild across the face with it.

"Ray, Ray! Use your head, before you lose it. You already know what I know, which is that you killed George and shot me, and that the FBI is looking for you. Now, let's go visit Rogers, get you paid for finding me, and as far as I'm concerned, you and your lady friend can be on your way."

"You ain't going to visit no Fred Rogers."

"That's a mistake, Ray. You left your car back at the lagoon. We can use it to get to Rogers' home in Lakewood."

"We're not going to Lakewood. You're not going anywhere. You're going to tell me what you know, and then I'm going to shoot you."

"I've already told you what I know, Ray. You weren't listening. I know that you shot poor George under that bridge since you have the .45 that was used and you're not denying it. Whomever it is that you think is your boss panicked when he found out I was looking into the murder, and because he was in a partnership with someone to rip off Lloyd's of London for a couple million bucks, he couldn't afford to have me nosing around. So he hired you again, to kill me.

"Now, you didn't know about the Lloyd's deal, did you? They're paying you practically nothing, and probably planning to kill you when you've killed me. There won't be any live witnesses, I can assure you. But with the information I can give you later, you can make a better deal. Think about that."

"I don't know nothing about any insurance claim, and I don't give a damn about it. I made a deal, and I'll get paid, and you'll be dead, and that will be the end of it."

"Ray," Fairchild interrupted, "think a second. You could get much more out of this deal if I'm alive. Or better yet, turn state's evidence against them in a trade-off with the federal prosecutors. You didn't know George, didn't know what he knew. They did.

"Sure it might cost you a few years, but would you rather do time in a nice federal pen, or down in what the state calls 'the big house' in Columbus.

It's a hell of a place, Ray. I've seen it, counseled guys sent there. The federal place is much better, but that's up to you. Give me your gun now, and I'll see that it's the FBI and not the Cleveland cops that get you."

"Like hell! You think I'm just going to hand you over this gun and turn myself in? Man, you're nuts!"

"Yes, I've always been a bit nuts, Ray. But, yes, you're going to hand me that gun. I suppose you may have killed someone before George. I don't know that. Probably the cops don't either, or you wouldn't be sitting here. That's bad, Ray, but it's not half as bad as either getting killed yourself by your so-called boss, or worse, killing me and then having to flee both your boss and the cops. It's up to you, Ray. Now, give me your gun."

"I'll give it to you, all right!" Ray exclaimed, swinging the revolver toward Fairchild's head. With that Fairchild ducked and lunged forward, crashing into Ingersol as hard as he could. The gun flew out of his hand, and fell with a loud thud to the deck. Ingersol quickly recovered, but by the time he had reached down and picked up the revolver again, Fairchild had dove over the port side of the cruiser and was in the water.

Ingersol ran to the side and looked over, prepared to shoot, but Fairchild had dived under the boat, and worked his way toward the bow. Ingersol ran to the starboard side, but Fairchild was not there, so he ran back to port. Fairchild surfaced near the starboard bow, and Sherri shouted, "Ray, he's over here."

Fairchild took a deep breath and again dived under the cruiser, and worked his way back, then, risking being seen, popped up for a quick breath. His clothing was weighing him down, and he was able to kick his shoes off. He could hear Ray at the port side again, and made a long dive that took him under the speedboat, and he again came up for air on its starboard side.

"He's over here!" Sherri shouted again, and Ray ran to the right side of the cruiser, but could not see Fairchild as the speedboat was in the way. Fairchild began rocking the speedboat as hard as he could, so that Sherri was unable to stand up without bracing herself.

"Damn it, Ray, he's trying to tip me over!" she shouted. She swung the wheel to the left and gunned the twin outboards, turning the speedboat around, and forcing Fairchild to dive under the bow and come up on the port side of the speedboat so that Ingersol could not get a shot at him.
"Ray, let's get out of here and leave him," Sherri shouted.

"Yeah, that'll do it. He told me enough so they'll know I got him. Gun your motors, and he'll probably get chopped by the propellers."

Sherri threw the throttle on the speedboat forward, again spinning the speedboat around, forcing Fairchild to kick away from the side. As he dove under the water again he could hear the twin propellers of the speedboat's outboards just above his head. Then he heard the roar of the cruiser's diesel engine as it, too, started forward. He came up for air, but the cruiser was still close. Ray Ingersol saw him, and started firing.

The first bullet hit the water just ahead of Fairchild, but by the time Ingersol fired the second time Fairchild was again diving. He felt the third shot nick his left arm, and he knew it was bleeding. Three more shots hit the water around him, so close he felt one brush through his hair, but Fairchild had to surface for air. He hoped that the revolver held only six shots.

As he came up, rather than swim, Fairchild floated hunched over, motionless, pretending to be unconscious or dead. His luck held. He heard Ingersol shout, "Got yah, yah bastard!" Then the cruiser roared away, following after the speedboat. Blood continued to ooze from the slash along the professor's left arm.

Chapter 13

Garrett Williams was sitting in his office at the back of the top floor of the Rogers Chemical Company building. His office overlooked the Cuyahoga River, which lay beyond the pipes and tanks of the chemical refinery. He was reviewing the entries the head bookkeeper had made showing the insurance recovery from London. He had already endorsed the check representing the hull and had sent it off to the bank in Detroit for processing of the loan cancellation. The balance would be returned to Rogers Chemical by a separate check. The bank would also forward title to the vessel. The letter from the insurers had instructed that the title was then to be sent to them, as they would be the owners in the event the ship would ever be recovered.

Williams had no trouble with that. He believed that the ship would never be found. Rogers Chemical had already set in motion the process of purchasing another vessel. Fred Rogers had gone to Greece for that very purpose, but so far a suitable ship had not been located. Williams, who had been assigned the marine department two years earlier as part of his duties as chief financial officer, had already turned down two tanker ships that had been offered for sale. One, he had said, was too large to be easily moved up the river. The other was too rusted. He had his own idea of where to get another ship.

While the insurance settlement would add cash to the Rogers assets, when another vessel was found and purchased, another loan would have to be negotiated. Interest rates had climbed a bit since the purchase of the *Chem Queen*, but were still fairly reasonable. In addition, he had personally negotiated an excellent deal for Rogers on the chemicals that had been lost when the ship disappeared. For over a week a tanker truck had made daily deliveries to replenish the supplies needed for manufacturing. If only Fred Rogers had known how good the deal really was, Williams thought to himself. He smiled, and leaned back in his chair, and his eyes scanned the sunny late July sky. The weekend was a day away, and with Eddie home from Yale, they were planning a long weekend visit to one of the state parks that had a resort hotel, leaving on Saturday morning.

* * *

Special Agent Thomas Morris was also sitting in his office in a building on Ontario Street that Thursday morning. He always had a backlog of cases under investigation, but one was particularly troublesome to him. He had just received a letter from a Canadian insurance investigator named Gunther Harcourt that informed him that the London insurers had paid off on the *Chem Queen* and its chemical cargo. That meant that Harcourt, too, had reached a dead end in his search.

He was tempted to place the file on a "investigation suspended" status since nothing new had been learned in almost ten months. But something nagged at him, something the hefty college professor who had heard about the crime had said. A connection. Something connected that professor's having been shot in a foreign country to the murder of a homeless man, and the theft of the Rogers Chemical Company vessel in Cleveland. But try as he might, he could see no links between the three.

Morris had not even opened the file, although he had pulled it out of the drawer and set it on his desk. With a shrug of his shoulders he shoved the letter from Harcourt into the folder and placed it back into his drawer behind the tab that said 'Pending.' Maybe, he thought, just maybe a break would come on the case and his investigation could move forward.

* * *

Ray Ingersol and Sherri Blake proceeded exactly as they had planned. Ingersol knew he could not have gotten the professor to deviate from the route to West Bass Island without force, and believed that they were far enough from shore that if Fairchild was not already dead, he soon would drown in the deep Lake Erie water.

The two boats sped side-by-side to a point beyond North Bass Island, also known as Isle St. George, in the channel between the Bass Islands and Pelee Island, in Canadian waters. Then they stopped, and Ingersol turned off the engine on the diesel cruiser, leaving the keys in the ignition slot. "At least there's no blood on board to clean up," he thought to himself as Sherri carefully manipulated the speedboat next to the *Castle Kent*. Ingersol then went around the cruiser with a cloth and carefully wiped everything he might have touched. He wanted no fingerprints. With Fairchild gone and the cruiser found drifting, there would be the assumption that he had either fallen overboard, or had committed suicide.

He was bothered, nonetheless, by what Fairchild had told him. Fairchild obviously knew he had killed the bum under the bridge, and had tried to kill Fairchild in Greece. Maybe the bit about the FBI tracing the gun wasn't a bluff. But it didn't matter. The gun was stolen, untraceable. He did not understand the bit about an insurance rip-off. Maybe there might be some dough in that bit of information. Perhaps Fairchild had told him more than he thought.

He used the rag to hold the rail of the cruiser as he climbed down into the speedboat as Sherri idled the motors and kept it along-side the cruiser.

"Not one print!" he told her. "Now, let's get this baby back to the marina and go collect our dough."

Sherri gunned the motors, and the speedboat took off across the open water. She followed a path that took them east of the Bass Islands and west of Kelleys Island, then around Catawba Point toward the Port Cleland marina where they had rented the boat.

* * *

"That's a bit queer," Mary MacIntosh said to her husband, Tom, as they stood in the observation deck atop the 352 foot monument to Perry's 1813 victory over the British at Put-In-Bay. She was looking through one of the high-powered telescope machines, into which she had deposited 25¢ a few moments earlier.

"What is, Dear?" replied Tom. MacIntosh was a naval history buff from York, England, and had always wanted to see where the famous battle had occurred. This was the couple's first vacation trip to the United States, and Tom had planned the itinerary so that he could visit several naval battle sites.

"Two boats, away off north where the ranger said was Canada. There was a big cabin cruiser, and a little speedboat. I could see someone climb off the bigger boat onto the little one, and they've just left the big one out there. It doesn't appear there is anyone on it."

"Let me see," Tom said, placing his own eyes in the slots where his wife's had been, and twisting a dial on the big silvery metal machine a bit to focus. "You mean that boat that appears to be coming this way?"

"Yes, very quickly. Maybe the man aboard the bigger boat was sick."

"I don't know. Oh! Damn! The bloody machine has shut off! Have you got another of those coins that are worth a shilling?"

"Aye, here's one," Mary said, digging into her purse.

Their conversation had interested the National Monument ranger who had earlier been talking with Tom about the battle. He came over to where Tom was inserting another quarter into the viewing machine, and asked, "What are you seeing?"

"There were two boats out there," Mary explained, "just south of that Canadian island you told us about, and someone got off the big one and got into the little one, and now they're coming this way. I thought perhaps maybe someone was sick or hurt."

"May I see?" the ranger asked, and Tom moved away from the machine and pointed to where the speedboat was now cruising, now just slightly northeast of South Bass Island. The ranger peered through the machine, then swung it around to scan the area north of North Bass, finally spotting the cabin cruiser. It had drifted a bit, and its stern was to the south. The ranger could barely make out the writing on the back, but was finally able to read '*Castle Kent*.'

"Oh, I know that boat," he said. "It belongs to one of the colleges near here. The previous owners are in prison for murder."

"Lord save us!" Mary exclaimed.

"Odd. There doesn't seem to be anyone aboard her. I think I'll go down and notify the Coast Guard." Before turning the telescope back over to Tom MacIntosh the ranger again swung it to the right, and followed the path of the speedboat. It sped to the east of Starve Island, then curved westward into the channel between South Bass and Catawba, heading in the direction of Port Cleland. With that the machine clicked off again.

"Oh, I'm sorry. I used up all your time on the machine," the ranger apologized to the MacIntoshes. He reached into his pocket and found another quarter, which he handed to Tom.

"Oh, that's quite all right," Tom replied, rejecting the coin.

"No, you keep it," the ranger insisted. He then moved toward the elevator to descend to the base of the monument where he had an office.

* * *

When he knew that the cruiser and the speedboat were beyond sight of him Fairchild turned over and began to float on his back. His arm was bleeding badly, and he was feeling lightheaded, as well as exhausted from his having to dive beneath the water. He had just put a clean handkerchief into his pants pocket that morning, and pulled it out. Although it was difficult to float while he moved, by making his body rigid he was able to lift his left arm close to his mouth, and using his right hand and his teeth, was able to tie the handkerchief around the bleeding gash in his arm and tighten it into a knot.

That morning he had also put on a fairly heavy camping shirt, the kind with several big pockets. He carefully manipulated his wallet from his left trouser pocket, and slipped it into the big pocket of his shirt, buttoning the top. If he did die, at least someone might find his corpse and discover who he was.

His trousers were weighing him down. He knew he had to get rid of them, and was grateful that he had put on a pair of under-shorts that had fasteners at the top. They would be about the same as swim shorts, he felt. He unfastened his belt, popped the buttons and unzipped the fly of the trousers, and felt them sink below him.

The activity had again exhausted him, and Fairchild again floated motionless. Despite the hot late July sun above, the deep water was cold, and that, too, was tiring. He knew he would have to swim if he were to keep from freezing in the water. Orienting himself toward the shore, he tried swimming on his back for a while. His arm throbbed and the stretching shot excruciating pains between his left elbow and shoulder, but at least the tightly tied bandage had stopped the bleeding.

He then rolled over, and tried to swim in a more natural position, but this too was painful and exhausting. He seemed to be making little progress. He would swim for a while, then float for a while, but the shoreline appeared to be no closer.

Fairchild calculated that the cruiser had been about half way between Port Cleland and West Bass when he had jumped overboard. That might put him a bit closer to the little fishing village at Long Beach, perhaps seven miles south of where he thought he was, as the shoreline curved to the north further west beyond Port Cleland. There were also reefs and a wildlife preserve that was little more than a swamp, probably full of snakes, if he came into shore too far east of Long Beach.

People had often swam far greater distances than seven or eight miles, he reasoned. But they were in better shape than he was, just recovering from a wounded right shoulder and now suffering from a deep gash in his left arm and loss of blood. Yet Fairchild was far too great an optimist to think negatively. Besides, his faith would carry him through, and he silently did what Ray had suggested, and prayed for help.

It was about an hour later. The professor had been swimming for perhaps ten minutes, and had just rolled onto his back to float and rest for a while. The sun continued to blaze down, and his watch, proving the correctness of the word 'waterproof' that was stamped on the back, showed it to be after 11 a.m.

While he floated he heard a roaring noise that appeared to be getting closer. He knew the sound was familiar, but for a few moments could not figure out what it was. It was not the sound of a boat motor, that he knew. Then he recognized it. It was the three engines of the old Ford Trimotor airplane of Islands Airlines, on its return trip from West Bass Island. He reckoned that its route would be almost directly above him, and began scanning the sky for the big "tin goose" antique airliner with its white fuselage, wide wings over the cabin, and red strip along the six passenger windows. The ancient plane, built in the 1920s as an early experiment into the aircraft industry by Henry Ford, was a lifeline to the outer Bass Islands, operating from its base in Port Cleland.

Fairchild quickly untied the handkerchief from his wound, which had now stopped bleeding, and, as he finally spotted the plane, flying well under a thousand feet above the water on its hop of perhaps no more than twenty miles between West Bass and the Port Cleland airport, started waving the limp wet rag.

If it had been dry it would have fluttered, he thought, but he waved it vigorously. The airplane was almost directly overhead now, and he could not tell if he had been seen or not. Then the plane flew on, and was almost out of sight. Fairchild felt disappointed. He knew there were no more flights to the island that day, in fact none until Saturday. He was about to re-tie the handkerchief around his wound, as it had once more begun to bleed, when he again heard the sound of the trimotor's three engines. The plane was circling around, and appeared to be coming back.

Again he frantically waved the cloth, remaining as rigid as he could to keep afloat with one arm raised. The big airplane circled completely around him, and then as it flew over him the door opened and an orange bundle fell from it, splashing into the water a few yards from where he was floating. The plane then flew southeastward and disappeared from his sight.

Whatever the orange bundle was, it, too, floated. Fairchild re-tied the soggy handkerchief around his left arm and knotted it before flipping over and swimming to the package. He was relieved to see that it was a life jacket, and he quickly pulled it on over his shirt, and, using a tube on the side, blew into it to inflate the airbags it contained. He felt he would no longer have to keep swimming, and the jacket now would keep him afloat without his having to remain rigid. However, he kept kicking his legs in order to keep warm in the cold water.

About twenty minutes later he heard another noise, this time obviously a diesel engine, and saw, approaching from the east, a white vessel. It was a small Coast Guard rescue boat. Within a few minutes it had come to a halt next to him, and two Coast Guardsmen hauled him aboard, wrapping blankets around him to help him warm up.

Petty Officer Ron Arbor was in charge.

"I recognize you," Fairchild said as the young Coast Guardsman stood over the seat onto which the professor had collapsed. "You were with Lieutenant Schifferman on the CG122 the day two years ago we arrested Fredrick Kolb, the German Nazi who was charged with the Coast Guardsman's murder back in the 1940s."

"Yes, I remember! You're a college professor, as I recall."

"That's right, at Fremont. My name is Richard Fairchild."

"What happened, Professor? I just heard on the radio that the Fremont College's yacht was found abandoned somewhere north of North Bass Island. Were you on that?"

"Let's just say I accidentally fell off."

"Really? The radio said some ranger at the Perry Monument saw two boats, and that someone had climbed off of the cruiser," Arbor said. He paused a moment to see if Fairchild would add anything else, then commented, "I think there is more to this than you are saying."

"No, I fell overboard, and the boat went on."

"Well, you are damned lucky. Some passenger on the Islands Airline plane saw you and told the pilot, and he came back to drop you that life jacket. He let us know where you were when he got back to the airport. But another storm is coming in. If that passenger hadn't spotted you, you'd have never made shore alive. What, were you trying to commit suicide or something."

"Heavens no! I've too much to live for!"

"We've got to take you to the hospital. I see you have been injured, and you probably have some exposure...."

"I don't think I need a hospital. I'd rather you take me to the Port Cleland lagoons so I can get my car and drive home for some clothes." Then he remembered that he didn't have any keys for the car. They were still in the boat's ignition when he had jumped.

"No, we've got to get a report from you first," Arbor replied. "This is a boating accident, and your cruiser was in international waters, so it has to be investigated. We'll get you some clean trousers and a shirt at the base. But we're going to see about that wound first."

Fairchild hoped that the Coast Guardsman would dock the boat at Port Cleland, but instead he headed to the larger base in Sandusky. An ambulance was waiting when it docked, and another Coast Guardsman accompanied Fairchild to it as Petty Officer Arbor insisted that he go to the Emergency Room. Fairchild was able to convince the ambulance driver to let them ride up front rather than on the stretcher in the back, and not to use the siren. "It's just a scratch," he insisted. Before they left, Arbor came out with a fresh shirt, trousers and some slippers, for which Fairchild was quite thankful.

Within a few minutes they were at the hospital, and Dr. Clayton Errington, a black physician, was examining the wound. "This looks like a bullet wound, Dr. Fairchild," he said. "How did you get it?"

Fairchild knew that if he now mentioned being shot that even more reports would be required, so he simply said, "I'm not sure. I guess I ripped my arm on something as I fell. It happened so quickly. I was trying to get a rope that had slipped off the side, and...." He waited, but the doctor did not press for further details.

"It's not too deep. I'll have to put some stitches in it. You've probably lost more than a couple of pints of blood, too. Have you had a tetanus shot recently?"

"Yes, just a month ago."

"I see a healing incision on your right shoulder. What was that?" the physician asked.

"An accident. It occurred when I was in Greece last month."

"You sound accident prone, Dr. Fairchild. You need to be more careful."

"Yes, that's what my wife, Esther, keeps saying."

"Wait a minute!" the emergency room doctor exclaimed. "I know you. You were in that car wreck two years ago."

"Yes, Dr. Errington. You testified at the trial on my behalf when I was almost killed in that set-up accident. You saved my life as well as my reputation, and I am very thankful that you did."

"I remember now," Dr. Errington responded. "They said at the trial that you were investigating some crime, and that you are some sort of detective. Is that what happened this time, too?"

"I'm not at liberty to say," Fairchild replied, trying to avoid sound too mysterious. The physician smiled and nodded his head. Then he filled a syringe with a pain deadening local anesthesia and injected it all around the wound so that he could begin to remove torn tissue and stitch it together.

An hour later the Coast Guardsman who had accompanied Fairchild to the hospital and had called for a car to return them to the base ushered the professor into the office of Lieutenant Peter Schifferman.

"Dr. Fairchild, good to see you again," Schifferman said, rising. "But under unfortunate circumstances, I understand. You say you fell off your cabin cruiser?"

Fairchild took a deep breath. "Lieutenant, I fear it is a long and complicated story, and as I am a bit tired from the ordeal and my arm hurts like blue blazes, I wonder if you would do me a favor."

"If I can."

"Good. Please call Special Agent Thomas Morris in the Cleveland office of the Federal Bureau of Investigation, and ask him if he can come to this meeting. I don't know his number."

"So, this sounds serious, Professor," the Coast Guard officer replied, reaching for a government agency phone directory from a shelf behind his desk. "Another gold treasure?"

"Maybe. Just maybe. Lieutenant Schifferman, were you involved at all in the search for the missing ship named *Chem Queen*?"

"Oh my God. Don't tell me you know about *that*!"

Fairchild did not answer, but waited while Schifferman dialed a number in Cleveland, and asked for Agent Morris. In a few moments he said into the phone, "Agent Morris, this is Lieutenant Peter Schifferman at the Sandusky Coast Guard base. I have a Dr. Richard Fairchild in my office who has just been rescued from Lake Erie, and he has asked that you be present for our interrogation. ... Yes. ... Unhuh, well, we found his boat. It was drifting in international water just south of Pelee Island. ... Okay, about an hour? Fine, we'll have some lunch and.... Yes, in the main building. Just ask for my office. Thank you," he said, hanging up the phone.

"I'll bet you're hungry, Professor," the Lieutenant said as he hung up the phone. "It's after two, and I doubt you've eaten, and I haven't either. Shall we visit the mess hall?"

"Sounds good to me, Lieutenant. Oh, by the way, there's no chance that the press will hear of this, is there? I sure don't want my wife to hear about it. She's already on the warpath about my getting involved in this mess."

"The press won't hear now! They sometimes follow up on radio distress calls, but we can tell them that it was just floating debris or something that the Islands Airline pilot spotted. Agent Morris said he would be here in a little over an hour, so let's have lunch."

Chapter 14

Later that same afternoon Raymond Ingersol and Sherri Blake sat together in the office of the man that had hired Ingersol. Keeping in mind what Fairchild has told him, Ingersol had his .45 revolver handy in case his employer refused to pay the agreed amount or tried to double-cross him.

"So this Fairchild guy says that he knows I plugged the bum, and that I also plugged *him* in Greece. Says the FBI traced the gun, but I think that's a crock."

"What else did he tell you?"

"He said you're making a bundle off some insurance company. Said I was probably being underpaid, compared to what you are gonna make. Is that so?"

"He said that? I was afraid he'd figured it out. Damn, I wish you'd have nailed him the first time. Who knows what or who he's talked to by now?"

"Well, he ain't gonna talk no more."

"You're absolutely certain he's dead?"

"Yeah, he's dead. But I want more money than we agreed upon because of the trouble. And we had expenses. That motel, and food, and renting a boat. Ten more grand should do it."

"That's far too much. I can't do that...."

"My keepin' quiet about the insurance deal, that's worth at least that much," Ingersol replied, leaning forward and giving a severe look into the eyes of the other man.

"Hell, you have no knowledge at all of any insurance deal. Just some babbling that nosey bastard told you."

"Yeah, but it's got something to do with Rogers Chemical. You told me that last night when you called. I know enough, and what I know is going to cost you."

"Okay, okay! But I can't get it right now. It will take a while," the other said. Then he reached into his drawer and pulled out an envelope. "Here's the amount we agreed upon. Let me know where you'll be, and I'll send you the rest. Or I can send it to that Post Office box you use."

"Like hell! Nobody knows where I am, or where I'll be. You have it here, tomorrow. By noon. I'll be by for it, and no funny business, or I'll shoot this place so full of holes you'll think it's Swiss cheese.'

* * *

Events moved quickly after the meeting in Lieutenant Schifferman's office that afternoon. Calls to the marinas between the Catawba Peninsula and Port Cleland, where the reports from the National Monument ranger and Fairchild's own impression indicated the speedboat might have come from, turned up the boat rental marina where a girl about twenty and a swarthy man had rented a fairly large twin outboard speedboat. A check of the record showed a local phone number, which turned out to be a Sandusky motel.

The couple had occupied rooms there for several weeks, but had moved out that morning. All payments had been in cash, and the motel registry slip showed the name Ray Southerland, the same name that had been given to Fairchild and that was on the reservations at the Castle Kent Inn. A call there revealed that Southerland had never shown up, which had been anticipated.

Erie County's Sheriff Department crime lab obtained a number of fingerprints from the motel room, and they had been sent to the FBI lab in Washington to identify, if a match could be made. Then that information would be sent to Agent Morris in Cleveland, but all that was not expected to occur for a couple of days. Photos would be airmailed to the Cleveland FBI office. Nevertheless, a bulletin was issued for the arrest of a dark, swarthy man known as Ray who used the alias of Southerland, and that of his girlfriend, a dark-haired woman in her early twenties, believed to be named Sherri.

* * *

Based on what he had learned, Richard Fairchild suggested that the FBI check with the Ohio Secretary of State's office to see who owned the T&W Marine, Inc. The records office was closed, and it was not until Friday morning that an FBI agent in Columbus was able to confirm that the company was registered to a Harry Taylor and a Garrett Williams, both of Cleveland. This was reported to Agent Morris in Cleveland.

Around two on Friday afternoon FBI Special Agent Morris, armed with a federal search warrant and accompanied by a U.S. Customs agent and two Coast Guard officers, went to the warehouse south of the chemical plant where Fairchild had predicted they would find the *Chem Queen*. The big warehouse turned out to be a very large old covered drydock, and inside a tanker was being torn down and its design changed. A sole welder was at work when they arrived. He had met Morris and the Coast Guard officers at the door with a gun in his hand.

"Nobody's allowed in here. What'd yah want?" the grimy, partially bald welder demanded.

Showing his FBI identification, Morris almost laughed at the man's expression as he quickly tried to replace the gun into his belt. "Trust you have a license for that thing," he said. "We have a search warrant," he added, drawing the folded document from his inside coat pocket and handing it to the welder. "What is your name?"

"Joe. Joe Price. What the hell's all this about?"

"Joe Price," Morris repeated, writing it in a notebook. "Is this vessel the *Chem Queen*?"

"Nah, it's just some old tanker some guys wanted restored. It's been here fer years."

"Oh, really. Well, Joe, we're going to have a look around. Then we'll have a little chat. If you are telling me the truth, you have nothing to worry about. If you are not, then let me warn you that anything -- and I mean *anything* -- you say may be held as evidence. You will be arrested and will be entitled to an attorney. If you cannot afford one...."

"Yeah, yeah, I know all about it."

Morris insisted that Price accompany the two Coast Guard officers and the Customs agent on their inspection. They had with them the specifications, photo and diagrams of the *Chem Queen* that had been obtained from the insurers in London. They first made an exterior inspection, but found that every place the name of the vessel had been painted had been sanded away. Moving next to the interior, they searched the various cabins and the pilothouse, eventually locating an old logbook in a bottom drawer. Although dated a few years earlier, it clearly identified the vessel as the *Chem Queen*, belonging to the Rogers Chemical Company.

"Who sanded off the names?" the Customs agent, Ricky Adams, asked.

"How should I know? They was off when I was hired to do some welding."

"When were you hired?" Morris asked.

"'Bout mid-October."

"Oh? Was anyone else working with you then?"

"Nah, just me."

"Interesting, Joe. Was part of your job to watch out for anyone who might be nosing around the building?"

Price looked that the FBI agent, thought a minute, then said, "If you're arrestin' me, I want a lawyer. I ain't sayin' nothin' more."

"I'm afraid we *are* arresting you, Mister Price," Captain Obelmann, the senior Coast Guard officer, said.

"What fer? Hell, I didn't know what this old ship might have been called, or anything about the damned boat." Price objected.

"You have the right to remain silent. You have the right to an attorney. If you can't afford one, to are entitled to...."

"Yeah, yeah. I know."

"What do we charge this as, piracy?" Adams, the Customs agent, asked one of the Coast Guard officers.

"I don't know. I've never written up a piracy charge before," he laughed. "Probably just insurance fraud."

Morris knew that the agent and the two officers did not know about the possible connection to the murder of George Antopholis. While one of the Coast Guard officers placed handcuffs on Price, the other three men walked around the inside of the covered dry-dock, noting the pulleys and cables that had drawn the large tanker out of the water and onto the wooden skids. There was a small office at the front of the building, but there appeared to be nothing in it of recent origin.

Morris anticipated that Joe Price would turn out to be an ex-con with a record, since he seemed to know all about his legal rights. It was doubtful that they would obtain much useful information from him, unless the federal prosecutor agreed to some deal to get Price to become a federal witness. With the information Richard Fairchild had provided, and the verification by the state of the corporate entity of T&W Marine, Inc., Morris was well on his way to solving the mystery of the disappeared vessel.

Although Taylor and Williams were common names, Morris knew from his earlier investigation that Henry Taylor was the insurance agent, and Garrett Williams the chief financial officer of Rogers Chemical. He wondered if Fred Rogers himself might be involved in the plot. He had never met the man, although Williams had spoken highly of him in some of their meetings about the lost tanker. He recalled that Fairchild had also identified Harry Taylor as the insurance agent for whom Sam Whitaker worked.

* * *

Ingersol had shown up at his client's office early that Friday. He thought at first that he was going to be ripped off when informed that his client was not there, but relaxed when the girl at the desk asked him if his name was Ray, and, upon confirming that it was, handed him an envelope. He quickly departed, and returned to the street where Sheri Blake was waiting in the car.

"Ha!" he laughed as he tore open the envelope. "The whole thing. I'll bet'cha there's even more money to be made off this sucker. Timings wrong. Let's wait a month or so and see how much more he might be willing to cough up to keep me silent."

* * *

Late that afternoon, about five-fifteen, Agent Morris, armed with both a search and an arrest warrant and accompanied by two Cleveland homicide detectives, went to the wharf and entered the second floor offices of the Taylor Marine Insurance Agency. Morris had met Taylor once before, although only briefly, at one of several meetings with Williams regarding the lost chemical tanker. Harry Taylor was still at his desk, although Sam Whitaker and the rest of his staff had already gone home.

"Yes?" Taylor said, as the three law enforcement representatives, each in plain clothes, appeared at his door. "Sorry my receptionist has gone home."

"That's all right, Mr. Taylor," one of the Cleveland detectives said. "You are Henry Taylor, are you not?"

"Yes. And you are.... Oh," Taylor stopped, looking at Morris. "You're that FBI agent who was investigating the theft of the Rogers Chemical Company's tanker, ahh, Morris, wasn't it? I met you at one of the meetings with Garrett Williams."

"That's correct, Mr. Taylor," the FBI agent replied, reaching into his inside pocket for two documents. "We have found the tanker, and this is a search warrant and also a warrant for your arrest for its theft. You have the right to remain silent. Anything you say voluntarily may be used against you. You are entitled to an attorney. If you cannot afford one, you will be provided one at the government's expense."

Although surprised, Henry Taylor surrendered without protest but refused to say anything, demanding to be allowed to call his attorney first. The closed Rogers Chemical File was removed from his file room as evidence. It was among the closed files, exactly where Richard Fairchild had told them it probably would be. In a desk drawer Morris also found a wooden plaque with the name *Chem Queen* painted on it. A fingerprint check several days later would confirm that it had been handled by a number of people including Joe Price, Taylor, and, making a direct connection in the state's murder charge, both George Antopholis and Raymond Ingersol.

While one of the Cleveland detectives took Taylor to the Payne Avenue police station for a federal hold, at which time Taylor phoned his wife and instructed her to contact his attorney, Morris and the other detective went to the home Garrett Williams, also placing him under arrest. Neither man had yet been informed that they were also under suspicion for the murder of George Antopholis. That would come during their interviews at the Cleveland police station, as it was a state rather than a federal crime.

By eight that evening both men had spoken with their attorneys, and had been advised to say absolutely nothing to either the federal or the state authorities. Both attorneys, also unaware of the state homicide charges, anticipated that they would have no difficulty obtaining a bond hearing for their clients. Once they were informed that their clients were also being held on suspicion of first degree murder, they realized that it was doubtful that the two partners would be released on bond.

Alvis West, the attorney for Henry Taylor, was somewhat more vocal than Jimmy Roberts, Garrett William's lawyer. "What's your evidence in this so-called murder?" he demanded of one of the detectives. "You haven't charged him, so I 'spect you've got no evidence," the heavy, chain-smoking feisty lawyer, who was nearly sixty and well-known to the Cleveland Police Department as a shrewd and successful criminal defense lawyer, shouted. "No evidence, no case, and you're going to look awfully silly when the *Press* and *Plain Dealer* get ahold of this. And this federal rap. Where's the evidence on that?"

Detective Sergeant Dick Mawson, who had been maintaining a file on the murder of George Antopholis since the homeless and deformed man had first been found shot to death, simply smiled at the two lawyers. He did it in such a way as to imply "you'll find out." He hoped that the plaque found in Taylor's office would prove to tangible evidence. The FBI had just confirmed the name of the shooter -- an ex-con named Ingersol -- but they didn't yet have Ingersol, and without him, it would be more difficult to make a case. He hoped that Taylor might rat on Williams, or Williams on Taylor. Or perhaps it was their boss, Rogers, who was behind it all. The professor didn't think so, but they'd find out soon enough. In the meantime, he had the right to hold Taylor and Williams for 72 hours without charging them, and, besides, they weren't going anywhere because of the federal charges. He did not inform them that Joe Price had also been arrested.

Just after eight Friday evening Mawson and Morris, accompanied by a City of Lakewood detective, arrived in two cars at the Forestwood Avenue home of Fred Rogers. While they did not have an arrest warrant, they did have a search warrant for the Rogers Chemical Company. Mildred Rogers answered the door, and the agents asked to speak with her husband. When he came to the door he had just finished showering and had on a bathrobe. The agent and detectives identified themselves, and the search warrant was served. Rogers was asked to accompany them to his offices. Mildred Rogers and Kelly, who was about to go out on a date that evening, were horrified by what was happening.

"What the hell is this all about," Rogers demanded. "What are you looking for?"

"We'll know when we find it, I guess, Mr. Rogers," Agent Morris replied. "The first place we want to visit, upon arriving at your plant on the Cuyahoga River, is the office of Garrett Williams."

"Gary should be there," Rogers stated. "I don't know what he keeps in there. He could tell you."

"Garrett Williams is in jail, Mr. Rogers," Morris replied.

"Jail? What the hell for?"

"Mr. Rogers, I must warn you. While you are not under arrest, you are under suspicion of the same crimes for which Garrett Williams and Harry

Taylor were arrested earlier this evening. Anything you say may possibly be evidence against you, and you may wish to consult with an attorney before saying anything."

"I've done nothing wrong, so what has -- oh, Taylor? He's that insurance agent, isn't he? What, he and Gary...."

"The current charges against them are marine piracy and insurance fraud. They are also being held on suspicion of first degree murder, attempted murder, conspiracy to murder, and conspiracy to kidnap. It will be a combination of federal and state charges."

"Piracy? What are you talking about?"

"We found your ship, the *Chem Queen*, this afternoon."

"Oh! Where was it?" Rogers asked, but Morris said nothing further, and asked no further questions.

The search at the plant continued well into Saturday morning. In a locked desk drawer in Garrett Williams office Morris and Mawson found a ledger-book. Morris, using a cloth, placed it in a plastic evidence bag for later analysis. Copies of other documents were also placed in evidence bags, along with Williams personal phone and address book. The search then moved to Rogers own office, where some of his records were also placed in evidence bags. Of special interest to Morris was a file entitled "Antopholis Shipping."

"You need not answer if you wish, Mr. Rogers, but I understand that you knew a George Antopholis, did you not."

"George, yes. Unfortunate poor guy, he was murdered. I see you are taking the Antopholis shipping file. We were considering buying one of their vessels to replace the *Chem Queen*. Did you know that George was related to that family?" Rogers asked.

"Yes, I did." Morris did not explain further, but his answer led Rogers to suspect that Morris knew much more than he was saying.

Chapter 15

Esther's return flight from Williamsport was due to arrive in Cleveland at 10:35 on Friday evening, aboard Allegheny Airlines Flight 377, a twin-engined Martin that had hopped across Pennsylvania from Newark and Philadelphia to Harrisburg, Williamsport, Bradford and Erie. Traffic was light around the new Cleveland Hopkins Airport terminal as Richard Fairchild parked his Ford station wagon in the airport parking lot, and headed inside. His left arm still ached from the stitches placed in the bullet wound.

He had wrestled with his conscience all day as to what he should tell Esther. He felt he could probably tell her the same story he had told Ron Arbor when he had been rescued, but that was a lie, and he could not bring himself to telling Esther a lie. Yet he knew what she would say when he told her that he had been shot, especially after being warned by the FBI to go away and be safe. She was already far too upset with him.

He also knew that if he did not tell her the truth, it would create a real problem when the man he knew as Ray Southerland was finally caught and tried. He would have to testify at the trial, and the wound would certainly be evidence of the attack Southerland had made on him aboard the boat. No, he thought, better to tell Esther exactly what had happened and get it over with as quickly as possible. Fortunately, there had been nothing in the newspapers about it. For that he was very grateful.

The Cleveland airport terminal was laid out like a **T** with several long concourses extending from a central ticketing and commercial area. Eastern Airlines had a handful of planes flying north and south, usually via Pittsburgh and to or from Detroit, at that time of night, as did United between Chicago and Washington, and Northwest Orient also had a late evening flight from Washington. TWA and North Central were shut down for the night, although Capital Airlines had a DC-6 Flight 875 scheduled to depart at 11:15 p.m. for Atlanta, with a transfer to New Orleans. In late July it usually flew with relatively few passengers, hence there were only a hundred or so people in the terminal as Fairchild entered. All but two of the concessions were already locked up for the night, but the coffee shop was still open.

It was well after ten o'clock, and although Fairchild rarely drank coffee in the evening, he anticipated that it would be nearly eleven before Esther's luggage would be available, and then there was at least an hour and a half drive back to Port Cleland. A cup of coffee, therefore, sounded good to him, and he started toward the coffee shop.

As he started to enter, he saw a young woman sitting at a table. It was her dark hair and thin, shapely shoulders that he noticed, and recognized. Although she was sitting alone, there were two plates and cups at the table. A second person obviously had been sitting with her.

Rather than enter the coffee shop Fairchild moved across from it to the area of one of the closed concession stands that was in a dark shadow. From there he could observe the girl at the table. She turned her head to look around for a moment, and he confirmed what he had suspected -- it was the girl in the speedboat.

About two minutes later the dark, swarthy man Fairchild knew only as Ray Southerland approached the table from the direction of the men's restroom. He picked up a briefcase that had been sitting on the floor next to the table, opened it, and placed something inside. Although he was saying something to the girl, Fairchild was too far away to hear what it was.

There was a central information board in the middle of the terminal, and it could be partially seen from the coffee shop. Fairchild carefully walked over to it, keeping an eye on Ray to be certain he wasn't seen, and went up to the man behind the counter.

"Yes, sir. Do you need a flight time?" The man asked.

"No, but I do see on the notice board that the Allegheny flight is going to be a few minutes late."

"Yes, we just got word. A mail delivery delay in Erie, I understand."

"Is there a police station in the Airport?" the professor asked.

"Yes, there's a small office down the back corridor, just beyond that door that points to the post office, but there's rarely an officer in it this late at night. He's usually wandering around somewhere."

"Can you page him?"

"Sure. You want him paged? Is something wrong?"

"Yes, very much so, but can you page him without using the word 'police'? Is there a code or something?"

"Well, yes, there is. A couple, one for an accident, and another if there's a theft or some crime."

"Use the crime one," Fairchild insisted, and looked over at the coffee shop. Ray and the dark haired girl were starting to get up. "Make it urgent!" he added.

"What's wrong, Mister?"

"Just do it!" Fairchild demanded. "Quick!"

"Well, okay, I guess," he replied, and picked up the microphone. "C.P.D. Murphy," he said. "Information desk, Code Orange."

Ray Southerland and the girl appeared to be walking straight toward the information desk. Fairchild pulled his hat down over the top of his face, and moved to the right side of the desk, where a doorway was located. The man at the information desk looked at him like he was crazy.

On Concourse B Sergeant Patrick Murphy had been checking locked doors as part of his regular rounds of the airport when he heard the page over the public address system. Code Orange -- a Code Red, crime in progress, with a "caution." What on earth was happening, he wondered as he started to run back toward the terminal.

The girl was studying the departure notices on the electronic board while Ray, holding the briefcase at his side, stood in front of the door where Fairchild waited. The girl started to say something as her eyes moved from the departure board, and swept toward the doorway where Fairchild was standing, He was turned sideways, his hat pulled down over his eyes.

She stopped what she was saying and stared at Fairchild for a moment, recognition finally coming. "Ray!" she shouted, and the swarthy man looked up. "Ray, it's that professor!"

"What?" he replied, then looked up to see Fairchild coming out of the doorway at him.

"Hello, Ray," the professor said, pushing his hat back on his forehead.

"You sonofabitch!" Ray muttered, then he hit the clasp on his briefcase, reached in with his other hand, and pulled out the .45 caliber pistol that was inside.

By this time Fairchild was fully in front of him. "Now, put that away, Ray," Fairchild demanded, but as the man he knew as Southerland began to bring the gun up to waist level, Fairchild pounded his right fist into Ray's belly, causing him to double up, and step back. Ray then swung the pistol sidewise toward Fairchild's head, striking him on the left cheek, and stunning him. Fairchild staggered a bit, but tried to reach for Ray's right hand that held the gun.

"Here, here, what's this?" an Irish-sounding voice shouted as the two men scuffled, and Ray again struck at Fairchild with the pistol in his fist. The man at the information desk, when Ray had pulled out the gun, had ducked beneath the black-painted counter.

Ray swung around at the voice coming from behind him and saw Sergeant Murphy starting to reach for his gun. Without taking much aim, Ray fired at the policeman, the bullet striking him in the right shoulder, and knocking him to the ground.

Fairchild lunged forward toward Ray, and, grabbing him around the waist in what resembled a football tackle, pushed him down on the floor and fell on top of him. As Ray hit the floor the gun was knocked out of his hand and skidded away from the two tussling men. Fairchild scrambled toward it, but the girl stepped over and picked it up, and aimed it at the professor.

"Let him up!" she demanded. Fairchild rolled to his side, and Ray scrambled to his feet. He stepped over to where the police officer had fallen on the floor and was now starting to recover from the shock of the impact to his shoulder. Ray reached down and took the policeman's revolver from his holster.

"You'll not need this!" he muttered, and then turned back toward Fairchild, who had also regained his footing. "You're a hard bastard to kill, Fairchild. How the hell did you survive out there?"

"It's a long story, Ray. Let's get some help for the policeman here, and then we'll go and talk about it."

"No, no more talk. I got my money, and thanks to what you told me, a bit extra. I don't give a crap about you, Fairchild, dead or alive." With that he stepped up to directly face Fairchild, raised the police revolver, and struck Fairchild as hard as he could on the side of the head. Fairchild was stunned, but not knocked out, although he allowed himself to crumple to the floor, where he feigned unconsciousness.

Ray and the girl looked around. The shot had attracted considerable attention, but no other police appeared to be around, and the two ran down some stairs toward where a sign pointed to taxies, taking the briefcase and the policeman's revolver with them.

Fairchild shook his head as he sat up, and found the man from the information counter standing over him. "Have you notified the police?" he asked.

"No, not yet, but we need to get an ambulance for Sergeant Murphy." He went back behind the counter, and made a call on his telephone. An ambulance was dispatched from the airport fire station, and within five minutes paramedics were lifting the wounded policeman onto a stretcher and rolling him out to the ambulance for the three or four mile ride to Fairview Park Hospital. A few moments later three squad cars pulled up outside, their red flashers reflecting on the darkened walls inside the terminal. One was from Cleveland and there was also a car from Brook Park and one from Berea, suburbs surrounding the Cleveland Hopkins Airport. Additional cars arrived, sirens screaming, a few minutes later.

Fairchild had been dazed and felt a slight headache, but his hat had softened the blow considerably. The barrel had struck just behind where he had suffered a concussion several years earlier that had required surgery to relieve the pressure. The medic with the ambulance had checked him briefly, shining a light into his eyes and asking him some questions before departing with Sergeant Murphy. Fairchild knew he was okay, and was grateful for that, knowing that Esther would be arriving in less than half an hour.

"That's the man, there," the information counter attendant was saying to the Cleveland police officer with whom he had been speaking, and pointed to Fairchild.

"What happened?" the officer demanded.

"You need to seal the airport, officer. Don't let that couple escape. They are wanted for murder," Fairchild said.

"We have closed the airport," he replied. "Anytime we get a report of an officer down, the area is sealed. If those two are going to get out of here tonight, they're going to have crawl down the Rocky River embankment at the other side of the airport. But who are you, and what happened here?"

"Officer, that guy hit me a pretty good clobber on the head. Could we move over to the coffee shop so I could get some coffee and an aspirin?"

"Yeah, sure." The two moved back to the coffee shop and Fairchild gave the officer a dollar to get him a cup of coffee and a packet of aspirin from a small clip post behind the cashier. He brought it to the professor, along with a cup of coffee for himself, and a small pitcher of milk.

"Officer Johnson," Fairchild said, looking at the policeman's metal name bar, and then taking a sip of the coffee to wash down the two tablets from the package of aspirin, "all I know for certain is that the man's first name is Ray. He has an alias, Southerland, but I don't know his real name. The girl, I think, is named Sherri. They are wanted by the Cleveland Police as suspects in the murder last fall of a homeless man named George Antopholis. I know there is a detective working on the case, but I don't know what his name is. Officer Andy Segretti is also familiar with the case."

"I know that name. He's in Central District. But who are you, and how are you involved?"

"I am Richard Fairchild. I live in Port Cleland, and am a professor at Fremont College. Because I found out a few things about the Antopholis murder, I was targeted to be killed as well, and was shot while I was in Greece this summer. When the bullet that killed Antopholis was matched with the one with which I was wounded in Corinth, the FBI got involved. Special Agent Thomas Morris is in charge of that case. He is at the Cleveland FBI field office."

"Yeah, I've heard of Morris. But this Ray guy... what happened tonight?"

"Well, gosh, it's a long tale! I'm here to pick up my wife. Her plane is due in about ten minutes. Can I tell you as we wander down to the gate?" Fairchild asked as he drained the last of his coffee.

* * *

Ray Ingersol and Sherri Blake had run out of the airport terminal at the taxi stand, and jumped into one of the cabs that were waiting at the curb.

"Take us downtown," Ingersol instructed the driver. "There's a train leaves just before midnight, and there's a big tip in it for you if you can get us there early."

"Okay, but ain't you got no luggage other than that case?" the driver asked.

"Nah, we were just here to see somebody off. Our stuff is already at the station," Ingersol replied. "But we need to hurry."

The cab pulled from the curb and around to the airport exit. As it reached the exit several police cars were racing into the entrance from the airport access road and main driveway, their red flashers and sirens giving warning.

"Wonder what's going on?" Ray said to the driver, although he knew very well what was happening.

"Don't know. Must be something big. Maybe some bigshot arriving on a plane. They always have a lot of police around for that sort of thing."

"Yeah, didn't I hear somebody say something about some politician coming in tonight, Sherri?"

"I think so," she replied, catching on to the notion quickly.

As the cab reached the entrance to the expressway the driver picked up the microphone to his radio and said, "Seventy-two. A fare to the Terminal Tower."

"Roger, Seventy-two," the radio squawked back. The cab continued on, while Blake and Ingersol relaxed in the back seat.

"There's a train out to Cincinnati just before midnight," Ray said softly to Sherri. "I've ridden it before. From there we can get a car, and ...."

The radio squawked again. "Car Seventy-two."

"Seventy-two," the driver replied, picking up the microphone.

"Seventy-two, weren't you just at the airport? Over," the dispatcher asked. Ingersol waited to hear what the dispatcher had to say, but slipped the briefcase open and put his hand on the grip of his pistol.

"Roger. Picked up a man and woman out front. Why?"

"Ah, Seventy-two, they've closed the airport, looking for someone. Where are you? Over."

"Just got on that new I-71 expressway, headed downtown. Over."

"Okay, roger, Seventy-two. Over."

Ray Ingersol, relaxed a bit, but kept the briefcase open as he drew out his hand. The cab continued toward the glow of downtown Cleveland, through the West 130th interchange, the City of Brocklyn, and toward the Dennison Avenue exits. Ahead Ray could see several police cars with their red flashers on.

"Get off at this exit," he ordered the cab driver, again reaching into his briefcase for his .45.

"But there's a police car blocking it," the driver answer.

"Ram it!" Ray demanded, pressing the gun barrel against the driver's head. "Ram it, and get us out of here fast, or I'll blow your brains out!"

The driver slowed slightly as he approached the freeway exit. Several police cars were at the side of the freeway on the overpass. There was just enough room behind the police car that was blocking the exit to get behind it if the cab went up over the curb, and the driver gunned the car forward and it bounced up the curb on the right two wheels, scraping the back of the police car and shifting it slightly sideways as the cab crunched its way around it. The three occupants bounced up and down inside the cab as it went up and over the curb, then dropped back down onto the pavement. Ray was tossed back into his seat from where he had been holding the gun against the driver's head, but quickly regained his position.

"Good boy. You do as you're told, and you won't get hurt," he told the driver as they pulled into Dennison. "Now, where the hell are we?"

"That's Fulton Road ahead," the driver said.

"Good. Take a left, and step on it."

The cab shot forward, and just caught the traffic light as it was changing to red. They swung around the corner as they heard sirens roaring down the wrong way from the expressway entrance. There was a dark side-street to the left, and Ingersol told the driver to up into it, go down to the end of the block, pull to the side and shut off his lights. The driver obeyed flawlessly.

"You're a good boy, Mac," Ingersol assured him. "What's your name? Your old lady don't call you 'Seventy-two,' I'll bet."

"Frank."

With that the radio sputtered again, and the dispatcher's voice said, "Seventy-two. Where are you now? Over."

"Don't answer him, Frank. Just get out, and start walking, straight ahead, not back to Fulton or Dennison. When you've walked ten or fifteen minutes and come to some nice place to sit down, then sit down and wait. Don't do nothin', and don't say nothin'. Yah got it?"

"Yeah," the driver said, opening the door. The radio again squawked "Seventy-two!"

Ray shot a bullet into it, and it sparked for a moment and was silent.

The driver ran down the street and behind a house to get as far away from the cab and its two occupants as he could.

"C'mon, Sherri, let's get the hell out of here," Ingersol said as they climbed out of the back seat of the cab. "Let's check some of these cars parked on the curb."

All of the houses on the street, a small working class neighborhood, were dark. It was after eleven, and unless someone might be in their back room watching the late news, it was unlikely that anyone would notice the cab parked on the street. As they walked back up the street they could see several police cars with red flashers rushing by on Fulton.

The third car they came to, a late model Buick, was unlocked. "Been awhile since I did this," Ray said as he slipped down on the floor on his back and felt under the dashboard for some wires. In a moment or two the car roared to life, and Sherri climbed in beside him. They drove up to the end of the street, turned right, and, upon reaching Dennison Avenue again, waited at the red light while yet another police car screamed through the intersection.

Ray turned left, drove a few blocks to the intersection with U.S. 42, and turned south. "Hell," he said. "We'll be in Kentucky by the morning. We was going to sit up all night on that flight to New Orleans anyway."

"What about our luggage?" Sherri asked.

"Ahh, forget it. I got the dough here, and there wasn't nothin' in those suitcases that we can't buy and replace." A few blocks further along they spotted a yellow taxicab stopped at the curb, with a police car pulled diagonally in front of it, red flashers going.

"Look at that!" Ray laughed. "Dumb idiots. They'll be pulling over taxis all night long! I wonder if that driver has gone back to his cab yet."

"No, I think you scared him too much, Ray, when you shot out that radio. Even if he did, he couldn't call anybody from it, and it would take him a while to find a phone in that neighborhood."

When they reached the intersection with I-71 in Middleburg Heights they stopped at an all-night doughnut shop. Ray couldn't turn the car off, as he had no keys, but Sherri went in and got them some coffee and doughnuts. Ray checked the gas. The tank was nearly full. A few minutes later they were southbound on the new Interstate to Columbus.

* * *

Esther's plane was about fifteen minutes late. The professor had finished telling Officer Johnson a brief version of what had transpired over the past two or three days, and supplied Johnson with all the particulars regarding his address and phone number so that city detectives might follow up the next day. Fairchild was still standing with Johnson as Esther came up the entranceway to the terminal.

"Esther!" Fairchild said in greeting. "Gosh, am I glad to see you! How was your flight?"

"Talk about a puddle jumper! We landed twice between Williamsport and here! I'm exhausted." Noticing the policeman, she looked at Richie and added, "What's wrong, Richie?"

"Nothing much," Fairchild fibbed. "There was a shooting in the terminal earlier. I was a witness, and...."

"Oh, Richie! Not again!" she moaned. "What on earth this time?"

"Well, it was the guy who shot me when we were in Greece. This time he shot a policeman."

"How do you know it was the man who shot you?"

"Well, as I was just telling Officer Johnson, here, ahh, the shooter tried to get at me again while I was on the boat, but I escaped, and...."

"Richie, will you never leave it alone? I was hoping this whole thing would be over by the time I got back."

"Well, it is, now."

"The police arrested the guy?"

"They're supposed to be doing that right now."

"They think he got away from the airport in a cab, Mrs. Fairchild," Officer Johnson said. "I just heard it on my radio, but they have the cab number and are going to stop it, so I'm sure they have the guy by now."

"Oh, Lord! I won't be able to sleep until he's in jail, Officer. This is the limit!"

"Don't worry, Mrs. Fairchild. We'll get him," the officer said in a reassuring manner. "Frankly, I think your husband is a hero."

"I don't *want* a hero, especially a dead or injured one," she replied. "I want a sane, sensible husband who doesn't go poking around in murders all the time, getting himself shot and beat up and involved with the police."

"Now, Esther...."

"Don't *'now Esther'* me, Richard Fairchild. You know I'm right and the next time you start messing around with criminals I'm going to ask Dean Harding to arrange for you to have your head examined."

"Yes, Ma'am," Fairchild replied, sounding a bit like a six-year-old caught with his hand in a cookie jar. He hoped that this would be the worst of what he had known was coming, and that by the end of the weekend Esther would have forgiven him.

Chapter 16

Once the documents taken from Garrett Williams' office had been completely dusted for fingerprints, Special Agent Thomas Morris opened the ledger and began to review it. It took him awhile to understand the system of entries that were made, but the ledger began to explain what had transpired. Williams had been siphoning off funds and recording phony expenses in the Rogers accounts, several hundred thousand dollars' worth, over the past year. It was necessary to match the ledger book they had found in Williams' drawer with the "official" account books that had also been collected the previous evening. In his plan to replace the stolen amounts he had arranged to have the ship hijacked, making sure that both the vessel and the cargo were insured.

Morris suspected that it was early in the plan that Taylor, the agent for the ship's insurance, had been brought into the conspiracy by Williams, and that the two had purchased the old dry-dock as a place to hide the vessel. Williams had probably discovered what the old building really was while dealing with some of the other old buildings that had once stood next to the dry-dock. Surely Fred Rogers must also have known what that building really was, Morris reasoned. After all, he had founded the chemical company and must have had some familiarity with the navigation on the river. Would he not have considered the dry-dock as a hiding place when the *Chem Queen* was first reported as stolen?

The tanker ship had arrived in Cleveland full of the expensive chemical. The secreted ledger showed that Williams had rented a tank truck and had unloaded chemicals from aboard the vessel into it whenever the chemical plant needed the chemicals. He'd even created a new corporation, T&W Chemicals, to be a supplier to Rogers. As Rogers' financial officer, he had the authority to authorize such purchases, which came at a very high price. He'd hired someone shown as *JP* to drive the truck around a bit, and then deliver the chemicals back to Rogers Chemical Company. Morris suspected that "JP" might be Joe Price, but he wasn't certain how he could prove that until Williams or someone else verified it. Williams had then used the profits from those chemical sales to restore the money he had embezzled, paying Rogers back with Rogers' own money.

In one of the other files removed from Williams locked desk there were some notes that indicated how else the two partners planned to steal from the company. The plan appeared to include modification of the ship, changing its outward appearance, and then somehow moving it back down the river and to some other lake port, where they would create a phony history for the ship, and try to re-sell it to Rogers. As the ship had ocean-going capabilities, if Rogers did not buy it, there would be plenty of other markets.

It appeared from the ledger that several others had been involved in the plot, but Morris could not tell if they were Rogers employees or men that had been specifically hired to assist in getting the ship from Rogers' dock to the dry-dock. All he had were initials. If they were Rogers Chemical employees, then this might also suggest that Fred Rogers himself was involved. Morris suspected he was, even though Fairchild said he doubted that. Morris calculated that it would be a lot easier to connect Fred Rogers to the piracy of his own ship, the federal charge, than to the murder of Antopholis, although Fairchild had certainly found enough connections. The homeless man had worked at both the chemical plant pulling weeds, and at Rogers' own home in Lakewood.

Morris was still looking for some indication in the files that would support Richard Fairchild's theory that George, while working around the old warehouses south of the Rogers Chemical Company plant, had stumbled across the covered dock where the *Chem Queen* was hidden. He probably had been observed by Price or Williams or some of the other employee in on the theft of the ship, and out of fear that he would tell someone what he had seen, either Taylor or Williams had arranged to have him murdered. But that would be the state's attorney's job to prove..

Later Saturday morning, while other FBI agents continued to search the Rogers Chemical Company, a federal judge issued an order freezing the Rogers Chemical Company bank accounts. About the same time Morris's phone rang.

"Morris, Dick Mawson here," the Cleveland homicide detective in charge of the case, said. "Did you hear what happened last night?"

"No. I was down at the Rogers Chemical offices all evening. Why? What happened?"

"Have you got a photo of Ingersol from that fingerprint identification yet?"

"Too early. We requested them Thursday, but it will be Monday before we can get the photo from the Maryland prison. But what happened last night?"

"Well, your professor friend was at the airport to pick up his wife and he spotted the guy he knew as Ray. Ingersol was with his girlfriend. Fairchild alerted the police out there, but it was late at night, and we had only one officer on duty. Anyway, the two of them confronted Fairchild, and they got into a fist fight or something, and when our officer arrived, Ingersol guy shot him...."

"Killed him?"

"No, just wounded him. He'll be okay. But then he and the girl beat it and jumped a cab for the train station. It left the airport just before we closed it down."

"You mean, you missed them."

"Yeah, but we had the number of the cab, and learned on the radio where it was headed, and set up a road block. The guy had the cabbie run it, and they tore out of there, and the patrol cars lost 'em.

"About an hour later the cabbie called in. They'd held a gun to his head, and made him get out and walk away. Then this guy, Ray, shot out his radio so the cabbie couldn't use it. It was some dark residential street near Dennison and Fulton. Anyway, a man in the neighborhood reported this morning that his car, a Buick, had been stolen. It was only a few hundred feet from where the cab was parked, so it looks like our two suspects stole the car and headed out somewhere. We have a bulletin out on the car, but...."

"You need a name and photo. I'll call Washington and see if we can't hustle the thing along. What were they doing at the airport? Skipping town?"

"Yeah, we found they had reservations under the name of Southman on a flight to New Orleans, through Atlanta. We were able to pull their luggage off the plane and have just finished going through it, but there's not much there of help."

"Hmm. Keep me posted, eh, Dick. Not much we can do on your murder charges against Taylor or Williams without the shooter."

"Yeah, tell me about it! Their lawyers are down here again this morning screaming their heads off."

* * *

By Sunday morning the FBI in Washington had the photos of Raymond Ingersol, age 32, last known address being a small hotel in Baltimore. He'd been a Marine in the Korean War, a specialist in weapons. He had served time in a Maryland prison for attempted murder, and was again being sought by authorities in Maryland as a suspect in several other crimes, including murder. Photos of Ingersol and his traveling companion, thought to be one Sherri Blake of Baltimore, were air-expressed to Cleveland, and put on the wire to all locations.

* * *

Mr. and Mrs. Raymond Webster boarded the Louisville & Nashville Railroad's Train Number 5, *The Hummingbird*, about six-thirty Sunday evening. The Pullman porter led them to one of the four double bedrooms on the middle of three sleeping cars to New Orleans. He helped Mrs.

Webster, a pretty young woman in her early twenties with dark hair, lift her brand-new appearing suitcase onto the shelf next to the opened lower bunk. Mr. Webster, a swarthy, dark-looking man, set his also new-appearing suitcase on the sofa that would later be opened as a second berth in the large room.

"That be all, Mr. Webster?" the porter, a black man about fifty, wearing a white jacket with a Pullman Company badge on it over his white shirt and black tie. "When you're settled, the diner-lounge car will be open shortly after we leave at seven. It's two cars forward. They drop it off in the middle of the night, and in Nashville we get a full dining car and a tavern lounge. I'll make up the room for you after we leave Lou'a'ville, 'bout ten thirty, if that's okay."

"That'll be fine," Webster replied, handing the porter a ten dollar bill.

"Oh no, Mr. Webster, no need to tip me," the porter replied, holding up his hand.

"Nah, you take it. We don't want to be bothered during the night, and I know you'll see to that."

"Yes, sir!"

"Are there many other passengers in the sleepers?"

"No, not too many headed south this time 'o year, just one other couple goin' to
N'Orleans like you. But we'll pick up a few more in Lou'a'ville, I 'speck."

"Okay, thank you." Webster said as the porter backed out of the room and Webster shut the door.

"Lounge cars, diners, this is going to be fun, Ray," Mrs. Webster said. "What time are we supposed to get to New Orleans."

"If the train's on time, about four tomorrow afternoon. It goes along the Gulf Coast from Mobile."

"I've never been to New Orleans, Ray. Is it as nice as they say?"

"I've only been there once. It's hot as hell in the summer time. But we'll only have a day or so to bum around. That freighter I'm going to try to get us on to Jamaica leaves Wednesday, providing that guy I called can come through with the passports."

"Kingston," the young woman giggled. "It sounds so romantic. ...*Met a little girl in Kingston town...*" she sang to herself. "Daddy took us to Canada once. That's the only other time, before Greece this summer, that I was out of the United States."

"Yeah, you told me that before. Well, we're going to see a lot of the world, you and I."

As the Websters unpacked a few of the items from the suitcases and set out things for the night, they hardly noticed that the train had started to move forward. By the time it reached the bridge over the Ohio River, it was moving fairly fast, but slowed again as it pulled into Covington about ten minutes later. The stop was very short, and soon the long train was moving forward again.

"It'll be a couple of hours before we get to Louisville," Ray said. "Let's go eat." They left their compartment and, following the porter's direction, turned toward the front of the train to move two cars forward to the dining car. There the steward, also dressed formally in a white jacket, placed them at a table for four on the right side of the car.

"You get a good view of the Ohio River on this side," he said, handing them each a menu, a small pad of paper and a pencil. "Just write down what you want and the waiter will bring it to you," he instructed. "There will be another couple at the table with you, if that is okay."

"Yeah, sure," Ray replied, "that's the way it works. I've been on these things before. Say, can we get a drink first, since this is also the lounge car?"

"Oh, I'm sorry, sir. It's still Sunday, and Kentucky law doesn't allow us to serve liquor on Sunday."

"Not even beer or wine?"

"I'm sorry, sir. The railroad has been arguing with the state about this for almost a hundred years. You'd think, in a state famous for its bourbon, that they'd welcome such sales, but...." He hesitated a moment, then explained, "This car is dropped off in Bowling Green around midnight, and in Nashville we'll pick up a full tavern car. It will be open tomorrow. Most nights we have a club lounge car right out of Cincinnati, except some Sundays."

After dinner, during which the Websters had enjoyed steak and a rich dessert, they walked forward to the next car, a coach, but the smoke was so thick that they quickly retreated to their room in the sleeping car. The sun was setting, casting an orange glow on the water of the river whenever it was visible along the side of the track.

There was a radio in the room, and they listened to music for a while. They'd not go to bed until they had left Louisville, when the porter said he would make up the beds for them. At Louisville the train became a bit longer as some additional baggage and mail cars from Chicago and Indianapolis were added at the front end of the train, causing a few bumps and thuds, but little real disturbance.

* * *

A break in the case came early Monday morning when the Buick that had been stolen on Friday night was found abandoned in the parking lot of the Cincinnati Union Station. While a number of passenger trains had left Cincinnati over the weekend, the FBI anticipated that Ingersol and Blake were on their way to Florida, and field offices along the several possible routes were alerted. The Cincinnati police dusted the car for fingerprints, but were unable to find any. As a courtesy Morris called Dr. Fairchild at his farm on the Portage River and advised that the suspects were now apparently out of the state and would probably not be considered a danger to him any longer.

"Tom," Fairchild said, calling the agent by his first name, "I wasn't really worried. The man held a loaded police revolver in his hand and had it pointed at me there in the airport. He said that now he had his money, and that what I had said had even helped him get more than he expected, he didn't care if I was dead or alive, so I'm not concerned about Ray any more. What did you say his name is? Ingersol?

"I was wondering, however," he continued, "if you had checked hotels in Corinth or Athens to see if a Southerland had been registered there when we were in Greece?"

"We did. We asked Interpol to check it, and they confirmed that a party of two, registered under the name of Southman, had been staying at a small hotel near yours at the time. That's the same name he was using for the flight they planned to New Orleans Friday night. They apparently have passports in that name that they are using. I wonder what other names he might use?"

"Well, I'll be happy to identify him, if you can catch him under any name."

"We will sure as heck try, Professor. Thank you again for your help on this case."

* * *

Sam Whitaker came to work early Monday morning to find a yellow "federal crime scene – do not cross" ribbon and public notice tacked across the door. Unsure what to do, he simply waited until the other employees arrived for work.

About nine o'clock that morning Officer Andy Segretti arrived at the agency. Whitaker and the other waiting employees greeted him as he came up the stairs to the insurance office.

"Andy, what the heck's going on?"

"I don't know the whole picture, Sam, but there must have been some excitement around here Friday night. Understand the FBI and our homicide guys arrested your boss on insurance fraud charges. Maybe murder, too."

"What! Whose murder?"

"Shoeless George's."

"George? Harry Taylor? You've got to be kidding. Why would Taylor have shot George?"

"As I understand it, he didn't, but he hired a paid killer who did. Apparently George found where some high-up guy running the Rogers chemical plant down in the Flats had hidden a tanker ship that was supposed to be missing. Taylor found out that George had been seen looking at this ship in some sort of inside dock, apparently while he was on some sort of clean-up crew for the city. Taylor was afraid George would talk about it, so he and the guy who had hidden the ship may have arranged to have George killed. Then when he discovered, apparently through you, that your friend, Fairchild, was looking into the crime, he tried to have him killed too."

"What? Is Richard Fairchild okay?"

"Yeah, he's been working with the FBI, and he almost caught the guy Friday night trying to board a plane to Atlanta and New Orleans, but the guy and his girlfriend got away. Must have been quite a scene. One of our officers was wounded. And I'll bet you didn't know that the FBI had a tail on you for the last week, too."

"Good heavens, no! But I've got to get into the office here to let London know about this. I heard the secretary say that they had paid the whole amount on that Rogers claim, and it was several million dollars."

"That's why I'm here. I'm to let you in with enough information so that you can let your insurers know what has happened, and then this office will be sealed." Segretti turned to the others waiting in the hallway, who were as stunned as Whitaker at what had just been said.

"Folks," the officer continued, turning to the other Taylor employees in the hallway, "I need to get each of your names and addresses. You're to go directly home, and Cleveland detectives, who will need to talk with you, will contact you later today. I hear the press is really excited about this story, but I'd suggest that you speak to no one about it until after the detectives meet with you. I'm afraid you're all going to be unemployed for a while."

"It won't be the first time," Whitaker mumbled, more to himself than anyone else.

"What did you say, Sam?" Segretti asked.

"I said, it won't be the first time. Only this time I hope I don't end up living in a post office box."

"You mean that was *you* living in that cupboard? Ha-ha!" Segretti laughed.

* * *

"And you're certain this is the man who purchased the tickets for New Orleans?" FBI agent Billy Farmer asked the ticket agent at the Cincinnati Union Station about eleven o'clock on Monday morning. He had two photos, one of a man in his thirties and another of a woman in her early twenties that he had just shown to the agent. Farmer had been dispatched when it was confirmed that the Buick found in the terminal lot was the same one stolen in Cleveland on Friday night. Farmer, a younger agent about twenty-six, was tall and lanky, and did not seem to fit into the dark gray suit he was wearing.

"Yep," replied the uniformed ticket agent, Quincy Radcliffe, an older man with white hair tufts extending from beneath his round Pullman Company cap. "Paid cash for a double bedroom suite, the one that has two lower berths. Name was Webster, though. I got it here on the Pullman log, Mr. and Mrs. Raymond Webster. She was a pretty little thing, dark hair and eyes. Said something about meetin' a boat or something."

"Unhuh. And the train left at seven?" Farmer asked.

The agent reached down and pulled out an L&N schedule folder, and opened it to the Cincinnati/New Orleans page.

"Yep," he said. "Let's see. Eleven a.m., that train, Number Five, would be pulling in tah Flomaton, Alabama. Goes from there to Mobile, about twelve thirty, and Gulfport about two. Now, that's Central Daylight Time, of course, an hour later than here. Arrives, or supposed to, anyway, in New Orleans about four this afternoon."

"Do you know which car they're in?"

"Well, it's marked as S-107. According to the lineup sheet, it would be the second sleeping car, and the second car from the end of the train. Those bedrooms would be at the front end of the car."

"Good. Thank you. We appreciate your cooperation, Mr. Radcliffe."

"Always glad to help the FBI. But they seemed to be a nice couple. What have they done?"

"Oh, can't say. I really don't know. I just got instructions to find out where they're headed, and that's what I'm doing."

* * *

After a seafood lunch in the large dinning car, served while the train was stopped in Mobile for almost twenty minutes, Mr. and Mrs. Webster moved back through the three sleeping cars to the tavern lounge car that had been added during the night at the end of the train. It was a handsomely designed car, L&N blue and silver metal fluting on the exterior, and designed like a comfortable living room on the inside. The rear of the car was curved, and a drumhead showing the train's name, *The Hummingbird,* with a small bird pictured on it, was mounted on the rear panel, which was a door and window. A large bar that served not only drinks but also sandwiches, snacks and playing cards, was located in the middle of the car. The Websters took seats on the left side of the car that gave them a view to the south, over the Gulf of Mexico whenever the train passed an area where the beach was visible.

Two men had boarded the train at Mobile along with a number of coach passengers headed for the Gulf Coast stops at Pascagoula, Biloxi, Gulfport, or Bay St. Louis, all scheduled stops before the train reached

New Orleans. The men moved slowly toward the back of the train, finally entering the tavern lounge car, looking around, and taking a seat across from the Websters. Both, similar in height and build, were dressed in dark suits and held their dressy-looking hats in their hands. They seemed out-of-place among the casually dressed first class passengers who were seated around the car. After a minute or two, however, they got up again as one of them said, "Let's get something to drink, and go on back to our coach seats. I don't like leaving the luggage back up there."

"Ah, it will be okay. Nobody's going to touch it. Let's sit at one of those tables. Get some cards."

The men looked over at the Websters, and the second man said, "Hey, want to play some cards?"

"What kind?" Raymond Webster answered.

"Gin rummy, poker, pinochle, whatever you like."

Raymond looked at the dark haired girl for her response.

"Nah," she said. "I'd rather read this book I got in Cincinnati. You go ahead and play, Ray."

Raymond Webster got up and joined the other two, who stopped at the bar and bought Coca-colas, a couple sandwiches and a deck of cards. Webster bought a bottle of Millers, which the white-jacketed porter poured into a tall glass for him. He also bought a pack of Camels, and lit one as soon as he sat down at the table in the front part of the car, on the shady side away from the Gulf. He offered a cigarette to the two men, but both declined, although one lit a cigarette of his own from a pack of Lucky Strikes.

"I'm Bobby," one of the men said, pulling off his coat as he sat down, setting it on the bench seat next to where he was sitting, his back to the window. He placed his hat on top of it.

"And I'm Jack," said the other, the man who had wanted to return to the coach, but he kept his coat on. He tore open the cellophane wrapper on the deck of cards, pulled them out and started to shuffle them, while puffing on the Lucky Strike.

"Ray," Webster said, knocking the ash from his Camel into the built-in ashtray in the floor-mounted table.

"How far are you going, Ray?" the first man asked.

"End of the line, New Orleans," he replied. "How about you two?"

"Yeah, us too."

They decided on gin rummy, and the second man dealt out the cards. No one said much, except about the game, as the train rolled westward. As the train approached Gulfport, Mississippi, the second man, still wearing his suitcoat, got up and stretched, and said, "I gotta get something out of my suitcase. I'll be back in a minute." Raymond and the other man continued to play. In about ten minutes the first man returned and rejoined the game, nodding his head to his friend from behind Ray.

The passenger train had lost a bit of time at the stop in Gulfport, and it was almost three when the train stopped in Bay St. Louis, about fifty-five miles east of New Orleans. Raymond checked his watch, looked at the schedule he had in his shirt pocket, and stood up. "Guys, we'll be in New Orleans in about an hour, if we're on schedule, or a bit thereafter, and the doll -- the wife -- and I have got to finish packing our stuff, so I'm going to cash out of this little game here. Sherri," he called to the girl, still engrossed in her paperback novel, "get your stuff. We need to finish packing."

"Bye," the first man said.

"Yeah, see yah around," Ray replied as he and the girl headed toward the front of the car.

The train did make up a bit of the lost time as it rattled across the trestles west of Bay St. Louis and into the fishing villages of Waveland and Clermont Harbor. The porter had already straightened up their room, and the two lower beds had already been made up for the night and folded back into their cabinets, transformed again into sofas. From a metal locker Ray pulled out his briefcase, looked inside, and closed it again, then set it on the floor next to his suitcase. Sherri completed re-packing hers, and Ray helped her close it up, setting it on the floor next to his so the porter could set them in the vestibule before reaching the station in New Orleans.

At about five to four the train made a brief stop at the Carrollton Avenue station, about fifteen miles from downtown New Orleans. Although they were sitting on the sofa looking out the window, the Websters did not observe two more tall men in dark business suits board the train a car ahead of the one in which they were riding.

The train again pulled out of the station, and quickly picked up speed as it clattered and clicked its way through the numerous industrial sidings and yards on the east side of New Orleans.

"Look at that!" Sherri exclaimed, pointing out the window. It was a cemetery where all of the graves were built in little stone buildings above the ground.

"I've heard of that," Ray said. "Something about the ground being so low that they can't dig graves, so they bury everyone in those little mausoleums. Some even have windows in 'em, I guess."

"Yeah, there's one with a stained glass window -- just like a little church!" Sherri said. "Oh, there, I see some of the downtown buildings."

With that the porter stuck his head in the door and said, "Is this all of your luggage, Mr. Webster?"

"Yeah, just take the two suitcases. I'll bring my briefcase. Thanks."

"You folks have a good trip, now," the porter said, removing the two suitcases and placing them in the alcove of the car to await arrival at the downtown terminal. Because the New Orleans station was a stub-end terminal, the train ran beyond it, then stopped, and backed into the station.

Ray had seen the train conductor headed for the rear of the train to direct the back-up procedure, a walkie-talkie in his hand. "Funny," he said to Sherri, "I never saw those two guys I played cards with head back to their coach. One seemed so anxious to do so. Hunh."

"Maybe they went by while we were busy packing," she replied.

"Yeah, probably."

The brakes of the train squealed a bit as it came to a stop inside the terminal train shed. As Sherri stepped out of the door of the compartment she almost bumped into the man who had said his name was Bobby.

"Oh, hi," she said.

"Hi," he repeated, turning sideways to let her pass in the narrow hall of the sleeping car. Ray picked up his briefcase and also stepped out into the passageway, his briefcase in his right hand.

The man who had called himself Jack stepped behind Ray, and Ray felt something clasp onto his right wrist. He turned, and started to lift his left arm when something was clasped around his left wrist as well.

"Raymond Ingersol, you are under arrest," Jack said, pulling his FBI identification from his suit jacket. "You have the right to remain silent. Anything you say may be used in court against you. You have the right to an attorney. If you cannot afford one, you will be provided one at government expense."

"What the hell?" Ray muttered. "My name is Webster."

"Yeah, and mine's Bo Peep," Bobby replied.

Sherri had already passed through the vacuum-operated door to the vestibule of the car where the porter had set the luggage. As she did so, two men in business suits stepped beside her and also handcuffed her, telling her of her rights, and showing their FBI identification. Another man was standing on the station platform awaiting their departure from the train. He had two New Orleans police officers with him.

* * *

Two weeks later a federal grand jury issued an indictment of Fredrick Rogers for conspiracy to defraud an insurance company. As president of the chemical company he had overall responsibility for what occurred in it, and if he did not know about the illegal action, the grand jury believed he ought to have known. It would be up to the federal prosecutor to prove the allegations, however.

The state's prosecutor was also considering indictment of Rogers in the murder of George Antopholis. He had called Richard Fairchild on the phone, and discussed that possibility. Fairchild suggested that unless they had some evidence stronger than what he knew about the matter, that he did not believe the charge would be provable. With the pending federal charge, the state prosecutor decided to place the matter on hold. Fairchild had been the one he had hoped would be his witness against Rogers, but that seemed unlikely, from what the professor had said.

Chapter 17

Esther's sister, Cecilia Carpenter, had fully recovered, and the Fairchilds had invited the Carpenters to join them over the Labor Day weekend for a cruise aboard the *Castle Kent*. Bob and Sally Merriam and the Whitakers had also been asked to join them for the holiday, and the cruiser's galley was stuffed with food and wine when Richard Fairchild backed the cruiser out of its Port Cleland lagoon dock and guided it into the channel, the drawbridge rising for it to pass.

The Carpenters had never been to Ohio's Bass Islands before, and the plan was to spend the first night in the protected harbor of Put-In-Bay, spend Saturday on South Bass, then motor over to the Castle Kent dock on West Bass for the rest of the weekend. Fairchild had been invited by his Kent Village friends, the Forrakers, to conduct the services at the small white framed church in Kent Village on Sunday morning, and had agreed. Normally a minister came to conduct services in the small chapel-like church only once a month, and only in the eight months when the island was not locked in ice.

As the cruiser easily slept ten, Courtney Whitaker had asked if she could bring a girlfriend along. Her school chum was Jill Conti, who was just slightly older than Courtney. The two young teenagers were propped in the bow of the boat, waving to people in their cars along Highway 2 as the diesel-engined boat burbled under the bridge. Carolyn had brought a big cake for the dinner, Sally a large salad, and Esther and Cecelia had prepared the rest of the meal in the kitchen back at the Fairchild's farm, packing it in a basket to bring aboard. They were busy in the galley getting it ready for when they would arrive in the harbor at South Bass Island.

Fairchild had never told Esther or the Merriams about his being shot at and abandoned on the lake a few weeks earlier. The gash on his left arm had healed, and even the ache in his right shoulder had dissipated. He felt no need to disclose any details of the event. Besides, it would have to be told in court, and it was best not to say anything before then.

"Do you come out here often?" Roger Carpenter asked the professor.

"Not as often as I'd like," he replied. "Not enough time. But Sam and his family were out with us this summer, and I had it out again a few weeks ago. Took it down to Cleveland, which was when I found that old dry-dock on the Cuyahoga River."

"I still can't figure out how Taylor was involved in that," Sam said.

"All the details will probably come out at their trial, but apparently Taylor knew about the old abandoned dry-dock. It had been there since the

1920s, but had not been used in at least twenty-five years. Garrett Williams, the financial guy at Rogers Chemical, had been dealing with Taylor for the insuring of Rogers' tanker, the *Chem Queen*. Now, which one of them cooked up the plan to hide the ship, sell the chemical cargo back to Rogers, and then try to re-sell the vessel to him as well, I don't know. Neither of them has given any sort of a statement, so it will be up to the federal prosecutors to produce the evidence to convict them."

"But why would Taylor have wanted poor George murdered?" Sam asked.

"Who is George?" Roger Carpenter asked.

"George," the professor explained as the boat proceeded out of the Port Cleland harbor and into Lake Erie in a direct path toward South Bass Island, "was a homeless man with bad feet. He was basically disabled and unable to do regular work, but the employment agency down in the Flats got him work pulling weeds or picking up trash, and he even apparently did some work for the Rogers family out in Lakewood. A few weeks after the *Chem Queen* had been hijacked and hidden in the dry-dock George was assigned to a job for the City picking up trash at a burned-out warehouse site next to the dry-dock. He apparently was working next to it, saw an open window and looked in, or he may actually have gotten inside. Of course, he had no idea what he was seeing, but he must have been observed looking in the window or entering the building by one of the men working on the vessel. He had also found the ship's nameplate. They apparently reported that to Williams, who in turn told Taylor, who arranged to hire Ingersol.

"Since they captured Ray Ingersol, the hired killer, there may be more details than I am aware of," Fairchild continued, "but from what Agent Morris told me, Ingersol has apparently admitted being hired by Taylor. He says he knew nothing at all about Rogers Chemical or Garrett Williams. I suspected that from when I had talked to Ingersol, and he didn't know about the insurance scam. He had just been told to find the wood nameplate."

"How did you meet Ingersol?" Bob Merriam asked.

"Bob, that's a long story I'll tell you some time, but I've been asked not to talk about it until Ingersol's trial next month. Suffice it to say that it was right here on this boat," the professor added with a chuckle.

"Wow," Sam Whitaker exclaimed. "And after he had already tried to kill you while you were in Greece. You're a lucky man he didn't try again." Fairchild did not respond to that, but simply chuckled.

"Where did they catch him?" Roger Carpenter asked.

"I don't know all the details, but from what the newspapers said, after he shot the policeman at the Cleveland airport he and the girlfriend got in a taxi and were headed for the train station. But the cab driver was able to advise his dispatcher where they were -- he didn't know why he'd been asked, of course -- and the police set up a roadblock. Ingersol basically hijacked the cab, ran the police roadblock, and got away. Then he disabled the cab radio and stole a car, driving to Cincinnati.

"There," the professor continued, "he and the girl boarded a train for New Orleans. When the FBI got the photos of him from Washington, based on the fingerprints at the motel where they were staying in Sandusky -- just a couple of blocks from your apartment, Bob -- they sent it to Cincinnati, and the Pullman agent was able to identify them. The train, at that time, was still on its way to New Orleans, and FBI agents boarded it in Mobile. I understand they actually played cards with him until additional agents got aboard, and they made the arrest in New Orleans."

"It wasn't a very good photo of Ingersol in the paper," Bob said, "but Sally said he looked somewhat familiar, but she couldn't say why."

"Maybe she'd seen them in Sandusky, perhaps at the store, while they were staying at the motel there."

"What was the girl like?" Bob asked.

"A pretty thing, in her early twenties, if even that old. Real dark hair, cut rather short, in a kind of cute style. Sherri Blake, I think her name is."

"Blake?" Fairchild's associate professor asked, and then his face turned white. "Oh my God!"

"What?"

"I know now why Ingersol's face looked familiar. Sally and I met the two of them at Cedar Point, riding on the Cyclone, and even had dinner with them. She said she was from Baltimore...."

"Yes, and he had been in prison in Maryland."

"The man, Ray, seemed real interested when he heard I knew you at Fremont College, and kept asking questions. I'm probably the one who told him how to find you."

"So, it's a good thing you did."

"No! I might have gotten you killed."

"But, Bob, you didn't. Somehow it all worked out for the best, and they are in jail now. Otherwise we might never have known who they were. However, now that you've told me that, I'm afraid that you are going to have to be a witness against the two of them. The FBI agent was wondering how they found out about this boat, and that explains it."

As the cruiser rounded the south end of the island, Fairchild had to cut back on the speed as a number of other pleasure craft were also approaching the island, along with one of the ferryboats. Rather than proceed to the village harbor at Put-In-Bay, he guided the cruiser toward the dock at the state park at Oak Point, pulling slightly to the side, and hollering, "Avast, ye mates! Drop anchor!" Bob Merriam and Sam Whitaker, knowing the routine, scrambled to the front of the boat and threw the heavy anchor over the side. The water was only about ten feet deep, and they secured the rope to a post on the bow so that the boat would not drift during the night.

* * *

Edgar Latimer sat in Tillman Farmer's office in the Guardian Building offices of Freeze, Farmer & Rivera. Farmer was explaining the details of the appeal filed by the Brothers of St. Vincent against the Probate Court's ruling upholding George's will.

"Look," Latimer said. "I've done a lot of thinking about this since the trial in Greece. What in heavens name am I going to do with a multimillion-dollar ship line? I know nothing about business, and, just to pay the taxes I'd have to sell off half the assets. Plus there's you and Sherling to pay.

"I'm pretty much content doing what I do," he continued. "The thought of running off to Greece to have to take care of a couple of villas holds no charm for me. I'm not angry that the Brothers filed their appeal. As far as I'm concerned, they can have the ship line, villas and all. I was working for them at the time, and they had a valid argument. Once I even considered joining that order, but I wasn't cut out to be celibate.

"George Antopholis was my friend. I didn't have any greed in mind when I first brought him up here to see if you could help get him some welfare benefits. You know that. Is there some way we can compromise with the Brothers on this, and they can take the bulk of the estate?"

"Is that really what you want?"

"Look, I'm not cut out to be a millionaire. If I had a few hundred thousand, clear of any taxes, from this, I could get myself a nice home, maybe up on the shore north of Boston so Terri, my girl in London, and I can get married, and have some money in the bank, and some stock to keep us going."

"Like stock in Cyprus-Hellenic Ship Lines?"

"Sure. That way, hey, if the Brothers had it, I could be on the Board. I don't know what board members do, but they all seem to be pretty well-off!"

"If it was set up as a Trust for the Brothers, you could also be a trustee."

"Sure, something like that, just to keep George's memory in it. Maybe there'd be enough cash to build a new chapel for the shelter, and we could call it the George Antopholis Memorial Chapel, or something like that."

"Well, if that is what you think you want, I'll talk to the other lawyers, and see what we can come up with. But just out of curiosity, what led you to this decision?"

"That professor, Fairchild. After I read in the Boston newspaper how he had figured out who had killed George, and why, I called him. You know, I'd met him before, in Athens during the trial. At that time he suspected me of having shot George, because of the will and the timing, and also because I knew Rogers, of whom he was also suspicious. I'd been a tenant of Rogers after I quit working at the shelter. Because of his suspicions I was prepared when the Greek government's attorney started asking the same questions. If Fairchild hadn't badgered me a bit first, I would not have been prepared to answer, and I might well have lost the whole thing.

"Anyway, I called him, and thanked him for finding George's killers. He invited me out to his farm, and I told him the next time I was in Cleveland I'd come visit him. This is the first chance I have had, and I'm going out there this afternoon. I didn't know until I read it in the papers that he was some sort of college chaplain.

"Seems odd," Latimer continued after a moment of thought, "that a religion professor would also be a detective."

"According to our papers, he's also an archeologist. Apparently it was by digging through the county plat maps that he figured out where that chemical tanker was hidden. Oh, that reminds me. The Marine Bank of Detroit that loaned Rogers the money to buy that tanker from your ship line sent the title on it to the insurers in London. Lloyd's would like to sell it back to you for the amount they paid on the claim."

"Gad. I guess I am in the ship business after all! I suppose we'd better talk to Ian Sherling about that one. But maybe I can sell it back to Rogers."

"He has been indicted," the attorney said.
"Yes, Fairchild told me when I called. But Fairchild doesn't think he's guilty."

* * *

Orientation week at Fremont College was always hectic. It included registration, the most frantic free-for-all of each semester, plus the first of the season's football games.

The residents of the Hayes Hall basement had seen it all too often, and were used to the turmoil that the opening of each new semester created.

Newspaper accounts of Fairchild's encounter with a professional killer, Raymond Ingersol, and his role in solving a murder and a ship piracy had expanded the professor's reputation as a skilled detective. But they also served as a further aggravation to Dean Harding, who believed that the criminology hobby of his Professor of Religions and Assistant Chaplain was bad for the college's image. Fortunately for Richard Fairchild, the college's Board of Trustees felt otherwise about their famous professor.

The federal trials of Taylor, Williams, Rogers, Ingersol and Blake were to come before their state murder trials. While Ingersol had not yet confessed to anything, he had admitted that he knew Taylor, but had never met Williams. The state attorney was attempting to get him to testify against Taylor and Williams in exchange for a reduced charge. Otherwise the charge might be capital murder.

Ingersol was suspected of murders in at least two other states besides Ohio. His arrest put the "closed" stamp on several murder cases, but none of the other states had sufficient evidence to have him extradited. Ohio prosecutors would have the first opportunity to try him, and they were certain of a conviction. If he ever reached parole, the other states would have their own opportunity to try him.

Fairchild asked that the state kidnap and attempted murder charge against Ingersol and Sherri Blake be dropped, but the federal prosecutor recommended to the state that it not do so. Only the federal charge of attempted murder of an American in a foreign country remained against her, and although there was not much evidence to support the charge, the federal prosecutor believed that by maintaining the state charge he had a better bargaining chip in his case against Ingersol.

A week before her trial Sherri Blake agreed to testify against Ray Ingersol, and the charge against her in federal court involving the attempt on Dr. Fairchild in Greece was dropped. She would still be subject to the state trial, however.

Ingersol, knowing he had little to lose and much to gain, then agreed to testify against Taylor, and the federal prosecutor agreed to consider a plea bargain on the federal charges. Ingersol insisted he had not known about Garrett Williams. He would tell the court that it was Henry Taylor who had hired him to kill both George Antopholis and Richard Fairchild, but that he did not know why the two were to be killed. He had no idea why he was supposed to find the nameplate from the *Chem Queen* in George's trash heap.

No early bargains were offered by the state's district attorney on the charge of the murder of George Antopholis, the kidnap and attempted murder of Fairchild in Lake Erie, the shooting of the Cleveland policeman at the airport, and the hijacking of the taxicab. The State of Ohio wanted him in prison for the rest of his life. In a final plea bargain Ray Ingersol was sentenced to life in an Ohio penitentiary with the possibility of parole after twenty or thirty years.

Esther had initially resented all the publicity and hounding by reporters. After a while, however, she began to realize that her husband was, indeed, a hero in solving the murder of the homeless man and discovering where a pirated ship had been hidden as well. She forgave him for the emotional trauma she had undergone. The two had packed a suitcase and driven up to Michigan, spending a long weekend in Petoskey.

Upon arriving home at their farm on the Portage River there was an envelope awaiting them from London. The Morris Staley Syndicate, Members of Underwriters at Lloyd's, London, was extremely grateful to

Fairchild for his efforts in resolving the claim of the Rogers Chemical Company, the letter said. They were inviting the Fairchilds to be the Syndicate's guests in London on October 17 for the presentation of a reward.

"When is that?" Esther asked.

"Let's see. There's a mid-semester break October 16, and we're due back on the twentieth. So I guess we would be able to go if we want to. I hope it's not cash. Our taxes are high enough without having to declare that, too."

"You're worrying about taxes?" Esther exclaimed. "Richard! You saved them millions!"

* * *

A week after the new semester began Richard Fairchild was sitting in his office when Sally Merriam knocked on his door. He looked up inquiringly.

"One of the students, a Miss Kelly Rogers, would like to talk with you, Dr. Fairchild," she said.

"Show her in." Sally turned and Kelly Rogers came to the door.

"Kelly! How are you?" the professor asked, immediately recognizing her from the summer tour.

"A bit depressed, I'm afraid. You know they arrested my father."

"Yes, Kelly, I do know. I fear I may have been partially responsible for that. When is the trial?"

"In a few weeks. I don't want to go to it. Mother said I should be there, but to have to sit through all that, I just don't want to face the shame of it."

"I don't believe you would be called as a witness, Kelly. So there is probably no official reason for you to go. But your dad will need all the support he can get. I understand that the charges against him are not as severe as against the others, and he had no involvement in planning for George's death. The insurance fraud charges are pretty serious, of course, and he could be sent to prison for a long time. But he maintains he did not know about the ship being hidden, and it is up to the prosecutor to prove the case. If he should be found guilty and sent to prison, he'll need your love if he is to survive there. He'll certainly need that love and care during the trial."

"I suppose. But there will be reporters and all, and I just...." Kelly began to weep.

"Kelly, I know your dad loves you an awful lot. I've only met him once, and he seemed to be a very honest person. I suspect the jury may think so, too. And I've also met your Mother, and she is going to need you at that trial, too. All of you are going to need all the love and understanding and prayers that can be mustered to get through it. When did you say the trial begins?"

"It's scheduled to begin October 16. They say it will last three or four days."

"That's the week of the semester break. Kelly, Esther and I are supposed to go to London that week, but I really have no desire to do that. How would it be if we agreed to sit with you and your mother during the trial? I can keep the reporters away from you, and you and your mother will be allowed to sit either with, or just behind, your Dad. Remember, your Dad hasn't pled guilty, so in the eyes of the law he is innocent unless the government proves he's guilty, and they may never be able to do that."

"But do you think he's guilty?"

"I don't know. Frankly, I don't think he is. All I know is that a certain tanker ship was hidden, and an insurance claim was made for it. It is up to the government to prove a relationship of any of that to your father. I don't know if they can. George, that very disabled poor homeless man who lived under a bridge in the cold was killed, apparently because of that ship. But I don't think your Dad had anything to do with any of it."

"He couldn't have, Dr. Fairchild. We all knew George and felt sorry for him. He occasionally worked at our home. But I guess you knew that." Kelly pulled a small linen handkerchief from her purse and blew her nose, wiping the tears from her eyes. "And you really will go with us to the trial?"

"Sure, Kelly. I'd be honored to sit with your Dad and help you give him the support he's going to need. Isn't that what we were studying in Greece, learning about how the Christian religion supplanted the pagan religions, because it had a new and unique belief? And what was that belief, Kelly?"

"Forgiveness, and love, you said."

"Your religious denomination is not important to us here at Fremont, but I've seen you attending the Sunday chapel services, so I can guess that you have been brought up in a church, somewhere. What is happening is exactly what that church and Christianity is all about. There has to be punishment from society for wrongdoing, but for us as individuals, we must express our love and forgiveness to any wrongdoer, and help that person. That may be why there were thieves and murderers up there on those crosses on Good Friday along with Jesus, and why our job is to remember those who are poor, or homeless, hungry or sick, or those who are in prison. It's not an easy task that Christianity sets for us, Kelly, but it's one we have to do. And besides, in this case, your dad may not have been a wrongdoer. He and his company were the victims."

"I suppose so, Dr. Fairchild. Okay, I'll go, if you'll go with Mom and me. Could you pray for us? And for Daddy?"

* * *

When Esther heard that Richard did not want to go to London in October she was relieved. "We've been to London, and I'm just as happy not having to go when it would only be for a day or two.'

"I'll call Staley long distance and tell him. Whatever it was they had, maybe they can mail it," he replied.

At nine the next morning, two in the afternoon in London, Fairchild reached the offices of Marcus Staley on Threadneedle Street in the City of London's financial district and advised that he and Esther would not be able to come to London in October.

"I'm disappointed, Dr. Fairchild," Staley said. "We wanted to have a reception for you in the Lord Nelson Room. You saved many of the Names a lot of money, Professor. Are you sure we can't reschedule it, perhaps over your Christmas holidays?"

"No, no," Fairchild replied. "I'm quite eager to forget about the whole thing. But really, the man you need to honor is Sam Whitaker."

"Taylor's assistant?"

"Yes, he's the key to the whole thing. He came across the *Chem Queen* file by accident, and told me about it. He is also the one who got the police interested in George Antopholis's murder. Sam's a really bright young man, and seems to have learned a whole lot about the marine insurance industry. Why, when he was out on our college boat a few weeks ago, he was telling me about some of the marine claims he's been involved in, and new business he has produced. But, of course, with Taylor in jail and the office closed, right now he's out of work."

"Whitaker is the one who notified us of Taylor's arrest. I talked to him myself," Staley said. "Yes, he does seem to be a good insurance man. But there is someone here in my office who would like to ask you some questions. His name is Gunther Harcourt, our American investigator."

"Yes, I've seen his name in the newspaper. I understand he will be a witness at Taylor's trial."

"Hello?" another voice said on the telephone a moment or so later. "Richard Fairchild?"

"Yes. Mr. Harcourt?"

"You are one heck of a good detective, Fairchild." Harcourt said. "How did you ever figure out where that ship was hidden?"

"A stroke of luck, I assure you. I understood that you had determined every place it wasn't. Therefore it had to be still up that river somewhere. The river's not deep enough for it to have sunk, so I checked the courthouse records for anything that might have been around the Rogers Chemical Company. Actually, I was looking more for something that might have triggered the murder of George Antopholis...."

"I heard about that murder while I was in Cleveland, but I never associated it with the loss of the *Chem Queen*."

"No reason to. I just happened to notice the back of that dry-dock that extended down into the water. When I sounded it with my pole, I realized that it was deep enough for a big ship to have been pulled in there, and the river just barely wide enough for it to be turned around. But it was the FBI that learned that T&W Marine was Taylor and Williams. From there it was easy to put the case together and also to connect them with the murder of George Antopholis."

Harcourt had several other questions, and then the conversation ended with Staley agreeing to mail the plaque they had prepared to Fairchild in Ohio. When it came, there was also a check drawn on a London bank for a considerable amount of money.

* * *

"Hello, Richie?" the voice on the telephone said that night when the professor answered. It was about a week later.

"Sam?"

"Yeah! Hey, I got some great news today. Marilyn Taylor got permission of the court to run the agency until her husband's trial. She called me, and asked me to run it for her, and I've been down there for the last few days catching up on all the stuff that's come in since August."

"Good."

"Yeah, but it gets better. Marilyn and Harry are going to need a lot of money to pay for his defense. He's hired a pretty high-priced lawyer, and the lawyer suggested that he sell the agency. I talked it over with Carolyn, and we went to the bank and they agreed to finance our buying the Taylors' interests in the agency. As of next week, it will be the Whitaker Marine Insurance Agency."

"Oh, that's wonderful news, Sam. Congratulations."

"Apparently you said something to Staley in London, I don't know what, but he has offered to give our new agency an exclusive managing agency account for the Great Lakes. That's Chicago, Milwaukee, Detroit, even Toronto, the whole works. Of course, it's just for his syndicate, not all of the Lloyd's business. I'm off to Chicago tomorrow to talk to some marine agents there. Carolyn is delighted."

"Sam, that's great! And to think that just a year ago you were living in a cupboard in a post office, afraid you'd never get your family back."

Chapter 18

The late October clouds had rolled in over Northern Ohio, and the first snow of the season had already fallen. Dr. Robert Merriam had agreed to cover Fairchild's classes while he attended the trial of Fredrick Rogers at the Federal Courthouse in Cleveland. Richard and Esther Fairchild were staying at the Cleveland Hotel on the Public Square during the procedure.

Although the U.S. District Attorney had interviewed Fairchild about his meetings with Rogers in Athens, he saw no need to call the professor as a witness, and the Fairchilds were able to keep their promise to Kelly to sit with her and her mother during the trial. Rogers was represented by Asa Bauer, a well-known Cleveland defense attorney. Bauer had also interviewed Fairchild about the case, and Fairchild had given him some information that he felt might be useful. Therefore, although the prosecutor would not call Fairchild, Bauer did.

Upon being sworn as a witness, Bauer wasted little time in getting to the point.

"Dr. Fairchild, I understand that you once visited the Rogers' home."

"Yes."

"Why was that?"

"I was trying to find out something about a homeless man, George Antopholis, who had been murdered a year ago. I learned that an Ed Latimer was the heir to the estate Antopholis had inherited just before his death. Latimer had once lived at an address in Lakewood, and that turned out to be the Rogers' home. I also knew that Antopholis had worked for Rogers, both at his home and at his plant on the Cuyahoga River, but at the time I visited their home, I did not know it was the same Rogers. It was just a coincidence that it was Fred Rogers' home."

"Did you see Rogers again?"

"Actually, I did not meet Fred Rogers on *that* visit. I only met Mrs. Rogers."

"Did you *ever* meet Fred Rogers?"

"Yes."

"Please explain, Dr. Fairchild."

"As I testified earlier, I am a college professor, and my wife and I often take students on a summer seminar to Europe for college credit. This past summer our tour was to Greece and Turkey, in connection with early church history events and places. One of the students on the tour with us was Kelly Rogers, the daughter of the defendant. Mr. and Mrs. Rogers stopped at the hotel where we were staying in Athens to visit with their daughter, and I was introduced to Fred Rogers at that time."

"Do you know why Fred Rogers was in Athens?"

"I didn't at the time."

"Have you since learned why he was there?"

"I've been told that ...."

"Objection," the U.S. Attorney, Don Selig said, rising to his feet. "Hearsay."

"Sustained," the judge replied. "Mr. Bauer, you may restate your question if you wish."

"Thank you, your honor. Dr. Fairchild, have you spoken with anyone about Fred Rogers since that meeting in Athens?"

"Not directly about Fred Rogers, other than agreeing to accompany his daughter."

"Did you discuss with anyone the chemical company Rogers owns?"

"Yes, sir."

"And who was that?"

"Two people, actually. One was Sam Whitaker, an insurance agent in the office of Taylor Marine Insurance, and Special Agent Thomas Morris of the FBI."

"What were those conversations?"

"Whitaker told me that he had accidentally seen a file involving the theft of a ship that belonged to Rogers Chemical Company. Agent Morris confirmed to me in a conversation a week or so later that he was investigating the theft of that ship. I also later was told by a Lieutenant Schifferman of the Coast Guard that he had also been involved in the search for that missing vessel, the *Chem Queen*."

"Morris testified for the prosecution two days ago. Did you hear his testimony?"

"Yes."

"He testified that you had provided information that led to the locating of that vessel. Is that correct?" Fairchild answered in the affirmative.

"Can you explain how that occurred?"

"Well, I'm a bit of a curious person -- I've been called nosey -- and...." There was a bit of laughter in the courtroom, and even the judge smiled, but then banged his gavel once to restore order. "...and I was curious about the murder of George Antopholis, whom I had met at a homeless shelter down in the Flats a year or so before he was murdered. I occasionally substituted for the shelter manager, being an ordained clergyman. There was a theory...."

"Whose theory?"

"Mine, I guess, maybe also Sam Whitaker's. We had a theory that George might have found something or seen something while he was working for the City on a cleanup project a few days before he was shot. So, while I had the college's boat in Cleveland, I went to the Cuyahoga County Recorder's office and checked the plat maps. Title to property that had once belonged to the Rogers Chemical Company had been transferred to the City. This apparently was a warehouse that had burned down. But just to the south of that parcel of property was another that had belonged to a company named Gooding. It had been transferred to another company called T&W Marine."

"Go on," Bauer said.

"I went on up the river to the Rogers plant, noted the vacant lot -- actually it looked like several lots -- and then observed the brick building on which there was still some faint wording that said Gooding. This structure was very high and wide, although it only had windows on the first floor level, and they were extremely dirty. I examined the back of the building from the river side, and noted that the rear wall, which had a rather odd appearance, extended down below the water line. With my sounding pole, I determined that the water was more than ten feet deep at that point in the river, next to that building."

"You say the building had an 'odd appearance'. Could you explain that?"

"Yes. Brick is usually laid in a manner where one brick will be placed with its middle across the two bricks beneath it, to give the wall strength. The bricks in this rear wall were laid that way, except for two vertical lines at each side, like it was some sort of a door that could be removed or moved upward."

"Did you hear Agent Morris testify that the dry-dock had such a door at the river's edge?"

"Yes sir."

"Did his explanation fit with what you observed?"

"Yes sir."

"Now, did the Cuyahoga County records show that either Rogers Chemical Company or Fred Rogers ever owned the property on which this dry-dock was built?"

"No. The plat map showed that it was the property north of that building that was owned by Rogers Chemical. That property was the vacant lot, where apparently a warehouse had once been located."

"Can you think of any reason why Fredrick Rogers would have known about that dry-dock, or...."

"Objection," Selig softly said, as he again rose from his chair. "Calls for a conclusion the witness could not possibly know."

"Sustained," the judge replied.

"Dr. Fairchild, have you any knowledge of your own that Fredrick Rogers, the defendant, knew that the dry-dock existed?"

"I have no such knowledge."

"Thank you. That is all the questions I have for now, Dr. Fairchild. Mr. Selig, your witness," Bauer said, sitting down.

"I have no questions of this witness, your honor," the U.S. Attorney said, and Fairchild was dismissed.

The trial continued one further day. A London shipping agent was called by the defense to testify that Rogers had been in Athens to see about purchasing another vessel to replace the *Chem Queen*. That ship had been purchased from the ship line belonging to George Antopholis's uncle, and Rogers had hoped to buy another used tanker from the line. This, Bauer suggested in his summary, was ample proof that Fred Rogers had absolutely no knowledge of the fact that his chief financial officer had arranged the theft of the boat, that it was being redesigned, and that it sat only a few thousand yards from the Rogers plant. Rogers, he told the jury, was the victim, not the perpetrator of this crime and should never have been indicted.

Attorney Selig's own summary had been very weak in its accusation. There was no tangible evidence at all that Rogers had known anything at all about the theft of his ship, and it was certainly not to his advantage to pay for chemicals delivered by Williams that he already owned. The best the government could suggest was that Rogers ought to have known he was being victimized, but he could not really find a label for such a crime. In the end, the jury took only about twenty minutes to reach a verdict that Fredrick Rogers was completely innocent.

That night Rogers insisted on treating Bauer, the Fairchilds and Kelly to dinner at a restaurant on Cleveland's "Gold Coast," Edgewater Drive, where it bordered on Lakewood, the next city to the west. Kelly then rode back to Fremont College with the Fairchilds for classes the next day.

* * *

It was late afternoon on the Tuesday of the following week and both Bob and Sally Merriam and Dr. Fairchild were busy in their basement office, preparing for the next day of classes

"It's snowing out there again," one of the students stopped in to say while on his way to a class on one of the upper floors.

"Why don't you two head home," Fairchild said to Sally Merriam, who was in her husband's small office placing a document he had just had her type on his desk. "I'll lock up here after this next class. That highway to Sandusky gets awfully skiddy in the snow."

"Yes, we're going to have to find something closer soon, I think," Bob Merriam replied. "Thanks for the offer. I believe we will head out."

The Merriams had just left when Fairchild's office phone rang. It was the college operator, advising that there was a long distance call for him.

When he answered, the voice on the other end sounded distant. "Hello, Dr. Fairchild?"

"Yes, who's calling?"

"Ed Latimer, from London. I don't think we have a good connection. Can you hear me?"

"Yes, go ahead."

"Dr. Fairchild, we're going to have a new chapel built at St. Vincent House, there in Cleveland, in memory of George. I want you to do the dedicatory service. It should be finished next spring."

"Sure, Ed. I'd be honored to do that."

"One more thing, Dr. Fairchild. Terri Brooks, my fiancée here in London, and I are going to get married next week in Cleveland, in the old St. Vincent House chapel. We'd like you to do the wedding. Could you do that?"

"You'll be required to have an Ohio wedding license."

"Yes, first thing we thought of. It's all arranged."

"Well, okay. May I bring Esther with me?"

"Sure! Amos Waterman is going to be my best man. Then we're going to Greece for our honeymoon. Seems Terri decided we ought to keep one of those Antopholis villas. You and Esther will always be welcome to use it."

"Thank you. Sure. Call me when you get to Cleveland and let me know the final details."

"Right. Cheerio, as they say here in London."

"Cheerio, Ed."

Richard Fairchild hung up the phone. And to think, he thought to himself, that all of what had happened over the past year had been because of George, a poor homeless man with disabled feet who couldn't wear shoes.

"Q"

Prologue to "Q"
Fremont, Ohio
February 6, 1962

"Forgiveness of others, including enemies, as a religious concept seemed to be new to many in Judea at that time, although there were many Old Testament references to forgiveness of iniquities. Perhaps it still is a *new* concept there – and here." Dr. Richard F. Fairchild, Professor of Religions and Assistant Chaplain of Fremont College, pointed to a map of Palestine as he told his Early Church History 217 class about some leaders of the Church, several of whom, like Stephen, had been accused of blasphemy and killed.

"Not everyone," he said, sitting down on the corner of his desk at the front of the classroom, "bought into a theology of forgiveness. Remember, Judea was very much under the oppressive thumb of the Romans, and the very idea of forgiving the conqueror was alien to Jewish thought of the day. Add to that the fact that these Galilean fishermen and their buddies were considered to be uneducated hicks by the religious intelligentsia in Jerusalem. But the church was growing. Matthias had already been selected to replace Judas as one of the twelve apostles -- by casting lots, no less -- and others, including both Stephen and another Philip, had been appointed as deacons. In those days deacons were primarily just food servers for the community meals the church held.

"People were coming to Jerusalem from all over the Empire, and even beyond it," he continued, pointing to Jerusalem on the wall map. "It lay right on the land trade route, and was very near the center of the Fertile Crescent. Those coming from the East, North, or West followed the trade routes to the port cities. To give you an idea how far some of the travelers to Jerusalem came, consider this passage from *Acts*:

"'A messenger,' many translations say 'angel of the Lord,' but that translates to a messenger, 'said to Philip,' not the apostle, but this new deacon, who was in Samaria at the time teaching, "'Get up and go toward the south to the road that goes down from Jerusalem to Gaza.'" See," Fairchild said, again pointing on the map to the area along the coast of the Mediterranean, a desert known as the Gaza Strip, "this is part of the Philistine lands those of you who were in the Old Testament class last semester were studying. So Philip packed himself off to the south as he was instructed. Now," again reading from his notes, "'There was an Ethiopian eunuch....' What's a eunuch?"

Several of the young women in the class giggled, but none of the students volunteered an answer. "Well, in those days, gentlemen," Fairchild smiled, addressing the men in the class, "in many Eastern countries, if you wanted to serve in government you had to be above reproach. Government service was costly, indeed. It was believed that if you had no sex drive, you would be more loyal to the monarch. So the highest ranking officials were castrated males. I can think of a few politicians today who might not have gotten themselves in so much trouble if they had been rendered in the same position. It certainly cuts down on the testosterone.

"But to continue the story, the Ethiopian -- his name may have been Ja'n Dereba -- was a high court official of the Candace, queen of the Ethiopians, and was in charge of her entire treasury. Now," Fairchild said, moving to another map showing a larger portion of Northern Africa, Western Asia and Southern Europe, and pointing to an area along the southeastern coast of the Red Sea, "this is Abyssinia. But it is also possible this official would have been Nubian, from the area south of Egypt," again pointing at the map, "not necessarily the area we know today as Abyssinia. Of course, we really can't be certain of that, and we do know that there was considerable communication between Judea and Abyssinia at the time. Travel to Abyssinia would probably have been by ship, and the Ethiopian would have headed to a Red Sea port from Jerusalem, rather than overland through Gaza. Our eunuch was undoubtedly a black man, but was not considered a Gentile. After all, Philip found him reading a Hebrew scroll. In those days all reading was done aloud, and there was probably at least one other person, the least the chariot driver and maybe also a guard, with him." Fairchild then continued to read from the text.

"'He had come to Jerusalem to worship, and was returning home. He was seated in his chariot, reading the prophet Isaiah. Then the Spirit said to Philip, "Go over to this chariot and join it."' They must have been at some village out there in the desert," the professor suggested. "Philip ran up to the chariot and heard the Ethiopian reading from the prophet Isaiah. "Do you understand what you are reading?"' he asked. The Ethiopian replied, "'How can I, unless someone guides me?" And he invited Philip to get in and sit beside him. Now the passage of the scripture that he was reading was this: "Like a sheep he was led to the slaughter, and like a lamb silent before its shearer, so he does not open his mouth. In his humiliation justice was denied him. Who can describe his generation? For his life is taken away from the earth.'"'

"Where does this passage come from?" Fairchild asked. No one volunteered an answer. "It is from *Isaiah* Chapter 53, verses 7 and 8, which are believed by many to be a direct reference to Jesus and the events at his trial.

"'The eunuch asked Philip, "About whom, may I ask you, does the prophet say this, about himself or about someone else?"'" Fairchild continued. "' Then Philip began to speak, and starting with this scripture he proclaimed to him the good news about Jesus. As they were going along the road, they came to some water,' -- and oasis, I suspect -- 'and the eunuch said, "Look, here is water! What is to prevent me from being baptized?"' Some texts add, 'Philip said, "If you believe with all your heart, you may," and he replied, "I believe that Jesus Christ is the Son of God."' However," Fairchild commented, "this is not in the standard text of Luke's book, and many scholars believe it was added later."

Fairchild then continued to read, "'He commanded the chariot to stop, and both of them, Philip and the eunuch, went down into the water, and Philip baptized him.'" Then the two of them went on their way, the eunuch back to serve his queen and Philip on to some towns in Caesarea.

"We usually think of Paul as being the great foreign missionary of the early Church, but as we note here, and in the next chapter of *Acts,* Paul -- then known as Saul -- was still busy trying to see that the early Christians, like Stephen, were stoned to death. Even after his conversion he wandered away into the desert for some twenty years before he began his missionary journeys. A lot of work was done throughout the Roman world by others during that period of time, but we don't often hear about it," Dr. Fairchild said.

At that point the bell rang, and the forty students in the room began gathering up their papers and notes to move on to the next class. Several came forward to ask the professor questions, which he gladly answered. The room was warm, and the professor, being somewhat plump and dressed in a sweater and brown sports coat, was often damp with perspiration at the end of his lectures. Occasionally he got so involved in his presentation that his brown-rimmed glasses fogged and he had to remove them to wipe them clear. As the last student departed, the professor, now in his mid-forties, collected his notes and headed for his office in the basement of Hayes Hall.

"Messengers!" he thought to himself. What had Luke meant when he referred to an "angel of the Lord"? The Greek physician had not been there. Who had told him this story? How did he hear it? What was it that sent this Philip, who was appointed as nothing more than a server of food at religious gatherings, all the way from Samaria to Gaza? Was there more to this story? Fairchild shook his head and consulted his watch.

Chapter 1

Ceobobo Monastery, South of Jima, Ethiopia
April 29, 1941, 11 a.m.

The mud brick chapel of the small Ge'ez monastery sat on a dusty yellow-brown ledge of a bluff overlooking the Gojab River and Mount Maigudo, which stood more than ten thousand feet high. Green patches of garden shared the relatively flat but narrow shelf with the chapel and a few surrounding huts. Below, the Gojab cut through more yellow-brown rock, with only occasional patches of green visible in the deep chasm. Cut into the yellowish rock face at the back of the ledge were a number of caves, several large enough for the monks to gather in for common meals and study. The rest were small, deep, and dark; each monk had his own where he spent many hours each day in silence and prayer. Most contained little but a straw mat, a table and stool where some document or book might be studied, and a small altar at which the monk could pray. Some of the younger monks lived in the small huts further down the ledge beyond the chapel. These, facing to the south, however, were hot and uncomfortable in the strong African sun; most of the monks favored the cooler caves as a refuge.

In the three years that Father Giulio Garmani had been in the Kafa region of Ethiopia he had learned enough of the local dialects to understand the Ge'ez chants and prayers of the monks who lived in huts and caves around the old chapel. Despite its mud construction, he recognized a beauty to the chapel that compared in many ways to the Baroque churches and cathedrals of his own heritage. The chapel's history was far more ancient than that of churches in Southern Switzerland and Northern Italy from where he had come. The round shape of the chapel, its high, curved dome and narrow nave with the ornately carved wood altar, give it elegance worthy of the treasure that the monks' legend said it contained. The chapel might easily have been two thousand years old, as the monks claimed it was.

The monks of Ceobobo, now only twenty-two in number and mostly aged sixty or higher, gathered in the chapel five times each day for prayer. Once there had been more than a hundred monks at Ceobobo, but the war had drawn many away to support their families or to fight for the independence of their nation. Emperor Haile Selassie had resisted the Italian invasion in October of 1935, but the Italian Army, invading from the east, had prevailed. British forces -- actually Indian and South African army troops -- had reclaimed the capital of Addis Ababa three weeks earlier. The British were moving quickly against the remaining areas of Italian control. It would not be long, thought Giulio, before he would either be dead or going home. The British bombing raids were coming closer each day. He had heard at the Italian Army camp that the rail line at Dire Daqua had been captured, but it had not been confirmed. Any escape would have to be by air or over the mountains into North Africa.

Father Garmani had no obligation to volunteer and serve as a chaplain in the Italian Army. He was a Swiss national, born in Tesserete, just north of Lugano, only a mile from the Italian border. But he had been studying in Rome in 1936 when a close friend of his father, the Duke of Aosta, was appointed to command the Italian forces in Ethiopia. The newly ordained Giulio saw the opportunity to go with the Duke as not only his duty as a priest, but also a chance to further his study of the Coptic and Ethiopian Ge'ez Christian Churches of Africa, a subject on which he was doing graduate study in Rome.

His curiosity about this unusual branch of the Christian Church had been rewarded when he had been assigned to the Italian forces in the Kefa region of Ethiopia. He learned about the Ceobobo Monastery and had made it a point to visit at every opportunity. While much of their worship seemed familiar to him, he was less tolerant of many of their rituals, superstitions and mythological beliefs. They alleged, for example, that their monastery had been founded by one of Jesus' disciples who had died at the monastery and was buried somewhere nearby. He had asked to see the grave, but the old monks refused his request, saying it was too sacred to touch. He doubted any such tomb existed, and certainly doubted that any of the Apostles had ever made their way to the mountains of Abyssinia.

The hot, dusty April morning was typical of the past few weeks. The troops had spread out along the roads from Jima in all directions, intent on holding back the British forces that were slowly retaking the countryside. Giulio had grabbed a ride up the steep valley with some of the soldiers after holding morning Mass in the camp, intent on spending another day with the monks. The officer in charge of the soldiers elected to use the monastery as his base for the day, deploying his troops and their trucks around it in anticipation that the British forces might proceed up the Gojab valley. If that occurred, the Italian forces would have the advantage of the high ground.

The bell that hung outside the chapel door called the elderly monks to worship. Each slowly left his individual cave or hut and proceeded to the chapel for the ritual prayers and chants. Giulio watched them enter and kneel, and was about to enter and join them when he heard a buzzing sound. The Italian soldiers also heard the noise and ceased their activity to scan the sky. Then they saw them, two British attack planes, approaching eastward up the Gojab River Valley.

"Take cover," the lieutenant in charge of the troops shouted, and the soldiers ran in every direction where some protection might be available, including inside the caves and the chapel. Several manned the guns mounted on their vehicles, and began firing at the approaching airplanes. Their vehicles, however, were still in the open, very visible from the air, and as the two single-engine aircraft roared overhead it was obvious that the vehicles had been targeted and the fleeing soldiers revealed to the pilots.

The two planes climbed and circled, now coming in from the opposite direction, the west, their machine guns blazing. The guns on the trucks were struck first, bodies and metal flying apart as the aircraft fire hit its mark. The bullets kicked up dust as they slammed into the yellow brown dirt on the plateau. Giulio's heart pounded in his breast as shells ripped into the army vehicles and the fleeing men around him. He ran to one of the dying soldiers, and began the prayers for the dying. Then he ran to another who was already dead. One of the planes was headed straight toward the door of the chapel near where he was standing. His panic almost paralyzed him, but at last he gained the strength and courage to run toward a rock escarpment at the opening to a cave just to the north of the chapel, shouting prayers to the Virgin Mary as he ran.

As the British plane flew over the roof of the chapel it dropped one of its bombs. There was no whistle -- the plane was too close to the ground for that. It exploded on impact. The force of the blast hit Giulio in the back as he was approaching the protection of the cave, blowing him off his feet and forward, his arms flaying wildly away in the air. Then a shower of debris hit him, and he fell to the ground unconscious. Dust and rubble enveloped his crumpled body, and blood gushed from a deep laceration in his scalp and gashes all over the rest of his black-clad body.

* * *

Vipiterno, Italy, South of the Brenner Pass
April 29, 1941, 2:45 p.m.

"Of course it won't stop them for long, but it will at least delay them," Damondo quietly responded. He spoke in thick Italian to the others gathered in the back of Damondo's little bakery shop in the village of Vipiterno, high in the Trentino Alto Adige below the Zillertaler Alps bordering Austria and Italy. "If we do it right, they may not be able to open it for months."

"It will only draw an attack on our village," Giovanni protested. He'd heard what the Germans did to saboteurs in other villages. Their wives and children had been lined up and shot, and the men were hauled away by the Gestapo for torture and painful death.

"Italy should never have joined forces with those bastards!" grumbled Alfredo, waving his hand. "Mussolini was a fool to ever trust the Nazis. But I agree with Damondo. We have to do *something*, and if we do it right, they'll be too busy to worry about finding out who did it."

"Wishful thinking!" Giovanni replied. "But let us hear your plan, Damondo."

"I walked the railroad last week just to see what the possibilities might be," the baker began. "Just a mile or so south of the pass there is a wide loop of the rail line to the west. Then it loops back to the east as it descends from the pass. That's to the north, just at the edge of the Isarco valley. There's a high rock cliff, a short tunnel, and a bridge. We have enough explosives to block the line from both the north and the south with rock from the wall above the track, then to collapse the tunnel from inside and knock down the bridge. It will take them a week or more to dig through the rubble from the rockslides, only to discover that the bridge is gone and the tunnel collapsed. That will take them months to repair."

"They'll send in troops to slaughter us!" Giovanni warned.

"Not necessarily. My cousin, Gimenici, works that rail line out of Brennero, right on the Austrian border. He says there are rockslides all the time up there, often caused by little earthquakes. What we need to do is to spread the word throughout the region that there was a massive earthquake up there. There are a few farmers' huts on the hillside, a couple of other structures, too. Perhaps we can't blow them up -- that would be too obvious -- but we could damage them the way an earthquake might, and then have the locals report a tremor."

"I've got some kin up there," Demetri interrupted. "I'm sure they would be glad to go along with that idea."

"Can you completely trust them?" Giovanni asked. "We'd be destroying their homes."

"Of course, of course!" Demetri replied. "But they hate the Germans as much as we do. I'll take them into my home, and we can rebuild theirs later."

"When do we do it?" asked Alfredo.

"Rumor has it that the Germans started supplying their North African forces through Italy early this spring. My cousin says that the Germans may put troops along the line to guard it, and he has already seen an increase in their trains coming south, so it is likely that those shipments will continue. I think we can be ready within a few days. Next Thursday is Ascension Day. Nothing will be open. So the night before would be best. It would be Friday before word gets around what happened."

"It better work," Giovanni responded in a pessimistic voice.

* * *

Ceobobo Monastery
May 1, 1941, 5 a.m.

As Father Giulio Garmani lifted his head, a searing pain shot through his left shoulder, causing him to let out a loud curse. Slowly reality began to return to him; he felt remorse over the curse and silently prayed for forgiveness. He could not lean on his left arm, so he rolled to his right side and tried to sit up. There was dust, and dirt and bits of wood and brick all around him. In his mind the priest pictured Job sitting in the ashes amidst all his troubles.

Although it was dark, there was a slight glow to the east. No sound could be heard. Giulio started to rub his left shoulder. It was not broken, not even dislocated, as far as he could tell. Apparently he had just been lying on it at an odd angle, and the muscle had convulsed into a hard mass. As he rubbed it the pain decreased and he was finally able to move it. He was very thirsty, but strangely not hungry.

As Giulio sat rubbing his shoulder and exploring the other wounds on his body with his fingers, the sky continued to lighten. Within an hour there was enough light to see around the immediate area. He could recognize nothing. He thought he knew where he was -- the monastery high above the Gojab River -- but this scene that was unfolding before him was unreal, unfamiliar, unnatural. There was nothing except some smashed and burned out army vehicles, with little piles of rubble all around. Where the chapel had stood now there was only a bit of mud brick wall and piles of debris. A stench of decaying flesh arose from it, and as Giulio listened he could hear the hum of thousands of flies, buzzing above the smashed building.

Slowly Giulio tried to stand up. New pains shot through him, and his right leg almost collapsed under him. A long split piece of wood lay next to where he had been, and he picked it up, using it as a cane to help steady himself. Each step was agony, and he had to stifle the curse words that started to spring from his mouth. "Need to pray," he kept repeating to himself. "Need to pray."

By the time he had shuffled over to where the chapel had stood, the sharp pain in his leg was diminishing. It, too, had been a cramped muscle or twisted nerve. Where the entrance to the chapel had been there were only traces of the foundation. A few yards away he saw the bell that had hung at the entrance. Now there was sufficient morning sunlight to make out the shapes and sizes of matter within the piled-up debris.

Some of the shapes were solid, stone, wood, mud brick. Some were soft, cloth and body parts. There were few bodies that were intact, and they were horribly mutilated. A smashed torso here, a crushed head there, each was barely recognizable as a former human being. Most of the cloth was the woolen robes of the monks, but here and there the green-gray uniform of an Italian soldier could be distinguished in the faint light.

Then Giulio began to cough. What he spit up was a combination of dirt and phlegm, and he realized his desperate need for moisture. The well, he thought. The well was near the huts. He turned to where the monks' huts had been, and started toward them, finally spotting the rounded stone opening to the well. The bucket that was attached to a rope was damaged, but not entirely broken. He lowered it into the well, perhaps twenty feet until he heard it splash, allowed it to fill, and pulled it back to the surface. Most of the water had run out, but there was sufficient for him to drink. After re-dipping the bucket several times, he was able to get enough to quench his thirst and wash most of the grit and grime from his face and arms.

It was clear from what he had seen around the damaged monastery that not all of the Italian soldiers had been killed. There were no bodies of the soldiers, except those bits and pieces inside the chapel. The survivors obviously had collected their fallen or wounded comrades and returned to their base in Jima. Because of where the blast had blown him and the debris that covered him, they had not noticed their injured chaplain. How long he had been unconscious he did not know. It might be the next day, or a week later. It was apparent, however, that the army would be pulling out quickly and would undoubtedly not return to the scene of this massacre. The British pilots had apparently not even realized that it was a monastery and not an army base that they had attacked. Giulio calculated that he was alone, on his own, and that his survival was now up to him.

Although alone, he was not helpless. If monks had survived for more than a thousand years up on this plateau, surely he could for at least a few days. There was bound to be some food around, maybe in the battered army vehicles. There was the monks' garden, and their bread oven was still intact. He had water. His faith would give him strength. When he was able and ready, he could walk down the valley, perhaps get a ride from Jima to Dabra Mark'os, and then into Addis Ababa. He was a Swiss citizen, after all, a neutral, and wore the uniform of the Church, not the army. His passport identification, however, was back at the army base. If he could not get home with the Duke's forces, he might get to Djibouti and find passage from there.

After resting awhile and cleaning his tunic as much as possible, Giulio moved to the front of the chapel, to where the wooden altar had once stood, hoping to at least find the stone cross that had stood upon it. He would offer prayers for the dead monks and soldiers. The altar was gone, as was the cross, smashed to bits by the British bomb. But where it had stood -- clearly visible in the now bright sunlight -- was a hole.

He had observed the ancient altar many times over the past months. It was a solid structure, firmly built and heavy. The chief monk, who acted as an abbot, had told him that the altar was very ancient, from the time when the chapel was first built many hundreds of years before. Now it was clear that the altar had been built over the hole, an opening perhaps three feet wide and almost as many long. More significantly, he could see that there was some sort of crypt or cave beneath, and some sort of steps down into it.

Giulio felt in his torn tunic pocket, searching for the box of matches he used to light the candles for Mass. The box was crumbled, but the matches were still intact. Carefully he struck one, and used it to light the end of a broken piece of wood. As the flame ignited the broken stick, he knelt down and looked into the hole, but he could see nothing in its deep blackness.

After gathering a few more sticks to burn, Giulio cleared the debris away from the edge of the hole, sat down on the cleared space, and slid his legs into the hole. He felt his foot hit the steps he had seen, and slowly, carefully, lowered himself with the lighted stick into the cavern. The flame flickered, and it took a few moments for Giulio's eyes to adjust to the darkness. Slowly an object began to take shape, a large, long object. Giulio moved toward it, and then could identify it -- a large sarcophagus with carvings on it. It was a burial crypt. This must be the tomb the monks had mentioned, and perhaps they did not know where it had existed.

As the first stick began to fizzle, Giulio lit the next, which, because it was more splintered, gave a brighter light. Now he could begin to make out several more objects in the dark. One appeared to be some sort of chest or box with a lid. Holding the torch in his left hand, Giulio pulled the box toward him. It was heavy, made of wood, but it did move. Slowly he dragged it over to the steps beneath the hole where he could examine it closer. There were metal bands around it, sealing it tight.

Giulio's torch was again about to go out, and he lit another, and then returned to the sarcophagus to see what else he might find. There was lettering carved into it, but he could not make the letters out, or read the inscription. There was nothing else, just the heavy stone burial container.

Giulio set down the torch next to the steps and again examined the box. He could see that it had a lid, but was not hinged. The metal straps held on the lid. They would not budge. He would therefore have to lift the box out of the hole if he were to get inside it, so he bent over and lifted. The box was heavy, at least sixty pounds. He slowly got it to the bottom step, then to the next, and on to the top step, which was still perhaps four feet below the opening where the altar had been.

Mustering all his strength amidst the pain of his leg and shoulder he stood on the third step and lifted the box up, finally tilting it slightly and sliding it over the edge of the hole onto the floor above. He felt exhausted, and the wound on his arm had begun to bleed again. Catching his breath, he climbed to the top of the steps, and hoisted himself out of the hole.

Despite what may have been hundreds -- perhaps even thousands -- of years in the dark hole beneath the chapel, the wooden box and metal straps were in excellent condition, with no evidence of mold, rust or rot. Giulio sat on the edge of the hole for a considerable time, resting and trying to figure out what to do.

He was torn between his religious and ethical belief that relics should honored and kept sacred -- perhaps left where they were found -- and his intellectual curiosity about what might be in the box. He had no money, no resources other than himself. At some point, he might need something with which to barter his survival. Whatever was in that box might help him accomplish that. Certainly he could not carry the box out of the valley; it was too bulky and heavy. But he might carry out whatever was in it.

Slowly Giulio got up, and began to hunt for something that would help him open the box. There was nothing in the chapel, nothing on the dead soldiers' bodies inside the chapel that he could use. He went to the first burned out army vehicle, then the next, and finally, in the third, found a tire jack with a sharp edge that could be used to break the metal straps and pry open the chest. In that same vehicle he also found several blankets, dirty and greasy, but that would be warm and comforting in the cool night, he thought.

Returning to the edge of the hole after getting another drink of water, he set down the blankets and began to work at the two metal straps around the box. The metal was thick and hard to penetrate. He had worked for more than an hour before the first snapped off. Beneath it he could see how the box had been assembled. It might be easier, he reasoned, to knock the end off the box than to undue the other strap, hence he began work on the seam where the box was nailed together.

Again it took nearly an hour, but at last the side fell downward, and the interior of the box was exposed. Giulio tipped it into the light and saw that there was a package inside, wrapped in some sort of a leather container. He was just barely able to slide it out. He carefully unwrapped the leather binding, and observed a scroll on some sort of animal skin that was tightly rolled inside. The lettering on the outside was faint, and the surface so brittle that he was afraid it would crumble in his hands. He looked at it and could make out some of the letters, but could not decipher them. The document, whatever it was, was not written in either Hebrew or Greek, for Giulio knew those two languages from seminary in Rome. It also was not Latin. He did not know what it was, except that it was very old. It looked like there might even be two different languages in the writings.

The document, unlike the box in which it had been contained, was light. Carefully Giulio returned it to the leather binding, and wrapped it in one of the greasy blankets, trying not to crush or smudge it. He anticipated that the blanket would help preserve the document, as well as help him conceal it as he attempted to return home.

Hunger was beginning to strike, and Giulio's mind turned to food. In the truck with the blanket he had also found a soldier's mess kit with some rations inside. They would be dry and tasteless, but would keep him alive until he could get away from this now reeking place of death.

* * *

Southern Command Headquarters, Munich
May 6, 1941, 9:02 a.m.

Major Kurt Kahler, Transportation Officer for the German Army's Southern Command, clicked his heels and saluted, his right arm extended at full length, as he entered the office of his commanding officer, Colonel Raphael Oberman.

"Heil Hitler," the Colonel softly replied, more wiggling his elbow rather than giving a full salute in return. "Come in, Kurt," he said in clear and precise German. "Have a seat here at this table where I have this map spread out. Undoubtedly you have heard the news."

"I heard that an earthquake has closed the Brenner to all rail traffic."

"*Ja!* Earthquake! Doubtful, but what can one prove? Anyway, it could not come at a worse time. Rommel needs all the supplies he can get, and with the Italians pulling out of Ethiopia, help from that quarter is impossible. Our trains are being blocked in the tiny yards around Innsbruck, and we have to get them down to Italy as quickly as possible.

"Berlin has been in touch with Bern, and they have reached an agreement to allow us to run our trains through the Bellinzona tunnels and into Italy south of Lugano. I'm putting you in charge of that operation. It's tricky. These are all military supplies and the Swiss are neutrals, so they should not be permitting such transit. We are going to call all the shipments food and medicine. But we need to be certain that everything gets through.

"Kurt, I want you to station yourself at Lugano and watch that border to be certain that the Italian resistance doesn't detect what we're doing, and either make a political case out of it in the world press, or, worse, create another 'earthquake' to block the route. Guard the line and the border. There are spiral tunnels on that route, and avalanches are not uncommon. Hitler wants those supplies in Africa by the end of the month, and that doesn't leave us much time."

"*Ja, Herr Colonel.* I understand. My men are well trained, and capable. Will they be permitted by the Swiss to run the trains?"

"No, but they will be permitted aboard to observe. The Swiss are particular. That line runs from German speaking cantons to an Italian one. Sentiments change when one crosses the mountains. I don't think you'll have too much trouble in the North, but…."

"I understand. We leave…?"

"This afternoon. We have arranged a special train for you and your men to get them into place. They are to dress as civilians until you reach Lugano, and the train will be Swiss, not German, from Zurich south. Once there they can put on their uniforms again, but they are to be cautious. We do not want an international situation here, Kurt."

* * *

Mota Italian Air Force Base, Ethiopia
May 9, 1941, 8:12 a.m.

The army truck in which Father Garmani had found a ride pulled up to the transport plane just as the door was about to be closed. The right engine had already been revved up, and the left one was coughing to life. It was the last truck to arrive in Mota, and the last plane to leave. Within a week the Duke would surrender the remaining Italian forces to the British. Giulio was grateful for a ride back to Rome.

He hopped out of the back of the truck with three other stragglers who had been found in the mountains south of Jima, and ran to the door of the twin engine plane, quickly climbing in, an object wrapped in a blanket as his only luggage. He was thin, gaunt and tattered, hardly recognizable as a priest, but enough black cloth of his tunic remained to identify him. But the base where he had been stationed had also been bombed. He had no passport or identification other than his tunic and his own word as to who he was, or that he was a Swiss citizen.

* * *

Seminary of St. Felician of Mentana, on the Outskirts of Rome
May 11, 1941

Giulio felt a wave of nostalgia as he arose from his knees following the morning Mass at his old seminary. Father Geovanni Bacalli had said the Mass, but only a handful of seminarians were in attendance. It had taken the young Swiss priest more than a day to make his way from the air base where the plane returning from Ethiopia had landed to Rome, and he had not arrived at the seminary until well after dark the night before. Buses and trains no longer ran on the schedules with which he was familiar.

Father Bacalli put his arm around Father Garmani as he walked to the back of the chapel. "I am glad to see that you have safely returned to us," he said in Italian. "There have been many changes since you were ordained and departed with the army, Giulio, and I fear that they are not at all good. Come to my office and let us talk. I know the other professors here are anxious to see you, but they are all teaching classes this morning."

The two priests proceeded down the hallway of the seminary, the last to be operated by a medieval monastic order of knights, a cool breeze blowing through the cloistered archways. Giulio had arrived in the same torn and filthy garb he had worn fleeing Ethiopia, and the lay assistant had obtained a new cassock for him. It did not exactly fit his tall, thin frame, but would do for the present.

"Brother Juniusi said you had practically nothing with you but some sort of bundle when you arrived last night, Giulio," the old seminarian said as they reached his office and sat across his desk from each other. "Tell me what has happened."

Giulio explained about the Ceobobo Monastery, the old Ge'ez monks there, and the bombing by the British in which he was almost killed. He then told his teacher and mentor about the document he had discovered in the crypt underneath the altar of the monastery's chapel. Father Bacalli rang a bell and summonsed the lay brother, Juniusi, and asked him to get the document from the room where Giulio had spent the night, and to bring it to them. While they were waiting, Father Bacalli brought his student up-to-date on what had been happening in Rome.

"Things are bad here, Giulio," he said. "The German generals apparently view Italy as a pawn rather than a partner, and with our defeat in Abyssinia they view our army as weak and ineffective, and have pretty much taken it over. Mussolini still controls the Italian government and military, but…. What can I say? Things do not look good for any sort of lasting peace. I fear that it will not be many months before there is a general, world-wide conflict, with battles right here in Italy."

"There seem to be so few students, Father."

"Yes, only twenty now, no new students this year. The young men are all being conscripted for the army or navy. Even some of our seminarians were taken."

"What can I do to help?" the young priest asked.

"You must return to your diocese in Switzerland, Giulio. We can offer you nothing here, and as you are not an Italian citizen, we cannot even offer you any safety beyond that of any priest, which under these German officers, means very little."

"I was hoping to get the aid of Father D'Amacic in determining what this document I found in Ethiopia might be. It would have been ruined by the weather without the protection of the altar and chapel above it, and no one was left at the monastery to care for it, no one in Ethiopia to take care of it, Father. I did not know what else to do but to bring it here."

"Let us see what you have," said the old professor when the lay brother returned with the bundle. Giulio carefully unwrapped the blanket, revealing a leather pouch inside in which was contained a very brittle old manuscript scroll on what appeared to be some sort of animal hide.

"I've only opened the first corner of it, Father. There appeared to be two different types of writing, two languages. The first may be some ancient form of Ge'ez, as far as I could tell. I could not read it."

"Hmm, yes. I see what you mean. Dameon D'Amarcio may be able to tell us. His class will finish by noon."

* * *

After the noonday meal which consisted of little more than a watery soup with some vegetables in it and bread, the three priests gathered in Father Bacalli's office. Professor D'Amarcio, a balding, dark-skinned man in his mid to late thirties, often served as an advisor on ancient languages to the Vatican. He carefully examined the manuscript as Giulio stood beside them and watched.

"This first," D'Amarcio said after several minutes, "is some very old form of Abyssinian Ge'ez script. I cannot read it. I doubt there is anyone in Rome right now who could. Perhaps an Egyptologist in Cairo, but.... Maybe also someone at the University of Geneva. You might try that, Giulio. This next is definitely Aramaic, as you apparently suspected. It seems to be some sort of list of instructions, like a code of law or something. The little pieces that have broken off, unfortunately, would have given us a better idea of what it says. But I do not think we should attempt to open this here."

"Why not, Professor D'Amarcio?" the young priest inquired. "I want to leave it with you here at the seminary."

"No, no! It would not be safe here, Giulio. We hear of other seminaries that have been taken over as barracks by the Germans, and their libraries pilfered. The Germans have always had a penchant for ancient buildings and documents, and it would not be many days before this ended up in a Berlin museum of ancient artifacts, lost to Rome forever. No, you must take this to Switzerland. Your bishop there can assist you in getting it into safe hands for translation."

"You cannot translate it here?"

"To translate it requires opening it. That is a very technical process, and must be performed slowly and laboriously, with each section of the scroll being preserved under glass. This is a fairly large document. It would take an entire room of tables with glass if we were to unroll it. We don't have an available room, and we don't have access to that much glass. We don't have the time or the chemicals, or even the knowledge of how to do this correctly. It requires experts. There are one or two at the other Vatican colleges, but, no, I would not trust even them to do this without fear of it being confiscated. I suspect that what you have here, Giulio, is a very valuable thing."

"What do you think it is?" Father Bacalli asked.

"I could suspect, I could conjecture. But that is all, for there is not enough of what we can see here to be certain."

"But...?"

The priest professor put his hand to his chin, and thought before answering Father Bacalli's question. "It is Aramaic, so it was written either sometime around the first century, or earlier. As it was in a Ge'ez monastery it is probably religious. So it could be some document of the early Church, maybe a copy of a Pauline letter. But it may also be nothing more than some copy of a code of laws, rules for the monastery, or something of that sort. But whatever it is, it needs to be protected. Father Giulio, you cannot leave it in Italy. You *must* take this to Switzerland with you and present it to your bishop there."

"As you know, Giulio," Father Bacalli added, "our Order has many lay members, our Knights, who assist us with matters such as this. But this war.... They have all been conscripted for the army, except a few who are so old and feeble they can no longer function and, bless him, Brother Juniusi, who is not really bright enough to assist you. You are going to have to make your own way. You said that you had, unfortunately, lost your papers in Ethiopia. There is no way that we can get you any sort of travel documents to get you back to Switzerland. I suppose the Swiss Embassy might help, but without any documents they will turn you away at the gates. Too many Jews have been trying to get the Swiss to help them get out of Italy. No, you must do this on your own."

"The Vatican...?" Giulio asked.

"Not even the Vatican, I fear. They, too, are crowded with Jews seeking asylum. We will give you a letter, of course," he continued, "but if you are stopped at the border, I am not sure whether it will be of much help to you. These days we even are required to have special permits to obtain a train ticket. We can perhaps get you such a pass to get to Milano. But from there it will be more difficult. We have heard that the Germans are running trains through Lugano because of damage on the Brenner Pass. It will be a difficult trip, Giulio, and our prayers will be with you."

* * *

Sancta Margherita, Italy, on the South Shore of Lago Lugano
May 28, 1941, 1 p.m.

Fantastico! Giulio thought as he stood on the high cliff overlooking the deep blue waters of the northeastern arm of Lake Lugano. He was nearly home. The Swiss border was less than a kilometer south of the pretty little shoreline village below him, and in another hour he would be across, able to get a ride to his adored Tesserte. Oh, to see his mother again, to hold his younger brothers and sisters close, and to taste his mother's cooking! It would be a wonderful reunion, a glorious surprise for them.

Father Garmani had been able to get a pass for a train from *Roma* to *Milano* after waiting several days. It was packed with people and military personnel moving about Italy from one place to another. It seemed that everyone's life was being disrupted by the war. As a priest and a Swiss national his travel request was not considered to be very significant to the Italian official who authorized passages. Perhaps, if Father Garmani had a few *lira* to slip him, passage might be granted faster. But all Giulio had was the ill-fitting cassock that he had acquired at the seminary in Rome, and his precious bundle.

From Milan Giulio had gotten a ride with a fisherman from Como, and from there had been successful in obtaining another ride up the west side of Lago di Como to Argegno, where he had only then to cross the mountains to the shore of Lago di Lugano. The road was steep and dusty, but he had, one by one, reached the valley villages, obtaining a bit of food from the village priests in several, and now had only to descend from the cliff to the little lakeside village below. There he might even find a boat to take him the mile or so across the lake, but he had heard from the villagers that the Italian border patrol boats were stopping all boats on the lake to keep smugglers from taking Jews or contraband into Switzerland.

Still, there was always a chance that as a Swiss and a priest .... No, he thought. How could he prove he was a Swiss. All his papers had been lost. He had the letter from the head of his seminary in Rome, but that, he had been warned, would be useless if he was stopped. His best hope was to avoid the border guards, for if he were to be apprehended he would probably be detained in Italy, and his manuscript would be confiscated. Yet, he hoped, perhaps on these back trails there would be no border guards.

The trail down the steep cliff to the tiny village of Sancta Margherita was difficult. It was not a road, just a goat herder's path, fit, thought Giulio, for goats or sheep, but not for humans. The views, however, of the city of Lugano and the shoreline villages opposite, Gandria and Oria, were spectacular. They, too, had steep cliffs rising from the lakeshore -- and behind those cliffs lay his beloved village of Tesserte.

Sancta Margherita, consisting of only a few red-tiled houses built along the edge of the shore and an abandoned villa or two on the cliff, was virtually empty as Giulio entered. There were no men at all in the village, as far as he could tell, only an occasional old woman or very young child. One called out to him in Italian as he passed. "*Padre, Padre!* Give us your blessing!" He had stopped, and said a prayer and benediction for the tattered old woman as she knelt before him.

"Where are your men?" he had asked.

"Conscripted and sent to the war," she explained. "Even the young women have gone to work in the factories in Milan and Torino. We have little food, just some fish from the lake."

"I will see what I can do when I get home," Giulio promised. He then moved southwestward along the shoreline trail toward the Swiss border. He had not gone very far, although far enough, he thought, to have actually entered Switzerland -- there was no formal border crossing, not even a marker, at this remote place -- when he stopped to take a drink from the flask of water he had been carrying with him. He saw some uniformed men approaching from the south, along the trail, and suspected that they might be Italian soldiers. He was, after all, still officially a chaplain in the Italian Army, an officer outranking most soldiers. He moved forward to greet them.

As he approached, however, he saw that they were German, not Italian. One raised his rifle and fired above Giulio's head. Fearful, Giulio turned, and began to run in the opposite direction. He heard the soldiers shouting something that sounded like "*walt.*"

* * *

Lugano, Switzerland
May 28, 1941, 3:27 p.m.

Major Kahler looked up from his desk as one of his sergeants and two of the sergeant's men stood at the door.

"*Ja? Was ist los?*" he asked.

"Herr Major," the Sergeant replied in his low German accent. "We, ahh, we …."

"You what?"

"We have shot a saboteur!" the Sergeant blurted out.

"You've done *what?*"

"We caught him sneaking across the border toward the railroad tracks. He was dressed as a priest, and was carrying a package we thought was a bomb or explosives. We ordered him to stop, but he ran from us, and we shot him."

"You shot him! My God, Sergeant, was that your orders, to shoot priests?"

"We were to stop saboteurs from damaging the railroad. We don't know that he was a priest. He had no identification on him other than some letter, which appeared to be a forgery, from a seminary in Rome."

"But he could have been a priest?"

"I suppose. How could we know?"

"This was on the Italian side of the border?"

"It was right on the border, Herr Major. He was crossing into Swiss territory, and would not stop."

"You addressed him in Italian?"

"My Italian-speaking corporal was sick today. We ordered the man to *halt*, but he ran."

"The Italian is *fermare*. No one shouted that?"

"We did not know that word, Herr Major."

"So you shot him. In the leg, I trust?"

"No. My man missed. He is dead."

"You *killed* him? And the bomb? I suppose it blew up and destroyed all the evidence?"

"No, Herr Major. It was not a bomb. It was some sort of scroll, Jewish, I believe."

"JEWISH?!! *Gute Gott*, Sergeant. We'll have the Gestapo all over us! That's the last thing I need now, with at least a dozen trains coming through here in the next eight hours. Where is this dead priest and his scroll? Surely you didn't leave him on the border for the Swiss police to find!"

"No. We hauled him back to our truck and put him, and the scroll, in it and came directly here. We weren't sure what else to do."

"Mmm. Yes. Well, let us have a look at this 'saboteur.'"

Major Kurt Kahler arose and followed the three soldiers out to their truck. In the back was a young man with a deep scar on his forehead, dressed in the black cassock of a priest. Around his neck was a rather unusual type of metal cross on a chain. It looked a bit like a Teutonic cross, but with three letters engraved on it. The General pulled it off to look at it, and then stuck it in his pocket. A bloodstain was evident at the upper back of the garment. Next to the body was a leather satchel wrapped in a greasy blanket. Inside it was an old scroll carefully wrapped in cloth. The writing on it was unclear, but did appear to resemble Hebrew.

"If your man aimed for his leg, he is terribly in need of target practice, Sergeant. Perhaps he will find it on the Russian front, for that is where he -- and perhaps you -- are headed!"

"Herr Major!"

"Aucht, what can I say? The deed is complete. Let us make sure he has no identity." The sergeant again rifled through the clothing, finding nothing. He then looked back at the Major.

"Who knows?" the Major continued. "Perhaps he was a saboteur, or a Jewish Italian trying to get into Switzerland, God help them. Who is to say? But we must never let this be known. Tonight, Sergeant, when it is dark and the Swiss border patrol has passed, take this body -- without its black garb -- and wrap it well in chains and dispose of it in the lake at a remote place. I will take this document, whatever it is, and get rid of it. Word of this must never -- *never*, I say -- come out. You saw no one. You shot no one. You know nothing about this. Is that understood, Sergeant?"

"*Ja, Herr Major. Jawohl, Ich verstehen ... und danke.*"

The Sergeant clicked his heels and threw out his right arm in the traditional Nazi salute, but the Major, who was career army and not political, did not respond. Rather, he grabbed the leather satchel, nodded glumly at his sergeant, and returned to his office to consider what to do about the scroll.

* * *

Locarno, Switzerland
May 30, 1941, 10:35 a.m.

Major Kurt Kahler was sitting in a soft leather chair at a desk in the Locarno branch of the Banca Lepontin di Locarno. He was dressed in the civilian clothes he had worn while traveling from Munich, and had taken the train to Locarno from Lugano. In his lap he held a large padlocked metal ammunition box, which he had painted white.

In his broken Italian he explained, "It may be a number of years before I can reclaim this artifact, but several friends have told me that you have a very good safe here, and would take good care of my property."

"I can assure you, Signore Kahler," replied the rather plump bank manager, "that our bank is very safe. For three hundred years we have been in business. Undoubtedly in three hundred years your treasure will still be here, safe and sound, if you do not claim it in the meantime."

"And the cost, for an unlimited time?"

"Eh, let us consider. For a year, a few score francs. Two years, perhaps double. But an indefinite time? Let us say the price of five years, paid up front, with the interest to accumulate to pay for any additional years needed. Should you reclaim your property before the end of five years, you would be entitled to all the collected interest, but not the deposit amount.

"We have done this same long-term arrangement for a few of our other customers, whose situations, they being Jewish, you understand, is, shall we say, *uncertain*. But I detect that you are not Jewish...."

"Of course not! I'm a Lutheran!"

"Certainly! Certainly, Signore! Here in Switzerland it makes no difference. Yet, one cannot be too careful. These are difficult times, no?"

The Major grunted, but did not reply. He was unsure of what the banker might do or say if he had known that he was dealing with a German officer. Instead he set the metal box on the desk and withdrew his wallet, counting out twenty-franc bills until the bank manager indicated that he had received enough.

"This box will fit inside your safe? It will not be opened?" he asked.

"It will fit very well, Signore Kahler. No one will touch it. Rest assured that your artifact is in safe and tender hands. Now, then, we need to draw up the documents, and you can be on your way."

An hour later Major Kahler awaited the southbound train at the station in Bellinzona, the junction between the Locarno branch and the Zurich to Milan mainline that ran through Lugano. He felt relieved that the scroll, probably some Jewish artifact, was safely locked up in a Swiss bank and not in his possession either in Lugano, or back in Munich, where he hoped to be within the month. The Gestapo could become very nosey about such matters.

Surely repairs on the Brenner Pass damage would soon be completed, he thought. He also hoped that a similar *earthquake* would not strike at any of the narrow passes around Chiasso, where the Swiss rail lines entered Italy. The most vulnerable place for such sabotage would be the railroad causeway across Lake Lugano at Bissone, and that is where he had deployed his troops. No, that line would be secure while he was there. Afterward....

But what would be afterwards? More war, more trains to the south and the north and the east and the west. More troop movements, more war material being shipped. If the Swiss remained neutral he might never see this place again. Still, it was a beautiful place, and he would miss it.

Chapter 2

"President Kennedy again expressed hope for a thaw in relations with East Germany in his press conference this morning," the announcer said on the noon news over the radio. "Ambassador Llewellyn Thompson met yesterday with Russian Ambassador Andre Gromyko in Moscow, seeking to end the stalemate over access to Berlin that is being denied by the East German government. West German Chancellor Conrad Adenauer said earlier today that his Christian Democratic Union party would do all it could to prevent an outbreak of hostilities over the border situation. At issue is the political standing of West Berlin, which NATO considers to be a part of West Germany. East German border guards have tightened the few remaining crossings within Berlin, and reports that the guards have fired on those attempting to cross the border illegally are becoming more frequent. In other news …."

* * *

Hayes Hall Basement, Fremont College, Ohio
April 18, 1962, 1:42 p.m.

Sally White Merriam, the department secretary, looked up as two tall men in dark business suits entered the offices of the Religions Department of Fremont College, located in the basement of Hayes Hall on the Fremont College campus. Her emerald green eyes met the brown ones of the taller of the two visitors.

"Good afternoon," he said, holding his dark felt hat and a briefcase in one hand. "I am George McCracken. You may recall I made an appointment yesterday to meet with Professor Fairchild."

"Yes, good afternoon, Mr. McCracken. Dr. Fairchild is expecting you. He seemed rather excited about your visit."

"We are old friends," the tall, dark-haired man replied. He was somewhat prematurely gray, but wore no glasses. He appeared to be slightly older than Richard Fairchild, who was now in his mid-fifties. His companion, who was a bit younger and rather blond, stood silently and said nothing.

Sally arose and went to the closed door of Fairchild's office, and knocked once. Her long, blond hair curled around her face, and she shook her head to swing it back into place. "Dr. Fairchild, your visitors are here. A Mr. McCracken and a companion."

"Well, send them in!" came the resonant voice from the other side, and Sally opened the door and ushered the two men inside.

"George! How are you?" Fairchild asked, rising from his chair behind a desk piled high with papers, and extending his hand. The portly professor, who tended to become a bit rotund each winter and then lose weight each summer, still bore his winter fatness, giving a jolly expression to his round, bespectacled face and bright eyes.

"Richie, it's good to see you. I hear great things about you, and the College. A great international studies program going, I understand."

"Yes, it was a brainstorming combination of the Religions Department, Dr. Simon's Geology and Geography Department -- he's our office partner here in the basement -- a few business and political science courses, and the Languages Department. Mark my word, George, some day we're all going to have to understand the intricacies of the different religions if we are to avoid more disastrous wars."

"You're probably right, Richie. We certainly learned enough about anti-Semitism in Europe during the War. Ahh, well. Oh, do you mind if we shut your door?"

"No, go ahead," the professor replied, sitting down again and nodding toward the two chairs in front of his desk. McCracken quietly shut the door, not that conversations from Fairchild's office could be heard in the outer office. The room could become stuffy with more than one person inside it.

"Richie, I want you to meet Mark Ahearn, a Central Intelligence Agency specialist on East Germany. I believe you know I stayed in the Intelligence Service after the War, and was there when Truman created the CIA." The second man nodded to Fairchild, who returned the nod. "We are here on official CIA business and to request your assistance, but we need to keep it very confidential."

"Oh, I don't know how I could help you, George. I've been out of the service for more than fifteen years now, and, remember, I was only a chaplain, not actually an intelligence officer."

"Richie, you were the best intelligence officer in the unit, even if you weren't 'official.' The CIA lost a great operative when you left to become a university professor. Besides, I understand you've made a local name for yourself as a bit of a detective."

"Pah! Just a bit of nonsense solved by nosey digging. You guys taught me how to do that."

"The way we heard it, you trapped a former Nazi spy and single-handedly broke up a terrorist ring."

"Press embellishment, I assure you," Fairchild replied. "The things were obvious. I simply got the balls rolling in the right directions."

"Be that as it may, we really do need your help."

"The CIA needs *my* help? Whatever for?"

"Mark, perhaps you can explain," McCracken said, looking toward the younger man sitting beside him.

Ahearn opened his briefcase and pulled out a folder. Inside it was a photograph of Richard Fairchild, several pieces of correspondence and a typed, stapled report. "Dr. Fairchild," Ahearn began, clearing his throat, "all of this must be kept extremely confidential. You do not have any sort of security clearance at present, but that is currently being arranged. Until then, we must hold you to a pledge of silence and nobody must know we were here.

"We are aware that each summer you take a group of students on a foreign tour as part of your religion program," he continued. "This year you applied to the State Department and to the East German Embassy take students into East Germany, and that you have already received special permission from both *State* and the Democratic -- ha! -- the East German government to visit Wittenberg, Luther's university, and some of the other East German Reformation places, as well as Leipzig and other locations associated with Bach. We understand that they have arranged for you and your students to stay at hotels in Erfurt and Wittenberg, and that you will be traveling primarily by train on your tour. Your group is to go from Frankfurt to Erfurt, and then on to Wittenberg and Leipzig by train. You've been scheduled to cross the frontier at Bebra and return to West Germany by the same route."

"You are very familiar with our plans, I see."

"Any travel behind the Iron Curtain attracts our attention, especially since you will be meeting with professors -- and maybe students -- from East German universities. I understand you will also have along some of your own faculty."

"Well, yes, just my assistant professor, Bob Merriam, and his wife, whom you met earlier. She assists in arranging the travel."

"And very efficiently, too. Or were the letters in *Deutsche* your work?"

"No, Dr. Merriam's. He is fairly fluent in German."

"I see. That is good news."

"The CIA does not want us to go? With this Berlin dispute...."

"On the contrary, Richard," McCracken replied. "We are delighted that you have arranged this tour. We'd love to send an operative with you, but believe that would be too easily detected. Rather, we need you to help us accomplish something, ahh, difficult."

Fairchild said nothing, but leaned back in his chair, his elbows resting on the chair arms, and placed his fingertips together, his eyes moving from one man to the other.

Opening the file, Ahearn pulled out a sheet of paper with some notes on it. "Dr. Fairchild," he began, "I should not be telling you this until we secure your agreement to help us, but George says that you probably would not agree to do anything until you know everything that it involves." The professor still did not reply nor even nod, but simply allowed his eyes to meet with Ahearn's.

"We have been contacted by someone in East Germany who we believe could be very important to us. This person wants to defect. We need your help in getting this person -- I'm not at liberty to tell you his or her name -- out of Germany. However, I can assure you that the person is very vital to the interests of the West."

"Hunh!" Fairchild grunted. "What, dress whoever it is up as one of our students?"

"No, it will not be *that* difficult, I can assure you. Besides, that would put you and your students at risk. We couldn't guarantee anyone any protection if this person were to be caught illegally leaving the country."

"Do you have a plan?"

"We cannot really place one in action until we know whether you would be willing to help us. If you are, then we have several possible scenarios in mind. The one we think is best involves a slight change in your itinerary, but it is one which would probably enhance your trip."

"Is the college board to know about this?" Fairchild asked, keeping in mind the possible reaction of Dean Harding if he heard that the professor was going to smuggle spies out of foreign countries using Fremont students as a cover. The Dean had already expressed considerable concern over the trip behind the Iron Curtain.

"Good God, no!" George McCracken responded. "That's the last thing we'd want. We know that your dean has given you trouble over some of your activities in the past. We *need* you; we don't want to get you fired!"

"But you cannot guarantee our safety?" Fairchild asked, although it sounded more like a statement than a question.

"Obviously there is risk any time any group goes into a Communist country, Dr. Fairchild," Ahearn answered. "Frankly, we do not believe that what we have in mind, if it works, will in any way increase that risk beyond normal risks of travel for your students."

"If it works ...," the professor repeated. "And if it doesn't?"

"If it doesn't, it is this person who will be in danger, not your students."

Dr. Fairchild sat silently for a few seconds, staring at his desk. Then he looked up and said, "I don't know, George. I'm going to have to think about this a bit. I'd have to hear the entire plan first, to see what is involved. I'm not sure, ethically, that I can risk putting either Fremont's students or the other faculty member and our families in any danger, or into a potential adverse political situation that might bring discredit on the college. I'm sure you understand.

"At the same time," he continued, "if there is no real danger, from what you say, this could be a very important matter that I would have to consider carefully. I could not possibly give you an answer, yes or no, without knowing the plan and having time to consider it."

"Obviously, we can't give you anything in writing about our plan," Ahearn replied, "but we can give you a bit of an outline of it. You may even have some suggestions of your own."

"Well, it's too warm in here. And I have a three o'clock class to teach. Gentlemen, let me call Esther -- she's my wife, George. You may recall meeting her that time we were up in Washington -- and see if we can rustle up some dinner out at the farm tonight for you two. Then we can spend the evening going over this plan you have, and I'll have something to consider. Okay?"

"You don't leave us much choice, Richard." McCracken answered. "Yes, I guess that is fair. But remember, no one is to know about our visit or what this is about."

"What about my assistant, Bob Merriam? He and his wife will be on the trip, and she's doing the travel arrangements."

"Not even them, Professor Fairchild," Ahearn replied. "You will be the only one to know. You can't even tell your wife who you are inviting home for dinner."

"Just tell her it's a couple of old Army buddies, Richard," McCracken added. "Now, how do we get to your place?"

* * *

It was about a week later when Dr. Fairchild called Sally and Bob Merriam into his office. He had taken a large map of Germany and tacked it to the wall, marking on it in green and red. The green showed the original route of the planned summer seminar in East Germany. The red showed a new route, southward from Leipzig, passing back into West Germany at Gutenfürst, and then jogging southward toward Nürnberg.

"I have some good news about our trip to Germany in June," Fairchild announced. "I didn't want to say anything about it earlier as I was unsure if it would be possible, but as it turns out, it is, hence our tour will be better than we expected.

"Bob," he continued, "you may recall that some of the students who signed up for this trip because of the Bach portion of it also sing in our chapel choir."

"Yes, at least three of them. Sally does, too. Two are music majors."

"Three, actually. Another had dropped out of the choir this year, but still likes to sing. And I spoke with Ross Johnson, the choir master, and he is going to get at least three more of the music majors who sing to join the tour."

"Why?" the tall, light-haired associate professor, Fairchild's assistant, asked.

"Look here on the map, Bob. It involves just a small detour through Nürnberg back to Frankfurt. That detour takes us through Bayreuth, where Wägner's Opera House is located. It just so happens that the Royal Dutch Opera Company is doing a special performance of Wägner's *Rienzi* on June 25, two days after we leave Wittenberg. Our choristers have been invited to join the chorus, which is always quite large in that particular opera."

"We're going to sing in an opera?" Sally sounded incredulous. "I've never heard of *Rienzi*. Are we to be in costumes, and act?"

"I doubt you'll be doing much acting, but, yes, you will be in costumes, and will have to memorize your music."

"What about those of us who don't sing?" Bob asked.

"Oh, there will be plenty for us to do, I assure you. Handling the costumes alone will be quite a chore. Of course, the opera house staff does all the stage work and lighting, but we will be responsible for our own singers and several different costume changes. It will be a lot of work. You might want to consider singing lessons!"

"Not me!" Bob laughed. "I'm not that fond of opera."

"What is *Rienzi* about, Dr. Fairchild?" Sally asked.

"I understand it was one of Wägner's earliest operas, and is quite long, around five hours or more. It is based on the life of Cola di Rienzo, supposedly the last Roman centurion, who lived in the twelfth century. He was some sort of papal notary at the time the papacy moved back to Rome from Avignon. He became a Roman senator, and tried to unite all of Italy into one state, but was murdered for his effort. In one report, he was said to be extremely fat -- 300 pounds or more -- but I suppose in the opera he will be some slim handsome tenor.

"The opera isn't performed often as some of the music from it was very popular in Nazi Germany. Exactly why the Dutch are doing it, I'm not sure, but I understand that another chorus from East Germany is also going to participate, so it will be quite an international event. I spoke with Dean Harding about it, and he agrees that it will be good public relations for the college, especially for our music department.

"Sally, the music, just the chorus part, is being shipped from Rotterdam later this week. There will be fifteen copies, one for Ross -- who is going on the tour with us -- one each for his choristers, one for you, Sally, if you will agree to sing, and one extra for Esther, who is about excited as anyone could be about joining the chorus. Bob, you will need to go through the music and indicate any pronunciations that might be difficult for our non-German-speaking singers. Think you could fit that into your schedule?"

"I can try," he replied.

"Good enough. Sally, you will need to contact the travel agent who is doing the trip, and advise of the changes. Here is the new schedule," Richie said, handing Sally a folded sheet of paper, "and the names of hotels in both Bayreuth and Nürnberg. We'll have to skip the three days we had planned for the Rhine River Valley in order to get the same return flight. She will have to make additional reservations for the four new people joining us. I've written down their names on that sheet, too, and they are in the process or ordering passports. We only have two months, but I think there is adequate time."

"This says 'Bay-rooth'," Sally said, looking at the sheet. "How is it pronounced?"

"Bye-royt," Bob replied. "Yes, I see why some word description will be needed."

"Mmm, yes. We do have our hands full." He hesitated a moment, and then added, "Sally, Ross said he would hold his first rehearsal Thursday night after the regular choir practice, providing the music has arrived by then. Can you attend that?"

"Sure. Bob can start working on the language explanations while we practice."

"Good. Esther will be there, too, so things should move along quickly. Thank you both for not getting upset by these last minute changes."

Chapter 3

As if there was not enough on the schedule, with the spring semester coming to a close in May and all the final exams, term papers and other matters to do, the Merriams were burdened with the added responsibility of practically translating hours of finely printed German script into readable pronunciations and planning costumes to fit a variety of scenes. In some of the sections only the men would be involved, in others just the women, and still others both. It would be quite a challenge to get it all accomplished before the June 15 departure for Germany. Commencement was scheduled for June 8; two of the returning choristers would be graduates by then.

Both took the additional work in stride, however, knowing that whatever their boss, Professor Fairchild, came up with would be very worthwhile. It was usually late in the evening before Bob and Sally got home to their one bedroom apartment in Sandusky, often stopping at the grocery store to pick up some items that Sally could quickly convert to dinner while Bob set the table and got the mail.

* * *

Hdq. *Grenztruppe der Nationalen Volksarmee*, Erfurt, East Germany
May 1, 1962

Although it was a national holiday, Major General Kurt Kahler, now a senior officer in the East German Army responsible for Border Troop operations on the Western front from Magdeburg to the border with Czechoslovakia, sat in his office headquarters in Erfurt. He was studying a large volume on his desk. It was the score of *Rienzi*.

Kahler hated singing. Although as a child he had been brought up in the strict Lutheran church of his home in Wirtz and had sung all of the hymns, he had no natural talent in music and preferred to be a listener. Nevertheless, he had worked hard to prepare something in his deep bass voice for the audition to the Army chorus. He had received orders to accompany the chorus to Bayreuth, across the border in West German territory, at the end of June. Border command anticipated defectors might use the chorus as cover, and Kahler was to prevent that by getting to know all the members of the chorus. To do that he had been forced to endure performing in the chorus's winter concert, a series of patriotic praises to communism and familiar folksongs. Walter Ulbricht, Communist ruler of the *Deutsche Demokratische Republick,* had attended. His stern face, more than sixty years of age now, remained unchanged by the performance.

There were melodies within the Wägnerian opera that pleased the General. They reminded him of military marches and songs of his youth when he had first joined the German Army. It was in the early 1930s, before Hitler had taken power, before Nazism and the war. In 1933 Ulbricht had seen what was coming and had gone to Russia.

Kahler had been trapped on the Eastern Front in 1945, by then a Colonel in the Transportation Corps, moving men and materiel back from the debacle in Russia and Poland to defend the Fatherland. Once, and only once, had he been involved in the rerouting of a Gestapo train to one of their infamous Eastern concentration camps. He had seen first-hand what the Nazis were doing there; it had sickened him.

He had been assigned to a railway center south of Berlin near bombed-out Dresden at the end of the war, and had remained in the army of the new eastern nation that had fallen under the control of the Soviets. He had been fortunate that Helga, his wife since 1935, had been staying with cousins near the Polish border when Germany fell to the Allies. She and Johann, their nine-year-old son, were at least in the same vicinity at the end of the war. They had eventually found each other. As he had been non-political during the war, the new Communist rulers had been quick to accept Colonel Kahler into the new East German Army. He was assigned to Erfurt and the Border Troops, primarily to guard any shipments that might move from East to West or West to East. But his role was also to prevent those in East Germany from crossing to the West. More than once his troops had fired at civilians attempting to cross the frontier.

Helga had joined him in Erfurt, and they had acquired a small house on the edge of town. His rank conveyed privilege, but that privilege did not include private education for Johann. The boy had seen little of his father during the war. After scarcely more than a year together with both is parents, Johann had to be enrolled in a state military school where he was properly groomed to become a staunch Communist. At age 19 he had entered the East German Naval Academy and was now a Captain. As Johann knew that his father was only outwardly loyal to the Communist Party, secretly disliking Ulbricht and all the Party stood for, Johann refused to have much to do with his father. In Johann's mind, his father might as well have been one of those capitalistic Westerners.

When Helga had died of cancer in 1959, Johann had returned for his mother's funeral. He had displayed little emotion at the graveside ceremony, and become angry when Kurt had mentioned a faith in God. "There is no God!" the young naval officer had yelled at his father. "The Fatherland is our god! It is the might of our military that will protect us, not some fairytale about deities and demons." He then performed an abrupt military about-face, clicked his heels, and marched from the cemetery to his waiting vehicle. Kurt had only seen him once since, at a military affair in Berlin. His son had introduced him to his companion, a very attractive professor of something or other at Halle University. The Major General had kept track of his son's successes in the Navy. Those successes, he realized, had probably benefited him as well, and he remained very proud that his son was advancing in the Navy.

General Kahler again looked at the score, envisioning what the scenes would look like on the mammoth stage at Bayreuth. He had seen that stage once when he was young, although he had not been much of an opera fan. As he spoke Italian, however, several of his fellow officers had enticed him to attend a Verdi opera there in 1939. He had thought it a bunch of silly nonsense. *Rienzi* struck him as much the same, a lot of words without much of a story.

His assignment for June included accompanying a group of American students who would be joining some of the East German Army chorus for the journey to Bayreuth to sing in the opera. He'd decided that it would be easier to join that chorus than to simply sit around all day while they rehearsed. Whether the opera was silly or not, he was memorizing the chorus parts and preparing for the presentation by the Dutch opera company. He was, after all, in charge of the American students' transportation into and out of East Germany, and for keeping track of them. He had assigned his Lieutenant to that task. Studying for the opera made time pass more quickly for Kahler.

Outside his office he could hear some of his fellow officers preparing for the May Day holiday. Several had already started drinking brandy, and Kahler anticipated that by the end of the evening there would be more than one who would require rescuing from a beerhall or wine cellar.

* * *

Sally Merriam had been working almost hourly with the Cleveland travel agent rearranging the plans to include the additional students who would be accompanying the tour group to East Germany. It was necessary for each to have special visas with entry and exit permits to cross the border, and several of the students had not yet received their passports from the State Department. Sally was in a near panic one mid-May afternoon as Bob locked the office and the two headed home to their Sandusky garden apartment.

"I'll never get those visas in time for the trip," she complained as they left the campus and headed northeast toward Sandusky in Bob's battered old Oldsmobile. "The State Department is just sitting on those last four passport applications, and the East German embassy has had the visa applications for three weeks now. Myrtle, at the travel agency, says that is not unusual, and not to worry, but...."

"She should know," her husband replied. "If she says not to worry, why are you worrying?"

"I'm worrying because of both you and Richie."

"Me? Why me?"

"Well, you were both in the Army, and Richie was in the Intelligence branch during the War. If the East Germans know that, they might hold up on your visas – and nobody else could go if you two don't."

"Oh, Pooh!" Bob laughed, using Sally's own familiar expression. "I seriously doubt that the East Germans have any record of who was in the American army during the War, or what they did. Perhaps if he had been a spy...."

"But he was a spy, wasn't he?"

"No! He was a chaplain assigned to an intelligence unit and served as a translator since he knew German. He interrogated German prisoners, but simply as a translator. Then he was taken prisoner, just before the Battle of the Bulge. While he was being held captive he learned that the Germans were very short of fuel, and then he managed to escape and report that information to the Americans. But he was not really a spy," Bob explained.

He could hear Sally let out a long breath. He glanced over at her and saw that there was a worried look on her face. "Why have you been so nervous lately?" he asked.

"Bob, you lunkhead!" she responded in an exasperated tone. "Can't you put two and two together? Remember that day a month ago when those two guys came to visit Richie?"

"No. What two guys?"

"Two men. They looked like government agents. Oh! That's right, you were teaching a class that afternoon."

"Two 'guys.'"

"Two guys. One Richie knew. Said it was an old Army buddy. Well, that means he was in Intelligence. Probably CIA or FBI or something now. Less than a week later Richie shows up with new maps of Germany, with our itinerary all changed around."

"But that had to do with the opera," Bob suggested. "The guy was probably a representative of the Royal Dutch Opera Company."

"Pooh!" Sally exclaimed. "He didn't look like any opera impresario to me! I think we're into something, but I don't know what."

"Well, sure, we're 'into something.' We're going behind the Iron Curtain into a very hostile country. We'll be far safer with the new plan than the older one. So, if they were government 'agents,' as you call 'em, they probably wanted only to add some protection for us."

By this time they were on the outskirts of Sandusky and Bob had to stop for traffic. "Besides," he added, "cultural and academic exchanges are taking place all the time. They're not all espionage affairs."

"I certainly hope not," Sally replied. "But with Richard Fairchild, who knows?"

* * *

The past year had been considerably duller for the residents around the Lakeview Garden Apartments. After their wedding the previous June, Max, their upstairs neighbor, and his bride, Margie Billings O'Berry, Sally's best friend, had moved to the Old Canal Inn in Lockhaven that Margie operated. Max had purchased land in the Cuyahoga Valley for a ski resort, resigning from his coaching job at a Sandusky high school to develop it.

Karen and Matt August, Bob and Sally's other friends, still lived across the court at the apartment complex, but they had spent their spring looking for a house in town. Karen was pregnant and they expected their baby in July, while the Merriams would be in Europe. They all still got together on weekend evenings, but Bob and Sally's own work at the college took up many other evenings.

Sally had been pestering Bob about also getting a house. They occasionally stopped to see new model homes or visited one that was marked "open" on a Sunday afternoon after the chapel service. Bob was not yet quite ready to take on the additional responsibility of a mortgage, however. He still had some of the money left from a book advance on an academic work he had published, but sales had not been as good as he had hoped for the history text. Any new royalties were charged against the advance. He wanted to have more money for a larger down-payment than what currently resided in their joint account before considering a house. They had also talked a bit about a family when they learned that Karen was going to have a baby, but both agreed that they needed to have a house and a bigger bank account before taking such a major step.

* * *

297 *Rue de Berne,* Genéve, Switzerland
May 5, 1962

"But this is not a Hebrew text, Maurice," Moshe Gelbstein, a small man with thick wire-rimmed glasses and a bald head, was explaining in French to another man, also short, but heavy and dark. Both were in their early sixties. Moshe wore a small woolen yarmulke atop his head. They stood at a counter in Gelbstein's small shop north of the main business section of Geneva, near the *Gare de Cornavin.* "I'm not sure what it is, but it is of little value to me. Perhaps some old Persian account book? Who knows?"

"You don't want it?" Maurice Ceveneau asked in a pained tone. "I thought you liked to deal in documents like this."

"Oy, I do, if they are marketable. But this? It's old, but it's junk."

"*Somebody* must have thought it was valuable."

"Who?" the Jewish antiquities dealer asked, knowing that Maurice did not know. "Where did you get this, anyway?"

"Now, now, Moshe, you know I can't reveal my sources. Let us just say that a bank was clearing out a lot of old stuff that they had acquired from depositors who had not come to claim their property. They do that after twenty years, you know. They can't keep things forever, can they?"

"Enhh, so you think this belonged to some old Jew who met his end in one of Hitler's camps? Perhaps there could be Jewish blood on this thing, courtesy of the Nazis. But then, what would a Jew be doing with this junk anyway? It's not in Hebrew. It's definitely not *Torah*."

"So you don't want it?"

"Oh, I suppose I could take it off your hands. Maybe I can find some old Persian or Arab who might be interested in buying it, but as far as I'm concerned, its trash."

"How much? I gave ninety francs for it."

"Ninety francs!" Moshe laughed, shaking his head and frowning. "Maurice, you were robbed!"

"I need a hundred and twenty. Moshe, you know you can sell it for twice that."

"In ten, twelve years, maybe. I should live so long? I'm an old man now, Maurice. My son, he's gone from the university to be a lawyer. He's not going to want all this junk in here. No. I'll give you eighty for it."

"Eighty? No, Moshe. I've got to get more than eighty. Say a hundred and five."

"It's not worth a hundred, even if I could sell it. Oh, Maurice, you paid too much! Ninety-five. That's it."

"Moshe, Moshe, we've known each other for so many years. I always bring you good things to sell. This too, I'll bet, is good. I've got to get more than five francs for my trouble."

"*C'est bien!* One hundred francs. *Oui?* I should go broke for what I am doing, Maurice. This will cost me dearly." Maurice smiled and the old Jewish antiquities dealer knew the bargain had been struck. Moshe turned toward his desk, opened a drawer, and withdrew a checkbook and ledger. He suspected that his friend, Maurice, had paid far less than he alleged for the document, but both knew how the game was played and he could not afford to alienate one of his better suppliers by rejecting the deal.

Carefully he wrote out the check, then made an entry in the ledger book. "Twenty years the owner left it, Maurice. In twenty years I'll be dead, and this thing, whatever it is, will still be on my shelf. You have no mercy!"

"Moshe, we both know you will unload it on one of those museum pals of yours within a week. What kind of a story are you going to put on it? Found it in Hong Kong? A friend in Berlin?"

"It's not Hebrew, but it's probably Mideast. We shall think of some good story for such a piece of junk, to see if someone will consider it. But if you think it is so valuable, Maurice, you can always have it back, as long as I have it, for the same price I now pay."

"So good of you, Moshe!" Maurice laughed, folding the check and placing it in his coat pocket. "Now, what about the other pieces I left with you last week, those valuable jeweled things?"

"That trash! Oy, Maurice. What can I say? Yes, some were Jewish pieces, but they won't sell here. Perhaps a South American dealer, or Far East? I might consider a piece or two, though."

Maurice smiled again, knowing that Moshe would buy enough of the jeweled pieces he had left with him the previous week to make his trip to Geneva successful. By late afternoon the transactions were complete, and Maurice was walking back toward the main railway station.

Shortly after Maurice Ceveneau left his shop Moshe Gelbstein picked up his telephone and placed a call to a number in Brussels. He leaned back in his chair behind his desk as the operator put the international call through for him. He took deep breaths to try to overcome his excitement.

"Alloh?" a voice on the line replied.

"Professor Gilles?" Moshe inquired.

"*Oui!*"

"Moshe Gelbstein, in Geneva, Professor. You may recall that we have provided you with some very good documents over the years."

"Documents, *qui*, very good ... *non!* Old does not necessarily mean good, *Monsieur Gelbstein*. Interesting, perhaps. Why do you call?"

"I have acquired a scroll. The seller thought it was in Hebrew, but it was not. I suspect it is Aramaic, but I cannot be certain. If it is, perhaps it has some historic value?"

"*Peut-être, Monsieur,* perhaps. How did you come upon this, ahh, scroll?"

"From another antiquities dealer, who did not know its value. He indicated that he had acquired it from a gentleman who thought it originated in the Mideast. From Persia, I believe. Or Syria."

"Syria would be more likely, if it is Aramaic. That was a Palestinian language. But we would have to have the credentials of its origin for us to consider it here at the *Institut des Arts et Métieres*. Only when we can verify the history of an object can it be presented to the *Musée D'Art Ancien*."

"*Qui*, Professor Gilles, this is not a problem. I will obtain the authentication of its source from the seller within a few days. Could you spare me a few moments next Tuesday, if I were to bring it to the Institute?"

"Certainly. Fourteen hundred hour, perhaps?"

"There is a connecting train in Paris, but it would be later, say fifteen thirty?"

"*Qui*, that would be fine. I will send a car to the station for you."

"*Merci*, Professor! That would be wonderful. Until Tuesday, then."

"*Au revoir, Monsieur* Gelbstein."

"*Au revoir.*" As Moshe Gelbstein replaced the telephone in its cradle, a smile crossed his face. Perhaps Damascus, or Amman, might be an appropriate place of origin for the scroll he had received. Some old fortress in the hills, perhaps. Moshe knew that fifteen years earlier Bedouin shepherds had uncovered some ancient scrolls from caves near Wadi Qumrân that had proven to be of great value. He must think of some source other than caves and shepherds. Periodically documents showed up in ancient Ge'ez monasteries, but he was too cautious to try that angle. Some fresh, new source for a Palestinian document must be created.

As he thought of a story he could use to sell the Professor on the authenticity of the scroll, the idea of telling him the truth -- that it was a document placed in a Swiss bank by a Jew who had then disappeared into a Nazi concentration camp -- began to form. It was logical, it was probable, and it left the Institute no way of trapping Moshe in untruthfulness. Many European Jews had possessed all sorts of ancient documents before the war, and this could easily have been one held in some Polish, German or Austrian -- maybe even Italian -- Jewish family for hundreds of years. Yes, he decided, this was indeed the truth, and the story Moshe would tell the professor the following week.

Chapter 4

"You're going to Paris and Brussels?" Miriam Gelbstein repeated when Moshe told her of his purchase. "This is *good* news. I have had a letter from my sister, Esther, in Paris, and she asks that we visit. You have wanted to visit Jacob for months. Such an opportunity!"

Moshe was, indeed, fond of his brother-in-law. They had been history students together at Sorbonne, part of the University of Paris, in the 1920s, wonderful days after World War I when art and music were greatly appreciated and business was profitable. It was Jacob Wiesenthal who had fallen in love with Esther Rubin, and Esther who had introduced Moshe to Miriam. Even in her mid-fifties Miriam was still a very attractive woman, thin and tall, with light brown hair. She wore glasses only for reading, and always, thanks to Moshe's generosity, dressed well. She and her sister were often taken for twins, as they looked very much alike. The Wiesenthals were always great fun. Jacob still worked for the Bureau of Antiquities in Paris. Yes, Moshe thought, visiting the Wiesenthals was an excellent idea.

"Send Jacob a telegram," Moshe replied. "Ha! He'll never suspect it is coming from me! 'You're too cheap to call on the telephone or send a cable,' he always says. We can take some of that smoked fish we bought, Miriam, and didn't you just bake some challah bread?"

"*Oui*, and some fresh butter I just got from Bern. This will be fun, Moshe!"

* * *

Moshe dearly loved his wife, and though they did not travel often, both were fond of visiting Paris where they had spent their younger years. They had been among the lucky few who immigrated to Switzerland in the early 1930s. When it appeared that Hitler would move his Blitzkrieg into France they had invited the Wiesenthals to their Geneva home. They had successfully sat out the horrible years that followed, doing what they could to rescue Jews across the French-Swiss border. Having a properly licensed and established antiquities dealership, Moshe was able to obtain travel visas for many of the Jewish students he and Jacob knew who had been trapped in France by the German invasion.

For those who were not overly Semitic in appearance Moshe was able to get a friendly Catholic priest, Father Damon D'Farra, to issue backdated baptismal certificates in common French names, and with the help of two friends in the passport office in Basel, many were able to return to France as Catholic Swiss citizens. It was to the elderly D'Farra that Moshe had taken the ancient manuscript, when Maurice first left it with him to inspect. D'Farra said he was not sure what it was, but suspected that it might be written in Aramaic. If so, he said, it might have some real value.

After the War Jacob and Esther had returned to Paris, where Jacob, having obtained his doctorate while in Switzerland, became an official with the Bureau of Antiquities, specializing in Mideastern archaeology. He had been in Persia in the late 1920s, and Moshe had joined him in a return visit in 1955, when they had together collected a vast number of artifacts and documents. Those that Jacob had not wanted for the French museums Moshe had been able to market to his long list of customers throughout Europe.

At 0730 that Saturday morning Moshe and Miriam entered a first-class coach of the through-train from Geneva to Paris via Lausanne and Vallorbe, the border crossing, arriving in Dijon by 1053, and *Gare de Lyon*, Paris a few minutes late, at 1335. Though Moshe watched his francs very carefully, he always rewarded himself with a first class ticket and a meal, if needed, in the train's diner. He was, after all, not a poor man as he had once been. Jacob Wiesenthal was waiting with open arms and a loud shout.

The Wiesenthal home was on the south side of Paris. Jacob, a rather fat, round-faced man with bright blue eyes and thick, snowy-white hair in his early sixties, loaded his guests and their luggage into his Peugeot sedan and pulled out of the railway station parking area into Boulevard Diderot. He then crossed the Seine at the Austerlitz Bridge, and drove southward on the Boulevard de L'Hospital. Moshe had placed the ancient scroll in a special container that was designed to protect and preserve such documents during transport. He was most anxious for Jacob to see it, but had made no mention of it in his cable.

It was not until after supper, while Esther and Miriam were in the kitchen, that he was able to tell Jacob about his purchase. He carefully opened the container and removed the scroll, placing it on the now emptied dining room table.

"One hundred francs you paid, Moshe?" Jacob repeated after being told how his friend had acquired the document. "You robbed the poor man."

"Maybe. But perhaps not. It is not in Hebrew, so most of my foreign customers would not be interested. I thought of the Institute in Brussels, and made the appointment for Tuesday, but you...."

"It's possible. Let us see what it is, first. The Bureau might be interested, but I, myself, would not have the authority to say." Jacob Wiesenthal turned to a sideboard, opened a drawer, and drew out a large magnifying glass, then bent over the corner of the scroll and examined the lettering on it.

"It appears to be written on lambskin," he said as he moved the glass over the surface of the scroll. "The ink, whatever it is, has lasted remarkably well. It appears that it must have been in a dry, but dark place. No molds or other destruction. Yes, I'd say it is definitely Aramaic, but I am unable to read it. I simply recognize the script as Aramaic."

"Is it Jewish?"

"It could be, Moshe. Many of the Jews in Palestine spoke Aramaic around the time of Roman occupation. It was a common language then. Who did you say owned it?"

"Maurice didn't say, but he made it obvious that he had obtained it from a bank where it apparently had been placed by some Jew who had disappeared in the Holocaust. He told me the bank disposed of such things if no one claimed them within twenty years. Probably some German or Austrian Jew put it in a Swiss bank, thinking it would be there after the War. It was, but he wasn't."

"Mmm. No. So tragic," Jacob agreed. "But there would be no way of finding the owner? He might tell you what it was."

"I would think that the bank would have tried to find him. But I don't even know what bank, or where. Maurice probably bought it at some auction. Wouldn't a bank have some obligation...?"

"Bankers are obligated to bankers, Moshe! Have you ever known a banker who gave a damn about anything other than money? Especially a Swiss banker. Good Calvinists they all are."

"No. I see your point."

"It's *Shabbat*, Moshe, but on Monday morning I will take you and this document to the Bureau and show it to Pierre Robeleiu. He is our specialist in ancient languages and perhaps he can tell us something more about this. It is worth a try. Then, if he thinks it is of value, we can show it to the Director, and see if the Bureau might have an interest in purchasing it."

"Oy, not so fast, Jacob! I do not intend to sell it to the first one who is interested. I have an appointment Tuesday afternoon with the Institute in Brussels, and I'd want their bid before I would say yes or no to the Bureau."

"Understood, Moshe. I didn't mean to rush you. But is it obvious that what you have here is most likely something of value. Whether of great or little value is the question, and the more we can find out, the better you can negotiate."

"True. So let us do that."

* * *

Pierre Robeleiu was a man about thirty-five, rather short and Mediterranean in appearance, with bushy black hair and black-rimmed glasses. He, too, peered at the old scroll through a thick magnifying glass, deciphering the ancient lettering.

"Definitely Aramaic, Jacob, except for that bit of scribble at the top. I can't say what that is. It might be some sort of African language, but I'm not sure." he said. "The rest of it appears to be some sort of lesson, and it sounds somewhat familiar, but I can't say what...."

"It's not just some old accounting record?" Moshe asked.

"No, no. No numbers or listings. Just instructions. 'You should do this, you should not do that,' and so on. It would take me years to translate this thing. Can you leave it with me?"

"No. I am taking it to the *Institut des Arts et Métieres* in Brussels tomorrow afternoon. Professor Gilles wishes to see it."

"Gilles?!! That old thief?" Robeleiu exclaimed. "He won't offer you a tenth of its value!"

"What do you feel it is worth?"

"Bah! In francs, who knows? But as a document of antiquity, it may well be priceless. Jacob, have you mentioned this to the Director?"

"Not yet, Pierre. We wanted your opinion first."

"I will go with you to the director. This scroll should stay in France!"

* * *

Moshe Gelbstein could hardly contain his joy as he boarded the 1140 non-stop express at *Gare Nord* for Brussels. The train would get him to his destination much earlier than he had arranged from Geneva, and he had made a telephone call to Professor Gilles to let him know of the arrival time. Gilles assured him that there would be a car to meet him.

Moshe settled into the comfortable first class coach seat, placing the special case containing the ancient scroll on the luggage rack above his head. The train was relatively crowded, and three other passengers shared the small compartment with him. One was a petite, almost feminine-appearing Frenchman in his forties, who wore a fine Italian suit, expensive shoes and a rich silk tie. He sat engrossed in some sort of novel even before the train left the station.

Sitting next to the window on either side was an American couple, obviously tourists, chattering away in English about their three days in Paris. Their luggage also occupied the racks above the seats. Moshe understood enough English to make them feel at home in the car. The conductor entered the car shortly after the train pulled out of the station, punched the tickets of each passenger, and moved to the next compartment. A few minutes later the American couple got up, asked Moshe which direction the dining car would be, and departed for it.

Esther had fixed a wonderful lunch for Moshe so that he would not have to go to the dining car. There was a small bottle of Bordeaux wine, bread she had baked that morning, spread with butter, and hunks of cheese and lamb, along with several large pickles, with some sort of almond honey tart for dessert. At noon Moshe opened the lunch parcel and slowly dined on the delicacies Esther had prepared for him. Although the Wiesenthals did not keep Kosher, they knew that Moshe and Miriam did, and Moshe knew that the meal had been prepared Kosher style. As good as it gets, Moshe thought to himself as the train sped through the station at St. Quentin, nearly 100 kilometers northeast of Paris.

About 1330 Moshe felt the need to use the car's lavatory before arrival in Brussels. The American couple had not yet returned from the dining car, and the small Frenchman in the expensive suit was still engrossed in his novel. Moshe took off his coat, placing it atop the case containing the scroll, and slid the door to the compartment open, then stepped a few compartments to the rear of the car to the lavatory, which was unoccupied. In less than three minutes he returned to the compartment. The Americans had still not returned, and the Frenchman was still reading his book.

Moshe entered the compartment and reached up for his coat. The coat was where he had placed it, but the container with the scroll was missing. He looked at the Frenchman and around the compartment, but the container was nowhere. Panicked, he shouted at the petite man, "Where's my container?"

"What?" the man replied.

"My container. It was under my coat. Who took it? I was only gone for a minute."

"I don't know. I was reading. You went out, someone came in and went out again. I paid no attention. I'm not your guard, Jew," he replied, returning his attention to his book.

Moshe ran out into the corridor, and went to each of the other compartments in the car, carefully looking at each luggage rack and other places where something as large as the scroll's container might be. In each car the occupants looked at Moshe with as much suspicion as he appeared to have himself, but nowhere was the container. Moshe's car was the second last on the train, and he ran back to the last car, and again examined each compartment carefully. The container was not in any of them. He checked the luggage rack at the ends of the cars. Nothing. He moved forward into the car ahead of his.

As he entered it, he met the American couple, returning from the diner. They recognized that Moshe was very agitated. "What's wrong?" the wife asked.

"Someone took my container. Did you pass anyone with a round, metal container about sixty centimeters long?"

"Centimeters?" the husband answered.

"Ahh, what, twenty, twenty-four inches?"

"Oh, no, we didn't see anybody."

As they passed, Moshe again raced from compartment to compartment, but saw nothing on the racks, and saw no one who had something that might hold the container. In the next car he encountered the train's conductor.

"I've been robbed!" he exclaimed.

"What?"

"Someone took my container from my compartment, the second car from the end."

"Who?"

"How the hell would I know? A thief! Stop the train!"

"We cann*ot* stop the train. We'll be in Brussels in a few minutes. The customs agent is aboard. Come with me and I will tell him of your loss, and perhaps he can help."

* * *

The Belgian customs agent reluctantly agreed to help Moshe Gelbstein report his theft to the authorities in Brussels. Moshe had ran back to his compartment for his coat, and then back to where the customs agent was stopping with each passenger to check their papers. Moshe hoped that by staying close to the customs agent, he might spot someone with his case.

All the passengers had been cleared by the time the train pulled into *Gare Midi*. Moshe quickly jumped off the train from the last car and stood watching each of the other passengers as they passed by him on their way into the terminal. Several had similar looking bundles, but none were exactly the same as his. He saw nothing that looked like it might have been his manuscript container. He saw no one familiar. At last the conductor and the customs agent left the train and Moshe joined them and walked into the terminal, where the agent led him to the police office.

"*Qui?*" a uniformed officer inquired.

Moshe quickly explained that there had been a theft, and that his manuscript was missing. The policeman extracted a form from his desk and began to fill it out. Name. Address, Business. Description of stolen item? All the details. Value of item?

"Value?" Moshe repeated slowly. "Who knows? Millions of francs, perhaps?"

"Millions?" the policeman questioned, looking up at Moshe. "How much did it cost you?"

"One hundred francs. But it...."

One hundred francs," the officer said, writing the figure on the report.

"It was worth much more -- a historic document!'

"A document?" the officer frowned, looking up. "If it was historic, what were you doing with it? Why was it being taken out of France?"

"I'm an antiquities dealer," Moshe explained. "I deal in such documents. It was to be inspected by Professor Gilles of the *Institut des Arts et Métieres*. It might have been considered for the *Musée D'Art Ancien*."

"Hmm, I see. But you said it was only worth one hundred francs."

"That's what I *paid* for it. It was worth much more!" Moshe responded in exasperation. Did this policeman not understand business? "It was an antiquity."

"And it came from Switzerland?"

"That is where I purchased it."

"Hmm. It wasn't stolen property, was it?"

"No, no! It had been in a Swiss bank for twenty years, but was not claimed by its owner. It was sold at auction."

"As it was on an international train," the office said, after a moment's pause, "it will be reported to Interpol. I'm sure they will keep their eye out for it."

"*Merci*," Moshe said.

As he turned he saw Professor Pierre Gilles standing in the police office doorway behind him.

"What has happened, *Monsieur Gelbstein*?" he inquired.

"The document was stolen from me on the train," Moshe explained. "I went to the restroom, and when I came back, it was gone. It was Aramaic. Paris confirmed that."

"But who would steal an Aramaic manuscript?" the professor inquired. "Who knew you had it, and that you were bringing it to Brussels?"

"Only my brother-in-law, Jącob Wiesenthal, who is employed at the Bureau of Antiquities in Paris."

"I know Wiesenthal," Gilles said. "He would not steal your document. But perhaps someone else who knew...."

"There was no one else. Just a language expert at the Bureau, who confirmed it was Aramaic. Oh, and the Director of the Bureau."

"So, it is a matter now for the police, and you have nothing to show me."

"Nothing, I fear. I will take the next train back to Paris. I am sorry to have inconvenienced you, Professor."

"If you recover it, *Monsieur Gelbstein*, let me know. I might still be interested."

With that Gilles turned and disappeared into the crowds in the railway terminal. A smile crossed his face. Perhaps, he thought, if this manuscript or scroll or whatever it was Gelbstein had really was valuable, he might obtain it cheaper through the black market than in a legitimate deal. Such was always possible, and he had an idea of where he might start inquiries.

* * *

"You were correct, my friend," Hans Schäfer said softly into the telephone. "It was indeed easy to get the document away from the Jew. I have it back at my shop now. How long do you think we must wait before we start to market it? Six months, a year? I think we should wait at least a year."

"A year?" blasted the other man. "I will not wait a year. You should make your first contacts right away. A week at most."

"But the old Jew reported it to the police. They will be watching for such an item to go on sale.'

"Bah! What are the police going to do? Nothing! You said he had no idea what it was, so how could they know what to lock for? Certainly it is not the only Aramaic manuscript in Europe. Common sense says he can't identify it without the leather case he was carrying it in "

"Perhaps. Yes, you may be right," Schäfer agreed. "We shall see. Just keep it safe for now."

"What do you think it is?"

"I have only a vague suspicion. The problem is that it is so fragile that if we open it to examine it further, it will deteriorate badly, and so will our profit. Better to let whichever museum purchases it open the scroll in their laboratories where it can be preserved. If I am right, however, there could be great value to it."

Chapter 5

Chapel Rehearsal Hall, Fremont College, Ohio
May 10, 1962

"Who is doing that warbling?" Dr. Ross Johnson, the college choir master yelled as he waved his arm for silence. "We can't have vibrato in the women's choruses. Keep your tone steady. Now, you second sopranos, you are to split on the first nine measures of the Chorus of the *Friedensboten*. Work it out among yourselves which of you will take the high or low notes. Let's start again, '*Ihr Römer, hört die Kunde des holden Friedens an!*' Römer -- not 'Roamer' ... Roeh-mer, heàart, not hooort. Com'on, folks, we've got less than a week to get this polished up." Johnson nodded to the accompanist on the piano, and the group of women again began the chorus, unaccompanied after the piano's introduction.

Everyone involved in the European tour was in a near state of frenzy. Instructions had arrived from Holland as to the type of costumes the students should prepare, and the travel agent called Sally Merriam to advise that all the visas had arrived. Nevertheless the students still had final exams, and the seniors would be graduating only a few days before the tour began.

In his office Richard Fairchild was reviewing the new itinerary he had approved with George McCracken. The Fremont group would enter East Germany on a train from Frankfurt, after visiting Worms and Heidelberg upon arrival in Europe. Their next stay would be in Erfurt, where Martin Luther had obtained his education. They would later return for a day to Eisenach, where Luther had first gone to school and Bach had been born. At Erfurt an East German officer would join their tour, traveling with them by train to Leipzig. A woman history professor would escort them to Wittenberg. Also in Erfurt they would practice with members of the East German Southern Command chorus, and cross back into West Germany at Hof, where they would transfer to buses for Bayreuth.

Dr. Fairchild suspected that it would be one of the East German officers joining them at Erfurt who might be the defector. His instructions were to have no political conversations with any of the military people who would be accompanying them on part of their trip, beyond what would be needed for the travel arrangements, and to act as nonchalant as possible with all of the East Germans. Several East German Army officers would be in the chorus. A high-ranking officer, probably higher up in the East

German intelligence service, McCracken thought, would probably travel with them to Bayreuth. None of the communications from the CIA agent had in any way hinted at who the defector might be, or even if it was a man or a woman.

* * *

University of Halle, DDR (East Germany)
May 12, 1962

Professor Hilda Von Werdau, director of Nuclear Physics at the University of Halle, was having lunch with her friend, Professor Maria Fergen, who taught history. Dr. Fergen was telling her about a group of American students who would be visiting Erfurt and Wittenberg. Since the early nineteenth century Wittenberg's university had been a part of the University of Halle. "They are interested in seeing all of the places where Luther taught and wrote some of his theology, but as we no longer have a theology department, I was appointed to be the instructor for this group. Fortunately, I speak enough English that this will not be difficult."

"What kind of an American university group is it?" Von Werdau inquired.

"The group contains both religious history students and, I understand, a number of music students who will be visiting Bach's home in Leipzig. Then they are going to join some Dutch opera company and perform *Rienzi* in Bayreuth before they return home to America. Actually, I am very excited about it, for the group's leader is a professor who is quite well known in the academic world for his treatise on monastic republics in France, which I read as a student."

"And they are singing in *Rienzi*? When"

"Toward the end of June. I heard that our Army's chorus will also sing in it."

"And this Army chorus will cross into West Germany?"

"So I understand."

"This is most interesting.... I like to sing. Perhaps I could join them. Maria, I wonder, when you take these Americans to Wittenberg, might I accompany you? I am fluent in English, you know, and I would like to meet this American professor. What is his name?"

"Fairchild. Richard Fairchild," the history professor answered. "There will be another young professor with him, and their university choral professor. But certainly. I would be happy to have you join us."

Their lunch finished, the two women professors arose from the table in the university dining hall and returned to their classrooms for the afternoon sessions. Hilda Von Werdau had a few minutes before the students would arrive in the room. She sat down at her desk, and her eyes wandered around the room, finally fixing on the trees outside the window which were now in full bloom.

Then, removing a key from her pocket, she unlocked the lower right hand drawer of her desk and withdrew a large envelope that had been addressed to her. It was marked *CCCP* at the top, indicating its origin in Soviet Russia. She had reviewed the material inside several times, but had yet to respond, beyond acknowledging receipt of the contents. Inside were a number of drawings and designs for a new type of nuclear engine for submarine use. Her review and suggestions were requested, as she was considered one of the top nuclear energy theorists in the Warsaw Pact. There was also an invitation for her to visit aboard the K-14, a Russian nuclear submarine that would be visiting the East German port of Warnamünde on June 18. Yes, she decided. She would accept that invitation and take along her camera. This might well enhance the plan that she had been making for several months.

* * *

Office of the Director, *Pergamonmuseum,* East Berlin
May 13, 1962

"My dearest friend Ezor," the letter Ezor Farnisch, Director of Ancient Antiquities for the *Pergamon* museum, had received began. "How nice to receive your invitation to visit sometime this summer. I do hope to accept and come to Berlin before next autumn.

"By coincidence," the letter continued, "a document is coming into our hands here that might be of some interest to you, and if so, perhaps a quick visit might be possible. It is a scroll on some type of animal hide, very fragile -- it has not been fully opened -- but appears to be in Aramaic. It has not yet been placed on the open market, but we are going to sound out some of our better customers in private communication to determine if they might be interested in reviewing, and perhaps purchasing, such a document.

"Although its exact origin is not known, it is believed to have belonged to a Swiss citizen sometime before the war, and was preserved by the Swiss until it became available for release to the public. I would like to bring it to Berlin for your review if you would be interested, but its present owner will not permit it. He is hopeful, however that you can meet with other possible customers to inspect it. It can be inspected at my shop, but will be sold on 3 July to the highest bidder. Please let me know. Claude."

Director Farnisch thought for a few moments, then called his secretary into his office. "Adelle, I want to send a reply to this letter I received today. Something simple and short. His address is on the letter," he said, handing her the letter. "Dear Claude, as you know we have a large Aramaic collection here, and I would be most interested in seeing whatever this document is that has been located, hopefully prior to public sale. If I can see my way clear to leave Berlin early next week I will let you know. I hope that you can come to Berlin sometime this summer. You are welcome to stay at my apartment here in Berlin if you wish. Our hotels, as you know, are excellent, but in the summer, perhaps a bit warm.... Make the usual closing, and I'll sign it. Thank you, Adelle." The secretary completed the notes she had taken in dictation, and arose from a chair to return to her typewriter.

* * *

Office of the Director, Antiquities Museum Library
Columbus, Ohio
May 22, 1962

Paul Sukhey re-read the letter he had just received from France, from someone he had met only twice before, Claude Immour. Sukhey knew the man to be somewhat of a shady dealer in antiquities, but the merchandise Immour handled was generally authentic and of great value. He was being invited to Immour's shop in Lyon to inspect and bid on a fairly large document which Immour believed to be written in Aramaic.

Sukhey was interested. The Library, frequented by students of ancient languages from some of the nearby universities, had several Aramaic texts, but nothing of any great significance. But there was no way he could attend. His wife, Martha, was scheduled for surgery in two weeks, and her recovery would take a minimum of six, during which she would need his help and constant attention. He anticipated being able to get to the office only a few times a week, and going to France to inspect a document -- based on as little information as Immour had provided -- was out of the question. Nor was there anyone on his staff who would be qualified to inspect a document possibly written in Aramaic.

Who could he trust? There was a professor of ancient languages at the Wesleyan University in Delaware, but he had indicated he was going to be traveling in the Mideast all summer. Dr. Raymous at Ohio State would be qualified, but he was getting married in June and would be on his honeymoon. He had told Sukhey that they were going to the Caribbean. There was one other possibility. He picked up the phone and asked the museum operator to get him a number in Fremont.

"Paul, good to hear from you," Richard Fairchild said when Sukhey identified himself as the caller. "How are you and Martha?"

"That's partly why I'm calling, Richie. Martha is going to have some major surgery in June, and will be a couple of months recuperating."

"Oh, I'm sorry to hear that."

"But why I'm calling is that I have been invited to inspect a document in France that will be sold in July, July 3, to be precise, to the highest bidder. Because of Martha's surgery I'm not going to be able to inspect the document, but the Library here might be interested in it. I know you usually spend part of the summer in Europe, and I was wondering if you could possibly get to Lyon sometime before July 3 and take a look at this document for us, and let us know if it is worth sending someone from the library to bid on it."

"What is the document?"

"I don't know, but it is supposed to be something in Aramaic. The man that is offering it is a bit of a sleazy character, but our experience has been that he only deals in very high-class goods. His customer list includes the British Museum, the Hermitage in Leningrad, and other museums and libraries all over Europe. God knows where he might have gotten the thing -- stolen somewhere along the line most likely -- but as far as I know nobody has ever pinned anything on Immour...."

"Is that his name?"

"Yes. Claude Immour. He has an antiquities shop in Lyon. A lot of the things he had unloaded in the past were probably Jewish property confiscated during the War."

"Is that all he's told you, that it is an Aramaic document?"

"Yes, so far."

"Hmm. Paul," Fairchild continued after a moment, "Esther and I are going to be in Europe in June, actually in East Germany. But perhaps at the end of our trip we might take a couple of days and go over to Lyon and take a look at this document for you. Could you let the dealer know?"

"Sure. When do you think it would be?"

"I can't say for sure at the moment. Toward the end of June or early July at the latest, but I'll give you time to get someone over here if I think the thing is worth bidding on. Has he given you a price range?"

"No. He never does. I doubt he had any idea what the thing is worth, and it may well be worth nothing. On the other hand, our universities here in Ohio are always looking for new documents to have their students work on, and this might serve that purpose even if it is valueless to us otherwise."

"Give me the name of the shop and the address in Lyon," Fairchild asked, writing it down as Sukhey gave it. This would give him a chance to get away from the students after the trip, he thought, and spend an extra week in Europe. With two other faculty members on the trip, he would not be needed for the return journey anyway. When he hung up he called Sally Merriam into his office to advise her of his need to change his return ticket. He'd ask Esther when he got home if she also wanted to stay the extra days.

* * *

Hdq. STASI, The East German Secret Police
East Berlin
June 2, 1962

Major Klaus Gärtner leaned back in his chair as he answered the telephone. But he quickly sat up straight and reached for a pen when he heard the voice on the other end of the line. It was Colonel André Rokovitch, head of the American section of the KGB, calling from Moscow.

"André, good to hear your voice," Gärtner responded in very precise Russian. "How is the family?"

"They complain, like all families. Not enough this, not enough that, too cold, too wet.... But it has been a wet spring here in Moscow. I hate to bother you, Klaus, but our contacts in Washington and Bonn have picked up on something. Unfortunately there is not much detail, but what they hear is that there will be some sort of defection occurring this month across your border."

"*Ein Mangelfehler?*" Gärtner exclaimed in German. "You have no other details?" he asked, again switching to Russian.

"None, I fear. One of our contacts in Washington simply heard that someone at the CIA had become very interested in a Dutch opera company. When we checked with our agent in Bonn, we learned that the company was scheduled to perform in Bayreuth in June. That is all we have. It may be nothing at all, but I did wish to alert you."

"*Da!* Thank you, Colonel Rokovitch. We will indeed follow up on this."

"Oh, by the way, Klaus, you have made the proper security checks for our new nuclear submarine that will be visiting your base near Rostock?"

"Certainly! Everyone involved is cleared for the highest top secret level."

"Good, good. Well, my best to your Anna."

Klaus Gärtner already knew about the Dutch opera company. It was his office that had approved their request for singers from the East German Army Chorus, based at the Army base outside Erfurt. But he had personally checked out each member. Most were enlisted men; only a handful of officers were in the Chorus, and most of those were of a low rank. True, there might be a desire among such men to defect, but if so they were of no consequence to the East German Command, for none had any special knowledge. They were foot soldiers who were also musicians -- that, and little else. He pulled a map from his desk and examined it. Bayreuth was south of Leipzig, in the Southern Border Troops territory. That was Kahler's area. He dialed the number he knew so well.

"*Ja, Herr Major,*" Major General Kahler said when Gärtner explained what the KGB had told him. "We have anticipated this. For that very reason I have elected to join our chorus and travel with them. One of my lieutenants will be with me, and I believe we can keep our eye on the men. Why don't you plan to join us? Don't you sing tenor?"

"Me? Tenor? Surely you jest, Kurt! My only singing was as a young man, in the beerhalls."

"But this is good patriotic music, Klaus. *Rienzi* -- good Wägner. But with that proverbial fat soprano to scream the final 'Ouch!' when the tenor sings '*Irene, Auf, durch die Flammen!*' and the tower in which they are standing collapses in flames."

"It sounds horrible! You are welcome to it, Kurt. But I may take you up on your offer. Where and when do you cross the border?"

"June 25, at Gutenfürst. We have arranged for two buses to take us from Hof to Bayreuth."

"Two buses? But there are only fifteen in your chorus."

"You forget, Klaus. There will be that American university group also traveling with us. I felt it better to separate the Army chorus from the students, even though they will be rehearsing together, those students who will also be singing in the opera."

"Oh, yes," he replied. "How many Americans?"

"I understand about twenty. Three professors, two with their wives, fifteen students. My lieutenant is assisting in their arrangements."

"I personally approved their visas. You have two former American Army men in that group. Did I not send you that record?"

"You did. The one is a well-known scholar. He had been an American chaplain during the War and had been a prisoner, but escaped. The other was an infantryman in Korea. They both speak some German, I understand, but I don't think that they can gather much intelligence hanging around old ruined castles and a former university town."

"Is that where they're going?"

"Yes. I've arranged for a professor at Halle to take them to Eisenach and Wittenberg, and some of them are also going to go to Leipzig. They are interested only in Luther and Bach."

"So they say, Kurt. But be cautious. You never know about old professors."

* * *

Lufthansa Airlines Terminal, O'Hare Field, Chicago
June 14, 1962

There were twenty people in the Fremont College group milling around the ticket counter of the German national airline. Lufthansa Flight LH431, a Boeing 707 jet, did not depart until nine in the evening, and it was only a bit after five in the afternoon. They had left Cleveland Hopkins Airport on United Flight #709, a Boeing 720 jet, at four that afternoon, but with the one-hour difference, had arrived in Chicago at shortly after four Central Daylight time. They had walked between the United and the International terminals with their luggage, which was now being checked in on the group's tickets that Sally Merriam held in her hand at the counter.

The uniformed ticket counter clerk, a girl in her twenties with short cut dark hair, spoke with a slight German accent. "Und you are certain, Mrs. Merriam, that each student does have his or her passport und visa?"

"Yes, we did a roll-call, and each was required to hold it up for inspection. The travel agent said it would be best to keep all the tickets together in this booklet, but that if anyone had to return earlier for an emergency, their return ticket could be removed and used separately."

"That is correct. Vee hope that will not be necessary, of course. It appears that all is in order. You should all be at the boarding gate, it will be Departure Gate Seven, I believe, by eight o'clock. You are scheduled to arrive at Frankfurt Rhine-Main at eleven twenty tomorrow, and a Lufthansa representative is to meet you there after you clear customs und direct you to your hotel. Der vill, of course, be dinner on the flight, vith vine of choice, but your group may vish to have some coffee und a snack before the boarding is called. The plane vill be arriving here in Chicago about five-thirty, so there is plenty of time for your group to shop und look around the airport. The duty free shops are all available to you "

"Thank you. Yes, some of our students do appear a bit hungry. Maybe we'd better feed them so they won't raid the galley on the plane."

"Raid the galley? ...Oh! Very funny. No, vee vouldn't vant them raiding our galley! But vee vill feed them vell enough."

"Thank you," Sally repeated, and turned to walk back to where the group was standing. While a few of the students had traveled before, this was a first transatlantic flight for most of them, including Ross Johnson, and thus was a mysterious adventure. That they would be going behind the Iron Curtain to East Germany made it even more so.

Sally explained to Richard and Esther Fairchild what the airline clerk had told her, and Fairchild made the announcement to the group. "Gather around, folks," he called. "The flight doesn't leave until nine, but we are to be at the boarding gate by eight, so we will all meet back here at seven forty-five. In the meantime, you can wander around the shops here in the terminal, and get yourselves a snack. The airline will be serving you a dinner, but it won't be until about ten tonight, which is eleven Eastern time, so your stomach will think this is lunch even though it is supper time." A couple of the students laughed at what Fairchild meant as a joke, but most just stared at him.

"Now, don't leave the International terminal and walk around the airport. This is a big place, and it is easy to get lost. Half the people here speak little or no English, and you won't be able to find your way back if you go hiking off someplace. Students have wandered off on previous trips, and we had to leave them behind.

"Another tip. Yes, you can use the duty free shops, but remember, anything you buy in them will be delivered to you aboard the plane, and you'll have to lug it around Germany with you for two and a half weeks. Even those of you over twenty-one, don't go buying booze. It comes in one, two and five liter bottles, and I can guarantee that you won't want to lug that around the Frankfurt airport when we get there. You'll have enough to carry through customs when we get there, and I doubt the East Germans will allow you to bring alcohol into their country.

"I believe all of you were instructed to try to get some Deutschemarks before the trip, at least $60 worth. You'll have to buy your East German currency at the border. If you did not get West German currency at a bank, then visit the international exchange here in the airport and get some so you'll have it for whatever you might need in Frankfurt and later in Bayreuth and Augsburg. It's generally a little cheaper here than at the hotels, but we won't have time for you to be running to the bank once we get there.

"Okay, now, we'll see you all back right at this very spot, at ... oh, wait a minute. Have you all set your watches back an hour? Its five twenty, Central Daylight time, here. Everybody check your watch, and if you didn't turn it back already, do so now. Okay, we will be here at seven forty-five. And watch out for pick-pockets. Keep a close watch on your wallets, purses, and your passports and visas. Things like that get stolen in airports, and if you lose 'em, you are not going to be able to go with us. Everybody clear on that?"

A few in the group nodded, and the rest continued to stare blankly at the professor, as if in a daze. He'd been through it all before, too many times. While the group might be college students at least twenty years old, they were really like a bunch of immature children. Slowly they broke up in to little groups and vanished into the complex of shops beyond the ticketing area.

Ross Johnson and Bob Merriam exchanged amused expressions, and Merriam asked, "Did you really lose someone and have to leave them behind?"

"No," Richie Fairchild replied, "but we came close one time at Idlewild. That place is a maze of terminals, too, and the airline we came in on at the domestic terminal had a different international terminal. One of the women students had seen a purse or something she wanted to buy at the domestic terminal, and didn't realize that our overseas flight would leave from the international terminal. By the time we found her they were making the last call for the flight. I vowed to never again let that happen. But it's usually the guys who wander off, not the women. They think they're big-shot international travelers, hike themselves into some bar, and get involved in whatever is on television and forget to watch the time."

At eight thirty the Lufthansa gate agent called for the Fremont College group to board. They had the five rear rows of the plane, two abreast on either side, and were the first to board after the first class passengers. Esther and Richard Fairchild followed Ross Johnson, a bachelor, and the Merriams into the plane, and took seats across the aisle from Bob and Sally. The students had sorted out who would sit with whom, and a bit of shuffling around was occurring in the seats behind them.

At nine, the sun still visible in the West, the gate was closed and the Boeing jet engines roared to life. As the plane started to taxi to the runway the captain began to speak on the intercom system. "*Guten Abend.* This is Captain Volfe. Velcome aboard Lufthansa Flight 431 to Frankfurt. Our flight path tonight vill take us northeast ober Canada and Labrador, possibly as far nort as Greenland, depending on the vinds, then over Scotland and Denmark. Vee should be right on time in Frankfurt, und the veatter there is reported as good. I understand vee have students aboard who vill be singing at Bayreuth in a Wagner opera. Perhaps vee vill ask them to sing for their supper, ehh? That vould be a treat! Until den, please relax and enjoy the flight." The message was then repeated in German, and within a minute the plane was turning on the east-west runway. It quickly accelerated and took off to the west, then circled around toward the northeast, giving the passengers on the right side of the plane at the windows a view of downtown Chicago and the orange-tipped waves on Lake Michigan as the sun began to set.

Chapter 6

June 16, 1962
Frankfurt-A-M, West Germany

Although Professors Fairchild and Merriam had attempted to arrange the tour to follow the chronological events of Martin Luther's life as closely as possible, timing and location sometimes made that difficult. Events that had occurred in the City of Worms were so important to the tour that it could not be left for a "last minute" visit at the end of the tour, but needed to be included while the student group was still in West Germany. Worms was located more than eighty kilometers from Frankfurt by rail, and a change of train would have been needed at Mainz, hence the travel agent had arranged for a bus to take the group on a more direct route by way of Darmstadt and Bensheim.

The eleventh-century city was located on the west bank of the Rhine in a wine-growing region. It was in Worms (pronounced *Vôrmz*) where Luther had been summoned by the Roman Catholic Church in 1520. A Papal Bull, *Exsurge Domine*, gave the theologian professor sixty days to recant his beliefs. Luther had responded with three papers, "To the Christian Nobility," "On the Babylonian Captivity of the Church," and "The Freedom of a Christian," defending his views. He then burned both the Papal Bull and a copy of the church canon. The following April, in 1521, Luther refused to recant his writings, and was excommunicated and declared a heretic and an outlaw.

It had been a busy year for Rome. Ulrich Zwingli was busy reforming the Church in Switzerland, clergy in Wittenberg had begun serving both elements, bread and wine, in Communion, and the Pope commended Henry VIII in England for his attack on Luther's viewpoint, little suspecting that the pious Henry would rip England from Papal jurisdiction thirteen years later. The same year the Anabaptist movement was growing in Central Europe, and Suleiman I became sultan of the Ottoman Turks. It was enough to do old Pope Leo X in, and Hadrian VI assumed the papacy in the Vatican.

Many of Luther's writings affect church doctrine to the present day, Fairchild told his students. In his treatise "On the Babylonia Captivity..." Luther stated, "I must deny that there are seven sacraments, and for the present maintain that there are but three, baptism, penance, and the bread. All three have been subjected to a miserable captivity by the

Roman curia, and the Church has been robbed of all her liberty." The students had been provided copies of the various documents prior to the trip, and these were discussed as the group toured the city and some of the locations where the events had occurred some 441 years earlier.

The lecture was presented during a visit to the cathedral in Worms, where some of the activities involving Luther had occurred. It had remained an episcopal see until 1806. The cathedral had been damaged in the War when the city was bombed and then captured by the Allies, but it had been restored. After the students had seen all there was to see in the cathedral square, including a statute of Luther, they proceeded to the Rhine River docks, where a tour boat was waiting. Once aboard, the crew served the students and faculty a lunch of sausages and sauerkraut, washed down with beer, and the boat sped up the Rhine toward Mannheim, where it then branched onto the Neckar for the fifteen mile journey to Heidelberg. Although no particular place in the city had a direct connection to Luther, he had attended a conference of followers in the city in 1517, and had been warned that he might be assassinated on the way. On the contrary, he had been highly received and had dined with The Count Palatine, who personally gave him a palace tour.

Most of the students made the long climb up the hill to the castle above the city while the older members of the tour group visited the shops below. They then gathered at dinner time at the *Schwartzschiff*, a hotel under the sign of a black ship, for a meal of pork, potatoes, cabbage and more beer. The bus that had taken them to Worms then returned them to their hotel in Frankfurt.

* * *

Bebra, West German
June 18, 1962

At 0845 European time, a quarter to nine in the morning by the students' watches, the students and their faculty advisors from Fremont gathered at the Frankfurt Main Bahnhof with their luggage. Costumes for the opera had been shipped ahead, directly to Bayreuth. Deutchebahn, the German Federal Railway, had reserved seats in a coach for the group aboard the #1457 Express to Leipzig, at least as far as their destination of Erfurt, 163 miles east of Frankfurt. Erfurt would be their center of activity for the rest of the week.

At 1110 the train rolled to a stop at the small village of Bebra, sixteen kilometers north of Bad Hersfeld, a forested area a few miles west of the frontier and the border with the DDR, the Democratic German Republic -- East Germany. A couple of the male students wisecracked a bit, but fell silent as two East German border guards entered the car at the front, shouting instructions in German. "*Achtung! Achtung! Zeigen irhe Pass, Vise und Gepäck, bitte!*"

Richard Fairchild, who was seated toward the front of the car, arose and spoke quietly with the guards in German, ascertaining that they did not speak English. He then turned to the group and announced, "Folks, they want to see your passports, your visa, and your luggage. If you have it locked, go ahead and unlock it, but don't open it until they come to your seat. You were all given a list of things that you could not bring with you, and if you have any of those items, you will need to turn them over." While he spoke, there was a slight jolt to the car, but not enough to knock those who were standing off balance.

"What's happening?" one of the female students, Andrea Morgan, asked.

"They are simply changing the locomotive," Fairchild responded. "The West German locomotive is replaced by one from the East German State Railway, the Deutsche Reichsbahn, and then we continue."

At the advertised 1127 the train again moved forward, although the guards had so far visited only about half of the students. About ten minutes later the train again slowed and stopped, and the students noted that there was a high double fence and a tall guard tower, and that they were passing through some sort of gate. Armed soldiers stood with their rifles in their hands as the train slowly moved forward.

"*Achtung! Achtung!*" one of the guards again shouted. "*Photographie ist verboten!*" The students needed no translation. They had been warned.

As a guard approached each student he would click his heels and nod, asking, "*Amerikaner?*" When the student answered, he would then take the student's passport and carefully review it against a list he carried, studying the face of the student and comparing it with the passport photo. He would then examine the visa, which was stapled inside each of the passports. Two of the students were Canadian, one of whom spoke fairly good German. He was able to assist the other, as their passports were different. They did not check every piece of luggage, but did check that of both Canadians very carefully. They seemed more interested in that of the adults and older students, although when one of the young women, Judy Yeary, who spoke German, attempted to start a conversation with them, they went through every bit of the contents of her suitcase and closely examined everything in it including her fancy underwear, much to her obvious embarrassment. It hadn't occurred to her that someone who spoke their language might potentially be a spy.

The train did not stop again until almost one o'clock at Eisenach, where a dining car was added to the train right behind the coach in which the group was traveling. The students and faculty then moved to the dining car. A light lunch had been arranged and was already awaiting them.

"Sauerkraut again!" several complained. They all liked the sausages, however.

"We will get a chance to return to Eisenach tomorrow," Fairchild told the group. "This is where Luther went to school in 1498. Just think as you look outside at this fairly modern city -- this place was thriving just six years after Columbus had discovered islands in the Caribbean and the American mainland was as yet unexplored."

An hour later the train came to a stop in Erfurt and the students got off, hauling their luggage. "No wonder they call it 'lug' - age!" one student joked. "You lug it on, you lug it off, you lug it to your hotel."

"Ahh, quit complaining, yeh big lug!" another replied, obviously seeking a laugh for his pun.

A uniformed East German Army officer, about thirty years old, was waiting at the end of the train shed as the students gathered around their professors with their baggage and other cases. He approached the group and smiled.

"Dr. Ross Johnson?" he asked Bob Merriam. "Professor Fairchild?"

"I'm Dr. Johnson," the choirmaster said, stepping forward, as did Richie Fairchild.

"Ahh, *Gute!*" he said, continuing in fairly good English. "I am Lieutenant Ernst Schuster. I vill be your guide, and your assistant vith our Army Chorus. And you are?" he said looking again at Merriam.

"Dr. Robert Merriam, Assistant Professor of Religions, and this is Dr. Richard Fairchild," he said, nodding to the elder professor.

"Dr. Fairchild! So pleased. Und your frau?" He stood at attention, clicked his heels together, and bowed to Esther Fairchild. "You have quite a following here among historians, I understand, *Herr Professor*. Some of our professors in Leipzig vish to meet you. You had a pleasant journey?"

"Very much so, Lieutenant Schuster. Our students are very excited about visiting your country."

"Vee are delighted to have you. Later I vant to talk mit you, Dr. Fairchild. I have a surprise, most pleasant, I hope. But for now, I vant to take you to your hotel, vitch is just a few steps from the Bahnhof. Is dat all right mit der students, a short valk?"

"Certainly," Ross and Richie both replied.

"Come along, den." He waved to the rest of the group, who then gathered up their luggage and began to tag along behind the three professors and the army officer. He led them outside the station, and down a street, but then paused for a moment at a corner while the ones at the back caught up.

"Velcome to all of you to Erfurt. I understand that many of you are interested in Johann Bach. If you look down dah street here you vill see dah spire of the Church of St. Augustine. In it is a 39-stop organ built by Johann Stertzing und Georg Schröter. In 1716 Johann Sebastian Bach came here and played it. But it vas actually Sebastian's brother, Johann Christoph Bach, who had more contact mit this city. Ven he vas fifteen he studied here mit Pachelbel for tree years at St. Thomas Church. St. Augustine organ was altered in 1753, but ve still have many concerts in these old churches."

The hotel was nearby, and the students were assigned their rooms, generally two or four to each room, depending on the size of the room. The students were given a large key that was attached to a round wooden ball, and instructed to turn the key in at the desk anytime they left the hotel. The Fairchilds had their own room, but Ross Johnson was assigned to the same room as the Merriams, as the room had a double bed and a single bed. When Ross offered to try to get another room Sally insisted that their sharing would not be a problem, for there were no bathrooms in any of the rooms -- a separate men's and women's bath and shower were down the hall. There were a few groans and moans from the girls, but the young men on the trip quickly offered to share their bath with any of the girls who didn't want to wait for the one assigned to the women. Whether the young men had an ulterior motive in their offer, the young women were not sure.

"I can see that this is going to be a very interesting trip indeed!" Ross said to Sally and Bob. "Have you had any, ahh, incidents on prior trips?"

"If you mean co-educational room sharing," Sally replied, "obviously we don't plan that unless a couple happen to already be married, but we have had a few students who have returned from these trips get engaged and married after they get home. I wouldn't be surprised at anything that might happen."

The dinner was scheduled for six in the evening in the hotel dining room, and all the students were present when the room was opened and they were led to their tables. The dinner was served in a sort of family style, with plates and bowls of dark bread, pungent meat, steaming potatoes and spicy red cabbage that were passed along the tables.

Lieutenant Schuster was seated at a table for eight by the window, and motioned for the professors and their family to join him. There was an elderly man sitting next to him. Schuster arose, and bowed slightly as Sally and Esther sat down, with Bob and Ross next to them, while Richard Fairchild sat next to the Lieutenant.

"Dr. Fairchild," the Lieutenant said, sitting down again," our records in Berlin show that you have been in Germany a number of times before."

"Yes, that is true," Fairchild replied. "Both before and after the War...."

"And during!" the Lieutenant added.

"Yes, in fact I was once a prisoner of the German Army, but I escaped. Actually, though, that was in eastern France."

"Our records show dat you vere a chaplain, and that you vere captured by some of the 12th Panzer Division near dah Belgium border, vere you became friends mit one of the German Army chaplains. My father."

"Yes!" Fairchild exclaimed. "Adolph Schuster!" He looked at the older man who was at the table, then spoke in German, "*Herr Schuster!*"

"*Ja! Herr Doktor Fairchild, es ist Ich!*" the old man replied. "*Siebzehn Jahrn!*"

"*Wie geht es Ihnen, Adolph? Es freut mich, Sie wiederzusehen!*"

"*Mmm, es geht.*"

"*Herr Captain Heintz, wie ist er?*"

"*Acht, Karl Heintz war toten ... 1945. Sehr traurig.*"

Fairchild nodded slightly at word that the tank commander who had taken him prisoner seventeen years earlier had been killed. Then he turned to his host. "Lieutenant Schuster, what a wonderful surprise! Many long discussions your father and I had while I was a prisoner -- I learned better German from him than at the university."

"He never forgot you, either. He no longer is a pastor of a church, of course, but he still does some counseling here in Erfurt. He is going to go vith us on some of your visits to Luther's, ahh, vas is it you Americans say, 'hang-outs'? He has been trying to learn some English, but *ist nicht sehr gute!*"

"Your father seems well, but, goodness, he must be in his late sixties."

"He's seventy-three, Professor. He vas in his mid-fifties during that final year in the var. My muttur und I vere afraid ve vould never see him again, but he got back just before the Russian Army took Berlin."

"Well, Lieutenant Schuster, this is going to be a wonderful trip."

"Please, please, you must all call me Ernst."

"You and your father will be joining us for the opera?"

"My father, no. But I, *Ja!* I have been practicing my tenor lines for months. Und my commanding officer, Major General Kahler, vill also be joining us. Please, do not laugh at his singing. He is not very *gute*, but he does sing softly, so no one vill hear!"

"We'll keep that in mind, Ernst," Ross Johnson answered.

* * *

Lyon, France
June 18, 1962

Claude Immour looked up from his desk where he had been reviewing some of the responses to his auction on the third of July. Three men had entered his antiquities shop and had inquired of the clerk whether Monsieur Immour was present.

"*Oui,*" he responded, then he opened the door to the rear office and spoke to the owner, who told him to send the men in. "*Entrez, S'il vous plaît!*" he said, pointing to the open door. Two of the men entered, while the third began looking at the various items displayed on the shelves in the shop.

"Good afternoon, Monsieur Immour," the taller of the two well-dressed men said in French. The antiquities dealer acknowledged the greeting with a nod. "I am Inspector Brun. We are from the national police," the man continued. "We understand that you know a man in Paris by the name of Pierre Robeleiu."

"*Oui,*" Immour replied. "His name is not unfamiliar to me. I believe he is a specialist in ancient languages, at the Bureau of Antiquities in Paris. Yes, he has, in fact, examined several documents we have had for sale in our shop, to verify their authenticity, you understand. We do not, of course, ever trade in documents where the authenticity cannot be confirmed."

"That is quite noble of you, Monsieur. I'm sure your customers are quite pleased to know that."

"You are from the police, you say? And you ask about Robeleiu. Is there some problem?"

"Perhaps. Robeleiu may be implicated in a theft. He tells us that you have been of assistance to him in disposing of documents he has handled in the past."

"Me? I have no knowledge of stolen documents. I deal only in legitimate artifacts. What kind of documents was stolen?"

"Ancient manuscripts, perhaps."

"But I have no ancient manuscripts, nothing that Robeleiu has given me to sell. Oh, once or twice he has known of some artifacts, but he simply gives me the owners' names, and I purchased from the owners, or act on their behalf, all perfectly legal."

"We would certainly hope so, Monsieur Immour. However, we have an order from the judge allowing us to verify that for ourselves. You are free to call your barrister if you so desire."

Claude Immour frowned, but did not reply, except to ask, "What kind of a document is it that Robeleiu is alleged to have stolen?"

"We are not at liberty to say," the policeman answered. "But the theft occurred from a train in Belgium from a Swiss antiquities dealer."

"So no crime has been committed in France?"

"International crime is under jurisdiction of Interpol. Yes, we have authority."

The police detective looked at the papers on Immour's desk, picked one up, and read the response. It was from a museum in the United States, advising that a representative would be present at the July auction.

"What is this?" the detective inquired.

"Simply a confirmation regarding an auction. We hold auctions all the time. It is how we do business. Certainly there is nothing illegal...."

"What are you auctioning?"

"Oh. A number of items. Egyptian mostly, or believed to be African." Immour knew enough about the document referenced in the letter to know it had some African origin, although he knew little else about it.

"No Mid-Eastern document, a manuscript, perhaps, in an ancient language?"

"Oh, many of our artifacts have ancient languages on them. I am no scholar, however. I must rely upon scholars like Robeleiu to interpret what they are."

"No manuscripts in a leather container?"

"You are welcome to search my shop, Inspector Brun. I believe that I can assure you that I have no ancient documents here in a leather container."

The three detectives carefully went over all of the items that were on display in the shop, and then asked Immour to open his safe. They reviewed all the items in it, but found nothing resembling the item that had been described to them.

Inspector Brun then started reviewing the files in Immour's desk, starting with the one on top. "What is this?" he asked, coming to a copy of the letters sent to various museums. "Here, this one to Ezor Farnisch, Director of Ancient Antiquities for the *Pergamon* Museum in Berlin. 'By coincidence,'" the detective read from the letter, "'a document is coming into our hands here that might be of some interest to you, and if so, perhaps a quick visit might be possible. It is a scroll on some type of animal hide, very fragile -- it has not been fully opened -- but appears to be in Aramaic. It has not yet been placed on the open market, but we are going to sound out some of our better customers in private communication to determine if they might be interested in reviewing, and perhaps purchasing, such a document.

"'Although its exact origin is not known, it is believed to have belonged to a Swiss citizen sometime before the war, and was preserved by the Swiss until it became available for release to the public. I would like to bring it to Berlin for your review if you would be interested, but its present owner will not permit it. He is hopeful, however, that you can meet with other possible customers to inspect it. It can be inspected at my shop, but will be sold on 3 July to the highest bidder. Please let me know. Claude.'"

The detective looked at the antiquities dealer. "Monsieur Immour, this sounds very much like the stolen document we are seeking. Yet you say you have no knowledge of such a thing? How do you explain this letter, and where is this document now?"

"Inspector, you gave me no information about what you were seeking. Something in a leather case, you said. I have seen nothing of the sort, nor do I have this document referred to in my letter."

"Where is it?"

"Its owner has it. I am simply the broker. He will bring it on the day of the auction and the attendees will examine it."

"Who is this owner?"

"You expect me to reveal my client?"

"I do indeed, Monsieur. I think you have been lying to me."

"To the contrary, Inspector Brun! I have been very truthful to you. I have no knowledge of what you seek, nor do I have anything here that has been stolen."

"We will search your home as well."

"I anticipate that. You are welcome to search whatever you please."

"And your client's name?"

"He is not in France."

"I don't care where he is, Monsieur! Give me his name. Tell me where he is, or you can go with us to our office and tell us there."

"Inspector, I do not know the owner of the document referenced in my letter. He has an agent in Zurich, one Hans Schäfer. It is true that Schäfer was referred to me by Robeleiu, but I have no knowledge of the origin of any artifacts that Schäfer markets through my shop. I deal internationally, as you can see from these letters. My clients trust me, and my customers trust me. That is my reputation -- one of trust, Inspector. I do not own this document, if it is indeed the thing you are seeking, which I seriously doubt. I have no knowledge of how the owner acquired it, or who the owner is. Perhaps Schäfer does, but you would have to ask him."

"And so we shall, Monsieur. You will give us his address."

* * *

Warnemünde Naval Base, Near Rostock, East Germany
June 18, 1962

The direct train from Halle to Rostock departed shortly after seven that morning and arrived at half past twelve that afternoon. It had carried only coaches and a car providing light refreshments. Professor Hilda Von Werdau, director of Nuclear Physics at the University of Halle, was met at the Rostock Bahnhof by Captain Johann Kahler, Naval Attaché for the Warnemünde Naval Base. He was a tall, handsome officer in his thirties, impressive in his Navy uniform. They had lunch at the train station restaurant, and then Kahler drove his guest to the base, where she was to inspect the new Russian nuclear-powered submarine, the *K-14*, that had arrived at the base two days earlier.

Hilda, who was twenty-seven, a tall, slender blond with deep blue eyes, picked at the salad the waiter has brought to her, while her companion, who was also tall, but dark, nibbled at an unappetizing cheese sandwich.

"You have reviewed the design specifications that the Russians sent and I forwarded on to you?" he asked in clear, precise German.

"*Ja, naturlich, Johann,*" she replied, continuing, "That is what you asked me to do, to advise on the design, and offer suggestions."

"I am not sure we should trust these Russian designers to build a safe vessel. They are too much in a hurry. German engineering is much better, don't you think?" Hilda nodded agreement.

Kahler and Von Werdau had been close friends -- finally lovers as well -- since their days at the Institute of Scientific Research in Berlin a year earlier, the naval officer attached to the procurement office, and the professor as an advisor to the Navy. Kahler was more politically-minded than she, but she was more dedicated to her science. Her father had been an engineer assigned to the Luftwaffe during the War. He had been captured by the British, but had died before being able to return to Germany. Hilda's mind was one of precision, orderliness and objectives. Kahler's was one of military discipline, political position, and advancement of the Communist cause.

"*Ja,*" she explained, "our nuclear design is much better. They should have several back-up systems that are not shown on these plans. The cooling system is inadequate, and there are too few monitoring devices to warn of potential malfunctions. Their tests do not show how much internal pressure the nuclear container can accept as the ship dives to lower depths. No, they have indeed pressed forward too quickly, I fear, Johann."

"We must be careful what we say to them at the base. They have some of their higher admirals visiting. Two arrived by train through Berlin yesterday afternoon. Admiral Peghnekoff is chief of submarine warfare at the Kremlin, and the entire nuclear program is named for his superior, Admiral Rostikovitch, who is also here. Our Admiral Jensen is under quite a bit of pressure to agree to accept some of these vessels for our fleet, and will be relying on your assessment."

"Johann, you know I must be honest in what I advise," she responded. "I have my reputation. I can appreciate the political pressure on Jensen, but .... Let's see how it develops when we get there. When are we to arrive?"

"They expect us at two. It is only ten kilometers, but we will need to get started. I will put your case in my car. You will stay at my apartment?"

"So I was hoping."

"Two nights?"

"If you don't throw me out."

Kahler's black sedan approached the guard booth at the entrance to the navy base and came to a stop. The guard scrutinized Kahler's pass and his passenger, then saluted and they proceeded toward the docks where the *K-14*, flying the red flag of the Soviet Union, was tied to the dock. Kahler parked his car, and the two approached the submarine. It was about ten minutes before two. Several high-ranking officers were standing on the deck of the vessel, and another officer stood in the conning tower high above them.

Kahler saluted the Russian and German admirals, one being Admiral Helmut Schmidt, his superior officer in Procurement, and introduced Hilda. One of the Russian civilians who were standing with the officers bowed, and said, "Professor Von Werdau, what a pleasure it is to meet you. I am Dr. Ivan Smernikov, one of the designers of the power source on this submarine. Your work in nuclear physics and engine design is well-known in Leningrad and Moscow. We are indeed honored that you have consented to visit the *K-14* and give us your assessment."

"Dr, Smernikov, yes. I appreciate your sending us the design plans, which I have had an opportunity to review prior to this visit." A frown crossed the face of Admiral Jensen upon her saying this.

"We had special permission from the Kremlin to send them, and anticipated that they might be reviewed by you. Your government speaks very highly of you, Professor."

"I understand that both our navy and our nuclear energy designers have been working closely together with your naval engineers. But I did not see where you had incorporated any of our suggested modifications on the U-327 thermonuclear reactor engine design, or the monitoring system...."

"No, we considered, but.... There were alternatives, which I will demonstrate"

The group then entered a hatchway on the side of the conning tower and descended the ladder into the interior of the submarine. The vessel's commanding officer, Captain Igor Vertovinsky, gave the German officers and Hilda a tour of the ship, from the forward torpedo and missile-launching pad to the crew galley and recreation area, finally arriving at the rear part of the submarine where the nuclear engine was located. While there was a radiation-monitoring meter outside the sealed hatchway, Hilda noted that the two crewmen who were monitoring the various controls were not wearing any sort of roentgen-accumulation badges. The crew opened the sealed hatchway to the engine room, and the group entered single file, Vertovinsky followed by Smernikov, who entered ahead of Hilda, with the other officers squeezing in behind them.

"There is not much room in here, I fear," Captain Vertovinsky said, pronouncing the obvious.

"Captain," Hilda asked in an inquiring voice, "when you are diving, what is the level of pressure within the submarine?"

The Captain responded with a figure, explaining how the pressure was increased to balance the outside pressure against the shell of the vessel.

"This increases as you dive?"

"Yes."

"What affect does an increase of pressure have on the engine? Could the increased pressure at a low depth impact upon the engine's valves or systems?"

"We do not believe so," Dr. Smernikov answered for the Captain.

"Has it been tested?" Hilda continued to probe.

"Just routine diving tests," the Captain admitted. Hilda glanced toward one of the East German admirals and made an expression of concern on her face.

"Explain to me how the cooling system functions, Captain," she continued, and Vertovinsky started to move further down into the belly of the vessel where the nuclear reactor was located, pointing out various pumps and pipes as he went. Water was dripping from one of these, and the Captain appeared embarrassed by the leak.

"What is the pressure level?" Hilda inquired.

"A maximum of 200 pounds."

"What happens if the pressure exceeds that level?"

"I don't see how it could, Professor. It is constantly monitored. The pump would automatically shut down."

"But if it did, and a pipe burst, is there a back-up cooling system for the reactor?"

"Redundancy was not necessary, Professor," Dr. Smernikov replied. "Besides, a reserve system, complete with reservoir, would take too much space. As you can see, the system is very compact."

"So, there is no back-up system?"

"None is needed, Professor."

Again Hilda glanced at the German admirals, trying to read their expressions while also trying to convey her own. "And are there no backups on the monitoring system either?" she asked. "What if one might default?"

"The crew would shut down the reactor," Smernikov replied.

"What is the training of this crew?"

"They are all veteran submariners," Captain Vertovinsky replied.

"Trained in nuclear physics?"

"No, but we have been trained by Dr. Smernikov, and he is establishing a new school for our nuclear mariners at Archangel."

"I see," Hilda replied. "And the loading? How are the fuel rods loaded onto the vessel?"

The Captain pointed upward, above the top of the reactor, to a hatch. "Through there," he said.

"And then, how are the rods raised and lowered into the reactor itself?"

"Ahh, that is what that series of chains and pulleys is for, Professor Von Werdau."

"And the crew that does this task, do they wear special protective gear?"

"Yes, we have two chemical suits that are worn during the loading processes. They are available at all times."

"Two *chemical* suits? Lead lined, I trust."

"No, but they are sufficient," the Captain replied.

"May I ask your background, Captain Vertovinsky?"

"Certainly, Professor. I studied electrical engineering at Moscow University before joining the Submarine Corps. My father was also a submarine officer, in the War."

"So you are not trained in nuclear physics?"

"No, that is why we have Dr. Smernikov to instruct us, until we are proficient."

"Thank you, Captain."

"What else may we show you, Professor."

"Where are the reservoirs for the cooling system?"

The tour of the nuclear vessel continued for about another half-hour. Finally around five that afternoon the officers and the professor climbed out of the hatch onto the submarine deck, and walked over the gangway to the dock.

"What do you think of our submarine, Dr. Von Werdau?" Captain Vertovinsky inquired.

"Oh, it is a very sleek-looking vessel. I'm sure it has tremendous armament capabilities."

"And the engine?" Smernikov inquired.

"Interesting, Dr. Smernikov. I shall be happy to file my report within a few days." He did not pursue the question further. Hilda turned to Johann Kahler and continued, "I've had a long train ride today, Captain Kahler. If there is nothing further, perhaps you could take me to my hotel?"

"We were hoping you would join us for dinner," one of the German admirals said.

"That is kind. But I am tired, and...."

"Perhaps in a few days when you have prepared your report, Professor, you will join us in Berlin?"

"Yes, that would be appropriate timing. June twenty-first, perhaps?"

"Very good," replied Admiral Schmidt.

"Thank you, Gentlemen."

Once back in Kahler's black sedan Hilda shook her head back and forth. "Get me away from here!" she exclaimed. "That damned ship is dangerous!"

"It's that bad?"

"It is worse than bad. Pray it does not have a meltdown in German waters! They have rushed it to production without any safeguards at all. Their basic concept is fine, but they must have a failsafe system, which they do not come close to demonstrating. The crew is totally unfamiliar with nuclear energy, and is under constant radiation exposure. Did you note the reading on that roentometer?"

"No."

"There will be some sick sailors before very long. Don't go back in that thing, Johann."

"No, I won't." The car stopped at the gate to the naval base, and the guard lifted the barrier while saluting the Captain. They then drove back into the city of Rostock to Kahler's apartment. After dinner in a nearby restaurant, by eight that evening the two were in Kahler's bed.

Chapter 7

"It was here at the University of Erfurt where Luther began his higher education in 1501," Dr. Fairchild was explaining to the Fremont students the following morning in a small room next to the hotel dining room. Ross Johnson had grabbed a seat at the rear of the group, but was scheduled to meet with Lieutenant Schuster and an East German General at ten that morning to review the plans to practice with the Army Chorus.

Adolph Schuster, the old Lutheran and former German Amy chaplain, stood beside Fairchild, adding a few comments in German which Fairchild translated for the class. The city, he had explained, had been the episcopal see founded by Boniface in 741, and the university dated from 1378, but had been pretty much closed down in 1816.

"Luther came here to study law," Professor Fairchild said, beginning his lecture, "and earned his baccalaureate degree a year later — as fast as the rules permitted — but he did not get his master's degree until 1505, at which time he went directly to the faculty of law. Luther loved academic debate and was so good at debating that he gained a nickname, 'the Philosopher.' His father, Hans, was very proud of his son, and paid for the rest of his legal education.

"But then, in July of that same year of 1505, something happened. Luther had made a journey to his home in Mansfeld to visit his family. On the way back to Erfurt, outside the village of Stotternheim, there was a terrible storm, and Luther, only 21 years old, was nearly killed when lightning struck the ground ahead of him. He screamed out, 'Help me, St. Anne, and I will become a monk.' His father had been a miner, and St. Anne was the patron of miners.

"Today, of course, we might well say, 'Ahh, the world was saved from yet another lawyer!' Perhaps we need more monks and fewer lawyers," he paused while a couple of the students chuckled, "but in those days there were far more monks than were probably needed. Hans Luther felt his son was wasting the fine education for which he had paid, including all his textbooks -- valuable items in those days -- and his lute, at which Martin was fairly proficient. Luther elected to enter the Black Cloister of the Observant Augustinians -- over there by the Church of St. Augustine that Lieutenant Schuster pointed out to us yesterday. His father was enraged, and remained unreconciled to Martin for many years." Fairchild paused, then asked, "Of whom does this story remind you?"

"You mean, about disappointing a father?" Mary Crawford, one of the women students, asked.

"Yes."

"Francis?" Judy Yeary asked. "Didn't he reject his father's wealth and give up being a knight?"

"Absolutely! If you recall from the Medieval History class, Giovanni Bernadone had come from a wealthy Umbrian merchant's family, and was expected to carry on the family trade. When he gave away his fine armor and horse, his father was angry, but Giovanni also rejected his father's wealth before the bishop, tore off his fine garments, and stormed off in little more than a rag. You *Bible* scholars, does this make you think of any verses?"

"Ahh," Jack Hornbet, a history student in his junior year, said, holding up his hand, "do you mean the one where Jesus says that he has come to bring division between father and son, mother and daughter?"

"Precisely! Very good. He said we had to love him more than father or mother. But that is often hard to do, and in many ways one might even think that it is counter to the commandment to honor your father and mother. But in Luther's case, perhaps it was a greater honoring in the long run than had he continued in the practice of law.

"Anyway," Fairchild continued, "later that month Martin presented himself as a novice. He probably could not have picked a more difficult order to join than the Augustinians, who were strict disciplinarians, despite somewhat of a reputation for their Rule being easy. But Luther was obviously a scholar, and perhaps it was clear early in his career as a monk that he would make a great professor. If anything, Luther became an Augustinian zealot. He himself later admitted, 'I was so drunk, so submerged in the doctrines put forth by the pope that I could have killed -- or cooperated with anyone who would kill -- whoever might take but a syllable of obedience away from him.' Of whom does this remind you?"

After a moment of contemplation, Andrea Morgan blurted out, "Oh! Saul, or Paul, on his way to Damascus to harass the Christians."

"Very good, Andrea!" Fairchild replied. "As we continue we will perhaps see other similarities between Luther and Paul -- perhaps one reason that Luther's theology was so heavily influenced by Paul's writings.

"As a monk," he continued, "Luther excelled. He spent hours confessing every little peccadillo that he could think of, seeking penances of vigils, prayers, fasting and various other punishments to the point where he became somewhat of an irritation to his confessor. I can just about hear him exclaim in frustration, 'Martin, go somewhere and commit a real sin so you'll have something to confess!' Remember Liza Doolittle in *My Fair Lady*? 'I'm a good girl, I am!' Well, that was Martin. I doubt at age twenty-two if he had as much as kissed a girl, let alone done anything that the church would consider sinful. But he took every word of Scripture literally. If he had looked at a pretty girl and had a natural male reaction, he probably would have ripped out his eyeball and thrown it at her. Luther later said of his days at the monastery here, 'I kept the rule of my order so strictly that I may say that if ever a monk got to heaven by his monkery, it was I!'"

"The fact that Luther was Augustinian played a role later in his life, especially at his trial before the Dominican inquisitors. Remember, this is the same time as the Spanish Inquisition, and the Church felt that torture was a wonderful way to persuade obstinate troublemakers. There was some animosity between orders. Perhaps there still is.

"It was Spanish Franciscans who accompanied the Spanish explorers of the New World with a missionary objective. Only a few Dominicans became missionaries, although a number of Jesuits did. But in France, there was greater rivalry between the orders to win converts among the natives. Some Recóllet Fathers came to New France, and Father Louis Hennepin did do considerable missionary work with the Native Americans in the upper Mississippi Valley. French Jesuits, -- Marquette and Joliet, also explored the Upper Great Lakes and down the Mississippi, even locating the later site of Chicago. Sulpician friars, including one who had studied for the priesthood, a French nobleman named Robert Rene Cavelier, sieur de La Salle, explored the Ohio and Mississippi in 1682, and two Sulpicians explored Lakes Erie and Huron. In Germany there may have been competition in scholarship and the reputation of universities.

"Let's try to picture how Luther might have appeared as an Augustinian monk. First, they spent a considerable time in prayer and study. They wore black cowls over white robes or surplices, and their heads were shaved in a tonsorial ring. After their novitiate they were known as 'canons' rather than as monks, although in England they were also known as Austin Friars or Canons. They followed the ancient monastic rule of Augustine of Hippo, perhaps the oldest rule in the Western Church, older even than that of Benedict. Augustine, along with some friends, formed a monastery in Tagaste in North Africa. There he first established the 'hours,' sometimes referred to as the 'offices' or the seven times for daily prayer. He later added a moral and theological base to his rule.

"Here, again," Fairchild continued his lecture, "we see how religious orders both built on and challenged the rules and practices of other orders. Benedict at Montecassino in Italy built upon the Augustinian practices regarding the hours, but added the divisions of the day between work, study and worship.

"By Luther's day there were more than twenty different orders in Europe. Many Augustinian houses established hospitals, schools, leper colonies or tended to cemeteries. This was especially true in the Black Death era. Still others, such as the house here in Erfurt, supported a bishop at a cathedral and in the surrounding diocese. Actually, it is surprising that the Dominicans, who became Luther's enemy later, were as harsh as they seem to us in the light of history, for St. Dominic built his order on the Augustinian Rule.

"Augustinian houses were common throughout both England and Germany. Their role was to support a diocese with whatever objective the house undertook, hence we find most Augustinian houses in urban settings rather than the remote mountaintops selected by those orders simply seeking contemplation. That was part of the Rule of St. Augustine -- it was outward-looking, service oriented, not aimed inwardly, as were the early Desert Fathers or some later 'cloistered' orders. However, there were a handful of Augustinian houses, even in Britain, that were quite remote from civilization. Many came to possess large parcels of land that often included vineyards. An Augustinian house -- as with many monastic enterprises -- relied heavily on patrons, such as a bishop or a local ruler.

"Two years after entering the monastery Luther was ordained as a priest. He then undertook the study of academic theology, and earned a new degree in Biblical studies. In 1510 a dispute arose within the Augustinian Order in Germany that required judgment by the Pope. Two canons from each Augustinian house were dispatched to Rome, and Martin was selected as one of the two representatives from Erfurt.

"The trip to Rome was very enlightening to Luther," Fairchild continued. "Pope Julius had engaged Michelangelo to paint the ceiling of the Sistine Chapel, and in 1506 had begun other restorations on St. Peter's at the Vatican. That restoration was going to cost a lot of money, and Julius had some great fund-raising ideas. Remember, this was medieval times, with medieval thinking, where visions of flesh-eating devils and roasting sinners were being portrayed by the Church to encourage proper behavior. The dead did not go to heaven; they went to Purgatory, where their souls might linger for millennium being cleansed before being able to enter heaven. Julius, however, provided a shortcut, by selling what were called Indulgences. When a penny hit the cup, a soul was released.

"The relics of saints were held to have mystical power. Simply looking at a saint's bones might provide a cure for an illness or heal an injury." Fairchild stopped and turned to Adolph Schuster, asking in German, "Were there any substantial relics here in Erfurt?"

"I don't believe so, unless it was of Saint Boniface," the old man replied, "but Pope Leo the Tenth declared that simply looking at some of the bones of saints in Halle would reduce one's stay in Purgatory by four thousand years."

Fairchild translated what Schuster had told him, then continued, "But what better relics might one find than those in Rome? Why, it was there that the bones of Peter and Paul were buried, those of Peter right in the Vatican. This is what made a pilgrimage to Rome so vitally significant in medieval times. The Vatican is still a draw in our century.

"Luther was struggling theologically. Like all Christians of his day he felt that he was so sinful that the only way to save himself was to work his way to salvation. He was of a pessimistic nature anyway, fearing God and damnation and the fires of Hell. A trip to Rome, as an official representative of his order more than just as a pilgrimage, was exactly what he felt he needed. Why, he'd reduce his sentence in Purgatory tremendously -- and maybe even reduce the sentence for his beloved parents -- just by looking at those saintly bones of Peter."

At nine-fifteen Ross Johnson slipped out of the room, and headed for the hotel lobby where Lieutenant Ernst Schuster was waiting. An Army vehicle awaited outside, and in ten minutes they had reached the headquarters of *Grenztruppe der Nationalen Volksarmee*, the National People's Army Border Troops, which was attached to the Headquarters of the Army's Southern Command, just outside Erfurt. There he was introduced to the unit's commanding General.

"Good Morning, Dr. Johnson," Major General Kurt Kahler said in unaccented English. "I trust the hotel where you are staying is comfortable?"

"Quite sufficient, General Kahler," Johnson replied. "The arrangements that you have made for us have been excellent so far."

"I hear that your group is taking the train back to Eisenach later this morning," the General said.

"Yes, it was supposed to be tomorrow, but the professor from Halle, Dr. Fergen, wanted to spend more time in Wittenberg, and has arranged for our students to visit the Wartburg Castle today."

"We have a bus that vill meet your students at dah Bahnhof," Lieutenant Schuster said. "Dey vill all be back in Erfurt for supper, a bit late, perhaps, but...."

"When will we get to meet with your chorus?" Johnson asked.

"That will be this evening, Dr. Johnson," General Kahler said. "While several of the singers are coming from units as far away as Leipzig, most are from the base here in Erfurt, and they are anxious to meet their American counterparts. I, too, have been practicing, and will be joining Lieutenant Schuster and the other chorus members on this unusual trip to Bayreuth."

"So I heard." Johnson replied. "Your English, I am afraid, is far superior to our chorus's German. But hopefully between now and the concert on June 25 our singers will learn the correct pronunciations."

"Who knows? Ve might have as much trouble mit der Dutch!" the Lieutenant laughed. "I can't imagine a Dutch accent to dose Wägnerian verds."

"Come," Major General Kahler said. "I want you to meet Sergeant Schlafer, who directs our chorus here. There is, of course, the principal Army Chorus in Berlin, as well as a Navy Chorus, but because of our proximity to Bayreuth and the fact that most of our singers are Border Troops, we were selected to provide singers for the Dutch company. They wanted to perform in Berlin and Leipzig as well, but, unfortunately we could not arrange for that as the opera house in Leipzig is under repairs, and the current politics between the West and our Warsaw Pact countries is such that this particular cultural exchange had to be limited. Your President Kennedy's stated positions on us and the Communist world, you know, made it difficult for these cultural exchanges."

"Who was it that arranged for our choir to join your chorus?" Ross Johnson asked.

"I suggested it," Lieutenant Schuster replied. "Ven I realized dat your Dr. Richard Fairchild was dah same man who knew my father, I brought dah idea to General Kahler. And my father, he suggested Dr. Fergen as your guide."

"It was an excellent idea. The timing was such that it worked well. This East-West political thing...." The General added. "Too bad, but we need to keep up the cultural contacts, Dr. Johnson, don't you think?"

* * *

Ross Johnson was unable to meet the Fremont group at the Erfurt Bahnhof for the westbound train that departed at a quarter after eleven that morning. Dr. Maria Fergen had arrived on a direct train from Halle at ten that morning, and had accompanied the students and faculty from their hotel back to the station, explaining the plans for the afternoon trip. There would be no dining car on the train, but the railway had arranged box lunches for each of the travelers on the tour.

Dr. Fergen, who was in her early thirties, spoke fairly good English, and spent several minutes telling Dr. Fairchild about how much she had enjoyed some of his published works. She was tall, slender, and dark-haired, with deep blue eyes, but she hid them behind thick glasses and under a rather frumpish hairstyle. She told Dr. Fairchild that while his books were no longer available in any East German bookstore, there were some copies in English in the university libraries. She explained that while the University of Halle had no separate religions department, religious history was taught as part of the History Department curriculum.

As the students wolfed down their lunches, consisting of bread, a piece of sausage, some hard, but very tasty cheese, and two small tart apples each, Dr. Fergen stood at the front of the railway coach in which they were riding and began to explain what they would be seeing that afternoon. A few other passengers in the car looked on with outward expressions of annoyance, but as the attractive professor continued, a few who understood English moved forward so that they, too, could listen to the lecture.

"Perhaps we are taking the story of Martin Luther a bit out of sequence," she explained. "It was to Wittenberg in 1511 that Luther went from Erfurt, reassigned to an Augustinian house in that city, and there he was made a professor of theology. Now no university is located there. But he made some statements that brought him to the attention of the church officials, his so-called ninety-five theses, in 1517, and the following year he was summonsed to appear before Cardinal Cajetan in Augsburg to recant his beliefs.

"He refused, of course, in his famous 'here I stand' defense of his beliefs, which put him in grave danger of being sent to Papal authorities for trial. It was Prince *Frederick, der Weise* who rescued him, but two years later, in 1520, he was called before the Diet of Worms -- I understand that you visited that city while you were in Frankfurt -- by Papal Bull. He was given two months to recant or be excommunicated. His response, in 1521, was to publicly burn the Bull. Hence, he was declared to be "a notorious heretic" and immediately excommunicated from the Church, and thus was basically an outlaw to be hunted to the death.

"Again," she continued, "it was Prince Frederick who came to Luther's rescue. Luther tried to escape back to Wittenberg, but the Prince arranged to have him kidnapped along the way, just outside of Eisenach. As he and a few of his companions entered the woods, the Prince's armed horsemen attacked along the way, and forced Luther to the ground with a lot of cursing and threatening. His companions fled, although they were apparently aware of the plot, and reports that Luther had been killed began to circulate among his allies around Europe. Luther, who was not aware of what was happening, was led around the forest until late that night, when his captors arrived at the massive gates of the Wartburg.

"As you shall shortly observe, this is a tall, massive fortress with a high watch-tower. The castle has three sections, the old medieval fortress, with its green copper roof, where kings and knights had once dined and wined, and where St. Elizabeth, the Hungarian Franciscan princess, had once stayed. The second section, above which the watch-tower stands, is somewhat newer, more gothic in design, with a black slate roof. The third section is a half-timbered wing at the top of the hill.

"But it was no place of luxury in Luther's day. His room, in the upper part of the castle, was already occupied by bats and owls, and at first he interpreted their actions as those of the Devil 'rolling casks down the stairs.' It is said that he threw an inkwell at the Devil, and there is an ink stain on the wall even today. A woodcut of the time shows Luther at his desk translating the *Bible* into German, a crucifix before him, armaments on the wall in the event of an attack on the castle, a stove behind for heat, and windows with round little panes common at the time. He may also have had a cat and a dog as companions. At the castle he took on the name of Junker George to hide his identity."

The train was slowing, and having made only one stop at the small town of Gotha, arrived in Eisenach a few minutes earlier than scheduled, about an hour after leaving Erfurt. Outside a rather old and decrepit-looking bus, belching black smoke from its exhaust, stood waiting. It sagged and squeaked as the students and professors climbed aboard it, but with a loud hiss and several bangs, it managed to pull out of the lot and into the main part of the village, stopping briefly in front of an old dilapidated building where Luther had attended school in 1498. They turned another corner and Professor Fergen pointed to an old, but impressive house. "That is where Johann Sebastian Bach was born and reared," she said. "In 1685. March, I believe. I wish we could visit, but currently tourists are not allowed."

The bus then turned south down a side street and started to climb into the Thuringian Forest, following the railroad tracks that led to the border. In a few moments the castle was visible to the left. Several of the students recalled having seen the castle from the train windows while on their way into Erfurt the previous day.

* * *

The first rehearsal of the Fremont choir members who would be singing in the opera with the East German Army chorus went about as well as Ross Johnson could have hoped. Lieutenant Ernst Schuster and his General were their only English-speaking singers. Sergeant Karl Schlafer spoke only a few English words, but he was able to make himself understood with Ross Johnson's help. While Esther Fairchild was one of the Fremont singers, Richard was not, and he elected to stay at the hotel.

Some of the Fremont students were surprised at how many women were in the military chorus. It was later explained that both men and women were subject to military service in East Germany. The rehearsal began with some vocal exercises, and then the women went off to a different room in the small theater on the Army base where the rehearsal was held, to practice an á cappella section from Act Three. After half an hour they returned, and the following four-part section was practiced. A young soldier with flame red hair accompanied them on a rather tinny sounding piano.

It was after eleven that night when a rattley old bus dropped the exhausted students back at their hotel in Erfurt. When they were told that the wake-up call would be at six the next morning for their drive to Leipzig, there were many moans and groans, especially regarding the shortage of bathrooms.

* * *

Office of Naval Procurement, East Berlin
June 21, 1962, 10:05 A.M.

Dr. Hilda Von Werdau had traveled from Rostock to Berlin with Captain Johann Kahler that morning after spending the night with him, and felt refreshed as the two proceeded to Admiral Helmut Schmidt's office in Naval Headquarters. She had her freshly typed report, along with two extra copies, in her case. She expected to find a number of officers awaiting her report, but as she and Johann entered Schmidt's office, only he was present.

"*Guten Morgan, Freülein,*" he said, not referencing her degree and position. "Please have a seat," he continued in polite German, pointing to a chair. Captain Kahler took the chair opposite her. "I see you have brought your report. May I see it?"

"Certainly, Admiral Schmidt. But I fear that it is not very complimentary to our Russian friends."

The Admiral slowly paged through the report, his eyes glazing over at some of the mathematical equations and technical items, but he said nothing for several moments.

Finally he closed the report, and handed it back to her.

"No, I anticipated this, Professor Von Werdau," he said at last. "It will not do. The decision has already been made here in Berlin to acquire two of these submarines. You are to revise your report and comment favorably on their quality. I must have such a report within the week."

"But Admiral, those ships are dangerous!" she exclaimed. "They could become deathtraps for their crews, or a hazard on the sea. If even the slightest problem were to arise, they have no backup system."

"Professor, there is much more than possible safety problems involved here. This is a political, not a scientific decision. You *will* revise your report, and have it to me by the 26th of this month. Johann, I want you to see that this is accomplished."

"But there is danger...."

"Professor! Listen to me. Your report is to be favorable. It will be copied and sent to the other Warsaw Pact nations, and to the Russians." He paused for a moment, and in a less harsh tone continued, "I understand your concern. It is admirable, and you have put a lot of effort into your report. Once these vessels are in our hands we can see about modifications, and you will be welcome to advise. Until then, my orders -- your orders -- from High Command are to provide a favorable report. Is that understood, Professor Von Werdau? Completely understood?"

"*Natürlich, Herr Admiral Schmidt!*" she said softly. "I shall proceed as directed."

"Good. Johann, be so kind as to see that the Professor gets back to Halle so that she can begin reworking her report."

"*Jawohl, Herr Admiral*," Johann said, arising from his seat, clicking his heels together and saluting the senior officer, who nodded a return salute.

Back in his official vehicle Kahler looked at the pretty young woman who sat beside him, obviously upset and near tears. "I'm sorry," he said. "I should have warned you. I did not know they had already made the decision, but these things are always decided on the basis of politics. If the Russians want to sell us bad armaments, we are willing buyers. It is no longer the Krupps who provide arms for Germany."

"Our sailors could die!"

"Keep your first report secret, but don't destroy it. You will undoubtedly be called upon to recommend modifications once the submarines are delivered. Can you have your report by the twenty-sixth?"

"Of course. But I must tell you that I am singing with an Army chorus the day before. I will have to send you my report."

"I will pick it up in Halle."

"No, Johann. I need time to prepare it. I will have it dispatched direct to the Admiral."

"But...."

"Johann, just drive me back to Halle, and return to Berlin or Rostock, or wherever you are to report. I need quiet to think about this. Please."

* * *

The trip to Leipzig was considered optional for the religion students. While Luther had conducted some serious debates at the Leipzig University with Eck and others, it was on this day that Ross Johnson and the Lieutenant were leading the music students to some of the locations associated with Bach. The Fairchilds elected not to go, and planned to spend the day exploring Erfurt. Sally Merriam also decided that, although the trip would be interesting, sleep sounded even more interesting, and with Bob and Ross Johnson departing early, she would have the room to herself to do some laundry and other tasks. Bob was eager to see Leipzig, but he understood his wife's desire to rest.

After a quick continental breakfast at the hotel, coffee and hard rolls with some cheese and sausages, the two professors and eleven of the students met Lieutenant Ernst Schuster at the Bahnhof for the seven-thirty train. It was a seventy-mile journey, taking nearly two hours with stops in three cities including Weimar, where Bach had first settled in 1708 with his young wife, Maria Barbara.

There he had been under the patronage of Duke Wilhelm Ernst, Ross Johnson had explained when they had walked to the station. "Unfortunately, Maria died after Bach left Weimar to accept a post under Prince Leopold in Cöthen. He remarried in 1723, moving to Leipzig, where he pretty much lived the rest of his sixty-five years. All told, he had twenty children, but only six survived, some also becoming well-known composers."

"Good morning!" Schuster greeted them as they entered the railway station. "Ve are in for a treat today. First ve are going to the University of Leipzig, ver dah professor of organ, Jacob Wilhelm, vill show us the organ that Bach himself examined and played in 1717. He vill then accompany us to several old churches, closed now, you understand, but vith operating organs that Bach once played. Dah Thomaskirche, und also dah Nikolaikirke. Many of dese organs ver built by Johann Scheibe, and Bach often recommended improvements to the organs.

"As you must know, Bach wrote many of his chorales and cantatas in Leipzig. He moved dere in May of 1723, und lived dere pretty much permanently until he died in 1750. It vas in Leipzig vere Bach developed his own style, so different from der Italian style in vogue in dah rest of Europe at dah time."

The Lieutenant's lecture continued, "Ven Bach moved to Leipzig in 1723 he vas hired as chief musician at the Thomasschule, associated mit dah Thomaskirche. He vas to rehearse dah singers for four different churches, direct dah choirs at any weddings or funerals, conduct a cantata every Sunday, and write oratorios ven deh vere needed. Dese ver mostly boys choirs. Bach complained dat very few of dah boys vere competent singers. It vas quite a job. Dere is a story -- perhaps Dr. Wilhelm can confirm it -- dat Bach had written into his contract dat he could leave dah church during dah long sermons to get a beer. Ha! Mit all dose boys in dah choirs, he must have needed a beer!

"Now Leipzig is associated mit many utter composers, too. Wägner, who wrote dah opera ve are singing, vas born in Leipzig, und Mendelssohn gave concerts der. Dah inn, from Goethe's *Faust* is dere. Ve vill visit dah cemetery at St. John Church vere Bach is buried, und see his tomb."

The group boarded the train as it arrived in the station, but most of the students curled up and napped. Ross Johnson, Bob Merriam and the Lieutenant reviewed the travel plans for the day. It would be late that night before they could return to Erfurt.

Chapter 8

Esther and Richard Fairchild had enjoyed their quiet day in Erfurt while most of the students were in Leipzig. The following day those students, along with Esther and Sally, who would be singing in the opera spent all day on the Army base in rehearsal with the soldiers and others in the chorus. They were joined by an attractive professor of nuclear physics from Halle University, a friend of Dr. Marie Fergen. Professor Fergen had accompanied her that morning on the train from Halle, and while the singers rehearsed, she spent the day in conference with Dr. Fairchild, planning for their stay in Wittenberg. That journey, the following day, would consume much of the day as the students had to pack, depart the hotel in Erfurt, and change trains three times to get to Wittenberg. Most of the Erfurt to Halle to Berlin trains went by way of Dessau, but Wittenberg was on a different mainline to Berlin, requiring a train change at Bitterfeld. Upon arrival in the old city, the students would transfer to their new hotel.

The students had been kept so busy that there was little opportunity for them to get into any mischief. The majority of them were in their early twenties, and while the beerhall down the street from the hotel did provide an attraction for a few of them, none seemed to over-indulge. "The people all seem so grim," Bob Lassiter, who would be a senior the next year at Fremont, commented to Dr. Fairchild. "I guess we Americans always picture the German beerhalls with their oompha-bands and Alpine costumes."

"That is what you will probably see in Bavaria," Fairchild had told him. "But this is Saxony, and life in East Germany *is* somewhat grim. In Frankfurt you saw a lot of restoration from war damage. Here, there has been little done to restore the damage. It is a very poor country."

"I wonder what they do for fun around here."

"Probably darned little, I suspect. There is mandatory military training for all young people, and tests from the time a child is six to determine his or her role in life. There is no such thing as choice. Remember, these people went directly from Nazism under Hitler to Communism under Russian rule. I guess one could wave a red banner for fun. Of course, there are sports. The East Germans have some of the best athletes in the world. And everyone enjoys soccer. That is probably their idea of fun."

* * *

Zurich, Switzerland
June 22, 1962, 9:30 a.m.

"I have no idea what you are talking about, Inspector," Hans Schäfer stated in a matter-of-fact Swiss-German accented voice. Inspector Gerhardt Mann of the Zurich Police and a detective from the Swiss Government CID had arrived unannounced at Schäfer's small shop on the Zollikon Road south of the main part of the city only ten minutes earlier.

"No, Schäfer, you know *exactly* what we are talking about. The Lyon dealer, Claude Immour, says that you are the agent for the owner of this document. Now, you will please inform us as to the owner."

"Inspector, I deal in many documents, old manuscripts, and many of them in ancient languages. You seem to have very little information about whatever it is you think was stolen. How can I assist you in finding the owner if you cannot properly describe to me this manuscript? Something in a Middle Eastern or African language in a leather pouch, you say? That could describe hundreds of documents on which I have been the agent."

"There can't be that many documents that you have been assigned in the past eight or nine weeks, Herr Schäfer. Just provide us a list of those individuals, and we shall be happy to check them out ourselves."

"I cannot -- I *will* not give you my list of customers. The private affairs of my customers are as sacred as the identity of those who hold bank accounts. In fact, several banks *are* my customers. But yes," he paused, as if in thought, "I did recently obtain an account on what was described a 'valuable ancient document.' I don't know if it could be what you seek or not, but you can go ask its owner. It's the Banco d'Milano."

"The Banco.... Surely you jest, Schäfer! Why would an Italian bank acquire such an artifact?"

"Banks often come into such possession. Foreclosures, liquidations, lots of items to dispose of in estates. Look around my shop, Inspector. You will see every type of document I hold for sale. Some I own, some I don't. But to simply demand that I know everything about some mysterious scribble in a leather pouch! Inspector, use common sense. That is impossible."

"What are your plans for the third day of July, Herr Schäfer?"

"July third?"

"Yes. Check your calendar and tell me what you have scheduled for that day."

"On the third of July my wife and I will be on holiday. To the South of France."

"Hmm, to the City of Lyon, perhaps?"

"Perhaps. It is on the way."

"Perhaps to the shop of Claude Immour?"

"I am familiar with Immour. We've done business together. I suppose that is possible."

"I suppose it is," the Inspector repeated. "And I suppose that you might show up with a certain document for inspection and sale?"

Schäfer did not reply, though he shook his head indicating no.

"No matter," the policeman said. "I'm sure Inspector Brun, my French counterpart, will also be present. But we have taken enough of your time, Herr Schäfer. Somehow I anticipate that we shall meet again. Until then, I bid you *auf Wiedersehen*."

Hans Schäfer watched as the two policemen returned to their car and drove away. Then he left his shop and walked down to the corner, where a pay telephone was located in a small café. He did not trust the police, and feared that the telephone in his shop and at his home might have been tapped. He deposited some coins, and dialed a number in Bern. It was simply too unclear what the police knew.

* * *

STASI Headquarters, East Berlin
June 22, 1962, 10 a.m.

Major Klaus Gärtner answered his telephone. It was André Rokovitch, calling from the American Section, KGB, in Moscow.

"André, how are you?" the German intelligence officer asked.

"Fine, Fine, Klaus. I called to see if you have any further information on the possible defection we discussed."

"Yes. I spoke with the commanding officer of that section of border, and he advised me that his unit had already anticipated that such might occur on this cross-border cultural exchange involving the Dutch. He and one of his officers are going to personally accompany the East German personnel who will be going to Bayreuth. He invited me along, and I shall also be present. Have you heard anything further?"

"No, nothing specific. However, we have learned that one of the CIA case officers who specializes in East German intelligence…"

"Specializes in us?"

"Yes, Klaus, *of course* they have such case officers,' Rokovitch laughed. "Oh, you are joking."

"Yes. We even know some of their names. Do you have a name?"

"Yes. His name is Mark Ahearn."

"The name is known to me, but we do not have a photo."

"Anyway, this Ahearn has a commercial flight scheduled to Frankfurt and will be arriving tomorrow. If you have an agent in Frankfurt, or nearby, you might have him pick up on Ahearn. He is fairly young, tall, speaks excellent German, I understand. There may be an older man with him. We don't have a name on him, but our contact says that he believes that the older man specializes in debriefing defectors."

"Well! But no one of importance is involved in this Bayreuth opera trip. Perhaps the defection will be in some other area, and the nonsense about the Royal Dutch Opera Company is to mislead us."

"Possibly. I thought of that. But you had better not take that chance, Klaus. Are you sure none of those Army singers is important?"

"None. The General has even joined this chorus himself in order to monitor it, and he has been known to have defectors shot. I did see the name of one civilian on the list, some university professor, probably of music. I will try to get more information on her before the group departs."

"Very wise. Oh, will we see you at the meeting in Warsaw next month?"

"Yes, I am looking forward to it. I will be on the overnight train."

"Good, good. Until then, Klaus."

* * *

Wittenberg, East Germany
June 22, 1962, 10:30 a.m.

Dr. Maria Fergen led the Fremont students and their faculty members and wives up a narrow street leading from the Elbe River. "It was here," she explained, "where Philip Melanchthon had his home. A contemporary and friend -- and often intellectual challenger -- of Martin Luther, Melanchthon was a scholar and Humanist. After Luther's excommunication and return to Wittenberg, Melanchthon was among the first to agree with Luther's translation and interpretation of the theology of Paul."

Fergen had traveled from Halle with the Fremont group the previous day. Her friend and fellow-professor at Halle, Hilda von Werdau, had joined them. She had met with Ross Johnson during the rehearsals in Erfurt the day before, and had asked Dr. Fairchild if she could join the Fremont group for the trip to Bayreuth rather than have to travel with the Army singers. "I have all the proper documents," she had explained to him. "I also have clearance from the Stasi, our national police, and I informed Lieutenant Schuster that I would prefer to ride with the students. He seemed to think that would be okay, and he, too, will be with your group from Leipzig."

"I'm sure that if it is okay with Lieutenant Schuster, it will be okay with us, Dr. von Werdau. I wish Dr. Fergen was going to Bayreuth with us, too."

"She does not sing," the attractive young professor replied. "I asked her to try, but she would not. She commented that, historically, Wägner's opera is a farce."

As the Fremont group had arrived in Wittenberg, their train slowly crossing the long bridge over the Elbe, the spires and rooftops of this medieval university town had glowed in the setting sun. Their hotel was only a few blocks from the Bahnhof, and the students were now used to carrying their own luggage.

The Hotel Modern lived up to its name in some ways, at least by East German standards, and appeared to have been built since the end of the War. Russian forces had captured the city on April 27, 1945, and although it was both a rail junction and a city where machinery, textiles, paper, leather, soap and schnapps were manufactured, it had not been as heavily bombed by the Allies as Berlin and Leipzig.

The Merriams had a room to themselves, with a small bathroom, as did the Fairchilds, and there were several larger bathrooms for the students to share. Even the food in the dining room was superior to that at the Erfurt hotel, perhaps attributable to the fact that the town was important both historically and economically to East Germany. It was also a bit of a holiday town, due to its location on the river.

"Wittenberg is a bit of a 'before and after' story for Luther, to compare with what you have already seen," Professor Fergen explained. "The city had only about two thousand residents when Luther was transferred to the new Augustinian monastery here in 1511. At the time some called the city 'the gem of Thuringia,' while others referred to it as 'a stinking sand dune,' a reference to its name -- white hill -- *witten berg* and the white sandy beaches on the river. The Augustinian cloister was at the opposite end of the castle church, just a few blocks north of the river.

"The new university had just been completed by Frederick, the elector prince, known as "the Wise," to compete with that of Leipzig. He invited the Franciscans and the Augustinians to each provide three professors for the new university, and Dr. Johann von Staupitz, vicar of the Augustinian order, selected Luther as one of their three. The next year, 1512, Luther was made a Doctor of Theology, and began his theological lectures at the university. Now, keep in mind that this was five years before he posted his famous ninety-five 'theses' on the church door, and that was only to publicly suggest debate.

"This is all before what occurred in Augsburg and Worms, and his exile at the Wartburg, but it was after his journey to Rome. Luther's role was as a theological scholar and he performed that task appropriately. The 'after' part of the story, however, is perhaps more significant, for it was after he left the Wartburg and returned to Wittenberg that he formed his new religion."

By this time the group had reached the Castle Church, which had been left open especially for the Fremont group. They all crowded inside, and Dr. Fergen continued her lecture. "Remember, at this time, 1512, you had a very serious person in this professor monk. He was afraid of his God..." Fairchild wondered if this woman was a believer or, to hold her university position, a declared Communist. He suspected that she might be one thing outwardly, and another inwardly, and was relieved that there were no party officials accompanying their visit on this particular day. Lieutenant Schuster would not join them again until the next morning. "And that fear," she continued, "lay at the heart of church doctrine of the day: God punished sinners, but partaking in the sacrament of penances and obtaining Indulgences could reduce that punishment beyond the grave. But Luther began to doubt, especially as he made an ever-increasing study of Scripture.

"It was a very sad and hopeless kind of doctrine. Only the Church could save. Only the Church possessed the knowledge of what was in Scripture, and that they kept to themselves, for few other than the monks and scholars could read, and there were precious few books to read anyway.

"But that was changing, wasn't it? Fifty years earlier, in Mainz, Johann Gutenberg had invented movable type, and the *Mazarin Bible* was published. Printing was to the 16th century what gasoline, diesel or electric engines are to our 20th century. It would not be many decades before a vast majority of the public could read and write, and monks would no longer be needed in scriptoriums to copy books.

"As Luther studied for his lectures and sermons, he began to see how the doctrines of the Church differed from what the Scriptures said. This led him to a number of questions: What is the true nature of God? By what mechanism are we saved? What was the purpose of the crucifixion? Where did the Church's authority come from? Were there too many sacraments? Was there really a Purgatory? Certainly Scripture did not mention such a place. How, Luther debated in his own mind -- at least at first -- could Indulgences sold by men to sinners possibly release a soul to Heaven? What, in deed, was Heaven? Remember, all this was concurrent with Copernicus and Galileo -- there was no general knowledge that the world was really round and spun around the sun, even though Columbus had discovered your continent using that exact theory nine years after Luther was born.

"But consider this: If Luther were to prove that the sale of Indulgences was a false doctrine and worthless, it would have a direct effect on his own university, which was supported by the sale of such Indulgences. Is this not what you Americans refer to as a 'pickle'? In 1517 it was a serious economic and political issue.

"Wittenberg being both a river port market and a university town, entertainment came in a variety of places. Like all medieval cities, it had its share of beerhalls and brothels, homeless wanderers and murdering thieves. But debate was also a great form of entertainment. Luther took the issues he posted in his theses very seriously, but to the public, such religious debate was as good as, say, a soccer game today. Debate was sport.

"So, when the Dominican, Johann Tetzel, arrived in town in 1516, Luther had had enough of Indulgences. Tetzel was an Indulgence salesman, using fear of the unknown as his hook. He had a jingle, 'As soon as the coin in the coffer rings, the soul from Purgatory springs!' Luther considered it fraud and a crime. When Tetzel was dying, Luther wrote to him to comfort him. 'You didn't start this racket,' he said.

"On All Saints Day, the end of October, 1517, Luther wrote out his nearly one hundred complaints on a paper, and posted it to the church door. He had declared war on the sacrament of penance and the sale of Indulgences. There were many who agreed with Luther, but the arguments he posed were in opposition to not only the Church, but also his own prince. It fell to a professor of theology at the University of Ingolstadt, a town in Bavaria, one Johann Eck -- who was actually an old friend of Luther's -- to debate him.

"The debate was held in Leipzig in 1519. The Leipzig town council provided Eck a bodyguard of more than seventy men. Luther arrived with two hundred students armed with battle-axes. The two scholars argued, but Duke George, a man with a long beard, stopped it for fear that if a fight erupted, people would be killed or injured.

"Eck, now opposed to Luther's thinking, sought Luther's condemnation at Augsburg. Luther retaliated by issuing a condemnation of the Church's position called 'Against the Execrable Bull of Antichrist.' The various sides in the debated issues gathered forces for the events at Augsburg, and later at the Diet of Worms. Most of Saxony supported Luther's position, but the towns and principalities to the west and south opposed him.

"Perhaps it was then, or perhaps it was later, after his translation of the New Testament from Erasmus's Greek, that Luther formed the real crux of his theology. He based it on texts from Paul's letters to the Galatians and the Romans, that sinners are justified by grace, through faith, not by the law or by human efforts, however good those are, or by magic such as the Indulgences."

She stopped for a moment, then concluded, "On this premise Luther proceeded to build his new religion. He fortified it with all sorts of writings, printed documents, and his German Bible, which all could read and judge for themselves. He challenged the Church on every point, including celibacy of the clergy -- whereupon he married a former nun. He preached thousands of sermons and wrote hundreds of documents, along with a few hymns, and he debated with fellow reformers on many points. Eventually the new religion led to war, and the bitterness of it still exists.

"Was Luther right? Theologically speaking, can one be saved solely by faith and belief? Or is what we do and how we live also a factor? Luther might reply, 'faith without work is dead,' but, alas, many think that simply giving lip service to belief is sufficient. That Luther stirred up a very difficult pot of stew is without question. This afternoon, after lunch, we will visit some other locations where Luther lived and created his new religion, and learn some more about it." She paused, looked at Richard Fairchild, and asked, "Dr. Fairchild, do you have any comments you would like to add, or would your students have any questions we might answer?"

Fairchild did have a few facts to add to what Dr. Fergen had said, and the students had many questions, but the discussion was curtailed shortly before noon so that the group could go to lunch at a nearby café that had been alerted to their coming. That afternoon they visited many of the places in the city associated with Luther, during which both Dr. Fairchild and Bob Merriam continued the lectures. Most of the students were ready for bed by the time they returned to the Hotel Modern that evening and completed packing for the journey back across the border the following day.

* * *

Columbus, Ohio
June 24, 1962, 9:30 a.m.

Paul Sukhey reviewed the cablegram he had just received. "Time and location of auction changed due to unforeseen complications," it read. "Contact Hans Schäfer, 327 Zollikon Road, Zurich, Phone 973-027-405, for new time and place, probably sooner. Claude." Calling Zurich was no problem, but how would he contact Fairchild? Then he remembered the copy of the college tour itinerary that the professor has sent him that included a list of the hotels where the group would be staying in West Germany. He had a vague idea what the complications referenced in the cablegram might be.

* * *

Studio of Monique LaDuc, Bern, Switzerland
June 24, 1962, 4 p.m.

"Yes, Hans, we have made the arrangements," the middle-aged dark haired woman said in French into the telephone. "The people from the museums may inspect the documents at my office in Arles, any time between the end of June and the first week in July. You have that address. The bids must then reach Claude by the end of July. I realize that delays the sale, but only by a few weeks."

"Good. Thank you for assisting in this. You know the circumstances of the document, and if it were not valuable, there would not be so much concern about it. Its owner is nervous, and wants to move it quickly."

"Tell him -- or is it a 'her'? -- to relax, Hans. It will be in good hands. I realize that Arles is a bit out of the way for some of the bidders, but they will enjoy the city. Now, what else do you have that we can handle for you?"

Chapter 9

Only one train, the *Ostsee Express*, ran directly from Berlin to Munich via Wittenberg, Leipzig, Gutenfürst and Hof, reaching the border shortly after three in the afternoon. However, it was an international express originating in Copenhagen and it did not stop in Wittenberg or Leipzig. The Fremont group, therefore, was scheduled to take a local train to Leipzig, where they would meet with the singers from the Army.

"Okay, folks," Dr. Fairchild said as the students gathered around their luggage in the lobby of the Hotel Modern in Wittenberg, "here is the plan. We will go down to the station. They have reserved part of a coach of us on the Leipzig train. When we get to Leipzig Lieutenant Schuster will meet us and take us to where the other singers are waiting. There is another coach on the Leipzig to Munich train. That train is joined with a through train from Dresden at a town called Plauen.

"Border guards will enter there, and you will again need to show your passports, visa, and the exit documents -- Dr. von Werdau, you indicated that you had these?"

"Definitely," she replied.

"Good. Now, as I understand it, those guards will get off at Gutenfürst, where the locomotive is switched to a West German one. We cross the border, then we will go through West German customs at Hof, where a bus will be waiting to take us all to Bayreuth. There were originally to be two buses, one for us and one for the Army singers, but Lieutenant Schuster advised me before we left Erfurt that only one bus will be provided. After we clear customs in Hof, it is less than an hour's drive to Bayreuth.

"We'll be taken to our hotel first, well, perhaps the Army singers will be taken to their hotel first, but the bus will pick us up again after supper and take us to the concert hall for our first rehearsal with the Dutch. We'll find out when we get to Bayreuth if this is a dress rehearsal, or casual. If it is in dress, those of you who are not singing, but are taking care of the costumes, will need to prepare quickly.

"I know some of you, probably most of you, still have some East German marks left. I do, too. They are no good in West Germany, so when we get to the train station, where there is a little souvenir shop, you may as well buy some trinket or postcards, and get rid of them. Anything you have left you will probably have to declare at the border. Any questions?"

Jack Hornbet raised his hand. "Dr. Fairchild, will there be a diner on the train?"

"Jack, I don't know. Probably there will be, as it is a Dresden to Munich express, but we won't have time to eat on the train. It may be a very late lunch when we get to the hotel in Bayreuth. I hope all of you ate your breakfast. If not, buy some candy or something at the train station. If there are no further questions, let's get down to the train station and find our coach."

It was starting to rain as they arrived at the Wittenberg bahnhof. It was typical of many East German railway stations built perhaps forty or fifty years earlier. It was black with grit and grim from the steam engines that still were in use on many of the non-electrified rail lines, and had a large open train shed. The terminal building itself had cracked windows, some broken seats, and was rather dilapidated in appearance. Both a north-south line and an east-west line converged on the station, which was on the north side of the main part of the city.

The professors, their wives, and the Fremont students walked the few blocks to the station. Dr. Fergen had already returned to Halle the night before, entrusting her friend, Hilda von Werdau to handle any language problem that might arise, although she realized that Fairchild was fluent enough in German that such help was unlikely to be needed. As the group approached the station, a rather nondescript man, shorter than six feet, in a gray overcoat and hat, stood at the entrance. As they got closer he stepped toward Richard Fairchild.

"Professor Fairchild," he said in clear English, and the group stopped as the professor nodded an acknowledgement. "I am Major Klaus Gärtner of the Stasi. I'll be joining your group all the way to Bayreuth, to assist you in crossing the border and making sure that everything is convenient for you and your students."

"Well, that will be very welcome, Major," Fairchild replied. "I gather that you are aware that we are meeting Lieutenant Ernst Schuster in Leipzig, and the Army singers?"

"Most definitely. Major General Kurt Kahler will also be traveling with the Army group, and, he has informed me, also singing with them and your musicians." Gärtner looked over the group, and then went directly to Ross Johnson.

"Dr. Johnson, I believe you met General Kahler at one of the Erfurt rehearsals."

"Yes, he introduced himself as 'Kurt.' I did not realize he was a general."

"He is a modest man. And you, Dr. von Werdau," he said, turning to the blond professor, "I understand are acquainted with the General's son, Johann."

"Yes. He lives near Rostock. I see him in Berlin on occasion."

"Interesting. We have about a half hour before the train departs, Dr. Fairchild, but the coach is already open, if your students would like to put their luggage aboard."

"That would be excellent, Major Gärtner. Then they need to do a little final shopping, postcards and such."

"Good. A little Western economic aid as well as cultural cooperation is always welcome, Dr. Fairchild."

The Stasi officer led the group into the station to a railway coach at the end of a train that was waiting. A locomotive had not yet been attached. The students and professors put their luggage inside, and then scattered around the station, some to a kiosk selling food, others to a newsstand that had postcards and souvenirs. Within twenty minutes they were back on the coach, and felt a slight jolt as a fairly large 2-6-4 steam locomotive was backed to the front of the train. They could hear the announcement of the train on loudspeakers in the terminal. "*Aufmerksamkeit! Personenzug Vierhundertzehn zu Bitterfeld und Leipzig, Gleis Drei.*" Other passengers scurried toward the train.

After some whistles, bells and blasts on the locomotive's steam whistle, the train slowly moved forward. The *Schaffner*, or conductor, had taken the tickets for the students from Dr. Fairchild as they had reboarded the train, and they were the only passengers in that particular coach.

Major Gärtner sat in a seat across the aisle from Richard and Esther Fairchild, next to Ross Johnson. The Merriams were seated further back, next to Hilda von Werdau. "This train will also stop at a few little villages," Gärtner explained as the train rattled across the iron bridge over the Elbe River and continued to gather speed.

"I am delighted to get to ride behind one of your steam locomotives, Major," Richard Fairchild said. "Almost none of our passenger trains in America are steam powered any more. They are mostly diesel electric."

"Please call me Klaus, Professor."

"All right, and I am Richie, and this is my wife, Esther. Ross you seem to already know."

"Ahh, you noticed. Yes, I have seen each of your faces before, on the visa applications. That is one of my duties at Stasi. We need more of these cultural exchanges, don't you think, Richie?"

"Yes, anything that can reduce tensions between East and West can only be good. I was not sure, when we first applied to bring our students into your country, that this would be permitted. As it has turned out, East Germany had been an excellent host to us, and we have learned much about both Bach and Luther."

"So I have heard. I am not an opera lover, but, living in Berlin, we do have our orchestra concerts and other musical programs, Bach's organ music and such. I hope to get some time in Bayreuth to visit the home of Franz Liszt. It is near the home of Wägner, I understand."

"Almost next door, I believe," Ross Johnson replied, joining the conversation. "I am hoping to take our students there the day after the concert."

"I will be, what is it you Americans say, 'out of your hair'? by then," the Stasi officer said.

"Will the Army singers be staying at one of the hotels in the city?" Esther asked.

"No, we have arranged for our soldiers to stay at a particular guesthouse nearer to the concert hall. The bus will probably stop there first. But you will see them again at the rehearsal this evening."

About an hour later the train arrived at the Leipzig Bahnhof. By this time it was raining quite heavily, but the large train shed covered the tracks where the Fremont group and their Stasi accompaniment left the train. Lieutenant Schuster stood awaiting their arrival. Fairchild introduced him to Gärtner, but it appeared that the Lieutenant half expected to see the officer from the secret police there.

"The General said you might meet us," Ernst Schuster said, "but I didn't anticipate your meeting the Fremont group in Wittenberg."

"It was on my way down from Berlin. You had provided a very good itinerary for the Americans, so I knew where they would be. I did not expect to find Dr. von Werdau with them, however. Was she not to join the singers here in Leipzig?"

"She is a close friend of Dr. Fergen. I understand she simply accompanied her friend down to Wittenberg as she had no classes to teach this week. She mentioned it at the last rehearsal with the chorus."

"Mmm, I see. Well, where are these other singers, Lieutenant?" the Major asked.

"Already at the track for the Plauen train. The General is with them."

The group moved forward into the terminal and over two tracks to an awaiting train of four cars, the last two of which would be switched onto the train from Dresden at the Plauen station stop. There was one intermediate stop at a town called Werdau. Fairchild wondered if the attractive blond professor's name somehow related to the little town when he saw the name posted on the railway marker, but never got an opportunity to ask her. As they arrived trackside she immediately went to greet the General, who was in his uniform as were the Army choristers standing beside him. They each had a small traveling case, and one of their members was in charge of a large box that contained the Army singer's costumes. Hilda von Werdau had brought her own costume with her.

As the Fairchilds passed, she called to them. "Dr. Fairchild, Mrs. Fairchild, I don't believe that you have had the opportunity to meet Major General Kahler yet. Dr. Merriam and his wife did, at the rehearsals, but I don't recall that you were there. I am a friend of General Kahler's son, Johann, and we met a few months ago in Berlin."

"How do you do, General Kahler," Dr. Fairchild said, as the General extended his hand. "Lieutenant Schuster has been taking excellent care of us, and I appreciate all of the steps you have taken on our behalf to make our trip so successful."

"That was easy, Dr. Fairchild," the tall, distinguished-looking military officer, his thick hair mostly gray, said. "Your reputation preceded you. Dr. Fergen at Halle University very much wanted to be your guide, and my Lieutenant's father said he knew you and wanted to meet you again."

"What is this?" the Stasi officer inquired.

"Klaus," the General laughed, "you told me that Fairchild had once been a prisoner of war. It was the Lieutenant's father who captured him. Ahh, but he escaped. It was actually in France, not Germany."

"It is a small world, Kurt," the Stasi officer replied, almost sounding sarcastic. "One big cozy family. You know Hilda von Werdau, who knows your son. Your Lieutenant's father knows the Professor here; next you will be telling me that Richard Wägner was your great uncle!"

"With my singing voice? I seriously doubt I have any musical bones in my body! But let us get our groups aboard the train before it departs. Lieutenant, have Sergeant Schlafer take the front part of the car reserved for us. Dr. Fairchild, perhaps your group could take the seats from the middle on back?"

"Certainly, General."

"Please, call me Kurt."

"And I am Richie," Dr. Fairchild replied as they moved forward toward the assigned railway car. This time Kurt Kahler sat next to the Stasi officer, and across from the professor from Halle. They conversed awhile in German, but as the Fairchilds had taken seats behind the Fremont students toward the back of the car next to the Merriams, they could not hear what the two officers were discussing.

"It seems unusual for a secret police official to be accompanying tourists," Bob Merriam said across the aisle to Richard Fairchild. "I guess, maybe because they have military people leaving the country, that concerns them politically."

"Perhaps," the older professor replied. "There is still a lot of tension between NATO and the East Germans. Even in a cultural event such as this, any incident could create a political crisis."

"I'm just glad that Dean Harding didn't come with us," Sally added. "Can you imagine how nervous he would have been crossing that border last week?"

"I'm surprised he let us come at all," Esther chimed in. "He has been pretty good about letting us plan most of our tours, but this is the first time we've gone into a Communist country."

"What I get amused at are the ladies who run the restrooms," Sally added. "Bob and I call them the 'poofnick ladies,' as you always have to put one of their poofnick coins in the basket in order to use the toilet. But I've yet to see a really clean toilet."

"Other than in the hotel, have you seen any soap?" Richard asked. "The whole place could use a good scrubbing."

"I always heard that Germans were so fastidious," Bob commented.

"Maybe just tedious...." Sally replied. "Remember that first rehearsal with Sergeant Schlafer? I thought, if we go over that same passage one more time, I'm going to scream. Dr. von Werdau didn't look very happy about it, either."

"Is she a good singer?" Esther asked.

"Yes, as good as our women, and of course, much better with the German words. She helped us quite a bit with the pronunciations."

With that the train started to move forward and pull out of the Bahnhof, clicking loudly as it moved from track to track over the station switches. Outside the heavy rain continued, and the city seemed to be sad and forlorn in the gray mist and fog. The lights remained on in the coach.

* * *

Plauen, East Germany
June 24, 1962, 11:45 a.m.

Some of the Fremont students chatted with each other as they rode toward the frontier, while others napped, read a paperback book, or wrote postcards to mail from Bayreuth. The train, electrically operated, sped southward along the Pleis River, stopping only twice in the journey of slightly over an hour and a half to the small city of Plauen. There the train halted, and the passengers could feel a few bumps and taps as the two coaches bound for Munich were disconnected from the other cars, and then, a few moments later, reconnected to a train that had pulled into the next track from Dresden.

Two border guards entered the car, but immediately came to attention and saluted as they recognized their commanding officer, Major General Kahler. Neither spoke English, but they were obviously nervous as they learned that the man sitting with Kahler was a Stasi Major, and that the back of the car was filled with American students. They passed out a form on which each passenger was to declare any purchases made in East Germany. Lieutenant Schuster translated the card to the American students, but few had much to declare on the form other than candy and postcards, although one of the Canadian students had purchased a cuckoo clock for her parents, which she intended to mail home from Bayreuth.

As had occurred in crossing the border at Bebra, the border guards carefully inspected each passport, visa, and exit authorization, examining the photographs carefully and being certain that each matched the bearer.

They then had each person open their suitcase or other baggage, but only examined the contents of one or two of the cases. Jimmy Higgins, one of the Fremont juniors on the tour, had been attempting to grow a moustache while on the tour, and his photo got a very careful review, resulting in a few wisecracks from other students.

"Hey, Jimmy," one joked, "that caterpillar on your upper lip is going to have to have its own passport and visa."

"Yeah, you should have shaved that thing off this morning!" another commented. One of the border guards leaned toward the other and whispered in his ear, and then both laughed. He was apparently translating some of the comments to the other. Both smiled at Jimmy, and moved on.

The guards moved from the back toward the front. When they reached Professor von Werdau they opened the documents she carried and reviewed them carefully, even though she was sitting across from their commanding officer. They said nothing, but simply refolded the papers and returned them to her with a smile. They never looked in her suitcase. They did the same with those of the Stasi officer, but barely glanced at those of Major General Kahler.

The train slowly moved forward, covering the remaining 21 miles to the border in about a half hour. At Gutenfürst the train again ground to a stop, and the passengers again felt a few bumps as the East German locomotive was disconnected and removed from the train, and a West German locomotive was attached at the front. The East German guards got off, and two West German customs agents entered the car.

Major General Kahler arose and met the agents at the front of the car. He had papers with him explaining the presence of East German soldiers in uniform, and presented them to the agents.

"Yes," they responded in German, "we were alerted that you would be aboard. Welcome to West Germany, General Kahler. We understand you also have some Americans in your group? They are the ones here in the car behind your soldiers?

"Yes, the man at the rear is their leader," Kahler replied. "A Dr. Fairchild, a professor, from Ohio in the United States."

"Ohio?" one of the agents said. "I have a cousin in Ohio. Perhaps he knows my cousin Wilhelm."

"Perhaps," the General answered, "But I've never been to Ohio, so I couldn't say."

"We hear that you are all performing at the *Festspielhaus* tomorrow night."

"That is correct. We are singing the chorus parts of *Rienzi*."

"Ahh, *Rienzi*! It is not performed very often. Too long, some say," the customs agent commented. "And who is the soprano?"

"I don't know," the General replied. "It is a Dutch opera company, and the lead singers are all from Holland."

"They will butcher our German language!" said the other agent, and Klaus Gärtner laughed loudly.

"It's one of those operas where the fat lady sings," he said. "I understand the whole thing takes about six hours."

"I don't think I'll go, Albrecht," the one agent said to the other. "I'd rather hear my music at the beerhall."

The two guards quickly glanced at the passports of the students and professors from the United States, although they paid a bit more attention to those of Hilda von Werdau and Klaus Gärtner, whose names were not on the list they had received. The train had again moved forward, and the students again observed the high gates and barbed wire fence as the train rolled slowly over the border into West Germany. It was only three miles from there to the station in Hof, and by the time the train stopped again the two customs agents had inspected each passport. While the sky was still gray, the rain had stopped.

"Okay, folks," Richard Fairchild announced to the Fremont students, having confirmed to the customs agent that he did not know the agent's cousin in Cincinnati, "this is where we get off. There were originally going to be two buses, but the tour agent could only arrange for one large bus. The Army singers will be dropped at their guesthouse first, so if you all don't mind, we'll take the back seats again."

"Is Hilda going to stay with us or the military group," Sally asked Richard Fairchild as they gathered up their luggage.

"I understand she will stay with some of the women in the Army chorus. I didn't talk with her about it, but I suspect that her movements outside East Germany would be rather restricted. I may be wrong though. She may be free to move about."

"Where is our hotel?" Bob Merriam asked.

"It's the *Alte Marktort*, right at the Old Market in the center of the city. The tour bus will be available to us for the two days we are here, before we move on to Nurnberg and back to Frankfurt."

As arranged, a large Mercedes bus awaited outside the train station. The Fremont students boarded first, moving to the rear of the bus, then the East German Army chorus members boarded, taking the seats toward the front. There was plenty of room in the bus for both groups. After all were aboard, and any oversized luggage stored in the luggage compartment below, the bus pulled from the driveway onto Highway 173 and headed northwest toward the main four-lane Autobahn that ran directly to Bayreuth through hilly countryside. For most of the East Germans, it was the first time they had been outside their country, except for a few who had participated in Warsaw Pact maneuvers in other Eastern Bloc nations.

* * *

Rostock Naval Affairs Office, East Germany
June 24, 1962, 12:45 p.m.

Captain Johann Kahler allowed the phone to ring at least twelve times before hanging up. He had been calling the number in Halle all morning to see how his blond lover was progressing with her report for his commanding officer. The Admiral had requested an update. Twice he had checked to be certain he had the correct number.

"She must be at the library," he muttered to himself. Then he thought of trying to get a message to her through her friend, Maria Fergen. He did not have that phone number, but was able to get it from the Naval Communications agent at the nearby base.

The number was an office at the University, and was answered by a clerk.

"Is Dr. Maria Fergen there?" he asked in German.

"No, I don't expect her back until later this afternoon. Is there a message?"

"Yes. Tell her I am trying to reach her friend, Hilda, but can't get any answer. Tell her to have Hilda call me. Tonight. It is urgent."

"Hilda?"

"Professor von Werdau."

"Oh, yes. And you are?"

"Captain Johann Kahler, in Rostock. She has my phone number."

"I shall pass on the message, Captain Kahler."

"Thank you."

* * *

Although the small city of Bayreuth dated from the 12th century, many of its ornate buildings in the center of the city had been built in the 18th and 19th centuries, including the highly baroque Margravial Opera House, built in the 1740s. Although beautifully decorated and acoustically accurate, the old opera house had been insufficient for the presentation of the elaborate and lengthy Wagnerian operas, and Richard Wägner arranged for the building of a much larger theater in 1872 in which to stage performances of his operas. The *Festspielhaus* sits on a wooded hill more than a mile north of the center city, surrounded by large residencies. Its stage is one of the largest in the world, and although nearly a hundred years old when the group from Fremont College arrived, as modern as any theater in the world.

The *Hotel Alte Marktort* was much more modern than its name might have indicated, and the street scene, with outdoor cafes and open plazas, resembled what some of the students thought Paris might look like. The bus delivered them to the hotel door, and they had moved their luggage inside, promptly been assigned their rooms -- each with its own bath -- which caused a loud cheer, especially from the young women. They were instructed to be in the dining room by five o'clock that afternoon for dinner, as the bus would take them to the theater for the rehearsal promptly at six. This would not be a dress rehearsal. That would be held the following morning.

As each of the rooms was assigned, any mail that had been forwarded to the hotel from parents or others was distributed. The Fairchilds were not expecting any correspondence, and were surprised when the room clerk said, in fairly good English,

"Herr Dr. Fairchild, here is a cablegram for you."

The professor looked at it, and saw at once that it was from Paul Sukhey in Columbus, dated June 23. "Richard, advised of change in time and location. New document auction to be held morning of July 1, *20 Blvd. Des Lices*, Arles, France, Studio of Monique LaDuc. Hope you can inspect it the day before. Will await your call. Paul."

Richard Fairchild had already changed his travel plans to reflect the first scheduled document examination in Lyon on July 3. While the Fremont group would be flying back to Detroit on June 29 from Frankfurt, he had rescheduled his flight out of Paris for the fourth of July. Esther had elected to return on the 29th as she was anxious to get home and did not want to "traipse all around France again," as she put it.

"Not even Provence?" he had asked her when they had received the first message from Paul Sukhey.

"Not Paris, Provence, or the French Riviera, Richard. I'll be tired of traveling and want to go home. There's a faculty wives' meeting in mid-July, and as sub-chairman I've got a lot of work to do to get ready for that. And the publisher of my latest children's book is screaming for the illustrations." Now, with the earlier inspection date, she reconfirmed her feelings. "Richard, stay in France those extra days and enjoy yourself. It will give me some peace and quiet, and I need to get that artwork finished and off. It's nearly done, but needs a few touches yet."

"You mean you haven't enjoyed the trip?" he inquired.

"No, not at all. It has been a wonderful trip, but tiring. Remember, Richard, we're more than twenty years older than these kids. You may still have the energy to run up and down stairs in old hotels where there are no elevators, hauling our luggage, but getting ready to sing in this six hour marathon tomorrow night is exhausting me. You might feel differently if you were singing with us."

"I'm no singer," he protested. "But I see your point. Maybe you should skip this rehearsal tonight."

"No, if I'm going to skip any of the rehearsals, it will be the one tomorrow morning. Having to wear that tight, crinkled costume all morning and again all evening is more than I think I can stand."

"Well, okay. I'll have to accompany the students both times, but...."

"Oh, I'll probably drag along, too. Why don't you change, take a bath, and we'll go down to that little café on the town square and have a glass of wine before supper. We didn't get much lunch, and I'm famished."

* * *

Festspielhaus, Bayreuth, West Germany
June 24, 1962, 6:30 p.m.

One thing the students had learned while traveling in Germany, both East and West, was that things happened on schedule. The group had just finished one of the best meals they had been served on the trip when the bus promptly pulled up outside the hotel at 1800 German time, which the American students still called 6 p.m. They all climbed on the bus, the singers carrying their thick folders of music. Because of the narrow streets in the city center, the bus headed west when it pulled away from the hotel with the students aboard, and circled around to the *Wittelsbacherring*, part of the ring road surrounding the old city. It then headed north on *Bahnhofstrasse* and *Burgerreuther Strasse*, circling around the ornate pink and white Festival Playhouse and stopping at a door that led to the stage.

A theater attendant met them as they climbed off the bus. He spoke no English, and Dr. Fairchild acted as translator for the group as it headed for the stage door and he led them inside. The East German Army choristers were already there, still in their uniforms. It was obvious that Lieutenant Schuster, the General and the Stasi officer were watching the men and women in the chorus very closely. Fairchild suspected that more than one of the singers -- many of whom were assigned to the Border Troops -- were prepared to act immediately if any of the others tried to hide or escape from the group.

"Hello," Hilda von Werdau said, walking over across the stage to greet Sally Merriam. "How is your hotel?"

"Oh, it is great, right on the city plaza," she replied. "How is yours?"

"Not very comfortable. It is really just a dormitory in an old boy's school building not being used in the summer. The seven other women and I are sharing the room, with bunk beds. I may see if I can transfer to your hotel. Is it full?"

"I don't believe so. I heard some of the students say that they had noticed some vacant rooms on the fourth floor. Are you required to stay with the Army singers?"

"Not really. I've traveled in the West before, and can pretty much go where I please as a party member. Party membership is required of the professors. I think I shall advise General Kahler and return with you."

A short, balding man with an odd accent seemed to be scurrying around the stage as the group from Fremont entered. After a moment he shouted, "Oll oof yooou! Over heeer," pointing to where the Army singers were waiting.

"Velcome, oll off yoooou, to Bayreuth und Festival Plaaayhooose. I be George Voorensen, Directooor of Royal Dutch Opera. Vee are oll going have goood time! Yooou singers, women stage left," he pointed to what Fairchild would have normally thought of as the right side, "und men, to right! Goood! Okaaay use music tonight, noot tomorrow."

With that a great, heavy curtain rose high into the ceiling of the stage, and the singers saw what clearly looked like a street in Rome. "Noow," shouted the little Dutch director, "vee vill doo it this vay. American men, yooou are Orsini's men. Orsini wants to abduct Irene, who is Rienzi's sister. Vemen ooff stage. Deutchers, *sie bein Colonna's Menchen*. Okay, Music!"

The Fremont students had not seen the orchestra in the pit below the stage up to that point. The strings began a lively tune as the soloist playing Orsini came out from the far side of the stage and began singing, "*Hier ist's, hier ist's! Frisch auf, ihr Freunde! Zum Fenster legt die Leiter ein!*" He then waved to the Fremont singers, who stepped forward, as Orsini sang yet another line, then they chimed in, tenors first, then basses, with "*Ha, welche lustige Entführung aus des Plebejers Haus!*" while the soloist playing Orsini sang out above them. They quickly learned that all the hours of rehearsal had been necessary -- and may have been insufficient.

The six Fremont students, four men and two women, who were not singing in the chorus joined Bob Merriam and Richard Fairchild in seats within the theater, about three rows from the front, where they could watch the rehearsal. The opera company also had chorus singers, and the extra women were not needed until Act Two. The first Scene was proceeding slowly. There was supposed to be a fight between the forces of the two parties, Orsini's and Colonna's, but it was clear that neither the Fremont nor the East Germans knew what to do in terms of acting out the fight.

The little Dutchman was beside himself. "*Nein! Nein!* Yooou moost look aggressive! Heeeer, prop-man, get them sooome clubs to wave threateningly. Und yooou singers, '*Orsini hock!*' Hoook! Not 'Orsini hawk!' Enunciate!"

Richard Fairchild leaned over toward Bob Merriam and whispered, "It's going to be a long night!"

* * *

Richard Fairchild and the others from Fremont in the audience were grateful to see that the director was only concerned with the parts involving the chorus, rather than doing the entire opera. That would come at the dress rehearsal the following morning.

During one of the breaks, Hilda von Werdau spoke briefly with Major General Kahler, advising that she would like to move to the hotel where the Americans were staying. He nodded his approval, and she came down into the audience and over to Dr. Fairchild, who was standing talking with Bob Merriam.

"Professor Fairchild," she said softly, immediately getting his attention. "I wonder if you could do a favor for me?"

"I could try, I suppose. What is it?"

"Professor Merriam, I spoke to your wife, Sally, earlier, and she said she thought that there are some available rooms at your hotel. As I am having to room with the women Army singers in a dormitory, I asked the General if I could move to your hotel, and he said that would be okay. Dr. Fairchild, I wonder, while we are practicing the third act if you could phone to your hotel and get me a room?"

"Well, certainly. But what about your things? Won't your case still be at the dormitory?"

"*Ja*, but Mrs. Merriam, Sally, said she would loan me a garment for tonight, and one of the Army singers will bring my case to me in the morning at rehearsal. I told the General that I might stay in Bayreuth a day or two extra. The Army singers, of course, will be returning to Leipzig and Erfurt on the morning after the concert, but I have no classes to teach right now and...."

"Certainly. Our group is also going to stay an extra day, as the music students want to visit Liszt's and Wägner's homes and the old Baroque opera house. You would be most welcome to join us."

"*Danke, Herr Professor!* I appreciate that offer."

"Gosh, I don't blame her for not wanting to stay in a dormitory with those six women singers," Bob Merriam said after the petite blond German had returned to the stage. "Only one of them looks half-way friendly. I heard some of them being really sarcastic to a couple of the men in their group. I guess they didn't realize I understood German when they were cussing them out."

"What about?"

"Well, most of the men, except two or three, are from the General's unit in Erfurt. They are border troops. Two of the women are, also. But the others are from some sort of artillery unit east of Leipzig. Some of the men from Erfurt wanted to get together with the women from the artillery unit, and the women turned them down flat. I don't know why. The guys aren't that bad looking, and neither are the women."

"Hunh," Fairchild grunted. "Maybe the moon wasn't full!"

"Yeah, maybe not."

Chapter 10

The bus again arrived at the hotel door promptly at eight thirty the next morning. This time large boxes of costumes were loaded into the bus first. The costumes had been shipped directly from Ohio to Bayreuth so that the travelers would not need to carry them along. They would change at the theater.

Dr. Fairchild had arranged a room near the Merriams for Dr. von Werdau, and she and the Merriams had sat together at breakfast. Fairchild had noticed several men in the hotel lobby. One looked somewhat familiar, but he usually was facing the other way or off in a corner somewhere so that Fairchild never got a good look at his face. One of the other men was always on the opposite side of the lobby, and seemed to be watching the first man. A large poster had been set up, advertising in German the performance of *Rienzi* by the Royal Dutch Opera Company, "assisted by the Chorus of Fremont College in Ohio and members of the Chorus of the East German Southern Command." When everyone was aboard the bus it again turned west and followed its circuitous route to the big opera house.

By shortly after nine the orchestra was tuning up, and the curtain rose on the scene of the Roman street where the forces of Orsini and Colonna would do battle. The East German Army singers had arrived from their dormitory already in their costumes. Fremont students who were not singing were back stage in the dressing rooms, four assisting the men with their costumes, and two assisting the Fremont women.

It was somewhat before noon when the opera got to Act Three. The Fremont students had all commented that this was their favorite part of the opera, beginning with a beautiful chorus of women, then moving to a loud and raucous battle hymn, "Arise, Romans, for freedom and the law. Be witness, O Earth, for these our greatest treasure.... *Santo Spirito cavaliere!*" Upon hearing it, Richard Fairchild knew why. He also knew why this was such popular music for the Nazis, who patterned some of the military marches after themes from the opera.

Shortly after noon the director called an intermission, at the end of the Third Act. He was not rehearsing the overtures or orchestrations that would be used between some of the acts of the opera, which reduced the rehearsal time greatly. All that would be heard that evening at the performance.

* * *

Rostock Naval Affairs Office, East Germany
June 25, 1962, 12:45 p.m.

"Captain Kahler, this is Maria Fergen."

"Yes, Dr. Fergen. Thank you for calling back. Were you able to reach Hilda?"

"No, I couldn't reach her by phone, so I stopped by her apartment this morning. She's not there. A neighbor said she was singing with the Army's chorus."

"Singing with the Army chorus? Oh, yes, she did say something about it. But where?"

"Did she not tell you? The Chorus of the Southern Command is singing in an opera in Bayreuth...."

"What! ... Bayreuth -- that's in West Germany!"

"Yes. She has been rehearsing for weeks. I though you would have known."

"When is she due back?"

"The concert is tonight. I suppose the Army group will be returning tomorrow."

"Do you know where they are staying?"

"No, she didn't say."

"What is this opera?"

"Wägner's *Rienzi*. They're doing it with a Dutch opera company, and our Army chorus is singing with a group of American college students. I was their guide while they were in our country."

"Americans? She's out of the country with a group of Americans? Oh, damn!" Johann Kahler hung up and placed a call to Naval Headquarters in Berlin. After a few moments he reached Admiral Helmut Schmidt, and explained the situation.

"This is certainly a serious breach of protocol," the Admiral said. "She should have known better. But we cannot assume that she is not going to return, or that her report will not be forthcoming shortly. I was very stern with her, and, well, you know how stubborn some people are if they are pushed. But I will contact Stasi and see what they know of the matter. Your father is high in Southern Command. He might know where they are."

"I will try to contact him. I have not seen him since that party here in Berlin."

"You should keep in better contact with your father, Johann. He is a very fine soldier."

"But a poor Communist. He even believes in God."

"A patriotic officer is a useful party tool, Captain. The state may not be the only god. The God in which your father may believe has a longer track record than the god in which you and I believe, would you not agree?"

"Yes, Admiral."

"Yes. Well, call him, and let me know. If anything goes wrong, you and I may well need his God."

Johann Kahler hung up and went to his address book to locate the number for the Southern Border Troops Command in Erfurt. He dialed the number and got a clerk. "Captain Johann Kahler here," he said. "Is Major General Kahler, my father, in?"

"*Nein,* Captain Kahler," the clerk replied. "He is out of the country with the Army Chorus."

"What?"

"He has gone to Bayreuth to sing in *Rienzi*. Do you want to speak to Colonel Hermann? He is next in command."

"No," the young Naval Captain said, hanging up. He then called the Admiral again, reaching him on the first ring.

"My father is also singing in the damned opera. He, too, is in Bayreuth."

"So, perhaps there is no danger. A Stasi Major, Klaus Gärtner, is traveling with them, I just learned. He is a friend of your father's, I understand, and they have other officers with them to watch for any possible defection. They are actually expecting such an attempt, so are very alert. I advised Stasi that our pretty professor is a high security risk. They were not sure that Gärtner knew that, and will cable him in Bayreuth. At least *he* is not going to be on the stage singing. Ahh, Johann! Once we get her back you'd better marry her so you can keep better track of her."

"We may be lovers but… I don't want to marry her. She's too bossy."

"All wives are bossy, Johann. Did your mother not boss your father?"

"I don't know, Admiral Schmidt. I wasn't there."

"Too bad. It is a drawback to our educational system. We should leave the children in their homes a bit longer."

* * *

Klaus Gärtner was at the theater when the cablegram from Stasi Headquarters in Berlin, prepared in code, was delivered. However, the clerk at the school dormitory decided that this message, which he did not understand, might be important, and had the school custodian deliver it to the theater. He found the Stasi officer standing off-stage behind the curtains.

Gärtner read and quickly decoded the message. He then moved over to where Major General Kurt Kahler was standing in his Roman townsman costume, waiting for the next chorus. "We may have trouble, Kurt," Gärtner said.

"What is it?"

"Our pretty professor. Did you know that she is one of our top nuclear scientists with detailed knowledge of Russia's new submarines?"

"No! I knew she has a top secret clearance. She's been to the West before."

"Yes, but she was supposed to be in Berlin today, delivering a report to the Navy on the Russian submarine."

"Oh."

"And you know she moved out of the women's dormitory at the school last night."

"But she asked my permission for that."

"And you gave it, naturally."

"I had no reason not to."

"She's going to defect. Wouldn't NATO love to get their hands on her!"

"You don't know that, Klaus. She has been practicing with our chorus for weeks. Never have I detected any unpatriotic comment or sympathy for the West in our conversations. She spends time with my son in Rostock, and he is a staunch party man. See, she is right over there with the women. If she was going to defect, do you think she would not have already done so?"

"What was in her luggage that Corporal Leon brought to her today?"

"I don't know. Anna Leon stands next to her in the chorus. She just said that Hilda wanted her to bring her case."

"You sing. I'll have a look."

Major Gärtner moved slowly away into the shadows, and descended a back stairway to the various dressing rooms. Each had been labeled in German and English for the singers, and in the Army women's dressing room he quickly spotted the suitcase that Hilda had been carrying when they had crossed the frontier the day before. He recalled that because she was sitting near their commanding officer, the Border Troop guards had not done a very thorough search of any of the luggage of the Germans on the train.

The case was not locked, and he quickly flipped it open. There was the dress that the young professor had been wearing when she arrived at the theater that morning, and a nightgown, a case with some cosmetics, some stockings, soft underwear, and a postcard of Wittenberg addressed to Captain Johann Kahler at an address just outside Rostock. It began, "Dear Johann," but the writing was a bit scribbled, apparently begun on the train, and the card was both unfinished and unstamped.

Gärtner felt all around the interior of the case for anything that might be hidden, assuring himself that there were no secret compartments in the case. He then put everything back in the case as it had been, closed it and returned it to the place where it had been sitting. He wished he had brought a signal transmitting device with him, but neither he nor the Stasi agent with whom he had met early that morning, and who had been following one of the Americans from Frankfurt, had one with them.

What the Stasi agent from Bonn had told him only served to heighten his concern. The agent, Tomas Bücher, had arrived at the Frankfurt airport prior to the arrival of the TWA flight from New York. He spotted the two American CIA agents immediately, and observed that they were escorted into the city by another American agent known to him. He watched their office, and observed the three depart in a large Mercedes sedan, and head west on the Nurnberg Autobahn. He followed at a discreet distance, and observed them exit east of Schlussefeld, taking a smaller road north to Highway 505, and then Highway 22 into Bayreuth. All three were staying at the same hotel as the American students, the same hotel where Hilda von Werdau was now staying. Gärtner was convinced. She was his defector.

* * *

Festspielhaus, Bayreuth, West Germany
June 25, 1962, 7:15 p.m.

The Dutch cast and the choruses had been served only a light supper in one of the larger halls below stage. Each of the major performers had his or her own dressing room, and the Dutch singers pretty much kept to themselves. Bob Merriam and Richard Fairchild had gathered in the room assigned to Fremont's male singers, along with the four students helping with their costumes. The men would require two changes of costume during the program, one on rather short notice.

Because of the length of the opera it was starting earlier than would be typical, and by seven that evening, 1900 by European time, Fairchild could hear the orchestra tuning up. Tension was building in the room. The non-singers would be allowed to observe the opera from the wings behind stage, as the theater was entirely sold out, with opera fans coming from as far as Italy and Norway for the performance. The theater had retained police officers to guard the staging areas, and there seemed to be police all over the theater. Dr. Fairchild anticipated that this might be because of the East German Army personnel participating in the opera.

At ten after seven a stage director led the men up a back stairway to take their positions as Orsini's men behind the curtain. The orchestra had stopped tuning, and there was a hush throughout the vast hall that could be felt even behind the curtain. Then there came a single note from a trumpet, loud then drifting off. The strings gave several quick, tension-building notes, then another blast came from the trumpet. The strings again responded, then with a final trumpet call the orchestra broke into the fast and furious overture, introducing and repeating some of the major themes from the opera. On some of the more famous themes the audience could hardly restrain themselves from shouting and cheering. Fairchild suspected that some of the Fremont singers had probably never heard the overture before, and hoped that its emotionalism would not cause them to flub when the curtain opened.

As the last note of the overture died away the curtain rose, and the baritone singing the role of Orsini rushed onto the stage in full costume, singing "*Hier ist's, hier ist's!...*" The men in the chorus came in perfectly on queue.

The opera moved along on schedule, with musical interludes between some of the acts, and intermissions during others. At the end of the intermission following the second act, Richard Fairchild and Bob Merriam took their place in the wings as the singers and actors got ready to start the third and longest act. It began with the principals and everyone in the choruses in a stage setting of the ancient Roman forum, with ruins of columns and collapsed temple arches. A bell, like a church bell, was tolling. As the curtain rose, the chorus, men and women, were milling around the stage, singing in German, "Have you heard the news? Protect your valuables! The nobles have already fled. Rienzi! Look for the Tribune...." Fairchild felt a presence beside him, and turned to find George McCracken standing beside him. McCracken put his finger to his lips and moved back into the shadows, with Fairchild beside him.

"It will be at the end of this act," the CIA agent whispered. "You have done a remarkable job, Richie, but it may not be over yet."

"So something is really going to happen?"

"Definitely."

"May I ask who it is? I've gotten to know these people pretty well."

"Whom do you suspect?" McCracken asked teasingly.

"Well, the professor, of course."

"Who?" McCracken sounded surprised.

"Dr. von Werdau. She's left the Germans and moved into our hotel, and wants to spend the day with us tomorrow, although the others are returning to East Germany in the morning. I'm surprised the Stasi officer who's been with us hasn't picked up on her yet."

"God, that's not who.... What is she a professor of?"

"Nuclear physics."

"Richard! You're kidding me!"

"Not at all, George. See the rather short guy with the gray hair standing over there on the other side? He has been watching her awfully closely."

"Yes, that's Major Gärtner. We knew he was here. We've also been followed by the Stasi since we arrived at the airport. They've been expecting us, I guess. But I know nothing about this professor. Who is she?"

"See the pretty blond, in the far corner over there. That's Hilda von Werdau of Halle University. Her friend, Dr. Maria Fergen, was our guide in East Germany."

"Well, we have a few German officers assigned to NATO with us, so we probably have them outnumbered, but I was not expecting to leave with two defectors, if, in fact, this professor is going to defect."

"I thought for a while it might be Gärtner who would be the defector," Fairchild said. "He just showed up at the train station yesterday morning and accompanied us across the border. In fact, he sat across from Hilda all the way from Leipzig. He told us that Hilda is a friend of General Kahler's son, Johann. I also thought that maybe it might be Lieutenant Schuster. I knew his father from the war."

"No, Schuster is gung-ho Army. So is Johann, a Captain in the Navy. We knew he had a lover, but were not sure who it was. It must be this professor. How did you know Schuster's father?"

"Remember when I was a POW? Schuster was the German chaplain assigned to guard me, and who let me escape. But you knew about Kahler and his son?"

"General Kahler is our target."

Fairchild said nothing. He did not know the General all that well. There he was, singing in the group of Germans, along with his Lieutenant, Schuster. Mark Ahearn came up behind them, along with another American, who was not introduced. McCracken quickly explained that they might have two defectors rather than one, and the men stiffened. They were not prepared for this.

*   *   *

The third scene of Act Three began with the ringing of bells and the clamor of the approaching battle between the nobles and the citizens of Rome. The entire chorus, dressed as townspeople and armed with swords and spears, with the women carrying banners, were on the stage. The Dutch members of the chorus were dressed as monks and priests, and they were all marching toward a Church. The tenor singing the role of Rienzi called them to battle, and the familiar theme of the battle hymn was sung by the men of the chorus. Then the women sang a high lyrical unaccompanied chorus that sounded more like it belonged in a church than an opera. Then the battle hymn occurred again, the orchestra worked to a frenzied pace, and with a final shout from the chorus of *"Zu End ist Sklavenjoch!"* -- *the yoke of slavery is broken*, the curtain came down to loud applause.

George McCracken stepped forward to the edge of the stage, and raised his arm, as if to signal. General Kahler turned and started walking toward McCracken. Hilda von Werdau seemed to be walking behind him.

"Ask her!" McCracken shouted above the noise to Fairchild, who then stepped out onto the stage, afraid they would raise the curtain for a curtain call, even though the opera was not yet over. Stage hands were busy moving scenery for the next act as Fairchild quickly stepped up to Hilda.

"That was beautiful, Hilda," he said. "But there is now an opportunity. Do you wish to defect? Do you want to come to America?"

"Yes!" she exclaimed, looking into his face with an expression of both fear and relief. "Yes, I want to go with you to America."

"Come quickly then." Fairchild took hold of her arm, and gently led her to the side of the stage where Mark Ahearn stood. "Hilda, this is an American officer. He will help you. Just do as he asks."

By this time Gärtner and the other Stasi officer, Tomas Bücher, who had been expecting all the East Germans to exit the stage on the other side as had been the practice all day, realized what was happening. They came running across the wide stage, headed particularly for Hilda von Werdau. As Gärtner approached, General Kahler drew the sword from the scabbard on his costume and confronted the Stasi officers. "No, Klaus, you will not have her, nor I," he said in German.

The second Stasi officer drew a gun, but before he could aim it or fire it Kahler brought the costume sword -- which was dull, but effective -- down on his wrist, and the gun fell and skidded across the stage. Bob Merriam quickly picked it up, and aimed it at the Stasi officer who was now holding his seriously injured wrist.

They were all suddenly surrounded by armed policemen. The East German singers had all left the stage with Lieutenant Schuster, as had the Fremont singers, and the stage hands seemed not to be paying any attention to what was happening around them. The police led the three CIA men, the two Stasi officers, Kahler, von Werdau, Fairchild and Merriam back behind the stage to an empty room, inquiring in German, "*Was ist los?*"

Two high-ranking West German officers approached, identified themselves to the American CIA men as their NATO contacts, and spoke to the police officers in German. One of the officers was sent to get a physician to see about the wounded Stasi officer. It was explained to the police captain who then came into the room what was taking place. He was asked to arrange transportation to the airport, six kilometers east of the outer ring road, where NATO had a jet waiting to take General Kahler, and now also Hilda von Werdau, along with the CIA agents, to Belgium.

"Why are we taking the woman?" one of the West German officers asked.

It was General Kahler who replied. "First, before you speak, get those two Stasi officers out of here. I'm sorry, Klaus. We've been friends, but your politics and mine do not match. You are too much like my son, as even Hilda will tell you."

"We will hunt the two of you down, you can be sure, Kurt. Always look over your shoulder, for the Stasi will always be there, and the opportunity will come."

"Go to hell, Major!" Kahler said, as the police clasped handcuffs on Gärtner and bandaged the other Stasi officer, Bücher.

"What do we do with them?" the police captain asked the West German Army officer, who then conferred with McCracken.

"Bücher is a spy. He's been operating in Bonn targeting NATO operations. Him you can throw in jail. Gärtner is here legally. He crossed the frontier with proper papers yesterday. You can throw him back across the border if you want, but why not keep him on ice for a couple of years," McCracken said. "He'll soon forget about his threats on General Kahler and the Professor he just made here. Come to think of it, isn't making a threat of harm a crime here in West Germany?"

"*Ja*," said the police captain, "I think it might be."

"Then that's grounds to arrest him, too."

"Can you deliver this message to my Lieutenant?" Kahler asked after the Stasi officers were removed. "He'll be like a lost sheep, and our singers are all loyal soldiers."

"What is it?" the captain asked.

"Tell him that I have become sick and have been taken to the hospital. He is to accompany the singers back to Leipzig in the morning as arranged. Tell him that Hilda von Werdau and Major Gärtner are going to stay here, and return with me in a few days. By the time he -- or Berlin -- figures out what has happened, we will be far away."

"General," Hilda von Werdau said, "perhaps the police could retrieve my case at the same time as they deliver your message. I don't wish to leave the theater in this uncomfortable costume, but we do need to take the costume with us."

"Certainly," the police captain replied, giving the command to his officer.

"May I ask why you want your costume?" Dr. Fairchild inquired, while the others were talking about the arrests.

"Yes," she whispered. "There are the design plans for the new Russian nuclear submarine sewn inside the costume. I thought you in the West might be interested. I have no money, and I have nothing but my knowledge to trade."

Fairchild later told his CIA friend. "Good God!" McCracken exclaimed. "She needn't worry. She'll be well taken care of."

* * *

None of the Dutch opera crew, the East German choristers or the Fremont students -- not even Esther or Sally -- had any idea of what had taken place, and Fairchild had no intentions of telling them. Even Bob Merriam was sworn to silence, at least temporarily. There was to be no news leaks about the double defection. The East Germans and Russians would find out soon enough.

On June 26 the Royal Dutch Opera Company packed up their costumes, scenery and singers and boarded a train headed for Vienna, where a new crop of extra choristers awaited the long, loud trumpet note. It was a day off for the Fremont students, and most of the music majors headed to Wägner's and Liszt's homes, and to the old baroque opera house in the city. The rest relaxed on the busy square, purchasing souvenirs, writing post cards and letters, enjoying the German pastries and other delicacies, and by mid-afternoon, the beerhalls. The East German Army singers had departed earlier that morning by bus to a different border station at Probstzella, a small village one hundred miles north of Nürnberg, where the rail line ran directly to Leipzig.

* * *

After learning of the travel plans from the clerk at Erfurt, Captain Johann Kahler stood awaiting the arrival of the Stuttgart to Leipzig train at 1613, a quarter after four that afternoon. The Erfurt soldiers, accompanied by his father, were to return to Erfurt from the Leipzig Bahnhof after dinner that evening. Johann planned to make an effort to be friendly to his father, and invite him to dinner, along with Hilda von Werdau, whom he would offer to drive back to Halle.

He was nervous as the train pulled into the station, and the East German soldiers, once again in their uniforms, climbed off one of the coaches in the center of the train. There were virtually no officers, other than some sergeants, other than one lieutenant, who disembarked from the coach. Johann went to him immediately.

"Pardon," he said, addressing Lieutenant Ernst Schuster in German, "but I am Captain Johann Kahler. My father, Major General Kahler, was supposed to be returning on this train, along with my friend, Professor von Werdau. Have you seen them? Are they still aboard?"

"Oh, Captain Kahler!" the Lieutenant replied in a pleasant voice. "No, I'm sorry. I'm afraid I have some bad news."

"What?"

"Last night, during the opera, your father became ill. They had to take him to the hospital there in Bayreuth, and both Professor von Werdau and the Stasi officer who was with us, went with him. He will be returning as soon as he is able to travel, I was informed. I hope that it is nothing serious."

"Oh, I do too. Thank you, Lieutenant."

Johann Kahler feared the worst. But the fact that the Stasi officer who had been with the group also remained in Bayreuth might indicate that his father really was sick. Still, there would be no reason for Hilda not to have returned. He found a telephone and placed a call to Admiral Schmidt. He knew that the senior procurement officer was awaiting word that all was well.

"Helmut Schmidt," the admiral announced when the operator rang his telephone at Naval Headquarters in Berlin.

"Admiral Schmidt, this is Johann Kahler. I'm in Leipzig."

"*Ja*, Johann. You have the Professor with you?"

"No, Admiral. I was informed that my father became ill last evening at the opera and was taken to the hospital in Bayreuth, and she went with him. There is apparently a Stasi officer with them."

"That is nonsense, Johann! She would not have gone with your father. She has defected. The NATO people were probably waiting for her, and that Stasi officer may already be dead."

"But we don't know that."

"Count on it, I fear. Johann, go to von Werdau's apartment in Halle and get those Russian submarine plans. If there is a report there, get it, too. If the plans are not there, then you can assume that she has them with her in her defection to the West."

"What then?"

"It will not take the Russians long to learn that their secret plans are in the hands of NATO. Both Stasi and the KGB are going to be all over us as to how they got out of our possession. Johann, you are a good officer, but you are the one who suggested that the plans be given to this professor friend of yours. I must protect myself. I cannot protect you, too, and I would not want to be in your shoes when either the Stasi or the KGB come hunting for you. It will not be pleasant, Johann. It could even be fatal."

"But you approved...."

"I will deny it. This was all your arrangements. My records here already reflect that. No, the blame will fall on you."

"But, Admiral Schmidt! What can I do?"

"Your career is finished. The best I could suggest is to go to Bayreuth, and if the professor is still there, which I doubt, kill her and get those papers back. If she's not there, hunt her down. What she knows is even more important than those drawings. If she is allowed to float around all over Europe and America, we are in deep trouble. No, *you* are in deep trouble. Find her and kill her."

"What about my father?"

"If he is really ill, you'll know soon enough. But chances are he, too, has defected. What a prize, Johann! A general officer in the border troops? Why, the West would love to know our border defenses and secrets. They've probably been tempting him for years. You yourself told me he was not a party supporter, just nominally in the party as are all our officers. He's probably a good, loyal soldier gone bad, and if he is not in a Bayreuth hospital, you'd better find him and kill him too."

"If I could do that, could I then return?"

"No. It is too late. You will be hunted by the Stasi and the KGB. They will consider you as much a defector as the others, but you will be targeted. Always watch over your shoulder, Johann.

"I will do this for you, but nothing more. Go to the Naval Intelligence Attaché there in Leipzig. I will cable to him an order for ten thousand West German marks and a civilian passport. Get it tonight, get some civilian clothing, and be out of East Germany by the morning. If, as you hope, both your father and this professor are in Bayreuth, get her back here, dead or alive, I don't care, as long as she has those drawings and plans with her. If she is not there, then you know what to do. Do it, and good luck." With that, the admiral hung up, and Johann Kahler stood looking at the telephone receiver in his hand.

Kahler returned to his automobile and drove to the office of the Leipzig Naval Attaché, which was near the Bahnhof. It took half an hour for the cable from Berlin to arrive. The Attaché, also a Navy Captain, said little as he counted out the West German currency and prepared travel documents and a false passport for Kahler in the name of Gerhardt Kalbmann. As a Naval Intelligence Officer, he knew that whatever mission Kahler was on was none of his business, and he simply acted as instructed.

Kahler then drove the thirty-five kilometers to Halle, broke into von Werdau's apartment, but could find neither the submarine report nor any other significant papers. He then drove south in his Russian-built automobile, after purchasing a shirt and a pair of trousers in Halle and disposing of his uniform. Once across the border he would have to get rid of the auto -- it was insufficient for travel in the West -- and by ten that evening he was at the border crossing at Gefell, on the direct road to Bayreuth.

Chapter 11

The Fremont students' last two full days in West Germany were largely spent touring. On the morning of June 27 they took the train from Bayreuth to Nürnberg, arriving about noon, and spent the rest of the day sightseeing. A bus had been arranged to give them a tour of the medieval Bavarian town, famous for its canals, buildings, churches, gated walls and Bavarian-style sausages, beer and pastries. Shortly after five the bus delivered them back to the Bahnhof, and they boarded an express train to Augsburg, arriving about an hour and a half later.

The group was to spend only one night in Augsburg, the last of the learning sessions about Martin Luther to take place the following morning. They would then return to Frankfurt later that afternoon. "What happened initially here in Augsburg," Fairchild explained to the students the following morning before they were let loose on the town to do their final shopping and beerhall visiting, "led up to the trial before the Diet at Worms. Prince Frederick negotiated with Cardinal Thomas de Vio Cajetan, the papal legate, to give Luther a hearing before the Diet to be held here in Augsburg in October of 1518, a year after he had posted his issues for debate. By this time Luther was a well-known theological scholar. Cardinal Cajetan was simply an Italian bishop and a general in the Dominican Order. Remember, they were the ones assigned the theological inquiries known as the Inquisition. Cajetan said he wanted to act as a father to Luther, not as a judge, but as the three-day hearing progressed, it was clear that this was not to be.

"On the first day Luther gave an indication of humility, prostrating himself before the cardinal, and being given a gesture of reconciliation. But then the cardinal informed Luther that he must recant -- deny -- the theological positions he had taken, especially regarding the Indulgences. Remember, this was an economic and political issue as much as a theological one, although Luther saw it only in a theological light. Keep in mind that the Turks were at Europe's back door, and the princes needed the Church's sanction for the raising of money to fight what was really the last Crusade.

"Luther refused to recant, realizing that it might result in his being burned as a heretic, although Frederick had obtained for him a promise of safety from Emperor Maximilian if he attended the Augsburg hearing. His primary fear was that if he were to be killed as a heretic he would disgrace his parents.

"The hearing was heated," Fairchild continued. "There was a lot of pomp and ceremony, characteristic of medieval pageantry, as especially practiced by the Church.

'Are you alone wise, and all the ages in error?' Cajetan inquired. Luther asked that the cardinal show him where his errors were. The cardinal replied that it was in Luther's denial of the Church's treasury of merit that had been announced by Pope Clement VI in 1343. The two sparred on the language of the document. Cajetan leafed through the document to the place where it stated that Christ, by his sacrifice, had *acquired* a treasure. 'Oh, yes,' Luther sarcastically countered, 'but *you*,' meaning Cardinal Cajetan, 'said that the merits of Christ *are* a treasure. This says he *acquired* a treasure. To *be* and to *acquire* do not mean the same thing. You need not think we Germans are ignorant of grammar.' Unfortunately, Luther's blustering and his theological points were not well aimed. The cardinal had interpreted the document correctly, and the whole issue fell to whether the 'keys of the kingdom' had indeed been assigned by Jesus to Peter, and thus to Peter's successors, the popes. If so, then this treasury of merit enhanced by the virtue of the saints was a treasury for the Church to use. Luther was trapped in the debate, even though he later declared that Cajetan was no more fit to try him than a donkey to play a harp. Nevertheless, the cardinal continued his efforts, through Luther's friends, to try to get him to recant.

"Keep in mind, however, that at this time Luther was still an Augustinian, and thus under a vow of obedience. He was in Augsburg with his order's vicar, John Staupitz, who had not only Luther to consider, but also the reputation of the entire order. Staupitz and Cajetan had dinner after the debate, and it became clear that Luther was unmovable in his position. Staupitz did not think that he could persuade Luther to recant, although he could technically order him, under the vow, to do so. Instead Staupitz released Luther from his vow, in effect, terminating his standing as a monk in the Augustinian order. Luther considered this as serious an act against him as excommunication itself.

"We hear much about Luther's *Augsburg Confession*. This is a basic statement of Luther's theology of 'grace through faith,' but it dates from some twelve years later, after the new church was well under way, not from the 1518 trial. It is a document of belief still actively in use by Protestant churches today. Luther's theology had an effect on all of Protestantism, from the Church in England to the Calvinists. There were differences, of course, but it was largely that stand by Luther against the excesses of the Church that led to the Great Awakening and the influences that continue to be reflected today.

"For example, the idea that salvation comes solely, or primarily, by one's belief, or faith, not by our own efforts, lies at the heart of a considerable amount of Protestant theology. Luther rejected much of the power of the clergy and many of the traditions and doctrines of the

Church, such as the veneration of saints and relics, the authority of Rome, the use of Latin only and celibacy of the clergy. At the same time he asserted the absolute authority of Scripture. Now, tell me what you think you have learned from our visits to Luther's centers of action and from the lectures you've heard about Luther."

It took several minutes and a few false starts before the students finally began to express what they had learned in some sort of logical format. Much of it was general in nature, such as the use of the Church's absolute power in a corrupt way, an idea that stirred debate between several of the students, including one of the Canadians who was a devout Catholic. "Luther," she said, "seems to have denied what the Gospels say Jesus said, that the keys of the kingdom were given to Peter, and that what was bound or loosed on earth was bound or loosed in Heaven. I don't think he had any right to do that."

"That's an excellent point, Kathy," Fairchild said. "Do any of you want to debate that issue?"

"Well, yes," Darrell Willingham, a history major, replied. "The Bible says Jesus said that to Peter. He didn't say anything about bishops of Rome."

"But Luther seems to rely more on the writings of Paul than the teachings of Jesus," Kathy Stewart countered. "It is like he was ignoring what Jesus taught. This seems evident in his suggestion that the Book of James, which seems to echo the three gospels more than Paul's writings, not be included in the Bible. I can't see where what Paul says, if it differs from what Jesus is supposed to have said, should take more emphasis in theology."

"I agree," Evelyn Woodbury, one of the choir members, said. "It seems to me that if the New Testament says anything -- of what Christianity really is -- is that one's actions speak louder than what one says or believes. Like James says in this Letter, faith without work is dead. Dr. Fairchild, doesn't he say something like, 'Even the devil believes, but what good does it do him?'"

"Close," Fairchild replied, "'Devils also believe, and shudder.' Anyone else?"

Jack Hornbet raised his hand. "But Luther's point wasn't just 'faith' or 'belief.' It was that we can't *work* our way to Heaven by just being good. He seems to be arguing that it takes God's love as expressed in the sacrifice of Jesus to win atonement."

"That's a very good observation, Jack," Fairchild said, "but would that argument not also support the arguments of Cajetan that such grace is for the Church to disburse?"

"Perhaps Luther's point was that one didn't need the Church to receive this grace," Jack replied.

"Then why do we still have a church?" Andrea Morgan asked.

"I was always taught that the church is just like a restaurant or a kitchen," Judy Yeary, a Lutheran from Pennsylvania, said. "We go there to receive the nourishment needed to go out into the world and do what we are called to do as Christians. It isn't the church itself, or the teachings -- the mental, or spiritual food, or, I guess as the Gospels would say, bread -- that is important, it is what we do with that sustenance."

"But doesn't that make church irrelevant?" Mary Crawford inquired.

"Not at all," Judy rebutted. "We need the church to give us the motivation and the authority to do what we should do as Christians."

"What about non-Christians?" Fairchild asked. "You may recall the lecture Dr. Fergen gave in Wittenberg on Luther's anti-Semitism. Although he rejected the Church's doctrine that sixteenth century Jews were personally responsible for the death of Jesus, he believed that it was the duty to Christians to proselytize and convert Jews to Christianity. You may remember that when Luther heard that some Christians were turning to Judaism in Protestant areas of Moravia, he recommended that all Jews be deported to Palestine, or at the very least be forbidden from serving as money lenders, and that their synagogues should be burned and their books confiscated. All this he published in one of his tracts, and don't think that it was ever forgotten. It was resurrected often by the anti-Semetics in Nazi Germany.

"We might try to defend Luther's position as being a theological one, not racist," the professor continued, "but in the long run that might not wash. He cited the authority of Paul, a converted Pharisaic Jew, who decreed in *Romans*, Chapter Ten, that the Jews were disobedient by rejecting Jesus as their Messiah, relying instead on the law, or *Torah*, although Paul thought that this rejection was perhaps only temporary.

"Luther's theology, heavily leaning toward Paul, further created a climate in Germany that also attributed to Nazism, and perhaps even in today's Communism. Look, for example, at what Paul says in the thirteenth chapter of *Romans*, 'Let every soul be in subjection to the higher powers,' meaning governments; 'for there is no power but of God, and the powers that be are ordained by God. Therefore he that resists that authority withstands the ordinance of God.' This implies the divine right of kings, and the authority of the state, demanding obedience. Could this be why so many Germans stood by and let Adolph Hitler come into power?

"What do you think our American writer, Henry David Thoreau, might say about this? Is Paul -- and thus Luther -- right? Is it wrong to oppose authority or government? Are monarchs given their authority solely by God? Remember, it is the Archbishop of Canterbury who placed the crown on Queen Elizabeth's head. It is often the Church hierarchy that supports monarchs. Does God alone determine the outcome of elections? Our Constitution makes provisions for impeachment of Presidents and others in high office if they commit crimes. Does this not go counter to what Paul seems to be saying regarding obedience to any civil authority? Joe, you told me that your dad is a Baptist minister, but that he supports the civil rights movement in Mississippi and Martin Luther King's practice of civil disobedience. You said that many in your dad's congregation had challenged him on the issue. On what did they base their arguments?"

"The Bible," Joe Williams, the Baptist from Mississippi answered. "But if it's in the Bible, shouldn't we believe it?"

"Martin Luther King, Jr. might question that when it comes to the authority of some small-town sheriff with a big dog, but the sixteenth century Martin Luther would certainly agree that we should, wouldn't he?"

"Why?" Kathy Stewart, the Canadian Catholic girl, asked.

"Perhaps because of the doctrine of infallibility of Scripture?" Joe answered. "'All Scripture is given by the inspiration of God,' I think is the verse."

"From Paul's Second Letter to Timothy," Fairchild confirmed. "Joe, what 'scripture' was Paul referencing?"

"The Bible. It's all God's word."

"What *Bible*? When Paul wrote that letter in around 67 AD it is not even certain whether John Mark had written his gospel yet. True, Paul knew John Mark, the author of that first gospel we call *Mark*, for the boy had accompanied Paul on his first missionary journey, but they had some sort of disagreement, we are told in Luke's *Acts of the Apostles*, and Paul sent him home. I would seriously doubt that, if John Mark had written anything by the time that Paul wrote that second letter to Timothy, he'd have considered Mark's writing to be *Scripture*. So, what 'scripture' would Paul be talking about?"

"The Old Testament?" Mary Crawford asked.

"Precisely. We might also question whether Paul would have considered his own writings to be "scripture.' I will grant that he had a high opinion of his own opinions and theology -- declaring that he got it all directly from God, as he so states in *Galatians* -- but I doubt that even Paul would have considered his own writings to be equal with *Torah*, the *Psalms* and the prophets. Do we need to look beyond Paul for a better authority?"

"To the books of the gospel? Is that what you mean, Dr. Fairchild?" Kathy answered. "I mean, God just didn't up and stop talking to us two thousand years ago. So why should the Church -- Rome -- not have just as valid a position as to the Word of God as St. Paul?"

"But can Jews be saved?" Joe Williams asked, returning to the earlier question. "I've always been taught that they can't, because they don't believe in Christ."

"Me, too," one of the other students added.

"How would Jesus answer that question?" Fairchild replied. "Would we assert that God's love is so narrow and limited that it can only be applied to those who believe in a certain form of theology? It seems to me that this is what Luther perhaps was saying, but in light of the last four hundred years of theological study, would we all be prepared to agree with him?"

"You mean just anybody can be saved, Dr. Fairchild, whether they are a Christian or not?" Andrea Morgan asked.

"That's not what my church says!" Evelyn Woodbury firmly stated.

"No, the concept of universal salvation is difficult for many to accept," the professor replied. "But then again, how do we define what a 'Christian' is? Is a Christian defined by what he or she thinks or believes, by what he or she does or does not do, by a combination of these, or by something else?"

"Professor Fairchild," Judy Yeary interrupted, "you said in the New Testament Class last year that the word 'Christ' is Greek for the Hebrew word 'Messiah,' which means 'the anointed one of God.' So a Christian would have to be someone that believed that Jesus was 'the anointed one.'"

"Okay, so would you say that belief that Jesus was the Messiah is key to being a Christian? Is that a correct interpretation of what you just said?"

"Yes."

"Do you remember the story we discussed in the class about the Transfiguration?"

"Yes."

"What was one of the main points in the story?"

"I don't remember!"

"Does anyone else?

"Oh," Jack Hornbet said, "You mean the voice of God being heard."

"Okay, Jack, and what did the voice say?" No one answered, and Fairchild continued. "'This is my son.... Listen to him.' Over and over in the gospels we hear Jesus say things like, 'Blessed are they who hear my words, and keep them,' or 'if you love me, you will keep my commandment to love one another.' If we believe that Jesus was the Christ, then to be a Christian must also mean that we are to keep his commandments to love one another, it seems to me."

"But can non-Christians go to Heaven, Dr. Fairchild?" Andrea Morgan again asked.

"I guess we'll all find out the answer to that question when we get there ourselves, Andrea. In the meantime, I'm not qualified to judge or say whom God will allow into Heaven and whom he won't allow. My own personal guess is that God has sufficient love for everyone." He hesitated, but the students had no further questions.

When Fairchild concluded the discussion he advised those that were interested in sites around the city where they might find remnants of the 16th Century world, but the students quickly scattered to accomplish their own agendas. Their luggage was already in the lobby, and they were to report back early so that they could catch the direct train to Frankfurt that left shortly after four-thirty that afternoon.

Before their departure, Fairchild met briefly with the other two faculty members, Bob Merriam and Ross Johnson. "As you both know, Paul Sukhey has asked me to inspect some ancient manuscript in France. It was supposed to be auctioned July 3, but was moved up to July 1, at a different location. I've not changed the reservation I have to fly back from Paris, but I've not mentioned the changes to any of the students, for fear that some of them might also want to stay over and fly home later. I don't think we want our group wandering all over Europe while they are under our jurisdiction. They can do that on their own if they want at some other time.

"Bob, you said you would record the grades for each of the religion students with the Dean when you get back, and I appreciate that. Ross, you said you'd record your music students' grades. I think they all participated with enthusiasm and willing attention, although there were a couple of our history students who had put some extra work into research before the trip, and I want to award them with an A. For some of them, a B is a gift, and we ourselves deserve an A for putting up with them.

"Anyway, Esther has decided not to stay, and will return with you to Detroit. Bob, would you mind dropping her at the farm when you get home? I'd appreciate it."

"No problem, Richie. We'll make sure everything is okay there before we leave her alone. But I trust you have left her a list of all the places you can be contacted."

"Yes, I have the hotels reserved, so she has some phone numbers for emergencies. Once I see this document that Paul wants me to inspect, I need to call him and find out if the museum in Columbus wants to place a bid. I should be home by the evening of July 4, just in time for fireworks."

* * *

The train that left Augsburg direct to Frankfurt that afternoon got the group to Frankfurt shortly after nine. The train had a dining car and the students were on their own, hence could order whatever they wished, or could afford. The hotel was near the Bahnhof, and the following morning, after checking out, a bus took them to the airport for their flight back to Chicago at two that afternoon. By five-thirty Central Daylight Saving Time they were back in the United States, and by midnight most were home in their own beds.

Richard Fairchild had gone with the group to the airport to make sure no problems arose, and to see Esther and the others off. He then returned to Frankfurt and caught a train at five o'clock for Strasbourg, France, where he spent the night. Early the next morning he caught an express train to Lyon, arriving in Arles early in the afternoon.

* * *

Robert Merriam had left his car in a long-term parking lot at the Detroit airport, as he and Sally had driven there to meet the students prior to the trip. The students had all taken various flights from Chicago to their homes, and only a few were returning to the campus in Fremont. Both Esther Fairchild and Ross Johnson rode back to Fremont with the Merriams, about a two-hour drive via Toledo and the Ohio Turnpike.

"That was some trip," Ross Johnson said after they had claimed their luggage and no longer had students tagging along. They headed out to the parking lot, where Bob's old Oldsmobile was sitting. "Some of the students said something happened after the third act of the opera, but nobody seemed to know what it was. I noticed that the East German general and that blond professor, Hilda, were not there at the end. What did they do, elope?"

Bob laughed, "Well, yeah, sort of, but I'm not supposed to say anything."

"Oh, Pooh! You can tell us," Sally insisted.

"Well, I was sworn to secrecy till we got home, but I guess we're home now. But, Esther, please don't tell Richie I spilled the beans before we actually got home. You know how he is about details."

"Don't worry, Bob, I'm as curious as the others. I thought something was up, but Richie wouldn't discuss it."

"Ross, I noticed you had an eye on that professor. What did you think?"

"Frankly, I thought she was very beautiful. I was wishing that she was on the faculty at Fremont. Don't forget, I'm still single. I understand she is, too, but from what I heard from some of the East German Army singers, she is engaged to the general's son. But what happened?"

"Well, a couple of months before we left Sally said she thought something might be developing with the American Intelligence community about our trip. You may not have known that Richie was assigned to an Intelligence unit during the War. Actually, the old German Army chaplain, Adolph Schuster, did not even know that Richie was in Intelligence when he was captured. The Nazis would probably have shot him if they had known. He was, as he has said, an Army chaplain, but he also served as an interpreter and interrogated prisoners. He spoke better German than he let on.

"Anyway, a couple of months before we left, two men, apparently from the CIA -- one of whom was Richie's old company commander in Military Intelligence -- came to the office. I didn't meet them, but Sally did. A week later all our plans changed, and Sally guessed that it had something to do with the CIA. Apparently you were right, Sally. Both the two you told me about, McCracken and Ahearn, were there in Bayreuth."

"They were? I didn't see them!"

"As far as I can understand the thing, the CIA and either NATO or Dutch Intelligence put together a plan to get Major General Kahler out of East Germany. He had somehow communicated to them that he wanted to defect. The idea of inviting East German soldiers to sing in the opera was devised as a means of his traveling to the West. Apparently the CIA wanted a major role for the Americans as well, so the idea of having our students also sing in the opera was implemented. I think it might have worked even without us, but we added some padding to the plan, giving the General and his staff some additional reason to travel to Bayreuth.

"The General, it turned out, knew Professor von Werdau -- who apparently was very close to the General's son, an East German Navy captain -- but nobody realized that she, Hilda, also wanted to defect. Maybe the General knew, but I don't think so. Richie suspected it, however, so when the moment came, the CIA got two defectors instead of just one." By this time the group had gotten into Bob's car and they had exited the parking lot, getting on the freeway headed toward Ohio.

"Richie was instrumental in that. He knew there was to be a defection, but he did not know whom. At one point, he told me, he thought it might be that Stasi major who met us at the train in Wittenberg. He thought the general was solid East German military. But if you recall, Hilda wanted to move to our hotel, and wanted to join our group touring the next day. Therefore, Richie thought she might be the defector. When he asked her, on the stage after the third act, if she wanted to defect, she said yes. But the Stasi -- there were two agents there opposite us on the stage -- already suspected her, because she apparently had a top secret clearance and knew some crucial nuclear information, and they came charging across the stage after her.

"The one Stasi agent pulled a gun to shoot her, and the general clobbered him with that costume sword he was wearing in the opera. It was quite a moment. The Stasi guy dropped the gun, and I picked it up, and the CIA and police took us all down to some room, where some NATO officers showed up to take General Kahler and Hilda away. They arrested the two Stasi agents, and cooked up some story about the General getting sick and being taken to the hospital. But that's all I know. Please, you mustn't say anything to anyone. The Communists may not yet know there has been a defection."

"I bet they do," Sally replied. "I'll bet when those German Army singers got back it was very clear that something was wrong. Who knows, they might come after us, too."

"Oh, I don't think so. But they might come after the General and Hilda. It's pretty embarrassing, I'm sure, to both the Russians and the East Germans."

"Gosh!" Ross said. "I hope Hilda gets to America. I wonder if there is any way I might contact her. Say, didn't Dean Harding say something at the last faculty meeting about needing another physics professor?"

"That's right, Ross. I think he did. When Richie gets back, I'll ask him what his thoughts might be on presenting the possibility of hiring Hilda at Fremont. By then she may have been given some new identity. But Richie's friends in the CIA might know how to reach her."

"I should have known something was up the night those two CIA guys came for dinner," Esther said. "Richie simply said they were old Army buddies, but the one guy was too young to have been in their unit in 1944. Richie was awfully quite after they left, and that is not like him."

"Do you think this inspection of a manuscript in France has anything to do with the CIA, Esther?" Sally asked.

"Oh, golly, I hope not. But I don't think so. He has known Paul Sukhey at the Antiquities Museum Library in Columbus for many years, and has made inspections for him before, so it isn't really all that unusual. No, it seems to be exactly what he said. I think he'll be home on the Fourth, Sally."

* * *

Colonel Par Nolensen, a Norwegian officer assigned to NATO in Brussels, leaned back in his chair and looked at the five other men in his office. Two were West German officers assigned to NATO, one was the Dutch Intelligence agent, named Nils Brinker, who had helped to arrange for the defection of General Kahler, and the other two were McCracken and Ahearn of the CIA. While Brussels would not officially become NATO Headquarters until five years later, many NATO activities were already occurring there. It was two in the morning, but none of them felt sleepy.

"This is all unbelievable!" Nolensen remarked. "Not only do we get the man who knows -- and helped to create -- the East German border defenses, we get the Russian nuclear submarine plans as well."

"As of this moment, there has been no indication that the East Germans or the Russians are aware of the defections," one of the West German officers, who had also been at Bayreuth, said. "But they'll wake up soon enough when they find Major Gärtner missing, along with their pretty scientist and their border general."

"What are you doing with Gärtner?" Ahearn asked.

"He's in a max cell in Stuttgart. They've got one of our guys over in Hungary. Maybe we'll work out a trade in a few months. Same with Bücher. He was a useless worm anyway."

"Can we believe everything von Werdau and Kahler told us?" the Dutch agent asked.

"I think so," George McCracken said. "The plans the professor brought out in her skirt appear pretty authentic, and match some of what we already suspected. She seems genuinely concerned that their submarines are dangerous and pose as big a threat to the East Germans as to the West. That, more than politics, seemed to be her motivation. She simply doesn't want a nuclear incident where we fail to understand the cause and respond with a nuclear missile or bomb."

"They'll hunt her down," the Norwegian said. "What do you propose?"

"New identity, new nationality," the Dutchman replied. "George, do you think you could arrange something in the States?"

"I'm sure we could try. She'd make a good professor for some university, maybe even Fremont College."

"I'd suggest Holland or Denmark," Brinker added, "but it's too close. They'd find her. She needs to be far away."

"What about the general?" Ahearn asked.

"It's going to take a week or more to finish his debriefing. He wants money and a new identity. Says he has some property in Switzerland he wants to reclaim, and then he may head for South America. He has some old German Army friends in Paraguay or Uruguay or one of those countries. A lot of Germans went there after the war," one of the West German officers said.

"He speaks several languages. He'll get along, but he needs to watch his back, too. The KGB will have their long knives out for him."

"All this might make it hard on his kid. The professor said the kid is the one who pushed her being made the East German advisor on the Russian sub deal, and then his father up and defects, too," Brinker commented.

"It could be the kid that they'll send after the two of them," Ahearn added. "He knows them both, and could get close. According to both the father and the girlfriend, he was gung-ho Communist."

"We've got to do what we can to keep them safe. We might need them again some time. You never know," Colonel Nolensen said.

Chapter 12

Würtrzburg, West Germany
June 28, 1962, 10 a.m.

Gerhardt Kalbmann stopped at a Shell station to fill the tank of the four-year-old Audi he had purchased at a used vehicle dealership just outside Würtrzburg. He had checked at every hospital in and around Bayreuth, and none of them had treated, or knew anything about, his father. Even the Bayreuth police at the big opera house knew nothing about the East German general or the pretty blond professor. The Dutch opera company had moved on to Vienna the following morning.

Kalbmann -- no longer able to call himself Captain Johann Kahler -- anticipated that the defectors would have been taken to NATO headquarters in Belgium, and that was where he was headed. He'd never been to Brussels, but there was the outside chance that he would spot one or both of them if he got there quickly and watched closely.

The Autobahn ran south of Frankfurt, and another curved northwest just outside Wiesbaden. Kalbmann had never seen these cities, but was surprised by the amount and speed of the traffic on the super highways, and elected to not attempt to drive in the cities until he became more used to heavy traffic. Several hours later he was east of Bonn and on a highway that skirted south of the main part of Köln, and headed west to Aachen. There he crossed the border into Belgium, and by late that evening was in Brussels. He found a hotel near the central railway station, and booked it for a week.

But Kalbmann had guessed wrong. It was not at the well-known NATO offices in the center city where the debriefing of defectors was conducted, but rather at a private residence in a Sterrebeek neighborhood east of the city near a horse race track. Although he had considered himself a sophisticated and intellectual German, Kalbmann was shocked by the opulence of the West, the quantity of goods in the stores, the freedom and light-heartedness of the people on the street -- a general absence of the grayness that permeated his former life in East Germany.

He was confused. These people seemed to speak two languages, French, which he did not know, and another, called Flemish, which he also did not know. He learned from his hotel clerk, who spoke some German, that there was also a third language, Walloon, but only a few spoke that one. He quickly came to recognize that he was easily identified as a German, and that this created a barrier between him and anyone he might speak with or ask a question. He concluded that people in Belgium were hostile to Germans.

On his third day he decided he needed a new wardrobe and visited a haberdashery shop. He could not believe the prices. The conversion of his German marks to Belgian francs had cost him some percentage points in value, but he could quickly see that the original ten thousand marks would not go as far as he had anticipated. Even though his rather shabby hotel was not overly expensive, even by East German standards, he had paid cash for the Audi and now had to pay to park it, and his food was expensive.

He got up early each morning to watch the NATO offices. He spotted a separate garage entrance in which he noticed high-ranking military officers entering and leaving, and carefully watched each vehicle. Twice he saw civilians with the military personnel, but in neither case was it either his father or his ex-lover. After a week he gave up in frustration, slept late, and checked out of the hotel. He had no idea where to go next. He anticipated that NATO might send the defectors to America, but he had no idea how to get there by himself. He had no skills outside of his naval training.

But that alone might be sufficient. He turned the Audi northeastward, and headed for the West German port of Bremen. With his West German passport and his maritime knowledge, perhaps he could get a job as a helper aboard a German merchant ship. He hadn't the papers to start as an officer, but there was the chance that his training might help him obtain promotions. As he drove across Holland and back into West Germany he thought up a story he could tell to explain his background.

* * *

Arles, France
June 30, 1962, 9:30 a.m.

Richard Fairchild walked from his hotel to the address Paul Sukhey had provided, the Studio of Monique LaDuc, *20 Blvd. Des Lices*, in Arles. Refreshed with strong coffee and a large croissant, the professor enjoyed the warm breeze off the Mediterranean as he walked past the ancient Roman ruins that still cluttered this small Provence town. He stopped along the way to look at some ruins, then proceeded to try to find the address shown in the cable he had received.

The address turned out to be a three-story building. The LaDuc studio was on the second floor, and was more like an office than an art or manuscript gallery. Dr. Fairchild climbed the stairs, and found the door open, with several other men inside, leaning over a table on which some sort of ancient scroll had been partially opened and placed under a sheet of heavy plate glass.

One of the men standing around the table looked up, and exclaimed in a deep voice with a strong British accent, "Fairchild! My word! I would never have expected to see *you* here."

"Well, George Morris! How are you?" Richard Fairchild replied. "Are you still with the British Museum?"

"Oh, yes. Dispatched to have a look at this item offered for auction. Have you seen it?"

"Not yet."

"Here, let me introduce you," Morris said, as the other two men looked up from the document. "Pierre, this is Dr. Richard Fairchild, a professor at a small college in America. Richard, Dr. Pierre Gilles is the director of the Museum of Ancient Art in Brussels." As Fairchild shook hands with the Belgian the other man also introduced himself, in German, as Ezor Franisch, Director of Ancient Antiquities at the *Pergamon* in East Berlin.

"Dr. Franisch," Fairchild repeated, again shaking hands. "I am just coming from East Germany," he said in German.

"What took you to our country?" the Director asked.

"We brought a group of our students from Fremont College into Saxony to visit the homes and universities associated with Martin Luther and Bach," the professor explained. "We were in Erfurt, Leipzig and Wittenberg."

"You did not get to Berlin?"

"I've been to Berlin, yes, but not on this trip. In fact, I very much enjoyed my visit to the *Pergamon*. Your Mideast collection is remarkable."

"This document also appears remarkable, Dr. Fairchild," he said. "Come and have a look at it."

With that a slender woman about forty, her dark hair done in a bun behind her head, entered the room from a side office. "You are *Monsieur* Sukhey?" she inquired in English.

"No," Fairchild replied, "but I am here to represent Paul Sukhey, who was unable to leave Ohio. I am Richard Fairchild, a professor at Fremont College in Ohio."

"Ahh, *bon*! I am Monique. Please have a look. Tomorrow we plan to sell."

"This thing is fantastic, Richard," George Morris said, moving to one side so that Fairchild could get close to the document. There was a large magnifying glass sitting on the table on top of the glass plate. Fairchild picked up the magnifying glass and began to study the document, a scroll with lettering on what appeared to be sheepskin. There were two different types of writing on it, one rather short in length, and inserted at the top, the other well-spaced and meticulously written.

"This at the top appears to be, what, maybe Ethiopian Ge'ez?" Fairchild said.

"Ge'ez! Yes!" the Belgian exclaimed. "I couldn't place it. Do you understand Ge'ez, Dr. Fairchild?"

"No, but I've seen it before, in Egypt. It was pretty common a couple of thousand years ago throughout Northern Africa. Undoubtedly some Egyptians may be able to translate it. Below that is...."

"It's obviously Aramaic," George Morris interrupted. "From what little we see here, it seems to be some kind of list of instructions or rules, but there are a few religious words as well. It could be anything. That was a Semitic language that flourished from perhaps 300 BC to maybe 200 or 300 AD. But it's not a copy of Hammurabi's Code. That was 2100 BC in Babylonia, and this is more recent. It seems to be some sort of religious or social code, though."

"Is the British Museum interested?" Fairchild asked.

"Oh, we'd like it for our collection, of course. We'll probably place a bid."

"And the *Pergamon*?" Fairchild asked in German. "Will they bid?"

"*Ja*, we're going to buy this document," Franisch replied in German.

"A religious document?" Fairchild asked. "Will your government approve?"

"It's historical, Professor! Do you think we are all a bunch of atheistic zealots? Our government is interested in culture, and this is cultural. It will enhance our historical collection."

"Most of which they stole," the Belgian said softly in French, knowing the German did not understand. "Those German so-called archeologists practically raped Egypt and Mesopotamia for their collection in Berlin. No, this belongs in Belgium, where we at the *Musée D'Art Ancien* can properly preserve and translate it."

The conversations continued for another hour, while the four men pored over the document. Fairchild asked Monique LaDuc if they were the only ones who had inspected the document.

"No," she replied. "We had a priest from Rome here yesterday who examined it, probably on behalf of the Vatican. An Egyptian gentleman is to take a look at it this afternoon. Neither Chicago nor the Metropolitan in New York elected to send a representative."

Once Fairchild had seen all that he could, he invited Morris to have lunch with him, advising that he would need to return to his hotel briefly to telephone Sukhey in the United States. He anticipated that getting an overseas operator would take a while, so they planned to meet again at one o'clock at a bistro near the studio.

Fairchild took a taxi back to his hotel, went to his room and asked the hotel operator, in French, to get him an overseas line. A half-hour later he was connected to Paul Sukhey.

"Yes, I do think it is authentic, Paul. It could be a real treasure. Then again, it may be little more than some scholar's homework."

"What do you think it is?"

"If it is what I suspect it might be, it could be the most important find since the Qumran Scrolls. But I have no proof, and the little bit that is showing of the scroll is insufficient to confirm what it might be. I just don't know what to tell you, Paul."

"How much do they want?"

"I asked LaDuc. She said that they would start the bidding at a minimum of two hundred thousand French francs. At five to a dollar, roughly, that's $40,000. But the others there represent big national museums -- Berlin, the British Museum, the Belgian Antiquities Museum, even Rome is going to bid, but both Chicago and the Metropolitan bowed out."

"The Vatican! How are we going to out-bid them?"

"I don't know. I'd love to have this thing myself, but if you get it, I trust you'll let me help translate it."

"If we get it, Richard, you will be the one to open it. Okay, now our board has authorized up to $60,000, but they really don't want to pay that much. That, they insisted, is the maximum, and it is totally reliant on your saying that the thing has value. But I think they'd go maybe another $5000 above that if it was absolutely necessary, but if the bidding exceeds that, drop out. Something else will come along."

"Okay, Paul."

* * *

Arles, France
July 1, 1962, 9:30 a.m.

The hotel at which Richard Fairchild was staying was close enough to the LaDuc studio that he could walk to it easily, which he again did after a leisurely continental breakfast at the hotel. As he approached the address on the *Blvd. Des Lices* he saw a large crowd gathering outside the doorway to the second floor studio. Certainly there will not be that many bidders, he thought to himself. It seemed like perhaps only five or six large museums might be seriously interested in the document. Could it be that auctions are some sort of crowd-pleasing sport in France? He did not think so.

When he reached the crowd he saw Ezor Franisch standing in the doorway talking in animated German with a policeman. Pierre Gilles was standing next to him, attempting to translate. He spotted the British Museum representative, George Morris, in the crowd and moved toward him. "What's happened?" he inquired, as Morris turned and acknowledged his arrival.

"Quite a bit," the Englishman answered. "The priest from Rome -- I assume he is the Vatican's representative, specializes in ancient languages.

He's a professor at one of the colleges in Rome. Anyway, he arrived about forty minutes ago and went upstairs. He found the door to Monique LaDuc's studio open, and went in. She was lying on the floor of her office unconscious, and her safe was open and empty. The table where the document had been was also empty. He used her phone to call the police, and an ambulance took her to the hospital. She'd apparently been hit on the back of the head, but will probably survive. He was coming back down the stairs when he met the Egyptian. The German and Gilles arrived a little later and the police are talking with them now. They'll probably want to talk with us next."

"The document was stolen?"

"Apparently. Of course, the police have not yet searched the studio. It could be that LaDuc rolled it back up and put it away somewhere until the auction. But even so, there won't be any auction today."

"LaDuc didn't own the manuscript. Do you know who does?"

"Richard, this is confidential. I don't want you saying anything to anyone about it, but there have been rumors that the manuscript was a stolen document, and that Interpol has been trying to trace it for a month or more. Allegedly it was stolen from a train in Belgium -- Pierre told me that he suspects that this is the same document that an antiquities dealer from Geneva was bringing to him to examine when it was stolen. That is why the Metropolitan, and probably Chicago, refused to bid."

"Why didn't the Bureau of Antiquities here in France have a representative?" Fairchild asked. "I thought that surely Paris would be represented."

"From what my superiors learned from Interpol, it is one of their employees who is a suspect in the theft, a man named Robeleiu. That is apparently why the auction was moved from Lyon to Arles, and the date changed. The seller was afraid Interpol might confiscate the document and hold it until they determined if it was the one stolen from the Paris to Brussels train."

"Paul Sukhey told me that Claude Immour was a questionable character, but that nothing had ever been proven. Does anyone know who is supposed to own the manuscript at present?"

"Obviously LaDuc knew," the British Museum representative replied. "I hope she isn't seriously hurt, but a blow to the head...."

"Yes, it could be a pretty serious type of injury. Even when she recovers, she might have problems. I was knocked out that way a couple of years ago, and suffered some temporary memory loss."

The crowd that had gathered when the police and the ambulance had first arrived started to disburse. Pierre Gilles was still talking with the police and translating German as Morris and Fairchild moved closer. Pierre nodded to them."

"*Monsieurs,* you had business here today?" one of the policemen asked in French.

"*Oui,*" Fairchild replied, also in French, "there was to be an auction at ten this morning. We were here to participate."

"And you are?" the other inquired.

"Dr. Richard Fairchild, Professor of Religions at Fremont College in Ohio," Fairchild answered. "And this is Dr. George Morris of the British Museum in London," gesturing to the man standing beside him.

"Yes, the Belgian gave us your names. I trust you can account for your whereabouts in the past eighteen hours?"

"I was at my hotel," Morris answered, also in fairly good French. "I had both lunch and dinner with Dr. Fairchild here, and Dr. Gilles joined us for dinner, at my hotel. Afterwards I returned to my room and read a book until going to bed."

"The hotel can verify that?"

"I'm sure they can. I received a telephone call about nine, what, twenty-one hundred, from my wife in Chelsea. The hotel may have a record."

And you, Professor Fairchild?" the policeman asked.

"After dinner at Dr. Morris's hotel I, too, returned to my hotel. I read awhile, watched some television, and went to bed."

"The hotel can verify?"

"I don't know. I received or made no telephone calls, but I'm sure the desk clerk could verify that I didn't leave the hotel again."

"We shall check. Now, how well did you know Madam LaDuc?"

"Just met her yesterday," Morris answered.

"And you, Professor Fairchild?"

"Yes, I only met her yesterday as well."

"Who advised you of this auction?"

"The British Museum received a notice of the auction from a dealer in Zurich," George Morris said. "I was dispatched as I am an expert in ancient languages."

"And you, Dr. Fairchild?" the other policeman asked.

"I was instructed to come here by Dr. Paul Sukhey, director of a museum in Columbus, Ohio. He could not attend as his wife is ill. I was to represent that museum at the auction. I do not know who may have contacted Dr. Sukhey about the auction."

"So you were not contacted by anyone in France?"

"No, Sir."

"Very well. We will need your passports, gentlemen, and verification of your addresses. You may pick them up again tomorrow, unless Madame LaDuc...."

"But I have reservations from Marseilles back to London this afternoon," George Morris protested.

"I am sorry, *Monsieur*. You will need to change your plans. You may stop at our office tomorrow morning."

The instructions did not upset Fairchild as much. His return flight on Lufthansa left Orly Airport in Paris at 11:30 on the morning of July 4, arriving in Montreal at a quarter after three that afternoon. He would have plenty of time to transfer to his Trans-Canada Airlines flight to Cleveland, and should be home by midnight.

"Is there any way to verify whether the document on which we were to bid might still be somewhere in the studio," Fairchild asked the policeman.

"Did you not know?" the policeman answered. "We found the safe in the studio open. That is where Madame LaDuc was found. There were no documents or any kind of manuscripts anywhere around. Father D'Amarcio, who found her, told us why he was there, and we confirmed that no such documents were in the studio."

"What about at her home?" Fairchild asked.

"We have not yet looked into that, *Monsieur Doktor Fairchild*, but we shall. We will know by the morning."

The interview on the street in front of the studio stairs was over, and the crowd had moved on. Fairchild looked at Morris and Gilles, and asked, in English, "What now?"

He then repeated it in German for Ezor Franisch.

"Fortunately I was not to return to Berlin until tomorrow," Franisch answered. "But if they do not return my passport and papers in the morning and allow me to catch my fight to Paris and Berlin tomorrow, my country will be filing a formal protest, I can assure them. The French! Bahhh!"

"Tomorrow, I suspect, it will be an Interpol detective who will be interrogating us, gentlemen," Pierre Gilles said. "I anticipate that they will suspect that this was a stolen document."

"Why?" Fairchild asked, anticipating the answer.

"Because I, too, suspect that this was the document that I was to inspect for Moshe Gelbstein, a Swiss antiquities dealer, two months ago. It was stolen from him aboard a train before he could show it to me in Brussels."

"Could it be the same one?"

"Gelbstein seemed fairly certain it was something written in Aramaic. Aramaic documents do not show up very often." He paused a moment, and then added, "You gentlemen are as astute as I, and you saw the document yesterday. The old Egyptian told me this morning that the first part does appear to be some ancient form of Ge'ez, but he could not decipher it. What do you think the manuscript is?" He repeated his question to Franisch in German as a dark-skinned man in his late fifties, dressed in black with a clerical collar, approached.

"Father D'Amarcio?" George Morris inquired in Italian.

"Yes, I am Dameon D'Amarcio" he replied in heavily accented English. "Are you the gentlemen from the other museums?" They each nodded an affirmation.

"You found Madam LaDuc this morning?" Gilles asked.

"Yes, she was unconscious. I assumed hit on the head. The safe was open."

"Why was the Vatican Museum interested in this document?" Fairchild asked.

"I did not know that they were, *Signor*."

"You're not here on behalf of the Vatican?" George Morris asked.

"No. I am professor of ancient languages at the Seminary of St. Felician of Mentana, just outside Rome. I am here on their behalf."

"We were told that the Vatican had sent a representative," Fairchild added.

"I don't believe so," the priest replied. "St. Felician is a very small seminary, a remnant branch of the Poor Brethren of the Hospital of St. John at Jerusalem. We have a number of lay brothers who conduct a variety of tasks for the Church and our Order. One of these men heard that an ancient document was going to be auctioned and told our seminary director to see if we would care to inspect it. The invitation came through our lay member, who passed it on to our director."

"Did you get to inspect the document before it was stolen?" Fairchild asked.

"Yes. I saw it yesterday."

"Do you know who owned it," Morris inquired.

"No, all I heard was that it was an Italian, perhaps someone from Milano."

"That is interesting. How did you hear that?" Fairchild asked.

"You are?"

"Oh, let us introduce ourselves," Fairchild said, and proceeded to introduce himself and Franisch. Gills and Morris introduced themselves. Morris inquired whether D'Amarcio had seen the Egyptian since the police had left.

"No, I think he said he was returning to his hotel, and I shall also be leaving very soon. Now, Dr. Fairchild, you asked what I had heard. I only know what I have told you."

"I see," Fairchild said, nodding. "And what do you think of the document? What do you think it is?'

"There was hardly enough of it to inspect to come to any sort of conclusion of that sort, Dr. Fairchild. It might be anything. There were some religious words, but.... I could not say for certain that it was any sort of a religious manuscript."

"Dr. Gilles, what do you think it is?" Fairchild inquired.

"Pahh, I, too, did not see enough to say. But my guess is that it is somewhere around eighteen to twenty-two hundred years old, probably Syrian in origin."

Fairchild asked the same question of Ezor Franisch in German. The man acted a bit flustered, but replied, "*Was ist es?*" he shrugged his shoulders. "*Ich weiss nicht. Vielleicht ein alt Staut, Vielleicht die Quelle? Vielleicht… Wer weiss? Nein, Ich weiss nicht!*"

"I don't know either," Morris agreed, "but you may be right. Perhaps it is just some old statute."

* * *

The following day Morris and Fairchild reported to the police station together. An Inspector Brun of the French National Police was awaiting them, and returned their passports to them, again reviewing what they had told the Arles policemen the previous day. Inspector Brun was very formal, but friendly, although he preferred to ask his questions in French, speaking English only haltingly.

"Yes, he said, "we spoke with the Italian priest yesterday and he has already returned on the train to Rome."

"How is Madam LaDuc?" Fairchild inquired.

"Oh, it is most interesting. She was not hit on the head as we suspected. Rather, she was rendered unconscious with chloroform, very carefully administered. She was not injured at all. The medical people suspected it from the odor when they found her."

"Did she say when she was attacked, or by whom?" Morris asked.

"I am not at liberty to say what she told us, *Monsieur* Morris. But it was not all that long before you arrived at her studio. The document was still in Arles at that time, but I fear it is probably long gone from here now.

"But we do not have any reason to detain either of you any longer," the Inspector continued. "We appreciate your cooperation. We have an address for each of you should there be further inquiries needed, and I wish you both *bon voyage*."

* * *

Cleveland Hopkins Airport, Brookpark, Ohio
July 4, 1962, 9 p.m.

Bob and Sally Merriam and Esther Fairchild were waiting at the Cleveland airport outside the U.S. Customs clearing zone as Richard Fairchild passed through. He looked tired after his journey, for although it was only nine in the evening in Cleveland, it was three in the morning in Europe.

"Did you win the auction?" Esther asked, after getting a welcome kiss and hug.

"There was no auction, I'm afraid. The document was stolen."

"You didn't get to see it?" Bob Merriam asked.

"Oh, we got to see it, all right. It's authentic, very ancient, and it is Aramaic, with an ancient Ge'ez introduction. But someone stole it before the auction the following morning."

"Stole it...?" Esther repeated.

"What do you think the document was?" Bob asked.

"Bob, I'm not sure. There was just a bit of it opened for display and inspection. It might be a copy of some old Syrian statute, or it could be a translation of a gospel, it's just impossible to say. There were representatives from Berlin, Belgium, the London Museum, and even Rome there, and we all agreed it was Aramaic and authentic. But nobody would commit themselves as to what it might be."

"Does Dr. Sukhey know yet?" Sally asked.

"Yes, I called him that morning. When we got to the auction the police were there. The priest, a professor from a seminary near Rome, had found the woman who ran the studio unconscious and the safe open. He notified the police, and they interrogated all of us, even kept our passports overnight. I understand that Interpol thinks that the manuscript was the same one that had been stolen about two months earlier from a Paris to Brussels train."

"It sounds like somebody thinks this document has real value," Esther said.

"Yes. Somebody certainly does. But I'm exhausted. Let's get home."

* * *

The Office of Dean Ralph Harding, Fremont College
July 8, 1962, 10 a.m.

"It sounds like your tour group had quite an adventure, Richard," the Dean said as he leaned back in his chair. Dr. Fairchild was seated in a chair across the desk from him. "This mess in Berlin between the Russians and the West seems to be getting worse. I was afraid that you might not be allowed into East Germany, but so far all the reports have been positive. Your trip was even mentioned in the *New York Times*. Ross tells me that everything went extremely well at the concert, and that the students really enjoyed singing in the Opera."

"Yes, it was an adventure, Ralph. But there is something that Ross may not have known. I believe that we advised you that there were some East German army personnel who also sang in the opera with us. We were on the same train from Leipzig. There was also a professor from the

University of Halle who was singing with the army choristers, and, well, when she got to Bayreuth, she defected."

"What! There was nothing in the news about a defection."

"No, I'm not even sure the East Germans were aware of it until several days after it occurred. Anyway, she was a professor of nuclear physics, and apparently was quite a catch for NATO."

"I can imagine!"

"I got a call yesterday from an old friend who is now with the CIA...."

"Yes, you were an intelligence officer once, weren't you, Richard?"

"Well, just a chaplain, assigned to an intelligence unit. Actually, the man who called me had been my commanding officer in the Army. Anyway, this professor is anxious to come to America, and my friend was wondering if Fremont College might need a nuclear physics professor. My friend, George McCracken, assures me that she is quite proficient in her subject."

"This is a surprise, Richard. But as you know, we have been considering taking on another physics instructor. Does this woman speak English?"

"Yes, we met her briefly while we were in Wittenberg, She speaks very good English. She was a friend of the University of Halle professor who was our guide there."

"Richard, are you sure there is not more to this story than you are telling me?"

"What do you mean?"

"Lord, with you, Richard, anything is possible! Knowing you, you probably talked her into defecting. But tell your CIA buddy that we might be interested in interviewing her. What is her name?"

"Hilda von Werdau. But I understand that she will be using a different name now, just to be safe, since she is a defector."

"Oh, what you get us into, Richard!"

* * *

Via della Posta, Locarno, Switzerland
July 21, 1962

Curtis Baldwin, a gray-haired businessman who spoke Italian with a heavy German accent, arrived at Locarno's main Swiss Federal Railway station on the direct train from Basle, via Bellinzona, at a quarter past one that afternoon, The station was near the Marina in Locarno. A large boat bringing tourists up Lake Maggiore from the resorts on the Italian side of the lake had just unloaded, and Americans, French, Italians, English, Japanese and Australian tourists were jamming into the shops along the hilly embankment of the town. Baldwin was traveling on a British passport, which neither revealed his former name nor high-ranking position with the East German Army.

Via della Posta intersected with the Viale al Lido. Although it was lunchtime, Baldwin was not hungry, and did not fight the crowd of tourists for a seat in one of the many cafes and restaurants near the marina. Instead he started up the sloping street, seeking an address, frustrated by twenty years of change since he had last been in this small Swiss city. He saw a policeman and went over to him.

"Pardon," he said in broken Italian, "do you speak German?"

"*Ja*," the policeman answered. "What do you need?"

Baldwin continued in German. "Twenty years ago there was a bank on this street, the Banca Lepontin di Locarno. Has it moved?"

"The Banca Lepontin? No, it was closed, about five years ago. They merged it with a bank from Bern."

"Does that bank have a branch here?"

"Yes. It is on the Angelo Nessi. *Bern Bankgeschäft*. About five blocks," the policeman answered, pointing toward the northwest.

About fifteen minutes later Baldwin found the Bern bank in a gray stone building on the upper street, and entered, asking to see a manager who spoke German. In a few moments he was escorted into an office, where a small man with a thin gray mustache sat behind a large desk.

"I am Herman Mueller. May we help you," the banker asked in excellent German.

"Yes," Baldwin replied. "Some twenty-one years ago I deposited a valuable document in the vaults of the Banca Lepontin di Locarno on the Via della Posta, and paid for its perpetual preservation. I now wish to recover my document."

"I see, Herr Baldwin. And you have an account number?"

"Yes," the former German general replied, removing a sheet of paper from an envelope in his coat pocket and handing it to the bank manager. "This is the contract with the account number. It was under the name of Kurt Kahler."

"You are not Kurt Kahler?"

"That was the name I used for the account. I was instructed at the time that it was the account number, not the name, that was important."

"Yes, for certain accounts that is true. Let us see. It will take me a moment. All of the accounts from Banca Lepontin were transferred, you understand, and we will need to see what became of your deposit." The banker arose from his desk and went into another room toward the back of the bank, where he apparently reviewed some filing cards, then returned with one in his hand. "Yes, we have the record of your deposit. Unfortunately it was transferred to our bank headquarters in Bern at the time of our acquisition five years ago. All of the accounts and locked deposit boxes were moved there if we were unable to contact the owners. Did someone not contact you at the time, Herr Baldwin?"

"Let us say that I was unavailable at that time, Herr Mueller. But I suppose that I must now go to Bern?"

"Yes, but I will prepare a letter for you to present that may assist you in recovering your deposit."

"That would be appreciated."

* * *

After weeks of debriefing at the NATO intelligence offices in Brussels General Kahler had been given a new British identity, and a very large cash account in a Luxembourg bank, sufficient to restart his life wherever he chose. He was, however, required to keep his Dutch intelligence agent contact, Nils Brinker, informed of his plans and travels. Kurt Kahler, *Kahl* being the German word for bald, had been transformed into Curtis Baldwin, a British businessman. He had advised Brinker that he wanted to take a short vacation to the Swiss Alps near where he had been stationed during the War, and would then report back to NATO on his further plans. He was fairly certain that he would accept the offer of a position as consultant to NATO on Warsaw Pact defenses.

Baldwin consulted the Swiss railway schedules, noting that he could get to Bern either by returning on the line through Luzern by way of the St. Gotthard Tunnel, or take the narrow gauge train over the Alps to Domodossola, Italy, and then northward to Bern via the Simplon and Lotschberg Tunnels. If he could make the connection at eight that evening, he could be in Bern an hour later.

Although the leisurely ride through the high Swiss and Italian Central Alpine Valley was scenic, Baldwin's mind was on other things than the pastoral scenes outside the windows of the small electric train. Although he had no idea what the manuscript he had locked away more than twenty years ago was, its presence had given him some reason to hope that he might once again see the beautiful Swiss and Italian Alps during the time he was doing service for a government he considered corrupt and evil. Because of Russian Communism he was despised even by his own son. He had few twinges of imagination and was realistic in thinking that the document was probably little more than some old Jewish *Torah* scroll, not worth very much even as an artifact.

It was not its monetary value he sought -- it was the mystery that had brought it to him and the freedom represented in its recovery now that enticed him to pursue his bank deposit. Had he ever really been free in his lifetime? He had rank and privilege, but it always came with duty, responsibility, and very little right to make personal decisions on his own. But was that not true of any military officer? The commitment must be total, like that of a monk to his order. He had no right to complain. Perhaps even now he still had no freedom.

Baldwin would be unable to get to the bank for several days due to the weekend. No one knew where he was, so he had the days to spend as he wished. There was no telephone to summons him to a meeting, no NATO officer to drive him from a safe-house to an interrogation session, no Stassi to question why he was crossing into Italy or back into Switzerland. His wallet was flush with cash. If he could only relax, he could enjoy himself as much as the tourists that surrounded him seemed to be enjoying themselves.

The following Monday morning Baldwin arrived at the bank in Bern shortly after it opened, and was escorted into the office of Wilhelm Obermann, First Vice President, who spoke fluent German. He presented his letter and British passport, and explained what he wanted while the bank officer patiently listened. The officer then excused himself while he went to check on Baldwin's deposit.

It was more than twenty minutes before Obermann returned, in the presence of another man, tall and a bit younger, who had a very concerned look in his facial expressions. "This is Stefen Page," Obermann said, introducing the second man. "He is a Senior Vice President."

"Herr Baldwin," Page said, bowing as Baldwin arose from his chair to shake hands. Page then nodded to the other two to be seated, while he sat down on the corner of Obermann's desk. "Herr Baldwin ... or is it Kahler?"

"It is Baldwin. As I explained, Kahler was just the name I used for the deposit."

"Yes, yes. Perhaps that was the problem."

"A problem? You do not have my document?"

"Herr Baldwin, as you are, I'm sure, quite aware, there was considerable chaos in the banking industry following the War. The bank in Locarno took in many deposits of German citizens in the 1930s and early 1940s. They did not know who you were, but you obviously were not a local Swiss when your deposit was made. They may have assumed that you were a refugee, perhaps even someone seeking asylum in Switzerland during the War. I cannot say what they thought.

"When the Bern bank took over the local Locarno bank five years ago, the building in which it was located was sold, and all of the contents, including safe deposit box accounts were transferred to our bank. We made a diligent effort to contact everyone whose deposit had been transferred, to come and have them renew their account with us."

"Diligent effort?" Baldwin asked.

"Yes, our records show that we wrote to the name we had, Kurt Kahler, in care of an address in Berlin, but our letter was returned, undeliverable. Here it is, stamped, *'unbekannt Mensch/adressieren.'*" Page handed him the letter, dated more than five years earlier. The address was that of the Third Reich's Transportation Corps Headquarters, which had been bombed into dust by the Allies in 1945.

"I see," Baldwin replied after studying the letter. "So, where *is* my deposit?"

"Our rule here on unknown accounts is twenty years, Herr Baldwin. The bank in Locarno had it more than fifteen years without hearing from you. When we received your deposit, we attempted to contact you, unsuccessfully, as you can see, but continued to hold your deposit another five years."

"And then...?"

"And then it was liquidated, along with a number of other deposits which had been unclaimed."

"Property of Jews, I supposed."

"Herr Baldwin! How would we know the race of our depositors?"

"No effort to find survivors or families?"

"Herr Baldwin, you gave us no information. A name, not your own, you say, with an address shown as unknown? What were we to do or think? Your deposit, it was not tiny, but a large and bulky white metal box."

"So what did you do with it? It cannot have been that long ago."

"You are correct. It was not. We use various agents for disposal of unclaimed deposits, depending on what they are. You had declared no value on your deposit, according to the Locarno records, or stated what was in the box, so we were forced to open it. We will check and see with which agent your deposit was placed. Perhaps he can trace it. The bank, of course, would be obliged to purchase it back for you."

"I would think so, Herr Page. When can we know?"

"It will take us awhile to identify and contact our agent, if he is in town. Many travel, you understand. We will try to have him here, say," he stopped and looked at the other officer, Obermann, "Wednesday morning, Wilhelm?"

"*Ja,* that should be time, I think," the other officer replied.

"Until then, Herr Baldwin, can you remain in town?"

"I seem to have no choice."

"You shall enjoy Bern at our expense, Herr Baldwin. Where are you staying?"

The bank arranged for Baldwin to move from the small tourist hotel where he had spent the weekend to a more luxurious one in central Bern near the bank, and provided him with letters to give to several high-class restaurants for meals on the bank's account. They also told him of some local places that he might enjoy visiting while he was in town. Instead Baldwin checked out of his hotel and took the train to Lausanne, booking a hotel room overlooking Lake Geneva.

When Baldwin arrived at the bank in Bern two mornings later Wilhelm Obermann escorted him directly to the larger office of Stefan

Page, where two other men were already standing beside Page's large polished wood desk. Introductions were made by Page.

"Herr Baldwin," he said, "this is one of our artifact brokers, as we discussed, Maurice Ceveneau. Maurice was involved in the sale of your deposit. This gentleman," he added, gesturing to a tall, plain-looking man in his forties who was dressed in a dark suit, "is Inspector Gerhart Mann of the Zurich CID. He represents Interpol."

"Interpol?" Baldwin replied in a surprised tone. "And how are they involved?"

"Perhaps I can explain a bit," Page replied, "as Maurice does not speak German very well. Maurice obtains items from banks such as ours, some on consignment, and some by direct purchase if he believes he has a market. The manuscript in your white metal container, Herr Baldwin, was believed by Maurice to be a Hebrew document. Having a market for such artifacts in Geneva, he purchased the document from us and presented it to his customer in Geneva, a Jewish art dealer named Moshe Gelbstein. Gelbstein confirmed that the document was not Hebrew, and that it would not appear to be of any interest to his own Jewish customers, but nevertheless he agreed to purchase it from Maurice.

"Gelbstein has a brother-in-law in Paris who works for the Bureau of Antiquities," Page continued. "He took the document to show to his brother-in-law, who then involved a researcher at the Bureau who confirmed that the document was written in Aramaic, an ancient Mideastern language. Gelbstein had an appointment to show the document to a professor at the Institute of Ancient Arts in Brussels. While taking it to Brussels on the train from Paris, the document was stolen. It was reported to Interpol, and they followed up, contacting Maurice Ceveneau here in Bern to try to determine what the document was or who might have stolen it."

"Has it been recovered?" Baldwin asked.

"Herr Baldwin, it is very complicated," the Zurich CID Inspector responded. "We heard of the sale of an Aramaic document to take place in Lyon, through a Swiss broker who occasionally deals in artifacts of questionable origin. The sale, however, was moved to Arles, and was to occur a few weeks ago through an arts dealer with offices there. It was inspected by a number of potential bidders from museums around the world, Berlin, Rome, America, even the British Museum, but the woman who was the arts dealer was attacked, rendered unconscious, and the document was again stolen. The professor at the Institute in Brussels says that the document he saw in Arles before that theft looked to be the same document that Gelbstein said was bringing him from Paris when it was first stolen."

"So where is my document now?" Baldwin asked.

"No one knows, Herr Baldwin," the Zurich policeman answered. "No one knows where it is, or what it is. When Maurice contacted us yesterday, as we had instructed him to do should anyone inquire about the document, we thought that you might have it."

"That I would have it? But if I had it, why would I be here trying to find it?"

"We did not know, Herr Baldwin."

"This is all very mysterious, gentlemen. It sounds as if the document might have some great value," Baldwin said.

"So it seemed, Herr Baldwin." Inspector Mann agreed. Then he looked directly at Baldwin and asked, "If the document belonged to you, as you claim, did you not know what it was or what it was worth? Could you tell us, sir, exactly how *you* came to be in possession of this document, what, twenty some years ago?"

Baldwin, very accustomed to thinking on his feet and acting with authority, responded immediately and forcefully. "No, sir, I cannot. I will tell you, however, that it came from Italy, and was being illegally brought into Switzerland when it was rescued by some of my employees. My possession of it was quite legal, I assure you."

"And these employees, Herr Baldwin," Inspector Mann continued, "we shall need their names and further information. Everything must be verified."

"You are not entitled to such information, Inspector," Baldwin again forcefully responded. "My employees were in Switzerland at the direct invitation of the Swiss government at the time, and...."

"And you, Herr Curtis Baldwin, *will* answer my questions."

"Inspector Mann, I was informed that my contract with the bank in Locarno was quite legal, and that it was also quite confidential under Swiss banking laws. By what authority do you now question me?"

"Inspector," Stefan Page interrupted, "Herr Baldwin is quite correct. His contract is confidential."

"So it may be. But if this document was acquired illegally by Herr Baldwin or by his 'employees,' that is not a matter for the Swiss banking laws, but rather for the CID. Herr Baldwin, your passport is British, yet you appear to be primarily a German speaker. What brought you to Locarno twenty-one years ago? And who *is* Kurt Kahler?"

Baldwin could see that this matter was not going well, and that he would need to be cautious in his approach to the situation. Technically the Zurich policeman was correct; he had no more right to the document than anyone else. His soldiers had shot -- perhaps murdered -- a priest and in effect the manuscript had been stolen and then hidden by him. A prosecutor could easily infer that he was as responsible for the murder and theft as were his men. Switzerland had been neutral in the War. They were not an ally. He and his soldiers had been nothing more than temporary guests with no authority on the Swiss side of the border. Who could he call? What could he do, or say?

Chapter 13

Dr. Hilda Waggoner smiled as she sat in Dean Ralph Harding's office during the second week in August, and signed employment papers. Officially she would be an instructor in the Department of Physics, but unofficially she would hold the title of Visiting Professor of Nuclear Energy and Engineering. Although her graduate work had been through the People's Institute of Nuclear Science in East Berlin and her doctorate from the University of Moscow, the resume that would be shown in the fall class catalog would list a doctorate from the University of Chicago and the Enrico Fermi Laboratory in Batavia, Illinois. Both institutions had agreed to the CIA's requests for the deception and the CIA had provided copies of the professor's scholastic papers from the Communist universities. How they got them the officials at Fremont College never found out, but similar arrangements had been made for other defecting professors.

Ross Johnson and Richard Fairchild had joined the Dean and Dr. Rayland Durrand, Chairman of the Physics Department, in the room. As the tall, blond German professor signed the last form, one providing her with health insurance, the four men applauded and welcomed her to the faculty of Fremont College. Ross Johnson had already offered to assist her in finding an apartment and in setting up her office on the fourth floor of the college's Science Building. It had been Ray Durrand's office for many years, and he was more than happy to depart the sweltering attic oven for an air conditioned one on the second floor.

Unbeknownst to Durrand, the Dean or the choral professor, Richard Fairchild had been again contacted by the CIA to keep an eye on the blond academic. Although her defection had been welcomed, and the information she had shared crucial to NATO, she was, nevertheless, an unknown to the intelligence community. Her defection might only have been a means of setting up operations as a spy, seeking American nuclear secrets under the cover of her college professorship.

It was partially for that reason that he and Esther had invited the new faculty member, Ross, and both Ray and the Dean and their wives to dinner that evening. By being socially close, Fairchild felt that he could better keep his eye on the attractive scholar. Frankly, he did not think she had staged her defection in order to become a spy, but with the heated tensions between East and West over Berlin -- tensions that had seemed to have been inflamed since their East German tour in June -- he realized that anything was possible. Had her defection not been real, why had the Stassi officer been prepared to shoot her? Had she known that the Army General who had accompanied them was also going to defect? He did not feel he could ask her these things, and it was doubtful that she would volunteer such information.

By seven that evening Johnson had located an apartment in Fremont for Hilda. It was near, but not within, his own apartment complex. Hers was near enough to the campus that she could walk to her office, the physics lab and her classrooms. He had already assisted her in setting up a checking account with a Fremont bank. She seemed unfamiliar with such accounts. She had also set up a savings account, and he had been shocked when he saw the amount that was put in it, apparently courtesy of NATO. Although she spoke excellent English, with only a trace of German accent, she was naïve about a number of American customs. Ross was more than willing to acquaint her with 1960s style American fast food, fast cars, and the joys of being American.

"Classes won't start until the second week of September," Esther said to Hilda at dinner that evening while Richard was pouring the wine. "What are you going to do over the next few weeks?"

"Dr. Durrand assigned to me two advanced classes, plus a survey class, to teach this semester. I must line up the textbooks I will use and become familiar with any American techniques that are different. There are quite a few. In nuclear sciences here, caution is exercised in the extreme. Dangers and caution are less commonly considered in the Eastern Bloc."

"Are you and Ross planning anything this weekend?" Fairchild asked.

"Ross has invited me to attend the college chapel on Sunday morning. He says you are going to be the... the priest? Pastor?"

"Just the preacher. Did he warn you that my sermon might put you to sleep?"

"Put me to sleep, Dr. Fairchild? Are you a hypnotist?"

Her question, asked in all seriousness as she did not understand the joke about sermons caused the others to laugh, and she looked bewildered.

"Oh, how I wish I *could* hypnotize them all and make them behave, Hilda. No, the reference was to becoming bored."

"Oh! Bored! No, he did not say you were boring, and I'm sure you are not. I enjoy theological discussions. There is, in theology, it is said, much in common with physics."

"Could it be that Dr. Einstein's theories also are laws in theology?" Ross asked.

"That's an interesting question, Ross," Fairchild answered. "Consider how often we refer to God as being Light. Maybe '$E=MC^2$' also equals God."

"If you preach on that, Richard, you'll get a lot of flak from conservatives in the congregation this Sunday," Dean Harding laughed. "Their favorite hymn is 'Give us that old time religion!'"

"I've never actually been to a real church service," Hilda said. "Our churches were used as museums, or for concerts. What is a service like?"

"At the college chapel, it's kind of formal," May Durrand explained. May was a tall, dark-haired woman in her early thirties. Her long hair was beautifully styled, and her make-up perfectly matched her coloring. In short, she was a very attractive woman. "There is a long procession, led by flags and banners and the choir, then the clergy. We sing loud hymns, and the choir sings anthems, and there are prayers and readings."

"And a twenty minute sermon," Ross added. "But both Richard and Dr. Boldt, the senior chaplain, are pretty good preachers. You've met many of the choir members, who were with us in Bayreuth."

"Oh yes! I'll be seeing them again, won't I," she said. "Did Kathy get her cuckoo clock back to Canada?"

"As far as I know she got it mailed from Bayreuth, cuckooing all the way!" Esther said, laughing.

"So, what is your sermon tomorrow, Richard?" the Dean asked.

"I think, in honor of Fremont's newest faculty member, it will be on freedom and love. Those are both good religious subjects, don't you think, Hilda?"

"Definitely, Professor Fairchild. I only wish one could practice such religion in my country. I think I shall like this America to which I have come. But I do have a question. I see on the calendar that the first Monday in September is called 'Labor Day.' I do not understand. Does it mean that you must work very hard that day? Or is that a day to do the autumn cleaning?"

"Getting Richard to do the cleaning on Labor Day would be hard work," Esther laughed. "But no, Hilda, it is a holiday to celebrate the labor movement in America, a day that all workers have off, to sort of extend the fun of summer before the coming of fall and winter. It is a day when no one goes to work, and the weekend is extended another day. A lot of people who travel in the summer use the time to come home and get ready for school and other activities that have shut down for the summer."

"Oh, like our May Day. Yes, I see."

"I know!" Richard interrupted. "Let's spend the long weekend on the boat! I'll get the *Castle Kent* loaded up, and we can cruise down to Fairport Harbor or Cleveland, have dinner at Jim's Steakhouse on Collision Bend Friday night, and visit the islands on Sunday. The boat easily sleeps eight. I don't think you've been on it, have you, May?"

"Ray and I drove down to see it once, but, no, we've not been on it. But I think our daughter, Ronnie, has some plans, since she'll be going down to Ohio State this fall, so she wouldn't be around that weekend anyway."

"We've got relatives coming," Ralph Harding said, "so count us out. I'd rather go on your cruise than deal with my brother and his six kids, but...."

"Now, Ralph," Sarah Harding interrupted, "you know you've been looking forward to Jack's visit. But we'll have to be excused, Richard. Perhaps some other time."

"Well then, Ross, can you plan to bring Hilda?"

"What is this *Castle Kent*, Dr. Fairchild," Hilda asked.

"It's a small battleship he acquired from the Texas Navy," Rayland joked.

"What?"

"Oh, quit teasing her, Ray," Ross laughed. "What he means is, it is a motor yacht that Fairchild won in court from a Texan who had planned to assassinate him and one of our civil rights leaders a couple of years ago. This guy had blown up a train, just outside the farmhouse here, one night in an attempt to kill Richard. When the guys responsible for that were caught, with Richard acting under cover for our FBI, he sued them and won the yacht, which he renamed for an island winery the college owns, and presented it as a gift to the college."

"The college owns a winery?"

"Yes," Ray confirmed. "Richard got that for the college, too, from some Nazi spy he caught."

"Nazi spy? You are joking with me again?"

"No," Ross said. "It was owned by some German corporation headed by this old Nazi. It was full of gold...."

"Oh, this is nonsense!" Hilda laughed. "I won't believe anything you say, now."

"Well, perhaps it really wasn't quite full of gold," May Durrand explained, "but there were several boxes of gold hidden in the old winery. It's quite a story."

"Dr. Fairchild, is all this true?" the German professor answered.

"Yes, Hilda. And, by the way, please call me Richie, like the others do. No titles are permitted off-campus. But anyway, yes, it was Bob Merriam and Sally who actually solved that little caper. Bob figured out about the gold, and Sally found it, and the college bought the whole island, except for the village on it, to use as a small inn for our hotel and restaurant management classes, and a new vintner course, which is taught, what, Ray, by the Chemistry Department?"

"Yes, I think it is Jones, over there in Chemistry, who teaches that. He'd been messing around with making wines for years."

"My father was a vintner," Hilda said. "He worked for a winery in the Rhine Valley before the war."

"Is he still alive?" Richard asked.

"Oh, no, he was put in the Army and was killed fighting the Russians in 1944. My mother moved to Berlin to live with her sister, her only surviving relative, and of course I was just a little girl. My mother and her sister were killed in one of the bombings, and I was brought up in an orphanage outside of Leipzig."

"So you have no relatives in Germany?"

"At one time I thought I had a cousin. It was another man named von Werdau. But it turned out he was simply from the small town called Werdau and took that name because his records were lost. I guess my father's family had once come from there, too."

"The War created so many tragedies," Sarah Harding said. "My brother was killed in the Pacific during the War. We never got over it."

"So it's agreed, then? We'll meet at the dock in Port Cleland on the Friday afternoon before Labor Day, and... I know! We'll spend Sunday night on the island at the inn. It has been open all summer. Maybe the Merriams can join us."

"Sounds great!"

* * *

NATO Headquarters, Brussels, Belgium
August 22, 1962, 10:12 a.m.

Nils Brinker leaned back in his chair and roared with laughter. "General Kahler, that Zurich CID officer thought for sure he had you when you said you knew that American professor, Fairchild, who had attended the auction of that document in France. When he pursued it further and the American CIA showed up to get you out of there, he thought he had triggered some international incident. They swore him to secrecy under a threat of death if he even told his own superior officers, and he went on sick leave for the next week.

"But, frankly, General, I wish you had let me know where you were headed and what you planned to do. Switzerland isn't a part of NATO, and not everyone there might feel the same as the rest of the West about the Eastern Bloc nations."

"The idea of freedom of travel was new to me. I see now that, while there is freedom, one must still be cautious."

"Did you know that Fairchild was interested in ancient documents, General?"

"No. During my interrogation by the Zurich police they asked me about a number of names, including one I recognized as a professor in Berlin. But then, when they said Richard Fairchild, an American religion professor, I thought, that has to be the man from Fremont College. How could he be involved with my document? When I said I knew him, they went berserk."

"Well, thank goodness you contacted us. We spoke with Fairchild, and learned that he was at the auction on behalf of some American museum, and had actually seen the document. Perhaps, since you have decided to accept the American offer of a position with their Pentagon as a consultant, you will have a chance to visit the professor in Ohio and see what he can tell you about your document."

"Yes. That would be interesting. And I leave for Washington...."

"Tomorrow afternoon's flight. Sabena's four o'clock flight to New York. A U.S. Department of Defense officer will meet you at Idlewild and travel with you to Washington. I understand that they already have a house for you in Virginia, near their Langley facility. I think you will like Virginia. It is hilly, and green, like Germany."

"Good. Again, I cannot thank you enough, Nils. Had I told those policemen how I had actually acquired that document, they might have charged me with murder."

"How did you get it?"

"My soldiers were to guard the Italian rail line crossing from Switzerland, as we were bringing trains through the St. Gotthart Tunnel as the Brenner Pass was closed, supposedly from an earthquake. Some priest was on a back trail, and had just crossed into Switzerland from Italy, carrying that document all wrapped up in a blanket. My men thought he was a saboteur who planned to blow up the railway, so they ordered him to halt, but when he ran, they shot him. Then they brought me the document.

"I thought it was probably a Hebrew document," he continued. "If the Gestapo found out, they'd harass my men and me, and we had work to do to get our trains south into Italy. So I took the document, put it in an old ammunition case, and took it to a bank in Locarno to keep until after the war. Unfortunately, I ended up in the East, and never could reclaim it until now."

"Well, I guess it's gone now. And you have no idea what it was?"

"I know now that it wasn't a Hebrew document. If it had been, it would not have been worth much. The policeman said it was Aramaic and apparently may be valuable."

"And you said it had first been stolen from a train? I wonder what happened to it between the time it was first stolen and when it was placed for auction?"

"According to that Zurich policeman, nobody seems to know. Maybe the art dealer in Arles knew."

"Well, good luck, General. Or should I say, Mr. Baldwin?"

"I need to develop a British accent, don't I. 'Oye say, mate, 'ave a jolly die, eh!"

* * *

Basement of Hayes Hall, Fremont College, Ohio
August 22, 1962, 11 a.m.

"Bob," Richard Fairchild called out from his office toward the small room used by his assistant professor. The offices were small enough that inter-office communication by shout was far easier than getting up and speaking softly.

"Yes, sir?" Merriam replied. His wife, sitting at her desk in the reception area between the two small offices, was used to the long-distance conversations.

"What do you know about the Knights Templar?"

"You mean, those fourteenth century Scots associated with Freemasonry?"

"No, the eleventh century original Knights of Solomon's Temple in Jerusalem."

"Oh. Not much. Weren't they dissolved by Philip IV of France for heresy? They had been building forts and protecting the roads into the Holy Land before the Crusades, but afterwards they seemed to get a lot of wealth. I seem to recall that their Grand Master, Jacques de Molay, was burned as a heretic. I'm not sure what happened to them. Why?"

"Just wondered." By this time Bob's curiosity over Fairchild's inquiry had drawn him from his office chair, and he went to the professor's doorway, leaning up against it with a coffee cup in his hand.

"Are you thinking of teaching another medieval history class, Richie?" he asked.

"No, there's nothing scheduled until the spring semester. But I came across some interesting information while I was in Arles, and thought I'd do a bit of research." He paused. Bob said nothing, but continued to look at Fairchild, waiting for him to continue. He anticipated that if he probed too much, Fairchild would say nothing.

"There were a number of military religious orders in the Middle Ages, Bob, including the Knights Templar, or by their correct name, the Poor Knights of Christ and the Temple of Solomon. There were also Knights Hospitaller of St. John of Jerusalem. Templars began as nine French monks digging in the ruins of Solomon's Temple. The Hospitallers provided lodging and medical care for pilgrims going to Jerusalem. But after the Crusades were lost, Templars and Hospitallers retreated first to Rhodes and Cyprus, and many Templars later back to France. There were other orders as well, the Teutonic Knights in Germany and others in Spain and Portugal. The Nazis tried to emulate the Teutonic Knights. For instance, their 'iron cross' was a Teutonic Knight's symbol.

"Anyway, these Knights, upon returning to Europe in the thirteenth century, had a lot of wealth, possibly due to some secret they found in the old temple ruins. They acquired a lot of land for their fortress monasteries. Ruins of the fortress headed by Fra de Molay still exist, not far from Arles. It might even be because of the Templars that the Papacy moved to Avignon, as one of the Templars' fortifications was built near Avignon. It was presented to Pope John XXII, who in turn passed it on to the Carthusians.

"At the time these guys had a lot of land planted in wine grapes. There's one story about a Templar fort that made a black wine so potent that it could be fatal to drink it straight. It was watered-down in a four-to-one formula. Apparently some of these vineyards still exist in various places, and a few are still in the hands of Knights."

"Really? Even now, in the twentieth century?'

"So I understand. The Knights of Malta, an Order that superseded both the Templars and the Hospitallers, have a Grand Palace in Rome. The Grand Master is considered a Prince, and his principality -- consisting of only that one palace -- is considered a sovereign state with diplomatic recognition by at least forty countries. They even issue their own passports."

"I've heard of the Knights of Malta. Don't they rescue royalty during wars or something?"

"Yes, they've been involved in such endeavors, I understand. Some historical theoreticians even suspect that they were instrumental in rescuing the Czar of Russia in 1917, but if so, like all their other activities, it has been behind the scenes."

"Why are you interested in them?" the young professor asked.

"When I was in Arles to inspect that Aramaic document for Paul Sukhey, one of the other persons there to inspect the document was a priest from Rome. We thought at first that he was representing the Vatican Museum, which would have a valid interest in such a document, but he told us that he was Father Dameon D'Amarcio, a professor of ancient languages at the Seminary of St. Felician of Mentana, outside of Rome. He told us that St. Felician was a small seminary, but that it was an ancient remnant of the Poor Brethren of the Hospital of St. John at Jerusalem. He also said that they had a number of lay brothers who conducted a variety of tasks for the Church and for their Order.

"I've done a little research since I got home," he continued, "and have learned that the seminary belongs to the Holy Knights of St. John of Cyprus. When both the Knights Hospitallers and the Templars got tossed out of Palestine by the Muslims for the last time at the end of the thirteenth century, they first went to Rhodes, and later to Cyprus and then to Malta. But a few remained in Cyprus, and it is apparently a remnant of that group that now runs the Seminary of St. Felician. But there's just not much information about this group anywhere in the modern literature."

"If there's anything I can help you research it, Richie, you know I'm happy to do so." Bob paused, and then added, "By the way, Sally and I are going to have to decline your invitation for Labor Day. Her family has a big picnic planned, and she doesn't want to miss it. She said, 'Oh, pooh, why can't we do two things as once!' It was very funny."

Sally had stopped typing when she heard her name, and listened while her husband explained to their boss about why they were declining the invitation. She regretted having to do so, but her cousin, Dexter, was going to be in town, and she did not want to miss seeing him.

* * *

Aboard the *Fräulein Weser,* Montreal, P.Q.
August 29, 1962, 11:15 a.m.

Gerhardt Kalbmann stood on the rear deck of the *Fräulein Weser,* a medium-sized freighter out of Bremen, a ship that until a year or two earlier had belonged to North German Lloyds, one of the major European shipping line. Now it was little more than a tramp freighter, but Kalbmann had been successful in convincing the captain that he had sufficient knowledge of maritime science to be of use aboard the vessel. He was basically the assistant to the third officer, but hoped that his status might improve and that he, too, could reach officer level soon.

The *Fräulein Weser* had left the Port of Bremen two weeks earlier. It had loaded a variety of cargo, including twenty Volkswagens, into its holds, and had made a stop at Southampton on its way to the St. Lawrence Seaway. The Volkswagens were being unloaded onto a pier along the river in Montreal. As it was not his assigned watch, he did not have to supervise the unloading.

Kalbmann had elected not to disembark with the other off-duty crewmen to visit the Canadian city. He had no interest in their drinking and story-telling. What money he had left from the amount Admiral Schmidt had allowed him he needed to save for the proper moments. He had, however, made a purchase while seeking work in Bremen -- a Luger semiautomatic pistol -- that he had hidden in his leather travel case in the room he shared with two other junior members of the crew.

The *Fräulein Weser* had originally been designed to carry up to twelve paying passengers, but the new owners did not wish the responsibility required of passenger-carrying ships and had sealed off the rooms. They were packed with cartons of third-class mail destined for the United States.

What cargo was left on the ship was destined for Great Lakes ports, first Toronto, and then, after the ship passed through the Welland Canal,

Buffalo, Erie, Cleveland, Toledo and Detroit. At each of these ports American manufactured goods would be loaded aboard for the return trip to Bremen. The captain envisioned at least four more round trips that autumn before weather on the Great Lakes made the voyages difficult. No, Kalbmann thought, there will be plenty of opportunities to see Montreal.

* * *

Fremont College
August 29, 1962, 11:35 a.m.

When Sally Merriam heard the name of the caller she immediately went and knocked on Richard Fairchild's office door, although he had told her he did not want to be disturbed.

"Dr. Fairchild, George McCracken is on the phone. I know you said you didn't want any calls, but...."

"That's quite all right, Sally, I'll certainly take George's call. Put him through."

Sally returned to her desk and transferred the call to the line in Fairchild's office.

"Hello, George," she heard him say, but she did not pick up much more of the conversation and was soon busy typing again.

"Richie, you are the most interesting character the CIA has ever dealt with," McCracken began. "You rescue people even when you don't know you're doing it."

"What do you mean, George? I haven't rescued anyone."

"You didn't know you did!" the old spy agency veteran laughed. "But it seems that our defecting general got himself in a bit of a fix with the Swiss police, and you were instrumental in getting him out."

"Me? I've not been in Switzerland...."

"No, but your name was. Let me explain," McCracken said. "After we got our man -- I won't say his name over the phone -- debriefed, and offered him a consulting position here in Langley, he said he wanted to take a few days to go to Switzerland, where he had been briefly stationed during the War. So, with his new identity, that of Curtis Baldwin, a British businessman, he set off for Locarno on Lake Maggiore. It seems that during the War, in 1941, he and his men had, well, shall we say 'acquired' some old ancient document from a priest. Our man, then in charge of trains crossing into Italy from Switzerland, and thinking the document was in Hebrew, he put it in a Swiss bank there. But then he ended up in the East, and this was the first chance he had to go get the document and see if it was worth anything.

"As it turned out, the bank in Locarno had been merged with one from Bern, and his document was sent there. They couldn't find him, as he had left no address, so they sold the document just this year to some antiquities dealer, who in turn sold it to another dealer who thought it might be worth something. Anyway, it got stolen, but then it shows up again at some auction in Arles, France, and you show up as one of the bidders."

"Yes, I did go to Arles, on behalf of one of our state museums."

"Right. Well, when our man shows up in Bern to claim his document and they realize that they sold it, they send out inquiries to try to buy it back, but instead they find that Interpol is investigating because the document was stolen a second time, in Arles."

"Yes, it was stolen the morning of the auction."

"Right. Well, the CID man from Zurich, who was investigating on behalf of Interpol, wanted to know how Baldwin, who's supposed to be British, but speaks better German, came to have this document in 1941. He refuses to disclose his identity, or that he'd been a Nazi officer, and they're really giving him the old rubber hose routine. They start questioning him about the people who had been at the auction in Arles, and he recognizes your name. That really puts them in a tizzy, and they're ready to throw him in a Swiss slammer for the rest of his life until he realizes that he'd better call for help.

"NATO got hold of our office there in Bern, and we hauled him back to Brussels and warned the CID guy from Zurich that if he even told his own boss what happened, he was toast. Scared the bejesus out of him."

"Where is he now, George?"

"We have him in a safe-house near Washington until we can set him up permanently. He's going to consult for us. But why I'm calling is this. He wants to meet with you, to see what you can tell him about his document, if in fact it really is his. I realize your semester will be starting after Labor Day, but...."

"No problem, George. I'd like to see him again, and I know Esther would, too, although none of them knew what was going on at the time. We're all going to go for a cruise over the Labor Day weekend on the college's boat, and there would be plenty of room for, what did you say his name was, Baldwin?"

"Curtis Baldwin. Right."

"Our new physics professor, Hilda Waggoner, will be on the cruise. Will that be a problem?"

"No. He knows about her. They knew each other in Germany, so he'll probably be glad to see her again. Okay, Richie, I'll have him call you, and you can set up whatever you want with him."

About two hours later the phone rang again Fairchild had left instructions with Sally to put any calls from a Mr. Baldwin through to him. He clearly recognized the voice as he heard the caller ask, "Herr Professor Fairchild?"

"Curtis Baldwin, I assume," Fairchild replied. "George said you would call."

"Yes. Did he explain...."

"Definitely! Can you join us next weekend for a cruise around Lake Erie?"

"That would be very pleasant, Professor."

"No, you must call me Richie, as do all my friends, Curtis."

"*Ja*, okay, Richie. I'm learning! So where do I come?"

"George says you are living south of Washington, so go to a travel agent and get a ticket on the Baltimore and Ohio Railroad from Washington to Fostoria. There's an overnight train that will get you in a little after noon, and I'll arrange for someone to meet you there. Get a sleeping car ticket. You will enjoy it.'

"Yes, I will do this. Did Herr McCracken, ahh, George, explain what I wanted."

"Yes he did. I think we will have a great discussion when you get here."

"Thank you, Professor Fair... Richie. I shall look forward to all this."

Chapter 14

Railway Terminal Dock, Cleveland
the Friday Before Labor Day, 1962, 6 a.m.

The *Fräulein Weser* had left the Port of Buffalo the previous evening. The ship's stop in Erie, Pennsylvania, had been postponed until their return as they were to pick up a large diesel electric locomotive for shipment to Finland. The captain had decided that the cargo would fit the holds better if they unloaded what was destined for other Lake Erie ports and Detroit before loading a large railway engine.

Just as the sun was rising to the southeast Gerhardt Kalbmann had come on duty. The old freighter was just slightly northeast of the entrance to the Cleveland harbor, and the first rays of the sun shone orange across the waves, with the tall outline of the Terminal Tower and other high buildings silhouetted in front. It was the third mate's command, and as the assistant, he was at his post to guide the ship safely to the dock.

According to the charts he and the officer had studied the previous evening, the Railway Terminal Dock was just east of the mouth of the Cuyahoga River -- the name of which Kalbmann could only try to pronounce. They would enter the harbor, approach the river mouth, then turn east; a tugboat would guide the large freighter to the dock.

Kalbmann had glanced at the cargo manifest. They would be unloading a variety of cargo from both holds, including some Farben electronics. Then they were to pick up a load of two hundred automatic coal furnace stokers from a company called Iron Fireman, for shipment to Germany. He considered how one of these stokers would be of benefit aboard the *Fräulein Weser*, as the fireman had to constantly shovel coal into engine Number Three. Engines One and Two had been converted to fuel oil, but for speed, the old coal-burning engine was still used. The unloading and loading would consume most of the day. Upon finishing, the freighter would sail to Toledo for a load of auto glass.

But word had circulated among the crew that because the following Monday was an American holiday, the *Fräulein Weser* would tie up in Toledo for three nights, not loading until Tuesday. Those crew members on duty during Friday who were not needed to get the vessel to Toledo could have the weekend off, as long as they were back aboard by Monday evening. At present Kalbmann had not intended to take advantage of the break. It would mean passing through U.S. Customs, which wasn't a problem, but he had no desire to see this dirty old American city that had a reputation of a filthy river. But so far, he had said nothing to his superior officer.

As the little red tugboat putted up beside the tall freighter, an exchange of whistles occurred, and ropes were tossed between the two vessels. The engines of the *Fräulein Weser* reversed, and the large ship was guided slowly backwards into the slip beside the railway dock. Just beyond, on a lift bridge over the river, a long, silver train of perhaps twenty cars, roared by. Gerhardt Kalbmann did not know it, but the New York Central's *Twentieth Century Limited* was several hours late, due to a freight train derailment in Indiana. Had he known, he would have expressed an inward pleasant emotion. German trains were never late. These Americans are *so* inefficient.

* * *

Port Cleland
the Friday Before Labor Day, 1962, 2:20 p.m.

Ross Johnson had readily agreed to meet Fairchild's "surprise guest" at the train in Fostoria, a town twenty miles southwest of Fremont. He had picked up Hilda on the way, and got to the station just as B&O's Chicago-bound train, *The Diplomat,* was arriving. It was actually early, the first of two sections of the train put on because of the heavy holiday traffic. Ross and Hilda were unsure of how they were going to locate their guest, whom they knew only as "Mr. Baldwin." Fairchild had told them, "You'll know him when you see him."

As a bewildered-looking former East German general descended from the third sleeping car, Hilda whispered, "It's the General!"

Ross, too, recognized the military man from his time spent in the chorus in Erfurt, and they were soon shaking hands and exchanging greetings. Ross placed the General's suitcase in the trunk of his car, and they headed north toward the Lagoons of Port Cleland where Fairchild docked the large cruiser, *Castle Kent.*

Rayland and May Durrand had arrived at the lagoon dock where the cabin cruiser was tied up just after one that afternoon. Esther and Richard Fairchild had already brought the food and drinks aboard, and had selected the lower rear cabin, normally considered the "crew quarters," for themselves, for although the ceilings were lower, the bunks were bigger. They awarded the Durrands the master cabin fore of the galley. Each of the other three would have one of the four small double-bunked cabins, although they would have to share the head with each other. The master stateroom had its own head, complete with a shower.

By two-thirty all were aboard. With the diesel fuel tank full, the *Castle Kent* pulled away from the dock, whistling for the drawbridge on the

Portage River. They were soon cruising around the north end of Catawba Island, which was not really an island at all, but a secondary peninsula on the Marblehead Peninsula. Although a cool breeze was blowing off Lake Erie, the seven sailors, each dressed in casual and light-colored clothing with canvass and crape-soled shoes, were warm within the main upper cabin, now enclosed with a thick clear plastic zip-in screening.

"Cap'n Richie," as he called himself aboard the cruiser when he donned his white soft-crowned captain's hat with the gold trim, was pointing out all the attractions, from the tall tower of the Perry Monument on South Bass Island to the old red and white Marblehead Lighthouse at the entrance to Sandusky Bay. "There's an island in the Bay that was a Union prison for Confederate soldiers during the American Civil War," he explained. "There's a ghost story to go with it. We'll come back into the Bay tomorrow, but need to hurry if we are to make our seven o'clock dinner reservations at Jim's.

"And look off there to the southeast," Fairchild continued. "Here, take the binoculars…. See the ramps and wheels and wooden structures on that peninsula east of the Sandusky buildings? That is Cedar Point. Ross, you'll have to take Hilda out there before it closes for the season later this month. It's what we call an amusement park. There are several very high roller coasters, other fast rides, and lots to do and see."

"We had no parks like that in Germany," Hilda said. "We heard about them, however. Tivoli Gardens in Copenhagen, the Prater in Vienna."

"I saw that once," Baldwin said. "Just before the end of the War. I was with a group returning from the Russian Front, and our train came through Vienna. Being in charge, I made sure we had a few days there before having to cross back into Germany."

"Do they have carousels?" Hilda asked. "With painted horses?"

"I think there are at least two at Cedar Point," Esther replied. "We also call them merry-go-rounds. They are about as wild a ride as I can manage these days."

"What else does one do in Ohio," the former general asked.

"Well, let's see," Fairchild replied. "Friends of the Merriams have opened a ski resort south of Cleveland. Do you ski, Hilda?"

"Yes. Maria Fergen and I went skiing a couple of years ago in the Polish mountains, and last winter Johann and I also went skiing at a place in Romania, but it was not very good."

"Is Johann a good skier," the general asked about his son.

"He doesn't get much practice. He was better than I, though."

The cruiser was now paralleling the shoreline, over an hour into their trip to Cleveland. The water was quite smooth, and the cruiser was able to run at around twenty knots. Esther went down into the galley to prepare some drinks and snacks, and brought them up to the top deck where they were all sitting, Cap'n Richie on a high stool behind the spoked wooden wheel and instrument panel. Although the twin diesel engines were running at near maximum, there was very little vibration, and hardly any noise.

Fairchild pointed out various towns and villages along the shore as they passed, Huron, Vermilion, Lorain, and Bay Village, advising that they would explore each of these harbors in more detail the next day on their return to West Bass Island, where they would spend both Saturday and Sunday nights. During one lull in the conversation, as Esther refreshed the drinks -- the Cap'n restricted to ice tea -- Fairchild said, "General, or should I say, Curtis?"

"Yes, I need to get used to being called Curtis, but I'm more comfortable with 'Kurt,' which I was told was a common nickname for Curtis."

"Kurt, then. I understand you had a little adventure in Switzerland."

"Yes, George McCracken said he had told you. I went to retrieve my package that I had placed in a Swiss bank, and found it had been stolen. I'd put it there in my real name, but they apparently thought that it was something some Jewish refugee had tried to preserve, and disposed of it."

"I imagine there was a lot of such disposal after the War," Ray commented. "What was in your package?"

"It was a document of some sort, an old scroll on animal skins. I thought it was written in Hebrew, but I have since learned that it was in Aramaic, an ancient Mideastern language."

"George said you had acquired it from your men, Kurt," Fairchild said. "What were the circumstances, if I may ask?"

"Certainly. Whatever the document was, it's gone now, so the story can be told. I was a Major in the Transportation Corps at the time, and because the Brenner Pass from Austria to Italy was closed -- supposedly due to an earthquake, although we suspected sabotage -- we needed to rush our supplies from Germany to Italy through the Gotthard Tunnel route via Lugano and on to Milan. I was put in charge of making certain that the trains got across the border into Italy without incident.

"If you are familiar with the area, Richie, you may recall that the rail line crosses Lago Lugano on a causeway and bridge just north of the Italian border. It would be an excellent location for a saboteur to cause damage and create delay, so my men were placed out in the hills to watch for any suspicious individuals, probably Italian under-ground, who might be approaching the rail line.

"It was near the end of May, 1941, and my men were on patrol. I tried to have at least one Italian-speaking man in each squad, but on this particular day the squad's Italian speaker was ill. They encountered a man, right at the Swiss/Italian border, dressed as a priest who was carrying a bundle, and ordered him to halt, but he started to run away. Thinking that the bundle might be a bomb, they shot him. The bundle, of course, was the scroll, and they brought it to me.

"We couldn't very well tell the Swiss police we had just shot a priest. We were guests of the Swiss government, after all, and they were neutral. Had it come out, it could have created quite an international incident, so my men disposed of the priest's body. I hid the scroll in an ammunition box and took it to a bank to keep until after the War. But then I ended up in the East, and this was the first chance I had to get back to Switzerland.

"When the Zurich policeman began to question me, I realized that, in their eyes, even though the priest had been shot on Italian soil, they would not see it that way, so I could not tell them how I had acquired the document. It really doesn't matter any longer as the document is gone. During the questioning, the policeman mentioned your name, Richie, and I said I knew you. I guess I shouldn't have said that, because then he really got excited. When they finally gave me permission to call someone, I called NATO in Brussels, and they sent someone from your Central Intelligence to rescue me. Later George McCracken said you had seen a document in France that might be the same one."

"Yes, I suspect it might be. Were there any letters or other documents on the priest? Any identification?"

"There was a letter, yes. I destroyed it, as it could have been evidence against us if the Swiss had found the priest's body. It was from some seminary near Rome. The priest was wearing an odd-looking cross on a chain, which I did keep, but I have since lost it."

"Really? What did it look like?"

"It was, well, here, let me draw the shape. It wasn't like a typical crucifix. Just a symmetrical cross." Esther gave him a pen and a piece of paper, on which the general drew the shape of a cross with three equal-length arms above a longer fourth arm in a tapered fashion, curved concave at the edges, and a small shield with the letters *S G C* in the middle. He handed it to Fairchild, who studied it for several moments.

"Do you remember the name of the seminary that was on the letter?" he asked.

"No. It was some saint I'd never heard of. But the Italians have so many saints."

"Yes, that's certainly true," Fairchild laughed. "But if those three letters stand for what I think they do, then, perhaps, Kurt, I have a hunch I may know where your scroll is." Fairchild said nothing further for a moment, then exclaimed, "Hey, look, we're down as far as the Rocky River already. It won't be long now until we're entering Cleveland's Harbor."

As the cruiser passed the long beach at Edgewater Park Fairchild picked up the microphone to the ship-to-shore radio that sat next to the controls and called the Cleveland Harbormaster, advising the identity of the cruiser, and their destination on the Cuyahoga River.

"How high is your cruiser, over," the Harbormaster inquired.

"We're a bit over twenty feet, with antennas and mast, over," Fairchild replied.

"NYC Number One is closed until six fifteen -- lots of pre-holiday rail traffic coming through, east and west. Just sit outside the mouth of the river. The B&O jack-knife will be open, as will the old Erie, but you'll have to signal for both the Carter Street Swing Bridge and the Columbus Road Bridge on Collision Bend. You familiar with the routine? Over."

"Yes, sir. Three blasts. Over."

"Right. You should get to Jim's with time to spare. They know you're coming? Over."

"Yes. We'll tie up at their dock. Over."

"Okay, *Castle Kent*, you're cleared to enter the harbor, but stay starboard of the *Aquarama* if it is coming out when you get there. Also, there's an ore boat, the *Duluth Princess*, that will be in the river coming out when that New York Central bridge opens. Stay clear of it. It's pretty wide. You can tie up at a Whiskey Island piling. Over."

"What's all that about?" Ross Johnson asked.

"It's a busy harbor! The passenger boat to Detroit will be leaving, along with one of those long boats that hauls iron ore, and they have to raise the roadway bridges for us to get under."

"What is 'Whiskey Island'? May Durrand asked.

"At one time," Fairchild explained, "the river wound around to the west of its current mouth, perhaps a mile or more. It was very swampy. Then when the old Ohio Canal got busy, they cut the new mouth to straighten the entrance to the river, and that made an island out of the land between the new cut and the old riverbed, which has now silted up, so that what was an island is now just land. There were at one time a score or more of saloons on the island, and the Irish laborers who worked unloading the ore boats dubbed it 'Whiskey Island.' There's a legend that the New York, Pennsylvania and Ohio Railroad, which became the Erie Railroad, used the initials NYP&O, which became an acronym for "nip and no, no nip, no work!" Today those big grasshopper-like steam shovels can unload a big ore boat in a few hours. I've taken the *Castle Kent* up that part of the river several times.

"So you've done all this before?" Ray asked.

"Sure. Last summer, when I was instrumental in helping to break up a piracy situation here on the river."

"What?!!" both of the Fremont professors uttered at once.

"I thought everyone knew...."

"You mean that homeless guy's murder you solved?"

"Yes."

"I didn't know it involved pirates!" Ross laughed.

"Yes, the one executive had pirated his company's ship in order to collect on the insurance and the homeless guy had part of the evidence, so that is why they shot him."

"What is this?" Hilda said, having just returned up the steps from the galley.

"Fairchild solves murders for a hobby," Ross Johnson said.

"Murders?"

"Got himself shot while he was in Greece last year, and the FBI -- that's our Federal Bureau of Investigation, Hilda -- identified the bullet as coming from the same gun that was used to shoot a homeless man who lived under a bridge."

"Right," Richard laughed. "He was found by another homeless guy who lived in a post office box."

"A post office box?" May Durrand repeated. "Oh, you're teasing us."

"No, that's where he was staying at night in the winter. It was warm in there."

"Where is that shelter where you were helping out, Richie," Ray Durrand inquired. "Isn't that where you met the old homeless men?"

"It's on the port side as we enter the river, just beyond the NYC bridge. I'll point it out, and I've arranged to dock there tonight. Maybe tomorrow we can tour the shelter and see the new chapel before we head west. The man that stayed in the post office," Fairchild continued, "is now an insurance executive. He and his family were on the *Kent* last year, and it's his firm that insures it now."

By this time the cruiser was approaching the wide space between the two lighthouses at the edges of the breakwater, a sandstone enclosure of the harbor. Fairchild reduced the speed on the cruiser, and they putted slowly into the open area of the harbor. The big passenger liner was still at its wharf to the east. Fairchild guided the cruiser to a point just outside the mouth of the river, opposite the Rail Terminal Docks. He shut the engine down and Ross tied the cruiser up to a piling along the east side of Whiskey Island. It was about four-fifty in the afternoon, and the Harbormaster said the bridge would not go up until a quarter after six, so they had nearly an hour and a half to wait. Across from where the *Castle Kent* was tied up the German freighter, *Fräulein Weser,* was being loaded.

"Now that we're off the Lake, Richie, it is getting rather warm in here," Esther said as she stepped up from the galley with another tray of drinks. "Maybe you should open the screens. We can close them again after supper."

"I'll give you a hand," Ray said, and both he and Ross began to unzip the thick clear plastic screening from around the exterior of the cabin. The soft breeze from the harbor pleasantly floated around them.

* * *

Aboard the *Fräulein Weser* Gerhardt Kalbmann had extended his watch to assist with the final loading. He stood on the starboard wing of the bridge overlooking the dock and the ship's mechanical lifting device, which was lowering the last five crates of furnace stokers into the hold. Because he spoke both German, the language of the crew, and English, the language of the longshoremen on the dock -- to whom he shouted by means of a portable loudspeaker -- the unloading and loading had gone quite smoothly, and the ship's crew knew that they would be finished before supper time. Already their cook was busy in the ship's galley.

A few of the off-duty sailors who had opted not to go ashore were loafing around the deck, watching activity on the railway bridges, in the river and on the harbor. About every thirty minutes a freight train would whistle and then rattle across the drawbridge a few hundred feet south of the mouth of the river. Although rumor said the river was heavily polluted, Kalbmann did not think that it was any worse than some he had seen in Germany, including the Weser, the river for which the ship was named.

As the final crate was lowered into the forward hold just before five o'clock, Gerhardt entered the bridge and blew the air horn twice, signaling completion of the loading. It also signaled the end of his time on duty for the day. The ship would move to Toledo, but he would have no further responsibilities until the following Monday evening. Perhaps he should have gone ashore, he thought. He might have found a book shop that sold books published in German. This was, he had heard, an American city in which there were many Germans.

As he contemplated what to do with his long weekend, two of his crewmates shouted to him from the deck below where they were standing by the port railing, looking across the river mouth. "*Ayy, Gerhardt, kommen sie hier! Wunderschöne Frauen!*"

From the bridge platform Kalbmann picked up a pair of binoculars and turned southward, toward the river. He saw the cabin cruiser tied up across the way, with several men and women aboard, and trained the powerful binoculars on them. The women had their back to him, but he could clearly see that one was older, perhaps in her forties, one, dark haired, perhaps thirty, but the third, a blond, seemed much younger. With that the blond turned toward the north and Gerhardt almost dropped the binoculars. "*Gott in Himmel!*" he exclaimed, although he believed neither in God nor heaven. He continued to scan the party aboard the cruiser, and expressed a second curse when he noted that one of the men on the other vessel was none other than his own father. So, he thought, it has to be Hilda. No two could look so much alike. They defected together, and are still together.

Kalbmann went to the door of the ship captain's stateroom, and knocked. Upon hearing a *Ja* he opened the door slightly. "*Herr Kapitan!*" he said in German, "Am I too late to request permission to leave the vessel?"

"You changed your mind, Kalbmann?" the vessel's commanding officer answered, also in German. "I thought you were never going to get off this boat. But you have put in extra duty today, for which I am thankful. The United States Customs agent has already departed, but I see no reason that you can't go ashore. All he would have done is look at your passport, since you are a crewmember. Take it with you, just in case. If you are not back tonight, we will be leaving just before midnight for Toledo. The ship will be docked at the ... let me look at the log ...." The Captain got out of his chair and went to his desk where he pulled out a rather large book, consulting one of the pages. "The Maumee Terminal Dock. You'll need to be aboard by eighteen hundred Monday."

"*Danke, Herr Kapitan,*" Kalbmann said as he started to turn.

"Oh, Kalbmann," the Captain said, calling him back into the stateroom. "Do you have any American money? The banks will be closed now."

"*Nein, Herr Kapitan!* Could you change a hundred Deutschmarks for me?"

"You may need more than that, Kalbmann. Here, let me give you two hundred and fifty American dollars. Use them as you wish. Then you can either pay me back in Deutschmarks, or I can hold it from your next pay, if you wish."

Gerhardt Kalbmann again thanked the officer and retreated to his own cabin, where he changed into the suit of clothing he had purchased in Brussels. He then slipped the Lugar into his pocket, and left the ship.

* * *

As the caboose of a westbound freight train rattled over the New York Central bridge at six ten that evening a signal light on the bridge turned to green for the river traffic, and the bridge slowly and noisily began to rise. As the harbormaster had advised, a long ore boat was poised to pass under it and out into the harbor. Richard Fairchild started the twin diesel engines on the cruiser, and as Ross Johnson unhooked the rope from around the piling post, freeing the boat, Fairchild slowly guided it to the port side of the freighter, and up the dirty brown river.

None of those aboard the *Castle Kent* observed a man with a cap pulled down over his eyes walking along Old River Road, parallel to the Cuyahoga. As they passed the back of St. Vincent House Fairchild pointed out the shelter where he had made so many friends over the years, and the dock at which they would spend the night.

"I've arranged with Brother Edward to allow us to tie up there overnight," Fairchild said. "It's a safe dockage, and cheaper than paying an overnight fee at the yacht basin. There shouldn't be much river traffic after eleven or so."

Beyond a little park where the Carter cabin -- Cleveland's first inn -- was set, the river made a rather sharp turn to the west, and then bent back to the south again. Fairchild had waited for the Carter Street Swing Bridge to open, and had then proceeded around the bend in the river, stopping again to await the opening of the Leonard-Columbus Road Bridge. The river then looped around to the east, and then the northeast, forming almost a circle. "Collision Bend," Fairchild told his passengers. "How the pilots on those long ore boats navigate around this bend every day is a miracle. Sometimes they scrape the bank, or if two of them get in the bend at the same time, well, you can understand the name of the place," he laughed.

The man with the hat had kept pace with the cruiser as it stopped for bridges, and had crossed the Center Street Bridge, putting him on the southwest side of the river. He did not know where the cruiser was headed, but could see that the river extended to the south and that there was an embankment to the east. On high level bridges and rail viaducts above him he could hear automobile and railway traffic. In the distance he could hear sirens. Now nearly seven in the evening, the sun was starting to fall toward the horizon, and deep, long shadows fell across the river valley.

As the man stood just beyond the Center Street Bridge as it rose to let the cruiser through, he could again see the people on the upper deck clearly enjoying themselves. There were seven of them. His father and his lover -- now both hated enemies -- a young man who appeared to be enamored with Hilda, and two other couples. As they passed, he could even hear their words -- all in English. It infuriated him.

As he watched, the cabin cruiser approached another wide bend in the river, where some sort of building sat on the point, hidden behind a truck terminal. There was a small grassy park, and he could see that there were pilings at a dock. It appeared to be a restaurant, and the cruiser was being docked at it. He continued up Carter Street toward the Eagle Street Bridge, and saw that the people aboard the cruiser were getting off at the restaurant, called Jim's Steak House. There was one other boat tied up at the dock, and a number of cars were in the parking lot along the east side of the restaurant.

Gerhardt Kalbmann was uncertain what to do, but he decided to wait until the seven people were inside the restaurant, and then to see if he could slip aboard in the dark. As the sun disappeared behind the west embankment of the river, the lights from the city above began to reflect in the oily, undulating water of the river. To the south was a faint orange glow -- almost like a sunset, but artificial. Kalbmann realized that the glow and the clanking sounds he heard were coming from a blast furnace. Also to the south he could see the high pipes and towers of an oil refinery, with a stream of flame shooting above several of the refracting and condensing towers.

Within twenty minutes it was nearly dark around the cabin cruiser, and he carefully moved forward from the side of a parked trailer toward the dock. Young men were at the entrance to the parking lot, opening doors for patrons and parking their cars for them. They were too busy to observe him skirting the lot along the side of the river.

On the rail viaduct high above the river to the northwest he saw several passenger trains and what appeared to be subway trains rattling toward or away from the lights of the city. Unobserved, he stepped up the short ramp and through the small gate into the main cabin of the cruiser.

The door to the galley was unlocked. Kalbmann, in the fading light, could make out some boxes of crackers, a tin of nuts and other snacks set on the counter. In the small refrigerator he found a plate of meat wrapped in plastic, and slipped a couple of slices off the plate in a way that their absence might not be noticed. He then grabbed a handful of the crackers, and wolfed down the meal, satisfying his hunger. He then explored the rest of the interior of the cruiser.

To the front of the galley was a large stateroom with its own head. It filled the entire front of the cruiser, but it provided no good hiding place, as the closet was too small to stand in. Behind the galley were steps down to the lower deck. Immediately to one side was another head, with a sink, toilet and small shower, less elegant than the one in the main stateroom. Off the center hallway were four small cabins, each with two bunks and a small closet. The second bunk in each was folded up into the wall. Each had one small porthole through which a bit of light still shown. He could see that three of these were being occupied, and recognized some of the clothing as that he had seen Hilda wear. He also recognized some of her personal items, such as her brush and comb.

At the back of the hallway was a ladder to a lower deck. He carefully switched on a button that lighted the hatchway. This bottom deck was not high enough in which to stand. There were several bunks, somewhat larger than those in the cabin above, and again he could see that the closet and drawers were being used. There was only a toilet and a sink, jammed tightly into a small nook. To the other side of the hatchway was a door leading to the engine room, where he observed two medium-sized diesel engines.

"This is some American millionaire's toy," he angrily thought to himself. "Our premier has nothing this fine." It was clear that the one cabin was not being used. His father and Hilda would be using two of the others, and one of the strangers, perhaps the young man he had seen talking with Hilda, would be in the third. He elected to wait in the fourth, unoccupied, cabin to see what would happen. Shutting off the light, he risked using the head, flushed it, then hid himself inside the fourth cabin, throwing the lock on the door.

* * *

It was nearly nine that evening when the Fairchilds and their guests returned to the *Castle Kent* and went aboard. May Durrand and Esther went below to use the head, but the others sat in the upper cabin while Fairchild started the diesel engines. Ross and Ray threw off the ropes, and Fairchild backed the cruiser into the river and turned it west, whistling almost immediately for the Center Street Bridge. Just beyond it they encountered the local party tour boat, the *Goodtime,* returning from its dinner cruise down the river and waiting for the next drawbridge to open. There was a lot of waving and helloing between the two vessels, and when the bridge opened Fairchild permitted the tourist boat to proceed ahead of the cabin cruiser.

When they had cleared the last bridge and entered the straight stretch of river leading to its mouth, Fairchild guided the cruiser gently toward the east bank, cutting the engines, and gliding to a gentle stop at the pilings behind St. Vincent House. Again Ross and Ray threw off the ropes and tied the *Kent* securely to the dock, which was lined with old tires to prevent rubbing of the boat against the wooden dock. The men all worked together to reattach the plastic screening around the deck, zipping it closed.

"Anyone want to stretch their legs ashore?" Fairchild asked. No one did, so he shut down all of the electrical navigation equipment except the marker lights and joined the others in the cabin.

"Anybody want anything else to drink or eat?" Esther inquired. Nobody did, as everyone had all they could manage at the famous riverside steakhouse.

"Richard," 'Kurt' Baldwin said as they sat together on the padded sofa in the cabin, "You said earlier that if the three letters meant something, you might know where my document went."

"Oh, it's just a hunch, Kurt," Fairchild replied. "But I have seen a picture of a cross much like the one you drew before, and there is a possibility that there could be a connection...."

"To what?"

"I suspect it is Latin or Italian, the *S* for *Sanctus* or *san,* and the *G* for Giovanni."

"And the *C?*"

"Perhaps *Cypri?* It's just a guess, Kurt."

"But if you are right about the letters, where is the document?"

"My best guess is that it is somewhere in Italy."

"Why Italy, Richie," Ross Johnson asked.

"Kurt, does the 'Seminary of Saint Felician of Mentana' sound familiar?"

"No, I can't say that it does. Who was Saint Felician?"

"A very obscure one. As far as I can trace, he was a medieval French knight."

"Is France where Mentana is?" May inquired.

"No, Mentana is just northeast of Rome. It's where the French defeated Garibaldi. I don't think there is any connection, but I'll try to find out for you. Well, enough of history, ladies and gents, how about a game of something? Poker? Scrabble? Charades?"

"Richie, I fear we'd have Hilda and Kurt at a disadvantage at Scrabble," Ross said, "but I'll bet they both can play a mean game of pinochle. I heard some of the German Army choristers talking about playing it."

"Pinochle, yes," Kurt replied. "Certainly we play pinochle. Hilda, you too?"

"Yes, I will join you."

"Richie, May and I have had a long day," Ray said." If it's okay with you, I think we'll turn in. I noticed a television in our stateroom. I assume we can get the local stations for the eleven o'clock news?"

"Oh, definitely."

"I'm going to turn in, too, Richie," Esther said. "I'm tired, and besides, pinochle is best played by four people.'

"Gosh, we're being abandoned! Well, let's get out the beer and pretzels, and have a hand or two," Fairchild said, getting up to open the card table and bring the cards from a cupboard while Ross poured some beer into a pitcher and brought it to the table with four glasses and a sack of small stick pretzels.

It was about eleven fifteen that evening when the team of Ross and Hilda declared themselves the victors over Richie and Kurt, drained the last of their beer, and bid each other good night. The three men waited while Hilda used the one bathroom, Richie using the time to inquire what the other two men would like to see the following day, and then Kurt and Ross descended through the galley to the lower deck. Kurt visited the head first, then went into his cabin as Ross followed him to the head. Richard Fairchild checked around the upper deck, putting away the card table and cards, and rinsing out the pitcher and the glasses to drain in the galley sink, then he also descended to the lower deck and disappeared down the ladder at the rear hatchway.

"Who won, dear?" Esther asked as she switched on the light over her bunk.

"Oh, Ross and Hilda. I think they were really enjoying themselves. They make a nice couple."

"The General seemed so relaxed. You'd never know he had just defected. He seems glad to be in America."

"He told me earlier that he had never been political, either with the Nazis or the Communists, but that his son was really a strict party-liner. They haven't gotten along well for years, especially after his wife died. Well, let me make a potty stop, and then I can get into bed too. I thought you'd be asleep by now."

"No, I read awhile. The boat would bump against the dock every now and then and I doubt I would have slept."

"Hmm. I don't recall any bumping. Maybe we were too engrossed in our card game. I do recall a couple of boats passing, but I didn't notice much wake."

In about two minutes both Fairchilds were in their bunks. Then there was some sort of commotion on the deck above them. There was a thud, and then a man shouted in German, "*Ihr bin Verrätern! Rache ver den Vaterland!*" As both Richard and Esther sat up, almost banging their heads on the low ceiling above them, two shots rang out, then two more, and finally two more. Then there was the sound of feet running up the deck toward the steps into the galley, and up to the main cabin.

"Good God!" Esther screamed. "What has happened?"

"I don't know!" Richard replied as he yanked on his trousers, hit the light switch, and bounded up the stairs. "It sounded like someone was shouting, 'You are traitors, vengeance for the fatherland.' Oh, my God!"

By the time Richie climbed up the ladder and hit the switch for the light in the lower deck hallway May and Rayland were standing in the galley looking down into the deck, and Ross Johnson was at his cabin doorway, just coming out.

"Some son of a bitch just shot a gun at me!" he exclaimed. "Hilda! Are you okay?" There was a moan from inside the cabin across from Ross's, and he grabbed the door handle, but it was locked from inside. "Unlock the door, Hilda, if you can."

There was no response. Meanwhile, Richie tried the door of the General's room, but it, too, was locked from the inside. "These locks will pop with a screwdriver," Richie said as he ran up the galley steps, returning moments later with a small Phillips screwdriver in his hand. He popped the lock on Hilda's room first, and Ross rushed into her cabin, finding her on the floor, blood pouring from a wound on her left shoulder.

He then popped the lock on the General's door. He was still lying in his bunk, but there was a deep gash on his forehead, and blood was also pouring from a second wound on his left thigh. "Get an ambulance!" Ross shouted, and Richie ran up through the galley to the ship-to-shore radio. In half a minute he had the harbormaster's office.

"This is the cruiser *Castle Kent*. We are docked behind the St. Vincent House on Old River Road. There has been a shooting aboard, and two of our passengers are seriously wounded. We'll need two ambulances and the police. Do you read?"

"We read, *Castle Kent*. We will notify the police dispatcher and the Coast Guard. Over."

"Hurry, please. Both victims are bleeding badly. Over."

"Understood. Joe," the Harbormaster spoke to another person, instructing him to notify the police. "Who did the shooting? Over."

"I don't know. Some German. Over."

"A German freighter is just clearing the harbor now. Was this person, what, male? Over."

"Yes. Over."

"Trying to hijack your cruiser? Over."

"No, I don't think so." As Fairchild signed off he could hear sirens coming down the St. Clair Street ramp. Soon two police cars, a fire department rescue squad, and two ambulances were stopped in front of St. Vincent House, and stretchers were being rolled around to the rear of the building.

The General was still unconscious as he was lifted up from the lower deck through the galley and placed on a stretcher on the dock. Hilda had briefly regained consciousness, said something that sounded like, "It was Johann," but passed out again when she tried to sit up. She, too, was lifted out through the galley and placed on a stretcher.

"Where will they take them?" Esther asked the emergency medic from the fire department.

"Either to Lutheran Hospital, or to St. John's," he told her. "They're both on the West Side. They'll go over the High Level Bridge."

Ross Johnson had yanked on his clothes, and said, "I'm going with them." He rushed out, and climbed into the back of the ambulance with Hilda and the medical technician. When they had asked who he was he had honestly told them he was Doctor Ross Johnson. It was only after they pulled up the hill that they found out he was a Doctor of Fine Arts, and not of medicine.

Chapter 15

There was little sleep for the four who remained aboard the *Castle Kent* that night. A Coast Guard cutter tied up next to the *Kent*, and two officers joined two Cleveland Police detectives around the dining table in the main cabin while Richard Fairchild made an attempt to explain what had happened. One of the Coast Guard officers recognized Fairchild, asking him to confirm if he was not the same man who had assisted in the recovery of the pirated *Chem Queen* the previous year and the arrest of two executives and a paid assassin for the murder of the homeless man. Fairchild also confirmed a relationship with Lieutenant Fochee, of the Cleveland Police Department, who had been involved with that case.

"So what does *this* shooting involve, Professor? And who are the two victims?"

"It's a long story, gentlemen. Last year it involved the FBI. This year, I'm afraid I may need to refer you to the CIA."

"The CIA?!! Com'on, Professor! Quit pullin' our leg," the Cleveland detective, Sergeant March, laughed. "Just give us some names."

"Okay, the woman is Hilda Waggoner. She is a Visiting Professor of Physics at Fremont College, and Dr. Rayland Durrand, here, is her department head."

"See, that wasn't so hard, Dr. Fairchild," the other detective, Mort Wilson, said. "Where's she visiting from, Dr. Durrand?"

"Ahh, I can't say."

"You can't say?"

"Ahh, well, she's from the University of Chicago."

"Oh. So what's the big deal?"

"Richard, what do we do here?" Rayland asked Fairchild.

"When we get to what happened tonight, they are going to have to know, I guess," Fairchild replied. "Look, as I suggested, this is complicated." Richard Fairchild reached into his pocket for his wallet, and extracted a card from it. "This is the phone number for George McCracken in Langley, Virginia. It is a secure line number at the Central Intelligence Agency, and even though it's the middle of the night, they will put the call through to him. I want you to call him and tell him that Curtis Baldwin and Hilda Waggoner have both been shot by a German agent, believed to be Johann Kahler. Tell him that I need his permission to discuss the case with the Coast Guard and the Cleveland Police. If he says okay, I'll tell you what you believe you need to know. If he says no, then I don't know what choice you are going to have. I suppose you can lock me up until he gets here."

"Dr. Fairchild, this is the craziest thing I've ever heard," Sergeant Marsh said.

"Just call him."

As there was no phone on the cruiser, only the ship-to shore radio, Fairchild and Durrand joined the two detectives and the Coast Guard officers aboard their cutter, where there was a phone. It took only five minutes to reach McCracken, who immediately comprehended the situation.

"Tell Fairchild I'll fly down there in the morning," he told the Coast Guard Officer, Lieutenant Liebowitzky, "but remember, anything he tells you tonight is highly confidential. Those two are vital to the nation's security. How are they doing?"

"We haven't gotten a report from the hospital yet, but the man's head wound did not appear too serious. However, they both seem to have lost a lot of blood. They should be okay," Liebowitzky told him.

"Let me speak to Fairchild," the CIA agent instructed. When the professor answered, McCracken said, "Richard, whatever you do, don't let the news media find out about this. You can give the police and the Coast Guard the basics, but use your best judgment. Refer anything you think you shouldn't say to me, and I'll be down there by noon tomorrow. Where will you be?"

"If they will release us, I'll take the cruiser back to Port Cleland. We don't have a car here in Cleveland, but will need to drive back to visit Kurt and Hilda at the hospital. At this point, we're not even sure which one they're in, but Ross Johnson is with them, and he'll let us know."

"Okay."

"God, I feel responsible, George. I planned this outing, and it's the college's cruiser. I can't see how Kahler could have found us. I mean, we're not even at a public dock."

"Richard, don't worry about it. There's no way you could have known what might happen. I'll see you somewhere this weekend. Fortunately Pricilla and I hadn't planned to go anywhere over the weekend. Maybe she'll fly down with me."

"If she does, have her plan to stay with Esther and me at the farm."

"Okay, we'll be in touch."

As Fairchild hung up, the four officers looked at him. "So, what's the story?" Lieutenant Liebowitzky asked.

"It's like this. Two months ago the older man, Baldwin, and the blond, Waggoner, were both very active in the East German government. McCracken can fill you in on their names, ranks and serial numbers, if they had serial numbers, if he wants to when he gets here. Our college choir and some of my religion students from Fremont were in East Germany visiting the homes of Martin Luther and Bach, and participating in a Dutch production of an opera, being performed in Bayreuth, which is in West

Germany. These two individuals were also to participate in the opera, and once in West Germany they elected to defect to the West. One was a professor, and she now holds a position at Fremont. The other was high up in the Army, and is now working for the CIA. You see why absolutely none of this can get into the newspapers or the radio. It affects NATO.

"Anyway, Baldwin's son, who is an officer in the East German Navy -- or was at the time – was engaged to the young woman professor, Waggoner. Apparently, because he knew them both, they must have sent him to assassinate the two defectors. That would explain what he shouted when he shot them, 'You are traitors; vengeance for the fatherland.' Hilda Waggoner recognized his voice. Now, how he located us – a d them – I can't imagine. Perhaps Russian or East German espionage agents here in America have been shadowing them. I just don't know. We were simply having a holiday cruise, with dinner at Jim's tonight. The son must have sneaked about the cruiser when it was docked at Jim's. There was an empty cabin, and he must have been hidden in it."

"And you say his name is Kahler? Johann Kahler?"

"Yes, but that is probably not the name he is using here in America. Oh, the Harbormaster said there had been a German freighter departed tonight. We had tied up across from it waiting for the New York Central Bridge to open. The *Fräulein Weser*, I think was the name. Maybe Kahler was on that ship, and saw us."

"It's possible," the second Coast Guard officer agreed. "We can stop it and search it for Kahler. But if he was on it and got off, he would have had to go through Customs, and they'd have a list of the crewmembers who got off. We can check that in the morning, but will check on the freighter tonight."

"I assume that Curtis Baldwin and Hilda Waggoner are not the real names of these two victims," Detective March said. "If the son's name is Kahler, the man's must be Kahler also."

"I'm not at liberty to confirm or deny that," Fairchild said. "But you can verify your conclusions with George McCracken tomorrow."

"What's the woman a professor of, Dr. Durrand?" Detective Wilson asked.

"Nuclear physics," Ray answered.

"As in nuclear power plants?"

"As in nuclear submarines."

"*Oh*. I see now...."

* * *

Gerhardt Kalbmann had been slightly disoriented when he first ran up to the deck of the cruiser and jumped to the dock. When he went around the side of the building housing the St. Vincent shelter he recognized where he was on Old River Road, and turned north, back toward the Rail Terminal Dock where the *Fräulein Weser* had been unloaded. It was less than a mile. But when he got there, he could see beyond the high wire fence and locked gate that the freighter had already been pulled from the dock by a tugboat. It was now in the middle of the harbor, headed for the opening in the harbor breakwater wall.

Hearing sirens coming down the hill to the river where the cruiser was parked, he quickly ran under a ramp off an overhead highway viaduct, and climbed up to one of the streets leading toward the center of the city.

Whereas at one time there were numerous flea-bag hotels and flop houses along West Sixth Street near St. Clair, now there were only the downtown higher class hotels. Walking in the direction of what seemed to be brighter lights, Kalbmann approached the Public Square, and noted that at one side of the high skyscraper was a sign that said *Hotel Cleveland*. He crossed the street and entered. By now it was well after midnight.

He entered the doors to the hotel, and climbed the wide staircase to the lobby, where he saw the reception desk. As he approached, the night clerk looked up and greeted him with a friendly gesture. "How can we help you?"

"I need a room for the night," Kalbmann announced. "You have one available?"

"Yes, despite the holiday, we have a few left. Is a single room sufficient?"

"A single... oh, yes, of course. I am alone."

The clerk handed Kalbmann a registration card and pen and asked, "Will this be on a credit card, or cash?"

"Cash," the German replied, looking at the questions on the card, one of which asked for a phone number. "I do not have a telephone. I'm traveling, and...."

"That's quite all right, sir. You may leave that blank. It will be ninety dollars a night. Actually, ninety-two eighty with tax. Will you be staying for more than one night, sir?"

"Ninety dollars?" Kalbmann thought. That's nearly two hundred Deutschmarks. This is an expensive nation. "No! No, just one night...."

"And your luggage, sir?"

"Ahh, it was delayed. Tomorrow I will get it."

"I see. We have a packet of items you may use, then, sir. A razor, and toothbrush, things like that. I'm afraid the shops in the Terminal are all closed by now, but our restaurant is still open, if you wish to dine."

"No, I am not hungry."

"Fine. It will be Room 1214. The bellboy can take you up if you wish."

"I can find it, I'm sure," the German replied. "What floor is it on?"

"The twelfth. The elevators are over there in that alcove," he said, pointing.

Kalbmann extracted the roll of American dollars his captain had given him and counted out five twenty dollar bills which he handed to the clerk, receiving some smaller bills and coins in return, along with a room key. He thanked the clerk and headed for the bank of elevators.

Room 1214 overlooked the Detroit-Superior High Level Bridge and the Cuyahoga River Valley. From his window he could see the stretch of river along Old River Road and the shelter where the cruiser had been docked. There was now a Coast Guard cutter tied up at the dock, and the red flashers from a police car on the street. He wondered if his shots had found their mark. Ultimately it did not matter. Whatever damage there was had already been done. He could never return to East Germany, but now he was not even certain he could return to the *Fräulein Weser*. Would they guess that he had been one of the freighter's crew? He knew he would have to find out.

Although he did not sleep well that night, it was not the fault of the bed or the room. The East German had never seen such a luxurious room. He enjoyed the big bathroom, with the fluffy towels on a heated rack, and the sack of items the hotel clerk had given him included everything he needed to be clean and comfortable. There were even some chocolates in the room. He would plan what to do the following morning.

* * *

Toledo, Ohio
Saturday Before Labor Day, 1962, 7:40 a.m.

The German freighter, *Fräulein Weser*, had sat outside the Toledo harbor until sunrise. A United States Coast Guard cutter from Sandusky had intercepted it about four hours earlier as it approached the passage north of the Bass Islands of Lake Erie, and had been in radio communication with the captain and officers, explaining that they wished to board the vessel when it docked in Toledo, and that no one was to disembark until then.

The Port of Cleveland U.S. Customs office had radioed the names of all of the crewmen who had disembarked in Cleveland, and who were not due back aboard again until Monday evening. There were only five such men on the list. The Coast Guard lieutenant in charge of the boarding asked the freighter's captain for a list of his officers and crew, and then asked the captain to hold a head count. The captain could clearly see what would happen, and said, in broken English, "Lieutenant, vee have a sixth man who vent ashore last evening after dah Customs agent had departed. He is not aboard now, but his name is also not on your list."

"And this man is...?"

"His name is Gerhardt Kalbmann," the captain confirmed. "He directed unloading and loading yesterday, and had not intended to leave dah ship. Den he came to me und asked permission to do so. I told him to take his passport mit him. He departed about seventeen hundred hours."

"Customs should have been notified, Captain."

"*Ja*, I know. But he is very intelligent young man, almost naval quality."

"What do you know about him? How long has he been on your crew?"

"Dis vas his first crossing mit us, Lieutenant. He joined crew in Bremen."

"You saw his papers?"

"*Nein*, he said he had lost them, but he obviously knew navigation skills needed for assistant mates."

"May we see his quarters?"

"Certainly," the Captain said, taking the two officers to the crew staterooms, and showing them the locker that had been assigned to Kalbmann. There was only his work clothes, plus a black winter coat and a pair of boots. One Coast Guard officer examined the boots carefully.

"Skoda!" he remarked.

"Pardon?" said the Captain.

"Skoda Leather Works. These were made in Czechoslovakia, most likely for East German naval officers. I would not be surprised to learn that your Gerhardt Kalbmann is really Captain Johann Kahler, of the East German Navy."

The freighter captain said nothing, though his eyebrows rose. He would be lucky if the Americans did not arrest him or detain his vessel for having violated U. S. Customs laws. He nearly shook with relief when, after interrogating the rest of the crew and matching names, he was instructed to contact the Coast Guard as soon as all his crew members reported in the following Monday, and to detain Kalbmann if he returned until they got there. He readily agreed, and the officers departed.

* * *

Dr. Ross Johnson had arrived back at the dock behind St. Vincent House at about four thirty that morning, having taken a taxi from St. John's Hospital on Detroit Avenue. The Durrands had gone back to bed, as had Esther, but Richard Fairchild was still sitting in the main cabin in the dark, unable to sleep or to concentrate on anything else. He was delighted to see the young music professor returning.

"How are they?" he immediately inquired.

"Both are awake and alert. Their wounds are serious, but not critical. Kurt's head wound was superficial, but the bullet was still in the muscle of his thigh, and they will have to do surgery to remove it. The bullet that hit Hilda's shoulder passed through the muscle and went on through the flesh of her back. Fortunately it did not hit any bones or organs, but she'd lost a lot of blood. They've given her antibiotics and stitched her up, but want to keep her over the weekend to be certain that she's okay. Good thing that she is under the college's medical plan. I was able to tell them who the insurer was."

"Yes, they always want to know that, first."

"What happened here after I left?"

"I thought they might lock us up when I told them I couldn't identify anyone until it was okayed by the CIA. They thought I was nuts until I got George McCracken, my friend from Langley, on the phone. Then they were impressed. When they heard that we suspected it was Johann Kahler who had shot his father and Hilda, it didn't take them long to figure out that Baldwin was a phony name, but I guess they're going to let us leave. I'd like to leave as soon as the sun comes up, and get back to Port Cleland to get the car. McCracken is going to fly in this morning and contact me at the farm. I guess we'll find out just how fast this old tub can go, because I'm going to run it at full throttle all the way back to the lagoon."

* * *

When Gerhard Kalbmann had awakened the following morning he realized that he would have to move quickly if he were to avoid detection. If anyone connected him with the German freighter that had been in port that day, the freighter would be carefully watched. He knew that Toledo was at the far west end of Lake Erie, and that the *Fräulein Weser* would already have reached the Maumee Terminal docks where it would wait for the American holiday to pass.

He gathered the few items he had, and went down to the hotel lobby. At the concierge's desk he inquired the best way to reach Toledo, and was informed that there would be both buses and trains, and that the train station was next to the hotel, down a ramp. He also learned that there were both stores and restaurants in the Terminal.

His first purchase had been a small case in which to put the few personal belongings he had. He then found a small restaurant where he had a breakfast of some flat crepes called pancakes, along with sausages that he could barely tolerate. He then found the railway ticket office, and learned that a New York Central train, *The Iroquois*, would depart at shortly after one-thirty that afternoon, and would stop in Toledo about an hour later. There was an earlier train, but it was fully booked. He bought his ticket, and wandered around the Terminal, finally finding a bookshop that had a handful of books in German, several of which he purchased.

Train 35, *The Iroquois*, carried many mail and package freight cars ahead of its three sleeping cars and three coaches. Kalbmann had a window seat on the right side of the train, which provided a view of the lakeshore for part of the trip, including the long trestle across Sandusky Bay. The train did not stop in Port Cleland, but as it crossed the Portage River Kalbmann was shocked to see that the highway drawbridge to the north was open and that a cabin cruiser, the *Castle Kent*, was passing underneath it. It was the same boat on which he had hidden himself the night before.

As the train slowly rolled into the Toledo Union Station over the Maumee River bridge Kalbmann spotted the tall German freighter now at its dock. He exited the station and walked in the direction he had seen the *Fräulein Weser*. It was tied up on the opposite bank. Behind it a U.S. Coast Guard boat was docked, and on the dock was a police car. Kalbmann did not need someone to translate these circumstances. He did not know how, but it was clear that they knew who he was, and would be watching for him.

He had only slightly more than one hundred American dollars left. There was not much chance of him finding work on this American inland sea. He would have to go to some large city and try to find work. He still had his passport. In a country this size there were probably hundreds of Gerhardt Kalbmanns. But he had heard from other crew members that in America one had to have something called a Social Security Number in order to get a job. He was unsure how to get such a number. All he knew was that he had to get out of this town, and that he could not go back to Cleveland. There was Detroit. There was Chicago… and, yes, there was Canada.

* * *

The Fairchilds received word on the following Wednesday that both Baldwin and Waggoner would be released from the hospital. George McCracken and his wife were still at Fairchild's farm as guests. George and Richard drove into Cleveland to collect the two recovering patients, and the six spent the next three days at the farm. The new college semester would begin the following Monday, and the McCrackens and Baldwin had reservations to fly back to Washington the prior Saturday.

The Coast Guard confirmed that the German sailor known as Gerhardt Kalbmann had not returned to the freighter, *Fräulein Weser*, hence they were fairly certain that Kalbmann was indeed Johann Kahler. All the other crewmen were accounted for and had been interviewed. A bulletin was posted for Kalbmann's arrest, with the warning that he was armed and dangerous.

The U.S. Customs Department considered filing charges against the ship's captain, but decided that it was not worth the effort. Even if Kalbmann had gone through Customs, there would have been no reason to detain him at that time.

Although stiff and still suffering some muscle pain, Hilda Waggoner was excited about beginning her new classes at the College. She felt well enough to tend to her new apartment in Fremont, and Ross Johnson assisted her in getting from Fairchild's farm to the campus and her apartment. With the start of the fall semester it seemed that the excitement of summer was becoming only a memory. Of that Esther Fairchild was extremely grateful.

* * *

Winery of the *Colli del Teramo*, Central Italy
September 13, 1962, 9:45 a.m.

Atop the vineyard-covered Abruzzi hill overlooking the Adriatic the high stone fortress with a round watchtower at the southeast corner and a square tower, slightly higher, at the northeast, seemed almost deserted. A much taller, square Italian Gothic tower sat above the fortress chapel; the square stone structure dated from the early thirteenth century. The vines on the hillside stood heavy with dark, almost black grapes -- the kind often used in better quality Chianti -- almost ready for harvesting.

The fortress winery, one of four holdings by the Holy Knights of St. John of Cyprus, served as both a winery, a summer campus for the order's Seminary of St. Felician of Mentana, outside Rome, and as a retreat for both the lay and ordained members of their military order. The order held possession of two former Carthusian charterhouses, one on the left bank in Paris, and the other near the Lambert Palace in London. Although primarily a Roman Catholic order, many of both its lay and ordained "knights," as they were known, were of other Christian faiths, including both Anglican and Orthodox. Their ordained members had, or would, serve as military chaplains.

While in retreat at the fortress the knights wore black tunics on which was emblazoned an oddly-shaped cross, tapered toward the center, with concave edges and a shield in the middle, bearing the letters *SGC*. In the Grand Hall adjoining the medieval chapel was a throne set up on a platform where the Grand Master, usually an Italian or French Cardinal or bishop, held the knighting ceremony for newly appointed members. This ceremony had occurred only rarely in recent decades, and often more than two years would pass without any new knights, lay or ordained, being inducted into the order.

Knights came from all over the world, and spoke many languages. Many of the Italian knights had served the Italian Army during the War, while those from France or England had served on the other side's armies. The War had decimated their ranks. Many of the ordained clergy knights were assigned by the order to various diocese or service entities, and in such cases only their bishops knew of their affiliation with the order.

Others in the order served the Church and governments in a variety of ways. Knights of St. John of Cyprus had smuggled hundreds of Jews to safety during the War. Several members of royal families of nations occupied by the Nazis had been secretly hidden in the fortress. Two knights who became members of the High German Command had been involved in an early plot to assassinate Adolph Hitler; their identity as knights was never revealed, even after their execution.

The Rev. Dr. Dameon D'Amarcio, an ordained knight who was also the professor of ancient languages at the Seminary of St. Felician of Mentana, had moved his office permanently to the fortress in July of 1962. There he had room to open, and the materials to preserve, an ancient document that had come into his possession. He had been aided in acquiring the document through several of the lay knights of the order, one in Milan, and another in Paris.

Although the police departments of Europe considered the document to be stolen, Father D'Amarcio knew it was not. It belonged to the Holy Knights of St. John of Cyprus, having been rescued by one of their ordained brothers and presented to the order in Rome in 1941. It had taken the order over twenty years to find it again, but now it was restored to its proper owners, and, when translated, due credit would be extended to the deceased Ge'ez monks who had preserved it during the prior two thousand years. D'Amarcio had already determined that none of the monks at the Ceobobo Monastery in Ethiopia had survived. War had obliterated all traces of the monastery high in the mountains south of Jima, ending a religious endeavor that had existed for nearly two millenniums.

Two letters had just been delivered to Father D'Amarcio. One came direct from an acquaintance in Alexandria, an expert on ancient Ge'ez languages. Father D'Amarcio had sent this expert, Haille d'Mosariff al Begetta, an exact copy of some wording he believed to be a form of Ge'ez. Al Begetta confirmed that it was as anticipated, and provided a literal translation of the wording.

It was the second letter, however, that intrigued him more. It came from an American professor at a small Ohio college, a man he had met briefly two months earlier in Arles, France. It had been sent to the seminary address in Mentana, and had been forwarded on to him at the fortress. It both puzzled and amused D'Amarcio, and he thought about how he would answer the letter. It read:

> Dear Rev. Dr. D'Amarcio:
>
> You may recall that we met on the morning of the auction, July 1, in Arles. You were representing your

seminary, and I a museum of antiquities in the United States. The document that we both had examined the day before had allegedly been stolen that morning, and the police were investigating. However, I have a theory that the document in question was not so much the subject of a theft as that of its return to the rightful owners.

Since returning to the United States I have learned something further about the document that I believe you may find interesting, but perhaps also a bit saddening. The document had, I have theorized, once been the property of a particular religious order, and had been partially examined at a location -- perhaps a seminary -- in Italy, perhaps during May of 1941. Due to political reasons, I have further theorized, it was decided to take this document to Switzerland. However, the courier, a priest whom I believe to have been of your knightly order, encountered German soldiers at the border and was killed. The document was then placed by a German officer, whom I am not at liberty to name, in a Swiss bank, where it remained for some twenty-one years.

When this officer attempted to reclaim the document this past July, he learned that it had been sold by the bank to an antiquities dealer in Geneva, from whom it was subsequently stolen. It was this document which I believe we both inspected in Arles, where it was intended to be sold by its unlawful owner to the highest bidder. Fortunately, in my theoretical opinion, it was reclaimed by its rightful owners for protection and preservation.

If my theories are correct and this document is now in the hands of its rightful owners, as an individual with a sincere interest in ancient religious manuscripts, I would very much like to assist in any project involving the translation and preservation of the document, entirely on a confidential basis. I believe that some of us who were present in Arles in July had a vague notion as to what the document was, although none of us had any idea of its origin. If these notions are confirmed, it will be difficult to maintain any degree of secrecy. But until such confirmation, I am committed to preserve absolute confidentiality about the document and the facts surrounding it.

If my theories are in any way correct, please advise if I may join in any endeavor to translate the document.

Richard F. Fairchild, M.Th., Ph.D.,
Professor of Religions,
Fremont College

Father D'Amarcio read the letter a second time, and shook his head. How could the man have learned all this? He had not appeared to have even heard of the document before the Arles auction, and had only seen it the day before. Father D'Amarcio tried to remember what he had said that might have revealed to this American college professor the connection of the document to the seminary. He had, he recalled, identified the seminary. What else had he said? Yes, he recalled, he had mentioned the Holy Brothers. But that was so little upon which this man had conjured up his "theories."

The seminarian arose and went to the fortress library. Somehow the name on the letter sounded vaguely familiar. He had not thought about it at the time. His mind had been elsewhere. Now? Yes, an Italian translation of a fifteen year old text, *The French Monastic Republics*, by R. F. Fairchild. The man was internationally known as an expert on religious orders. *That* was how he had figured it out. D'Amarcio returned to his office and began writing a letter.

Dear Dr. Fairchild:

Your letter addressed to our seminary in Mentana has been forwarded to my current quarters at our order's retreat in Abruzzo Province. You no doubt will learn of this location. Being familiar with your scholarly work on the French monastic republics, we are honored by your inquiry. Your identity ought to have been recognized by me in Arles, and I apologize for my failure in doing so.

I am not at liberty to either confirm or deny the accuracy of your theories. The matter is still under investigation by the international police, and whether or not the present location of the document to which you refer is with its legal and rightful owners is not an issue we are prepared to pursue. The information you have provided, however, is most welcome, and might well become evidence for a claim of document ownership in the international courts, should such legal action become necessary

Our order did not know what had happened to either Father Giulio Garmani, who was a Swiss citizen, or to the document he had brought with him from Ethiopia, where he had served as a chaplain to the Italian Army based there. I will tell you that the document came into his hands in the form of a rescue, and that its previous custodians were all killed in an unfortunate attack during the War in Ethiopia. We have verified that there would be no valid Ethiopian ownership. Perhaps it was within God's plans that the document came into Father Garmani's possession, and perhaps also within His plans that the document should someday become known. But that is not for me to say. Father Garmani's family near Lugano will be advised of the information you have provided.

All that I can say at this moment is that I want you to contact the Rev. Reginald Forebusher, at Willingcroft Charterhouse, Albertbank Street, London. He will be alerted to your contact. If your theories are confirmed and your request is to be granted, you will have to work out details with the Rev. Forebusher. That is the best I can offer you at this time. I thank you for your letter.

Yours in Christ,
Fra Dameon D'Amarcio, KSGC

Chapter 16

Cold weather struck Northern Ohio early that autumn. Temperatures dropped to near freezing in September, and by mid-October the first snow had fallen. The Fairchilds and the Merriams had made one short weekend trip to West Bass Island to help with the grape harvest, but no other outings, other than to college football games, were planned. Ross Johnson and Hilda Waggoner had gone along, although Hilda still did not have the strength to do much grape harvesting.

Repairs to the interior of the cruiser had taken about a week. The bullets had shattered three cabin doors that had to be replaced, blown out the porthole in the cabin that Ross had been occupying, and the other two mattresses had been soaked in blood and had to be replaced. A second bullet was found lodged in the wall just above where Hilda's head had been, and they left it there as a *souvenir* of the adventure. The total cost was slightly less than the deductible on the marine insurance policy on the vessel, and Fairchild had not submitted a claim. As he felt responsible for the damage, even though he had given the college title to the cruiser when he had first won it in a court battle against the domestic terrorist who had owned it, he also elected not to turn the bills over to the college. Esther had agreed that they should bear the expense.

George McCracken promised to let Dr. Fairchild know if and when Kalbmann was found. The CIA did not believe that there would be a second attempt to kill either Hilda or Baldwin, although McCracken asked Fairchild to continue keeping an eye on the young blond German nuclear scientist, both for her own safety and for any signs that her defection had been staged.

The routine of events in the Hayes Hall basement offices of the Religions Department was comforting to Richard Fairchild. He taught only classes he enjoyed, participated weekly in the college chapel services, noting that Hilda had joined the college choir, and counseled students as needed. On the farm his cattle had been brought into the barns for the winter, and one of the beefy steers had been butchered. Esther's freezer was full of meat for the rest of the season.

It was toward the end of October that a package arrived for Dr. Fairchild from London. It was in response to a letter he had written in September. It contained a questionnaire, which the professor completed and was ready to return. So far he had said nothing to Esther about his theories or letters, but she had been curious about the London package, and had asked him if he knew why he was being contacted.

"Yes," he replied. "I believe this has to do with some letters I wrote last month, Esther. It's possible that we may have to make a trip to Europe again sometime this year, but that remains to be seen."

"To London?"

"Maybe. Let me explain. Do you remember when Paul Sukhey asked me to inspect a document in Arles, France, on behalf of his museum, and attend the auction of an old historic document? As it turned out, the document was the same one that Kurt Kahler -- or Baldwin, as he's now known -- had placed in a Swiss bank in 1941. The bank had sold it when they couldn't locate the owner, and then it got stolen, so the police were watching. They apparently were not aware of the auction or the document's location until after it disappeared a second time.

"You may recall, in our conversations with Kurt on the cruiser that day before he was shot, he told us how he had come to acquire the document -- from a priest who was shot bringing it from Italy across the Swiss border. When he described the small cross the priest wore, it explained something to me. That cross represented a particular religious order, and it was the same order as one of the participants at the Arles auction, a seminary professor from the outskirts of Rome.

"If you remember, I asked Kurt about what the priest had with him, besides the document, and he mentioned both that cross, and a letter from a seminary. He could not remember the name of the seminary, but had destroyed the letter. It was probably from the same seminary as this religious order, quite probably in Latin, and was probably addressed to the priest's bishop in Switzerland, explaining about the document. Thanks to the Germans, it never got to the bishop, and the priest probably ended up at the bottom of Lake Lugano. I've since learned the priest's name, Giulio Garmani, and he had family in the Lugano area."

"Good heavens, Richard! You've been so busy, how have you had time do follow up on this?" Esther asked.

"Well, if what I suspect is true, this religious order reclaimed the document in Arles, and took it to some fortress they have in Italy. There I anticipate they are going to open and study the document. I think I know what the document is, and if I am right, I want to be in on the translation of it. It could be the greatest archeological find of the century, perhaps of the last thousand years."

"What is it?"

"Esther, I'm not certain, but I think it is a copy of the so-called *Quella*, or 'source document,' from which both the gospels of Matthew and Luke were written. There is so much common material about the teachings in their work, which we know was also based in part on John Mark's gospel. There had to be a number of copies of that document. Paul may have acquired one at some point, and copies may have existed elsewhere in the Roman Empire. The copies may not have all read the same way, however.

Look, for example, at the differences between Matthew's Chapter Five and Luke's Chapter Six. Was this editing by Matthew or Luke, or were the sources they were using different?

"But I can't be certain it's a copy of the '*Q*' until I see the document. If it really is in the hands of this religious order in Italy, it may not be made public for decades, perhaps even a century or more, because they are so secretive. I'm nearly fifty, Esther. How long could I wait?"

"So what is this package from London?"

"I'm not sure. I wrote to the seminary in Rome, and the letter was forwarded to some location in Abruzzi, where the priest I had met in Arles wrote back to me. He would neither confirm nor deny my theory, but was grateful for knowing what had happened to his young priest twenty-one years ago. I was referred to some clergyman in London, and this packet is in response to that inquiry. As I understand it, I would have to be cleared by the order -- probably sworn to secrecy -- before they would let me see the document or help in its translation."

"Goodness. It all sounds so bizarre," Esther said. "What is this religious order?"

"The official name is the 'Holy Knights -- or Brothers -- of St. John of Cyprus.' Like the Knights of Malta, it is a remnant of the Knights of St. John Hospitaller, dating from the time of the last Crusade. It's a very secret international organization, as far as I can determine, and it has both lay and ordained members, not all Roman Catholic, but all very dedicated. They've been involved in a lot of daring rescues, including Jews during the War, royalty during takeovers of governments, and similar acts of mercy. I understand that they fund hospitals, orphanages and other institutions around the world, all behind the scenes."

"So, do you think they'll let you see this document?"

"I suppose there is always blackmail -- I could threaten to go to the media if they don't cooperate, but, Esther, you know I'd never to that. Perhaps if I return these papers and answer all their questions, they might reconsider my request. All I can do is hope."

* * *

Gerhardt Kalbmann had taken a bus from Toledo to Chicago, and found a large community of German immigrants on the near North Side. He had followed their advice, and with their aid had found a job in a small electronics factory. He hated the work, but the pay was more than he had earned as either a naval officer or a freighter crewman, and with the low weekly rent at a boarding house where German was the primary language, he felt comfortable for the time being.

But he knew that he would be unable to stay there long. At the Chicago Public Library he had read about Social Security, and that everyone had a nine-digit number. He made up a number when hiring on at the electronics factory, but anticipated that when income was reported to that number, it would not be long before the government would follow up on his identity. When he had saved up several thousand dollars he took a train to Seattle, crossed into British Columbia, and asked for Canadian immigration status. Although his German passport was in the name of Gerhardt Kalbmann, he told them that his name was Kolmann, and that the passport was simply typed wrong. He hoped that the Canadians would not check further, and they did not. With the immigration papers in the Kolmann name he was able to apply for work legitimately, and was soon hired as a mate's assistant on a Canadian freighter transporting lumber to Japan.

* * *

The letter from Reginald Forebusher at Willingcroft Charterhouse, London arrived a few days before Thanksgiving, via air mail, to the Fairchild farm. Esther called Richard at his office, and he asked her to open it and read it to him over the telephone. It read:

Dear Dr. Fairchild:

Professor George Wiggins of Oxford sends his regards. George confirms what you had stated in the biographical information you provided to us, and what we had learned through other outside investigation -- that you are indeed an internationally known scholar of religions, with a legitimate interest in historical and archeological documents.

A copy of your earlier letter to Dameon D'Amarcio in Mentana was forwarded to the Charterhouse for review and consideration. Father D'Amarcio was uncertain how you reached your theoretical conclusions, and obviously is reluctant to either confirm or deny them. As you are apparently aware, our order, the Knights of St. John of Cyprus, is an international organization. It is not totally under the auspices of any Church, neither the Roman, Orthodox nor Anglican, but functions both officially and unofficially as a self-governing diplomatically- recognized political institution. As such, access to any of its facilities must be limited to those who are granted knighthood and are thus under sworn vows of obedience to the Grand Master, currently the Right Reverend Pierre Montclaire.

Such status is solely by invitation, coming only after approval by a majority of the Body of Knights. Those under consideration for induction must grant their permission for such consideration. Your name has been placed in nomination as a lay, married member. That fact may not be disclosed to anyone, other than your wife. If it is, the nomination will be considered withdrawn immediately. If you grant permission for the nomination, however, it will be placed before the Body at the next meeting in Italy, and if they vote agreement, your invitation will be extended.

If you agree to these terms, please so advise me as soon as possible, as a meeting of the Body will be held prior to Christmas. If you do not agree, or would have any hesitation to swearing an oath of allegiance and obedience to the Grand Master and the Order, no response is necessary. However, if such is the case, your request to visit and assist with any documents held by the Order will be considered as denied. We prayerfully await your reply.

Reginald Forebusher, KSGC

As Esther finished reading the letter she paused a moment, then said, "Richard, I know you well enough to anticipate what your initial response will be. I don't know what this organization is, but it is apparently more than just some Masonic Lodge that holds a parade and a barbecue once a year. I can't imagine you swearing an oath of obedience to some foreigner, but neither can I imagine you walking away from what you think might be a lifetime achievement. What are you going to do?"

Esther could hear her husband exhale. "I don't know, Esther. Everything I do know about this organization is positive. Apparently George Wiggins, my professor at Oxford, is a member. I'll certainly consult with him before deciding. I'd say the only thing we can do at this time is pray about it. I realize, on first look, that it appears to possibly be an issue of "God *or* Country." But perhaps it is more an issue of "God *and* Country."

After Fairchild's afternoon class he went to the college chapel. Sitting alone he thought about the options placed in front of him, his obligations to Esther, the college, and others, and his obligation to his own professionalism. If he was correct, and so far there was no indication that he was not, the opportunity to assist in translation of the manuscript was truly a providential gift. Could he decline such a gift and live with himself afterwards?

* * *

On the Monday of the week before the Christmas holiday break Bob and Sally Merriam arrived at the basement office of the Religions Department in a state of excitement. It was very evident to Richard Fairchild as he sat in his office preparing for his nine o'clock class lecture on Old Testament Prophets. "What are you two up to?" he inquired.

"We bought a house over the weekend!" Sally replied. "It's here in town, so we won't have to commute to Sandusky in the snow all winter."

"Oh! Congratulations. Is it a one or two story house?"

"It's two stories, built, oh gosh, probably fifty years ago. It's over by Spiegel Grove, the Hayes Presidential estate." Bob answered. "There's a tree-lined sidewalk in front, big houses all around, and it has just recently been modernized, new wiring and plumbing. Even a new furnace."

"Sounds great. Had you been looking for a place?"

"I didn't think we could afford one," Bob replied, "but with just a small down payment, the mortgage is actually going to be less than our current rent and gasoline costs driving back and forth to Sandusky. My dad is loaning us the money, so we won't be paying the full mortgage rate that a savings and loan might charge.'

"Of course, that means that we have to pay our own property tax and insurance," Sally added, "but the best part is that there is a little garage apartment -- perfect for one person -- and we can rent that out. It would just about cover the monthly payment."

"Well! Any prospective tenants yet?"

"Hilda mentioned to me at the last choir practice that she was not real happy with her apartment, because there are students next door who are into rock and roll music," Sally replied. "Apparently the 'thump-thump-thump' goes on late into the night. I can't wait to tell her about this, and see if she might be interested. The rent might even be cheaper than where she is."

"But you two could get noisy, too, I'll bet."

"Us, Dr. Fairchild?" Sally laughed. "Oh, pooh, we're about as noisy as goldfish!"

"No, I can see it now. First will come the barking puppy, then three squalling babies, then Bob will start a machine shop in the garage, and next thing your tenant will be accusing you of disturbing the peace."

"Oh, pooh! We will not!"

"When do you move in?"

"We're signing the paperwork this week, and take possession on the first of January," Bob explained, "but the current owners have already moved out, and said we could move our stuff in any time after the closing. Our lease in Sandusky can be terminated at the end of the month, so I think we'll actually be moved in by Christmas."

"I hope we can get a Christmas tree put up, and have a big party New Year's Eve," Sally added. "But we'd better not send invitations until after the closing."

"We're going to have a professional mover do the furniture, but that reporter from the *Fremont Blade*, Jack Grady, just bought a truck and is going to help us move the other stuff," Bob explained.

"Grady's still working for old Sam Bostitch, eh?" the professor asked.

"Yes, he said he didn't think there was any place he could go where he might get as many exclusive stories as you create for him, Richie. You know, that interview he did with you after the homeless man's murder was solved last year almost won him a prize."

"When Esther read it, about my little adventure in Lake Erie, it almost won me a prize as well -- grounds for marital aggravation. I didn't tell him about that, but then he interviewed the Coast Guard officers who were involved, and they blabbed it all."

"You could have been killed, Dr. Fairchild," Sally said.

"When? By the murderer, or by Esther?" he laughed. "It's life on the edge, all right! But let me know what Esther and I can do to help you get settled in your new home. We'll look forward to seeing it."

* * *

The Merriam's New Year's Eve party was a bigger success than they could have imagined. In addition to Sally's parents and one of her brothers and his wife, the Fairchilds, Hilda and Ross, the Durrands and several other faculty members responded to the invitation, which was also a "house warming party," as Esther called it.

The movers had also stopped in Norwell and picked up Sally's old piano, which fitted very snugly in a corner of the living room. She had it tuned, and Ross kept the party singing until well after one in the morning. Just before the party broke up, Ross Johnson said, "Folks, Hilda and I have an announcement to make."

That quieted the crowd, and, Ross, with his arm around Hilda's waist, and a big smile on her face, said, "Hilda has agreed to be my wife! Our wedding will be at the college chapel in June. Richard, will you do the service for us?"

"If I'm able to, sure," Fairchild replied, thoughtfully. "Do you want it in German or English?"

Everyone laughed, and Bob called for another round of drinks, suggesting that if anyone needed one, he'd be happy to call a cab. Dean Harding had renewed his annual holiday party program that he called "the

Rickshaw Rebate." If anyone went to a party, enjoyed him or herself to the point of inebriation, he or she had to use a taxi, ferryboat, train, plane or rickshaw to get home -- mandatory -- but the college would reimburse the fare. In the three years it had been in effect, there had not been one faculty or student auto accident on or before any holiday.

By two a.m. the crowd had disbursed and the Merriams had jammed the dirty dishes in the sink and taken out the trash. They were exhausted as they climbed into the big double bed on the second floor of their new home.

"What a night," Bob exclaimed. "I think everyone really enjoyed themselves."

"I think so too," Sally replied. "But when Ross asked Richie to do their wedding, did you notice the hesitation?

"Now that you mention it, yes, 'If I'm able to,' he said. I wonder what he meant. Why wouldn't he be able to marry them?"

"I can't imagine. You don't suppose he's sick, or something."

"Ho, I certainly hope not," Bob said as he wrapped his arms around his wife's shoulders and pulled her close to him.

Chapter 17

Office of the Dean of Administration, Fremont College
February 7, 1963, 12 p.m.

"Come in, Richard," Dean Ralph Harding said as his Chairman of the Religions Department appeared at his door. "My secretary is at lunch. She told me you had called for an appointment."

"Yes, I appreciate your seeing me."

"How's Esther?"

"Oh, fine. Busy as ever. She has another deadline to illustrate yet another children's book, and has been working steadily in her studio."

"What is this one about?"

"Airplanes or something. I'm not sure of the title. It will be geared for junior high school level, so she's having to do a bit more research on the subject than for the books for younger children. How's Sarah?"

"Oh, she's also well, and busy. She's been pestering me to be sure she gets a cruise on that boat of yours this spring when the weather gets better."

"It's a sheet of ice out there now. She could probably walk to West Bass Island. I saw where they were driving the mail across from Catawba to Put-in-Bay on the ice again. They're not able to do that every winter."

"What brings you to see me, Richard?" the Dean asked after a momentary lull in the conversation.

"I need a short leave of absence, Ralph."

"What?" the dean said, sounding shocked. "Whatever for? Are you sick? Do you need surgery?"

"No, no, nothing like that. You may recall that I turned down your offer of a sabbatical a couple of years ago. Didn't need one, didn't want one. But an opportunity to do some really important religious archeological research has arisen in Europe, and I don't feel that I can professionally decline."

"What kind of research?"

"Ralph, it's very important. I'm not at liberty to disclose what it is, or may be, but it could possibly be one of the greatest historical discoveries of the century. I realize that this may throw a kilter in the winter/spring semester plans, but...."

"Where is this research, and how long would you be gone?"

"I have to be there March 15, it is in Italy. I would be gone six weeks."

"Six weeks, Richard! What about your classes?"

"That is obviously the problem. I know Bob Merriam can take over most of them. He knows the subjects and is quite capable. But there is a schedule conflict for two of them, the Islamic Studies 308 course, and History of Denominations 212. I spoke with Dr. Abram al Shim, our Arabic language instructor, who is here twice a week, the same days as my Islamic Studies class, and he is very interested in teaching that class, if you approve."

"Yes, he'd certainly be qualified. He knows the far *Koran* better than you do."

"Much better. Jim Jackson, who graduated last year with a major in Religions, and who is working on his Masters down at Bowling Green, would certainly be qualified to take over the Denominations class for a couple of months. I've not asked him yet, but did sound him out on his schedule, and he has no conflicts."

"What if I don't approve of this, Richard?"

"This is important to me, Ralph. I'd have to resign."

"Oh God, no! No, we'll work something out. It sounds like you already have done so. But tell me more about this project."

"I can't."

"You can't? What do you mean?"

"Information about this archaeological find is highly confidential. If I disclose anything about it, my invitation to participate in the project will be withdrawn. Ralph, you are going to have to take my word that this is a very important thing. I don't know if the project will ever be publicized. It may not. But the opportunity to participate is a 'once in a lifetime' situation. I can't turn it down."

"Hmm. I see. When do you leave?"

"Esther and I have reservations for the tenth of March to Rome. I can be contacted through a seminary there, although this project takes place elsewhere. I don't know exactly where yet. We have return tickets for May first. We fly out of Boston on Alitalia. Esther will spend most of her time in Rome."

"Well, golly, Richard. It sounds like something very exciting. Will we be able to hear about it when you get back?"

"I can't promise that. I don't know."

* * *

Winery of the *Colli del Teramo*, Central Italy
March 21, 1963, 11 a.m.

Dr. George Wiggins, KSGC, was Richard Fairchild's sponsor at the ceremony that would occur at noon. Other participants included Reginald

Forebusher, an Anglican priest, Professors Dameon D'Amarcio and Geovanni Bacalli of the Seminary of St. Felician of Mentana, and the Right Reverend Pierre Montclaire, Bishop of Lucien, Grand Master of the Holy Knights of San Giovanni of Cyprus. Fourteen other Knights from all over Europe were present in the Chapel. Esther Fairchild, under a dark veil and wearing a dark-colored dress, was the only woman present. Bishop Montclaire was conducting the service, which was not a Mass but rather a chanted litany of prayers, with many hymns.

The Grand Master was dressed in a red and gold robe and cape, with the cross symbol of the Order emblazoned on the cloak. All were bareheaded. Each Knight wore a black robe with the cross symbol of the Order on the front and back, and a sword at the left side. Only Fairchild was dressed in a common business suit.

At the end of the service there was a loud fanfare on the chapel organ, and those in the chapel proceeded to the Main Hall, led by a Knight carrying a cross and a thurifer. The pungent odor of incense filled the Hall. Esther was provided a chair at the rear of the Hall where she could observe the ceremony.

The Grand Master proceeded to the throne chair on the raised platform, turned, and sat down. One of the Knights stood beside him with a heavy iron sword.

Escorted by Wiggins and Forebusher, Richard Fairchild, at the rear of this procession, was led to the foot of the platform. The two escorts then stepped aside.

"State your name," the Grand Master said in English with a strong French accent.

"I am Richard Francis Fairchild."

"State your desire."

"I desire to become a Knight of the Holy Brothers of Saint John of Cyprus."

"State your reason."

"I desire to assist the Knights in all of their holy endeavors."

"Have you allegiance to any other religious orders?"

"Although ordained, I have no allegiance to any other religious order."

"Sir George, Sir Reginald, have you investigated the qualifications of this applicant?"

They both stepped forward and responded in unison, "We have, Grand Master."

"And have you found him suitable?"

"We have, Grand Master."

"Richard Francis Fairchild, step forward." Dr. Fairchild stepped up to the first level of the platform.

"Do you solemnly affirm, before God and this Body of Knights, allegiance to the Holy Brothers and to the authority of the Grand Master, to obey in all manner required any commission from the Grand Master in matters other than conscious sinfulness?"

"I so affirm," Fairchild said.

"Kneel." As the professor knelt before the Grand Master, the Knight to his left handed over the sword, which the Grand Master held high above his head. "Father, may it please the Holy Trinity to accept this, our brother and fellow-servant, Richard Francis Fairchild, to be a Knight in your Holy Order from this time forward unto death, to obey the rules of this Order, to preserve the secrets of this Order, and to serve only this Order as You, our Heavenly Father, may show us to be the True Path of Christ, your Son, and the Holy Spirit." The others all answered, "Amen."

The Grand Master then touched the blade of the sword first upon Fairchild's left shoulder, then upon his right shoulder, and then upon the top of his head. "I dub you Sir Richard, Knight of the Holy Brothers of San Giovanni of Cyprus, in the Name of the Father, the Son, and the Holy Spirit. May God preserve your soul and grant that you may be a worthy servant." Again the Knights responded "Amen."

"Arise, Sir Richard!" the Grand Master instructed. As Fairchild arose, the two English members of the order, Wiggins and Forebusher, came forward with a black robe, which was placed around his shoulders. On it was the cross symbol of the order. Another Knight then stepped forward with a highly polished sword. He bowed, handed it to Fairchild, and said, "May you never use this sword in anger, but only for the defense of God and His Kingdom." Wiggins and Forebusher then attached a belt around Fairchild's waist, and the sword was inserted into a sheath at his left side.

"Congratulations, Sir Richard!" George Wiggins said, shaking his hand, and the others cheered the initiation of their newest member.

"And now, Sir Richard," Father D'Amarcio said, coming forward to shake hands with Fairchild, "after our noonday meal, at which your lovely wife is most welcome, how would you like to see the document about which you have been so curious."

"Oh, yes! I would like that very much!" Dr. Fairchild replied.

* * *

"There are a lot of gaps in the opening portions of the manuscript, Dr. Fairchild," Dameon D'Amarcio explained, as he led the American professor into a large room near the top of the fortress after the lunch. George Wiggins and Reginald Forebusher had returned to Rome with some of the other Knights, and Esther had gone with them. She had signed up for a three week tour of Italy, followed by a two week Mediterranean cruise, after which she would meet Richard in Rome for their return to the United States. After seeing and hearing the ceremony, she was pleased that her husband had accepted the invitation, and knew that he was very excited about being allowed to participate in what he believed would be a great academic project. However, she still had no idea what it involved.

"When we first opened the manuscript we saw what you had also observed in Arles, that there were some holes in the skin on which the manuscript was written. It may be impossible to fill in some of the gaps those create," Father D'Amarico continued, "but it may not matter, as it appears to have been some sort of instruction to readers regarding how the manuscript was to be understood. The real heart of the text does not start until one goes beyond the place where the manuscript was opened for our inspection.

"It appears," he continued, "that the manuscript was opened several times after it was completed. We theorize, since it was brought to us from Ethiopia, that when it first arrived there Aramaic was an understood language, but that after a few decades those who understood the language died, and then no one was able to read or interpret this document, hence it was hidden away as a treasure, and the dry climate helped to preserve it until now."

"Do you know where it was?" Fairchild asked.

"Yes. It was in a crypt under an altar in the Ceobobo Monastery, south of the city of Jima, in the mountains. The monastery was located on a ridge in the mountains overlooking a valley to the south. According to Giulio, our brother priest, who was serving with the Italian Army as a chaplain, the handful of monks in the place were old, and seemed to have no plans for preservation of their monastery. There were only twenty or so of them, and they apparently did not even know about the crypt under their altar, or the existence of this document. All they had were legends of something important that had been entrusted to them. For now this discovery cannot be disclosed. With current world tensions, timing about the release of what this document is and what it contains must be cautious. Italy at present has many Communist advocates. Further, the Church is in a state of flux. Who knows what may come of this Second Vatican Council? Perhaps nothing, perhaps very vital and necessary change. There is resistance, even among some of the Knights, to proposed changes. No, this is not the time to reveal the contents of this treasure. God will guide us as to the proper moment."

"How much has been translated so far?"

"Of what we can see, perhaps a quarter to a third of the document. As we have slowly opened it, we have tried to preserve each section and then translate it. I have four seminarians who have learned Aramaic assisting in the project. With your help, it may go even faster."

"May I see what you have translated so far?"

"Certainly, but it is in Italian. Do you read Italian?"

"Not well, but with your help, Father Dameon, I'm sure I can understand it."

As they entered the room, which was brightly lit from both overhead electric lights and large windows overlooking the Adriatic Sea, four black-robed seminarians looked up. "Giuseppe, Armando, Julio, and Alfredo, thank you for attending our initiation of our newest member today. This is Dr. Richard Fairchild. He has joined our order solely to assist us in the translation of the manuscript upon which we are all working. He will only be here for five weeks, and must then return to America, where he is a professor at a college there. He is a Protestant clergyman, but he is most knowledgeable about medieval history, and is the author of our text on monastic republics, a copy of which is in our library here. Professor, may I call you Richard?"

"Certainly."

"Thank you. Richard, you are welcome to join us in this endeavor. You will get to know these four students well in the coming weeks, and undoubtedly will be of great assistance to us. Come, I will show you what we have accomplished so far."

As the four students returned to their work, Father Dameon led Fairchild to another desk, where some papers in Italian were set. He explained that this was as literal a translation of the document as they had been able to make.

This is the fifth copy of (blank) of the scribe who was (larger blank). He instructed that the Rabbi Jesus said that the words had many meanings, and should not always be taken literally. The (blank) had instructed that Holy Scripture was to be understood by the heart as well as the mind. His followers had many (blank) and the rules they imposed on themselves were severe.

He spoke on many things, and (blank) about himself, the Law and Holy Scripture, and interpreted the commandments. In (blank) was love and forgiveness. (Blank) in the style of the Prophet, of blessing and woe, as Jeremiah said, "Woe to the man who builds his house on the gains of unrighteousness and injustice." (Blank) the joys he proclaims:

Blest are you who are poor; for God's Kingdom is yours. Woe, though, be unto those who have unrighteous gain and wealth that becomes their god, for that is all to which they may be entitled.

Blest are you who must mourn; God shall provide comfort. But woe be to mockers and those who are scornful, for their merriment shall turn to grief.

Blest are you who are meek and humble; you shall inherit the land justly. Woe to those who dominate and are haughty; what they gain in pride shall be lost.

Most blest are you who are hungry or athirst, for satisfaction shall come. But for those who fatten themselves with gluttony and drink, that may be their only fulfillment.

And blest are you who give mercy, for you shall receive in like kind. For the unforgiving and unmerciful, the cruel and hateful, be woe, for the lack of (the absence of?) mercy shall be their lot forever.

Blest be you who weep, for joy shall come, but woe to those who laugh with false merriment; their time to weep shall also come.

Blest are you who retain purity, for only in such purity may God be seen.

But for the deceitful and impure, they shall not find God.

And blest be those of you who work for peace and justice, for you are the true sons of God; it shall become as (undecipherable) to those who rebel and seek to make war and argument, for by it shall they perish.

And fear not, for you are blest when you are rejected by men and punished for the good that you proclaim; bear the false accusations and rejoice that you are in the company of the prophets who likewise suffered before you. But be cautious, for woe shall be the lot of those of whom men speak well and praise as great, when they are but false prophets. Fear such praise and (undecipherable).

"Oh my goodness!" Dr. Fairchild exclaimed as he read, with Father Dameon's assistance. "You can see where both Matthew and Luke got their texts. Do you think this is what Jesus actually said?"

"From the rest of what we have deciphered, yes. This seems to best set the tone for the other teachings. Here, note this section."

The blest are like saltiness, but if the salt has lost its flavor, how can it be restored? It gets thrown out, and tramped into the ground.

The blest are as a light, a beacon on a hill, but not to be hidden under a basket. Children, you must be as salt, to savor the world with goodness, and as light to illumine the darkness. And it is by your good deeds that you shall be known as my children.

"Is there anywhere else, besides in the introduction, where the writings identify the teacher as Jesus?" Fairchild asked."

"Yes, and that may also be in the parts at the beginning that were missing. Here:"

The Master from Nazareth spoke in stories (parables) and sometimes his followers did not understand. He said to them, 'Be thankful that the Father, Lord of Heaven and of Earth, has hidden understanding from the wise, but revealed truth to those who are as infants, as is God's will. But all knowledge has been given to me by the Father, and none know the Son but the Father, nor the Father but the Son and those to whom the Son shall reveal the Father. That knowledge of the Father is restful to those who labor and are burdened, so take that yoke of knowledge upon you, for I shall give you rest for your soul. My yoke is easy, and the burden light.'

'Everyone who hears my words and keeps them shall be like the wise man who built a house upon rock, so when the rain fell and the floods flowed, and the winds blew against it, it did not fall. But if you hear my words and do not do what I say, you will be like the man who built his house upon sand, and when the rain fell and the floods overflowed, and the wind blew against it, it fell mightily. 'For it is not peace that I have come to bring to you, but rather a sword between you, for a man will oppose his father, and a daughter her mother, and a daughter-in-law against her mother-in-law, for a man's enemy shall be in his own household for the sake of these teachings. He who loves a parent more than God is not worthy to be my follower, for unless he loses the life he knows for the sake of God he cannot save it.'

"Most amazing, Father Dameon," Fairchild said. "Is this as far as your translation has gotten?"

"No, we are somewhat further. We found a section where it appears that the Ten Commandments are restated. That is the section that the seminarians are currently translating. Although we found them in one section, it is interesting that in both gospels they are scattered and stated somewhat differently. Here:"

God alone shall you serve, for no man can serve two masters. He would hate one and love the other, or be devoted to one and not the other. Consider all the false gods, like wealth. You cannot serve both God and wealth.

You have the law that said to the men of old, 'You shall not swear falsely, nor take the name of God in vein, but shall perform what you have sworn.' But I say, do not swear at all, by either Heaven, the seat of God, or by Earth, His foot rest, or by the great city of the King, Jerusalem, nor even by the hair of your own head, the color of which you cannot control, but simply say 'yes' or 'no' and do as you have promised.

Remember that the Son of Man is Lord of the Sabbath day, which was made for man, not man for the Sabbath. For which of you, if your sheep were to fall in a pit upon the Sabbath day, would not go rescue it and lift it out? Is man of not more value than a sheep, or shall it be unlawful to do good on the Sabbath?

God commanded, 'Honor your father and your mother. He who speaks ill of his father or mother shall surely die.' Yet you have said that if one tells his parent, 'what you have given me is given to God,' he need not honor the parent. So for the sake of tradition you have annulled the word of God. Yet I say, those who hear the word of God and keep it shall be my parents and my brethren.

You have heard that it was said to the men of old, 'You shall not kill, and whoever does kill shall be liable to judgment.' But I say even more, that whomever is angry with a brother without cause shall be liable to judgment; whoever insults a brother and calls him a 'bastard' or 'fool' is worthy of the fiery garbage pit at Gehenna. Hence, when you are angry, and you take your offering to the altar, leave it there and go and make peace with that brother with whom you are angry, and be reconciled, and then come and offer your gift.

And you have heard it said, 'You shall not commit adultery.' But I say that whoever of you shall look upon a woman with lust in your heart has already committed adultery. It would better to be blind. I say to you that everyone who divorces his wife, except on the ground of being unchastely, makes her an adulteress, and whosoever shall marry her commits adultery.

Take heed, and beware of all covetousness, for a man's life does not consist of the abundance of his possessions. Prepare, rather, your treasure in Heaven, where thieves do not break in and steal, nor rust corrupt.

"That's as far as we've gotten with this section. It hasn't been easy, Richard. We have tried to translate as literally as possible, but there are the influences of knowing how the Gospels have been worded, and even our own prejudices in the selection of just the right word, where several may apply."

"It certainly shows the genius that the Gospel writers used in their translations." the professor commented. "They also appeared to have struggled with the prejudices if they had these same sources, Matthew, of course, for the Jewish reader, Luke for the Greek. What language references do you have?"

"There are no Aramaic dictionaries, of course. We have several books that have been translated and which show the Aramaic on one side and Latin on the other, and that, of course, gives us wide options as well."

"What about the words in Ge'ez at the beginning? Were you able to get any sort of translation of that?"

"Yes, Richard. We sent an exact copy to an expert on ancient Ge'ez language who lives in Alexandria, Haille d'Mosariff al Begetta. His translation arrived here the same day as your letter. It was an exciting day for us, finding out what had happened to our priest, Father Garmani. Here, I will show you the letter."

* * *

Dear Dr. D'Amarcio:

As you have anticipated, the words you have sent me are of Ge'ez origin, but of a very ancient form used only formally in the south, which would include Abyssinia. I have seen it only several times before, on official court documents.

The writer states he is of the royal Ethiopian house of Candace, an official of the royal treasury. He says he is a believer in *Yahveh* and that he had been in Jerusalem for the Passover. On his return while in Gaza, he says he encountered a young man who told him of the one anointed by God as the sacrifice for salvation, and who gave him this scroll of teachings when he agreed to a ritual washing. He said the young man's name was Philip. He presents the document to his royal masters. I could not completely decipher his name, though it appeared to be something like 'Ja'n De Reba.'

This is all the document says. I appreciate your allowing me to assist in its translation. Best wishes to you and your brothers,

Haille d'Mosariff al Begetta

"So you can see, Richard, the position we are in. If we were to announce that we have such a document, and that its origin has been verified, the world's news media, both academic and secular, would descend upon us like a plague of locusts. Any real value of the document might be lost in the publicity of it. But we can finish our translation here, with your help, and then gradually allow bits and pieces of this great work to disseminate. It may take five years -- it may take fifty. But whatever time it takes, we will have a better understanding of the joy that these words, brought to us in the Gospels, have had on mankind, and of the truth of Christ's teaching that the Church has preserved."

"So be it, Father Dameon," Richard Fairchild replied.

Sandusky Bay

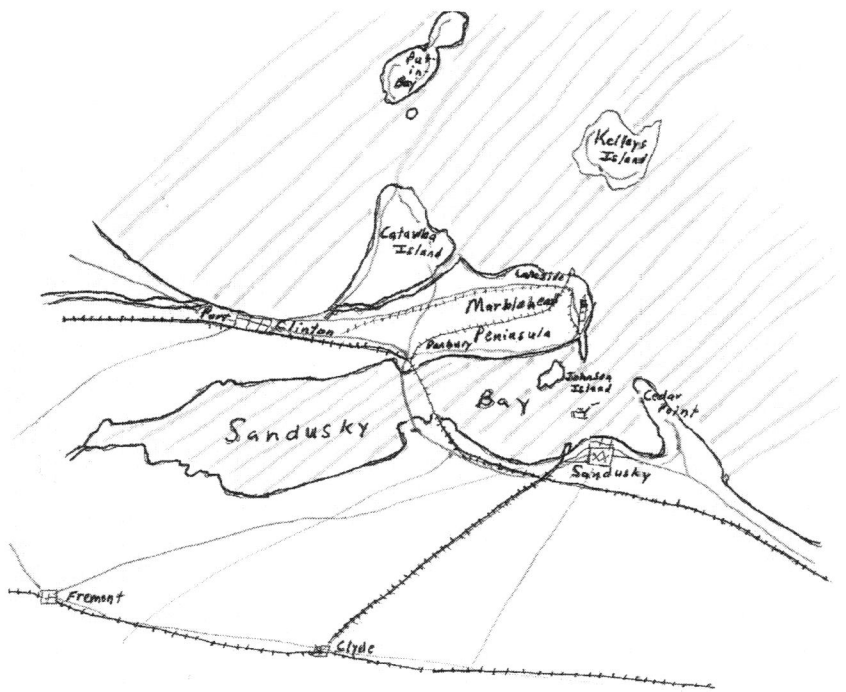

Prologue to Sandusky Bay

In that vast inland sea known as the Great Lakes lie many large and small bays, islands, harbors and ports. Because four of the larger lakes also form an international border with America's neighbor to the North, Canada, international commerce, political agreement and disagreement – even war and espionage – has occurred over the centuries.

But Canada is not America's only neighbor. To the east lies Bermuda, a British colony even in the 21st century, and to the south Cuba, and Mexico. These places also have interacted with the United States over the centuries.

The role played by our international neighbors, and by those nooks and crannies of bays and islands in the Great Lakes, are the source of many true and intriguing stories. Many such stories center on Lake Erie, especially in its western edges where bays and islands form a broken link between two nations. From the time of its settlement by various Native American tribes and its discovery by French Sulpician friars in the 17th century to its modern-day role as a wine-growing fruit basket agricultural center and recreational vacationland, the waters of Sandusky Bay and the islands surrounding the Marblehead Peninsula have been a source of such stories.

Since the days of the Revolutionary War in America Northern Ohio has played a key role in the nation's history. From the decisive Battle of Lake Erie in the War of 1812 to the role played by Ohioans and the region in the days leading up to and during the Civil War, Sandusky Bay and the surrounding islands have been the scene of great adventures, intrigue and even bloodshed.

In the 21st century commerce tends to whiz by the region without notice. A few railway trains may still cross the Bay, but they no longer are bring the tourists or travelers to the region. Super highways bypass the ports and islands, and travelers can barely get a glimpse of the blue waters of the Lake. If tourists come at all it is to ride the coasters at Cedar Point or guzzle beer or wine at local restaurants. Few remember, or care to know, the fascinating history of the place.

Yet the story of Sandusky Bay is unequaled elsewhere in America. There are, perhaps, more picturesque places along the Great Lakes, places with equal attraction for tourists and commerce. There are larger cities than those on Lake Erie, equally or greater flows of traffic and people and business. Yet those places along the shores of Lake Erie and Sandusky Bay are perhaps the heart of America, where attitude and heroism and political interaction helped cement the nation into what it is today.

Chapter 1

April 14, 1911
Office of the Suwannee & Gulf Railway & Steamboat Co.
Waycross, Georgia

"Jack, what the heck is *this*?"

William Dubose was looking at the company ledgers. As the comptroller, he was responsible for overseeing the various assets of the company, but had just found a book of additional properties owned by the company that had been kept by James Fitzgibbons, the company's longtime president, who had died three months earlier. His son, Jack, had taken over the transportation firm, and was now president.

"What you got there, Bill?"

"It appears to be a listing of some properties we own that aren't on the regular register. Some I knew about, like the hotel out there on the Gulf, but what the heck are we doing with real estate up in Ohio?"

"Oh, that!" Jack Fitzgibbons, a tall, light-haired man about thirty-five, dressed in a dark suit with a high, stiff collar, replied in a deep Georgia accent. "I'd almost forgotten about it. Yeah, that's ours. A couple of properties up around Sandusky."

"Okay," Dubose acknowledged, rubbing his balding head and looking over his round-rimmed thin wire glasses, "but what are they?"

"Just two houses we own. They're rented out, and the rent sent directly to a bank up in Atlanta. That's the Citizens Bank account you were asking me about last week. One's a farm out on a peninsula up there, the other's in the center o' town, right on one of the streets that makes a compass and square."

"Compass and square? You mean it's a Masonic town?"

"Might 'a been at one time. Guess the guy who laid the streets out was. It was jest a hellhole port full of saloons an' drunks before Daddy went up there in '58. That's when Daddy bought that first property in town. About five years later he bought the other one on the peninsula. Later he transferred ownership to the company so that the taxes on 'em could be covered. He was afraid they'd get lost in the mail comin' here an' not get paid." "So it's just two houses?"

"A house in town, and a farm, right on the Bay. Actually, it's a very pretty place. Y'know, I'd forgotten about it. Think I'll take young Forrest up there this summer and let him see the place. He might like tah take a holiday there sometime. Better'n this old swamp on the Okeefenokee."

"What was the old man doing up there in Ohio?"

"Hee, that's a long story, Bill. He was what they called in those days, an 'agent.' Had accounts from all over South Georgia. Was up there when the War began, 'n that's when he went off to Hamilton. It wasn't until after the War that he took over his brother's rail line to Branford an' bought his first steamship to run out on the Gulf. His brother, Zebulon, you know, was killed in the War up in Atlanta."

"Yes, I recall now. Your old man must o' been quite a guy, Jack. I heard rumors about James Fitzgibbons years ago, how he almost got killed trying to get money for the Confederates, but I never had the courage to ask him about it."

"You should have. He'd a' told you. Damned proud James was about it. I don't know all the details, but I do know that he had arranged for a loan payment to come through Suwannee in '64. A Union blockade gunboat sunk it. Far as I know, that wreck's still layin' out there in the Gulf somewhere. The Yankees had no idea what was in it when they sunk her."

"You know where?"

"Nah. One report said the steamer and its escort tried to outrun 'em while headed up toward Hog Island, but it never was confirmed. Most likely it was in deep water, like so many of these wrecks out there."

Dubose resumed analysis of the financial records as his boss, Jack Fitzgibbons, turned to the daily operations report. The office occupied the south side of a brick depot alongside several rail lines, the S&G curving off toward the south from its interchange with the Atlantic Coast Line that continued west to Valdosta. It was sunny in the small room, and both men sat behind roll top desks containing various pigeonholes for papers, train orders, freight bills and other necessary accounting records for the transportation company. With the new Interstate Commerce Commission rules, bookkeeping had become a full time task. The Suwannee & Gulf continued to operate its railroad between Waycross, White Springs and Branford, Florida, where the train met the company's fleet of riverboats for the remaining sixty mile trip to the Gulf. Until the 1880s tiny Waycross had been called Tebeauville, and it was not incorporated until almost 1890, as "crossing of the ways" of several rail lines. From Suwannee steamships transported both passengers and cargo to ports further south in Florida, to Cuba and the Caribbean, and to Mexico and the Gulf Coast. At Branford the line connected with the competing Atlantic Coast Line, and carried a Coast Line through-coach from Savannah to Tampa. Its main business, however, was hauling lumber, turpentine and sugar, although some passengers booked fishing trips operated by the company's hotel on the Gulf of Mexico at the mouth of the Suwannee River. Commissioned by the two states in 1851, the S&G had been a lifeline to the communities of North Florida during the Civil War and the decades after it.

* * *

Forrest Fitzgibbons, twenty, was a student at Georgia College in Milledgeville. He was tall with light brown hair, and had only a slight trace of a well-manicured moustache. Having grown up in one of the finest houses in Waycross, he was popular with other young men at the college and with the young women in the town. While being the son of the president of a small railroad and steamboat company was less prestigious than a few of the other students from wealthy families, Forrest was able to hold his own in most activities, from boxing to drinking. But he was also a studious person, and took his studies seriously. He had traveled to Europe and South America with his grandfather, John, and spoke several languages fairly well. As he knew he would someday take over the company business, his knowledge of both Spanish and French would be useful in making international contacts for trade. He had already suggested to his father that they consider purchasing at least one or two passenger-carrying steamships for the Latin American trade, to operate from their docks on the Gulf of Mexico.

When Forrest returned home for the summer and his father told him that they would make a trip to Ohio, Forrest was quite intrigued. He had never been in that part of the country, and did not know that the company owned property there. While their trip would take only a bit over a week, for the young man it was still an adventure.

It was a Tuesday morning in early June when Jack and Forrest Fitzgibbons boarded the local Atlantic Coast Line train for Jessup, arriving in time for the 10:30 a.m. *Florida Special* on the Queen & Crescent Route. They had booked a berth on the sleeping car all the way through to Cleveland, scheduled to arrive at 3:15 the following afternoon. Jack had made reservations at the Forest City Hotel there for that evening, and the following day they would take the Lake Shore & Michigan Southern, one of the New York Central lines, to Sandusky.

The following morning at breakfast in the hotel's dining room Jack consulted the New York Central schedule while awaiting their coffee and meals. "Ah was hoping we might get a train that stopped at Danbury," Jack explained, "but it looks like we'll have to go to Port Clinton and take the trolley. That might be better anyway, from what ah hear, Forrest, 'cause the trolley line jest opened a spur down to Bay Point, an' that's less than a mile from the farm. We can get back to Sandusky either by that ferryboat or by the local train to Danbury."

A streetcar delivered the two travelers to the Union Station down along the waterfront about two hours later. Train 133, an express to

Detroit carrying a parlor car, left shortly after noon. It sped west with stops in Elyria, Vermilion, Huron and Sandusky, crossing Sandusky Bay on the causeway the LS&MS had reopened in 1872, reaching Port Clinton about two that afternoon. A few minutes after arrival there the two men transferred to a Toledo, Port Clinton & Lakeside Railway trolley car for the one hour trip through Marblehead to the ferry dock at Bay Point.

The electric trolley, with its high curved windows rattled eastward at a fairly high speed, stopping only briefly at a gypsum factory wedged between the trolley line and the LS&MS mainline. After it passed the Danbury siding, it curved northeastward through farm fields, and then skirted some quarries as it approached the Methodist summer camp at Lakeside. While most of the remaining passengers exited there, or at the next stop less than a mile down the track at Marblehead, a handful of passengers also boarded in order to transfer to the ferry at Bay Point. As the car rounded the curve at Marblehead, Jack Fitzgibbons pointed out the white and red lighthouse on the rocks at the point of the peninsula. At Bay Point the two Georgians left their luggage at the small wooden depot to claim later, and started down the forested dirt roadway toward the west.

After walking about a quarter of an hour Jack stopped at a driveway that led south. Beyond the trees along the road were some fields planted with various crops, undeterminable this early in the summer, and a peach orchard. "This is a mighty fine area for fruit trees, Forrest," Jack said. "An' grapes, too. My Daddy always said that the wine they made up here was the best in the world. Guess it still is. Lots o' good lime in the soil's what does it. You probably saw those cars loaded with stone when we came through Marblehead there, where ah pointed out that old lighthouse. They quarry the stuff, ship it all over. Probably a pile of it under this farm, too."

There was no gate on the driveway, although a painted wooden sign read Bayview Farm. The two men headed back toward the large stone farmhouse that sat on a bluff overlooking Sandusky Bay. There were several out-buildings — a barn, a couple of sheds, a coach house, and what appeared to be a covered vat. The house was two stories, with an attic and basement. Jack said it had been built in 1863 out of Marblehead limestone, and that after the War the interior had been reworked with walnut paneling. The primary focus of the house was to the south, so that the approach from the drive was actually to the rear of the structure. Rows of tall trees made a semi-circle around the house, giving it the appearance of a small fortress.

About a mile to the south was a small island. "Johnson's Island," Jack explained to his son. "Quite a story about that place. I'll tell you tonight. Right now, let's see if anyone's at home."

A knock on the door brought an elderly woman from inside the house, inquiring who was there.

"Miz Lambert?" Jack asked. "You're Miz Jessie Lambert?"

"Yes," the gray-haired woman acknowledged.

"How do, Miz Lambert. I'm Jack Fitzgibbons, and this here's my son, Forrest. We're your landlords! I know you pay through the bank in Atlanta, but we actually own the place."

"Jack Fitzgibbons!" the woman repeated. "Why, yes! I remember your father when Jacob and I first rented the farm back in 1882. You were just a boy when you came up with him, How is James?"

"Oh, my Daddy died about six months back, now, Miz Lambert. This here's *my* boy, Forrest. He's a college man, down in Georgia. Same one I went to. Don't think he even knew about this place till our company comptroller found it in the records and reminded us we owned it. How is Jacob?"

"Jacob died about ten years ago, Jack," the old lady explained. "My two sons helped me run the place until they went off, one in the Army, and the other to work on the railroad, but they come back each spring to plant, and in the fall to harvest, so we do okay. My daughter, she's in school in Cleveland. I send the rent every month. You're not planning to move me out, are you?"

"Oh, no, Miz Lambert. Not at all. You're takin' good care o' the place, and we appreciate that. I just wanted you to meet my boy, here, and to let him see the farm. It's more beautiful than ever!"

"You're welcome to look around. Don't keep any cattle now other than one old milk cow down in the barn. Used to press some grapes back there in the vat room, but, well, after Jacob died and the boys went off – both married now – no sense going to all that work for a few bottles of wine I can buy just as cheap at the store."

As they talked Jessie Lambert led the two men around the house, which was decorated in Victorian style, with newly installed electric lights illuminating the dark corners. The kitchen had been remodeled with a gas stove and interior plumbing, including a large upstairs bathroom, so a long, cold walk outside was no longer needed. "My Daddy always said that was the best wine in the world, Miz Lambert." Jack continued. "But the place sure looks good. I see they're still quarryin' stone up north of here, by Marblehead. Place seemed busy."

"Yes, it is. The Methodist's opened that summer camp there at Lakeside quite a while back, and people come from all over the state to spend part of their summers. Then they've built that new amusement park out on Cedar Point, east of Sandusky, and the ferry line runs one of their steam launches over there from Bay Point a couple of times a day for the tourists. Some folks even building cottages out on Kelley's Island, from what I hear, and they're running a ferry from Marblehead over there, and to South Bass." "What about Johnson Island?" Jack asked. "Anything happening over there?" "No, they had a bunch of Italian stone cutters over there for a while, digging up stone, but otherwise there's not much there but snakes and that old cemetery."

"Yeah, they're lots o' snakes around here, Forrest. Water moccasins up in the rocks along the shore, rattlesnakes by the bushel. Got to watch where you're a-walking, that's for sure. But, Miz Lambert, down there in the Okeefenokee where we live – that's where the Suwannee begins – we got all sorts of poisonous snakes, an' alligators! Some o' those brothers are about twenty-five feet long!"

"Oh, Jack!" Forrest – who always called his father by his first name – interrupted. "I never heard of one that long!"

"No? Well, you jest ain't been far 'nough up in that old swamp, then, Son," Jack replied, utilizing his Southern drawl to give the story emphasis with a touch of humor. "Ah even heard mah Daddy tell 'o one what was thirty feet long. They tried to ketch him for a zoo, but he done ate their boat!"

"Nonsense!" Jessie Lambert laughed. "But that sounds like a tale your father would have told. He was quite a character. Wish I'd have known him when he was living around here."

"Yes, he spoke well of you and Jacob, too, Miz Lambert. Well, if Forrest and I are going to see the place an' get back to Sandusky tonight, we'd better be getting' on. Thank you again for taking good care o' the place."

After the two men had wandered around the farm for a while Jack Fitzgibbons looked out across the Bay and saw the steam ferry moving southward. "I spect that's the last ferry this afternoon, Forrest. We'd better hustle if we want to catch that last steam train to Danbury. Have to get our luggage at Bay Point first."

The father and son quickly walked back to the trolley station at Bay Point, where the last ferry from Sandusky was just arriving. They collected their luggage and bought tickets to Lakeside, where they transferred to the Lakeside & Marblehead Railroad, a rural rail line much like their own down in Georgia and Florida. The L&M was only eight miles long, but its first mile southwest of Lakeside ran beside open stone quarries with sidings where large slabs of rock were being loaded into railcars, and an 0-6-0 Brooks steam engine was waiting to pull the cars to the stone crusher at Marblehead. The quarries had the appearance of a moonscape – large craters dug in odd shapes and depths for the rich lime and mineral deposits that original settlers had thought was marble.

The two Georgians joined a handful of other passengers traveling the seven miles to Danbury, the junction with the Lake Shore & Michigan Southern, aboard the L&M's new Fairbanks-Morse gasoline motor car, which resembled the trolley car on which they had traveled earlier that day. Jack commented that the gasoline car was a good invention, and one that the S&G ought to consider for its lightly traveled local daily train. "Just think, Forrest," he said, "with one of these, we could run it with just an engineer and a conductor, and wouldn't need a whole crew. No need for a steam engine or tender."

West of the quarries the line ran through rich farmland and orchards, making two stops, one at a rural farm crossroads called Picolo, and another at a point where the railroad met the trolley line at another crossroads where the sign read 'Violet.' The entire trip took only twenty minutes.

A LS&MS mail train that ran between Toledo and Cleveland, making all stops, had them in Sandusky by 6:30 that evening, and by seven they had registered at the Bay House Hotel and were sitting in the dining room about to order their dinner.

"Do you know the people living in the Sandusky house as well, Jack?" Forrest inquired.

"No, they're new since Daddy an' I were up here last. The bank had a real estate agent arrange for them. Last I heard, the tenant's name was Haber or something like that. The local agent makes all the arrangements. We'll check there first in the morning."

"Mrs. Lambert seemed awfully nice," Forrest said.

"Yep. Daddy once told me that if he'd met Jessie before he met my Mama, she might'a been your granmama. But, of course, they were both married before that. Not much before, though. Your Aunts Jenny and Juney weren't born 'til '74 and '75. Oh, I guess it was awhile after all. I was probably fourteen when Daddy brought me up here."

* * *

The following morning the two men walked up the slight hill from the waterfront hotel where they had spent the night to a small real estate office on the main business street about a block from the town square. The sign read Firelands Rental and Estate Sales. "What's 'Firelands'?" Forrest asked.

"Way I heard it, Son, was that after the Revolutionary War most of Northeast Ohiah was reserved for veterans from Connecticut. The best farmland, out here where the soil was black and rich, went to the men who had been under fire in the War, so they called it 'Fire lands.' Another version I heard was that this good land went to farmers whose farms were burned by the British. Either way, though, the name had to do with the Revolutionary War," Jack explained as they entered the office.

"May I help you?" a young man in a dark suit, wearing thick glasses and seated at a desk, asked as he stood up.

"Yes, is Mistah Websteh' in?" Jack replied, immediately re-instituting his Southern accent.

"I'm David Webster," the young man replied. "Are you looking for my father, Dan?"

"Yessir. Dan-yel. But you'll do fine, Son. I'm Jack Fitzgibbons, and this here's my boy, Forrest. We own that big house over on Hue-ron Avenue that you rent out for us."

"Oh, yes, Mr. Fitzgibbons. I know that account. The place is vacant right now. Sometimes it's hard to keep tenants in there, but we think we have a new family that may move in at the end of the month."

"What? Hard to keep tenants? Why's that?" Jack asked. "It's a good house, and the rent's cheap enough. Ought to be higher then it is."

Well, yes, it's a good house, all right, but, well, maybe when my Dad gets here he can explain the problem."

"Problem?"

"I ... I'm ... ahh, I really can't say, Mr. Fitzgibbons, but.... Oh, here comes my father now!" The young man looked relieved as an older man, also in a dark suit and wearing glasses, entered the office. "Dad," David Webster said, "this is Jack and Forrest Fitzgibbons, visiting from Georgia. They want to know about the house over on Huron."

"Oh, well, Mr. Fitzgibbons! This is a delight. I've heard so much about your dad. Only met him once – why, yes, *you* were with him, just a boy you were! How is James?"

"He died awhile back, Mr. Webster, about six months ago."

"Gosh, I'm sorry to hear that. He was quite a well-known figure around town at one time, I've heard. But, please, call me Dan," the older man insisted. "What can we do for you? Are you planning to sell the place on Huron? Might get a right good price for it, you know," the real estate agent said.

"No, we're quite happy to keep it rented. But your son, here, David, says there's a problem renting it."

"Oh, no, Mr. Fitzgibbons, no problem. Just that a couple of tenants have moved out earlier than their leases required. But they paid the rent due, or we found other tenants. So, there's been no problem. Right now the house is vacant but we have a prospect who may move in at the end of the month."

"Why did the previous tenants move out?" Forrest asked.

"Well, it's ... ahh ... it's hard to say, really. Number of different things. One got transferred, another didn't like the place – probably a problem with the neighbors, it was too big or something, nothing serious."

"I'd like my boy, Forrest, here, to see the place if we could. If nobody's living there...."

"Certainly, certainly. I've got my Ford out front and we can drive over there. David, you stay here, and we'll, well, we'll be back before lunch and we can all dine down at the hotel, if you gentlemen are not in a hurry."

"Nope, we're staying the night, Dan. Forrest hasn't been up here before, so I want him to see the town."

"Good, good! I'll be glad to show you around. Say, maybe this afternoon, Forrest, you and David could take the boat over to that new amusement park on Cedar Point. They've got a ride over there that'll scare the pants off you!"

"A ride?" Forrest Fitzgibbons asked. "What kind of a ride?"

"It's called a roller-coaster," David Webster explained. "You get into this little rail car, and a chain hauls it up, oh, a hundred feet or so in the air, and then it rolls down the hill and around a bunch of curves. It goes real fast with a lot of noise, and makes the girls scream! There'll be lots of them over there this time of year."

"A rolley-coaster," Forrest repeated. "I've ridden on a lot of trains, but never one that goes straight down a hundred foot hill. Wonder how it keeps from derailing?"

"Ahh!" the younger Webster replied. "That's the exciting part!"

Webster led the two Georgians out of the front door of the office to his Model T that was parked at the curb, and the two guests climbed up on the machine. Webster turned the crank, the engine coughed, and the vehicle began to shake as Webster stepped in, released the brake and headed south on Columbus Avenue.

"Gotta get me one o' these here machines!" Jack Fitzgibbons shouted above the noise the automobile was making. "There's getting to be quite a few of 'em down in Waycross now. Our banker's got him one, and the undertaker, why he's just bought some fancy new one to take the place of his old glass-windowed hearse. Heard he was even going to sell his team of matched back horses that used to pull it out to the cemetery."

"New models coming out every year now, Mr. Fitzgibbons," Webster shouted back. "By next year they'll be much better than this noisy old flivver. Not many roads, I would guess, are paved outside Waycross, though, are there? We only have a few here."

"No, none at all. I can walk from my office to the house, so I don't really need a motor car yet. But wouldn't it look grand, pullin' up in front o' the Baptist Church each Sunday in some fine motor carriage!"

"Take a look at the Winton, Jack. Old Alexander Winton makes a real sturdy and good looking motor car over in Cleveland. I got one on order, and hope to pick it up in a couple of weeks."

"Winton? Is that the guy who drove his car from San Francisco to New York back about eight years ago?"

"No," Webster shouted back over the noise, "that was some physician named Horatio Nelson Jackson. From Vermont, I think. But he did it in a Winton motor carriage. Doing that's not quite as big a deal any more. But you'd like a Winton, Jack. A fine, well-made automobile."

At Adams Street Webster turned left, then at a street running diagonally southeastward he turned right, drove half a block and pulled up in front of a large three-story house with a wrought-iron fence and a yard that was full of large elm trees. The house was made of a dark stone, much like the house at Bayview Farm, but was quite a bit larger. There was a long porch that surrounded two sides of the house, and a driveway through a large gate that led to a two-story carriage house at the rear.

Forrest Fitzgibbons jumped out of the back seat of the Ford and opened the gate while Webster drove the Ford into the driveway and shut off the engine.

"Great place, Mr. Fitzgibbons. My boy, David, comes over and mows the grass once a week to keep it looking good for potential renters."

"Yes, David and you said something about difficulty keeping tenants," Jack replied. "What seems to be the problem? Can't be the rent. It's too low now."

"No, no, as I said, there is no problem, Mr. Fitzgibbons, but...."

"But what?"

"Well, let's go on in and look around, and I'll explain."

The three men climbed up the steps to the front porch and Webster removed a long gray key that was on a metal ring with a smaller key from his pocket and inserted it in the lock on the front door. It was a fancy leaded glass and carved wood double door with stained glass panels around the clear glass. Inside was a small foyer, leading into a large parlor. From there several rooms led toward the back of the house, and a long, curved stairway led to the second floor.

"So?" Jack questioned.

"Maybe it's just the age of the place, Mr. Fitzgibbons. This house was built almost sixty years ago, now, and, well, old houses have strange noises. You may recall that about five years ago we had one of those new coal-burning furnaces installed down in the cellar. They had a hard time fitting it in the corner near the outside entrance where the coal could be delivered, and then they ran flues up through the walls to registers in all the rooms. It makes the place real nice and warm in the winter, and winters are very harsh up here on the lake."

"So the furnace makes noise?" Jack sounded puzzled.

"Yes, I'm sure that's all it is, but, well, you know the history of this place ... I mean, there's still people around here who remember, and neighbors will be neighbors and tell stories that probably aren't true and are pretty exaggerated, and some of the tenants, since that new furnace went in, said that there's just something different about this house. Something creepy."

"Are you saying the house is haunted?" Forrest interrupted.

"No, no!" Webster replied. "Just things they hear at night – probably just that furnace heating up the flues and pipes, or the indoor plumbing banging. You know how pipes'll bang if there's air in the line. Folks around here come from farms where they only had fireplaces and outdoor plumbing – it's just new to them, that's all."

"Well, damned if that don't take all!" Jack Fitzgibbons laughed. "Folks skeert of the sounds of an old house! Dang, you Yankees are dumb! No offense, Dan, but just tell folks up front that the furnace and the plumbing are noisy, an' that there ain't nothing to those tales about what my Daddy did in this house."

"Well, I heard those stories too, Jack, that your father, James Fitzgibbons, came up here to find runaways," Webster said.

"Oh, I'll admit he did do a bit 'o bounty hunting for a while, mostly south of here, from what I heard him tell, and it was perfectly legal, too. And my Uncle Zeb hired them to work on the railroad, and paid them. Those tales that got around after the War just weren't true. He never killed anybody, black or white. You mark my word, Dan, those stories are all nonsense."

"Well, I'm glad to hear it, Jack. Come on, and let's show your son the rest of the house. He'll be interested in that new coal furnace down in the cellar, too."

Three days later the Fitzgibbons were back in Waycross.

Chapter 2
January 22, 1963
Beverly, Massachusetts

Elias Ward sat in the library of his suburban Beverly mansion overlooking Massachusetts Bay reviewing a log book he had set on his table months earlier. Since his grandfather had died in June of 1962 he had inherited a considerable collection of papers and documents, along with most of the Ward fortune. It was his great grandfather, Stephenson P. Ward, who had started the Ward Coastal Steam Packet Line, which had later been purchased by the American Export Lines for millions of dollars. Many of the old papers dated to his great grandfather's career as a Boston shipping magnate, and some even earlier than that.

Elias picked up a heavy leather-bound volume. It was a ship's log, dated 1864. Captain Stephenson P. Ward had commanded a Union gunboat, the *U.S.S. Providence,* part of a small armada of naval frigates under the theater command of Admiral Farragut, based in Mobile and Pensacola. The *Providence* was based in Tampa, but patrolled from the small Fort Dade at the entrance to Tampa Bay on Egmont Key. Elias Ward's eye caught an entry dated June 28, 1864. "Ten, morning watch. On blockade patrol, Anclote Keys to the Cedar Keys. Spotted armed steam corvette that appeared to be accompanying a smaller cargo steamship on a heading of northeast by east. No sails showing, but both producing gray smoke. Appear to be headed for Suwannee Sound. In pursuit."

The next entry was at noon. "Vessels sighted us, increased speed. Changed heading to due north." An hour later there was another entry. "Close enough to observe flags. Corvette carries French; the smaller ship appears to carry Mexican flag. They have rounded north end of Hog Island. Suspect they may wait for us there, and perhaps attempt evasion or fight."

The next entry was made about two hours later. "Entered Suwanee Sound to southeast of Hog Island. Spotted the foreign vessels sitting to northeast of Hog. The corvette was turned facing northeast, apparently prepared to fire upon us had we followed to the north of the island. As we approached, I ordered our cannoneers to prepare for battle, and to fire warning shots across the bow of both vessels. Lieutenant Garver prepared his Marines for boarding. Upon spotting us the corvette, on which we could then clearly see the name, *C.S.S. Biloxi,* quickly turned, and immediately after the firing of our warning shots, her cannons opened fire upon us. Our cannoneers responded. A mortar apparently found the powder bunker, and the *Biloxi* exploded in a great flash of fire and noise. Many crewmen not killed or wounded immediately abandoned ship and began swimming toward the island, which was only several hundred yards away.

"The other vessel, now observed to be the *M.S.S. Austrian Princess*, approximately a twenty ton freighter, raised steam and passed through the debris of the corvette, picking up only a handful of survivors. We pursued, again firing our cannons and preparing to board if we got close enough. As we were already at full steam, we quickly caught up with the freighter, and again fired upon it. She was hit below the water line, and began at once to take on water and list to starboard. Two small boats aboard were lowered and the crew – there appeared to be no more than a dozen – abandoned ship. One headed south toward Hog Island. The other was immediately captured, and seven prisoners taken.

"The *Austrian Princess* sank in less than ten fathoms approximately one to one and a third nautical miles north northwest of Hog Island. We reversed course and sent the Marines onto Hog Island, where sixteen other sailors and two officers, as well as one civilian, were captured. Eight of the sailors and one officer were severely injured by the explosion on the corvette, and may not survive passage to the infirmary at Ft. Desoto on Mullet Key. May put in at Cedar Key for medical aid."

The next entry was several hours later. "Captured officers and crew refuse to reveal nature of the cargo aboard the freighter. We suspect guns. Its captain, a Lieutenant Helmut Hubler, an Austrian operating on behalf of the Mexican government, will be charged with blockade running as the steam corvette bore both French and Confederate flags and was therefore an enemy vessel. Its surviving officers and crew will be considered prisoners of war. The civilian was aboard the freighter. He speaks English, and is carrying a Canadian passport. He states he was a paid passenger and demands release. The name on his passport is James Farthington. I doubt he is Canadian, but will turn him over to the Union commandant at Ft. Dade for decision. Two crew of the corvette died of wounds before reaching Cedar Key. Two more serious wounded men were left there with the old doctor who lives in the town. I doubt either will survive." The log continued for a number of pages. The *Providence* arrived at Tampa Bay the following morning, and the civilian passenger and the less injured officer and sailors were turned over to the naval commandant. The remaining prisoners were transported to the Union prison on Dry Tortugas, west of Key West, and the *Providence* resumed blockade duty. All entries were signed S. P. Ward, Capt., U.S.N.

Elias Ward closed the volume and leaned back in his chair. He had been surprised to find the log among the papers as most Navy logs were secured by the command and eventually sent to Washington. As an amateur historian he had studied the Civil War blockades and knew that the South was desperate by 1864 for any sort of aid. A French corvette with an obvious Confederate States name, and a cargo vessel from Mexico – what could it mean? Probably not food or other staples. Most likely it would be armaments, perhaps foreign currency to help support the South's war efforts. That might be in the form of gold or silver. Most ship captains attempting to run a blockade would turn away if spotted by a Union vessel. These two did not. That the cargo vessel was accompanied by an armed corvette that was willing to fight suggested to Ward that the cargo must have been quite valuable. Perhaps his great-grandfather had thought the same thing, which is perhaps why he had kept the log.

* * *

Junius Plunkett, a dark, rough-looking man, short but stocky, was in his office on the second floor of a Boston Harbor wharf and warehouse a week later when his phone rang. Having no secretary, he answered it himself. "Eastern Dredge and Salvage. Hello?"

"Plunkett?" the voice on the line inquired. "Yeah, this is Jay," he said in a voice with a strong "Bahston Irish' lilt. "Who's callin'?"

"Plunkett, this is Elias Ward. You may remember doing some work for me a number of years ago on an old freighter we had go aground off the Cape."

"The *Sturbridge*. Yeah, I recall. Why? What's up? Got another grounding?" "No, no, nothing like that. But I have come across some information that might interest you. Perhaps a, ahh, joint venture?"

"Joint venture? That requires dough. Lots of it. You got the wrong guy!"

"Not so fast! You have equipment, and that's what I need."

"So, what is it?"

"I have information on what might just be a sunken ship that has a lot of valuable stuff on it. It's probably easily accessible, but it is within the three mile limit."

"Sunken treasure?" The way Plunkett said the word it sounded more like *treas-ah*. "Who d'yah think I am, Captain Kidd? I suppose there are pirates and pretty maidens all in a row as well?"

"No, this is for real. I've done some research down in Washington at the National Archives, and I don't think anyone knows about this. I can't give you any details until I know if you are interested."

"So where is this 'treasure' ship?"

"Florida's Gulf Coast."

"Florider, ehh? Well, it's cold as hell up here right now, and I ain't got anything much on the burnah at present. Why don't you come over and I'll see what you got?"

"Okay, I'm just north of Salem. How about tomorrow, about ten?"

"Yeah," Plunkett chuckled. "I think I can fit you into my busy schedule. Yah know where we are?"

"You still at the warehouse off of Northern Avenue?"

"Yeah, same old place. See yah then, Ward."

* * *

Even though the U.S. Navy had been involved, Florida law applied to any archaeological finds involving shipwrecks within three miles of shore. Beyond that, however, it was a "finders-keepers" legal principle. For abandoned vessels admiralty law applied, but Ward reasoned that if the federal government had not acted in almost a hundred years, it was not likely to take much interest in the vessel now. As to the state, he anticipated that what they did not know would not bother them. After all, he had no intent to raise the vessel – simply to explore it and remove any valuables he might find. They could always deal with the tax man later.

Junius Plunkett reviewed the log that Captain Stephenson Ward had written, and poured over several charts of the Suwannee Channel that Elias Ward had brought with him. "Doubt that ship is still where your great granpappy says it is, Ward," he said. "From this chart it looks like the channel of the river flows right over the probable site, if that log is accurate. That would push it to the northwest, and probably, in a hundred years, cover it with a lot of silt. But that's not too deep to dive in, there. You dive?" "I've been down a few times, SCUBA diving. Yes, I definitely plan to go down with you."

"I'll have to put together a crew. At least four more guys, unless you're with us." "I've done some sailing. Got a Coast Guard certificate. Sure, that old tugboat of yours isn't much different from a motor launch."

"Hell of a lot different, Mister, but I suspect you'll learn," Plunkett replied. "I've got no other jobs lined up this winter. But once the Gloucester swordfish season opens again in the spring, I gotta be back. I'll give it six weeks, but you've got to stay with me. No flyin' home if we come up empty out there. An' you finance the whole damned thing. If we find something we split the profit fifty-fifty. You can take your costs out of your half. My contribution's the boat. Deal?"

"Deal."

Within three days Plunkett had outfitted his salvage tug, the *Roberta II*, named for his mother, and hired three men who had worked with him for a number of years in the season, and they were ready to start the voyage down the coast toward Florida.

The three crew members Plunkett had hired had all worked with him before. One, Jimmy Garth, a pimple-faced ex-con about twenty-five who was balding prematurely, was a deep sea diver, used to diving underneath stranded or disabled vessels to hook tow lines or free debris. He had served time in Connecticut for assault, the result of a drunken brawl in which he had nearly strangled another sailor.

Vinny Noveti was also about twenty-five. The son of an Italian fisherman, he had grown up on his father's cod boat out of Gloucester, and spoke English with an Italian accent. He was single with thick black hair, and the physique of a Greek god. Vinny's ventures with the girls of Boston kept the crew, including Ward, enthralled for the entire trip down the Atlantic Coast.

The third man was Plunkett's cousin, Rick Sands, a sort of younger version of Jay, with the same accent and short, stocky stance. He was quiet, moody, and read a lot, mostly magazines or pulp novels. Rick was the only married man on the crew, but Jay trusted him the most at the helm when any navigational hazards arose.

It took over a week to reach the Florida coast, with the *Roberta II* staying starboard of the Gulf Stream. Another three days south brought them to Key Largo, and they then followed the Inland Coastal Waterway into Florida Bay, around East Cape, and northward again through the Ten Thousand Islands. To that point they had had perfect weather, sunny and, for early February, warm. Off of Marco Island a storm formed to the west, and for two hours the tug rolled in heavy waves.

The rolling motion of the tug made Ward seasick, but he stayed in his cabin and did not let the other crew members see his reaction. They were used to far worse than this on the Grand Banks. The storm subsided, and Plunkett increased speed, heading into the deep harbor at Boca Grande for diesel fuel and other marine supplies.

"That should keep us goin' for a couple weeks, Ward," he said. "But hell, we still got hundreds of miles up this damned Gulf Coast to go yet. You're on watch tonight, Ward, for there's too much heavy traffic – coal and oil barges, tankers, banana boats, freighters, dumb tourist fishermen -- heading in and out'a Tampa Bay for one guy in the pilothouse to watch out for. We can relax once we get there."

For all his gruffness, Plunkett knew navigation. He had been a Navy petty officer, both as a helmsman and as an engineer, and had grown up in a family of merchant marine sailors. His father had been on a tanker that was sunk by a German submarine in convoy during the War about two months after Jay had volunteered for sea duty in the Navy. His own ship had been torpedoed, but had not sunk, although it was necessary for it to limp into Iceland for repairs. After that he had been transferred to the Pacific, where he was a chief engineer on a destroyer. That ship, too, had been attacked, but had survived. Plunkett had no fear of the sea, nor of those upon it.

On the evening of February 9 the *Roberta II* entered Suwannee Sound and anchored for the night. About two miles to the northeast they could see the lights of the little fishing village of Suwannee. "I don't think that river mouth or the little harbor at the marina in the town, there, is deep enough for the draft of this tug," Plunkett told Ward. "When we need stuff, we can send one of the men into the village there in the small boat. If we can find this damned wreck of yours, we'll just stay anchored out there." "There's probably a lot of fishing boats, charters and such, coming in and out of the harbor," Ward replied. "Think they'll get nosy about what we're doing?"

"I thought o' that, Ward. Let's just tell 'em you are Professor Pete Wadsworth, an Oceanographer at MIT if anybody asks. You're doing research on fish or something. You make it up, whatever you want. They'll leave you alone if they think you're going to bore them with some long lecture. In fact, that's not a bad idea... Tell 'em you're studying the depletion of the game fish in this area of the Gulf. That'll scare 'em off. That's all they want out there anyway are marlin and tarpon, maybe some bass."

About twenty minutes after they had anchored they felt something bumping against the side of the boat. Fearing that heavy debris from the river was drifting against it, they rushed to the starboard rail and looked over. Huge fat sea creatures were pushing against the side, almost in a playful way.

"Funny-looking dolphins!" Rick Sands said. "What are they? Whales?"

"No," Jay Plunkett answered. "I read about those things in a book once. They're called manatees. Some call 'em sea cows. Old time sailors used to think they were mermaids, but they'd make damned ugly mermaids."

"After a few months at sea," Vinny Noveti laughed, "I suppose some of those guys might have tried to make love to anything female."

"Gad, I'd hate to get in the water with one of those things," Rick replied. "But they're probably harmless."

"I don't think they'll do any damage to the boat," Plunkett added, "unless they were to get tangled up in the propeller. If they're still banging around in the morning we'll have to be careful not to run over one. I imagine they're protected by law. Last thing we need is some game warden nosing around!"

For the next ten days the *Roberta II* crisscrossed the sandy Gulf north of Hog Island, carefully watching the screen of the mini-sonar device that Ward had purchased in Boston to search for underwater metals. Several times they had received echoes, but most had turned out to be junk or trash. On the eleventh day they found a large wreck buried deep in the sand and silt. It was spread widely, almost in a circle, no more than forty feet below the surface of the water.

"That's probably the French corvette," Plunkett said. "Let's go down and dig around it a bit, see if we can confirm that. If so, and if you're theory is right, Ward, the valuable stuff is probably on the freighter, so we shouldn't waste our time on this thing unless there's some interesting guns or something. Think that underwater metal detector thing you got will work?"

"It better," Ward replied. "It's the best on the market."

The two donned wet-suits and SCUBA gear and splashed over the side. Garth assisted them, holding a long rope with a bucket on it to use in the event they found anything. Rick Sands had dropped the anchor so that the tug would not drift. Plunkett and Ward used the anchor chain to descend down to the sea floor, where they could see bits of debris poking up through the sand and silt.

Their plan was to find the stern and see if a name or other identification could be found. From Captain Ward's log it was likely that the corvette had been facing northeast when it exploded, hence the stern should be to the southwest of the debris field. Once their eyes adjusted to the shadows and shade of the cloudy greenish water Ward could make out a large chunk of metal protruding at an angle out of the water. He pointed at it and Plunkett nodded. The two moved toward it and around to the far side where it became clear that it was the bow of a large iron-clad ship. A mound of sand had drifted against it like a snowbank against a barn in a blizzard.

Sand had been anticipated, and Ward returned to the surface for the air hose that would blast the sand away from the wreck. Vinny cranked up the compressor, and Ward submerged to the sea floor with the hose. It had a nozzle that would blow a strong stream of air, controlled by a button on the nozzle. Returning to where Plunkett was trying to push sand away, Ward began spraying the air over the sand, pushing it back and away from the metal plating. He concentrated on the center of the plate, finally exposing a large portion of it. The plate sat at an angle, tilted to the southwest. At last some faint lettering appeared: a small 'xi,' then an 'o.' To the left of what might have been an 'l' was a gaping hole. It confirmed, however, that they had, indeed, located the *Biloxi*.

While they still had air in their tanks the two men used the air hose to blow through the sand and silt in other areas of the wreck that might have proved interesting. The silt clouded the water so badly that it was difficult to see anything, or to get any idea of what might be buried deep beneath the sand. They returned to the surface and agreed that if they could not find the *Austrian Princess* that they would return and explore the *Biloxi* a bit further.

In the Civil War log Captain Ward had said that the Mexican ship had steamed past the French corvette and had picked up some survivors of the explosion. They had been close enough to Hog Island that other survivors had swum to it, where they were later captured by the Marines. On the chart Plunkett penciled-in the location of the *Biloxi* and calculated what might have been the wreck's drift over nearly a hundred years from its probable location when it exploded. He was surprised at how far it had moved, but noted that the movement was almost due north rather than northwest, no more than two miles from the shore.

From that calculation the two men then penciled-in a possible pathway of the Austrian/Mexican freighter to where it might have been sunk, and calculated the drift it might have taken over the last century. That is where they resumed their underwater sonar search.

For two days the *Roberta II* ran slowly back and forth over several square miles of the Gulf. Twice the sonar indicated large objects. One turned out to be the wreck of an old fishing boat, perhaps no more than thirty years under water. Another was the fuselage of an old World War II bomber that apparently had crashed into the sea. As it was largely still intact and several hatches were open, it was apparent that the crew had escaped. Ward made a mental note to research the crash when he got back to Boston.

The next day dragged on slowly, the sonar virtually silent. In the morning a mild storm had passed over them, soaking the tug and everything on it, but the sun had quickly dried it again, but the storm had brought frigid temperatures, and the breeze made it feel about fifteen degrees colder than it really was. Even though the sun set about six fifteen each evening, they were able to continue their sonar search in the dark.

About seven thirty that night the sonar began picking up several large objects beneath the waves. The objects, whatever they were, were separated by as much as twenty feet, but were in a fairly straight line. Vinny unhooked the anchor cable, and it fell perhaps thirty feet into the sea, preventing the boat from drifting further. They were about a mile and a half from the shore, which was just a mangrove wilderness perhaps six or seven miles northwest of the small village of Suwannee. There was no habitation at all along the coast at that area.

Shortly after sunrise the next morning Ward, Garth and Plunkett all pulled on wet-suits and SCUBA gear, and armed with the air hose, descended to the floor. Here, well out of the channel of the Suwannee River, the water was crystal clear. The three divers swam to the southern-most of the areas they had seen on the sonar, and could see debris sticking out of the sand. Even with the air hose blowing the sand it did not cloud the water as the silt had on the wreck of the *Biloxi*.

Again they searched for the stern to try to find an identifying indication that this was the *Austrian Princess*. Captain Ward's log had not described the vessel except as a freighter, but from the shape of the debris on the sonar it appeared that it might be a side-wheeler, and that the mid-section of the ship was lying on its port side.

The bow was fairly intact, and after about twenty minutes of working with the air hose and pushing away sand with a bucket some lettering appeared. It was in German script, *Österreicherin Prinzessin*, although more than half the lettering had been worn away by the sand. Ward thought it odd that his great grandfather would have recorded the vessel's name in English rather than as it appeared.

The three then moved to the tilted starboard deck. The iron rail, framing for cabins and decks were still visible, although all the wood planking had largely disintegrated or rotted away, as had most of the wooden hull. The port side was buried deep in sand. Large groupers had taken over portions of the area where cabins had been located, the big, rather homely fish looking bug-eyed at the three divers. In one of the cabins the frame of a bed remained, and on a shelf were some personal effects – a shaving mug, razor, and ivory handle to a brush with all the hairs gone. It apparently had been a passenger cabin. The interior wall was missing, and through it Ward could see into the opposite port cabin. He switched on his underwater torch and poked his head through the opening. Again there was the frame of a bed and the remains of a dressing table and chair, but little else, and no personal items that he could see.

Garth had found an open hatch to the lower deck and had submerged down into it, ascertaining with his torch that the wooden ladder was rotted away, but that the area below was open. He popped back up, and signaled to Ward and Plunkett to follow him. Below was one of the holds. In the front part appeared to be a coal bunker, but only bits of coal remained, and the torn front half of this part of the vessel was buried in the sand. To the rear were long cases, largely still intact and bound with some sort of iron seals. There was printing on them that could barely be seen, and the words were in French. The port side of the hull had been torn away, and only about twelve of the cases were still stacked there, six high in two rows. Smaller boxes were also scattered around the hold. They searched each corner, then ascended through the hatch, returning to the surface.

"Find anything?" Rick asked as he and Vinny pulled the three divers aboard.

"Yeah," Garth replied, "but it will be a bitch of a job getting it out of there – up a hatch that's tilted forty degrees to port."

"You think that stuff is what we're after, Ward?" Plunkett asked.

"The long crates are probably guns. Don't know what's in the other boxes, and none of us tried to move them to see if they were heavy. If they are, they could be gold. Or just ammunition. I saw one barrel near the port side hole that might have been gun powder. Or flour. Impossible to say."

"Instead of trying to snake a rope to pull that stuff out the hatch, what would you say to just pulling the starboard side out of the hull – the little planking that remains there anyway – and bringing the stuff out the side?"

"A real archaeologist would be offended," Ward replied. "But what we're intent on doing probably is illegal anyway, so...."

"That siding'll probably be rotted away in a few years regardless," Garth interrupted. "It would be real easy to get those crates out through an opening in the side, which is tilted upward anyway. That's what I'd do."

"Makes sense," Plunkett agreed. "Let's refill our air tanks and go for it. Vinny, bring out those extra ropes so we can haul those crates aboard. Rick, see if you can find us a couple of axes or claw hammers we can use to tear that planking loose."

"We need to fill that big tub we brought with us with sea water," Ward said, "so that we can stick the stuff we bring up in it until we open the boxes and see what's inside. Otherwise some of it might deteriorate. I read that this was how they were preserving the stuff they found on that big wooden battleship that sank on launching in Sweden."

"Yeah," Plunkett agreed. "I looked that up when you told me about it, and how we'd need that tub. Thing was so big that when they launched it the damned thing sank right there at the dock! What was it, the *Watership*, or something?"

"The *Vasa*, built in 1628. Of course it had been under water three hundred years when they raised it. This is just a hundred years. Nevertheless, best not to take chances, if there's anything of value," Ward replied.

The three divers again descended to the wreck and began ripping out a larger hole where the starboard side of the hull opposite the hold already was opened by damage. The water-soaked planking was remarkably firm, and the wood amazingly thick. The axes and hammers had almost no effect on the wood. Exhausted they returned to the surface.

"We need some sort of power saw," Ward said.

"Hell, by the time we'd find one that would work under water it would be next winter!" Plunkett exclaimed. "Those crates went in through that hatch. We'll just have to bring them out the same way."

Again the three descended into the hold through the hatch. Taking turns two would move and push each crate upward through the open hatchway while the third held the torch so they could see in the black water. It took them most of the remaining air in their tanks to simply get six of the long crates out the hatchway.

After replenishing his air Garth returned to the ship with the ropes and tied three around the first of the six crates they had pushed out of the hold. The four men on the deck of the tug then pulled it upwards, and carefully lifted it out of the water. The crate, along with whatever was inside, was full of water and extremely heavy. They tried to knock a hole in it with their hammer, but this wood, too, resisted the blows. With a final struggle the heavy box fell on the deck with a thud.

"Won't fit in that tub, Ward," Plunkett said.

"Ahh, to hell with it, we'll just open it up and stick whatever's inside in the tub."   After resting awhile the three divers returned to the black hold of the ship, pushing the remaining crates and the boxes through the hatch. One of the boxes split open while being moved, and hundreds of brass rifle shell casings spilled out into the black water in the hold. Ward also stopped back at the cabins on the upper deck and picked up a few of the personal items that had been abandoned when the ship sank. Plunkett and Ward returned to the surface and joined Sands and Noveti in hauling the remaining crates and boxes to the surface.

Once Garth was back aboard they got tools to pry open the crates. On several the wood was like mush, and gave way with little effort. Others were encrusted with barnacles and had to be sawed open. As anticipated, the crates contained rifles, apparently of Mexican or Spanish manufacture. They had an odd-colored barrel and firing mechanism, but the wooden stocks were in reasonably good shape.

"I suppose these will bring some sort of fairly good price from an arms dealer or collector," Plunkett said. "But I doubt they're going to bring enough to cover your costs, Ward."

"No, but let's do what we can to preserve them so we get the best results," he replied, pulling out several and putting them in the tub of seawater. "And if those other boxes are just cartridge casings, they're not going to bring much either."

The boxes and two small barrels that they had hauled to the surface were opened after all the rifles were soaking in the tub. The barrels contained what might have been food at one time but was simply mush now. Of the boxes, six contained more cartridge casings, worth little more than the scrap value of their brass. The rest, except one, held what appeared to be blankets and uniforms, one also containing boots, now fairly rotted. The final box contained various military medals, each stamped with the words of a campaign, the symbols and wording of the Army of the Confederate States of America.

"Do you think if we went back toward where the *Biloxi* was we might find some of the rest of what was in that hold that must have fallen out as the ship drifted north?" Ward asked.

"We sure didn't see it on that sonar," Plunkett answered. "Yeah, there's probably stuff out there, but what the hell, time is money, and we're not getting any richer with this junk. Even if we took a week to find it, it's probably just more guns and blankets and barrels of flour. Not worth it, Ward."

The exhausted men sat looking at their recovered treasure as the sun began to set over the Gulf. Rick Sands, who acted as their cook, finally arose and headed into the galley, and began preparing steaks for their dinner. Plunkett had insisted that Ward pay for only the best food for the venture, which he had gladly agreed to do. They had been dining well so far on the voyage.

The next morning Plunkett had the anchor drawn up, and they moved to the middle collection of wreckage the sonar had shown. The shape of what they were seeing appeared to have some sort of wheel, and the debris was almost sixty feet down.

"Your great granddaddy didn't say what kind of steamship he was following," Plunkett said. "Looks like it was a side-wheeler. That means the engines will be in this part. Probably no cargo hold."

The three divers again pulled on their wet-suits and descended to the wreckage. This time it was lying on its port side, with the starboard side facing the surface. It was, as Plunkett had suggested, a side-wheeler, with the planking around the metal frame of the wheel shroud entirely eaten away. The starboard side of the hull was still mostly intact, but there was a gaping hole right behind the wheel frame, probably the place where the cannonball from the Union gunboat had entered, causing the engine room to flood and the ship to sink.

Garth located a passageway inside the front part of the wreckage, and the three lit their torches and moved down what was intended as a stairway to the engine room. The boilers were still in their same position, and the two steam engines, although encrusted with barnacles, looked otherwise undamaged. The engines and boilers took up most of the interior of this section of the ship, and they found nothing of any value in it to haul to the surface.

On the upper deck were several additional small cabins, each with what appeared to be a built-in bunk and table. Ward anticipated that these would have been the cabins for the crewmembers. He looked around each for personal items, but saw none of any value. The walls did not back up to cabins on the pot side, as the stacks for the engines were in the center of the hull, and the port cabins were buried in the sand.

Once back on board the decision was made to move forward to the northernmost location of wreckage and, guided by the sonar, Plunkett had the anchor drawn in and slowly moved the tugboat forward and slightly to the northeast. When they were directly over the wreckage the tug was probably no more than two miles from the shore, which was just palmettos and cypress trees, no beach, and no habitation. The sonar indicated that this debris was about forty-five feet below the surface.

Plunkett had taken off his wet suit, and said to Ward and Garth, "I got some paper work to do. You two go down and have a look, see what's down there. If it looks promising I'll go down with you tomorrow.

Otherwise, I've got to be thinking about getting back to Boston. When we were in Boca Grande fueling up I called a couple of my customers. They say the fishing season may start early this spring, due to the higher prices for cod and swordfish, so I can't waste my time out here lookin' for buckets of bullets or some damned thing."

Elias Ward and Jimmy Garth refilled their air tanks and splashed over the side. The water here was warmer, and crystal clear, being well out of the channel of the Suwannee River. How or why the wreckage had drifted this far was not clear, but what they immediately saw was that the bow of the ship, including the front cabins and pilothouse, were sitting flat on the bottom, not tilted to either side.

Ward was delighted to see how well preserved the wreckage seemed to be. He and Garth began to look for a hatchway or entrance to the front cargo hold, and Garth finally located one about half way between the wall of the pilothouse and the bow rail. They both struggled with the tools they had brought down with them to pry the hatch open, but at last it gave way, and Garth switched on his torch to descend into the blackness below. Ward lit his torch and held the light just ahead of where Garth was moving, until Garth had moved far to the back and out of Ward's sight.

It seemed like several minutes, but at last Garth came back to the hatch and up through it, shaking his head to indicate that there was nothing there. With his hands he motioned that the bottom of the hull had been torn out, and there was nothing holding up the wreckage but the sides of the hull. A wave of disappointment sloshed through Ward. Unless there was something of value in the cabins or the pilothouse with the ship's wheel in it, the trip was going to be a waste of time and money.

The two divers explored the wheelhouse next. Ward was surprised that the glass in the windows and doors was still intact, although one window was cracked. The port door, however, was open, and all of the interior, including the brass compass and engine signal bell frame were covered with barnacles. The spoked wheel at the helm had held its shape, but sea worms had eaten large holes in it. Fish were swimming in and out of the open door, occasionally bumping into the windows and looking much like fish in a glass aquarium. A door led down some steps behind the wheelhouse, and Ward lit his torch and descended into what had apparently been the captain's cabin.

In the light of the torches Garth and Ward could see that the furnishings in the cabin had once been quite elegant. There were two exterior doors, both jammed with barnacles, but the glass in the round portholes was still intact. A number of personal items still remained in the room – a jug and basin for washing, a small mirror above the table on which they sat, some fish-eaten bits of uniform in a closet, and a locked drawer in a desk. With his claw hammer Garth broke open the hasp on the lock, and inside was a small wooden box with metal straps.

Ward returned to the outside of the ship and signaled on the rope to lower the bucket for loading things. In a few moments he had the large plastic bucket and pulled it into the open door of the pilothouse. He and Garth then loaded all of the personal items and the small chest from the locked drawer, then yanked the signal to draw it up. They then moved around to the next cabin, the port door of which was ajar. It was the dining room, with tables and chairs all scattered about. Through a door in the back, again with their torches lit, they found the galley, complete with some sort of cooking stove and shelves for provisions, most of which had disintegrated or been eaten by fish. Ward found some china, but in examining it, found that it was just a simple type of pottery, not fine Dresden porcelain as he hoped. In a closed cupboard, however, he found another set of china and some silverware. This china was much finer than that apparently reserved for the crew. Garth signaled again for the bucket, and the china and silver was sent to the surface. In another drawer was the ordinary flatware, a pewter-like metal, but the drawer had been partially open and the metal, whatever it was, encrusted with barnacles.

Only part of another cabin remained behind the dining hall. It had apparently been torn apart when the front and mid sections of the ship separated, and there was nothing in it except what appeared to be a mirror nailed to the wall. Finding nothing else, Garth and Ward returned to the tug, and eagerly awaited the opening of the wooden chest they had found in the captain's cabin after they had dried off and gotten back in their clothes. Rick had spent the afternoon fishing, and had caught several large groupers which he had dressed and was preparing for their dinner. But Garth and Ward wanted to open the box they had found first.

The box was about six inches high, with a square top, perhaps eight inches long and five wide. There was a hasp with a metal lock, and two hinges on the back. Without a key Ward feared that they would have to break open the box, until Jimmy Garth said, "Let me have a go at it." He took out his pocketknife, opened a small, rounded blade in it, and inserted it in the keyhole. After probing for several minutes there was a faint 'click.' The lid did not move, but Garth was able to run the larger blade on his knife between the two halves of the lock, then, with a twist, the lid popped open. The box, lined with some sort of cloth, was empty.

* * *

It was the fifth of March when the *Roberta II* chugged into Boston Harbor and tied up at the wharf on Northern Avenue. On the way back Plunkett and Ward had compiled a list of every item recovered from the wreckage. The day after they got back Ward was sitting in Plunkett's office.

"Who d'yah think's going to buy all this stuff," Plunkett asked, adding, "a buyer who ain't going to ask a lot of questions?"

"Any suggestions?"

"I don't, but I asked Jimmy, and he said his cousin knows some guy who deals in art and jewelry and stuff like that, of, well, to quote Jimmy, 'of questionable origin.' He's going to ask his cousin for the name of this guy. We might try him. I'm out the time, and the wear on the boat, but, Ward, you're out a bundle for the crew's pay, and all our expenses, and don't forget, half of whatever we get is mine."

"I won't forget, Jay. The trip was worth it to me. We can't go broadcasting it, because of the location in state waters, but it was well worth the effort. Besides, I can probably write off any loss on my income tax and stick Uncle Sam with the bill."

"You rich bastards are always sticking some poor sucker with a bill!" Plunkett laughed. "You're right. It was worth the effort. Guys pay big bucks to take a cruise like that and go wreck-diving. The only bad part is that Jimmy told me he's not going to crew with me this spring. Said he had another cousin who had a better job for him with a lot less risk and labor."

"Garth seems like a good man," Ward said, "despite his background. I hope he does well. And I hope that cousin of his can get us some decent prices for this stuff." "Yeah. Me too. Com'on, I got a bottle of good bourbon here. Let's have a toast to your great grand-daddy who sank those two wrecks. I'd bet he had some plan to go back and look at 'em himself, and never got to it."

"I'll drink to that, Plunkett. I don't doubt but you're right. To Captain Stephenson Ward, United States Navy. Damned right."

Chapter 3

April 15, 1963
Office of the Department of Religions and Geography
Fremont College, Ohio

The telephone rang on the desk of Sally Merriam, the department secretary in the basement office of the old Hayes Building on the campus of Fremont College. Sally pushed her long blond hair aside as she placed the receiver to her ear.

"Department of Religions and Geography," she announced. Her husband, Dr. Bob Merriam, was upstairs in one of the building's lecture halls teaching a class normally taught by the department chairman and assistant chaplain, Dr. Richard Fairchild. Professor Fairchild, however, was on a sabbatical in Italy for a few months and his exact whereabouts were unknown even to the college dean and board. Fairchild was known to operate with an aura of mystery, and his suddenly requested sabbatical certainly did little to alter the myth.

"Long distance call for a Mrs. Sally Merriam," an operator announced, indicating a person-to-person call.

"This is she." Sally replied.

"Sally?" the voice on the line inquired.

"Dexter!" she exclaimed, immediately recognizing his voice. "How are you? Where are you calling from?"

"Atlanta. Sally, I've got some news!"

"What? *What*?!" Dexter Atwater was Sally's first cousin, the son of her mother's sister. The two had grown up together, were about the same age, and had always been close. Dexter had gone to medical school at Western Reserve University in Cleveland and had further training at the Cleveland Clinic. He was completing his last year of residency in cardiology at a large Atlanta hospital.

"Well, it's a long story, but I've been offered a partnership in a practice up in Sandusky with several specialists. One is Dr. Ledfelder, whom I believe you may know." "Yes, he was Richie Fairchild's neurosurgeon when he had that head injury a couple of years ago."

"Well, Ledfelder is on the board at Memorial Hospital there, and says that the town needs a good cardiologist. I'm going out to Houston for a month to train with one of the famous heart surgeons there, and when I finish I'll take my boards as a surgeon. So I'll be returning to Ohio about the middle of June. Could you and Bob maybe put me up for a week or so until I can find a place in Sandusky?"

"Sure! We'd love to have you. We commuted to Sandusky for years before we got our house here in Fremont. Maybe you could get our old garden apartment in Sandusky."

"Maybe so. But there's more...."

"What?"

"I'm engaged! I met a nurse here at the hospital. She's from some town in South Georgia, pretty as a picture, and we're going to get married as soon as I pass my boards and get settled back in Ohio."

"A nurse! What's her name?"

"Peggy. Actually it's Patricia, but she goes by Peggy. Peggy Fitzgibbons. She's an only child, and her dad has spoiled her rotten, but she is delightful, and really excited about coming to Ohio. You and Bob are going to have to come to the wedding, which will be down here in Georgia."

"Wild horses couldn't keep us away, Dexter! Let us have all the details."

"I'll write. Have to go now, but if I can bunk with you guys for a few weeks, that will be one worry solved."

"I'll count the days! Gosh, I've missed you, Dexter. Do you realize that the last time I saw you was *our* wedding, and that was only for a few hours at the reception?" "You were a beautiful bride, Sally. But Peggy is also going to be a beautiful bride. I can't wait until you get a chance to meet her."

* * *

When Associate Professor Robert Merriam returned to his office, his wife was bubbling with excitement at the news of her cousin's return to Ohio and his engagement. Bob Merriam had been puzzled by Cousin Dexter since he had first heard his name from another of Sally's cousins, Mary Black, who suggested that Sally tell Bob of some "ancient history" of her own, which she had always refused to do. Bob suspected it was an event that happened when the three cousins were growing up together, and Mary had said it had something to do with Dexter's decision to become a physician, but he had never been able to learn the secret. What Bob imagined was probably far removed from what had really occurred.

Now that the Merriams were residing in Fremont, avoiding the daily drive of nearly thirty miles each way to Sandusky, they had greater opportunities to join in campus and town activities. However, the big Victorian house they had purchased required a lot of upkeep, and Bob found that he was spending nearly every weekend doing minor repairs or working in the yard. Having grown up in a large Philadelphia "Mainline" home where there were servants, he found the tasks both relaxing and rewarding, although the work also kept him from his favorite pastime, reading.

Hilda Waggoner, the college's new professor of physics and former nuclear energy advisor to the East German Navy, had moved into the Merriam's garage apartment until her own wedding. She was marrying Dr. Ross Johnson, the college's choral director, whom she had met when defecting from East Germany the previous summer. After their wedding the Merriam's guesthouse would again be vacant.

"When is he coming?" Bob asked as Sally explained her cousin's phone call.

"I don't know, exactly. He said he'd write, but he has to go to Houston for a while and said it would be mid-June. Hilda and Ross's wedding is June 8, so the guesthouse will be vacant by then. But if it's just for a few weeks, he could use the guest bedroom."

"Sounds okay to me," Bob replied. He was usually cooperative with any of his wife's plans, and in several years of marriage they had yet to have a real quarrel.

* * *

The Fitzgibbons holdings had expanded considerably after the Depression. The railway and steamboat operations had evolved into an international shipping enterprise, and the firm had purchased several paper mills near forested land it held in South Georgia and Northern Florida. Their hotel on the Gulf, now over one hundred years old, remained open, but construction of a planned resort there had not yet been started. The family still resided in Waycross, although old Jack Fitzgibbons had died in 1956.

Forrest Fitzgibbons had only met his future son-in-law once when Dexter drove down to Waycross with Peggy for the weekend. It had been on that trip that the two had become engaged, and Forrest gave his blessing. He had been surprised when, about a week later, Peggy had informed him of Dexter's offer of a practice in Sandusky. Peggy had been just as surprised by her father's response, as she had expected him to be opposed to the idea.

"Sandusky?" he had asked. "Up on Lake Erie! Yes! Peggy, I'll bet you did not know that we own property up there."

"We do?" she replied. "You mean the company has some holdings there?"

"No, well, it's run through the company books, but actually those properties – there are two of them – are held in the Fitzgibbons name, not the S&G's. If this Dexter of yours does take that position up there, Darlin', you'll have to take a look at them. One currently has a tenant, but the other – the one in town – has been vacant for a few years. I thought about selling it, but it would be good to have someone there to take care of the place and, heck, to pay the taxes on the thing!"

"Dad! You mean you'd give it to us?"

"Well... maybe. Let's wait and see."

* * *

In May the wedding announcements arrived and Sally and Bob began their planning for the trip to Georgia. Hilda and Ross Johnson's wedding was two weeks earlier, and Hilda would be vacating the garage apartment in time for the Atwaters to move in after their honeymoon, someplace on the Gulf of Mexico that was owned by Peggy's family. Two of Sally's brothers planned to fly down to Jacksonville and rent a car to drive to Waycross. After conferring with the Whites, Sally's parents, it was agreed that George White, who had just purchased a new Buick sedan, would drive down and he and Bob would take turns driving. Mary Black, who was still single, also would go with them on the trip.

The following weekend Sally and Bob drove to Toledo to shop for wedding gifts. Sally had the gifts for Peggy and Dexter sent to Waycross, but the one for the Johnsons they brought back to Fremont. Sally was to be Hilda's maid of honor in the wedding that would take place in the Fremont Chapel, and Dr. Fairchild had written from Italy, where he was on a short sabbatical, that he would be home by the first of June and would conduct the service.

At the end of May Dexter flew up from Houston to Cleveland, and the Merriams picked him up at the Hopkins Airport and drove him out to their home in Fremont, which was in the same neighborhood with Spiegel Grove, the Rutherford B. Hayes Presidential estate. Hayes had been the 19th President of the United States, elected from Congress in 1877 with less than 50% of the popular vote, though he ran a relatively successful term. Peggy had not yet informed Dexter about the property in Sandusky, and he wanted to size up the garage apartment as a temporary home. He was scheduled to take his Ohio medical board examinations the following week in Columbus, and, while happy to be with Sally and Bob, spent most of the few days in Fremont with his nose in a book.

* * *

Spanish moss hung from the live oak trees on the wide avenue in front of the large pillared antebellum Fitzgibbons home in Waycross. Two blocks away a red brick church that looked like an amphitheater inside was being decorated with white and pink flowers for one of the largest weddings seen in the town in several years. Dexter guessed that as much as a tenth of the town's population must have been related to the Fitzgibbons as he had met scores of aunts, uncles and distant cousins – many on

Peggy's mother's side of the family — and he suspected that an additional ten percent of the town had been invited. The church was nearly full, although his own family occupied only two pews.

After the liquorless reception held in the church basement following the ceremony the large Cadillac sedan driven by one of Forrest Fitzgibbons' employees delivered the newly married couple to the railway depot where the S&G business car sat on a siding, hooked to the local S&G train. It would deliver them several hours later to the dock on the Suwannee River, where the company's cabin cruiser, complete with a captain and steward, would transport them overnight downstream to the Suwannee Hotel at the river's mouth. Peggy's gift from her father was the deeds to two properties in Ohio.

* * *

The Suwannee Hotel was about a hundred and fifteen years old. It had been built in the early 1850s in a brief boom in the area when lumber, sugar and turpentine were shipped down the Suwannee from the northwestern interior of the state to the docks where sail and early steamships transported the goods to New Orleans and other Gulf of Mexico ports. At the time the Florida Railway had not yet been completed from Fernandina to Cedar Key, running only as far as Gainesville. The river was the only means of travel to the northern interior of Florida, connecting with the S&G's track, originally at White Springs, and later at Branford, thus avoiding a nearly one hundred mile loop of the river. By 1855 cotton and other products from Georgia were also being shipped from the tiny port, and passengers from along the S&G line used the hotel to await passage to other Gulf ports, such as Tampa, Pensacola, Mobile, New Orleans or Galveston. Wealthy plantation owners often used the hotel as a base for fishing as the hotel owned a small steam launch that took the men out beyond Hog Island, which sat at the entrance to the harbor, for game fishing.

By the 1960s, however, the hotel had fallen on hard times. Although the small hamlet and its few shops were somewhat protected from storms by the islands in the harbor, nevertheless gales off the Gulf had rendered the old, three-story hotel building weather-beaten and gray. Each floor had a long porch at the front overlooking the street and the harbor, with old, sometimes torn and useless rocking chairs on which to view the sunsets. Modern plumbing and electricity had been added in the 1920s, but the pipes were nearly forty years old, and produced rusty water in rooms that were not used frequently for the first few minutes after the taps were opened.

Nevertheless, there was still an old-fashioned elegance to the place, and fishermen continued to use it as a base for deep-sea fishing. A number of charter boats now lined the few remaining docks where steamers once had loaded cargo. The sunsets remained beautiful, and the fresh seafood served in the hotel dining room was still excellent. Otherwise, the tiny port village was little more than a ghost town, with only a handful of shops.

There was a small stretch of sandy beach north of the village reachable by boat, and someone had cut a trail into the mangroves and forests to the northeast behind the village where visitors could hike and view the wildlife of the area. Thousands of songbirds, aquatic birds, turtles, alligators, snakes, deer, wildcats, and even bears inhabited the area. At night the bears would raid the hotel's garbage pit, but the villagers had learned to coexist with them. In the river a large colony of manatees had prospered, and the state had posted warning signs that these marine mammals were a protected species, not to be harmed.

Peggy and Dexter settled into the largest of the hotel's rooms on the second floor at the front, where they had a great view of the harbor and sunsets. Their six honeymoon days were spent on the nature trail, or aboard the company's cabin cruiser fishing. Dexter managed to hook a large marlin, which a local taxidermist agreed to mount for him and arrange to have it shipped to Fremont.

"It's *not* going in the living room!" Peggy insisted. "My things are all Victorian, and there's no place for a big fish!"

"Don't worry! I'll keep it in my office," Dexter laughed, still infatuated enough with his bride that he would have agreed to throw the fish into the ocean if she had asked. Their time went quickly, and soon the week they had planned for their honeymoon was up, and it was time to take the launch back to civilization. The newlyweds arrived back in Waycross on a Wednesday afternoon, and spent the night at the Fitzgibbon home while Peggy prepared what was left of her wardrobe for shipment to Ohio. The next evening they boarded the Atlantic Coast Line's *Dixie Flyer* as it arrived from Jacksonville at eleven, and bedded down in their double bedroom in an L&N Pullman car that would deliver them the following morning to Atlanta. From there they flew from Hartsfield Airport to Cleveland Hopkins Airport on a Capital Airlines Viscount propjet, where Bob and Sally met them for the drive back to Fremont.

"I'm going to have to get a car right away," Dexter said as they pulled out of the Airport drive and circled around to head west on Brookpark. "I don't think I can afford a new one yet, and we'll probably have to get one for Peggy, too."

"There are a few used car lots in Fremont, Dexter," Bob replied, "but your best bet is Toledo. That's where I got this hunk of junk we're riding in. I'd thought about getting a new one, but with buying the house last winter, it just didn't work out. I'll go with you next week and we can look at some. You'll need a reliable one if you're called out at night for emergencies."

"I'm hoping I can get a job as a nurse at the hospital in Sandusky, too," Peggy said. "If so, if we're on the same shift, I could ride with Dexter."

"I won't be at the hospital all the time, Dear. But maybe at first, until I get established in the office...."

Chapter 4

June 28, 1963
Sandusky, Ohio

Although it had been less than a week that the Atwaters had occupied the guesthouse, they had already established a routine. Bob and Dexter had traveled to Toledo one afternoon the previous week and Dexter had purchased a three-year-old Dodge that was in very good condition. He had met with several other Sandusky physicians, and had been invited to join the practice with two general practitioners, with the promise that he might be able to buy into their partnership at some future time. He had taken the Ohio medical board exams a few days before the wedding, and received notice in the mail that he had passed, and was being issued a license to practice in Ohio. With this notice, he was able to start work at Memorial Hospital, but as the hospital was currently short on emergency room physicians, he was asked to take the night shift that included weekends until additional personnel could be found. Hence he was leaving for Sandusky about nine every evening except Tuesday and Wednesday, and arriving home about eight each morning. Dexter and Peggy had dinner with Bob and Sally each evening before Dexter left for Sandusky, and the four young people were becoming close friends. It was about a week later that the phone rang in the Religions Department office, and Sally answered.

"Mrs. Atwater?" a voice inquired.

"No, that's my cousin, who is currently staying with us. She does not yet have a phone. Is there something I can do to help you?"

"No, just tell her that her shipment has come in, and is down at the Railway Express Agency here in Fremont, at the old freight depot."

"Okay. Is it something that will fit in a car trunk? Maybe I could pick it up."

No, I doubt it, lady. It's about seven feet long. Think you'll need a truck."

"Goodness! What is it?"

"Danged if I know, lady. It's all crated up. Must weigh a hundred pounds or more. The agent in Cincinnati said there was another shipment for Atwaters coming in tomorrow, too. A bunch of stuff. You can leave this here till then if you want, and get them all at once."

"Oh. Okay, well, we'll see what we can arrange."

Sally hung up, and puzzled over what the shipment might be. She did recall that Peggy had said that her clothes, presents, and a few furnishings were going to be shipped up from Georgia, and anticipated that this was what would be at the freight depot. There was not very much storage room in the guesthouse, but if Bob left his car outside, large boxes could be kept in the garage. The Atwaters had arranged to have a telephone installed at the guesthouse, but it wouldn't be put in for a few days yet.

With only a handful of summer courses, plus the planned Religions Department summer tour the last week in July and the first of August, the office was not as busy as during the regular school year, and Sally was able to leave about four that afternoon. "A long, heavy box?" Peggy said, when Sally told her about the call. "I can't think of what that might be. I do have two antique chairs that were carefully packed by the S&G's shipping agent for me, and a dresser, but that doesn't sound like this. Where can we get a truck to pick up this stuff?"

"Richie Fairchild has a truck at his farm. Maybe he'd let Bob borrow it for an hour when the other stuff comes in, and we can move the things into the garage."

"Do you think he'd mind? I've not met your Professor Fairchild yet. Dexter said, from what he's heard from you, that your boss is quite a character."

"That he is!" Sally laughed. "But he and his wife, Esther, are going to be out of the country on their summer tour with about eighteen students at the end of July, so maybe we can get the use of the truck then, too, if your place in Sandusky is available. When are we going to go see it?"

"Dexter has Wednesday off, so maybe we can drive over then. Could you get that day off?"

"I'll try. The summer tour this year is to Rome, to some seminary where Richie spent part of the spring, so the travel arrangements are not as difficult as they were last year to go into East Germany. Bob has no afternoon classes on Wednesdays, and Dr. Simon only has one that morning. Maybe I can talk them into giving me a day off. I don't take many, and hardly ever take a sick day."

"Good. Daddy gave me the directions for the two properties and the realtor's phone number, and I'm anxious to see them. Where is this 'Marblehead Peninsula' where the farm is located?"

"Oh, that's a place across from Cedar Point, with an old lighthouse on it that forms the north shore of Sandusky Bay. It's kind of flat, with quarries and farms and little resorts along the shore. You can go by way of Port Cleland, up past Dr. Fairchild's farm, or by Bayview, across the causeway. It is south of Catawba Island, and from Marblehead you can take the ferry over to Kelley's Island. It's a fun place."

* * *

Fairchild's old Ford pickup truck barely held all the boxes that were waiting at the New York Central freight depot. The springs in the passenger seat of the old truck were pushing up through the upholstering, so Sally, Dexter and Peggy had followed in Bob's '51 Oldsmobile. As Bob and Dexter loaded the boxes, the long, heavy box that had arrived separate from the rest puzzled Dexter at first. It had been shipped from Gainesville, Florida. Suddenly he realized what it was and began to laugh. "It's my fish!" he said.   "Your what?" Sally asked.

"My marlin. I caught it on our honeymoon, and had it stuffed. I promised Peggy I'd not put it in the living room. But right now, it wouldn't fit in my office either, so I'll have to just store it until I get a bigger office."

"I'll be anxious to see it, Dex. Let's get this stuff to the garage so we can head over to Sandusky and see your new house. Maybe there will be space for it there, other than in the living room," Bob said, as the last box was shoved into the back of the truck.   After unloading the boxes into the Merriam's garage, the four climbed into Dexter's Dodge and headed for Sandusky. Peggy had called the real estate agent, David Webster, and he had agreed to meet them at the house on Huron Avenue with the key. "I've met your Dad a few times," he told her. "First time we went over to Cedar Point. He's an interesting guy, Mrs. Atwater. Told me to get the place fixed up a bit for you. Had it repainted inside. Hope you like white."

"I'm sure it will be very nice," she assured him.

The homes along the tree-shaded street all appeared to be at least a hundred years old, Victorian or earlier in appearance, and very large, with lots of large trees in the yards and between the street and the sidewalk. The Fitzgibbons house still had a wrought iron fence around it, and the realtor had already opened the gate at the driveway so that Dexter could pull in. Webster's own car was parked in front on the street. He appeared to be a man in his sixties, although he was a bit older than Peggy's father.

Although it was a bright, sunny day, the dark stone of the house and the deep shadows from the tall, thick elm trees gave the house somewhat of a foreboding appearance. But the long, wide porch that ran around the front and driveway side of the house had been painted white. A glider swing hung from hooks on the ceiling. Toward the back on the driveway side the porch had a second floor extension.

"That upper part of the porch is attached to the big upstairs bedroom," David Webster said. "It runs all the way to the back, and overlooks the garden."

"There's a garden?" Peggy asked.

"Yes, not much in it this year yet, though. It's kind of gone to seed the last couple of years. But we've kept the weeds down, and the lawn mowed. It needs a green thumb." Dexter was interested in seeing the two-story carriage house that would serve as a garage for their cars. "Maybe I can make an office upstairs."

"That would be a good place for your fish!" Sally suggested.

"Topical fish?" Webster inquired.

"No, a stuffed marlin I caught on our honeymoon," Dexter explained.

"Let's see the house first, Dex," Peggy insisted. The real estate agent gave her the key, a long gray metal one that supposedly fit all three of the outside doors, including the leaded glass front door. Peggy pushed the doorbell button, but there was no sound.

"Power's off," Webster explained. "I have the number for Ohio Edison to get it turned back on, but since it has been vacant, and nothing electrical running in the house, we've kept the bills down for your dad."

"What kind of heat does it have?" Dexter asked.

"More than fifty years ago we had a coal-burning furnace put in, with new venting all over the house. About ten years ago, however, your father-in-law asked us to arrange to have an oil furnace put in to replace it. We got one that will burn either oil or natural gas, just by changing a few dials, and the folks who were living here then said it did a good job of heating in the winter. It's not air conditioned, but with all the trees, and the breeze off the Bay, I doubt you'll really need much air conditioning. Maybe in that carriage house apartment.... It probably gets hot up there in the summer."

"Daddy said there were some tenants one time that said there was a ghost, but it was just noises," Peggy said. "Is it still haunted?"

"No, Mrs. Atwater, there's no ghosts that I know of. I think it was the metal flues for that old coal-burning furnace that made noises when they heated up."

"It is kind of spooky looking," Dexter commented as he climbed up the porch and joined the others in the foyer, just inside the door. The foyer led to a small parlor at one side, and a more formal living room on the other side, with a large mantled fieldstone fireplace. There were no furnishings in the house, but there were drapes and curtains at all the windows. The oak floors were all bare. A bay window in the living room jutted out a few feet into the porch.

"Last owner left those," Webster explained. "Said they wouldn't go with their new house, which I'd sold them myself, and I know they had a decorator put these in, so they should be good quality."

"Yes, they're nice," Peggy commented, and Sally concurred. They all moved forward through the living room to a very formal dining room, with a crystal chandelier hanging from the cove ceiling and a wainscoted wall with a chair rail and two built-in china cabinets. There was also another fireplace. Through a swinging door was the kitchen, which had fairly modern looking appliances, a gas range, large refrigerator, with the door open, and a small chest freezer in a large shelved pantry. Several doors led off the pantry, including one to the outside of the house.

Another room ran between the kitchen and the parlor. It backed to the dining room and shared another fireplace with the dining room, open to both rooms. Book shelves lined the wall on either side of the fireplace. A side door led onto the porch on the driveway side of the house.

"A library!" Dexter exclaimed. "This will be a great place to entertain."

"Don't be getting any ideas about hanging that fish in here, now, Dexter!" Peggy warned him.

One of the doors off the pantry led to a built-on addition that had a laundry sink and water hookup and plugs for a washing machine and dryer. Another door led to the steps down to the cellar. A small powder room, with a door to both the dining room and to the laundry room had been added in the corner. "We had the house re-plumbed about six years ago. Replaced all the old lead pipes with copper," Webster explained. "Brand new bathroom in the big bedroom upstairs, but the other bathroom up there is from about the 1890s. You may like it, though. It's kind of unique. European in a way, if you've ever been to Europe. All white tile and large fixtures."

"Let's see the upstairs!" Sally said, and they returned to the foyer, where a wide, somewhat curved stairway with a curved oak banister led to the upstairs. On a landing half way up was a stained glass window with a geometric design.

"That closed door in the kitchen," Webster said, "is another stairs to the second floor. It's handy to the laundry room, or for a midnight snack, Dr. Atwater."

There were four large bedrooms upstairs, plus a large sitting room at the top of the main stairway. Three of the bedrooms shared a large, oversized bathroom that, as Webster had advised, looked like something from the Gay 90s in Paris, with a large tub standing on four feet, a large white pedestal sink, a big window overlooking the other side of the house, and a large closet for linens, robes, or whatever might be needed. Each of the bedrooms also had large walk-in closets, and there was an extra-long closet in the middle of the hallway. At the back was another door. Dexter went to it and turned the handle, but it was locked.

"To the attic," Webster said. "I don't think the front door key works it, but this smaller key on the chain may. I've not been up there since I was a kid. There's still some old trunks and things up there, probably things that belonged to your great grandfather, Mrs. Atwater. We always kept it locked for that reason, when the place was rented out. Didn't want the tenants up there messing around with your family's stuff.

"We can see that some other time, then," Dexter said, as the group moved into the main bedroom, a large, bright room with windows on two sides, and a fireplace on the third wall. It also had a large walk-in closet, and a large, very modern bathroom with a modern tub and shower, plus two sinks connected with a marble counter top and drawers.

"Wow!" Sally exclaimed. "You'll really enjoy this, Peggy."

"I won't, until we get it furnished. It's going to cost a fortune!"

"I was afraid of that," Dexter laughed.

Sally had been looking out the door to the porch, and suddenly exclaimed, "Look! You can see the harbor! Just above the trees to the left. Oh, this is going to be wonderful when you get it furnished, Peggy."

"Anybody want to see the cellar?" Webster asked.

"Sure," Dexter said, but the two women elected to stay in the large bedroom and plan the furniture, so Bob and Dexter accompanied the real estate agent back down the rear stairway and to the door off the pantry that lead to a dark set of steps. The realtor had a flashlight and turned it on to show Dexter where the furnace, water heater, and other items were. It was a large basement, and there were several empty rooms off the main furnace room. One had been the old coal storage area. A few lumps of coal still remained in one corner of it.

* * *

As it was getting close to noon Webster suggested that he drive them out to the farm on the peninsula, and treat them to lunch on the way. He had a large late model Cadillac, and it easily held five people. They headed west, going along some side streets rather than back to the downtown area, and came to the main road at a corner where there was a large church. The two-lane highway then went west, with Sandusky Bay to the north. A marsh separated the highway from the double-tracked New York Central railway, and there was marsh along the south side as well.

"Great place for duck hunting in the fall," Webster said. "And the fishing in the Bay, here, is excellent. Even in winter. You'll have to get yourself an ice fishing shanty, Dr. Atwater."

"No, think I'll stick to deep sea fishing in Florida. Ice fishing doesn't sound attractive to me."

The road made a turn to the northwest at Bay View, and started across a causeway with a drawbridge in the middle. At the other side the roadway climbed a hill, crossing over the railway, then curved slightly toward a couple of intersections. "Normally I'd turn here, for Danbury and take the lower back road to Marblehead – the farm is just off that road – but we'll go on to the Gables and have lunch and then come back," Webster told them. At the intersection with another state highway he turned right, and continued across another intersection. "Cheese Haven," he said, as they passed a large store on the southwest corner. "Best place around for good party food. Boaters like to stock up there." After crossing Route 163 and a small stretch of land onto Catawba Island, the realtor explained, "This really isn't an island now, but it used to be. They've filled in for the road in several places. But this is a wonderful farming area, especially for fruit and grapes, and there are lots of wineries out here, and fruit farms. There are a lot of fruit trees on that farm of yours, Mrs. Atwater. But I don't think anyone has taken much care of them for the last few years. You may have to do a bit of pruning to get them back in shape. Gosh, it would be good to have someone keep up that place. It is really nice."

"I thought there were tenants there," Peggy replied.

"Well, it's a long story. Jesse Lambert lived there most of her life. When she got to be quite feeble her daughter, Jessica, and her husband, Jim Wilson, came out to take care of Old Jesse. The two brothers helped when the fruit trees needed picking in the fall, but they moved away, and the Wilsons stayed on until old Jim Wilson died, about eight years ago. Your daddy never raised their rent, and Jessica stayed on until about a year ago, when she went into a nursing home over by Toledo, but she arranged to pay the rent until she died, so she could keep her things here. She'll come back a few times in the summer, but only stay a night or two. Last time I saw her, I didn't think she'd live long. Her own daughter and grandchildren live in Chicago, so they don't want the place or anything in it."

The dining room at The Gables overlooked a small bay and some docks where large cabin cruisers and fishing boats were docked. Webster recommended the Lake Erie walleye, and Bob seconded the recommendation. With a local white Catawba wine and some local cherry pie for dessert, the meal was excellent.

"I can see I'm really going to enjoy this area," Peggy said to Sally as they got back into Webster's Cadillac. "It's beautiful out here, and not as humid as Waycross."   "Almost always a breeze out here," Webster said, as if he was building up the area for a sale. "Even mild in the winter."

"I'll bet!" Dexter laughed. "I've been out on Marblehead in the winter, Webster. Don't forget, I grew up in Northern Ohio. I've seen snow six feet deep out here, and the Lake all frozen over."

"Good for ice fishing!" the optimistic realtor replied. "But, yes, it can get cold sometimes." Webster turned east on Route 163. Traffic was fairly light, and they covered the six miles to Marblehead in about ten minutes. The real estate agent pointed out the road to East Harbor State Park, and the Lakeside Resort, then the Neuman ferry dock to Kelley's Island. When he got through the little village of Marblehead, he pulled in at the driveway for the old lighthouse and parked so that the four young people could see the historic old white and red structure, the oldest operating lighthouse on the Great Lakes. In the far distance to the east Webster pointed out the amusement park at Cedar Point. After a few minutes at the water's edge the group climbed back into the Cadillac and Webster continued south to Bay Drive, then exited on a back road, finally coming to a driveway with a weather-beaten sign reading Bay View Farm. The gate was open, and he drove down the weedy driveway until the stone farmhouse came into view, with Sandusky Bay and a small island visible just beyond it. The barn and other outbuildings seemed somewhat dilapidated.

"What a view," Bob exclaimed. "This place looks fantastic."

"Although a bit run down," Peggy added. "But I can see why the family never sold it. It's such a great location."

"That it is, Mrs. Atwater," the realtor replied as he pulled up in front of the house.

"Come on and see the inside. I have the key here."

* * *

Jimmy Garth sat on the edge of his bed in the Seashore Motel on Clearwater Beach, planning his next move. He'd been with Elias Ward and Jay Plunkett when they had found the wrecked Mexican cargo vessel that had attempted to evade the Union blockade at Hog Island. Ward and Plunkett had found nothing of much value, just some crockery, a few boxes containing ammunition, some crates of a Spanish designed rifle, but they all doubted that they would be of much value. Plunkett and Ward seemed quite philosophic about the gamble, and Ward felt his money in the venture was worthwhile. Plunkett had resumed his dredging and salvage business, and Garth had found an excuse to quit, at least for the spring fishing season.

What neither Plunkett nor Ward knew was that Garth had indeed found what Ward suspected might be on the Mexican vessel He'd told Ward that the bottom of the bow hull had been ripped out of the wreck, and that the hull was sitting in sand. That was true. But he had seen some sort of shelf at the back of the hold, up high out of Ward's sight, where a number of casks were stored. Part of the shelf had collapsed, and one of the casks had fallen in the sand and cracked open. Garth had seen that it contained coins, probably, he guessed from the discussion, Mexican gold pesos.

Now he had about completed his plans for retrieving the kegs or barrels, whatever they contained. He had leased a motor launch from a marina in Tarpon Springs and had purchased the necessary diving gear, a motorized winch, and other equipment. He was almost ready to head for the Hog Island location, but a slight infection on his foot had caused him to delay.

* * *

It was about two weeks later. Sally had finished up all of the arrangements for Dr. Fairchild's summer tour group to Europe, and she had invited Richie and Esther Fairchild to join Bob and her and the Atwaters for dinner that evening, a Friday. Peggy had been in Toledo selecting furniture for the Sandusky house, having borrowed Bob's car, and got home just a few minutes before Dexter returned from a day at the hospital in Sandusky.

"Thank goodness I didn't have to work late tonight. It was surprising for a Friday afternoon. Usually there are a lot of accidents with people piling out to the islands for the weekends. I guess the rainy weather forecast for this weekend kept them home."

"Maybe, but don't count on it, Dex," Bob replied. "Are you on call?"

"Only for a heart attack or stroke case they can't handle. I'd better go get dressed if you're having company for supper, Sally. Who did you say was coming?"

"Dr. Fairchild and his wife – our boss at the college," Sally replied. "You may have met him at our wedding – he's the one who assisted at the service."

"Oh yes, I recall now. Distinguished looking man. I'll get going here, and Peggy and I will be down as soon as possible."

The Fairchilds arrived before Dexter and Peggy came down. They had brought a couple bottles of Chateau Kent wine from the college's winery on West Bass Island. Bob had just opened one of them and was pouring six glassfuls when the Atwaters entered the room, and he introduced them to Richard and Esther. "This is some of our West Bass wine, Dex," Bob explained. "You're probably used to French wines, but...."

"French? I couldn't afford Thunderbird!" Dexter replied, tasting the yellow wine in the tall stemmed glass. "Say, this is good. A bit on the sweet side, but tasty."

"What is West Bass?" Peggy inquired.

Sally replied, "It's an island in Lake Erie about eighteen miles northwest of Catawba Island, and the college has an inn and winery out there. We'll tell you that story some time, about how Bob and Dr. Fairchild found skeletal remains and a Nazi spy ring, and the pot of gold at the end of the rainbow out there a few years back."

"What!" Peggy laughed. "You're kidding."

"Well, no, not really," Esther answered. "All four of us were there when it happened."

"I remember something about that," Dexter said. "The old mansion on the cliff was owned by the railroad or some outfit as a resort, and the college bought it after the owners were arrested. Wasn't the gold from the War of 1812, or something."

"Yes, that's basically it. A German metallurgist had found records of a sunken British ship with a cargo of gold while doing research at Cambridge, and used it to finance fascist enterprises. Bob's really the one that turned up the facts in his own research at Oxford, Cambridge and at Lloyd's, in London."

"Sally said you were some sort of detective, Dr. Fairchild. Do you do a lot of detective work?" Dexter asked.

"First, Dexter, forget the 'doctor,' or I'll have to call you 'Doc Atwater'! All of them call me Richie. But to answer your question, no, I'm not much of a detective, but I'm curious about things, so I occasionally stumble on something that may have involved a crime. But I have to be careful, or Esther and Dean Harding at the college with have my toy tin badge taken away."

"He's constantly getting shot at or beaten up, or someone's breaking into the house," Esther confirmed. "It's a real nuisance. But I might as well try to turn him into a puppy dog as to get him to quit digging into old mysteries he encounters."

"Peggy," Sally said getting up from her chair, "tell Richie and Esther about your two houses while I check on that roast in the oven."

Peggy started her story explaining about her family and the S&G Railway, and how her great grandfather had owned two houses, one in Sandusky, and the one on Marblehead. Fairchild listened very intently, and asked a few questions about the houses and their locations. By the time Peggy finished he story, Sally had the dinner on the table, and the others moved into the dining room. Dr. Fairchild said the blessing, and they started passing the dishes, several of vegetables, mashed potatoes and gravy, and a big pork roast around the table.

"That Johnson Island, just beyond your farm on the peninsula, is an interesting place. Lots of legends about it," Richard Fairchild said.

"Wasn't it a prison or something during the Civil War?" Bob asked. "I seem to recall some legend about the cemetery."

"Yes," Fairchild replied. "There's about two hundred Confederate soldiers buried out there. There's a bronze statue of a Confederate soldier in the graveyard. Most of the Marblehead peninsula was owned by a man named Johnson, including that island. He was one of the partners in the stone quarrying business that grew on the peninsula – it's still in operation, and even expanded over to Kelley's Island. Well," Fairchild continued, after chewing a bite of meat and noting that he had an audience, "after the Civil War the island just sat there, but around the turn of the century a resort was opened on it, with a little boat that took people there. Then the quarry company decided to quarry some of the stone on the island, and sometime after 1910 the company hired some Sicilian stone cutters to work out there. During one fierce storm in March – it may have been, oh, 1912 or 1915, I'm not sure – the stonecutters were afraid their barracks was going to blow away, and they went out to the cemetery.

"They were gathered around the statue when they heard a bugle call, and saw the ghosts of the Confederate prisoners rise up out of their graves and march across the Bay to the South."

"Oh, go on!" Dexter laughed. "You're making that up!"

"No, that's the story I heard, too," Bob confirmed. "The stonecutters left the very next day and refused to return."

"Somebody later went and got over 200 Georgia granite stone markers for each of the graves," Fairchild added, "but of course the troops had gone home by then...."

"Oh, pooh!" Sally said. "But I, too, recall some tale about the island during the Civil War. Something to do with John Brown."

"Yes," Fairchild said. "I'd forgotten that story. It's a long one. Let's wait until after supper, and I'll see if I can remember the details."

The conversation switched to the food Sally had prepared and her recipes. A big apple pie and coffee followed the dinner, and the three women insisted on the men moving to the living room while they cleaned up the dishes. Finally they all gathered in the living room, and Dexter reminded the professor that he was going to finish the story about Johnson Island.

"Okay," Richard Fairchild said, "but I may be off on a few of the dates and names. Actually, there are a number of stories, and I suspect that what I've heard or read may well be a combination of some of them. Anyway, after the Civil War began and the Union troops started to make some progress against the Confederacy, they captured some officers and their men. Most of these were wealthy plantation owners, not professional soldiers like Lee, but they were very important to the South. Union contracts to build a prison on the island were drawn in the fall of 1861, to be finished within a year. It was then decided to put any captured officers or civilian spies in the Johnson Island prison, because it was to be considered almost impossible to escape from it. Nevertheless, there were many attempts, and many plots, and, I understand, more than a few successful escapes. While the winters were dangerous because of the cold, once the ice froze, one could actually walk ashore from the island. Hence there were an awful lot of guards posted there. It was an Ohio Volunteer Infantry company, as I recall, that was assigned to guard it. Later the Navy also sent a gunboat to help guard against any plots.

"I don't recall exactly when John Brown's son moved to the islands, but sometime after his father's famous slave revolt attempt at Harper's Ferry in 1859, John, Junior, moved to Put-In-Bay. Because of his martyred father, he was quite well known around Northern Ohio, and was often called on as a speaker. He apparently was a friend of Jay Cooke, and lived at Cooke's estate on Gibraltar Island in the Bay. Anti-slavery sentiments ran high in Northern Ohio.

"As I said, there were a number of plots to free the prisoners on Johnson Island. In one, the prisoners were to be armed after escape, and operate as a raiding force southward through Ohio on their way back to the Confederacy. But the best known of the plots was that involving the steamship Philo Parsons, and the plan to capture the Union gunboat Michigan that guarded Sandusky Bay. A Confederate major, I think his name was Cole, came to Sandusky and got a room at a big house there called West House. There he met with two co-conspirators, a woman named Annie, and a man named Beall. Beall was some sort of officer in the Confederate Navy. He, in turn, met with some Scotsman named Burley, who supposedly had brought plans for a submarine from Scotland. He was also known to be familiar with the mining of harbors.

"Cole became friendly with a Captain Carter, who commanded the Union warship, Michigan. He spent a lot of money on food and wine for the crew, and was given free run of the vessel in return. But the plan involved three vessels, not just the Union gunboat. The Parsons ran a regular route between Detroit, the Lake Erie islands, and Sandusky. Beall and the Scotsman, Burley, boarded the Parsons at Detroit, and booked passage to Kelley's Island, which is just north of Marblehead. However, Burley told the captain that he wanted to stop at a Canadian port on the way to meet some friends. The captain agreed, but said they couldn't bring any luggage, as there were no Customs agents at Kelley's Island. However, one brought a large box with him.

"The Parsons stopped at Put-In-Bay and then Middle Bass Island next. While there, Burley informed the captain, who was going to leave the ship in command of his first mate, that he decided to go to Sandusky instead of Kelley's Island. Meanwhile, a small ferry that served the islands and also transported prisoners out to Johnson Island, the Island Queen, was approaching. Burley and the men picked up in Canada opened their chest, which was full of guns, and commandeered the Parsons. When the Island Queen came close, they captured it as well, forcing male passengers into the hold of the Parsons, releasing the women and children. They shot one of the crew members when he refused to surrender. Later they scuttled the ferryboat, but it grounded on a reef and was salvaged later.

"Meanwhile, Cole was aboard the Michigan. The plan was that following the big dinner party he had given for the crew, with lots of wine, when Cole saw the Parsons he was supposed to light a signal, then take over the gunboat. However, Captain Carter had received a telegram earlier warning that there might be a plot, and he had sent an officer to inspect Cole's room at the West House. The officer returned with some papers that Carter considered suspicious, so he had Cole arrested before he could give the signal.

"By now it was after ten at night. Beall and Burley awaited the signal from Cole, but it never came. Beall considered going ahead with the plan anyway, but procrastinated. What he did not know was that John Brown, Jr., had witnessed some of what was happening at Put-In-Bay, and had rowed over to Marblehead, crossed the peninsula, and rowed another boat to Johnson Island, alerting Colonel Hill, who was then commander of the prison, that there might be a prison break planned. The prison guards were ready, but the attack never came. Beall abandoned the Parsons, and the passengers were released unharmed. Cole got to Johnson Island all right, but as a prisoner. Beall was captured at Niagara Falls and was later hung as a spy at Governor's Island in New York. Burley was arrested in Canada and extradited to the United States, but was never tried. What happened to Annie, nobody is sure."

"Good heavens, Richie," Dexter exclaimed, "that's quite a tale. How do you remember it all?"

"About ten years ago I gave a talk to a local historical society in Port Cleland, and they wanted to know something about the islands, so I researched that story and told it."

"That calls for a drink," Bob said. "Brandy, everyone?"

Chapter 5

It was a Saturday, about a month later. Peggy, with Sally's assistance, had selected most of the furnishings for the big Sandusky house, and after what carpeting was to be installed and new rugs put down, the furniture was being delivered. The Fairchilds were still out of the country, and Bob had the professor's permission to borrow the truck to transport the items Dexter and Peggy had at the Merriam's to their home in Sandusky. The Atwaters were now ready to move into their new home

While Bob and Dexter moved the last few items up to the master bedroom, Sally and Peggy went to the grocery store for all the things Peggy would need in her kitchen, including enough for a dinner that evening.

"We'll need to get a barbecue grill for the back," Peggy said, as they stacked four steaks in the basket. "These would be a lot better grilled over charcoal."

"They'll still be good, and I'll whip up a salad for us," Sally replied.

After Bob and Dexter completed their tasks and Dexter had unloaded all the clothes from their suitcases and Peggy's steamer trunk, Dexter said, "I guess we should put the luggage in the attic." He got out the key to the doors, and tried the smaller one Webster had given him in the door at the back of the hallway closet. A click indicated that the real estate agent was correct.

Both men expected that there would not be much light in the attic, except for that from two dormer windows at the front of the house, but were surprised to find an electric light switch. There were several lights in the large room at the top of the stairs extending from a beam in the ceiling. At the back of the attic, opposite the two dormer windows, were several cots. There were only two small, narrow unopenable windows on that side of the attic, but there were iron bars across them.

"It looks like this was used as a bedroom or a dormitory," Dexter said. "Perhaps there were children, and Old Fitzgibbons was afraid they'd fall out."

"Interesting," Bob answered, looking around at the sparse room, which had only a table with no drawers in it. "Whoever lived up here must not have had much clothing. There's not even a place to hang up a shirt."

"Yes. Let's see what else is up here." On the other side of the attic by the dormer windows was a large chest. There was a combination padlock on it. The chest was heavy and the lock quite secure. "I doubt we'd ever find the combination to that lock," Dexter said. "Let's carry the chest downstairs, and get Peggy's okay to open it."

The two men struggled a bit to get the chest down the attic stairs and out into the hallway. Then, before turning off the lights, they carried the steamer trunk and suitcases up and put them in a handy corner of the attic. They did not lock the attic door again as they came down, but carried the heavy chest down to the parlor. The two women arrived just as they set the chest down.

"What have you two been up to?" Sally asked as she and Peggy carried bags of groceries into the kitchen, and the two men went out to the car to retrieve the remaining bags. "You look all dusty."

"We've been exploring the attic," Bob replied. "It's dusty up there."

"What did you find?" Peggy asked.

"It's like a dormitory," Dexter answered. "Four cots without bedding, and a table. But there are bars on the inside of the dormer windows. It's at the back. There's not much in the front part, but we found a padlocked chest. We hauled it down and put it in the parlor."

"What's in it?" Peggy inquired.

"We don't know. We were waiting for your permission to break the lock off." "Well, sure! Why don't you two get the lock off while Sally and I get dinner? Then, after we eat, we can see what's in there."

One of Dexter's possessions was a fairly extensive tool kit. After examining the lock and hasps for it he decided that it would be best to saw off the lock rather than tear off the hasps, perhaps damaging the chest. The chest itself was wood, with brass straps and hinges, and was in excellent condition.

"It's probably well over a hundred years old," Dexter said. "At least as old as the house."

"No doubt. It looks like one of those old sea chests you see in pirate movies. Maybe the old man was a pirate, like some of the stories you've been hearing about him. Perhaps his ghost is up there in that attic!"

"I don' know. Maybe he was a pirate. After all, he had that hotel down on the Gulf of Mexico, and supposedly traveled a lot. Bob, you know a lot about the history of this area. Were there any pirates around here?"

"Oh, I'm sure there were. The Lake has been a channel of transportation and shipping for a couple hundred years, so it is likely that a bit of piracy has occurred. Just a couple of years ago Richie Fairchild was involved in a case that turned out to be piracy."

"Really? What happened?"

"Some corporate executive was stealing money, the way I understood it, and arranged to have the company's tanker ship stolen and hidden so that he could somehow profit from the chemicals aboard it and make an insurance claim. It resulted in the murder of some poor homeless guy with bad feet, and Richie solved the whole thing and found the stolen ship, but he almost got killed himself."

"Good heavens! I don't think Sally told me about that. I did hear about the Nazi gold you guys found on some island, however. Well," Dexter added, "let's get to work." The two took turns sawing at the loop of the lock, which was made of brass and quite thick. When they had sawed about three fourths of the way through Dexter took a sharp screwdriver, put the point in the cut, and hit it with a hammer. The metal cracked, and the lock split open. At that very moment Sally called that dinner was ready.

* * *

The sun was close to setting when the four young people finished the dishes and got back to the parlor to explore the contents of the chest. Peggy got some rags and wiped all the dust off it, revealing a fine wood finish underneath. The lid, however, seemed stuck. Examination of the hinges on the back showed that they were slightly rusted, and with a little machine oil, Dexter was finally able to pry open the top. Inside were several old, worn blankets, eight sets of what appeared to be leg irons with locks attached, an envelope with small keys to the locks in it, a second small envelope, a leather holster with a Colt revolver and a box of bullets, two large ledger books, and a packet of letters wrapped with a string.

"Good heavens!" Peggy exclaimed when she saw the contents. "Whatever was he doing up there?"

"Maybe these letters or the ledgers will tell us," Bob suggested. He opened one of the books and found in easily readable handwriting a listing:

May 14, 1858 "Roger" for Henry Mawson, Douglas, $125 if sound
May 22, 1858 "Jim" and "Joe," for Jack Dawson, Bristol, $250
May 28, 1858 "Jingo," (14, house boy) James Blake, Alma, $75
June 1, 1858 "Charlie," Jackson Willson, Waycross, $180
June 7, 1858 "Billie + Sal," Geo. Perrin, Bickley, $160 the pair
June 8, 1858 "Dessie," (cook), Daniel Argile, Talmo, $80
June 12, 1858, $150 Capt. Harper

The list went on, page after page, but ended in November of 1859. There were fewer entries during the months of November, 1858 through March or 1859. The second ledger book was similar, but with dates between 1857 and 1858.

In the back of the newer of the two ledgers was an envelope, labeled The Bank of Hamilton. Inside was a small key.

"I wonder what that is for?" Dexter said.

"Maybe Daddy knows," Peggy answered. "I'll write him tomorrow and ask." "What do you suppose those entries in the ledger are?" Sally asked.

"I remember Granddad saying that his father had been some sort of agent," Peggy said, "but I can't imagine what this would be."

"An agent?" Bob said. "He was from Georgia?"

"Yes, Waycross."

"These dates are all prior to the Civil War," Bob said. "They stop in late November of 1859, and the firing on Fort Sumter was in April of 1860, so maybe it had something to do with the War."

"When was the Dred Scott decision, Bob?" Dexter asked.

"I believe it was in 1857. After that it was legal to transport captured run-away slaves back to their owners. It was quite a defeat to the abolitionists, and there were plenty of them around this area."

"Maybe that's what all this represents," Sally said. "Peggy, maybe your great grand-father was taking runaway slaves back to their masters in Georgia."

"That would certainly fit with the dates and names and places," Peggy agreed. "And it would explain the leg irons and locks."

"Hey," Bob exclaimed, having just turned the envelope with the small key in it over, "what's this scribbled on the back?" The lettering looked like $\delta\Phi\Sigma\Omega\gamma\lambda\sigma\psi\beta\pi$. "It appears to be Greek."

"Do you read Greek?" Dexter asked.

"No, but Richie does. If he were here, he would probably be able to deduce much more from all this."

"It must explain about the key," Peggy added. "Maybe it is to someplace in Greece."

"Maybe the letters will tell us what all this is about," Sally suggested. Peggy agreed, and opened the first, which was addressed to James Fitzgibbons, Peggy's great grandfather. The date was June 3, 1859. She read it aloud.

> Dear Jimmy,
>
> I have missed you so very much since you have been up North. I look forward to each of your trips down once a month, and now that Delbert is home from the Academy, we are looking forward to going back with you next month. I'm sure it will be much cooler there than here.
>
> Silas, at the office, says that you are getting lots of new orders, and all at good prices, too. The crops are good this spring, and the men will be needed. But everybody thinks that if things don't change, there might

be a war. Delbert says he'd definitely fight if it came to that.

Nanny Sue said she heard that Farnsworth Gilbert's houseman and the woman he lived with had fled north, but only got to Macon before they were caught and sent back. Nanny Sue said Gilbert said he hadn't the heart to whip them, but I don't think they'll try it again. Don't know how so many make it as far as Ohio.

Jimmy, Silas says that progress on the new line to Branford from White Springs is nearly finished. Says you'll be able to dedicate it next time you're down. I know you're anxious to open that new stretch.

Margaret Mae said to tell you Auburn Hendricks broke his leg when his horse threw him a week ago. The doctor set it, but he's hobbling around town on a stick. You'll want to pay him a visit when you get back down.

I'll get this off in the post, now, Jimmy. Oh, how I miss you and wish you were here with me. I count the days until your next trip down.

All my love, Annamarie

"I seem to recall that Annamarie was my great aunt, his sister," Peggy explained. "What she says sure seems to support our theory that he was bringing back runaways." "I wonder who Delbert was," Dexter added.

"I'm not sure, but I remember hearing about some relative named Delbert who was killed in the Battle of Atlanta. I don't think my great grandfather was married then, or old enough to have a teenaged son in 1859, but it might have been a younger brother, or maybe Annamarie's and James's cousin."

"You have quite a family tree, Peggy," Bob said. "I'd like to hear more about it." "I'll write to Dad and Mom tomorrow and see what I can find out. Bob, maybe you could show that envelope and key to Dr. Fairchild, and see what he says about it."

* * *

Richard and Esther Fairchild were exhausted after their European trip with sixteen students. Their return flight from London had been delayed by fog, and was eight hours late in arriving in Chicago. By then they had missed their 6 p.m. United connecting flight from O'Hare to Toledo, and elected to return by train. New York Central's Train 90 left Chicago at 9:30 that evening, but arrived in Toledo at three in the morning. By the time they had located a taxi that would take them to the airport where their car was parked, the sun was already rising. It was four days before the Professor returned to his office to officially write up the tour.

Sally waited a few more days before showing the strange envelope full of keys to Dr. Fairchild. "It's definitely Greek letters," he agreed. "But it isn't a word or phrase. It's just gibberish. Where is this Bank of Hamilton?"

"We don't know," Sally replied. She had explained to him about the ledger books and the letters, and the contents of the trunk, including shackles, and he agreed with their theory that Peggy's great grandfather may have been in the business of returning run-away slaves. "It could be a bank in Hamilton, Ohio, or maybe in Canada. Isn't there a Hamilton, Ontario?"

"Yes, and the Confederates did have a number of Canadian contacts." Fairchild placed the envelope on his desk and reached over to his bookshelf for an atlas. He paged to the index, and added, "But there is no Hamilton in Georgia. A bank in Southern Ohio doesn't seem to make much sense. Of course, the bank could be named for a person, like Alexander Hamilton. Hmm. Sally, your cousins' house intrigues me. I've got a few weeks' vacation due. If you had any additional information I'd take a look into the situation to see what I could find. But there are just not enough details."

"I think Dex and Peggy would appreciate that. Peggy wrote to her dad about what we found, but he had no information at all. He said he didn't think his grandfather kept any of his old records in Waycross, but that there might be some in the old depot at the dock in Branford, Florida. He said he'd look the next time he was down there, and send Peggy anything he found."

* * *

It was three weeks before any further information was received, in the form of a package Peggy from her father containing a number of old documents and letters that he said he had found in his grandfather's desk in the old railroad depot. That weekend the Merriams and the Atwaters again got together, and reviewed the material in the package. There were a few letters similar to the ones that had been in the trunk, but the only item that might have had any bearing on the envelope was an old steamer routing ticket booking passage for two persons from Halifax to Bermuda, beginning November 28, 1864. The voyage was booked in first class aboard the British Atlantic Line's Castle Harbor. There was no further indication of any travel from Bermuda.

"Bermuda," Bob said. "The capital of Bermuda is Hamilton. Maybe that is where the bank is."

"And the key is to a lock box?" Dexter added. "But would it still be there a hundred years later?"

"Won't know if we don't check," Bob replied. But can any of us take the time to fly out to Bermuda to look into this?"

"Dr. Fairchild said he had some vacation time and would like to look into this if we had more information. Maybe this is something he'd be willing to investigate."

"He really does investigate things?" Peggy asked.

"Yes, and he sometimes draws Sally and me into his digging around as well. He calls it research! He's been shot and beaten and everything else because of his investigating, but I can't see how he'd get hurt on this kind of a puzzle."

"Shot?" Peggy exclaimed. "Good gracious!"

Chapter 6

**August 11, 1963
Toronto, Ontario, Airport**

"Richie, I never thought you'd want to fly anywhere else this summer," Esther Fairchild said as the two travelers stood in the line to have their passports checked. "You're really making this trip just to please Sally's cousin?"

"Well, no, not entirely. A week on the beach at Southampton will be relaxing before the semester begins again. And besides, we both deserve a treat. You work as hard as I do on those class trips."

"That's true enough," she said as she handed her green U.S. passport to the customs agent. He looked at it, and his eyebrows went up.

"You've certainly been traveling, Mrs. Fairchild," he said. "Even East Germany!"

"When you're married to a professor who can't sit still for ten minutes, yes, one does a lot of travel," she laughed.

"And you're the professor?" the agent asked as he took Fairchild's passport, noting identical entries. "Where do you teach?"

"Fremont College, in Ohio," the professor answered.

"Really! I have a cousin who went there. She took a trip last year with a group of religion students to East Germany. By any chance...."

"Kathy Steward?"

"Yes! So you're that professor she fell madly in love with?"

"She did?" Esther asked. "More likely it was either Bob Merriam or Ross Johnson, the choral director, who was single then. Kathy did sing in the opera."

"It is a small world indeed!" the agent laughed. "Yes, she can't stop talking about being on the stage for that opera. It must have been an exciting moment."

"More than she'll ever know!" the Professor replied, not telling the agent that it was also the scene of the defection of two high-level East German officials.

* * *

Lunch was served aboard the 10:40 a.m. Trans-Canada flight, which arrived at Bermuda's airport near St. George by two that afternoon. A tourist bus transported the Fairchilds and their luggage westward over another island to their hotel on Southampton, and by five they had unpacked and taken a stroll down to the beach.

Sally had given Richard Fairchild the envelope with the key in it. The following morning he and Esther boarded the local bus and rode into the town of Hamilton. While Esther went shopping along the waterfront and King's Square, the Professor looked up banks in the phone directory. There were a number of British and other European banks, a few American branch banks, the Royal Bank of Bermuda, and a Bank of Hamilton, located on Duke of Clarence Street. He asked directions, and soon found an old building that appeared to be at least early 19th century. The door was locked, but he could see people inside, and tapped on the glass.

"I'm sorry, we don't open until eleven this morning," a clerk said through the glass. It was still half an hour. Fairchild turned and wandered down the street to kill time. Sharply at eleven he was back at the door, and the same clerk, an elderly, balding man, was just unlocking it. "Sorry to have made you wait," he repeated. "But most of our business is by appointment. If you're looking for foreign exchange, I'm afraid I'll have to refer you to the Royal."

"No," Fairchild replied. "Actually I'm looking for information about a possible account that might have existed here about a hundred years ago."

"One hundred years ago! Good Lord, man! Why on earth...."

"Your bank didn't exist then?"

"Well, yes it did, but...."

"So may I see a manager and discuss it with him."

"Certainly. And whom may I say is inquiring?"

"Dr. Richard Fairchild. I'm a college professor in Ohio."

The clerk led the professor into the bank, which had only one old-fashioned caged window, and tapped on a glass paneled wooden door that had a name painted on the frosted glass – George Cliverson. A younger man, also balding, dressed in a shirt and tie, but wearing Bermuda shorts and long stockings, arose, conversing with the clerk.

"Dr. Fairchild? I'm George Cliverson, the vice president of the bank. What may I do for you?" he asked, pointing to a wooden armchair that sat in front of his desk. The elderly clerk turned and moved toward another office.

"Mr. Cliverson," Fairchild began, removing the small key from his shirt pocket, "I have some reason to believe that this key may be to a lock box at your bank. It may date to the year 1864. I wonder if you could verify that for me."

"Gracious! Our records go back a long way, but.... Here, let me examine the key." He took the small key in his hand and turned it around several times. On it was embossed a tiny number, '472-C.' "By Jove," he remarked, "I believe this might be one of our keys. I've never seen one before, but I heard that prior to the Great War in 1914 that we had coded accounts that were accessible only by a key and a code word selected by the customer. But those records are all in storage in our vault. Perhaps if you could come back this afternoon, or better yet, tomorrow morning, I will have one of the clerks look into it."

"Certainly," Fairchild replied. "My wife and I will be here for several days, and that would be convenient. I do appreciate your agreeing to look into this."

"May I ask how you acquired this key?" Cliverson asked.

"It belongs to the cousin of one of my associates. They have asked me to look into the origin of this key that they found in an old house they inherited in Sandusky, Ohio."

"Most interesting. And Harold said you were a professor? Also in Ohio?"

"Yes, I am Professor of Religions at Fremont College."

"You have been to Bermuda before?"

"Several times. The first time was during the War, when our Army transport landed here for refueling. I vowed to come back and enjoy what I saw from the air."

"I, too, was in the War, Professor. We are a British colony, you know, and had our own regiment in France under Montgomery. Why don't you, and your wife, if you wish, come at eleven tomorrow, and perhaps we can go to lunch and talk about our experiences? And if we can find any trace of your account, there may be other things to discuss as well."

"Fine. Tomorrow, at eleven," Fairchild agreed, arising from the chair and extending his hand to the bank official.

* * *

From their agreed meeting place for lunch the Fairchilds elected to take a bus to the town of St. George's Harbor rather than to risk riding the narrow roads on motor scooters. They walked along the shops on the harbor, and visited the ruins of an old church. It was after six when they returned to their hotel on Southampton, but the sun was still shining and they went for a swim in the warm ocean before dressing for dinner.

Promptly at eleven the next morning they were back at the bank, being escorted into George Cliverson's office. Cliverson was a tall man, and rose to shake hands.

"I have some good news, perhaps," he said.

"Perhaps?" Fairchild inquired.

"Yes, we found a coded account with the number 472-C, but the lock boxes in which those accounts were kept were stored only by a code selected by the customer. It was a security measure used at the time, apparently due to political reasons. Sort of like the Swiss numbered accounts today. We would have to have the secret code to find the actual box or container, and that is not on the card with the numbers."

"Was there a name on the account?"

"Yes. James Fitzgibbons."

"That is the name of owners of the key. Might it be under the name 'Fitzgibbons'?"

"We checked that. There was no such box. No 'J.F.' either."

Fairchild had written the Greek letters that were on the envelope that held the key on a separate slip of paper. He removed it from his pocket, and handed it to the banker who looked at it: $\delta\Phi\Sigma\Omega\gamma\lambda\sigma\psi\beta\pi$. "Could that be the code?" Fairchild asked.

"It might be," Cliverson replied. "Let's go down to the vault and look. There are quite a few containers left there, but I seem to recall seeing one with Greek letters." A back stairway led down to the basement. There were a number of rooms along a hallway, and Cliverson unlocked a door behind which was a large vault with several layers of steel plating. It appeared the door simply enclosed a large room built into the foundation, but the plating may have also surrounded the floor, ceiling and walls. There were a number of additional safes inside the vault. At the very back of the room on shelves were stacked a great number of locked containers of various sizes. It was dark in that part of the vault and Cliverson turned on a flashlight he had brought with him to review the various containers. In a second row, toward the bottom he spotted what he was looking for, and exclaimed, "Here!" The fading lettering on the identification label was partly worn away, but the first part was "$\delta\Phi\Sigma\Omega...$," just like the Greek letters on the envelope. The container was not extremely large. But it was necessary to move all of the other containers on top of it to get at it. Fairchild assisted Cliverson, and in a few minutes the container was free. Cliverson lifted it and said, "It requires two keys. I have one, and if the key you brought yesterday fits, then you may open the container. We have a room where you may do that. Let's carry the box there and try our keys."

Cliverson led the Fairchilds to a small room with a table just outside the door leading to the vault, which he again locked, and placed the box on the table. Cliverson put the bank's key in the double lock; it easily turned. He then took the key Richard Fairchild had provided and inserted it in the lock. He slowly twisted it, and with a click the lid partially opened.

"So far, so good, Dr. Fairchild. It looks like this is your container. I will leave you now to review the contents. When you have finished, just push that button on the wall, there," he said, pointing at what appeared to be a doorbell. "We'll come let you out. But I fear I may also have some bad news for you."

"Bad news?" Esther Fairchild repeated.

"Yes, there may be a few pounds rent due."

"Ahh, yes. I had anticipated that," the Professor replied. "I hope whatever is in this box will be worth it."

As Cliverson closed the door and returned to his office Fairchild lifted the lid on the container and looked inside. There were several journals, some very similar to the type of journal that Sally's cousin had showed him in Sandusky, and in the same handwriting, but they were written in French. There were also several official-appearing documents, with wax seals, now slightly crumbling. Two were in French and one in Spanish. The only other item in the box was a copy of a receipt, also in French, and a single sheet of music, folded in a blank envelope. On several of the documents were the words, The Confederate State of America.

"Esther, it's going to take months to translate and decipher these things properly. Let's ring the bell, go to lunch with Cliverson – perhaps we can talk him out of his rental charges – and take these back with us. I'm going to need some sort of leather case to put them in. I don't want to just pack them in my suitcase. I have a feeling that these are some very valuable papers. I wonder what the music is."

* * *

Once back in Ohio Fairchild presented the material to Dexter and Peggy Atwater with his offer to translate the journals, if they so wished. They were delighted with the offer, and asked that he proceed. They also offered to reimburse the Fairchild's their travel expenses and the $182 dollars in bank storage charges they had paid, but the Professor refused. Fairchild began the task of translating the journals at his farm. He suspected that they had been written in French to keep them confidential. Many educated Southerners had been trained in French, Greek and Latin in the nineteenth century, he knew, and it was likely that this was a foreign language in which the writer – if it was Fitzgibbons – may have communicated with any foreigners. But Fairchild was not certain. Perhaps there was another reason that French and Spanish were the languages of the documents. Fairchild knew he could easily translate the French documents, but he got Peggy Atwater's permission to refer the Spanish document to the Fremont College Spanish professor, Dr. Anna Garcia. The French was clearly written. Where the author had not known the French word he had substituted English.

Chapter 7

August 27, 1963
Dr. Fairchild's Office
Fremont College

Richard Fairchild began work on the journal and document translations, but quickly realized that with the amount of detail they contained, it would take months. The school year was about to start, and both he and Associate Professor Robert Merriam were busy lining up their classes for the semester. Classes were scheduled to start September 14, and there was always a lot of work to do before Labor Day.

In the morning mail letters arrived for both Fairchild and Merriam from the National Association of Religion Academics, in Boston, Massachusetts, of which both were members and Fairchild an officer. They were dated the previous week.

Dear Fellow Professors and Instructors:

The NARA Board of Directors, in an emergency meeting last Tuesday attempted to respond to inquiries from a number of members regarding how to instruct and advise students on the recent translations of the Qumran Library. This is a problem that affects many of our members, and the Board has elected to hold a special open session on the issue prior to the start of the current academic year.

We realize that this is late notice for many of you, and that you probably already have plans for your Labor Day weekend, however, that was about the only time that we could arrange for such a gathering.

Accordingly, the special session will be held in the Alachua Auditorium on the University of Florida campus September 5 beginning at 10 a.m. We apologize for the late notice, but are hopeful that a majority of our members will be in attendance.

Sincerely,
Robin Harper Morris, Ph.D.
Director, NARA

"This is certainly short notice!" Bob Merriam said as he stood in Fairchild's office doorway, the letter in his hand. "Do we go? And if so, how?"

"Yes, I think we should go. Neither of us need another Labor Day picnic. As an officer – I think they elected me vice president of something or other this past year – I feel obligated to be there. And you may as well go, too. We can fly down and rent a car at Tallahassee or Jacksonville or someplace."

"Will the College pick up the costs?"

"Yes, I'll con Dean Harding into it somehow. Let me worry about that. Have your wife book us a flight and car, and maybe a couple nights hotel in Gainesville, the fourth and fifth. That's a holiday weekend, so it will probably be busy."

Sally had overheard the discussion, and had already seen her husband's copy of the letter. She got out her airline guide and found that Eastern Airlines had a flight from Cleveland through Charlotte to Tampa, but not to Jacksonville or Tallahassee. Delta had a connecting flight from Toledo to Atlanta, and on to Jacksonville, and Capital had a Cleveland to Jacksonville flight arriving shortly after noon, with a plane change in Atlanta. A return flight was available at ten in the morning. At $58.70 each way, Fairchild felt that the fares should not bankrupt the departmental budget.

A rental car was also arranged, but finding a hotel was a problem. "There's not a hotel room within fifty miles, the travel agent told me," she explained to Dr. Fairchild the following morning. "There's a big pre-season football game in Gainesville that weekend, and it's also when the parents are bringing the new freshmen for orientation and moving them into their dormitories. But I do have some good news. I talked with Peggy last night, and she called her cousin who runs the hotel down in Suwannee. He said that they will have lots of vacancies that weekend, and that you and Bob are welcome to stay free."

"The Dean would like that price, but isn't that on the coast? It must be a long drive from there to Gainesville."

"Peggy said it was about sixty miles, but the roads are not crowded, and they are all paved. She said it might take you an hour and a half at most each way. Of course you might chance finding a motel somewhere south of Jacksonville, but that is just about as far away."

"Not much choice," Fairchild agreed. "So go ahead and tell Peggy and her cousin we'll stay there, but will still expect a bill."

* * *

The flight to Jacksonville aboard the Capital Viscount prop-jet was comfortable and on time. By the time the two travelers had grabbed a bite of lunch at the airport and signed up for their Avis Rent-a-Car, it was one thirty in the afternoon. Bob agreed to do the driving. The map showed that the best route was west on Route 90 to 301, then south to Gainesville, where they would hunt up the auditorium for the following morning, then west on State Routes 26 and 349 to Fanning Springs, Old Town, and Suwannee.

The North Florida early September heat seemed to create steam as the two religion professors proceeded southwest across the scrub pines and open areas of Duval and Bradford Counties. Part of Route 301 was divided highway, and they stopped at Starke for a Pepsi. By three they were on the University of Florida campus, an expanse of beautiful Florida-style buildings, open areas and green lawns, and had located the auditorium in an older building on the west end of the campus not far from the downtown area. The campus was busy, all the parking lots full, and people seemed to be milling around everywhere. They saw a few banners reading "Go, Gators!"

"Make's Fremont's laid-back campus look puny!" Richard Fairchild commented. "Our freshman orientation doesn't draw crowds like this. Of course this is a state school, so they have to accept all applications."

"And our football games don't attract so much attention, either," Bob replied. "Did you see that van that said 'CBS Sports' on that side street near the stadium? Can you imagine national television covering a Fremont game?"

"Not unless the team was made up of turtles or mice or something."

"Girls?"

"Ha-ha! Someday, Bob, there will be a girls' football team. You watch. Men aren't always going to be the rulers and the athletes. Well, we'd better head for the coast. Looks like a few clouds building to the west."

Bob quickly located Route 26 in the downtown area and headed west, crossing under the new Interstate 75 that ran south from Georgia to the Florida Turnpike. As they passed through Newberry high cumulus clouds gave way to cumulonimbus thunderheads, blocking out the afternoon sun. By the time they turned right onto U.S. 19 at Fanning Springs, crossed the Suwannee at Old Town, and turned south on State Route 349, the sky was almost back, and bolts of lightning were shooting around them.

"Gracious!" Dr. Fairchild exclaimed. "See if you can get anything on the radio."

Merriam fiddled with the dial, getting mostly static. At last he picked up a station out of Ocala, but the voice was frequently blocked by static. "…[I]n the Gulf thirty- five to forty miles northwest of Cedar Key, with sustained winds up to fifty miles per hour and gusts to sixty or higher… [static] easterly direction at twenty to twenty five miles … [more static] …Bureau has issued gale warnings from Anclote Key to Apalachee Bay. The Coast Guard has issued a small craft advisory, and warns commercial shipping to be alert for the possible formation of this tropical storm into a hurricane. The eastern edge... [static] ... and may make landfall by this evening. Heavy rain is... [static]. Stay tuned to WOKL for further bulletins. We return you now to our studio for...."

"Looks like we're in for it, Bob," Fairchild said as a few drops of rain began to hit the windshield. The two-lane road was fairly straight, and Bob accelerated, hoping to reach the hotel before the heavy rains might hit. The road ran mostly south, curving off slightly to the west, with the river never far from the left side of the car. The area surrounding the raised roadway was mostly marsh and swamp, and not infrequently Bob swerved slightly to avoid running over some dead animal or snake that had met its end on the roadway.

"Bet there's lots of alligators out there," he said.

"Yes," Fairchild replied. "The University doesn't call their team the Gators for nothing, I suspect." With that the rain started to fall quickly, drenching the car in wind-blown streams as if shot from a high-power fire hose. Bob turned the wipers on at full speed, and also turned on the headlights, slowing to a crawl as he could barely see the road for the heavy rain and water."

"Can't stop," he said. "This might go on for hours, from what they said, and we ought to be about there."

The road jogged slightly to the southwest, and the rain came at more of an angle toward the car, improving Bob's view very slightly. He had slowed to less than twenty miles per hour, and could feel the car, a new two-door Chevrolet sedan, being buffeted by the winds.

"There's a house," Dr. Fairchild said, pointing to the right side of the car. "We must be getting close." Soon other buildings appeared, and they crossed a small wooden bridge, noting that the water was almost up to the level of the roadway. The road turned to the right, and they found themselves on the main street of the little hamlet. At the far end they saw a sign, HOTEL.

"That must be it," Bob said, pulling up before what appeared to be a ramshackle three-story building with a porch around three sides, and on the two upper levels. "I packed an umbrella, but it's in the luggage in the trunk." "We'll just have to make a dash for it. Be sure to turn off the lights – don't want a run-down battery in the morning," the older man warned. "We can get the luggage later."

Both of them were nearly soaked in just the brief dash from the car to the hotel porch, but the humid air was warm and the interior of the old hotel dry and inviting. An older man met them at the door. "Hell of a storm headed this way, I hear. You gents must be the two from Ohiah my Cousin Patricia said needed rooms."

"Yes," Bob replied. "But you look familiar. You must be Simon. I think I met you at the Fitzgibbons Atwater wedding in Waycross."

"Yep, Simon Fitzgibbons. I remember now. You're Dexter's cousin or something."

"My wife is. He's quite a guy. Getting a good medical practice going in Sandusky."

"Here, let me get you both some towels." Fitzgibbons said. "I've got some shirts upstairs you can try on till yours dry out. We'll get some rain gear and fetch your things later. You kin leave your car there for now."

"Only got a couple other guests this weekend," Fitzgibbons continued as he brought a couple of towels and old shirts down from the second floor. "Couple of fishermen, and some guy from up North who was doin' some diving north of Hog Island and got chased in by the storm warnings."

"Do you get many storms like this?" Fairchild asked.

"Couple gales a year. This'n they think might become a hurricane, but I doubt it will get that strong. Too early in the season. Of course, 'Hurricane Beulah' took a good swipe at the East Coast a week back, but those Atlantic storms usually head out to sea. Our Gulf storms usually go north or west. Almost always something cookin' out in the Gulf at this time of year. Yeah, a few come in shore, but usually blow themselves out quickly," he explained.

The lights were on inside the hotel, and they flickered slightly. "Don't worry," Fitzgibbons continued, "if the power lines come down, as they're apt to, we've got us a big old generator that will keep things runnin'. And the cook stove's gas, so dinner should be right on time. Hope you boys like fish."

"You're singing our song!" Fairchild laughed.

* * *

Clad in a rubber poncho and bare feet with trouser legs rolled up, Bob had gotten back to the car and retrieved the two suitcases from the trunk. He then pulled the car around the side of the hotel to the small parking lot, and paddled his way back into the lobby. After drying himself off and carrying the cases upstairs to the two rooms they had been assigned, he took a hot shower and felt much better.

It was just before dinner that the power failed, and Fitzgibbons moved through the darkened hotel to start the generator. In about five minutes the lights were back on, but with a much lower glow that before. Three other men and a woman were also in the dining room. Two of the men and the woman sat at one table, and the other man, young but rather rough looking with an unkempt beard, joined Fairchild and Merriam at theirs. Fitzgibbons also served as waiter, but there had been no menu. It was either grilled grouper, French fries and cold slaw, with apple pie and coffee, or a hamburger. While the other man selected the hamburger, both of the professors elected the fish dinners.

"Some storm," the man said as they waited to be served. "Like some Nor'easters I've been in."

"Are you from up North?" Bob asked.

"Boston. Did I hear old Fitzgibbons say you two were from Ohio?"

"That's right," Fairchild replied. "This is Bob Merriam, and I'm Richie Fairchild. We're on the faculty of Fremont College, and are scheduled to participate in a meeting in Gainesville tomorrow, but I'm beginning to have my doubts."

"Garth, Jimmy Garth," the man said, introducing himself. "You're professors? Of...?"

"Yes, religions. Religious history, that sort of thing," Fairchild replied. "You're doing some fishing, Jimmy?"

"Oh, you might say that, I guess. Been doing some SCUBA diving. But I had to dock the motor launch I chartered until this storm passes. If it had been my own boat I'd a ridden it out, but it's a charter, and the owners called me on ship-to-shore and said to dock it till the storm blew out." "Looking for anything specific?" Bob inquired.

"Nah, just having fun. Been out there a week or so now, and think I'm about to head home again. Couple of days ago one of them manatees came up and tried to get romantic. Ugly damned things, but playful. There have been a few porpoises around, too."

"Is there a reef out there?" Richard Fairchild asked.

"Nah, just mostly a sandy bottom. Bit of junk occasionally."

"I take it you're single," Fairchild continued.

"Divorced. I was out on the boats more'n half the year and she got bored waiting around for me. She remarried and has several kids now." Garth said. "Normally I'd be working on a tug hauling in stranded fishing boats this time of year."

"It sounds like an interesting line of work, Jimmy." Fairchild said as Fitzgibbons brought their plates to the table.

"Any of you guys want a beer? Or coffee?" he asked. Only Garth said yes to a beer and the proprietor went to get it.

"Just curious," Garth asked, "but did I hear Fitzgibbons say something about you guys being cousins?"

"Not exactly," Bob explained. "His cousin married my wife's cousin," Carrying the beer in one hand and a cup of coffee for himself in the other, Fitzgibbons returned to the table and pulled up the fourth chair.

"How is Patricia? Y'know, they honeymooned down here at the hotel." he added.

"Happy and busy, as far as I can tell," Bob answered. "You probably know about that big house in Sandusky her father gave her and Dexter.

They've completely redecorated it, and it's quite a showplace. My wife, Sally, was as excited about it as Dexter and Peggy were."

"Sally. Long blond hair, green eyes?" Fitzgibbons said. "Beautiful gal. Like one of our Southern belles! Yes, I remember her from the weddin', too."

"Simon," Dr. Fairchild asked, "do you know anything about a James Fitzgibbons who lived in the 1860s?"

"Old Uncle James. Oh, he was dead long before I was born, but he was sort of a legendary member of the family. He's who bought those houses up there in Ohiah."

"Did he ever stay here in Suwannee?"

"Oh, he probably did, Richie. He took over the railroad and steamboat line after my Great-grampa Zebulon was killed in the War, and arranged for the building of half this little village. I've never come across anything 'o his here, though. Why? How d'you know about him?"

"Your cousin found some of his papers in the old house in Sandusky, and mentioned it to us," Fairchild explained, making a point not to reveal too much of what he had learned. "Bob and Sally told me about the railroad and this hotel, and I just wondered if he might have been down here too."

"Old papers?" Garth asked. "What sort of papers?"

"Oh, just old letters and lists. What sort of legends have you heard, Simon?"

"Hee, if even half of them were true I'd be shocked. You know how those family stories get better with each generation. Why, the way I heard it, he ran special missions for Jefferson Davis himself, but I doubt that. I heard he wasn't even in the country during most of the War. Hid out someplace, maybe Canada, so I don't think he was any hero."

"What did he do before the War?" Fairchild asked.

"What I heard was that he was some sort of 'agent,' whatever that meant, for various Georgian planters. Sounds bad these days, but I suspect he was bringing back runaways. Some said that's why he was up in Ohiah."

"After that Dred Scott case, that would have been legal," Bob said. "I guess the slaves were worth a lot of money."

"Alive," Simon Fitzgibbons said. "But those days are long gone now. Thank goodness. Never believed in it myself. A man's a fella' human being regardless of the color of his skin, I always thought."

"A good thing to think," Fairchild confirmed.

* * *

The storm raged all though the night. Bob tossed in his bead, but despite the howl of the wind and the banging of shutters, doors and the occasional tinkle of broken glass he managed to fall asleep about two in the morning. When he awoke at six, the storm had passed, and there was the faint glow of dawn outside his second floor window. He quickly arose, shaved and dressed.

Simon Fitzgibbons was already busy at work in the dining room when Bob and Richard Fairchild came down about seven. A radio was on, and they stopped to listen to the news. Most of it was about the storm.

"The heart of the storm, on an east northeast path, came ashore north of Cedar Key, and passed directly over Gainesville, spawning several tornadoes. One partially tore the roof off an auditorium, another toppled the steeple of Shiloh Baptist Church, and two stores were badly damaged when their wooden facades were blown loose. Billboards, falling trees and other debris damaged homes and automobiles, and power is still out for about a third of the city. The University stadium, however, was not damaged, and the game scheduled for this afternoon will take place. Further south in Ocala the van of two tourists at Silver Springs was overturned and several trees were blown down. Our news will continue after these messages.

"Charlie's Automotive is offering a three-day post storm special on...."

"I hear there are several trees down on the road to Old Town," Simon said, turning the radio down. "Doubt you fellas'll get to Gainesville today."

"If that auditorium that was damaged with the one where our meeting was, there wouldn't be any meeting anyway. Any way to find out?"

"Telephone lines are down, but we've got ship-to-shore here, so after breakfast I'll make some inquiries for you. Cook wants to know if ham 'n eggs'll do you fellas?" "Sure," Bob replied. "Sounds good to me." Fairchild concurred.

"Has Garth come down yet?"

"The Yankee? Oh, he left about six this morning. Said he'd eat on his boat. Been living on it more'n a week. Apparently anxious to continue his diving."

"Interesting man," Fairchild commented.

After the meal was complete Simon Fitzgibbons made a few radio calls. It was confirmed that the Alachua Auditorium had been damaged by the storm. He also learned that the County was working on clearing the highway to Old Town, but that part of it near the river was still flooded. "You boys will have to enjoy the pleasures of our town," he told the two professors. But you should be able to get out of here in the morning. High water usually dissipates in less than a day."

The two worked on class schedules for an hour or so, and then took a walk around the little village of Suwannee. There were only a couple of commercial establishments, small stores geared to serving the needs of boaters and fishermen, and a marina. Fairchild considered renting a boat and going out to see if he could find Garth, but the surf was still quite strong, and he quickly rejected that idea. They poked around the streets for about an hour, then returned to the hotel and spent the rest of the day with some books they had brought with them.

"Don't think either of us intended to teach much about the Dead Sea Scrolls this year anyway," Fairchild commented, remembering the topic of the Gainesville conference. "From what I've seen of the translations I don't think it adds much to the literature. Maybe a bit to our knowledge of the Essenes."

"I've heard some stories suggesting a connection been Jesus and the Community. But I'd be more likely to associate it with John the Baptist. Richie, have you ever heard of that community of Mandaeans that trace their heritage to the Nasorean sect?"

"Yes, they're a small group somewhere in the south of Iraq. Their beliefs are similar to Christianity, but they trace their origin to Yahia Yuhana, or John the Baptist. It's more likely that some of the writings will be found to relate more to Gnostic beliefs, the ritual washings, secret knowledge, and so forth. It is surprising to me that more scholars have not picked up on the fact that John was a Nazirite. His description is like that of Samson, long hair, wild ways, living in the wilderness. It's based on Torah, from the Book of Numbers. Here," he said, opening a small Bible he had in his briefcase, "Chapter Six. 'When men or women make a special vow to be a Nazirite, separate and consecrated, they shall drink no wine.... No razor shall come upon their head; they shall let the locks of their head grow long.... They must never go near a corpse....'

"The same is held true of any of the Hebrew priests," Fairchild continued. "This is what gives a different interpretation to the parable of the Good Samaritan. Remember, it was both a priest and a Levite who came along and found the injured man, and passed by on the other side of him. Why? Because if they were Nazirites, they could not touch human blood or be near a corpse. It was unclean, a taboo, for them. It was this taboo that Jesus was criticizing in his parable. Hence, to these Nasoreans, Jesus would have been somewhat of a heretic. Remember the story about John's disciples coming to interview Jesus, and what he told them to tell John?"

"Yes. But didn't the Nasoreans use symbols, sort of as a code."

"Surprisingly, yes. One, for example, was a fish. It's interesting that the early Christians also used the fish symbol for Jesus, based on the Latin word for fish. But I suspect there may have been a more subtle reason that particular symbol was selected, and it may have had nothing to do with Latin. But I doubt we'll ever know."

Chapter 8

December 12, 1963
Fremont College
Journal and Document Translation

As was typical, the academic year began furiously and got busier with each passing day. The Department of Religions had seven courses that fall, four taught by Dr. Merriam and three by Dr. Fairchild, who was also busy with student counseling and as assistant chaplain. Dr. Mawson, Professor of Geography, continued to share the basement offices in Hayes Hall, and as the joint departmental secretary, Sally Merriam was kept as busy as the academics themselves. Dr. Mawson had moved out several years before.

Fairchild found that it was only on a rare evening or Sunday afternoon that he had any time to devote to translation of the journals and documents he had acquired in Bermuda. The task was fairly easy, but the journals were lengthy, with considerable detail. But the story the journals revealed was beginning to gel. They were basically diaries or business logs like the one found in the Atwater's attic. But they were also like an autobiography, written, said their author, for his family in the event of his capture or death, but otherwise to be kept secret.

It was only after the first few sections had been translated that Richard Fairchild had conferred with Peggy Atwater, again seeking reassurance that she wished him to continue, regardless of what the journals revealed regarding her ancestral family. He explained that these were historic documents and warranted publication if they revealed new information. She did not disagree, and in effect gave consent for exactly that.

The sheet of music was puzzling to Fairchild. He had tried to plunk out the single treble cleft notes on the piano in the living room at the farm, but the tune had made no sense. He studied the notes carefully, noting a repeated three-note sequence that periodically appeared. Suddenly it dawned on him what he was seeing. It was a code. He tried matching letters with notes. He knew that the most common word in the English language was 'the,' and thought that the three-note combination might apply. At first that did not seem to be the case. He tried other three letter words, but none seemed to fit. As midnight approached he gave up and went to bed.

* * *

It was late December before Dr. Richard Fairchild completed his translation of the Journals and documents he had acquired in Bermuda. At first he was concerned that he could not find a Tebeauville in Georgia. He asked Peggy Atwater about it, and she said that she believed that was the original name of Waycross before the 1880s.

Fairchild had carefully written out the English on note pads. He did not think that he'd be justified in asking Sally Merriam to type the contents as part of her secretarial work for the college, but approached her with an offer to pay her for her time in typing up the translations. She protested and offered to do it for free, but he insisted on paying her, because, he said, the documents were historically and academically significant, and he wanted it done right, which he knew she could do. She took the handwritten translations home and began typing them over the Christmas/New Year's break.

The Journals also contained various accounting records, many involving purchases and shipments of locomotives, rail cars and supplies, and more lists of names and locations, at least up until 1959. The Professor had Sally type those lists separately from the autobiographical material in the Journals.

* * *

May 20, 1864, Hamilton, Bermuda

> I, James Fitzgibbons, Agent of the Confederate States of America, enclose these Journals and Accounts, prepared in the French language in the event of my demise and any eventual need of the reports and information contained herein for diplomatic or legal purposes on behalf of the Confederacy. Keys and the code necessary to retrieve them from the lockbox at the Bank of Hamilton have been provided to four individuals, in addition to my own set: Col. Pierce Heber, CSA, Assistant to the Confederate States of America's Ambassador to France, Pierre Hallon, Consul General of France, Hamilton, Bermuda, Samuel Winston, Consul General of the Confederacy, Hamilton, Bermuda, and, via Col. Heber, Zebulon Fitzgibbons, my brother, President of the Suwannee & Gulf Railway and Steamboat Company, Tebeauville, Georgia, Confederate States of America. Nevertheless, much in these journals is personal, and should not be revealed unless it is absolutely necessary in the best interests of the Confederacy.

Journal One
April 7, 1857
Tebeauville, Georgia.

The Fugitive Slave Law was passed in 1850. By 1857 there had been some legal clashes between the State of Ohio and the federal government over the law. Federal marshals in May of 1857 arrested several Ohio citizens for aiding runaways. Ohio had passed its own law, the so-called Personal Liberty Laws that barred slave-owning in the state, and also barred the kidnapping of Negroes. It was repealed in 1858. The state then passed a law that anyone at least half-white would be entitled to vote as a white citizen.

It has been more than a year since Chief Justice Roger Taney issued the Scott v. Sandford decision, returning the Negro slave, Dred Scott, from Illinois because he was not found to be a citizen with a legal right to sue in federal court. I was approached by a number of planters in and around Ware County who knew of my frequent travels north purchasing iron rail, locomotives and cars for my brother's new railroad and other railroads in Georgia. They wanted me to see if I could arrange to locate and return to them some of their runaways.

There seemed to be some sort of pattern in these desertions. Two or three of the Negroes would disappear. They apparently found help somewhere along the Satilla and Ocmulgee River Valleys, and then up in the North Georgia mountains to reach Tennessee and Kentucky, where Quaker farmers helped them reach the Ohio River. Threats to the Quaker farmers seemed to be useless, and once across the Ohio, there seemed to be some truth to the tales we heard about an 'underground railway' that escorted the Negroes and allowed them to cross to Canada. It was fairly certain that they wouldn't be riding any real railroads up there.

Rumor had it that most of their crossings were from Lorain or Sandusky, Ohio, or at Detroit. We saw that Taney's decision in effect nullified the Missouri Compromise. It appeared that the Southern point-of-view regarding our property rights would be supported by the government against the abolitionists. That gave us the legal right to reclaim our property and return it to Georgia.

First thing I needed to do was get a place where I could work up North. Sandusky seemed the most likely place to find these runaways, so I met with a business broker up there and purchased a house in the town near the harbor. Figuring that I might have to keep some of the runaways for a few days, I fixed up the third floor to hold them. The question was how to get them back down south. Depending on which car builder my brother and I purchased from, we used several routes to get our cars down to Georgia. There was no bridge at Cincinnati, or over in Indiana, so all railcars crossing the Ohio were put on ferries at Cincinnati or Louisville. South of Cincinnati the line ran to Louisville, and then down to Nashville on the L&N. Sandusky also made more sense as three or four different rail routes ran there, and there were none to Lorain.

As I had attended Yale College up in New England and knew several languages, I was able to speak without sounding too much like a Southerner. That was helpful, and I soon was being invited to participate in the social life of Sandusky. It was a Masonic town, and as I was a thirty-two degree man many of the lodge members welcomed me into their homes. One was the Reverend Silas Dobbins, a Congregational minister who also had attended Yale. His church was just down the street from my house, and I frequently saw Negroes being brought there in wagons. They would only be there a few days before they were gone.

Another lodge member was Mackinsey Harper. Harper was owner of a small fleet of steamships that ran from Sandusky over to some of the islands, including the Canadian one, and on to Detroit and Windsor, Ontario. I had brought a case of good Tennessee whiskey with me, and invited Captain Harper over one afternoon when he was in town for a chat. He told me that Dobbins, and another local preacher, Harwood Maxwell at the Presbyterian Church, would bring him runaway slaves and pay him $50 to take them to Canada. He'd take three or four a month.

Harper was a friendly old guy, but I could tell he was not of an abolitionist mind. His interest was strictly business. I said, "Harper, I got a better idea. You know I need good men to help me get our railroad, down in Florida, built. I'm willing to hire those Negroes and pay them as workers, and that would be a lot better for them than going to Canada. You can still collect the $50 from Dobbins and Maxwell, but I'll pay you for letting me look them over, and select a few to hire. $25 for each one I take." We shook on it, having a deal.

There was a small firm just east of Lima, Ohio, that was making wooden boxcars. My brother had arranged with some of his fellow railroad owners in Georgia to allow me to act as agent and purchase boxcars Lima-built locomotives for them. We used some of the boxcars ourselves, and sometimes we'd get orders from other rail lines for boxcars or passenger coaches, as there was a coach-building company over in Cleveland, so I was constantly getting locomotives and cars. It was easy to fix the boxcars to transport the Negroes back down to Georgia.

It wasn't long before Captain Harper came to me and said he had five Negroes he'd been paid to take to Canada. I went down to the dock and looked them over. One was a man and wife from Alabama, both fairly old. They'd been house slaves. Another was from Mississippi. The other two were from around Albany, on the Flint River. I said I'd take those two, and paid Harper $50. The other three he took to Canada. I'd heard tales told that some of the steamer captains simply dropped their cargo off in the middle of the lake if Canada was out of their way. Harper seemed an honest type, and I doubt he did that.

The two Negroes I had acquired were young, healthy males who had been working cotton for Jackson Alderman on a plantation east of the Flint River. They were obviously scared, and said they didn't want to go back down South, even if they were to be paid to work on a railroad, as Aldeman's foreman would kill them if he caught them. It soon became clear that they would not go back peacefully. I enticed them to the house, fed them, gave them some whiskey, and when I got them to the third floor, drew a gun on them and shackled them to their bunks.

When they sobered up a bit I said I'll let them loose if they would tell me who had helped them escape north up the Flint River Valley. The one boy, named Johnnie, said there was a Negro preacher in Drayton who had taken them up to Macon where a white Anglican preacher had arranged to get them up somewhere north of Athens. That information was going to be worth my investment.

I had arranged for a small three-foot gauge Shay locomotive to be built in Lima. It was geared rather than piston-operated, designed to work better in the mountains for lumbering. Two wooden boxcars were to accompany it south. The builders brought the locomotive and the two cars up from Lima to Toledo, and then over on the Lake Shore to Monroeville, on two flatcars. From there I was to escort them down to Cincinnati, put them on the ferry to Covington, and then down to Louisville, and on to Nashville. From there it would be routed to Chattanooga, and put on a river barge to haul over to the mountains. I'd continue south with my two runaways to Albany.

I arranged for a wagon and team to take me to Monroeville the night the locomotive and cars were to be delivered. I brought to two Negroes down, well shackled, and locked them into the bed of the wagon, covered them with a blanket and headed south. Monroeville was about fifteen miles south of Sandusky. I got there about four in the morning. I spotted the small locomotive and cars sitting on a siding, and climbed up on the first car. I'd brought along a shackling rings and plates, which I screwed tightly into the wood siding of the car. They were solid enough that the boys could not pull them out, having been designed for farmers taking cattle to market. Then I unchained the two Negroes from the wagon, hoisted them up into the boxcar and shackled them in. I gave them plenty of water and food – they would be valuable cargo, and I intended them to arrive back in Albany in better shape than they'd left.

I rode in the boxcar with them. At each junction where one railroad turned the cars over to another, I had the papers for the two flatcars, and no one ever considered climbing up to look inside. I'd fetch fresh water and food along the way. Even when the cars were rolled onto the ferry at Cincinnati there was no fuss. It was as if the two Negroes, Johnnie, and the other, Mose, accepted their fate. They still held hope that I was going to give them jobs working on the rail line, which, if their owner, Alderman, didn't want them, was exactly what I would arrange.

The trip was long and slow, with the freight trains sitting for hours on sidings awaiting passenger trains. I realized that it might be as fast by river packet, down the Ohio, and up the Tennessee to Chattanooga, for future trips. At last we reached Chattanooga, and at long last I was able to cross into Georgia on the Western & Atlantic occupying a decent coach seat, with my two runaways stowed securely in the baggage car. No one would question Negro prisoners here.

It took another couple of days to get from Atlanta to Albany. I kept my two runaways in the city jail while I contacted Alderman and told him what I had. He said he'd already replaced Johnnie and Mose, and that he wasn't interested in paying me for them – I wanted $100 each – and that I could shoot them if I wished.

There being no train to Tebeauville, I bought a team and wagon, and the three of us started for Tifton. I had told those two boys that I'd be good to my word that they'd be paid to work on the railroad, and on the trip south they'd come to trust me until they realized I was taking them to Albany. But when Alderman didn't want them – and I was glad he didn't – they agreed not to try to run away again. Zeb agreed to put them to work at a fair wage. As far as I know, Johnnie and Mose are still working on the Branford line.

While I was in Albany I had met with several of the planters, and told them what I'd learned about how their runaways were escaping up the Flint River to Macon. They indicated they'd put a stop to that.

* * *

October 30, 1858
Sandusky, Ohio

It was clear that if I was to make any money on bringing runaways back it would have to be on a specific order basis and that I'd have to get help to transport the Negroes back to Georgia. I also had orders for new locomotives and cars as well. Zeb had put out word around the area plantations of what we were offering, and we got a number of requests. Of course, we knew we couldn't find most of them. Not all the runaways that made it to the Ohio would go north to Sandusky. Some might go to Cleveland, Lorain or other towns along the lake, or go up by Detroit and swim over to Canada, if they could swim at all. But Zeb didn't need me right then to help run the S&G, so I headed back to Sandusky with about twenty orders; Zeb said he'd telegraph to me others he received.

We arranged for car or locomotive shipments every two months through December. Runaways hardly ever made it in the wintertime, and as the lake froze over, none would come to Sandusky anyway. We had a cousin, Billy Morgan, who was a big bulky man, quite strong and fierce-looking. Billy said he'd like to join us in our runaway salve business, so we arranged to have him accompany future locomotives and cars south from Ohio. The Atlantic & Gulf that ran through Tebeauville was building a line all the way from Savannah to Bainbridge, eventually with the intent of reaching Tallahassee. They were running a line south to Live Oak that crossed the S&G, and we had arranged to bring a number of cars and locomotives down for them during the autumn of 1858.

Not all our captured runaways survived. Occasionally one would believe our story that we wanted to hire them for the railroad, but most said they'd sooner die than go back south. Several managed to escape during travel back. One tore loose and jumped off the ferry when it was crossing the Ohio. He probably drowned. Another managed to kill himself up on my third floor. He somehow wrapped his chains around his neck and basically hung himself. Billy helped me load the corpse into a wagon and we dumped him in the bay. One old couple was already quite ill when we got them, and both died before we could get them south. For the most part, though, we got them far enough that we could stop hiding them.

I was surprised that the whole time we were returning runaways nobody in the town of Sandusky figured it out. Sometimes some of these Negroes would start to singing or shouting up there, and I expected that the neighbors would inquire. They never did, but I heard there was talk. Every Sunday I went over to Silas Dobbins church to hear his sermons and see if he mentioned anything about his abolitionist actions. He came up to me one Friday night at Lodge and said, "James, I hear you occasionally have Negroes at your house, that you bring them in and take them out at night. Are you bringing them up from the South to get them to Canada?"

"No," I told him. "They're freemen that I've been hiring to work on the railroads. I represent several railroads out West, and they need workers."

"That's good of you, James," he said, believing every word. "Keep it up!"

It was fortuitous that Dobbins believed that I was hiring the blacks to work on railroads. In September of 1858 a runway was being helped by some abolitionists in Oberlin, but the abolitionists were in violation of the federal fugitive slave law. A federal marshal arrested the runaway, John Price, and took him by train to a jail in Wellington. The abolitionists got a mob together, went to Wellington, and rescued Price, sending him away, probably to Canada by way of Sandusky. He was not one that I had an order to find. The federal law officers then arrested almost forty men from

Oberlin and Wellington for violation of the federal law. Had it been known that I was simply operating under the federal runaway slave law, I might well have been lynched.

* * *

February 2, 1860
Tebeauville, Georgia

In October of 1859 I was about to shut down our business operations in Sandusky for the winter when news came of some abolitionist attack on a federal arsenal at Harper's Ferry, Virginia. Some crazy man who had led an Indian uprising in Kansas, named John Brown, had fostered the raid. He'd been captured and hung, but his raid had been seen very favorably in Ohio, and it turned out that his son came to live somewhere in the area of Sandusky. I got a telegram from Zeb telling me that I needed to return to Georgia, and that I should come back as soon as possible. Billy and I shut up the house in Sandusky and, with one additional runaway we had purchased from Captain Harper, we boarded a standard gauge coach we had purchased used from the Lake Shore & Michigan Southern, and headed for Cincinnati.

The further south we went the more we heard about how angry people were over politics. The Democrats seemed split between Stephen Douglas and John Breckinridge, and there was now some new party, calling themselves Republicans, who were pushing the Whig Congressman from Illinois, Abraham Lincoln. There was serious talk of secession of some of the Southern states from the Union.

When we got back to Georgia and delivered the railway coach we'd brought we took our runaway down to Tebeauville and collected from the planter whose slave he was. Zeb invited me over to his house. "James," he said, "things are going to be happening soon, I suspect, especially if this man Lincoln is elected next year. Plans are already in the works for Georgia to secede, and I hear that the same is true for Alabama and the Carolinas. Don't know about Florida yet, but I'd not be surprised if they went along with us.

"Now, if that happens we can expect that this man, Lincoln, may start a war over it. If so, we need to be prepared. You've been passing yourself off as a Yankee for a couple of years now, and if there is a war and secession, we're going to need men with your knowledge of the North. I've been talking to Henry Taylor up in Macon, and he's been in touch with that Mississippian, Jeff Davis, and they would like to meet with you."

It was about two weeks later when I arranged to meet with Taylor at a hotel in Savannah. He had a fellow named Alexander Stephens with him.

Stephens related that he was strongly opposed to secession, believing that by taking control of Congress through Democratic support, they stood a far better chance of obtaining the laws they desired.

Taylor said that they understood what I'd been doing up in Sandusky, but that they were afraid, with all the tension after the Brown raid, that if I was caught bringing back runaways, I might just be lynched. Nevertheless, they wanted me to return to Sandusky the following summer and wait to see what happened in the 1860 election. If there were secession, and a war, they'd provide me with instructions. If there wasn't, it was possible the Supreme Court might reverse Scott and the fugitive slave law. It might then be illegal to return runaways.

In the meantime, they had a job for me. Whatever happened, the South was going to need lots of financing. Because I spoke several languages, Taylor told me they wanted me to sail to France and make some contacts to see what money might be raised to finance the purchase of armaments. They had also sounded out the British Colony of Bermuda, which lay about seven hundred miles east of the Carolinas. It would be a neutral place where transactions might take place. Taylor suggested that I travel there, perhaps from Canada, and arrange for some small house that might be used if needed, and to set up a bank account that could be used in the event of secession.

Zeb agreed that I would not be needed to help run the S&G, even though great progress on the extension to Branford was being made. That stretch of rail, from White Springs to Branford, would eliminate many miles of necessary navigation on the weedy and slow-running Suwannee, and gain faster access to the Gulf and foreign markets for Georgia cotton. If, in fact, secession did occur, those markets would be even more vital.

* * *

August 20, 1860
Paris, France

Billy did not accompany me back to Sandusky that spring. I arrived in April, and at the first lodge meeting I detected a lot of political feeling about what was going on in the nation. Many of the Ohioans said they did not care whether new territories were to be for slavery or against it. What they did fear was that, with the rise of industry along the Great Lakes, cheap labor in the form of Negro runaways would take jobs that their own sons might need. If slavery were to be abolished, it would have a great impact on the Northern economy. For factory owners this was a good prospect, but for many sons of farmers who might not inherit the land that would go to their elder brothers, and who were not tradesmen or shopkeepers, the prospects of competing with Negroes for jobs was not pleasant. Already there were hundreds, if not thousands, of Irish and German immigrants who had come to work on the canals and railroads who were also seeking jobs. These, if they were citizens allowed to vote, would take up the Democrats position. But the majority of those who would have the vote seemed drawn to the Lincoln Republicans, opposed to any secession by the South.

I stayed in the big house in town for several months, sounding out the political situation and making a few railcar and locomotive purchases for my railroad clients. With some of the escape routes out of Georgia being shut down, once we learned who was aiding the runaways, I would have had very few clients that year anyway. If agents from other Southern states were at work in the town I never heard. Unless they also dealt with old Captain Harper, I probably would not have come across them. More likely they were attempting any intercepts further south, at Ripley, Portsmouth, Marietta or Cincinnati.

The Grand Trunk Railway of Canada had opened a line from Niagara Falls to Toronto, on to Montreal, and from there to Portland, Maine. From there one could get a steamer to Halifax, and from Halifax to Bermuda or Europe. From Monroeville I caught the Lake Shore & Michigan Southern, which took me through Oberlin and Cleveland, to Buffalo, and then took Vanderbilt's New York Central across John Roebling's new suspension bridge to Canada. Within five days I was in Halifax and aboard a steamer bound for Bermuda. There I found a small house on the Parlaville Road, and purchased it. I also opened an account at the Bank of Hamilton. For the accounts of foreigners they required a code. I had begun to keep my journals in French to keep them confidential, but I used a series of random Greek letters for the bank code.

This took about a month. I thought it might also be wise to see if I could obtain a British Colonial passport, and made application. Advised that my request would take several months to process, I returned to the harbor and found a steamer headed to Southampton.

I'd met several French students at Yale, including Claude Roget, whom I knew was now affiliated with the French finance bureau in Paris. Upon arrival in Cherbourg I sent him a telegram and received an invitation to meet with him. His title was Deputy to the Citizenry of the Treasury.

Claude was a handsome man, exactly my own age, and he seemed delighted to see me. We spoke a combination of French and English, as I knew slightly less French than he English, but by the end of the week very little was being misunderstood between us. Claude was aware of the political situation in America, and said that the Europeans rather expected that there might be some sort of civil conflict as a result. They, too, were undergoing similar problems of clash between rural agriculture, demanding cheap labor if prices were not to become exorbitant, and the rise of industrial cities, drawing excess labor to jobs in factories. As in American first the canals and now the railroads and telegraph were making transportation and communication easy. The world was changing, Roget agreed, and that change would bring conflict.

My concern was what the French government might do if the American South should secede from the United States and set up a separate nation. It would be a slave nation, hence the agricultural products of the south, primarily cotton, lumber and indigo, would remain cheap. France had, like Britain, given up slavery except in a handful of their colonies. However, they still utilized prisoner labor, as did the British, and many Frenchman worked as hard as slaves under various forms of bondage.

Obviously Claude could not speak for the French government, which was in a bit of a political turmoil itself at the time. He understood that if there was secession the South would need both armaments, financial aid, and perhaps even troops. He agreed to sound out some of the higher officials, and let me know. Meanwhile, he suggested I enjoy the pleasures of Paris, and tour a bit of France.

* * *

March 15, 1861
Sandusky, Ohio

Since the Revolution earlier in the century France seemed to be having a renaissance of sorts. Arts, drama and what seemed to be a lot of glitter was energizing Paris. The efforts of Napoleon III to unify the empire and gain back the support of the Catholic Church and expand French influence seemed to provide a liberal intellectualism that suited the French well. Yet France's relationship with its neighbors, ranging all the way from the Crimea to the return of the Papal States to Rome, limited its view beyond the Atlantic.

It was mid-September before I was able to meet with Claude again. He reconfirmed that he understood our situation, but that the politics of the moment prevented his government from taking any position vis-à-vis a potential secession of any states or of any future relationships with either side in the slavery dispute. Perhaps, he suggested, when the situation developed a bit further, he could again approach some of the French politicians regarding help for the slavery states.

I returned to Bermuda by way of London, and tried to get a feel for the attitudes of the British toward the possible secession of Southern states. There was practically no mention of the United States in the British press. Industrialism, the new railroad lines being opened, and the colonies around the globe were their concerns of the moment. They had their own sources of cotton, hence potential fluctuations in supply were not then of any major concern.

By the time I returned to Hamilton my request for a colonial passport, providing the benefits of citizenship, had been granted. In effect, although I maintained my American passport as well, in the event of a war I would be able to travel between the North and South as a foreigner. At the time I had no idea how valuable that would be.

By the end of October, 1860, I had sailed to New York, and took the train back to Sandusky. Seldom had there been an election that stirred the public as much as this one. Although there were many in Ohio who were strongly for Douglas, Republican promises of a strong tariff to protect the coal and iron businesses gained many advocates for that party's candidate. In the election even strongly Democratic Cincinnati voted for Lincoln.

Ohioans had hoped that the election of Lincoln would silence the secession movement in the South. But it was the opposite that occurred. I returned to Georgia after the election, and was there on December 20 a convention met in Charleston and voted for secession. They declared, "The union now subsisting between South Carolina and other states under the name of the United States is hereby dissolved." Some, including Davis and Stephens, argued that the South should give Lincoln a chance to see what his administration might do to help the South on the slavery issue, but the public was so fired up over the issue that by the first of February in 1861 all the states west and south of South Carolina had also seceded, including Texas. Davis was then elected president, and Stephens vice president at a congress of the seven seceding states held in Montgomery a few days later.

* * *

June 30, 1861
Tebeauville, Georgia

Events transpired quickly. In April Virginia – except for the western part along the Ohio River – voted to secede. In May Arkansas and Tennessee joined them. North Carolina had at first voted down secession, but finally joined the other Southern states. Kentucky remained neutral, and Maryland stayed with the Union, but Missouri seemed split between whether to join the South or stay with the Union. Many of the Indians joined with the South. It was on April 12 that South Carolina militia fired on the Union fort in Charleston harbor, and war was declared.

The planters living around Tebeauville were well aware that the war would curtail their sale of cotton to the textile mills in New England. This had been a major product for the Suwannee & Gulf in South Georgia, bringing in carloads of cotton for transfer to the Atlantic & Gulf. Now textile mills were being opened throughout Georgia and the Carolinas, guaranteeing that our railroad business would continue strongly. There was still no connecting line between Savannah and Charleston. Cargo before the war was often shipped from Savannah to Charleston by coastal steamer, or sent all the way north by ship, as the rail route was from Savannah to Atlanta, on to Chattanooga, and from there to Knoxville and up the Shenandoah Valley through Virginia.

Timber, pine tar and turpentine from North Florida were now desperately needed for new railroads, telegraph lines, mounts for cannons, and other war materiel. We let word that if any of the planters were going to cease production while they fought in the war, we needed their Negroes to help on the railroad and our steamboats on the Suwannee. Most of the planters who joined the Confederate Army, however, continued to work their plantations leaving a foreman in charge. Most of us anticipated a quick victory, believing that Lincoln had no heart for a long fight.

Chapter 9

Journal Two
March 2, 1862
Paris, France

With Virginia's addition to the Confederacy, Jefferson moved his government to Richmond. Robert Lee was appointed as the chief general of the South's army, and he quickly put together a fierce military force that sent the Union Army scurrying back across the Potomac after their run-in with General Thomas J. Jackson at Bull Run Creek. But the war was progressing slowly, and our hopes that it would be over by 1862 faded. Immediately after Fort Sumter fell Lincoln imposed a naval blockade of every Southern port. However, the Union forces had neglected to fortify Norfolk before the war, and it quickly fell to the Confederates, giving us access to a naval force. But with Union gunboats sitting outside Norfolk, Wilmington, Charleston, Savannah and Jacksonville, and, soon thereafter, Tampa, Pensacola, Mobile, Biloxi and New Orleans on the Gulf, it was clear that any goods coming in would be very expensive.

Many captains were quite willing to make a good profit running the blockades. One port that the Union did not bother blockading was our small hamlet at the mouth of the Suwannee. With completion of the rail line from White Springs to Branford, and two additional steamboats on the Suwannee, we were able to ship out cotton and bring in whatever goods we needed that could be purchased overseas.

In November of 1861 I was summoned to Richmond where Stephens introduced me to Colonel Pierce Heber. Heber, who had thick black hair, was a Cajun about my age from New Orleans. He spoke fluent French, and had the stature of a diplomat. My instructions were to get him to France, as he was to be the Confederacy's liaison to Paris, in hopes of getting financing and weapons. Stephens had my report on my meetings with Roget, and wanted us to work together to try to win France as an ally.

We were given our instructions and official papers to present to the French from Davis, but were left on our own as to how to get to France. We could go to a Southern port and try to get passage on a ship running the blockade. We could go back to Tebeauville and down to Suwannee and get a blockade-runner from there, but there was no guarantee we would ever get to France.

A better idea was to get back into Ohio, establish some Union purpose for Heber, and try to get a ship for France out of Montreal.

Although Lincoln had appointed George McClellan General-in-Chief, he seemed to be doing nothing. That suited us, and we used the Chesapeake & Ohio Railway to get from Richmond to Covington, the end of rail. From there we were able to travel overland to the Kanawha, where we were able to get a steamboat up to the Ohio. From Marietta we got a canal packet north to Cambridge, and from there by the Baltimore & Ohio to Columbus, and on to Sandusky. I had brought a good supply of Union currency, which I placed in my Sandusky bank.

It was the first winter I had experienced in Sandusky, having always closed up the big house in town and returning to Georgia. Although Heber was Catholic, he agreed with me that it would be wise to pass himself off as an Anglican, and go with me to the Lodge. I introduced him to Dobson, Harper and the others as a fellow railroader from out West, without being too specific. Heber had many pre-war contacts with businessmen in Baltimore, New York and Boston, and with many of these names being known to the Ohioans, he was accepted as a Confederacy-hating Yankee.

Between Christmas and New Year's we took the Lake Shore & Michigan Southern train to Buffalo, caught another across the Roebling suspension bridge at Niagara, and in a week had reached Montreal. There Heber was able to arrange to obtain a Canadian passport, telling the British officials there that he was from a small town in Northern Quebec. We then found a small sailing vessel that was going to Marseilles, and set out across the North Atlantic.

How I wished we had waited for a steamer, or at least until spring. North of the Belle Isle Straits we encountered a fierce gale that blew us far off course. Fortunately we picked up the Gulf Stream, and slowly sailed northeasterly until we were somewhere west of Ireland. This was far north of where the captain was headed, but we convinced him to put in at Cobh, and from there we caught a steamship to Cherbourg. However, we were both ill with temperature, and upon arrival we found a hotel and arranged for a doctor. He prescribed large doses of cognac, and in a few days we had both recovered sufficiently to travel on to Paris.

While my friend, Claude Roget, was happy to see me again, he did not hold out great promise for our interests. Both England and France, he explained, had been building up their cotton supplies in anticipation of the American conflict. Britain had other cotton sources as well. Europe in general was now opposed to slavery, and there was little support for the Confederacy on a philosophical basis. As the French Ambassador to Washington did not anticipate that the war would go on very long, with the South being defeated, France had not much interest in assisting the Confederacy. However, he told us, individual French industrialists were quite free to do as they pleased.

Claude did suggest that if the war went on for any great length of time that the situation might well change. Although Britain had other sources for cotton in the Middle East, from Egypt and parts of Africa, the French had fewer such sources. If their supplies dwindled, they would not want Britain taking over their textile markets. Roget then provided us with a list of ship builders, cannon manufacturers and armaments dealers who might be very willing to sell to the Confederacy, if the money was available.

* * *

May 4, 1862
Tebeauville, Georgia

Heber and I agreed that he would stay in France and try to arrange for the purchase and shipment of arms. I was to return to Richmond and advise Stephens and Davis of the situation. I crossed back over to England and got a steamer for Halifax that went on to New York, but it was late April before I was able to cross back into the South and get to Richmond. There my instructions were to return to Tebeauville and await developments, but also to see if better dockage for blockade-running vessels could be built along the Suwannee.

Word was coming to the South that the British were softening a bit on their attitude toward the Confederacy. The war had dragged-on a year longer than anyone had anticipated, and it was likely that England's cotton inventory was beginning to dwindle. In November President Davis had dispatched two diplomatic agents, J. M. Mason and John Slidell, to the British Court. They were aboard a British mail steamer, H.M.S. Trent. On November 8, 1861, Captain Wilkes, in command of the U.S.S. San Jacinto, stopped her at sea and removed the two Southerners. As Britain was officially neutral, the Trent's captain could have been arrested, but the steamer was allowed to proceed to Southampton. When word reached Parliament that the Union Navy had boarded a British vessel and removed passengers Lord John Russell drafted a demand for an official apology from the Union, to be sent by the newly laid transatlantic cable. The British reinforced their army in Canada. London's press demanded war for violation of the Queen's Proclamation of neutrality. Prince Albert intervened, and fortunately the cable had temporarily quit working, so the heated dispatch was not received.

Still, the situation was tense. The American press made much of the boarding incident, and, despite Lincoln's strong desire to keep the two Southerners prisoners, on Christmas he was convinced by his cabinet members to release the two and allow them to go to England. It was as close to another war with Britain that the United States had come since 1814.

* * *

October 30, 1862
Sandusky, Ohio

    Admiral David Farragut captured New Orleans in April of 1862, and the Union was able to patrol the entire Gulf of Mexico under his command until the end of the war.

    My role changed significantly in the spring of 1862. As the Union forces were making greater progress in the war than they had in 1861, they were capturing many prisoners. We learned that they had purchased half of a small wooded island that was located in Sandusky Bay, perhaps five miles from the town of Sandusky, and maybe half a mile south of the Marblehead Peninsula. The west end of the island was low and swampy, but there was a rise on the eastern end and a Union representative arranged to purchase it as a location for a prison. By midyear there was a stockade, barracks, a hospital, and houses for the quartermaster and commissary. It was a rugged place. I knew it from my various steamer trips out of Sandusky, and I knew that the water was quite deep all around that island.

    Many prisoners of all types were being sent there, usually by railway to Sandusky and by steamer out to the prison. The Union dispatched the gunboat U.S.S. Michigan to guard the Bay. I received a letter from Richmond instructing me to return to Sandusky and report on the situation. This time I used a route through Tennessee and Kentucky, crossing into Indiana west of Louisville, and then on to Sandusky by railway.

    I arrived back in Sandusky in May, and again took up residence on Huron Avenue. Each morning I would walk down to the harbor and, if he was not off on a voyage to one of the islands, Detroit or to Canada, visit with Captain Harper. "Mack," as the Lodge members called him, was one of the boat owners commissioned to ferry Union soldiers and prisoners from Sandusky to Johnson Island.

    Some of Mack's crew members had joined the Ohio militia or the Army or Navy, and he kept complaining to me that he was shorthanded. I said, "Mack, I'm not getting many railroad car orders right now. Why not take me on as a crewman. I can help load and unload cargo for that prison camp out there on Johnson Island, and I really don't need a lot of pay."

    "Oh, I'd pay you," he said, but he agreed to put me on. The tree rail lines coming into Sandusky at that time included a branch of the Lake Shore that ran from Amherst, but it was just a local line, with no trains operating from further than Cleveland. Most prisoners were brought into town on the Cincinnati, Sandusky & Cleveland, running from Dayton through Tiffin, or the Sandusky, Mansfield & Newark that connected with the Pittsburgh & Columbus at Newark. Both ran to the docks just west of the town, and Mack would take one of the smaller steamers down there on days that a coach load of prisoners was brought in, so they could be unloaded directly onto the boat.

During most of that summer and fall the prisoners were young recruits, mostly infantrymen who had been captured doing picket duty or caught as deserters. They were a straggly bunch from all over the South. I did not see any that I recognized from Georgia, but I made it a point not to converse with them, as the Union guards were trying to impress the prisoners with their authority over them. There was a lot of cussing and swearing at them, but for the most part I did not see any real brutality by the guards.

The food we took over there was not always the best produce, but it was as good or better than what I recall the slaves getting to eat on the plantations. Every now and then a black prisoner would come through. I asked one if he was really a 'Johnnie Reb,' and he just shrugged and nodded yes. There were tales of many of the Negroes taking up arms and fighting for the South, and, like any soldiers, they were sometimes taken prisoner. We'd also heard of a number of Negro soldiers fighting for the Union.

* * *

June 1, 1863
Sandusky, Ohio

That winter a number of the prisoners got ill and died. A cemetery on a short bluff overlooking the Bay was started. Some in the town feared it might be smallpox or typhoid, but neither Mack nor I saw any indication of that, and the guards said that most of those who had died had been there during the summer, chopping wood out in the swampy part of the island and had caught swamp fever. Whatever it was, it took a lot of lives, but it never claimed any in the town.

By the following spring we noticed that most of the prisoners being brought in then were officers. It soon became apparent that Johnson Island was going to be maintained as the lead prison for captured higher rank officers. They were from many different units, some in Lee's main force, but most in various state units that acted almost independently of the rest of the Confederacy.

It was also that spring of 1863 that I decided to see what I could do to rescue some of those officers. At the time there were only a handful of farms out on the Marblehead Peninsula. Thomas Dyar was the lighthouse keeper at the time. He lived down the road on the north side of the Peninsula from a stone quarry that had been dug. There was also a dock where boats from Kelley's Island, just to the north of the Peninsula, could tie up. There were perhaps a hundred and fifty people on the Peninsula, but none of them had farms along the swampy south shore. There was, almost opposite Johnson Island, however, one rather high hill. To the east of that was a relatively flat area. While Sandusky was the seat of Erie County, the Marblehead Peninsula, including Johnson Island, was in Ottawa County. The courthouse was at Port Clinton, and the county included all the outer Bass Islands that had been inhabited since before the 1813 Battle of Lake Erie.

I got Mack to have one of his Detroit steamers drop me off in Port Clinton one day and found someone familiar with land on the Peninsula. The Clemons family owned much of the land, but I found a parcel of perhaps a hundred acres on the south shore east of the hill that was unowned. I inquired of the county clerk how I might obtain it and was referred to a Judge Martin. For a fee (of which I'm sure a considerable amount went to the Judge) he arranged for me to purchase it from the county. I did not argue about the price. Land was then going for about $25 an acre. Martin wanted more, but we agreed on $30, and I was given a formal deed and the purchase was duly recorded in the county records, along with my first tax payment of $5.

I got a ride over to South Bass Island, and the Island Queen picked me up on its way to Sandusky from Detroit and I was home that evening. The following day I met with a contractor who agreed to build a house on my property, along with a dock, a barn and a couple of sheds for animals or crops. He said that stone could be obtained from the quarry that was already in operation out there, and we agreed on a price for the buildings. I told him the type of house I wanted, overlooking Johnson Island. One of the things I wanted was an ice house that could be entered through the basement of the main house. I explained that when I used the farm, it would be great to have a place to store fresh meat. The prison was on the southeastern side of the island, not visible from Marblehead, but it could be seen from a point of land that extended south from just east of my land. I could also see most of the Bay from the location where I wanted the house constructed, including the buildings in Sandusky. The contractor promised to have it finished by mid-October, and I agreed to pay him extra if he met that date.

* * *

September 7, 1863
Sandusky, Ohio

It was in early June while I was unloading some supplies from a railcar at the depot that the train from Dayton and Cincinnati came in. One of the passengers that got off was a very attractive young woman, perhaps in her early twenties. She was wearing a gray dress, and had long blond hair rolled up underneath a matching gray hat. It was appropriate dress for travel. She seemed somewhat unsure of what to do, and was standing on the platform with two pieces of leather baggage. I went over to her and asked if I could help her. The minute she answered I knew she was from Georgia.

"You're from the South, I detect," I said.

"That's right," she replied. "I'm a reporter for the Washington Weekly News, sent by my editor to learn about conditions at a Union prison that is supposed to be around here somewhere. You wouldn't know about such a place, would you?"

"Ma'am, the supplies I'm loading on that wagon are for that prison, and will be taken out there by steamer in the morning. But I don't know if they'll let a lady go in."

"Maybe you could help me? Of course, first I'll need a hotel room. Are there any hotels in this town?"

"There's the West House, and the Portland House, but I heard that they might be full. I'll be glad to take you there and see if I can help you get a room."

"I'd be obliged," she replied in that Southern voice that I so missed, and smiled. I finished loading the wagon and put her two bags in the back, then lifted her onto the seat. We clattered down the street toward the harbor where one of the hotels was located. She told me that her name was Livia Parkens, and that she was from Savannah, but had been in Washington when the war began.

As I had expected, the hotel was full, as was the Portland House. There were two or three others, but I said, "Ma'am, I really couldn't recommend that you stay at either of those. They're, well, not really for ladies, or shall I say not for nice ladies like yourself."

"But I've got to stay somewhere," she protested.

"Miss Parkens, I do have a suggestion," I said. "I have a big house here in town, and you are most welcome to stay there as long as you need. There's an old German lady in the neighborhood who comes in a couple of times a week to keep the place tidy, and if you like, I could ask her to come and stay, too, so you would not be alone."

"Why, Mr. Fitzgibbons," she answered. "I couldn't put you out like that."

"The house has plenty of room, Miss Parkens. It's nearby. You can see it and then decide. If you can stand it, then I'll get Mrs. Gelbermann to come over and assist you and spend the night. She often does if I have a guest, so she can make us a big breakfast. She's a wonderful cook."

When Parkens saw the house and all the big bedrooms upstairs she agreed that this would be better than staying in one of the old hotels, which were little more than brothels with saloons attached. I carried her bags up to the guest room and walked over two blocks to a smaller street where Mrs. Gelbermann lived. She was a heavy-set widow lady near sixty who spoke with a thick accent. I had always paid her well, as she kept the house for me during the winter months when I was away. Of course, I never had her in whenever there were runaways there, so she knew nothing of the activities that occurred in the house.

She said she'd be delighted to help, and would be over in about an hour to plan our dinner. I told her that would not be necessary as I would probably take Miss Parkens out for dinner, but that we would want her to spend the night, and perhaps several. As she lived alone, she agreed that would not be a problem.

"Frankly, I've never heard of women newspaper reporters before," I said that evening as we had dinner in one of the restaurants in town. "Isn't that rather unusual?"

"Probably, Mr. Fitzgibbons. But I had a friend who worked there, and when he joined the Union army I talked to his editor, told him I was a good writer, and he agreed to hire me. I even covered one of the battles, but mostly I write about the military posts, the officers' families or the hospitals for the wounded soldiers. When I heard about this prison here in Ohio I asked if I might come and write about it, and the editor agreed."

"Do you have any sort of letter from the military that might help you get in?" I asked. She did not, and the more we talked, the more I suspected that she was lying to me. She mentioned some places and forts I'd never heard of, and I had followed the war pretty closely. Then I asked her about her home in Savannah, and if she knew any of the names of the officers of the Atlantic & Gulf Railway. She did not, but she did know one of the officers of the Central Railway of Georgia, which also owned the Augusta & Savannah. She'd never heard of Tebeauville, however.

On the way back to the house I confronted her with my suspicions. "Miss Parkens, please don't take offense," I said, "but I somehow doubt that you are here to report on a prison for any Washington newspaper."

"Oh, but I do work for the newspaper!" she quickly answered.

"Yes, so you may, but there are so many other Union prisons that are far closer to Washington, and easier to reach, than this one. I suspect you know someone there."

She did not reply for a long moment. I glanced over at her, and could see tears in her eyes.

"Is it a husband?" I asked.

"No," she said. "I'm unmarried. But...."

"Yes?"

"You are correct. My brother, Major Albert Parkens, was captured in Virginia. I heard he had been wounded, but that they sent him here. I just want to see him, and let him know that we're praying for him. I also have to tell him that Father died, and I'm not looking forward to telling him that, for they were close."

"I see," I replied. "Well, let me see what I can do for you. For now, you maintain that story about writing for the newspaper. When I go out there tomorrow on Captain Harper's steamer I'll talk to the commandant and see if we can arrange something for you. Maybe you can even get to see your brother."

Frau Gelbermann was waiting for us when we returned. She and Miss Parkens went upstairs while I sat in the parlor and drank some French cognac I had brought back to America with me. I had only met Major John Eddelstone, the prison commandant, once, but I had learned that he was a Mason, and had been invited to Lodge meetings in town. But many of the prisoners were also Lodge men, and I thought that might be a possible entrée, better than that of news reporter, who might make negative comments about the prison.

In the morning, after dining on Frau Gelbermann's kuchen and coffee and she went off to straighten out Miss Parken's room, I asked if her brother, by any chance, might be a Masonic man. She confirmed that he was, and I explained my plan to her. While she stayed at the house, I took the freight out to the island and met with Major Eddelstone. I explained that one of the prisoner's sisters was trying to get in touch with her brother, who as a good Masonic man, and wondered if, as a fellow Mason, he might allow for them to meet briefly. Eddelstone looked doubtful, but said he would let me know in a day or two, asking for the name and rank of the prisoner.

The prisoners all wore similar cotton uniforms, with blue and white stripes. Any officers at the prison served as supervisors for enlisted prisoners, under the protective eyes of the guards, when they went into the swampy forest on the island to gather wood for the kitchen or stoves. That way the rank and file soldiers felt that they were under the command of their own officers, and less likely to rebel. Many of them had been there far longer than the officers, however, and knew much more about the island and both the successful and unsuccessful escape attempts. The previous winter, for example, the ice had frozen between the island and Marblehead. Five prisoners simply walked over to the Peninsula, but without food or shelter, had died before they could even reach the neck of the Peninsula. It was so remote that the Peninsula, surrounded eighty percent by water, was a prison in its own way.

That evening I sat down with Miss Parkens, who insisted I call her Livia, and said we would hear from the commandant in a few days. She feared the answer would be no, but I tried to encourage her to be hopeful.

"Why are you helping me?" she asked.

"Why not?" I asked, not wishing to explain anything to my very attractive guest, especially not that I, too, was a Georgian and a Confederate agent. I had an ulterior plan, and Miss Livia was part of it.

Two days later, when I took some more freight out to the prison on the steamer I stopped by Major Eddelstone's office. He greeted me warmly, and said that he would agree to allow Major Parkens to meet with his sister the following Sunday evening, if she would attend the service at the prison chapel. They could have twenty minutes after the service, but could not sit together during it. I inquired who would lead the service, and learned that it was another fellow Lodge member, the Reverend Jack Thornesbury, a Methodist preacher.

Upon returning to town I contacted Thornesbury, explained about Major Parkens and his sister, and asked if we could ride out to the prison with him on the ferry, and he agreed. With only two days to plan, I had much to do. First I went to the town hall and inquired where indigents were buried. I was advised that there was a small cemetery west of town, beyond the railroads, behind an old abandoned Quaker meeting house that the city used for paupers.

Next I went to a marine dealer and arranged to purchase a small steam launch. It was only about twenty four feet long, and the steam engine took up the entire stern of the boat, but it was easy to maneuver, and would suffice for moving around the Bay. I then stopped at the coal depot dock and purchased a good load of coal, filling the bunker on the launch, and steamed over to Marblehead to where the contractor was working on my house. Already he had it framed and the roof on, but it was otherwise still open.

I anchored the launch at the dock the builder had built for his own boat, which was not where I wanted my own dock to be built. He had not yet started on it, and the location I wanted was in some weedy cat tails at the base of a slope down from the house. I got a long, round pole and a sledge hammer from one of the workers, went down to the water and drove the post in as far as I could, to show where I wanted my dock to be built. The builder was at the site that day, having to bring his crew and the supplies over each day, and I arranged to have him build my dock where I had placed my post. I wanted it built by Saturday. He frowned, but agreed to the price I offered if he finished it by then.

I then steamed westward up the Bay to the mouth of the Sandusky River. It was a swampy area, but as long as I stayed in the main channel of the river I was able to get perhaps a mile up-stream before hitting a shallow sandbar. I then steamed back to Sandusky, having arranged with Captain Harper to dock my launch with his vessels. It was just after dark when I returned to the house, and found that Frau Gelbermann and Livia had already had dinner.

On Saturday I again took the steam launch out, with both Frau Gelbermann and Livia as passengers. We crossed the Bay to Cedar Point, where a hotel was being built, and then crossed the open mouth of the Bay to the rocky ledge on which was built the tall white and red lighthouse.

Frau Gelbermann had brought along a basket of sausages, cheese and bread, and I had purchased a bottle of one of the local wines, and we had our lunch along the shore under the lighthouse.

It was a warm afternoon, but the breeze off the Lake made it comfortable. On the way back to Sandusky I went around the long point just east of the prison. The gunboat Michigan, was laying at anchor, and on our approach we could see the crew come to an alert, but we simply waved, and returned to the wharf in town.

That evening at dinner in one of the restaurants in town I asked, "Livia, does your brother speak or understand any languages?"

"Only Latin," she answered. "He studied it at the academy as a youth so that he could go to the university. I don't know if he studied anything further there, as the war began, and he joined with other Georgia boys to fight the Yankees. He's only twenty, three years younger than I am."

This was helpful. I'd forgotten most of my Latin, but had several books in my library, and that evening I sat up late with an oil lamp, pouring over them and composing a short letter. If my plan failed to work, I might well end up a prisoner on Johnson Island myself. But if it worked....

As Livia said she was an Anglican, on Sunday morning I drove her to the Anglican Church, but waited for her outside. That afternoon we walked over to the Methodist Church and joined the Reverend Thornesbury, riding with him in a carriage to the ferry dock, where one of Captain Harper's steamers would take us out to the prison.

The prisoners had already gathered in the dining hall when we got there. There were some hymn books scattered on the table, and one of the prisoners banged out a tune or two on an ancient piano that sat in the corner while the men sang some of the hymns that were familiar to me from my youth in Georgia. Livia looked quite lovely in a blue dress with a wide skirt, a big white bow in the back, and a blue bonnet. We sat toward the back of the room, and the prisoners all looked at Miss Parkens with obvious desire in their eyes. One tall young man toward the front nodded as we came in. Major Eddelstone sat with us, and other guards and Union officers joined in.

The Reverend Dobbins was longwinded, but not half as much as Thornesbury. His sermon was well over an hour, but at last he called for a final hymn, gave the blessing, and the prisoners filed out of the room. Eddelstone moved us to a far corner, waved his hand to Major Parkens, whose uniform had a red stripe on the sleeve, and he came over, hugging his sister tightly. I had asked Livia to wait until the end of her visit with her brother before introducing me to him. Meanwhile I chatted with Eddelstone about supplies I would be delivering that week, and what else the prison might need.

At the end of twenty minutes we could tell that Thornesbury was getting anxious to go out to the ferry. Livia gave her brother another hug, and then brought him over to where Eddelstone, Thornesbury and I were standing, and introduced us to Albert Parkens. I had a small piece of paper in my hand, and as we shook hands I moved the paper into his. He looked strangely into my eyes, but as I took my hand away he closed his over the paper, and I saw him transfer it to his pocket a few moments later. None of the others had noticed any of this. By the time the sun set, we were back in Sandusky.

On Monday night just before sunset I took the steam launch down toward the railroad docks and up a creek next to the old Quaker meeting house. I had a shovel with me, and found a fresh grave, which I dug, finding a simple pine box a few feet under the ground. I pried it open, but found that it was a woman. I closed the box and the grave, and tried another, which turned out to be an old man. On the third attempt I found a younger man who had roughly the same coloring as Albert Parkens. I pulled the body out of the box, closed it, and covered the dirt back over it, hauling the stinking corpse down to the steam launch.

I crossed the bay to the back of where my new house was being constructed, and found that the contractor had kept his word, completing the dock as ordered. I hauled the body out of the boat, dragged it up through some weeds, and hid it under a canvas tarp, covered with weeds, in such a manner that wild animals would not find it. I then steamed back to Sandusky. By the time I arrived, the lingering odors from the decaying body had disappeared.

I slept late Tuesday morning. Livia and Frau Gelbermann had already had breakfast when I came down from my room. There was no cargo delivery scheduled for that day, and after breakfast I said to Livia, "Thursday you will leave. I will go with you for the first part of the journey." She looked surprised, but said nothing.

That afternoon I left her and the Frau and took the steam launch out to my new house on the Marblehead Peninsula. I had loaded a few things in it earlier. I had now gone putting past the U.S.S. Michigan often enough that they no longer sounded the alarm when I approached. I tied up at the dock, and awaited sunset.

When it was almost dark I untied the launch and climbed in, waiting to see in which direction it would drift. It hardly moved at all, but in the distance, toward the island, I could hear the baying of hounds. I knew the time to move had come. I started the engine and putted off in the dark in the direction of the island, approaching from the north, then curving around toward the west. I came in as close to the shore as possible, and watched. Soon I saw a man waving his arms, and moved as close as I could. He splashed into the water and swam out to the launch, and I pulled him in.

Albert was soaked and his striped uniform clung to him as he fell exhausted into the boat. We could still hear the dogs baying in the woods behind him on the island. I turned the boat around and ran as quickly as I could back to the dock. While we went I instructed Albert to take off his prison uniform and put on the clothes I had brought for him that were in a satchel in the bow of the boat, but to not throw the uniform away. He had completely changed when we got back to the dock, and I shut the engine gears down.

We then climbed up the bank, went to where I had hidden the corpse, and pulled it down to the launch. What little clothing was on it was stripped away, and we put Albert's uniform, complete with the red officer's stripe on it, and, in the tarp placed it back on the steam launch. I then fired up the engine again, and we putted back toward the far side of Johnson Island.

We could still hear the dogs as we reached the far western point of the island. There I brought the launch in as close as possible to the shore, and we rolled the tarped body up on the gunwale, slid it over the side, and I slashed into the water, dragging it to the shore. I made sure that it was well tangled in weeds and would not float off on its own. I anticipated that it would be at least a day or two before it was found.

Back in the launch, we steamed at full speed westward. There was only a slight moon that night, and it was difficult finding the mouth of the Sandusky River, but once in it we putted upstream as far as we could, and I shut off the engine.

"Why are you doing this?" Albert asked.

"I have reasons," I answered.

"Livia?" he asked.

"No, not really, although she is a lovely lady, your sister."

"What is going to happen?"

"First we are going to sit here until morning," I said, opening a box with some food and a jug of water inside. "Then I'm going to get you out of this boat and have you slog through this swampy river about four miles to a road that runs south. That's why the big heavy boots you have on now will be needed. Once you reach that road, get rid of the muddy boots and trousers and put on these in this sack. Then you'll walk about ten miles south to a little village named Clyde. Two railroads intersect there. Find someplace to hide for the night. There are no hotels.

"In the morning dress in the clothes in this satchel. There's a frock coat and hat, and dress shirt, and a bit of money. There will be two southbound trains. The first is a mail train. The second is a passenger express train that runs about a half-hour later. When the first train goes by, start out for the depot, and wait there. There will also be freight trains going in both directions, and trains on the east and west line, but watch for that mail train about nine-forty. I'll be on the ten-fifteen. If you're not there, I'll not wait."

He said he understood. We were both tired, and it was the middle of the night. He curled up in one side of the boat and I in the other. The sun was already high in the sky when we awoke. We both ate some more food, and he started off over the sandbar and into the swampy marshes at the river's east side. I hoped that he would find higher dry ground soon, but knew that the marshes could go for some distance. I'd given him a long-sleeved shirt and some netting, as the bugs and mosquitoes were very thick in those marshes. When he was out of sight I started the engine and putted back into the Bay and eastward to Sandusky. I could see the Michigan prowling around Johnson Island.

I had stopped at the coal dock on the way back to refill the bunker on the launch. Some of the men were talking, and mentioned that they had just returned from taking a load of coal out to the prison.

"Yeah," one was saying, "I heard they haven't found him yet, but expect to soon. His body will show up somewhere along the shore, you can be certain. There's no place to go out there, even if you got off the island."

"What happened?" I inquired.

"Some Johnnie Reb's trying to escape again. They never learn, those Rebs. What's he think he's going to do, swim to Canada?"

"Yeah, four of 'em froze to death last year trying to walk across on the ice. I know you can walk to the islands on the ice some years, or so I've heard – never tried it – but you can't walk to Canada."

"It's like some of those runaway slaves that used to come through here," the first said. "Try to get someone to take them to Canada, and their bodies would end up floating ashore on Kelley or South Bass. All that trouble, then to be murdered."

"Well, hell! The Canadians didn't want 'em," the other said. "All those slaves knew how to do was pick cotton or tobacco."

"They've got tobacco in Canada," I said. "Some of those Ontario farmers were paying the abolitionists to get them up there. They needed the labor."

"That so? I didn't know that."

I steamed on back to the Harper docks, tied up, and returned to the house. Livia said very little that afternoon, but I told her to be packed and ready to leave by eight the next morning. Frau Gelbermann said she'd be up and have an early breakfast for us. I had arranged for a carriage and driver to pick us up. What I didn't have yet was a plausible story as to why I would leave town with a beautiful young lady, and I knew word of it would spread around town. Most of my Lodge friends already knew that Livia was from the South and had visited her brother in prison. "Why is she staying with you?" Captain Harper had asked me.

"Why not?" I had replied with a wink. He asked nothing further. But implying any impropriety would be foolish. I couldn't pass her off as a distant cousin, so I simply let it be known that she had other relatives in the area and I was going to take her to them. I hoped that would quiet the speculation.

Thursday morning was sunny, and our carriage arrived right on time. We rode to the Cincinnati, Sandusky & Cleveland depot, where I had found Livia, and I purchased two tickets to Clyde. That was not unusual, as it was the junction with the Lake Shore line, which sold its own tickets.

Livia Parkens and I boarded the train, which left only a minute or two late. At about a quarter after ten it pulled into Clyde and we climbed off with Livia's two pieces of baggage. Albert was waiting. I had warned both Livia and Albert not to do or say anything at the depot, as there were almost always Union soldiers around, and many in the area now knew that Livia was from Georgia and had visited her brother at the prison.

I nodded to Albert, and we entered the station, which was operated by the Lake Shore line. The next eastbound train from Chicago was due at a little after noon. I purchased two one-way tickets for Buffalo, and Albert followed the instructions I had given him to also purchase a ticket for Buffalo, but to make it a round trip ticket. He had seemed puzzled by this until I explained that if anyone questioned who he was, having a return ticket would be considered less suspicious. I then went across the street to a small shop and purchased some food and a jug of water.

Once aboard the train I gave the Parkens final instructions. They were to go to Buffalo, cross into Canada, take the train to Montreal, and get on a ship bound for Bermuda. I gave them the name of a friend in the town of St. George who would help them find a blockade running vessel for Charleston or Savannah. Then I gave Livia a letter to give to the agent.

"I'll miss you, Livia," I said as the train approached Cleveland. "After the war, if you are back in Savannah, may I call upon you?"

"Well, certainly, James," she replied. "But I still can't understand why you have done all you did for Albert and me. After all, you're a Yankee, and...."

It was risky, I knew. But I could not resist the temptation. I leaned over, kissed Livia on the cheek, and whispered in her ear, "I'm a Georgian, and a Confederate agent. You must tell no one. Absolutely no one."

She looked at me and smiled. I'll never forget that smile. The train rattled over a bridge into Cleveland, and I got up to get off. As I stepped toward the vestibule of the car Livia came and stood beside me. I turned, and she put her arms around me and we kissed. The train came to a stop, and I climbed down.

I waved at the two siblings as the train moved on a half-hour later. Then I bought a ticket and took a westbound train back to Clyde. That evening I was home again, alone and lonely, with many thoughts about the lovely Livia.

Chapter 10

Journal Three
November 1, 1863
Sandusky, Ohio

The plan had worked well. I now knew that I could successfully rescue officers from Johnson Island. Two days later I was out there with freight. Major Eddelstone called me into his office. "That young woman you brought out to visit her brother," he started.

"Yes?" I said, not sure what Eddelstone would say.

"If she's still in town, I'm afraid I have some bad news for her."

"Oh, what happened?"

"Well, the son of a bitch tried to escape two nights later. He got lost in the woods. When we found his carcass it was pretty much torn up by animals and birds. Hardly recognizable. We buried him in the cemetery. She was a pretty thing, and I think she was really devoted to her brother. He seemed a decent lad, very knowledgeable."

"Oh? I'd just met him at that service. Seemed a typical Southern bastard to me," I said. "And she was a pain. Very demanding. I'd not be surprised they were really husband and wife."

"Really? I guess that's possible."

"She went off on the train a couple of days later. Don't know why she hung around."

"I heard she stayed with you."

"With the old German lady who cleans and cooks for me, really. It's a big house, Major Eddelstone. Say, why don't you come over for the Friday night Lodge meeting and spend the night with me? You're a single man, and I'll bet I could scare up a few local ladies who might like to meet you."

"Why, thank you, Fitzgibbons. I might just do that. I get tired of living out here with these prisoners all the time, eating the same stuff they do, getting up at the same awful hour, and listening to that bugle all day long."

"You probably heard that I bought a farm over on Marblehead Peninsula," I said, sounding him out.

"I did hear something about that, yes. Just opposite the island, here. Captain Carter on the Michigan said he'd seen you on a small steam launch going back and forth, and that you seemed to be building a big stone house out there."

"It's about finished, or will be by autumn. Next spring I'll get some of the land plowed and planted, and see what will grow. If this war is still on, let me know what you need, and maybe we can do business."

"Always need cabbages, if you can grow those. And potatoes, onions, stuff like that. You going to have any cattle?"

"No, too much work," I said. I offered to steam out and pick him up on Friday, but he said he'd come in on the ferry.

* * *

March 8, 1864
Marblehead, Ohio

The prison was filling quickly, mostly with officers or a few non-commissioned officers. In July the Union had won battles both at Gettysburg and Vicksburg, and in September of 1863 Rosecrans had taken Chattanooga, and it was clear that the plan was to overwhelm the South in Georgia. Word reached me to Zeb had escaped capture during the battle at Vicksburg, and had managed to make it back home to Tebeauville. I was anxious to get back south, but knew my duty was to stay where I was.

By mid-October the house and barn were completed and I moved some furniture into the new house on the Bay. With so few neighbors I decided to spend the winter in Sandusky, but to visit the farmhouse every week to check on it. The winter of 1863-64 was one of the coldest in many years, old-timers in Sandusky told me, and by mid-January the Bay was frozen solid all around Johnson Island and in the harbor. At that time there was only one road on the Peninsula, running from Port Clinton to Danbury, a point on the south side of the Peninsula, and from there to the quarry and dock opposite Kelley's Island, by the lighthouse.

One morning a load of freight – they appeared to be new prison uniforms – arrived at the train depot. I needed news of what was happening out there, so I agreed to take the boxes on the roads to get there. It was a long trip, and I hired two sturdy horses and a wagon at the livery stable. The trip was over twenty-five miles to Fremont, where I stopped for the first night, then another twenty to Port Clinton, and then on the third day another twenty beyond that to my farm. From there I loaded the boxes on a sled, and with just one horse, ventured out onto the ice. It held nicely, and Major Eddelstone was delighted to receive his cargo.

I heated up the fireplaces and stoves in the house, and spent the next three days out there. On the second night there was a blizzard. I went out to the barn to check on the two horses and to make sure they had plenty of feed, and I heard the hounds baying on the island. It was obvious that someone had escaped, and might try to cross over to the Peninsula on the ice. I made my way through the wind and snow to the dock and looked out, but in the driving snow I could see nothing. I went back into the house and got a lantern, which I filled with oil and lit. Returning to the dock, I hung the lantern at the back of a post, so that it could not be seen from the island, but might be seen up and down the shoreline.

About midnight I heard some rattling downstairs. I thought it was probably the wind, but grabbed my revolver anyway, and crept down the stairs to the main room below. I heard voices, obviously Southern voices, of at least three men. "Don't see much food," one was saying.

One had brought the lantern in with him, and as he walked into the room where I was standing at the foot of the stairs and saw me with the revolver in his hand, he almost dropped the light. "Be careful," I said. "I don't want a fire out here. Tell your friends to come in here and sit down. I'll get you food in a few minutes."

The other two men slowly entered the room after being coaxed by the first. All three had the red stripe on their uniforms indicating they were officers, as were almost all the prisoners on Johnson Island. "Welcome, gentlemen, to my farm," I said. "You must be cold and tired after your journey on the ice."

One of the officers recognized me. "You're that man that brings supplies out to the prison all the time. In fact, I saw you there today."

"That's right," I said. "And I don't see any reason for you three to have to go back there," I added. "The problem is, as soon as this storm lets up, the guards will cross over the same way you did and find us all here. Now, that wouldn't do, as it would look like I'd helped you to escape, which I didn't. But I did hang out that lantern in case you came this way."

"It led us right here," one of the enlisted men said. "We brought it into the house in case those damned bloodhounds they've got over there tracked us across the ice."

"First, tell me who you are," I said, "and then we'll decide what to do." The senior officer spoke for the other two. All three were members of the Georgia Volunteer Infantry who had been captured at Vicksburg the previous summer. The leader was Captain Lawrence Harder, of Thomasville. He later told me he knew Zebulon, and confirmed that he had escaped when the others were captured. One of the junior officers was Lieutenant Billy Jones, also of Thomasville, and the third man Reginald White, of Albany. I looked at the third man and asked, "You know a planter named Alderman there, a Jackson Alderman?"

"Uncle Jack? Sure! How the hell d'yah of know him? He was killed at Vicksburg. A Captain, like Captain Harder, here. But how...."

"It's not important for you to know who or what I know, Lieutenant. It's just important for your commanding officer, here, to get you safely back home and into the war. That's his job, and I don't want to stand in the way of any man doing his job," I said.

The problem was, how would I help these three to escape? I hadn't any corpses to dress up, and I didn't even have extra civilian clothes for them to wear. But I did have blankets, and I soon got them something to eat and got them bedded down for the night.

Early the next morning the snow was still falling, which meant that any scent the dogs might have been following would dissipate. I had also thought of a plan — although not a good one — of how I might fool Major Eddelstone. I had each of the three give me parts of their uniforms, a prison cap, and shirts with their red stripe. These Jones and I took as far west down the shore as we could manage to walk in the deep snow. I found several large rocks, and from the bank we threw each as far out onto the ice as we could until finally one broke through the ice. I then took the uniform parts, soaked them in the icy water, and made sure they were frozen into the surface of the ice so that it would appear the men had broken through thin ice and had drowned. Meanwhile Harder and White had been fashioning blankets into coats that they could wear.

Early the next morning I harnessed the two horses, hooked up the wagon, and we started down the path toward the road to the Kelley's Island dock and Port Clinton. There I had the men hide in the back of the wagon until I could purchase some warm clothing for them. It was already evening, but we started south toward Fremont as the snow had stopped blowing, and the roadway was well packed from other traffic during the day. The men were lighter than the freight I'd hauled up, and we arrived in Fremont early the next morning, cold and hungry, but safe.

I took the horses and wagon to the livery for food and water, and arranged to have them sold. I then got hotel rooms for the four of us, and we dined in the dining room. "Don't say anything," I warned them. "Your voices will give you away. Let me do any talking." I needed to get these three men to Canada as quickly as possible. Captain Harder had the least Southern-sounding voice, and my plan was simple. I'd put them on the train to Buffalo, as I had with the Parkens. If no one spoke to them, they were not to speak to others. I gave Harder my revolver, and went down to the hardware store and purchased a set of shackles. In the morning, when the three boarded the train, the two junior officers were to be shackled together. Harder could explain that he was a federal marshal and was taking the two captured Rebs for a trial in Buffalo. Once there, they could toss the shackles and cross into Canada, making their way to Montreal and on to Bermuda. I hadn't much money with me, but gave them all I had. I also had a couple of contacts in Toronto, and gave their names to Harder.

Whether the three made it back to Dixie I don't know. I got back to Sandusky the same day, stopped at the bank for some cash to pay the livery bill, and went back to the big house on Huron to plan my strategy. It was clear that men would attempt escape from the prison any way they could. If I were to use the same strategy I had used with Parkens,

I'd need a good supply of cadavers, fresh clothes and food. My own horse was not capable of the trip to Marblehead, and I would need a sturdy wagon. I went back to the livery stable, and arranged to purchase two fairly strong horses worthy of the task. The cost, with my own horse traded, was less than the cost of one single workhorse. I then visited a wagon dealer and got a sturdy wagon with an enclosed seat, then stopped at several stores to purchase supplies, food, clothing and other things I thought I would need. As many of the shopkeepers were Lodge members who knew that I had purchased a farm out on the Peninsula, it was easy to explain that I was simply moving from my house in town to the farm temporarily.

Well loaded down with hay, oats, food, clothing and other things, I waited until nightfall, returned to the town cemetery, and found four fresh graves with young or middle-aged men in them. The ground was frozen solid, and the work of digging the dirt hard and heavy labor, but by sunrise I had the corpses wrapped up in the wagon and had started down the road to Fremont. While the bodies in the back were now frozen, any heat during the day would easily turn them rancid, so I bypassed the town, and went toward Port Clinton. A few miles north of Fremont I found a secluded spot to hide the wagon for the night, so I unhitched the two horses and rode one, leading the other, into town, where I put them in the livery stable overnight, and returned to the hotel.

"Back again?" the clerk said, recognizing me from two nights earlier.

"Yes, I'll probably be passing through town every so often," I said.

"Who were your three buddies?" he asked, in reference to the three soldiers who were with me on that previous visit."

I leaned over the counter and whispered in the clerk's ear. "I'm not supposed to say, but that was a federal marshal and two Johnnie Reb spies he'd caught. But it's a secret, and if you were to say anything, even to your boss here at the hotel, you'd be in violation of a federal security law, and they'd have to arrest you."

"God, Mister! I promise I won't say nothing." he exclaimed, a frightened look in his eye. I told him that was good, and that I'd be leaving early the next morning. I knew that by saying what I had, he'd not try to probe me for information about who I was.

By late that night I had my wagon load of supplies and bodies at the farm. I had encountered no one on the journey, and had not made any stops in Port Clinton, except briefly outside the town to feed the horses. I stabled them in the barn, got them bedded down and fed, and went into the house to get the fireplaces and stoves going for heat. That night it started to snow again, and by morning I could barely make out the barn from the upstairs window.

My first job was to find a secure place to keep the pauper cadavers I had brought with me. I needed to keep the bodies as fresh as possible, so I went down to the water, cut some large slabs of ice, loaded them on the sled I had out there, and got one of the horses harnessed to pull it up the embankment. I then stacked the four well-wrapped bodies in a corner of the icehouse I had the contractor build for me as an addition to the main house, and packed the ice around it. The floor of the icehouse was at least ten feet below the ground level, with a drain off to the water's edge. I calculated that the ice would keep those bodies frozen solid until well into late spring.

The days were long, but I had brought some books with me, and continued writing these journals, so my time was not wasted. Each afternoon and evening I would go outside after taking care of the horses, and listen for the dogs. Twice, several weeks apart, I heard them baying, and knew that a prisoner had gotten loose on the island, and would probably try to escape over the frozen Bay. By then I had made a wagon path between my farm and the high hill to the west of the farm, extending the road that went east toward the lighthouse. I would hang a lantern on the dock post so that it could not be seen from the island but could be seen from along the shoreline. Then I would hike up to the hill and with a small sea-captain's telescope I had purchased, watch the ice to see if I could spot the escapee.

Both times the men were successful in getting to the shore before the dogs located their scent in the frozen woods of the island's southwest end. Both were officers. I found each, usually hungry, half frozen, and scared, and brought them to the house. We would retrieve a corpse from the ice house, dress it in the escapee's uniform, and haul it back down the shore far enough that it was out of sight of the dock at the farm. Then, from the hill, I would watch until guards, venturing out on the ice, spotted the body in its prison uniform, and crossed to make sure the prisoner was dead. Our only fear was that the guards would recognize that the body was not that of the escapee. But in one case the officer said he'd only been on the island since a week before the Bay froze and had kept clear of the guards, hence he doubted they knew what he looked like. The second one the guards simply hauled back onto the ice, found the body too heavy to carry, and broke a hole in the ice and shoved it through.

Rather than risk the long wagon trip to Fremont or Toledo with the two officers, I simply kept them at the farm until the ice would break up on the Bay and we could get the steam launch, which was in dry-dock in Sandusky. Several times I walked across the ice in the daytime to the prison and visited with Major Eddelstone, once borrowing some flour and coffee from the commissary, and asking when he though the ice would break up and the ferry could operate again. I said I'd heard the dogs baying a couple of times, and asked if there had been escapes.

"Yes, several this winter, since the ice froze, but they all died of exposure. Three of them fell through the ice, and the other two only made it to the shore."

"Is there anything I can do to help?" I asked.

"Just keep a lookout. If you see anyone in one of our prison uniforms trying to escape, just shoot him. Don't try to be a hero." I promised to do just that.

* * *

It was nearly April before the ice was sufficiently thin that the ferry could resume operations to the island prison. It had been nearly three months since I had delivered the load of supplies, and the prison commissary needed almost everything. During the winter a number of the prisoners had died, many of wounds they had sustained before being captured. On one of the first trips out to the island, the ferry had brought Army guards with twenty more prisoners.

I had a small rowboat at the farm, and rowed over to the prison dock to meet the ferry on the second day of its operation. I warned my two guests, one of whom was a Colonel from South Carolina and the other a Major from Tennessee, to stay hidden in the house until I returned, regardless of who might stop. I took the ferry over to Sandusky, arranged with Captain Harper to get my launch out of storage, went uptown to check on the house there (where the widow Frau Gelbermann had spent the winter, it being more comfortable for her than her own small house), and then took the launch to the coal dock to fill the bunker and get a good supply of coal for my stoves at the farm. I then steamed back to the harbor, docked, got more supplies at the various shops in town, and steamed back out to the Peninsula, arriving just before sunset. That evening my guests and I dined well. It was about time for them to move on.

Neither man had enough of a Northern accent to be able to pass themselves off as anything other than from the South. My little steam launch was not sufficient for a trip to Canada, nor even to some of the outer islands. I did think I could manage a trip over the open water as far as Kelley's Island, however. From there, they could take the Island Queen ferry to Put-In-Bay and on to Detroit, but they would need to be cautious. I gave them some money, and gave each a pistol I'd gotten them in Sandusky. Once at Detroit, they were to cross into Canada, and try to get to Bermuda if they could.

The following morning we watched until we saw the Island Queen steam out of Sandusky on its scheduled trip to the islands and Detroit. I fired up the boiler on the launch and steamed out ahead of it, running the tiny vessel as fast as its little rear paddle-wheel would turn, arriving at the Kelley's Island dock well ahead of the much larger and faster ferry. My two passengers disembarked, and waited for the ferry while I headed westward well out of the ferry's way, then crossed back to the Peninsula. I anticipated that my steam launch might be recognized, but hoped that I had kept far enough ahead of the ferry that the captain would not recognize me and later ask who my two passengers had been. Captain Harper had hired several new men, and I remained hopeful that the ferry crew might be some of the newly hired.

By noon I had rounded the point on Marblehead and steamed on across the Bay to Sandusky, deciding to spend the night in town. It was a Friday, and I had not been at a Lodge meeting for months. As usual, there was talk of little else but the war. The North was winning, some said. The South was winning, said others. The newspapers told of battles and sieges, but little was decisive. General Sherman was mounting an attack in North Georgia, having successfully claimed Tennessee the previous November in the Battle of Missionary Ridge at Chattanooga.

* * *

May 20, 1864
Marblehead, Ohio

I stayed in town all the following week, catching up on the news and ferrying supplies out to my farm. As I no longer had a horse in town, I either carried things down to my boat, or had the shops deliver goods there. I had to make a trip to the farm each day to take care of the horses. I received practically no mail, but did check periodically at the post office. When I had first come back to town there was a tax bill awaiting me, and I promptly went to the bank to draw a check to pay Erie County. I wanted no hassles with the tax collector. I planned to return to the farm the following Saturday, after Friday night Lodge. That afternoon I again checked at the post office, and found a large envelope, mailed from Bermuda and sent via Canada. I opened it and found a sheet of music.

I knew what it was. We had arranged a code based on the scale. The key signature would indicate where "A" began, and the letters would then be sequential. I folded it and stuck it in my coat pocket, knowing that it would take hours to decipher. I could do that at the farm. Before I left the following morning I gave Frau Gelbermann a large amount of money, and told her that it might be that I would be doing some traveling, and she was to keep the house in good shape for me until I returned. She seemed delighted that her stay in the big house was to continue, and I knew it was in good hands.

That afternoon I sat at my desk at the farm and started to translate the music. It would have made no sense if played on a piano – just a lot of random notes. But every few measures the key would change, and the translation was tedious. There was no greeting, no closing, not even a date. It simply read:

Col. Pierce Heber captured at Norfolk. Transported Johnson Is. in December
Desperately needed in Richmond. Rescue and transport to Hamilton.
While there, meet French corvette, escort to Veracruz for cargo. Escort
Suwannee, Savannah. High caution. Up to you now. JD

It was April 20, and the Bay was now totally clear of ice. The ferry was bringing supplies and new prisoners over to Johnson Island almost daily. I no longer accompanied the freight, but I did stop over every few days to visit Major Eddelstone, and took him over to Sandusky for Lodge meetings. A day after translating the message I decided that a bold move was needed. I steamed over to the prison and waited in Eddelstone's office while he reviewed some formation of guards and prisoners. He seemed glad to see me when he came in, and offered me a glass of whiskey.

After a bit of chat about Lodge I said, "There's a rumor you got some sort of French mercenary here."

"A Frenchman, what, a spy?" he answered, looking puzzled. "You mean a man that's not a Confederate?"

"Oh, I don't know what he might be, or say he is. It's just a rumor I heard a day or so ago when I was down in Fremont. Some French officer was caught in a blockade at Norfolk or some other Southern port, and sent up here in December."

"If he'd have been a spy, they'd have hung him," Eddelstone said. "We got some officers they send up from Virginia in December, but they were all uniformed Southern officers as far as I know. What else have you heard about this mercenary?"

"Oh, nothing else. It probably isn't even true. You know how rumors are. But is there any chance I might get to meet some of those officers who came in last December? If one really is French, and maybe even a spy, I'd like to be able to say after the war's over that I met a real French Confederate mercenary!"

"You want to meet the prisoners?"

"Oh, no, not all of them. Maybe just the ones you got in December."

"Odd request, Fitsgibbons, but I certainly don't care. Sergeant," he called to one of his guards, "look in the register and see how many officers we received as prisoners in December from Norfolk or any other blockaded port, and have them report outside."

"Yes, sir," the guard replied, and moved to a large log book on another table, where he started writing down names. Meanwhile, I changed the subject, and the Major and I talked about the quality of beef the prison was receiving. I said I would see what I might to do get them a better quality.

About twenty minutes later the sergeant came back in and said he had the officers lined up. I had known both the sergeant and Eddelstone long enough to know that neither spoke any foreign languages, although Eddelstone, as a military academy graduate, had a vague familiarity with Latin. Most military schools had their students study Roman battles in the original Latin. Eddelstone accompanied me outside, and we looked at the pathetic, scrawny men standing before us in their prison uniforms, each with a red stripe on the shoulder. Many appeared ill, others were bandaged, and two had missing arms.

Pierce was in the middle of them. He had grown a full black beard, and his hair was long and stringy, and I hardly recognized him. I could tell from the look in his eye that he was shocked to see me, but he did not let on. "Gentlemen," Eddelstone said as we went out, "this is our nearest neighbor, James Fitzgibbons, who has a farm nearby. Said he wanted to meet those of you who arrived in December. He's the man who brought out the uniforms you're wearing, and the blankets you use at night, and the food you ate this past winter, and what coal we had. Hauled it on a sled over the ice. He told me he'd heard that one of you was a Frenchman. Are any of you men French?" Nobody responded.

"Guess the rumor was wrong, Eddelstone," I said, interrupting. "But I traveled in the South once, down to New Orleans. Any of you from or been to New Orleans?"

Haber knew I meant for him to answer, and he raised his hand. "J'espère vous revoir bientôt," I said in French, telling him I hoped to see him. None of the other prisoners seemed to understand, so I continued, looking directly at Eddelstone. "Dois-je tourner au nord, ce soir, minuit." Turn north tonight at midnight, I said for Pierce.

"Oh, I don't understand French," the Major laughed. "I don't think that fellow from Louisiana does either."

"No, these Southern fellows aren't very well educated. What's the name of that man from New Orleans?"

"Sergeant?" Eddelstone asked. The sergeant consulted his list.

"Morgan, sir. A Lieutenant Pete Morgan. His record says he was a cannoneer on a Confederate ship that was trying to run the blockade at Norfolk. Six of these guys were on that same ship."

"Thank you, Sergeant," Eddelstone said. "You want to meet any others?" he asked me.

"No, they're a sorry-looking lot. I wouldn't want your job, Eddelstone," I replied.

"Dismiss the men back to their work duties, Sergeant," Eddelstone ordered, and the prisoners filed off back toward the barracks. The Major and I went back into his office to finish our whiskey.

After eleven that night I took the rowboat out from the dock and quickly crossed the channel between the farm and the island. It was a dark night, just a new moon, and thick clouds that hid it. In the distance I could hear thunder from an approaching storm. I pulled the boat into the low trees and weeds along the north embankment and waited. Several times I thought I heard someone crashing through the woods, but the first time it was only a fox chasing a rabbit. The second time the sound stopped, and in the distance I could hear some shouting from the prison. The rustling in the trees continued again, and then I heard the baying of the hounds as they picked up the scent of the escaped prisoner.

"Here!" I said as loud as I dared, and I heard the frantic rustling getting closer. Then Heber was at the water's edge and I grabbed him and pulled him into the boat and rowed as hard as I could back to the dock at the farm. We had no sooner tied up than the Michigan steamed up the middle of the channel. It was barely deep enough for the gunboat, but by staying in the middle of the channel it could make passage completely around the island. I could see the crew, all standing on the starboard side, carefully surveying the north shore of the island. In the distance the dogs were still baying as they chased the scent Heber had left.

"My God, that was close!" Pierce said. "How on earth did you find me?"

"It was luck, I guess, but I got a message that you had been captured and brought here. I'm afraid I had to make up some story about a possible spy in order to get to see you, and I know it was a risk to speak in French, but I knew Eddelstone, the commander, did not know French, nor any of the other guards I've met.

"None of the other prisoners I came in with do, either," he replied. "But what the hell are we going to do?"

"You're going to be shot," I said.

"What!"

"Don't worry about it. I've already rescued six men off that island and got them out of the country. We have orders to get to Hamilton, and for you to get to Richmond, Colonel. Only your corpse will still be here."

"I don't understand."

"You will," I replied. The storm that had been brewing to the west over the lake now hit with full fury. We drank some whiskey and then I took Heber to a room on the second floor and got him out of his uniform and into bed. The uniform I hid until the morning, just in case the guards might come to inquire. At this point I could only hope that they did not yet make a connection between the escaped prisoner and the man from New Orleans to whom I had spoken French earlier that day.

Both of us were up early the next morning. I had laid out fresh clothes for Pierce, hoping I'd judged the sizes correctly, and he said I had. After we had some breakfast and coffee, I told him that he was going to have to shave, and that I'd cut his hair, but that he was not to throw the hair he shaved off away. Again he looked puzzled, but agreed. I got him a kettle of hot water and a basin, and a small basket to put the thick black hair in. Then I led him down through the basement to the ice house and moved the blocks of ice out of the way, exposing the two wrapped cadavers. One was a bald man, but the other had dark hair, but no beard. The corpse appeared to be about our same age. I could see that he had been shot to death, probably in a bar brawl, since he was in the pauper's cemetery, and that would be useful. We hauled the cadaver up the stairs, dressed it in Pierce's prison uniform, burning a small hole at the same location as the dead man's wound, and then, using some mucilage, carefully stuck the black beard Pierce had shaved off that morning onto the face of the corpse. I had previously tested the glue in water and knew it would not easily wash off.

We waited until near evening. The gunboat was still patrolling the channel, and we could still hear the bloodhounds baying on the island. Just before dark Pierce and I carried the still-frozen corpse down toward the sandy point at the end of Marblehead and lodged it between several rocks. Then I fired my revolver several times in the air, hoping the shots could be heard at the prison. We then returned to the house and got ourselves something to eat. I fed and bedded down the horses, and we talked until very late.

The next morning I took the steam launch over to the prison and went up to Eddelstone's office. The sergeant nodded as I came in, and I waited until the Major returned from wherever he had been.

"Oh, Fitzgibbons! Back again, I see."

"Yes. I'm afraid I've gone and shot one of your prisoners?"

"What?! You did?" he exclaimed. "Where? We had one escape the other night, the same one you spoke to in French, some gunnery officer."

"Is that who it was? Well, I was down along the Point checking some traps I'd set out, and this prisoner of yours jumps up and throws a big rock at me. He started to charge at me, and I did as you said and shot the bastard. He's out there now, somewhere down on the rocks along the Point. It was getting dark, and he probably thought I was one of the prison guards. I couldn't see his face very well, but I think he had a beard."

"Yes, that's Morgan, all right. Morgan the Pirate, some of the others called him. Well, well. I guess we owe you for the bullet, James. Will you bill the Army?"

"Ha!" I laughed. "One less Johnnie Reb isn't going to hurt my feelings. My pleasure, Major. But while I'm here, I wanted to tell you that I was taking my team and wagon over to Toledo for some things. I'll be gone probably a few weeks, and will leave the steam launch at my dock at the farm, though I may go into Sandusky by train a few times before coming back here. So if you see it docked over there, don't be concerned."

"That's fine, James Fitzgibbons. You have a good trip. If you happen to come across some of that good Canadian rye whiskey, though, I'd sure like to have a few bottles." I told him I'd see what I could do.

The next morning I watched the channel, but never did see a boat go out toward the Point to see about the body we had hidden there. We loaded up the wagon, including the remaining frozen corpse, and closed up the house. I had Pierce stay in the back of the wagon until we were well out of sight of the channel. Then he moved up onto the driver's bench and we continued down the dirt road past the lighthouse, the quarry and dock to Kelley's Island, and on toward Danbury and Port Clinton, reaching the town about dusk. Along the way we dumped the frozen corpse into a swamp. While Pierce, who had no Southern accent, arranged for rooms at the hotel, I took the horses and wagon down to the livery stable. I asked for the owner, but was told to come back in the morning.

After breakfast the next day I returned to the livery stable and spoke to the manager. I told him that I was going to be joining the Army and wondered if he would buy my team. It was a good strong and healthy team, and I had taken good care of them. He agreed, gave me a fair price – I might have taken even less – and I offered him the wagon as well. Back at the hotel I met Pierce Heber, and we walked down to the docks and learned that a Cleveland to Detroit steamer would be stopping that afternoon. We bought our tickets, and by evening were steaming up the Detroit River.

The ferry to the Windsor Great Western Railway terminal left Detroit at eight-thirty the next morning, and the train for Hamilton departed at nine, arriving in Hamilton that afternoon about four. An accommodation train arrived in Toronto about nine that evening, and we stayed at a hotel near the station. The following morning we departed for Montreal, an all-day trip of more than three hundred miles. Many in Montreal spoke French, and we soon found a packet steamer bound for Martinique in the Caribbean that agreed to drop us in Bermuda on the way.

It was the end of the first week in May before we arrived in St. George Harbor, and we had encountered a fairly strong squall off the Georgian Banks on our way south. On the way Heber had explained the urgency of his mission and the possible complications that might well result from his delay by having been captured. Since 1862 he had been tempting the French to oppose the Union blockade so that Confederate cotton could go to both England and France. In November of that year the French Ambassador had suggested to Secretary of State William Seward that it was time to recognize the independence of the South, and end the war, but there was no official statement as Napoleon III was awaiting a similar suggestion from the British. The French also tried to get the Russians to intervene, but an armistice was rejected by Parliament.

The following year, 1863, had proven to be much more productive for Confederate interests abroad. The Confederate Navy had won several battles, and orders were placed in both Britain and France for armed iron rams that could break through blockades and allow cotton shipments to get out. But Southern finances were running thin and credit was hard to find.

In June of 1863 Napoleon III had invaded and captured Mexico, installing Maximilian of Austria as the Mexican emperor. The French leader saw this as an opportunity to restore French influence in the West, and the Confederate emissary, Slidell, offered Southern support to Mexico. Thus in January, shortly after Heber had been captured, the French proposed a truce between North and South, but Secretary Seward rejected the offer again.

Heber had been bringing word of negotiations with the French and with Maximilian to Richmond when he was captured. It remained vital for him to report developments. He had arranged with a Bordeaux shipbuilder to construct several steam corvettes and two armed rams, which were to be delivered in Hamilton by mid-May. The French were bringing some official documents, and Heber was to be the courier.

Although slavery had been abolished in Bermuda in 1834, sentiment among the populace was strongly for their Southern neighbor to the west. Bermuda had become a trading center with warehouses full of cotton being shipped to Britain and France that had managed to avoid the Union blockade, and armaments from Europe headed for the South. The problem was finding enough blockade runners to deliver the guns to the Confederate Army, now spread between the Mississippi and Virginia.

Sam Winston was our Confederate contact in Bermuda. He had lived in Hamilton when I had first purchased the house on Parlaville Road, which is where Pierce and I stayed when we first arrived, but Sam had moved to St. George, running several warehouses filled with Southern cotton awaiting European markets. He confirmed that two fully-armed corvettes and a ship of the Mexican Navy – which he understood was under Austrian control – would be arriving within a week or two. Two Confederate Navy crews were being billeted somewhere between Hamilton and St. George, awaiting the two corvettes. Their French sailors would return to France, and the Southern crews take command of the warships, although a French officer would remain aboard each to instruct the Confederate officers on the technicalities of the steamers and their guns.

Winston had with him two documents in French that had been given to him by a French agent to pass along to the Confederacy, but Sam spoke no French and did not know what they were. The documents proved to be in duplicate, a common practice, Heber told me, in the event a courier was about to be captured and was forced to destroy the document.

Upon opening and translating the documents we found that they were simply the titles to the two Bordeaux corvettes, financed on credit of 50,000 francs each by the Julius Marchaud Banque d'Paris. We wondered if Winston had enough cotton in his warehouses to pay for that, but at present that was his, not our problem. Heber kept one set to take to Richmond, and I placed the other in my box at the Bank of Hamilton.

Winston also had new passports for us, in the event of our capture. They were issued as Canadians, Pierce becoming Pierre Hoenig of Montreal, and I became James Farthington, a newspaper reporter from Toronto. I had been there often enough that I could easily describe the city, should anyone question my origin.

Nine days later the three vessels steamed into the harbor at St. George. One of the corvettes was towing a large fortified iron ram that could be mounted at the bow of the ship. Both the French crews and Winston were grateful that Heber and I spoke French, and while the crew enjoyed a day or two of shore leave, we firmed up our plans.

The Austrian ship, operating under a Mexican flag, was to be my responsibility. Heber would accompany the first corvette with the ram to Norfolk, and run as far up the James River as possible, completing his mission of six months earlier. I would accompany the second corvette and the Mexican steamer to Veracruz. The Mexican representative of Maximilian presented me a document in Spanish promising a loan of three million Confederate dollars in Mexican gold pesos, to be repaid upon legitimate establishment in the international community of the Confederate States of America. The document, also in duplicate, was signed by Archduke Maximilian, Emperor of Mexico, who was the brother of Austrian Emperor Francis Joseph. It was also countersigned by Napoleon III of France. I have kept one copy for presentation to Davis and Stephens in Richmond, and am placing the other with the two French documents in my bank lockbox.

May 20, 1864.
James Fitzgibbons, Tebeauville, Georgia,
Confederate States of America.

Chapter 11

October 28, 1963
Boston, Massachusetts

Jimmy Garth was frustrated and angry. Usually his anger was expressed in a flash of temper and a blow to someone's nose, but this time there was no one to strike, nothing on which to take out his frustrations. He sat on the side of his bed in his small apartment in the west end of Boston just off Commonwealth Avenue, wondering what to do. The six casks – round wooden barrels -- of coins he had found on the shelf of the bow hold of the wreck of the Austrian Princess did, indeed, contain gold coins. He had gone to the library before he left Clearwater Beach and had found a book on restoration of sunken merchandise, and had followed the instructions on how to preserve the value of metal objects such as coins. He'd even gathered up a few of the loose coins that had spilled from the cask that fell off the shelf, but had no idea how many casks there might have been originally. For all he knew there might be millions of dollars in gold scattered along the floor of the Gulf north of Hog Island. He had hidden the casks in the back of the pick-up truck that he had parked at the charter boat dock in Tarpon Springs, and stopped at the first military surplus store he found to buy two lockable footlockers and secure padlocks.

Once out of town he had stopped in a secluded place and transferred the coins to the two footlockers, and drove, almost non-stop, back to Boston. He had taken one of the cleaned-up coins to his cousin's friend, but the man had told him that he had no interest in trying to unload even one coin, let alone a bunch. He had suggested that Garth take the coin to a coin dealer he knew, a Sam Mittlestein. Garth had found him in a little shop in Brookline and showed him the coin.

"Mmm, Mexican, I see," the old gray-haired coin dealer had said. "And minted in 1864. Where'd you get this?"

"My old man had it. Picked it up somewhere during the War, I guess. I got it when he died."

"Yeah? Well, this isn't near mint condition; it shows some flaws," Mittlestein said, studying the coin under a magnifying glass. "I'd give you forty, eh, forty five bucks for it. Had it been in better shape, maybe fifty."

"Fifty bucks? Hell, my cousin says gold's going for two, three hundred an ounce, an' this is at least half an ounce. Bull! I ain't as dumb as you must think I am!"

"So take it elsewhere. I don't need more coins to unload right now anyway." "Don't worry. I will," Garth had muttered. Now he sat on his bed wondering what to do next. If gold was several hundred dollars an ounce, he had a couple hundred pounds of it. He had read where gold was measured in some sort of 'troy' measurement, a troy ounce was half a troy pound. Exactly how much that was he was uncertain, but even if it took a dozen troy ounces to make a real pound, he still had more than half a million dollars' worth of gold. But if the coins were rare, their real value might exceed their worth as just gold.

Where could he turn for help in making the best of his investment? He couldn't go to Plunkett nor any of the crew, nor to any of his old fishing boat buddies as word would quickly get back to Plunkett, and he didn't want to mess with Jay when Jay was mad. He'd seen him nearly kill guys before, and Plunkett had almost thrown him off the boat in the middle of the ocean once. He thought about his ex-wife's new husband, who was some sort of an insurance man, but then he thought that anyone he might tell, even ask, would want to be in on the deal. No, this was his gold. He found it. No one else.

His first task was to protect it. He didn't have much cash, but he had hauled the two footlockers up to his apartment, and didn't like having them sitting there. He wanted a more secure place, like a bonded warehouse so he looked in the Yellow Pages, found a couple, but on hearing what they charged, decided to risk leaving the lockers where they were. It was damned sure nobody was going to run off with a box weighing more than a hundred pounds, and the locks he had purchased were secure.

Then he thought of Danny. Danny Martin had been his schoolyard buddy for years before they both dropped out of high school. Jimmy had gone to work on the boats, but Danny had turned to crime. First was a bit of auto theft, but Danny evaded getting caught, even after one police chase in which Danny had wrecked the stolen car, but had managed to escape by swimming a drainage ditch. He had then turned to burglary, but had been caught inside a store with a silent alarm and had gone to prison for a year and a half. Garth tried to remember where Danny went after he got paroled. He recalled that Danny had been living with his mother, and perhaps she was still around. He looked her up in the phone book and found a number for the address where Danny and he used to hang out.

"'Lo," a wheezy voice said after several rings.

"Mrs. Martin?"

"Yeah. Who's dis?" she asked. He detected that she had been drinking, and perhaps was drunk.

"Mrs. Martin, this is Jimmy Garth, Danny's school buddy."

"Oh, yeah.... Jimmy. Been years. What'cha been doin' with yourself?"

"Working on boats, mostly, Mrs. Martin. Say, listen, is Danny in town?"

"Danny?" she asked, sounding like she'd never heard of him. Of course, she'd had six kids, and Danny was never one of her favorites. "No," she continued. "After he got out of the Pen he went west. The parole officer was looking for him awhile back, too. Last I heard he was in Cleveland."

"Cleveland? Ohio? You have an address?"

"I don' know. Lemme look," she answered, slurring her words. It was more than a minute before she returned. "Dis, maybe. 1481 Abbey, ahh, that's A-b-b-e-y. But it's been a few months since he wrote. Maybe he's not there now."

"I hope he is. Thanks, Mrs. Martin. You doin' okay?"

"Hell, no! The old may ran off with some twerp, an' I can't even pay the rent here. My youngest girl's still in school tryin' to get herself pregnant, and the older ones don't send me nothin'. No thought of their old mother. But you know how it is, Jimmy. You all've got your own lives to live."

"Yeah, I guess. So, if you hear from Danny, tell him I'm trying to find him. Bye."

Cleveland. It was a long-shot, but he'd nothing to lose, so he dialed information and asked for the Cleveland name and address. Amazed, he got a number, had the operator ring it, but there was no answer.

That night he tried again, but there was still no answer. At four the next morning he was awake, and decided to try it again. After six rings a grouchy voice answered, "Damn, it's the middle of the night. Who the hell is this?"

"Danny? Danny Martin?"

There was a pause, as if the person on the line was not sure. "Who's calling?" "Danny, it's me, Jimmy Garth. Your mama gave me your address."

"Jimmy! How the hell.... How are yah?"

"I'm fine. How about you?"

"I do okay. Where are you? Boston?"

"Sure. But there's nothing cooking here. I couldn't reach you yesterday or last night. Thought I'd try early."

"Dang it, Jimmy, you always were a night owl! But if you ain't doing nothing, why not come on out here, and see what we can get ourselves into, eh?"

"I was thinking that. Got a pick-up truck, but it's falling to pieces. Let me see what I can arrange, and I'll get back with you. What time do you usually get home from work?"

"Work? Ahh, well, depends. Sometimes I'm here all night, other times I ain't. Just keep callin'. But, Gees, don't do it at four in the damned morning!"

Garth's old pick-up truck had made it to Florida and back, but he was unsure it would make it to Cleveland. But then, he'd never been to Cleveland, and did not know what might be involved. There had been a map in the glove compartment of the old truck when he bought it, and he dressed and went out to get it. It was a New York map. He saw that there was a toll road from Albany west, but lots of other free roads. He guessed that it was probably around six to seven hundred miles. No, he'd need a new vehicle.

He had no love of anything in his apartment. That he would just abandon. The lease was about up, and the landlord could do as he wished. No sense paying another month's rent when I could move out. But he'd need dough, and he hadn't worked since Ward had paid the crew on the tug at the end of winter. He'd just been living on that for half a year, and now the dough was gone.

But if a crooked coin dealer would offer him forty bucks for a coin, maybe a more honest one would offer more. After he ate some breakfast he began calling dealers around Boston, and finally found one who said he'd take a look at the Mexican coin. He had told the dealer that he "had several." He'd dump eight or nine, enough for another truck – a panel truck this time, he thought, one he could sleep in if needed – and a bit of spending money until he could unload the coins for a real pile of dough.

The dealer offered him a hundred fifty each for two of the coins that were in pretty good shape, and a hundred each for six more that were badly stained. He'd been put through the same "where'd you get these" questioning and suspicious looks and didn't press his luck too far. He took the offers and left. Whether he had been chiseled or not he didn't know, or at that point care. The coin shop was over on the Cambridge side of the river, and on the way back to his apartment he saw a used car lot and pulled in. "What can we do for yah?" the salesman asked in a cheerful voice when he saw Garth looking over a 1957 Chevrolet panel truck. The sticker on the window read $699.

"This heap ain't worth no seven hundred," Garth replied. "Does it run?"

"Of course it runs!" the salesman answered. "Here, let me get the key and you can start it up. It's been tuned recently. It belonged to the phone company. They just used it to haul tools around, and had it repainted blue before they sold it to us. It's well maintained. Phone company does a good job of keepin' their stuff clean and in tiptop condition."

The salesman jogged over to his little shack and returned with a set of keys. He unlocked the door of the panel truck, popped the hood lever, and showed Garth how nice and clean the engine was. He started it up, and Garth walked around it, listened to the engine, checked the tires and looked in the back, which was empty.

"Give you four and a quarter for it," he said.

"Oh, I couldn't take that!" the salesman replied. "I might get my manager to come a tad off the seven hundred, but not that much."

"Yeah? Well go ask him. Tell him it's cash. No loans, no hassling around."

The salesman went into the shack and made out like he was pleading Garth's case. Garth doubted there was anybody else in the shack, or that the salesman had spoken to anyone, in person or by phone. Soon the salesman was back.

"No, he says the best he can do is six hundred even."

"Yeah, well, I think he can do better'n that if he tries. Look, I'll give you four fifty and that truck of mine over there. Got the title in the glove compartment, all free and clear, no loans. It's a good truck. Just needs a tune-up, and maybe a new tire."

"I don't know...."

"The hell you don't! Come on, you know it's a good offer. Let's go into your little shack there and tell the boss we've struck a bargain."

"He's at the other lot. I had to call him."

"Sure. He leaves you here with no authority to buy and sell? Don't gimme that!"

"Oh, all right. Four fifty and your truck. Plus tax, tag transfer, and we can write some insurance on it for you."

"Don't need no damned insurance. Just a bill of sale."

By six the next morning Garth was on the new Interstate, headed for Springfield in the panel truck. In the back were several cartons of his possessions and the two heavy footlockers. He'd called his sister, Marsha Garth, who lived in Brockton, and told her he was leaving town again and might not be back for a long time. She was surprised to hear from him, and didn't even know he had been away from, or back in, Boston. As far as she was concerned his departure meant little. He left her Danny's phone number, but she simply wrote it down, stuck it in her address book, and wished him well.

* * *

The following Sunday a small article appeared in a local news section of the Boston Globe:

Rare Mexican Gold Coins Marketed

Eight Mexican coins containing slightly more than half a troy ounce of 22 karate gold were purchased earlier this week by a Cambridge coin dealer who reported that he was amazed when he determined the history of the coins. Silas Coverdell said that a young man had entered his shop Wednesday and offered to sell the eight coins, indicating that he would accept their market value as gold. He apparently was unfamiliar with numerology, and said only that he had acquired the coins from his father, who had obtained them during World War II.

Two of the coins are in near mint condition, and the other six are in marketable shape, Coverdell said. "When I first looked at them all I saw was a face on one side, and an eagle standing above a wreath. But with a better reexamination of the face and wording, it read, in Latin, 'Emperor Maximilian of Mexico, 1864,' and 'Five pesos' in Spanish. The earliest previously noted Maximilian pesos were from 1865, and were the first Mexican coins called 'pesos,' as prior coinage used the Spanish denomination of 'escudo or real' representing an eighth, the so-called 'pieces of eight' on which stock market quotes are still given. A small letter v was visible to the left of the eagle."

Coverdell conferred with several other local dealers, who concurred that the coins are extremely rare, and that they might have been minted in Veracruz Province for some special occasion. The dealer is researching records to see if prior samples of the coin can be found for comparison, and to alert the world market to their existence.

* * *

Elias Ward's phone rang about ten o'clock on Monday morning. He answered and found a very angry Junius Plunkett on the line.

"Damn, Ward! What are you trying to pull?"

"What do you mean?"

"Vinny called me this morning, He'd read in the paper yesterday that somebody had been selling rare Mexican gold coins from 1864, and thought we were holding out on the crew. He was F.O.ed at me, and I don't know a damned thing about it. Now who would know about Mexican gold coins? You're the only one I know."

"Jay, I don't know a thing about this. What newspaper?"

"The Globe. I went and got a copy and it says some guy wandered in to sell eight coins, two in mint condition, apparently minted in Veracruz. That sounds a hell of a lot like the coins you said were in that ship. You found stuff and kept it to yourself. Why, those coins might be worth thousands."

"Jay, I know nothing about this. We found nothing down there. Hell, you were with me. Maybe you found the coins and are accusing me to take the blame of yourself." "Like hell, Ward. This ain't no coincidence. The timing is too close, just nine months from when we were down there."

"Well, it's not me, Plunkett. I don't know where the coins would have come from, but I'll go back through the paper — I was just reading it now anyway — and see what I can find out. If I learn anything, I'll call you."

* * *

It had taken Jimmy Garth three days to get to Cleveland. The panel truck had blown a water hose in the Berkshires, and he had to leave it by the roadside while he thumbed a ride to a service station where he could by a new hose and clamp. Fortunately he had packed his tools, and was a good enough mechanic to know what to do. The next night he was outside of Erie, Pennsylvania, and was tired driving so he had pulled into a parking lot and crawled in the back of the truck for a nap. It was daylight when he awoke.

It was already early afternoon when he finally got to Cleveland, bought a map, and located Abbey Avenue, on the city's west side, just above a narrow curve in the Cuyahoga River. Danny Martin's apartment was above a small bakery, and Jimmy bought himself a big pastry and a cup of coffee for his lunch before he went up the stairs to bang on Danny's door.

After several minutes of silence Danny asked who was there. When he heard it was Garth he opened it a slit and looked out, making certain it was Garth. It was dark inside, and the blinds were tightly drawn. He looked like a ghost when he finally opened the door and let Garth in.

"You look like you just got up!" Garth said.

"Yeah, I did. Was out all night. Here, let me get a light on." Martin hit a switch and an overhead light came on, illuminating the room dimly. It was packed with boxes and cartons of cameras, televisions, hi-fi systems, art work, sets of silver and drawers of smaller items, including jewelry.

"Gez, Danny! What the hell is all this stuff?"

"Merchandise." Martin answered. "I'm sort of a middle man."

"Holy K-rist! It's like a warehouse! What do you do with all this ... this junk?"

"It's not junk, Jimmy. It's the best."

"But...."

"Come on in, Jimmy. There's a sofa in here somewhere. I'm awake now. You want a cup of coffee or something?"

"No, I just had a cup. Just got into town, and looked you up first thing."

"Got a place to stay?"

"Not yet. I was hoping I could bunk with you for a few days, but it looks like you're full up."

"You can sleep on the sofa if you want for a few nights. It's not real comfortable, but it'll do till you find something. In fact, I think there's a vacant apartment next door. I'll ask the old Hungarian who runs the bakery downstairs and owns the place."

"Okay, but what do you do with all this stuff? Where do you get it?"

"Ha!" Danny gave a quick laugh. "Here and there. Maybe you don't want to know. I'm workin' the far Westside right now. I skip around, hit the suburbs."

"Yeah, you're right. I maybe don't want to know. Danny, you could get caught again. I thought you hated prison."

"Nah, I ain't going to get caught. I got a good system. Sometimes I can even work in the daylight. I got this big truck, see, and maybe it says 'Jones Furniture Delivery' on the side, and I find some place out in the suburbs where there's nobody at home in the daytime, and back into their driveway. Neighbors think somebody's getting something new. Of course, they ain't. Then when I get back here, off comes 'Jones,' and on goes 'Ace Appliances.' I never use the same sign twice, and the truck is easy to spray-paint. I park it in the lot at the back, and nobody's ever back there. Hittin' different suburbs, each with their own police department, they never catch on."

"But what do you do with the stuff?"

"There's a guy in a town out west of here who deals in second-hand stuff. He'll buy anything if he thinks he can get rid of it. It's sixty, seventy miles from here, and I'm due to take this stuff out there. Hey, let's bum around today, and tomorrow we'll load up the truck and you can ride out there with me. But enough about me, Jimmy. What are you up to these days?"

Garth did not want to reveal what he was doing except to say that he had acquired some items that might have some value and wanted to pawn them. He guessed that Danny would assume he had stolen whatever it was, and suggested that the fence, who was located in a town Danny called Sandusky, might be able to help Garth unload whatever it was he had. Garth agreed, but said he wanted to see if he could find some place to stay for a week or so first, and arranged to meet Danny for dinner. Danny said he knew some girls that might like to join them, and Garth was not opposed to the idea. After a few phone calls Garth found a motel on Superior Avenue and booked it for a week. He still had a few hundred dollars from the coin sale, but tore the listing of local coin or gold dealers from the phone book in the motel room, shoving it in a pocket just in case. Then he filled the tank of the panel truck, moving only the things he would need for a few nights into the motel room, and went back to Martin's apartment.

Martin took him out back to show him the truck, which had "Eddie's Appliances" painted on the side. Parked next to it was a brand new black Pontiac sports car. "Whose is this?" Garth asked. "The baker's?"

"No, Jimmy, my boy! That's mine!" It's souped up, too. It'll do a hundred, hundred twenty flat out. I've outran the cops twice now."

"Danny, don't ask that baker about the apartment. You live too dangerous a life for me!"

"Ahh, don't worry! I won't be caught. Hey, how about helping me load some of the stuff upstairs into the truck so we can hit the road first thing in the morning. I could use some help with those TV sets. Besides, I heard it was going to rain tonight."

Chapter 12

December 28, 1963
Fremont, Ohio

"Have you read these?" Sally Merriam asked Bob the evening after she had finished typing the translations of the James Fitzgibbons' journals.

"No. Is there anything significant?" he inquired.

"Just a spy story, one of the best I've ever read," she replied. "I'm surprised Richie didn't say anything to you while he was working on the translations."

"He probably forgot."

"Oh, pooh! He didn't forget. But he knew that this was a remarkable story, and it will get a lot of publicity for the college if it is handled correctly. Wait until Dexter and Peggy read what's in this thing."

"Are the documents really important ones?"

"I don't know. The journals might be, but the others are just basically invoices." "Invoices?"

"Yes, for two ships and some ram."

"Oh. Ram? You mean a male sheep?"

"No! Some sort of floating iron ram."

"Here, let me read it before you have to give it back to Richie," Bob said, and Sally handed him the stack of papers she had just transcribed. Bob spent the rest of that evening, late into the night, finishing the story.

As instructed, Sally had made several carbon copies of the transcription. She typed one final page, a title page. It stated, "This is a transcription of journals written in French in 1864 by James Fitzgibbons, an Agent of the Confederate States of America. They were discovered in a bank vault in Bermuda, and translated in 1963 by Richard F. Fairchild, Ph.D., Fremont College, Fremont, Ohio."

Fairchild returned the originals and the top translation copy of the journal and documents, which he had also had translated, to Peggy Atwater. He advised her that he had kept a copy, and that he would like her permission to investigate the journals further, and perhaps publish them. She, as the owner of the journals and documents, however, would have complete control over them, including any copyright.

He also advised her that the journals and documents, especially the Mexican one, would be considered very valuable historical artifacts, and that she should arrange to secure them in a bank vault, and perhaps even insure them. If she had been somewhat unconcerned about the items in the Bermuda bank previously, that suggestion obviously got her attention.

"How much should I insure them for?" she asked.

"At least a couple hundred thousand dollars, I'd say. The signatures on that Mexican loan document alone would bring at least that amount at auction. If you have this published, I'm sure the royalties over the years will be significant, but without the actual journals, should they be lost or destroyed, it would be difficult to verify what they actually state."

"Dr. Fairchild, you asked me if you could investigate the journals. What did you mean? How would you investigate them?"

"First, I'd want to verify what happened to the French corvette and ram when it reached Norfolk, and determine whether Pierce Heber ever got back to Richmond. Your family may have some old letters in Waycross that might show correspondence between your great grandfather and some of the men he rescued, or even with Heber.

"Then I want to find out what happened to the second corvette and the Mexican ship that steamed to Veracruz. Did it make it? If so, did it ever get to the Suwannee? I seem to recall your mentioning a story that a valuable shipment was sunk by the Union Navy. Was this that shipment? Obviously your great grandfather survived and got home again, but where was he after he left Bermuda?"

"How could you find all that out?" Peggy asked.

"Oh, I imagine many of the blockade records are still available somewhere, probably in Washington."

"Of course you are welcome to research it all, Dr. Fairchild... Richie." Peggy said, remembering that he had asked her to call him that. "That's what I would want you to do, and to also get the honor of publishing whatever you find."

* * *

Over the New Year's holiday Peggy wrote to her father in Waycross and sent him a copy of the translated journals. She asked if he had any information about his grandfather, particularly just before the end of the War. Forrest Fitzgibbons sent her a packet of correspondence that his father had stored in a dresser in the family home. He said he'd never read the letters and other papers and wasn't sure what they contained, but that his father, Jack, had told him that James had kept them in a roll top desk in the Branford depot until just before he died.

That February Peggy invited the Fairchilds and the Merriams to their Sandusky home for Saturday dinner, asking that they come early so they could go over the letters and see what they might reveal. They were all written in clear English, but some were in the same format as the French journals had been.

October 7, 1864
Tebeauville, Georgia

    Running the Suwannee & Gulf has kept me busy since returning to Georgia, for I learned upon returning that Zebulon had been killed at Kennesaw Mountain prior to the Battle for Atlanta. Delbert and Annamarie have been trying to run the line with Billy's help since then but with the ports at both Suwannee and Savannah now cut off by the Union Navy, little is coming up the line other than some lumber and a bit of sugar.
    Why the Union did not blockade the Suwannee previously was not entirely clear to me. They had been watching Cedar Key, but the rail line from Jacksonville has not yet been completed to the island, and everything coming in there has to be portaged beyond Otter Creek, almost to Archer. They must have thought we were too preoccupied to think of using the river.
    With our French corvette escort, which Captain Handley promptly renamed for his hometown, Biloxi, I sailed on the Austrian Princess, a side-wheeler, to Veracruz. There I took possession of twenty kegs of freshly minted Mexican gold pesos, for which the Confederacy had pledged an equal value in cotton and tobacco or other products, to be delivered by the end of 1867. The Mexican government had a copy of the same document I had placed in the bank in Hamilton, which I signed on behalf of Jefferson Davis, as were my instructions received through Heber.
    On June 26, 1864, we steamed out of Veracruz and headed northeast, attempting to stay away from the coast until we were near the Suwannee. Sail was hoisted for most of the journey until we came near the coast, at which time we used only steam so that the sails could not be seen by any gunboats watching for blockade runners. Unfortunately, the quality of coal we had was such that it put out a dark gray smudge on the sky.
    About one that afternoon we realized that we had been spotted by a Union ship, which seemed to be headed our way at a good speed, intending to intercept. It took us almost two hours to reach the Suwannee channel. We steamed north of Hog Island and waited to see if the Union ship would follow or whether it would continue up the coast. It surprised us by coming between Hog Island and the river's mouth, whereupon it fired upon us. The Biloxi immediately returned fire, but a Union shell hit their armory, and the corvette exploded, killing or seriously wounding most of the crew.
    Our Austrian captain immediately moved forward, and we picked up as many of the crew from the Biloxi as we could, the other survivors swimming toward Hog. Then this Union gunboat, the Providence, began firing at us, despite our showing the Mexican flag, that of a nation not at

war. A ball must have hit below the water line, mid-ship, and we immediately began to sink. We took to the boats, but were captured. Some Union Marines went ashore on Hog, and captured those who had reached it, and we were then transported south.

The Union captain, named Stephenson Ward, agreed to put the most injured of the Biloxi's crew off at Cedar Key, where there was a physician, but I seriously doubt several of them survived, poor devils. We had no ship's doctor, but fortunately none of the crew of the Princess had been injured, except an engineer's mate cut when the ball splintered the hull behind the engines. Captain Ward quizzed our Austrian captain about our cargo. He told him we had nothing aboard, proclaiming that the ship was empty and was simply going to pick up a load of cotton and sugar to take back to Mexico. We had agreed on that story prior to capture, in such an event. I presented my documents as James Farthington, a Toronto journalist, trying to get to Georgia to cover the anticipated battles there. This was the story I told the commandant at Fort Dade, when we reached it just before sunset. The uninjured passengers were stockaded at a fort on an island across from Fort Dade, which is at the entrance to Tampa Bay, and I heard that they were all transported to the Union prison on Dry Tortugas a few days later.

The commandant wasn't quite sure what to do with me. I showed him some news articles Heber and I had printed up in Hamilton, purporting to be from a Toronto newspaper, with my name as the reporter. He finally agreed to put me on the next ship going into Tampa, whereupon I was finally able to move north to Branford and get home.

At that time I still have no idea whether Heber made it to Richmond. He, too, had fake newspaper clippings backing his false identity as a reporter from Montreal. It wasn't until a month later that I heard that he had gotten ashore somehow near Charleston. I've not heard yet whether the ram and the corvette have been able to break into the blockade. With Sherman having taken Atlanta and pillaging all the way to Savannah, I fear the Confederacy's cause is doomed. What that will mean for the future is unclear. Certainly peace will be good for the S&G, with commerce restored. New railroad lines are bound to open, but it is hard to guess what the North will impose upon us. I will keep my properties in Ohio, for they could prove useful again, or could be rented for goodly sums as they are fine houses, well built and of good location. I shall also need to determine what happened to the many prisoners I helped escape, and what became of Livia Parkens and her brother.

* * *

In other correspondence James had reported to Vice President Alexander H. Stevens, through William Johnston in Macon that the aid from Mexico had been lost to the Union Navy. It was a serious financial blow to the South. By the time he had gotten back to Tebeauville Sherman was on his devastating march across the state, and further action in South Georgia was deemed impossible.

In that fall of 1864 President Jefferson Davis appointed Captain Charles H. Cole to try to arrange a prison break from the Union Prison on Johnson Island and rescue the officers who were desperately needed in the war. A plot was arranged to hijack one of the ferryboats at South Bass Island and to capture the Union gunboat Michigan, and free the prisoners. The plan was foiled and Cole became a prisoner on the island himself. Beall and other conspirators escaped to Canada, although one was captured and hung. The Union never discovered the earlier successful escapes from the notorious prison, aided by James Fitzgibbons.

In another letter in 1865 a friend commented that James Fitzgibbons had said it was ironic that when Stevens had attempted to meet with Lincoln prior to the end of the war to negotiate a peace and was rebuffed, the only offer Stevens received was from Secretary of State William Seward. Seward had suggested that the Confederacy join the Union in an attempt to expel Maximilian from Mexico. It made clear why Maximilan was willing to help keep the Confederacy going.

Peggy remembered that her great grandmother had been called 'Liv,' and that she was from Savannah. Among the letters in the drawer of the old dresser in the family home her father had also found some old letters between James and Livia in 1865. Livia and her brother had stayed in Canada until the end of the war, writing news articles for both the Washington and several Southern newspapers. In February Peggy went down to Waycross and reviewed the Ware County records. In them she confirmed the marriage of her great grandfather, James Fitzgibbons, on May 7, 1866, to Livia Parkens.

Chapter 13

Fremont College
March 28, 1964

The last part of the spring semester did not resume until the second week of April. Over the spring break Richard Fairchild had conferred with Esther and canceled plans to attend the ground-breaking ceremony for a new building on the campus and a dinner with Dr. Boldt, the college chaplain, and his wife. Instead, on the Thursday they drove down to Bowling Green, where they caught the Detroit to Washington B&O Ambassador, managing to reserve the last double bedroom on the overnight train. It was snowing when they awoke outside Harper's Ferry, but the train arrived on schedule at nine thirty that morning. Fairchild placed Esther in a cab with the luggage for the Mayflower Hotel on Connecticut Avenue where they had a reservation, while he caught another cab for the National Archives on Constitution Avenue.

Washington seemed deserted. Congress was not in session, and the nation was still reeling from the assassination of John Kennedy four months earlier. President Lyndon Johnson was spending the holiday week at his ranch near Austin. Although the Archives were scheduled to be closed the following day and again on Palm Sunday, Fairchild believed he could find what he needed quickly.

At the Archives, a massive pillared building, he explained who he was and what he wanted. But he was directed to the Naval War Records Office, secluded in a small building east of the Washington Channel north of Fort McNair. He phoned Esther meet him later at the hotel, and then he took a cab to the NWRO. The gray-haired clerk in the Records Office seemed annoyed when he asked about the Gulf Blockade Squadron records from 1864. But when she determined that he was an academic doing serious research, she brightened her smile and agreed to see what she could find for him.

"Some of those records may not be here," she warned. "A few have been transferred to the Naval Academy Library in Annapolis, and there may be others at the Library of Congress. It will be open tomorrow, but not the next day, I heard. There may also be some at the Navy Museum down by the Navy Yard on M Street at Ninth, or even the museum in Annapolis, but let's see what is here, first."

He thanked her and waited. About twenty minutes later she brought a folder of hand-written reports, stored in a box entitled 1864 Gulf of Mexico Naval Commandant Records. The contents were all out of any sort of order. There were some mixed in from various Gulf ports the Union Navy had captured, from Texas to Mississippi. There were a few from Pensacola, and a handful from Key West, all of which he carefully reviewed for any reference that might be connected to Fitzgibbons or the summer of 1864. Finally he found a jumble of papers from Fort Dade, located on Tampa Bay, but the dates were all mixed, a few in January, some in November, and others containing notes from several months. It was apparent not much was happening on the Gulf Coast that year.

In the papers he found an entry that related to what he knew about the two ships. It was dated June 30, 1864:

> U.S.S. Providence docked; Captain S. P. Ward had prisoners, some with wounds. Had destroyed two blockade-running vessels including C.S. Navy gunship. Two officers from steamer Austrian Princess, believed to be a Mexican vessel, but they were German-speaking. The wounded were taken to either a doctor at Cedar Key or the infirmary. Civilian prisoner, James Farthington, presented a Canadian passport, claimed to be an innocent passenger. Says he's a journalist from Toronto. No reason to hold him. Uninjured sailors from Confederate vessel dispatched to Fr. Jef'son. German-speaking crew from Mexican vessel and their officers held for further orders from Naval Command, Key West. Ward requested notice to Farragut, Gulf Forces Commander aboard the Hartford.
>
> Wilbur Morris, U.S. Commandant, Ft. Dade

Fairchild continued to hunt through the records, but could find no indication of a response being received by the commandant from Key West. For all the records show, the Austro-Mexican crew might still have been sitting in some damp brig in Tampa Bay. He suspected that prisoners charged with blockade running were probably released at the war's end. He also thought that somewhere might be records of prisoners kept at the infamous island prison Fort Jefferson on Dry Tortugas, but did not consider that important enough to pursue at the time. At least he had confirmed that the ship's captain was named Stephenson Ward. Perhaps at the Library of Congress he might find some information on Ward.

The clerk could find nothing else. He asked where ship's logs might be kept. She researched her catalog for those of the Providence, but could find none for the months of 1864 that Fairchild wanted, although there were some previous to that, and several after then. She said that she knew there were no logs from that era at the National Archives, but that some might either be the Naval Academy Library, the Library of Congress, or, as was occasionally the case with nineteenth century commanding officer's logs, kept by the officer as personal property. The more popular ones were from around World War I and thereafter, with perhaps a few from the Spanish American War.

It was late afternoon when Fairchild completed his review at the Records Office. He thanked the clerk, paid her for the thermofax of the page he had found, and left the building. It was snowing again, and the streets were deserted when the cab pulled up in front of the Mayflower Hotel. He and Esther relaxed in their room for an hour, enjoying a bottle of wine he had purchased in a shop outside the hotel, and then they went to dinner. "I think we're not going to be able to wrap this trip up as early as I had anticipated," he told Esther. "I found some interesting information today that ties in completely with the French journals, even to the name of one of the persons, an alias for Peggy Atwater's great grandfather. I've also confirmed the name of the captain of the Union gunboat, but we need to try to find out something about him."

"Really! Well, that's something."

"Yes, but there's something else. I'm not quite sure what, but something about this bothers me. I can't put my finger on it, but I keep wondering why the log for the date of the sinking of the Austrian Princess isn't with the other logs. The clerk thought it might be in a library in Annapolis, or that the captain kept it. But if Captain Ward did keep it, did he have some special reason to do so? Tomorrow I'm going to the Library of Congress, and I may be able to find something there."

"I've always wanted to see that building and all the genealogy books," Esther replied. "I'll go with you."

By ten the following morning the Fairchilds had arrived at the Library of Congress and were each pursuing different areas of the many floors and stacks. Esther Fairchild was interested in looking up records on some of her ancestors. The professor asked about naval ship logs, and was directed to a section that had several, but none were from the Civil War era. He then asked about biographical information on Civil War Naval officers, and was directed to a section where he found Esther pouring over thick volumes of names.

"Come to help me?" she asked.

"No, I need to look up one myself. Where might I find something on the name 'Stephenson P. Ward'?"

"In the Ws, I suppose," she answered, "but that clerk over there might tell you."

Fairchild went to the clerk and they spoke briefly. She then led him to a section far in the back of the room, and he came out from behind the high stack with a thick, heavy volume that he placed on a table, sat down, and started turning pages.

About thirty minutes later he found what he was looking for, and started scribbling notes frantically. He had found reference to Captain Stephenson Perry Ward, U.S. Navy, commander of the U.S.S. Providence, from June of 1862 until April, 1865, assigned to enforce the Union blockade from Key West to the Mississippi Delta. Ward was part of a fleet of gunboats under command of Admiral Farragut. They were placed in strategic harbors such as Tampa, Pensacola Bay, Apalachicola, Biloxi and other potential Confederate ports.

But in reading further, he found that Stephenson Ward had founded the Ward Coastal Steam Packet Line in Boston in 1869. Fairchild thought for a moment, and looked further down the Ward family records in the big volume. There was S.P. Ward, Jr., who took over the Ward Line in 1890, and S.P. Ward, III, who joined the company in 1920, and was key in its sale to the American Export Line in the late 1930s. But Commander S. P. Ward IV, U.S. Navy, had been killed in World War II in the Pacific. The remaining heir was his brother, Elias Ward, of Beverly, Massachusetts. But the volume was twelve years old. Fairchild wondered whether Ward would still be in Boston.

"Elias Ward!" Fairchild said aloud, surprising himself and another lady looking at a large book who was sitting at the same table. He scribbled some notes, and closed the volume, following instructions to leave it on the table for the librarian to return to the stacks. He then went over to where Esther was paging through a book and said, "If you're about through, let's get out of here and go to lunch. I think we may need to change our plans."

"Why? What did you find?"

"I'll tell you later," he answered.

Chapter 14

March 29, 1964
Beverly Massachusetts

Back at the Mayflower Hotel Richard Fairchild contacted the Boston area directory assistance and obtained a telephone number for an Elias Ward. He then had the operator place a person-to-person call, anticipating that he would not find the man, if he was the right Elias Ward, home. He was surprised, however, when the person answering the phone, apparently a maid or secretary, asked the operator to hold, and in a moment a man came on the phone, confirming that he was Elias Ward.

"Mr. Ward," Fairchild said when the operator announced that the party was on the line, "my name is Richard Fairchild. I'm a professor at Fremont College in Ohio, doing some historical research. I am trying to find the Elias Ward who is the great grandson of a Civil War Naval Captain, Stephenson P. Ward, who commanded the U.S.S. Providence in 1864. Would that be you, by any chance?"

"Yes," the man said. "What can I do for you? What do you want to know about my great grandfather?"

"I'm trying to locate one of his ship logs from 1864," Fairchild replied. "By any chance would you know if any of Captain Ward's papers or ship logs are still available, besides those at the Naval War Records Office in Washington?" There was a long silence, and Fairchild began to wonder if they were still connected. "Hello?" he asked. "Are you still on the line?"

"Yes, Fairchild. Ahh, my great grandfather's ship logs? He started a steamship line. Perhaps those logs or records might be available. Would those interest you?"

"No, I don't think so. I'm more interested in trying to find the logs of his ship, the Providence, for the summer of 1864. I thought that perhaps you might happen to have some of those logs."

"Oh. How did you come across such information?"

"At the Naval War Records Office. I'm in Washington at present. In fact, I was wondering, if you have any such logs, whether I might visit you the day after tomorrow, unless you're going to be out of town."

"No, I'll be here. Ahh, I suppose I can look around through my family's old records and see if there are any such logs. Yes, you're welcome to visit if you wish. My home is on the Coast Road, just northeast of Beverly. You can get a train from North Station, but take the Gloucester train, and get off at Montserrat. There will be taxis. What time may I expect you?"

"Would around ten thirty be convenient? My wife, Esther, will be with me." "Certainly, Professor Fairchild. I shall look forward to meeting you."

* * *

As Elias Ward hung up the phone he wandered into his living room and collapsed into a well-stuffed leather chair. He wondered what this professor, if that's what he was, really wanted. Some college in Ohio. He could look that up. But what on earth would have tied him to his great grandfather's ship? What did Fairchild know, and how would it affect what he had discovered in Florida, and the artifacts he had either already sold or had stored in his home that were unknown to anyone but himself. And Plunkett.

If his find became public there might briefly be some publicity about the discovery, but what he had recovered was within Florida's three mile limit jurisdiction, hence subject to all the state's archaeological laws. They might prosecute him for having taken property without the proper license. And then there was the Internal Revenue Service. But so far he had made no money, and what he did have would not come near to covering his costs.

Yet there was that business of the gold coins that had mysteriously shown up in a Cambridge coin dealer's shop. He didn't think Plunkett had cheated him, but the coincidence was so great that there had to be a connection to their venture. That, too, might attract the attention of state or federal authorities. He thought it might be best to sound out this nosy professor, see what he knew, and then, if he knew too much, do something about it.

But that was not his way. It would probably not bother Plunkett at all. He'd probably left more than one man at the bottom of the sea during his long career. He'd have to inform Plunkett of the inquiry by this professor, and get rid of this nuisance if he could. It all depended on what the professor needed or wanted. He decided that for the time, there was nothing to do but wait until Fairchild came and to see what he knew, and what he wanted.

* * *

The Fairchilds checked out of the Mayflower early the following morning and took a taxi to Union Station. They traded in their first class return tickets on the B&O for first class seats on the Pennsylvania Railroad's Colonial, which departed at nine that morning and arrived in

Boston at a quarter to seven that evening. The parlor car had day roomettes and a bar lounge as well as a grill car, and the Fairchilds rode comfortably through the snowy white landscape of Maryland, Pennsylvania, New Jersey and New England. They had reserved a hotel near the North Station, where the Boston & Maine commuter train would leave the following morning.

Hardly anyone was on the three-car Gloucester train the next morning, and as Ward had predicted, a taxi was waiting outside the station. Fairchild gave the driver the address, and in about ten minutes they were driving up a wooded drive toward a very large house that sat on the side of the Salem Harbor part of Massachusetts Bay.

Elias Ward had sent his housekeeper home for the day, and met the Fairchilds at the door himself when they arrived and rang the bell. He acted very graciously toward his guests, inviting them into the large living room that overlooked the Bay from a high bluff and serving them coffee that he had prepared in anticipation of their arrival.

That served as ground-breaking conversation, along with the Fairchilds' comments on the beauty of the scene outside the window – the snow-covered lawn sloping down toward a large boathouse on the water. They were soon on a first-name basis with each other, the friendly manner of the Fairchilds easily countering any anxiety Ward had about the professor's research.

Esther inquired if there was a Mrs. Ward.

"No," he replied. "I'm divorced. A long time ago. She's remarried, and has several kids now. It was more a business deal than a marriage, I guess," he explained. "Jane's father was big at American Export Lines, and I had Ward Coastal Steam Packet, the old Ward Line. They wanted to buy us out, and Jane was part of the deal. I did okay money-wise, but the marriage never worked. After a year and a half we agreed to split.

"So," he continued, "I started another little venture, the New England Transfer Line, mostly coastal freight, down to Nassau, the Caribbean, places like that." Ward then inquired how Fairchild happened to have come across his great grandfather.

"It's an interesting story, Elias," the professor began. "Sally Merriam is our department secretary at the college, and her cousin, a physician, married a girl, a nurse, from Waycross, Georgia. Her name was Fitzgibbons. Her family owns a railroad that runs from Waycross – which used to be called Tebeauville prior to the 1880s – to a small town on the Suwannee River. At one time there was also a steamboat line on the river that ran out to a harbor at the mouth of the river, which is now just a little fishing village called Suwannee. But at one time it was a port for ocean vessels."

Ward nodded, his expression indicating that he was intently interested in what Fairchild was saying. Mention of the Suwannee and a port having been at the mouth of it explained a lot about the two wrecks they had uncovered.

"Some of the family holdings included a house in Sandusky, Ohio, not far from Fremont College. After the wedding, the couple moved into the house, and in the attic discovered an envelope and key, with a code on it written in Greek letters. The envelope was from a bank in Hamilton, but it didn't say where Hamilton was.

"From other information we suspected that it might be Hamilton, Bermuda, and Esther and I went there, and confirmed it, finding some other documents and journals. These Journals were written in French, which I translated last fall. Some of the other documents were in Spanish."

"But what has this to do with Stephenson Ward, my great grandfather?" Ward asked.

"From an historical point of view, quite a bit. Let me explain," Fairchild replied. "The author of the Journals that we found in Bermuda was a Confederate agent. He had instructions to accompany two vessels that left Bermuda in May of 1864 bound for Veracruz, Mexico, where a shipment of money was to be transferred as a loan to the Confederacy. The Confederate agent was James Fitzgibbons, the great grandfather of the nurse my secretary's cousin married in Georgia last spring. Fitzgibbons traveled on this voyage under a false name, James Farthington, and the destination of the loaned Mexican money was the small port of Suwannee, where the Fitsgibbons' steamboat and railway would transport it into Georgia and get it to the Confederacy.

"But the Mexican steamer and a French-built corvette that was accompanying her never made it to Suwannee. Somewhere along the Gulf Coast, possibly somewhere around Cedar Key, the two vessels were spotted by your great grandfather's ship, the Providence, and destroyed. A number of prisoners were taken, including Farthington, who was really James Fitzgibbons. The only records in Washington are from the Naval Commandant at Fort Dade, which I believe was at the mouth of Tampa Bay, across from the present day Fort De Soto. While he reports that Captain Ward sank the two foreign vessels, he does not say where."

"But what has this to do with me, now?" Ward asked, although he feared the answer.

"At the Naval War Records Office I tried to find the logs from the Providence. There were a few, but none from the summer of 1864," Fairchild explained. "But unless they are at the Naval Academy in Annapolis, they may have been destroyed after the Civil War, or, and this is why I am here, they may have been kept by the ship's captain, your great grandfather, Stephenson.

"If you have the logs, or know where they are, I would ask you for an opportunity to study them to see if they indicate where the Providence may have encountered and sunk the Mexican ship, the Austrian Princess.

It is part of the story of James Fitzgibbons, the Confederate agent, -- which is being published as an academic historical record -- and therefore the log would be a significant document, probably of great value, which, of course, would be yours, if you had the log. Besides that, there was apparently quite a valuable cargo of Mexican currency, probably in the form of gold coins, on the Princess. With modern recovery capabilities, both treasure hunters and the government, who knows, maybe even the Mexican government might launch some sort of expedition to see if it could be found and reclaimed. As far as I know, it was not an insured cargo."

"Ahh, I see," Ward said. "So you don't know where the attack occurred, and it might be anywhere in the Gulf of Mexico. Do you know what this cargo of coins was?"

"Elias, according to the Mexican document in Spanish that was in the Bermuda bank vault, Emperor Maximilian was loaning the Confederacy over three million dollars' worth of Mexican gold pesos. God only knows what those would be worth today – certainly far more than three million.

"The Mexican document that confirms this will become known early next year, as it is historically significant, and publication is already underway. The fact that your great grandfather sank the ship carrying that gold will also become known. Undoubtedly treasure hunters from all over the globe will scour the Gulf Coast for the wreck, and historians will descend upon you seeking your great grandfather's ship log, if it is still in existence. Frankly, Elias," the professor said, pausing a moment, "I suspect it is."

Ward said nothing for a moment, and then asked Fairchild to explain what he meant. Fairchild smiled, then said, "Elias, it seems odd to me that all or most of your great grandfather's ship logs are at the Naval War Records Office except the ones for the summer of 1864. The logs that are there are not numbered – just dated – so I don't know if there is just one missing log or several. But why would Captain Ward have kept that one log, if he did keep it? Of course, as they told me in Washington, the log could be in Annapolis or in some other museum, but I doubt that. Why this particular log?"

"Someone researching Admiral David G. Farragut might have obtained the log, as Stephenson Ward was under his command," Fairchild continued, "I have not had an opportunity to look into that possibility. But I would anticipate that if such were the case, there would have been some indication of it at the Records Office. Now why would Captain Ward have kept the log? Perhaps because it does reveal where the Austrian Princess sank, and Ward had some reason to want to keep that location secret? If the ship sank in shallow water, he might have had some intent of returning to it someday."Ward thought for a few moments and then said, "What you are saying is that the existence of this shipwreck will definitely become known, as will its contents and how it came to be wrecked."

"That's correct," Richard Fairchild replied. "If the wreck is within three miles of the Florida coast, as I understand maritime and antiquities laws, the state has authority over it, and any treasure hunters would have to be licensed to search for it. And any findings would be taxable if they provided income," he added.

"Of course," Fairchild continued, "if someone just pleasure diving, say, someone like you, were simply to come across the wreck by accident and find something valuable aboard it, they would have to report the find to the authorities."

"And if they didn't?"

"Well, in this case, I can't imagine what would happen if Mexican gold coins from the 1860s were to show up on the market. The authorities would be all over that situation in a hurry."

Ward did not reply, and Fairchild said nothing for several minutes, fixing his gaze on the scene outside the window. Ward thought about what he had read in the Boston Globe about just such coins being traded. Someone had found such coins, but where, and how, and how many? If they had been in the holds of the Austrian Princess, he certainly had not seen them. All he had found in the cabin he and Plunkett's diver had entered they had recovered and either already sold to antique armament dealers, or he had paid Plunkett for his share and had them in his home.

Fairchild, he knew, was correct. Once word of the wreck became known treasure hunters would be bound to find it in the shallow waters off Hog Island, if they hadn't already. He would be unable to sell any of the remaining artifacts without revealing their source, but then he did not intend to sell what he had anyway.

He leaned back and said, "Dr. and Mrs. Fairchild, there is an excellent seafood restaurant just up the road apiece. It is almost noon. Why don't we go to lunch, and then we can talk further when we get back?"

His guests agreed, and Ward led them to the garage and backed his late model Buick out and turned it in the driveway.

* * *

During the meal, for which the professor insisted on paying, Ward had said little. As they sat over coffee he made his decision. "What would happen, Richard, if someone did find the wreck and reported it to the authorities?"

"Oh, I suspect he would make a lot of money from the find," Fairchild answered. "Really? How?"

"Well, the documents and the story about what they involve are going to trigger a lot of public interest. While there might be Mexican coins on the vessel, there might be other things, too, maybe arms – guns destined for the Confederate Army – who knows what. By turning the find over to authorities the finder would reserve the rights to photograph anything found, and to publish any official records that relate to the find. For example, your great grandfather's story, if it were fully known, would make an excellent book. Someone like yourself could write it, or you could have a historian work with you on it. It would undoubtedly get a lot of public interest.

"Some organization, say, like National Geographic, or the Smithsonian, would be bound to take an interest. The finder would have certain rights, and those rights could have great value. Of course, besides the monetary interests, great as they might be, the pleasure of making a find such as that wreck public would be rewarding in and of itself."

"That's true," Ward said slowly, rubbing his chin with his right hand. "What would be your interest in it?"

"I'm a historian, Elias. It's the academic aspects of a find such as the Journals I translated, and the documents that excite me. My secretary's cousin holds full rights to the Journals and documents we found, but I'm assisting her in publishing them through the college press. The reward I receive is not financial, but in satisfaction of scholarship." "What are your thoughts, Mrs. Fairchild?" Ward asked.

"I was with Richie when we opened that metal box in the Bermuda bank vault. It was a treasure hunt, but until he translated the Journals I had no idea what kind of treasure he had found. I've read his translation. It's quite a story, involving a pre-Civil War bounty hunter, prison escapes, and what is basically international political intrigue. I think anything connected to that story is going to become important. But the Gulf of Mexico is a big sea. Who knows what's at the bottom of it?"

"Richard," Ward said, "I did find my great grandfather's log recording the sinking of a couple of ships somewhere near the mouth of the Suwannee. Let's go back to the house, and I'll show you the Navy log you're seeking, and also something else that will perhaps surprise you."

Once back at Ward's home on the Bay he took the Fairchilds into his library, and pulled a leather case out of a drawer of a chest. Inside were several old ships' logs, each with the name of a vessel and the dates covered by the logs. "My grandfather commanded several vessels in the 1860s," Ward explained. "The U.S.S. Providence was only one of them. He had several commands prior to that, but was on the Providence until he left the Navy in 1868. He founded his shipping company the following year, and it passed down through the family until the 1940s, when my grandfather and I sold it and I wound up with Jane. I told you that story.

"My grandfather, we called him Steve, died in 1962," Ward continued. "My father was already dead. I think my brother's being killed in the Pacific during the War was more than Dad could stand. Anyway, I inherited all my grandfather's papers, including these logs. There was quite a mess of stuff, to be quite honest. We Wards seem to have a habit of keeping everything. It took me months to sort through all of it.

"In February of last year I came across these ships' logs, and realized that this one was from my great grandfather's days in the Civil War. I was reading through it and came across for...." He stopped, reached into his pocket and pulled out a pair of reading glasses which he placed on his nose and ears, and paged through one of the logs. "Here. June 28, 1864. He describes spotting two ships and following them up the Gulf Coast from around Cedar Key. They engaged each other, and the gunboat – apparently the French vessel – was hit and exploded. The other one then steamed off, with my great grandfather in pursuit, and he fired on it and sank it just north of Hog Island, which is at the mouth of the Suwannee River.

"When I discovered that, I met with a salvage operator I knew in Boston, and agreed to finance a diving expedition to see if we could find the wreck, anticipating that there might be some armaments or something else of value on it. Over the century the currents had shifted the wreck northward and covered much of it with silt, but we found it, but didn't find anything much of value aboard it.

"Or at least that's what my partner and I thought. We had SCUBA equipment, and I was able to find a few undamaged things, china, crystal, some Spanish rifles, but no gold coins. I'd financed the trip, and my partner thought it was a waste of his time.

"But a couple of months ago I got a phone call from Junius Plunkett, my partner on the deal. He started accusing me of cheating him, and referred me to an article in the Globe. Here's a copy. Somebody had sold eight Mexican gold coins dated 1864. He swears it wasn't him, and it sure as hell wasn't me. I contacted the coin dealer, but he wouldn't tell me anything more than what the paper says."

"Was it just the two of you, you and Plunkett, who were on the expedition?" Esther Fairchild asked.

"Plunkett and his crew. They rescue damaged fishing boats on the Grand Banks. Say, maybe he could bid on the salvage operation." Fairchild nodded that such was always a possibility. Ward continued, "Plunkett had a diver named Garth who went down, too, but I was with him the whole time he...."

"Jimmy Garth?" Richard Fairchild interrupted.

"Jimmy! Yes. How the hell did you know that?"

"Well, Elias, by coincidence my associate professor, Bob Merriam – it's his wife who is cousin to the husband of the Waycross girl – and I were in Florida for an academic meeting last September. Because of a football game in Gainesville we stayed at a hotel owned by the Fitzgibbons family out in Suwannee. A storm blew in from the Gulf, and a young man, sort of rough looking, partially balding, was at the hotel, too, riding out the storm. He said he was doing some SCUBA diving 'for fun,' and told us his name was Jimmy Garth. From what you've said, I think he may have found your gold."

"Garth! I never thought of Garth."

"How can we find him? If he has already sold some of the coins, he might be in violation of Florida law."

"If Plunkett hasn't taken his tug back to sea yet, maybe he knows. Let me give him a call."

Ward looked in his desk directory and dialed the number for Plunkett, who answered on the second ring.

"Jay, Elias Ward here. Remember accusing me of finding gold coins on the wreck?"

"Yeah, Ward. I still think you're holding out on me!"

"No, no, it's the other way around. It's one of your guys."

"Wha'd yah mean? What one of my guys?"

"Jay, I'm sitting here with a history professor who was in a hotel in Suwannee last September and came across a young guy SCUBA diving out in the Gulf – by the name of Jimmy Garth."

"Garth?" Plunkett repeated. "Garth quit me right after we got back to Boston. Said he had some other job. I guess the hell he did!"

"How do we find him? He may have a whole bunch of those coins."

"Gad, I don't know. Let me look in the personnel file." There was a silence on the line, broken only by the sound of a drawer on a metal file cabinet being opened. "Here. I got his address, out off of Commonwealth, but I don't think he's there. I mailed him his W-2 in January, and it came back to me marked 'moved, no forwarding address.' Ahh, let's see. Family, ahh, here's a sister. That's all I've got."

"Give me her name. We'll try to find him. This professor says there may be some historical value in our find, and I don't think we need to tell anybody about those rifles."

"What rifles?" Plunkett laughed. "But find that SOB Garth. I've got to have a word with him."

"Me, too. Oh, and by the way, Plunkett, this professor thinks that if the authorities in Florida may want to resurrect those wrecks. You might want to bid on the project on behalf of Eastern Dredge and Salvage Company. Who knows, maybe the state university might agree to help finance the project."

Ward hung up and explained to the Fairchilds what Plunkett had told him that Garth had a sister, Marsha Garth, who lived in Brockton. He called directory assistance and obtained a phone number. A man answered, but he said he would get Marsha to the phone. Ward explained to her that he was trying to reach Jimmy Garth, and wondered if she knew where he might be. She said she didn't, but then remembered that he had left her

Danny Martin's phone number, which she thought was in Cleveland. She found it in a drawer and read it to him. Ward thanked her and hung up.

"So," he asked. "Where do we go from here, Professor?"

Three days later the Fairchilds were back in Fremont. The professor explained to Bob and Sally Merriam what he and Esther had discovered, and that it appeared that the young man named Jimmy Garth had acquired some gold coins off the vessel, but they had no idea how many. The Merriams were having dinner with Peggy and Dexter the following weekend, and agreed to bring them up-to-date on the situation.

Chapter 15

Winter and Spring, 1964
Sandusky, Ohio

Jimmy Garth had accompanied his friend, Danny Martin, with the truckload of stolen merchandise, and had been introduced to Pappy Sanchez, a Puerto Rican from New York who operated a big appliance store on the southwest side of Sandusky called Pappy's Place. Sanchez was in his late fifties, balding with a grizzly beard and piercing dark eyes. It was full of very high-class appliances, televisions, hi-fis, cameras, jewelry, silver, furs and other items.

Sanchez was a friendly guy who asked no questions. He looked over the items Martin had in the back of his truck, offered him what Martin thought was a fair price for the items, and then got two Spanish-speaking employees to help Martin and Garth unload the things and carry them into the storeroom at the back of the large square building. Martin introduced Garth, and Garth had showed Sanchez one of the cleaned-up coins, advising him that he had a few more of these, but wanted a good price for them, more than just their value as gold.

Sanchez closed his mouth and puffed through his lips. "Son, that might be a bit difficult. But leave this coin with me, and I'll check around, maybe Detroit or Chicago. Give me a few weeks. You said you have more? How many?"

"Ahh, quite a few, actually," Garth replied, "But they're not with me right now."

"Where are you staying?" Sanchez asked.

"Right now I'm looking for a place. There's no room at Danny's, but coming out here I saw a lot of little towns that remind me of Gloucester and Massachusetts Bay, so I may move out into this area."

"When you get yourself situated, Garth, get back with me, and maybe I'll have some news. I don't know a damned thing about coins, but this looks like it is unusual, and I see a date of 1864 on it, so some dealer might be interested. Are they all like this one, or different?"

"They seem identical."

"Okay. Well, my fee is twenty percent plus any expenses. That okay with you?"

Garth had looked at Danny, who nodded that it was the standard price. "Guess it will have to be, won't it," Garth replied.

* * *

When Garth had arrived in Cleveland he had planned to pal around with his old school chum, Danny. But once he learned what Danny did for a living, he felt very uncomfortable and decided that he would be far better on his own. Garth had been careful not to let Danny see the two footlockers full of coins that he still had hidden in the panel truck. He and Danny drove back into Cleveland, and two days later Garth had moved out of the motel on Superior Avenue and headed west out the Lake Road beyond Lorain and Huron. He found a cheap motel on the east side of the town, and signed up for a few days until he could find some place more permanent. Then he decided he did not want Danny to have his new address. He could keep in contact with Sanchez on his own.

Danny and his lifestyle scared Garth. Living with a cat burglar, outrunning cops at over a hundred miles an hour, and hanging around with type of girls Danny had introduced him to the night he arrived was not for him. Garth was no choirboy, but except for that unfortunate event a few years back when he had been drinking he had managed to stay out of trouble. It was just a matter of time until Danny either got caught or got killed. After a couple of days of looking at small efficiency apartments in Sandusky Garth found one that suited him, and signed a lease. He still had enough money from the coin sale in Cambridge for the deposit and first month, but his cash was running low. A week later he went back to Pappy Sanchez, but the dealer had no news yet. Garth feared that Sanchez was stringing him along, maybe looking for a sweeter deal for himself, but he said nothing. Sanchez was his best bet for getting rid of the coins. If he only sold a few here and there to dealers for whatever he could get, it might take him years to sell all of them, and dealers were nosy about the origin of the coins.

One January day Garth had stopped at Pappy Sanchez's store. Sanchez was with a customer, but signaled to Garth to meet him in his office, a cluttered broom closet affair at the back of the store. After a few moments Sanchez came in and motioned Garth to a chair, while he sat on a rickety old office chair that looked quite ancient.

"Got some good news for you, Garth. My contact in Detroit says he has a dealer in Canada who was fascinated by the coin, and would like to buy ten more, if you have that many, and if they are as good shape."

"Only ten?"

"Well, how many you got?"

"More than that. But yes, I've got some in even better shape. How much is he offering?"

"He said he assumed you didn't have any papers on the coins, showing authenticity, so the most he's agree to was $170 each, a total of $1700, less my twenty percent and about a hundred for my expenses running up to Detroit."

"So $1260 is the best you can do?"

"Beggars can't be choosers, Garth."

"Yeah, well, okay, but tell him I got some really good ones, and find out if he'll take more of them. I need the dough."

"Sure, sure. So bring in the ten coins – in fact, if you've got more, bring me twenty, and I'll see if he'll take them. Bring good ones, nice and clean."

"Yeah. I will."

* * *

On the afternoon of April 7 Danny Martin had been sitting on his bed when the phone rang. He rarely received calls, and answered cautiously. "Who's this?"

"Mr. Martin, Mr. Danny Martin?"

"Depends on who's calling," Martin cautiously answered.

"Mr. Martin, My name is Richard Fairchild. I'm a professor at Fremont College." He assumed he had Danny Martin, but asked to confirm it.

"Yeah, my name's Martin. What'd yah want?"

"Mr. Martin, I'm trying to reach a man named Jimmy Garth."

"Garth?" Martin repeated. "Yeah, he was here a few months back, but left again. I don't know where the hell he is now. He never said and never contacts me."

"Do you have any idea how I might contact him?"

"No," Martin replied emphatically, although he could have suggested that this professor guy might try to reach him through Pappy Sanchez. "Why d'yah want him?" "I suspect that Garth has something of great value, and he may not know how valuable it is." Fairchild didn't want to say too much, but might have to say enough to get Martin to tell him how to contact Garth.

"Yeah? Valuable, eh. What sort of thing?"

"Sort of like a coin."

"A coin, eh?" Martin replied, recalling the coin he had seen Garth discuss with Sanchez. His mind now turning to how he might get in on this valuable coin. "Well, I can't help you. I don't know where Garth is, or care. Bye."

Martin had hung up before Fairchild could inquire further. Martin then thought to himself, "Well, well! So that coin Jimmy had was valuable. Wonder where he got it." He then placed a call to Pappy Sanchez's, and told the old man that he was trying to contact Jimmy Garth."

"He comes in occasionally," Sanchez confirmed. "Next time I see him, I'll tell him to get you a call. Okay?"

"Yeah, that will have to do, if he hasn't given you an address."

"I don't want no addresses, for either you or him," Sanchez replied.

* * *

The ten coins the Detroit dealer had sold in Canada brought about twice what he had paid Sanchez for them. When Sanchez took him twenty more the dealer said he'd do what he could to sell them, suggesting to Sanchez that they were hard to get rid of, but Sanchez didn't go for it. "Look, you old chicken thief, I know them damned coins are worth more than $170 each. I want $250 each for this batch, because they're in better shape. You can get twice that much easily."

"Not so easily, Sanchez, but I can go to $210 for the best of these, $200 for the others."

"$225 for the best, $215 for the others," Sanchez insisted, and the dealer shook his head. The Detroit dealer had heard that the first coins he had sold had made quite a stir in the coin market. There was a report that several identical coins had shown up in Boston a few months back, and dealers all around the world were looking to buy, but he did not let Sanchez know that.

"No," he said. "$220 for the best ones, $210 for the others. That my top figure, Sanchez. Maybe I can do better if you can get me some more of the better quality ones. I have to clean these up to put them back in good shape. How many can you get me?" "I don't know how many the kid has. He won't say."

"Well, send him up to see me and...."

"Hell, no! You deal with him through me!"

"And you call me a chicken thief, Sanchez! I know what you're doing – you're telling that kid these ain't worth nothing and robbing him blind."

"Hey, I'm just an honest business man. I don't know coins from Shine-o-la! I'm fair with the kid."

When Garth returned to Pappy Sanchez's store the following week Sanchez told him he had good news that he had gotten the dealer in Detroit up to $200 for the best of the coins, and $190 for the others. "And I had to go to Detroit anyway, so my expenses are only $50 this time, Garth. And the best news is, he wants some more. How many more you got?"

"Would he take two, three dozen?"

"You got that many! Gawd-a-mighty, Kid. Where you keepin' those things? They should be in my safe here at the store."

"They're safe enough, Pappy, don't worry."

Garth accepted the cash Sanchez had for him and agreed to bring him more coins the next day. He then left the big store and got into his panel truck and headed back to his apartment, pleased with himself about the way the coins were turning into real money with no taxes being taken out, as it had been when he worked on the tug. He did not notice a sleek black Pontiac sports car following behind him as he turned right on one street and then left on another, pulling up into the parking space in front of his apartment. Danny Martin sat in his car on the street outside the apartment complex for a few moments trying to decide what to do. He could con Garth out of some of the coins, he could offer to become a partner, or he could just steal them. But he didn't know how many coins Garth had, or where he kept them. He sat looking at the blue panel truck. He had noticed that Garth kept it locked. Maybe that was where he had the coins.

He decided to wait and find out that night, so he pulled away and found a bar where had had a few beers and listened to music until that evening. Then he went and had a steak at a local restaurant, and after it was dark drove back to Garth's apartment. The panel truck was gone, so he parked across the street and waited.

Garth had gone to dinner and then to a movie, so he had not arrived back at his apartment until around ten that evening. He parked the panel truck and locked it, then went into his apartment and had a beer while he watched some television. Martin left his Pontiac hidden across the street from the apartment complex and made his way quietly to the back of the panel truck, on which the two doors opened outwards. Locks were no hindrance to Martin, and in less than a minute he was inside the truck with the doors closed, exploring the interior with his flashlight. There was a tool kit, some diving equipment that Garth had in a big carton, and two locked footlockers.

The locks on these were not the type that Martin could easily pick, though he spent five minutes trying. He then tried to move the foot lockers, but found them extremely heavy. He raised one enough that he could shake it, and could faintly hear the rattle of coins inside.

"Holy Toledo!" he exclaimed under his breath. "There's got to be thousands of coins in these."

He crept back out of the panel truck, not relocking it, and crossed back over to get his Pontiac. Then he slowly drove the sports car into the apartment complex and parked it next to Garth's panel truck. He got out, opened the trunk, and hoisted the first of the foot-lockers out the back and lowered it to the ground. He pulled it over to the back of his car, and with all his energy concentrated, lifted it into his truck. He could see that there was not going to be room in the trunk with the lid closed for the second locker, but he thought he might be able to maneuver it into the back seat of his car.

As he was lowering the second footlocker from the panel truck it slipped and hit the pavement with a thud. The noise was loud enough that Garth heard it inside his apartment and stuck his head out the door to see what was happening. Another neighbor also heard the sound and looked out, and a third neighbor was just driving in at that moment. In that car's headlights Garth saw the back door of his panel truck open, and came charging out, hollering, "Hey! What the hell are you doing?" He did not see who was there, but he recognized the Pontiac.

Martin ducked behind the truck and pulled out a pistol. As Garth ran around the front of the truck Martin fired, and Garth fell to the pavement. Martin then picked up the second footlocker, set it on top of the first in the trunk of his Pontiac, although he was unable to close the trunk, and tore off with a squeal of tires. He drove around a few back streets of Sandusky until he could find a dark lot where he managed to get the second footlocker out of the trunk and wrestled it through the right passenger door into the back seat of the sports car. He then drove back to Cleveland.

* * *

Within minutes the apartment parking lot was filled with emergency vehicles from the fire department, the police, and an ambulance that rushed Jimmy Garth to Memorial Hospital. He had been hit in the chest, and was bleeding profusely. The emergency room physician on duty that night was Dr. Dexter Atwater. Garth was unconscious, and Atwater immediately arranged for emergency surgery, and had the nurse notify the thoracic and pulmonary surgeon on call. Garth's wallet was still in his trousers, but there was little in it except a Massachusetts driver's license and a lot of cash. It was nearly four the following morning when the two surgeons retrieved the bullet from Garth's right lung; it had missed the heart and a vital artery by only a quarter of an inch. Garth would survive, but a long recuperation would be needed. It was only later, when Atwater was filling out the surgery report that he noticed the patient's name, James P. Garth, of Brookline, Massachusetts. He had heard that name recently, but it took him a few minutes to recall where.

It was now after sunrise on a Friday morning, and Dexter picked up the phone and called his cousin, Sally, in Fremont. Bob answered, and Sally got on the extension. Dexter explained that he was at the hospital. "Do you recall, awhile back, Sally, you said that Dr. Fairchild had identified the man who had been selling those Civil War coins as a 'Jimmy Garth'?"

"Yes, Dex, that was the name."

"I've met him," Bob added. "Young fellow, balding, kind of rough looking." "Well, we got a gunshot victim in here last night, shot in the chest. This morning I saw his identity, a James Garth of Brookline, Massachusetts, which is a suburb of Boston. I think it may be your man."

"I'd know him if I saw him," Bob said. "I've got classes this morning, but if he's still there this afternoon I could come over and meet him, and see if it is the same guy." "Oh, he's not going anywhere soon, Bob. He was in surgery nearly five hours. He almost bled to death. In fact, if you have

Type O blood, we could use some more for him. But he might be awake by then, so come over and have a look at him."

* * *

Danny Martin had gotten back to his apartment on Abbey Avenue about midnight. He had driven carefully, as he did not want to attract police attention, not with the two footlockers in the car. But he was in a quandary. He didn't know if any of the witnesses who had shown up at the wrong time might have gotten an identification of his car, and he didn't know if he'd killed Jimmy. He didn't want to hurt him, but it was likely that if Jimmy did survive, it would not take him long to figure out who had stolen the coins. That would blow Danny's operation wide open, including that of Pappy Sanchez. Plus he couldn't stay where he was. If Danny was alive, he knew Danny's address. And then there was that damned professor who had phoned inquiring about Jimmy. With his phone number, it wouldn't take the cops long to find where he was living. No, he had to move out, immediately.

At daylight he transferred the two footlockers to the big truck, packed his personal possessions in the apartment – there were not that many – and abandoned some of the heavier stolen items he had collected since his last delivery to Sanchez. In a spirit of good will he stopped down in the Hungarian bakery, bought some pastry and coffee for his breakfast, and paid for the next month's rent. "Anything in there you want, just keep. There's some good stuff up there." He bid the baker so long, and departed, leaving the black sports car in the lot, but driving the truck to a nearby vacant lot where he parked it behind an abandoned building. Then he walked back and got the Pontiac and started down the hill into the Cuyahoga River Valley. It was time to change his general location.

Once across the Columbus Road Bridge over the Cuyahoga he stopped at a small convenience store in the old warehouse section of the Flats and purchased a local area advertiser-type newspaper that usually listed temporary rentals. He circled three, and by four that afternoon had rented a small two-room apartment off Lorain Avenue, but the parking lot was not big enough for his truck. He had also found a small warehouse off West Third, along the edge of the Cuyahoga and had rented eight hundred square feet on the third floor, next to a freight elevator, where he could store the things in the truck. Then he took the Rapid Transit train to the 25th Street Station near where he had parked the truck. By seven the truck was parked at the warehouse, and the Pontiac was in the lot at the new apartment.

Danny thought about driving out to Sandusky to get a local newspaper to see if it reported the shooting, but was afraid that if the police were watching for a black Pontiac, he might get stopped. No matter.

Without Sanchez to fence the stuff, he was going to have to find a new outlet for his goods. Maybe somewhere south, where he could get rid of the coins. But that, he realized, might be a bigger problem than he anticipated. He remembered that Jimmy had told him that coin dealers wanted to know the origin of the coins, and, if as that professor had said, these were especially valuable, they would be difficult to sell. Yet, he rationalized, well worth the effort.

* * *

Bob Merriam had told Fairchild about the call from Dexter Atwater, and Fairchild suggested that he and Sally take the afternoon and go into Sandusky and see if this Garth was the same man they had met in Suwannee. It took them a little less than an hour to reach the hospital. Dexter Atwater was off duty, but Peggy was working on the critical care ward, the same one Garth was one.

"He hasn't totally come out of the anesthesia yet, but he was moving around enough that they released him from recovery," she said. "A police detective was here to talk with him, and I'm supposed to notify him when Garth comes around."

"I suppose they want to know if he knows who shot him, or why. Would it be possible to just take a look at him?" Bob asked. "If he is the same man Richie and I met in Suwannee at your uncle's hotel, we might want to talk with the detective, too."

"Sure. I've got his card here, ahh, 'Detective Sergeant David Wilkerson, Sandusky Police Department, 784-2206, Extension 47. Come on, but you will have to suit and mask up. This is an open chest wound and we're taking special care."

Bob donned the white cover and put the white facemask over his nose and mouth, following Peggy into the room. It had two other beds in it, but only the one patient. Sally waiting outside in the hall. He needed only a glimpse to know that this was the same man that they had joined for dinner in the Florida hotel, the acne-scarred young man who said he was doing some SCUBA diving. The man was in a deep sleep, and did not stir while they were in the room.

"I don't imagine he will be doing much diving with a hole in his lung," Bob said as he came out of the room with Peggy.

"Oh, I don't know. That will be up to the doctors, but Dex is a pretty good surgeon and he and Doc Willoughby, the thoracic specialist Dex called in probably put him in better shape than he might have been in before. One good thing, they said, they don't think he was a smoker."

"Well, he's definitely the man we met in Florida, so I can anticipate that if he had any gold coins from the wreck of that Mexican steamship, that's probably why he was shot. But, of course, it's another thing to prove it. Is there any chance you or Dex, or even Richie Fairchild, could be here when the detective interviews him?"

"I don't know, but I can ask."

"Better yet, I'll have Fairchild give the detective a call. He might want to have some information before he talks to Garth."

Richard Fairchild agreed to give the detective a call that afternoon, and caught the detective just as he was leaving for the weekend. Fairchild explained who he was, and that he had confirmed through another professor that James Garth was someone he knew.

"I talked to the hospital people about half an hour ago, Professor, and they said Garth was going to be in there for a long time, so I said we'd either have another detective who is on duty this weekend stop by, or I'd come out first thing Monday. How do you happen to know this guy?"

Fairchild tried to make the story brief, but when he got to the business of the gold Civil War era coins showing up in Boston shortly after he and Merriam had met Garth in Florida the detective became quite interested. "If robbery was the motive, Detective Wilkerson, those coins may have been what the thief was seeking. Were there any indications of a theft?"

"Yes, the back of Garth's panel truck was open, and the only things inside were a tool box and a carton of SCUBA diving equipment. We sure didn't see any coins. But he wouldn't have kept coins in a truck, would he?"

"Depends on how many there were. If he only found a handful of them down there, not knowing what they might be worth, why would he bother going back down on his own? He might have found a whole chest full of coins down there, and he's sure not going to haul those around in his pocket."

"Professor, it sounds like you're talking about a whole lot of gold!"

"Well, what would three million dollars in 1864 value be worth today?"

"Ha! That would settle the national debt! How do you know all this?"

"This is not for publication, Sergeant, but that nurse you spoke with earlier is the great granddaughter of the Confederate agent who was bringing the coins from Mexico. And I had dinner a few months back with the great grandson of the Union gunboat captain who sank that Mexican ship. Fremont College is in the process of publishing the historical records on this little adventure. And we are quite interested in acquiring any of those coins that we can – they technically belong to either the United States government or to the State of Florida Department of Antiquities, but it will probably take a court battle to figure that out."

"Fairchild, are you that same professor who helped catch a bunch of Texas terrorists a year or so ago?"

"Well, I did aid the FBI a little," Fairchild smiled, just a bit amused.

"Okay, I buy your story. I think I'll just go interview Garth myself in the morning. Want to be there?"

"Sure, if you'll allow me."

"What else can you tell me about this Garth?"

"Not really too much. He was a diver aboard a salvage tug called the Roberta II, out of Boston, and has a sister in Brockton. It was from her that I got a phone number for a fried of Garth's who was living in Cleveland, ahh, let's see …. Oh, yes, a Danny Martin. I have that Cleveland phone number in my office. According to the sister Garth and Martin were buddies in school; both dropped out early, and both had been in prison."   "Garth has a record?"

"Just for assault, as far as I know. Ward told me it was apparently a drunken brawl or something – typical fishing boat stuff, he called it. Martin, apparently, is a much harder case."

"You think it might be Martin who shot Garth?"

"I don't know, Sergeant. It is a possibility. If I can find that phone number and you can match it to an address, you could see if there are matching fingerprints on Garth's truck."

"Yeah, get me that number, Professor, and we'll contact Cleveland and see what we can find."

* * *

There was almost a crowd in the critical care ward the following morning when Detective Sergeant David Wilkerson, Ike Wallender. an attorney from the Erie County District Attorney's office, Dr. Fairchild, Dexter and Peggy Atwater, all wrapped in white with face masks, gathered around Jimmy Garth's bed. Ward's bed was in a semi-sitting position, which made breathing easier.

Dexter Atwater had been in the room before the others arrived to check on the wound, and he assisted Peggy in changing the dressings. Now he said, as the others gathered, "Gentlemen, Mr. Garth has a very serious wound to his lung, but he is very lucky. The bullet came very close to a key artery from the heart, but we recovered it, and, Sergeant Wilkerson, you said you wanted it for evidence. We have secured it, and Nurse Atwater, here, will provide it to you later.

"Now, Jimmy," Dexter said, looking at his patient, "these men are investigating your shooting, and want to help you. But I don't want you getting excited or exhausted. Speak as little as you can, until you get full use of your lung back. If you begin to get tired, just indicated that, and any of this can be completed later." Garth nodded, but looked very uncomfortable. Dexter introduced the two lawmen and Fairchild. Garth seemed puzzled by the professor, knitting his brow like he was trying to remember.

"Jimmy, we have met before. Do you remember the night of the storm on the Gulf of Mexico, when we had dinner together at the Suwannee Hotel?" Garth smiled and nodded. "You said you were from Boston, and I thought you might need a friend here in Sandusky."

"Can you state your name?" Wilkerson asked.

"Jimmy Garth..., James Paul."

"Where do you live, James?"

"Ahh, the Shoreview Apartments, here in Sandusky. Number Seven."

"Where did you live prior to that?"

"An apartment in Boston, right on the line with Brookline."

"Are you currently employed?"

"Ahh, no. I work on boats when I can."

"What kind of work?"

"Deck hand, salvage diver, that sort of thing."

"James, do you own a blue Chevrolet panel truck, Massachusetts tag Y8772ZX?"

"Yeah, I don't know the tag number, but that sounds about right."

"James, on Thursday evening was that panel truck parked outside your apartment at the Shoreview Apartments?"

"Yeah."

"Was it locked?"

"Yeah."

"May we ask you what was inside the panel truck?"

"Ahh, yeah, I guess. The bill of sale and a map were in the glove compartment. I had a tool kit in the back, and, ahh, yeah, a carton of diving gear."

"Anything else?"

"Ahh, yeah, two locked footlockers. They were full of stuff."

"What kind of stuff?"

"Ahh," Garth hesitated, and looked at Fairchild as if to ask whether he had to answer that question.

"Sergeant Wilkerson, why don't you come back to that question in a few minutes," Fairchild suggested, sort of nodding toward Wilkerson. He suspected that the District Attorney's man was not aware of what Fairchild had told Wilkerson. "James, when the police arrived on the scene you had been shot, and the back of your truck was open. There were no footlockers inside." He hesitated, and could see Garth clench his teeth and lips in resignation to the fact that he'd been robbed. "Do you have any idea who might have done this?" Wilkerson continued.

Garth took a deep breath, sort of nodding his head to indicate "no," but he didn't say anything.

"No idea at all?" Wilkerson pressed. Garth still did not answer. Was there, indeed, honor among thieves, Fairchild wondered to himself. But Garth was obviously afraid. If he told the police he knew exactly who it was, and had known from the second he had ran out the apartment door and saw Danny's black Pontiac sports car, then he had to tell all about Danny, who was a burglar, and about Pappy Sanchez, the fence, and what it was that Danny was stealing. He could be arrested as an accomplice, even though all he had done was to help Danny load the big truck with the stolen items and ride from Cleveland to Sandusky with him.

"James," Wilkerson then continued. "do you know a Danny Martin?"

"Ahh, Da ... Danny? Well, I do know of a Danny Martin."

"A Danny Martin that lives in Cleveland, but used to live in Boston?"

"Ahh, yeah, that Danny."

"Did Danny shoot and rob you Thursday night?"

"Ahh.... Yeah! How the hell did you know?"

"James," he continued, "were there gold coins in those two footlockers?" Wallender, the Assistant District Attorney, looked as surprised as Garth at that question. "Oh, God! How the hell do you know this? Have you caught Danny?"

"No, but we will. The Cleveland Police are checking now. If we can match finger prints from him to the back of your truck, will you help us convict him?"

"Sergeant, Danny was a friend," Garth said. "But he's turned into a rat. The Cleveland Police need to catch him. He's a burglar. That's how he makes his living. He has a place above a Hungarian bakery on some Cleveland street called Abbey Avenue. That's where he keeps the stuff he's stolen until he gets a load, and then he brings it up here to Sandusky to sell. When I found out that's what he did, I refused to have anything further to do with him."

"Where does he sell the stolen items?" Wallender asked.

"I wouldn't have known, except that ... well, you guys apparently know I had some gold coins, but I assure you, they were not stolen from anybody. I needed a place to market them, and before I knew what Danny was doing, I rode with him one day with a load of his stolen stuff to some place west of here, called Pappy's."

"Pappy Sanchez?" Wallender asked.

"Yeah, Sanchez. He was helping me sell a few coins. I was to take him some the next day, hey, what day is today?"

"Saturday."

"What happened to Friday?" Garth asked, and they all chuckled.

"Look, guys, I don't want to get in trouble, or get Danny or Pappy in trouble, but Danny drives crazy, and he's dangerous. I just wanted to sell the damned coins and go home...." Garth began to cry.

Dexter Atwater leaned over and asked if he was okay, and held his hand on Garth's shoulder. "Gentlemen, do you have many more questions? I think my patient is exhausted."

"May I ask one or two?" Richard Fairchild inquired of the officers. They nodded that it was okay. "Jimmy," he began, "let me tell you a little story. It involves your nurse, here, Mrs. Atwater." Both Garth and Ike Wallender looked surprised, as did Peggy.   "Mrs.   Atwater's   great grandfather was an agent for the Confederacy during the Civil War. As you may or may not know, at the time there was animosity between the Union and Mexico under Emperor Maximilian, and Maximilian agreed to help finance the Confederacy with a loan of three million dollars' worth of Mexican gold pesos. The French sold the Confederacy two gunboats, called corvettes, and one accompanied a former Austrian ship assigned to Mexico to Vera Cruz to pick up a cargo of various items for shipment to the Confederacy, to be delivered to the port of Suwannee, at the mouth of the Suwannee River. But the two vessels were spotted by a Union gunboat operating on blockade duty under Admiral Farragut, and the two vessels were sunk in the Gulf of Mexico, just north of a little village called Suwannee.

"That wreckage probably may lie beyond the three-mile state jurisdiction, hence anyone who locates it would be entitled to the salvage rights, although the federal government might also have a right of claim on the coins. If the wreckage is within three miles of the state, then the State of Florida would also have a right of claim. But in either case, it is the historic value of those coins and what they represent as a national historic treasure that makes them important.

"Jimmy, I know you were on an expedition paid for by an Elias Ward, because you were on the crew of the Roberta II, under Captain Jay Plunkett. The three of you found the wreckage, but did not find anything of value. I suspect that you wanted to be sure, to double check, and see if you might have missed something on that first expedition, and that is when my associate, Bob Merriam, and I met you during a gale at an old hotel in that village of Suwannee.

"Jimmy, I think you did find that Mexican shipment, and rescued it from future pillage. To finance your venture I believe you had to sell a few of the coins, but that you were probably unaware of their real significance or value until just now. But what it means, if those coins can be found, is that you are going to be honored by the historical artifacts community, and that could be worth a lot more than trying to sell a few coins here and there.

"And, Jimmy, although I cannot speak for these officers here, it sounds to me as if they could use you as a prosecution witness in what may have been a very expensive criminal ring. I think you're going to come out of this like a hero. It was those gold coins that were in the footlockers, wasn't it?"

"Yes, Professor. It was. I didn't know what to do with them. Just their value as gold had to be something, but I suspected they might be worth more than as just gold. But now they're gone, I'm shot, and I haven't any money or a job or anything." "Jimmy," Peggy Atwater said, "finding that gold brings to conclusion a very long and interesting story about my great grandfather, who lived right here in Sandusky and had two houses, one of which Dr. Atwater, here, and I live in at present. But the other one is currently vacant. It is over on the Marblehead Peninsula, and is a farm that could use some upkeep on the buildings. Dex, do you think Jimmy might be able to do some of that work until he recuperates fully? That way he'd be available to assist the officers here?"

"I don't see why not. And Jimmy, I wouldn't get rid of that diving equipment just yet. I think you'll be as fit as ever soon, and I don't believe you are a smoker, which is what makes your healing so much easier."

"Doc, I don't know what I'm hearing! Am I dreaming? I think I may pass out!""You go back to sleep, Jimmy," Dexter said. "You're not dreaming, but you're in good hands and I don't think from what I'm hearing that you are in any trouble."

Chapter 16

Cleveland, Ohio

The Cleveland Police located the apartment above the Hungarian bakery with no difficulty after matching the phone number Fairchild had provided to an address, confirmed by Garth's description. But it was clear that Martin had departed. Descriptions of both the black Pontiac sports car and Martin's big van truck, which was apt to have the name changed frequently, was distributed to law enforcement agents around Ohio and neighboring states, but there was no sign of Martin. Fingerprints from the apartment matched not only those on Garth's panel truck but also at the scene of numerous burglaries throughout Cleveland suburbs.

When Jimmy Garth was released from Memorial Hospital Peggy had a day off, and drove Jimmy back to this apartment to collect his personal belongings. The police had suggested that Garth not stay at his apartment, for it was probable that Martin had already determined that he had not killed Garth, and they feared that Martin might return to finish the job if he anticipated that Garth would testify against him if he was ever caught. Garth felt well enough to drive the panel truck a short distance, and having put his personal things inside it, he followed Peggy to the big house in Sandusky. Dexter had fixed up the room above the garage as a temporary office and small apartment, and Peggy agreed to check on Garth each day to be sure he was okay, and following her husband's strict instructions for his recovery. She had also gotten Dexter to prescribe a skin medication for Garth's acne, and after several weeks his face cleared up considerably. It was agreed that once he was able to do some light work that they would take him out to the Marblehead farm and let him move in there. That occurred about three weeks later, and when Garth saw the farm he was delighted.

"It's like Marblehead, Massachusetts!" he exclaimed. "And that's only for rich folks who can afford to live on the bay."

"Yes, and I expect you will make it look even better, Jimmy," Dexter said. "Now, just take it easy until you get settled in. We have had the power turned on, and the town has hooked up the water system, so you don't need to worry about a well. The phone company said they'd hook you up sometime this week, so you can call us if there is any need. The heating and range is gas, but I think there's a quarter tank still, and we'll set it up for routine service. Don't think you'll need much heat now that summer is here, but it can be damp in the mornings, I imagine, in this old stone house."

They walked around the various barns and buildings to the east of the house, and both Dexter and Peggy saw a number of things that they hoped Jimmy would be able to do. "Now, I don't want you repainting the barn and sheds until you are fully recovered. I'll tell you when you can start that," Dexter said.

In one of the sheds they found an eighteen foot fishing boat with a small cabin. It was pulled up on a rack, and looked to be in fairly good condition. It had a gasoline motor, but the tank was empty.

"Well!" Dexter said. "Jimmy, you're a sailor, you say. Think you could get this thing fixed up and running?"

"You bet I could!" Garth replied. "Of course, it will take a bit of time and money for a good coat of marine gel and paint, but...."

"You let us know what you need, and we'll either get it for you and bring it out, or give you the money and you can arrange to buy it. There are lots of marine supply houses around, both out here on the Peninsula and in Sandusky. And whatever you need for the work on the farm, either let us know, or keep receipts."

"Doctor Atwater, I don't know how to thank you and your wife enough for all you have done for me."

"Jimmy, we were going to have to hire someone to work out here anyway. This is good for both of us. You have a home; we have an employee – for we will pay you for your labor – and someone to make this place livable. Besides, there's good perch and walleye in the Lake if you're a good fisherman. We can work the wages out later." Garth began to laugh. "My pot of gold was stolen, but what I've found at the end of this rainbow is far better."

Erie County authorities delayed any move on Pappy Sanchez, whom they had long suspected of receiving stolen goods. Without Martin, however, they had little concrete evidence beyond Garth's statement and their suspicions, but kept a close watch, hoping to spot the van truck Garth had described. At Fairchild's recommendation ads were placed in several newspapers in Cleveland, Lorain County, Toledo, Akron and other towns where Martin might have gone, seeking "historic Mexican coins." On the assumption that Martin would have opened the two footlockers, at least studied the nature of the coins, and pondered what to do with them, Fairchild hoped that Martin might respond to the ad. The only response was from a Canadian coin dealer who has seen the ad and advised that he had purchased several such coins through a Detroit dealer a few weeks earlier, but Garth believed these may have been the coins that Sanchez had sold for him. Fairchild offered to purchase the coins, for which the dealer wanted $700 each. After considerable negotiation, he was able to arrange to purchase two for $1150, which he did on behalf of the Atwaters and Fremont College.

By the end of the Spring Semester, with Graduation Day approaching, the normally frantic pace of the Religions Department at Fremont College was starting to slow. Jimmy Garth had moved into the old house across from Johnson Island and was working on repainting the barn and sheds. Dr. Atwater's private cardiology practice was growing to the point where Peggy was able to quit her job at the hospital and work as Dexter's office nurse full time. Bob and Sally had agreed to take the summer tour to Europe this year, to visit church-related sites in England, Wales and Scotland, ranging from Canterbury to Iona.

The Fairchilds were planning a quite summer at home. That ended with a morning telephone call two days after Commencement Day. Esther had answered the phone. "I'm responding to an ad about some gold coins. Is this the right number," a voice at the end of the line with a slight Boston Irish accent inquired.

"Oh, you want my husband. Let me go get him."

"Hello?" Richard Fairchild said, a few moments later.

"Yeah, I'm trying to reach the guy who placed an ad in the Cleveland papers a couple weeks back, looking for old Mexican coins."

"Do you have such coins?"

"I might know how to get some, if the price is right."

"Well, I'd have to see them, Mr. ...."

"Ahh, Daniel. Just call me Daniel."

"Yes, Mr. Daniel. Is there someplace we could meet? Are you in Cleveland?"

"Yeah, at present. Where are you?"

"A bit west of there. But I'd be happy to arrange a meeting and can drive into town to meet you there if you wish."

"I could come out to your place. Just tell me where, and...."

"No, I don't think we could meet here, too many people here. We need someplace where we can see what you have, and talk about it."

"Yeah, yeah, don't want too many people around. That's a good idea. So, ahh, maybe half way, somewhere."

"Are you familiar with Sandusky?" Fairchild asked.

"Sandusky? Yeah, sure. I've been there. That where you want to meet? Where?" "Well, there's a little coffee shop on the main street, just a block up from the docks on the west side of the street. Say about two or two-thirty this afternoon? Would that give you time to drive out from Cleveland?"

"Yeah, I think so. Okay, but, and what did you say your name was?

"I didn't. Call me Richard."

"Listen, Richard, this is just the two of us, no coin club or nothing like that. I only want to deal with individuals. I see you with others, I don't even come in. What'cha look like?"

"Late forties, horn-rimmed glasses, a blue jacket."

"Okay, two o'clock."

* * *

Jimmy Garth, who was growing a fairly thick black beard since moving to the farm, had fixed up the fishing boat, replacing damaged wood where necessary, putting in all new railings, varnishing all of the wood paneling both outside and within the small cabin, and overhauling the gasoline motor, installing a twenty-five gallon tank. With Dexter's help they had hauled it down to the old dock behind the farm house and had launched it into Sandusky Bay. The engine immediately started, and the two had cruised around Johnson Island before bringing it back to the dock.

"Hey, this is great, Dr. Atwater. I think it will be faster for me to get to Sandusky in this than to drive. Is there a place over there I could dock it, if I came in for supplies?"

"Well, you could try the municipal dock. I see private boats in there occasionally. I don't know what they charge, but if you're picking up supplies for the farm repairs, I'll reimburse you whatever it is. Of course, if you've got some girl out to see the moonlight on a cruise over to Cedar Point, then you're on your own!"

"I haven't met any girls yet. What do you suggest?"

"Gosh, Jimmy. Let's see. There's no college in town, so no college girls your age. You might get a good Sunday suit and try one of the churches in town."

"I've not been in a church since I was a little kid. But your friend, Professor Fairchild, invited me to come to their Fremont Chapel service sometime. Is he the preacher there?"

"Assistant chaplain. Yes, he's the Religions Professor at the College. Take him up on it. There will be lots of girls there, single ones attending summer courses. You might try taking a few courses, too. How was your high school record?"

"D.O., I'm afraid, Dr. Atwater. Dropped out. Maybe I can find some classes around Sandusky to finish my high school. Don't you have to take a test or something to get into college?"

"Yes, but many people are successful in doing just what you described. Oh, you might join the military and get your education there."

"I thought of that. I was in prison for a few months for beating up a guy in a fight. Think they'd still want me?"

"Isn't that what the military does? Fight?"

"Ha! I guess so."

It was a week or so later that Garth needed some additional paint and a longer ladder to start painting the barn at the farm. He had noticed a hardware store on the main street in Sandusky, and thought it would be easier to bring the supplies over by boat than to drive his panel truck, as the ladder would stick out the back unless he tied it to the roof. He and Dr. Atwater had selected a color, not a bright red, but more of a tan, the same color as the rock house, and he had phoned the hardware store to see if they could mix paint to the color he wanted.

It was a sunny June day and Garth wore his tee shirt and a brimmed sailor hat as he putted across Sandusky Bay from the farm, and tied up at the dock at the foot of the hill on the main street of Sandusky. He thought he'd get a bite to eat at the small coffee shop across from the hardware store before he made his purchases and carried them back to the boat. He'd left the farm about noon, and it was almost two o'clock already.

* * *

As soon as Martin had hung up Richard Fairchild phoned the Sandusky Police Department and asked for Detective Sergeant Wilkerson. Wilkerson was out on a case, but the clerk in the Detective Unit agreed to have him call Fairchild back. Within about ten minutes the phone at Fairchild's farm rang.

"Martin has made contact," he told the detective. "I'm to meet him at the coffee shop there on the main street up from the docks at two o'clock. He made a point of my being alone to see the coins."

"Good. The timing is good, too, for I've got three other men available, all plain clothes, so we'll be ready. Are you to meet him inside or on the street?"

"We didn't say. Which would you prefer?"

"Outside, I think. Meet him just to the north of the doorway. I'll have a man inside watching, and a couple others you won't notice. You're taking a risk, you know." "Oh, I don't think so. I'm anxious to see this guy off the streets. He might want to burglarize me next."

"Well, let's get him locked up. Two o'clock."

Esther wanted to accompany her husband. He tried to talk her out of it, but she said she had things to buy in Sandusky anyway, and would be far away from the coffee shop when the time came. He knew he could not convince her to stay home, so the two drove into town and parked a block away from the coffee shop.

At five minutes to two Fairchild was standing a few feet north of the doorway to the coffee shop when a sleek black Pontiac sports car roared up the hill and parked in front of the coffee shop. The young man driving it got out, slammed the door and started over toward Fairchild, who was dressed as he said he would.

"You Richard?"

"Yes! Mr. Daniels? You are right on time."

With that a black bearded man in a sailor cap came running across the street, shouting, "You sonofabitch! Damn you, Danny, you tried to kill me!"

Garth ran to the right side of the Pontiac as three other men also appeared from seemingly nowhere, and a fourth came out the coffee shop door. Danny quickly pulled a pistol from his pocket and stepped behind Fairchild, aiming the gun at Garth.

"What is this, a trap?" he snapped.

"Drop the gun, Martin," Wilkerson barked.

"Like hell!" Martin shouted back. "Jimmy, get in the car, the driver's seat."

Garth hesitated, but Danny shot a bullet between his legs and Danny slowly moved to the left side of the Pontiac as the four detectives moved closer.

"No, no, fellows," Martin said. "Move any closer and this man here dies. By the way, who the hell are you, Richard?"

"Richard Fairchild."

"Oh yeah, the guy who called me last April, trying to find Jimmy Garth — well, there he is! Now get in the car, and lean forward — I'm getting in the back."

By this time several police cars had arrived, and the ends of the street were blocked off.

"Swing around, Jimmy, and head down that hill to wherever you parked your truck."

"I didn't come by truck. I came by boat!" Garth replied.

"Oh, better yet! So go to wherever your boat is tied up."

As the car backed around and started down the hill the police shot out all four tires. Martin instructed Garth to keep on driving, and they banged around the police car blocking the intersection and rumbled down the hill to the dock, the police running on foot behind them.

When they reached the dock, Martin ordered the professor and Garth out, and he stepped beside the professor and put his left arm around Fairchild's neck, pressing the pistol against the side of his head so that the police could clearly see that Fairchild was being held hostage.

"Into the boat!" Martin ordered, keeping Fairchild between himself and the police. "Now get this thing moving!" he ordered, and Garth threw off the docking ropes and started the engine, putting out into the water and away from the dock. Meanwhile Martin barricaded himself in the cabin, still behind Fairchild, who faced outward. Garth piloted the small boat out into the main channel and away from the dock. The ferry from

Cedar Point was coming in from their starboard side, but was far enough away that it did not block their escape.

"Okay, now, wise guy," Martin said to Fairchild as they cleared the harbor and entered the Bay, "what the hell is all this about? And Jimmy, what the hell are you doing here?"

"Long story, Danny, but Dr. Fairchild here really was interested in those coins you stole from me."

"Yeah? What's he going to do with them? If I can't pawn the damned things it's a cinch he ain't going to be able to get rid of 'em."

"Danny, those coins are worth more than gold. But they've brought trouble to everyone who has possessed them, and they will for you, too."

"Oh, sob away!" Martin came out of the cabin to look around. They were now out in the Bay. "Where we going?"

"No place to go, Danny," Garth said. "This is the end of the line. You can't get to Canada in this thing – not enough gas. You could get out to the islands, but what would you do there? The Coast Guard'll pick us up in less than half an hour. They won't hesitate to shoot like the cops did."

"Yeah, well, we'll see. "Canada, eh? What? Due north? This thing have a compass?"

"Right there," Garth replied, pointing at the flat device above the steering wheel. "And I don't think you'll need me!" he exclaimed and jumped over the side. Martin ran to that side and looked over, but Garth was already swimming back toward the harbor. Martin decided not to shoot.

As he turned around Fairchild clobbered him with a life preserver that had been stowed under a seat, knocking the gun from Martin's hand. He then shoved the life preserver into Martin's face and pushed him back against the railing as Martin swung and struggled to strike Fairchild and regain control. Fairchild then brought his knee sharply up between Martin's legs, and Martin gave a shout of agony.

Fairchild again renewed his forceful push, leaning Martin back over the railing. By this time the boat had started to curve around, and was starting to head back toward the harbor. Fairchild brought his knee up again as Martin slid lower against the rail, and rammed it into Martin's stomach. Again Martin groaned in agony. Fairchild then kicked Martin's legs apart, and Martin fell to the deck. Fairchild again clobbered him with the life preserver, then stepped back and picked up the pistol, sticking it in his pocket. Martin sat in a stupor, but when he started to regain his senses Fairchild rammed the side of a fishing kit into his jaw, and Martin collapsed onto the deck unconscious.

Fairchild quickly looked around, and saw where Jimmy Garth was swimming. He'd left his hat in the boat, but it was clear that his clothing was weighing him down. Fairchild maneuvered the boat up next to Garth, and, using the docking rope, helped him pull himself aboard.

"Damn!" Garth exclaimed. "I must have missed one hell of a good fight, Professor. Didn't kill him, did you?"

"I sure hope not, Jimmy! But I think I see a police boat coming. Why don't you go below and get out of those wet clothes. You got any others in there."

"Yes. My wetsuit. I was thinking of doing some diving, but not the type I did do!"

* * *

Esther, who had heard the gunfire and had rushed to the scene, was terrified when she heard that Richard had been taken hostage. She was at the dock when the police boat escorted the little fishing boat in, and was relieved to see Richard behind the helm. By the time they had docked Martin was starting to regain consciousness. An ambulance, escorted by two police cars, took him to the hospital for examination, but Garth said he had no need of any more medical, and was just fine. Someone went to get him some dry clothes so he wouldn't have to go around in his rubber wetsuit, and the police took a complete statement from Fairchild. By this time a local newspaper reporter and photographer had arrived on the scene, along with the local radio news reporter, and Garth was upset that his picture had been taken dressed in a rubber suit.

From papers inside the Pontiac the police found the address in Cleveland where Martin had been staying. The large van truck was parked in the rear, and inside were the two footlockers, still full of gold coins. These were taken by armored truck to a vault at the Cleveland Trust Company, and the following day the headlines blazed Civil War Era Mexican Gold Coins Recovered in Arrest of Local Burglar.

The next evening Fairchild placed a call to Elias Ward. "Yes," he said after explaining that the coins had been recovered and were now secure in a bank vault, "it was quite a little adventure. Jimmy Garth turned out to be the hero, although for a while it looked like he had messed up the arrest. The important thing is that the coins are safe." "So what happens now, Fairchild?"

"I suspect things will pick up when the Journals are published. Peggy Atwater has just gone over the galleys, and publication should be by September. I've written an introduction to them, and have just brought it up-to-date as to the finding of the gold and the wreckage of the two vessels in the Gulf. As we discussed, your great grandfather's role in the story is covered completely, but I did not reveal where the ship's log was. I'm sure others will be in touch with you."

"Well, Professor, I guess it ends well. I plan to come out to Ohio sometime soon, and will give you a call. Perhaps I can meet the Atwaters."

"I'm sure they'd enjoy that."

Solemn Evensong

Part One – A Death in the Cathedral

Chapter 1

Sunday, April 12, 1959
A Large City in Southern Ohio

Heavy rain was falling as John Morris drove the mile and a half from his small apartment toward the towering neo-gothic cathedral building that occupied an entire side of the central city square. The Cathedral of St. Matthew had been built in the 1880s by some of the city's prominent industrialists as a monument to their own glory. It was they who had made this south central Ohio city so prominent. Their factories continued to belch smoke, employ thousands, and produce boxcar after boxcar of products for the entire world.

The swish-swash of the wipers on Morris's ten-year-old Buick provided a slow rhythm, and few other cars were on the street. The gray, misty gloom of the storm matched the gray-haired tall sixty-three-year-old's mood as he passed under a few trees just starting to bud for the first time since fall had depleted them of their leaves. It was not that Morris disliked spring rains, nor did he dislike the massive church structure at which he was a regular usher at the Sunday afternoon Solemn Evensong service. It was a service he loved, based on ancient texts and sung by the ten professional singers that the cathedral employed. It was, in fact, Morris's second service of the day as he had attended the early morning Eucharist, which was still festive two weeks after Easter.

He always felt revived by the festive morning services, chanting along with the choir and the congregation in the various parts of the liturgy, and singing the hymns with his gusty baritone voice during those morning services so full of pageantry and ritual. He had enjoyed Dean Williams' sermon, associating God with love and light, and suggesting that perhaps Albert Einstein's theory – $E=MC^2$ -- might just be an explanation of creation and life, making all of us brothers and sisters in the light of Christ, just as the Creed stated: God from God, Light from Light.

But light was not on Morris's mind as he drove through the rain. What was, on this gloomy afternoon as the rain fell heavily as he neared the Cathedral, was his recollection that it was Canon Augustus Packard who would be the priest officiating at the Evensong service that afternoon.

Packard had been at St. Matthew's only three years. His rotation to the Solemn Evensong service came only about once a quarter, but it was once a quarter too often for John Morris. He knew he should respect and honor the sixty-eight-year-old balding and nearsighted priest, but only a dry crusty callus existed on his heart for the old clergyman. He'd known him too long.

Twelve years before, when John and his much younger wife, Melissa, had lived in the Lockfield County suburb of Park Grove and had attended the Church of the Atonement, Father Augustus Packard had arrived as the new priest to assist the aging rector, Father Bill O'Day. Morris was an operations executive at the Wilson Company, a job that required him to travel frequently to other Wilson factories and sales offices across the country, and even to Europe. He had occasionally been able to take Melissa with him, but most often she was left at home with only her reading and a neighborhood bridge club to keep her busy. She had once worked as a nurse, but disliked the hours required by the hospital, and with John's salary, a second income was not needed. The home was paid for and the Morris family had no debts. But they had no children either, one infant having died soon after being born. Melissa had never fully recovered from that death. It had left her bitter, disappointed and quite often depressed. They had been unable to have other children, and, with John's frequent travels, had been rejected several local agencies for an adoption. Melissa had been lonely.

That had been the start of the problem, but it blossomed when Augustus Packard arrived in the parish. He was announced as a wonderful counselor, and many in the parish had sought meetings with him. While John had been on an extended trip to Minnesota one winter, Melissa had made an appointment with Packard. They'd met first in his office, and regular meetings had turned into something more – John was never sure what – but when he had returned from the Minnesota assignment, the weekly meetings had become nearly daily meetings, often in John Morris's home.

Melissa had encouraged John to join in her counseling sessions with Packard, and he finally agreed to meet with the priest, as Melissa was increasingly depressed. It quickly became clear to John what was happening. There was some sort of romantic attachment that Melissa had to the older priest, more than just a father-daughter or priest and communicant situation. In his mind John could still picture the man, then only partially bald, leaning back in his chair in his black suit with his clerical collar, peering at John over the top of his glasses. The relationship with Packard was tearing Melissa apart, and it was evident that the priest was doing nothing to prevent the growing attachment between the two.

A few days after that first joint conference John had to travel to New York for a meeting. It lasted three days. When he returned home, Melissa was gone. He contacted her elderly mother, who had no idea where Melissa might be. He called her sister, Joan, but she also could not explain Melissa's disappearance, although she told John that she and Melissa had had a long conversation about a week before, when Melissa was in extreme distress.

She said that Melissa had told her that while she still loved John as a husband and provider, it was no longer love warranting their continued marriage. She had praised the priest, Packard, and told Joan that he was encouraging her to divorce John and leave him to find a new life for herself. Packard, who was not married, said he would help her, and Joan anticipated that either Melissa was already in an affair with the priest, or was planning to enter one.

John had angrily phoned Packard, demanding to know where his wife was, but the priest said he did not know. The priest responded with his own anger when John accused him of alienating his wife from him, and had hung up on John. John then phoned Father Bill, the rector, telling him of Melissa's disappearance and the conversations with Joan and Augustus Packard. Father Bill was supportive of his assistant priest, but could offer John no suggestions.

John was frantic. He called every place he could think of where Melissa might have gone, every one of her friends, her cousins, even the hospital where she had been a nurse, but no one had any idea of where Melissa might be. John was due to make another trip, and went to his office, clearing up some paperwork on his desk and writing a letter to the vice president of operations advising that he needed some time off to find his wife, suggesting that his assistant make the next business trip. He left the letter on his boss's desk, and drove home, arriving about eleven fifteen that evening.

He could see a car in the driveway as he approached the big two-story house, and hoped it was Melissa's. But as he got closer, he saw that it was a police car, and that two officers were standing by his front door. John parked on the street and rushed up to the two officers.

"Are you John Morris?" one asked.

"Yes! Have you found my wife? She left a few days ago and I've been searching frantically for her."

"Well, yes we have found her," the other officer replied. "But perhaps we could discuss this better inside."

John unlocked and opened the door and turned on the lights in the living room, asking the two policemen to sit wherever they wished, expressing his concern for his missing wife and asking if he could get them anything before he, too, sat down.

"No," replied the first, a Sergeant Robby. Then he said, "You say your wife has been missing for more than a day. Have you filed a missing person's report?"

"No," John replied. "I thought she had gone to stay with her mother or sister or someone while I was out of town on business, and I only got home last night. I've called everyone I can think of, but so far none of her friends or relatives has any idea of where she might be. I hadn't thought about filing a missing person report yet, as I thought I'd soon locate her. But you say you found her?"

"Yes, we found her," the other officer, a Lieutenant Jacobs, replied, "But I'm afraid the news is not good." He paused, while Morris stared at him, his mouth slightly open, unsure what to anticipate.

"What? Where is she?" he asked.

"Your wife owns a blue Chevrolet, is that correct?"

"Yes."

"License number 742-AY?"

"I'm not sure of the license number, but that sounds like it."

"Do you own a gun, Mr. Morris?"

"No."

"Did your wife own a gun?"

"Ahh, I don't think so. She discussed buying one about a year ago when I was traveling quite a bit, just for security around the house, but I don't think she ever did. Why? What has happened?"

"We found your wife's car at the Forest Oaks Cemetery this evening. She was sitting behind the wheel with a gunshot wound to her head, and a small pistol in her hand."

"Oh my God! She's dead?"

"Yes," Sergeant Robby answered. "By appearances she shot herself, but we are investigating."

"There was a note," Lieutenant Jacobs continued. He opened a file folder, and showed the note to Morris, but would not let him touch it. "We have not yet dusted it for finger prints, but we do anticipate finding only your wife's."

"What did she say?"

Jacobs read the note aloud. "John, I am so sorry. I just can't go on, and am torn by what is right and what I know would be wrong. I've always loved you, but lately that love has died. Nothing filled the gap in my heart after Johnnie died until I started meeting with Auggie. I didn't want to hurt you, but I couldn't do what was wrong, either. There is no other way out. I can't go home to mother – you know her situation. Joannie has her own family to worry about, and there's no one else. If only Johnnie had lived…."

"She didn't sign it," Jacobs added. "Does this look like her handwriting?"

"Yes, it's a bit of a scribble – a style she acquired as a nurse."

"Can you get us some other samples of her handwriting?"

"Sure, but I'll have to look around the house for them."

"Who is 'Johnnie'?" Jacobs asked.

"John, Junior, was our son. He died shortly after birth. He's buried at Forest Oaks. That may explain why she went there. But how long had she been there?"

"At least two days. She'd parked the car in a wooded area, and the cemetery people hadn't noticed it until today. We traced her through the license number and the information in her purse, which we will return to you after our investigation is complete."

"Yes, there was a little woods near where our infant was buried. Melissa was never the same after Johnnie died. She visited the grave frequently."

"Who is 'Joannie'? Robby asked.

"That's Melissa's sister, in New Jersey. They'd been close, but...." John began to weep.

"Who is this 'Auggie'?" Jacobs asked.

"I don't know him by that name, but I'm guessing it is Father Augustus Packard at the Church of the Atonement. Melissa had been counseling with him. I'd even gone once, and it was clear to me that their relationship was something very unusual. She was seeing him frequently."

"Frequently? How frequently?"

"Well, it was supposed to be just a weekly counseling session, but I was out of town on business a lot, and I guess, from what I sort of picked up from her, that it had become more frequent. And no, I don't think they were having an affair ... yet."

"I see. Well, Mr. Morris, I hate to have you do this, but you will need to come down to the coroner's office tomorrow to identify the body. Then you can make your funeral arrangements."

"You think it was suicide?"

"It looks like it," the Lieutenant replied, "but we do need to be certain. Rule out any other cause, although there does not seem to be any. It does not appear that anything was taken from her purse."

"What was in her purse?"

"One thing we noted," Sergeant Robby answered, "was a receipt from Ralph's Gun Shop dated last week for the pistol that was in her hand. Can you account for where you have been in the past few days?"

"Well, yes! I just flew in from New York last evening. My associates there can confirm that I'd been there at meetings for three days, and I'd stayed at the Roosevelt Hotel. Here," Morris answered, fishing in his suit pocket, "here's a copy of the hotel bill. I forgot to turn it in on my expense account this afternoon when I was at the office. Why do you ask? Am I a suspect in her death? God, I loved Melissa. I never would have harmed her."

"No, no!" Jacobs answered. "But we just need to verify everything. You know how that is, Mr. Morris. This is a difficult time for you, I know, and we'll be on our way. But we'll give you a call in the morning about visiting the coroner's office."

* * *

John Morris called Father O'Day the next morning and explained what had happened. He asked for a quiet funeral service, but insisted that the Rev. Packard have absolutely nothing to do with it. John explained why, and O'Day responded, "So I've heard, so I've heard. But I don't know if it is fact or not that Augustus got carried away with some of his lady clients. You know how church rumors can be. Difficult to verify."

After identification of his wife, Morris had arranged with Patrickson's Funeral Home for a closed casket burial – Melissa's face was too torn apart to make it presentable. Joan and her mother flew in from New Jersey for the service, and burial was at Forest Oaks next to John, Junior. The memorial service at Atonement was brief, the few family members, and neighbors and friends of Melissa. There was no mention in the newspaper of the cause of her death, and Morris resisted all inquiries, just advising that it had been sudden and unexpected.

It quickly became clear to John that he would need an attorney, not because he was a suspect in his wife's death, but because she had no will, and the house was in both names, along with other accounts that would be tied up until the state probate court could release the assets. It was the company attorney who recommended Bob Willingham to Morris, and the two met in Willingham's office a week after the funeral.

After Morris explained the entire situation, Willingham, a man almost John's age with thick white hair, leaned back in his black padded leather chair and looked at Morris for a moment. "You need to sue," he said.

"Sue? Sue who?"

"The priest, of course. Clear case of alienation of affections. Malpractice on the part of a counselor. I can think of a dozen good allegations, although most might not survive a summary judgment. Are you angry enough to do that?"

"I don't know what I am, Mr. Willingham. Yes, I hate the bastard, but I guess I was partly at fault because I was away from home so much, and Melissa needed me after the baby died. What would a lawsuit involve?"

"Simple, actually. We file the suit and a motion to produce the list of all his female clients. He has legal privilege – the priest and confessor thing – but the suit itself might bring some of the other women he's counseled forward on their own. Get one or two to confirm that his style doesn't conform to professional standards, and, who knows, you might even get him defrocked, or at least recover the cost of the funeral in damages."

"Well, let me think about it. I don't know if he has any assets or not. He drives a big car, but the church pays part of that."

"We won't know until we try. Doesn't cost much to file the suit, and let's see what happens."

* * *

Willingham's suit, *Morris v. Packard,* generated more heat and excitement than either Morris or the lawyer had anticipated. The local newspaper picked up on it, but the result was that Melissa Morris's suicide was disclosed. Packard voluntarily resigned from Atonement and went off to some monastery in Michigan for a few years. At that point Morris had Willingham drop the suit. Morris then sold his suburban home and moved to a small apartment near the downtown area, where he transferred his membership to the Cathedral parish. While bitter about Packard, his bitterness did not extend to the church.

But then, ten and a half years later, after Morris had just retired from Wilson, Packard was hired by the Cathedral as Canon for Pastoral Counseling, one of seven clergymen under Dean Williams. Morris had been surprised and unhappy about encountering the old priest again, but they were able to keep their distance from each other. It was only on a rare occasion that they met, other than briefly passing each other in the hall, except when Packard drew the Solemn Evensong assignment.

The rain was still increasing as Morris drove into the parking lot and into one of the five slots reserved for ushers. He thought to himself that there would not be many attendees at the service due to the weather, and attendance was always light after Easter anyway. "Twice a Year Christians," Dean Williams called them. Christmas and Easter. For some, the highly liturgical solemn service was boring – all medieval plainsong and Latin anthems. The homilies were short, and the Eucharist service even shorter. Normally perhaps fifty might attend. As many members also disliked Packard's so-called sermons, which were often overbearing and loaded down with minor theological points, he doubted that there would be more than a dozen attendees. But Evensong was a tradition, and, being an Anglican cathedral church, tradition meant everything.

Morris pushed open his umbrella as he stepped out of the car, and hurried toward the side door to the atrium where he could hang his raincoat and collect his boutonnière indicating his status as an usher, picking up a second for Will Smithers, who would be his co-usher that afternoon. A few other cars were already in the lot, a big Mercury parked in one of the slots assigned for clergy, and seven or eight others that were probably either choir members or acolytes. It was about forty minutes before the service would start.

Morris's first task was to go to the basement print shop and pick up the bulletins for the service. He would then have to identify the two or three hymn numbers that would be sung by the congregation as well as the choir during the service, and post the numbers on the hymn board on the front left pillar next to the chancel. As he scanned the bulletin his eye caught the title of the homily for the service: "Why Someone Who Commits Suicide Cannot Go To Heaven." Canon Packard knew who the ushers would be. He had an odd way of getting even. Morris thought to himself.

Chapter 2

Down the hall in the choir room Morris could hear the small group rehearsing a chanted Psalm for the service. It sounded as if a few of the members were missing – the high notes sounded overwhelmed by the altos and bases. Dr. Ripple, the choirmaster and organist, stopped after a few lines, and Morris could hear him asking if one of the altos would mind switching to the soprano part. As paid professional singers, most of the Evensong choir – a select group who acted as section leaders in the big Cathedral Choir – was able to sing almost any part. When the Psalm began again, it was in better balance and the basses less powerful.

The ten paid singers, Morris knew, were also unhappy with Canon Packard. He had been lobbying Dean Williams to do away with paid singers and make the choir totally voluntary. Too much of an expense, Packard had argued, adding that what Ripple was paid, despite his national reputation as an organist, was certainly not in keeping with church tradition. Undoubtedly some of the choir, knowing Packard would be participating in the late afternoon service, had elected to claim any excuse to avoid coming, even if it cost them their weekly honorarium. Most of them were highly paid professionals in other fields anyway – a physician, an attorney, an accountant, two local music teachers, and several well-known local business people – but the small weekly payment was considered to be an honor, just as it was named, and it imposed a sense of responsibility as well.

Returning upstairs, Mrs. Gilfrey, a member of the Alter Guild, had just arrived and had unlocked the chancel sacristy, turning on the light. Morris entered, greeting her, and retrieved the necessary numbers for the hymn board, returning to one of the front pillars with a short step ladder, which he opened and climbed to insert the numbers. While the hymn numbers were also printed in the bulletins, it was tradition to also post them on the board, along with the Psalm number, so that the congregation could follow the choir's chant. The entire service was tradition, from the verger's leading the procession of incense and cross to the vestments worn by the clergy.

When Morris returned the step ladder to the sacristy Mrs. Gilfrey was busy preparing the chalice, paten and other silver items for the elements for the Eucharist service that would follow the Evensong. He chatted with her for a few moments, then took the collection plates from the cabinet which Mrs. Gilfrey had unlocked so that he could place them next to the entrance doors, as a few parishioners who might not stay for the entire service often left their offering before the service. He walked back down the side aisle of the cathedral nave, passing beneath the beautiful stained glass windows that made the tall neo-gothic building with its multiple pillars and side aisles shimmer in color when the sun was shining. But in today's rain, the windows were dull, the Biblical scenes and historical figures barely recognizable. He placed the stack of bulletins on a table to be handed out as worshipers arrived and placed an offering plate on a small table next to the central doors.

In a side hall off the narthex were two rooms. One was the vestry, where the vestments and some of the various items used in the service were kept. The other was the vergers' office. George Watson was the head verger, but tonight one of the assistant vergers would be in charge, a man who had served for a long time as a verger in another church, Bill Parkenson. Morris had known Parkenson for a few years as he had been a member of the Church of the Atonement back when Packard was also there. Morris had no idea what Parkenson thought or knew about Packard until he arrived at the vergers' room and found him putting on his black verger's cassock.

"I see that damned Packard is serving this afternoon!" Parkenson said.

"You don't like our good Canon Augustus Packard, Bill?"

"He's the reason Margaret and I left Atonement. The S.O.B had tried to break up our marriage just as he did yours. Why the Chapter ever hired him to serve here I'll never know. You and I should have warned them what kind of a man he was."

"Well, Bill, he's near retirement age now. Perhaps he'll be gone soon to some church in a warmer climate, and...."

"I can think of a very warm climate where that bastard belongs!" Bill interrupted. "He's enough to make anyone lose what little bit of faith they have left."

"I know what you mean. For example," Morris said, handing Parkenson one of the bulletins, "look at his homily title for tonight. Packard knows damned well that I'm one of the ushers tonight, and that Melissa died a suicide. That's hardly an appropriate subject for the day's Gospel reading anyway."

"There must be a lot of hate in that man. By the way, how many acolytes are we going to have this afternoon?" Parkenson asked, and Morris checked the roster.

"There's supposed to be three. One of the older teens from the morning list, Jeff Marchington, one of the adult acolytes, and Jim Slade, the other adult. Will Smithers will be the other usher."

"Oh, that explains the message the secretary put in my mailbox. Slade called in sick Friday, and said he was unable to get a substitute, and would be unable to make it this afternoon."

"Ouch! That leaves us one short. Neither that teenager nor Marchington know how to be thurifer. Packard will be livid when he finds out, as he's such a stickler for 'proper liturgical tradition,' as he calls it. But I'm not going to do it."

About that time Will Smithers came into the room, still shaking the water off his coat. Smithers was a short man, over seventy years old, and a bit awkward in his ways as well as a bit forgetful. He'd often forgotten to show up on a Sunday afternoon.

"Hello, Will," the two greeted him. "Still pouring out there, I see."

"Only a few cars in the lot. Suspect it will be a small congregation tonight," the old man said.

A few minutes later Jeff Marchington and Robert Crofton, an eighteen-year-old high school senior – an honor student, from what Morris had heard – arrived, and greeted the others. As they put on their white acolyte robes with blue sashes Parkenson explained that Jim Slade, who was a trained thurifer, would be absent.

"I know the routine," Will Smithers said, "but I haven't done it in years, probably a decade or more ago. Who's the celebrant?"

"Packard."

"Oh no! " Smithers replied in a dejected tone. "Oh well, it can't be helped. I'll never meet his standards! Is he here yet?" Smithers moaned.

With that the five men saw the light in the vestry room go on, and the door slammed shut. Packard had apparently been in his office on the second floor of the church parish hall prior to coming down for the service. "He's here!" Parkenson replied.

"Well, I don't know how to do it," Morris said. "And wouldn't, for him, even if I did. Who's going to break the news to Packard?"

"I guess I have to," Parkenson said. He crossed the hall and knocked on the closed vestry door. A dull roar sounded from within and Parkenson entered. There was a brief but loud reaction from the priest, and Parkenson retreated as quickly as he could. "He's willing to have you do to it, Will. You'll have to load the thurible in the vestry. It's hanging there on the stand."

"Why didn't you bring it out with you?" Will asked.

"There's a ritual to its lighting – Packard will do the whole nine yards of it, of course, probably telling you about all those years he was a monk."

"Yeah, I've heard all about those years! Okay."

* * *

By ten minutes before the five o'clock service about fifteen people had shown up for the service. Three were regulars that Morris knew by name, who rarely missed the Sunday afternoon Solemn Evensong. Morris had no idea of their feelings toward any of the clergy, but he had heard two other attendees mutter "Oh no! Packard!" when he had handed them the bulletin. There were two men in their twenties who always showed up, rain or shine. Morris did not know their names, but knew that they lived together and were musicians who enjoyed the music of the service. He had heard Canon

Packard comment about them about six months earlier, saying something to the effect that "the Church ought to throw those kind of people out! They've no business being here." Morris had not replied, and none of the other clergy seemed to have any objection to anyone who came to services, black, white, Oriental, Hispanic, married or otherwise.

There were only seven in the choir as they lined up for the procession, which would be accompanied only by a slow minor melody on the organ. When Will Smithers had entered the vestry to get the incense lighted, there had been some loud grumbling and shouts from behind the closed door, and Morris had heard only part of the words. "I don't know where the stuff is. Look in that cupboard!" Packard had shouted. Later, he had bellowed,

"Look out, you clumsy ox! You're spilling it!" Somehow the thurible had gotten blessed and lighted, and pungent smoke was pouring from it as Will took his place behind Bill Parkenson, swamped in the large borrowed white acolyte robe, and ahead of the two cross and banner-bearing acolytes and the choir, dressed in their own blue robes. The Reverend Canon Augustus Packard, vested in a black robe with academic hood and white stole, would march at the rear of the smoky parade. Parkenson pressed a button on the wall that signaled the organist that they were ready, and the slow music began as Parkenson led the procession slowly down the aisle and into the chancel, his verger's staff in his hand, as tradition dictated – verging a path for the clergy.

The Cathedral of St. Matthew was in the traditional English Gothic design, with a deep chancel and high altar, then parallel rows of choir seats ornately built into the wall. The two sections of the organ protruded above them, in matching ornate organ cases designed in wood and brass pipes that formed matching geometric patterns. There was also a division of the organ in the high balcony at the back. The organ console sat in a low pit, almost hidden behind the choir seats, and it was from there that Dr. Ripple directed the choir. The lower altar, from which the Eucharist was served, was surrounded by a low wooden rail on a raised platform, with needlepoint kneelers, and an open center gate that the acolytes would close and then reopen before and after the Eucharist. To the right was the high pulpit, and on the left a speakers stand from which the Old Testament and the Epistle were read. A high cross hung above the high altar, surrounded by stained glass windows depicting the events of Holy Week.

High pillars extended to the faux-vaulted ceiling sections. There were small balconies at the top of each of the two transepts, indented, but allowing open stained glass windows below them. The transept balconies were entered by doors from the inner part of the passages that extended to the right and left of the chancel area. Above the crossing, or the area between the nave, chancel and the two transepts, was a high square bell tower that also contained stained glass windows allowing natural light during the daytime services. A carillon in the tower was played from the organ console on Sunday mornings, and automatically rang the hours during daylight. As there were no flying buttresses supporting the outer walls of the long nave, side aisles on either side of the nave allowed stained glass windows between each set of pillars supporting the roof. In sunlight the windows depicted various Biblical scenes from the New and Old Testament and from the history of the Church. John Morris loved the building and the services that were conducted in it, and always marveled at the beauty of the place.

Morris stood at the large wooden doors at the center of the rear of the nave, ready to close the doors when the procession had entered. As Canon Packard passed Morris, he leaned toward Morris and whispered, "Leave the collection plate in the …." Morris did not hear the final word. Packard proceeded into the nave; Morris shut the doors, taking a position by a side door near the entrance for any late comers. There were none. He left the side door open so that he could hear the beautiful chants, hymns and anthems, but closed it when Canon Packard arose to give his sermon. Morris could only anticipate that the priest would be watching for Morris's angry face at the rear of the nave. He did not want to give the priest that pleasure.

As the sole usher and with so few in the congregation, taking up the offering took only a few minutes, and the plate was then taken to the sacristy, as was the usual procedure, where Mrs. Gilfrey locked it in the cupboard where the silver communion vessels were kept for the cathedral treasurer to retrieve in the morning. Morris had already taken the second plate back to Mrs. Gilfrey as Will Smithers had to serve as an acolyte. He then returned to the nave as the final part of the service, the Eucharist, began, with the Canon again censing the altar. The altar had first been censed during the singing by the choir of the ancient *Magnificat*. Will Smithers had awkwardly brought the smoking thurible to the priest, but had turned to return it to the temporary stand in the sacristy before censing the priest himself, which was due, Morris suspected, as much to Smithers dislike of Packard as to unfamiliarity with the ritual of the incense.

As the elements were prepared, Morris guided the handful of worshipers to the alter rail, waiting while they took communion and returned to their seats. Although he usually also participated as the last communicant, today he chose not to. He then returned to the rear of the nave, and opened the doors for the recessional that followed a final hymn. It proceeded in silence up the central aisle of the nave, in the same order as the processional, Will Smithers swinging the thurible back and forth, the smoke pouring out of it over the nearly empty cathedral pews.

Morris waited at the door as a few of the congregation would turn their bulletins back to him for paper recycling, and Packard stood in the narthex, shaking hands with a few of those who had attended, while others used the side door to escape that task. Jeff Marchington used the opposite side aisle to return to the chancel to extinguish the altar candles. Will Smithers had carried the still smoking thurible back to the vestry, and was there when Canon Packard entered it. Morris was returning to the vergers' room after again closing the doors and dimming the lights. Just as he was entering it he heard Packard shout, "Morris, get in here!"

As John Morris approached the open vestry door he saw Will Smithers standing with the thurible on its chain, asking the priest, who was just lighting a cigarette, what to do with it.

"Damn it, don't you know? Oh, hell, just hang it there and I'll take care of it later. Now get the hell out of here." Smithers hung the still smoking thurible on the stand and quickly left the room as Morris entered, shutting the door behind him as Packard had instructed. Before the door closed, the priest yelled, "Morris, where is that collection plate? I distinctly told you to leave it in here!"

"You whispered something as you passed, but I did not hear what you said," Morris replied as the door clicked shut.

"I said for you to bring it in here. You didn't. Where is it?"

"The same place it is always placed after Evensong – in the locked cabinet in the sacristy."

"That's not where I wanted it, damn it. Go get it and bring it here."

Morris could not believe what he was hearing, but left the vestry, closing the door behind him. "What does he want?" Parkenson asked from the vergers' room as Morris passed the door.

"He wants the collection plate. They're always left in the locked cabinet in the sacristy."

"Better hurry then. Mrs. Gilfrey usually closes up quickly."

Morris hurried back through the side door to the front of the tall arched-ceiling cathedral, opening the left front side door and moving to the sacristy. The hall was dark, and the door already locked. Morris had no key to the sacristy, nor to the cabinet within. He reluctantly turned and returned to the vestry. He knocked on the door and heard a bellow from within, and entered.

"The sacristy was already locked, and I don't have a key for it or the vessels cabinet where the collection plate was put."

"Well, here's my keys – the one with blue is to the sacristy door, the little one to the cabinet. Go get that plate. I want to see a note I saw someone place in that plate."

"Yes, sir," Morris replied, returning through the dark cathedral toward the sacristy. Outside he could hear more thunder and the pounding of rain. He turned on the sacristy hall light and found the blue key that opened the door, then turned on the sacristy light, moved to the locked cabinet, and, using the smaller key, opened it, retrieving the collection plate. He then relocked the cabinet, turned off the light, locked the sacristy, and turned off the hallway light, returning to the narthex in the dark, lighted only by an occasional lightning flash glowing through the stained glass windows.

By this time the vergers' room was locked and everyone else had left the Cathedral. Morris knocked on the vestry room door, and was ordered in. He entered, and the priest was in the process of removing his cassock from over his head. "Put it on the table over there, and get out of here. I'll put the plate back in the sacristy later. Leave my keys on the table, too, and close that door behind you."

Morris was happy to retreat. He went to the coat closet and got his raincoat and umbrella, then moved to the outside door, which had a crash-bar that would lock behind him as he left. All the lights in the atrium had been turned off by the custodian who had already departed, and as John Morris splashed through the rain to his car, he noted that only his and Packard's black Mercury were still in the lot.

It was a quarter to seven. Usually Morris stopped at a diner for supper on his way home after Solemn Evensong, but with the heavy rain falling, and the ill taste in his mouth from his encounter with Canon Packard, he was in no mood for a meal. He headed home to his apartment, and finished a bowl of soup that was in his refrigerator.

Chapter 3

It was about three the following afternoon as John Morris sat in his living room reading a novel. The rain was still falling heavily, and the noon news had advised of some local flooding due to a low pressure system that seemed to hang over the city. Morris had also heard another local news report: "Local police advise that the body of a clergyman was discovered this morning in a prominent local church. The police released no details, advising that investigation was continuing. We hope to have further factual information by the six o'clock news. In national news, President Eisenhower told several prominent Senate Republicans at a meeting in the White House this morning that...."

Morris's apartment intercom buzzed, and he got up to answer the wall speaker. He was not expecting any visitors, and rarely had any. "Yes?" he spoke into the microphone.

"John Morris?" a man's voice answered.

"Yes, I'm John Morris. What can I do for you?"

"Well, let us in the door, for one thing. This is Lieutenant Clark of the police department."

"Oh," Morris replied, pressing the button on the speaker device that unlocked the front door to the apartment house. By the time the two plain-clothed officers had climbed the stairs to the second floor, Morris had the door open and stood waiting for them. He invited them in as they showed him their identification and gold detective badges.

"What is all this about?" Morris inquired.

"Did you hear about the death at the cathedral on the news," the second man, a Sergeant David Roderick asked. He was a large man, somewhat bald, with a round face dressed in a rumpled brown suit with a gray hat in his hand.

"There was something about finding a clergyman dead, but the church was not identified. You say it was a cathedral? The Cathedral of St. Matthew?"

"Yes, St. Matthew's. And the clergyman was one Augustus Packard. Do you know Augustus Packard?" the Lieutenant asked. Linus Clark was younger than Roderick, with a full head of dark hair and round glasses, much more trim and neat in his dark blue suit. He also held a hat in his hand.

"Certainly! I was with him yesterday evening. You say he's dead? How?"

"His body was found this morning in the vestry room," Roderick said. "He had been suffocated. We understand that you were one of the people who were involved in the service yesterday evening."

"Yes, I was the lead usher. There were a number of us there. In fact, I suspect I was the very last, other than Canon Packard, to leave."

"Why was that?"

"Well, Packard made an unusual request. He wanted me to bring him the collection plate. It was locked in the sacristy, and he gave me his keys to go get it for him. Seemed odd."

"Why would that be odd?" Lieutenant Clark asked.

"The collection plate is always locked in the vessels cupboard in the sacristy after the Evensong service on Sundays. Packard had whispered something to me at the start of the service, which I had not heard. It was to bring the collection plate to him, rather than put it in the sacristy. He told me he wanted to see a note someone had put in the plate during the collection, but that didn't make any sense, as he said he'd told me to bring it to the vestry before the service, and the collection wasn't taken up until the middle of the service."

"Maybe he just wanted to count the take," Roderick said.

"That's the treasurer's job. He always retrieves the plates Monday morning."

"Was there a note in the plate?"

"There may have been. I didn't notice. There weren't many in the congregation, so the plate was not very full, but I don't recall seeing anything except some cash and a couple of offering envelopes some of the congregation use. People sometimes put money in the plate before the service if they don't intend to stay for the entire Evensong. If there was a note, I didn't see it."

"Who else was present yesterday evening?" asked Lieutenant Clark, as Roderick got out his notepad to write down the names.

"Gosh, let's see," Morris said, thinking back over all those who had been there. "There were somewhere between fifteen and twenty in the congregation. I counted twenty during the first part of the service, but a few always leave early before the Eucharist – the communion part of the service. I don't know the names of most of them, but most are regulars. Very few regulars were there yesterday afternoon because of the rain. The only ones I know by name are Dr. and Mrs. Levitt. They were there. And of course Mrs. Schuster, who never misses. There were two young musicians who always come, as they like the music, but they always leave before the Eucharist. I didn't see them leave, but I assume they did. I don't know the names of the others in the congregation, but some of the other participants may know some of their names."

"Who were the other participants?" Clark asked.

"The verger was Bill Parkenson...."

"Verger?" Sergeant Roderick asked.

"Yes, it's an honorary traditional position. The verger is basically the lay person in charge of making sure the service runs as it should. He leads the procession in, a role in medieval times to verge the crowds for the clergy to enter, in the centuries before there were pews George Mitchell is the head verger, but he wasn't there yesterday."

"Who else?"

"There were supposed to be three acolytes and another usher, Will Smithers, a man in his mid or late seventies. But one of the adult acolytes, Jim Slade, who usually acts as thurifer, was out sick."

"What is a 'thurifer'?" Roderick asked.

"Oh, you must not attend a church that uses incense, Sergeant! The thurifer swings the thurible – the censer containing the incense – and proceeds behind the verger in the procession. The nickname is the 'incense slinger,' and some of them really wind that thing up and around to get great clouds of smoke pouring out! Smithers wasn't used to doing it, though, so there was not the occasional theatrical slinging yesterday."

"So you were the only usher, then?" Clark asked.

"Yes. With such a small group, that was no problem. It happens occasionally. The acolytes were Jeff Marchington and Robert Crofton, an eighteen-year-old high school senior, who usually serves in the morning services. They carry the cross and a banner in the procession, and assist during the Eucharist, or communion, as you may call it "

Roderick read his list. "Parkenson, this head guy, Smithers, the incense guy, Marchington and Crofton, the acolytes. You have any addresses for these men?"

"I have a church directory. Most of the members are listed in it, but it's a couple of years old, my only copy. I can see what's in it," Morris said, starting to get up.

"Don't bother, Morris. We'll get one from the church," Clark said. "Now, who else was there besides the five of you and the clergyman?"

"The choir, of course. Dr. Ripple is the choirmaster and organist. There are usually ten singers, the staff singers, for Evensong, but three were missing yesterday. Oh, and Mrs. Gilfrey, of the Altar Guild. She was back in the sacristy, but had left, as I said, before I did."

"This Dr. Ripple, he's a physician, a dentist, or what?"

"Professor of music, I think, at one of the local universities. He travels a lot on concerts. His assistant wasn't there yesterday."

"What's his first name?" Roderick asked.

"I think it is Neal, but I'm not certain."

"Do you know the choir members names?"

"No, but they're listed in the church directory, as they are paid staff singers."

"They pay people to sing for twenty persons in the congregation?" The Sergeant asked, sounding confused.

"That service is held in churches and cathedrals all over the world – whether there is anyone there or not. I once attended an Evensong at St. Paul's in London, and there were only three of us in attendance, along with the boys' choir and the clergy."

"Really! That's some tradition!" the Sergeant remarked.

"Could anyone have still been in the building, besides Packard, when you left? Someone in the choir, or someone who was hidden or in a restroom?" Lieutenant Clark asked.

"I suppose that's possible. Oh, the custodian, I just know him as Jim, he had been there, but had already turned out the lights in the atrium and departed before I left. He would have checked the restrooms and turned off any lights in them, I'm sure, before he left. But what happened to Canon Packard?" Morris asked. "Who...."

"We're still investigating, Morris. The church secretary gave us your name as the head usher, and said you would know who had been there, which is why we're contacting you first. It looks like foul play, frankly, but the coroner will have to confirm the cause of death before we can say what happened. By the way, we were told Packard was single. Do you know if that was correct? Did he have any family that you know of?"

"Lieutenant, I've known Packard for many years, first at a church in Park Grove where he was an assistant. He was single then, and when he left there he went to some monastery in Michigan for a few years before showing up at St. Matthew. He's never been married as far as I know, but I don't know if he has any relatives anywhere. We were not friends."

"You say that like you were maybe enemies, Morris," Sergeant Roderick said.

"No, we were not close by any means. I admit I did not like the man, but my feelings were not bitter toward him nor did I hate him. We just did not get along well. I think you'll find he was not all that popular at St. Matthew. But I really don't know much about the man."

"Thank you for being candid with us, Morris," the Lieutenant said.

"May I offer you some coffee, gentlemen?" Morris asked. "It's such a cold, miserable day out there."

"No, thank you anyway. I think we need to be going. You have been most helpful, and we appreciate the information you have provided us. Once we get a church directory we should be able to find the others we'll need to talk with," the Lieutenant replied.

* * *

The next morning John Morris opened his newspaper, the *Morning Sentinel*, to read the following:

Local Clergyman Believed Murdered In Cathedral

City homicide detectives believe that a local clergyman was murdered in the Cathedral of St. Matthew Sunday evening after performing a service at the prominent downtown church. The coroner has determined that death of the Rev. Canon Augustus Packard was caused by asphyxiation, placing the time of death at about 7 p.m. on Sunday evening. Various items of religious vestments were found near the body, and the police believe they may have been used to snuff out the life of the 68-year-old priest, who was single and lived alone in a house near the downtown area.

Investigation is continuing, with the police contacting all of the various persons who both participated in the service or were known to have attended the service, a traditional Solemn Evensong, chanted in plainsong by the priest and the choir. They request that any persons who may have attended the service as part of the congregation contact Lieutenant Linus Clark of the Homicide Division at the Central Station at 472-8221.

The Very Rev. Joseph Williams, Dean of the Cathedral, told the *Sentinel* that Canon Packard was planning to retire in the next year, and his duties at the Cathedral were already being reduced at the time of his death. A requiem service will be held this Friday at noon for the deceased clergyman, conducted by the Right Rev. Simon Shillinger, Bishop of the Diocese.

Packard had resided in the area for a number of years, and had served for about five years as an assistant clergyman at the Church of the Atonement in Park Grove. He was a licensed marriage counselor, and served in that capacity at the Cathedral. After leaving the suburban church, Packard spent a number of years at a monastery in Michigan, but the *Sentinel* has been unable to reach anyone there yet who recalls Packard.

The police are uncertain of the motive for the murder. A collection plate was found in the small vestry room – a room where the clergy put on their vestments for the service – where the clergyman's body was found Monday morning, but nothing appeared to have been stolen from it, although the exact amount of money in the plate had not yet been recorded. There is some early indication that

Canon Packard was not as popular at the Cathedral as some of the other clergy, but investigation is continuing.

Augustus Packard is survived by a cousin in Indiana and a niece, Gloria Smith of Urbana, the daughter of his brother, Simpson Packard, of Cincinnati. In lieu of flowers, those interested are asked to make contributions to the Cathedral Memorial Fund.

Morris re-read the article, shook his head, and finished his breakfast. He thought about what the others who had been participants in the service might have told Clark and Roderick. Who, he wondered, would have a reason to murder the old priest. Certainly nobody he knew liked Packard, but that would not seem a reason to kill him. In his mind he went back over every step he had taken after the service, from the two times he'd gone to the sacristy to when he left Packard alone in the vestry with the door closed. There had been no one in there with him – the room was not that big – unless they were hidden in the large cupboard where the vestments hung. He did not think it high enough for someone to hide in, though.

Could someone have hidden in the cathedral or the atrium, or any of the classrooms or other rooms, he wondered. There would be hundreds of places to hide, from the basement to the second floor offices of the cathedral and the diocese. Like most cathedrals, St. Matthew had many secret passages, including some to the roof area and into the ceiling above the organ pipes and into the bell tower. There were many cupboards and closets where one might easily hide.

Morris had no intention of attending Packard's funeral. He saw no reason to do so, and the following Sunday afternoon he heard all the details from Bill Parkenson, who was again the Evensong verger, and who had assisted Watson, the head verger, at the requiem Eucharist service two days earlier. This time all the scheduled ushers and acolytes were present, Will Smithers and the adult acolytes, Jeff Marchington and Jim Slade. Jerry Winston, another of the older teen acolytes, would serve as thurifer.

"I met Packard's brother, Simpson, after the service," Parkenson said. "I don't think there was much love lost between him and our Canon, from what he said. He lives down in Cincinnati, and as the closest relative had to make certain arrangements, but he didn't seem very happy about it."

"Were there many at the service?" Morris inquired.

"No, a few regular attendees, some clergy from the diocese, and of course the entire funeral committee. None of the choir sang. I suppose if they had, the 'Hallelujah Chorus' would have been appropriate."

Morris and the others laughed at the joke. "Seems nobody liked Packard," Morris said. "By the way, the police stopped by to talk with me. I guess I was the last person to see him alive. I find it hard to believe that someone would have been hiding in the cathedral and murdered him after we all left."

"They visited me, too," Will Smithers said. "Said you'd given them my name as one of the participants in the service."

"Yes, I got a visit, too," added Parkenson. "They asked a lot of questions about you after they learned we had both been at Atonement when Packard was there. I gave them the name of the rector there, but didn't really tell them much about Packard. Why speak ill of the dead?"

"They'll probably get around to me, too," Jeff Marchington replied. "But I'll be like the three monkeys – hear no evil, see no evil and speak no evil."

"Well, if they plan to interview the entire congregation to see who was at the service, they're in for heck of a job. A lot of people who attend this service aren't members, and a lot of the members hardly ever come to Evensong. By the way, who is officiating this afternoon?"

"Canon Richards, I believe," Morris answered, having just glanced at the bulletins he'd brought up from the basement print shop. "It sounded like the entire choir was there, too. Last week just over half of them were there."

"I'm glad I missed the excitement," Jim Slade said. "Packard should have retired a couple of years ago. The Dean told the newspaper that he was going to retire soon, and was cutting back on his schedule."

"He was still counseling love-torn women, wasn't he?" Smithers asked.

"As far as I know," answered Parkenson. "After he left Atonement he should not have been permitted to continue that nonsense. He's probably broken up far more marriages than he ever saved."

"He sure broke mine," Morris said, but didn't say much else as only Parkenson knew the story, and he did not want to go into any details of Melissa's death.

* * *

It was about three weeks later, early on a Tuesday afternoon, while Morris was putting away some groceries that his phone rang. He quickly answered it.

"John Morris?"

"Yes."

"This is Lieutenant Clark. You may recall that Sergeant Roderick and I stopped by a few weeks ago to talk with you about the death of Canon Augustus Packard?"

"Certainly I remember."

"Well, there are a few points that are not clear to us about the event, and we wonder if you would mind coming down to the headquarters on

Fifth Street this afternoon and see if we can clear up some of the questions we have."

"Oh, I don't know what more I could tell you, but, certainly, I'll be glad to come down. I should just ask for you?"

"That will be fine. I'll alert the desk sergeant to send you upstairs."

Morris finished putting away his groceries, and then locked the door and went down to his car, which was parked behind the apartment. It was only a short drive to Fifth Street, but he had to look for the station, as he had never been there before. There was a visitors parking lot on one side of the building, and he parked and went in the main door.

The sergeant at the desk called the Lieutenant to advise Morris had arrived, and pointed to a stairway. Clark met him at the head of the stairs.

"Thank you, Mr. Morris, for being so prompt. We appreciate that. Ahh, let's go into one of the smaller rooms where it will be a bit quieter than at my desk," Clark said, and gave a wave to Sergeant Roderick to join them. The room was the type Morris had seen in television shows where criminals were interrogated. Roderick had his pad and pen along, but Clark asked all the questions.

"Mr. Morris, you told us when we visited that you were not a friend of Canon Augustus Packard, and indicated that you did not like him."

"No, I was not fond of the man. I suspect a lot of people were not fond of him."

"Why would that be?"

"Oh, I don't know. Maybe it was his personality. He was a bit of a perfectionist, and would scold any of the service participants if they didn't do things exactly as he wanted them to."

"You told us, Mr. Morris, that Packard had served at the Atonement Church before coming to the Cathedral of St. Matthew."

"Yes. I think I told you I'd known him there."

"That's correct," Roderick said.

"But you did not tell us that you had left the Atonement Church because of Packard."

"There were a number of reasons I left there. For one thing, I moved downtown after my wife's death."

"A suicide, I understand."

"Yes."

"Was Packard counseling your wife prior to her suicide?"

"Yes, but that had nothing to do with Packard's death at the Cathedral."

"Do you recall the title of Packard's sermon at the Evensong service that afternoon?"

"Yes, of course. I handed out the bulletins on which that sermon title was printed."

"Did that title upset you?"

"It was something typical of Packard. I sat in the verger's office until the sermon was over, so I didn't hear what he had to say."

"Did anyone see you waiting there?"

"I would doubt it. I had to check his progress several times, as the collection is taken up at the end of the sermon, so I occasionally opened the door to see if he was near the end of his sermon."

"How would you know, if you didn't listen to it?"

"Well, at Evensong, sermons usually last only ten or fifteen minutes. They're short, and having heard hundreds of sermons, it's usually easy to judge when it will end."

"About the collection plate. There was just the one plate used?"

"For the small number in the congregation, that was all that was needed, and I was the only usher."

"Would you object to our taking your finger prints?"

"No, but it would be obvious that my prints would be on the plate. I was the usher who handled it."

"Yes, but we have found a number of different prints, and want to try to identify them."

"You mean, you think someone tried to steal the collection?"

"We have to check every possibility. You said you were puzzled by why Canon Packard wanted the plate after the service, as that was not the usual routine."

"Yes, I think I told you he said he'd seen a note being put into it, but that didn't make any sense as he says he'd told me to bring him the plate just as the service began."

"Why do you think he wanted to have the plate?"

"I've no idea."

"Can you think of the names of any other people who were at the service?"

"No, I told you all that I recalled."

"Do you know if Canon Packard was doing any counseling at the Cathedral?"

"I don't know from my own experience, but he was listed as a counselor in the church directory, and I had heard that he was doing some counseling."

"Do you know anyone he might have counseled?"

"No, but the Dean might."

"Have you heard any comments about his counseling at the Cathedral."

"I don't recall any."

There was a long pause as Clark looked over his notes and Roderick completed the notes he was placing in his notebook. Finally Clark said,

"Well, we do appreciate your coming down this afternoon, Mr. Morris. Now, if you will go with Sergeant Roderick, he will assist you with the finger printing and get you some soap and water."

Morris complied with the sergeant's request, and after being led to a men's room where he scrubbed his hands, he was back home before four that afternoon. He wondered if they had called Parkenson back for further interviews or finger prints, but anticipated that he would find out the following Sunday.

As he mulled over the questions Clark has asked, the policeman seemed to be trying to make a connection between Packard's counseling of Melissa and the sermon he had preached that afternoon. Was there a connection? Was he a suspect? He couldn't imagine it – a suspect in a murder case simply because he had been an usher. But then maybe Packard was counseling others at the Cathedral and there had been similar problems to those both he and Parkenson had experienced at Atonement. Maybe some jealous or outraged husband or wife had sought revenge. He shook his head, and turned on the television to see what might be on.

Chapter 4

It was about a week later. Although it was early May, springtime growth was just beginning to come into full bloom, perhaps helped by the heavy rains of April. John Morris had been thinking about a vacation, and had driven to a near-by travel agency to pick up some brochures on various cruises that he might consider. He had never been to Hawaii, and one of the brochures showed a picture of a Matson Line cruise ship arriving in Honolulu. But he also looked at some other cruises as well, including one to South America or to the Mediterranean Sea. He agreed with the agent to review the brochures and consider where he might want to go.

As he drove down the street and pulled into the drive to the apartment parking lot, he was surprised to see Lieutenant Clark and Sergeant Roderick standing by the front door of his apartment building. He pulled into his parking space and as he was getting out of the car with the brochures in his hand, the two policemen came running around the corner of the building. Morris locked the car door and turned to greet the officers.

"John Morris," Lieutenant Clark said in an authoritative voice, "we have a warrant for your arrest for the murder of Augustus Packard. You have the right to remain silent. You have the right to an attorney. If you cannot afford an attorney you will be provided with one."

"But there must be some mistake," Morris started to say, but was interrupted by Sergeant Roderick, who stepped behind Morris and placed a handcuff on his left wrist, then brought his right hand behind him and fastened the other cuff to that wrist.

"Best to say nothing for now, Morris," Roderick said, taking the travel brochures from Morris's hand. "Anything you say can be used against you. You'll have plenty of time to explain later. I see you are planning a trip," he added, handing the brochures to Clark, who placed them in a bag he withdrew from his pocket, then briefly frisked Morris to see what was in his pockets. He allowed Morris to keep his wallet, but took the keys and placed them in the bag.

"We will obtain a search warrant for your apartment, and will need these keys," Clark said. "Do you keep personal property at any other location?"

"No," Morris said, then added, "Oh, I do have a lockbox at the bank, but it's just my personal papers and some stocks and bonds and insurance policies."

"Okay, let's go." The two officers led Morris back to their unmarked police car and placed him in the back seat. The handcuffs made sitting uncomfortable, and Morris complained that the angle at which he was sitting was hurting the arthritis in his right shoulder.

"It's a short ride. We'll take them off at the station," Roderick replied, placing a red flasher on the roof of the car, and turning on the siren so that he could get to the headquarters building faster. Upon arrival, Roderick drove the car into a garage under the building, and Clark opened the rear door and assisted Morris out of the car. They moved to an inside door, and went up two flights of stairs to the offices where Morris had been interviewed several weeks before. Clark went to his desk and began working on some paperwork.

Roderick unlocked the handcuffs and led Morris to his own desk where he started to fill out some papers. "You'll be booked into the city jail until your preliminary hearing, which should be in a day or two. If the judge permits you to post bond, we'll return all your property to you at that time, except those travel brochures, Morris. I'm afraid those will become evidence."

"But I..."

"Better not say anything until you get an attorney, Morris. Do you have one? You're entitled to one phone call."

"The only attorney I know is Bob Willingham, but I don't know his phone number."

"Here's a phone book, Morris. You can call him on my phone, here."

John Morris looked up the phone number, and placed the call to Willingham's number. The firm was Jones & Partridge, and Willingham was not in. Morris asked to speak with his secretary, and was put through. She told him that Willingham would not be back that day, but would call in before five for any messages. Morris said, "Well, this is urgent, so be certain he gets this message today, even if you have to call him at home. This is John Morris. Bob handled a case for me a few years ago, so he should recognize my name. Tell him I have been arrested for a murder I did not commit and know nothing about, but I'm being put in the city jail until a preliminary hearing, and I desperately need his help. I don't know the routine here, or who he should call. A Lieutenant Clark is in charge of the case, along with a Sergeant Roderick, at the main police headquarters. I don't know if this is where the jail is or not...."

"It's two floors up," Roderick said, looking up from the forms he was completing.

"The Sergeant says it's here, two floors up from the second floor. I don't know what the rules are, as to when Bob can see me."

"I'll see that he gets the message, Mr. Morris," the secretary said.

"Thank you," Morris said as he hung up the telephone.

"Come on, Morris," Roderick said, getting up from his desk. "We already have your finger prints, but we need a photograph and some preliminaries to get you comfortable in our little hotel here." He led Morris to a small room in the back of the building where Morris had to stand in front of a wall marked with various heights. Roderick took a small black board with ridges on it and filled in the letters of John's name and age, handing it to Morris. Morris was to hold the board in front of his chest for the first photograph, and in front of his face in a side profile photograph.

When Roderick had completed the photos, he set the board aside, and led Morris up two more flights of stairs where another police officer was sitting at a desk. "Give the old gentleman a cell by himself if you have one, Billy," Roderick said. "He's being booked on a homicide charge, don't know if it will be first or second yet, but he called his lawyer, so there may be somebody stop by later or tomorrow to see him. That will be okay. He'll be arraigned in the next couple of days, I suspect – preliminary bond hearing."

"Okay, Dave. I'll make him comfortable," the officer said as Roderick returned to the stairway. "What's your name?" he asked Morris.

"John Morris."

"Okay, John. For now, keep your own clothes, but take everything out of your pockets and put them on the counter here, and I'll make a list."

"Lieutenant Clark has my keys, and all I have is my wallet and a handkerchief. Oh, and my wrist watch."

"Okay," the officer said, writing down the wallet, containing $47 in cash. Morris had no change in his pocket. He then wrote down the Timex watch, and placed the wallet with the cash in it and the watch in a bag, and labeled it with Morris's name. Next he ordered Morris to take the shoe laces out of his shoes, and he placed the laces on the list and put them in the bag. "Here," he said, sliding the form with the three items listed over to Morris, "sign that line there."

Morris signed the form. Then the officer led him down a hallway to an empty cell that contained a bunk, a sink and a toilet, and when Morris had entered it, he closed the barred door, and said, "We serve dinner about six in the evening, and breakfast about seven. The rest of the time is yours, John. We'll keep in mind the old rule that you are innocent until we prove you're guilty."

* * *

It was after ten the following morning when Bob Willingham and another young man arrived at the police station and asked to see John Morris. A different sergeant named Michael Terry had come on duty about seven that morning, and had served Morris his breakfast, a rather tasteless scrambled eggs, bacon and toast, with coffee. He unlocked the cell and had Morris follow him to a small room, similar to the interrogation rooms on the second floor, where Willingham and the other man were waiting.

"I'm sorry we couldn't get here any sooner, John, but I didn't get your message until yesterday evening, and when I phoned down here they said there was no use coming as there would have to be a preliminary hearing before any bond could be set."

"Bob, I do thank you for coming. I just don't know what to do. They're accusing me of murdering old Packard, and I swear I had nothing to do with it. He was perfectly fine, which for him means crabby, when I left him in the vestry room."

"Are they treating you okay here?"

"It's not the Ritz, but no one has hurt me, and I've been pretty much left alone since yesterday afternoon, except for meals. But how do I get out?"

"Well, that's the problem, John. I spoke with Lieutenant Clark before coming up here, and he said they would oppose a bond hearing for you as you had some travel brochures with you when you were arrested. Were you planning a trip?"

"I'd been thinking about a vacation this summer, maybe a cruise somewhere, and had stopped at a travel agency. But they're making it sound like I was trying to escape or something. I never dreamt that I was a suspect in Packard's death."

"They've dug up that old lawsuit we filed against Packard, and are digging into Melissa's suicide. That gives them a potential motive. You had opportunity. They have to prove you did it, but they may have a hard case for you to break. John, that's the problem, and I brought Jack Higgins with me. Jack, John and I go back quite a few years.

"The problem is this, John," Willingham continued, "because I was the attorney who filed the lawsuit against Packard, it is most likely that I will be called as a witness in the case to testify about that lawsuit and your feelings about Packard. That would put me in a conflict situation. Besides, I'm not a criminal attorney. I don't keep up with all the decisions that affect criminal law in the state. Jack is a new attorney with our firm, but he came to us from the District Attorney's office, and he specializes in criminal law at Jones & Partridge. I've asked him if he would be willing to take your case on, and he said he would."

"Bob, I'm not a rich man, as you know. I can't afford a high-priced lawyer. This thing, this arrest, I just don't understand it. I didn't dislike Packard enough to kill him, or even hurt him. What happened was in the past, and while not forgotten, certainly didn't fester within me. I'm not guilty, and I can't imagine who would be. You may remember Bill Parkenson, who was at Atonement when Packard was there. Well, he was the verger at the Cathedral that night, and certainly he can tell you that I wouldn't have done anything bad to Packard."

"At this point, don't worry about the bill. I'm a senior partner at the firm, and have the authority to waive the retainer fee. Jack is just an associate, so his hourly rate is far less than mine would be. For now, we're just here as friends. Clark has gotten a time for the preliminary for tomorrow afternoon at two. We'll both be there when they bring you into the courtroom. When the judge asks you how you plead, you just say, 'I am not guilty, your honor,' and that's all you have to say. Jack will take it from there and try to get you released on bond. Jack, you had some questions you wanted to ask John."

"Yes," the younger man, tall, slim and dressed in a dark blue suit, slightly balding with thick glasses, said. "John, you've told us you are innocent, and that is the basis on which we will proceed. First, can you think of anyone else who may have had a grudge against this Canon Packard?"

"Anyone? Maybe half the congregation, for all I know. The staff singers were upset with him because he was trying to get them to work voluntarily, the choir master wasn't happy with him, he was nasty to a lot of the lay people, like myself, who assist in the services. He was openly hostile to anyone he thought was homosexual. He may have been counseling couples.... Marriage counseling was his main position, I guess, in the parish. He may have upset some people like he did Parkenson and me at Atonement...."

"This Atonement you mention. What is it?"

"It's called the Church of the Atonement, a parish in Park Grove where Packard was an assistant priest and did counseling about fifteen years ago. It turns out he was basically trying to start affairs with some of the women he counseled. I guess it happens a lot with psychologists and psychiatrists. My wife had gone to him after our baby died. I was away from home a lot on business, and I blame myself as much as Packard, who would come to our house to see Melissa when I was away. I can't prove that anything ever happened, but he upset her and apparently tried to convince her to divorce me. That's when she shot herself."

"You blamed Packard for her death?"

"Bob suggested I sue him for alienation of affection and malpractice, and I did, but Packard left the church and went to some monastery in Michigan when some of the other church members also complained about him, and we dropped the lawsuit."

"You never pursued it?"

"Why bother. He had no assets, and he left town, basically disgraced but not defrocked."

"I see. Well, if that is Clark's 'motive,' it is certainly a weak one. I suspect we'll have you out of here by tomorrow evening. Was Packard single?"

"I don't know if he'd ever been married, maybe before he came to Atonement. I never heard anything about a wife. I don't know where he lived, or, really, much about him. I tried to stay out of his way, but I usher at the Evensong services, and he was the assigned priest on rotation, so we had to work with each other occasionally."

"What's this thing about the collection plate that Clark mentioned."

"That's a puzzle, Jack. Packard said something to me as the procession began, but I didn't hear it all. He wanted me to bring him the collection plate after the offering. But he said later that he wanted it because he saw someone put a note in it. That didn't make sense, as he says he told me to bring him the plate before the service, and the collection plate didn't go around until the middle of the service."

"Clark says your finger prints were on the plate when it was found next to Packard in this vesting room."

"Of course they were. I was the usher that took up the collection."

"He said that Packard's prints weren't on the plate, so if he had wanted the plate, why didn't he touch it? Was there a note in it?"

"I saw no notes. A couple of offering envelopes, some cash, and that was it. It was a rainy night, and there were not many people there, not even all of the Evensong choir."

"That's all the questions I have for now, John, but after tomorrow we'll get together and plan our defense strategy. I think they've got a lot to prove and a difficult task doing it."

"Thank you, Jack, and you too, Bob. I just hope I didn't leave a coffee pot on at the apartment or anything. Is there any way I could get a change of clothes before that hearing tomorrow?"

"We'll see what we can do. Clark has your keys, and apparently has a warrant to search the apartment, but we'll ask," Willingham said.

* * *

The preliminary hearing did not go well. Morris pled not guilty, but the assigned state prosecuting attorney, Jim Harper, a tall, dark-haired man in his mid-forties, very athletic-looking, called Lieutenant Clark to the stand in his argument that bail not be allowed as the case involved first or second degree murder, and, as travel brochures had been found on Morris when he was arrested, the state believed Morris to be a flight risk.

The county judge, Wilhelmina Huffmiester, a gray-haired woman in her fifties, with large round glasses, reviewed the file, and agreed to set bond at $2 million, an amount she knew Morris would never be able to raise. Therefore, unless he posted the bond, he was to be bound over to the county jail, and trial in the criminal court was to be set for mid-July. Morris was escorted from the courtroom by the bailiff, who turned him over to the city jailer who had brought him to the county courthouse, who then delivered Morris to the county jail, where he was processed and issued a county jail uniform, which was white, with several blue strips on the sleeves and legs.

Jack Higgins immediately filed an appeal of the bail bond amount, as no local bondsman would issue such a large bond on a murder case, but to no avail. The motion to appeal was rejected by the court, and a further appeal to the state court was also rejected. Morris would therefore have to remain in the county jail until the trial date.

Chapter 5

Judge Jorge Alvarez scheduled the Morris trial for mid-July, giving both sides plenty of time to prepare for prosecution and defense. During the first two weeks Morris sat in the county jail he did not hear from either David Franklin or Willingham, but later learned that they had been busy on his behalf, obtaining a copy of all of the police records, the coroner's report, and reviewing what documents or other evidence the prosecutor had from the search of Morris's apartment.

Because the charges against John Morris were for a capital offense he was not allowed to participate in the county jail's work projects, but had to remain in his cell, except for a special exercise period each day when he could walk around the jail's basketball court, escorted by a guard. His meals were brought to his cell, and he was not allowed to meet with or talk with other prisoners who were either awaiting their own trial or were serving a county sentence.

He was allowed visitors, however, and was delighted when, one afternoon, Bud Williams, the Cathedral Dean, arrived, and Morris was escorted by the guard to a small visitation room. Although the guard closed the door, he stood watching the two visit through a window in the door, making sure that each remained on his own side of the table and that nothing was passed between them.

"How are you holding up?" Dean Williams asked.

"As well as could be expected, I guess, Sir. It is totally beyond my belief that I am in this situation. Dean Williams, I swear before God that Canon Packard was alive and healthy when I left the Cathedral that evening. I did not touch the man. I just can't see how they can prove that I did anything to him."

"You are on our daily prayer list, John," the Dean replied. "None of us, especially those who were there that evening, think you did anything to Packard. I certainly don't know what happened, but I've known you long enough to believe that you are innocent."

"That's a comfort," Morris replied. "I didn't know what anyone thought. I know the police interviewed everyone who was there that evening that they could find. I admit that I was not fond of Packard – even told the police that – but I certainly didn't hate him enough to murder him! And I don't think I was the only one there that evening who was not a friend of Packard, not that I think any of them would have harmed him."

"Yes, he seems to have made a few enemies in his lifetime. I recall your telling me one time that you had known Augie when he was at Atonement, and had counseled your wife."

"Perhaps that is why I'm here, Dean Williams. Yes, Packard did counsel my wife when he was an assistant at Atonement, and apparently they fell in love. She was torn by her duty to me and attraction to him, and killed herself, shot herself near the grave where our only baby was buried. She'd been depressed when the baby died, which was why she went to see Packard. Plus I was traveling a lot on business, and was out of town far too much at the time. After she killed herself, I brought a suit against Packard, and that's when he left and went to that monastery in Michigan."

"Oh, I see. And maybe that explains why the police wanted a copy of the Evensong bulletin from that service. They wondered if I had a copy of Augie's homily. I was surprised when I saw the title of it. His notes were in the vestry, and I guess the police have them. Most were simply Biblical references."

"I didn't listen to his sermon. When I saw the title, I figured he was trying to get even with me for having sued him, even though I dropped the suit when he left town. It may have cost him his position at Atonement, but nothing else. I wasn't even angry about it, but of course the police will probably cite that as a motive for murder."

"John, I'll be happy to testify for you as a character witness, if your attorney wishes. But there was one thing that puzzled us when we found Packard's body. Why was the collection plate in the vestry room?"

"That was a mystery to me, too, Dean Williams. Packard tried to tell me something before the service that, due to the procession already starting, I did not hear.

When the service ended, he said he had told me to bring him the collection plate after the service. He actually seemed angry about it. He said he'd seen someone put a note in the plate, and he wanted to see the note. It didn't make any sense. The collection was in the middle of the service, so if he saw someone put anything in the plate, how could he have alleged to have told me to bring it to him before the service began? I'd already put it in the cupboard in the sacristy. He sent me there to get it and bring it to him, but the door was already locked by Mrs. Gilfrey, and I had to run back to Packard to get his keys to unlock the sacristy door and the cupboard to bring him the plate. I think Bill Parkenson must have heard him yell at me about the plate, but when I finally got it to Packard, Bill and the others had already left. You know, Bill Parkenson was at Atonement the same time Packard and I were. He knew Packard pretty well, too."

"Meaning?"

"Well, I don't know the details, but Bill told me Packard had been counseling his wife, too, along with a number of other women in the church. There was a whole fuss about it that led up to Packard's departure from Atonement. I don't know if the Bishop knew about it or not, but Father Bill O'Day would know."

"Now that you mention it, I don't recall seeing any sort of report from Bill O'Day in Packard's file when we took him on as a canon at the Cathedral. Maybe I'll go back and take another look. But for now, John, are you okay here? Are they treating you well?"

"They feed me, and I've got a bunk and a toilet and sink. Somebody comes around occasionally with books, so I'm able to spend some time reading. But I've not seen a newspaper in weeks, and I'm not allowed a radio, so I've no idea what's going on in the world." With that, the guard tapped on the window, and pointed to his watch, implying that our time was up. "Would you say a prayer for me, Dean?" John asked.

* * *

It was a week later when David Franklin came to the jail to talk with Morris. Again Morris was led to the small interview room, and again the guard remained by the door. Neither Morris nor Franklin said anything until the guard closed the door.

"Good news?" Morris asked, eagerly looking into the younger man's face.

"News, I suppose, but it depends on what it means, Mr. Morris. As we had all anticipated, they know all about your lawsuit against Packard, and the fact that he was basically fired from his position as a result of it. Then when they found out what the topic of his sermon was that afternoon, they believe that gave you a motive to kill Packard."

"But I told them I didn't even listen to it."

"That will be difficult to prove, with only your word, unless someone saw you while he was preaching."

"No, I've tried to remember if anyone was around the narthex, but I was all alone."

"They also found a few things in your apartment that they're considering evidence."

"Like what?"

"Your gun, for example."

"That was my wife's gun. She bought it just before she shot herself. I should have thrown it away – it certainly had no sentimental value to me, and I never touched it since then, except when I moved into the apartment and put it in a drawer."

"I don't know what they'll make of it. Maybe nothing."

"What else did they find?"

"Your Army commendation."

"That! How is that evidence of anything?"

"Do you remember what it said?"

"Of course, even if it was in 1917 in the First World War. I jumped a bunch of Germans, and killed them. It was just a lucky event, as they were lobbing shells into our trenches and killing our guys, and I snuck out at night and caught some of the bastards sleeping. Five or six of them."

"Eight, to be exact, according to the citation. And you got away with it by smothering them."

"Well, I couldn't make any noise or shoot them or I'd have been killed myself. I throttled a couple and knifed a few of them."

"And ended up a war hero."

"I didn't feel very heroic at the time."

"The problem is, you obviously know how to kill a person by smothering them, and it was Packard who was your battalion's commander."

"He was? I didn't know that!"

"He's the one that signed your commendation. By the way, did Packard smoke?"

"Smoke cigarettes? Yes, he did. He was smoking one after the service. Why?"

"Oh, just some comment in the coroner's report about a substance on Packard's lungs. He attributed it to tobacco."

"It sounds like you are saying things are not going well, Mr. Franklin," Morris said, seeking some reassuring response.

"Knowing the opponents ammunition is always helpful, John. We have to know their strategy if we are to counter it. So, yes, progress is being made, by understanding their arguments, and finding ways to counter them. Oh, one other thing. There was a note found next to Packard's body. It complained about the topic of his sermon, something to the effect that Packard was responsible for the writer's wife's suicide. Did you see such a note?"

"No, but there was some money in the plate when I took it to take up the collection. Maybe there was a note in there that I didn't see. But I certainly didn't put it there. Maybe that is what Packard was referring to. What about finding the person who really did kill Packard? Any progress there?"

"We don't know yet. I've scheduled depositions of all of the witnesses the police have, including Clark and Sergeant Roderick. That will take a while. I'll ask Bob Willingham to stop by now and then to keep you posted. I know mid-July sounds like a long time from now, but believe it or not, that is barely enough time to prepare."

"It's long enough from my point of view, Franklin. I simply did not do it. What real evidence do they have that I did?"

"Frankly, none. It's all circumstantial. From their point of view you had a motive. You had opportunity. And knowing how to kill, you had the means of doing so. But they have to have more than circumstantial evidence to prove that you did it beyond the shadow of a reasonable doubt. It's not just preponderance of evidence, as in a civil case."

* * *

John Morris did not sleep well that night, nor any night thereafter until his trial. The morning the trial began Morris was transported in a sealed vehicle to the court house and placed in a holding cell. Bob Willingham had brought his suit from his apartment, and Morris was allowed to dress in it, rather than wearing his jail uniform in the trial.

The entire morning, while Morris waited in the holding cell, Willingham, Franklin and Jim Harper, the state's prosecuting attorney, selected a jury. Morris did not get to hear the selection process, but when he was finally brought into the courtroom after lunch he saw that there were nine men and five women in the chairs of the jury box, two being alternates. Two of the men appeared to be as old or older than Morris; the others appeared younger. The older men and two of the others were dressed in suits, while the remaining five wore only shirts and no ties. The women were of various ages, some with gray hair, and one, who appeared to be about thirty, with long red hair. Looking around the courtroom, Morris saw a lot of familiar faces, and some that he did not recognize.

Dean Williams, Bill Parkenson, Jeff Marchington and Will Smithers were there, along with Neal Ripple, the organist/choir master and a couple of the paid singers from the choir. He recognized a couple of other people he'd seen in the congregation quite a few times, but did not know their names.

The court's clerk sat at a table along with the court stenographer. Morris was led to a table on the left of the high judge's bench, while Jim Harper and Lieutenant Clark sat on the right at another table. Although dressed in his suit, the bailiff had placed handcuffs on Morris. At the table he unlocked them, but placed an ankle cuff on Morris's right foot and locked it to a steel hook on the table leg. The bailiff then took his place beside the door through which he had brought Morris. A bell, like a doorbell, rang, and the bailiff announced, "All rise. The Honorable Jorge Alvarez is presiding."

A dark haired tall man with thick glasses, wearing a black robe, entered the high platform from a door behind it, and looked out at the audience before him. "Please be seated," he said, and everyone sat down.

The clerk arose to read the charges. "Your Honor, this is the case of the State of Ohio, in and for Lockfield County, versus John Alfred Morris. The charge is murder in the first or second degree of the Reverend Augustus Packard, and the defendant has pled not guilty."

Judge Alvarez looked down at Morris and motioned for him to stand up, which Morris did. "Do you wish to change your plea?" the Judge asked.

"No, your Honor, I am innocent. I did not harm, hurt or kill Canon Packard, or...."

"That's sufficient, Mr. Morris. You may sit down. This Court will consider you to be innocent until the gentlemen representing the State of Ohio prove otherwise. Are you prepared, gentlemen?" he asked, looking at Jim Harper."

"We are, your Honor."

"Then let us have your opening statement," the Judge replied.

Harper got up from the table with a few pieces of paper in his hand and walked over to the jury box, where he looked each member in the eye before beginning his explanation of the case. "Ladies and gentlemen, the State of Ohio contends that on the evening of Sunday, April 12, 1959, the defendant, John Morris, willfully and with malice of forethought did viciously suffocate and asphyxiate the Reverend Augustus Packard, age sixty nine, in the vesting room of the Cathedral of St. Matthew here in town. The State will endeavor to prove that the defendant, John Morris, had a motive for killing the Reverend Packard, that he had the opportunity to do so, and had the knowledge and means of doing so. In the course of this trial we will present evidence to prove each of these factors so that you may determine without any reasonable doubt that John Morris intended the death of the Reverend Packard, and did cause that death. We will also present witnesses who will testify as to the state of mind of the defendant on the evening in question and the circumstances that led up to the action taken by the defendant. We believe that you will have no doubt of John Morris's guilt when you have heard and have thoughtfully considered all of the evidence we will present. Thank you."

As Harper sat down, Judge Alvarez looked at David Franklin and Bob Willingham and asked, "Are you prepared to present your opening statement, gentlemen?"

"We are," Franklin replied, but it was the older man, Willingham, who arose and approached the jury box.

"Good afternoon," he began. "I know, from our interviews this morning when you were each selected to serve on this jury that you are all fine and intelligent and honorable people. Mr. Harper has told you that he will present evidence to prove that my client, and my longtime friend, John Morris, murdered Augustus Packard on April 12 of this year by asphyxiating him. You will find out that I was the attorney representing John Morris as a plaintiff in a lawsuit against the Reverend Packard a number of years ago, which lawsuit was dropped at the request of the defendant, John Morris. The State will attempt to convince you that it was that lawsuit and the facts surrounding it that provided a motive for murder. I trust that you are all intelligent enough to see that such an alleged motive is pure nonsense on the State's part, despite other aspects that they will attempt to use to convince you otherwise. As to opportunity,

John Morris, to the best of his knowledge, was the last person to see Augustus Packard alive. When he left the Cathedral of St. Matthew that evening, Packard was alive, sitting in his vesting room, smoking a cigarette. The State will not present you any evidence to the contrary. The State will then attempt to convince you that John Morris, because he was a soldier in the First World War, and was commended for his service in risking his own life to kill enemy soldiers who were killing his own American fellow soldiers, had the physical means and knowledge to commit the crime of murder. This combination of circumstantial situations that the State will attempt to use to convince you is pure speculation and totally without any real evidence. You must remember that in order to convict John Morris of murder, you must be convinced without the shadow of a reasonable doubt. I have no doubt that you will be unconvinced. Further, you will be asked to find that John Morris intentionally and with planned forethought did this act of which the State has accused him. He did not, and the State's case is without any substance of proof. Rather than finding the real killer of Augustus Packard, the State has simply abandoned their investigation and has directed all their energy to proving a false allegation. Therefore, I am convinced that you will find John Morris totally innocent of this crime, as he has himself stated. Thank you."

As Willingham sat down, Judge Alvarez looked at Harper and said, "Mr. Harper, you may call your first witness."

Harper arose and said, "I call to the stand Lieutenant Linus Clark, Homicide Division of the city police." Clark arose from the table, walked to the stand and turned while the bailiff, holding a Bible on which Clark placed his hand, promised to tell the truth. As he sat down, Harper began by asking Clark to fully identify himself and his profession, which he did. Harper then asked, "Lieutenant Clark, would you describe for the jury what you and Sergeant Roderick found upon arrival at the Cathedral of St. Matthew on the morning of April 13, 1959?"

"Certainly," Clark began. He'd been through this routine many times before and showed no nervousness in his presentation. "I was contacted about nine o'clock that morning, advised that a body had been found at the church, the cathedral. Apparently the body was found by one of the priests who had gone to this vesting room to get some garment to wear for a morning prayer service. My assistant, Sergeant Roderick, and I arrived about nine thirty. We were met by several of the clergy, a Dean "Bud" Williams, who is apparently the head clergyman, and a Canon Jones, who had found the body. They led us to this vesting room."

"Did they say if the door was open or closed when Canon Jones had found the body?"

"Yes, he told me the door was closed, but not locked, which surprised him, as it is normally kept locked."

"Please describe for the jury what you found," Harper said.

Turning in the direction of the jury box, Clark continued, "The room is small. There was an open closet door with various colored vestments in it. On the back of one chair was some sort of a cape or sash that apparently the deceased had taken off. However, there was a white cloth garment made of a relatively thick material, with a white rope belt, that was partially covering the upper part of the deceased's body. We removed it, after taking photographs, and found the body of the deceased, identified by the lead clergyman, a Dean Williams, as that of Canon Augustus Packard, age sixty nine.

"Were there any marks on his body that you observed?"

"We examined his neck. There did seem to be some bruising, but we were unable to tell if it was related to his death. The coroner's office dispatched an investigation team, which arrived about ten that morning, and they estimated that the clergyman had been dead about fifteen or sixteen hours, give or take a few. So we estimated the time of death as sometime around six the previous evening or shortly thereafter."

"What else did you find in this room, Lieutenant Clark?"

"The deceased was sitting in a chair, and as I mentioned, had this white garment over his head. There was a table nearby on which a collection plate with money in it was sitting, and a stand where various things apparently used in their services were placed."

"What sort of things?"

"Oh, crosses on top of poles, candle holders on poles, several banners with printing on them, a stand with some sort of gold object hanging on chains, things of that sort, the kind of things one would expect to see in a very formal type of service. We took photographs of the scene."

"Those photographs will be placed into evidence later. What else did you find?"

"On the floor next to the deceased's chair was a piece of paper with a note on it."

Holding up a piece of paper, Harper asked, "Is this the note you found?" Clark looked at it and affirmed that it was, and Harper turned to the judge. "Your Honor, the State wishes to submit this note as Item of Evidence Number One." The judge nodded, took the note from Harper's hand, looked at it, and handed it back. Harper took the note to the defense table where it was examined, then turned to Clark and said, "Please read the note to the jury."

Clark took the note and read, "'You bastard.' There are three exclamation marks after that, then it continues, "You know my wife committed suicide – and after meeting with you for help, too. I won't listen to such nonsense.' Then there is another exclamation mark. The note was printed, and was not signed." Clark handed the note back to Harper, who took it to the jury box and allowed each member to look at it.

"What did you do with this note?" Harper asked.

"We carefully placed it in an evidence bag, and later examined it for fingerprints."

"Did you find any?"

"There were some smudged prints, and one or two, later identified as those of Augustus Packard."

"Are these the photographs of the body and the room?" Harper asked, holding up a series of enlarged photos. Clark identified each, and they were individually entered into evidence, and then shown to the defense team and the jury. Harper then asked, "Did you find anything else in the room?"

"Yes," Clark replied. "There was a glass ashtray with two cigarette butts in it, and a brass collection plate with money and collection envelopes in it."

"What did you do with the money and envelopes?"

"The money and envelopes were carefully removed from the plate without touching it, and the plate was secured in an evidence bag for later examination. We also recorded the names of those who had used envelopes, as they obviously had been at the service, and would be potential witnesses. The church's financial man then took the money and envelopes."

"Were any fingerprints found on the plate?"

"There were a number of prints, some smudged, but most of the prints were those of the defendant, John Morris."

"I see," Harper said, nodding his head toward the jury box. "What did you do next?"

"Well, the coroner's team arrived and took the body to the morgue for autopsy. We inquired who had been assisting at the service the previous afternoon. The secretary gave us the defendant's name and address as he had been the head usher, and he gave us the other names and we contacted each person who had been there."

"Who was on the list?"

"There was a William Parkenson, who was what they call a 'verger,' who leads the procession when it enters or leaves the cathedral. He's sort of the head organizer of the service. Then there were what they call 'acolytes.' One was an older teenager, who usually serves in the morning services, named Robert Crofton, age eighteen. We found out later that he had left the church with his father immediately after the service. There was supposed to be two adult acolytes, Jeff Marchington, and a Jim Slade. Slade had reported that he would be out as he was ill. There was supposed to be two ushers, a Will or William Smithers, and the defendant, John Morris. But because Slade was not there, Smithers had to take his job as the third acolyte, we later learned. Hence John Morris was the only usher at that afternoon's service. There was also a Mrs. Gilfrey, who was on what they call the 'altar guild,' who prepares the bread and wine for the service. She was in a room at the front of the cathedral, and left shortly after the service."

"Were there any other participants you were able to identify?"

"Yes, the choir master organist, a Dr. Neal Ripple, had been there," Clark said, consulting his notebook, "and about five members of the choir." They all left the church after returning to their choir room and removing their robes, and on contact, each said he or she had left the church through a hallway in the basement that has a door directly to the parking lot. It was raining heavily that afternoon and evening, and they were anxious to get home."

"Were you able to contact any of the people in the congregation?"

"Yes, we contacted each of those whose names had been on the envelopes. William Parkenson also gave us the name of several of the parishioners that he knew had been there that afternoon. We interviewed each of them, but they all told us that they had left the church immediately after the service, as quickly as possible due to the heavy rain. None knew anything about what had happened to the deceased, although a few said they had stopped to shake his hand and say a few words with him at the end of the service as he waited in what they call the 'narthex,' before he went to this vesting room."

"Did they say what they had talked about?"

"Most said they didn't recall, but that they usually just wished whomever was the clergyman a good evening, or maybe commented on the music."

"Did you interview this Dr. Ripple, or any of the choir members?"

"Dr. Ripple gave us the names of the choir members who had been there that afternoon, and we contacted each. He also said he had left immediately after the service, locking both the choir room and his office, and using the basement exit."

"Did you interview William Parkenson?"

"Yes, it was Parkenson who confirmed that John Morris was probably the last of those who had participated in the service to depart."

"There were no custodians or janitors there?"

"Yes, one called 'Jim' had been there after what they call this 'solemn evensong' service but he told us he had left after checking the restrooms and turning out the lights. The ushers or clergy usually turn out any remaining lights, and the doors are self-locking after they exit."

"What else did this William Parkenson tell you?"

"The verger's office is directly across the hall from this vesting room, and he overheard the deceased yelling for the defendant, John Morris, after he had returned to that room and the congregation had departed. He said that Will Smithers was also in the vesting room at the time, and that the deceased ordered him to get out. He then heard the deceased say something about the offering plate, and he saw the defendant, John

Morris, return into the now-darkened cathedral to get the plate, but by that time he had taken off the black robe that he wears in the procession, and had hung it in the closet. Will Smithers came in and hung his white acolyte robe next to the other robes, and, along with Jeff Marchington, the three left the church together, before Morris had returned to the vesting room. As far as he knew, by that time only Morris and the deceased were left in the church."

"Did you interview Marchington and Smithers?"

"Yes. Marchington confirmed that he had heard the deceased call for the defendant to come into the vesting room, and Smithers also confirmed that he was in that room when the defendant entered, and the deceased told him to get out and close the door. He said he heard the deceased yell at the defendant, 'Morris, where is the collection plate. I told you to bring it here,' or something to that effect."

"Did he hear Morris's reply?"

"No, by then he told me he had closed the door."

"Why would the deceased have wanted the collection plate?"

"None of those we talked with had any idea. The plate is usually locked in the room next to the altar area after the service."

"Did you interview the defendant?"

"Yes, John Morris was very cooperative with us. He seemed surprised that the clergyman was dead. He told us that the deceased had asked him to bring the collection plate because, he said, the deceased said he had seen someone put a note in it. He had not heard the instruction at the beginning of the service because of the organ playing, and by the time he got back to what he called the 'sacristy' Mrs. Gilfrey had already departed and locked the door. He had to go back to the defendant to get the keys for the room.'

"Were the keys returned?"

"We did find a set of keys in the deceased's pocket."

"Did Morris have an explanation of what the deceased wanted with the plate?"

"He said he was puzzled by it, as the deceased said he had instructed Morris to bring him the plate after the service, because he'd seen someone put a note in it. That, said Morris, couldn't have been, as the collection was only taken at the middle of the service."

"Did you ask him if he had seen a note?"

"Yes. He said he hadn't. But I suppose someone could have placed a note in the plate before the service began."

"What else did he tell you?"

"I have my sergeant's notes." Harper had the notes entered as evidence, and asked Clark to read from them. Clark continued, "Roderick wrote down what Morris said. He wrote, 'I've known Packard for many years, first at a church in the Park Grove suburb where he was an assistant.

He was single then, and when he left there he went to some monastery in Michigan for a few years before showing up at St. Matthew. He'd never been married, as far as I know, but I don't know if he had relatives.' This was in answer to my question of whether Morris knew of any family of the deceased. Then Roderick writes, and I recall hearing Morris say, 'We were not friends.' Asked if this meant they were enemies, Morris said, 'No, we were not close by any means. I admit I did not like the man, but my feelings were not bitter toward him nor did I hate him. We just did not get along well. I think you'll find he was not all that popular at St. Matthew. But I really don't know much about the man.'"

"Lieutenant Clark, did you find out what Morris might have meant by this?"

Franklin arose, and said, "Objection, Your Honor. This calls for a conclusion...."

The judge asked Clark if he had actual evidence, which he said he did, and the judge overruled the objection, but had Harper rephrase the question."

"Lieutenant, do you have any evidence regarding why the defendant may have disliked the deceased?"

"Yes, sir. Plenty...."

"Objection!" Franklin shouted, jumping up from the defense table.

"The jury will disregard the term 'plenty,'" Judge Alvarez said, sustaining the objection.

Clark coughed, then consulted his notes and continued, "We learned that John Morris had previously resided in the suburb of Park Grove, and had attended a church called 'Atonement' there. That is where he was referring to in his statement to us, as the deceased, Augustus Packard, had been an assistant priest at that church. We contacted the Park Grove Police Department and learned that Morris's wife, Melissa Morris, had apparently committed suicide. She had been receiving counseling, according to the Park Grove Police, from Reverend Packard. We then checked the county court records and found that there was a suit filed in May of 1947 entitled *Morris v. Packard*. We obtained a copy of that lawsuit."

"Is this a copy of the suit?" Harper asked, holding up a legal file, which Clark examined.

"Yes it is, sir," Clark replied, and the file was entered into evidence, and shown to the defense and the jury. Harper then asked Clark to read parts of the lawsuit, pointing out that the attorney for Morris in that action was none other than Robert Willingham, the attorney for the defendant in this case, John Morris. "The allegation of the lawsuit reads, 'Count One. In that the Defendant represented himself to be a professional marriage counselor, and at various times during 1946 and 1947 did offer professional counseling to Melissa Morris, the deceased wife of the Plaintiff, and did induce her to reject the romantic advances of the Plaintiff in an unprofessional manner, the Defendant thus committed malpractice of his alleged profession. Count Two. In that over the course of months the Defendant made romantic advances toward the late Melissa Morris, causing her to sustain psychological confusion regarding the status and stability of her marriage to the Plaintiff, the Defendant was the primary cause of the self-inflicted and fatal gunshot that killed Melissa Morris, and the Plaintiff was a primary cause of her wrongful death. Count Three. Because of the romantic advances toward the Plaintiff's now-deceased wife, which took place not only at the Defendant's office at the Church of the Atonement in Park Grove, Ohio, but also in the Plaintiff's own home when the Plaintiff was out of town on business, the Defendant had caused an alienation of affection between the Plaintiff and his late wife that is mentally anguishing and emotionally disturbing to the Plaintiff. Count Four. The inappropriate and unprofessional actions of Defendant has led to considerable damage to the Plaintiff, not the least of which includes costs incurred for the funeral of his deceased wife, Melissa Morris, embarrassment in his community, and loss of time from his employment, all of which constitute compensatory damages. Count Five. As a result of Counts One through Four, Defendant has caused damages to Plaintiff, in amounts to be shown at trial, and has, as a result of his unprofessional gross negligence, caused damages which warrant the imposition of punitive damages as well as compensatory damages.'"

"Did you learn anything else about the defendant and his lawsuit in 1947, Lieutenant?"

"Yes, we reviewed the Park Grove Police Report. It alleges that the defendant, John Morris, had been in New York on business, and had returned to find his wife missing. Nevertheless, he did not report this to the police, but rather made telephone calls to his wife's mother and sister, attempting to locate her, then he went to his office at the Wilson Company, where he was employed. During that time employees of Forest Oaks Cemetery in Park Grove found the defendant's wife's automobile, with her body inside. The police believed the death to be a suicide, noting that the deceased, Melissa Morris, had purchased a pistol several days before, and had left an unsigned note for her husband. The police file still contained the note, which read 'John, I am so sorry. I just can't go on, and am torn by what is right and what I know would be wrong. I've always loved you, but lately that love has died. Nothing filled that gap in my heart until I started meeting with Auggie. I didn't want to hurt you, but I couldn't do what was wrong, either. There is no other way out. I can't go home to mother – you know her situation. Joanie has her own family to worry about, and there's no one else. If only Johnnie had lived....' We determined that this 'Johnnie' was an infant that had died shortly after birth, and the location of the deceased's automobile was in a wooded area very near where the infant was buried in the cemetery. We further learned that the reference to 'Auggie' was to the Reverend Augustus Packard, the deceased in this case. The Park Grove police confirmed that the defendant had, indeed, been in New York City in business meetings at the time of his wife's death, which was ruled by the coroner to be a suicide. The suicide note was to become evidence in the lawsuit that Morris filed against Packard, but later dropped when Packard left the state.

"Thank you, Lieutenant," Harper said. "Tell me, was any further investigation made of the defendant, John Morris, in the homicide of Augustus Packard?"

"Yes, sir. We learned that the title of the sermon that Augustus Packard preached at the service that afternoon was entitled, 'Why Someone Who Commits Suicide Cannot Go To Heaven.' As Packard knew that Morris's wife had committed suicide, we believed that Morris reacted to the sermon and committed the crime. When we went to arrest him to bring him in for further questioning, he had with him travel folders for cruises, and we therefore considered that he was contemplating fleeing the city. On that basis his bond was placed at an extremely high level, which he was unable to post. We then obtained a search warrant for Morris's apartment."

"And what did you find in the apartment, Lieutenant?"

"Along with pictures of his deceased wife, who was a very beautiful woman, we found a pistol, which had the same registration number as the one Melissa Morris had purchased and used in her self-inflicted fatality. We found a number of papers regarding Morris's employment at Wilson Company and his subsequent retirement. He is not yet old enough for Social Security, but has a substantial pension and large investments."

"Objection, Your Honor," Franklin said, interrupting the Lieutenant. "This is all immaterial and has no bearing on the case."

"Over-ruled. Please continue, Lieutenant," Judge Alvarez quickly replied.

"We also found a certificate dated October 14, 1917, commending Private First Class John Morris, U.S. Army, for his action in battle."

"Is this that certificate you found?" Harper asked, holding up a yellowing document.

"Yes, it has my initials on the back."

"Would you read it for us?"

"It says, 'Private First Class John Morris, U.S. Army, is commended this date, October 14, 1917, for his bravery and action in battle in France when he voluntarily slipped out of his sheltering trench in the dark of night, crawled toward an enemy artillery placement, and, finding its crew sleeping, did strangle, smother or knife to death eight of the enemy German troops. He then disabled the two guns at the placement by removing the firing pins, and crawled back to his own lines.'"

"Did you verify the authenticity of this certificate, Lieutenant?"

"Yes, we did. We contacted the Army Records Center at Fort Benjamin Harrison and obtained a copy of the original investigation."

"Is this that report?" Harper asked, holding up a file. When the Lieutenant confirmed that it was, it, too, was entered into evidence and shown to the defense and the jury. "What did you find in the report, Lieutenant?"

"We read the entire file. Two factors were evident from the investigation made by Morris's Infantry Captain, Rowland Fabre. Fabre sent his report to the regional battalion commanding officer, advising that Morris had acted on his own out of frustration of the constant shelling from the enemy emplacement, had acted heroically, and should be awarded a medal of at least a silver star, if not higher, and given a field promotion to at least two higher grade levels."

"The certificate does not mention that, Lieutenant."

"No. And the reason was that Captain Fabre's commanding officer was one Lieutenant Colonel Augustus Packard, who replied to Fabre that Morris was no hero and ought to be court-martialed for acting without orders."

Franklin leaned over to Morris at the defense table and whispered, "Did you know about that?"

"I knew that my Captain's request for a medal had been rejected, but I certainly did not know that Packard was Fabre's commanding officer, or that he rejected Fabre's request. I had no idea. I was just nineteen at the time, practically a raw recruit."

"Lieutenant," Harper continued, "Do you believe that John Morris was the author of the note that you found on the floor beside the deceased?"

"Objection, Your Honor. That calls for a conclusion the officer would be unable to make."

"Sustained. Do you have any further questions for Lieutenant Clark, Mr. Harper?"

"No, Your Honor. Mr. Franklin, your witness."

Chapter 6

"Thank you," David Franklin said, arising from the defense table and approaching the witness stand. "Now, Lieutenant Clark, I do thank you for a very clear and precise description of your investigation to date, but I wonder what other investigation you have conducted since the arrest of my client, John Morris."

"What do you mean?"

"Mr. Harper asked you if you thought John Morris was the author of the note you found on the floor beside the deceased. I objected before you answered, as it called for a conclusion. But the question is valid. Did you believe John Morris wrote that note?"

"We thought it probable. We had asked Dean Williams if he knew of any other parishioners whose wives had committed suicide, and he did not."

"What about any of the other clergy in the Cathedral?"

"Well, Sergeant Roderick and the district attorney asked them about that."

"And what did they say?"

"None of them knew of any other suicides."

"Tell me, Lieutenant, how many murders in this county have you investigated?"

"Oh, gosh, dozens, but there are not all that many in Lockfield County."

"In those investigations, have you ever known a murder suspect to leave incriminating evidence at the scene?"

"We do find incriminating evidence, but usually a criminal will try to remove such evidence."

"Would it be logical, if, for conjecture's sake, John Morris did harm Augustus Packard because, as you have implied, he hated Packard because Packard was allegedly the cause of his wife's suicide, for Morris to leave a note – signed or unsigned – on the floor if that note could be construed as a motive for murder?"

"No, but it could have happened. In his haste he...."

"Just answer the question, Lieutenant. You say that no, that would not be logical. Now, if John Morris would not logically have written that note and left it beside the deceased's body, is it not probable that someone else wrote that note?"

"No, we don't think so."

"You testified, I believe, that Morris told you that Packard told him to bring the collection plate because he had, and I quote, 'seen someone put a note in it.' Is that correct?"

"Yes."

"Now, Lieutenant, if Packard had observed Morris put a note in the collection plate, would he not have said 'I saw you' rather than saw 'someone'? Morris, if he had written the note, would have removed it before bringing the plate to Packard, would he not?"

"Objection!" Harper shouted, jumping to his feet. "That calls for conjecture."

"Sustained. Please rephrase your question, Mr. Franklin," Judge Alvarez said.

"My point, Lieutenant, is to ask if you or Sergeant Roderick ever considered whether some other party might have either written the note, or committed the crime of which John Morris is accused."

"No, we do not think anyone else did it. Morris was the last one to be known to have been seen with the deceased."

"Did you obtain a sample of John Morris's handwriting?"

"Yes, we obtained several samples of his writing at his apartment."

"Did you have the note analyzed by a handwriting expert to compare it with those samples?"

"No. The note was printed. Morris's samples were all in writing"

"Did you not think that analysis would have been a good idea?"

"We frankly thought – were convinced – that Morris had printed the note."

"Thank you. Have you toured the Cathedral of St. Matthew?"

"To some extent, yes."

"Are there places where someone could hide, undetected, until everyone had left?"

"I'm sure there are."

"But you did not look into anyone else's background to see if they, too, might have had a motive for killing Augustus Packard?"

"We do not have any other suspects."

"Lieutenant Clark, you testified that John Morris told you that he did not believe Canon Packard was well-liked at the Cathedral of St. Matthew. Is that correct?"

"Yes."

"Well, then, did you determine if that statement was true or false?"

"We asked Dean Williams, but he said he did not know who liked or disliked all of the various clergy."

"Do you believe John Morris's statement was false?

"I don't know."

"You don't know. Did you know, for example, that the deceased was opposed to paying the staff singers and wanted the choir to be entirely voluntary?"

"No, I did not know that."

"Did you know that he believed that the organists were overpaid?"

"No."

"Did you obtain a list of people that Augustus Packard was counseling, and interview them?"

"No, but their conversations would be privileged communications, priest and confessor."

"Did you interview the pastor of the Church of the Atonement where Augustus Packard had previously served to find out why he left that church to go to a monastery?"

"No."

"Are you telling me, Lieutenant Clark, that you simply decided that because John Morris had once sued Augustus Packard because his wife committed suicide, you decided he had to be the guilty one, and you conducted no other investigation?"

"We believe Morris had both motive and opportunity. He has a citation for having suffocated people, so he certainly knew how to do so."

"But you investigated no one else?"

"No, we saw no need to do so."

"Thank you, Lieutenant. Your Honor, I would like to reserve the right to recall this witness later if necessary."

"So granted," the judge replied, adding, "Mr. Harper, call your next witness."

"I call Dr. Samuel Fleming." A distinguished man arose from one of the benches in the courtroom and stepped through the gate in front of the judge's bench. The bailiff stepped forward and swore in the witness. Fleming was introduced as the assistant county coroner who had performed the autopsy on Packard's body. "And what did you find as the cause of death," Harper asked, after several preliminary questions.

"It was evident from the blood tests and other tests we conducted that the deceased suffocated, and died of asphyxiation. In other words, his brain and body were robbed of oxygen. When he was found he had a heavy cloth garment of some sort over his head. We did not observe any signs of trauma indicating strangulation, nor were there other signs of trauma."

In the autopsy, were the deceased's lungs examined?" Harper asked.

"Yes, we examined the various organs, especially the lungs. They appeared consistent with asphyxiation. There was also some evidence of smoke, and we found two cigarette butts in an ashtray near the deceased's body. He apparently was a heavy smoker."

"Could his cigarette smoking have caused asphyxiation?"

"Oh, I would highly doubt it. Never heard of such a situation. It might have given him lung cancer or emphysema eventually, but wouldn't cause sudden asphyxiation where the oxygen was basically sucked out of his body."

"Could Augustus Packard have died of natural causes?"

"None that we could find."

"Could he have died at his own hand?"

"Suicide? No, not the way he appeared when found. That would be extremely doubtful."

"Do you therefore conclude, Dr. Fleming, that Augustus Packard was murdered?"

"That was our finding, sir."

"Your witness, Mr. Franklin."

David Franklin arose and walked to the witness stand. He looked at the assistant coroner and then asked, "You are one hundred percent certain that Augustus Packard was murdered?"

"Perhaps not one hundred percent, Mr. Franklin, but we did not find any other logical cause of death. The blood samples taken showed a clear lack of oxygen."

"Thank you, Dr. Fleming."

Jim Harper then called Bill Parkenson to the stand. Parkenson confirmed that he had been the verger at the Evensong service, and that afterwards he had heard Packard calling to Morris to "Get in here," referring to the vestry. On cross examination Parkenson testified that he had known Morris when they were both residents of Park Grove and both attended the Church of the Atonement. He confirmed that he was aware of Morris's suit against Packard, and also said that he anticipated being called as a witness in that suit, as his wife had also been counseled by Packard, and that she felt Packard was trying to start some romantic relationship out of the counseling sessions. He confirmed that he had left for home before Morris had returned with the collection plate, which he had found an unusual request, but had not known about the note that was supposedly in it.

Will Smithers was also called as a witness, and testified that he had to serve as the thurifer that evening as the third acolyte, Jim Slade, who usually did that job, was ill. He said that he was not overly familiar with the routine, and knew he had angered Canon Packard by the clumsy way he had used the censer during the service, but that when he returned it to the vestry room and Morris entered, Packard had ordered him out, and he had gone home. He confirmed on cross examination that he heard Packard ask Morris where the collection plate was, and that he had said, "I distinctly told you to leave it in here." He'd closed the door and left.

Harper's next witness was Simpson Packard, the deceased's brother. He testified that he and his older brother had not gotten along well, and that he knew Augustus, whom he also called Auggie, had a reputation for establishing romantic – perhaps even occasionally sexual – relationships with younger women he would counsel. When several members of the Church of the Atonement had come forward with such allegations after Morris had filed his lawsuit, he said Auggie had decided to "clear out, as he put it, and go live in some monastery for a few years until things blew over." On cross examination Franklin asked if Simpson knew anything about his brother's Army career or the threat he had made about Morris's commander's recommendation for a medal. He replied, "No, I don't know much about his Army days. He went in as an officer from college, and I was just a kid at the time. But it sounds like Auggie. He didn't think anybody could do anything right but himself."

"Was your brother ever married?" Franklin had asked.

"Yes, after the First World War he married some girl from Pennsylvania that he had gotten pregnant. But the baby died, and she divorced him, claiming mental cruelty. It sounds like Auggie. He could be a cruel son of a bitch. After that he went back to graduate school and seminary, and I never saw much of him for years. He came home when our folks died, and we stayed in touch, but not much else."

"Did the church know about his divorce?"

"I doubt it. It was pretty hush-hush, and I doubt he ever told anyone about it."

"Thank you, Mr. Packard.

At that point the judge called for an adjournment until the next day. Harper indicated that he had no further witnesses, and Judge Alvarez said to Franklin, "Be ready to go by nine. I'd like to wrap this up by tomorrow afternoon." The bailiff unlocked the chain from Morris's foot, replacing the handcuffs, and led him back to the holding cell to be transferred back to the county jail.

* * *

The next morning Morris was locked to the table leg before the trial resumed. Both David Franklin and Bob Willingham felt that the trial was going well, and hoped that by that afternoon Morris would be a free man.

The defense had only a few witnesses to call. They had already cross-examined all the prosecution's witnesses, and believed they had achieved what they wanted. The first witness called was Father Bill O'Day, who was now retired, but still lived in town. Father O'Day wore a black shirt with a white clerical collar. He was short and his gray hair was thin, and he wore thick round glasses that sat low on his nose. He was sworn in, and sat in the witness chair.

"Father O'Day," Franklin began, "I understand you knew both the defendant, John Morris, and the deceased, Augustus Packard."

"That is correct," he replied with a slight Irish accent, having been born in Ulster and brought up in the Church of Ireland.

"Were you aware that the defendant had sued the deceased when both were at your Church of the Atonement?"

"That I was," Father O'Day answered.

"What was your understanding of that dispute?"

"Well, John, your client over there, was married to a lovely lady named Melissa. They had a baby, but the baby died and was buried. Melissa was very upset by the baby's death, and came to me for guidance. I suggested that she might use some counseling from Augustus Packard, my assistant, as he was a professional therapist. She started seeing him, and, well, as I understand it, some romantic attachment resulted. That distressed her greatly...."

"Objection, Your Honor," Harper shouted. "That calls for a conclusion not established by evidence."

"Sustained," Judge Alvarez replied. "David, please guide your witness better."

"Yes, sir. Father O'Day, did Melissa tell you of any romantic advances that Augustus Packard may have made toward her."

"No, not directly."

"Did any of your other congregants tell you directly about any romantic moves that the Reverend Packard had made toward them."

"Not until after Melissa Morris shot herself. Then, when John filed his suit, several women, with some of their husbands along, came to me and said that Packard had been making advances toward them as well."

"Objection, your Honor," Harper interrupted. "There is no basis for the 'as well' implication."

"Sustained," the Judge replied, looking toward the jury. "The jury will disregard the 'as well' comment of the witness."

"Do you have the names of these persons?" Franklin continued.

"Well, I don't now. I recall a few. Bill Parkenson, sittin' over there, and his wife were one of the couples that complained about Packard. Another couple also came forward, but they left the church soon after and I don't recall their names or where they moved to."

"Did you confront your assistant priest with the accusations?"

"Aye that I did, and at first he denied it, but when he heard that others were sayin' the same, he said he'd resign his position and go to a monastery. That way he could avoid being brought before the bishop and perhaps bein' defrocked."

"Was what he did a basis for being defrocked?"

"Aye, that it might have been, but when he left John dropped his lawsuit, and we didn't pursue it further with Packard. He was gone, and good riddance. He could be a nasty cuss."

"In what ways?"

"Well, all the kids that served as acolytes were scared to death of him. He'd rant at them after the service, and even cuss sometimes. He'd been in the War, so I attributed his attitude to that."

"Thank you, Father O'Day. Jim, your witness."

"No questions, Your Honor. Go ahead and call your next witness, David."

David Franklin then called his senior partner, Bob Willingham, to the stand. Willingham testified that he had encouraged Morris to file a lawsuit against Packard, not out of any real animosity, but to prevent the old priest from breaking up other families as that was what seemed to be happening. He confirmed that Morris was not really all that angry with Packard because he felt partially responsible for his wife's taking her own life, as he had been traveling on business so much and should have been more attentive with her after the baby died. Morris, he said, blamed himself for the problem more than he blamed Packard. Franklin then presented a copy of the suit dismissal as evidence, which was entered and shown to the jury. Harper then asked a few questions of Willingham, considered recalling Parkenson to the stand, but then decided against it.

Franklin's next witness was Mildred Thurman, a travel agent. She confirmed that John Morris had come to her agency the afternoon of his arrest simply to seek some ideas for a vacation, not necessarily outside the country, but something like a cruise, or a trip on one of the new streamlined trains. She had given him some brochures to review, and he said he was not in any hurry to leave, and might wait until the late summer or fall to take his vacation. Harper had no questions for her.

Franklin's final witness was Dean Joseph "Bud" Williams, a tall, stately looking man with thick graying hair. Dean Williams was sworn in, wearing a purple clerical garment appropriate for a Cathedral dean. He explained his job and title, and was asked if he knew the defendant and the deceased.

"Certainly, I've known them both for years," he replied.

"Dean William," Franklin asked, "when was Augustus Packard hired by the Cathedral of St. Matthew?"

"We needed another clergyman about three years ago, as two of our prior canons had taken jobs with other parishes. Packard had been in a Michigan monastery, and responded to a notice put out by the diocese, as he had once served at Atonement. He was interviewed by the chapter, and, due to his age and probable retirement within a few years, was hired basically on a temporary basis, but that ended up covering three years."

"What did you know of his background?"

"Actually, in hindsight, not very much, and certainly not as much as we should have known. We knew he had served at Atonement, but Father O'Day was traveling in Ireland visiting his relatives at the time, and we did not contact him. There was nothing in the diocese records that indicated anything negative about Augustus, and he had a good report from the monastery. We needed someone trained in counseling, and he fit that requirement, as he had a graduate degree in counseling as well as being ordained. The chapter voted to offer him the position, and he took it."

"What have you heard recently since his death?"

"Well, of course his death came as a shock. But then I heard that John Morris had once sued him when he was at Atonement, and that others had also complained. I contacted some of the people Packard was counseling, and, of course, our conversations were confidential, but they seemed to confirm that he was prone to both being crabby with the men and somewhat forward with the women, especially the younger ones. He was single, and not bad looking for a man almost seventy, so it's hard to say what it all meant. But had I heard this before he was killed, I suspect we would have brought the issue before the chapter."

"How long have you known John Morris?"

"Oh, many years. He has served as our lead usher at the Solemn Evensong services for years, and also helps out at the Sunday morning services. He has taught classes, and works in the kitchen, is on several committees, and, gosh, he's a very faithful person. You can always count on John doing what he says he'll do."

"Do you believe him capable of murder?"

"Objection!" Harper shouted.

"Sustained. Mr. Franklin, please rephrase your question."

"Dean Williams, knowing John Morris as you do, do you think he might have reacted to Canon Packard's homily in some unforeseen way?"

"I can't imagine it, but then, if as was said yesterday, he was brave enough to crawl out of a trench and throttle some of the enemy, it's hard to say what is in a man's heart or mind."

"Thank you, Dean William. Mr. Harper, your witness."

"Dean Williams," Harper asked, "prior to the evening of April 12, 1959, had you heard anything negative about Canon Augustus Packard?"

"The only thing I noticed was that when he was the preacher, the attendance was less. But he tended to be a perfectionist and his homilies were technical, theologically speaking, so perhaps a bit boring to many in the congregation. But, actually negative, no, I don't recall anything much. Now that I think of it, some of the older teenaged acolytes were often absent when Canon Packard was the celebrant."

"Thank you."

* * *

Franklin and Willingham elected not to put Morris on the stand to testify in his own defense. Rather they petitioned Judge Alvarez for a dismissal on the basis that the prosecution had failed to prove that John Morris had murdered Augustus Packard.

The Judge denied the motion, and called for the attorneys to sum up their cases. The prosecutor, Harper, began first, reviewing for the jury all the negative connections between Morris and Packard, from denial of his Army medal to the suicide of his wife, and the topic of Packard's sermon that evening, emphasizing that Morris was admittedly the last one to see Packard alive.

Bob Willingham summed up the case for the defense, insisting that the jury remember that they had to have a finding that did not have even the shadow of a reasonable doubt of Morris's innocence, and that all of the evidence the prosecution had presented was totally circumstantial and proved nothing.

"The prosecution," he told the jury, "has no facts at all. They have conducted no investigation, and once they found John Morris, they went no further. As you have heard, there were lots of people in that congregation who did not like the deceased. There was no absolutely no investigation made as to whether someone could have been hiding in the church and murdered the old priest after John Morris went home. The prosecution has simply failed to prove their case and you have a duty, ladies and gentlemen, to find my client, John Morris – an honest and upright gentle man who has a strong faith and excellent morals – innocent of the state's accusation. Thank you."

Judge Alvarez then charged the jury to bring in a verdict, to be made without the shadow of any reasonable doubt. The jury was to answer two questions. First, did the jury find that John Morris suffocated Augustus Packard on the evening of April 12, 1959. If the answer to that question was yes, then did they find that John Morris did so with malice of forethought and premeditation for his action. The jury was then taken to the jury room for lunch and deliberation, and Morris was returned to the holding cell. The Judge called for adjournment for lunch, with trial to resume at 1:30 pm to await the jury's verdict.

At 3:40 that afternoon the jury entered the courtroom again, indicating that they had reached a verdict. John Morris was brought back into the courtroom and the parties assembled at the table. The benches behind the fence were full, including both members of the press and members of the Cathedral. The foreman handed to the bailiff the paper on which was written the two questions. Judge Alvarez looked at it, and then looked at the jury, each one in turn, studying their eyes.

"Mr. Foreman," he said, addressing the man that the jury had selected as foreman, "how do you find to question one, 'Did John Morris suffocate Augustus Packard on the evening of April 12, of this year, 1959?'"

"Your Honor, we find the defendant, John Morris, guilty."

"Jury members, do you all agree?" Each responded "yes."

"Mr. Foreman, do your find that the defendant, John Morris, acted with malice of forethought and with premeditation."

"Your Honor, we could not find that there was any forethought or premeditation, at least not without reasonable doubt."

"Jury members, do you all concur in that finding?" Again, each answered yes.

Judge Alvarez then thanked the jury for their service to the State of Ohio, and dismissed them. He then called John Morris and all the attorneys to the bench.

"Normally we schedule sentencing for a later date, but the jury has spoken, and I see no reason not to proceed with sentencing at this time. John Morris, you have been tried and found guilty of second degree murder. You will be bound over to the state penitentiary system for incarceration for the rest of your life. You may become eligible for parole after twenty-five years."

*　*　*

It was over. The defense team was incredulous. Franklin and Bob Willingham promised immediate appeals, and motions for retrial. As it turned out, none of these were successful, and Morris was taken back to the county jail, to await transfer to the infamous gothic Ohio State Reformatory in Mansfield. Both he and Willingham had hoped that due to his age Morris would be assigned to a minimum security prison farm, but such was not to be the case. Morris ended up in a small cell with a Polish man from Cleveland who had tried to rob a bank, on the third level of the prison. From his cell he could see the outside from a window that was opposite the cell but the view was only of a barbed wire field.

Part Two

Chapter 7

February 7, 1963
Office of Dr. Charles Rule, Professor of Biochemistry
Larken Hall, Fremont College, Fremont, Ohio

"John, this thesis of yours is fascinating. I know you're working with Dr. Myland at Western Reserve Medical School, and will be admitted there when you graduate this spring," Dr. Rule said, leaning back in his chair behind his desk and looking at his 22-year-old student in a side chair, "and I think your paper reflects the amount of research you have put into it. The notion that fragrances can trigger allergies is not new, but you have honed in on just how significant the problem can be."

"My chemical experiments here in the lab have shown that different fragrances have different chemical compounds. It only seems to make sense that some of those compounds could trigger skin or respiratory system histamines that would be irritating. My dad smokes a pipe, and when he uses certain aromatic tobaccos, it drives my head crazy! There's one that has a maple smell to it that is especially nauseating to both my mother and me."

"Does cigarette smoke do the same to you?"

"Sometimes," John Booker replied. "It depends on how close I am to the smoker, or whether there is ventilation in the room. But some perfumes are so strong that they can actually affect the chemical balance in others around the person wearing it. I guess that is where the notion of a love potion comes from – human smells that are attractive to the opposite sex."

"Ha! I don't think the girls on campus need much of a love potion to attract the men around here. They seem to be doing well enough whether they wear perfume or not. How about that redhead that you are dating? What does she wear?"

"Gail usually doesn't wear perfume, but when she does, she smells like a dish of vanilla ice cream! I asked her what it was, and she said it was French, Shalimar or something. Gosh, for her birthday I thought I'd buy her some of it, and went to the perfume counter down at the drug store, but it was like $35 for just a tiny bottle of it."

"Flowers or candy can be cheaper," the professor laughed. "But what is it in perfume that you think might be able to trigger a physical reaction?"

"From what I've studied, Dr. Rule, it seems to be compounds such as aldehydes or other substances that respond to the body's heat and release vapors that can travel several feet before completely disintegrating in the air. It's the same with tobacco. Volatile organic compounds are released when the heat reaches the interior of the tobacco leaf, producing substances ranging from benzene to toluene."

"Your research, John, pointed to a large number of chemicals, such as boron, cyano, chalcogen, polycyclos, and carbonyl. Have you been able to identify any of those in your perfume studies yet?"

"No, but I'm hoping that Dr. Myland may be able to assist me with that. So far I've been able to identify a number of natural products that are used in making perfume, and I'm guessing that each will be found to contain all sorts of individual chemicals. Gosh, they're making perfume from spices, fruits, vegetables, petroleum, even animal substances like musk. I can imagine perfumes from flowers and things, but vegetables? I can see walking into a department store and asking for a bottle of 'Essence of Beets!' And yet...."

"It's not so far-fetched, John. There is a lot of sugar in beets. But perfumes, I understand, are also made from resins and minerals. Have you looked into anything like those 'joss sticks' that the Chinaman who runs the Chinese restaurant downtown sells?"

"I know it's a form of incense, but I'm not sure how they make it. Do you know anything about incense?"

"No, not much, but perhaps one of the religion professors might be able to guide you in that area. I think Bob Merriam was teaching a class on Oriental religions this semester – the Buddhists use a lot of that sort of stuff. Maybe he could help you."

That's an idea. Where's his office? Over in Hayes Hall where the religion classes are taught?"

"I think so. His wife's the secretary there. Maybe she can set up an appointment for you."

"Thanks, Dr. Rule. I've got some time this afternoon, and think I'll wander over there before my next class. I really appreciate the time you've taken to help me on this project. Your help in contacting Dr. Myland in Cleveland was really great. He's put me in touch with those in the administration at Reserve to help me get a head start on my Master's program. Fortunately I had a pretty good score on the Graduate Record Exam."

"Very good, I heard, John. I predict you will make a fine biochemist someday."

* * *

John Booker walked across the Fremont campus toward the dark stone Hayes Hall that was located near the campus chapel. There were a few steps up to the main entrance, and inside he consulted the directory, noting that the offices of the geography and religions departments were in the basement. He went down the wide cement stairway, passed the entrance to the furnace room and the two restrooms, and found himself in the reception area with several offices around it.

At her desk typing, Sally Merriam looked up at the tall young dark-haired man, stopped typing, and asked, "May I help you?" As she did so, she threw her head slightly sideways to shift the long blond hair that was hanging over her forehead, revealing her deep green eyes and beautiful smile.

"Yes," Booker answered. "I'm looking for any of the religion professors that might be able to assist me with a technical question. I'm John Booker, a biochemistry major graduating this June, and am working on a research project I hope to complete in graduate school next year."

"Biochemistry?" Sally replied. "Is your question about religion or chemicals?"

"Actually both. I understand that Dr. Merriam taught a class in Oriental religions last year, and I was hoping he might give me some insight as to how various religions use things like incense in their practices."

"Oh. Well, Bob's in his office right now grading some papers, but maybe he will take some time to talk with you. Let me ask him."

Dr. Robert Merriam, Assistant Professor of Religions, had his office door closed, but responded immediately to his wife's knock. She quickly explained what Booker wanted, and he said to have Booker come in. Sally motioned to Booker, stepped aside, and Bob motioned to a chair facing his desk. "You're John Booker, aren't you?" Bob Merriam asked.

"Yes. I took a freshman religions survey class with you years ago. You have a good memory."

"You were a good student, as I recall. A lot of the students in the class that year were somewhat disappointed in their grade, but you got an A as I remember. So, you are a senior now, and going to graduate school?"

"Yes, Dr. Rule has assisted me in getting a fellowship to Western Reserve in biochemistry. I'm going to be working with a Professor Myland there. I'm working on a thesis that fragrances can trigger allergic reactions, and need to quantify which chemical compounds in various substances react with certain bodily functions."

"But how can I help you? I'm not a chemist, and don't have any allergies that I know of," Bob chuckled.

"Yes, but you may know about one substance that would logically fit into my subject. Incense."

"Oaah! I see. Yes, perhaps the most ancient of all fragrances, the frankincense of the Bible. The incense burned at temples all across Asia. Yes, the history of incense is, well, thousands of years old. Originally it was used to cover up bad odors, such as those that developed when animals were sacrificed in the temple on the altar. Temples could be smelly places, and the Temple in Jerusalem was full of animals being bought and sold for sacrifices. There were sayings like, "Let our prayers rise like incense," perhaps with thoughts that prayers would waft up to heaven in a cloud of smoke along with the sacrificed goat, dove or sheep. Or in some cases, a captured enemy's carcass."

"What were the ancient incenses made of?" John asked.

"Hmm. Well, at least five thousand years ago there was what was known as the 'Frankincense Trail," a trade route from the southern areas of the Arabian Peninsula – areas such as Oman, Aden and Yemen today – where resins of certain trees were tapped. These resins were hardened, sometimes mixed with herbs and spices, and sold throughout the Middle East. The Queen of Sheba may have gotten her wealth and power from the sale of the resins, and it was a very valuable commodity. The trail led up the west side of the Arabian Peninsula, then up the Gulf of Aqaba and through the trading centers of the Nabateans, to their trading center of Petra, then it was distributed throughout the entire region. If you remember the Christmas story, one of the Magi was supposed to have brought frankincense, and another myrrh, which was of equal value with the gold brought by the third. Considering how hot and stinky those guys got under the garments, one can imagine why something that smelled good was valuable."

"You mean, like the cost of perfume today! I went to buy some for my girlfriend and couldn't afford it!"

"I know what you mean. That stuff Sally wears costs a fortune! Actually, the incense used in the Far East didn't arrive until around 200 to 300 A.D. They made a lot of it using local substances such as resins, spices, flowers and things, even wood. But what is it especially that you are researching, John?"

"My study is on how various fragrances or substances, if burned, can trigger allergic reactions. Have you ever heard of a situation where someone had a reaction to incense?"

"No, I can't recall of ever hearing about such a thing. The biggest incense burner in the Western world is in northwest Spain at the cathedral of Santiago de Compostela, where James the Greater, the brother of John, is supposed to have been at one time. The James who was the brother of Jesus was later beheaded in Jerusalem in 44 A.D. It is so big it swings from chains hung from the ceiling, back and forth, filling the place with smoke. Dr. Fairchild is taking his summer study group there this year, in fact.

"But in most Christian churches that still use incense," Merriam continued, "they just fill a small ball-like thing, like what one would use to put tea leaves in a teapot, and swing it around to make a bit of smoke during a procession. A lot of people don't like the smell, or may sneeze, but I've never heard of anyone becoming ill. That's not to say it hasn't happened. I doubt this is helping you much with your research."

"On the contrary, Dr. Merriam, it tells me where to look. I recall hearing about a monastery somewhere in Switzerland where someone had carved a Madonna hundreds of years ago. Over the centuries from the candles and incense the Madonna had turned black. When they cleaned it up years later, making it white again, people were so upset that they had to paint the Madonna black again."

"Well, I hadn't heard of that, John, but it sounds logical. People like what they are used to, I guess. Are you looking forward to graduation?"

"Very much so. My family is in Cleveland, so I can commute to graduate school, and the fellowship will help pay my tuition with a bit left for food and fun."

"Good! Best wishes for your success, John, and let us know how your research project turns out."

Chapter 8

February 7, 1963
Basement of Hayes Hall, Fremont College

Dr. Richard F. Fairchild, Professor of Religions at Fremont College, was sitting in his office studying a map of Spain. Fairchild, known to his friends and colleagues as "Richie," was somewhat of an institution at Fremont, a liberal arts college with a number of graduate level courses, on its way to becoming a university. Fairchild had created an International Studies Program that drew students from all over the nation. It combined various language studies with political science, history, economics, geography and religion courses designed to prepare students for service in international businesses or government work.

Many years earlier Fairchild had begun conducting international summer sessions for some of his upper-level religion department majors, visiting European and Mideastern countries to visit religious centers. With the creation of the International Studies program, the summer sessions were extended and opened to all of the students in the program, and the focus was no longer only on religious studies, but on other political and geographical factors as well.

One previous year Fairchild had taken his group into East Germany. Along with his religion major students were several in other fields, including a number of music majors, as the college had been asked to join a Dutch opera company in a production of Wagner's *Rienzi*, accompanied by members of the East German Army Chorus on the big stage at Bayreuth, in West Germany. During the event two prominent East Germans had defected. One was a General in the East German Army – a major prize for NATO as he was in charge of maintaining security along the Southern part of the East German border. The other was a beautiful young nuclear scientist who brought with her the plans of the new Russian nuclear submarine.

She was now a faculty member in the physics department at Fremont, and was married to the music professor and chorus director whom she met when she accompanied the East German Army Chorus across the border to the West. The General was the father of her former boyfriend, an East German Naval Officer, who, after the defection, had tracked her and his own father to Ohio and had attempted to assassinate them.

The year before that Fairchild had been shot at and wounded while leading a student group in Greece. Believed at the time to be an accidental stray shot, it turned out that Fairchild was indeed a target of a killer because he was investigating the murder of a homeless man who had bad feet and who lived under a Cleveland bridge. Fairchild had a reputation – one not particularly favored by the stern Dean Harding of Fremont College – of delving into mysteries that involved old, unsolved crimes. He had been beaten, shot, and almost drowned for his troubles, but had managed to secure for the college not only an entire island in Lake Erie as a hotel and viniculture training center, but also a large yacht for the college's use in navigation training.

Richard Fairchild, the perfect image of a portly middle-aged and bespectacled professor in a tattered sports coat, maintained that his curiosity about unusual events stemmed from his years in the Army during World War II, when, as a chaplain fluent in German, he had been assigned to an Army Intelligence Unit, where he assisted in debriefing captured German officers. He had then been captured by a German Panzer Unit and befriended by the unit's own chaplain. He had learned some of the German Army's plans just before the Battle of the Bulge, and had managed to escape, bringing what he had learned to Patton's Armor Division, which was on its way to relieve the Americans trapped in Bastogne. As he had trained along with the Intelligence officers, he was as well versed in investigation as he was in theology. After the War he had written the definitive text on Europe's Monastic Republics, and had completed study at Queen's College in Belfast before becoming Professor of Religions at Fremont

But Dean Ralph Harding was not the only one who disapproved of his Religion Department Chairman's side business in crime detection. Esther Fairchild, who always accompanied Richard on his international trips, was likewise dismayed at the ventures that risked their lives because of the professor's curiosity. The two owned a farm on the Portage River, raising a few cattle for their own use, and where they entertained both students and faculty frequently. Esther was an author and illustrator of children's books and was well-known on her own behalf, working from her studio in the old farmhouse near the river. Together Richard and Esther, who had been unable to have children, planned their trips, assisted by Richard's Associate Professor of Religion, Dr. Robert Merriam and his beautiful blond, green-eyed wife, Sally, who had been Dr. Fairchild's secretary even prior to the arrival of Merriam.

This year the various professors who made up the International Studies Program had selected Spain for their summer studies tour. Eighteen students and four professors and their wives would be accompanying the Fairchilds. Six of the students would be History or Political Science majors, two Economics majors, three Spanish language majors, and seven Fairchild's upper level religion students, two of whom were Muslims and four Catholic.

Under General Francisco Franco Spain had not been considered a popular tourist attraction, although with the beginning of the *desarrollo*, or so-called "Spanish Miracle," Spain was beginning to withdraw from its Post World War II isolationism. Fascism had kept Spain a U.S. enemy during the War, but in the post-war period the anti-communist nation was then seen as a potential ally against Russia in the Cold War. In 1953 the U.S. and Spain had signed the Pact of Madrid, a series of international agreements that assisted Spain economically, and allowed for the creation of U.S. bases in Spain, including a Naval Station at Rota in 1955, and Spain was admitted to the United Nations. That same year it entered a *Concordat* with the Vatican, Catholicism being in effect the state religion. There were, in effect, no Protestant churches in Spain, and certainly no Jewish synagogues or Muslim mosques except as museums.

In 1958 Spain was admitted to the World Bank. Yet it was an impoverished nation, with little industry and a peasantry that seemed largely backward in their ways. Strict censorship had been in force until around 1960, and minor spats between the various provinces of Spain still raged around the nation. Basques wished to form their own nation, the Catalunyans spoke a different version of Spanish from those in Aragon, Andalucía or Castillo, and Franco, although a Galician, decreed Castilian Spanish as the official language, in effect isolating Barcelona from the western part of the nation, with but one train a day making a connection.

Plans had already been formulated and reservations made for the trip, which would require the Fremont students to make their own way to Idlewild International Airport in New York for Iberia Airlines Flight #952 to Madrid, leaving on Wednesday, June 12, at 7 p.m. and arriving in Madrid at eight the following morning. The return flight two weeks later, also on a Wednesday, June 26, would involve two stops enroute, one in Lisbon, and another at Santa Maria in the Azores, a Portuguese island. Within Spain the group would travel by bus on what promised to be fairly primitive roads. Fairchild's map had circles on many of the cities. Salamanca and Avila to the west of Madrid, Toledo to the south, and Zaragoza in the center. The college's travel agent in Cleveland was making the arrangements, and Sally Merriam, as usual, was organizing the students to be certain each had a passport and had filed the forms for Spanish visas. Fairchild was grateful that his associate professor's wife was as efficient as she was in making the travel arrangements. This year they again would be joining on the tour, and both the Fairchilds and the Merriams were brushing up their Español.

* * *

The telephone at Sally Merriam's desk rang. She received all the incoming calls for both Fairchild and her husband, and also for Dr. Simon, Professor of Geography and Geology, who shared a basement office with the Religion Department. Sally knew those with whom the professors would wish to speak, and those who might only be salesmen seeking to market some new textbook, calls she would handle herself. For this call she arose and knocked on Fairchild's open door.

"It's Bill Winters, Dr. Fairchild. Would you want to talk with him now, or call back later?"

"No, I'll take the call, Sally. Put him through."

Sally advised the caller of the transfer, and pressed a button on the phone. Fairchild answered, "Hello, Bill. How are things in Mansfield?"

"Fine," the other man replied. "But I may need your help again, Richie, in April."

"What's happening?"

"Well, the Association of State and Federal Prison Chaplains has a conference in St. Louis, and the warden here has authorized my attending. Susan is going with me, and we plan to maybe go on out to California for a few days to visit our daughter in Santa Monica, and we were wondering if any of that might correspond with the Fremont's spring break."

"The break is April 8 through the 19th this year. Does that correspond with your dates?"

"Yes. Now the big question. Would you be able to spend a few days a week down here doing some counseling, and conduct the Sunday services on the 14th and 21st? The guys really enjoyed your visits the last times you were here."

"Let me look at my calendar," Fairchild answered, pulling out his schedule book. "Aah, I'm scheduled for our chapel service on the 21st, but Dr. Boldt will be here, and I'm sure I could switch a Sunday with him. Sure, I'll put it down and keep you posted. Anything current or exciting happening?"

"Not since the 1957 riot, but that was quickly controlled. We've had a few celebrity guests, including one of the Brinks robbers, but other than that, it has been pretty routine."

"Routine in a prison is exactly what you need, I guess, Bill. As you know, I'm against capital punishment – I don't think it defers anyone from doing capital offenses – so I hope there are no executions scheduled while you are away."

"No, we had one man sent down to Lucasville – that's where the chair is – a couple of weeks ago, but I don't think any are coming due in April. But I know what you mean. That long walk from death row to the sealed van that transports them to the death chamber is one of the worst parts of this job. And like you, I don't think it accomplishes a thing."

"I've never understood how Christians can think in terms of revenge or a final punishment. To my way of thinking," Fairchild continued, "Christianity stands for forgiveness and restitution. Where did society get this notion of the need for a pound of flesh?"

"Some of these guys deserve it, though, Richie. That one a couple of weeks ago, Roberts, Jack Roberts, he was one tough guy. He'd raped and murdered twelve women over three years – God only knows how many more that we didn't know about – and when I went to see him he was laughing about each of the ones he'd killed. He was an animal. I know you could argue that he was crazy, and use that as an excuse, but there's no curing that kind of crazy. The Governor said that reading Roberts' file made him sick, and he refused any sort of commuting of the sentence."

"You've got a lot of lifers down there, I hear."

"Too many. But getting to know them, I can see why they got life instead of a death penalty. You'll meet them. Some are rather friendly and helpful. I'll put the word out to a couple of them to ask to see you when you come."

"Fair enough. Say, when are you and Susan going to come up to the farm for a weekend again? We sure enjoyed your visit last year."

"Well, not until after this St. Louis trip, but I know Susan would love to spend more time with Esther. Let's discuss it when the St. Louis trip is over. Are you going to Europe again this summer?"

"Yes, Spain this time. The group will only be less than half religion students, the others language or International Studies students. It will be the usual hassle, passports, visas, tickets, vaccinations, etc. Going to France or Italy is easier, or West Germany. The last trip was East Germany, and that was really something."

"Yeah, I heard something happened, but didn't hear what."

"I'm not at liberty to tell all of it, but when you and Susan are up to the farm next time, I'll tell you about it. It tied into the shooting on the college cruiser."

"You were wounded, weren't you?"

"No, not on that venture. I was, the year before. Twice, once in Greece, and once out on the Lake. And got bopped on the head at the airport as well! Say, one of those guys involved in that caper may be down there in Mansfield. Do you have an inmate named Ray Ingersoll down there?"

"Ingersoll? Young guy, killed some homeless man under a bridge or something?"

"Yes, that's him."

"He's one of the lifers – when Ohio gets through with him, meaning after he dies before he's eligible for parole, then the feds get to have him – doubt they'll follow up, though. How do you know him?"

"He's the guy who tried to kill me twice. Just struck me with a gun barrel the third time. That should make an interesting visit."

"I'll arrange it for you. Anyway, Richie, I really appreciate it. Let me let you get back to whatever you're doing."

"Okay, bye."

* * *

Office of the Chaplain, Mansfield Reformatory, April 9, 1963

The gray stone walls of the 1886 prison, which took ten years to build, resembled some sort of medieval castle dungeon at the end of a long driveway. At one end of the long multi-story cellblock was a three-story Victorian-style building that looked every bit the part of a prison to which it served as an entrance. Built initially with the intent of providing humane treatment of those convicted of crimes, the high stone walls with gun turrets on each corner had become a death house for many, with complaints of less than kind treatment of inmates in recent years.

Although it was a drive of over fifty miles from Fairchild's farm to the Mansfield prison, the professor's commute was less than an hour and a half each way, and he did not arrange for local temporary quarters. Chaplain Winters' office was on the second floor, and consisted of two rooms, one an office where he kept and worked on individual files for each of the incarcerated prisoners. The second room, on the other side of a locked, steel door, was a conference room with three comfortable chairs where Winters could conduct interviews and do counseling. Next to this room was a rather large high-ceilinged chapel with several stained glass windows, although one could easily see the steel bars on the outside of the windows when the sun shone on that side of the chapel. A series of stone pillars lined either side of the chapel, with inlaid panels behind the altar. It served several religions, and a local Catholic priest came four times a week and again on each Sunday to offer Mass. A Conservative rabbi also came each Friday night.

As Richard Fairchild was cleared through the double steel-door entrance and his arrival announced to Winters, the chaplain came down to the entrance to meet him, and reintroduce him to the warden, Sam West, whose office and much larger conference room was on the first level of the old Victorian-style center of the prison.

"Richie, the warden and I really appreciate your agreeing to fill in for us for a couple of weeks again," Winters said. The warden, a short, balding man in his mid-fifties with a no-nonsense attitude, nodded agreement. He advised Fairchild that he was welcome to join the staff for lunch if he wished, but Fairchild said that he had enjoyed having lunch with the prisoners the last time, and asked if that would be okay. "That's what I do, too," Winters said. He then led Fairchild to the wide, straight stairway toward his second-floor office.

"Warden West remembers how popular you were with some of the old timers," Bill Winters was saying as they sat down in his office and Winters began showing Fairchild some of the files that would be coming up over the following two weeks. "I pulled Ingersol's file and asked him if he would like to meet with you, and he said he would, so that is scheduled for this afternoon, after lunch.

"There's another older gentleman here who works as my assistant. He runs errands for me, notifying inmates of their appointments, keeping the chapel clean and prepared for the different types of services, and passes out the hymnbooks at the Sunday services. He's a lifer, sentenced for murdering an Episcopal priest in some down-state cathedral four years ago. His name is John Morris. You'll get plenty of time with him, and he's a friendly guy. He maintains he's innocence, but doesn't seem bitter about it."

"Do you think he was guilty?"

"Oh, after a few years here you get to hear that they are all as innocent as lambs! Not a guilty one in the entire cellblock! It's hard to tell. Morris seems to be honest about it, says he didn't like the priest, but that he sure didn't smother him as he was accused of doing. But he's not the first to be in here based on circumstantial evidence. His jury was unanimous, and he lost all his appeals."

"I remember something about that case," Fairchild said. "But I don't remember why he said he didn't like the priest."

"Morris says he'd known him at a prior parish several years before, and that the priest, a Reverend Packard, as I recall, had counseled his wife, and apparently was trying to have an affair with her. He traveled a lot on business, and after returning from one trip found out she'd committed suicide, mentioning her confusion by this Packard guy in her suicide note. Morris sued the priest, who then left the state for a while, but later showed up at the cathedral where Morris was an usher at the afternoon service. I heard that the clincher for the jury was that Packard's sermon was on why suicides can't go to heaven. The jury figured the sermon had just angered Morris so much he smothered the priest and left him there. The jury didn't think it was premeditated, so he got a second degree murder conviction, but I doubt he'll live long enough to come up for parole."

"That must have been some priest!" Fairchild commented. "Not very sound theology either."

"Morris says he never even listened to the sermon, and that Packard was alive when he left, but there were other factors, too. It turned out Packard had stopped an award of a silver star to Morris when he was Morris's commanding officer in the Army. Morris was to be commended for sneaking over to the German trenches in World War One, and smothering an entire German artillery unit. Morris said he had not even known that it was Packard who was the commanding officer, but Packard's name was on the citation in Morris's room, and the fact that he knew how to strangle someone convinced the jury he was guilty."

"Are you convinced?"

"Richie, I don't know. Sure, there have been a few innocent men sent here, but whether Morris is one of them I just don't know. He'll be your assistant while you are here, and I'm sure he'll tell you his story. Most of the men like to tell why they are here, whether they brag about their crimes, or claim innocence. But anyway, your helping us out for these two weeks is really great. The pay isn't so hot, but there's always a bit of excitement around here."

"Let's hope not too much excitement! I get enough of that with our undergraduate students."

"Where did you say you were taking your group for the summer seminar this year?"

"Spain. I've only been to Barcelona before, but we are going to do Western and Central Spain, visiting both religious and historic sites. Only about half of the group will be my religion students. The rest are in the International Studies Program, some in political science, some in Spanish language, and others in history. Should be an interesting trip."

"It sounds like it. Wish Susan and I could tag along. When is it?"

"June 12 through the 26th, from New York."

"Heck! I don't get vacation until August. But I know you'll have a great time. Any chance you can come down to the house for dinner tonight? We don't leave until the morning."

"That should be possible. I'll give Esther a call and let he know. Is the number here still the same?"

"Yes, same extension too," Winters relied

"Okay. Are the boys going with you to St. Louis? Gosh, how old are they now?"

"They're fourteen and twelve, and will be staying with Susan's parents while we're away as they have school next week. Both are eating us out of house and home, too. Billy was on the junior football team, but Jimmy is more into music. Plays saxophone in the school band. They miss their sister since she got married and moved out west. What is Esther doing these days?"

"Oh, busy on another children's book, as always. I think she thrives on deadlines."

"Not me. I hate the pressure of a deadline." About that time a bell rang in Winters' office. "Oh, that will be Ingersol showing up. Let's move into the conference room and let him in." The chaplain unlocked the steel door, showing Fairchild how the combination lock and key system worked. The key alone would not unlock the door, as someone could easily overpower the chaplain and escape. Winters gave the professor the combination, and suggested that he not write it down anywhere.

Once inside the conference room Winters moved to the other locked door, slid the metal screen off the small window, and opened it for the man on the other side. Ray Ingersol looked in, saw Fairchild standing by the other door, and said, "The Holy Joe said you wanted to see me," a slight cast of sarcasm in his voice. Ingersol was thinner than Fairchild remembered him at his trial and earlier, and the gray prison uniform sort of hung on him in a rather unfitted way.

"I've a couple of guys I want to see on the block," Winters said, "so I'll leave you two alone for a while." He left through the same door Ingersol had entered, locking it behind him.

"So, Professor. You've come to gloat," Ingersol said. Fairchild motioned to one of the chairs, and sat down in one of the others.

"Not at all, Ray. I hold no animosity against you at all," Fairchild replied. "If I couldn't forgive, then I'd have no business being in a 'Holy Joe' job, as you call it. But how are you doing? You look thinner than I remember."

"Yeah. They don't serve as many steaks down here as I was used to. Then I had a bit of pneumonia this winter. Was in the infirmary for a week, but I'm over that now. How about yourself? Have all your wounds healed?"

"Oh, I get a twinge in my shoulder now and then, but it might just be arthritis. It goes with age, I guess. I hear that Taylor was down here for a while, too."

"Yeah, but not for long. The feds wanted him in their lockup. Yah know, I got a laugh out of it. He and that other schmuck he was working with got both murder and the federal piracy charges against them. As I was a part of that, I was charged with abetting piracy, too. Guys ask me what I'm in for, and I tell them I was a pirate! They look at me like I was crazy. I get a kick out of it. Me, the pirate!"

"Well, hijacking a ship was piracy, and that's what they had done. And you pirated the college cruiser, too. I had the Coast Guard drop those charges against you and Sherri Blake. You had enough on your hands with the murder of George...."

"You did?" Ingersol interrupted. "I didn't know that. By the way, who was that bum under the bridge that was so important? At the time I thought I was doing the city a favor getting rid of him."

"George Antopholis. He was basically a cripple, as he had deformed feet. That's why he lived under the bridge, because he was too noisy when he stayed at the shelter, paddling around in boxes he used for shoes. But, Ray, he was much more than that. As it turned out, George was heir to a Greek shipping fortune. If you hadn't killed him, he would have been one of the richest men in the world."

"No kiddin! That old bum?"

"That old bum, as you call him. But he was loved by all that knew him. If you had asked, he'd have given you that piece of wood off the *Chem Queen* and never asked any questions. He was like that – always wanting to give things away."

"Hnah. Yeah, like Chaplain Winters says, I'm supposed to feel remorse. I don't feel that, though. Just anger at myself for getting caught."

"Both remorse and anger are similar emotions, Ray. We all feel them at various times. It's the way we're made, I guess. But what is key is forgiveness. Unfortunately society, through the state, seeks revenge and punishment, and is not very forgiving. Forgiveness is a personal thing, Ray. One of the hardest jobs all of us have is forgiving ourselves. We can't move on to other emotions such as love or devotion until we've cleared the blame from within ourselves, even if the rest of the world never forgives us."

"So how do you do that?" Ingersol asked.

"Did you truly love Sherri Blake, or was she just convenient for the moment."

"Ahh, she had google eyes. I heard she was out of the pen already. She thought that trip to Greece was like a honeymoon, food, sex and all. But she could be a pain in the ass. Nah, I never loved her. Never loved anyone."

"Including yourself," Fairchild stated.

"Never thought of it that way. Ain't lovin' yourself kind of selfish?"

"In Greek mythology there was a handsome young man named Narcissis who fell in love with a nymph named Echo, but she loved another she couldn't have, and pined away until only the sound of her voice was left. Then Narcissis fell in love with his own image that he saw reflected in a pool of water, and he, too, pined away until he died. People who love only their own image are like that – unable to love anyone else. But in Christianity we learn that there are three levels of love. First we must love God, and do so with all our mind, strength and soul, and then we must love our neighbor to at least the same extend that we love ourselves. So, yes, we do have to learn to love ourselves before we can ever learn to love someone else."

"Well, there sure ain't no guys in here that I want to love!"

"How about loving yourself? How might you do that?" the professor asked.

"How would I do it? I don't get yah, Fairchild. I'm in here for the rest of my life, and I ain't thirty yet. I'm supposed to love *that*?"

"That's your situation, but it isn't you yourself. Everyone has both good and bad characteristics in their life, including me. I can irritate the hell out of my wife sometimes, because I'm driven and find relaxation hard. But anyone can take an assessment of their life and see what's good and what's bad in it. That's the starting point."

"Nah, there's nothin' good about me. I was a rat as a kid, and I'm still a rat. Knocked a guy up against the wall the other day for lookin' at me funny. Almost knocked his teeth out and nearly wound up in solitary for a week, but the guard didn't see it. I never thought twice about shootin' either you or that bum, or that cop at the airport."

"Ray, I'm willing to bet that you have more good qualities than bad. I know that Winters, or the psychologists here at the reformatory, have some personality tests, and I'd like you to take them, so you can get a better understanding of yourself.

"Do you remember the day that you and Sherri were at Cedar Point and met a young couple like yourselves on the roller coaster, and had dinner with them?" Fairchild continued.

"Yeah, something like that. He told me how to get in touch with you."

"Both of them work with me, Bob as a professor, and his wife as our secretary. They said that you were a very nice man, and that they had enjoyed being with you. They are both good judges of character, Ray. Even though they didn't know what you were up to, when you aren't busy being bad, you have good qualities, too. Those are what we – you – need to find in yourself, and give them power over all those bad characteristics. Who knows – lives have been improved in the past, and they could be again."

"You sayin' I might get out o' here? Ha! You're a damned fool if you think that! I ain't goin' nowhere. There ain't no parole for murder one."

"But there are ways of making being here easier, aren't there?"

"I wouldn't know. I work in the shop where they hammer out license plates and state highway signs. I suppose it keeps my mind off getting stuck in the cell all day. Look, Fairchild, you ain't never been a prisoner, so...."

"That's where you are wrong, Ray. I was a prisoner of war during World War Two. But I learned how to make the best of it."

"No kiddin'! What happened?"

"I escaped! I knew German and learned things that helped us win the war. Now consider, Ray, that you are at war, too. You're a prisoner of that war, and it's a war against yourself. Do you think you can win that war? Or do you think you can escape that war? I don't think you can win it, but I do think you can escape the war within yourself. You are your own worst jailer, but you can change that jailer. It could make a world of difference in your life."

"Yeah? I suppose you want me to start coming to Holy Joe's services here. I came once. They sing and pray and listen to stories, but that's not for me. I'd rather hang out in the library."

"Oh, that's interesting. What kind of books do you like?"

"Mysteries. They don't have many in there – mostly big clunky novels or self-help books. But occasionally some mystery will show up. But they're never the type with sex or murder in them. Always the good guy wins. An' that ain't real, Fairchild. Good guys finish last."

"You seem to be in last place right now, Ray. So, you must have been one of the good guys – at least at one time."

"Ahh, bull! You're wasting your time and mine, Fairchild. All that 'love and self- forgiveness' stuff is bull, and you know it. Frankly, I don't give a damn if you forgave me for shooting you or not. I can't forgive myself for missing. Twice. You're a hard damned bugger to kill, Fairchild! No wonder you aggravate your wife!"

"Well, there's one good characteristic you have, Ray. A sense of humor! You could be a funny guy."

"Yeah, a real ball of laughs. That's me, all right." With that, the door opened and Chaplain Winters returned.

"You two getting along okay?"

"Ah, Fairchild's a BS artist like yourself. Says I gotta start lovin' myself. Imagine! Me lovin' anything!"

"He's right, Ray. It all starts within yourself."

"Bill, do you or the psychologists have any sort of aptitude or personality trait tests? I'm willing to bet Ray ten dollars that he's got some characteristics that are far better than he thinks he has. I think he has some talents that could be more useful around here than hammering out license plates. Ray, would you be willing to take my bet and take those tests?"

"For ten bucks? Make it twenty, and you're on!"

"Okay, twenty, assuming Bill has them available for while I'm down here."

"Yes," answered Winters. "There are always a bunch of tests administered when inmates first arrive, but the scores usually change over the first few years. Ray can take a new set now if he wishes."

"It's lunch time. Can we do it this afternoon? I'd have to get a pass from my press foreman."

"I'll arrange it, Ray," Winters replied. "Come on, we'll join you in the dining room."

Chapter 9

April 10, 1963
Hayes Hall Basement

Richard Fairchild sat at his desk reviewing the file of Ray Ingersol, including both the initial tests taken when he was first incarcerated, and the ones he had completed the previous afternoon. As he had anticipated, Raymond Ingersol had intelligence well above normal, and an aptitude for clerical rather than mechanical tasks. His personality profile had modified considerably from when he was first brought into the reformatory, with his depression lessening, but his hostility rising. The profile indicated that he had strong feelings of inadequacy and self-loathing, and these had remained about the same over the four years he had been imprisoned. What was positive was that he saw himself as having leadership capabilities and a desire for knowledge.

His record showed that his parents were probably dead. His father had abandoned his mother when Raymond was five, and his mother disappeared about four years later, leaving him with an unmarried aunt who was strict and punishing. She had forced him to go to Sunday school, but he often had slipped out of the class and smoked cigarettes before his aunt came to get him to go into the local church. It was a church with strong fundamentalist beliefs – spare the rod and spoil the child – and threats of hell and damnation were unleashed at the unrepentant boy every Sunday morning and Wednesday evening. There was no doubt in Fairchild's mind that Ray knew all about religion; he had seen the worst of it.

At fifteen Ray had ran away from his aunt's home and joined a gang on the streets of Baltimore, living with several other boys in various houses where the owners were absent. He had been arrested at age sixteen for car theft and burglary, but his sentence of three months in the Maryland juvenile reform program served only to encourage him in a life of crime. There were several gang murders in which Ray's name was mentioned, but insufficient proof to indict. Supposedly he had gotten several girls pregnant by the time he was twenty, but without a high school diploma he had found it difficult to find a job of any sort, and had stolen most of what he had, usually without getting caught.

In his spare time, however, Ray had started reading. Mostly it was pulp fiction, semi-pornographic novels or true crime stories, but occasionally, according to the list of books he had shown on one of the reports, a few "how to" instructional books, some fairly good literature, and a variety of spy and mystery books. He'd met Sherri Blake at a Baltimore dance hall, and they had driven around the Northeast in a stolen car, having out-run the police on several occasions. They had wound up in Cleveland, where Ingersol had acquired a reputation as the "go to" guy for tasks no one else would touch. That was how he got the contract to find and kill old Shoeless George Antopholis.

Fairchild considered how he might approach Ingersol again when he returned to Mansfield two days later. Technically the professor had won the bet that Ingersol had more talents than he thought he did, and that his attitude was holding him back. But maybe conceding the bet might be a better approach. He knew that the Richland County School System had a high school completion program active at the reformatory, and that Ray had not joined in the program. He also knew that Ohio State University also was offering college-level courses for the inmates. If he could talk Ray into joining in those programs, he believed he might help improve Ingersol's life behind bars.

Three other conferences had been scheduled for the morning when Dr. Fairchild returned to the chaplain's offices two days later. The first was a young man who had been in the Army, but had been dishonorably discharged over a drunken fight he was in during which another soldier was seriously injured. The young soldier had served six months in the base stockade at Ft. Knox, Kentucky, but then had returned to his home in Marion, Ohio, and, finding no work, had robbed a liquor store. He was sentenced to five years, and had been in Mansfield for just over a year. He'd received a letter from his father that his mother had died, and he was blaming himself for her death.

Fairchild listened to the man's story, and made a few inquiries. It turned out that the mother had had cancer for the past six years, long before the prisoner's problems in the Army developed, and Fairchild tried to explain that the prisoner's self-inflicted guilt was misplaced. He left the conference somewhat more cheerful, and agreed to come again the following week, after reading a book Fairchild had given him.

The next two were brought up from solitary. They had been in a fight together, and sent to solitary for two weeks. Fairchild had learned that all prisoners in solitary confinement were required to be seen by the chaplain or a psychologist at least once a week, and, visiting with each separately for about half an hour, Fairchild was fairly certain that they were holding up under the punishment as well as could be expected. Neither were religious, but agreed to attend chapel services after being released from the solitary cells.

It was about forty five minutes before the lunchtime meal when Ray Ingersol arrived for his scheduled appointment. He looked somewhat happier than he had previously, but still snarled and made sarcastic remarks as he entered the conference room. "Well, Fairchild, do I win the bet?" he asked.

"Technically yes, Ray," Fairchild answered, handing Ingersol a twenty dollar bill. "But I was right. You have talents you didn't know you had."

"What? A better left hook with my fists?"

"No. Better than that. You're no genius, but you're not dumb either. Did the psychologists not tell you about your intelligence scores?"

"Nobody tells you nothin' around here."

"That's a shame. Ray, you have a good brain in your head. I read your file, and I can see where your problems arose. Weren't very fond of Aunt Sully and her Church of the Grand Redemption, were you?"

"Haw! More Holy Joes like yourself, telling fairy tales and saying that you had to be dipped in the blood of some sheep or something or you'd burn in hell. Hell's right here."

"Well, yes, that last is right. Hell *is* right here. And that is exactly what you have a good possibility of escaping."

"Escaping? How?"

"I'll bet you've heard about the high school diploma program that the Richland County Schools sponsor here at the reformatory."

"Yeah, some of the guys signed up for that. Had to learn a bunch of nonsense and take a bunch of tests. Most of 'em flunked out."

"You would not, Ray. You've got the capability of passing those courses and getting your high school degree, and then going on to college."

"College! You're bullshittin' me again, Fairchild. I ain't goin' to no college!"

"Why not? The courses are offered here every other weekday evening."

"So I heard. But none of those guys are lifers. They won't take lifers."

"Want to bet?"

"I've already got your twenty bucks, Fairchild. What are you trying to pull?"

"My bet is that if you get your high school diploma, Winters will help you get into that Ohio State program. Whatever you study, it will put you into a better job around here than hammering out license plates."

"Yeah? But no guarantees, I'd bet."

"No. No guarantees – because it would be entirely up to you. You know, Ray, I'd also bet that you know more about the Bible than most of the guys in here. Those 'fairy tales' you mentioned. That's only one kind of religion – the kind that makes you frightened. Your Aunt Sully was afraid of God, wasn't she?"

"Yeah, she was always bellyachin' about 'the fear of the Lord and his wrath on Judgment Day,' stuff like that."

"I brought you a book that I want you to read. I think you will enjoy it. You can keep it or give it to someone else here, but I think you'll find both your Aunt and yourself in that book, and in a much different way than you suspect. It's not a religious book, nor any kind of textbook. Just one that I think will surprise you. If you'll read it, and talk to Chaplain Winters about that high school program, I think you'll find life around here a lot more pleasant. You have great skills. They're not mechanical, Ray, but you'd make a fine leader, like a teacher in some of the classes offered here."

"Yeah, so you say, Fairchild. Okay, gimme the book, but I make no promises."

"Nor do I, Ray. Now, let's go have lunch."

* * *

That afternoon Richard Fairchild met John Morris. As Fairchild was returning from the dining hall he heard some clattering sounds in the chapel and entered to investigate. A rather thin older man with gray hair, sort of balding with thick glasses, was setting up chairs in a semicircle in front of the altar.

The man stopped and looked up as Fairchild said "Hello." The man nodded a greeting, and continued moving chairs around. "You must be John Morris," Fairchild said, and the man stopped, straightened up, and looked at him.

"Yes, I'm Morris," he said quietly. "And you must be that college professor that the Reverend Winters said would be taking his place for a couple of weeks."

"That's right, John. I'm Richard Fairchild. I hear you are a good assistant to Chaplain Winters."

"It's easier work than the stamping plant, or scrubbing floors, and it keeps me out of mischief."

"Why are the seats in a semicircle?"

"Rabbi Goldstein prefers it that way. He only has a dozen or so that come, and he likes to get up close and personal with them. That service is tonight, then tomorrow I'll put the chairs back in rows for the Sunday service. Will you be the one conducting that, Sir?"

"Yes, and as long as we'll be working together for a while, why not call me Richie, like my friends and family do?"

"We're not supposed to call staff by first names, Sir. But I could call you Professor Fairchild, I guess."

"That would do. May I help you set up the chairs? I plan to stay until this evening in order to meet Rabbi Goldstein. I know his service won't begin until sunset."

"That's right, probably about seven, this time of April. I'm usually here, too, in case he needs anything. But I'm about through here."

"I don't recall seeing you at lunch, John."

"No, I came in early, ate quickly, and then came up here. I like it up here better. It's quieter. I don't like the rock and roll music that many of the guys blast on their radios. I'm surprised the Warden allows it."

"Do you have some time this afternoon? I'd like to get to know you better, John. Bill Winters was telling me something about your situation.'

"I certainly don't have anywhere else to go, except back to my cell or the library. I know you had a couple of appointments this morning, at least those two guys down in solitary. I've known them quite a while. Hard cases."

"Come on in the conference room awhile. I hope you don't mind my calling you John."

"No, that's my name! What else would you call me? 40724? That's my prison number."

"You seem to have a good sense of humor," Fairchild said as he unlocked the conference room door and the two men entered. Morris stood until Fairchild nodded toward one of the chairs, then they both sat down.

"What else do you do here at Mansfield?" Fairchild asked.

"I'm sixty seven now, Professor. A couple of years ago I had a bit of a heart attack, so they took me off heavy work, and allowed me to work in the library and here in the chapel. I enjoy that, because I can attend all the services, and be an usher, which is what I was before I was arrested."

"That's what I heard, John. Can you tell me about it?"

"I've told Chaplain Winters. I was the usher at that Sunday evening service. The other usher had to serve as thurifer because one of our regular crew was sick. Canon Packard was the celebrant, and he was in a foul mood. But that wasn't unusual for him. I'd known him before, and he was always a sour type of guy. I'm surprised they let him be a priest. Anyway, they found him dead the next morning, and as I was apparently the last one out of the cathedral, they blamed me for killing him. But I swear to you, Professor, I did not touch the man. I won't say I liked him. I had good reason to hate him. But not enough to kill him.

"Actually, it's not too bad here," Morris continued. "After my wife died – she had killed herself, supposedly because of Packard – I was a lonely cuss. Activities at St. Matthew's were about the only thing that I enjoyed. They had interesting classes, dinners, a men's group and an annual barbeque, things like that. After I retired early from the company where I worked I hadn't much to do – no close relatives around, which is why I moved from Park Grove in Lockfield County downtown, and started attending services at the Cathedral. I'd been one of those 'cradle Episcopalians,' brought up in the church as an acolyte and singing in the boys choir. I suppose I was sort of like that Pharisee in the parable about him and the tax collector at prayer. I could beat my chest and say what a good boy I was, always attending church, and paying my ten percent. But it was a good investment. I worked in the kitchen, helped the gardener keep the grounds nice, and ran the library on Sunday mornings, always ushering at the evening service. Otherwise, it was a lonely existence."

"Where had you been employed, John?"

"I was with the Wilson Company there in Park Grove. I'd started in operations right after graduating from college in Gambier, and was a vice president at the time our baby was born. But I had to travel quite a bit, and was away when the baby died, and that was what upset my wife. She sought counseling from Packard, who was at our little church in Park Grove at the time, and I was away more than I was at home. It was my own fault what happened, and I'm really responsible for Melissa's death. She was young, and beautiful. I still miss her, and remembering how she was has helped me get along here. I can live out my days, I guess."

"You seem to have a positive attitude, but blaming yourself and feeling guilty isn't always the best way to handle a situation. There are so many reactions one might have to a story such as yours. Anger, resignation, revenge. Were there no other suspects in the case?"

"Oh, plenty! I doubt there were ten people in the congregation who liked Canon Packard. The choir was mad at him, he wanted to cut the salary of the choirmaster, he had the driest and most boring homilies of any of the clergy, but was such a stickler for details that he was a nuisance to those of us who had to work with him. Fortunately his turn at Solemn Evensong came up only every six weeks or so."

"Sounds like St. Matthews had very traditional services."

"Yes. On our honeymoon Melissa and I went to England, and visited a number of the larger cathedrals there. She'd been Baptist, but enjoyed the pageantry of the Anglican services, so after we were married she joined Atonement there in Park Grove and was confirmed. I had been thinking about a trip back to Europe when Johnnie died. John, Junior. That changed everything."

"Thank you for telling me your story, John," Fairchild said. "It is a rather sad one, but you seem to be making the best of it. I gather you do a lot of reading, if you also work in the prison library."

"Yes, it beats sitting in the cell all day, and since the guards know I'm not one of the trouble-makers, they pretty well leave me alone. But of course, prison life can be difficult. They guys are always fighting. Drugs are smuggled in – I don't know how. Occasionally one will get hold of a gun and start shooting. They're always talking about escape. Over the wall. Under the wall. Hiding in a food truck. Most of them are nuts. There are a few smart ones in the bunch – too smart for their own good, which is why they're here. White collar crime, they call it. Forgery, fraud, cooking the books.

"There was a guy at Wilson who was keeping two sets of books. I was the one who detected it when parts shipments that were supposed to have been sent never arrived. I had the auditors look into it, and the guy was caught and sent here for five years. He'd threatened to kill me if he ever got the chance, but he was out of here and I was in before he got the opportunity. I'd not be surprised but what he had a good laugh when he heard I'd been sentenced to life in prison and ended up here. He must have come out about the same time I came in. But tell me something about yourself, Professor. Chaplain Winters told me that you are some sort of detective or something, as well as a professor. What do you teach?"

"Religion. I'm also the assistant chaplain at Fremont College. But I think Bill exaggerated if he said I'm a detective. There have been a few situations where I was able to assist the authorities in resolving some dead ends. Do you know Raymond Ingersol here at Mansfield?"

"I know of him. He thinks he's a tough guy, but he likes to come to the library to read, so I got to know a little about him. Killed some homeless guy under a bridge or something, he told me. They call him 'the Pirate.'"

"Yes. I was looking into that case, and he shot me twice, too, but I survived."

"No kidding! Shot you twice?"

"Once in Greece, when I was leading some students on a tour, and again aboard the college's cruiser out in Lake Erie. It seems that the homeless man, George, had found evidence of a pirated ship on the Cuyahoga River, and the men responsible hired Ray to find that evidence and shoot George. If I hadn't gotten involved, he probably never would have been caught, at least for that crime. I've met with him a couple of times this week."

"Yes, he came up on his own. Usually the Chaplain sends me down after the guys who are scheduled for a conference. So you are an ordained clergyman?"

"Yes, but our college is non-denominational, so I'm fairly generic, I guess you'd say. But like you, I enjoy the liturgical services."

Morris looked over at the clock on the wall and said, "Professor, I'm supposed to work in the library this afternoon, so I need to move on there. But you said you'd be here this evening for the Jewish service?"

"Yes, and Sunday morning as well. I hope we get another chance to talk, John. I will certainly keep you in my prayers, and you keep a hopeful attitude. Without hope there is nothing worth considering."

"Okay, Professor, I'll do that. Thank you."

* * *

The remaining week and a half of service at the state reformatory had kept Richard Fairchild busy. He conducted several services including two each Sunday, counseled four new inmates, met again with the two men in solitary, and conducted a funeral of an inmate who had committed suicide, but he had not had another opportunity to talk with either Raymond Ingersol or John Morris.

In between, he had been preparing for the final exams in his courses at Fremont and boning-up on what the study group would be doing in Spain. The trip would depart shortly after graduation ceremonies, at which Fairchild was to give the Invocation as Dr. Boldt was going to be out-of-town.

Graduation time came quickly. Final exams had to be graded and the grades entered into the new computer Fremont College had purchased. This year Fairchild had issued no failing grades. The college's growing international reputation had resulted in a high caliber of students, and most were dedicated to learning rather than to four years of frolic, as often was the case at many other colleges. The student speaker at the graduation was John Booker, who was graduating *summa cum laude,* with the highest grade point average in the college. He was already involved in graduate work at Western Reserve University in Cleveland, which, Fairchild had heard, was about to merge with its campus neighbor, the Case Institute of Technology, making it one of the finest schools in the nation. Booker's address was short, and did not touch on the subjects on he would be working, but he gave much of the credit for his accomplishments to his academic advisor, Dr. Charles Rule, in the biochemistry department.

Chapter 10

June 12, 1963
The Departure Lounge of Idlewild International Airport
New York

As he had been on so many of the foreign seminar trips before, Richard Fairchild was amused as he surveyed the bewildered look of the eighteen students gathered before him. Only two had traveled to Europe previously, and to the others, the entire process was a mystery.

"I want you to listen carefully," Fairchild was telling them. Esther and the Merriams, and Dr. Jose Ambrose, Fremont's Professor of Romance Languages, who were accompanying Dr. Fairchild on the trip, stood behind the students. "To a few of you international travel is old hat, but for the rest of you it will be a new and exciting experience. It will be about two hours before our 7 p.m. flight departs, but boarding will start well before then, at least by 6:30. This will be an Iberia Airlines DC-8 jet, and will arrive in Madrid at around eight tomorrow morning. I understand there will be a stop in Lisbon on the way, but we will not deplane there. Hopefully you'll still be asleep when we land there at a little after six. You will be served dinner on the flight soon after we leave New York, and breakfast probably after we leave Lisbon, although it is only an hour flight. On our return flight in two weeks I understand the plane will make a stop at Santa Maria in the Azores, which is a Portuguese island, so you will have an opportunity to see a bit of Portugal from the air.

"Do not leave the Iberia Terminal here. Idlewild is a large airport, and if you go wandering around, you may get lost. Mrs. Merriam has all your tickets, and you each have your own passports and visa, right? Take them out and hold them up." A few of the students scrambled in carry-on luggage or purses, but after a few moments each held their green passports up for the professor to see. "Good. If you had forgotten them, you'd not be going with us.

"Now, some of you know each other, and some of you don't. I want those of you who know or speak some Spanish to move to the right." About a third of the group did so. "Okay, now the rest of you find one of these travelers who knows Spanish and team up with them. As in all countries, there are many dialects, and the textbook Spanish you've heard at home or in a class at Fremont may be different from what you will hear in Spain. Unlike some parts of Europe, most Spanish do not speak English, at least not in the parts of Spain where we will be going. So stick close or you could get left behind.

"How many of you obtained some Spanish currency before arriving in New York?" A few hands went up. "Okay, for those of you who did not, there is an international currency exchange here in the Terminal. Go there and purchase perhaps $25 worth of Spanish currency, in small amounts, so you will have something for souvenirs, snacks or whatever you may need once you are there. You don't tip on the plane, but for any other service you receive, a small tip is considered polite. I know most of you are over age 21 and legally able to drink. I suggest, however, that you stay out of the bar here in the Terminal. You'll probably be served Spanish wine on the plane, and you don't need to buy hard liquor or beer. In the meantime you have an hour to spend here in the Terminal. Yes, there is a duty free shop, but anything you buy will be delivered to you on the plane, and you don't want to be carrying a few liters of booze around with you on the trip. Besides, you need your ticket to purchase anything there, and Mrs. Merriam has those. Don't fill up on snacks. Even though we are going economy class, there is usually a very adequate evening meal. Enjoy it, and then try to go to sleep. We won't have much time for you to catch up on jet lag once we arrive in Madrid.

"Dr. Maria Espinosa, of the University of Zaragoza, is going to meet us after we clear customs, and take us to the tour bus that we will be using on the trip. I doubt it will be anything like an air conditioned Trailways or Greyhound, so I hope you brought some cooler clothes. And, no, for those of you who have not yet asked me, we will not be going to any bull fights! The only fights we need to watch out for are pick pockets. Gentlemen: If you are carrying your wallet and passport in your hip pocket you are going to lose them. Use your side pocket, or better yet, in one of the shops here in the terminal buy an inside cloth pocket that fits over your neck and shoulder and zips shut. They're just a few dollars, and they'll keep your wallet and passport safe. Okay, now let's synchronize our watches." Fairchild looked down at his, and said, "Five thirty seven. Set your own to that. And be back at this very spot at ten after six. If you're not here we are going to move on to the departure gate without you. Understood?"

As expected, a few blank faces peered back at him, one or two cracked a joke, and the rest mumbled and walked away.

"Good God!" Jose Ambrose said as the students departed. "Are they always like this? It's like they were in a daze."

"Yes, this is typical. But after a few days, and they get rid of their jet lag, you'll find them fairly alert. For some, this is the biggest adventure in their lives. For a few, it is old hat and a big bore. The first few days are like corralling cats, but then they fall into the rhythms of the trip, and things go pretty well. But expect the unusual."

"I heard something big happened on your trip to East Germany," Ambrose said. "It was all hush-hush or something."

"Yes, a little excitement. During the opera at Bayreuth we had two defections, one of an East German general and the other of a nuclear scientist, but the CIA won't let us tell any of the details."

"Did you know in advance?"

"Do you think Dean Harding would have let us go into a Communist country if we had known there were going to be defections?"

"No, I see what you mean. He'd have blown his stack!"

"Precisely. Well, it's a half hour to kill. Want to join the Merriams and Esther for a cup of coffee?"

* * *

The Madrid Airport seemed more like an armed fort to many in the Fremont College group. Francisco Franco was still the dictator of Spain, and ruled with fierce response to any challenges to his power. The Spanish customs agents scrutinized each passport and visa carefully, and listened intently while Dr. Ambrose explained why the students and professors were there.

"Ahh, si!" the customs agent finally said, adding in Spanish that he had heard that a professor from Zaragoza was waiting for their arrival. That helped clear the path, and soon the group was being escorted to the luggage retrieval area and to a rickety-appearing diesel bus that waited at the curb. So far, Fairchild thought to himself, there have been no hitches.

"Buenos dias!" Dr. Espinosa greeted the group as they assembled at the bus door with their suitcases and other baggage. "Welcome to Spain. I trust you have had a pleasant flight? They fed you well on Iberia, yes? Si, of course!

"I know some of you will be tired – it is hard to sleep on the airplane sometimes, but we do have a shorter day today, and tomorrow a bit longer. We are east of Madrid, and will stay in a hotel near the Plaza de Mayor, and should be there in an hour or so. It is near the Prado Museum, for any of you who wish to see the Goyas or other art this afternoon.

"But tomorrow we will leave early, about eight thirty, for Salamanca. It is a university town, very ancient, with a twelfth century cathedral. I understand several of you are musicians, and I have arranged with the cathedral organist to allow those of you who play to climb up to the organ and play it. Jimenez, the cathedral organist, will give you more details tomorrow, but only those who play may go up, as the organ is very old and valuable.

"We will stop in Avila on the way, and have lunch there. It is a walled city, and I believe you will enjoy seeing it. Here are some printed pages of our itinerary. From Salamanca we will go due north to near the coast and visit in Santiago de Compostela, a very ancient city. We will spend several days there, and then return through several cities to Madrid, where we have arranged for you to tour the government offices and the old palace. Spain once had a king, you know, and many hope that one day again there will be a royal family, but, not quite yet. The time is not yet come for that. But I believe you will find it interesting. We will also visit Toledo, and will take a train to Seville for a day, but will not have time for the palace of Granada, I fear. But I think you will enjoy your stay. Are there any questions?"

The group was silent, but as the driver opened the luggage compartment, they each dutifully placed their cases inside and climbed on the bus. Most were too tired to talk on the road into Madrid, but as they entered the city, they became more lively.

Compared to the desert-like browns and yellows outside the airport, the city was lush and green. Near the central rail station the bus pulled into a narrow alley, and the students and their faculty disembarked, claimed their luggage from beneath the bus, and entered the hotel. Rooms had been assigned, and there were only two slight mix-ups, where male and female students had been paired, but the switch was easy to accomplish.

The Fairchilds knew better than to tour that day, and after a light lunch in the hotel dining room, retired for a nap. The Merriams decided to visit the Prado, and several of the students and Professor Ambrose joined them. He had been in Spain several times before, and spoke fluent Spanish, including both the Castilian and Catalonian dialects, as well as French, Italian and some German.

* * *

The smoking diesel bus was waiting in the alley the following morning as the students slowly left the hotel with their baggage. Some of the men had nicknamed the bus "Old Stink Bomb," but once everything and everyone was loaded, the driver, Pasquale, who spoke no English, maneuvered the bus skillfully through the narrow streets of Madrid until reaching the main highway to the west. Once outside the city, the landscape again turned to browns and yellows, with occasional patches of green where farmers had planted crops. The land was rolling, but not mountainous. After a couple of hours the bus approached Avila, to the south of the main highway, and turned into another road leading to the walled city that sat atop a hill. The bus stopped at a wide area on a lower street with several shops around it, and a stairway leading upward.

"This is as far as the bus can go," Dr. Espinosa explained. "We will go up these steps and through the east gate to the city, which is next to the cathedral. If you will look up at the wall of the cathedral, which is built into and is a part of the city walls, you'll see the nests of storks, which are considered to be a very good omen by the locals. This town was here when the Romans came through, and is one of the best preserved walled cities in Spain. Try to stay together as a group, for we will be having lunch at one of the cafes near the wall in about an hour, and then will move on to Salamanca."

The students and their faculty companions climbed out of the bus and started up the stairway. It was not long before they encountered some souvenir shops, and a few drifted behind the group. The rest climbed up to the gate, many stopping to take photos along the way. Indeed, storks were nested along the cathedral wall, and some of the students entered the cathedral to see the elaborate gold altarpieces.

Lunch and shopping completed, the students again gathered just inside the east gate in the wall, and a headcount confirmed that all were present. They then returned to the bus, which had, during the time the students were inside the city, been turned and was now facing toward the main highway again. It was only about an hour until they arrived at the larger city of Salamanca, and again the bus let them off near steps and walkways to the center of town.

"This is a university city," Maria Espinosa explained, "and has been since soon after Roman times. It was also occupied for a brief time by the Visigoths, who were chased out of Spain by the Moors in the Eighth Century. Archaeologists have found materials dating back thousands of years in this part of Spain, and, as we will learn tomorrow as we drive through Zamora and Orense, the area was also settled by Celts who moved through Europe from somewhere in Asia. But it has been a Christian city for nearly fifteen hundred years, and records show that it became a diocesan see by at least the year 589, more than a hundred years before the Moorish era of Spain, when the city was dominated by Moorish leaders.

"What had stood as a cathedral before the Moors was converted to a mosque, but Christians were tolerated, and services held along the River Tormes, near the Vega Monastery. Even at that early time there was a Premonstratensian college, which was later ceded to the Dominicans, who became very active in the period of the Inquisition. That early church of St. John the White, unfortunately, was destroyed in a flood."

As the group reached the upper level of the city, slightly west of the central plaza, they stopped in front of the massive Spanish Gothic cathedral. Dr. Espinosa explained, "There are two cathedrals here, the old one dating to the late twelfth century, and the new one – perhaps the last of the Spanish Gothic style – built in the sixteenth century, although it was not finished until 1733. Many new additions and changes have been made over the centuries, but we have some brochures for each of you, and you are welcome to browse through both the old and new cathedrals. However, it is a long way up to the bell tower, and I doubt any of you will have time to climb it. While the view of the city is spectacular from there, the steps are narrow, dangerous, and I cannot recommend it.

"Now I understand three of you are organ students, and we have obtained permission for you to play briefly on one of the two main organs that are hung above the choir. One was built in the sixteenth century, the newer one in 1745, but it has been well maintained and parts reconstructed over the years. The entrance to the stone spiral stairs is through a door in the choir, and I understand that Jimenez, the cathedral organist, will be up there to assist you after he plays something for the entire group. Only one of you will be able to go up at a time, as there is very little room at the keyboard. If the rest of you want to listen, just sit in the choir. But note the elaborate carvings on both the organ chest and the choir stalls, each depicting some historic person, saint or event.

"Also note, as you walk around the cathedrals, the various side chapels, many containing paintings or sculptures. Be sure to visit the Chapel of the Christ of the Battles, which is very elaborate, with lots of gold ornamentation on the pillars."

"Where did the gold come from?" Jim Hastings, one of the history students in the group asked. "Is it gold from the Americas, stolen by the Conquistadores?"

"Yes, you might say it was taken, or stolen, from gold that the Spanish found in their explorations. That, we now view, was a period of Spanish history, like that of the Inquisition, that is a bit shameful for us now, but at the time it was seen as a faithful act in reverence to the Church and to our royalty."

"Why was the old cathedral abandoned?" Dr. Fairchild inquired.

"The old cathedral was built on a Visigothic site in the Romanesque style. You will recall that the cathedral in Avila was also of the Romanesque, which, due to the narrow spaces left for light, made for dark and dreary interiors. The two cathedrals share a common wall, but, basically, the city outgrew the old cathedral, and with growing wealth in the sixteenth century, the decision was made to build a new one. Structurally, they are both sound, however."

The group entered the cathedral, and Dr. Espinosa led them around the various chapels and then into the choir. The organist was up above, and spoke to them in rather broken English, but explained a bit about how the organ is now used only for large ceremonial events. He then played a baroque Spanish piece, using some of the large trumpets for which Spanish organs are noted, and then the first organ student, Michelle O'Brian, was led to the open door in the choir, and gasped when she saw the stone spiral steps that would take her up to the loft. "Gad! I hope I don't fall!" she exclaimed. Other students stepped over to see what these stairs looked like.

As each of the three musicians had their turn and the students wandered around the two cathedrals and the museum, purchasing postcards of views from the bell tower and of various art and chapels within the cathedral, it soon was time for the group to depart again. A head count confirmed that all of the group were present, and they walked back down the hill to the waiting "Old Stink Bomb."

The two-lane highway ran due north to Zamora, then curved to the northwest along the northern border of Portugal to Orense, entering the ancient province of Galicia, then again due north over some Atlantic Ocean inlets to Santiago de Compostela. It was nearly dark when the bus pulled up in front of a large building in the center of the town.

"Tonight you are in for a treat!" Dr. Espinosa announced before the group left the bus.

"This is the Hotel Hostel dos Reis Catholicos, which is perhaps the oldest hotel in the world. It was built originally in 1499 as the Royal Hospital, but even then provided shelter for pilgrims coming to Santiago. It has been redesigned as a parador, so it has all the modern conveniences to which I'm sure you are accustomed, and after you have found your rooms and unpacked, we will meet in the dining room at eight o'clock. You will note that the basilica is just across the square, and I will tell you about it tomorrow. But I am sure you are tired after this long day, and are anxious to relax. After dinner, you might wish to wander around some of the cloisters, as there is some quite interesting art on display."

The students filed off the bus, and they and the faculty members claimed their luggage from the bus storage area, and entered the hotel through a high open stone archway that led into a beautiful lobby. A manager was standing by, ready to assign the room keys, and the group quickly dissolved up the stairs to their rooms. At eight the group was gathered in the dining room, and a salad with some of the thinly sliced Spanish ham awaited at each plate. The Fairchilds, Merriams, Dr. Ambrose and Dr. Espinosa sat together at one of the tables, while the eighteen students, now paired up with others as Fairchild had suggested, sat at other tables of six.

"I think the three organ students really appreciated your arranging for them to play the organ in Salamanca today," Richard Fairchild said to Maria Espinosa. "I noted that even some of the non-music students waited to hear all three before moving on."

"Yes, I noted that. Some of them would have enjoyed climbing up there, or up to the bell tower, which is separate from the cathedrals, but there just wasn't enough time. But as we'll be here for two nights, tomorrow they will have plenty of time to wander wherever they want."

"I hope you weren't offended by Jim Hastings' inquiry about the source of the gold in the cathedral," Bob Merriam said.

"Not at all, Bob," Maria replied. The Spanish Church has many good characteristics, but it also has a tarnished history, I fear. A lot of what is claimed is difficult to confirm. Legends become believed history. We're a nation that has seen many wars over the centuries, with one racial group replacing another. Our Civil War was a disaster for Spain, and we have not yet fully recovered. But we are survivors, and our culture is one of survival."

"How did St. James come to be associated with this city?" Sally Merriam asked. "Wasn't he the brother of John?"

"That's correct," Maria Espinosa answered. "Perhaps you know the story, Professor Fairchild?"

"Well, there are legends, myths and history, and they're all sort of mixed together in the case of the two sons of Salome and Zebedee. James was apparently the older of the two brothers, and they, like their father, were fishermen on the Sea of Galilee. It's possible that they may have even been cousins of Simon Peter and Andrew, but that is not known for certain.

"Supposedly, after the experience at Pentecost, the fifty days after Passover, Peter, who became the leader of the group of Christians, dispatched the Apostles all over to spread the word of Jesus as the Messiah. Thomas is believed by some to have gone to India. Peter ended up in Rome, Andrew, well, the Scots claim him, but nobody is sure. John, apparently being the youngest, remained with Mary somewhere around Ephesus. There were two disciples named James, just as there were two Simons and two Judes or Judases. That is probably why Jesus called the one Simon 'the rock.'

"Anyway, according to the legend – and there does not appear to be any historical collaboration – James the older, or greater as he became known to the church, somehow got over to the continent and arrived in Galicia to convert the Celts there. His exact route is only theorized, but he then returned to Jerusalem around A.D. 44, and was caught by Herod Agrippa, the First, and beheaded. Tradition says that his disciples took his remains back to Spain where they were buried and lost for a number of centuries, and mythology says his body was transported by angels back to Spain. Take your choice, I guess!

"According to the legends, some monk in the middle ages apparently rediscovered his remains and brought them here, where they were declared relics by one of the popes. Have I explained it accurately, Maria?"

"That's about the way I heard it. His original tomb was abandoned in the third century, probably under Roman persecution, and was rediscovered in the ninth century by a hermit monk named Pelayo, who supposedly saw lights in the sky telling him where it was. The Church recognized this as a miracle, and that is when the remains were first brought here, to a chapel that was constructed on the site. In Spanish his name is Saint Jazo."

"And in Hebrew," Fairchild added, "It is Yakob, or Jacob."

"Do you think the legends are true?" Jose Ambrose asked.

"It's difficult to know what is actual fact and what might be just legend when one is dealing with a situation that occurred almost two thousand years ago," Fairchild answered. "But it is interesting that Paul seems to make reference to the story in the fifteenth chapter of his letter to the Romans when he says that he had completed the preaching of the gospel from Jerusalem to Illyricum, which was the Adriatic peninsula, noting that he wanted to bring the gospel where it had not been heard, but did not want to build on another's foundation, although he planned to stop in Rome on his way to Spain.

"Spain was not unknown to those in Palestine," Fairchild continued. "You may know of the legend that Joseph of Aramathea was a tin dealer who traveled – presumably by ship, to Devon in England. Another legend suggests that he was an uncle of Mary, hence may have been related to Jesus. If, as the Glastonbury legends maintain, Joseph brought the cup used at the last supper by Jesus to England, it could be entirely possible that James could have been with him, and stopped in Galicia. We saw how many little harbors there were south of here."

"This legend of Glastonbury of which you speak, Professor Fairchild. I am not familiar with it," Maria Espinosa said.

"Well, that's really all it is, is legendary stuff. Supposedly the cup used in the upper room – perhaps even with some of Jesus' blood in it – ended up somewhere in the swampy area of Devonshire, where the legends of King Arthur take place, searching for that cup. Supposedly it is at the bottom of a well that has reddish radioactive water in it that became a health spa in medieval times. There is even a thorn tree there, near the ruins of an old Cistercian monastery, that allegedly grew from a thorn stick that Joseph brought and stuck in the ground. The Church of England maintains the place, but it is also a center of Druid worship, so it is hard to tell how much is Druid legend and how much is Christian mythology. Supposedly King Arthur's grave is also there, but there's really no documentable evidence that there ever was a King Arthur."

* * *

The following morning the group gathered outside the stone entrance to the hotel, preparing to enter the basilica. Maria Espinosa was explaining the significance of this combination cathedral and basilica to the students. She explained about the legend that St. James the Greater was buried there, telling much of the story that the professors had discussed the previous evening.

"The cathedral was started in the late eleventh century, around 1075," Dr. Espinosa explained, "on the site of an early church that had been destroyed by Al-Mansur Ibn Abi Aamir, the commander of the caliph of Cordoba. It is a large building, and you will find a number of pilgrims worshiping inside. Please do honor their privacy in their devotions, and keep as quiet as you can.

"Two things you will want to see include the basilica. One is the crypt, which is below the main altar. It is where the remains of St. James are supposedly located, along with relics of his two disciples, St. Theodorus and St. Athanasius. The reliquary is silver, but it was only placed in the crypt in the 19th century.

"The other thing you want to see is the botafumeiro, which is a very large and heavy gold thurible created by a goldsmith in 1851. It is one of the largest censers in the world, and during important religious services is swung across the nave on chains attached to pulleys. It is kept in the library when it is not in use, but is worth visiting. When it is in use, such as on St. James Day and other holy days, or for ordinations, it takes eight red-robed 'tiraboleiros' pulling ropes to make it swing over the transept, pouring out the pungent smoke. Supposedly the use of a lot of incense started about 700 years ago, to cover the stench of all the unwashed pilgrims who had ventured here from all over Europe, following what became known as the St. James Way.

"So enjoy the morning, and meet back here at twelve thirty for lunch. You will have all afternoon to visit the town if you wish," she concluded, as the group started to break up and head into the basilica.

"I definitely want to see that thurible," Bob Merriam said to Fairchild. "I was telling John Booker about it a few months ago."

"John Booker?" Fairchild replied. "The student who gave the graduation speech?"

"Yes. The study he is going to be doing at Western Reserve is on the effects of fragrances on allergies. He and Dr. Rule were talking about it, and the subject of reactions to incense came up, so he came to me to find out something about incense. I'd never heard of any problems with it."

"No, neither have I, although a lot of people don't like the smell of it. Interesting. Well, shall we go see the big thurible? It's one of the things this place is famous for."

Chapter 11

The remainder of the trip was active and busy for the students and their faculty. The "Old Stink Bomb" bus almost broke down on some of the roads through the Asturian Mountains along the northern coast and back south along the Ebro valley. It took half a day to reach León, where the group had a late lunch. A brief stop was planned in Segovia, and by the time the bus returned to the hotel in Madrid the group was ready for a relaxing evening of little activity, although a few of the older students decided to join the Spanish tradition of eating late and partying until after midnight.

For the next few days the group stayed in Madrid, visiting the Royal Palace, and having an audience with the Spanish Minister of Culture, who spoke English quite well, and explained about the Spanish government and its relationship with the rest of the world since becoming a member of the United Nations. Another day was left open for the students to do as they wished, and many took advantage and went to the Prado Museum, including the Fairchilds, Jose Ambrose and the Merriams.

On the following day the bus again pulled up in front of the hotel, and the students and faculty loaded for a day's journey to Toledo. Dr. Espinosa was not with them on this trip, but Jose Ambrose had been to Toledo before and acted as guide, explaining about the history of the giant gothic cathedral atop the hill, the El Greco paintings, the role of Toledo in the war with the Moors and during the Inquisition, and other aspects of the hilltop town. Again the bus let them off outside the city, and they had to climb the narrow streets to the top.

Dr. Espinosa did join them for the next two days, a train trip to Cordoba and Seville. They had to rise and have breakfast early as their non-express train left the Atocha Main Railway Station, not far from their hotel, at ten to eight in the morning, and traveled the 442 kilometers, a little over three hundred miles, to Cordoba, arriving about one thirty in the afternoon. A bus tour of the took them around the town, and shortly before three thirty they were back at the train station for the remaining 190 kilometer trip to Seville, where their hotel was again near the train station.

Seville, located on the Rio Guadalquivir, was packed with Moorish architecture, some converted after the Moors left to Christian buildings. Both houses and gardens were designed to provide as much shade from the summer sun as possible, and the group heeded Maria Espinosa's advice to stick together as they roamed the narrow streets. Most of the students had brought cameras with them, and were soon inquiring where they could purchase film. It was not difficult to find in a city designed for tourists.

In the evening the group enjoyed snacking on tapas and the strong Andalusian coffee, then joined crowds in restaurants around ten in the evening for a dinner of local specialties, dining outside beneath the twelfth century Giralda, which had begun its life as a minaret to a mosque, and was now a 322-foot bell tower. Some of the students had climbed it earlier the day, and were glad to get back to bed around midnight. The return trip to Madrid left Seville shortly after lunch the following day, arriving back at Atocha Station shortly before ten in the evening on the second class train, which, unfortunately, did not have a dining car. The famished students ate at Atocha Station before returning to their hotel. They all bid farewell to Maria Espinosa, who was returning to Zaragoza the following morning, after spending the night with her sister in Madrid.

* * *

The Iberian Airline flight back to the U.S. arrived on time, after its stop in the Azores, and the students departed for various flights to their homes, although most were returning with the Fremont faculty members to Cleveland. The summer seminar was over, and all three professors agreed that the students had learned more than they had anticipated on the trip, and planned to award grades accordingly.

Jose Ambrose had left his car at the Cleveland Hopkins Airport long-term parking, and the five Freebooters returned to the campus where they had left their own cars. The Merriams had only a short drive to their new home in town, but the Fairchilds had about a twenty minute drive to their farm.

Richard Fairchild had no summer classes scheduled, and planned to spend most of his time working on fences on his small farm on the Portage River. Esther had an approaching deadline for the children's book she was writing and illustrating, and was anxious to get it completed. "Well, at least nobody shot you on this trip," Esther commented as they drove back to the farm. "And let's hope nobody has blown up the house again!"

"No, once is enough. No diaries to investigate, no operas to sing, no defectors to help relocate, no pirates this year!" he laughed. "Speaking of pirates, I met that young man that shot me when I was down at Mansfield. I believe I told you of my interviews with him. Anyway, he said that he tells the other prisoners that he was a pirate. He really was, but he gets a kick out of it. Apparently, from what I heard, that's his nickname down there, 'the Pirate!'"

"Maybe you should get him a black patch to put over his eye!" Esther laughed. "Make him look like a real swashbuckler. Say, that might be a good theme for another children's book, maybe something about a good pirate who helps people. Were there any?"

"Depends on your politics. Morgan was a hero in England and hated by Spain. Funny, that never came up on the trip. I guess the Spanish Armada was not part of Maria's specialty in history."

"No, but she was well informed on what we did see. A nice young woman. How did you contact her?"

"I didn't. Jose knew her. He put me in touch with her, and we both worked with her on the plans for the trip."

Chapter 12

July 6, 1963
West Bass Island, Ohio

One of the navigation students was kept busy running faculty and family members from the Port Cleland dock to the Fremont College facilities at Castle Kent on West Bass Island in Lake Erie aboard the college's cabin cruiser. The Fairchilds and Merriams had been out there over the weekend preparing for the annual faculty picnic and barbeque, and even though it was only mid-day, they were fairly exhausted. Many bottles of the previous year's vintage of Chateau Kent had already been opened and consumed.

Bob and Richie were out on the lawn firing up a great barrel-shaped barbeque full of charcoal, with a slotted grill on top, and slowly roasting pork ribs, chickens and steaks. The event, now an annual ritual for the college staff, was fully paid for by the college, and all the directors were among those most enjoying the event.

As Fairchild slowly turned a long rack of ribs over on the grill and basted it with sauce he asked, "Bob, remember when we were at Santiago de Compostela you mentioned to me that John Booker, the graduate speaker, had asked you about incense, and whether it could cause allergic responses?"

"Yes. He said he would be working with some professor at the Western Reserve Medical School on the research."

"Do you remember that professor's name?"

"Hmm. I think he just mentioned his last name. Miles, or Myland or something. But Charles Rule would know. He's the one who put John in touch with him."

"Are Charles and Gloria here at the picnic?"

"I'm not sure. They may be. I think he had a summer class, so they were probably in town. Want me to check?"

"If you don't mind, I'd like to talk with him."

* * *

It was several days later when the professor said to Esther, "How would you like to take a little ride downstate. You said awhile back that you'd like to visit that little town of Dublin, Ohio, and maybe stay at that old inn in Lebanon, and come back through Amish country. We could use a few days to ourselves."

"What are you up to, Richie? I can tell you have something more on your mind than honeymooning at some place where Charles Dickens once stayed!"

"No, not at all. I just want to stop at the newspaper and courthouse in Lockfield County for a few minutes, maybe look at some records, but it shouldn't take long."

"Knowing you, it will take a longer time than you think. But, okay, I'm game."

"Good. We'll go down U.S. 23, then take some back roads around Dayton to Lebanon. I'll call and make some reservations. Let's see. What is it called, the Golden Lamb, or something? Lots of good shopping in the town, I hear."

Fairchild spent the rest of the day on the phone, and three days later after packing the station wagon he and Esther headed south. The highway, mostly a two lane rural road, took them through Fostoria, Upper Sandusky and Marion, where they had lunch near the McKinley Memorial before moving on to Dublin, a suburb of Columbus, finding a little hotel in the town for the night. Because of its name, the town tried to present an Irish atmosphere, with an Irish Pub and Irish linen and pottery shops.

About eleven the following day they drove on south, arriving in Lebanon about four and checking into the Golden Lamb Inn for three nights. The Inn, which dated to the early 1800s, was one of the oldest in the state, and was famous for its dining, of which the Fairchilds took full advantage, then strolled around the town after dinner before retiring for the night.

The next morning, while Esther was lounging around in the room before the stores opened, the professor drove over to the county seat of Lockfield County, slightly to the northeast, and stopped at the small newspaper office called *The Morning Sentinel.* He inquired about old copies of newspapers, and was directed to an office in the basement where he was able to review copies of papers between April and July of 1959. He obtained photocopies of several articles he wanted, which provided him with other names, and then checked the local phone directory for numbers. One was for an attorney named Bob Willingham. The attorney's office was in Park Grove, about eight miles outside of Lockfield, on the second floor of a bank building.

"What can I do for you, Mr. Fairchild?" Bob Willingham, a man in his sixties, said as his secretary led Richard Fairchild into his office.

"First let me thank you for allowing me to visit on such short notice. As I said on the phone, I am Richard Fairchild, a professor at Fremont College in Fremont, Ohio, as well as assistant chaplain of the college. This past spring I was assisting a friend who is the chaplain at the Mansfield

Reformatory for a few weeks, and met one of your clients, John Morris, an inmate there. I understand that it was your firm that represented him in his murder trial."

"Yes, ahh, Professor Fairchild. Or is it Reverend?"

"Well, I usually go by Dr. Fairchild, but call me Richie, as my friends do. Anyway, John told me a little bit about his situation, and I remembered the event when it happened – not too many murders of clergymen these days, except in an Agatha Christie mystery – and I obtained some of the newspaper articles on the case, and the trial this morning at the *Sentinel*."

"I'm not a criminal attorney, so it was actually one of our associates at the time that conducted the defense. I simply did the opening and summary to the jury. David Franklin was the lead attorney. He's moved to a firm in Cincinnati now. Jones & Partridge was the firm that represented Morris's employer, the Wilson Company, which is why he called on me."

"I understand. But with Morris being convicted on only circumstantial evidence, I'm surprised the courts did not allow an appeal."

"Oh, we appealed, as far as we could. The appellate court reviewed the case, and sustained the trial court decision. The state Supreme Court refused to hear the case. Unless we had new evidence, there wasn't much chance of getting a new trial."

"Do you have a copy of the trial transcript, Mr. Willingham?"

"Call me Bob, and yes I do. Let me get it for you." He picked up his phone, pressed a button, and directed his secretary to pull the *State v. Morris (1959)* file. In a few minutes she delivered the thick file to Willingham.

"May I review it?" Fairchild asked.

"Certainly. But I was there during the entire trial, so perhaps there are some specific questions I might be able to answer for you."

"Maybe. I understand that the coroner did an autopsy, and testified."

"Yes. He confirmed that the cause of death was asphyxiation, but that the old priest did not appear to have been strangled. He noted some coloration in the lungs, but attributed it to the fact that Packard, the priest, smoked."

"Was Packard's medical records ever introduced in the trial?"

"No, I don't believe so. The state didn't obtain them, or testify on them. Neither did we. Why?"

"Well, as I said, I met Morris at Mansfield, and over the years I've gotten to be a pretty good judge of character. I don't see him as being guilty, although he does blame himself for his wife's suicide. The newspaper articles seemed to leave some questions as to the facts of what happened.

"Two months ago I led a student seminar to Spain. One of the places we visited was Santiago de Compostela. My associate professor, Bob Merriam, happened to mention that one of the Fremont students, who is now in graduate school at Western Reserve in Cleveland, had asked him about incense, as he is doing research on whether fragrances or aromas can trigger allergic reactions. Later I got to thinking about John Morris. It was a Solemn Evensong service, and I believe that the Cathedral of St. Matthew uses incense at that service."

"Yes, there was some testimony about incense. One of the men who was supposed to usher had to do the incense, and left it in the vestry where Packard died."

"Yes, that was mentioned in the newspaper reports. I contacted the Western Reserve professor of medicine and biochemistry that our student is working with, a Dr. Jordan Myland, and asked him if incense, or a combination of incense and tobacco smoke in a small, closed room could trigger an allergy attack, and he said that it could, and might also trigger an asthma attack if the person was subject to asthma. The smoke could cause the bronchial tubes to swell, in effect suffocating the patient."

"My God! We never thought about that! If we get Packard's medical file and it shows allergies or asthma, we might have a basis for a new trial."

"That's what I thought, too, Bob. John is doing okay in Mansfield. He works with the chaplain there, and in the library, and ...."

"Yes, I know. I try to visit him occasionally, and take him things that he likes and that are allowed in the prison."

"Don't mention this to John until you've got Packard's records. Can you obtain them, or would you have to get a subpoena?"

"Oh, we'll get them one way or the other, Fairchild. I'm ashamed that we didn't think of it sooner."

"I'm surprised the prosecution didn't obtain them."

"You know, maybe they did, and didn't share them with us. That could lead to another cause for a new trial, and, if they knew and didn't reveal it, maybe a wrongful conviction charge. It has happened before."

"Bob, I won't take these records with me now, but I will leave you Dr. Myland's number in Cleveland. If you can get a hold of Packard's records, have him review them. He could be your expert witness. In the meantime, I'm going to pay a visit to St. Matthews and see the scene for myself."

"Good idea. Let me know if you come up with any new ideas. But, boy, this one is a dandy."

Fairchild left the offices of Jones & Partridge and drove back to downtown Lockfield, and quickly found the Cathedral of St. Matthew. At an information desk he inquired about any clergy that might be available, handing over his business card. He was informed that Dean Joseph "Bud" Williams was in his office, and after a brief phone call, the person at the information desk directed Fairchild to a second floor office overlooking a cloister and the side of the gray stone cathedral.

"Dr. Fairchild," the Dean said, rising from his desk chair as the Professor appeared in the open doorway, the Dean's secretary standing behind him. The Dean was dressed in black, except for a purple clerical shirt and white clerical collar, and was a balding man in his fifties with large black-rimmed glasses. "What may I do for you? Coffee, perhaps?"

"Yes, I'd enjoy a cup of coffee if you are having some." The Dean's secretary responded at once, turning and shortly bringing two cups of coffee and a plate with sugar and packages of creamers. "I appreciate your agreeing to meet with me, Dean Williams. As the lady at the information table told you, I am Dr. Richard Fairchild, Professor of Religions at Fremont College here in Ohio, and the assistant chaplain at the college. This spring I substituted for a friend, who is the chaplain at the Mansfield Reformatory, and had occasion to meet...."

"John! John Morris!"

"Correct."

"I try to get up there to see him whenever I can. I feel so sorry that he was convicted. I never believed he murdered Canon Packard."

"Nor do I. In fact, I believe that there may be enough new information that could lead to a new trial. I met this morning with his attorney, and also got the newspaper reports of the trial."

"They tried all sorts of appeals. I don't know why they were unsuccessful. There was no real evidence against John."

"One thing that didn't come out was Canon Packard's medical records. Would you happen to have any records on Packard that might indicate any medical conditions?"

"Medical records? I don't understand. There was an autopsy."

"Yes, but it only confirmed that Packard was asphyxiated. He suffocated, but was not strangled. One of our Fremont students is doing graduate work at Western Reserve in Cleveland, and that research is on whether fragrances, such as perfumes, or maybe even incense, might trigger an allergy or asthma attack. If Packard had a history of allergies or asthma, it might give basis for a new trial for John."

"Good gracious! I know a lot of people here don't like incense, but most enjoy the ceremony, and I've never heard of anyone having an allergic attack from it."

"Nor have I, but, it is one aspect of Morris's case that wasn't covered, at least during the trial. Would it be possible to see the vestry room where Packard died?"

"Certainly. Let's finish our coffee, and I'll take you down there. Are you staying around here somewhere?"

"Yes, my wife and I are staying at the Golden Lamb in Lebanon. She's probably out shopping this afternoon. We have one more day in the area. Sunday."

"Sunday? Could you attend our services? Say, would you like to give the sermon at one of the morning services?"

"Yes, we could attend, but I'll pass on preaching. I get enough of that with the college chapel services. But I've not been to a formal Evensong service in years."

In the next few minutes while Fairchild finished his coffee Dean Joseph Williams went to a file drawer and withdrew a thick envelope. "This is Packard's file," he said. "The state's attorney subpoenaed it, but sent it back to us after the trial. You are welcome to look through it."

Fairchild opened the clasps on the envelope, and slid out the thick manila folder inside, paging through it. There were various pieces of correspondence, communications from the monastery in Michigan where Packard had gone after leaving the Church of the Atonement in Park Grove, and letters, pro and con, from members of the Cathedral of St. Matthew. Among the pay stubs were some personal notes from Packard to the Dean, and a copy of the Dean's reply. On one was a note regarding Packard failing to show up for a weekday service. Packard had responded with an apology, saying that he had been suffering a respiratory problem of long standing, and had been at the doctor's office and forgot about the service, but would not have been able to officiate anyway. He said that Dr. Victor March would be able to confirm it. There was also a copy of Packard's application to the monastery in Michigan, which contained the question, "Do you have any health problems?" Packard had answered, "No, except an occasional asthma attack."

"This is important, Dean Williams. Close it back up and keep it. I will suggest to Bob Willingham that he subpoena the file. If the state's attorney had it and knew that Packard suffered from asthma, he failed to reveal it at the trial. That could be a crucial factor in getting a new trial."

"Yes, I can imagine. Well, come on downstairs and I'll show you the vestry room." The two men descended a back stairway, entering the narthex through a side door. The big wooden doors to the cathedral nave were open, and Fairchild stood and looked in for a moment.

"Beautiful! I'd love to study the windows and other art here. It's so bright and welcoming."

"Yes, it is a wonderful place. Unfortunately, our congregation is small, and we have a hard time financing the upkeep. But here is the vestry," he said, removing keys from his pocket and unlocking a door. The room was very small. There was a long floor to ceiling closed cupboard along one side where the vestments were kept, and a few drawers below a shelf where there was a mirror. In one corner were stacked some crosses on poles, banners and other items, and hanging on a brass rack was a thurible on a series of chains. A chair sat in the middle of the room with a small table next to it. The room appeared to be about six feet by eight, including the closet where the vestments were kept, and the door closed tightly when locked.

"Has the room been changed any since 1959?" Fairchild asked.

"No, it has always been like this. Various colored vestments for different liturgical seasons and such. The altar clothes are kept in the sacristy, but the vestments are here."

Pointing to the chair, Fairchild asked, "Is that where they found Packard?" The Dean nodded yes. "Where is the incense kept?"

The Dean went over to the second drawer beneath the shelf and opened it, allowing Fairchild to look in. There were several metal containers or canisters. One was an old coffee can. Fairchild removed the plastic lid, and noted that it was full of crumbled charcoal. "We saw the giant thurible at Santiago de Compostela. It takes forty kilograms of charcoal to get it fired up," Fairchild said. "It is near the crypt where the remains of St. James the Older, the brother of John, is supposed to be buried, but that is the legend. Who really knows?"

"I've heard of it. Thank goodness ours doesn't require more than an ounce or two."

"What's in this tin?" Fairchild asked, removing a small round tin.

"That's one of three types of incense we have. Those two tins at the back are the others. One was a present from a parishioner who had been in Oman, and contains some of the resins used in frankincense, so we reserve that for Christmas and Easter. The other is some I purchased in Italy when I was there, and it has some rare spices in it. This other we get regularly from a church supply store in New York."

"Is that what would have been used the night Packard died?"

"Probably. You'd have to ask Will Smithers, who was the thurifer that night."

"What's in this other can?" the professor asked, pointing to an oblong metal container that was in the corner of the drawer.

"Moth balls!" the Dean answered. "We put them in the cupboard to keep the vestments from getting moth eaten."

"Would they have been there in 1959?"

"I suppose. They've been there as long as I have been here," the Dean answered.

"Could Will Smithers have gotten confused and put them in the thurible instead of incense?"

"Gosh, I wouldn't think so, but I suppose it would be possible. He only did that job occasionally, and usually when others were around."

"Thank you, Dean Williams. This has been most helpful. Perhaps Esther and I will come over on Sunday. What time is Evensong?"

"It starts at five in the summer, when most of the choir is away. Are you sure you won't come in the morning and participate in the service?"

"No, I'll take a rain check on that. But if John gets a new trial and is exonerated, I'll come down and preach the best sermon I can for you."

"That's a deal I will look forward to! Thank you, Dr. Fairchild. You have given me the best hope I've had in years."

Chapter 13

September 22, 1963
Lockfield County Court House

Events moved quickly over the following six weeks. Attorney Willingham contacted Dr. Myland at the Western Reserve Medical School and, as Fairchild had suggested, subpoenaed Canon Packard's file from the Cathedral with the notes about the asthma in it. Dr. Victor Marsh was contacted, and agreed to testify if his medical file on Packard was subpoenaed. Willingham then contacted Judge Roger West of the appellate court, and explained what new evidence had come to light. Judge West reviewed the appellate file, and granted an Order for Retrial. Jim Harper, the original prosecuting attorney, was still with the Lockfield County District Attorney's office, and was not pleased by the order. David Franklin, who had served as Morris's lead defending attorney, agreed to come up from Cincinnati to again serve on the defense team with Willingham, who was still with the Jones & Partridge firm.

The subpoenas were issued, and a retrial date set for September 22. Two days before, Morris was transferred to the Lockfield County Jail from the Mansfield Reformatory. Judge Alvarez was again the trial judge, and over a two day period a new jury was picked. Classes had resumed at Fremont, so Dr. Fairchild was unable to attend any of the proceedings down state. He did call his friend, Bill Winters, at the Reformatory and filled him in on what was happening.

"Yes, I heard," Winters said. "They came and got Morris a couple of days ago. I'm without an assistant now."

"Why not ask Ray Ingersol? I think he might turn out to be a good surprise."

"Ingersol, the guy they call 'The Pirate'? I doubt it, but I'll ask him if he's interested."

*　*　*

The district attorney presented the same evidence that had been presented in the first trial. Morris was the last to leave the cathedral. He knew and disliked Packard, and blamed Packard for the suicide of his wife. Further, it was Packard who had denied Morris a silver star during the war. Added to that was the fact that Packard's sermon was geared to be upsetting to Morris. Then there was the mysterious note. The fact that Morris knew how to kill from his wartime experiences, said the state's attorney, was sufficient to know that Morris had murdered Packard. Jim Harper's first witness was Lieutenant Linus Clark, whose testimony was the same as he had given in the first trial.

On cross examination, Franklin wasted no time getting into the basics of the defense's theory. "Lieutenant Clark, when you began your inquiry into the death of Augustus Packard, did you determine if, when he was found, the door to the vestry room was open or closed?"

"Yes, we learned that it was closed."

"Did you examine the door?"

"Well, the door had a lock, but the priest who found the deceased said that it was unlocked when he entered it."

"But did you examine the door to determine if it closed tightly, or whether there was space around the top, sides or bottom?"

"Nah, we didn't look at it that closely. Can't see how it would have made any difference."

"No? Well, did you measure the dimensions of the room?"

"No."

"The State's Exhibit 3 is a photograph of the room," Franklin said, handing Clark the photograph. "Would you disagree if you were told that the room was eight and a quarter feet long, six and a half feet wide, and the ceiling was seven and a half feet high? Those measurements include the cupboard or closet, which shows as closed in the photo, which is two and three quarters feet deep, floor to ceiling. That is roughly three hundred and seventeen cubic feet of open space."

"Yeah, I suppose that sounds about right."

"When you examined the small vestry room at the Cathedral of St. Matthew, you told us what you found. One item was a brass thurible that was supposed to have contained incense. Is that correct?"

"Yes, sir. It was hanging on a brass rack by some chains."

"Did you examine the contents of that thurible?"

"Well, we looked in. It was full of ashes."

"Did you have those ashes analyzed chemically?"

"No. We saw no need to do so."

"Did you look in any of the drawers or cupboards in that room?"

"Yeah, we looked in. There were a bunch of religious vestments, robes and things, in the tall closet, and some sashes or whatever they were in a top drawer, all different colors, and some tins in a second drawer."

"Tins? Tins of what?"

"We asked one of the priests. He said that the big one was the charcoal and the others were incense for the services."

"Were there other tins?"

"Yeah, all about the same size. More incense, I guess."

"You guess. Did you open the tins and examine them?"

"No. The priest told us what they were."

"So you did not open the tins. Is that your testimony?"

"Yeah."

"Lieutenant Clark, would you be surprised to learn that one of those tins contained moth balls, a product that contains naphthalene and paradichlorobenzene?"

"Yeah, if that was the case. The priest didn't say anything about moth balls."

"That *was* the case. We will present witnesses who will testify to these facts. Now, given that information, do you now think that analysis of the ash in the thurible might have been a wise investigation?"

"I suppose so."

"You suppose so. Lieutenant Clark, you testified that there was a table next to the chair in which Canon Packard's body was found, and on it was an ashtray with several cigarette butts in it. Is that correct?"

"Yes."

"Did any of the cigarettes appear to have been left unfinished, perhaps with a long extension of ash, as if it had burned for quite a while before being extinguished?"

"I don't recall. It might show up in the photos we took."

"Here is the photo that was entered in the first trial as evidence, marked Prosecution Exhibit 4. Would you examine that photo for us?"

"Yeah, oh, yeah, there is one of the cigarettes with a long ash on it."

"Could that ash indicate that the cigarette was still lighted and giving off fumes at the time that Canon Packard was suffocating?"

"Objection!" Harper shouted, jumping up from his table. "This calls for a medical conclusion that the policeman is unable to render."

"Sustained," said Judge Alvarez. "Please rephrase your question, Mr. Franklin."

"Yes, sir. Lieutenant Clark, in your investigation did you determine if there was still heat and smoke coming from the brass thurible that was hanging on the brass rack?"

"No."

"Did you seek any medical records for Canon Augustus Packard?"

"No, we had an autopsy report. It said he was asphyxiated."

"Is that the same as suffocating?"

"Yeah. About the same."

"Are there medical reasons why one might suffocate or be asphyxiated?"

"Objection!" Harper shouted again, and the Judge sustained again.

The courtroom was jammed with people who knew Morris or had heard about the case, and several reporters were present. There was a rustle of sound from the room, and Judge Alvarez banged his gavel. Franklin said, "That's all for now, Lieutenant, but I will reserve the right to recall you later."

Jim Harper next called Dr. Samuel Fleming, the Lockfield County Assistant Coroner to the stand, and again reviewed with him the information that he had presented in the first trial. On cross examination, Franklin again focused on the contents of the thurible, the cigarette smoke and the size of the room. "How much oxygen would burning charcoal and a lighted cigarette consume in a room with three hundred and seventeen cubic feet of air, Dr. Fleming?" he asked.

"I would need to study that issue before I could give an answer."

"That's fair enough, Dr. Fleming," Franklin replied. "But why was it not considered at the time of the first trial? Were you unaware of what was in the room?"

"No, I was with the crime lab staff when the body was removed, but I did not make any measurements."

"Did you consider any cause of death by asphyxiation other than someone smothering the deceased?"

"Well, we hadn't performed an autopsy yet, so no causes were considered at the time."

"What about later? You testified in the first trial that there was some discoloration in the victim's lungs, which you attributed to his smoking. Could there have been other causes for asphyxiation?"

"Such as?"

"Such as an allergic reaction or an asthma attack?"

"Yes, I suppose that would be a possibility. But we did not consider it."

"Why was it not considered, Dr. Fleming?"

"The police had a suspect, and there seemed to be enough evidence that he had murdered the old priest, so we didn't consider other factors. Perhaps we should have."

"Yes, perhaps you should have. Thank you, Dr. Fleming. That's all for now."

Everyone, from Judge Alvarez to the jury, were shocked when David Franklin asked the judge if he could call a rebuttal witness before it was the defense's turn to cross-examine. The judge agreed, and Franklin called the prosecuting attorney, Jim Harper, to the stand. Harper objected, but was overruled by the Judge, and was duly sworn in as a witness.

"Mr. Harper," Franklin began, "how long have you been a prosecuting attorney here in Lockfield County?"

"Eight years."

"And during those eight years how many murder cases have you prosecuted."

"We have about four a year. This isn't a high crime area, so there's not a lot of killing going on."

"In your investigation of a murder, do you ever investigate the victim as well as the suspects?"

"Sure. That's standard procedure."

"Did you investigate Canon Augustus Packard, after he was found dead?"

"Of course we did."

"Would you describe that investigation for us?"

"Well, we got his file from the cathedral head priest, Dean Williams. We visited Packard's apartment in town. We looked into the lawsuit that the Defendant, Morris, had filed against him, and things like that."

"Things like that," Franklin repeated. "And what did you find in the file that you obtained from Dean Williams?"

"I don't recall now."

"Your Honor, the Defense would like to have entered as Defense Exhibit One the file on Augustus Packard which was obtained by subpoena from the Cathedral of St. Mathew." The file was handed by the clerk to the judge, who looked it over, and handed it back to the clerk, who handed it to Franklin. "Mr. Harper, is this the file you examined?"

"It looks like it. Yes, there are my initials on the back."

"Would you please look through the file, and tell me what you found that might have related to your prosecution of John Morris?"

"We didn't see anything in there that we felt would help us."

"Did you advise me, as the defense counsel for John Morris, that you had this file?"

"I saw no reason. There was no evidence of importance in it."

"No? I have placed several orange tabs on some of the pages in the file. Would you please open the file and read those items to the jury?"

"Okay. Here's one. Some sort of memo from Dean Williams to Packard inquiring why he missed some service he was to conduct."

"Is there an answer to that?"

"Yes, the next page says that he had been sick and went to the doctor."

"What does it say, specifically?"

"It says, 'I apologize for missing the service, Dean William. I was suffering a respiratory problem of long standing, and had been at the doctor's office and forgot about the service, but I would not have been able to officiate anyway. Dr. Victor March will be able to confirm that I was sick.'"

"Did you contact Dr. Marsh?"

"No. So he was sick? So what?"

"'So what?' He says he had a respiratory problem 'of long standing.' A man suffocates who has had a respiratory problem, and you see no possible connection?"

"No, I don't."

"What else is in the file, Mr. Harper? What does the next tab show?"

"It appears to be an application to the Monastery of St. Philip in Michigan."

"Would you please read the twenty second line?"

"'Do you have any health problems?'"

"How did Augustus Packard answer that?"

"He said, 'No, except an occasional asthma attack.'"

"Do you know what asthma is, Mr. Harper?"

"It's some sort of breathing problem, I guess, but I object as I'm not a physician...."

"Don't worry, Mr. Harper, I'll not pursue the matter. We have a few doctors available – you had an opportunity to depose them, and chose not to – who will be able to advise us very well what bronchial asthma is, and will also testify that well over ten thousand deaths from it occur each year.

"They will also testify that incense, when burned as it presumably was in that thurible in the vestry of the Cathedral of St. Matthew – unless it was moth balls in that thurible – that incense smoke contains carbon monoxide, sulfur dioxide, nitrogen dioxide, ketones, aldehydes and other volatile organic compounds that can both trigger allergies and asthma.

"Your Honor, I wish to submit the report confirming those facts into evidence as Defense Exhibit Two." The clerk again handed a folder containing a report to the judge, who reviewed it, and handed it back to the clerk, who handed it to Franklin, who then handed it to Harper, giving him time to look it over.

"Now, Mr. Harper, do you want to reconsider your answer as to your not advising me, as John Morris's defense attorney, of what you had found in this file when you examined it?"

"No."

"Your witness, Mr. Harper."

The silence of the courtroom seemed to explode in a gasp. Franklin turned to the judge, and asked permission to approach the bench. Judge Alvarez agreed. "Your Honor, the Defense requests a directed verdict in the case of *Ohio v. Morris* of 'not guilty.' To continue this trial would be a waste of everyone's time. Further, your honor, the Defense wishes the record to show that the prosecuting attorney, Mr. Harper, withheld evidence in the first trial of John Morris that might have led to his exoneration at the time. Instead John Morris has spent the last four years in the Mansfield Reformatory for a crime of which he was totally innocent.

"Mr. Harper, please approach the bench." Harper left the witness chair, and stood beside Franklin. "Mr. Harper, do you have any real evidence at all, other than the circumstantial evidence that you have placed into evidence here, that John Morris did in fact murder Augustus Packard?"

"No, Your Honor."

"Then I declare that the evidence presented here today by the Defense exonerates John Morris, and hereby declare him innocent of the charges against him."

A cheer arose from the courtroom, and from the jury.

Chapter 14

May 18, 1964
The Fairchild Farm

Esther was walking in from the mail box at the road, sorting through some letters and envelopes that had been delivered as Richard Fairchild sat in the kitchen enjoying a cup of coffee on that Saturday morning.

"Goodness, I wonder what this is?" she said, looking at a square, narrow envelope. "The Richland County School Board. It's addressed to you."

Fairchild took the envelope and used a butter knife to slice it open. Inside was an invitation to a high school graduation.

"Who do we know in high school in Richland County?" Esther asked.

"Well, let's see what it says. 'You are cordially invited to attend the graduation of the Class of 1964 at the Mansfield Reformatory, Mansfield, Ohio, May 26, 1964, at 2 p.m. in the Reformatory Chapel. The speaker will be the valedictorian, Raymond Ingersol. RSVP Chaplain William Winters.' Well if that isn't a wonder!"

"Who is Raymond Ingersol?" Esther inquired.

"He's the guy who shot me in Greece, and then made a second attempt to shoot me out on the Lake. Weren't you with me at the trial, where he turned state's witness against the other two guys in that insurance fraud case and got life instead of the death penalty?"

"No, but I remember your telling me about it now. So he's graduating from high school at the prison?"

"I guess so. I'm the one who talked him into taking the high school program – he's a pretty smart guy."

"Are you going to go?"

"I wouldn't miss it. Go with me. You know Winters, and his wife will probably be there, too. Let's see. That's a Sunday. I think Dr. Boldt in preaching that week, so I should have the day off."

"We should get him a present. What would you get a man in prison? Gosh, he must be, what, around thirty?"

"Late twenties, I think. Hmm. Not much you can take into a prison. A good book, perhaps. I know! He's been to Greece. Let's get him a book on the history and scenery in Greece. It might give him some pleasant memories. I think I may have won a bet with him, but we never shook on the amount. I bet him he could finish high school – he'd dropped out at fifteen – and go on to college. Ohio State has a program there at the prison. He said that they didn't let lifers in, but I bet him that there was a chance for him if he would work for it. I'll give Bill Winters a call tomorrow and advise that we'll come down." Fairchild was still shaking his head as he drained his coffee and headed into his library with the invitation.

* * *

It was raining on May 26 as the Fairchild's station wagon entered the long driveway to the Reformatory, and pulled into the parking area. Esther and Richard both carried umbrellas and a plastic sack with a wrapped gift inside as they made their way to the reception room. The guard on duty recognized Fairchild, and, showing the invitation, said, "Welcome back, Professor. I suspect you know the way to the Chapel. There will be a guard on duty up there clearing the guests – mostly family and some of the Richland teachers – who are coming. By the way, I hear you had something to do with John Morris's release. We actually miss that guy."

"Yes, he didn't murder anyone and got a new trial that exonerated him. Next time I'm filling in for Bill Winters I'll tell you about it. But actually, I wasn't at his new trial. I had to work. I got all the details, however."

The Fairchilds climbed the wide staircase to the second floor. Another guard who also recognized Fairchild stood by the separate door to the chapel, where a crowd was gathering inside. "Dr. Fairchild, Chaplain Winters said to have you come to his office when you arrived. Just knock on the door."

"Richie! And Esther," the prison's chaplain exclaimed when he opened the door to Fairchild's knock. "I'm so glad you came. I can't believe what all has happened since you were here last year. Your new trial for John Morris left me without an assistant, and, as you suggested, I asked Ray Ingersol if he would be interested in the job. He agreed, and has turned out to be an excellent assistant. He'd already taken your advice about completing high school, and started with the classes that are offered here three nights a week. Got straight 'A's, and commendation from all his teachers. I can't tell you how pleased Sam West – he's the warden, Esther – is with Ingersol. He's become a real inspiration around here for many of the guys. He's even teaching them a Bible course.

"I read about Morris's re-trial, Richie," the chaplain continued. "One thing I didn't understand. Who wrote the note found in the vesting room?"

"That was a bit of an unsolved issue, but about a week after the trial Morris's attorney got a letter from a man in Kentucky, I forget his name, who said that his wife had received some counseling from the priest, Packard, and that she had been complimentary of him. They were not members of the Cathedral.

"She had some serious depression problems, and had committed suicide a few months after ceasing counseling with Packard, and he had notified Packard. The wife had signed up for the weekly Cathedral newsletter, and this man saw that Packard would be conducting the Sunday afternoon service, so he decided to go and hear him, since his wife had thought so highly of him. When he saw the title of the sermon he got angry, scribbled an unsigned note, stuck it in one of the offering plates and left. He didn't realize that Packard saw him as they did not know each other. He'd not heard about Packard's death or Morris's arrest, but saw a newspaper article on the re-trial."

"So all the loose ends were tied up," Winters replied. "I had been puzzled about that point. But enough jabber. The warden and I will be on the platform along with the principal of the high school and the head of the Richland County School Board. Richie, would you like to give the Invocation?"

"Thanks for the invitation, but I'd rather sit in the audience with Esther and listen, if it's all the same with you."

"Oh, that's okay. The thing will start in about twenty minutes. Let's go on in. There are going to be about three hundred people present, so the chapel is a bit packed. Wish I could get that many on Sundays."

"This is a Sunday!" Fairchild laughed.

"Well, yeah, but you know what I mean." Winters unlocked the side door to the chapel and the three of them entered. Richard and Esther found some chairs in the middle of the room and sat down. Another inmate was to their left, and a black woman who was probably the wife of a graduating inmate was to their right.

Shortly before two o'clock several men, including the warden, the chaplain, and Ray Ingersol, moved from a side aisle and took the seats on the platform where the altar usually was located. Warden West approached the podium and welcomed everyone to the graduation ceremony. He introduced the principal and school board director, and then signaled to an inmate who sat at the chapel organ. Two rows of chairs remained empty at the very front of the chapel, and as the chapel organist played the traditional Elgar march, *Pomp and Circumstances,* fourteen inmates marched in and sat in the two front rows. Bill Winters then stood up, and went to the podium.

"I, too, welcome you all to our chapel for this wonderful occasion. I know some of you are parents or wives or maybe just friends of the fifteen men we are honoring this afternoon. One of them has been my assistant for about half a year now, and he set up all these chairs for us after the morning service. He will tell you his story shortly. But first, let us ask the Lord's blessing on this event, each in his or her own way, with a moment of silence, and then the Lord's Prayer, if it is your custom."

The audience maintained silence, and then most of them joined in the prayer, with a smattering of "debts" or "trespasses" here and there, and a final Amen. Winters then turned toward Ray Ingersol, and said, "Ladies and gentlemen, I am proud to introduce to you Mr. Raymond Ingersol, our valedictorian."

Ray got up and went to the podium, and looked out over the audience, spotting Richard and Esther Fairchild in the middle of the group. "Thank you for coming. I want to say a special thank you to one man who is out there among you. He's a professor at Fremont College, and I'm standing up here because he made me a bet that I could stand up here and accomplish something. Dr. Fairchild, thank you for coming.

"Now for the rest of you who do not know me, I'm known around here as 'The Pirate.' That's because I am, or I was, a pirate! I robbed and stole, and I shot a homeless man to death under a bridge in Cleveland because someone paid me to do it. I later learned that the man I'd murdered would have been rich if I hadn't killed him. But I wasn't through with murder yet. Twice I tried to kill Richard Fairchild, that man sitting out there today. Damn, Fairchild, you're one hard sonofabitch to kill!" The audience laughed at that.

"Yes. Once I shot him when he was leading a group of his students in Greece. Another time I pirated a cabin cruiser that I'd tricked him into letting me on out in Lake Erie. I still don't know how in hell he survived that one!" The audience again laughed. "Then I shot a cop and bopped Fairchild with the gun barrel at the Cleveland Airport when my girl and I were trying to escape. Didn't kill him that time, either. I guess I wasn't a very good pirate after all!

"Of course I wound up here, and here I'll be for the rest of my life, I suppose. It was looking like a pretty grim life a year ago when Fairchild showed up. I thought he'd come to gloat, but instead I got challenged. He said I was smarter than I thought I was, and if I'd take the high school classes that the Richland County School offers out here, I could graduate, and maybe go to college. Ohio State offers classes here, but not to lifers on a murder one sentence like me. But Fairchild said, 'don't be too sure.'

"Well, for the first time in my dumb life, I took some advice, and signed up for the high school. Then I got a prison job working with Chaplain Winters, and that was better than hammering out license plates down in the foundry. I did my studying in the library. History, mathematics, government, literature, geography, all the classes I could take. It opened a new world I didn't know was there. I took all the tests, and I guess I must have passed them all, because they said I was their best student. Imagine! Me, the Pirate! A student!

"Well, the Holy Joe here, as we inmates refer to Chaplain Winters, got to me, and he talked to Warden West, and they talked to the guys at Ohio State who teach here, and now I'm going to get to take those classes too. All because of that bet I made with the Professor out there. Fairchild, you won. Why, the Holy Joe here even has me teaching a Bible course once a week. My Aunt Sully is sitting out there, too. Stand up, Aunt Sully." An elderly woman in the back of the chapel stood up, and everyone looked at her.

"See, I thought those Bible stories about miracles her preacher was always telling were fairy tales. I listened, but I didn't believe them. Maybe they are just fairy tales, but sometimes even fairy tales have a bit of truth in them. That's what I've learned in the last year. And that I'm standing up here and not down in my cell this afternoon is a miracle, one I never thought could occur. So thank you all, those of you who were my teachers, my fellow Richland County students, Warden West, Chaplain Winters, and, damn it, Fairchild, I owe you twenty bucks! Will you take an IOU until I get my college degree?"

Ingersol sat down, and everyone applauded. Then the principal started handing out diplomas to the graduates as they filed in front of the audience. The last one was Ingersol's. "And Raymond Ingersol. Congratulations, Ray. You were one heck of a pirate, but a much better scholar. Good luck in your future."

Fire & Ice

Author's Note: This is a work of fiction; while there is a NASA facility at the former Plum Brook Arsenal near Sandusky, Ohio, where a small reactor was once in operation, the events and persons in this story are entirely from the author's imagination. There is no Fremont College in Ohio.

Chapter 1

September 28, 1968
Staten Island, New York

"... and my conclusion is that the fire was from an electrical spark igniting a gas leak, and not incendiary." Lieutenant Jim Roberts, FDNY, sat at his desk in his Staten Island office finishing the report on an Island fire on which he had just completed his investigation. Although the fire had initially been suspicious as the homeowner was "out of town" and had taken a number of valuable possessions and his two dogs with him, the cause of the fire was traced to a leak in a gas line that obviously had not been caused by the owner.

Jim leaned back, his hands behind his head, and reviewed in his mind what lay ahead for the next seven weeks before he could retire after twenty years with the City and return to Erie County, Ohio, moving into his parents' old farmhouse on Mason Road now that they were both deceased. Neither Jim's remaining brother, Jack, nor his sister, Ellen, had wanted the farm, and had moved to other cities over the past two decades. James Roberts, Senior, had given up actively farming the 200 acres about five years before Jim's mother, Sarah, had died, and now that James was also deceased, no one was living in the old New England-style farmhouse.
Jim's auburn-haired wife, Jayne, was looking forward to the move. She, too, had grown up on a farm. Their small apartment on Staten Island was cramped, expensive, and overlooked industrial docks – the best Jim had been able to afford on his salary as a fire inspector. Now that Jimmy had graduated from Bowling Green University, married and was living in Toledo, there was no reason for the Roberts to stay in New York City.

But it had been an adventure. When Jim had graduated from Milan Canal High in Huron in 1941 he had elected to give up working on his father's farm and had joined the Navy, barely six months before Pearl Harbor. After training at Great Lakes Naval Base north of Chicago he had been assigned to the Pacific fleet as a ship's fireman, and got his baptism of fire on that fateful Sunday, December 7, when the destroyer on which he was stationed took a direct hit from a Japanese bomb, exploding the ammunition below one of the turret guns, setting the ship ablaze. Jim and his fellow firemen had extinguished the fire, saving the ship, and it had survived the remaining five years of the war, although frequently under attack.

Jim had returned briefly to the farm after the war, but it was his younger brother, Bill, who really wanted to be a dairy farmer, and the prospect of repeating all the chores he had done as a kid did not suit his need for excitement. He had also been able to continue his education on the G.I. Bill, obtaining a degree in chemistry and physics at near-by Fremont College, commuting from the farm. After marrying Jayne, who had also attended Fremont, Jim and Jayne moved to New York City. With his degree and experience in the Navy, he got a job with "New York's Finest," being assigned at various times in all of the boroughs, and eventually earning a Master's Degree in Fire Science and Chemistry at Rutgers University.

Jim had applied for the job of arson investigator, having no desire to be a chief or higher ranking officer, and was glad he had made that decision as he enjoyed the investigations and his law enforcement status. Now was an opportunity to retire, even though he was still young, and sustain himself on his pension until he found something to do in Ohio that would suit his taste, along with what he might do with the farm. All the livestock had been sold when Bill had been killed in an auto accident and James, Senior, had continued farming only with a few cash crops of hay, corn and soybeans.

Jim stood up, stretching his six foot two lean body with his arms above his head, and looked at his watch. It was just a little over five minutes past noon, and Jim thought about perhaps going home for lunch. In his dark blue uniform his brown hair and eyes kept him looking youthful. The office, which sat just above the fireboat dock, faced toward Manhattan's lower side from the New Brighton area of Staten Island. As Jim gazed out over New York Harbor he saw a flash in one of the Wall Street area highrise office buildings. Lower Manhattan was part of his territory, along with the harbor, and within what seemed like seconds the bells and horn on the radio were signaling units that were to respond to the fire at 34 Water Street. Jim's bell was included, and he reached for his round white lieutenant's cap and raced down the dock to the fire boat that was already starting its engine to take him across the harbor.

Marine 2 crossed the misty harbor and quickly docked at Pier A at the northern edge of Battery Park. A red fire department battalion car was waiting, and a fire cadet rushed Jim toward the Wall Street business area with siren blaring and red flashers opening the way through traffic, until they reached Beaver and Pearl, which was entirely blocked by fire trucks. While Jim had been crossing the harbor a second and third alarm had sounded, and fire equipment, pumpers, ladder trucks and chiefs' cars were all over the streets. Jim thanked the cadet, who had said his name was Charles Young, and started walking toward what turned out to be a twenty-story building built in the early 1900s. Flames were shooting from some of the upper floors, and Jim quickly found Battalion Chief Brad Rogers, who brought him up-to-date on the situation.

"It's an older building, Jim, and was scheduled for demolition in a few months. A handful of businesses remained, however," Chief Rogers explained. "The building had originally been fitted with natural gas, but that had supposedly been shut off around 1938, although some of the original gas lines were still in place. The explosion apparently was caused by gas, as far as the initial responders can tell – on the seventeenth floor. We shut off the gas main here on the street," he said, pointing to a manhole cover lying beside an open hole. "One file clerk was in the back room, which they used as a lunch room, when the explosion occurred. She was killed, and the guys had a hell of a time getting her body out, as the flames were spreading upward. I'd suspect this one is going to be a total loss.

"Fortuitous, if the building was to be torn down anyway," Jim replied. "What kind of business was using the offices where the explosion occurred, Brad?"

"Near as we can tell from the directory and what was on the door, some sort of finance and insurance company. There are a lot of insurance companies in this area, being so close to Wall Street. We got the elevator operating up to the fourteenth floor, but you're going to have to hoof it up the stairs from there, and it's pretty smoky. Get one of the guys to give you a SCBA mask and tank. The fire's still out of control on the upper floors, and all but one was vacant, and they managed to make it down the stairs before the fire extended. A couple of the other women in the office where the explosion occurred were injured in the blast and flames and have been transported to the hospital. The other chief, Brannigan, has their names and addresses."

Leaving the cadet, Charles, to watch the action, Jim walked over to a near-by ladder truck and requested turn-out gear, a ceiling pike and a breathing device. After donning the heavy tan and yellow fire coat and helmet, he strapped the tank to his back, but did not turn it on until he had entered the building and taken the elevator, which was being operated by a fireman, to the fourteenth floor. Quickly finding the stairway, he climbed to the seventeenth floor, turned on the oxygen and placed the mask over his nose and face. While Jim did wear glasses for reading, he had good vision otherwise, so the mask did not disturb his vision.

Jim could easily see where the fire had been, as black soot completely surrounded the door, which was now hanging from one hinge. He pulled a note pad from his uniform pocket and examined the door. "Manhattan Insurance & Finance Company" was painted on it. Jim entered and surveyed the smoky mess inside the offices, which consisted of a reception area, a larger area where four desks and typewriters sat, apparently used by the clerks or secretaries, a small room jammed with metal file cabinets, several other small offices that appeared empty, an open room with the blown-out windows through another door to an inner office that had been locked, although the firemen had hacked it open to check for flames. It held a large desk, a few chairs, including a swivel executive chair, and several file cabinets. Jim went to the desk, which had only a lamp and a leather desk pad and calendar on it, and tried the drawers. They were all locked. He then tried the file cabinet drawers, but these also were locked.

Jim then moved to the break room where the explosion had occurred. He found a large hole in the floor below the windows, definitely showing blast evidence. He picked up several larger slivers of the wooden floor that had been broken in the blast, and placed them in a plastic evidence bag he carried in his uniform. Then he removed a flash camera from a case on his equipment belt and began taking pictures of the hole and the rest of the office, including the ceiling above the blast area and the blast hole. One factor that drew his attention was the direction of the shattered and burned wood around the blast hole: it all bent upward, indicating that the blast had come from below. He then started to collect scrapings of the soot and damaged wall area, also placing these in a plastic bag for later chemical analysis.

Jim saw, next to the burned hole in the floor, several charred boxes that appeared to have contained files. With a ruler he found on one of the secretarial desks he poked through the charred remains, but most of the files were burned beyond any recognition. Only one, at the far end of the box, remained fairly unburned, and this Jim fished out and found a larger plastic bag to put it in. He could tell from the pattern on the floor where the woman who had been killed in the blast had been found and dragged out of the room. The room contained a table, some chairs, and as counter with what was left of a coffee maker and a small refrigerator on it. In a cupboard were some cans of coffee, filters and various other items one would expect in a break room, and in the small refrigerator, a couple of paper bags, apparently employees' lunches.

Knowing that there was not much more he could do immediately until he spoke with whomever the occupant of the executive office might be, getting permission – or a subpoena – to inspect the records, Jim left the office and descended the stairs to the sixteenth floor, moving to the office that would have been directly beneath the blast hole. The door had been smashed open, but Jim anticipated that it was the firemen who had been checking to see where the blast had originated. It was a large vacant office. Jim moved to the back wall that corresponded with the break room above, and again took photos of the ceiling, the blasted out windows and debris on the floor. There was quite a bit of debris, and he selected several pieces, placing them in plastic bags, and writing "16th Fl" with a black marker on it. He noted that the edges of the hole in the ceiling bent downward.

Rummaging around in the rooms, he found an old chair, and moved it to the hole in the ceiling. Climbing on it, he could barely see into the crawlspace between the floors, and used his camera to take a number of photos of the interior of the crawl space and the hole above it where the blast had occurred. There were a number of wires – the building's electrical system, telephone and a few other wires – air ducts and a broken lead pipe, which bent upward toward the hole in the seventeenth floor above it. This was apparently the old gas line, and he could see where the blast had broken the pipe at a joint where the pipe bent.

Again he swept some of the debris under the pipe into a plastic bag, marking it "blast area." Straining upward on the chair Jim could see how some wires stretched toward the center of the building below an air duct. He poked away some of the ceiling a few feet to the side of the blast hole with the ceiling pike until his tool touched something that was loose.

Climbing down, Jim moved the chair a few feet to where he thought the thing he had touched might be, and using the ceiling pike, pulled down enough of the ceiling to get his head close to the space between the ceiling and the floor above. With his flashlight he peered into the gaping hole and saw what looked like a telephone. One wire ran toward the blast area, and the other appeared to be spliced into other telephone cables in the ceiling area. He took a number of flash photos of the telephone and the wires, but left them for further inspection by a police crime lab technician.

Knowing that there was not much more he could do at the time, he went back down to the fourteenth floor and took the elevator to the lobby. Chief Rogers was standing with Captain Brannigan, a big Irishman, well known in the Department. Brannigan was talking with an older man in overalls, and Jim went over to them to see if this was the building custodian. "Jim," Brannigan said, "this is Sam Parker, the building custodian. He tells me the gas has been shut off since the 1920s, and he can't figure out how there could have been a gas explosion on the 17th floor."

"Can we get to where the old gas line entered the building?" Jim asked, sliding the SCBA gear from his back, sliding off the tan coat with yellow stripes on it and replacing the heavy helmet with his lieutenant's cap.

"Well, its way down in the bowels of this place, but if yah don't mind getting' that white hat o' yours a bit dirty, I can get you there," Parker replied.

"Keep that turn-out coat from the truck, Jim, and the helmet. I'll hold your hat," Brannigan ordered, and Jim went back to the nearby truck to return the SCBA gear, then returned to the building. The old custodian, who must have been about sixty, led Jim to a doorway and stairs leading to the basement. Both held flashlights as the power to the building had been cut off, and from the basement the custodian led Jim down yet another stairway, amongst an array of pipes and conduit, to a remote, cluttered part of the sub-basement where pipes entered from below the street level.

"This one here's the gas line," Parker said, and both flashlights focused on it. "The valve is over here," the custodian said, leading Jim to a spot about a yard away, but the valve was up about nine feet above their heads.

"Look here!" Parker exclaimed "Someone's moved this box right below the valve." Jim climbed up on the box and reached for the valve.

"It's loose! Someone must have opened it."

"Would have been a hell of a job," Parker said. "That valve was tight as a drum. Had to check it every few years when the building when the building was inspected."

"Well, it's loose now," Jim replied, getting out his camera and taking several flash photos of the valve, including a close-up. "I can see some marks on it – like someone used a big wrench to open it."

"But why?" Parker asked. "Ain't been no gas heat or light in this buildin' since the Twenties."

"'Why' is exactly the question, Parker. In the ceiling between the sixteenth and seventeenth floors it looks like someone intentionally bent a lead pipe upward, right where it broke, and that was probably the gas line right below where the explosion was."

"Ahh, hell!" the old custodian exclaimed. "You tellin' me this weren't no accident?"

"That's the way it is looking right now. Who would have known about this location down here where the old gas line came in?"

"None o' the tenants, far as I know. Ain't many left now, mostly on those upper floors."

"Who owns the building?"

"The City. The owners lost it for back taxes about five years ago. It's supposed to be demolished as soon as the final leases run out."

"So who employs you, Sam?"

"The City. When they took it over, I'd been here so long they just kept me on. I'm lookin' forward to the thing goin' down so's I can retire."

"Well, that may be sooner than later now, I'd bet. We both work for the City, and I'm about to retire too! But I'll have to figure this mess out first, though," Jim said as they headed back to the main floor entrance.

"Find anything?" Captain Brannigan asked as they got back to the entrance and Jim unloaded the turn-out coat and helmet.

"Yes, mark it 'highly suspicious,' as I'm pretty sure someone did this deliberately."

"The owners?"

"Not hardly! It's owned by the City – taken for back taxes five or six years ago. But somebody turned on the gas and set some sort of detonator in the area between the sixteenth and seventeenth floor, and, I suspect, set it off with a phone call."

"Huh!"

"We're going to need the help of the police on this one, Captain Brannigan, maybe the federal ATF guys, too. This was obviously an intentional act. If the call was placed to the phone that detonated the blast at a time when someone knew there would be people in that break room where the explosion occurred, then I'd even guess that we're looking at pre-meditated murder. So where were the injured employees taken?" Jim asked.

"Beekman, I think. That's the closest."

"There's not much more I can do here for now, Chief, so I think I'll go see if I can find those employees. Do you have their names?"

"Lieutenant Carter has them. He's just outside directing men." Jim had left his SCBA gear and evidence bags in the lobby and got those, returning the SCBA gear and pike to the truck from which he had borrowed it, and the turn-out gear and helmet to the other truck, then spotted Carter on the sidewalk partway down Water Street talking to the cadet, Charles.

"Hi, Jim," Bob Carter, a tall black man, called as Jim approached. "Big enough mess for you until you cash out, short-timer?"

"Big enough, I'm afraid. Looks intentional. Understand you have the names of the deceased and the two employees who were taken to Beekman."

"Yep, here they are," Carter replied, writing three names and addresses on a note pad. "Weisnewski's got some bad burns, and Jacoby got a broken leg in the blast. Threw her clear across the room, Weisnewski said. Jacoby was too much in pain to talk, and both were upset that Markowitz, Judy Markowitz, was killed. If this was arson, then it's big time stuff."

"Big time is right," Jim replied. "What information do you have on this Manhattan Insurance and Finance outfit?"

"Not much. Weisnewski said the guy who runs it was away in Connecticut today. She didn't have his address, but his name is Lester Minsk. Lives somewhere on the Upper East Side, the ritzy area, she said. She didn't know the address."

"Did she know where he was going in Connecticut?"

"No, but she said it was to one of their reinsurers – apparently insurance companies lay off part of their risk to other insurers or something. Said it was probably Travelers, Aetna or maybe The Hartford – they're all headquartered in Hartford."

"Huh, well, thanks, Bob. Now, I'm glad that cadet that brought me over here stuck around," Jim said as he and Charles started back to where the red fire department officer's car had been parked.

"Beekman is up around Fulton," Jim said, and the cadet driver nodded, replying that he'd been there a couple of times and knew where it was.

* * *

Beekman Downtown Hospital was an old institution in Lower Manhattan that served the financial district, but was falling on hard times, given its 19th century origins. The cadet driver was disappointed that Jim didn't want to arrive with the siren and lights going, but found a parking spot outside the Emergency Room to wait. Jim told him to leave the car and come in with him, and to take notes.

Their FDNY uniforms got attention at the reception desk, and the clerk directed them to a Dr. Horowitz in a small office down the hall. Horowitz, in his white coat, thick glasses and black bushy hair, looked the part of a trauma surgeon. He glanced up from his paperwork as Jim knocked on the door. "About those two brought from the explosion, I bet," he asked.

"Right. Any chance of talking with them?"

"Weisnewski's in surgery for her burns, both legs and one arm with third degrees. She'll need skin grafts. Damned painful stuff, I'm afraid," Horowitz said, shaking his head. "Judy Jacoby has a compound fracture of her left femur. She's in surgery, too. I'd say it will be tomorrow before you can talk to either. They'll be here quite a while."

"That's too bad, their injuries, I mean. But thank you, Dr. Horowitz. I guess we'll go look for their boss instead."

"Good luck. The Jacoby girl said he'd been gone all week. To Hartford, Connecticut, she said."

"We'll find him, somewhere, I guess. Thanks again," Jim said, turning to the door with the cadet right behind him. "Charles, let's stop by the reception and see what else we can find out."

The receptionist referred the two firemen to the business office. An older woman with glasses set in almond-shaped frames was seated behind a desk, looking over some papers as Jim knocked on her door. She looked up and motioned them to some chairs in front of her desk. "Inquiring about those two girls brought in from the explosion?" she asked.

"Yes, Weisnewski and Jacoby. I already have their addresses, Miss Jamison," Jim answered, reading the name board on her desk.

"It's Mrs. But this is going to get interesting, I'm afraid. The Jacoby girl said she was certain that their workers compensation insurer was New

York Industrial. We deal with them all the time when it's an employment-related injury, but when I called, about a half an hour ago, they told me that the policy on Manhattan Insurance and Finance had been cancelled three weeks ago when their check bounced and the insured, a Lester Minsk, gave them some run-around, but never made the payment."

"Do they have other insurance?"

"That's what I'm checking. They both had Blue Cross group insurance cards, but I've not confirmed that those are valid yet. It may take a while. Is there some place I can call you to let you know?"

"Sure, here's my card," Jim said, handing her a card from his wallet. "But I'll be back tomorrow to talk with Jacoby, at least, and Weisnewski, if she's able, so I'll stop back here if you are on duty tomorrow."

"Paah! I'm *always* on duty, or so it seems! But, yes, I'll be here tomorrow," Mrs. Jamison replied. Jim and Charles thanked her and left the office. Back in the car Jim radioed the department headquarters for an address check on Lester Minsk, and in a few minutes the two were headed up Roosevelt Drive toward Midtown.

The Carson Arms Apartments was a thirty story building on the east side of Second Avenue, obviously a plush place with a canopy to the street and a liveried doorman. Charles stopped the car in a spot with a sign, "loading zone," knowing that no one would bother the FDNY officers' car. Jim told Charles to come with him, and they approached the doorman. "Do you know a Lester Minsk?" Jim asked him.

"Yeah, he moved out a week or so ago," the doorman answered, in a Brooklyn accent.

"Moved out? You mean furnishings and all?"

"Quite a bit. I understand some of his stuff is still up dare, but he had a lot of boxes dat some guy in a truck picked up last Saturday. Plus furniture outfits came tah claim stuff."

"Did he say where he was going?"

"Not to me. Yah might ask deh manager. His office is just off dah lobby. Should be dare, he don't go tah lunch 'til latah."

Easily finding the manager's office, Jim looked in and inquired if the man at the desk was the manager. "Yeah, what'd yah need? I'm Joe Lozano. I think all our fire stuff is up-to-date, though."

"No," Jim replied, "it's not about fire codes. We're looking for a Lester Minsk."

"Ha! You, and half of New York City, I understand. He moved out last week, three months behind in his rent, and two furniture companies have already been here to reclaim their stuff. What do you want him for?"

"His business had an explosion this morning."

"You mean that one down by Wall Street? Heard about that on the news. So that was Minsk's place?"

"Did he leave a forwarding address, Mr. Lozano?"

"Not even a clue as to where he was going. His mail's been piling up, and I told the Post Office to just return it all to the senders. But people have been phoning, too, looking for him. Apparently they were expecting monthly checks or something, and didn't get them."

"Really! It seems a bit fishy."

"Yeah, his place was the Fulton Fish Market, if you ask me. He had a lot of luxurious stuff up there, but the place is a mess now. I'm going to have to hire a crew to clean it out. Good thing he paid a healthy deposit."

"May we see his apartment?"

"Yeah, sure. Let me get the pass key," Lozano said, reaching into a drawer in his desk. He got up and led the two firemen back into the lobby to a set of three elevators, and in silence they rode up to the seventh floor. Lozano led them down the hall to a door marked 7-D, unlocked the door, and stepped back. There was sufficient light from the windows to show that the apartment was in disarray, a few pieces of furniture here and there, some boxes with linens and towels in them, and in the bedroom a king-sized bed stripped to the mattress. In the bathroom the medicine cabinet was empty, and in the kitchen there was only a tin of coffee and a couple of boxes of crackers and cereal in the cupboards. The refrigerator was running, but was empty except for two cans of beer.

In what might have been an office there were some cartons, but they were empty. Jim took a few photos, looked around for some potentially hidden spots, and sighed. "Not much here to go on. Thanks for letting us in."

Chapter 2

Jim sat in the office of Florian Madeira, Assistant District Attorney of the State of New York. Madeira was sharing information from a file on his desk. "We think he was operating some sort of Ponzi scheme, getting new investors to put in money, and using that money to pay insurance claims and monthly benefits to the earlier investors. That search warrant we served on his office on Water Street turned up a big zero. Both the desk and the file cabinets were empty. The crime scene team got the telephone, and lifted some good prints off it; they matched those we had from Minsk's apartment. He had no record here, but the FBI said there was a record of a "Rudy Minsk" in Detroit, and we think it may be the same guy."

"Weisnewski said she and Judy were on the phone when the explosion occurred. Normally they would have been in the break room with Hamilton, the girl that was killed, so it looks like pre-meditated First Degree to me. What leads do you have on Minsk?" Jim asked.

"The contents of that partially burned file you rescued showed that he had no reinsurance on the insurance policies he was selling, so the chances that he was in Hartford that morning are practically none," Madeira replied. "A check of the airlines shows that a man traveling with an American passport in the name of Minsk flew to Caracas, Venezuela at 4:30 the afternoon of September 28, on Re-al Airlines Flight 809 from Miami, arriving about 10:20 that evening. We contacted the Venezuelan police and they verified that he arrived and checked through customs, but have no further information on his location. I think he probably flew on from there to God knows where, as there are a number of international flights from Caracas.

"We did get the Miami police to check the Miami Airport phone records, and at the time of the explosion, 12:07 p.m., there was a call placed to the number that corresponded to that telephone between the two floors," Madeira continued. "The electrical charge that would normally have rang the telephone instead set off the dynamite beneath that broken pipe, igniting the gas that had accumulated beneath the break room floor in the explosion. I'm surprised the three women hadn't noticed the smell of gas by then."

"But it does suggest that they had some knowledge of Minsk's activities, although they really did think he was going to see reinsurers in Hartford," Jim suggested.

"Just as soon as Weisnewski and Jacoby get out of the hospital we're going to depose them and find out just what they did know. It had to be enough that Minsk wanted them dead."

"Will the feds take over the case now that the federal explosives and the FBI guys are involved and Minsk has skipped?"

"New York will maintain the arrest warrant for arson and murder, but it will have to be the feds that go after Minsk, if they can find him. My suspicion is that he had millions stashed away on some off-shore island – maybe somewhere near Caracas – and will change his name and disappear. Hell, he might even end up back here in the U.S. under some other name. If that Rudy Minsk in Detroit was him, or even a relative, he may have an incentive to come back. We're having a hellova time getting a photo of him. I couldn't recognize anybody from that passport photo the State Department sent us."

"What about his state insurance license? Or the banking authorities?" Jim asked.

"His license to sell insurance policies expired a couple of months ago. The state is behind on their license enforcement and hadn't gotten around to his case yet, but they had a whole file full of complaints against him. So did the banking commission. The SEC was about to subpoena him to come in and explain his investments, they had so many complaints. Now they're just advising those who call that they're investigating, but not to get their hopes up. It's a real mess, Jim."

"Is there anything my department can to do help, Flo?"

"Do you speak Spanish? You could always go down to Venezuela and look for him," the D.A. asked, jokingly.

"No, I'd not be much help there. I would like to be in on the depositions of the two survivors, however, if you'll keep me posted. The arson is FD business, even if the state gets the murder angle. If either of them knew what Minsk was doing, they could be accomplices."

"Yeah, we thought of that. That's probably why he wanted rid of them. But I'll keep you posted."

"Thanks, Flo. I'll be retiring before Thanksgiving, moving back to Ohio, but I'd like to get the Department's end of this wrapped up by then."

"I heard you were going to hang up your fire hat, Jim. You really want to do that? Look at all the excitement you'll be missing."

"If you think crawling through soot and cinders is exciting, you've got an odd sense of excitement," Jim laughed. "No, Jayne and I are anxious to get home. We're both from there, and since Staten Island has gone Hispanic lately, at least in our part, well, I really do need to learn Spanish! If I'd been staying, the Department would have required me to learn it."

* * *

The depositions were taken at the hospital a few days later. Weisnewski was a relatively new employee of Manhattan Insurance, and knew very little about its operations. She had been hired primarily to handle the growing number of phone calls from clients seeking payments, and she herself had not yet received her first paycheck, which she had hoped to get the day of the explosion. As she was still heavily medicated, her words were a bit hard to understand.

Judy Jacoby had worked for Manhattan Insurance for about half a year. She was primarily a receptionist, and in charge of putting any official posters on the bulletin board, which is why she had known who the workers compensation insurer was supposed to be. She said that Sheila Hamilton had been the one that knew the most about Minsk's operations, as she was pretty much the office manager. Jacoby and Weisnewski were instructed by Minsk to tell callers who inquired about checks that there was a problem at the bank, and that their checks would be issued in a few days. But so many calls were coming in that both she and Weisnewski had to take phone calls when they usually would have been in the break room for lunch. Jacoby said that it was Sheila who had told them that Minsk was going to Hartford to meet with reinsurers, and that they were the reason the checks were delayed.

Neither Jacoby nor Weisnewski knew anything at all about either the insurance or the finance business that Minsk was running. Hamilton had told her that a year ago there was a full staff of workers sending out policies or contracts and handling claims, but they had all been terminated before Jacoby was hired. Minsk had said that all that work had been contracted to another company. She did recall that Minsk had mentioned that his attorney was a Brad Nichols, but when the D.A. had checked, there was no such attorney in New York. There was such an attorney in Detroit, however.

By Mid-November Jim Roberts had completed his reports for his successor, a young black lieutenant named Bill Washington, and classified the file on the Manhattan Insurance & Finance Company as "pending." It was dependent, alright, on finding Minsk, on whom an arrest warrant for arson and murder had now been filed. Jim rejected a retirement party by the Department, and agreed that, if Minsk was ever found, he would be happy to come back to testify at his trial. As Jim had constantly been on call as an arson investigator, he'd been assigned a red FDNY officers' car for his use on the island. This he gladly turned over to the new lieutenant, along with his small office by the fire boat dock, and then packed the Roberts' Ford for the trip home.

As snow was predicted across Northern New York before Thanksgiving Jim and Jayne decided to take the New Jersey, Pennsylvania and Ohio Turnpikes back to the farm in Milan Township. The moving van had picked up what furniture and other property they were sending home two days before the holiday, and the Roberts arrived the day ahead of the van, spending the night in a motel.

Jayne was busy sorting out where china, linens, clothes and silverware would go, and Jim was helping re-arrange the furniture to Jayne's plan. They had arranged to have their mail transferred, and there was a stack of it that the mailman brought to the door the Monday after they had moved in. After that, they would have to walk down to the mailbox at the road Jayne had always loved the farmhouse, which she had known from when she and Jim had dated prior to his going in the Navy, and had a good idea where she wanted things to be placed. She planned to keep some of Jim's parents' furniture, including a super-sized dinner table intended to feed both family and farm hands.

Among the mail, a few bills, flyers and some "welcome home" letters from friends in Ohio was a folder from the Fremont College Alumni Association. "Next weekend is Home Coming," Jim read aloud from the folder. The football team is playing Bowling Green State University. I'll bet Jimmy will want to attend that game. Let's give Suzie and him a call and see if they'll join us Saturday."

"Okay. It's not much of a drive from their place in Toledo, so let's make dinner reservations at the hotel in Fremont and have a family reunion. Gosh, it has been over a year since they were up in New York, and I'll bet Trice is getting bigger all the time." Jim and Suzie had named their son James IV, but as the current third James the family nicknamed him "Trice."

Plans made, Jim called ahead for reserved tickets to the game. The early December Saturday was cold, but clear, and wearing all their warmest clothes Jim and Jayne started off for the stadium on the Fremont College campus. Jimmy and Suzie, with a well-wrapped Trice, now four years old, met them at the gate, and they found their seats on the Fremont side, somewhat beyond the 25 yard marker. "I ought to be on the other side, yelling over at you guys how you're going to lose," Jimmy said. "How about a bet, Dad?"

"I've not been following the Fremont team for a while so I don't know how good they are – hopefully better than they used to be. But, yes, I'll risk a ten spot on them." Father and son shook hands, and started up the concrete steps to the row where their seats were. It put them next to another bundled-up couple, a man younger than Jim but older than a student, and a beautiful blond, green-eyed girl wrapped in a parka.

"Alumni?" the man asked Jayne.

"Yes, both Jim and I graduated from Fremont in '48, then Jim went with the Fire Department in New York. Our son, Jimmy, went to Bowling Green, so he expects them to win. Are you alumni, too?" Jayne asked.

"I'm not, but Sally is," the man said, turning to his blond wife. "Class of 1961. I'm a professor here, and Sally is the Department's secretary."

"Oh, a professor?" Jayne replied, turning to introduce Jim, Jimmy and his family. "In what department?"

"Religion. Dr. Richard Fairchild is the head of the department. I'm Bob Merriam."

"Religion?" Jim repeated. "Is Dr. Boldt still the chaplain?"

"Yes, and Richie Fairchild is Assistant Chaplain. In fact, he's holding the chapel services tomorrow morning. He's a great preacher and scholar. I'm sure you'll enjoy the service. Sally still sings in the chapel choir, so we'll have to be there, rain or shine. Do plan to come."

"Thank you for the invitation, Professor ...."

"Bob. No formalities allowed on weekends!"

"Bob. What do you think, Jayne, for old times? We were married by Dr. Boldt in the Fremont Chapel."

"So were Sally and I," Bob said. "I don't remember much about it as I was too scared to death! When the organist turned on those trumpets I about jumped out of my skin!"

"Yeah, I was pretty shook too. I seem to recall reading in the Alumni News that your department does summer trips with upper-class students. Are you involved in that, too?"

"I'm afraid so. Sally is in charge of all the arrangements, and Richie and I take turns doing the trips. Last summer we were in Israel. Jayne, did I hear you say that Jim was with the New York Fire Department?"

"Yes, he just retired as a Lieutenant. He was an arson investigator. He inherited the family farm on Mason Road in Milan, so we'll be doing some farming, I guess."

"Oh, I'll need some sort of job as well. I've not done farm work since I was a kid."

"We have a great Ag Department here. Maybe they can give you some tips on getting started. But as a fireman, there should be lots of opportunities. If I see Rayland Durrand, the head of the Physics Department here today I'll introduce you to him. He may have some ideas for a job. If he's not here, and he may not be as his wife is not a football fan, visit him in his office in the Science Building next week, and I'm sure he'll be glad to help. You know where the Science Building is?"

"Sure. I was a chemistry major, and got a Masters in it at Rutgers, courtesy of the FDNY. The old red brick building with the observatory on it."

"Same place." By this time Sally had moved next to Jayne and Suzie, and they were deep in some discussion. Jim took her seat next to Bob as the game started to loud cheering and a stand-up for the National Anthem played by the Fremont Marching Band and the Fremont College ROTC Color Guard flag presentation.

Jimmy won his $10 as Bowling Green beat Fremont by ten points. Jim invited Bob and Sally to join his son's family and Jayne at the hotel for dinner, and they agreed. After Jimmy, Suzie and Trice headed back to Toledo the Merriams invited Jim and Jayne to their home in Fremont, near the Hayes Presidential House, Spiegel Grove, for coffee. Having no better place to go, the Roberts agreed, and it was after midnight when they finally started down the highway toward Milan.

Much of the conversation had been about the Merriam's boss, Richard Fairchild, and how he had been involved in so many complex mysteries. It had been more than a year after the trip into East Germany that Bob and Sally had finally learned that Richie had known about the defections that occurred on the stage of the Opera House at Bayreuth, when both General Kurt Kahler of the East German Army and the Halle University Physics Professor, Hilda von Werdau, had both been given CIA's assistance. Hilda was now also a professor at Fremont, married to the Choral Director, Dr. Ross Johnson. Then Bob told about how the college had acquired both an island in Lake Erie and a big yacht due to Fairchild's escapades, and the Roberts were anxious to meet this famous professor who solved mysteries as a hobby.

"I'll bet he could help the New York Attorney General's office find Lester Minsk," Jim said, explaining, "He's the guy who set up an explosion to kill his employees with a phone call from Miami, blowing up his office on the seventeenth floor of a Wall Street area building. The whole building is now being torn down."

"How did he do that?" Sally asked.

"Well, he got a gas leak started in this old office building where the gas had been shut off since the 1920s, and set a bomb below the employee's break room wired to a telephone. He expected all of his employees to be in the break room when he called the number from the Miami Airport, and the call to the phone inside the floor below set off the bomb. Only one employee, the one who may have known about a Ponzi scheme he was running, was killed, but the other two were badly injured. Then this guy, Minsk, who may have been from Detroit, took off on a South American airline to Venezuela, probably with all sorts of money he had stolen and put in some off-shore bank – the D.A. traced part of it to the Bank of Sark, wherever that is -- and he disappeared. If they ever catch him, I'll be glad to go to the trial and testify on the arson."

"Golly, you sound like as much of a detective as Fairchild," Bob said. "What other cases have you investigated?"

"Oh, heavens! Hundreds over the years. I have a pretty good conviction rate, too. Some were arson for profit, insurance deals. Over-insure the house, then as the saying goes, 'sell it to the Yankees,' meaning the insurance companies. Surprisingly though, most of the arson cases involved kids, either playing with matches or with some psychological problem that made them want to burn property or their parents. Two of those cases were really sad. Five dead in one family with the ten-year-old ending up in a state institution. Another with six dead, including the teenager that set the fire. Quite a few were just homeless guys trying to keep warm in the winter in old abandoned buildings."

"What did you do, Jayne, when Jim was off chasing fire bugs?" Sally asked.

"I was a music teacher at an elementary school on Staten Island," Jayne explained. "I had them from kindergarten up through sixth grade. Once a year we'd take them on the ferry and the subway to Carnegie Hall for a concert – now that was always an adventure. Eighty fifth graders, some of them on their first subway ride. Talk about herding cats!"

"Believe me, Jayne, college students are just as bad! On some of the foreign trips they get lost in the airports and we have to hunt them up before our flights leave. On that trip to East Germany that Bob was telling you about, we were on trains crossing the borders, and I think the kids were scared to death."

"You weren't too happy yourself, as I recall," Bob added.

"No, both you and Richie had been in the Army and I thought the East Germans might detain you."

"The Army?" Jim asked. "When?"

"I was in Korea during the early part of the fifties. Infantry, believe it or not. But Richie was a chaplain with an Intelligence unit and worked as a translator as he knew German pretty well. He got captured by a Panzer Unit, and escaped with some vital information, and was picked up by Patton's units about the time of the Battle of the Bulge. He underwent the same training as the Intelligence guys, and the CIA later tried to hire him, but he chose teaching religions instead," Bob explained. "I think that's what gets him so interested in any little mystery that comes along, even though it sometimes drives Esther Fairchild nuts when he gets into danger."

"Danger?" Jayne asked. "What happens to him?"

"Well, he got shot a couple of times on one adventure, once in Greece, and another time when the college yacht was hijacked. That yacht was another of his adventures. It was a bunch of fanatics who were planning to murder Thomas Jefferson Singletary, the civil rights leader, at a symposium at Fremont. Fairchild acted as a spy for the FBI and got the whole bunch arrested."

"Then there was the Nazi ring that owned the island that the college now owns," Sally added. "Richie figured out that the island played a role in the Battle of Lake Erie in 1813, and, well, the college got a castle on the island and the vineyards that went with it, and it is now our viniculture department and hotel management center in the summer."

"Good heavens!" Jim exclaimed. "I want to meet this guy."

"Well, come to the chapel service tomorrow at ten and we'll introduce you before the service. Rayland Durrnad and his wife are usually there, too. Maybe save you a trip back on Monday.

Chapter 3

Bob Merriam was standing with a distinguished-looking older man in clerical and academic stoles and robe near the entrance to the Fremont College Chapel as the Roberts entered. "Sally's not with you?" Jayne asked as they approached.

"No," Bob replied. "She sings in the choir, and they are downstairs rehearsing."

"I know that room well!" Jayne said. "I sang in the Women's Chorale for two years when I was a student here."

"Hot Dog! A new choir member!" the man in the robe exclaimed.

"Jayne, Jim, I want you to meet Dr. Richard Fairchild, head of the Religions and International Studies Departments here at Fremont, and our assistant chaplain."

"How do you do, Dr. Fairchild?"

"Not very well, unless you call me Richie," Fairchild replied with a smile. "Only the students are allowed to call me Professor or Doctor. Otherwise, I get all nervous and start looking for my grade book! Bob tells me that you were with the Fire Department in New York, Jim, an arson investigator."

"Yes, and Jayne was a teacher. We lived in Richmond, which is the Borough of Staten Island. I covered the Island, the Harbor and Lower Manhattan for the last twelve years. Did a lot of commuting by fire boat!"

"Ahh, a sailor! You'll have to take a cruise on our college cruiser. It's docked in Port Clelland. And Bob tells me you were in Pearl Harbor on December 7. You've had an exciting life."

"I understand you have, too, Richie, that you're the local Sherlock Holmes!"

"Ha! Hardly that. I'm just a curious SOB. But I understand you want to meet Ray Durrnad, our Head of Physics and Astronomy. His wife is downstairs with Bob's and my wife, as they sing in the choir, but Ray is in Cleveland today visiting his parents. I'm sure he'll be glad to meet with you tomorrow sometime. Just call the college and ask for the Physics Department and if he's not available his secretary will schedule an appointment. Jim, I've got to go now to get ready for the service. It's liturgical Protestant – I hope that is okay with you?"

"My wife and I are Methodists, but we were married here in this chapel and attended when we were students. We're both looking forward to the service."

With that the organ began the Prelude, a Bach Fugue, and Bob led the Roberts to a pew toward the front. As it was the first Sunday in Advent and many of the students were probably sleeping off their Homecoming Day celebrations, attendance at the service was not all that heavy. An usher had handed them a folder, and they all opened the hymnal to the first Processional Hymn, "Sleepers Awake."

As the Prelude ended there were some bells ringing in the bell tower, and as they ended, the organ trumpets blasted a fanfare and the congregation rose as the ROTC Color Guard led the verger, one of the Senior Class officers carrying the college mace, a crucifer and two acolytes down the aisle followed by the choir in blue robes and velvet academic berets, followed by Dr. Fairchild in his academic hood and clerical stole. Jim leaned over and whispered in Jayne's ear, "A lot more formal than our little church on Staten Island. I think we're going to enjoy this."

After the service Dr. Fairchild and the man who had led the choir came back into the sanctuary accompanied by an older woman and three beautiful blonds, one of whom was Sally Merriam. Fairchild brought them over to where Bob and the Roberts were standing. "Jayne, Jim, I know you've already met Sally, but this is my wife, Esther, who writes and illustrates children's books, May Durrand, Ray's wife, and Hilda and Ross Johnson, the choirmaster. Hilda is also a physics professor. I'm afraid I 'spilled the beans' and let Ross know that you had been in the Chorale when you were a student here, Jayne. I think he's going to twist your arm to join the choir."

"Oh, I don't know if I'm that good now. I've not sung in years," Jayne replied.

"I'm so glad you came," Sally said. "We're having a buffet brunch and we want you two to come. My cousin, Dexter and his wife, Peggy, are driving over from Sandusky. They're probably there by now, and you can follow us over if you don't recall where it is from last night. Dexter is a cardiologist, and was on duty this morning at the hospital, but got off at eleven. Peggy is a nurse at the hospital. Usually they attend here on Sundays."

"Gracious!" Jayne replied. "But you weren't expecting...."

"Yes, I was!" Sally interrupted. "We often end up at Richie's farm on the Portage River, and it has been our turn to host brunch and we usually have a gang from somewhere, so you will be most welcome. It's all just a cold lunch, not the delicious steaks Richie grills when we go there. That's a treat you'll have to experience. Steak and a little Chateau Kent."

"Chateau Kent?" Jim asked.

"It's the name of the wine grown on West Bass Island," Dr. Fairchild explained. "The college acquired the island and the vineyard – except for the little village on it – a few years ago when we were able to purchase it from the German company that owned it. Not many colleges have their own winery, but it's run by our Chemistry Department. It's a long story. Have Bob tell you about it – he and Sally were involved, too."

"Another mystery! Bob, you've got to tell us this afternoon. This is becoming a real Home Coming for us. Thank you for the invitation," Jim said.

* * *

It was 2:30 on Tuesday afternoon when Jim parked his Ford outside the Fremont College Science Building and climbed up the steps to the entrance. Rayland Durrand, Ph.D., had an office in the basement, as did Dr. Hilda Johnson, whom the Roberts had met on Sunday. The door marked *Department of Physics and Astronomy* was open, and a young pretty dark-haired secretary, Darlene Smathers, according to her name tag, who appeared to be a student, looked up as Jim entered.

"Mr. Roberts?" Smathers asked and he nodded. "Dr. Durrand is expecting you. Just knock on the door, the second to the right."

"Thank you," Jim replied, doing as he had been instructed. Inside, a balding man with horn rimmed glasses who appeared to be about forty-five years old, stood up and extended his hand. "Thank you for agreeing to meet with me, Dr. Durrand. I met your wife, May, Sunday at the Merriams. She's very delightful."

"Yes, she told me. But please, call me Ray. Sit down, I'm sorry that chair isn't as comfortable as it might be. It is usually some student sitting in it, and it is made for squirming! I understand you're a retired fireman looking for a job."

"I inherited my family farm in Milan Township, and plan to do some farming, but that and my pension from the City of New York won't keep me occupied most of the time, so I'd like to find some way to use my talents."

"I understand you have a Master's Degree in chemistry."

"Yes, from Rutgers. I got it so that I could become an arson investigator. That requires a bit of chemistry knowledge."

"I can imagine. It must have been an exciting career."

"Sometimes too exiting, but usually just a lot of digging through cinders and ashes."

"I think I might have something that would interest you. I got a flyer a week or so ago from the National Aeronautics and Space Administration, NASA. They've taken over the old Plum Brook Arsenal south of Sandusky, and are looking for a specialist in property security. The job would seem perfect for a fireman with chemical knowledge as I think they are doing various experiments there. Something to do with cryonic research."

"I know that area. Actually, it's just down the road a bit from my farm. I recall the War Department created it from farmland to make ammunitions just after I joined the Navy."

"May said you'd been in Pearl Harbor on December Seven."

"A fireman aboard a destroyer. It was hit a couple of times, but we saved it. Our training paid off that Sunday."

"Sure did! I, too, was in the Navy, as a Reservist during Korea, but I never got called up for active duty. Lucky, I guess. But I was in Grad School at Case, and was allowed to finish. Anyway, here's the flyer I got. There's a phone number, but no name. You might give them a call and see what the job is about.

"But I have another idea too," Durrand continued. "Earlier this semester we were talking with Dean Harding – he's the head of faculty – about adding a fire science course to our science program. Would you be interested in teaching here at Fremont? I understand you're an alumni. It would only be very part-time, maybe one or two courses a semester. Have you done any teaching?"

"Yes, I taught at the Fire Academy, mostly preliminary arson, for the last eight years. I'd have to talk with Jayne about it, but I can't imagine that she's object. It would be daytime classes, I would guess."

"Weekdays, if the program is approved, and I think it will be. It would start with the new semester at the end of January. Keep it in mind when you talk with whomever at NASA. I'll talk with Dean Harding, and see if we can get the Board to approve it. I'm afraid it won't pay much. One or two three-hour credit courses. You'd be part of the Science Faculty, but not required to attend all the faculty meetings, graduations and such. For that, I would envy you."

"These are all great ideas, Ray. I thank you very much for the offer – depending, of course, on the Board, but also for the information on NASA. That sounds really promising."

"Great. I'll talk with Harding this week. We'll need a transcript from Rutgers. We'll already have the one from here when you were an undergrad, what, on the G.I. Bill?"

"Yes. It enabled me to get my degree in three years, as I got some credit for my Navy training. By the way, I was told that Hilda Ross was also a physics professor here. She seems to have a slight accent, perhaps German?"

"Jim, I'm not allowed to tell the whole story, and I'm not even sure I know all of it. But yes, she was the head of the physics department at Halle University in East Germany, a specialist in nuclear physics. Richie Fairchild was involved. Maybe he can fill you in on the details."

"From what I hear he is quite a character."

"You don't know the half of it!" Durrand laughed.

* * *

Later that afternoon Jim called the number on the flyer, and spoke with a Colonel Josephs, who said he was an Air Force officer. Josephs agreed to an appointment the next morning, and Jim spent the evening discussing the Plum Brook possibilities and Rayland Durrand's offer of a teaching job with Jayne, who was very enthusiastic about both.

The main gate to the Plum Brook Lewis Lab was off Bogart Road in Perkin Township. Jim drove west on Mason Road to U.S. 250, then north about a mile, and entered the property coming to a gate in a high fence where an Air Force military policeman stepped out of a small guard shack and brought Jim to a stop at a barrier. Jim rolled down his car window.

"I have an appointment with Colonel Josephs at ten," Jim explained.

"Jim Roberts?" the uniformed corporal asked, consulting his clipboard, and Jim affirmed it, showing his New York driver's license. "The Colonel is expecting you. Drive to the third building straight ahead and park in one of the unoccupied spaces. There's a glass door. Just go in and up to the second floor. His secretary will meet you there. I'll let her know you have arrived."

Jim thanked him, and followed the instructions to the third building. Off in the distance to his right he could see what looked like a high concrete dome. He parked, entered the building and climbed the stairs to the second floor, where another glass door read "Command Center." Another uniformed Air Force corporal, slender and trim in her blue Air Force uniform with a short dark hair style, rose from her desk and ushered Jim into a small, cramped office not much bigger than the corporal's.

Colonel Jeffrey Josephs, a tall, balding man about fifty, was dressed in civilian clothes consisting of a white shirt and tie, his suit coat hanging on a hat rack next to his overcoat and hat. He stood up, and offered his hand to Jim, who shook it, introducing himself, and then sat down in a chair beside the Colonel's desk that the officer had indicated after hanging up his coat.

"Had a talk with some folks in New York this morning. They say they wish they had you back. Either you paid them for all the compliments they dished out, or you were one hell of an investigator. Seeing you, I suspect the latter. Jim," the Colonel began after a moment, "this is a NASA facility, but we have Air Force support for the time being. It should be NASA's own folks, but NASA hasn't gotten around to setting up its own police and security yet, so they're borrowing from the military for the time being. That's part of what we need here, someone to both head up physical security and to act as a chief head of risk.

"Now exactly what that means is complicated," he continued. "You may have noticed a domed structure as you drove in. That is a nuclear reactor, the first one for NASA. They are doing a variety of experiments here, some chemical, some just plain physical like the wind tunnel, testing upper-stage rockets, ceramics for re-entry use, tests for cryological resistance – don't ask me to explain as I don't understand half of this stuff. But in short, there are tank cars of all sorts of stuff arriving almost daily – oxygen, nitrogen, various gases, nuclear stuff – and that's part of our problem. Word got out that there is an atomic reactor here, and even though it is a small one, with all this Cold War talk, there has been some public reaction of a very unpleasant type. Who knows what some of these kooks might try.

"Jim, I'll be honest with you. I need a take-charge kind of guy to oversee that all this stuff is kept safe so the scientists and engineers can do their work in preparing parts for a rocket that will get men to the moon. Could you be that guy?"

"Colonel Josephs, if you spoke with anyone in New York who knew me, you already know that I've investigated every type of explosion a city can sustain, worked with the ATF, the FBI, state and local police, and had police training for arson crimes. But I have only a layman's knowledge of anything nuclear – I really wouldn't know uranium from mud or gravel!"

"You wouldn't need to. The engineers and egghead scientists and engineers take care of that sort of stuff. It's the physical plant security we're concerned about. They bring stuff in by train, and then use mobile cranes to lift it into the reactor building. Some of those guys are independent contractors with top secret clearance, as are many of the engineers and scientists who work here. They know what they're doing, I don't. But someone has to watch to make sure they're using all the proper safety equipment. There's an Atomic Energy Commission rule book that has to be followed to the letter.

"But I suspect you'll also have to find out and know about all the various experiments that go on here. If you take the job, you'll have one of the highest classifications of secret clearance, and will be on twenty-four hour call seven days a week. This is no forty hour a week job, Jim, it's a major pain in the ass job. I'm not trying to talk you out of it, but if you say you are interested we'll start your clearance today and get you assigned a weapon. But you don't have to wear a uniform, unless you really want to. I should, I suppose, but in dealing with the eggheads and engineers, it's easier if I don't."

"Well, Colonel Josephs, I...."

"Call me Jeff. It's just the Air Force cops that call me Colonel and have to salute. Actually, I try to keep it relaxed around here. I can retire in a couple of years and having you to take some of the burden of running this shop would be a damned good way to spend them."

"Jeff. I think I would be very interested. Twenty-four hour call is old hat, and I only live about five miles away in Milan Township, and I have my own service revolver from the FDNY. But Dr. Durrand at Fremont College asked me if I'd be interested in teaching a fire science course there in the Spring Semester, if he can get the dean's approval for it. It would probably only be two or three mornings a week, or afternoons, depending on the schedule."

"Fremont College? Well, this is better yet! They've got this physics professor over there that I'm supposed to keep an eye on. Hilda von something-or-other, who I learned from Air Force Intelligence is from East Germany."

"Hilda Johnson," Jim replied. "I met her Sunday. She's married to the choir conductor."

"You met her? But hell yeah, that's her all right. Apparently she's under some sort of CIA protection, and the FBI has their twit in a fiddle since she's some sort of nuclear specialist. I suspect its inter-agency rivalry, but I imagine you're familiar with all that sort of political fun and games."

"Sure. The NYPD always wants to take over if an arson has a death in it, and they don't know beans about arson investigation. But being on the inside of the department I could keep an eye out for any indication of a problem. I don't know the story, but I heard Sunday that she had been a defector."

"So, Jim, do you want the job?"

"I figured it would be something like this, and talked with my wife, Jayne, about it. She encouraged me to take it, if it was something I would enjoy doing. I really do think I would be good at what I understand the job is – though it will take a while to really know what it is – so, yes, I would be interested."

"Good. Now, these Air Force guys are pretty good. They are on three shifts, eight hours, around the clock, five teams of three. One mans the main gate, where you came in, one wanders around the buildings making sure they're secure, and one drives the perimeter of this place, which is nine thousand acres. But NASA only uses about sixty-four hundred of them. Do you know the history here?"

"It was built as an arsenal after I went in the Navy, but I heard from my folks and high school friends that a contractor operated it to manufacture explosives, TNT and stuff, and that there were bunkers out in the fields to hold the stuff until it was shipped."

"That's basically it. They did some testing of various explosives out in what we call 'the prairie,' a natural area of land that never was farmed. For all we know there could still be un-exploded stuff out there, and that, too, will be your job to find. When can you start?"

"I suppose when you get my clearance."

"Ahh, to hell with that. That could be weeks. Come in tomorrow at eight-thirty and I'll get you a locker downstairs, which is also the Air Force barracks, and get whoever is on duty to drive you around the place to see it. Then when your clearance comes, I'll get one of the engineers to take you around that reactor."

"Anything I should study besides the AEC regulations?"

"Yeah. You might look into crowd control if the anti-nuclear bunch get rambunctious. It's usually on the weekends they show up. So far, just parading around outside the grounds with signs, but you never know with a mob what they might do."

* * *

On his way back to the farm Jim drove around the roads that bordered the facility. There was little to see but fence and trees, but he could see two tracks of a dirt road that must be what the Air Force patrols used, with cameras mounted at various spots and what looked like air raid sirens on high posts at corners of the fences. At the southwest side he crossed some railroad tracks that led to a gate in the fence that was padlocked, then led through the trees toward the center of the facility, and at the north side there were more railroad tracks and a gate through the fence. When he got to Columbus Road he had completed circling the facility, and headed home to inform Jayne that he had accepted the job.

The following morning a different armed Air Force guard checked his identity and again directed him to the third building. This time the young female Air Force corporal, Alicia McQuinn, met him as he entered the second floor office, and led him downstairs to the dormitory, which consisted of individual rooms and a mess hall, day room and showers. Jim would have a small room of his own, even with a cot if he needed a nap or had to stay over-night, and a locker where he could store whatever he needed. "Are you sure you don't want a military weapon?" the attractive dark-haired corporal asked.

"No, I have my FDNY revolver, and I'm more comfortable with it. What other weapons do the guards have?"

"I don't have a key to the weapons room, Mr. Roberts, but the Colonel said he would get you one. I've only been in there once, but it seemed well-stocked with automatic rifles, tear gas and other anti-riot gear. We're hoping we never have to use it. Of course, the guys each have their side weapons and holsters. Each is responsible for his own gun."

As they left the barracks room, Corporal McQuinn led Jim to a box beside the stairway, and started to pick it up. Jim saw it was heavy, and reached over to take it, lifting it into his arms. "Where do you want this taken?" he asked.

"To your car," she replied. "We don't have any extra vehicles right now, but you may be assigned one if we get some more. Until then I'll need to add some things to your car." She led him outside to his Ford, and he set the box on the ground next to the driver's door. Then she opened the box and pulled out a small square NASA-emblazoned card with his name already printed on it, and taped it to the lower left inside of the front windshield. "That is your pass for the gate here and at our main facility in Brookside, where you may need to go occasionally." Then she brought out a round red magnetic roof flasher with a long cord. "Just stick it on the roof of the car and plug this into the cigarette lighter when you need to use it. I'm sorry we don't have a siren, but you can use your horn, I guess, if you're on an emergency call." She then hauled a walkie-talkie out of the box, and stuck a holder for it below the radio in the center of the dashboard. "This has a ten mile range. You should keep your car locked at all times when not on the facility. These things are signed out in the Colonel's name, and he doesn't want to lose them. Now, are you familiar with a beeper?"

"Sure. Had to wear one at the Fire Department."

"Good. This one has a fifty mile range. If it goes off, call the number on this card, which you should keep with you at all times. Now, come back upstairs and I'll take your picture for your identification badge."

Photos taken and papers completed, Jim was, by noon, a federal government employee at GS-11 level, sworn to uphold the Constitution and the Government Secrets Act. He was given several manuals to study, and then, after lunch in the "mess hall" downstairs, a young sergeant, Jason Warbish, took him around the facility in one of the two Air Force cars.
The buildings all had letter or letter and number names, and Jim noted each on a diagram of the facility. K-Site was the Cryogenic Propellant Tank Facility, and next to it was the Cryogenic Components Lab. B-2 was for Spacecraft Propulsion – rocket – Research, and HFT was the Hypersonic Tunnel Facility. Sgt. Warbish explained that there was a wind tunnel at the Lewis Lab behind the Cleveland Hopkins Airport, but it was not powerful enough for testing air-breathing propulsion systems at speeds exceeding five times the speed of sound.

Next they visited the Space Power Building, home to the world largest space environment simulation chamber, where parts for rockets would be tested. Following that was the largest vacuum chamber in the world, designed to test equipment that might carry astronauts or other equipment into space. Then Warbish drove over to the domed building Jim had seen earlier – the nuclear reactor. "What do they do here?" Jim asked.

"I've no idea!" Warbish answered. "But if you find out, let me know. As far as the rumors around here go, it simply provides power for the Space Power Facility and the HFT, which suck up a lot of energy. It is surprisingly quiet, and the non-radiated water is drained to a cooling pond out in the woods. It's fenced off, but even though it is supposed to be just fresh water, I wouldn't want to swim in it. We'll drive over there and you can see it. Actually, I think it is that pond, as much as the reactor itself that has the demonstrators all in a dither. There are a lot of wells around here on the farms, and people are afraid of ground water contamination. NASA has assured the people through press releases that the chance of any nuclear explosion or water table contamination is next to nil."

"'Next to nil,'" Jim repeated. "But not 'nil' itself."

"From what I hear, the answer to that is supposed to be *your* worry!"

"Oh, thanks, Jason! Colonel Josephs didn't tell me *that*. I thought the sales pitch was a bit too pleasant," Jim laughed.

"You said you'd driven the outside perimeter yesterday. Want to see the perimeter fence from the inside?"

"Sure. I noticed some cameras along the way. Is it monitored twenty-four hours a day?"

"The cameras are motion-sensor activated. Any movement starts the camera, and a beeper sounds in the guard shack. Ninety-nine times out of a hundred it's a deer or rabbit or crow that sets it off, and if that is detected on the camera we don't investigate. If the camera does not show an animal or bird or does show an intruder, we respond with both cars. Doesn't happen often, but we've caught a few teenagers, and one guy with a protest sign he was going to hang somewhere in the facility. The teenagers we just scare the devil out of, but the guy with the sign was prosecuted for trespassing on federal property, though we threatened him first with violation of the espionage act. I think he got a $500 fine and ten days in the clink."

"Colonel Josephs mentioned something about a prairie – some sort of open area. What and where is it?"

"It's over by the pond. I'll show you," Warbish said as he turned the car to the right and down a track between the trees to a hidden area of perhaps a hundred and fifty acres of open land. "There are supposed to be a lot of native plants in here, things that no longer grow in other parts of Ohio. I'm not a botanist, but occasionally one will request permission to explore this area. We have to accompany them, and they have to sign a release, as this was a testing area when the facility was used for explosives, and there could be unexploded materiel in here. We've never seen any, but you might want to get a metal detector and hunt around for some."

Warbish then drove back to the perimeter trail, and turned east, coming to a gate where more railroad tracks entered the facility. He turned on a road beside the tracks and followed these a few thousand feet to where they split into about six tracks, then one continued back into an area that appeared to be bunkers, and split again into about eight tracks, each with a loading dock.

There was a shed with a small gasoline-powered locomotive in it, used to move cars around the various tracks. "Most of these will probably be taken out soon," Warbish said. "This is where they used to load the explosives into boxcars and seal them for transport to Atlantic and Pacific ports for transfer to Navy vessels that took them to the war zones during World War Two. I've been told that all the bunkers are empty now, but I've seen activity around one or two recently, so I don't know what's really in them. I imagine you will find out."

"That should be fun," Jim commented jokingly. "What other surprises are around here?"

"That's about it. Corporal McQuinn said that the Colonel wanted to see you before you headed home, so if there's nothing else, I'll take you back to the barracks."

Alicia McQuinn waved Jim into Colonel Josephs' office as he entered the second floor door. Josephs, still dressed in civilian clothes, but wearing reading glasses now, was sitting behind his desk reviewing some papers, and looked up as Jim entered.

"Warbish gave you the grand tour, I hear, and McQuinn gave you homework to study," he stated, and Jim nodded. "Your position has needed filling for over a year, well, two or three years, really, ever since we expanded with the reactor. I'm not a safety or security guy, but was stuck with the job until I could find someone, and you seem to fit the bill. Tomorrow morning at nine I'm holding a monthly meeting with the enlisted men – all of them. Corporal McQuinn will man the gate during that time, and I want you present to meet all the guys. Then I will take you around all the facility buildings again to meet the engineers and eggheads who run them. They need to know who you are, and why you will be prowling around their buildings.

"Jim, you've been assigned a rank as high as most of the engineers, scientists and technicians around here, which means you have as much authority as I do to act as you see best," Josephs continued. "It means you make your own schedule, and as you will see in all those booklets McQuinn gave you, all the responsibility for making this place safe. In some ways it is like any civilian factory, and many of the engineers and scientists and such are employed by contractors, not by the government. But you still will have authority over them if it involves safety or security. You'll be making your own rules and regulations. Occasionally some bigwig from D.C. may come down to look things over, and the head guys at other NASA facilities usually stop by when they come to Lewis Labs down in Brookpark. They may look over your plans, but I doubt they'll give you any guff.

"The mission is to get men into space as quickly as possible with the least amount of trouble doing it. That's your mission as well – just keep that objective in mind and things should go smoothly. As you've probably noted, things are fairly laid back here, no rigid military rituals or other falderal. We formally raise the flag in the morning and take it down at night, and the guys keep their uniforms clean, so as far as I'm concerned, the Pentagon has forgotten we're here! Any questions?"

"I'm sure I'll have dozens, but for now there is one thing I'm curious about. Alicia had me sign the Government Secrets Act Agreement. So far I've not seen anything that I would consider so secret I couldn't describe it to Jayne, my wife. I mean, the public already knows that you have a nuclear reactor here. So, what am I to keep secret?"

"Right now, nothing. But remember, we're in a space race with Russia. You will be learning things that need to be kept under your hat. You'll know soon enough what's secret."

Chapter 4

Jayne was surprised when Jim got home about a quarter to four. But when she saw all the material Jim had to read that afternoon and evening, she left him alone after he had told her about his day, and the amount of authority he was to have. "It is more than the authority of a Chief in the Fire Department," he said. "There's thousands of acres and millions – maybe billions – of dollars' worth of scientific equipment and stuff out there, and if anything happens to any of it, apparently it's my responsibility. It seems all laid back and chummy, but I suspect you'll be spotting a few gray hairs on my head over the next few months. I can't even guess at what might come up. Riots, picketing, law suits, spies! If one of the contract engineers is a Russian spy, I guess I'm supposed to find that out."

"Good heavens, Jim!" Jayne responded. "Are you sure you want this job?"

"Oh yes! It will be a challenge, and I think I'm up to it. I guess, from what Josephs said, I basically have the entire space agency and the Pentagon to back me up. But the job is to avoid having to call for help."

* * *

The next day brought more surprises. Jim was to report the following morning for a physical – procedural, of course, and also had to review some government insurance program options. Both he and Jayne would be covered for health and hospitalization, and there was a life insurance policy, disability and other benefits to which he would be entitled. After meeting the fifteen enlisted men who supplied the security team Colonel Josephs took Jim to each of the major facilities and introduced him to the engineers, scientists, technicians and clerical staff.

Jim learned that each facility had a safety officer who was familiar with all the operations in that facility. At one time there had even been a fire truck on the base, but because of the many computers water could not be used to fight most fires. Rather, halon extinguishers that stopped the oxygen were available. Each of the safety officers had several books on safety for their particular project, and Jim was given a copy of each to study. Colonel Josephs then took him to an office in the Spacecraft Propulsion lab to meet Dr. Bernard Ruhl, the Director of the Plum Brook NASA Facility.

As he moved from facility to facility he made notes of all the materials each used or had on hand. For each he knew that there was a National Fire

Protection Association regulation or code that he would have to get and study. He was beginning to see why he needed a room in the barracks for his materials. It would be his base of operations. Jim also obtained several diagrams of the entire area and of each individual facility. He inquired about the bunkers near the rail yard, but no one, including Colonel Josephs, seemed to know much about what was there. It had snowed the previous evening, and Jim drove over to where the final rail yard and loading docks were located, and wandered around. There seemed to be fresh activity, at least within the past month, but nothing appeared unusual.

* * *

Sally Merriam and Esther Fairchild had talked Jayne into joining the choir at the college chapel, and Thursday evening Jim drove her there for the seven o'clock rehearsal. Jim had decided that they needed a second vehicle for Jayne, and planned to get one before Christmas. The choir was getting ready for the Christmas Eve service. The men tried to talk Jim into joining, but he was no singer and declined. Richie Fairchild was also present, but not singing, and asked Jim if he had found any extra employment yet.

"Most definitely!" Jim replied. "Ray Durrand gave me a lead on a job for NASA at the old Plum Brook Arsenal, and it is going to be quite a job. In charge of security for the place."

"That would be quite a job. I hear they've gone atomic."

"Apparently, but I don't know all the details. Oh, and Ray wants me to teach some Fire Science courses here at the College."

"Yes, I heard about that at the Dean's Meeting. He's certain the Board will approve it. I might sit in on that meeting, even though I'm notorious for being a truant! Interesting subject."

As the rehearsal came to a close Esther and May Durrand came over to talk, along with Sally and Hilda. Esther said to Jayne Roberts, "What are your plans for Christmas Day?"

"Well, we've pretty much got the house arranged like we wanted, and Jimmy, who Bob and Sally met at the Bowling Green game, is hosting a friend, I understand. His wife is from Norwalk and they're having Christmas Day dinner at her parents."

"So you really have no plans for Christmas Day?" Esther asked. "How about joining us at the farm. It's traditional and you already know most of the folks who will be there."

"That's a great plan!" Richie Fairchild added. "The farm's easy to find, right on the Portage River, south of Port Clinton."

Jayne and Jim protested, but when the others joined in the invitation – only gag gifts of under $5 permitted – and Jayne could bring her best mince pie that she had mentioned during one of the rehearsals – the deed seemed done. Christmas was two weeks away, and part of the Plum Brook facility would be closed for the holiday week, as would the college except for the chapel, where many of the local staff and professors attended, as well as students who lived in Fremont or the surrounding areas and other people from Fremont.

December was more than half way through as Jim became ever more familiar with the facility and its routine operations. He had obtained NFPA specifics and recommendations on each of the chemicals and other material that entered or was created in the various buildings, and had finally received his "top secret cryptic" clearance. As head of security at the facility, he established a schedule of meetings with each of the individual unit safety officers, and started with a joint meeting of all of them together. There was, in one of the other buildings, a conference room that he was able to secure for that meeting, although the individual meetings would take place in each of the buildings where the safety officer was located, so that Jim could learn the processes performed there and learn of any particular hazard.

He was most concerned about the nuclear reactor building, and the safety officer in charge of it was a William Hallister, known around the facility as Bill. Hallister took Jim all around the reactor building, showing him all the areas and safety devices that were in use, along with the redundant systems that would protect against any emergencies. "Actually," Hallister explained, "this reactor isn't that much bigger than what is used on a nuclear submarine. There is an engineer on duty at all times, and about the only time there is any open exposure to the fuel rods is when they are brought in on a special rail car from Hanford, Washington, and transferred by crane through the reactor dome, and the old fuel rods exchanged. Each of the rods is filled with pellets of fuel, mostly uranium 235 and oxygen, and are sealed during delivery. There is a hatch in the dome and once the individual spent fuel rods are removed, each is replaced with a fresh rod, lowered by a special crane. We'll be making an exchange December 27. The rail car is coming from the AEC Hanford plant, and should arrive a few days earlier, before Christmas. The rail route by-passes most large cities and the car is unmarked so no one knows what's inside it."

"What about the heated water that runs the steam turbine. I understand that there have been protests about ground-water contamination," Jim asked.

"The rods are suspended in water, producing the heat, but that water is recycled within the reactor and never is exposed outside. The steam is condensed as it leaves the turbine, and much of it is also recycled after cooling down. Excess water is drained to the pond you visited, but that pond has a concrete bottom and sides, it's basically a basin and can't leak into the ground, but there is no radioactivity in that water anyway, so even if it did leak it couldn't harm the water table. But you can't convince the local farmers that there is no danger. They see danger because they don't understand the system.

"I think that you already have visited the pump and shop building and saw the water pond. It's a different system. Much of that water is pumped to other facilities that use water in their work, like the steam-powered altitude exhaust system, designed to reduce the pressure at the exhaust nozzle exit of each rocket test stand. Those steam accumulators can store up to 42,000 gallons of steam and water. The pressure is controlled at the valve house."

"What happens to contaminated water that isn't recycled?"

"It's piped out to the rail yard and pumped into special tank cars that take it back to Hanford for reprocessing, as are the spent fuel rods. The pipes are completely surrounded by concrete between the reactor and the rail yard, and the pump is in a sealed container out there that has radiation monitors on it that would sound an alarm and stop the pump if radiation reached a certain level. The pump is in one of the old World War bunkers in the back part of the rail yard. The contaminated water is then pumped into special heavy-duty rail tank cars for shipment back to Hanford. The reactor will be shut down over Christmas as new fuel rods are going to be installed January 2."

"That must explain the activity I noted around one of the bunkers in that rail yard. Bill, on my first tour around here I noticed what looked like air raid sirens at several points along the perimeter. Are those related to the reactor?"

"Politics, Jim. In order to get both state and local cooperation in installing the reactor, we had to agree to put in an alarm system. It has only been tested once, but the shriek it gives would deafen a horse! The county wants it checked annually, but it hasn't been done in a couple of years. You'll probably find some nasty letters in your files when you get into them. But for now, I'll introduce you to some of the engineers who run the reactor."

Although Jim had a fairly good memory for names, he has started a notebook in which he kept the name, job and phone extension for each engineer, technician and scientist he met. Most of the safety officers were technicians of some sort, but one or two were also safety engineers, checking various safety systems that would be used on the rockets being built. He learned that the facility had been in charge of the design for the fuel system for the X-33 rocket, and that while some of the rocket systems being developed used nitrogen, they also used a lot of oxygen, making the combination a potentially explosive fuel.

The following week Jim made a trip to Brookpark to the NASA Lewis Research Center, located on the east bank of the Rocky River behind the Cleveland Hopkins Airport. His meeting was with Jeff Hunter, head of security for both Lewis and any related facilities, including Plum Brook. Hunter, a tall man with thick gray hair, about age fifty-five, was a retired

Army Military Police Colonel, who had the highest praise for Colonel Josephs – obviously no inter-service jealousies in NASA. He did note that Jeff Josephs had a humorous sense of sarcasm for things governmental, and hoped that Josephs had not been sarcastic to Jim, which Jim assured him had not been the case. Jim was given a tour of the Lewis Lab and the gigantic wind tunnel, although it was minuscule compared to the Hypersonic Tunnel at Plum Brook. He was introduced to many of the engineers and technicians whose counterparts he had met at the Sandusky facility, and began to have a better understanding of what the role of the two facilities was. He added all the names and numbers to his notebook.

Jim saw little of Colonel Josephs over the next week. The Air Force had sent in several new military police to temporarily replace half of the regular crew that were receiving leave over the Christmas holidays. Sgt. Warbish and Jim set their schedules and ran them through the basics of what they would be doing until the regular team returned. Even the Colonel was planning to be off the facility during the holidays.

Chapter 5

December 25, 1968

Jim and Jayne Roberts arrived at the Fairchild farm about eleven on Christmas morning. They had attended the Christmas Eve service at the Fremont College Chapel the evening before, and as Jayne was now singing in the chapel choir, Jim had sat with Bob Merriam, his wife's cousin, Dexter Atwater, who was a surgeon in Sandusky and his wife, Peggy, and Rayland Durrand while their wives and Hilda Johnson had been in the procession up to the choir loft. It was a very formal candlelight service and Jim was quite impressed by it.

After Richard Fairchild had given Jim a tour of the farm and the cattle he raised, they were all gathered in the Fairchilds' parlor, which contained a massive Christmas tree and other decorations, enjoying eggnog, punch, wine or anything they wished while delicious aromas emanated from the kitchen. Each of the wives had brought something to contribute to the feast, which was scheduled for two that afternoon. Jim had cornered Richie Fairchild and demanded to hear some of the stories that he had heard about from Bob or Ray. Fairchild made light of most of them, describing himself as "just a nosey SOB that was like the cat that got too curious." Hearing that, Esther shouted out from the kitchen that one day his curiosity would get him killed if he wasn't more cautious.

"Nonsense!" he laughed. "But I will admit that I was a bit nervous when I had that DUI charge and had to go to court with no memory of what had happened."

"How did that come about?" Jim asked.

It was Bob that answered. "Richie was headed home from the college one night and was hijacked by a couple of thugs who drugged him with vodka and put him into his car, then pushed the car into a bridge abutment intending to kill him, but although he had a concussion and resulting temporary amnesia, he survived. Some kids from around Tiffin found him and got him an ambulance to the hospital in Sandusky where Dexter and Peggy now work. Turned out these hijackers were working for some ex-Nazi who owned the West Bass Island winery where Richie and I had found a skeleton of some Nazi spy who had accidentally been killed during the War. Richie was following up on what happened, and the ex-Nazi, who was in West Germany, hired these two characters to kill Fairchild."

"Why?" Dexter asked.

"Well," Fairchild said, "it seems that the big castle-like house on island was full of gold ingots that the Nazi was using as collateral for all sorts of his investments."

"There was gold on the island?" Jim asked.

"A ton or two. It had been on a British ship sunk during the Battle of Lake Erie in 1813."

"I remember that story now," Jim said. "The British had gotten the gold from some Indians in Canada and were taking it to Toronto or someplace, and when Perry attacked at Put-In-Bay, they scuttled their ship. Records of it were in London or something."

"That's right," Bob added. "The German, Frederick – I've forgotten his last name – tore the description of where the ship was scuttled out of the insurance records at Lloyd's, and that's how we got his name. Was it 'Kolb'?"

"Yes," Fairchild confirmed. "He had been studying metallurgy at Cambridge and had come across the mining of gold by the Indians in Northern Ontario and the shipment by way of Ft. Mishlemackenac. The island winery was not being used during the War, and was owned by a railroad that was a Kolb subsidiary, so the Nazis brought in diving equipment, found the gold, and after the war used it as collateral for a number of businesses. Eventually the College acquired the island except for Kent Village, and the winery, which the Chemistry Department uses for its viniculture courses, and the big castle is operated as a hotel by the College's Hospitality Department. The following year I acquired a big cabin cruiser in another little adventure, and that became the college's Marine Department."

The stories continued for another hour or so until finally the call to dinner came, and the families gathered around a festive table where a massive prime rib roast was set in front of Dr. Fairchild. He asked the blessing, and then began carving the roast while plates were passed around the table and filled with roasted potatoes, Yorkshire pudding, squash and several kinds of greens, gravy, cranberry sauce and other delights. Before sitting down Fairchild poured wine into everyone's wine glass. "Chateau Kent," he said. "This is the wine grown on West Bass Island, Jim. These bottles are from the mid-1950s, before the College took it over. They've not quite perfected the same quality yet, but they're getting close, wouldn't you say, Ray?"

"It all tastes good to me!" the physics professor replied, but Hilda is the best judge of wine, being German."

"Oh *Ja!*" she responded in German. "*Ist sehr gute wein!* Of course it doesn't match a good German Riesling, but it will get there some day. Jayne," she continued, "each September we all go out to the island to help harvest the grapes. I hope you and Jim will join us next year."

"That sounds like fun," Jayne replied. The conversation then turned to the roast beef and other goodies, and then to still other topics of interest to the bunch around the table. Jim was thinking how lucky he was to be considered part of a group like this when there was a rumbling sound off in the distance.

"Was that thunder?" Ross Johnson asked. "It was a nice clear day when we got here. It must have clouded up."

"No," Esther replied. "The sun is still shining."

Within a minute Jim's beeper went off, sounding a loud blatt until Jim shut it off. "Holy smoke!" he exclaimed. "Something must have happened at the facility. Richie, can I use your telephone? I have a number I am supposed to call when there is an emergency."

Fairchild led Jim into his library, which the professor used as his office, and Jim called the number on the card, speaking with Sgt. Warbish, who had answered immediately, explaining what had happened. Jim hung up and went back to the dinner table.

"Folks, I'm afraid I'm going to have to miss dessert! There's an emergency at the facility and I guess I'm the one in charge. Dexter, could you and Peggy see that Jayne gets home? I may be tied up for hours – maybe days – on this. Jayne, I'll try to call you this evening if I'm going to be late. I may have to stay at the facility."

"Sure, Jim. We'll get Jayne home," Peggy answered. "I hope no one was hurt. If so, Dex and I may also be called in to the hospital."

"I'm sorry this breaks up this wonderful day, and I do want to thank you, Esther and Richie, for the best Christmas we've had in years, but I've got to hurry."

* * *

It was the first time Jim had had to use the red flasher, which mounted on the roof of his Ford by a magnet with the wire running across the dashboard to the cigarette lighter. He anticipated that the Turnpike would be his fastest route to Plum Brook, and traffic would be light in the middle of Christmas Day. Although he stopped to get a card when he got on the Ohio Turnpike, the toll-taker at Route 250 waved him through, noting the NASA identification in the front windshield.

As Jim drove up the road to the entrance gate he found it jammed with all sorts of red flashing lights. One NASA security car was stopped next to two Erie County Sheriff's cars, a state highway patrol car, and a Perkins Township police car, along with squad cars from both Milan and Huron, the towns closest to the facility. Sgt. Warbish was in the guard house as Jim pulled up next to it.

"Glad you got here so quickly, Jim" Warbish said.

"What happened, Jason?"

"We're not entirely sure yet, but pull your car on around the gate here, as there are more fire trucks on the way." Jim pulled his flasher off the roof of the car and unplugged it, then went back to the gatehouse. There was blood on the floor.

"It was some kind of attack. Alicia McQuinn was manning the gate house while the three guards were at lunch. She was shot, and the gate crashed through, then whoever it was headed for the rail yard. As far as we can tell, they set off some explosive, dynamite or TNT or something, under the two tank cars of oxygen that blew them sky high, and started fires all over the place. The blast blew the sealed car with the new nuclear fuel rods in it on its side, but we don't think it split open. Won't know until the technician Bill Hallister left in charge gets back with his Geiger counter."

"What about Corporal McQuinn."

"She has a chest wound, and was taken to the hospital about ten minutes ago. I hope she'll be okay. The problem is, we don't know if whoever it is did this is still in the facility with more explosives or if they left. Perkins Township response was really quick, and all the MPs got here before I did, so I don't think anyone got back out this gate – one of the MPs and a couple of police are driving the perimeter now to see if there is any evidence of fence cutting. Here, you can see the rail yard on the remote camera."

Although it was just a small black and white television, the remote camera that constantly monitored the rail yard showed the devastation of the two tank cars, the overturned special flat car with the high metal center containing the fuel rods, fire in surrounding trees and other places, with several fire trucks working on the fires.

"Fortunately Hallister had shut down the reactor last week, in preparation for the fuel rod exchange, but if there is a target, that reactor may be it," Jim said. "Has anyone notified Brookpark?"

"I called Jeff Hunter, the head security guy, right after I set off your beeper, but that was at least ten minutes after the explosion. He wasn't there, but their security guy said he would call Hunter at home."

"This is a federal facility. That means the FBI will have primary jurisdiction," Jim said. "Have they been notified?"

"Not yet. I wasn't sure where to call."

"I've got a number at my office. I'll call from there. In the meantime, get those fire trucks to the blast area and you and the highway patrol guy keep this gate closed to all but official traffic. The rest of the officers here we'll organize for a complete search of the facility."

Jim drove to his office, called the FBI number he had in Cleveland, and explained to the special agent in charge what had happened. He then drove to the reactor building, and found the technician just coming out with a lunchbox-size box in his hand. He knew the technician, Wilmer Patrick. "Will, is that the Geiger counter?"

"Yeah, it was locked up and I had to find the key."

"Well, stay here for a few minutes until I can round up some of these local police to guard the reactor building, which may be the primary target, then we can check on the overturned rail car. How sensitive are those rods to heat or banging around."

"They're not too fragile, but you don't want to mess around with them, either. The car was just delivered yesterday afternoon. The two cars of oxygen came in the morning before. None had been moved to the back unloading area yet. We have a little locomotive for that job."

"So if anyone had been watching the place, they could have seen the deliveries?"

"I guess so."

While Patrick waited at the reactor Jim quickly drove back to the gate and found two Milan police officers and had them follow him back to the reactor building. He then explained what the building was, and why it needed to be guarded in the event the intruders were still on the facility and this was their ultimate target. "Keep your weapons loaded, but make sure it's an intruder and not someone supposed to be here. Shoot, if you must, to wound – whoever did this, we want alive." The two officers nodded, and parked their squad car at the reactor entrance.

Roberts and Patrick then took Jim's car over to the rail yard, where fires were still burning in some of the trees and grass around the area. Jim had brought his camera from his office, and took a number of photos of the demolished oxygen cars and the reactor rod car lying on its side. Then he had Patrick show him how the Geiger counter worked, and had Patrick wait while he walked toward the overturned railcar, listening to the clicking on earphones. The clicks were a bit louder as he approached the car, but did not register in the danger area of the dial. He then walked around to the other side of the car where the lead container for the rods were lying, still inside the flat car, but on its side. The clicking sound increased a bit, but still remained in the safe area of the dial. He then called Patrick over to where he was, removing the earphones from his ears, and handing the box and earphones to the technician.

"What do you think?" Jim asked. "Is it safe enough, or should we be cordoning off this area and keeping people away?" Wilmer Patrick also walked around the car, listening, and watching the dial. At one point he set the box into the railcar, next to a crease in the top of the lead container and noted the needle jump up into the danger zone.

"It's probably leaking, and it's hard to say if it will get worse. Yes, I think we need to seal this area off until guys with the white space suits can get in and see what's happening inside the chamber. Where we are standing now is no more hazardous than flying in an airliner, but up close, well, we don't want to do that!"

"I need to organize the search of the premises. Come back to my office. I've got some red fire department 'keep away' tape, and maybe you have some radioactivity danger signs, and we can post the area."

"Yes, there's a couple of those yellow triangular signs in the reactor office. I'll get them, stop by your office in the barracks for the tape, and get some posts at the utility shed."

"Okay, if I'm leaving before you get there, I'll leave the tape on my desk," Jim replied, and they both got back in Jim's car and drove to the reactor, where Patrick had left his own personal car.

For the next two hours Jim organized the various police officers who had joined the scene in a manhunt through all the facilities, the woods, around the perimeter, and any other place someone might be hiding. Two of the larger facilities had been closed and locked for Christmas and there was no sign of breaking and entering. Half way through the search Jim's walkie-talkie squawked and Sgt. Warbish reported that two FBI agents were at the gate. Jim turned his car and headed there.

FBI Special Agents Bret Leonard and Aaron Greenspoon were out of the Toledo office, closer than Cleveland, and were totally unfamiliar with the NASA facility, although both had heard of it. Jim explained as best he could what had transpired, what was currently being done, and what yet needed being done. It being a federal facility, he knew that the FBI would now be in charge of any investigation outside the facility, although Leonard said Jim would need to keep them informed of any information learned at the facility.

"Any thoughts on the perpetrators?" Special Agent Greenspoon asked.

"There have been a lot of local protests about the nuclear reactor and the cooling pond, although I'm told both are perfectly safe. But I can't imagine local protestors who usually just picket the place shooting a guard and using explosives."

"Do you have any experience with explosives?" Special Agent Leonard asked.

"Yes, quite a bit. I was an arson investigator with the New York City Fire Department for twenty years. Handled many industrial explosions, and was on a murder by explosion case when my retirement hit."

"Do you have sufficient equipment to identify the explosive here, or do you want us to send a crime lab crew?"

"I think I have what I need, or can get it at the college where I'll be teaching Fire Science next semester, but if I run into problems, I'll let you know. As for other forensics, yes, I think an FBI team would be very helpful."

"Who else might be suspect?" Greenspoon asked. "Any employee problems? Union problems?"

"None that I know of, although I've only been here since November. I've not heard of any problems, and I've met with all the safety technicians who would have mentioned something like that to me. So would Colonel Josephs."

"Who is Josephs?"

"Air Force Colonel Jeffrey Josephs. He's in charge of the Air Force MPs that guard the facility, at least until NASA gets their own security service. He's off for Christmas, but has been notified, and I suspect he will be here tomorrow, if not tonight, as his 'right-hand girl,' Corporal Alicia McQuinn, was the guard shot by the intruder or intruders.'

"How is she?"

"I've not heard yet. She was taken to Sandusky General, shot in the chest, but I've not had time to follow up yet."

"Any other suspects?" Greenspoon asked.

"Considering the activities that go on here, even though none of it is top secret as far as I've been told, one might suspect a competitor. An industrial competitor? Maybe, but doubtful. A foreign competitor? Much more likely. Now, who is in the space business that competes with the U.S.? Russia is an obvious answer, but there could also be others. But my guess would be an international competitor, either trying to gain information or cause delay in what NASA is doing. What are your thoughts?"

"I, too, would be surprised if it was local people," Leonard answered. "What can we do right now to assist?"

"With that railcar of nuclear fuel rods on its side apparently leaking radiation, I would anticipate that the AEC is going to be on the scene. The technician I was without there is sealing off the area with tape and signs until the AEC can inspect the overturned car. Could you notify and work with them?"

"Yeah, they're probably off for the holiday, but we can contact them tomorrow and see what they want to do. What about the railroad? They delivered the two tank cars that blew up, and the fuel rod cars."

"The tracks are NASA's beyond the gate, and it wasn't touched by the intruders. I'll need to determine who owned the two cars and notify them. We'll probably need the railroad's help re-righting the car that is on its side. I'll take care of that tomorrow. Right now I'm concerned about Alicia and would like to call the hospital to see how she's doing."

"Okay. We'll stay here and see what these local police have done, or if they find anyone. Come back to the gate after you check with the hospital. We'll make the gate our operations point for the time being."

Jim had to look up the phone number for the hospital, and used his best authoritative voice to get past the typical holiday help on the hospital switchboard. "This is James Roberts, chief of security for NASA here in Erie County. This afternoon an Air Force corporal, Alicia McQuinn, was brought in to the Emergency Room. I need to know her condition." It was effective, and he was connected immediately to the E.R., where a nurse also responded to his introduction.

"Oh, Mr. Roberts – or it is Commander or something?" Jim replied that Mr. Roberts was sufficient. "Corporal McQuinn was unconscious when she arrived. She's in stable, but critical condition with an open chest wound. We have called in two of our surgeons, Dr. Atwater and Dr. Errington, and they are preparing for surgery at present."

"Dexter Atwater?" Jim asked.

"Yes! Do you know him?"

"I had dinner with him earlier today, before the accident. But Alicia McQuinn is military. Will that affect her stay in the hospital?

"We have no near-by military hospitals, so for the time being, she should be staying here. But we don't know how to contact her family."

"I'll take care of that. Here is my phone number. There is an answering machine, so please have the surgical staff and Dr. Atwater keep me posted on her condition." Jim left his number, and quickly returned to the gate. The two FBI agents were busy fending off questions from a number of reporters, a television news car from Toledo and two TV trucks from Cleveland, plus others that had just arrived and were clamoring at the gate. Jim recognized that the agents were not familiar with dealing with the press.

"Agent Greenspoon," he said, "perhaps I can help. Press relations is part of my job description here. Gentlemen," he announced in a loud voice, and the crowd gathered around while the television cameras rolled, "there was an incident here earlier this afternoon, and one of the Air Force security team members was injured. I've just spoken with the hospital and her condition is stable, and I was assured that she is receiving the best of care. We are looking into the cause of the incident, which involved two railroad cars within the facility, but have no further information for you at this time. I will try to have a further bulletin in time for your evening news tomorrow afternoon at three. Until then, we request that you all return to your stations or offices so that we can keep this area open for emergency vehicles. Thank you."

"What's your name, mister?" one reporter shouted.

"James Roberts. I'm head of security here at the Plum Brook NASA facility."

"This place has a nuclear reactor on it. Is that what exploded?" asked another.

"Indeed not! The reactor was not in any way involved. It had been shut down temporarily before the holidays. There is no concern regarding the reactor, gentlemen. I'll have more details tomorrow." The questions kept coming, but Jim turned to the two agents who gave him a nod and smile. The broken gate parts were dragged into place, ending the session.

As the reporters and television crews departed Jim inquired from Sgt. Warbish if his men and the police had found any trace of the persons who had broken in. Apparently he had already told Agents Leonard and Greenspoon, but repeated the non-news that they had found nothing. "But how is Alicia?" he asked. "'Stable condition' really doesn't mean much."

"She apparently is in surgery at this very moment, from what I was able to learn. Her condition is critical, but stable, and I happen to know the surgeon they called in, so I think that she is in good hands. I also got a call from Jeff Hunter at Lewis in Brookpark and informed him of the situation. He may come out tomorrow, but for now we are on our own. Agent Leonard," Jim said, addressing the nearest FBI agent, "is there any chance of getting a forensics team here tomorrow to really examine the scene. They'll need to get the bullet from the hospital if the surgeon was able to extract it from Corporal McQuinn. I can get some of the explosive debris and do chemical analysis, but my suspicion is plastics explosives, probably with a timer so that whoever it was had already left before the explosion. I doubt we'll find any fingerprints, unless we can find the timer and they didn't wear gloves – and I doubt that's the case.

"The rails within the facility are NASA's, but we'll need to get what the railroads call 'the big hook' out here to turn that overturned car back onto the tracks, but we'll probably have to do it under AEC supervision."

"What's 'AEC'?" Jason Warbish asked.

"The Atomic Energy Commission. They investigate any accidents involving anything nuclear. They may even have some ideas about who did this."

"What about the two cars that blew up?" Greenspoon asked.

"I only got a brief glance when I went with the reactor technician to the yard, but it appeared to me that the cars were specially built stainless steel high-pressure cars for carrying liquid oxygen. They were probably owned by whichever company manufactured the oxygen. Someone must have been watching them being delivered by the Baltimore & Ohio on the B&O branch from Sandusky and knew that they were oxygen and not nitrogen. It's not that explosive. But for whatever experiments are going on, fuel-wise, that oxygen would be crucial. This isn't simple vandalism. Jason, do you know what time were those cars brought in?"

"A Corporal Gibbons was on duty when the call from the NYC in Toledo came about midnight that they had two cars to switch to here, and to open the gate when they arrived. He called me at the barracks as he is one of the replacement men and didn't know about railroad tracks or gates, so I had to get up and dress and open the gates. It was about one in the morning when I got there, and about a half hour later when the switcher engine brought in the two cars. The gate was closed until then, and as soon as the cars were delivered and the switcher changed tracks around them – the track between the two tank cars and the car with the fuel rods was empty – the switcher backed out the gate again and I locked it up. I sure didn't see anyone around watching at two in the morning."

"It's starting to get dark," Agent Greenspoon commented. "Not much more we can do here tonight. Can you get some of those police departments to stick around? Maybe ride shotgun with your men who run the perimeter, and one or two here at the gate, Sgt. Warbish?"

"Yeah, I think they'll agree. This is Perkins Township and Erie County, so between the township and the county we should be able to get three or four guys to stay their shift and get the next shift out here."

"I'll be here, too, Jason," Jim said. "I'll call my wife from the guard house and let her know. Actually, it was the surgeon operating on Alicia and his wife who were to bring Jayne home from the dinner we were at. Have you and your men had dinner yet?"

"One of the off-duty guys made some sandwiches for us. Yeah, we're okay."

"Tomorrow I'll have Sgt. Warbish get a couple of his guys to go through the neighborhood north of the facility and see if they have any damage from the blast. I'd be surprised if there weren't a few broken windows," Jim said.

* * *

Jim called home from his office. Jayne had just arrived, and Peggy Atwater was still with her. "Dr. Atwater stayed at the hospital, so Peggy drove me home. Do you want to talk with her?"

"Sure do!" Jim answered, and Peggy soon came on the line. "Thank you, Peggy, for getting Jayne home. I'm afraid NASA has interrupted both your and Dexter's as well as our Christmas. But I know the Air Force corporal – how is she? The hospital told me Dexter was one of the surgeons."

"I think she'll be all right, but it will take a while. She was in recovery when Jayne and I left the hospital. Dex is going to stay there to make sure she is stable, until I get back. He said the bullet just missed the heart and a major artery, but collapsed one lung. They got it functioning again, and the thoracic specialist is going to check her later this evening. Dr. Errington was on duty in the ER when she arrived. He saved Dr. Fairchild's life one time, and is an excellent physician and surgeon."

"That's good. The Air Force guys here were all anxious to hear. I hope Dexter saved the bullet."

"Oh, that's quite routine in a shooting. But we don't often have military wounds. Will she get a Purple Heart or anything like that?"

"I don't know. She should get some sort of medal. I don't suppose you heard if she said anything."

"No, she was unconscious when they brought her in, and the hospital called Dex. It will probably be a day or two before you can visit her. Here's Jayne; she wants to ask you something."

Jayne came on the line and asked if Jim would be home that night. He explained that the facility was still being searched and was basically under FBI orders, so he would spend the night and call her the next morning.

As he hung up, he sat and thought for a moment to decide what to do next. Everyone who should be notified had been, except Corporal McQuinn's family. Her file was in Colonel Joseph's office and Jim had a key, but he hoped that the Colonel would report back either that evening or by early tomorrow, and felt that it was the Colonel's responsibility to notify McQuinn's family. Besides, by tomorrow they would know more about her condition.

The next thing was to try and determine if anyone associated with the facility might have a desire to delay whatever tests were pending. Jim wasn't sure which of the facility units was planning on using the oxygen. If it was a unit that was operated by a contractor, a competitor of that contractor might have reason to cause a delay. The contracts usually had strict time requirements, and any delay could cost the contractor penalties, perhaps allowing a competing contractor an opportunity to take over. But this was just conjecture.

An international competitor seemed equally possible. Russia obviously had a space program, but so did the French and British, and probably Red China. The Chinese had, after all, invented rockets centuries before and knew quite a bit about explosives. But Jim could only guess until he knew more about where the oxygen was to be used.

Perhaps, he wondered, it was not the oxygen but the nuclear fuel rods that had been the target, and the intruders hit the wrong cars. If they had exploded the fuel rod car, it would have been a national disaster, not just the equivalent of an industrial incident. But the shipment and exchange of the fuel rods was not well-known or publicized. If that had been the target, it would have to be an "inside" job of someone who knew when, where and what would be taking place. Jim suspected that the blast overturning the fuel rod container car was not the intent of the sabotage. Nevertheless, he would have to check it out. He chuckled to himself as he suddenly realized that what Colonel Josephs had said was true: he'd know what to keep secret when the time came. What had happened this afternoon was certainly going to create a lot of secrets.

He was also unsure of what reporting would be required. If this was the FDNY, a report in triplicate would be expected as soon as possible, with formal captioning. Force of habit made Jim insert paper into the typewriter he had been provided and start such a report. But to whom? Colonel Josephs? Jeff Hunter? The FBI? He simply typed, "To Whom It

May Concern – Confidential, December 25, 1968, Plum Brook NASA Incident."

Chapter 6

The rest of the holiday week and the first week of 1969 were hectic for Jim. His thoughts about contractor competition were demolished when he learned that the cars of oxygen were destined for a unit that was entirely staffed by NASA employees, with no independent contractors involved. While the oxygen was crucial to the work that unit was doing, they had an ample supply on hand and would not be delayed in their research.

The unit and Colonel Josephs put Jim in charge of notifying the B&O Railroad to help move the demolished tank cars, once the FBI and AEC investigations were complete, and notifying the oxygen company, O-One, Inc., of the destruction of the cars and the need for replacement. The tank car mess was not cleaned up until after New Year's Day. Each afternoon Jim met reporters at the gate, but there was little news to give them. Colonel Josephs had notified the McQuinn family the morning after the explosion, and they had driven to Sandusky from their home in Michigan to be with their daughter as her condition improved.

The overturned nuclear fuel rods car was much more of a challenge. An inspector from the Atomic Energy Commission had arrived the day after Christmas and found that the leak from the container was severe enough that something would have to be done to stabilize the rod-carrying lead shield casing before the car could be turned back on its wheels. Further, the wheels, which Jim knew were called "trucks," on the left side of the flatcar were so bent and twisted by the blast that they would have to be removed and replaced before the car could be transported to the back part of the rail yard where the rods would be unloaded. As the explosion had happened on NASA property and tracks, the railroad would be charging NASA for all of the involved costs.

This got Jim to wondering if it had really been the car containing the nuclear rods, and not the two chemical cars, that had been the target of the sabotage. He contacted the security officers at both the Hypersonic Tunnel Facility and the Propulsion Research lab and inquired whether they had any projects that would be delayed by the inability to bring the new fuel rods to the reactor, the source of power for the two facilities. Indeed, he learned, that for the HTF this was the case, that the lack of power would delay a very strategic test that was needed so that other units could proceed with their work. Half of the technicians who worked the HTF were contractors, employed by Gearmone Engineering, a French company that had contracted with NASA to assist in various wind tunnel tests.

Jim then inquired whether Gearmone Engineering was the contractor on any of the related projects, and learned that they were also involved the Spacecraft Propulsion Research lab, and that two of the contractor's engineers had come from France and were in charge of dealings with the other contractor employees.

Jim requested and received the personnel files on all of the employees, both contract and NASA, at both the HTF and SPR, and all of the employee personnel files that NASA had on all of the Gearmone employees, regardless of where they worked. It was a stack of twenty-eight NASA files and thirty-seven Gearmone employees. All of the NASA employees were American, all graduates of various universities with several graduate degrees, and all had signed the government secrets agreement, meaning that they had already been screened by the FBI.

Twenty-eight of the Gearmone employees were Americans, who had also signed the secrets agreement. Seven were French, and had been educated in either France at the Sorbonne or, in the case of two, at McGill University in Montreal, each possessing at least one doctorate. Of the other two, one, Pierre Beye, was Swiss, and had been in America since 1936, married to an American, and was a graduate of Case Institute of Technology in Cleveland. He had been the Gearmone engineer who had recommended Gearmone to NASA, and was highly respected by NASA, and was the Gearmone employee in charge of the others. He, too, had signed the secrets act agreement, and had been cleared by the FBI.

The final Gearmone employee was Rolfe Reübrich. He had arrived from France only in mid-October of 1968, and spoke English with a German accent. He had not yet received his FBI clearance, but was permitted to work at the Spacecraft Propulsion Research lab as he was a specialist in hypersonic rocket design and came highly recommended by the negotiators for Gearmone, who had an office in Boston. Several of the Gearmone employees had also worked at the Lewis lab in Brookpark, but not Reübrich. Jim called the SPR security chief, Harold Tibbs, and asked him to stop by Jim's office. Tibbs arrived a few minutes later.

"Harold, what do you know about Rolfe Reübrich?" Jim asked.

"Not much, really," Harold replied. "He arrived a couple of months ago, highly recommended by the Gearmone people in Boston. Pierre Beye did not know him, but when he arrived he seemed to know what he was doing and was very quiet, not socializing much with the other Gearmone contractors or with the NASA guys, except to the extent it involved his work. He speaks English with a German accent, and some of the NASA guys believe he may have been a German scientist who was brought to France after the War. He's supposed to be brilliant."

"He hasn't received his FBI security clearance yet, according to his personnel file."

"No, we submitted the papers after he got here, but have not had any response yet. Why are you concerned about Reübrich?"

"I'm just curious about him. Do you know anything about the French space program?"

"No, I just know they have one, but it's not very advanced yet. Some of their labs and such are somewhere in Africa."

"Are any of their operations being conducted by Gearmone?"

"I don't know. I wouldn't be surprised if they were. Oh, I see what you're headed. You think he might be a French agent who would like to see our operations delayed?"

"Maybe. It's just a theory. You've not seen any evidence at SPR?"

"No, none at all."

"Not being an engineer, I don't fully understand the hypersonic design or what it entails, but whatever your team is doing at SPR is going to be delayed until we get the reactor operational again. Will there still be work for the design team to do during the wait?"

"Yes, plenty! Actually the delay is helping us catch up on some backlogged items preliminary to the tests we are anticipating, but I wouldn't think anyone at SPR would want to intentionally delay the projects."

"Well, that's good to hear, if there is any good to come out of this explosion."

"By the way, how is that Air Force girl that was shot?"

"Doing okay. She'll recover fully, and has the full use of her left lung back. Colonel Josephs got back the day after Christmas and notified her family – she's single, of course – and they drove down from Michigan and are staying in town until she is released, and then will take her back to Michigan for recuperation. I agreed to pick up their hotel bill. Problem is, the Air Force hasn't sent a replacement for her, temporary or permanent, so I've had to take over some of her duties, and the rest of the AF gang are helping out, too. She must have been an octopus to accomplish all she did on a regular basis: answer the phone fifty times a day, set the work schedules for the Air Force MPs, type Colonel Josephs' correspondence, and fetch his coffee, you name it and she did it!"

"I'm surprised a good looking kid like her is still single," Tibbs said. "I hope they send her back here when she's recovered."

"Her doctor, Dexter Atwater, whom I know, told me she wanted to come back to work even before she was released from the hospital, but he insisted she take at least three weeks before doing any work. I met her parents. They are very nice, and I can see why she is, too."

Despite Harold Tibbs lack of doubts about the French contractor with the German accent Jim wondered why, if his security clearance had come through in a matter of days, Rolfe Reübrich's was taking months. After Harold left Jim's office to return to the HTF Jim dialed the Toledo FBI office and asked for either Agent Greenspoon or Leonard. It was

Greenspoon, the Special Agent in Charge, who answered a few seconds later, and Jim explained his concern about Reübrich's security clearance and what Harold had told him about Reübrich's having possibly been a German scientist during the War. Greenspoon was unfamiliar with the security clearance request and had Jim hold while he checked to see if the Toledo office had a file on NASA clearances.

"No," Greenspoon said when he came back on the line, "the security clearances are handled out of Cleveland. I'll forward an inquiry on Rolfe Reübrich and see what's holding it up. Do you really think someone – contractor or government – was targeting the nuclear fuel car by exploding the two oxygen cars?"

"There was no reason to destroy the oxygen. There was plenty already on hand, so that did not cause a delay. But if the fuel rods were the target, why not attack that car directly? This wasn't just local vandals or protesters, not using plastics and shooting a military policewoman. I couldn't think of any other reason, but Tibbs says that the nuclear power being temporarily out isn't causing any problems. So what was the objective?"

"The forensics team found nothing except one possible print, which they are checking now," Greenspoon replied, "and the AEC guys said they could find no damage to the nuclear fuel car other than it being blown over by the oxygen blast and the wheels bent. But they're going to have a hell of a time getting the container sealed and the car back on the track right-side up, and the car can't be moved."

"Yeah, a couple of guys in their space suits – what are those things, lead? – are out there trying to figure out how to inspect the rods and seal the container before the railroad can bring in the equipment to lift the car. They offered me a suit if I wanted to watch, but with that young Air Force corporal in the hospital, I've ended up with much of her duties. But I do need to get with them this afternoon. Well, if you find out anything on Rolfe, let me know."

Chapter 7

Dr. Hilda Johnson, Professor of Physics at Fremont College, was in her office planning for her next class the following day when her phone rang. She answered, and heard a man's voice on the line. "Dr. Johnson, Dr. Hilda Johnson?"

"Yes, who is calling?"

"Dr. Johnson, my name is Julius Blanski. I'm a senior engineer with the Atomic Energy Commission in Washington. I understand your former name was von Werden."

"I'm married to Dr. Ross Johnson, the choral director here at Fremont. My maiden name was Waggoner."

"Yes, yes, I know all that, but I understand that you are a nuclear engineer familiar with nuclear fuel rod transfers, including to submarines."

"I don't understand...."

"Dr. Johnson, we need your help. I believe you are aware of an explosion of some rail cars at a National Aeronautics and Space Administration south of Sandusky called Plum Brook."

"I have heard about this, yes. The news said it was two cars of liquid oxygen."

"Yes, that is correct. But the news did not report the rest of the story, and it is in regards to that where we need your help. Might I stop by your office in the morning and discuss it with you?"

"I have a class to teach at nine-thirty, but after eleven I could meet with you. Do you know where my office is?"

"The Science Building basement?" Blanski asked.

"Yes. I will be here."

Hilda was curious about the call. No one, except Ross, the Fairchilds and Merriams, plus Dean Harding and the department head, Ray Durrand, knew her real name or that she had been a consultant to the East German Navy. Several near nuclear accidents involving the transfer of fuel rods in Germany, Poland and the Ukraine had become a part of her professional biography, but only the American CIA was supposed to be aware of that. Then she recalled a small item in *The New York Times* about three days earlier that a number of U.S. AEC engineers, scientists and technicians would be attending a two-week conference at the U.N. Nuclear Energy Agency, the International Atomic Energy Commission, in Vienna. This, she reasoned, might have something to do with the phone call.

The following morning after her hour and a half lecture on the role of the electron in an atom, she returned to her office to find two men in dark business suits, one about sixty, tall and gray haired, the other younger, slightly balding with thick glasses. "Professor Johnson?" the older man asked, and Hilda nodded, ushering them into her small office next to Dr. Durrand's. The younger man closed the door.

"As I explained yesterday on the phone," the older man said, "I am Julius Blanski. This is Dr. Rod Thurmond, and we are investigators for the Atomic Energy Commission, based in Washington, although we have been in Ohio for most of the past week. We have a problem, and believe you may be able to help us."

"How did you get information about me?" Hilda asked.

"From the Central Intelligence Agency. They were reluctant to let us see your file, and after reading it, I can understand your reluctance to talk with us," Blanski said. "But under the circumstances they broke their own rules and let us review your file. You are a very brave individual, Dr. Johnson. But let me explain.

"As you probably know from the news," he continued, "two tank cars of liquid oxygen exploded in the NASA rail yard at Plum Brook on Christmas Day. What was not reported was that the person or persons committing the sabotage – probably at least two or more – also shot the Air Force MP at the gate, crashed it, and set plastic explosives under the two tank cars of oxygen. Their motive is unknown. Anyway, the explosion caused another rail car two tracks to the west to be blown over. That car had just arrived from Hanford AEC facilities in the State of Washington, and contained fresh nuclear fuel rods that were intended for replacement in a small nuclear reactor located on the Plum Brook facility. The force of the blast caused the heavy sealed container for the fuel rods to split open, and unacceptable levels of radiation are escaping from the overturned car. We can't get the railroad to come in and turn the car right-side up until we can be certain that the leak is stopped and even more radiation will not leak in the process."

Rod Thurmond then said, "Our problem is that the two experts we have on this type of fuel transfer problem are attending a conference in Vienna, and both are key to that conference and can't be brought back. We sent an inquiry, and somehow they learned that there had been an East German scientist who was an expert in such problems who defected a few years ago to the U.S. They had no names or details, but we contacted the CIA and they reluctantly gave us access to your file. Will you help us?"

"If you will allow me to verify what you are saying – and I have no reason to disbelieve you, but I must be cautious, as you may recognize from my file – I would feel it my patriotic duty to do whatever I can to help you."

"How soon?"

"I have another class this afternoon, but after that I am free tomorrow, but not again until Saturday. I should be able to give you an answer this afternoon. Go have lunch and come back here before one-fifteen."

Immediately after the two men left her office Hilda called the Religions Department. Sally Merriam answered, and Hilda asked if Dr. Fairchild was in and could see her as soon as possible. "Yes, Hilda, he just came in from a class and won't have another until this afternoon. Come on over, or do you want to talk with him on the phone?"

"No, I need to see him. Don't let him leave for lunch until I get there. It's just across the campus." She hung up, and, grabbing her winter coat, hurried from her office up the stairs and across the college quadrangle toward the chapel and Hayes Hall, where Fairchild's office was located. Fairchild met her as she came in the door and led her to his office, shutting the door as he had no idea what to expect. Was she having a problem with Ross, or a student? He could not guess what might make her sound and appear so frantic. But when she explained the visit from the two AEC technicians, he understood her concern. No one was supposed to know that she was a former East German scientist that the Stasi had already attempted to murder her once, aboard the college cabin cruiser on the Cuyahoga River in Cleveland.

Hilda explained the visit from the two AEC engineers, but said she needed verification. Richard Fairchild dug through the clutter on his desk and found his address book. He had a direct line to his friend, George McCracken, at the Central Intelligence Agency in Langley, Virginia. McCracken had been Fairchild's commanding officer in an Army Intelligence Unit operating behind enemy lines during World War Two; Fairchild was the unit's chaplain, but his ability to speak German also made him their interpreter, and after the War McCracken had tried to recruit Fairchild for what was to become the CIA as he had been trained as an intelligence officer as well as being a chaplain. Fortunately his call caught McCracken just as he was leaving for lunch. Fairchild explained what Hilda had told him, and McCracken asked to speak to her.

"Hilda, I hear you are doing a great job at Fremont and married that choir director. I'm sorry I couldn't get to the wedding. Now, I understand your concern, and you are absolutely correct to be concerned, but in this case Dr. Blanski and Dr. Thurmond are definitely Atomic Energy Commission employees and, as I understand their need, definitely do need your help. Blanski is tall, gray-haired, about sixty, right?'

"Yes, that's a good description. Thurmond is younger, balding, wearing glasses," she replied.

"Okay, those are the two I met yesterday morning. The AEC's own experts are in Vienna, as they told you, and heard about a defected nuclear scientist in the U.S., so in cross-referencing other experts they came across your credentials from the University of Chicago which we had placed in the records, and that led them to me, and me to you. I should have called you to alert you they would be coming, and I apologize for not doing so. But I do hope you can help them."

"I'll certainly do what I can," Hilda answered. The two spoke for a few more moments and then Fairchild spoke to McCracken again before hanging up.

"Hilda, I think McCracken was testing you by not calling to warn you that the AEC would need your help, and, if I'm right, you passed perfectly. The CIA does stunts like that, but if George says it's okay, then I'd certainly agree with him. Want to stop at the campus cafeteria for a bite of lunch before you meet with the two technicians again."

"Thank you, Richie, but I have a sandwich at my office, with some fruit, so I'll just wait for Blanski and Thurmond there. If I'm going to be going to Sandusky for who knows how long I need to get my class schedule in order in case Ray needs to take one of my classes."

* * *

That evening when Ross heard what Hilda had agreed to do, he got concerned for her safety. "Even though those two guys are cleared by the CIA, you shouldn't be messing around with leaking nuclear fuel rods," he scolded.

"You're not supposed to know about this!" she laughed. Technically, I wasn't supposed to tell you, but I know you can, what is it you Americans say, 'keep it under your shirt'?"

"Hat. Keep it under my hat. In other words, keep it secret. 'Keep your shirt on' is the expression meaning not to get excited But it's going to be hard to 'keep my shirt on' if I have to keep the fact that you are going into something dangerous 'under my hat!'"

"So do it anyway," she replied. "I'll have a protective suit and won't be in any danger. Besides, I understand that Jim Roberts is the person in charge of this operation, he, and an Air Force colonel named Josephs. Remember Jim and his wife, Jayne, from the Christmas party?"

"Yeah, the New York fireman. He seemed to be knowledgeable, but nevertheless, you be damned careful around that nuclear fuel car. If I didn't have the chorus rehearsal tomorrow I would insist on going with you."

"I doubt they'd let you. But don't worry. There is no danger of explosion. It's just puzzling to them why the oxygen cars were blown up, but not the nuclear fuel car. That young woman guard is still in the hospital recovering from her bullet wound."

* * *

"Jeff," Jim said to Colonel Josephs as they waited at the gate for the team that the AEC was sending to inspect the car and arrange for its lifting, "when you hired me and learned that I knew Professor Johnson at Fremont, you said you wanted me to keep an eye on her. Well, I just learned this morning from Dr. Blanski that the person who is going to direct this operation will be none other than your Professor Hilda Johnson."

"What?" he exclaimed. "You're puttin' me on!"

"Nope. You said she was some sort of nuclear specialist, and I understand this sort of thing is that specialty. Apparently she did this sort of thing all over the Iron Curtain countries before she defected, and someone from Poland mentioned it to the AEC guys at some conference in Vienna. She defected during an opera, from what I've been able to pick up from friends at Fremont."

"She was at an opera?"

"No, she was singing in it!"

"Good God! Well, I see a couple of vehicles coming. I hope it's the AEC team."

Jim rode with Colonel Josephs and Sergeant Warbish and led the three vehicles from the gate after they had received passes to the rail yard. In a black sedan were the AEC engineers, Blanski and Thurmond, and Hilda Johnson. In a large white van was the rest of the AEC team and the third held their equipment, including special white radiation-protecting head-to-toe suits with built-in breathing apparatus. Upon arrival at the rail yard the van parked far away from the overturned flat car with the encased fuel rods, and the other two vehicles parked next to it. Because of the radiation leak the two destroyed oxygen cars remained where they had been Christmas Day after the blast; the railroad refused to allow its crews on the facility as long as the nuclear fuel was leaking.

Five technicians in the white van set up some sort of tent with a shower and a tank of something, then assisted Blanski, Thurmond, Johnson, the colonel and Jim in putting on the white suits and adjusting their breathing equipment. A few days earlier Blanski and Roberts had performed the same dressing up for the AEC's first look at the car. Johnson and Blanski were handed special Geiger counters, and only when the technicians had carefully checked each suit were the five allowed to approach the overturned railcar.

Although the sound was muffled by the suits, by shouting they were able to hear each other. "When we were here a few days ago, Dr. Johnson, the main area of leakage seemed to be coming from the top of the container, and there appeared to be a crack in the lid," Julius Blanski said. Rod Thurmond had a strong light and beamed it on the area Blanski had described, and Hilda moved forward with her Geiger counter, which clicked like a printing press, the dial spinning into the red zone.

"I don't see a crack, but I do see where the two parts of the top of the container have separated," Hilda said. "It appears to be hinged on both sides. I've not seen that type of container before, but it is a very good design. Do you have the diagrams of the container that Hanford sent?" Thurmond had them in his hand and gave them to Hilda to study.

"Yes," she continued. "See, each of the rods is suspended on lead brackets for transport, with individual shielding so they can be lifted out and installed in the reactor. The two halves of the top fold upward and are then pressed together and sealed for transport. When the car was blown over, one of the brackets may have broken, and the weight of a rod casing rolled into the right side of the top, breaking the seal and allowing the top right half to open downward. It is from there that the radiation is leaking.

"While the radiation is high from the fuel pellets in the rods," she continued, "I don't believe, from the way the brackets and casings are designed that the rods could possibly touch each other. That would be disastrous. From what I see and from the diagrams what we need to do is jack the right half of the top of the container back into place and seal it again, which should stop the radiation leakage, then brace the container while the rail car is righted.

"According to the diagrams from Hanford there are lifting loops on both ends...." She stopped momentarily and walked to each end of the container, seeking the loops, which were about two-thirds up from the bottom of the container. "Yes, that's right. The container can be braced when the car is turned back up, and then it can be lifted by crane and transferred to another flatcar. Julius, you said Hanford was sending both a lifting crane designed for this purpose and another flatcar, is that correct?"

"Yes, it had reached Chicago yesterday, and should be here Saturday."

"*Gute*! Now, we need to get the two halves of the lid jacked back together and sealed. Hopefully, when the car is righted, the loose rod will slide back into its brackets where it should be, and the container will remain stable."

"What if the bracket is broken?" Jim asked.

"Let's look at the diagram, Jim. According to this, each rod of fuel pellets is stored in a separate encasement. From the diagram I can't see how, even if the curved bracket was broken in the blast and jolt of overturning, that the rod could escape from its individual containment area to come into contact with any of the other rods. These containers, I would imagine, are designed for rail transport and thus for accidental overturning. Trains derail and overturn all the time, so the rods should be reasonably protected. At least that is what the diagrams show. Julius, I trust these are accurate."

"That is what the engineers at Hanford assured me."

"Do you have jacks and soldering equipment on your van?" Hilda asked.

"I believe so. Rod, go check." Thurmond trotted over to the white van and questioned the technicians. Then he returned and advised that they had jack equipment, but no welding equipment, oxygen and acetylene."

"We should have that here," Jim said, "at the maintenance shed. Jeff, could Jason go and get it?"

"Yeah, I'll send him for it. He'll probably need a truck, but there is one at the maintenance yard." Colonel Josephs went over to where Sgt. Warbish was waiting and sent him in the Air Force car to the maintenance shed. He then came back to where the two AEC engineers were discussing how best to jack the lower half of the container lid up to the upper half. "What I want to know," the colonel asked, "is whether these fuel rods are going to have to be shipped back to Hanford and replaced, or whether we can go ahead and load them into the reactor? I mean, the reactor can't run without fuel and that power is needed for the HTF."

"What is the HTF?" Julius Blanski asked.

"The Hypersonic Tunnel Facility," Josephs replied. "It's a special wind tunnel to test air-breathing engines that operate at five times the speed of sound. Takes a lot of power, which is why the reactor is so vital. It's also needed for the propulsion lab."

"If the container can be sealed and the car turned right-side up, I think you should be able to use those fuel rods without difficulty. Even if one was bent, the others could be used, and the bent one returned to Hanford. Would you agree, Dr. Johnson?"

"Rolling off the brackets, unless the rod hit something inside the lid and bent, should not cause it any damage. Uranium is a metal, after all. But how do you do your transfer, Colonel?"

"We bring in a crane to lift the container off the railcar in a separate rail yard down that track over there," he replied, pointing to a rail line running into a grove of trees. "Then it is put on a special wagon and hauled down a concrete pathway to the reactor building, where the engineers have another crane device to open the container and lift the rods through a movable slab in the concrete dome of the reactor. The old rods have already been removed when the reactor was shut down a couple of days ago. I think they were sent to Hanford on a car similar to this one in the same type of container. But I wasn't a witness to it being done. You'd have to talk to those eggheads that work there – no offense, ladies and gentlemen – the engineers, I mean, as to the exact process."

By the time Sgt. Warbish got back with the truck and the welding equipment two of the technicians had also suited up in white safety suits and were starting to apply the portable jack to the lower half of the container lid. By fractions of an inch it was pushed upward, and Rod Thurmond kept monitoring the clicking on his Geiger counter.

"It's going down by the minute," he announced. As the two lips of the lid met, four wide metal straps were welded onto the bottom half of the lid, brought over the lips of the lid, and welded onto the exposed left side of the container, completely sealing it. "Just normal readings now, from radiation on the car itself," Thurmond said. "I think it is ready for the railroad to turn the car right-side up. If the new flatcar from Hanford gets here Saturday, and the car is up-righted, perhaps the container can be transferred using the same crane."

"No, Rod. If the railroad uses the kind of crane they use on derailments, it will have to be a different type of crane to lift the container to the other car, I suspect. However," Julius Blanski said, "this railcar and the remains of those two chemical tank cars will have been contaminated by the leak. That's the radiation you were picking up when you first came out here, Jim. They will have to be cut up and taken back to Hanford in pieces. Colonel Josephs, as NASA is federal, as is the AEC, I think you can bring in an experienced contractor to do that job. I'll contact Hanford and see who they recommend."

Colonel Josephs looked at Jim, still in his white safety suit, and said, "Jim, can you arrange with the Baltimore & Ohio to bring in their whatever-they-call-it to turn the car over? I imagine you AEC guys will want to be here when that happens to check the container again," he said, addressing Julius Blanski.

"Definitely," Blanski agreed. "We had planned on that. However, I don't think you will need to be present, Dr. Johnson, unless you want to be."

"Frankly, I'd sooner miss eating for the next week than miss that!" she said with a chuckle. "Saturday or whenever, let me know and I'll be here."

"Good. We appreciate that. Your insight into this situation has been most helpful," Blanski said. "Don't you agree, Colonel Josephs?"

"Yeah, it's a good thing you got her to help," he conceded. "Dr. Johnson, I confess I was concerned when I heard you were coming, as I'd received a notice that there was some former Commie over at Fremont College and to make sure you weren't some sort of spy that might try to find out what NASA is doing here. But I think that was FBI nonsense."

"I understand, Colonel. I *was* a Party member at Halle University. All the professors were, but none of us believed in Communism, and most of us hated the government, even though we worked for it. The information I provided to NATO when I defected was vital, and proved accurate. It involved Russian submarines, and that they were dangerous ships. But I didn't defect to be a spy for the East; that I can assure you.

"I wonder, Colonel," she continued, "if I might witness the transfer of the container to the reactor and the installation of the fuel rods. That can be a dangerous operation, and I've supervised similar operations a number of times in Poland and the Ukraine."

"Well, I'm not in charge of that, thank goodness," he replied, "but I will inquire and see what can be arranged. I'll let you know. Now, let's get the hell out of these damned suits!"

"Hold on, Colonel!" Thurmond said with a laugh. "That suit is contaminated. We all have to go into the shower tent over there – it's a special liquid to decontaminate the suit – only then can you take it off. Dr. Johnson, I'm sure you are familiar with the routine."

"That's what scared me about the Russian submarine – they had no such suits."

* * *

Arriving back at his office with the two AEC engineers and Hilda Johnson, Jim had just sat down behind his desk when the phone rang. It was Aaron Greenspoon from the Toledo FBI office. "Roberts," he said, "we were finally able to get a statement from Corporal McQuinn, and also got the report back from forensics on the video tapes taken December 25."

"I visited Alicia a few days ago, but she was still too medicated to make much sense. How is she doing?"

"Doctor Atwater says she'll make a full recovery. We got the slug and it was sent to Washington. She says that there were three men in a black car, a Lincoln, she thinks, who pulled up at the gate, and when she went out to register them, they shot her before she could even get a look at them. That knocked her back into the guardhouse, where she hit her head. By the time she gained enough sense to get up, they had crashed through the gate. She saw the car in the rail yard on the camera screen, and sounded the internal alarm. When the blast went off, she also hit the red nuclear alarm – guess it scared the neighbors half to hell and back! About two minutes later the black car sped out through the gate they'd broken through so fast she hadn't time to react. She was so weak from the wound that she collapsed again.

"The video all confirms what she said," he continued. "The camera at the gatehouse really didn't show much except the arrival of the car and a hand coming out the window with a gun. The bullet appears to be a .357, but Washington will confirm that. The film on the rail yard shows that the three guys in the car surveyed the three cars carefully, and then placed the explosives on the two cars of oxygen directly opposite the nuclear fuel car so that the blast was certain to turn it over. That was intentional. You can tell from the video when Corporal McQuinn set off the alarms, because the three guys all stopped momentarily and looked around, then hustled to finish setting the explosives and sped away in the car. It was a black Lincoln, but they'd spread mud on the license plate, so none of the videos showed any of the car's plate. What's happening with the nuclear fuel car?" Greenspoon asked as he finished telling Jim what the video had shown.

"I've got the two AEC engineers with me here in the office right now. We have sealed the fuel container, and now the railroad can come in and turn the car right-side up, although it will have to be cut up and sent to Hanford, Washington, as both that car and the two oxygen tank cars are contaminated with radiation. Want to watch that operation? We've got lots of really comfortable space suits you can wear! Even a shower of some white goo to clean them."

"I'll bet! Nope, I think I'll pass on that." Jim did not mention that Dr. Hilda Johnson had assisted in the operation, knowing that it was the FBI that had warned the Air Force, and in turn Colonel Josephs, about her months earlier. He was afraid that information would wave red flags if they knew, but anticipated that they'd eventually find out. Greenspoon finished his conversation and hung up.

"I didn't mention your being involved, Hilda, as I think the FBI and the CIA don't get along very well right now. But at some point you will probably need a security clearance, so it will be necessary for them to raise a little cane then."

"When did you defect?" Julius Blanski asked Hilda.

"In 1962. I hadn't really planned on it, and it is all supposed to be a secret, but from what was said out at the car, you know I was an East German professor of nuclear physics. It was the summer of 1962. Fremont College was sponsoring a trip into East Germany to visit the homes of both Bach and Luther, and to sing in a production of Wagner's *Rienzi* at Bayreuth with a Dutch opera company, in which the East German Army Chorus would join the Fremont chorus. I enjoy singing, and joined the East German Chorus. I'd traveled on a number of occasions outside what you Americans call "The Iron Curtain," the Warsaw Pact countries, so no special permission was needed for me. At the time my boyfriend, his name was Johann Kahler, was an East German Naval Officer and his father, Kurt, was an East German Army General, actually the person in charge of the arrangements for the Fremont tour and coordination of the two choruses for rehearsals. My good friend, Professor of History at Halle University, Maria Fergen, was their tour guide, which is how I heard about the opera. Kurt and his son didn't get along very well as Johann was a staunch Communist, and was in the procurement unit of the Navy.

"Johann had arranged for me to make an inspection of a new Russian nuclear submarine, the *K-14,* at Warnamünde Naval Base on the Baltic," she continued. "I did, and found it to be a very dangerous design. I wrote a report pointing out all the hazards of this new submarine, and Johann's superior officer was angry with the report and ordered me to write a report favorable to the submarine's design. I could not in good conscience do that, so when I got to Bayreuth, West Germany, with the chorus I asked for asylum. As I brought the plans for the submarine with me, NATO was happy to have me, and I ended up being Hilda Waggoner, as I told you on the phone, Dr. Blanski. The professor from Fremont College who led his group East Germany got me a professorship at Fremont, and I married their choral director, Ross Johnson. Johann was sent to hunt down his father and me and kill us, and he made one attempt to do so, but I was only wounded. So I owe much to the American CIA, and want to help as much as I can."

"That's quite a story, Hilda," said Rod Thurmond. "I'm glad your boyfriend wasn't successful. When was the attempt made on your life?"

"In the fall of that year. We were aboard the college's cruiser on the K-oga – how do you pronounce it?"

"Cuyahoga," Jim answered.

"*Ja!* That's it ... river, and Johann was on a German freighter in the harbor when he spotted us and followed us, boarding the boat while we were at dinner. It was quite an adventure. He escaped, and I guess the FBI is still looking for him, maybe Interpol, too."

"Your English is better than that of most Americans, I must say," Julius Blanski said. "If anything, it sounds slightly British, no German accent at all."

"I had good English teachers, and occasionally taught English at Halle University as well, so that was not a problem."

"Do you speak other languages, too?" Jim asked.

"Russian, Polish, and French. Just a bit of Spanish, but it was Cuban Spanish, from a vacation there with my friend, Maria Fergen."

"I better call the railroad and get them over here with their 'big hook,' as they call it, for moving overturned railcar," Jim said. "Right now there's not much we can do until that is done, so I'll give you all a call when I know the schedule. Meanwhile they have to bring in that empty flatcar from Hanford. It should be here soon, but my experience with railroads, although limited, is that railroad time is not always the same as the customer's time."

Chapter 8

It was the following Tuesday before three empty flatcars were delivered, spotted on the empty track west of the overturned car. The first would be for the container, once it was right-side up, and the other two would be for the remains of the two blasted tank cars and the contaminated flatcar. Hanford also send four experienced technicians who would suit up and cut the cars into pieces for the crane to lift into the empty flatcars.

Wilmer Patrick, the technician at the reactor who had accompanied Jim in the initial inspection of the overturned car said he was not surprised that Hanford had sent their own techs to cut up the cars. "If contaminated metal got into the scrap metal industry it could contaminate any number of products if they contained that metal. We've used a local scrap yard for non-contaminated stuff in the past, and my boss, Jeff Hunter, down at Lewis Labs in Brookpark, was surprised the other day when he got a call from a Toledo scrap yard called the Brodasky Brothers wanting to bid on the metal from the rail cars. Don't know how he even found out rail cars were involved. I don't think the press mentioned it."

Jim was not surprised, therefore, when FBI Agent Leonard called the next day and told Jim that the FBI crime lab had gotten a lead on several suspects from finger prints. He said that they had checked with the O-One firm and ruled out any of their people, and any on file for the Penn Central, but that one matched a welder who worked for a Toledo scrap firm.

"Brodasky Bothers?" Jim inquired.

"Yeah, how'd you know that?"

"Seems they've done some welding and scrap metal purchasing here before, and called the head of security, Jeff Hunter, at Brookpark wanting to bid on the job, but didn't say how they knew there would be scrap metal available."

"I think we may have our culprit. We're running a sheet on Boris Brodasky right now, and will pick him up for questioning. Want to sit in?"

"I'd love to, Rod, but things are so hectic here right now that a trip to Toledo would be counter-productive. They're installing the fuel rods tomorrow, and I should be here."

"Okay, I'll keep you posted on the Brodasky Brothers."

Jeff Hunter arrived early the next morning to observe the fuel rod transfer. A heavy crane had been brought in to move the container from the damaged flatcar to a heavy-duty trailer that would be hauled by tractor to the reactor. The crane was mobile, and would also move to the reactor to lift the lead shields out of the container and into the reactor. Hilda Johnson arrived about ten, just as the first lift was taking place.

The AEC was actually in charge of the transfer, and she stood with their agents who were specialists in this procedure, and, Jim learned later, had offered several suggestions that made the job faster and safer. In fact, Jim heard that the AEC engineers and NASA's engineers were so impressed with Hilda that they offered her a job as a part-time consultant.

Colonel Josephs, when he heard that, commented, "How the hell are we going to get a security clearance on her?" Jim said he had an idea, spoke to Hilda about it, and then called Richard Fairchild. Fairchild agreed to contact his CIA friend. George McCracken, and arrange for an FBI security clearance. Josephs responded with a laugh: "Guess it's better with the camel in the tent looking out, than the camel outside the tent looking in! The FBI told me to watch out for her, and this way I certainly can."

The following day Jim got another call from FBI Agent Leonard. "The guy was shocked when we asked to see him. He has a black Lincoln, and another one of the print sets matches one of his employees. Tried to give us some song and dance about noticing and touching the two tank cars when they came through the Toledo rail yard and were set out for Plum Brook as he'd done work for NASA there before, but in the end his story fell through, and we have all three of the guys in a holding cell, awaiting a federal hearing. We've asked the federal attorney to see if he can get the judge to denial bail for them as I think they are prone to run if given the opportunity. Jim, your help on this case was really great."

"Thanks. There's something else coming down the pike that you'll probably hear about. Are you familiar with the name Hilda Johnson, a physics professor at Fremont College?"

"I've heard the name. I think it was Julius, the AEC guy, who was running down that lead. Why?"

"NASA may hire her as a nuclear consultant, and I anticipate that the CIA will be putting pressure on you guys to give her a security clearance."

"Wait till Aaron hears that! Have you met her?"

"I've been at two parties with her husband, Ross, and her, and she sings in the college choir with my wife, Jayne. Yes, I know her, trust her, and know that the AEC was glad for her help in securing that leaking nuclear fuel container. Apparently when she defected, she brought plans of a new Russian submarine with her, and NATO was delighted."

"I doubt Aaron will be as delighted, but I'll give him a heads up. How do you know all this?"

"Ever hear of a Professor Richard Fairchild?"

"Fairchild? Oh, yes! He's helped us on a number of occasions. Why?"

"I suspect he'll be one of her references. He was the one who literally 'staged' her defection, during an opera."

"Figures. Well, I'll keep you posted on the Brodasky Brothers situation. Suspect, with damage to federal property, shooting an Air Force MP and everything else we can charge them with, they'll be in the clink a long time."

Chapter 9

It was about three and a half weeks later when Hilda Johnson's security clearance was approved, and she was officially authorized to be a consultant to NASA, to be paid only for whatever time she might actually spend in a consulting role at the facility. When it arrived Colonel Josephs called Dr. Johnson at Fremont College to let her know, and asked her if she would like a tour of the entire NASA facility. She heartily agreed, and a date was set for the following week. He also let Dr. Bernard Ruhl, the Director of the Plum Brook Facility, know so that he could plan to meet with Hilda and formally welcome her. He had met her only briefly during the crisis with the rail car.

Hilda arrived at Plum Brook appropriately dressed for an inspection of a scientific facility. It happened to be Alicia McQuinn's first day back on full duty after her recuperation, and, as had occurred with Jim Roberts, she had to sign a variety of papers in the Colonel's office, have a NASA identification badge made, and an id sticker placed in the left corner of her car windshield so that she could enter the gate without any confusion. She was not, however, issued a beeper or flashing roof light, as her role would not normally include emergency response.

The Colonel had alerted Jim that she was coming, and asked if he would conduct Hilda's tour for him since they already knew each other. Jim agreed, and began with the cryogenic propellant and components laboratories, with the assistance of their security officers to explain the technical questions that Hilda had, and she had many such questions. Hilda was already familiar with the nuclear power reactor, so after lunch with the Air Force MPs at the barracks, Jim took her to see the hypersonic wind tunnel and rocket propulsion facilities next, with which she was quite impressed.

"There are so many new ideas being put into practice here," she said to Jim, "that what we are teaching at Fremont will need to be to be updated if our graduates are to be prepared for the future types of employment they will seek. I think we need to add advanced courses on astro-physics in the department. Maybe some of these NASA scientists would be interested in teaching such courses."

"I have a directory of all the scientists and engineers, and if Fremont is interested, I'll be happy to contact some of them and inquire. My own class in fire science starts on Thursday next week. I've received sufficient copies of National Fire Protection Association Handbook that we can get right into the meat of the subject quickly. What classroom has Ray assigned for that class?"

"You had twenty-two enrollees, so you'll get to use one of the classrooms on the third floor of the Science Building, I think the one below the observatory. It's not used during the day, so should be a quiet location for your class."

"Sounds great. I'm really looking forward to it," Jim said as they left the wind tunnel building and crossed to the propulsion research lab, where Harold Tibbs was waiting to escort Hilda on a tour of the facility. He explained the mission statement of the lab, and all the various projects that were taking place to test the capability of full-scale rocket engine firings for the spacecraft vehicle launch systems necessary to get humans into space.

As they walked around one of the rocket engine assembly areas Jim noticed one man who seemed to be studying Hilda with greater than normal attention. Of course, he reasoned, she was a beautiful woman, and most men might give her a second glance, but this seemed more than just a sexual attraction look. Hilda had been looking at something Tibbs was showing her, but did glance up, and momentarily locked eyes with the man who was staring at her. Then she quickly looked away again at what Tibbs was explaining. By three in the afternoon the tour was complete and Jim was walking Hilda back to her car.

"Are all the employees here NASA?" she asked.

"No," Jim answered, "I understand that a number are contractors employed for specific jobs. A French company, Gearmone, has several dozen engineers and scientists here, as do some of the American aircraft companies, Grumman, Boeing, and a few other technical outfits. I confess I'm not fully familiar with all of them or what they do, but I have copies of the contracts. Why do you ask?"

"Well, I thought I recognized one of the men working in the propulsion lab. But I could be mistaken. Doesn't matter. I just wondered." They had reached her car, and Hilda headed back to Fremont.

* * *

Unknown to even Ross Johnson, Hilda had another appointment that afternoon with a physician in Fremont. She had seen Dr. Tilden two weeks earlier, and was anxious to hear the results of some tests he had made. She arrived early for her four o'clock appointment, and sat in the waiting room with several other women awaiting appointments either with Dr. Tilden or one of the other two obstetricians in the office. Soon her name was called by the nurse, and in twenty minutes she was leaving the office with a very large smile on her face. The baby would be due sometime in late August or early September, so Hilda knew she would have to take a leave of absence from teaching for at least two or three semesters. She would also have to avoid wine and other treats she enjoyed, and would probably not be able to partake in the annual grape harvest on West Bass Island that fall.

She drove home to the house on Ontario Street in Fremont that she and Ross had purchased two years earlier, and prepared a dinner of Ross's favorite foods. The doctor had given her a prescription to help quell the morning sickness bouts she anticipated, hoping that they would not upset her teaching schedule at the college. She also hoped that she would not experience the same problem that Bob and Sally Merriam had – two separate miscarriages, and a diagnosis that Sally would probably not be able to have children – but they had overcome their grief as best as they could. Bob had suggested adoption, perhaps of an older child, and had spoken with an agency about it, but had not yet had a response.

To say that Ross was delighted with the news that evening would be putting it mildly – he was ecstatic! Since their marriage he had wanted children, not caring whether it was a boy, a girl, or several of each. The next day he sent her a big bunch of flowers, to be delivered at her office in the Science Building in the morning. By mid-afternoon word had spread all around the campus of the news that the Johnsons were going to have a baby. Sally made a special trip from Hayes Hall to the Science Building to congratulate her, and at choir rehearsal that evening someone brought a big cake. That evening Jim got the news from Jayne, but surprised her as he had already heard that afternoon at the Science Building. Sally said that they would need to plan a baby shower for Hilda sometime in May or June. While May Durrand was also delighted with the news – she and Ray already had two children – Ray was less enthused; he anticipated having to hold some of Hilda's classes when she was sick during the current semester and teaching some of them for a year or more after the baby arrived. Then he recalled something Hilda had said after her tour of Plum Brook, that there were quite a few Ph.D. scientists there who would make excellent teachers if the department needed them. Hilda's becoming a NASA consultant might have hidden benefits for Fremont College.

* * *

Rolfe Wolfmann, known to Gearmone Engineering and NASA as Rolfe Reübrich, placed a call to a number in Chicago. A man with a strong German accent answered in Russian. "*Волк* {volk} here," Rolfe said, using his Russian code name, *wolf*. "Vee haff edier trouble or opportunity," he added in thick German accent, then continued in Russian. "Today I saw a woman I recognized from Moscow School of Science at the plant. Hilda von Werdau. I inquired. She is to be a nuclear consultant. But she is vulnerable, no?"

"Do you think she recognized you," the Chicagoan asked, switching from Russian to German.

"I don't know," *Volk* answered in German. "She looked at me momentarily, but then looked at what someone else was showing her. She was with the new security officer."

"We will check up on her. What is her current name?"

"She came to Ohio using the name Waggoner," Reübrich said, "and I learned that she is now professor of physics at Fremont College, married to another professor, Johnson, so she is now Hilda Johnson," Reübrich continued in German.

"Johann knows this woman! I've heard him speak of her. We will see if this is trouble or not, Wolf. Do nothing for now. We'll take care of it," came the reply in German. Reübrich hung up and had his dinner.

* * *

Sally Merriam was busy over the next two months arranging the International Tour for the Religions and International Studies Juniors that Bob and she would be conducting that summer in the British Isles. She had to make sure that each of the twenty-two students who had signed up for the credit course had valid passports and sufficient funds for the costs of the tour, which would include air fare from Chicago to Manchester, England, returning from London, Britrail Passes for travel within England and Scotland, plus some chartered buses for side trips, hotels for each night, and most meals. After doing these arrangements for ten years Sally was familiar with the process, but it was usually Professor Richard Fairchild who led the tours, not Assistant Professor Robert Merriam. Bob had led a couple, and knew what a chore it could be, not only keeping the students from wandering off whenever they felt like it, but also preparing lectures at each location that was factual and in keeping with the course curriculums.

Because the tour was not just about religion but also politics, sociology, history and geography, Bob had been spending his spare time studying English history, British politics and the uniqueness of each part of Britain that they would be visiting. He was thankful that the tour was only for two weeks, which meant that they could not include politically volatile places such as Northern Ireland.

The plan was to begin, after landing in Manchester, with a train trip to York and a tour of Yorkminster, home of the second archdiocese of England. From there they would travel by special coach to Lindesfarne, an island with an ancient monastery in the North Sea, and from there to Edinburgh, visiting the castle and learning of the relationships over the centuries between England and Scotland. The next trip would be across Scotland to the island of Iona, where St. Columba had established a colony of monks who Christianized Scotland and the North of England in the sixth and seventh century. Arranging overnight there in June had proved to be the biggest problem Sally had encountered, as there were precious few rooms available on the island. They had finally settled for a hotel on the Isle of Mull.

From there they traveled back through the Lake District and Yorkshire to Oxford, for a three night stay as a base of operations for Stratford-on-Avon, the Cotswolds, Worcester Cathedral and Blenheim, where Winston Churchill had been born, as well as an escorted tour of the University. Then they would travel southward to Wells, visiting Glastonbury and spending the night in Salisbury. The five remaining nights would be spent in London, with two side trips, one to Hastings and Canterbury, and one to Hampton Court Palace, associated with King Henry VIII. They would have a tour of Parliament, a concert at the Royal Albert Hall, a visit to the British Museum, and tours of Westminster Abbey, St. Paul's Cathedral, the Bank of England on Threadneedle Street, and the Tower of London.

"If they're not exhausted after all that, they'll deserve an 'A' each for endurance," Bob had commented as he reviewed the arrangements. "Getting them to Victoria Station for the ride to Gatwick Airport will probably be enough to make them sleep all the way back to Chicago."

"Their plane leaves from Heathrow," Sally said, "not Gatwick. I've arranged for a bus to pick us up at the hotel across from Green Park. Just getting them all out of bed and fed some breakfast will be chore enough."

"At least they won't be exhausted by a wedding night like we were on our first night in England," Bob said with a chuckle. "Remember that awful bed and Mrs. What's-her-name, always asking 'isn't it, deary?' like we were expected to answer 'most definitely' every time she spoke."

"Yeah, but just start re-enforcing 'Mind the right, now,' every time you see one of them. One of this gang of Midwesterners is bound to forget and step out in front of some car driving on the left. I'll have to spend the whole flight over warning about the left-handed driving."

"It's a shame we couldn't include Cambridge in the tour, or some of the big houses. But these kids are young. They can go there on their own. Will Parliament be in session when we visit?"

"In June? I doubt it, Bob, but the building is interesting enough anyway. Some of the girls asked if there would be a chance to visit Harrods's or Selfridges. I put a free afternoon in the schedule so that they could. I'll probably go with them."

"We have a couple of Methodists who want to see Aldersgate and Epworth Chapel; maybe I can go with them there. It's not far, but not in the best part of London. And one of the journalism students wants to visit Fleet Street. Maybe you can find out something about a tour there that he'd enjoy."

"I'll look into it. What's your next class this afternoon?"

"Introduction to Eastern Religions. They're going to have an exam on some of the Hindu gods and goddesses next week, so I'm sure they will all be there today," Bob replied. "What's Richie teaching this afternoon?"

"Different sects of Muslims. I never realized how many different types there were until I started typing up his notes and making copies for the students. Sunni, Shiite, Alawaite, Druze, Sufi, Yezidi, even Dervish. The ones in Indonesia are as different as Quakers and Catholics from the ones in Morocco. Yet they all believe in the same Allah and the same *Koran*. I'll bet Richie's exam in that class will be a lulu!"

"All his exams are 'lulus,' my dear. That's why he's so popular. You have to pay attention in his class lectures – there is no way to cram for one of his tests. I heard him say that one of the tours in a couple of years would have to be to the Middle East. Arranging that will be a real picnic for you."

"Oh, Pooh. He'll probably assign that trip to you."

"I'd just take them all on the Hajj to Mecca!"

"You can't do that unless you're Muslim."

"We'll all wear turbans! I think it would be fun to throw stones at the Devil."

"The Devil might throw stones back at you, silly!" Sally replied. "Now, go prepare for your class while I call in this hotel reservation."

Chapter 10

May 7, 1969
Fremont

Hilda Johnson was sitting at her desk in the basement of the Science Building grading some papers from an intermediate physics class when the pretty, dark-haired department secretary, Darlene Smathers, an elementary education junior year student, put through a phone call to her.

"Dr. Johnson," she answered.

A deep voice replied in German, "Hilda von Werdau. You will listen carefully. Write nothing down. Do exactly what you are told, and no harm will come to you, that baby you are carrying, or your husband, or anyone else you care about."

"Who is this?" she demanded.

"Never mind who we are," the voice continued. "Mind who you are, what you were taught and pledged long ago in Moscow. You will do as you are told, like a good little East German Freülein. You wouldn't want harm to your family, or your friend, Maria Fergen, who wants to leave Halle. She has written to you to ask for your help, is that not correct."

Hilda did not reply. She remained silent, terrified by the voice and what it seemed to be suggesting. Someone knew an awful lot about her. She knew this was no joke.

"You need not reply," the voice continued, "but you will do as instructed. You disobeyed once. You will not do so again. Do you understand?"

"I can understand that you are evil and that I will do nothing for you!" Hilda replied in English.

"That is, you think, up to you," the voice answered in clear English, then switched again to German. "But you are mistaken. You will do as instructed, or the first casualty will be your beloved Ross. Now, you would not want anything unpleasant to happen to Ross, would you, Hilda von Werdau?" Hilda remained silent, and the voice continued. "You have no class to teach next Tuesday. You have a doctor's appointment in the morning. After that, you had planned to do some shopping. But that is not what you will do.

"Instead," the voice continued, "you will drive to the NASA plant at Plum Brook. But first, you will stop at a Sunoco gas station on Route 4 just north of the intersection with Route 113 east of Bellevue – it is the way you usually go to Plum Brook – we have observed you. There you will find, under the sink in the women's restroom, a large box with handles on it. It should be easy for you to lift without difficulty. Place it in your car on the floor of the back seat, and say nothing to the Air Force guard who signs you in. He will not question you as you have NASA identification. Upon entering the plant, drive to the rear railroad yard. There you will see a silver colored tank car, just the one car, awaiting unloading. It is full of liquid nitrogen, which you know is not explosive. You will take the box out of your car, and place it behind the left rear wheels of that railroad car. Then get back in your car, drive to the far end of the plant, turn around, and drive home. Do you understand, or do you want me to repeat this?"

"I understand," Hilda said, "but I will not do it."

"If you do not, then you will be planning a funeral for your husband the next morning. Do you understand that?"

"You are a fool, a damned fool, whoever you are!"

"You may call me whatever you wish, Hilda von Werdau, but this is what you will do, and you will tell no one, do you hear me? No one. You do not want to raise your baby as a widow. If you speak to anyone about this, we will know. Your husband will be the first victim, Maria the second, your baby the third. By then you will have learned to do as you are told."

The phone went dead, and Hilda listened for a moment before hanging up. Someone certainly knew a lot about her. She was frightened. If someone was watching or listening, she could not communicate with anyone at NASA. She picked up the phone and dialed the number for Sally Merriam.

"Religions and International Studies," Sally said, answering the phone.

"Sally, it is Hilda. Is Richard in?"

"He's teaching a class at the moment, but should be back in about twenty minutes. Do you want him to call you?"

"No! No, I'll walk over. I need to talk with him."

"You sound upset, Hilda. Are you okay?"

"Physically fine. I just ... please don't let him leave until I get there."

"Sure. Come on."

Hilda wrapped a sweater around herself. It was not all that cold out, but she felt an inward chill. She climbed the basement stairs, and as she reached the door it opened and Jim Roberts came in as he had an afternoon class. She was tempted to tell him about the phone call, but thought she better talk to Dr. Fairchild first.

"Hello, Hilda!" Roberts greeted her cheerfully. "How's everything in the Physics Department?"

"Oh, fine, fine. I hear your students all are enjoying your class."

"Well, most of them, anyway."

"I must run. I have an appointment," Hilda explained as she rushed out the door before it closed, heading across the campus toward the Hayes Hall building.

* * *

FBI Special Agent Bret Leonard was at his desk in the Toledo field office preparing a report on an attempted bank robbery in Lima. Despite the would-be robber's threats, the male teller at the bank had simple stonewalled the robber, dropping to the floor behind the window and pressing the alarm. The robber ran away. According to the teller, who was the only one on duty behind the windows although others were in their offices in the bank, the robber looked to be about eighteen or twenty, and was more frightened than the teller. He said he had a gun, but never showed it, and the teller doubted he did. Leonard was alone in the office as Special Agent Aaron Greenspoon was in a meeting at the Detroit field office.

When his phone rang, Bret was surprised when the voice at the other end introduced itself as a Central Intelligence Agent calling from Langley, Virginia, and Bret quickly wrote down the name the agent gave, George McCracken. He could verify that later, he thought.

"What I hear from Congress, Bret," McCracken said, "is that any counter-espionage is FBI territory. Assuming Congress hasn't changed their mind, I guess that puts you special agents in charge of catching spies."

"I guess it does. Why, do you have one in mind?"

"We think so. Have you ever heard of a Fremont College professor named Fairchild?"

"Richard Fairchild? Certainly have. Special Agent Slade, who was here before Aaron Greenspoon became the Special Agent in Charge had numerous contacts with Fairchild, who was extremely helpful, so I heard, at his own expense and risk."

"That's Richie Fairchild, all right. Gets in the middle of a lot of pickles."

"Certainly he's not your spy, is he?"

"No, no! Of course not. But he thinks there may be one at the NASA facility at Plum Brook, south of Sandusky."

"We just had an incident there last Christmas, Mr. McCracken. It was a contractor looking for business."

"Call me George if we're going to work together on this, Bret. I know about that. You may recall a young, pretty physics professor from Fremont who helped analyze the risk for the Atomic Energy guys."

"Certainly. Hilda Johnson. We got a request from CIA – who, you? – for a top secret security clearance for her about a week later. I did the research. She was East German, studied in Moscow, she'd stolen some nuclear submarine plans when she defected."

"NATO is still grateful to her for those," McCracken confirmed. "But they sent someone to kill her and the East German general who defected with her. Maybe you heard about that."

"Yes, it was before my time in Toledo, but the assassin had been an officer on a West German freighter that docked the next day here in Toledo. What, has he shown up again?"

"We don't know. Maybe, although I personally doubt it. Here's what has happened," McCracken explained, telling how Hilda had come to Fairchild all upset by a phone call that threatened her life, as well as that of her husband, a friend in East Germany and her baby that's due in August.

"Basically, next Tuesday she is supposed to pick up a box at a gas station and take it to the NASA facility and place it behind the wheels of a tank car of nitrogen that will be parked on the rear rail yard. You may know where that is from the previous explosion. We presume that the box will be a bomb of some sort. She has NASA clearance, hence can get onto the facility without any difficulty. She's afraid that if she does not do what she is told, whoever is doing this will murder her husband, who is also a professor at the college."

"Does she have any idea of who this person is, or that it might be a joke."

"No, she's sure it is no joke. This person knew too much about her, including her friend at Halle University who also wants to come to America. The person called her by her real name, which is not a part of her American record. We brought her into the U.S. under the name Waggoner, which was given her by NATO, and even her husband does not know that Hilda had been working with the East German Navy before defecting. In fact, he barely knew her at all, as she was singing with a chorus from the East German Army.

"But she does have one suggestion," McCracken continued. "While receiving a tour of the spacecraft propulsion lab she saw a man looking at her. She just got a glimpse of him, but believes she recognized him from somewhere, maybe the Moscow Science and Technology Institute. He apparently works for one of the independent contractors authorized by NASA, but is the only one of their employees who has not yet received his security clearance. You might want to look into that."

What's his name?"

"Rolfe. Rolfe Reübrich."

"Reübrich? Yes, something crossed our desk the other day asking for a check on someone with that name. I'll check with Aaron, Special Agent Greenspoon, and see what he has on Reübrich. Anything else?"

"You might give Fairchild a call and have him go over what Dr. Johnson told him, like the location of the gas station where she is to get the box, that sort of thing. Today is Thursday, so you have a few days to plan something. Hilda sings in the college chapel choir, and will be at their rehearsal tonight, which is conducted by her husband. I think she'll feel safe there. Here's her phone number and address, and Fairchild's number. You or Aaron may want to talk with her, let her know what to do. Fairchild thinks she's really scared, but that she will cooperate fully. Please also keep me informed here at Langley. I'll give you my direct line. Fairchild has it, too. But don't leave a message if I'm not in. There are big ears around here."

"I understand, George. The FBI has big ears, too!"

* * *

Sally noticed that Hilda still seemed somewhat upset at choir practice that evening, but anticipated that it was due to her pregnancy, and said nothing about it, even though she had been curious about Hilda's urgent meeting with Fairchild that day at noon. Fairchild had said nothing to her or Esther about Hilda, so she decided to mind her own business. At the end of the rehearsal they all headed home, and Bob, who had not seen Hilda's visit to Fairchild that afternoon, chatted away about something else on the short drive home.

"You know, we really need to get a second car," Bob commented. "I certainly don't mind waiting all evening, as I had plenty to do in my office, and as we both work in the same office, two cars usually wouldn't be practical, but sometimes it would be nice for you to have more freedom to go when and where you need without my tagging along. Next week why don't you drive me home for supper, and just drive yourself back to the rehearsal?"

"I read where Fremont might get a local bus service. Maybe that would be the answer."

"Mmm, possibly. I rode the buses and trains in Philadelphia growing up, so that wouldn't bother me. Another car was just a thought."

"Keep it in mind. I do have a birthday coming soon."

"Oh, yeah! You want a Cadillac or a Lincoln?"

"Why not one of each, brand new, too?" Sally joked. "Or I could ride the bus."

"No way! Not at night, even if it is just a mile or so. But keep the thought of another car in mind. Something just to putt around town in."

"Okay." By that time they were home. As they had eaten supper at the college cafeteria neither was hungry, so they relaxed for a half hour and then went to bed. Sally did not mention how Hilda had seemed upset at the rehearsal and had met with Fairchild that afternoon.

* * *

Friday morning Corporal Alicia McQuinn received a call asking if both Colonel Josephs and Jim Roberts were in. They were, and she connected the caller, who had not identified himself, with Colonel Josephs.

"Colonel, this is FBI Special Agent Aaron Greenspoon. You may recall our meeting last January prior to the arrest of the Brodasky Brothers, and the explosion of the two oxygen cars."

"Yes, certainly, Agent Greenspoon. You remember that the federal attorney subpoenaed Jim Roberts and me to testify at the trial. What can I do for you?"

"Could Special Agent Leonard and I meet with you later this afternoon, say about three?"

"I know Jim's in the office. Don't know his schedule, but I'm sure he will stick around if you are coming. What's up?"

"We'll explain when we get there. Just have Roberts wait until we do. We'll appreciate it," Greenspoon said, then hung up.

Josephs called Jim Roberts' number and told him of the FBI request.

"Sure, I'll be here. Three, in your office?"

"Right. Wonder what's up?"

"Don't know. Maybe Brodasky's appeal was successful. I'll alert the MP at the gate so they can come on through."

At five minutes to three the two FBI agents parked their car outside the barracks building, entered the glass door, and climbed to the second floor, being greeted heartily by Corporal McQuinn, who immediately recognized them. "The Colonel and Jim Roberts are expecting you," she said. "Please go on in."

"Any residual discomfort from that wound you got?" Bret Leonard asked.

"No, nothing. I'm fine now. The Colonel even arranged for me to get a special medal as I was on duty and wounded in the attack."

"You are a brave young woman, Corporal McQuinn. I know your parents are proud of you."

Jeffrey Josephs and Jim Roberts both stood up when the two Special Agents came through the door, and shook hands. Bret Leonard closed the door behind him. The small office was crowded, and Jim had brought an extra chair up from his office so that they could each sit during the meeting.

"What's up?" Colonel Josephs asked as they all sat down.

"In short, Colonel, we think you have some sort of Communist agent working here at the facility, and there may be a plan for some sabotage."

"Really?" Colonel Josephs replied, sounding somewhat skeptical and flippant, which was his usual attitude toward authorities. "Commies here in the plant, eh?"

"Either Russian or East German," Special Agent Greenspoon replied. "Jim, you followed up on the Gearmone Engineering employee, Reübrich, for whom you could find no security clearance. The Cleveland district office never answered your inquiry because they could find nothing on Reübrich. He may or may not be involved, but the Boston office is checking with Gearmone's people, and if that turns up nothing the CIA will check with their Paris headquarters. He works in the space propulsion lab, I understand."

"The German guy," Colonel Josephs answered. "Yeah, I had a chat with him when he first arrived, about a year ago. There was some rumor that he had worked in rockets for the Nazis during the War, and I asked him about that. He said he had worked in rocket propulsion, but that it was for a West German firm in Essen after the War. Then he said he was hired by Gearmone."

"We have no evidence that what he told you was not true. But we are concerned, as your consultant from Fremont College, Dr. Johnson, believes she recognized him, perhaps from the Moscow Science Institute."

"Isn't it more likely that she's your spy?" Colonel Josephs said.

"No, we don't think so, but we need your help. Are you expecting delivery of a tank car of nitrogen, Colonel?"

Josephs looked at Jim, who said, "Yes, it is supposed to be delivered tonight, about two or three in the morning. The MPs on duty then will open the gate for the delivery. Then tomorrow our little locomotive will move it to the rear rail yard for unloading next Wednesday."

"That confirms what we've learned. Is the nitrogen intended for the propulsion lab's use?

Jim answered. "Both the propulsion lab and the two cryogenic labs use nitrogen. It might be for either. We get shipments of nitrogen all the time."

"Okay. Colonel, next Tuesday afternoon there will be an attempt made to blow up that car. We need your help to not only prevent it, but to identify the parties responsible."

"You're not kidding, then," Colonel Josephs replied, with a more serious sound in his voice.

"No, we're not kidding. We think lives are at stake, including Dr. Johnson's. But we have to get your assistance in order to trap the perpetrators. Jim, I think you are aware – and Colonel Josephs, you may be also – that Hilda Johnson defected from East Germany six or seven years ago; I don't have the exact date. The CIA arranged her professorship at Fremont. There are certain details that only she – and the CIA – would know, like her real name and that of her close friends in East Germany.

"An anonymous caller with an Eastern European accent and speaking German, contacted her yesterday and threatened to kill her husband, and others, including her, if she did not do as they instructed," he continued. "We can't risk her not doing what they want, so next Tuesday afternoon she is to pick up a box, which we believe will contain some sort of explosive device, and bring it onto the facility here. She has ample identification to get through the gate, and will place the box as she has been instructed. Then she will leave and return home.

"Now," Special Agent Greenspoon continued, "early Tuesday morning we will bring a team of explosives experts in and place them in the rear rail yard, well hidden. Jim, clear that with the MPs – the truck will be unmarked, but they will have FBI identification, but tell them to keep quiet about it. We suspect someone, either Reübrich or someone else, will be observing to make sure Dr. Johnson does as instructed. Hopefully we will spot whoever it is, but will wait until he – or she – leaves the area. Then we will defuse whatever the device may be. We will then set off another explosion – nothing like the two oxygen cars – but enough that anyone inside or outside of the facility will think that it is a major explosion. We're hoping that the plotters will believe that Dr. Johnson has done what she was supposed to do. But of course, once they learn that the explosion did not do what was expected, they'll probably either try again or find some other mischief for her to do."

"We will be observing all the various steps of the operation," he explained. "Hopefully this will give us a lead on who is involved. While we suspect it might be Reübrich, we have no proof of that yet, so we don't want you two to say or do anything here that might tip off whoever it is that we are onto the plot. Jim, if you could very discretely observe Reübrich for us that afternoon it would be appreciated. Maybe just some minor excuse to be in the propulsion lab where he works to see if he leaves at any time. When the explosion does go off, have the alarms sounded. Assuming local fire departments will respond, we'll leave enough burning debris around to give them something to do.

"Now, obviously, you must not discuss this with anyone, not the MPs, nor your commanding officers or Dr. Ruhl, the director here, Colonel, or any of the other NASA people. If any questions arise later, refer them to us," Special Agent Bret Leonard said. "Are you clear on what we said, Colonel?"

"Oh, yes! I understand now. Jim, you once asked me what secrets there were around here to keep. I guess this is another one for you."

"I guess so," Jim replied. "I can anticipate a long Tuesday night, but I won't alert Jayne that I might be late until after the alarm."

"Good. Thank you, Colonel Josephs, for your time and understanding. We hope this will be a successful operation, and if so, we'll see that some credit goes to the Air Force."

Chapter 11

Jim Roberts had not hunted in years. The only gun he had, besides his FDNY service revolver, was his dad's old shotgun. But Jayne said she had seen many deer in the field behind the house, and large birds, so when hunting season opened, Jim got a license and hunted on his own property, bagging a number of pheasants and one young buck, noting that there were several that had been competing for the heard. He found it relaxing, with the turmoil that was going on at the facility, and felt rested by Tuesday.

Tuesday afternoon Jim and Colonel Josephs sat in the Colonel's office. They had just returned from a brief inspection of the various labs, and had not noticed anyone, including Rolfe Reübrich, missing or acting unusually nervous. From the Colonel's office window they were able to watch the roadway that ran to the rear rail yard. They also knew that two other railcars had arrived the previous evening and were being switched by NASA's little locomotive to the rear rail yard. Jim had notified Aaron Greenspoon of this, and he seemed to consider it good news. What he did with the information he did not say.

Three o'clock passed with nothing happening. Then three thirty, three forty-five, and four o'clock. "Maybe it was all a practical joke after all," Jeffrey Josephs said, although his voice sounded concerned. At ten after four there was a terrific boom, with smoke coming from the rail yard. The Air Force MP set off the alarms, including the nuclear alarm – guaranteed to scare the neighbors and their cattle, pigs and chickens half out of their skins – and within a few minutes the air was filled with the sound of sirens; Perkins Township Volunteer Fire Department and Sandusky's Municipal Fire Department responded, as did the Erie County Sheriff. Jim and the Colonel rushed down the stairs and used Jim's car to race to the rail yard. The other two MP cars were already there.

There was burning debris scattered around, but the car of nitrogen sat undamaged on a different track than it had been on. Where it had initially sat was a blast hole with broken ties and bent iron rail. If there were FBI agents surveying the scene Jim was unable to see them, but he suspected that not only were they watching from some hidden point, but also filming who showed up. He also suspected that other agents would be hidden outside the facility watching to see if anyone else was waiting for the explosion.

"Hot Damn!" Colonel Josephs exclaimed. "They didn't blow up the nitrogen car. What damage is here will be easily repaired. Okay, Jim, I guess your German girlfriend, Hilda, did what she was told."

"Girlfriend? I barely know her."

"Well, as long as you don't know her 'barely!'" Josephs laughed at his own pun. "Oh, hell! Tell her thanks when you see her. Are you going to tell NASA about this, or that it was the FBI that blew a hole in our rail yard?"

"My report will be silent as to what really happened. I'll have to think up some explanation for what did explode, because I'll bet the neighbors are already on the phone to their Congressman to bitch about this facility. Two explosions within six months ... Washington isn't going to like this."

"Yeah, neither is the Air Force. But you're the security guy now. Think up something good for that report."

By this time the two fire departments – a total of four engines – had the small fires extinguished. The fires had done no damage at all. The Colonel looked around and asked, "By the way, Jim, I understood that the FBI was going to bring a bomb unit in after the bomb was put in place by the German woman. I never saw them come in."

"It was last night. When the B&O delivered those other two cars and the MP went to open the gate I took over the guard house, and that's when they came in with their van. I guess it's hidden in the woods there, or was, anyway, and they must have slept in it all night." Bret Leonard arranged it with me yesterday morning. I should have told you today."

"Glad you didn't. I'd have been even more nervous. Well, I don't see much more that we can do here. Let's go and have a slug of bourbon in my office and hope that the FBI catches the bastards."

"Me, too. Yes, I could use a drink, but just one. I was here most of the night and don't want to fall asleep on my way home."

* * *

That evening Hilda had just finished washing the supper dishes while Ross was planning some music for the Thursday evening choir rehearsal when the phone rang. Hilda answered. "Freülein von Werdau," the low voice spoke in German. "You did not do as told. The railcar was not damaged. This is bad news."

"No, I did exactly as you said," she replied in German. "But there was a small locomotive switching cars in the rail yard. It must have also moved the car of nitrogen after I left. I placed the box exactly where you told me to."

"The car was moved? Yes," the voice continued in German, "that would explain the bent track and blast hole. So, if you did as told we will not harm you. If we learn otherwise, you will be sorry."

"I...." Before Hilda could say more, the man hung up, and Hilda replaced the phone.

"Who was that, Honey?" Ross called from his small office near their bedroom. "It sounded like you were speaking German."

"I think it was a wrong number, but they sounded German, and I asked in German if they were, and they hung up to call the correct number."

"Oh. Say, are you familiar with the Brahms *Requiem*? I'm thinking of using part of it in a couple of weeks."

"Yes, I know the work, but only from records. I've never heard it performed."

"We won't do all of it. Just some of the choruses. You'll enjoy it."

"*Ja*, Brahms is enjoyable," she replied, wondering if she would ever hear from the man on the phone again.

* * *

The mid-June trip to England and Scotland were upon Bob and Sally Merriam faster than they had expected. The spring semester was barely over, and the only blessing of the early date for the trip, necessary in order to get the hotels they wanted, was that Bob would have to miss the graduation ceremony at the college, an event he had learned, as Dr. Fairchild had predicted, to hate. It was usually either steamy hot or raining, and the necessary outdoors parade to the main auditorium in their heavy robes, hoods and academic caps was tedious. Even if the chosen speaker was interesting, the long list of graduates coming forward for their diplomas seemed to take forever.

But with the house locked and their car parked at the Toledo Airport they were soon in the air to Chicago and the overnight flight to Manchester. While Sally had always been able to sleep almost anywhere, Bob was not able to sleep during long flights, and anticipated a big headache when he got to England. Fortunately the students on the trip acted in a mature manner, and when they reached the hotel in York, everyone was alert, well-behaved, and ready for bed.

* * *

In the Russian Embassy in Washington KGB Major Sergi Kolnekov was discussing the Plum Brook situation with Johann Kahler. Kahler, a former East German Navy officer, had fled East Germany under the name of Gerhardt Kalbmann. The reason Captain Kahler had fled was his fiancée, Hilda von Werdau, Professor of Nuclear Physics at Halle University. She had been with him on an inspection of a Russian submarine and had found it dangerous, but Kahler's commanding officer had instructed her to write a report favorable to the submarine's design, and she had refused. Instead she defected to NATO with plans for the submarine sewn into the costume she was wearing in the opera being performed at Bayreuth, in West Germany. Kalbmann, now again able to use his real name and again in good standing with the Warsaw Pact and Russia, had made an unsuccessful attempt to assassinate both his father, an East German general who had also defected, and his fiancée aboard a cabin cruiser on the Cuyahoga River in Cleveland. He had escaped a manhunt, but after three years had contacted the KGB and retrieved his reputation and position, albeit as a KGB officer in the U.S. His fiancée's predictions about the dangers of the Russian submarine design had proven to be correct.

"*Volk* was careful not to go to the rail yard to see where the explosion had occurred," Kahler was telling Kolnekov in German-accented Russian, "but learned from co-workers that it had been exactly where the rail car had been parked, but that the car had been moved during the afternoon to an unloading station. The railcar and its contents were unimportant, but it shows that von Werdau did as she was told, and undoubtedly will again when we put our plan into action."

"And you are absolutely certain that she was not being observed or that the Americans had no agents spotted in the area of the pick-up?" Sergi asked in a Russian accent indicting his peasant upbringing.

"I was watching. I saw no one else, either at the gas station where she collected the bomb or at the rail yard. Of course, I was unable to get into the facility, but was observing from near the gate where the tracks enter the plant."

"And from there you could see the railcar that was to be blown up?"

"No, there is forest between the two yards, but the explosion was exactly at when the timer was set."

"No one was watching *Volk*?"

"He says not. Of course when the alarms sounded they all had to vacate the building. He remained outside it, not going to see what had happened as many others did, in order to not draw attention to himself."

"Has *Volk* gotten most of the information he needs yet?"

"He says he is nearly finished. He needs about three weeks yet. Then we can proceed with the plan to contaminate the facility sufficiently to put the Americans five years backwards in their research."

"How will you know when the winds are correct for the explosion?"

"The winds are always from the west northwest," Kahler replied. "There are sufficient summer storms that we will have at least twelve hours advance notice, sufficient time to act."

"This Hilda, what is her American name, Johnson?"

"Yes."

"She is pregnant. How will we know that she is not off having a baby when the time comes for her to act?"

"According to what I've been able to learn, her baby is not due until late August. *Volk* should have what he needs well before that, so I don't think it will be a concern."

"Good. Now, how is your contact at the Fermi Labs south of Chicago doing? Anything of value there yet?"

"Nothing of real value yet, but Klaus is hopeful."

"He better be. Moscow is getting anxious, Captain Kahler. They do not like failure."

"Nor do I," Kahler replied. The meeting at a close, Kahler arose from the chair in Major Kolnekov's office and saluted.

* * *

It was mid-July and Hilda Johnson had heard nothing further from the mysterious voice instructing her to do anything at the NASA facility. The Merriams were back from their trip to England and Scotland, and Sally had organized a baby shower for Hilda that was to be given in early August. Hilda had, however, received several requests from Bill Hallister and Wilmer Patrick, the head engineer and the technician who served as the security engineer at the nuclear reactor. A new experiment was taking place at the spacecraft propulsion lab that required some modifications to the reactor to produce an additional amount of electricity for the lab. Hallister had directed the initial modifications, but was uncertain of the specific changes being made and asked Hilda to stop by the next time she had no class, which was most days in the summer.

She had checked Hallister' figures and plan, made several suggested improvements, and had become interested enough in the project that she was spending several days a week at Plum Brook. As Ross was conducting a choral workshop at Frankenmuth in Michigan, he had purchased a newer car for his use so that Hilda could use the car that had the NASA identification on it.

Hilda had recruited two of the scientists from the NASA labs, both with Ph.D. degrees in physics, and they had been approved by the Fremont College Board to temporarily substitute for Hilda during the fall semester, each with the title of guest lecturer. Hilda and Ross agreed to work out a reasonable plan for the baby's care in the spring semester when the time came.

On one Tuesday afternoon in early August, four days before the planned shower, Hilda had just returned home from a doctor's visit with her obstetrician and was taking a nap after lunch. She had been asleep for several hours, the Chevrolet she drove parked on the quiet+ street in front of the house, although the large trees in the front yard blocked any view of the car from the house. Ross had completed the workshop in Michigan but was at the college working on the new semester programs that would begin in September. His office was at the rear of the college auditorium where various concerts were performed throughout the year. The phone ringing woke Hilda, and she got up, uncomfortably, and moved to the kitchen where the telephone sat on the counter. "Ross residence," she answered.

"Dr. Hilda Johnson?" a voice she did not recognize asked.

"Yes, with whom am I speaking?" she asked in her best English grammar.

"This is Joe, one of the technicians at the NASA reactor. Hallister gave me your number and asked me to call you. They have an emergency and need you to come and help them. Can you come within an hour? It's really important and they need you."

"I can try. I'll need to notify my husband, and then I'll leave, but it often takes an hour to get there if traffic is heavy." She did not recall a technician at the lab named Joe, but he sounded urgent, so she called Ross's number and told him she had to go to the NASA facility as they had some sort of emergency at the reactor. He told her to be careful – it was her eighth month and she had been instructed by the doctor to not get stressed.

"I'll be careful," she promised. "Don't worry."

As Hilda closed the door to the house and rushed toward her car, parked on the street in the shade of the trees, her next door neighbor, Mrs. Maude Baldridge, came out on her porch and called to Hilda to come over. Hilda replied, "I'm just on my way to some emergency. Maybe I can stop by later, Maude."

"No, I need to tell you something now, before you drive away." That got Hilda's attention and she walked hurriedly over to the Baldridge porch.

"Hilda," Maude said as she approached, "I saw some men tampering with your car about an hour ago. Did you have some work done on it?"

"No! The car has been fine. Someone did something to it?"

"It was very subtle," Maude said. "A van pulled up next to it and two men got out, and went to the back of your car, then crawled under it. I was expecting a package to be delivered and had been watching for a van, but this wasn't a delivery van. It was white, with no name marked on it. I thought about calling the police, but then thought that maybe this was some repair you had ordered, and waited to ask you when you left."

"I'm glad you told me. I'm not sure what to do. I'd better call Ross. Maybe he planned some work on the car and forgot to tell me."

Hilda returned to the house and immediately called Ross, but there was no answer. He had apparently left his office for a moment. Then she thought she had better let Bill Hallister or Wilmer Patrick know that she was running late and dialed the number for the NASA reactor office. It was Patrick who answered.

"Wilmer," she explained, "one of your technicians, Joe, called a few minutes ago and said that there was some emergency and that Bill Hallister had asked that I come in immediately, but…."

"Hilda," Patrick replied, "there's no emergency here, and we don't have a technician named Joe. I think someone is pulling a practical joke on you."

"I don't know. My next door neighbor says that two men put something under my car, and now I'm frightened."

"Well, you're not needed here right now, so let Ross check your car so you can relax. The project you helped us with is wrapping up, so I don't think we'll need you again for a while."

Unable to reach Ross on her second try she instead called Richard Fairchild at his office in Hayes Hall and told him what her neighbor and the NASA reactor security technician had said. "I'm frightened. Why would someone want me to go to the NASA reactor if they didn't need me?"

"Get a hold of Ross," Fairchild directed, "and tell him what you just told me. Stay in the house with the doors locked until Ross gets home. I'll make some calls for you."

As soon as Hilda hung up Dr. Fairchild called George McCracken in Langley. McCracken agreed that the matter was serious and told Fairchild to call either Bret Leonard or Aaron Greenspoon at the Toledo FBI office. McCracken had their direct phone numbers. Special Agent-in-charge Greenspoon was out, but Bret Leonard was in, and when Fairchild identified himself and explained what had happened. Leonard said he would be on it immediately. Fairchild told Leonard what he suspected, given that Hilda had already been used to transport one bomb to the NASA facility, that a powerful bomb had been attached to her car. If she parked it near the reactor, the bomb might damage the reactor enough that it would leak radiation over the entire NASA facility. It was a windy, rather rainy afternoon, and that could spread radiation over the entire area. Leonard agreed, and said he would notify the Fremont Police and Fire Departments. As it was uncertain whether the bomb, if it was a bomb, was on a timer or would be activated by a remote phone call, a bomb squad would be needed.

Leonard first called Hilda and told her that he was on his way. He asked if the house had a basement with an outside entrance, which she said it did. He instructed her to go to the basement, as far to the rear of the house as possible, and wait there until the police came to evacuate her, but to call her husband first and tell him not to come home until he was notified to do so by the Fremont police. This time Ross answered the phone, and Hilda explained what was happening and that he was not to come home until notified.

Leonard then called the Fremont Fire Department, and explained to them what was happening. The nearest bomb disposal team was in Toledo, and the Fremont Fire Department agreed to notify them. Then Leonard called the Fremont Police Department, again identifying himself and requesting that they block off the area around the Ross home and evacuate all the neighbors, allowing no one in until the Toledo bomb squad arrived. He explained what he had instructed Hilda Ross to do, and that she was to remain in the basement until they evacuated her, hopefully in the opposite direction from the parked car.

Leonard then placed a call to Jim Roberts at the NASA facility and suggested, after explaining what was happening, that the facility be placed on a close watch. But he also asked Jim to find out if Rolfe Reübrich was at work that day. Leonard then left a message for Greenspoon and headed to his car to drive to Fremont, notifying the Cleveland FBI field office of the incident he was investigating and that he and Aaron might need backup.

The Johnson home was on Ontario Avenue, just off of West State Street, U.S. Route 20, slightly northwest of the town center. Within minutes sirens were blasting their way to the address, and the police were broadcasting the evacuation of the neighborhood over loudspeakers, and calling homes in the area. Hilda had called Maude Baldridge and told her what she had been instructed to do by the FBI, and Maude agreed to come over and stay with her in her basement, which had a rear exit. In about ten minutes a policeman was banging on the basement door, and the two women joined him, crossing through back yards and over to the next street, then to the one beyond that. Hilda began to feel ill, and the policeman, fearing that perhaps Hilda's baby might be on the way, called for an ambulance. It arrived within minutes and Maude rode with her to the hospital.

It was about an hour and fifteen minutes after Hilda had received the phone call from the "Joe" telling her to drive to the NASA reactor facility. Both Special Agent Leonard and the Toledo Fire Department Explosives Disposal Unit were racing down U.S. Route 20 toward Fremont when they saw a black cloud suddenly appear in the sky west of the city limits. The bomb had detonated with a force at least twelve times greater than the one Hilda had placed in the rail yard at the NASA facility.

The blast had demolished the trees and the entire front of the Ross house, and had blown the porch off the Baldridge house, shattering windows of homes all along Ontario Avenue and for several streets in all directions. Hilda's car was a smoking pile of rubble with parts scattered for hundreds of yards in all directions. The trees in the front yards of homes on the street were on fire, and the fire trucks moved in to control the blazes. Fire was also seen inside the Ross home, and the firemen attacked that blaze as well. The fire hydrant a few hundred feet down the street had been blown over and water was shooting into the air. The fire pumpers had to draw from their tanker truck until a functioning hydrant could be located and the water shut off to the broken hydrant.

Special Agent Leonard arrived ahead of the bomb squad, and carefully dodged burning debris in the street as he pulled his car as close to the

Johnson home as possible. A policeman approached him, and he showed his identification, inquiring, "Was everyone evacuated?"

"As near as we can tell, yes. Are you the agent that told us that a Mrs. Ross would be in the basement?"

"Yes. Is she safe?"

"Well, the officer that got her and her neighbor out of the basement got them a couple of streets away, but Mrs. Johnson, being pregnant, got sick, and an ambulance took them to the hospital. But I heard she's okay and that it wasn't that her baby was coming."

Another car approached, stopped by another policeman, and the man inside got out and ran toward the house. "Good God!" he exclaimed. "My wife was inside!"

"Ross Johnson?" Leonard asked.

"Yes!"

"She's fine. Not hurt. We had the area evacuated before the bomb went off. But they took her and your neighbor to the hospital as a precaution. You might go there and get her. I don't think she'll be cooking your dinner for you here tonight."

"Oh, God! The house is a mess! What on earth happened?"

"We're not totally sure yet, Dr. Johnson. But we will need to talk with you and Mrs. Johnson later. Do you have friends with whom you might spend a night or two, or a hotel that you want to use? I'm sure your insurance company will also assist you."

"I'll go to the hospital first, and get Hilda," Ross Johnson said as Leonard gave him one of his cards with his name and number on it, along with the FBI emblem embossed on it.

Retrieving Hilda at the hospital and driving Mrs. Baldridge back to her home, Hilda suggested calling the Merriams and seeing if they could use the small apartment above their garage for a night or two until they figured out what to do. Sally was delighted to hear that Hilda was safe. She had been in Dr. Fairchild's office when Hilda had called him and knew the story. She and Bob had also felt the blast, which shook houses all over town, but they had no damage. Sally was more than happy to have the Johnsons use their garage apartment for as long as they needed it.

While Special Agent Bret Leonard remained at the Johnson residence, directing additional help from the Cleveland FBI office that had arrived and the Fremont police in searching for any parts of the bomb, Special Agent-in-charge Aaron Greenspoon called Jim Roberts and Colonel Josephs at the NASA facilities and asked them to await his arrival. He had asked if Rolfe Reübrich had been at the rocket propulsion lab that day. He had not, and had not been there the day before, either. Roberts had also notified Jeff Hunter, head of security at the Brookpark NASA facility, and both Hunter and Greenspoon arrived at the main gate about the same time. Being on high alert, three Air Force MPs guarded the gate, with the others patrolling around the Plum Brook facility. Harold Tibbs, the security technician for the Spacecraft Propulsion Research lab, had already joined Jim Roberts and Jeffrey Josephs in Josephs' office when Greenspoon and Hunter arrived. Carrying all the file material NASA had on Reübrich, they moved to the conference room in the Vacuum Chamber building. One of the Gearmone Engineering rocket contractors also joined them.

"Okay," Greenspoon began the meeting, "what do you know about this Rolfe Reübrich?" No one replied. Greenspoon summarized what he thought they knew: "He was supposed to be from West Germany, around Essen, but the Boston Gearmone office knew very little about him as he was hired in France. We asked our contacts at Interpol to find out what they could about him, and that report just came into the Cleveland FBI office this morning.

"It seems we've had a spy among us, gentlemen," Greenspoon continued. "Rolfe Reübrich was originally from Essen, that part was true, but he worked under Wernher von Braun in the Nazi rocket development program during the War, and his real name is Rolfe Wolfmann, a well-trained KGB agent recommended highly by the Stasi, East Germany's secret police. We can only presume that his mission here was to gain information on the American rocket technology, and since he has disappeared, he probably had what he needed. What do your records show as his local address, Colonel Josephs?"

"A small apartment in Sandusky," the Air Force colonel replied. "When Special Agent Leonard asked us to find out if he'd been at work today and we found he had not, we contacted the Sandusky police and asked them to check the address. The apartment was empty, with the rent paid in full. No one there knew when he'd left or where he was going."

"There were obviously others involved," Greenspoon responded, "although we don't think any of the other Gearmone Engineering personnel were part of the plot. We're guessing that some members of the KGB outfit on this operation planted the high explosives under Hilda Johnson's car and then tried to get her to come to the NASA facility, specifically to the nuclear reactor building, with the timer set to go off probably within minutes of her arrival. They were trusting she would respond quickly, and that it would take her about an hour to get here from the time she left her home in Fremont. If she was late her car would have blown up on the highway and no one would know where she was headed. Had the explosion occurred at the reactor building, it presumably would have damaged the reactor and contaminated all of the facility buildings, rendering them useless, a wonderful cover-up for the KGB's theft of your rocket plans, gentlemen.

"We have an all-points bulletin out for Wolfmann, who is known in the KGB as 'the Wolf,' or 'volk' in Russian," Greenspoon continued. "But as he was not acting alone, undoubtedly whatever plans he has are probably already in the dispatch case from the Russian Embassy in Washington, on their way to Moscow. However, our initial concern has to be that they may yet make an attempt to contaminate the facilities here to stop your further research. What do you suggest, Colonel Josephs, to fully secure the facilities?"

The military officer was ill-prepared to answer that question, and looked at Jim Roberts with an expression of pleading for help. Jim responded. "Colonel, what I would suggest, given the potential exposure, severe in the short term and moderate in the long term, is that we get the Air Force to supply us with at least two dozen more MPs to guard the facilities day and night, and then get the NASA politicians in Washington to get to work on establishing a NASA security team for all its facilities, perhaps using Air Force training facilities, but eventually having our own uniformed and armed security force here and at all NASA facilities, like the AEC does. Would you not agree, Mr. Hunter?"

"I've been after NASA to do that for years," the Brookpark NASA security head replied. "Yes, that would be a good plan. Would you have further suggestions, Agent Greenspoon?"

"No, that seems reasonable for now. How soon do you think you can get more MPs here, Colonel?"

"Ahh, well," he hesitated. "I'll call command headquarters today, and maybe by the end of the week...."

"Not soon enough!" both Jeff Hunter and Aaron Greenspoon responded at the same time. "Get them here by tonight, if possible, or tomorrow morning at the latest," Greenspoon added.

"I'll contact NASA in Washington and explain our problem," Hunter said. "We'll get some Congressmen to twist a few arms at the Pentagon and have them flown in tonight. But we'll also need air cover, in case the bastards would think about dropping a bomb on the reactor from a plane or helicopter."

"One thing is certain," Jim Roberts said. "Once word of this gets out, the good folk of Erie County are going to be clamoring at our gates to shut down operations. There have already been some nasty editorials in the local papers after that second explosion in the rail yard and the sirens being set off."

"That's exactly why we need more MPs," Jeff Hunter added, and Colonel Josephs nodded his agreement. Hunter continued, "But we don't want any word of what has happened to get out. There's no need for the explosion in Fremont to be connected to Plum Brook."

"Harold," Greenspoon said to Tibbs, the SPR security technician, "can you find out precisely what information Wolfmann, or Reübrich, as he was known here, had access to or what he was doing. Any of his own work would be suspect and should be reviewed by other engineers and technicians, as it probably would cause damage if used. But keep track of the costs involved, as those can be charged to the contractor, who was it, Grumman?"

"No, Gearmone Engineering," Roberts corrected.

"Oh yes, Gearmone. I suppose Wolfmann could have been acting for the French, but I doubt it. This, according to Interpol's information, is pure KGB. Now, let's get to work."

* * *

Matthew August, Adjuster-in-Charge for Hallmark Fire & Casualty Co., was at his desk planning his day's itinerary when he received a call from one of Hallmark's agents in Fremont. "Did you read the paper this morning?" the agent asked.

"Yes, why? Is Hallmark in the news?"

"Not yet, but you read about the explosion in Fremont that wrecked a house and car and damaged half the neighborhood?"

"Yes, wasn't that something!"

"Well, Matt, that something is yours now! Hallmark insured both the house and the car, plus about another six houses in the area that had their windows broken. One insured is even claiming that the explosion scared her pet cat to death, but I told her the homeowner's policy doesn't cover pets. She wants to sue someone, so find out if any subrogation is possible."

"The paper was vague. Said the police, the FBI and the Alcohol and Firearms Authorities were investigating. Sounds like something fishy. Who's the insured?"

"Two professors at Fremont, your old alma mater. Drs. Ross and Hilda Johnson, 327 Ontario Street, just off Route 20 west of town. They're holed up with a Bob and Sally Merriam, at ...."

"I know their address. We were neighbors in Sandusky and I've known them for years. I suppose somewhere in this we'll find Richie Fairchild investigating, too."

"You know the Fairchilds? They're my clients, too."

"I know. Remember the train accident back in 1960 that half demolished their house? I got subro on that, too!"

"Yeah, that's right. Well, this one should be easy. The Fremont Fire Department has condemned the Johnson house, so it will have to be demolished. Most of the contents were damaged by either the blast or the subsequent fire, so it will probably be a policy limits case. Same with the car. The FBI has impounded the debris for analysis, so there won't be any salvage. Stop by my office and I'll give you a list of the insureds with broken glass claims."

Matt placed a call to Sally at Fremont College, confirmed that the Johnsons were okay, and headed out for his car.

Chapter 12

Darlene Smathers, the student secretary in the Physics Department, walked from the Science Building to Hayes Hall and down the basement stairs. Sally Merriam was away from her desk for a few minutes, but Dr. Fairchild was in his office with his door open and a fan outside the door attempting to catch what little cool air might blow in on the hot August day. Darlene knocked lightly on his door. She knew him from having taken a Freshman Basics of Religions class with him a few years before.

"Dr. Fairchild, do you have a moment? I need to ask you something," Darlene said.

Recognizing her, Fairchild answered, "Yes, Miss Smathers – Darlene, isn't it? – come on in. If it is something personal, feel free to close the door, although it is rather warm in here."

Darlene responded by closing the door and sitting down in one of the chairs across from Fairchild's desk. She remained silent for a moment, as did Fairchild as he searched her face for some sign of emotion. "Dr. Fairchild," she finally said, "I think I've done something terrible. I don't know what to do about it."

Fairchild smiled, and said, "There's not too many problems that don't have some sort of solution."

"I know," she replied. "But this is...." Then she began to cry. Fairchild kept a box of Kleenex near his desk for just such occasions, and handed her several.

"Tell me," he said. "You know you can speak with me in confidence, Darlene."

"Yes," she sobbed, wiping her eyes and nose. "I know. But I fear I almost got Dr. Johnson killed."

"Good gracious! You mean the explosion yesterday afternoon? You certainly weren't involved with *that*, I'm sure."

"Not directly, no. But I met a man about five months ago when a friend and I went to a movie in Sandusky. He was older, at least thirty, I'd guess, and spoke with a German accent. My friend had to get back to campus here, and this man said he'd drive me back if I stayed and had dinner with him. I had no reason not to, and he said he knew a little about Fremont College, and mentioned Dr. Hilda. When I said I worked for Dr. Hilda and Dr. Durrnad he became especially interested in what I did, what classes I was taking, my thoughts about politics and the world, and other things, very friendly. He took me to dinner at a very nice restaurant, and

745

then immediately brought me back to the campus. I live in the women's dorm.

"I thought nothing much about it," Darlene continued, "but about a week later he called me and asked if I would go to dinner with him again. I agreed, and he picked me up at the dorm, and we went to Port Clinton to a seafood restaurant there. I told him about the college cruiser and our island in Lake Erie, and he seemed very interested, but he didn't tell me much about himself, except that he had been a sailor once. Again he brought me straight back to the campus, but called again the following week. I had other plans, but he asked me about my work for the Physics Department, and the two professors. He seemed especially interested in Dr. Hilda, and I said that she was expecting a baby toward the end of August. He asked me more about her, and I told him what I knew, that she was married to Ross Johnson, the choral director."

"Did he give you his name?" Fairchild asked.

"He said his name was Johann, and that he had been born in Germany. I don't remember his last name, Caleb or something, as I wasn't really interested in him – he was far too old for me, but he was nice and took me to dinner."

"Could it have been 'Kahler'?"

"Yes, something like that. I just don't remember. But when I heard this morning that Dr. Hilda's home had been bombed yesterday and then a rumor that she and Ross and the baby that is due had been threatened by some man with a German accent, I realized that I had been the one who had told this German guy, Johann, all about Dr. Hilda! That makes me responsible for what happened to her yesterday."

"Oh, I don't think so, Darlene. I think I know who this Johann is. What you have just told me solves a big mystery, and I'm glad you did tell me. He would have done what he did – if he is the one who did it – regardless of what you may have said. Do you know where he was living?"

"No, I never asked."

"Do you think he might contact you again?"

"I don't know. I doubt it if he was the one who destroyed Dr. Hilda's home."

"But he might," Fairchild said. "And if he does, and wants to meet you again, I want you to not say no, but to let me know immediately. Here is my number at the farm. Call me and let me know what he wants you to do. Say, are you going to join the gang on West Bass Island for the grape harvest next week? I know Dr. Johnson, both of them, will not be there this year, but if this man calls you, tell him you are going to the grape harvest and invite him along. He might just agree. Then let me know right away. Okay?"

"I wasn't planning on going to the grape harvest, but why would you want him to go if he's the man who blew up Dr. Hilda's car and threatened her earlier."

"Because if he is that man, he needs to be caught, and you might help with that. But whatever you do, even if you agree to go with him, don't. Just let me know and then stay in the dorm. Where is your parents' home?"

"Near Columbus."

"Well, at the time you are to meet him, you be with your parents in Columbus, and leave the rest to me, okay?"

"Okay, Dr. Fairchild. Thank you. I'll do as you ask."

As soon as Darlene had left his office Fairchild picked up his phone and called the Toledo FBI office, reaching Special Agent Leonard. He began by asking if they had any leads on the man known as Rolfe Wolfmann, or any of the other KGB agents that might have been involved, and learned that there were no leads – they had seemingly disappeared. Fairchild then explained the visit he had received from the secretary in the Physics Department, which explained how the KGB agent that had contacted Hilda Johnson knew so much about her, and why Fairchild felt certain that he knew who the man was.

Fairchild concluded, "And we suspect that one of those agents, besides Wolfmann, was Johann Kahler, the former fiancé of Hilda von Werdau, the man who attempted to kill her aboard the college's cruiser on the Cuyahoga River in 1962. If he contacts Miss Smathers again and she arranges a meeting with him somewhere and lets me know, you should be able to grab him."

"This is all good information," Leonard replied. "But I seriously doubt, given what has transpired, that he will contact her again. Kahler may have been the one we filmed putting the box with the bomb in it at the gas station, and again filmed outside the railroad gates at Plum Brook awaiting the explosion, but we were unable to track him. Yet, it never hurts to try."

* * *

Rolfe Wolfmann, the *volk*, sat at a desk in the motel room of Johann Kahler in Vermilion, about twenty-five miles east of Sandusky, working on his notes and translating many of them into Russian. "I wish I had been able to get more information on what the Americans were doing at the cryogenics lab," he said to Kahler in German. "There are actually two labs there, and they are working on some project that affects how a space capsule will react in the extremely low temperatures beyond the atmosphere."

"Could the Russians not get a cryogenics expert in there through Gearmone?" Kahler continued the discussion in German.

"They tried, but Gearmone Engineering does not work in that field. But at least the Americans are using the metric system in their research."

"That is probably due to Wernher von Braun. The Americans got him after he was arrested and before the Russians came in. He was a dedicated scientist, and although a party member was not much of a Nazi, so he was hustled off to America to help them build their rockets, just as Teller was taken to help build thermonuclear bombs." Kahler explained.

"Yes. I had been a communist before the war – the Nazis never found that out – so I was able to defect to Russia when their troops were still in Poland," *Volk* said. "They put me to work in the Science Institute. When the Russians had trouble with their nuclear subs and you were able to get back in the good graces of the Stasi, that's when they teamed us together to see what we could learn from the American space program. Currently Russia is ahead, but…."

"I know. I know. Major Kolnekov was very angry with me when he learned that Hilda von Werdau had not driven her car to the reactor building and let it explode at her house."

"You and Klaus were certain that she would follow through. What changed her mind?"

"We're not sure. We think a neighbor saw the two of us tampering with her car and told her. Apparently she survived the explosion, and she and her husband moved in with another professor until her baby is born. You know, I guess, that I was once engaged to her."

"No! I did not know this. What happened?"

"My commanding office demanded that she alter her report on the Russian sub, and she said the sub was too dangerous and refused to do so, so she defected. Even though I was initially thrown out of the East German Navy and told to track her down and kill her – along with my father, who also defected – I missed by inches. It was here, in Ohio, down in Cleveland. She and my father were on a big cabin cruiser. I wounded her, but the wound was not serious. I barely escaped, and had to change my name and escape into Canada for a couple of years before I got my East German citizenship back. By then she was married to the music professor, Johnson."

"Ehh, so that's the story. What about this new girl you've befriended who gave you the details about this Hilda?"

"Aww, she's just a child, a student working in the office of the Physics Department. But I may keep in touch with her. Hilda seems to have good contacts at the Plum Brook facility. In fact, their security officer, Jim Roberts, is teaching a fire science course at the college, so there is always a chance I might get another opportunity to get in there with another bomb."

"You think that is possible? Sergi Kolnekov wanted to know what else we might try. He even suggested spraying something from an airplane, but the first rain would dilute anything toxic, hence that would not help any. Besides, planes are easily traced. Maybe you could get a bomb into this Roberts' car. If so, use a remote trigger."

"Yes, I have been thinking that might be possible. We'll see," Kahler replied.

"You are certain that the American FBI is unaware of your presence in this?"

"I'm sure that if they were, I'd already be in jail. Certainly nobody was watching when I placed the first little explosive in the gas station for her, and she did exactly as instructed. Coming from East Germany, she knows fear and that my threats were real. I disguised my voice so she would not recognize it. Of course, she'd know me if she saw me. I imagine there is still a warrant for my arrest for attempting to kill her and my father."

"What is your father doing now?"

"He's back in Europe, working with NATO, I understand. He was their intended defector at that Wagner opera in Bayreuth – but they got Hilda as a bonus."

"Of course, now that I have disappeared from Plum Brook," Wolfmann said after a moment's pause, "they will be watching for me, suspecting that I was a spy and stole vital information. What I got is good stuff, and I should have it fully translated into Russian by mid-September so I can get it to Kolnekov to send to Moscow in the diplomatic pouch. Then I'll be back in Russia to put what I learned into the Russian programs. I just wish that we could find some way to shut down the American rocketry program. But what they are doing here in Ohio is nothing compared to the facilities at Vandenberg Air Base in California, Houston, Huntsville in Alabama or Cape Canaveral – what do they call it now, Cape Kennedy after their President who was assassinated?"

"*Ja*. Cape Kennedy. They are making too much progress. But no doubt the KGB has agents at those facilities as well, either sabotaging or gathering information. Look at what the KGB was able to learn at Los Alamos and Oak Ridge."

"We need a plan, in the event we are spotted by the authorities. I've been thinking about it, and if either of us suspect we've been detected, our best bet is to abandon this place and the autos, and get to Chicago as quickly as possible."

"That is wise. There are some buses from here to Toledo or Cleveland, and trains from there. I think we should avoid airports, but we need to get to Chicago where Klaus can help us get the data you've prepared to Washington."

"What has Klaus learned at the Fermi Lab?" Wolfmann asked.

"So far not much. He has an agent inside the Lab associated with one of the universities in Chicago, but their role in the space program is limited. They're work is more in applied physics and nuclear research."

"Surely something will show up." *Volk* said. "How safe are we here at this motel? Any questions about what we are doing here for a month?"

"The desk clerk stopped me the other day and asked. I told her you were a writer working on a book about the vineyards around here, and that I represented the publisher and was trying to hurry you along. She seemed pleased, and said to tell you to take your time and sample all the vineyards around here."

"Vineyards! I know nothing about vineyards. What if she asks me?"

"Ha! Rolfe, you are a German! You know more about wine than any ten Americans."

* * *

Hilda's baby shower had been held at the Merriam's home, and had been quite successful. Although Hilda and Ross had lost everything except some of Ross's collection of music literature in a room in the back of the house, Matt August, their insurance company's adjuster, had arranged for removal of all the debris. Rather than rebuild, Ross and Hilda had found another house in the same neighborhood for sale, a house that was larger than the one that had been destroyed, and which had an extra bedroom that Hilda fixed up into a nursery after the baby shower. Matt August had helped them find the house, and, with the old mortgage paid off, the amount of settlement was more than a down-payment on the newer home, with a much lower mortgage. The value of the vacant lot, now available for new construction, would probably be enough to pay off that mortgage, leaving the Johnsons in better shape than before the fire. The settlement on the Johnsons' contents also was enough for Hilda to select new furnishings, although many of their wedding presents had been lost in the fire. The insurer even reimbursed the Merriams for the two weeks Ross and Hilda had stayed in the garage apartment, although both Bob and Sally had protested to Matt that they didn't want to be paid.

A week after moving into the new home – with deliveries of furniture, bedding and other things an almost daily routine – Ross had rushed Hilda to the hospital on the twenty-ninth day of August, where she had given birth to a baby girl they named Heidi. That weekend was also Labor Day weekend, the weekend of the grape harvest on West Bass Island, but the Johnsons would not be able to go – baby feedings at four each morning would leave them with enough to do without having to pick grapes in the hot sun.

Dr. Rayland Durrand had met with the two physics scientists from Plum Brook and had assisted them in selection of textbooks they wanted to use and with class schedules. The books were ordered with plenty of time to be stocked in the college book store. The text for Physics 101 was the same one that Hilda had used the year before, so there were a few copies, including a few used copies from non-science majors, available in the bookstore. A newer text had been selected for one of the more advanced courses, and a new course in astrophysics was to be taught jointly by one of the Space Power Facility scientists, Dr. Bill Rubenstein, and Fremont's own professor of astronomy, Dr. George Whitmore. When the new course was announced, the local newspaper picked up the story, and it gained mention in *The New York Times*. Fremont College was again making headlines.

The Annual Grape Harvest and Barbeque would take place over the three-day Labor Day weekend. The Fairchilds had invited Jim and Jayne Roberts to attend, and with the new Air Force MPs at the facility on round-the-clock patrol, Jim felt that he could afford the three-day weekend before the facility got busy and he again started teaching at Fremont. So far the technicians, engineers and scientists at the Spacecraft Propulsion Research Lab had been unable to detect any data that Rolfe Wolfmann had stolen – although they couldn't be certain what he might have copied – and they had found nothing that he might have sabotaged. He had been a well-trained rocket scientist.

The college's small Marine Navigation Department, consisting of a retired Coast Guard Commander, Joshua Philby, and eight students, was in charge of ferrying students, staff and guests to West Bass aboard the *Castle Kent* for the grape harvest and barbeque. It was the large cabin cruiser that Richard Fairchild had won in a lawsuit against its prior owner, a Texas millionaire now in prison for murder and conspiracy to kill the civil rights leader, Thomas Jefferson Singletary, who was to be a speaker at a Fremont College symposium.

The Hospitality Management Department, again a small college department run by Joyce Philby, Commander Joshua's wife, who had previously been a manager of a small hotel in New London, Connecticut, would put the grape harvesters up at the Chateau Kent, although the Fairchilds planned to stay in Kent Village with the Forracres. Forracre – if he had a first name nobody remembered it or used it – and his wife, who was also named Hilda, were the primary residents of Kent Village, a small hamlet on the north end of the island. Hilda ran a small store that also served as the post office for the village, and Richard Fairchild had agreed to hold a service in the small village church; about the only times there were services was when either Richie or some other preacher would come to visit.

While the lake steamers no longer called at Kent Village, Islands Airline continued to operate a small plane to the island twice a week (or daily if there were any school-age children who needed transport to Port Clinton, a service paid by the county). The airline operated an old Ford

1923 Tri-motor "tin goose" airplane that had a short take-off and landing ability, but was considering selling the antique. It now also used a slightly larger but more modern aircraft. For the grape harvest festival the airline would also offer a shuttle service from its base at Port Clinton Airport for those who didn't want to use the college's cruiser. As Jim had to be back at the Plum Brook facility on Monday, despite the holiday, he and Jayne would fly back Saturday evening, although they would ride the college's cruiser to the island on Friday night in a special group Richard Fairchild had planned, spending the night aboard the cruiser.

Chateau Kent had been a millionaire railroad baron's mansion on a cliff above the vineyards on the west side of the island. The large mansion had been turned into a small boutique hotel and restaurant where hands-on classes in hotel and restaurant management were taught by Joyce Philby, who had a Master's degree in hospitality management. Tents had been set up for the overflow of people coming to the harvest, and the management students would run the barbeque. The winery was in the basement, where grapes would be pressed and put in barrels for later bottling by the Vintners Club of Fremont College, a non-credit group of eager young wine-makers under the direction of Dr. Charles LaDue, Professor of Chemistry, who had grown up on a winery in France. Chateau Kent wine had not yet reached prize-winning status among Ohio wines, but was getting better with each season's vintage.

On the same day that Heidi Johnson was born Darlene Smathers was kept busy with phone calls from people wanting news of the new baby. Darlene was almost as excited as Ross Johnson, who had promised that Heidi would be taught to call her Aunt Darlene when she learned to talk, as neither Ross nor Hilda had siblings. Rayland Durrand had gone to the hospital with a bouquet of flowers for Hilda, and Darlene was alone in the Physics Department answering the phone. A few calls were from students inquiring what the textbooks for the next semester courses would be. Then Darlene got a call she had been fearing. She'd answered the phone, "Physics Department."

"Darlene? Darlene Smathers?" asked the German-accented voice.

"Yes, this is Darlene...."

"This is Johann. I was wondering if we might get together again for lunch or dinner?"

"Oh, Johann. How are you? I wondered if I would ever hear from you again."

"Why, yes. I wouldn't forget the wonderful times we had. Oh, and how is Dr. Johnson? Wasn't her baby due soon?"

"Ye-yes, it was born about noon today. A little girl they are going to name Heidi."

"Why that's wonderful!" Johann said, although he felt a pang of jealousy as that baby ought to have been his. "And can we maybe have dinner to celebrate her birth tonight?"

"Ah, no, no, I can't tonight, Johann. Ah, but... Tomorrow is the grape harvest on West Bass Island and I'd enjoy going with you to that."

"A grape harvest? What and where is it?"

"Well, ah, the college, Fremont here, owns an island, well, at least most of it, except a small village on the north side, in Lake Erie. There's a hotel the college runs there, and a vineyard and winery. Each year over Labor Day weekend college staff and students and other guests go out there to pick the grapes, and a group of chemistry students make the wine to sell. It's a lot of fun, and you could go as my guest."

"Oh, thank you, Darlene. That would be fun. I picked grapes as a child in Germany. But I would assume that Dr. Johnson will not be there."

"Hardly!" Darlene replied with a laugh. "Not with a brand new baby!"

"What time may I pick you up at the dorm?"

"No! No, Johann, I'm going to ride to the boat with friends. I'll meet you there. Remember the night we had dinner in Port Clinton and I pointed out a boat in the lagoon?"

"Yes."

"That's the boat to the island. I'll meet you on the dock at, oh, we'd have to be there by nine-fifteen to catch the first trip. There won't be another until nearly eleven. It's about a fifty minute trip over there."

"The nine-fifteen trip will be okay, Darlene. I have to drive about thirty miles or so."

"Yes, it will be fun, Johann."

"Good. I'll see you at the dock then, before nine fifteen. I shall look forward to it. Bye."

"Good-bye, Johann."

As soon as Darlene hung up she called the Fairchild farm. Esther answered, and when Darlene explained who she was and why she needed to talk to Dr. Fairchild right away Esther agreed to go out to the barn and get him. Within two minutes Fairchild came on the phone and Darlene explained what had happened, then remembered to also tell him about Hilda's baby.

"Wonderful, Darlene. You did exactly the right thing. Were you planning to go to the grape harvest?"

"I went last year and got such a bad sunburn I decided never to do it again, so, no, I'll catch a bus to Toledo and on to Columbus to stay with my folks."

"Great. Tell me a little about what Johann looks like."

"I'd guess he's about thirty-five, blonde hair with a blonde moustache, and doesn't wear glasses. If anything, he's under-weight, but tall. Has a distinctive German accent, pronounces a 'w' as a 'v,' that is really all I know about him."

"Well, that's enough, Darlene. You be careful to catch the first bus you can, and if you see Johann anywhere, hide."

"I will, Dr. Fairchild. I hope you can get the FBI to arrest him."

As soon as Darlene Smathers hung up Fairchild phoned the Toledo office of the FBI. He was in luck, and Special Agent Leonard answered.

"Johann Kahler has made contact with Darlene Smathers," Fairchild explained after identifying himself. "She arranged to meet him at the dock in Port Clinton at nine-fifteen tomorrow morning to go to the grape harvest on West Bass Island."

"She's not going to meet him, is she?"

"No, she's going home to Columbus this afternoon. But I'll meet him. She described him to me and I'll tell him that she got sick and couldn't come in the morning, but will come later and that he should go on to the harvest and she'd meet him in the vineyard. Will you be there?"

"Yes, probably both Greenspoon and I will be there, but we don't want to arrest him yet until we find out where Wolfmann is, and undoubtedly he knows. After he parks his car, we'll put a tracer on it, and when he returns to it, follow him. How long will all of you be on the island?"

"I'm staying for the weekend, but I think Johann will only stay part of the day once he figures out that Darlene is not going to be there. I've also invited Jim Roberts and his wife to the grape harvest, but they are returning Saturday evening. I'll alert him that you and Greenspoon will be there and that I will be with one of the suspects so that he doesn't react if he sees you."

"Good idea. He's a smart guy, and is doing a great job there at the NASA facility, but if he saw Aaron or me there he might say something that would tip this Johann off."

As soon as Fairchild hung up from talking with the FBI he called Roberts. "Jim, this is Richie. We'll still take the cruiser out to the island Friday evening, have dinner aboard and spend the night, but I need to get back to Port Clinton before nine-fifteen Saturday morning for the first trip to the island. Something important has arisen. Johann Kahler has contacted Smathers at the Physics Department, and she invited him to the harvest and barbeque. He agreed, and is to meet her at nine-fifteen, so he'll be on that trip too."

"Surely she's not going to go with him!" Jim exclaimed.

"No, she's on her way to her parent's home in Columbus for the weekend. But I needed to alert you, as the two FBI agents, Leonard and Greenspoon, will be there, and you're not to let on that you know them. They're going to put some sort of tracking device on Kahler's car and try to get him to lead them to Wolfmann."

"Wow! This is a real break. Do they think Wolfmann is still in the area?"

"I think they've got a watch on the airport, and maybe trains, but he has not turned up yet, so he may still be around here somewhere."

* * *

Shortly after nine Saturday morning Richie and Esther Fairchild were standing on the dock where the *Chateau Kent* would dock as a late-model car drove into the parking lot and a blonde-headed man with a small moustache got out. He was wearing a light jacket and a baseball cap. He looked around, and then walked toward the dock. As he approached, Fairchild took a step or two toward him and said, "Are you Johann, Darlene Smathers' friend?"

Looking somewhat apprehensive, Kahler answered, "Yes. Where is she?"

"Johann," Fairchild replied, "she got sick in the middle of the night, and called me early this morning to see if I would meet you and take you to the island. She thinks she will be better soon and will able to come in a few hours and hopes to see you there, taking a later trip. In the meantime, I know you will enjoy the ride to the island – Darlene said you had told her you had been a sailor – and we do have a good time there," Fairchild continued. "This is my wife, Esther."

Kahler looked at Fairchild as they shook hands and said, "You look familiar. Are you one of the professors at the college?"

"Just one of several who will be at the grape harvest," Fairchild answered.

"Well, if you think Darlene, Miss Smathers, will be along later I guess I may as well go with you rather than wait here," Kahler said.

Others had gathered on the dock for the trip, and a group of about twenty, including a man wearing brown jacket, a floppy hat and sun glasses joined the group on the dock. He had arrived with another man wearing a suit and hat who didn't look properly dressed for a harvest and barbeque, and who remained in his car. Most crowded aboard the boat. Within a few minutes the cabin cruiser, filled with students, faculty and friends, departed for the harbor from the dock.

"There's coffee and donuts in the galley, folks," a student crewman of the boat, a senior who had received his Coast Guard certification, said. "And the heads – that's the bathrooms for you landlubbers – are down below. You're welcome to explore the vessel as we make our way to West Bass. It's about eighteen nautical miles, about a fifty-minute trip."

The man in the jacket and cap boarded last. He stood off by himself and watched as the students who served as crew members threw off the ropes and the cruiser headed into the lagoon, blasting the horn for the highway bridge to open for their passage.

Upon arriving at the dock by the Chateau on the west side of the island, another student was waiting to direct them to the vineyards. "Each of you take a basket and clippers," she instructed. "Pick only the bunches of grapes that appear ripe, probably less than half of them. The winemaking class will pick the rest of them in a few weeks when the rest are fully ripe. When your basket is full, bring it around to the back of the chateau here, I'll show you, and dump them in the big vat, then return to the vines. At noon we'll bring you sandwiches and drinks. The barbeque will begin at six this evening."

Everyone followed her, collecting their basket, and she led them around the back of the old mansion turned hotel to an outside doorway and steps to the cellar, telling them that was where the vat was. Then she led them down the hillside to where others were already picking grapes and bringing them to the vat.

Kahler looked around, and not seeing anyone watching him, went ahead and started to fill his basket. When it was full he took it to the vat. Noticing the student who had directed them to the vineyard, he asked, "Does the boat take people back to Port Clinton whenever they want?"

"Oh sure!" she said in a youthful voice. "People will be coming and going all weekend. Some will stay just for the day or only one night, others both nights, depending on the weather, so you'll see different people all weekend."

By two o'clock Darlene Smathers had not yet arrived, and Kahler took his half-filled basket to the vat and watched as the cruiser docked and people began coming ashore. He had decided that if Darlene was not in this bunch he would take the boat back to Port Clinton. She was not among those who disembarked, and he asked if he could ride back. Several others were also going to return, including the man in the jacket and floppy hat. Kahler boarded, and went below to the head, then wandered around the vessel a bit.

He examined several of the cabin doors below deck, noting that several had been repaired. The last door, the one he had once hidden behind before attempting to kill Hilda von Werdau and his father, General Kahler, was much as it had been seven years earlier.

He remained on deck until the cruiser was back in Port Clinton, but noticed that the man in the jacket and hat had been watching him as he came up from below decks. When the boat docked, he waited until that man disembarked, then slowly left the boat, watching him. The man went over to another car, where a man in a suit was waiting. He also noted that Darlene was not on the dock, awaiting the next trip to the island.

Rather than return to his car, Kahler walked up the walkway to the highway and crossed the drawbridge beyond the lagoon where the Portage

River and the lagoon met. This led him into the town of Port Clinton, and he watched as traffic passed. The car into which the man in the cap had entered with the man in the suit drove past him and onward, but it turned into the town a few streets beyond where Kahler was walking. There was a hotel on the corner, and Kahler entered, seeking a telephone. He called a number in Vermilion, and deposited sufficient coins.

"Yes," a German-accented voice answered.

"Wolf, it is Johann. I think I have been spotted," he said in German. He had been watching the street outside of the hotel and saw the same car with the two men in it drive by at least twice. "Get out of there as soon as you can. Grab a couple of shirts and socks for me and my razor – the rest of the stuff we can leave – and take the next bus to Sandusky to the train station. Buy two tickets to Chicago. The schedule I studied showed that the train's next stop after Sandusky was Port Clinton, so I will board here without buying a ticket, and you'll have one for me. I've got to get to the station without being spotted. I think there's a back door to this hotel, and I'll work my way around and not get to the platform through the station. I'll need to kill a couple of hours here first, but make sure you catch that train. Then we'll get off a few stations before Chicago, and get Klaus to pick us up. Okay?"

"*Ja!* I see it on the schedules. A bus in half an hour, and the train leaves Sandusky about five. I'll be on it. Be careful," Wolfmann replied in German.

Johann Kahler left the hotel through a rear door to a parking lot, and walked along a back street toward the railroad tracks. There was a bar on one corner, and he entered, ordered and paid for a beer, and sat in a seat at the back where he could watch the street and anyone that entered. After about fifteen minutes he saw the same car with the two men in it drive by slowly, and then park. He quickly found a rear exit and left the bar, unseen by the bar tender.

Special Agent Leonard entered the bar and asked the bar tender if there had been a blonde man in a jacket who had come in.

"Yeah, some guy came in a while ago and ordered a beer. I don't see him now. He must have left."

"Did he have a German accent?"

"German, yeah. That might have been what it was. Why? You lookin' for him?"

"Yes. If he comes back in, call this number," Leonard said, giving the bar tender one of his cards on which he wrote a special mobile telephone number.

"FBI? You really *are* lookin' for that guy, eh?"

"Yes, we'd like to talk to him."

"He paid for the beer, but I see he left half of it, so if he comes back, I'll let you know. Of course he may just have gone to the restroom. Yah might look in there before you leave."

Leonard doubted Kahler would be in the restroom, but he looked anyway, then returned to the car. "He was there, but must have seen us," he told Greenspoon, who was waiting in the car. So he's in town somewhere."

"Unless he's going to go back and get his car, how can he get out of this burg?" Greenspoon commented. Let's find out where the bus station is, and the train station. Those would be his best ways."

"I saw the bus sign by that hotel. It probably just stops there as it goes through town. Drop me there and I'll check the schedule. Then we can check the train station."

Agent Leonard got a schedule from the hotel clerk who also sold bus tickets, and learned that the next bus would be a westbound in about forty minutes. The two agents then drove toward the railroad tracks and spotted the Penn Central depot, which was at street level, although the tracks were up above the street. There were two passenger trains due, an eastbound in about forty minutes, and a westbound at about five-thirty. Greenspoon drove Leonard back to the hotel to watch for the bus, and Greenspoon parked in front of the train depot where he could view the entrance.

A Trailways bus arrived on schedule, tooted the horn, but no one came out to get on it, and only an old woman with some bundles got off, then started walking east toward the residential part of town.

Kahler had found a wooded area that led to a slope up to the two sets of railroad tracks through town. In the distance he heard a train whistle, but it came from the west. There was another thicket of trees and bushes on the other side of the tracks at the bottom of the slope, and he slithered down through the grass and waited, well hidden in the brush. In a few minutes there were more train whistles, and a Penn Central passenger train slowed as it entered the depot area and came to a stop. Kahler couldn't see the platform, but imagined that it was about a hundred yards from where he was hidden. The train paused for only a minute, then slowly rolled out of the station, its horn blasting for a crossing.

About fifteen minutes later Kahler heard another train whistle from the west. He climbed up the slope to watch the platform, and saw the man in the suit standing there, watching. The noise of the approaching train grew louder, and soon a fast freight train with three locomotives on it roared into view and through the depot without stopping, whistling for the next crossing. Kahler was concerned. If the man in the suit, probably an FBI agent, remained on the depot platform Kahler would be unable to get to a coach door when the westbound train arrived. Then he heard another train whistle. It was only four-fifty, so he thought it couldn't be the passenger train yet – if it was, Wolfmann would not have had time to catch it.

He worked his way along the side of the slope until he came to the underpass for the road beneath the tracks. From here he could see that there were two brick-lined platforms, one next to the stairs down to the depot and the other in the middle of the two tracks. He recalled that both of the eastbound trains had used the south track, and, as this westbound train approached it was moving very slowly. If it was ahead of the passenger train, there was the possibility that the passenger train would arrive on the east-bound track, using the platform between the two tracks so that when it left it would pass the freight train.

Just as a caboose of the freight train came into view the freight train began to stop, with a hiss of air and squeal of brakes. The caboose stopped opposite the stairs down to the depot, and one of the crew got off with some papers and started down the stairs. Kahler reasoned that this meant that the westbound passenger train would pass the stopped freight on the eastbound tracks, giving Kahler an opportunity to hide underneath the freight train until the passenger train stopped, where he might get aboard without the man in the suit seeing him.

Kahler waited about half an hour until he heard a whistle from the east, indicating the arrival of the passenger train. He quickly darted across the eastbound tracks, well out of sight of the man in the suit, and moved slowly toward the rear of the freight train. Within minutes the Penn Central passenger train slowed as it entered the depot area. There were two locomotives and several express and Railway Post Office cars, and some sleeping cars ahead of the coaches. Kahler moved down the platform, still next to the freight train, and saw the Dutch door of one of the sleeping cars open, and a porter in a white jacket standing there. Kahler approached and indicated he wanted aboard, and the porter opened the door and started to set out the step box, but Kahler grabbed the safety bar and pulled himself aboard. He shot a quick glance back toward the rear of the train where a conductor was assisting a passenger off, and two were waiting to board, and saw that the man in the suit had not seen him.

"Thanks," Kahler said to the porter. "I thought the coaches would be up front, and I didn't want to run all the way back down there," he said, reaching in his pocket and handing the porter a five dollar bill.

"Oh, that's okay. I don't mind lettin' you on, but if you have a coach ticket, you'll have to go back through four cars, this and the next Pullman, the diner, and the first coach you come to which is a special group, then that next one where the conductor will collect your ticket."

"Oh, thank you again," Kahler said, as he headed back through the maze of bedrooms and roomettes toward the diner. He felt the train start to move and hoped that the man in the suit had not seen him."

At last reaching the second coach as the train was picking up speed, after passing the stopped freight train and switching back to the westbound track, he spotted Wolfmann in a double coach seat, and sat down beside him as the conductor approached. Wolfmann handed Kahler his ticket, and Kahler gave it to the conductor who punched it. "The diner will be open in a few minutes if you want dinner," the conductor said as he moved on. He had apparently seen Kahler boarding at the front of the train.

"Did you see a man in a suit at the depot, watching?" Kahler asked.

"Yes. He seemed very puzzled that the other passengers, a small family group, did not include you. I think you managed to avoid being seen. But I expect they will go over the car and try to trace it."

"What time do we get to Elkhart?"

"About eight-thirty, I think. That's a good place to get off. If they suspect you were on the train, they'll be watching in Chicago."

"It was a close call, Wolf. I'm glad to get out of here."

"Yes, but your mission is still to disrupt the research at Plum Brook, and mine to get the information I have to the Embassy. We must work smarter next time. Your girlfriend will not be able to help this time."

* * *

Greenspoon picked up Leonard at the hotel after the train left and said, "I'm afraid he's gotten away, but not by train or bus. We should notify Chicago to watch for the arrival of that train just in case, though. I'll bet he's stolen a car and is heading to Canada or someplace. Let's check with the local police and alert them that if there are any reported car thefts, we want to know."

"Good idea. But I also agreed to let that professor, Fairchild, know if we got him so he can let the girl know if she'll be bothered again by Kahler. Good thing he tipped us off to where Kahler would be. You got good photos?"

"Yes, a number of angles. We'll have his face in every FBI and police office across the nation by tomorrow night."

"Well, let's hope we catch him. Let's go examine his car and see if we can figure out where they were staying."

A search of the car turned up enough evidence to show that Kahler had been staying in a motel in Vermilion. A check at the motel showed that two men had been staying there, but the room now appeared abandoned, although a number of personal items remained. From these the two FBI agents collected a number of fingerprints, and added additional information to their file.

Chapter 13

Dr. Bernard Ruhl, the Director of the Plum Brook facility, was sitting at his desk in his office in the Spacecraft Propulsion lab when the phone rang. It was the Air Force MP at the main gate advising that a U.S. Marshal was there demanding to see the Director. "Well, if he has proper identification, tell him where my office is and let him in."

In a few moments the federal marshal arrived, and, upon asking Dr. Ruhl for his name and position, handed him a summons and complaint entitled Jerry Summers et al. v. The Plum Brook Facility of the National Aeronautics & Space Administration, a Federal Agency. "What on earth is this?" Ruhl asked, but the marshal said he was just the delivery man and had no knowledge of what the lawsuit was about. It was filed in the Federal District Court of the Northern District of Ohio, and contained about thirty pages.

When the marshal left with a signed receipt, Ruhl began to read the document, but after the first page or two picked up the phone and called Jim Roberts and Jeffry Josephs to join him in his office. They arrived within minutes.

"As we feared, gentlemen," Ruhl said, "our neighbors have sued us, and want the facility declared a public nuisance! Listen to this: 'Count 1. The defendant facility possesses and maintains a dangerous nuclear reactor without license and without clearance from the U.S. Environmental Protection Agency, the Ohio Emergency Management Department or any other state or federal agency that has authority over such installations. Count 2. Dangerous substances including nuclear fuel rods, liquid oxygen, liquid nitrogen and various other hazardous chemicals and compounds to be identified at time of trial are routinely brought into the facility by rail without any guarantee of safe transport. Count 3. At various and sundry times various alarms have been sounded from the perimeter of the facility that exceed county noise control limits and which disturb the peace of residents within a ten square mile range of the said facility, including the peace and tranquility of farm animals, including chickens, thus reducing their production, and even threatening the wildlife in the area, part of which has always been a nature preserve. Count 4. On December 25, 1968, criminals managed to breach the inadequate security of the facility and set off an explosion that produced sound waves sufficient to break windows, crack residential walls, cause fires and smoke within the facility and frighten the general public, which was forced to respond through its taxpayer-supported police, fire and other Erie County facilities. Count 5. On or about May 27, 1969, a second explosion of lesser volume occurred on the facility further causing damage to neighboring homes, including those of Plaintiffs 1 through 12, and upsetting farm animals of Plaintiffs 13 through 18, also triggering the afore-said alarms which resulted in reduced production from said farm animals and chickens. Count 6. On or about August 24, 1969, the home and auto of one of the facility's contract consultants, identified as Defendant Doe, was bombed in Fremont, Sandusky County, believed to be connected to the Defendant facility, with further proof to be shown at time of trial.'"

"How the hell did they make that connection?" Colonel Josephs stormed. "There was nothing in the press that related that bombing to NASA."

"I know," Ruhl replied. "But wait until you hear this," he continued, flipping through several more pages of less innocuous counts, "'Therefore the afore-stated Plaintiffs seek an injunction against the Plum Brook NASA Facility and an Order from the Court that the afore-said Facility be immediately shut down and its operations ceased and desisted permanently.' In addition to about two million dollars in compensatory and another million in punitive damages," Ruhl summarized, "they want us shut down!"

"They can't do that!" the Colonel exclaimed. "This is a federal governmental agency!"

"Let's hope they can't, Jeff. But for now, we have to get this to Brookpark and into the hands of the attorneys for NASA to file an answer and oppose this litigation. Jim, I'm placing you in charge of doing that. Let Brookpark know first, then contact NASA in Washington and have them get us good counsel here, not some kid just out of law school, either. Undoubtedly the press is going to pick up on this immediately, and I suspect by tomorrow there will be television trucks and reporters clamoring at our gates demanding details. Jim, you're job includes being the publicity man, so better get a good night's sleep tonight, for I fear you are going to be busy for a few weeks."

* * *

Klaus Kravitz was enjoying his coffee after breakfast in his apartment near the University of Chicago south of downtown, and was reading The Chicago Tribune. "Hey, Johann," he shouted in German to one of the two men sharing the apartment with him temporarily. Johann Kahler came out of the bedroom to the small kitchen in response. "Look at this!" Kravitz said, pointing to an article in the newspaper. "You may not have to blow up that reactor after all. All the neighbors of the place have filed a 'cease and desist' injunction against the facility, and the court is to hold a hearing today. They may just shut the operation down."

"Somehow I doubt that," Johann replied in German. By this time Rolfe Wolfmann had joined them in the kitchen and was reading the article in the newspaper.

"I agree with Johann," he said in German. "That place is too important to them getting a man into space – maybe to the moon – to shut it down. Is there not some law in America about 'eminent domain'? NASA could just buy the neighborhood and that would be the end of it."

"Maybe the results of the court hearing will be on the television news tonight," Klaus said. "Or in tomorrow's newspaper. The court is in Cleveland, so we can get a Cleveland paper tomorrow and read about it."

"Johann," Rolfe said after a pause, "make me another cup of coffee. The translation part I'm currently working on is boring but important, and I need to get it right. I should have the translation finished by next week."

"Have you thought about how we're going to get it to Washington?" Klaus asked.

"Ja! By train. My picture will be all around the country by now, so Johann will take it on the Chicago to Washington night train, boarding at Gary in Indiana, and getting off a couple of stops before Washington. I doubt the FBI ever watches those little stations."

"But if those two FBI agents got your photo, too, Johann, you will be as vulnerable to being spotted."

"It's a risk I've got to take. I thought of going to our embassy in Canada, but that means going through U.S. Customs. Best to go directly. Rolfe, alert me a couple of days before you finish so I can arrange with the embassy to have them pick me up wherever I get off the train."

"I wish our man in the Fermi labs had something concrete to send with you, but he seems to be finding only routine physics experiments, nothing Russia does not already know."

"Any way to louse up their science?" Rolfe asked.

"We thought of that, but he says there's not really anything that would slow them down much, short of blowing the whole place up."

"Too bad they can't get a lawsuit going against that place as well," Johann laughed.

* * *

Although reporters and television crews waited impatiently outside the Federal Court House in Cleveland, the initial hearing of Jerry Summers v. NASA, as the case had come to be called, took less than fifteen minutes. The government's motion to dismiss was postponed, but the court's judge, Eric Slidell, denied the plaintiffs' injunction and set a trial date about six months in advance, guaranteeing that for at least the next six months the Plum Brook facility would continue as it had for longer than the last half-dozen years, and also guaranteeing that there would be an appeal to the Sixth U.S. Circuit Court of Appeals.

Hilda Johnson, identified only as "Doe" in the lawsuit, had never been served and other than what had appeared in the newspapers had not been affected by the lawsuit. Although she was still on maternity leave in October, Bill Hallister had called her on the first day of October to visit the reactor and confirm something they were planning. She gladly complied, as Ross had that morning off from any classes and could take care of Heidi.

In the basement of Hayes Hall Richard Fairchild was preparing a lecture on the Synoptic Gospels, including the newly discovered second Gospel of Thomas from the Nag Hammadi cave in Egypt in 1945. The first such Gospel was deemed a Gnostic document. He was comparing some of the Coptic texts with those he had seen in the Q Document in Italy several years earlier, which were still being kept secret, when Sally Merriam put a phone call through to him.

"Richie?" a familiar voice asked. Fairchild immediately recognized it as that of George McCracken, the CIA agent who had been so helpful with Hilda Johnson.

"Yes, George. What can I do for you?" Fairchild answered.

"Quit teaching and come join us!" George said, teasingly. "I know, you'd never do that, but it's a shame we lost you to the academic world. I just heard what you and your Toledo FBI buddies did last month. They have all-points bulletins out on this Johann Kahler and Rolfe Reübrich, whom we identified as Rolfe Wolfmann, former Nazi rocket scientist turned KGB. I don't think you've ever seen him, have you?"

"No, but I've seen Kahler enough that I could spot him easily."

"That's what we thought. Here's our problem. The National Security Agency has been watching for any transfer of space program data from the U.S. to Russia by encrypted code since Wolfmann left the NASA facility there in Ohio. They have seen nothing yet, and believe that whatever Wolfmann has is still in the U.S., perhaps being translated into Russian before it is sent in the diplomatic pouch. If so, Wolfmann and Kahler are hiding out somewhere. The FBI scoured their motel room in Vermilion, but came up with very little, except that Kahler had received two phone calls from Chicago. We suspect that is where they are, preparing to transfer to Washington.

"There are lots of ways they could come," McCracken continued. "Drive to Milwaukee and fly to Baltimore, fly from Chicago Midway or O'Hare via some obscure route, drive, or take the bus. But as winter is approaching in Chicago, we anticipate that they are most likely going to come by train. There are several ways they can do that. Both the Pennsylvania and the B&O have direct trains via Pittsburgh. The C&O has several via West Virginia and Charlottesville, which gives them cover off the main lines. Via Cincinnati there are several other ways. We can't watch all of these."

"So, what do you want me to do?" Fairchild asked.

"Our counter-intelligence guys think that the Chicago-Washington B&O route is the most logical for them to use, if in fact they are in Chicago. You seem to have a good knowledge of the trains there in Ohio, and lots of friends in the industry. We're going to send you a bunch of photos of these two guys, and ask that you visit the crew change center at Willard and pass the photos around among the crews that handle passenger trains, and if they spot one of these two guys to let you know, and you let me know. That way we'd know what train they are on, and board it before it gets to Washington in case they get off early."

"George, this sounds far-fetched, to be honest. It's a one-in-a-thousand chance it would work, that they would take the Washington train, or be spotted. But, if that is what you want, I'll do it. But really, why?"

"Same reason as always. It's the FBI's game to catch these guys. CIA can't operate in their bailiwick, and the FBI is of the opinion that whatever Wolfmann and Kahler have is already in Russia. We don't think so. Counter-intelligence is also FBI's job, but other than turning up those two Chicago phone calls – which they were unable to trace – they have no leads. You we can trust; them we can't rely on. J. Edgar probably told his guys it's a dead end, and if Hoover says to forget it, they will."

"Okay, George. It's a long-shot. But I'll talk to all the passenger crew guys in Willard, even the ones who get on in the middle of the night, and maybe something will happen. Now, that won't include the porters or cooks, who go the entire route, just the conductors and brakemen. But it would be better to talk to the crews in both Chicago and Pittsburgh as well, for all the Chicago to Washington trains...."

"We have, Richie, and they are already watching for the guys. But they are busier there than at the Willard location, which is why we thought of you. Isn't Willard just southeast of your college?"

"Yes, a few miles, but close. Okay, I'll do it over the next few days, starting tonight. I'll have to let Esther know."

Although he doubted that much would come from meeting with B&O passenger train conductors at the crew-change office in Willard, a town just east of Fostoria that was famous for its glassware, Fairchild dutifully drove down to Willard each evening after classes and met with the crews that were either just coming off trains or about to get on one. He left photos that McCracken had expressed to him of the two men, Kahler and Wolfmann, and asked the conductors he met with to show the photos around to other crews, so that by the third evening he was certain that all the crews traveling between Chicago and Willard, or Willard to Pittsburgh, would have seen the photos and have Fairchild's number to call if either man was spotted. Just to be certain, he also drove down to Crestline, Ohio, the crew-change point on Chicago-Pittsburgh Pennsylvania Railroad passenger trains and left photos and his business cards there as well. His cost was a tank of gas and his time, but Fairchild was as anxious to see the saboteurs caught as was the CIA.

Just after he got home on the third night he got a call from FBI Special Agent-in-Charge Aaron Greenspoon. "I hear you are doing some work for the CIA," Greenspoon began. Fairchild was uncertain if Greenspoon's knowledge of what he had been doing was good or bad for his FBI relationship. It turned out to be good. Greenspoon continued, "What McCracken wanted you to do was an excellent idea. We can watch the Chicago rail terminals, but, as you undoubtedly know, there are five stations and dozens of ways Kahler and Wolfmann could get through without being spotted by anyone. We simply can't keep a twenty-four hour watch on all five terminals, and Hoover has decided this is a low priority mission."

"Well, frankly, Aaron," Fairchild replied, "I fear it's a fool's errand. I told McCracken I doubted it would bear fruit, but, what the hell, it is worth a try, and only cost me ten gallons of gas. He specified the B&O, but I also put some of the photos and my number at the Pennsylvania crew change center in Crestline as well. The B&O was only a wild guess."

"It may not come to anything, but if the details of what Wolfmann was doing at Plum Brook are not already in Moscow, I'd be surprised," the FBI agent said. "Nevertheless, we'd love to catch the buggers! Who knows what else they may be up to, and Chicago has a lot of government labs. Let me know if you get any bites on this fishing line you've established. You've got my office and home numbers, so don't be afraid to ask for help."

"Don't worry, Aaron. I won't."

* * *

That same day Jim Roberts, Dr. Bernard Ruhl and Colonel Jeffry Josephs had been sitting in the Sandusky office of Attorney Martin Schwartz, who represented all the homeowners, farmers, and others who were suing NASA and attempting to shut down the Plum Brook facility. Each of the three were being deposed, and Palmer David, an assistant deputy federal solicitor-general for government agencies, was assisting the witnesses being deposed. As a courtesy, Dr. Ruhl had been the first to undergo grilling, but he had basically less information than the other two and could testify only to the nature of chemicals and other materials brought onto the facility periodically by rail or truck, without adding much detail about when or how much or how hazardous any of the materials might be. Neither Roberts nor Josephs were able to hear what Dr. Ruhl had said in his deposition, and when it was over Dr. Ruhl returned to the facility.

Colonel Josephs was next. As Jim had anticipated, given the Air Force Colonel's volatile temper, it was all that Palmer David could do to keep him from socking Schwartz in the nose as Schwartz asked the same questions over and over in different ways, trying to trip the officer up in his story. It was frustrating for all three involved, and Jim heard the court reporter, who was taking down the testimony, ask several times if he should include the expletives in the transcript. Schwartz was generous and said no.

After Colonel Josephs was finished the two attorneys agreed that a lunch break was in order, and Josephs was warned not to discuss his testimony with Roberts until after Roberts had been deposed. Jim had undergone depositions many times in his role as an arson investigator and arresting officer for the FDNY, and knew what to expect. The federal attorney suggested that the three of them go to a nearby restaurant, and it took Colonel Josephs a good half hour to cool down from the rant he had put up during his deposition.

"Those goddamned bastards!" Josephs exclaimed as they left the attorney's office. "Don't they know that what we're doing there at Plum Brook is key to America's survival and our best chance to beat the Russians in space? Why, they're a bunch of unpatriotic pinkos, if you ask me. And that Schwartz. What a cocky son-of-a-bitch he is. What did he take me for, a bloody idiot? I'd answer one question and he'd ask the same thing again in different words."

"That's the way it works, Jeff," Palmer David said. "The plaintiffs' time will come, and when it does Schwartz will be so busy producing the documents we've demand that he won't know what day it is."

"What sort of documents?" the Colonel asked.

"To start with, it is the plaintiff's job to prove every allegation. They allege that the blasts broke windows and cracked walls. They'll have to produce invoices for glass repairs, or testimony from a glass repair shop operator as to how much glass was replaced. They claim their walls were cracked. We'll want photos, and a seismic engineer's report that any cracks are due to blast damage, which is quite different from settlement cracks. According to our own expert, who also will testify, this whole area is karst topography, with potential sinkholes, hence there are lots of settlement cracks in houses around Plum Brook. For example, there's a park in Castalia called 'The Blue Hole.' That's a sinkhole, leading to caves underneath the ground. We will have seismic analysis of the area of the two oxygen cars' explosion to determine if any underground shock waves were produced.

"And then," David continued, "there's the alleged damage to farm animals. We'll be demanding income tax records and current income documents to see if cows gave less milk or hens laid fewer eggs after the blast than before it. When it comes to the so-called mental anguish aspect of the neighbors, we'll demand psychiatric evidence. I believe they will get the message quickly that they've taken on more than they can chew. Most of them won't be happy about producing their income tax records, because we will have those gone over by the IRS, and who knows what they'll find."

"Hell, if I'd known all that, I wouldn't have gotten so angry with Schwartz," Josephs said. "Now you got me feeling sorry for the bastards!"

"Palmer," Jim Roberts said, "I've been through dozens of depositions of this sort, usually in criminal cases, but sometimes with insurance companies as well, where they're trying to prove an arson when there was no real evidence of it. I think I'm prepared for Schwartz's interrogation, so I'm going to enjoy lunch, which I trust Uncle Sam is buying for the Colonel and me, and be fortified for this afternoon."

Martin Schwartz had not really expected as much difficulty from the Colonel. He munched on a sandwich his secretary had brought up for him, along with a tall cup of coffee, while he reviewed the courtesy copy of the Motion to Produce that Palmer David had filed in the court the day before. He was glad that he had agreed to represent the multiple plaintiffs in their lawsuit on an hourly basis, as the demanded documents and evidence would be a nightmare for his clients to produce. But perhaps he might turn up something helpful in the testimony of Roberts, the security chief. His research so far had turned up few details about him.

At one o'clock Roberts, David, the Colonel and the court reporter were again gathered in Schwartz's office, and the court reporter swore in Jim Roberts, having him state his name, address and position with NASA. Schwartz looked up from his notes and stared at Jim for a minute, then said, "Mr. Roberts – Jim – are you from around here originally?"

"Yes, I grew up on that farm on Mason Road in Milan Township, and went to Huron Canal High."

"I thought I recognized you! You married that cute little redhead, ahh, Janet, was it?"

"Jayne. Yes, but only after I'd been in the War."

"I remember! Yes, I was in the class behind yours. Oh!" he said, looking at the court reporter, "Don't take any of this down," then he continued, "But I remember a report in the paper when I was a senior that you had been a fireman on one of the ships at Pearl Harbor or something, and had saved the ship. Weren't we in Four-H together?"

"Yes, I recall now. We called you 'Marty the Dutchman' because your parents were originally from Holland and we attended parties at the Lutheran Church where your dad was the preacher. But you were in the War, too, weren't you?"

"Mostly stateside, but in Germany, too, after the war as I spoke Dutch and a bit of German, albeit very badly. Hey, let's get together sometime after this case is over, okay?"

"Sure. Now, fire away. I'm ready." Schwartz nodded to the court reporter and started asking Jim questions. It came out that he had been a lieutenant with the FDNY, had a graduate degree in chemistry, was teaching a fire science course at Fremont, and had been on the scene after the two oxygen cars were blown up.

"Now, there was a third railroad car there, is that correct?" Schwartz asked.

"Yes."

"Tell me about it."

"That's too broad of a question," Palmer David said. "Can you be more specific?"

"There was a car containing nuclear fuel rods that was overturned in the blast, is that not true?" Schwartz rephrased the question.

"Yes."

"Was that car damaged?"

"The car was blown over onto its right side, the left wheels twisted, and the lower or right half of the heavy lead lid of the container fell open by gravity," Jim replied.

"Was the car checked for radiation leakage?"

"Yes, almost immediately upon my arrival, the technician on duty – this being Christmas Day and the reactor being shut down – brought a Geiger counter, and we checked the area."

Schwartz asked for the technician's name and some other details, then inquired, "Was there radiation leakage?"

"Within eighteen to twenty inches, maybe a yard, of the open lid there was some indication of increased radiation, but in the general vicinity, the radiation level was no higher, according to that nuclear technician who was in a position to know, than that experienced flying in a commercial airliner, and far less than that of a chest X-ray."

The questioning continued for another hour, and Colonel Josephs managed to keep his cool when Schwartz tried to quiz Jim about the second explosion. The federal attorney, Palmer David, knew that it was the FBI that had actually set off that explosion, but did not want that information revealed in the deposition. Jim carefully, but truthfully, by-passed the details, and even had brought photos of the blast hole and broken track to show that the explosion had caused little damage. No reference to Wolfmann or the FBI's investigation, or Dr. Hilda Johnson's involvement came up, and Schwartz was apparently unaware of her assistance in the initial Christmas Day explosion beyond Jim's confirmation of information Schwartz already had that the Atomic Energy Commission had been in charge of righting the overturned railcar containing the nuclear fuel rods and that an outside nuclear expert had been called in to assist.

By three o'clock Colonel Josephs and Jim Roberts had departed the law office, leaving the two attorneys to discuss what would occur next. "Glad that's over," the Colonel said. "How about that turning out that you and Schwartz knew each other. I'm glad I didn't bring a gun and try to shoot the bastard!"

"I'm glad you didn't either, Jeff," Roberts replied with a chuckle as they drove back to the Plum Brook NASA facility.

* * *

It was just before five o'clock the following afternoon as Dr. Fairchild was sitting in his study reviewing some lesson plans on his farm north of Fremont when the phone rang, and he answered it. "Is this Richard Fairchild?" the voice of what sounded like an older man asked. Fairchild acknowledged it. "I'm Greg Craig, and I've only got a minute. I'm the conductor on the B&O's Capitol Limited. We pulled out of Chicago's Grand Central about an hour ago, and are at the station stop in Gary, Indiana. The guy in the photo that you were showing some of the fellows in Willard just boarded the Washington sleeper. His ticket is to Washington, but he asked me to confirm that there were stops before Washington in Maryland. He's got a room in the sleeper – there's only one from Chicago these days, plus one that comes down from Detroit. It's the car ahead of the diner lounge and the two coaches. Anyway, he's on the train, and I gotta run, as the engineer just blasted the horn." The man hung up, and Fairchild looked at the clock. He didn't know the schedule, but figured that the train would get to Willard in about three to four hours.

He picked up the phone again and first dialed the number for the Toledo FBI office, but it was the Detroit field office that answered, advising that both Greenspoon and Leonard were away on a case, but they promised to notify the Pittsburgh office and see if they could get an agent aboard the train when it stopped there. Fairchild then called a Washington number, and George McCracken answered. "George," Fairchild said, "I'm amazed, but it worked. One of the two guys, I'm not sure which, is on the B&O train to Washington. He boarded at Gary, Indiana, and the conductor just called me, but had to hurry back to the train. He has a room in the Pullman car. I notified the FBI and they may have an agent board at Pittsburgh."

"Hell, I never thought it would work, either," McCracken said. "We'll stake out the Washington Union Station and watch for him."

"The conductor said he had inquired about other stops in Maryland, so he may get off before he gets to Washington, just as he boarded after the train left Chicago. I've got time to drive down to Willard, and I'll get a coach ticket for Washington and if I spot him getting off before Washington, I'll do what I can to delay him, if the FBI doesn't get someone aboard in Pittsburgh."

"I think that train stops in Silver Springs. Maybe I'll get over there in the morning before it arrives and see who gets off, and if one of our guys doesn't, I'll get on and ride into town."

"Good idea. Better go armed. Either of those two characters could be dangerous."

As soon as Fairchild hung up he called to Esther that he had to go out, and that he'd not be back until the next day. She knew about the photos he had distributed at Willard, but was upset that he was going to drive down there and take a train to Washington. "Call Sally in the morning, and have her have Bob cover my Introduction to the New Testament class. Tell her my notes for the class are on my desk there at the office," he said as he changed his clothes and got ready to depart.

Fairchild checked his wallet for sufficient cash for the ticket and whatever else he would need, and headed outside to his car as Esther locked the door behind him. It was a little over an hour's drive to Willard, but at this hour of the night there was little traffic, and he arrived before nine o'clock, more than an hour ahead of the train. The ticket office was closed, but the conductor who would be boarding at Willard to Pittsburgh said he'd get Fairchild a ticket when he boarded. The conductor, Gil Walters, recognized Fairchild from when he had been distributing the photos and inquired if something had occurred.

"Yes," Fairchild said, "Greg Craig called me from Gary and said one of the two men in the photos had boarded there with a ticket for Washington and had a room in the sleeper. The FBI may board in Pittsburgh and someone is going to board in Silver Springs and ride into Washington Union Station and try to get the guy, but I suspect whichever of the two it is may get off before that. Oh, I need to make a phone call to the FBI. Is there a pay phone near here?"

"Use that one on the desk over there, if it's to a government agency." Fairchild thanked Walters and dialed the number for Aaron Greenspoon again, waking him up as it was late and advising him of what was happening and that the Detroit office was going to try to get an agent aboard in Pittsburgh, if possible.

"Boy, it was a long shot, but maybe we'll catch the guy. I'll contact Pittsburgh and Washington and pass along the word, and tell them that your CIA friend may be there to assist."

In about forty minutes, after the passage of a westbound freight train that also exchanged engine and caboose crews at Willard and a through-southwest-bound Nickel Plate freight, now a part of Norfolk and Western, that did not stop as it crossed the B&O tracks, Fairchild saw the light of an approaching train.

Conductor Gil Walters was standing next to Fairchild. "I'll introduce you to Greg as he gets off. Maybe he can tell you more about which man boarded the train," he said. As the train blasted its horn for a crossing and slowly glided past the depot, stopping near where the freight agent was waiting with a cart for any off-loaded mail sacks or other freight from the baggage cars behind the diesel engines, the coach stopped where Fairchild and Walters were standing, and the conductor, brakeman and flagman prepared to climb off.

"Greg," Walters said to the conductor as he stepped off the stool and handed a packet of papers to Walters, "this is Mr. Fairchild, the guy you called from Gary. Anything else you can tell him about the guy he's looking for?"

"Oh," Craig replied. "I didn't expect you to be here. Yeah, the guy got on at Gary, and had a couple of cases with him. Nothing suspicious-looking about him, but he had a reservation for a bedroom in the Pullman, and the porter took him there with his luggage."

"What did he look like?" Fairchild asked.

"Oh, I'd say he was in his mid-thirties, blond, well dressed. Had an accent, maybe German?"

"Did he have a name on the reservation?"

"Yeah, Gil, it's in those papers. Bedroom B." Walters looked through the packet that Craig had given him, and found the sleeper reservation. The name was Joseph Braun. "Is that the guy you want?" Craig asked.

"His name is probably Johann Kahler, but I won't know until I see him. But Mr. Craig, you have done a great service to the nation tonight. Thank you."

Fairchild boarded along with the new crew and two other coach passengers who already had tickets. Walters sold Fairchild a round-trip ticket to Washington, and found him a seat in the darkened coach, which was only about half full. The Detroit section of the train, a coach and one sleeping car, were being hooked to the rear of the train. Cars from Cleveland used to be added at Akron, the next stop, but the Cleveland cars had been discontinued as most passenger train service was just a remnant of what it had been ten years earlier.

Fairchild managed to go to sleep, sleeping through the stop at Akron, but shook himself awake as the conductor called out the stop at Pittsburgh. No one who appeared to be an FBI agent boarded. Fairchild again slumbered until the new conductor called out the stop at Cumberland, from which point the train would basically follow the Potomac River into Washington. As they left Cumberland Fairchild, who had no luggage, moved forward one car into the diner-lounge. It was too early for breakfast, but the car was open and lighted. About forty minutes later the dining crew arrived from the crew quarters and started to prepare the diner half of the car for breakfast. A few minutes later some of the sleeping car passengers entered the diner from the front of the car, and were seated at tables and given a menu and pad on which to write their order. To Fairchild's surprise, about ten minutes later Johann Kahler also entered the diner and was given a seat at a table just in front of the small kitchen. Fairchild waited until he had filled out the order pad, then got up from the lounge seat and moved into the dining section of the car, indicating with his hand to the waiter that he would sit with Kahler.

"Why, goodness!" Fairchild said in a surprised voice. "Johann! What a surprise seeing you again. I was in Kent Village during the grape harvest and didn't see you there later. Did Darlene find you?"

"Oh," Kahler said, almost as a groan. "No, she never showed up. I left mid-afternoon and went back to Port Clinton. Where are you headed?"

"Just a meeting. We college professors have to attend far too many meetings these days. How about yourself? Going all the way to Washington?"

"Oh Ja. I, too, have meetings." At this point the waiter arrived with a menu and Fairchild filled out the pad requesting oatmeal and coffee. He knew the oatmeal would be from a package and totally tasteless, but the waiter had also brought Kahler's breakfast, bacon, eggs, toast and coffee, which would take him a while to eat. Kahler drank his coffee and the waiter refilled his cup. By this time one or two others had come into the diner, either from the coaches or the Detroit sleeper, but fortunately they were seated at other tables, and the two remaining seats with Fairchild and Kahler remained empty.

"Did you enjoy the grape festival?" Fairchild asked.

"It reminded me of my youth in Germany, but would have been better if Miss Smathers had shown up."

"Gosh," Fairchild replied. "She must have really been sick, as I know how much the students enjoy that festival."

"Your university is interesting, Professor," Kahler said. You have a big boat and a hotel and a winery as well as science courses. Not many universities have a cabin boat like the one there at Port Clinton. Was it given to the school?"

"Sort of, Johann. It had belonged to a Texas oilman who had planned to assassinate the civil rights leader, Thomas Jefferson Singletary, at a symposium at Fremont College. We're not a university yet, but hope to be soon. Anyway, the courts awarded his big cruiser to the college, and we established a marine navigation class and use it to ferry guests out to the hotel on West Bass Island and, of course, for the grape harvest festival."

"The hotel – it was also donated?"

"It was owned by an international corporation and the college arranged to purchase it. It's a long story. You wouldn't happen to have heard of a Frederick Kolb of Weisbruden, would you?"

"Kolb? No, I do not know that name."

When Kahler finished his breakfast and consulted his watch, he paid the waiter for his breakfast and excused himself, returning to his sleeping car. When the waiter came to collect Fairchild's bill, Fairchild asked, "Are there any further stops between here and Silver Springs?"

"Yes," the waiter answered. "But they are only for passengers to leave the train – no new passengers to board. Usually we stop at Harpers Ferry, and tonight will make a stop at Brunswick, Maryland, to unload any upfront freight. A few passengers disembark there, but that is also a commuter train stop, so no new passengers ever board there."

"Thanks," Fairchild said as he replaced his wallet in his left pocket and arose to return to the coach. He had been on this train before, and as it was now daylight he recognized various locations along the line. The train whistle sounded, but the train slowed as it passed through a short tunnel and rattled over a bridge for a scheduled stop at Harpers Ferry.

From his seat in the coach Fairchild could observe the alcove between the coach and the diner-lounge car. After about twenty minutes, with the train running quickly along the valley, he saw the porter in a white jacket bringing some luggage to the vestibule, a usual procedure if someone was going to be getting off the train. He quickly jumped up and got to the porter as he was entering the diner-lounge car.

"Excuse me," Fairchild said, touching the shoulder of the black porter, "but is it the man in Bedroom B, Mr. Braun, who is going to get off at the next stop."

"Yes, Sir," the ported answered, rather surprised at the question. "He's booked to Washington, but wanted to get off at Brunswick. That's not a usual stop unless we have freight for there."

"Thank you," Fairchild said, and the porter went on toward the sleeping car. Fairchild returned to the coach and hunted up the conductor, who was sorting papers in the next coach.

"Excuse me," Fairchild again said, "but I understand that the train will make an unscheduled stop at Brunswick. Is that true?"

"Well, yes, we have some express freight for there, and one of the passengers decided he wanted to get off there. Why?"

"That passenger – I know him and had breakfast with him, so I know who he is – is a KGB spy wanted by the FBI. They're waiting to arrest him when the train gets to Washington; only he won't be on it by then if he gets off here. We need to delay him somehow. Do you have a radio?"

"Yes."

"Can you contact the station agent at Brunswick and have them get the police to the station as quickly as possible. I'll try to delay this man if I can, but I suspect that a car from the Russian embassy will be waiting for him, and once in that he will have diplomatic immunity."

"Are you puttin' me on, mister?" the conductor asked, looking doubtful.

"I certainly am not," Fairchild replied, opening his wallet and handing the conductor one of his Fremont College cards with his identity on it and also Aaron Greenspoon's FBI card. "That man is not Joe Braun, as your list shows, but Johann Kahler, wanted by the FBI for espionage, sabotage, attempted murder and probably a dozen other charges. Please, contact the station master if you can. I'll get off with Kahler and try to hold him until the police arrive. I don't think he suspects that I know who he is, but if you want clearance, the stationmaster can contact Special Agent-in-Charge Aaron Greenspoon of the FBI in Toledo at the number on this card that I'll write on the back of my card. But please hurry."

"We're running a bit ahead of schedule, so it will be only a few minutes before we get to Brunswick. Okay, I'll do it, Fairchild – if that's who you are – but if this is some stunt, you're violating federal law."

"I assure you, every word is true." The conductor then picked up his hand-held radio and called for the stationmaster at Brunswick, telling him what Fairchild had said about there being a spy on the train and the FBI awaiting him in Washington. There were some squawking sounds, and then a voice, saying "Roger," and that the Frederick County Sheriff would be notified. Satisfied, Fairchild returned to his seat in the first coach and sat watching the vestibule door, which operated pneumatically.

In about ten minutes Fairchild saw Kahler enter the vestibule between the two railcars from the diner-lounge, and the conductor passed through the coach and also entered the vestibule, opening the Dutch-door top half of the outside left-side door and lifting the floor panel, revealing the two steps to the exit. The train had apparently switched to the left track so that it would be next to the station platform.

As the train began to slow and the locomotive horn could be heard through the open door Fairchild arose and walked toward the vestibule. The train glided to a stop at the station platform, which was at ground level, and the conductor opened the bottom half of the door and grabbed his step box to set on the ground for the passenger getting off. The porter was behind Kahler and said, "You get off, sir, and I'll hand you your luggage. And thank you for traveling with the B&O." Kahler said nothing, but looked angry when he saw Fairchild also in the vestibule.

The conductor got off first, and then Kahler. Fairchild stepped in front of the porter and got off next, before the porter could hand the first suitcase down to Kahler. "Here, let me give you a hand with that, Johann," Fairchild said, taking the suitcase from the porter as Kahler reached up for it. The porter handed Kahler the second case, by which time Fairchild had moved away from the doorway, and was in the middle of the platform.

"Here, give me that, Fairchild!" Kahler demanded, but Fairchild held on to the case.

"What's in here?" Fairchild asked. "The details of what Wolfmann stole at Plum Brook?" Kahler looked shocked at the question, and grabbed for the case Fairchild was holding. The conductor stood watching, fascinated.

"Who the hell do you think you are?" Kahler demanded. "I don't know any Wolfmann."

"No? Even after spending weeks with him in that Vermilion motel, you don't know Rolfe Wolfmann? And I suppose you know nothing about the explosion of Dr. Hilda Johnson's car, either, do you? The game is up, Kahler."

Kahler made a lunge for the suitcase in Fairchild's hand, but Fairchild brought it up quickly, hitting Kahler right below his chin, knocking him backwards. Kahler regained his equilibrium and made another lunge toward Fairchild as two men jumped from a black Lincoln sedan and ran toward where Kahler and Fairchild were fighting. At the same time another car pulled into the station lot with red flashers swirling around and reflecting off the side of the train. People in the coach were looking out the window at the scene as the two men, dressed in dark clothes, ran toward Kahler and Fairchild, and two deputy sheriffs also ran toward the scene.

"Vitch vun ov you ess Kahler?" one of the two men from the Lincoln demanded in a gruff voice.

"Ich bin!" both Fairchild and Kahler responded, confusing the man. Fairchild continued to swing the suitcase at Kahler, and Kahler continued to grab for it as the two deputies ran up.

"What's going on here?" the taller deputy with sergeants' stripes demanded.

"Watch out for these two Russian agents," Fairchild shouted at the second deputy. "This man who is trying to get his suitcase from me is wanted by the FBI for espionage. NASA documents are probably in his case." The first deputy took the suitcase from Fairchild and held it while the other deputy drew his revolver and stepped back. The conductor came over and whispered in the first deputy's ear, then that deputy took the second suitcase from Kahler as the man who had been driving the black Lincoln backed away from the platform, preparing to run back to that car. The second deputy saw him, and motioned with his revolver to get back with the others. He apparently did not speak much English, and said nothing.

By this time the sergeant was on his radio calling for back-up, and the conductor was back on the train, with the Capitol Limited pulling out of the station. A small crowd had gathered on the platform to see what was happening. In about five minutes two more Frederick County Sheriff cars had arrived, lights flashing and sirens blowing, along with two Brunswick Police cruisers. One of the cars contained a city police lieutenant, who asked what was happening. The sergeant from the sheriff's department said, pointing at Fairchild, "This man says that blonde man is a KGB spy wanted by the FBI, and that there may be secret documents in the suitcases. The conductor says it was this man who instructed the station master to call for police."

"Well, let's take 'em all down to the County Building until we figure out who is who," the lieutenant said. "If this guy's the spy, who are these other two birds?"

"I expect they are from the Russian Embassy," Fairchild answered, "and they'll be hollering about diplomatic immunity pretty quickly. Did the station agent give you the FBI agent's name and number, sergeant?"

"Yeah. Someone was calling him when we left to get here," he answered, then explained to the city police lieutenant what the conductor had told the station master. The lieutenant decided that if federal crimes were involved that the Sheriff's deputies should be in charge, taking Kahler and the two Russians to the Sheriff's Office in Frederick, the county seat, and he would follow in the city police car with Fairchild. When Kahler protested being taken anywhere the sergeant read him his rights and put him in handcuffs, shoving him into the back of his sheriffs' car, while the two Russians were escorted to the other as one of the city officers retrieved the keys from the parked black Lincoln.

Twenty minutes later they were all at the Frederick County Building, and the desk sergeant advised that two FBI agents were on their way from Washington. Richard Fairchild asked the sergeant to call the Silver Springs B&O station and ask for George McCracken, and tell him that Dr. Fairchild and Johann Kahler were in Frederick at the County Sheriff's Office.

Neither Kahler nor the two Russians would say anything, either to the sheriffs or to each other, beyond a brief discussion between the two Russians in Russian that none of the others understood. They were all moved into a large interrogation room where they could all sit around a table, with the city policeman and the two deputy sheriffs standing guard, Kahler still in handcuffs. It was about twenty minutes before George McCracken arrived, and the two FBI agents from Washington, both special agents in counter-intelligence, arrived about ten minutes later. They knew McCracken and had worked with him previously, and George allowed them to take the lead. The two special agents, Bill Blatt and Harry Cook, had a briefing report from Aaron Greenspoon and knew what the situation was, but were careful not to discuss it in front of Kahler or the two Russians.

"We can't open the two cases without a warrant," Blatt said, "and we're trying to get one this morning. But we can interview Kahler. Dr. Fairchild, you seem pretty familiar with this situation – I'm not clear on how that came about – but if you wish to sit in on our interrogation of Kahler, you are welcome."

"Thanks," Fairchild replied. "But I've got to get back to Ohio today; I've got classes to teach tomorrow. George can fill you in on how I'm involved, if, in fact, I am involved besides being a nosy SOB."

Kahler was escorted to a smaller room, and Special Agent Cook began by asking Kahler his name. Kahler refused to respond. Cook then asked

Kahler why he had gotten off the train in Brunswick if he had a ticket to Washington. Again, Kahler said nothing, nor did he demand an attorney.

In the next room Special Agent Blatt was attempting to get information from the two Russians. They were each carrying diplomatic passports, but neither would say anything. The passports showed that the one who spoke practically no English was Vlad Koshinskovitch. The other was Alexis Brodasky. Blatt advised Cook of the two names, and Richard Fairchild reacted by repeating the name, "Brodasky? That's interesting. I wonder if he has relatives in the scrap metal business in Toledo, Ohio."

"Why?" Blatt asked.

"Because Greenspoon and Special Agent Leonard arrested two guys named Brodasky for blowing up two railcars full of oxygen at the NASA Plum Brook facility Christmas Day and shooting a young Air Force corporal at the gate. They almost caused a nuclear incident. They claimed they just did it in an attempt to get a contract to collect the scrap metal, but that sounded fishy to me. When you talk with Aaron Greenspoon and get someone who speaks Russian to press these two characters, you might find they have more to do with this attempted sabotage than just collecting scrap metal and giving Kahler a ride to the Embassy."

By two that afternoon the federal warrant had been signed by a judge in Washington, allowing the FBI to open the two suitcases. The first contained only Kahler's personal items, most of which were new as he had abandoned most of his things when he and Wolfmann fled to Chicago. The other was full of drawings, diagrams, photos and detailed logs in Russian, but the papers obviously showed rocket engine designs. The reports were signed by Wolfmann.

The two Russians had been allowed to call their Embassy, and it had dispatched an attorney to try to get them released. As they were probably going to be charged with aiding and abetting espionage, a hearing would have to be held, and they were to remain in federal custody until that time.

Around noon Fairchild had asked George McCracken to drive him back to the B&O station so he could get back to Willard. "Richard," McCracken said on the short drive, "if Kahler had gotten those documents to the Embassy, it could have greatly aided Russia's space program. What you did this morning is amazing, but then I always said you were a born intelligence agent. Are you sure you won't give up teaching and come join the CIA?"

"No way, George. When those two FBI agents asked how you knew me and you said you'd been my commanding officer in an Army Intelligence Unit operating behind Nazi lines, but were really the company's chaplain and now a college chaplain and professor of religion, oh, and a cattle farmer, I thought they'd flip. But I'll probably flip when I have to show up for the depositions and trials."

"Listen, you need to send us a bill for your services...."

"No, any good citizen would do the same...."

"Nonsense. Let us at least reimburse you the train ticket and gasoline."

"Well, okay on that, George, but do keep me posted. I've got personal skin in this game now, having to be pleasant to that damned Kahler after he shot up my boat and tried to kill both Hilda and his own father."

Chapter 14
October 20, 1969

Jim Roberts heard from Aaron Greenspoon later that day that one of the KGB agents, Johann Kahler, had been caught along with two employees from the Russian Embassy in Washington, with Richard Fairchild being the detective who rounded them up. Jim was amazed, but considering what he'd heard about and from Fairchild, he decided he shouldn't be too surprised. What did surprise him was Fairchild's suggestion to the FBI that the Brodasky brothers might be more than just scrap metal dealers – and the FBI was checking on their background, for they, too, might be part of the KGB operation at Plum Brook. Agent Greenspoon asked Jim to research whether it was true that the Plum Brook facility had used the services of the Brodasky Brothers in the past, as they had claimed. Jim could find no record of it.

"So they planned to cool their heels in prison for a few years on little more than a glorified vandalism charge, then walk out and go back to Russia?" Jim asked.

"If they're part of Russia's spy agency, they'll be re-tried for espionage and sabotage and could be handed a death sentence. But we won't know until our investigation is finished," Greenspoon replied.

Later that day Jim called Dr. Fairchild's office, but he was in a class. Sally Merriam agreed to have Fairchild call him back. So far word of what he had done in Maryland had not reached Fremont, and Jim felt it was not his place to blab the news.

About two that afternoon Fairchild returned Jim's call. "Busy night, I hear you had!" Jim said.

"How did you hear?"

"Aaron Greenspoon called. Told me what he'd heard from the agents in Maryland, and also mentioned that they were doing background checks on the Brodasky boys. Gad! This place sure did need security! Hopefully we'll get some action now from Washington.

"But Richie, that's not why I called. Since we got here from New York we've really not had time to do much with the farm. I don't want any activities that require daily work, like dairy cows or chickens, but you seem to do well with beef cattle, and planting the acreage in corn or beans would only involve minimal activity and the purchase of some new equipment, tractors and combines, a truck, things like that."

"Or you could arrange to have someone plant and harvest the land for you," Fairchild said. "That's what Esther and I did, and Jack also watches out for the cattle when we are away, although when they're in the pastures in summer, they really don't need much looking after."

"That's a thought. What I wonder is whether you and Esther might join us Friday night for dinner so we can talk about possibilities. Besides, I want to hear more about your adventure this week and some of your other crime-solving tales."

"I'll ask Esther, but as far as I know, we don't have any other plans. And I want to hear about some of your arson cases, too. I'll check with Esther and let you know. Thanks for the invitation."

Action from Washington did begin later that day for Jim Roberts when he got a call from the Brookpark NASA supply officer that a brand new squad car, labeled NASA Law Enforcement had just been delivered and had Jim's name on it. It was a special blessing for Jayne, as she had no car when Jim's was not available.

He and Jayne drove down to Brookpark that evening and picked it up, with Jayne driving the Ford back home and Jim following in the black car bristling with antennae and flashers. It, too, was a Ford, top of the line, much like the FDNY chiefs drove, and Jim knew he'd have to get a big bottle of car wax to keep it shiny as he had no garage at home or at the facility. Colonel Joseph gave him a big smile that afternoon when Jim told him about the car, and then told Josephs about the arrest in Maryland and the possibility of the involvement of the Brodasky brothers as KGB spies.

"Damn!" Josephs exclaimed. "I gotta meet this professor friend of yours."

"Well, we've invited the Fairchilds for dinner Friday evening. Why don't you and your wife join us?"

"Gosh! Oh, but Friday night is her bridge night. But I'd love to come. I'll tell her tonight as she always fixes something for me when she goes out with her friends on Fridays."

Jayne was delighted that Colonel Josephs would be joining them as well, and had prepared a special recipe of walleye with various vegetables and spices that she had found in an Ohio cookbook. Colonel Josephs arrived about five fifteen and the Fairchilds about five thirty. Esther had brought a cake for dessert and Josephs an expensive bottle of single malt Scotch. Jim, Jeffry and Richie sat in the living room enjoying the Scotch while discussing various types of beef cattle that Jim might consider raising, how to acquire young steers and breeding cattle in order to keep the herd growing, and how to care for them in winter. There was a barn on the farm that had not been used in many years, and Fairchild had some recommendations as to what the various parts of the barn, which was laid out as a dairy, could be used for various purposes needed for raising beef cattle, including what food they would need in the winter.

At supper Richie Fairchild said, "Jim, you said something about a case you were working on when you retired involving an explosion and murder. Can you tell us more about it?"

Jim was usually not shy about telling of his cases, but asked if he should with Esther and Jayne there, as it had some gruesome details. The two women insisted that they wanted to hear the story, too, so Jim related his Lester Minsk and the Ponzi scheme story, which was exciting enough without any embellishments. He mentioned that the only connection to Minsk seemed to be in Detroit, with an attorney and someone else named Minsk there, but that the NYPD had been unable to make any headway in the investigation since Minsk had fled the country, and was apparently not in Venezuela. "Have you ever heard of the Bank of Sark?" Jim asked.

"Sark?" Richie answered. "I think it is a tiny island near Jersey in the English Channel, but I don't know anything about their bank. Of course, so many of those off-shore islands are havens for cash raised by criminals, so that is probably one of those types of places. Why?"

"Don't get Richie too curious about it," Esther laughed, "or he'll be finding some reason to fly off to England to find it. Like the time we spend half our time in Bermuda in the vaults of the Bank of Hamilton, on nothing more than a vague reference to such a bank, not knowing if it was Hamilton, Ontario or Hamilton, Ohio."

"What was in the Bermuda bank vault?" Jayne asked.

"The diary of a Confederate spy who had been rescuing Confederate officers from Johnson Island in Sandusky Bay, and the papers regarding a shipment of gold coins from Mexico and the transfer of two French vessels to the Confederacy."

"Good Heavens!" Jayne exclaimed. "What did you do with them?"

"Published the diary, and located the coins…."

"I remember that!" Jim interrupted. "Some kid from Boston had dug them out of a ship wreck off the Florida Coast or something, and didn't know what he had."

"He knew he had gold coins, but he didn't know how to get rid of them as it was illegal for him to have them. I ended up in a squabble in a boat in Sandusky Harbor with a guy who had been committing burglaries in Cleveland and …."

"And almost got yourself killed!" Esther exclaimed. "Richard Fairchild, you'll be the death of both of us yet! But it turned out okay. The boat belonged to the Atwaters, who were having the kid from Boston live at their farm on the Marblehead Peninsula that the Confederate spy – an ancestor of Peggy's – used as a base of operation. The Confederate spy also had a big house in Sandusky that the Atwaters live in now."

"It's handy, since both of them work at the hospital," Jayne continued. "Peggy invited us over sometime when she brought me home on Christmas Day when Jim and Dexter were both called in due to that shooting, and

I've never had a chance to follow up. She's not in the choir, so I don't see her often."

"We need to finish that Christmas Dinner sometime soon," Richie Fairchild said. "With both you, Jim, and Dexter getting called away, the party fell apart. Next time, Jeffry, you and your wife, Mary, will have to join us. It's an annual tradition."

"What fell apart was that beautiful crown rib roast you put on our plates. That was absolutely delicious."

"You'll soon be having your own roasts and steaks, Jim, if you raise beef cattle."

* * *

The FBI Chicago field office had no leads at all on the Russians or Rolfe Wolfmann. They had pressed Johann Kahler for information on the Chicago connection, but he had stone-walled every attempt to give up information on the operation. The FBI Lab had gone over everything in Kahler's luggage and the documents looking for any clue that might lead to the rest of the KGB operations, but with no positive outcome. They had also had the documents in Russian translated back into English and certified the translation, which initially appeared to have been made in German, not English.

The FBI also began looking into Gearmone Engineering, for whom Wolfmann had worked, suspecting that their screening of employees assigned to U.S. operations had not been very thorough, but no further indication of espionage through the French firm was found. The attorneys for NASA did file a lawsuit against Gearmone for some of the costs that the three incidents had cost the government, and Gearmone paid the demanded sum rather than fight the lawsuit and perhaps jeopardize their contract with NASA.

The two Russians from the Embassy had denied any connection to Kahler and had told the FBI, via the attorney sent by the Russian Embassy that they had simply been stopped at the Brunswick train station to have a cup of coffee and saw two men fighting and ran to help stop the fight. The Embassy denied all knowledge of Kahler and the documents, and Kahler was saying nothing.

Klaus Kravitz and Rolfe Wolfmann had moved to a new location near Northwestern University in Evanston, not knowing whether Kahler might have revealed the old Chicago location and activities in the interrogations they anticipated he was undergoing. They had heard from the KGB contacts in Washington that Kahler had been arrested with the Russian translations of the NASA rocket plans. Wolfmann had already started on a new translation from his notes.

Chapter 15

Two mornings later the phone rang and Kravitz, a short, bald-headed man with black-rimmed glasses, picked up the phone. The voice on the other end asked, "Volk?"

"Nyet," Kravitz answered, continuing in Russian, "He is not here."

"Go to 'C,'" the voice said in Russian. It was the KGB operation Control, a voice Kravitz knew well. "Twelve minutes."

"C" was a phone booth in a Walgreen's Drug Store a block from the new location that Kravitz and Wolfmann had rented. The KGB team had scouted out four public telephone booths where they could be reasonably certain that the phone had not been tapped by the FBI as they were unsure whether Kahler might have revealed any information about them, and were exercising extreme caution. Kravitz exited the building by the rear door in case the apartment house was being watched, and walked quickly to the drug store.

A minute after he arrived at the booth just inside the store the phone rang and he picked it up. The conversation, in Russian, was short and to the point. "Klaus, Volk must re-translate his notes again."

"He knows," Kravitz replied. "He has already started."

"Next time he will deliver the document himself. No public transportation. Private car. He has an American driver's license, but we are sending him new identity. It will be delivered next week. You will be told where to pick it up, and make damned sure you are not observed. Instructions as to his contact in Washington will follow. Then you will close down your operation. Your next job will be to complete what you and Kahler were unable to do with von Werdau's car. This time steal a van and load it with nitrate fertilizer – you know the formula – and blow up that reactor, even if you have to blow yourself up with it. Do you understand?"

"Da!" Kravitz understood what Control meant alright. The phone went dead and, using back streets, Kravitz returned to the apartment, where Rolfe Wolfmann had returned and was working on his translation. "New instructions," he told the Wolf in German. "You will receive new identity papers next week and drive the report to Washington yourself. You'll be instructed where to meet your contact before you leave. I'm to finish the job at Plum Brook."

"How?" Wolfmann asked, still in German. "That professor won't fall for the emergency rush again. She's not stupid."

"No, and neither am I. Control said to use nitrate fertilizer and succeed 'even if I have to blow myself up with it.' I'll figure a way. But when you finish what you are working on, draw me a diagram of where things are at that Plum Brook facility, especially the reactor."

"Jawohl, Klaus, I will show you how to get in."

* * *

While the National Security Agency had been unsuccessful in tapping into any of the KGB's secure phone lines, they had been able to identify several of the agents by voice via long distance listening devices. The quality of the recordings was poor, but sufficient for the CIA's Russia Desk to identify several individual agents and decipher the gist of what they were doing. Most of these agents simply referred to themselves as "Control," thus it was difficult to isolate any one operation. They were, however, able to determine where calls from the Embassy were directed. When they detected calls to three different Chicago numbers, one near the University of Chicago on the south side and two in Evanston on the north side, they referred the information to the Chicago FBI Field Office try to locate the phones. One was found to be a phone booth in a Walgreens drug store. The other two were to apartments, but upon investigating, both had been abandoned, and the landlords were looking for the tenants for back rent. The FBI scoured both apartments for any information they could find. The telephones and other items had been wiped to destroy any lingering fingerprints, however, and nothing of value was found.

About two days later the NSA tracked a fourth call to Chicago, again to a phone booth. There was nothing there by the time the FBI arrived, and again all fingerprints had been wiped away. The booth was in an area of Chicago with a number of cheap hotels, but using the FBI photos of the man they believed to be Rolfe Wolfmann taken at Port Clinton in late August, a canvass of the hotels turned up very little. One desk clerk said he thought he recognized the man, but that man and another who had also checked in at the same time had checked out that morning. The names on the registration were Philip West and Gerald Tradeau.

Late that evening NSA detected a conversation in the Embassy between a Control and someone on a phone traced to a gas station phone booth in Northern Indiana. The NSA Russian translator sent what he was able to decipher from the recording to FBI Headquarters: "Volk, the meet will be at Great Falls Park, Virginia side. Noon. The Overlook. Control will be wearing a red scarf. Take your time, don't speed."

The FBI now had the place and time, but not the date. However, they knew that the Russian word for wolf, volk, was the codename for Rolfe Wolfmann. If he was in Northern Indiana he was probably using the Turnpike System, from which he would have to divert somewhere in

Pennsylvania to get onto the Virginia side of the Potomac. As a snow storm was blowing east from Chicago it was likely that The Wolf would stop somewhere for the night, and that driving would be slow on the snowy highways. It could be as early as the next day if he drove all night, although that was doubtful, or any day for the next three. A team was prepared to stake out the Park and make an arrest, anticipating that The Wolf would have retranslated his notes and would have a duplicate of what Johann Kahler was taking to Washington.

At the same time as the conversation between Control and Wolfmann was taking place Klaus Kravitz was in Joliet, Illinois, stealing a mid-sized Dodge paneled van that had no windows beyond those in the front and passenger seats, including no windows in the back. Klaus had opened the van at the used car lot after picking the lock on the car dealer's door and finding the correct set of keys, using a flashlight. As it was a Friday night, and an early snow storm hit Northern Illinois that evening, it was four days before the used car lot realized that one of their vehicles had been stolen. Although it had no tag, Kravitz remedied that by stealing one from an old junker parked on a back street in South Chicago. He then headed east on U.S. 6.

Rolfe Wolfmann did stop for the night, somewhere around Goshen, Indiana. He had a late supper, and watched television until he fell asleep. About six the next morning when he awoke there was about two inches of snow on the ground and his rental car. He returned to the nearby restaurant for breakfast, and then got back on the Indiana Turnpike and headed east. The snowfall had melted by the time he reached Ohio, but by the time he reached the Pennsylvania state line it had again started to snow, and traffic on the four-line toll road through the Allegheny Mountains was slippery and slow. It was late evening when Wolfmann finally exited the Turnpike at Harrisburg and found a motel for the night. Again he found a restaurant for a late night dinner, and went to bed, exhausted from the difficult drive.

Arising at five the next morning, Wolfmann packed his two cases, one with his clothes and the other with the newly translated NASA rocket research data, and put them in the trunk of the car while he had breakfast and coffee at a small all-night diner. The snow had not stuck to the roads, and Wolfmann headed southeast, entering Maryland and then following the Potomac River until crossing into Virginia. It was about ten-thirty. He checked the map he had purchased, and found it was about twenty miles to the park where he was to make contact with Control.

Three Special Agents had set up a watch about eight that morning, making sure that no one else was watching the Falls Overlooks where the meeting was to occur. Two or three other cars arrived on this cold, rather dreary Sunday morning, but did not stay long. They waited patiently. About eleven-thirty a black Mercedes pulled into the parking lot, just beyond the toll booth, and the driver turned off the motor and remained in the vehicle. From his viewpoint one FBI agent could see that the driver was wearing an overcoat and a red scarf. Twenty-five minutes later another car, a blue Chevrolet, also pulled into the parking area and parked. The man in the blue car sat for a few minutes, then got out, went to the trunk of the car and removed a leather case. He then walked toward the first of the three overlooks. When he arrived at it the man in the Mercedes also got out of his car, and the agent noted that there was a second man also in the car, who remained there while the man with the red scarf walked toward the overlook.

One of the FBI agents was at the second overlook. His radio signaled that the meeting had started. The third agent was hidden in some trees near the first overlook, and was closest to the fenced in area above the rocky falls. Both agents started toward the first overlook, trying to look casual, despite their being dressed in suits and overcoats. The third agent warned over their radios that there was another man in the Mercedes, but that he had not left the car. As the third agent left his hiding place and moved toward the overlook, and the other two agents closed in on the two KGB agents, the man in the Mercedes blew the horn three times. However, Wolfmann had already handed the leather case to the KGB Control agent in the red scarf.

As the three FBI agents announced their arrest, with guns drawn, the third man started the Mercedes and drove away. The first agent had already gotten the license number, and two FBI cars were awaiting outside the park entrance to stop any escapes, alerted by radio that the Mercedes was leaving.

Neither Wolfmann nor the Control agent gave any resistance to their arrest, although they verbally argued with the FBI agents. "What is this about?" Wolfmann demanded.

"And your name is…?" the lead FBI agent asked.

"You have no right to ask me!" Wolfmann almost shouted, although the Control agent sort of shook his head, indicating that The Wolf should say nothing.

"It wouldn't happen to be Rolfe Wolfmann, of Gearmone Engineering of Paris, would it?" the second FBI agent said, comparing a photo in his pocket to the taller of the two men. "Do you have your passport with you?"

"It is in my car, in my luggage."

"Let's go see it," said the agent, slipping handcuffs on Wolfmann, who did not resist. "And your name?" the agent asked the Control, who was rather short with a round red face.

"Nyet!" the Control said, muttering something in Russian.

"No English?" the agent asked.

"Nyet! No Anglush. I diplo immune," he said, indicating something in his coat pocket as the handcuffs were placed on his wrists. The agent reached into the pocket and extracted a red U.S.S.R. diplomatic passport. It showed the man's name as Vladimir Kolinsky."

"Well, let's go look at Mr. Wolfmann's passport," the agent said after reading Wolfmann his rights to remain silent and to have legal counsel. "We already have a search warrant, by the way," he added, approaching the blue car and extracting the keys from Wolfmann's overcoat. The keys indicated that the car was owned by Hertz Rent-a-Car. Inside the trunk was a leather suitcase. The agent popped the case open, and a French passport was on the top. Opening it, the agent saw that it was in the name of Rolfe Reübrich.

"See if there is anything else in the car," the lead agent said to one of the other agents, "and if not we'll leave it here, take the keys and drop them off to Hertz and tell them where to get their vehicle. Hope you paid by credit card, Rolfe." The agent searching the car found the rental contract. It was in the name of Gerald Tradeau, with a Chicago address. "Lots of names, Rolfe. This will make an interesting case."

By this time one of the other agents had opened the leather case that Wolfmann had handed to the Russian Control. Inside were papers and diagrams that clearly indicated that they were the NASA rocket designs at Plum Brook. In addition to the Russian translation were Wolfmann's original notes. It confirmed that they had the right men. They loaded them into their black van that had been hidden in the trees, exiting the park on their way back to Washington.

By three that afternoon Rolfe Reübrich or Wolfmann and Vladimir Kolinsky were booked into federal custody and charged with espionage. Other charges would be added later. The third man, in the Mercedes, was stopped, photographed, identified, and then allowed to leave. He, too, spoke little English. By four o'clock attorneys representing the Russian Embassy were at the FBI Headquarters attempting to get the two prisoners released, but they were out of luck. Neither prisoner would say anything. Now there was just one member of the Chicago KGB group focused on Plum Brook that was missing, and it was unclear who he was or where he was, or what he was doing.

Chapter 16

Palmer Davis was sitting in the Sandusky office of Martin Schwartz discussing the Jerry Summers suit against NASA. When most of the plaintiffs had heard what information the government was going to demand from them in proof of their claim, much of their anger switched from Plum Brook to the legal system. Davis, a week earlier, had offered a small settlement to any of the plaintiffs who believed they could actually prove damages to their homes or livestock if Schwartz would drop the mental anguish and punitive damage charges, but the plaintiffs had all agreed to continue the lawsuit. The Court had scheduled a preliminary hearing at the Cleveland Federal Courthouse on Superior Avenue, and demanded that all of the plaintiffs appear, prepared to answer questions.

"Martin, do you really believe that Judge Eric Slidell is going to go along with your 'absolute liability' theory?"

"Certainly. It's res ipsa loquitor, Palmer. Nuclear fuel rods, tanks of oxygen, a single guard opening the gate for the railroad at night. The thing obviously speaks for itself. I'll give you that my clients may have a hard time proving that their chickens laid fewer eggs or their cows gave less milk, but even your own seismic engineer agreed that the nearest house had a shattering appearance to the cracks, not the kind due to settlement. And your own witness, Jim Roberts, said in his deposition he heard the blast, and he was thirty miles away," Schwartz continued.

"But where is the evidence of mental anguish?" Davis countered.

"Have you been around when those sirens go off? I can hear them here in my office in Downtown Sandusky, so what must it be like for a mile around the facility?" Schwartz countered. "Just be sure you warn the Colonel to keep his temper under control tomorrow or Judge Slidell will find him in contempt and throw him in jail."

"I'll put Jim in charge of the Colonel," David laughed.

The following morning Jim and the Colonel drove into Cleveland in Jim's new NASA vehicle, being permitted to park in the "Federal Vehicles Only" section of the courthouse parking lot. The plaintiffs had chartered a bus, and all arrived together. It was the first time that Jim had actually met any of the plaintiffs, although Jeffrey Josephs recognized several from when they had come to his office to complain about the sirens in the past, but they were not on a first or last-name basis. "That short, fat guy in the tee-shirt is Jerry Summers, I think," the Colonel whispered to Jim as they sat at the defense table with Palmer Davis, the federal agency attorney.

Summers was sitting next to Martin Schwartz at the plaintiff's table, and a court reporter sat in front of the judge's podium. There was no jury present as this was just a preliminary hearing. The rest of the plaintiffs sat in the seats behind the rail in back of Schwartz.

After a few moments a door behind the bench opened, and the bailiff announced, "All rise." There was a clatter as the group of plaintiffs arose and Jerry Summers squeaked his chair on the floor as he pushed it back before standing up. Judge Slidell, a tall man about sixty with thick gray hair and wire-rimmed glasses wearing a black robe, motioned for everyone to sit down, and opened the file on the platform bench. "This is a preliminary hearing," the judge announced, "on Case 69-72884, Jerry Summers, et al v. The National Aeronautics and Space Administration, et al. Gentlemen," he said looking at Davis and then at Schwartz, "are all your 'et als' here?"

Martin Schwartz arose and said, "Your Honor, two of the original plaintiffs have withdrawn from the action and I have filed an amended complaint deleting their names. One of my clients, Mrs. Josephine McGonagall, is elderly and suffers from severe crippling arthritis, and I have filed a motion with the Court requesting that her presence not be required."

"Yes," Judge Slidell answered. "I read that and the supporting document from her physician. She is duly excused from attendance at this or future hearings, and may respond to any questions from the defense or this Court by affidavit. Now, gentlemen, you have stated your claims and defenses clearly in the documents. Mr. Davis, I have carefully considered your motion to dismiss on the basis of federal immunity. There are cases here in the Sixth U.S. Circuit on such issues before, and they go both ways. The admitted facts are that this NASA facility is in a reasonably rural to suburban area with homes and farms around it, and that periodically railroad cars full of various hazardous materials must be switched on a siding from the Penn Central in urban Sandusky, on a lengthy spur of the Baltimore & Ohio from its Sandusky branch on which Penn Central had trackage rights, through residential areas to the facility. Were this facility located in a remote area without close proximity to farms or homes, it being a duly legislated branch of federal government, I would agree that it should be immune from civil actions such as the plaintiffs have presented in their lawsuit.

"However," the judge continued, "the location of Plum Brook does create exposures that would not exist were the facility out in the desert somewhere. Its mission is vital, and to move it, or close it down, would not be beneficial to the nation which is in a so-called 'space race' with the Soviet Union. On that basis I rejected and continue to reject the plaintiffs' motion for an ordered injunction to shut the facility down. It exists, and will continue to exist. But I see no basis to affirm that just because the facility is owned and operated by the federal government and because of its very nature hazardous materials are on occasion brought into the facility that it should be exempt from civil litigation for any harm that the plaintiffs allege and are in a position to prove to this Court. Therefore I must deny the government's motion for summary judgment on the basis of governmental immunity.

"Now, Mr. Schwartz, it appears from the file that the government has provided you with all of the documentations requested in your motion to produce, with the exception of a complete listing of all materials, hazardous or otherwise. Further, the government has filed a motion that such a listing should not be submitted to this Court due to the potential revealing of confidential data that the government considers classified. In return I ordered that the listing be submitted to me in camera for my review and consideration of the government's motion. I have done so, and agree that, beyond the listing of chemicals and other products, such as nuclear fuel rods, referenced in the plaintiff's complaint, there is no reason, no need, for the plaintiffs to have such a list of substances to support their allegations. I therefore grant the government's motion to not produce that list as a part of the court's record. Should any of the items on that list later be shown to be necessary as an item of evidential proof, the Court will review such requests on an individual item basis for further consideration.

"Mr. Schwartz," Judge Slidell continued, "I gather you have advised your many clients that the burden of proof of their allegations in the lawsuit is theirs, is that correct?"

"Yes, Your Honor. They understand that they must prove their allegations."

"Some of those allegations are specific, and some are rather broad and non-specific. Mr. Davis has presented you with a Motion to Produce. I understand that he has not yet received a complete response to that motion. Can you advise this Court when you anticipate being able to completely comply with the defense motion?"

"Yes, Your Honor, my clients should be able to fully comply within the next three weeks."

"Now then," Judge Slidell said, again addressing Martin Schwartz, "your clients allege in Count One that 'the defendant facility possesses and maintains a dangerous nuclear reactor without license and without clearance from the U.S. Environmental Protection Agency, the Ohio Emergency Management Department or any other state or federal agency that has authority over such installations.' So far, in the evidence submitted to the Court I have not seen any indication of proof of this allegation. Will such evidence be forthcoming, Mr. Schwartz? The defense has submitted documents from the Atomic Energy Commission that includes an environmental impact statement in the authorization when the reactor's construction was approved. Does that not supersede EPA or OEM regulation?"

"At present, we are seeking an answer to that question, Your Honor. If we cannot provide it within sixty days we will withdraw the count."

"Thank you, Mr. Schwartz. Now, as to Count Three your clients allege that 'at various and sundry times various alarms have been sounded from the perimeter of the facility that exceed county noise control limits and which disturb the peace of residents within a ten square mile range of the said facility, including the peace and tranquility of farm animals, including chickens, thus reducing their production, and even threatening the wildlife in the area, part of which has always been a nature preserve.' The defense has provided documents showing that it was the Erie County Commission that insisted upon the installation of those sirens, and that their volume in decibels is mandated by the Atomic Energy Commission. They admit that if any fault lies with the sirens it is that they have not been tested as routinely as the AEC recommends. In other words, if the defendants were testing the sirens as often as they should be, say every month or six weeks, or at least quarterly, would your complaint not be better directed to the Atomic Energy Commission?"

"Your point is well taken, Your Honor, but our complaint and request for an injunction and a cease and desist order, which Your Honor denied, was intended to ban all use of the sirens."

"But if the presence of the nuclear reactor is deemed legal, then the emergency sirens are for the benefit of the citizens of Erie County, and periodic testing would be mandatory, would it not?"

"Your Honor, in our amended complaint we again requested the cease and desist order. If that is granted, the reactor would be removed and there would be no need for sirens."

"That request is denied. Mr. Davis, instruct your clients that they should follow the directives of the Atomic Energy Commission. Now, Mr. Schwartz, in Count Four your clients allege that 'on December 25, 1968, criminals managed to breach the inadequate security of the facility and set off an explosion that produced sound waves sufficient to break windows, crack residential walls, cause fires and smoke within the facility and frighten the general public, which was forced to respond through its taxpayer-supported police, fire and other Erie County facilities.' This is a statement in background, but does not state a claim. Please amend your complaint again to state precisely what your claim is. If it is that there was insufficient security to prevent such intrusion – and I understand that an Air Force corporal at the gate was shot by the aforementioned criminals gaining entry, then state that. If your claim is for tax money spent by the emergency services for which you pay taxes, should that claim not be brought by the involved agencies? I must read into the complaint that your clients seek restitution for broken windows, explosion damages to their structures, and 'fright,' or mental anguish to both themselves and their livestock. Please clarify this for the Court, and also do so for Court Five."

"Yes, Your Honor."

"Now we come to Count Six, which alleges that 'on or about August 24, 1969, the home and auto of one of the facility's contract consultants, identified as Defendant Doe, was bombed in Fremont, Sandusky County, believed to be connected to the Defendant facility, with further proof to be shown at time of trial.' Have you identified this Defendant Doe?"

"Yes, Your Honor. In the depositions of James Roberts and Jeffry Josephs, this defendant was identified, but we were advised that for national security reasons we could not subpoena nor depose this individual. The event, which occurred in Fremont, Ohio, does have bearing on the case in that it again represents a security issue at the NASA facility, but as the matter is still under investigation by the Federal Bureau of Investigation, we have been limited in what we could produce to only the Fremont Police report and the report from the Fremont Fire Department and the Toledo Fire Department's bomb squad."

"Is this true, Mr. Davis?"

"Yes, Your Honor. The matter is under FBI investigation."

"Can either of the two gentlemen sitting with you shed light on that for the Court?"

"The defense would request that such an attempt not be made at this time. May we approach the bench to explain?"

"No, instead I shall call a fifteen minute recess and we can meet in my office. Does the defense have any objection to Mr. Swartz joining us?"

"No, sir."

The bailiff again called out for all to rise, and Jerry Summers and the other plaintiffs slowly wandered out into the courthouse hallways to seek restrooms or drinking fountains. Jim and the Colonel joined the two attorneys in the judge's office, where the chairs were a bit more comfortable. Introductions were made of the two NASA representatives.

"Two explosions within a six month period in the Plum Brook rail yard," Judge Slidell began, "seems fishy to me. Have there been other explosions in the past, Colonel Josephs?"

Not that I know of, Your Honor. There were protests when the nuclear reactor was first constructed, but those were outside the gates and handled easily by the Air Force MPs."

"Any arrests?"

"We prosecuted one man who broke through the perimeter fence to post a protest sign, and we threatened some teens with arrest, but that was about all."

"You were in charge of that, Mr. Roberts?"

"No, Your Honor. I was only hired in November last year."

"So nothing much was happening at the facility until after you were hired?"

"I'm afraid it was bad timing, Your Honor. But there was only Colonel Josephs and his team of MPs for security, along with the cameras along the perimeter, so part of my job was to analyze and improve security."

"So what explains these explosions, including the one in Fremont that has the FBI involved? What is so 'confidential' and 'classified'? Is it so secret that Martin Schwartz ought not hear about it?"

"No, Your Honor," Jim replied. "Martin already knows part of the story, but it is confidential, and we would not want the media to find out about it. Briefly, there was a man, Rolfe Reübrich, although his real name was Rolfe Wolfmann, who was employed as a contract worker in the spacecraft propellant lab. He was an employee of a French contractor, Gearmone Engineering, but was German. As it turns out he had been a rocket scientist for the Nazis during the war, but was East German, and was employed as a spy by the KGB. He had taught at the Moscow Institute of Sciences.

"A professor at Fremont College, Hilda Johnson, was brought to the U.S. by the CIA after defecting. She was a specialist in nuclear energy and transfer of nuclear fuel rods. When the December 25 explosion occurred, as the testimony shows, two cars of oxygen were exploded and knocked over a third railcar containing fresh fuel rods for the reactor, which was shut down for the holidays. The Atomic Energy Commission experts were at a conference in Vienna, and Dr. Johnson was called in to give advice on the situation. She was then hired as an occasional consultant to NASA on their reactor.

"About a week or so after her first visit to the rail yard where the Christmas Day explosion had occurred she was given a tour of the entire facility. While in the spacecraft propellant facility she recognized Wolfmann from when she had been a student at the Moscow Science Institute. He apparently recognized her, too, and one of his KGB confidants, one Johann Kahler, who had once been engaged to Hilda Johnson in East Germany where he was an officer in the East German Navy, contacted her. He threatened her husband, and the baby she was about to have, and got her to pick up an explosive device and deliver it to NASA to blow up another rail car. But she went to a friend, Dr. Fairchild, and he put her in touch with the FBI, and while she did pick up the explosive device, the FBI had a bomb crew on the facility to disarm it, then set off a very minor explosion to convince the KGB that she had done as instructed."

"Richard Fairchild, the religion professor?" the judge inquired.

"Yes. Do you know him?"

"He solved a big insurance fraud case here in Cleveland about nine years ago. I hear he's quite a detective. His testimony helped convict a couple of guys for murder. I was the judge that sent them to prison for piracy, the federal part of their crime."

"Yes, that sounds like Richie. Anyway, on August 24 Kahler and another KGB agent put a bomb under Dr. Johnson's car and then faked a phone call from the NASA facility, telling her to drive quickly to the reactor as they were having an emergency. A neighbor had seen the men tampering with her car, and the FBI suspected it was a plot and had the neighborhood evacuated. Her car and house blew up, but she was safe. That's the connection with NASA, and the FBI wants to keep it confidential until they round up this KGB team."

"Have they caught any of them yet?"

"Yes, Johann Kahler. It's a long story, but Richie Fairchild tracked him down on a Washington-bound train and got him arrested. He had the plans from the NASA rocket propulsion lab with him."

"Fairchild again, eh? So I can see why NASA doesn't want this tried in court. Okay, let's go back out," Judge Slidell said.

When the plaintiffs had all taken their seats again, the judge began by issuing an order instructing that Count 6 be withdrawn from the lawsuit in the plaintiffs' new amended complaint. He then had all of the plaintiffs stand, and asked each their name and where they lived in relation to the Plum Brook facility. Then he thanked them, and adjourned the hearing.

* * *

The Port Clinton Feed & Fertilizer Company store was on the west side of the little port city, just beyond the last of the restaurants and motels that catered to the tourists who flocked to the area in the summer. But the store was less busy on this late fall Saturday as homeowners did not need grass seed, weed killer or lawn fertilizer until the following spring. Richard Fairchild had brought his sixteen head of Aberdeen cattle into his barn toward the end of October, before the first snow storm of the season. His neighbor, Jack Ralston, had baled Fairchild's and his own hay that summer and Fairchild's barn held enough hay to last until the cattle went back out onto the pasture. But they needed more than hay, and Fairchild was in town with his pick-up truck to purchase grain and other feeds that he would need to keep the cattle healthy and happy – a recipe for good steaks and roasts when the time came to select one of the beasts for butchering.

As Fairchild was discussing his order with Bucky Thompson, the owner of the store, he noticed a short, balding middle-aged man with dark-rimmed glasses examining bags of fertilizer and reading the contents. "Something I can help you with?" Bucky asked him.

"Not yet. I vunt dah kind mit dah highest level of ammonium nitrate. My soil is very poor, and I vus told it vould help it produce better crops," the man answered with a distinctive German accent.

"Well, these are all about the same level," Bucky said. This one, Mono-West, is pretty good, a bit cheaper, but just as high in quality. How much you need?"

"About, oh, about fifteen fifty pound bags, I guess."

"How many acres you got?"

"Ahh, about a hundred."

"A hundred? At a little less than 240 pounds an acre, you'll need about 450 fifty pound bags."

"Oh! Nein, I'm just going to fertilize a couple of acres for now. Fifteen bags should do me."

"You got a spreader?" Bucky asked.

"Oh, Ja, I borrow my neighbor's"

"I think probably ten bags would be sufficient for a couple of acres, wouldn't you agree, Richie?" Bucky said, addressing a question to Fairchild.

"Ten or less, this time of year. Spring's the usual and best time to spread fertilizer. If you put it down now, the snow melt could wash it off and pollute a creek somewhere," Fairchild answered. Then he added, looking directly at the man, "Sie bin aus Deutschland?"

"Ja!" the man answered. "Five years now, but new to this area. New to farming."

"Welcome, then. Around here we're always glad to help someone new to farming, right Bucky?"

"Yes, we're all neighbors in the country."

"I'm Richie Fairchild," Fairchild said, extending his hand to the bald-headed man.

"Ah, Klaus," the man answered, shaking Fairchild's hand. "I planned to get dah fertilizer now for use in spring, Ja? Best to plan ahead."

"I guess so," Bucky replied. "Let me finish with Richie's order here, and then we'll get you the fertilizer."

"Dunke," the man replied. Richard Fairchild completed his order, which Bucky would deliver to Fairchild's farm later in the week. He then helped the German man with his order, inquiring if he wanted Bucky to deliver it to his farm.

"Oh, nein, I'll put it in my truck now," this man who called himself Klaus answered.

"Bring it around to the back, and we'll load it in for you," Bucky said.

"I'll give you a hand," Fairchild said, and started toward the storage area with Bucky as the German man went out front to get his truck. When he backed it up to the loading dock, rather than a pick-up truck, he had just a mid-sized dark brown Dodge panel van, the kind used by small businesses without rear windows. He came around and opened the rear doors as Fairchild came out the back door of the store with about five bags on a four-wheeled cart. He looked into the back of the van, which contained several barrels and a lot of electrical wiring and gear and said,

"Gosh, Klaus, I'm not sure we're going to be able to get fifteen bags in there with all that other stuff. Why don't we put these five in your van, and load the other ten on the back of my pick-up and I'll follow you to your farm and help you unload them."

"Nein, nein!" Klaus said briskly. "I'll move dah barrels forward. We get it all in now."

"Well, okay," Fairchild said as Bucky came out with five more bags. Together Fairchild and Bucky were able to push and shove the whole order into the back of Klaus's van, and the German man slammed the two doors together. Fairchild made a mental note of the license plate, an Illinois number.

"Where is your farm, Klaus?" Fairchild asked.

"Oh, on Route Six."

"Well, safe journey, Mr. ...?" Bucky said, holding out his hand to his customer.

"Klaus," the German replied. "Herr Kurt Klaus. Dunke." He climbed into the van and started the motor, then pulled out of the store lot, but instead of heading west or south, turned east into the town.

"That's a strange one," Bucky said to Fairchild as the truck left the lot.

"Most definitely," Fairchild agreed. He then returned to his own truck, and also turned east into Port Clelland. He drove quickly through town and passed the Port Clinton Airport, heading toward the Bay. As he started across the Bay Bridge he could see the back of the dark brown van at the far end of the bridge. There were no other cars between the van and Fairchild's pick-up truck, and he maintained the distance. At the village of Bay Bridge Fairchild anticipated that Kurt Klaus, if that was his name, would turn right on the state road that would lead to Route Six, but instead the van continued on toward Sandusky.

Maintaining a distance Fairchild followed the van as it approached the outskirts of Sandusky, continuing on toward the town center. Just beyond a large Catholic Church the van turned down a side street and came to a stop in front of an old house that had a garage apartment. The van was then backed up to the garage, and, watching from a safe distance, Fairchild saw Klaus get out, open the garage door, and back the van inside. He then closed the garage door from the inside. Fairchild moved forward, noting the address of the house and writing it down alongside the Illinois tag number.

He then drove on, re-tracing his path back to Port Clelland and on to his farm near Oak Harbor on the Portage River. It was about noon, and Esther was preparing lunch.

"You were longer than I anticipated. How's Bucky doing?" she inquired.

"Oh, he's fine. Have I got time to make a phone call before lunch?"

"Sure. It will be ten or fifteen minutes yet. Go ahead."

Fairchild entered his library, serving as his office at home, and picked up the phone, dialing the number for the Toledo FBI office. A young woman answered, and advised that neither Aaron Greenspoon nor Brett Leonard were in, but she had an emergency number for both. Fairchild wrote down both numbers, and called Aaron Greenspoon, catching him at lunch at his home in Perrysburg.

"I apologize for interrupting your day off," Fairchild began, "but I think this may be urgent."

"Fairchild, if you think something is urgent, by all means interrupt anything you want. What has happened?"

Fairchild explained about the incident at the fertilizer dealer's and what he saw in the back of the panel van. Then he explained how he had followed the van into Sandusky and observed it being parked inside a garage, advising that he had an Illinois tag number for the Dodge van and the address in Sandusky.

"And you suspect something?" Greenspoon asked.

"Well, November is not the time to fertilize, and 750 pounds of ammonium nitrate fertilizer, properly prepared and attached to some sort of timer, would make one hell of a bomb."

"Yes, that's the same conclusion I would have, Richard. I'll check out this Illinois plate number and get working on a search warrant for the address in Sandusky, and keep you posted."

Fairchild heard nothing the rest of the day, and the following day being Sunday, he was busy all morning at the chapel, although it was Dr. Boldt who had the sermon. That afternoon the Fairchilds passed on the usual Sunday Brunch at one of the choir member's home and returned to the farm. There were no calls that afternoon or evening, other than a call from Esther's sister in Pennsylvania.

Monday Fairchild had classes all morning, and was at his desk in the basement of Hayes Hall reviewing term papers when the phone rang. It was Special Agent Brett Leonard.

"Your hunch was on target," he began. "That Illinois tag was to a 1958 Chevrolet and the registration had expired two years ago. It must have been stolen from some abandoned jalopy in South Chicago. Then we got a report of a stolen Dodge van in Joliet a week ago Friday night, although with the snow storm, the theft wasn't discovered until the following Tuesday.

"The house in Sandusky is vacant, but is listed for rental. Whether this German guy, Kurt Klaus or whatever his name is, actually rented the place or is just using the garage and the upstairs apartment we're not sure. We had the Sandusky Police go with us to the place with a search warrant, but the garage was empty. There was evidence that someone was living in the upstairs apartment, however, so we have an 'all points' out on the van. From stuff in the garage, gasoline and other liquids, trimmed wires, etc., we think your belief that this is a bomb is accurate. There was even an empty box for a two-way radio set. The question is, what is the target, and when will it be targeted?"

"Were do you suspect?"

"Where would you suspect, Fairchild?"

"The NASA reactor, on a damp, breezy day. But unless the guy is suicidal, how would he get in. I don't think they would try using Hilda Johnson again. Wolfmann could have provided some suggestions as to where the perimeter is most vulnerable, like one of the railroad gates."

"Yes, we thought of that, and alerted Roberts not to let any of the MPs open the railroad gates unless they were certain that it was an expected delivery. Oh, by the way, we caught Wolfmann passing the plans for the rocket facility operations to his KGB Control. They were both arrested at the Great Falls Park in Virginia earlier this week."

"That's good. If this Klaus guy is the other Chicago KBG guy, you'll have them all."

"It's an 'if,' but we think it's probable. Where do you think this guy might try to get in?"

"Gosh, Brett, I don't know. I've never really been on the Plum Brook facility, so I don't know where it is most vulnerable. Jim Roberts would be your best bet on that. But I seem to recall that there are two railroad gates, one at the north end where most of the deliveries are made, and another coming from some back-woods branch line, to the southwest. My guess might be that the southwest gate is the vulnerable one."

"I'll run that by Roberts and see what he thinks."

"If that van has been converted to a bomb, I'd get an Army tank out there to blast it the minute it breaks through the perimeter fence. Maybe a bazooka would do!"

"Thanks! I don't think we can borrow a tank, and we don't really want another explosion. The neighbors are already suing for the first two. We'd rather catch the guy before he acts."

Chapter 17

Carl Mitchell at NSA was on the listening line late Tuesday evening when he picked up a conversation between one of the Russian Controls and a field operative named Klaus. The call appeared, from what Mitchell could determine, to be made from somewhere in Northern Ohio, probably from a public phone. He recorded the conversation, which was extremely brief, and immediately notified the Russia Desk at CIA Headquarters in Langley, Virginia, transferring the recording electronically to their translators.

Within an hour the CIA had transcribed the conversation, and notified the FBI in Washington, which in turn notified the Cleveland and Toledo FBI field offices. The conversation, in Russian, was hard to decipher as the one making the call had a strong German accent. But from what they were able to make out, this person had said, "It is ready. I want to go tonight." The Control had told him to proceed as planned. Then the conversation ended.

Special Agent in Charge Aaron Greenspoon understood completely. Brett Leonard had already gone home, but was contacted and told to meet Greenspoon and five agents coming from Cleveland at the Plum Brook main gate as quickly as possible. Greenspoon then called Jim Roberts and alerted him to the phone conversation picked up by the NSA, and asked that he get Colonel Josephs to the facility as soon as possible, and alert the Air Force MPs. The full contingency would be needed as no one was certain how this KGB agent intended to enter the facility, although they could guess the target.

As it happened, delivery of a tank car of liquid nitrogen was expected that night, about three in the morning. Roberts had advised Greenspoon and Leonard of this earlier in the day, and the Baltimore & Ohio Railroad, which would be bringing the car through the southwest gate, was also notified. The nitrogen was needed for some of the cryological experiments NASA was conducting, considering the iciness beyond earth's atmosphere.

Roberts had still been up, reading a book, when the call came. He told Jayne he had to go to the facility urgently, and was at the gate before any of the others, including Josephs, arrived. All the MPs were rounded up, most, except those on duty, from their bunks, and Josephs unlocked the armory and issued each man both a side arm and an automatic rifle, smoke and flash grenades and Chemical Mace. Some of the FBI agents had bullet-proof vests. They had all been briefed on what the FBI suspected would be an attack on the reactor, and when Greenspoon arrived, he updated them about the NSA recording.

Surprisingly, Colonel Josephs, after consulting with Aaron Greenspoon, advised Jim Roberts that Jim was to be the person in charge of the operation. Jim therefore got up on the step of his car in front of the MPs, FBI agents and two Coast Guard medics that the FBI had brought with them. "Gentlemen!" Jim began, speaking loudly so they could all hear him. "As you have been briefed, there is a strong likelihood that there will be an attack tonight targeting our atomic reactor building. A major explosion beside it could create a serious radiation leak, and with the damp breeze tonight, it would potentially contaminate this entire facility and all the employees currently working in them. We have elected not to evacuate them, as it would disrupt the major projects on which they are working. The engineers and technicians at the reactor building have been briefed, and, if there is a breach, they are to be notified by radio, at which time they will do an emergency shut down of the reactor.

"There is the added problem that a railway delivery of a tank car of liquid nitrogen is expected, perhaps around three in the morning, on the track from the south that winds around the west side of the facility and then into the rail yard. That gate is on the southwest side of the perimeter. When I get notification from the railroad that the car is within five miles, I'll go to that gate to open it, but that may be a crucial moment if our suspect either knows about the delivery or discovers that the gate may be opened for the railroad. Sergeant Warbish and his FBI companion will also be watching that gate, but that may not be the target location where the intrusion will occur.

"The problem," Roberts continued, "is that if there is an attack we will not know where it will be made or how the suspect plans to detonate his explosives. It could be by means of suicide, by a timing device, or by a radio signal. As the suspect recently purchased a two-way radio set, we anticipate that remote detonation will be the method, but that is not guaranteed. What is clear is that we want to catch this son-of-a-bitch alive. Now, that is going to be difficult, as he will probably try to detonate his explosives if he is cornered. As the FBI found the box the two-way radio came in, we know its radio frequency and will attempt to jam the signal, but there is no guarantee that such an attempt will work.

"We don't want to endanger any of you, but if we are to take this bastard by surprise we can't sit around the perimeter with our headlights and red flashers on, so we need to proceed basically in the dark until something happens – if something actually does happen. It could be a long night and come to nothing. But you must keep your radios on and every ten minutes we'll do a count. Each car will have a number, and an FBI agent with each MP. You will all be armed, but we're hoping to catch this guy alive. This is not for anyone outside this group, and you are all sworn to the state secrets act, but we believe this is a KGB operation, and there is no doubt they are good at what they set out to do. But, guys, we're a hellovalot better!

"Take a look at the papers I gave each of the MP drivers. It shows where we want you to locate, places selected because your vehicles won't be visible from outside the perimeter. Then in the upper left corner is a number. That is your reporting number. Next is a chart of the facility, showing where each number is located. If the suspect – he's driving a dark colored Dodge panel van – approaches the perimeter, immediately identify yourself by your number. The cars on either side of that number should then prepare to go to that numbered location, but only after the suspect has broken in. Is that clear to everyone?" There was a mumbled affirmative response.

"Now, if you are in danger, or if you suspect that this guy is going to attempt to detonate his explosives, don't hesitate to use your weapons, whatever you believe is justified. This is a dangerous situation, and every caution is needed. Okay? Now, head out, and keep us posted."

* * *

Klaus Kravitz sat in the Dodge van in which he had arranged the 750 pounds of ammonium nitrate and other chemicals to the formula he had been supplied by the KGB in Moscow. It was after midnight, and he had parked the van in a grove of trees near a creek that flowed north toward the east side of Sandusky. That afternoon he had been driving on U.S. 20 after having lunch in Bellevue, and when he reached Monroeville he had noted a silver tank car sitting on a railroad siding just south of where the rails crossed the highway. He pulled into a lot near the tracks and walked over to the tank car. There were several cardboard markers or plaques on the car, and one read "Liq. Nitrogen for P.B. via Wilmer," with tomorrow's date on it. Kravitz knew from Wolfmann's map and diagram of the facility that Wilmer was on the west side of the facility, and that most of the rail deliveries occurred at night. He checked the road map he had purchased the previous week at a gas station, and found the road that seemed to parallel the railroad. All he had to do was wait, and perhaps the gate would be opened for him. It was about ten miles from where the tank car was parked to Wilmer.

Kravitz drove the route until he found the grove of trees near the creek where he could await the train. Then he drove back to Bellevue for dinner, and walked around the town, which was a major rail town for the Norfolk and Western. He did not know which railroad owned the tracks he would be following. About eight that evening Kravitz drove back to Monroeville and found a place where he could observe the parked tank car. It was nearly eleven when he heard a diesel locomotive horn, and observed a railway signal light on the north side of the highway turn from red to green.

A train of about seven cars pulled by a switch engine slowly rocked into the town sounding its horn for the highway and street crossings, also crossing some east-west rails. After the last freight car cleared the end of the siding Kravitz saw a man with a lantern and a hand-held radio standing by a switch, then unlocking it and pulling it toward himself. The train then backed up, and the rear car entered the siding and backed to the tank car. The man with the lantern then spent a few moments connecting the two cars, and, as he climbed up a step on the side, the train again moved forward, stopping when the tank car had completely cleared the siding. The man with the lantern then climbed down and reversed the switch, locked it again, and the train backed up until the locomotive was opposite the man so he could climb aboard it. The train then proceeded north at perhaps fifteen to twenty miles per hour.

Kravitz got back in his van and drove to the grove of trees where he could observe the train when it passed. He heard the locomotive before he saw the headlight, but as it rattled and swayed past the grove. Kravitz started the van and drove up the road toward Wilmer, passing the train as he went. At Wilmer he had spotted the switch to the spur line that ran into the Plum Brook facility, and, although there was no road to the gate, moved the van into some weeds so that he had a clear view of where the two halves of gate would open outward for the locomotive to enter the facility.

The train soon came into view, and rolled past the switch to the spur track, where the man with the lantern and hand-held radio again had climbed off the locomotive and unlocked the switch, moving it to the side. The man then climbed onto the freight car ahead of the silver tank car as it backed up, with the silver tank car coming to the gate first. On the other side of the gate was a NASA security car, and a man was unlocking and opening the gate for the train.

The gate was too narrow for the van to enter beside the railcar, but Kravitz realized that, as the gate had opened outward, the man from the security car would have to go out to close the gate, and that would be his opportunity to drive through it. He would try to knock the man down with the van, but if that didn't work he had his revolver sitting on the seat next to him, and his windows were down. He started the van, but did not turn on the lights.

The locomotive pushed the train of cars through the gate, and they curved around toward the north following the track, which crossed the interior perimeter road. As soon as the locomotive had passed through the gate and the guard, Jim Roberts, started out to close the two halves of the gate Kravitz gunned the van forward toward the security guard, missing him, but firing a shot at him. He saw the perimeter road that Wolfmann had drawn on the map of the facility and turned left or north on it, traveling perhaps a little over a thousand yards. But immediately about four sets of headlights came on, temporarily blinding Kravitz, and he saw in his side view mirror that the gate behind him was already closed. He fired the revolver at one of the cars that was directly in front of him on the perimeter road, as another pulled up behind him and men were running toward him with guns. A smoke grenade was thrown in his window and startled him when it exploded with a bang, but he was uninjured as he had on a heavy coat.

Voices instructed him to get out of the vehicle and put his hands up. At this moment the last car on the train, the silver tank car, was passing the right side of the van. Kravitz slid over to the right door, threw it open and jumped out, running to the opposite side of the tank car. Men started closing in around him, and one appeared from the back of the second last car of the train, shining a bright light on Kravitz. Kravitz swung the revolver in that direction and pulled the trigger. The bullet hit a valve on the upper side of the silver tank car, and with a whoosh a cloud of icy nitrogen blasted out of the side of the railcar hitting Kravitz like a block of ice. His hand holding the revolver seemed frozen, and he fell backwards screaming. Two men behind him pulled him out from the jet of nitrogen spewing on him and yanked the gun from his frozen hand.

Kravitz was hardly breathing as the men carried him to the perimeter road, and an MP car with the two Coast Guard medics pulled up about a minute later. His face was starting to thaw, but any exposed part of his body had what appeared to be third degree burns or frostbite.

The train stopped, and one of the men on the locomotive came back with a toolbox, and knowing how to seal the damaged valve, stopped the release of the nitrogen. He later estimated that no more than a quarter to a third of the liquid had vaporized. The railroad crew then completed the delivery of the silver tank car of liquid nitrogen to the rail yard, and the train departed again, locomotive first. This time it was Sergeant Warbish who opened the gate for the locomotive and train.

Two FBI bomb specialists climbed into the van and quickly figured out how to disarm the explosives. The entire van was the bomb, and in the back of the van was a motorcycle on which Kravitz had intended to escape.

Kravitz was suffering badly as Special Agent Leonard read him his rights, and then two FBI agents accompanied him in the ambulance that had been called from Perkins Township to take him to the hospital in Sandusky. The nitrogen in the tank car had frozen any live vegetation around the side of the track, but no other harm had occurred. The emergency was over, and Kravitz would be arraigned from his hospital bed later that day for espionage, conspiracy, sabotage in Fremont, attempted sabotage at Plum Brook, attempted murder and damages to federal property, as well as trespass on federal property.

* * *

Media relations again fell to Jim Roberts. He did not know how they had found out, but by ten o'clock the following morning reporters and television news crews were at the main gate demanding information about what had occurred in the middle of the night. Jim had just gotten off the phone after talking with Dexter Atwater at the hospital about the suspect's condition. The FBI had confirmed that his name was Klaus Kravitz, a Stasi agent from Dresden, East Germany.

Roberts approached the gang at the gate as flashbulbs went off and the whirr of television cameras and shouted questions was a cacophony of noise. "Please! Please, gather around and be quite and I'll try to advise you what we know," Jim started. As he spotted several women reporters in the group, he did not start by saying "Gentlemen." Rather he waited until there was silence, and then began.

"As you probably know from previous events here at Plum Brook NASA facilities, our mission is to assist NASA in advancing our nation's space program. That being the case, we are obviously in competition with other nations that also have a space program, primarily that of the Soviet Union. We learned within the last month or so that we had a Russian spy who was employed by one of the contractors doing work here in the space propulsion research facility. I have been authorized to tell you that his code name was 'the Wolf,' but am not at liberty to tell you more about him as he and others of his associates have been arrested, and none of the information he had collected reached its intended destination.

"There was a sub-plot, however," he continued. "As many of you may be aware – it is certainly not a secret – there is a small nuclear reactor here at Plum Brook to supply power for several of the testing facilities that require high amounts of energy, such as the supersonic wind tunnel. An earlier plot to place a bomb next to the reactor was foiled about three or four months ago, but the FBI anticipated that another attempt would be made. Information was received that such an attempt would be made early this morning, and NASA, the Air Force, which provides our Military Police, and the FBI were here awaiting that attempt, which occurred simultaneously with the arrival of a railroad tank car of liquid nitrogen, which as I'm sure you all know, is not explosive. It is hazardous, if exposed to air, however.

"The man attempted to drive an explosive-laden vehicle into the facility when the perimeter gate was opened for the train delivering the tank car of nitrogen. He has been identified as one Klaus Kravitz, that's spelled with two 'Ks,' K L A U S   K R A V I T Z, of Dresden, East Germany. In his attempt he fired his gun at NASA, Air Force and FBI personnel who were prepared to stop him and disarm the explosives. Unfortunately for

Mr. Kravitz one of his bullets hit a valve on the tank car, and he was sprayed with vaporized nitrogen, which has an extremely low temperature and causes immediate frostbite burns. He was arrested and rushed to Sandusky Memorial Hospital. I spoke with one of the physicians there a few minutes ago, and was advised that Mr. Kravitz has third degree burns on his face and hands, and second and first degree burns on other parts of his body. He will be transferred to the Cleveland Clinic for initial burn therapy, and then to a federal prison hospital where skin grafts will be used on his face and hands. We are hopeful that he will recover reasonably well before his trial.

"Mr. Kravitz has been charged with espionage, sabotage – that in connection with another explosion not at but related to Plum Brook – attempted murder and other federal crimes. Thankfully he was not a very good shot and no one but himself was injured this morning. This is all the information I am authorized to release at this time, but I will attempt to answer any further questions you may have, and I will also issue a later bulletin with this same information and any updates by three o'clock this afternoon for your evening news cycle."

"What's your name and position, Mister?" one of the reporters shouted.

"I'm Jim Roberts, director of security here at Plum Brook."

"Was this Kravitz guy working for the Russians?" another called out.

"Kravitz, as far as we have been able to learn so far – and this is preliminary and not yet verified – was an East German Stasi agent, working with the KGB."

"Do you think there will be other attacks on the facility here?" shouted another reporter.

"Well, we certainly hope not! While there are obviously secret processes and experiments occurring here, and have been occurring here for years, this is not a secret NASA facility. We even offer occasional tours of our facilities to the public and our engineers and scientists are proud of the contribution they are making to America's space program."

"Were any shots fired at Kravitz?" the same reporter asked.

"The only thing fired at Mr. Kravitz was a smoke grenade. We wanted the man alive."

"Who was the spy you said was called 'the Wolf' working for here?" asked another reporter.

"We have a number of contractors working here on various projects. As the Wolf's case is still pending in federal court I'm not at liberty to reveal his contractual relationship, but that may become public at some future time. Now, folks, I've been up all night and want to get a bit of rest before the three o'clock briefing, so please return to your papers or stations and await further bulletins. Okay?"

The crowd slowly dispersed and Jim returned to his office to call Jayne. Then he lay down on his cot and slept for a couple of hours.

Chapter 18
December, 1969

Jim Roberts was in a conference with Colonel Josephs when Corporal McQuinn put through a phone call initially intended for Jim. Jeffrey Josephs answered, and began to smile. "Good!" he said. "That's great news. Yes, I'll tell Jim. Thanks, Aaron."

Jim knew that the call must have been from Special Agent-in-Charge Aaron Greenspoon in Toledo. Josephs explained, "The Brodasky Brothers were both in the United States illegally. When you were unable to find any records that they had ever done work here before, the FBI followed up, and found that they were members of the Secret Service of Poland, doing work for the KGB. Our little Christmas Day blast was not their first. They'll face espionage and sabotage charges now, so this apparently wraps up the loose ends of our Plum Brook attacks."

"Well, I thought there was something fishy about their story," Jim said. "But I wonder why they didn't go after the car with the nuclear rods rather than the oxygen cars?"

"Probably because they didn't realize what the car with the rods in it was, and they knew oxygen would be explosive. Neither spoke very good English as you may recall."

"So we were just lucky. Let's hope there is no 'next time' event."

"Amen to that, Jim."

* * *

Martin Schwartz was on the telephone with Jerry Summers explaining that Jerry was going to have to attend the mandatory mediation that Judge Slidell had ordered for the following Wednesday. It would be held in the office of Attorney Brian Wilson, a federally approved mediator, in Lorain, about thirty-five miles east of Sandusky. Jerry was instructed to advise all his fellow plaintiffs, and to have as many as possible of them attend, as there would probably be offers made that they should consider. Schwartz said he would speak for the interests of Mrs. McGonagall, but that all the others should be there or they might lose their opportunity to present their lists of damages.

At the same time Palmer Davis was advising Jim Roberts and Colonel Josephs of the mediation, and that they would be expected to attend. Jim wrote down the address of Attorney Wilson's office. He had been to mediations before and knew how they worked, but, again, he was advised to have Colonel Josephs keep his temper from flaring if the negotiations got hot.

Wednesday turned out to be a damp, cold Northern Ohio wintery day, with snow flurries, but no heavy snowfall. It was, suggested Palmer Davis, a good time for a mediation, coming before the Christmas holidays, when people were generally in a better mood. But not all of the attendees were preparing to "get it over with," get some offer and bail out of the lawsuit that had caused them to reveal much of their private business in response to the government's Motion to Produce. Stacks of documentation had been sifted through at Palmer Davis's Cleveland office by three young attorneys in his federal department, and they had produced quite a list of questions for each of the plaintiffs.

When all of the attendees had arrived, with only one of the plaintiffs besides Josephine McGonagall not present, the parties were seated around a large conference table. Davis and one of his assistant attorneys sat next to Jim Roberts and Jeffrey Josephs, Brian Wilson sat between Martin Schwartz and Davis, and Jerry Summers and the other plaintiffs filled in the other seats around the large tables.

Wilson began by making them all welcome, and advising the rules for the mediation. After the opening session, both sides would retire to separate conference rooms to discuss what was said, where there would be coffee and snacks. They would have half an hour, or longer if needed, and would then return to the main conference table to discuss what they had decided. If the matter could be resolved at that point, they could all go home. If it had not been, then they would return to their conference rooms, and sandwiches would be brought in from a shop in the next block from Wilson's office and discussion would continue while they ate lunch, then they would return to the conference table again. This would be repeated until some consensus was met, or the mediation failed. The mediation costs would be borne equally by both sides.

Wilson then began with a summary of what he understood the issues to be, and asked the plaintiffs to correct any misunderstandings he had. Roberts thought Wilson did a good summary, but Jerry Summers immediately took issue with some of what Wilson had said. He was wearing the same tee shirt as he had on at the earlier court hearing.

"The problem is on-going. Just a week ago there was a hell of a racket going on over there, with police and ambulances and God-knows-what raising a ruckus, then the next day there were reporters and television crews all over the place yelling and shouting through the gate."

Wilson had a large map of the facilities and surrounding neighborhoods. "Could you show me, on this map, Mr. Summers, where your home is located?" Jerry Summers pointed to a house in a subdivision perhaps a third of a mile from the entry road to the facility and at least a mile from the main gate, which was not at the actual perimeter of the Plum Brook property.

"So you are about a mile from this Main Gate? Is that correct, Mr. Summers?"

"Yeah, I guess, about a mile. But the whole damn place is a hellovalot closer."

"You saw or heard these reporters yourself?"

"Yeah, when I saw television trucks heading in there I went in to see what the heck was happening."

"But if you had not gone onto the facility property, Mr. Summers, would you have heard the reporters from your home?"

"No, but they were all on television that night, including that guy there, sitting next to Mr. Davis," he replied, pointing at Jim Roberts.

"Do you believe this event you have described, an ambulance coming to the facility and reporters at the interior Main Gate, has direct bearing on your lawsuit, Mr. Summers?"

"Yeah, it sure does. From what this guy, what, Roberts? said there had been some clown trying to get in in the middle of the night to blow up the reactor, and they used grenades to stop him. Imagine, our families exposed to grenades going off all around us! It only proves that that place ought to be shut down."

"But hasn't Judge Slidell already ruled on that, Mr. Summers?"

"Yeah, well, I think Schwartz, here, ought to appeal that. The Judge was wrong."

"Mr. Summers," Wilson said, "that may be an issue for another day. What we are here for today is to determine who had real damages from prior incidents, not from incidents occurring after you filed your complaints. Now, what damages did you actually suffer, Mr. Summers?"

"In that blast last Christmas I got three broken windows, and there's a big crack in my chimney. The blast was so loud my dog crapped on the floor. Hellova mess to clean up."

"Did you sustain any additional damages in the August blast?"

"Well, no new broken windows, anyway. I don't know if my cracked chimney was made worse or not."

"And your dog?"

"Naw, the dog's fine."

Wilson looked at Palmer Davis and asked, "Do you have an engineering report on Mr. Summers' chimney?"

"Yes, Northern Ohio Engineering Company examined all of the homes claiming damage in early January. They did detect what they believed to be blast damage to the home of Mrs. Josephine McGonagall, who lives closest to the rail yard where the Christmas Day explosion occurred, and determined that the damage could be repaired for $3100. She also had seven broken windows, and we have agreed with Mr. Schwartz to a settlement of $3800 with her, is that not correct, Martin"

"Yes, and her three neighbors that also suffered broken windows have already been reimbursed their costs by the government. Two have signed releases and have been removed from the plaintiff list. The third also plans to sign a release. She is not here today."

"Thank you, Mr. Schwartz. Now, I understand that each of the rest of you have submitted evidence of your damages to Mr. Schwartz and Mr. Davis, is that correct?" Heads nodded affirmatively around the table. "Have any offers been made to you regarding those damages by the government?"

Mr. Schwartz answered for his clients, "The individual offers were passed on to each of the plaintiffs. Each said the amount was insufficient as it just covered their actual damages, nothing for the fear and fright that my clients felt when the Christmas Day blast ruined their holiday celebrations. They have countered with a demand of $50,000 each, in addition to any actual material damage to their homes."

"Mr. Schwartz, your original and amended complaints allege loss of income for those of your clients who operate farms. Have your clients presented any evidence of loss?"

"No, while they believe that there was a reduction in milk and egg production for a few days after the Christmas Day blast, there was no actual reduction in income noticeable in their financial records. But they do believe that the blast was a disturbance to both their livestock and their own peace of mind."

"Has the government made any offer to settle these "peace of mind" claims of the plaintiffs?"

"A paltry amount of $500 to $1000, depending on the plaintiff's proximity to the rail yard where the blast occurred. The government argues that as the blast was caused by criminals, that under Ohio tort law an owner cannot be held liable for damages caused by a criminal over whom they had no control. We contend that as the Plum Brook facility has hazardous materials on and brought into their property that this is an issue of absolute liability. The government had a duty to keep criminals out, and they breached that duty when criminals did get in and caused damage to both the government and my clients."

"Thank you, Martin. Now, Palmer, how does the government respond to this allegation?"

"As Mr. Schwartz stated, Ohio law, which we believe the federal court will recognize in this case, does indeed hold that an individual cannot be held liable for damages caused by a criminal over whom that individual had no control. We have cited several Ohio and Sixth Circuit cases in our summary, which I believe you have before you. Further, we argue that the government did take all reasonable and prudent steps to prevent an invasion of its property. There is a very strong fence, locked gates, surveillance cameras, and a platoon of U.S. Air Force Military Police stationed permanently at the Plum Brook facility which should suffice to keep criminals out of the facility. However, as the documents will show, these criminals, which we now have come to believe may have been retained by a foreign government, did not break down the fence or enter at any unobserved gate. Rather they drove through the Main Gate barrier which was guarded at the time by an Air Force corporal who was shot and wounded in the invasion. Fortunately she has fully recovered. Given all that, we see no negligence at all on the part of the government for the intrusion that occurred and the subsequent explosion of two tank cars of oxygen. If there is no negligence, then there would be no liability for any damages, although we have agreed to reimburse any actual physical damage that did occur."

"Thank you, Palmer. Given that certain operations at your client's facilities are top secret and that hazardous and dangerous materials are frequently within or brought into the facility, as Martin has stated in his summary, the situation speaks for itself – the protections provided were insufficient. Would you not agree?'

"What would you suggest, a tank or a cannon?"

"Well, I believe these plaintiffs would suggest something more than one female unarmed Air Force corporal manning the gate. Tanks and cannons would not be practical. As such, do you believe your offers to date have been sufficient?"

"We believe that under Ohio law they are."

"Martin, would your clients agree?" Wilson asked.

"Absolutely not!"

"Then, since it appears that the government is willing to offer something, but not enough to meet your clients' demand, that we adjourn to the conference rooms for you attorneys to talk with your clients and see if there is any basis for movement in your offers and demands."

The two groups went off to their separate conference rooms. Within a few minutes Jim could hear shouting coming from the other room, and the voice sounded like that of Jerry Summers. Palmer Davis looked at Colonel Josephs and said, "Jeffry, he sounds a little upset!"

"He's the same son-of-a-bitch who has been stirring up trouble among the neighbors for years. I wouldn't offer him a penny."

"Well, an offer has already been made of more than one cent, but their trouble is not worth any $50,000 each. There's ten of them left, and that's half a million. Jim, what would a $5000 offer each do to your NASA budget?"

"You told me to be prepared to offer some serious money. I talked with the folks at Brookpark and they talked with the head guys in Washington, and decided that $12,500 each would be the maximum limit.

Why don't we start below $5000 and go up in $2500 increments if necessary?"

"Okay. I have some interesting opening comments first that might get their attention," Davis replied. "What do you think, Colonel?"

"It's not the Air Force's problem. We've already beefed up the number of men, but our little outfit is at the bottom of the feed line, and I don't think it will improve."

"Martin had a point about the guards being unarmed. Could a concession be made for them to carry side arms, with perhaps a rifle or shotgun in the guardhouse at the Gate?"

"Well, the MPs have always had a side arm. That was in my original orders, but I can go to the Pentagon and suggest rifles in the guardhouse. Hell, I'll demand it! I've plenty of reasons now. It was just unfortunate that it was McQuinn, who doesn't carry a weapon, was on duty during the men's lunchtime. Next time she'll have one, and know how to use it."

"Good. Well, let's see if the other side is ready to try again," Palmer Davis said, when there was a knock at the door. It was Brian Wilson.

"I've been with the plaintiffs and I think they're ready to move down a little. I suspect the government will have a little maneuvering room, but you're going to have to be serious about it. That you've offered anything at all tells me that you, too, think there is some exposure."

"Some, but not much," Palmer Davis agreed. "Are they ready?"

"Yes, let's go back in."

Once everyone was seated around the table the mediator, Wilson, had a few opening statements presenting a positive approach and hopefulness for an agreement. Then he turned to Palmer Davis for any opening remarks he might have. Palmer stood up and drew the big map of the area that was in the middle of the table toward him. On it he had circled in red each of the homes of each plaintiff. Most were in the subdivision to the north of the facility, and Mrs. McGonagall's was the closest to the north railroad gate. Two or three were just east of the B&O branch leading into the facility. The rest were east of that, except for a few farms on the south and west side. The east side was highway and some commercial properties, none of which had joined in the lawsuit.

"Mr. Schwartz, do you know when this subdivision where most of your clients live, was first constructed?"

"No, I'm not sure."

"I checked the Erie County records. The project was started in 1955 and completed in 1961. Mr. Summers, when did you purchase your home?"

"Ah, I think it was in 1963."

"In 1963, about five or six years ago?"

"Yeah, that's about right."

"Did you or you and your wife and family, drive around the area before purchasing your home?"

"Yeah, I suppose we did. I was workin' in Lorain at a steel mill, and the wife, she liked the area."

"But you didn't look around the neighborhood yourself?"

"Yeah, sure I did."

"What did you see?"

"Well, there were some railroad tracks that led up to a fence on the other side of the road that is at the south end of the subdivision. And other homes around."

"Did you know what was behind the fence?"

"I knew it was some government outfit. There was a sign that said to keep out."

"How old are you, Mr. Summers?"

"Thirty eight. Born in 1931."

"Where did you grow up and go to school?"

"Here in Sandusky. Why? What's this got to do with my claim?"

"Oh, quite a bit, Mr. Summers. Tell me, when you were growing up in Sandusky did you ever take a ride south of town?"

"Sure, lots of times."

"Did you ever see the fenced area before the subdivision in which you now live was built?"

"Yeah, it was farmland, and then the Army built an explosives factory in there. They made ammunition for the war. It was called the Plum Brook Arsenal then."

"Do you know when NASA took over that arsenal for their space research?"

"Eh, I'm not sure. Sometime in the late 1950s or early 60s, I think."

"So you knew what it was when you purchased your home, is that correct?"

"Yeah, but so what? Dat don't give the government no right to disturb the peace."

"Have you ever been aware of any other attempts to break into the government facility?"

"None that I know of. Why?"

"Do you have children, Mr. Summers?"

"Yeah, a couple of boys."

"Is one named Randy?"

"Yeah...."

"So you are aware of an attempt to break into the facility, then, are you not, Mr. Summers?"

"Randy didn't get in."

"That's right. Why didn't he get in?"

"The MPs stopped him before he got over the fence."

"So the perimeter is pretty secure then, eh?"

"What you drivin' at, Mister...?"

"The Erie County Sheriff's report does indicate that the fence was not breached, but that an attempt was made, in June of 1967. It was the next month, in July of 1967, that you began a neighborhood protest against the facility, is that correct?"

"I don't remember no dates."

"But if you purchased your home in 1963 and knew that there was a NASA facility here, and it was well known that there was a small nuclear reactor there at that time, and you did not protest until 1967, a month after your son was almost arrested for trespassing on government property, I just wondered about these coincidences. Mr. Schwartz, would you please explain to your clients the Ohio tort law defense called 'assumption of risk,' and Ohio's law regarding contributory negligence?"

"I think I see where you are headed, Mr. Davis," Wilson interrupted. "The plaintiffs all had to be aware that this was either an Army ammunition factory or a NASA facility before they purchased their homes. Therefore they had to assume that there might be risks, and that purchasing their homes meant assuming that risk. But I would also argue that assuming a risk, while a defense and mitigating factor, is not an act of negligence. However, I think that we need to discuss damages a bit more."

"Fine," Davis answered, "but first I want to ask each of the plaintiffs that live in the subdivision north of the facility whether, on the day after Christmas, an Air Force MP came to their door, or left a note, in order to inquire if they had sustained any damages, and if they had, to get repair estimates for government reimbursement." There was a brief muffle of voices in the room among the plaintiffs, and nodding of heads indicating that this was true.

"The government appreciates that you, its neighbors, do have to put up with some nuisance because of our facility," Davis continued. "There are trains that come through your neighborhood at night, and some noise if the supersonic wind tunnel is in operation. In fact, before the subdivision in which you live was built, the government offered to purchase that tract of land, but a developer already had it and wanted to build the homes most of you now occupy. Nevertheless, although we do not believe there is any legal liability on the part of NASA, we are willing to offer $2,500 to each plaintiff in addition to any actual costs of repair or damages they sustained."

"Mr. Schwartz," Wilson said, "would your people be willing to accept such an offer? Or do you need to conference with them again in private?"

"Wait a minute," Jerry Summers exclaimed. "Schwartz, you said we had a good chance of a nice recovery here. Instead this son of a ... ah, this gentleman from NASA insults me an' my family, and offers a pittance of twenty five hundred bucks? That ain't fair. I'm the one that rounded up all these people for you. I deserve more than that!"

"How much do you think is 'fair,' Mr. Summers?" the mediator asked.

"Well, at least ten grand."

"Then I'd suggest, Mr. Schwartz," Wilson continued, "that you go back to your conference room and poll your clients for their thoughts on the offer. As I remember you all waived a jury trial, so it will be Judge Slidell who will make the decisions if you cannot reach an agreement today and must go to trial."

Jerry Summers began to rise from his chair, but the other plaintiffs began a whispered conversation among themselves. Finally one lady raised her hand and said, "Mr. Wilson, I think the rest of us have reached a decision. Isn't that right?" she said, looking around at the others, who all nodded their heads in approval. "We want to settle for the twenty-five hundred and go home. Mr. Summers had us believing that we were going to be made rich if we joined his law suit, but it has been nothing but trouble. Personally, I don't think Jerry Summers deserves any money, the stink he has been putting up over nothing. And had we known that he only did it after his kid tried to break into the place – why, his kid has been in and out of trouble for years. Those occasional trains don't bother us much. One or two cars, and a toot or two."

"Mr. Summers?" Martin Schwartz asked, looking at his lead client.

"Oh, all right. I'll settle, but I want the money today.'

"But that's not possible," Schwartz replied. "Remember the contract with me that you all signed? Now, I've tried to keep my expenses at a minimum, and they will be a lot less than had our contract been on a contingency of one third plus expenses, and I would imagine that the government will issue individual checks payable to each of you with my name as your attorney, and you will have to sign releases before they can be cashed." Palmer Davis leaned over and whispered something to Jim Roberts and the Colonel, and they shook their heads.

"Martin, my clients and I have discussed your expenses," Davis said, "and if you and your clients are willing, the government will agree to pay your expenses including your half of today's mediation costs separately to you, if that is agreeable to you and your clients."

"Thank you, Palmer. My clients are not wealthy, and I think they will be good neighbors to Plum Brook." Then, looking at his group of clients he asked, "Is that agreeable to all of you?" They unanimously agreed, except Mr. Summers, who said nothing, but did nod his head.

Hands were shook all around, and Schwartz invited Brian Wilson, Palmer Davis, Jim Roberts and Jeffrey Josephs to join him for lunch before they headed back to Sandusky. The case was settled over a glass of Firelands wine.

* * *

Jim Roberts turned the table on everyone's Christmas plans. Instead of everyone that had become part of the Roberts' "gang of friends" in the year they had been back in Ohio going to the Fairchilds' farm, the Roberts invited all of them to their farm for Christmas Day, promising a dinner of pheasant, wild turkey and venison – Fairchild's roast beef was only a close second fiddle to an offer like that! And so it was agreed that all the choir members – both Peggy and Dexter Atwater had now become members – the Durrands, Fairchilds, Merriams, Atwaters, Ross and Hilda Johnson, Jeffrey Josephs and his wife, Martha, and Jimmy, his wife and Trice would come to the farm on Mason Road on Christmas Day.

As the Fairchilds were driving from their farm to Fremont on Christmas Eve for the late evening service, Richard was listening to Station CKLW in Windsor, Ontario. He knew that what the current weather there was going to be the weather in Northern Ohio the next morning. The station had the usual CBC Christmas stories, storms in the western provinces, politics in Ottawa, and so forth. But one of the stories caught the professor's attention: "The RCMP fraud division advises that they have closed down the London, Ontario, office of Minsk Investments, and have issued a warrant for Rudy Lester, who ran the operation, which was a Ponzi scheme. Minsk Investments, headquartered in the British colonies of the Turks and Caicos Islands, has also been targeted by Scotland Yard, and their assets in the Bank of Sark impounded. RCMP officers visited Lester's home in Kingsport but were unable to find him, and have posted a bulletin for him, suspecting that he might have crossed into the U.S. They have also alerted both the U.S. Federal Bureau of Investigation and Interpol. In other province news, the Windsor Curling Team has moved toward the finals with their win last evening...."

The Christmas Eve service was lightly attended as most of the students had returned to their own homes for the holiday. To help out in the choir, even Jim, Rayland, Dexter and Bob Merriam agreed to don choir robes and sing in the choir, as most of the student members were missing. Jimmy, his wife Suzie and Trice were in the congregation, although the Josephs were Catholic and attended a church in Sandusky. After the candlelight service they all returned to the Durrand's home in Fremont for eggnog and cookies. As Jim was now a part of the Fremont College faculty, he and Jayne felt right at home.

The following afternoon everyone had gathered at the Roberts' farm on Mason Road. Heidi, at four months old, was properly "ooo'ed and "ahh"ed by the adults. Each family had contributed something to the dinner, as was the tradition, and aromas of roasting wild turkey, pheasant and venison rolled from the kitchen while the men sat in the Roberts' living room enjoying various drinks. Dr. Fairchild had brought six bottles of Chateau Kent for the dinner.

"Oh, by the way, Jim," Fairchild said during a slight lull in the conversation, "if I remember correctly you said that the man who caused that explosion in New York that killed his office manager and injured his other two employees was named 'Minsk,' Lester Minsk?"

"Yes. He fled the country. Why?"

"Well, last evening when Esther and I were driving from our place to Fremont we were listening to the news on the Windsor, Ontario, radio station, and they were describing a situation in London, Ontario, involving a Minsk Investments, and a man named Rudy Lester, who was running some sort of Ponzi scheme. Scotland Yard was also involved, and had frozen Minsk's accounts in the Bank of Sark. The company was based in the Turks and Caicos Islands."

"That sure sounds like my Lester Minsk all right. Did they arrest him?"

"No, they're hunting for him, but think he may have crossed into the U.S., so they notified the FBI and Interpol. The Royal Canadian Mounted Police fraud unit is investigating."

"What did Minsk do?" Dexter asked.

"He rigged a bomb under his office lunchroom, flew to Miami, and set off the bomb by calling the phone to which the bomb was attached," Jim answered. "Then he flew to Venezuela and disappeared."

"Boy, that's one crook Dad would like to catch!" Jimmy Roberts said.

"Darned right. Maybe after the holiday I'll call Aaron Greenspoon and see if he knows anything about it."

"Who is Greenspoon?" Ray Durrand asked.

"He's the Special Agent in Charge of the Toledo FBI office, and was involved with capturing the third KGB agent, Klaus Kravitz."

"Oh yes. He's the agent who came down from Toledo when those KGB guys blew up Hilda's car, wasn't he?"

"I think so," Jim answered. With that the women in the kitchen started carrying the food to a long dining room table that had been in the farmhouse for over seventy-five years.

"Dinner time, boys!" Jayne called. Richard Fairchild was again asked to give the blessing, and they all sat down to a fabulous Christmas dinner.

***

With information Jim Roberts was able to supply the Toledo and Detroit offices of the FBI, within two weeks they were able to track down Rudy Minsk, residing with a relative in Detroit. Rudolph Lester Minsk was arrested. He had already planned his escape by way of Miami. A request for extradition to Ontario was received, along with one from the State of New York, after Jim notified Florian Madeira, Assistant District Attorney of the State of New York.

Ontario officials agreed to a quick trial and disposition of the Rudy Lester Minsk case, believing that most of the assets he had stolen in his Ponzi scheme would be recovered from the accounts in the small island bank in the English Channel, and then New York could have him for their murder and arson trial. It took until April for Ontario to bring Minsk to trial and find all of his hidden assets, which far exceeded what he had acquired in Canada. The rest would be available for Minsk's victims in New York.

Minsk was then transferred to Rikers Island Jail in New York to await his trial on murder, arson, fraud and conspiracy. The trial was scheduled for early June, and Jim Roberts agreed to return to New York, at the City's expense, to testify against Minsk. Jayne went with him, enjoying the week of the trial shopping, visiting friends on Staten Island and attending plays in the evenings with Jim. The trial of Minsk for the murder of Judy Markowitz, the arson, and attempted murders of Weisnewski and Jacoby took only four days, aided by Jim's testimony. The trial of Minsk for fraud was going to take another week, and Jim was not needed for that portion of the trial, so the Roberts returned to Ohio. They heard the following week that Minsk had received a life sentence, and if he ever became eligible for parole, which was doubtful, he would be returned to Ontario to serve their twenty-five year sentence. In short, Minsk was a goner.

Although his attendance was not required at the college commencement ceremony, Jim was surprised when he was asked to be one of the commencement speakers, along with Senator Whitfield. "But why me?" he demanded of Dean Harding.

"Why not you?" the Dean replied. "You're the guy who helped capture some KGB agents who intended to contaminate half of Erie County. And that New York arson murder story would make an excellent story to encourage our graduates to be good citizens."

"Well, Richard Fairchild did more than I did. He actually did capture the KGB guy on the train, and found out where the third guy was building his bomb. And he tipped me off as to the New York arsonist, too."

"Fairchild has enough on his mind with his upcoming trip this summer to India. Besides, we think your work at NASA makes a good example for our students here. You are our star alumni, and Fremont is grateful."

"But I'm no public speaker. I just teach a couple of fire science courses for you."

"Too late," the Dean replied. "We've already ordered your robe and cap. And it's going to have three red stripes on the sleeves."

"What?"

"The Northern Collegiate Academy of Arts and Scientists has just agreed that Fremont is to become a credited university, effective immediately, and you will be our first Honorary Doctor of Letters. You have more accomplishments that most Ph.Ds. And maybe some sunny day you'll get that, too."

"But...."

"No 'buts" to it, Jim. You're going to be Dr. Roberts, like it or not!"

Made in the USA
Lexington, KY
07 November 2017